The Treasury of Allan Quatermain Vol II

The Treasury of Allan Quatermain Vol II

by H. Rider Haggard

Allan and the Holy Flower
Finished
The Ivory Child
The Ancient Allan
She and Allan

Allan and the Holy Flower

Table of Contents

Brother John

I do not suppose that anyone who knows the name of Allan Quatermain would be likely to associate it with flowers, and especially with orchids. Yet as it happens it was once my lot to take part in an orchid hunt of so remarkable a character that I think its details should not be lost. At least I will set them down, and if in the after days anyone cares to publish them, well--he is at liberty to do so.

It was in the year--oh! never mind the year, it was a long while ago when I was much younger, that I went on a hunting expedition to the north of the Limpopo River which borders the Transvaal. My companion was a gentleman of the name of Scroope, Charles Scroope. He had come out to Durban from England in search of sport. At least, that was one of his reasons. The other was a lady whom I will call Miss Margaret Manners, though that was not her name.

It seems that these two were engaged to be married, and really attached to each other. Unfortunately, however, they quarrelled violently about another gentlemen with whom Miss Manners danced four consecutive dances, including two that were promised to her fiancé at a Hunt ball in Essex, where they all lived. Explanations, or rather argument, followed. Mr. Scroope said that he would not tolerate such conduct. Miss Manners replied that she would not be dictated to; she was her own mistress and meant to remain so. Mr. Scroope exclaimed that she might so far as he was concerned. She answered that she never wished to see his face again. He declared with emphasis that she never should and that he was going to Africa to shoot elephants.

What is more, he went, starting from his Essex home the next day without leaving any address. As it transpired afterwards, long afterwards, had he waited till the post came in he would have received a letter that might have changed his plans. But they were high- spirited young people, both of them, and played the fool after the fashion of those in love.

Well, Charles Scroope turned up in Durban, which was but a poor place then, and there we met in the bar of the Royal Hotel.

"If you want to kill big game," I heard some one say, who it was I really forget, "there's the man to show you how to do it--Hunter Quatermain; the best shot in Africa and one of the finest fellows, too."

I sat still, smoking my pipe and pretending to hear nothing. It is awkward to listen to oneself being praised, and I was always a shy man.

Then after a whispered colloquy Mr. Scroope was brought forward and introduced to me. I bowed as nicely as I could and ran my eye over him. He was a tall young man with dark eyes and a rather romantic aspect (that was due to his love affair), but I came to the conclusion that I liked the cut of his jib. When he spoke, that conclusion was affirmed. I always think there is a great deal in a voice; personally, I judge by it almost as much as by the face. This voice was particularly pleasant and sympathetic, though there was nothing very original or striking in the words by which it was, so to speak, introduced to me. These were:

"How do you do, sir. Will you have a split?"

I answered that I never drank spirits in the daytime, or at least not often, but that I should be pleased to take a small bottle of beer.

When the beer was consumed we walked up together to my little house on which is now called the Berea, the same in which, amongst others, I received my friends, Curtis and Good, in after days, and there we dined. Indeed, Charlie Scroope never left that house until we started on our shooting expedition.

Now I must cut all this story short, since it is only incidentally that it has to do with the tale I am going to tell. Mr. Scroope was a rich man and as he offered to pay all the expenses of the expedition while I was to take all the profit in the shape of ivory or anything else that might accrue, of course I did not decline his proposal.

Everything went well with us on that trip until its unfortunate end. We only killed two elephants, but of other game we found plenty. It was when we were near Delagoa Bay on our return that the accident happened.

We were out one evening trying to shoot something for our dinner, when between the trees I caught sight of a small buck. It vanished round a little promontory of rock which projected from the side of the kloof, walking quietly, not running in alarm. We followed after it. I was the first, and had just wriggled round these rocks and perceived the buck standing about ten paces away (it was a bush-bok), when I heard a rustle among the bushes on the top of the rock not a dozen feet above my head, and Charlie Scroope's voice calling:

"Look out, Quatermain! He's coming."

"Who's coming?" I answered in an irritated tone, for the noise had made the buck run away.

Then it occurred to me, all in an instant of course, that a man would not begin to shout like that for nothing; at any rate when his supper was concerned. So I glanced up above and behind me. To this moment I can remember exactly what I saw. There was the granite water-worn boulder, or rather several boulders, with ferns growing in their cracks of the maiden-hair tribe, most of them, but some had a silver sheen on the under side of their leaves. On one of these leaves, bending it down, sat a large beetle with red wings and a black body engaged in rubbing its antennæ with its front paws. And above, just appearing over the top of the rock, was the head of an extremely fine leopard. As I write to seem to perceive its square jowl outlined against the arc of the quiet evening sky with the saliva dropping from its lips.

This was the last thing which I did perceive for a little while, since at that moment the leopard--we call them tigers in South Africa-- dropped upon my back and knocked me flat as a pancake. I presume that it also had been stalking the buck and was angry at my appearance on the scene. Down I went, luckily for me, into a patch of mossy soil.

"All up!" I said to myself, for I felt the brute's weight upon my back pressing me down among the moss, and what was worse, its hot breath upon my neck as it dropped its jaws to bite me in the head. Then I heard the report of Scroope's rifle, followed by furious snarling from the leopard, which evidently had been hit. Also it seemed to think that I had caused its injuries, for it seized me by the shoulder. I felt its teeth slip along my skin, but happily they only fastened in the shooting coat of tough corduroy that I was wearing. It began to shake me, then let go to get a better grip. Now, remembering that Scroope only carried a light, single-barrelled rifle, and therefore could not fire again, I knew, or thought I knew, that my time had come. I was not exactly afraid, but the sense of some great, impending chance became very vivid. I remembered--not my whole life, but one or two odd little things connected with my infancy. For instance, I seemed to see myself seated on my mother's knee, playing with a little jointed gold-fish which she wore upon her watch-chain.

After this I muttered a word or two of supplication, and, I think, lost consciousness. If so, it can only have been for a few seconds. Then my mind returned to me and I saw a strange sight. The leopard and Scroope were fighting each other. The leopard, standing on one hind leg, for the other was broken, seemed to be boxing Scroope, whilst Scroope was driving his big hunting knife into the brute's carcase. They went down, Scroope undermost, the leopard tearing at him. I gave a wriggle and came out of that mossy bed--I recall the sucking sound my body made as it left the ooze.

Close by was my rifle, uninjured and at full cock as it had fallen from my hand. I seized it, and in another second had shot the leopard through the head just as it was about to seize Scroope's throat.

It fell stone dead on the top of him. One quiver, one contraction of the claws (in poor Scroope's leg) and all was over. There it lay as though it were asleep, and underneath was Scroope.

The difficulty was to get it off him, for the beast was very heavy, but I managed this at last with the help of a thorn bough I found which some elephant had torn from a tree. This I used as a lever. There beneath lay Scroope, literally covered with blood, though whether his own or the leopard's I could not tell. At first I thought that he was dead, but after I had poured some water over him from the little stream that trickled down the rock, he sat up and asked inconsequently:

"What am I now?"

"A hero," I answered. (I have always been proud of that repartee.)

Then, discouraging further conversation, I set to work to get him back to the camp, which fortunately was close at hand.

When we had proceeded a couple of hundred yards, he still making inconsequent remarks, his right arm round my neck and my left arm round his middle, suddenly he collapsed in a dead faint, and as his weight was more than I could carry, I had to leave him and fetch help.

In the end I got him to the tents by aid of the Kaffirs and a blanket, and there made an examination. He was scratched all over, but the only serious wounds were a bite through the muscles of the left upper arm and three deep cuts in the right thigh just where it joins the body, caused by a stroke of the leopard's claws. I gave him a dose of laudanum to send him to sleep and dressed these hurts as best I could. For three days he went on quite well. Indeed, the wounds had begun to heal healthily when suddenly some kind of fever took him, caused, I suppose, by the poison of the leopard's fangs or claws.

Oh! what a terrible week was that which followed! He became delirious, raving continually of all sorts of things, and especially of Miss Margaret Manners. I kept up his strength as well as was possible with soup made from the flesh of game, mixed with a little brandy which I had. But he grew weaker and weaker. Also the wounds in the thigh began to suppurate.

The Kaffirs whom we had with us were of little use in such a case, so that all the nursing fell on me. Luckily, beyond a shaking, the leopard had done me no hurt, and I was very strong in those days. Still the lack of rest told on me, since I dared not sleep for more than half an hour or so at a time. At length came a morning when I was quite worn out. There lay poor Scroope turning and muttering in the little tent, and there I sat by his side, wondering whether he would live to see another dawn, or if he did, for how long I should be able to tend him. I called to a Kaffir to bring me my coffee, and just was I was lifting the pannikin to my lips with a shaking hand, help came.

It arrived in a very strange shape. In front of our camp were two thorn trees, and from between these trees, the rays from the rising sun falling full on him, I saw a curious figure walking towards me in a slow, purposeful fashion. It was that of a man of uncertain age, for though the beard and long hair were white, the face was comparatively youthful, save for the wrinkles round the mouth, and the dark eyes were full of life and vigour. Tattered garments, surmounted by a torn kaross or skin rug, hung awkwardly upon his tall, thin frame. On his feet were veld-schoen of untanned hide, on his back a battered tin case was strapped, and in his bony, nervous hand he clasped a long staff made of the black and white wood the natives call *unzimbiti*, on the top of which was fixed a butterfly net. Behind him were some Kaffirs who carried cases on their heads.

I knew him at once, since we had met before, especially on a certain occasion in Zululand, when he calmly appeared out of the ranks of a hostile native *impi*. He was one of the strangest characters in all South Africa. Evidently a gentleman in the true sense of the word, none knew his history (although I know it now, and a strange story it is), except that he was an American by birth, for in this matter at times his speech betrayed him. Also he was a doctor by profession, and to judge from his extraordinary skill, one who must have seen much practice both in medicine and in surgery. For the rest he had means, though where they came from was a mystery, and for many years past had wandered about South and Eastern Africa, collecting butterflies and flowers.

By the natives, and I might add by white people also, he was universally supposed to be mad. This reputation, coupled with his medical skill, enabled him to travel wherever he would without the slightest fear of molestation, since the Kaffirs look upon the mad as inspired by God. Their name for him was "Dogeetah," a ludicrous corruption of the English word "doctor," whereas white folk called him indifferently "Brother John," "Uncle Jonathan," or "Saint John." The second appellation he got from his extraordinary likeness (when cleaned up and nicely dressed) to the figure by which the great American nation is typified in comic papers, as England is typified by John Bull. The first and third arose in the well-known goodness of his character and a taste he was supposed to possess for living on locusts and wild honey, or their local equivalents. Personally, however, he preferred to be addressed as "Brother John."

Oh! who can tell the relief with which I saw him; an angel from heaven could scarcely have been more welcome. As he came I poured out a second jorum of coffee, and remembering that he liked it sweet, put in plenty of sugar.

"How do you do, Brother John?" I said, proffering him the coffee.

"Greeting, Brother Allan," he answered--in those days he affected a kind of old Roman way of speaking, as I imagine it. Then he took the coffee, put his long finger into it to test the temperature and stir up the sugar, drank it off as though it were a dose of medicine, and handed back the tin to be refilled.

"Bug-hunting?" I queried.

He nodded. "That and flowers and observing human nature and the wonderful works of God. Wandering around generally."

"Where from last?" I asked.

"Those hills nearly twenty miles away. Left them at eight in the evening; walked all night."

"Why?" I said, looking at him.

"Because it seemed as though someone were calling me. To be plain, you, Allan."

"Oh! you heard about my being here and the trouble?"

"No, heard nothing. Meant to strike out for the coast this morning. Just as I was turning in, at 8.5 exactly, got your message and started. That's all."

"My message----" I began, then stopped, and asking to see his watch, compared it with mine. Oddly enough, they showed the same time to within two minutes.

"It is a strange thing," I said slowly, "but at 8.5 last night I did try to send a message for some help because I thought my mate was dying," and I jerked my thumb towards the tent. "Only it wasn't to you or any other man, Brother John. Understand?"

"Quite. Message was expressed on, that's all. Expressed and I guess registered as well."

I looked at Brother John and Brother John looked at me, but at the time we made no further remark. The thing was too curious, that is, unless he lied. But nobody had ever known him to lie. He was a truthful person, painfully truthful at times. And yet there are people who do not believe in prayer.

"What is it?" he asked.

"Mauled by leopard. Wounds won't heal, and fever. I don't think he can last long."

"What do you know about it? Let me see him."

Well, he saw him and did wonderful things. That tin box of his was full of medicines and surgical instruments, which latter he boiled before he used them. Also he washed his hands till I thought the skin would come off them, using up more soap than I could spare. First he gave poor Charlie a dose of something that seemed to kill him; he said he had that drug from the Kaffirs. Then he opened up those wounds upon his thigh and cleaned them out and bandaged them with boiled herbs. Afterwards, when Scroope came to again, he gave him a drink that threw him into a sweat and took away the fever. The end of it was that in two days' time his patient sat up and asked for a square meal, and in a week we were able to begin to carry him to the coast.

"Guess that message of yours saved Brother Scroope's life," said old John, as he watched him start.

I made no answer. Here I may state, however, that through my own men I inquired a little as to Brother John's movements at the time of what he called the message. It seemed that he *had* arranged to march towards the coast on the next morning, but that about two hours after sunset suddenly he ordered them to pack up everything and follow him. This they did and to their intense disgust those Kaffirs were forced to trudge all night at the heels of Dogeetah, as they called him. Indeed, so weary did they become, that had they not been afraid of being left alone in an unknown country in the darkness, they said they would have thrown down their loads and refused to go any further.

That is as far as I was able to take the matter, which may be explained by telepathy, inspiration, instinct, or coincidence. It is one as to which the reader must form his own opinion.

During our week together in camp and our subsequent journey to Delagoa Bay and thence by ship to Durban, Brother John and I grew very intimate, with limitations. Of his past, as I have said, he never talked, or of the real object of his wanderings which I learned afterwards, but of his natural history and ethnological (I believe that is the word) studies he spoke a good deal. As, in my humble way, I also am an observer of such matters and know something about African natives and their habits from practical experience, these subjects interested me.

Amongst other things, he showed me many of the specimens that he had collected during his recent journey; insects and beautiful butterflies neatly pinned into boxes, also a quantity of dried flowers pressed between sheets of blotting paper, amongst them some which he told me were orchids. Observing that these attracted me, he asked me if I would like to see the most wonderful orchid in the whole world. Of course I said yes, whereon he produced out of one of his cases a flat package about two feet six square. He undid the grass mats in which it was wrapped, striped, delicately woven mats such as they make in the neighbourhood of Zanzibar. Within these was the lid of a packing-case. Then came more mats and some copies of *The Cape Journal* spread out flat. Then sheets of blotting paper, and last of all between two pieces of cardboard, a flower and one leaf of the plant on which it grew.

Even in its dried state it was a wondrous thing, measuring twenty-four inches from the tip of one wing or petal to the tip of the other, by twenty inches from the top of the back sheath to the bottom of the pouch. The measurement of the back sheath itself I forget, but it must have been quite a foot across. In colour it was, or had been, bright golden, but the back sheath was white, barred with lines of black, and in the exact centre of the pouch was a single black spot shaped like the head of a great ape. There were the overhanging brows, the deep recessed eyes, the surly mouth, the massive jaws--everything.

Although at that time I had never seen a gorilla in the flesh, I had seen a coloured picture of the brute, and if that picture had been photographed on the flower the likeness could not have been more perfect.

"What is it?" I asked, amazed.

"Sir," said Brother John, sometimes he used this formal term when excited, "it is the most marvellous Cypripedium in the whole earth, and, sir, I have discovered it. A healthy root of that plant will be worth £20,000."

"That's better than gold mining," I said. "Well, have you got the root?"

Brother John shook his head sadly as he answered:

"No such luck."

"How's that as you have the flower?"

"I'll tell you, Allan. For a year past and more I have been collecting in the district back of Kilwa and found some wonderful things, yes, wonderful. At last, about three hundred miles inland, I came to a tribe, or rather, a people, that no white man had ever visited. They are called the Mazitu, a numerous and warlike people of bastard Zulu blood."

"I have heard of them," I interrupted. "They broke north before the days of Senzangakona, two hundred years or more ago."

"Well, I could make myself understood among them because they still talk a corrupt Zulu, as do all the tribes in those parts. At first they wanted to kill me, but let me go because they thought that I was mad. Everyone thinks that I am mad, Allan; it is a kind of public delusion, whereas I think that I am sane and that most other people are mad."

"A private delusion," I suggested hurriedly, as I did not wish to discuss Brother John's sanity. "Well, go on about the Mazitu."

"Later they discovered that I had skill in medicine, and their king, Bausi, came to me to be treated for a great external tumour. I risked an operation and cured him. It was anxious work, for if he had died I should have died too, though that would not have troubled me very much," and he sighed. "Of course, from that moment I was supposed to be a great magician. Also Bausi made a blood brotherhood with me, transfusing some of his blood into my veins and some of mine into his. I only hope he has not inoculated me with his tumours, which are congenital. So I became Bausi and Bausi became me. In other words, I was as much chief of the Mazitu as he was, and shall remain so all my life."

"That might be useful," I said, reflectively, "but go on."

"I learned that on the western boundary of the Mazitu territory were great swamps; that beyond these swamps was a lake called Kirua, and beyond that a large and fertile land supposed to be an island, with a mountain in its centre. This land is known as Pongo, and so are the people who live there."

"That is a native name for the gorilla, isn't it?" I asked. "At least so a fellow who had been on the West Coast told me."

"Indeed, then that's strange, as you will see. Now these Pongo are supposed to be great magicians, and the god they worship is said to be a gorilla, which, if you are right, accounts for their name. Or rather," he went on, "they have two gods. The other is that flower you see there. Whether the flower with the monkey's head on it was the first god and suggested the worship of the beast itself, or *vice versa*, I don't know. Indeed I know very little, just what I was told by the Mazitu and a man who called himself a Pongo chief, no more."

"What did they say?"

"The Mazitu said that the Pongo people are devils who came by the secret channels through the reeds in canoes and stole their children and women, whom they sacrificed to their gods. Sometimes, too, they made raids upon them at night, 'howling like hyenas.' The men they killed and the women and children they took away. The Mazitu want to attack them but cannot do so, because they are not water people and have no canoes, and therefore are unable to reach the island, if it is an island. Also they told me about the wonderful flower which grows in the place where the ape-god lives, and is worshipped like the god. They had the story of it from some of their people who had been enslaved and escaped."

"Did you try to get to the island?" I asked.

"Yes, Allan. That is, I went to the edge of the reeds which lie at the end of a long slope of plain, where the lake begins. Here I stopped for some time catching butterflies and collecting plants. One night when I was camped there by myself, for none of my men would remain so near the Pongo country after sunset, I woke up with a sense that I was no longer alone. I crept out of my tent and by the light of the moon, which was setting, for dawn drew near, I saw a man who leant upon the handle of a very wide-bladed spear which was taller than himself, a big man over six feet two high, I should say, and broad in proportion. He wore a long, white cloak reaching from his shoulders almost to the ground. On his head was a tight-fitting cap with lappets, also white. In his ears were rings of copper or gold, and on his wrists bracelets of the same metal. His skin was intensely black, but the features were not at all negroid. They were prominent and finely-cut, the nose being sharp and the lips quite thin; indeed of an Arab type. His left hand was bandaged, and on his face was an expression of great anxiety. Lastly, he appeared to be about fifty years of age. So still did he stand that I began to wonder whether he were one of those ghosts which the Mazitu swore the Pongo wizards send out to haunt their country.

"For a long while we stared at each other, for I was determined that I would not speak first or show any concern. At last he spoke in a low, deep voice and in Mazitu, or a language so similar that I found it easy to understand.

"'Is not your name Dogeetah, O White Lord, and are you not a master of medicine?'

"'Yes,' I answered, 'but who are you who dare to wake me from my sleep?'

"'Lord, I am the Kalubi, the Chief of the Pongo, a great man in my own land yonder.'

"'Then why do you come here alone at night, Kalubi, Chief of the Pongo?'

"'Why do *you* come here alone, White Lord?' he answered evasively.

"'What do you want, anyway?' I asked.

"'O! Dogeetah, I have been hurt, I want you to cure me,' and he looked at his bandaged hand.

"'Lay down that spear and open your robe that I may see you have no knife.'

"He obeyed, throwing the spear to some distance.

"'Now unwrap the hand.'

"He did so. I lit a match, the sight of which seemed to frighten him greatly, although he asked no questions about it, and by its light examined the hand. The first joint of the second finger was gone. From the appearance of the stump which had been cauterized and was tied tightly with a piece of flexible grass, I judged that it had been bitten off.

"'What did this?' I asked.

"'Monkey,' he answered, 'poisonous monkey. Cut off the finger, O Dogeetah, or tomorrow I die.'

"'Why do you not tell your own doctors to cut off the finger, you who are Kalubi, Chief of the Pongo?'

"'No, no,' he replied, shaking his head. 'They cannot do it. It is not lawful. And I, I cannot do it, for if the flesh is black the hand must come off too, and if the flesh is black at the wrist, then the arm must be cut off.'

"I sat down on my camp stool and reflected. Really I was waiting for the sun to rise, since it was useless to attempt an operation in that light. The man, Kalubi, thought that I had refused his petition and became terribly agitated.

"'Be merciful, White Lord,' he prayed, 'do not let me die. I am afraid to die. Life is bad, but death is worse. O! If you refuse me, I will kill myself here before you and then my ghost will haunt you till you die also of fear and come to join me. What fee do you ask? Gold or ivory or slaves? Say and I will give it.'

"'Be silent,' I said, for I saw that if he went on thus he would throw himself into a fever, which might cause the operation to prove fatal. For the same reason I did not question him about many things I should have liked to learn. I lit my fire and boiled the instruments--he thought I was making magic. By the time that everything was ready the sun was up.

"'Now,' I said, 'let me see how brave you are.'

"Well, Allan, I performed that operation, removing the finger at the base where it joins the hand, as I thought there might be something in his story of the poison. Indeed, as I found afterwards on dissection, and can show you, for I have the thing in spirits, there was, for the blackness of which he spoke, a kind of mortification, I presume, had crept almost to the joint, though the flesh beyond was healthy enough. Certainly that Kalubi was a plucky fellow. He sat like a rock and never even winced. Indeed, when he saw that the flesh was sound he uttered a great sigh of relief. After it was all over he turned a little faint, so I gave him some spirits of wine mixed with water which revived him.

"'O Lord Dogeetah,' he said, as I was bandaging his hand, 'while I live I am your slave. Yet, do me one more service. In my land there is a terrible wild beast, that which bit off my finger. It is a devil; it kills us and we fear it. I have heard that you white men have magic weapons which slay with a noise. Come to my land and kill me that wild beast with your magic weapon. I say, Come, Come, for I am terribly afraid,' and indeed he looked it.

"'No,' I answered, 'I shed no blood; I kill nothing except butterflies, and of these only a few. But if you fear this brute why do you not poison it? You black people have many drugs.'

"'No use, no use,' he replied in a kind of wail. 'The beast knows poisons, some it swallows and they do not harm it. Others it will not touch. Moreover, no black man can do it hurt. It is white, and it has been known from of old that if it dies at all, it must be by the hand of one who is white.'

"'A very strange animal,' I began, suspiciously, for I felt sure that he was lying to me. But just at that moment I heard the sound of my men's voices. They were advancing towards me through the giant grass, singing as they came, but as yet a long way off. The Kalubi heard it also and sprang up.

"'I must be gone,' he said. 'None must see me here. What fee, O Lord of medicine, what fee?'

"'I take no payment for my medicine,' I said. 'Yet--stay. A wonderful flower grows in your country, does it not? A flower with wings and a cup beneath. I would have that flower.'

"'Who told you of the Flower?' he asked. 'The Flower is holy. Still, O White Lord, still for you it shall be risked. Oh, return and bring with you one who can kill the beast and I will make you rich. Return and call to the reeds for the Kalubi, and the Kalubi will hear and come to you.'

"Then he ran to his spear, snatched it from the ground and vanished among the reeds. That was the last I saw, or am ever likely to see, of him."

"But, Brother John, you got the flower somehow."

"Yes, Allan. About a week later when I came out of my tent one morning, there it was standing in a narrow-mouthed, earthenware pot filled with water. Of course I meant that he was to send me the plant, roots and all, but I suppose he understood that I wanted a bloom. Or perhaps he dared not send the plant. Anyhow, it is better than nothing."

"Why did you not go into the country and get it for yourself?"

"For several reasons, Allan, of which the best is that it was impossible. The Mazitu swear that if anyone sees that flower he is put to death. Indeed, when they found that I had a bloom of it, they forced me to move to the other side of the country seventy miles away. So I thought that I would wait till I met with some companions who would accompany me. Indeed, to be frank, Allan, it occurred to me that you were the sort of man who would like to interview this wonderful beast that bites off people's fingers and frightens them to death," and Brother John stroked his long, white beard and smiled, adding, "Odd that we should have met so soon afterwards, isn't it?"

"Did you?" I replied, "now did you indeed? Brother John, people say all sorts of things about you, but I have come to the conclusion that there's nothing the matter with your wits."

Again he smiled and stroked his long, white beard.

The Auction Room

I do not think that this conversion about the Pongo savages who were said to worship a Gorilla and a Golden Flower was renewed until we reached my house at Durban. Thither of course I took Mr. Charles Scroope, and thither also came Brother John who, as bedroom accommodation was lacking, pitched his tent in the garden.

One night we sat on the step smoking; Brother John's only concession to human weakness was that he smoked. He drank no wine or spirits; he never ate meat unless he was obliged, but I rejoice to say that he smoked cigars, like most Americans, when he could get them.

"John," said I, "I have been thinking over that yarn of yours and have come to one or two conclusions."

"What may they be, Allan?"

"The first is that you were a great donkey not to get more out of the Kalubi when you had the chance."

"Agreed, Allan, but, amongst other things, I am a doctor and the operation was uppermost in my mind."

"The second is that I believe this Kalubi had charge of the gorilla- god, as no doubt you've guessed; also that it was the gorilla which bit off his finger."

"Why so?"

"Because I have heard of great monkeys called *sokos* that live in Central East Africa which are said to bite off men's toes and fingers. I have heard too that they are very like gorillas."

"Now you mention it, so have I, Allan. Indeed, once I saw a *soko*, though some way off, a huge, brown ape which stood on its hind legs and drummed upon its chest with its fists. I didn't see it for long because I ran away."

"The third is that this yellow orchid would be worth a great deal of money if one could dig it up and take it to England."

"I think I told you, Allan, that I valued it at £20,000, so that conclusion of yours is not original."

"The fourth is that I should like to dig up that orchid and get a share of the £20,000."

Brother John became intensely interested.

"Ah!" he said, "now we are getting to the point. I have been wondering how long it would take you to see it, Allan, but if you are slow, you are sure."

"The fifth is," I went on, "that such an expedition to succeed would need a great deal of money, more than you or I could find. Partners would be wanted, active or sleeping, but partners with cash."

Brother John looked towards the window of the room in which Charlie Scroope was in bed, for being still weak he went to rest early.

"No," I said, "he's had enough of Africa, and you told me yourself that it will be two years before he is really strong again. Also there's a lady in this case. Now listen. I have taken it on myself to write to that lady, whose address I found out while he didn't know what he was saying. I have said that he was dying, but that I hoped he might live. Meanwhile, I added, I thought she would like to know that he did nothing but rave of her; also that he was a hero, with a big H twice underlined. My word! I did lay it on about the hero business with a spoon, a real hotel gravy spoon. If Charlie Scroope knows himself again when he sees my description of him, well, I'm a Dutchman, that's all. The letter caught the last mail and will, I hope, reach the lady in due course. Now listen again. Scroope wants me to go to England with him to look after him on the voyage--that's what he says. What he means is that he hopes I might put in a word for him with the lady, if I should chance to be introduced to her. He offers to pay all my expenses and to give me something for my loss of time. So, as I haven't seen England since I was three years old, I think I'll take the chance."

Brother John's face fell. "Then how about the expedition, Allan?" he asked.

"This is the first of November," I answered, "and the wet season in those parts begins about now and lasts till April. So it would be no use trying to visit your Pongo friends till then, which gives me plenty of time to go to England and come out again. If you'll trust that flower to me I'll take it with me. Perhaps I might be able to find someone who would be willing to put down money on the chance of getting the plant on which it grew. Meanwhile, you are welcome to this house if you care to stay here."

"Thank you, Allan, but I can't sit still for so many months. I'll go somewhere and come back." He paused and a dreamy look came into his dark eyes, then went on, "You see, Brother, it is laid on me to wander and wander through all this great land until--I know."

"Until you know what?" I asked, sharply.

He pulled himself together with a jerk, as it were, and answered with a kind of forced carelessness.

"Until I know every inch of it, of course. There are lots of tribes I have not yet visited."

"Including the Pongo," I said. "By the way, if I can get the money together for a trip up there, I suppose you mean to come too, don't you? If not, the thing's off so far as I am concerned. You see, I am reckoning on you to get us through the Mazitu and into Pongo-land by the help of your friends."

"Certainly I mean to come. In fact, if you don't go, I shall start alone. I intend to explore Pongo-land even if I never come out of it again."

Once more I looked at him as I answered:

"You are ready to risk a great deal for a flower, John. Or are you looking for more than a flower? If so, I hope you will tell me the truth."

This I said as I was aware that Brother John had a foolish objection to uttering, or even acting lies.

"Well, Allan, as you put it like that, the truth is that I heard something more about the Pongo than I told you up country. It was after I had operated on that Kalubi, or I would have tried to get in alone. But this I could not do then as I have said."

"And what did you hear?"

"I heard that they had a white goddess as well as a white god."

"Well, what of it? A female gorilla, I suppose."

"Nothing, except that goddesses have always interested me. Good night."

"You are an odd old fish," I remarked after him, "and what is more you have got something up your sleeve. Well, I'll have it down one day. Meanwhile, I wonder whether the whole thing is a lie, no; not a lie, an hallucination. It can't be--because of that orchid. No one can explain away the orchid. A queer people, these Pongo, with their white god and goddess and their Holy Flower. But after all Africa is a land of queer people, and of queer gods too."

And now the story shifts away to England. (Don't be afraid, my adventurous reader, if ever I have one, it is coming back to Africa again in a very few pages.)

Mr. Charles Scroope and I left Durban a day or two after my last conversation with Brother John. At Cape Town we caught the mail, a wretched little boat you would think it now, which after a long and wearisome journey at length landed us safe at Plymouth. Our companions on that voyage were very dull. I have forgotten most of them, but one lady I do remember. I imagine that she must have commenced life as a barmaid, for she had the orthodox tow hair and blowsy appearance. At any rate, she was the wife of a wine-merchant who had made a fortune at the Cape. Unhappily, however, she had contracted too great a liking for her husband's wares, and after dinner was apt to become talkative. For some reason or other she took a particular aversion to me. Oh! I can see her now, seated in that saloon with the oil lamp swinging over her head (she always chose the position under the oil lamp because it showed off her diamonds). And I can hear her too. "Don't bring any of your elephant-hunting manners here, Mr. Allan" (with an emphasis on the Allan) "Quatermain, they are not fit for polite society. You should go and brush your hair, Mr. Quatermain." (I may explain that my hair sticks up naturally.)

Then would come her little husband's horrified "Hush! hush! you are quite insulting, my dear."

Oh! why do I remember it all after so many years when I have even forgotten the people's names? One of those little things that stick in the mind, I suppose. The Island of Ascension, where we called, sticks also with its long swinging rollers breaking in white foam, its bare mountain peak capped with green, and the turtles in the ponds. Those poor turtles. We brought two of them home, and I used to look at them lying on their backs in the forecastle flapping their fins feebly. One of them died, and I got the butcher to save me the shell. Afterwards I gave it as a wedding present to Mr. and Mrs. Scroope, nicely polished and lined. I meant it for a work-basket, and was overwhelmed with confusion when some silly lady said at the marriage, and in the hearing of the bride and bridegroom, that it was the most beautiful cradle she had ever seen. Of course, like a fool, I tried to explain, whereon everybody tittered.

But why do I write of such trifles that have nothing to do with my story?

I mentioned that I had ventured to send a letter to Miss Margaret Manners about Mr. Charles Scroope, in which I said incidentally that if the hero should happen to live I should probably bring him home by the next mail. Well, we got into Plymouth about eight o'clock in the morning, on a mild, November day, and shortly afterwards a tug arrived to take off the passengers and mails; also some cargo. I, being an early riser, watched it come and saw upon the deck a stout lady wrapped in furs, and by her side a very pretty, fair-haired young woman clad in a neat serge dress and a pork-pie hat. Presently a steward told me that someone wished to speak to me in the saloon. I went and found these two standing side by side.

"I believe you are Mr. Allan Quatermain," said the stout lady. "Where is Mr. Scroope whom I understand you have brought home? Tell me at once."

Something about her appearance and fierce manner of address alarmed me so much that I could only answer feebly:

"Below, madam, below."

"There, my dear," said the stout lady to her companion, "I warned you to be prepared for the worst. Bear up; do not make a scene before all these people. The ways of Providence are just and inscrutable. It is your own temper that was to blame. You should never have sent the poor man off to these heathen countries."

Then, turning to me, she added sharply: "I suppose he is embalmed; we should like to bury him in Essex."

"Embalmed!" I gasped. "Embalmed! Why, the man is in his bath, or was a few minutes ago."

In another second that pretty young lady who had been addressed was weeping with her head upon my shoulder.

"Margaret!" exclaimed her companion (she was a kind of heavy aunt), "I told you not to make a scene in public. Mr. Quatermain, as Mr. Scroope is alive, would you ask him to be so good as to come here."

Well, I fetched him, half-shaved, and the rest of the business may be imagined. It is a very fine thing to be a hero with a big H. Henceforth (thanks to me) that was Charlie Scroope's lot in life. He has grandchildren now, and they all think him a hero.

What is more, he does not contradict them. I went down to the lady's place in Essex, a fine property with a beautiful old house. On the night I arrived there was a dinner-party of twenty-four people. I had to make a speech about Charlie Scroope and the leopard. I think it was a good speech. At any rate everybody cheered, including the servants, who had gathered at the back of the big hall.

I remember that to complete the story I introduced several other leopards, a mother and two three-part-grown cubs, also a wounded buffalo, and told how Mr. Scroope finished them off one after the other with a hunting knife. The thing was to watch his face as the history proceeded. Luckily he was sitting next to me and I could kick him under the table. It was all very amusing, and very happy also, for these two really loved each other. Thank God that I, or rather Brother John, was able to bring them together again.

It was during that stay of mine in Essex, by the way, that I first met Lord Ragnall and the beautiful Miss Holmes with whom I was destined to experience some very strange adventures in the after years.

After this interlude I got to work. Someone told me that there was a firm in the City that made a business of selling orchids by auction, flowers which at this time were beginning to be very fashionable among rich horticulturists. This, thought I, would be the place for me to show my treasure. Doubtless Messrs. May and Primrose--that was their world-famed style--would be able to put me in touch with opulent orchidists who would not mind venturing a couple of thousands on the chance of receiving a share in a flower that, according to Brother John, should be worth untold gold. At any rate, I would try.

So on a certain Friday, about half-past twelve, I sought out the place of business of Messrs. May and Primrose, bearing with me the golden Cypripedium, which was now enclosed in a flat tin case.

As it happened I chose an unlucky day and hour, for on arriving at the office and asking for Mr. May, I was informed that he was away in the country valuing.

"Then I would like to see Mr. Primrose," I said.

"Mr. Primrose is round at the Rooms selling," replied the clerk, who appeared to be very busy.

"Where are the Rooms?" I asked.

"Out of the door, turn to the left, turn to the left again and under the clock," said the clerk, and closed the shutter.

So disgusted was I with his rudeness that I nearly gave up the enterprise. Thinking better of it, however, I followed the directions given, and in a minute or two found myself in a narrow passage that led to a large room. To one who had never seen anything of the sort before, this room offered a curious sight. The first thing I observed was a notice on the wall to the effect that customers were not allowed to smoke pipes. I thought to myself that orchids must be curious flowers if they could distinguish between the smoke of a cigar and a pipe, and stepped into the room. To my left was a long table covered with pots of the most beautiful flowers that I had ever seen; all of them orchids. Along the wall and opposite were other tables closely packed with withered roots which I concluded were also those of orchids. To my inexperienced eye the whole lot did not look worth five shillings, for they seemed to be dead.

At the head of the room stood the rostrum, where sat a gentleman with an extremely charming face. He was engaged in selling by auction so rapidly that the clerk at his side must have had difficulty in keeping a record of the lots and their purchasers. In front of him was a horseshoe table, round which sat buyers. The end of this table was left unoccupied so that the porters might exhibit each lot before it was put up for sale. Standing under the rostrum was yet another table, a small one, upon which were about twenty pots of flowers, even more wonderful than those on the large table. A notice stated that these would be sold at one-thirty precisely. All about the room stood knots of men (such ladies as were present sat at the table), many of whom had lovely orchids in their buttonholes. These, I found out afterwards, were dealers and amateurs. They were a kindly-faced set of people, and I took a liking to them.

The whole place was quaint and pleasant, especially by contrast with the horrible London fog outside. Squeezing my small person into a corner where I was in nobody's way, I watched the proceedings for a while. Suddenly an agreeable voice at my side asked me if I would like a look at the catalogue. I glanced at the speaker, and in a sense fell in love with him at once--as I have explained before, I am one of those to whom a first impression means a great deal. He was not very tall, though strong-looking and well-made enough. He was not very handsome, though none so ill-favoured. He was just an ordinary fair young Englishman, four or five-and-twenty years of age, with merry blue eyes and one of the pleasantest expressions that I ever saw. At once I felt that he was a sympathetic soul and full of the milk of human kindness. He was dressed in a rough tweed suit rather worn, with the orchid that seemed to be the badge of all this tribe in his buttonhole. Somehow the costume suited his rather pink and white complexion and rumpled fair hair, which I could see as he was sitting on his cloth hat.

"Thank you, no," I answered, "I did not come here to buy. I know nothing about orchids," I added by way of explanation, "except a few I have seen growing in Africa, and this one," and I tapped the tin case which I held under my arm.

"Indeed," he said. "I should like to hear about the African orchids. What is it you have in the case, a plant or flowers?"

"One flower only. It is not mine. A friend in Africa asked me to-- well, that is a long story which might not interest you."

"I'm not sure. I suppose it must be a Cymbidium scape from the size."

I shook my head. "That's not the name my friend mentioned. He called it a Cypripedium."

The young man began to grow curious. "One Cypripedium in all that large case? It must be a big flower."

"Yes, my friend said it is the biggest ever found. It measures twenty- four inches across the wings, petals I think he called them, and about a foot across the back part."

"Twenty-four inches across the petals and a foot across the dorsal sepal!" said the young man in a kind of gasp, "and a Cypripedium! Sir, surely you are joking?"

"Sir," I answered indignantly, "I am doing nothing of the sort. Your remark is tantamount to telling me that I am speaking a falsehood. But, of course, for all I know, the thing may be some other kind of flower."

"Let me see it. In the name of the goddess Flora let me see it!"

I began to undo the case. Indeed it was already half-open when two other gentlemen, who had either overheard some of our conversation or noted my companion's excited look, edged up to us. I observed that they also wore orchids in their buttonholes.

"Hullo! Somers," said one of them in a tone of false geniality, "what have you got there?"

"What has your friend got there?" asked the other.

"Nothing," replied the young man who had been addressed as Somers, "nothing at all; that is--only a case of tropical butterflies."

"Oh! butterflies," said No. 1 and sauntered away. But No. 2, a keen- looking person with the eye of a hawk, was not so easily satisfied.

"Let us see these butterflies," he said to me.

"You can't," ejaculated the young man. "My friend is afraid lest the damp should injure their colours. Ain't you, Brown?"

"Yes, I am, Somers," I replied, taking his cue and shutting the tin case with a snap.

Then the hawk-eyed person departed, also grumbling, for that story about the damp stuck in his throat.

"Orchidist!" whispered the young man. "Dreadful people, orchidists, so jealous. Very rich, too, both of them. Mr. Brown--I hope that is your name, though I admit the chances are against it."

"They are," I replied, "my name is Allan Quatermain."

"Ah! much better than Brown. Well, Mr. Allan Quatermain, there's a private room in this place to which I have admittance. Would you mind coming with that----" here the hawk-eyed gentleman strolled past again, "that case of butterflies?"

"With pleasure," I answered, and followed him out of the auction chamber down some steps through the door to the left, and ultimately into a little cupboard-like room lined with shelves full of books and ledgers.

He closed the door and locked it.

"Now," he said in a tone of the villain in a novel who at last has come face to face with the virtuous heroine, "now we are alone. Mr. Quatermain, let me see--those butterflies."

I placed the case on a deal table which stood under a skylight in the room. I opened it; I removed the cover of wadding, and there, pressed between two sheets of glass and quite uninjured after all its journeyings, appeared the golden flower, glorious even in death, and by its side the broad green leaf.

The young gentleman called Somers looked at it till I thought his eyes would really start out of his head. He turned away muttering something and looked again.

"Oh! Heavens," he said at last, "oh! Heavens, is it possible that such a thing can exist in this imperfect world? You haven't faked it, Mr. Half--I mean Quatermain, have you?"

"Sir," I said, "for the second time you are making insinuations. Good morning," and I began to shut up the case.

"Don't be offhanded," he exclaimed. "Pity the weaknesses of a poor sinner. You don't understand. If only you understood, you would understand."

"No," I said, "I am bothered if I do."

"Well, you will when you begin to collect orchids. I'm not mad, really, except perhaps on this point, Mr. Quatermain,"--this in a low and thrilling voice--"that marvellous Cypripedium--your friend is right, it is a Cypripedium--is worth a gold mine."

"From my experience of gold mines I can well believe that," I said tartly, and, I may add, prophetically.

"Oh! I mean a gold mine in the figurative and colloquial sense, not as the investor knows it," he answered. "That is, the plant on which it grew is priceless. Where is the plant, Mr. Quatermain?"

"In a rather indefinite locality in Africa east by south," I replied. "I can't place it to within three hundred miles."

"That's vague, Mr. Quatermain. I have no right to ask it, seeing that you know nothing of me, but I assure you I am respectable, and in short, would you mind telling me the story of this flower?"

"I don't think I should," I replied, a little doubtfully. Then, after another good look at him, suppressing all names and exact localities, I gave him the outline of the tale, explaining that I wanted to find someone who would finance an expedition to the remote and romantic spot where this particular Cypripedium was believed to grow.

Just as I finished my narrative, and before he had time to comment on it, there came a violent knocking at the door.

"Mr. Stephen," said a voice, "are you there, Mr. Stephen?"

"By Jove! that's Briggs," exclaimed the young man. "Briggs is my father's manager. Shut up the case, Mr. Quatermain. Come in, Briggs," he went on, unlocking the door slowly. "What is it?"

"It is a good deal," replied a thin and agitated person who thrust himself through the opening door. "Your father, I mean Sir Alexander, has come to the office unexpectedly and is in a nice taking because he didn't find you there, sir. When he discovered that you had gone to the orchid sale he grew furious, sir, furious, and sent me to fetch you."

"Did he?" replied Mr. Somers in an easy and unruffled tone. "Well, tell Sir Alexander I am coming at once. Now please go, Briggs, and tell him I am coming at once."

Briggs departed not too willingly.

"I must leave you, Mr. Quatermain," said Mr. Somers as he shut the door behind him. "But will you promise me not to show that flower to anyone until I return? I'll be back within half an hour."

"Yes, Mr. Somers. I'll wait half an hour for you in the sale room, and I promise that no one shall see that flower till you return."

"Thank you. You are a good fellow, and I promise you shall lose nothing by your kindness if I can help it."

We went together into the sale room, where some thought suddenly struck Mr. Somers.

"By Jove!" he said, "I nearly forgot about that Odontoglossum. Where's Woodden? Oh! come here, Woodden, I want to speak to you."

The person called Woodden obeyed. He was a man of about fifty, indefinite in colouring, for his eyes were very light-blue or grey and his hair was sandy, tough-looking and strongly made, with big hands that showed signs of work, for the palms were horny and the nails worn down. He was clad in a suit of shiny black, such as folk of the labouring class wear at a funeral. I made up my mind at once that he was a gardener.

"Woodden," said Mr. Somers, "this gentleman here has got the most wonderful orchid in the whole world. Keep your eye on him and see that he isn't robbed. There are people in this room, Mr. Quatermain, who would murder you and throw your body into the Thames for that flower," he added, darkly.

On receipt of this information Woodden rocked a little on his feet as though he felt the premonitory movements of an earthquake. It was a habit of his whenever anything astonished him. Then, fixing his pale eye upon me in a way which showed that my appearance surprised him, he pulled a lock of his sandy hair with his thumb and finger and said:

"'Servant, sir, and where might this horchid be?"

I pointed to the tin case.

"Yes, it's there," went on Mr. Somers, "and that's what you've got to watch. Mr. Quatermain, if anyone attempts to rob you, call for Woodden and he will knock them down. He's my gardener, you know, and entirely to be trusted, especially if it is a matter of knocking anyone down."

"Aye, I'll knock him down surely," said Woodden, doubling his great fist and looking round him with a suspicious eye.

"Now listen, Woodden. Have you looked at that Odontoglossum Pavo, and if so, what do you think of it?" and he nodded towards a plant which stood in the centre of the little group that was placed on the small table beneath the auctioneer's desk. It bore a spray of the most lovely white flowers. On the top petal (if it is a petal), and also on the lip of each of these rounded flowers was a blotch or spot of which the general effect was similar to the iridescent eye on the tail feathers of a peacock, whence, I suppose, the flower was named "Pavo," or Peacock.

"Yes, master, and I think it the beautifullest thing that ever I saw. There isn't a 'glossum in England like that there 'glossum Paving," he added with conviction, and rocked again as he said the word. "But there's plenty after it. I say they're a-smelling round that blossom like, like--dawgs round a rat hole. And" (this triumphantly) "they don't do that for nothing."

"Quite so, Woodden, you have got a logical mind. But, look here, we must have that 'Pavo' whatever it costs. Now the Governor has sent for me. I'll be back presently, but I might be detained. If so, you've got to bid on my behalf, for I daren't trust any of these agents. Here's your authority," and he scribbled on a card, "Woodden, my gardener, has directions to bid for me.--S.S." "Now, Woodden," he went on, when he had given the card to an attendant who passed it up to the auctioneer, "don't you make a fool of yourself and let that 'Pavo' slip through your fingers."

In another instant he was gone.

"What did the master say, sir?" asked Woodden of me. "That I was to get that there 'Paving' whatever it cost?"

"Yes," I said, "that's what he said. I suppose it will fetch a good deal--several pounds."

"Maybe, sir, can't tell. All I know is that I've got to buy it as you can bear me witness. Master, he ain't one to be crossed for money. What he wants, he'll have, that is if it be in the orchid line."

"I suppose you are fond of orchids, too, Mr. Woodden?"

"Fond of them, sir? Why, I loves 'em!" (Here he rocked.) "Don't feel for nothing else in the same way; not even for my old woman" (then with a burst of enthusiasm) "no, not even for the master himself, and I'm fond enough of him, God knows! But, begging your pardon, sir" (with a pull at his forelock), "would you mind holding that tin of yours a little tighter? I've got to keep an eye on that as well as on 'O. Paving,' and I just see'd that chap with the tall hat alooking at it suspicious."

After this we separated. I retired into my corner, while Woodden took his stand by the table, with one eye fixed on what he called the "O. Paving" and the other on me and my tin case.

An odd fish truly, I thought to myself. Positive, the old woman; Comparative, his master; Superlative, the orchid tribe. Those were his degrees of affection. Honest and brave and a good fellow though, I bet.

The sale languished. There were so many lots of one particular sort of dried orchid that buyers could not be found for them at a reasonable price, and many had to be bought in. At length the genial Mr. Primrose in the rostrum addressed the audience.

"Gentlemen," he said, "I quite understand that you didn't come here to-day to buy a rather poor lot of Cattleya Mossiæ. You came to buy, or to bid for, or to see sold the most wonderful Odontoglossum that has ever been flowered in this country, the property of a famous firm of importers whom I congratulate upon their good fortune in having obtained such a gem. Gentlemen, this miraculous flower ought to adorn a royal greenhouse. But there it is, to be taken away by whoever will pay the most for it, for I am directed to see that it will be sold without reserve. Now, I think," he added, running his eye over the company, "that most of our great collectors are represented in this room to-day. It is true that I do not see that spirited and liberal young orchidist, Mr. Somers, but he has left his worthy head-gardener, Mr. Woodden, than whom there is no finer judge of an orchid in England" (here Woodden rocked violently) "to bid for him, as I hope, for the glorious flower of which I have been speaking. Now, as it is exactly half-past one, we will proceed to business. Smith, hand the 'Odontoglossum Pavo' round, that everyone may inspect its beauties, and be careful you don't let it fall. Gentlemen, I must ask you not to touch it or to defile its purity with tobacco smoke. Eight perfect flowers in bloom, gentlemen, and four--no, five more to open. A strong plant in perfect health, six pseudo-bulbs with leaves, and three without. Two black leads which I am advised can be separated off at the proper time. Now, what bids for the 'Odontoglossum Pavo.' Ah! I wonder who will have the honour of becoming the owner of this perfect, this unmatched production of Nature. Thank you, sir--three hundred. Four. Five. Six. Seven in three places. Eight. Nine. Ten. Oh! gentlemen, let us get on a little faster. Thank you, sir--fifteen. Sixteen. It is against you, Mr Woodden. Ah! thank you, seventeen."

There came a pause in the fierce race for "O. Pavo," which I occupied in reducing seventeen hundred shillings to pounds sterling.

My word! I thought to myself, £85 is a goodish price to pay for one plant, however rare. Woodden is acting up to his instructions with a vengeance.

The pleading voice of Mr. Primrose broke in upon my meditations.

"Gentlemen, gentlemen!" he said, "surely you are not going to allow the most wondrous production of the floral world, on which I repeat there is no reserve, to be knocked down at this miserable figure. Come, come. Well, if I must, I must, though after such a disgrace I shall get no sleep to-night. One," and his hammer fell for the first time. "Think, gentlemen, upon my position, think what the eminent owners, who with their usual delicacy have stayed away, will say to me when I am obliged to tell them the disgraceful truth. Two," and his hammer fell a second time. "Smith, hold up that flower. Let the company see it. Let them know what they are losing."

Smith held up the flower at which everybody glared. The little ivory hammer circled round Mr. Primrose's head. It was about to fall, when a quiet man with a long beard who hitherto had not joined in the bidding, lifted his head and said softly:

"Eighteen hundred."

"Ah!" exclaimed Mr. Primrose, "I thought so. I thought that the owner of the greatest collection in England would not see this treasure slip from his grasp without a struggle. Against you, Mr. Woodden."

"Nineteen, sir," said Woodden in a stony voice.

"Two thousand," echoed the gentleman with the long beard.

"Twenty-one hundred," said Woodden.

"That's right, Mr. Woodden," cried Mr. Primrose, "you are indeed representing your principal worthily. I feel sure that you do not mean to stop for a few miserable pounds."

"Not if I knows it," ejaculated Woodden. "I has my orders and I acts up to them."

"Twenty-two hundred," said Long-beard.

"Twenty-three," echoed Woodden.

"Oh, damn!" shouted Long-beard and rushed from the room.

"'Odontoglossum Pavo' is going for twenty-three hundred, only twenty- tree hundred," cried the auctioneer. "Any advance on twenty-three hundred? What? None? Then I must do my duty. One. Two. For the last time--no advance? Three. Gone to Mr. Woodden, bidding for his principal, Mr. Somers."

The hammer fell with a sharp tap, and at this moment my young friend sauntered into the room.

"Well, Woodden," he said, "have they put the 'Pavo' up yet?"

"It's up and it's down, sir. I've bought him right enough."

"The deuce you have! What did it fetch?"

Woodden scratched his head.

"I don't rightly know, sir, never was good at figures, not having much book learning, but it's twenty-three something."

"£23? No, it would have brought more than that. By Jingo! it must be £230. That's pretty stiff, but still, it may be worth it."

At this moment Mr. Primrose, who, leaning over his desk, was engaged in animated conversation with an excited knot of orchid fanciers, looked up:

"Oh! there you are, Mr. Somers," he said. "In the name of all this company let me congratulate you on having become the owner of the matchless 'Odontoglossum Pavo' for what, under all the circumstances, I consider the quite moderate price of £2,300."

Really that young man took it very well. He shivered slightly and turned a little pale, that is all. Woodden rocked to and fro like a tree about to fall. I and my tin box collapsed together in the corner. Yes, I was so surprised that my legs seemed to give way under me. People began to talk, but above the hum of the conversation I heard young Somers say in a low voice:

"Woodden, you're a born fool." Also the answer: "That's what my mother always told me, master, and she ought to know if anyone did. But what's wrong now? I obeyed orders and bought 'O. Paving.'"

"Yes. Don't bother, my good fellow, it's my fault, not yours. I'm the born fool. But heavens above! how am I to face this?" Then, recovering himself, he strolled up to the rostrum and said a few words to the auctioneer. Mr. Primrose nodded, and I heard him answer:

"Oh, that will be all right, sir, don't bother. We can't expect an account like this to be settled in a minute. A month hence will do."

Then he went on with the sale.

Sir Alexander and Stephen

It was just at this moment that I saw standing by me a fine-looking, stout man with a square, grey beard and a handsome, but not very good- tempered face. He was looking about him as one does who finds himself in a place to which he is not accustomed.

"Perhaps you could tell me, sir," he said to me, "whether a gentleman called Mr. Somers is in this room. I am rather short-sighted and there are a great many people."

"Yes," I answered, "he has just bought the wonderful orchid called 'Odontoglossum Pavo.' That is what they are all talking about."

"Oh, has he? Has he indeed? And pray what did he pay for the article?"

"A huge sum," I answered. "I thought it was two thousand three hundred shillings, but it appears it was £2,300."

The handsome, elderly gentleman grew very red in the face, so red that I thought he was going to have a fit. For a few moments he breathed heavily.

"A rival collector," I thought to myself, and went on with the story which, it occurred to me, might interest him.

"You see, the young gentleman was called away to an interview with his father. I heard him instruct his gardener, a man named Woodden, to buy the plant at any price."

"At any price! Indeed. Very interesting; continue, sir."

"Well, the gardener bought it, that's all, after tremendous competition. Look, there he is packing it up. Whether his master meant him to go as far as he did I rather doubt. But here he comes. If you know him----"

The youthful Mr. Somers, looking a little pale and *distrait*, strolled up apparently to speak to me; his hands were in his pockets and an unlighted cigar was in his mouth. His eyes fell upon the elderly gentleman, a sight that caused him to shape his lips as though to whistle and drop the cigar.

"Hullo, father," he said in his pleasant voice. "I got your message and have been looking for you, but never thought that I should find you here. Orchids aren't much in your line, are they?"

"Didn't you, indeed!" replied his parent in a choked voice. "No, I haven't much use for--this stinking rubbish," and he waved his umbrella at the beautiful flowers. "But it seems that you have, Stephen. This little gentlemen here tells me you have just bought a very fine specimen."

"I must apologize," I broke in, addressing Mr. Somers. "I had not the slightest idea that this--big gentleman," here the son smiled faintly, "was your intimate relation."

"Oh! pray don't, Mr. Quatermain. Why should you not speak of what will be in all the papers. Yes, father, I have bought a very fine specimen, the finest known, or at least Woodden has on my behalf, while I was hunting for you, which comes to the same thing."

"Indeed, Stephen, and what did you pay for this flower? I have heard a figure, but think that there must be some mistake."

"I don't know what you heard, father, but it seems to have been knocked down to me at £2,300. It's a lot more than I can find, indeed, and I was going to ask you to lend me the money for the sake of the family credit, if not for my own. But we can talk about that afterwards."

"Yes, Stephen, we can talk of that afterwards. In fact, as there is no time like the present, we will talk of it now. Come to my office. And, sir" (this was to me) "as you seem to know something of the circumstances, I will ask you to come also; and you too, Blockhead" (this was to Woodden, who just then approached with the plant).

Now, of course, I might have refused an invitation conveyed in such a manner. But, as a matter of fact, I didn't. I wanted to see the thing out; also to put in a word for young Somers, if I got the chance. So we all departed from that room, followed by a titter of amusement from those of the company who had overheard the conversation. In the street stood a splendid carriage and pair; a powdered footman opened its door. With a ferocious bow Sir Alexander motioned to me to enter, which I did, taking one of the back seats as it gave more room for my tin case. Then came Mr. Stephen, then Woodden bundled in holding the precious plant in front of him like a wand of office, and last of all, Sir Alexander, having seen us safe, entered also.

"Where to, sir?" asked the footman.

"Office," he snapped, and we started.

Four disappointed relatives in a funeral coach could not have been more silent. Our feelings seemed to be too deep for words. Sir Alexander, however, did make one remark and to me. It was:

"If you will remove the corner of that infernal tin box of yours from my ribs I shall be obliged to you, sir."

"Your pardon," I exclaimed, and in my efforts to be accommodating, dropped it on his toe. I will not repeat the remark he made, but I may explain that he was gouty. His son suddenly became afflicted with a sense of the absurdity of the situation. He kicked me on the shin, he even dared to wink, and then began to swell visibly with suppressed laughter. I was in agony, for if he had exploded I do not know what would have happened. Fortunately, at this moment the carriage stopped at the door of a fine office. Without waiting for the footman Mr. Stephen bundled out and vanished into the building--I suppose to laugh in safety. Then I descended with the tin case; then, by command, followed Woodden with the flower, and lastly came Sir Alexander.

"Stop here," he said to the coachman; "I shan't be long. Be so good as to follow me, Mr. What's-your-name, and you, too, Gardener."

We followed, and found ourselves in a big room luxuriously furnished in a heavy kind of way. Sir Alexander Somers, I should explain, was an enormously opulent bullion-broker, whatever a bullion-broker may be. In this room Mr. Stephen was already established; indeed, he was seated on the window-sill swinging his leg.

"Now we are alone and comfortable," growled Sir Alexander with sarcastic ferocity.

"As the boa-constrictor said to the rabbit in the cage," I remarked.

I did not mean to say it, but I had grown nervous, and the thought leapt from my lips in words. Again Mr. Stephen began to swell. He turned his face to the window as though to contemplate the wall beyond, but I could see his shoulders shaking. A dim light of intelligence shone in Woodden's pale eyes. About three minutes later the joke got home. He gurgled something about boa-constrictors and rabbits and gave a short, loud laugh. As for Sir Alexander, he merely said:

"I did not catch your remark, sir, would you be so good as to repeat it?"

As I appeared unwilling to accept the invitation, he went on:

"Perhaps, then, you would repeat what you told me in that sale-room?"

"Why should I?" I asked. "I spoke quite clearly and you seemed to understand."

"You are right," replied Sir Alexander; "to waste time is useless." He wheeled round on Woodden, who was standing near the door still holding the paper-wrapped plant in front of him. "Now, Blockhead," he shouted, "tell me why you brought that thing."

Woodden made no answer, only rocked a little. Sir Alexander reiterated his command. This time Woodden set the plant upon a table and replied:

"If you're aspeaking to me, sir, that baint my name, and what's more, if you calls me so again, I'll punch your head, whoever you be," and very deliberately he rolled up the sleeves on his brawny arms, a sight at which I too began to swell with inward merriment.

"Look here, father," said Mr. Stephen, stepping forward. "What's the use of all this? The thing's perfectly plain. I did tell Woodden to buy the plant at any price. What is more I gave him a written authority which was passed up to the auctioneer. There's no getting out of it. It is true it never occurred to me that it would go for anything like £2,300--the odd £300 was more my idea, but Woodden only obeyed his orders, and ought not to be abused for doing so."

"There's what I call a master worth serving," remarked Woodden.

"Very well, young man," said Sir Alexander, "you have purchased this article. Will you be so good as to tell me how you propose it should be paid for."

"I propose, father, that you should pay for it," replied Mr. Stephen sweetly. "Two thousand three hundred pounds, or ten times that amount, would not make you appreciably poorer. But if, as is probable, you take a different view, then I propose to pay for it myself. As you know a certain sum of money came to me under my mother's will in which you have only a life interest. I shall raise the amount upon that security--or otherwise."

If Sir Alexander had been angry before, now he became like a mad bull in a china shop. He pranced round the room; he used language that should not pass the lips of any respectable merchant of bullion; in short, he did everything that a person in his position ought not to do. When he was tired he rushed to a desk, tore a cheque from a book and filled it in for a sum of £2,300 to bearer, which cheque he blotted, crumpled up and literally threw at the head of his son.

"You worthless, idle young scoundrel," he bellowed. "I put you in this office here that you may learn respectable and orderly habits and in due course succeed to a very comfortable business. What happens? You don't take a ha'porth of interest in bullion-broking, a subject of which I believe you to remain profoundly ignorant. You don't even spend your money, or rather my money, upon any gentleman-like vice, such as horse-racing, or cards, or even--well, never mind. No, you take to flowers, miserable, beastly flowers, things that a cow eats and clerks grow in back gardens."

"An ancient and Arcadian taste. Adam is supposed to have lived in a garden," I ventured to interpolate.

"Perhaps you would ask your friend with the stubbly hair to remain quiet," snorted Sir Alexander. "I was about to add, although for the sake of my name I meet your debts, that I have had enough of this kind of thing. I disinherit you, or will do if I live till 4 p.m. when the lawyer's office shuts, for thank God! there are no entailed estates, and I dismiss you from the firm. You can go and earn your living in any way you please, by orchid-hunting if you like." He paused, gasping for breath.

"Is that all, father?" asked Mr. Stephen, producing a cigar from his pocket.

"No, it isn't, you cold-blooded young beggar. That house you occupy at Twickenham is mine. You will be good enough to clear out of it; I wish to take possession."

"I suppose, father, I am entitled to a week's notice like any other tenant," said Mr. Stephen, lighting the cigar. "In fact," he added, "if you answer no, I think I shall ask you to apply for an ejection order. You will understand that I have arrangements to make before taking a fresh start in life."

"Oh! curse your cheek, you--you--cucumber!" raged the infuriated merchant prince. Then an inspiration came to him. "You think more of an ugly flower than of your father, do you? Well, at least I'll put an end to that," and he made a dash at the plant on the table with the evident intention of destroying the same.

But the watching Woodden saw. With a kind of lurch he interposed his big frame between Sir Alexander and the object of his wrath.

"Touch 'O. Paving' and I knocks yer down," he drawled out.

Sir Alexander looked at "O. Paving," then he looked at Woodden's leg- of-mutton fist, and--changed his mind.

"Curse 'O. Paving,'" he said, "and everyone who has to do with it," and swung out of the room, banging the door behind him.

"Well, that's over," said Mr. Stephen gently, as he fanned himself with a pocket-handkerchief. "Quite exciting while it lasted, wasn't it, Mr. Quatermain--but I have been there before, so to speak. And now what do you say to some luncheon? Pym's is close by, and they have very good oysters. Only I think we'll drive round by the bank and hand in this cheque. When he's angry my parent is capable of anything. He might even stop it. Woodden, get off down to Twickenham with 'O. Pavo.' Keep it warm, for it feels rather like frost. Put it in the stove for to-night and give it a little, just a little tepid water, but be careful not to touch the flower. Take a four-wheeled cab, it's slow but safe, and mind you keep the windows up and don't smoke. I shall be home for dinner."

Woodden pulled his forelock, seized the pot in his left hand, and departed with his right fist raised--I suppose in case Sir Alexander should be waiting for him round the corner.

Then we departed also and, after stopping for a minute at the bank to pay in the cheque, which I noted, notwithstanding its amount, was accepted without comment, ate oysters in a place too crowded to allow of conversation.

"Mr. Quatermain," said my host, "it is obvious that we cannot talk here, and much less look at that orchid of yours, which I want to study at leisure. Now, for a week or so at any rate I have a roof over my head, and in short, will you be my guest for a night or two? I know nothing about you, and of me you only know that I am the disinherited son of a father, to whom I have failed to give satisfaction. Still it is possible that we might pass a few pleasant hours together talking of flowers and other things; that is, if you have no previous engagement."

"I have none," I answered. "I am only a stranger from South Africa lodging at an hotel. If you will give me time to call for my bag, I will pass the night at your house with pleasure."

By the aid of Mr. Somers' smart dog-cart, which was waiting at a city mews, we reached Twickenham while there was still half an hour of daylight. The house, which was called Verbena Lodge, was small, a square, red-brick building of the early Georgian period, but the gardens covered quite an acre of ground and were very beautiful, or must have been so in summer. Into the greenhouse we did not enter, because it was too late to see the flowers. Also, just when we came to them, Woodden arrived in his four-wheeled cab and departed with his master to see to the housing of "O. Pavo."

Then came dinner, a very pleasant meal. My host had that day been turned out upon the world, but he did not allow this circumstance to interfere with his spirits in the least. Also he was evidently determined to enjoy its good things while they lasted, for his champagne and port were excellent.

"You see, Mr. Quatermain," he said, "it's just as well we had the row which has been boiling up for a long while. My respected father has made so much money that he thinks I should go and do likewise. Now I don't see it. I like flowers, especially orchids, and I hate bullion- broking. To me the only decent places in London are that sale-room where we met and the Horticultural Gardens."

"Yes," I answered rather doubtfully, "but the matter seems a little serious. Your parent was very emphatic as to his intentions, and after this kind of thing," and I pointed to the beautiful silver and the port, "how will you like roughing it in a hard world?"

"Don't think I shall mind a bit; it would be rather a pleasant change. Also, even if my father doesn't alter his mind, as he may, for he likes me at bottom because I resemble my dear mother, things ain't so very bad. I have got some money that she left me, £6,000 or £7,000, and I'll sell that 'Odontoglossum Pavo' for what it will fetch to Sir Joshua Tredgold--he was the man with the long beard who you tell me ran up

Woodden to over £2,000--or failing him to someone else. I'll write about it to-night. I don't think I have any debts to speak of, for the Governor has been allowing me £3,000 a year, at least that is my share of the profits paid to me in return for my bullion-broking labours, and except flowers, I have no expensive tastes. So the devil take the past, here's to the future and whatever it may bring," and he polished off the glass of port he held and laughed in his jolly fashion.

Really he was a most attractive young man, a little reckless, it is true, but then recklessness and youth mix well, like brandy and soda.

I echoed the toast and drank off my port, for I like a good glass of wine when I can get it, as would anyone who has had to live for months on rotten water, although I admit that agrees with me better than the port.

"Now, Mr. Quatermain," he went on, "if you have done, light your pipe and let's go into the other room and study that Cypripedium of yours. I shan't sleep to-night unless I see it again first. Stop a bit, though, we'll get hold of that old ass, Woodden, before he turns in."

"Woodden," said his master, when the gardener had arrived, "this gentleman, Mr. Quatermain, is going to show you an orchid that is ten times finer than 'O. Pavo!'"

"Beg pardon, sir," answered Woodden, "but if Mr. Quatermain says that, he lies. It ain't in Nature; it don't bloom nowhere."

I opened the case and revealed the golden Cypripedium. Woodden stared at it and rocked. Then he stared again and felt his head as though to make sure it was on his shoulders. Then he gasped.

"Well, if that there flower baint made up, it's a MASTER ONE! If I could see that there flower ablowing on the plant I'd die happy."

"Woodden, stop talking, and sit down," exclaimed his master. "Yes, there, where you can look at the flower. Now, Mr. Quatermain, will you tell us the story of that orchid from beginning to end. Of course omitting its habitat if you like, for it isn't fair to ask that secret. Woodden can be trusted to hold his tongue, and so can I."

I remarked that I was sure they could, and for the next half-hour talked almost without interruption, keeping nothing back and explaining that I was anxious to find someone who would finance an expedition to search for this particular plant; as I believed, the only one of its sort that existed in the world.

"How much will it cost?" asked Mr. Somers.

"I lay it at £2,000," I answered. "You see, we must have plenty of men and guns and stores, also trade goods and presents."

"I call that cheap. But supposing, Mr. Quatermain, that the expedition proves successful and the plant is secured, what then?"

"Then I propose that Brother John, who found it and of whom I have told you, should take one-third of whatever it might sell for, that I as captain of the expedition should take one-third, and that whoever finds the necessary money should take the remaining third."

"Good! That's settled."

"What's settled?" I asked.

"Why, that we should divide in the proportions you named, only I bargain to be allowed to take my whack in kind--I mean in plant, and to have the first option of purchasing the rest of the plant at whatever value may be agreed upon."

"But, Mr. Somers, do you mean that you wish to find £2,000 and make this expedition in person?"

"Of course I do. I thought you understood that. That is, if you will have me. Your old friend, the lunatic, you and I will together seek for and find this golden flower. I say that's settled."

On the morrow accordingly, it was settled with the help of a document, signed in duplicate by both of us.

Before these arrangements were finally concluded, however, I insisted that Mr.

Somers should meet my late companion, Charlie Scroope, when I was not present, in order that the latter might give him a full and particular report concerning myself. Apparently the interview was satisfactory, at least so I judged from the very cordial and even respectful manner in which young Somers met me after it was over. Also I thought it my duty to explain to him with much clearness in the presence of Scroope as a witness, the great dangers of such an enterprise as that on which he proposed to embark. I told him straight out that he must be prepared to find his death in it from starvation, fever, wild beasts or at the hands of savages, while success was quite problematical and very likely would not be attained.

"*You* are taking these risks," he said.

"Yes," I answered, "but they are incident to the rough trade I follow, which is that of a hunter and explorer. Moreover, my youth is past, and I have gone through experiences and bereavements of which you know nothing, that cause me to set a very slight value on life. I care little whether I die or continue in the world for some few added years. Lastly, the excitement of adventure has become a kind of necessity for me. I do not think that I could live in England for very long. Also I'm a fatalist. I believe that when my time comes I must go, that this hour is foreordained and that nothing I can do will either hasten or postpone it by one moment. Your circumstances are different. You are quite young. If you stay here and approach your father in a proper spirit, I have no doubt but that he will forget all the rough words he said to you the other day, for which indeed you know you gave him some provocation. Is it worth while throwing up such prospects and undertaking such dangers for the chance of finding a rare flower? I say this to my own disadvantage, since I might find it hard to discover anyone else who would risk £2,000 upon such a venture, but I do urge you to weigh my words."

Young Somers looked at me for a little while, then he broke into one of his hearty laughs and exclaimed, "Whatever else you may be, Mr. Allan Quatermain, you are a gentleman. No bullion-broker in the City could have put the matter more fairly in the teeth of his own interests."

"Thank you," I said.

"For the rest," he went on, "I too am tired of England and want to see the world. It isn't the golden Cypripedium that I seek, although I should like to win it well enough. That's only a symbol. What I seek are adventure and romance. Also, like you I am a fatalist. God chose His own time to send us here, and I presume that He will choose His own time to take us away again. So I leave the matter of risks to Him."

"Yes, Mr. Somers," I replied rather solemnly. "You may find adventure and romance, there are plenty of both in Africa. Or you may find a nameless grave in some fever-haunted swamp. Well, you have chosen, and I like your spirit."

Still I was so little satisfied about this business, that a week or so before we sailed, after much consideration, I took it upon myself to write a letter to Sir Alexander Somers, in which I set forth the whole matter as clearly as I could, not blinking the dangerous nature of our undertaking. In conclusion, I asked him whether he thought it wise to allow his only son to accompany such an expedition, mainly because of a not very serious quarrel with himself.

As no answer came to this letter I went on with our preparations. There was money in plenty, since the re-sale of "O. Pavo" to Sir Joshua Tredgold, at some loss, had been satisfactorily carried out, which enabled me to invest in all things needful with a cheerful heart. Never before had I been provided with such an outfit as that which preceded us to the ship.

At length the day of departure came. We stood on the platform at Paddington waiting for the Dartmouth train to start, for in those days the African mail sailed from that port. A minute or two before the train left, as we were preparing to enter our carriage I caught sight of a face that I seemed to recognise, the owner of which was evidently searching for someone in the crowd. It was that of Briggs, Sir Alexander's clerk, whom I had met in the sale-room.

"Mr. Briggs," I said as he passed me, "are you looking for Mr. Somers? If so, he is in here."

The clerk jumped into the compartment and handed a letter to Mr. Somers. Then he emerged again and waited. Somers read the letter and tore off a blank sheet from the end of it, on which he hastily wrote some words. He passed it to me to give to Briggs, and I could not help seeing what was written. It was: "Too late now. God bless you, my dear father. I hope we may meet again. If not, try to think kindly of your troublesome and foolish son, Stephen."

In another minute the train had started.

"By the way," he said, as we steamed out of the station, "I have heard from my father, who enclosed this for you."

I opened the envelope, which was addressed in a bold, round hand that seemed to me typical of the writer, and read as follows:

"My Dear Sir,--I appreciate the motives which caused you to write to me and I thank you very heartily for your letter, which shows me that you are a man of discretion and strict honour. As you surmise, the expedition on which my son has entered is not one that commends itself to me as prudent. Of the differences between him and myself you are aware, for they came to a climax in your presence. Indeed, I feel that I owe you an apology for having dragged you into an unpleasant family quarrel. Your letter only reached me to-day having been forwarded to my place in the country from my office. I should have at once come to town, but unfortunately I am laid up with an attack of gout which makes it impossible for me to stir. Therefore, the only thing I can do is to write to my son hoping that the letter which I send by a special messenger will reach him in time and avail to alter his determination to undertake this journey. Here I may add that although I have differed and do differ from him on various points, I still have a deep affection for my son and earnestly desire his welfare. The prospect of any harm coming to him is one upon which I cannot bear to dwell.

"Now I am aware that any change of his plans at this eleventh hour would involve you in serious loss and inconvenience. I beg to inform you formally, therefore, that in this event I will make good everything and will in addition write off the £2,000 which I understand he has invested in your joint venture. It may be, however, that my son, who has in him a vein of my own obstinacy, will refuse to change his mind. In that event, under a Higher Power I can only commend him to your care and beg that you will look after him as though he were your own child. I can ask and you can do no more. Tell him to write me as opportunity offers, as perhaps you will too; also that, although I hate the sight of them, I will look after the flowers which he has left at the house at Twickenham.--

"Your obliged servant,

ALEXANDER SOMERS."

This letter touched me much, and indeed made me feel very uncomfortable. Without a word I handed it to my companion, who read it through carefully.

"Nice of him about the orchids," he said. "My dad has a good heart, although he lets his temper get the better of him, having had his own way all his life."

"Well, what will you do?" I asked.

"Go on, of course. I've put my hand to the plough and I am not going to turn back. I should be a cur if I did, and what's more, whatever he might say he'd think none the better of me. So please don't try to persuade me, it would be no good."

For quite a while afterwards young Somers seemed to be comparatively depressed, a state of mind that in his case was rare indeed. At last, he studied the wintry landscape through the carriage window and said nothing. By degrees, however, he recovered, and when we reached Dartmouth was as cheerful as ever, a mood that I could not altogether share.

Before we sailed I wrote to Sir Alexander telling him exactly how things stood, and so I think did his son, though he never showed me the letter.

At Durban, just as we were about to start up country, I received an answer from him, sent by some boat that followed us very closely. In it he said that he quite understood the position, and whatever happened would attribute no blame to me, whom he should always regard with friendly feelings. He told me that, in the event of any difficulty or want of money, I was to draw on him for whatever might be required, and that he had advised the African Bank to that effect. Further, he added, that at least his son had shown grit in this matter, for which he respected him.

And now for a long while I must bid good-bye to Sir Alexander Somers and all that has to do with England.

Mavovo and Hans

We arrived safely at Durban at the beginning of March and took up our quarters at my house on the Berea, where I expected that Brother John would be awaiting us. But no Brother John was to be found. The old, lame Griqua, Jack, who looked after the place for me and once had been one of my hunters, said that shortly after I went away in the ship, Dogeetah, as he called him, had taken his tin box and his net and walked off inland, he knew not where, leaving, as he declared, no message or letter behind him. The cases full of butterflies and dried plants were also gone, but these, I found he had shipped to some port in America, by a sailing vessel bound for the United States which chanced to put in at Durban for food and water. As to what had become of the man himself I could get no clue. He had been seen at Maritzburg and, according to some Kaffirs whom I knew, afterwards on the borders of Zululand, where, so far as I could learn, he vanished into space.

This, to say the least of it, was disconcerting, and a question arose as to what was to be done. Brother John was to have been our guide. He alone knew the Mazitu people; he alone had visited the borders of the mysterious Pongo-land, I scarcely felt inclined to attempt to reach that country without his aid.

When a fortnight had gone by and still there were no signs of him, Stephen and I held a solemn conference. I pointed out the difficulties and dangers of the situation to him and suggested that, under the circumstances, it might be wise to give up this wild orchid-chase and go elephant-hunting instead in a certain part of Zululand, where in those days these animals were still abundant.

He was inclined to agree with me, since the prospect of killing elephants had attractions for him.

"And yet," I said, after reflection, "it's curious, but I never remember making a successful trip after altering plans at the last moment, that is, unless one was driven to it."

"I vote we toss up," said Somers; "it gives Providence a chance. Now then, heads for the Golden Cyp, and tails for the elephants."

He spun a half-crown into the air. It fell and rolled under a great, yellow-wood chest full of curiosities that I had collected, which it took all our united strength to move. We dragged it aside and not without some excitement, for really a good deal hung upon the chance, I lit a match and peered into the shadow. There in the dust lay the coin.

"What is it?" I asked of Somers, who was stretched on his stomach on the chest. "Orchid--I mean head," he answered. "Well, that's settled, so we needn't bother any more."

The next fortnight was a busy time for me. As it happened there was a schooner in the bay of about one hundred tons burden which belonged to a Portuguese trader named Delgado, who dealt in goods that he carried to the various East African ports and Madagascar. He was a villainous- looking person whom I suspected of having dealings with the slave traders, who were very numerous and a great power in those days, if indeed he were not one himself. But as he was going to Kilwa whence we proposed to start inland, I arranged to make use of him to carry our party and the baggage. The bargain was not altogether easy to strike for two reasons. First, he did not appear to be anxious that we should hunt in the districts at the back of Kilwa, where he assured me there was no game, and secondly, he said that he wanted to sail at once. However, I overcame his objections with an argument he could not resist--namely, money, and in the end he agreed to postpone his departure for fourteen days.

Then I set about collecting our men, of whom I had made up my mind there must not be less than twenty. Already I had sent messengers summoning to Durban from Zululand and the upper districts of Natal various hunters who had accompanied me on other expeditions. To the number of a dozen or so they arrived in due course. I have always had the good fortune to be on the best of terms with my Kaffirs, and where I went they were ready to go without asking any questions. The man whom I had selected to be their captain under me was a Zulu of the name of Mavovo. He was a short fellow, past middle age, with an enormous chest. His strength was proverbial; indeed, it was said that he could throw an ox by the horns, and myself I have seen him hold down the head of a wounded buffalo that had fallen, until I could come up and shoot it.

When I first knew Mavovo he was a petty chief and witch doctor in Zululand. Like myself, he had fought for the Prince Umbelazi in the great battle of the Tugela, a crime which Cetewayo never forgave him. About a year afterwards he got warning that he had been smelt out as a wizard and was going to be killed. He fled with two of his wives and a child. The slayers overtook them before he could reach the Natal border, and stabbed the elder wife and the child of the second wife. They were four men, but, made mad by the sight, Mavovo turned on them and killed them all. Then, with the remaining wife, cut to pieces as he was, he crept to the river and through it to Natal. Not long after this wife died also; it was said from grief at the loss of her child. Mavovo did not marry again, perhaps because he was now a man without means, for Cetewayo had taken all his cattle; also he was made ugly by an assegai wound which had cut off his right nostril. Shortly after the death of his second wife he sought me out and told me he was a chief without a kraal and wished to become my hunter. So I took him on, a step which I never had any cause to regret, since although morose and at times given to the practice of uncanny arts, he was a most faithful servant and brave as a lion, or rather as a buffalo, for a lion is not always brave.

Another man whom I did not send for, but who came, was an old Hottentot named Hans, with whom I had been more or less mixed up all my life. When I was a boy he was my father's servant in the Cape Colony and my companion in some of those early wars. Also he shared some very terrible adventures with me which I have detailed in the history I have written of my first wife, Marie Marais. For instance, he and I were the only persons who escaped from the massacre of Retief and his companions by the Zulu king, Dingaan. In the subsequence campaigns, including the Battle of the Blood River, he fought at my side and ultimately received a good share of captured cattle. After this he retired and set up a native store at a place called Pinetown, about fifteen miles out of Durban. Here I am afraid he got into bad ways and took to drink more or less; also to gambling. At any rate, he lost most of his property, so much of it indeed that he scarcely knew which way to turn. Thus it happened that one evening when I went out of the house where I had been making up my accounts, I saw a yellow- faced white-haired old fellow squatted on the verandah smoking a pipe made out of a corn-cob.

"Good day, Baas," he said, "here am I, Hans."

"So I see," I answered, rather coldly. "And what are you doing here, Hans? How can you spare time from your drinking and gambling at Pinetown to visit me here, Hans, after I have not seen you for three years?"

"Baas, the gambling is finished, because I have nothing more to stake, and the drinking is done too, because but one bottle of Cape Smoke makes me feel quite ill next morning. So now I only take water and as little of that as I can, water and some tobacco to cover up its taste."

"I am glad to hear it, Hans. If my father, the Predikant who baptised you, were alive now, he would have much to say about your conduct as indeed I have no doubt he will presently when you have gone into a hole (i.e., a grave). For there in the hole he will be waiting for you, Hans."

"I know, I know, Baas. I have been thinking of that and it troubles me. Your reverend father, the Predikant, will be very cross indeed with me when I join him in the Place of Fires where he sits awaiting me. So I wish to make my peace with him by dying well, and in your service, Baas. I hear that the Baas is going on an expedition. I have come to accompany the Baas."

"To accompany me! Why, you are old, you are not worth five shillings a month and your *scoff* (food). You are a shrunken old brandy cask that will not even hold water."

Hans grinned right across his ugly face.

"Oh! Baas, I am old, but I am clever. All these years I have been gathering wisdom. I am as full of it as a bee's nest is with honey when the summer is done. And, Baas, I can stop those leaks in the cask."

"Hans, it is no good, I don't want you. I am going into great danger. I must have those about me whom I can trust."

"Well, Baas, and who can be better trusted than Hans? Who warned you of the attack of the Quabies on Maraisfontein, and so saved the life of----"

"Hush!" I said.

"I understand. I will not speak the name. It is holy not to be mentioned. It is the name of one who stands with the white angels before God; not to be mentioned by poor drunken Hans. Still, who stood at your side in that great fight? Ah! it makes me young again to think of it, when the roof burned; when the door was broken down; when we met the Quabies on the spears; when you held the pistol to the head of the Holy One whose name must not be mentioned, the Great One who knew how to die. Oh! Baas, our lives are twisted up together like the creeper and the tree, and where you go, there I must go also. Do not turn me away. I ask no wages, only a bit of food and a handful of tobacco, and the light of your face and a word now and again of the memories that belong to both of us. I am still very strong. I can shoot well--well, Baas, who was it that put it into your mind to aim at the tails of the vultures on the Hill of Slaughter yonder in Zululand, and so saved the lives of all the Boer people, and of her whose holy name must not be mentioned? Baas, you will not turn me away?"

"No," I answered, "you can come. But you will swear by the spirit of my father, the Predikant, to touch no liquor on this journey."

"I swear by his spirit and by that of the Holy One," and he flung himself forward on to his knees, took my hand and kissed it. Then he rose and said in a matter-of-fact tone, "If the Baas can give me two blankets, I shall thank him, also five shillings to buy some tobacco and a new knife. Where are the Baas's guns? I must go to oil them. I beg that the Baas will take with him that little rifle which is named *Intombi* (Maiden), the one with which he shot the vultures on the Hill of Slaughter, the one that killed the geese in the Goose Kloof when I loaded for him and he won the great match against the Boer whom Dingaan called Two-faces."

"Good," I said. "Here are the five shillings. You shall have the blankets and a new gun and all things needful. You will find the guns in the little back room and with them those of the Baas, my companion, who also is your master. Go see to them."

At length all was ready, the cases of guns, ammunition, medicines, presents and food were on board the *Maria*. So were four donkeys that I had bought in the hope that they would prove useful, either to ride or as pack beasts. The donkey, be it remembered, and man are the only animals which are said to be immune from the poisonous effects of the bite of tsetse fly, except, of course, the wild game. It was our last night at Durban, a very beautiful night of full moon at the end of March, for the Portugee Delgado had announced his intention of sailing on the following afternoon. Stephen Somers and I were seated on the stoep smoking and talking things over.

"It is a strange thing," I said, "that Brother John should never have turned up. I know that he was set upon making this expedition, not only for the sake of the orchid, but also for some other reason of which he would not speak. I think that the old fellow must be dead."

"Very likely," answered Stephen (we had become intimate and I called him Stephen now), "a man alone among savages might easily come to grief and never be heard of again. Hark! What's that?" and he pointed to some gardenia bushes in the shadow of the house near by, whence came a sound of something that moved.

"A dog, I expect, or perhaps it is Hans. He curls up in all sorts of places near to where I may be. Hans, are you there?"

A figure arose from the gardenia bushes.

"*Ja*, I am here, Baas."

"What are you doing, Hans?"

"I am doing what the dog does, Baas--watching my master."

"Good," I answered. Then an idea struck me. "Hans, you have heard of the white Baas with the long beard whom the Kaffirs call Dogeetah?"

"I have heard of him and once I saw him, a few moons ago passing through Pinetown. A Kaffir with him told me that he was going over the Drakensberg to hunt for things that crawl and fly, being quite mad, Baas."

"Well, where is he now, Hans? He should have been here to travel with us."

"Am I a spirit that I can tell the Baas whither a white man has wandered. Yet, stay. Mavovo may be able to tell. He is a great doctor, he can see through distance, and even now, this very night his Snake of divination has entered into him and he is looking into the future, yonder, behind the house. I saw him form the circle."

I translated what Hans said to Stephen, for he had been talking in Dutch, then asked him if he would like to see some Kaffir magic.

"Of course," he answered, "but it's all bosh, isn't it?"

"Oh, yes, all bosh, or so most people say," I answered evasively. "Still, sometimes these *Inyangas* tell one strange things."

Then, led by Hans, we crept round the house to where there was a five- foot stone wall at the back of the stable. Beyond this wall, within the circle of some huts where my Kaffirs lived, was an open space with an ant-heap floor where they did their cooking. Here, facing us, sat Mavovo, while in a ring around him were all the hunters who were to accompany us; also Jack, the lame Griqua, and the two house-boys. In front of Mavovo burned a number of little wood fires. I counted them and found that there were fourteen, which, I reflected, was the exact number of our hunters, plus ourselves. One of the hunters was engaged in feeding these fires with little bits of stick and handfuls of dried grass so as to keep them burning brightly. The others sat round perfectly silent and watched with rapt attention. Mavovo himself looked like a man who is asleep. He was crouched on his haunches with his big head resting almost upon his knees. About his middle was a snake-skin, and round his neck an ornament that appeared to be made of human teeth. On his right side lay a pile of feathers from the wings of vultures, and on his left a little heap of silver money--I suppose the fees paid by the hunters for whom he was divining.

After we had watched him for some while from our shelter behind the wall he appeared to wake out of his sleep. First he muttered; then he looked up to the moon and seemed to say a prayer of which I could not catch the words. Next he shuddered three times convulsively and exclaimed in a clear voice:

"My Snake has come. It is within me. Now I can hear, now I can see."

Three of the little fires, those immediately in front of him, were larger than the others. He took up his bundle of vultures' feathers, selected one with care, held it towards the sky, then passed it through the flame of the centre one of the three fires, uttering as he did so, my native name, Macumazana. Withdrawing it from the flame he examined the charred edges of the feather very carefully, a proceeding that caused a cold shiver to go down my back, for I knew well that he was inquiring of his "Spirit" what would be my fate upon this expedition. How it answered, I cannot tell, for he laid the feather down and took another, with which he went through the same process. This time, however, the name he called out was Mwamwazela, which in its shortened form of Wazela, was the Kaffir appellation that the natives had given to Stephen Somers. It means a Smile, and no doubt was selected for him because of his pleasant, smiling countenance.

Having passed it through the right-hand fire of the three, he examined it and laid it down.

So it went on. One after another he called out the names of the hunters, beginning with his own as captain; passed the feather which represented each of them through the particular fire of his destiny, examined and laid it down. After this he seemed to go to sleep again for a few minutes, then woke up as a man does from a natural slumber, yawned and stretched himself.

"Speak," said his audience, with great anxiety. "Have you seen? Have you heard? What does your Snake tell you of me? Of me? Of me? Of me?"

"I have seen, I have heard," he answered. "My Snake tells me that this will be a very dangerous journey. Of those who go on it six will die by the bullet, by the spear or by sickness, and others will be hurt."

"*Ow?*" said one of them, "but which will die and which will come out safe? Does not your Snake tell you that, O Doctor?"

"Yes, of course my Snake tells me that. But my Snake tells me also to hold my tongue on the matter, lest some of us should be turned to cowards. It tells me further that the first who should ask me more, will be one of those who must die. Now do you ask? Or you? Or you? Or you? Ask if you will."

Strange to say no one accepted the invitation. Never have I seen a body of men so indifferent to the future, at least to every appearance. One and all they seemed to come to the conclusion that so far as they were concerned it might be left to look after itself.

"My Snake told me something else," went on Mavovo. "It is that if among this company there is any jackal of a man who, thinking that he might be one of the six to die, dreams to avoid his fate by deserting, it will be of no use. For then my Snake will point him out and show me how to deal with him."

Now with one voice each man present there declared that desertion from the lord Macumazana was the last thing that could possibly occur to him. Indeed, I believe that those brave fellows spoke truth. No doubt they put faith in Mavovo's magic after the fashion of their race. Still the death he promised was some way off, and each hoped he would be one of the six to escape. Moreover, the Zulu of those days was too accustomed to death to fear its terrors over much.

One of them did, however, venture to advance the argument, which Mavovo treated with proper contempt, that the shillings paid for this divination should be returned by him to the next heirs of such of them as happened to decease. Why, he asked, should these pay a shilling in order to be told that they must die? It seemed unreasonable.

Certainly the Zulu Kaffirs have a queer way of looking at things.

"Hans," I whispered, "is your fire among those that burn yonder?"

"Not so, Baas," he wheezed back into my ear. "Does the Baas think me a fool? If I must die, I must die; if I am to live, I shall live. Why then should I pay a shilling to learn what time will declare? Moreover, yonder Mavovo takes the shillings and frightens everybody, but tells nobody anything. *I* call it cheating. But, Baas, do you and the Baas Wazela have no fear. You did not pay shillings, and therefore Mavovo, though without doubt he is a great *Inyanga*, cannot really prophesy concerning you, since his Snake will not work without a fee."

The argument seems remarkably absurd. Yet it must be common, for now that I come to think of it, no gipsy will tell a "true fortune" unless her hand is crossed with silver.

"I say, Quatermain," said Stephen idly, "since our friend Mavovo seems to know so much, ask him what has become of Brother John, as Hans suggested. Tell me what he says afterwards, for I want to see something."

So I went through the little gate in the wall in a natural kind of way, as though I had seen nothing, and appeared to be struck by the sight of the little fires.

"Well, Mavovo," I said, "are you doing doctor's work? I thought that it had brought you into enough trouble in Zululand."

"That is so, *Baba*," replied Mavovo, who had a habit of calling me "father," though he was older than I. "It cost me my chieftainship and my cattle and my two wives and my son. It made of me a wanderer who is glad to accompany a certain Macumazana to strange lands where many things may befall me, yes," he added with meaning, "even the last of all things. And yet a gift is a gift and must be used. You, *Baba*, have a gift of shooting and do you cease to shoot? You have a gift of wandering and can you cease to wander?"

He picked up one of the burnt feathers from the little pile by his side and looked at it attentively. "Perhaps, *Baba*, you have been told--my ears are very sharp, and I thought I heard some such words floating through the air just now--that we poor Kaffir *Inyangas* can prophesy nothing true unless we are paid, and perhaps that is a fact so far as something of the moment is concerned. And yet the Snake in the *Inyanga*, jumping over the little rock which hides the present from it, may see the path that winds far and far away through the valleys, across the streams, up the mountains, till it is lost in the 'heaven above.' Thus on this feather, burnt in my magic fire, I seem to see something of your future, O my father Macumazana. Far and far your road runs," and he drew his finger along the feather. "Here is a journey," and he flicked away a carbonised flake, "here is another, and another, and another," and he flicked off flake after flake. "Here is one that is very successful, it leaves you rich; and here is yet one more, a wonderful journey this in which you see strange things and meet strange people. Then"--and he blew on the feather in such a fashion that all the charred filaments (Brother John says that *laminae* is the right word for them) fell away from it--"then, there is nothing left save such a pole as some of my people stick upright on a grave, the Shaft of Memory they call it. O, my father, you will die in a distant land, but you will leave a great memory behind you that will live for hundreds of years, for see how strong is this quill over which the fire has had no power. With some of these others it is quite different," he added.

"I daresay," I broke in, "but, Mavovo, be so good as to leave me out of your magic, for I don't at all want to know what is going to happen to me. To-day is enough for me without studying next month and next year. There is a saying in our holy book which runs: 'Sufficient to the day is its evil.'"

"Quite so, O Macumazana. Also that is a very good saying as some of those hunters of yours are thinking now. Yet an hour ago they were forcing their shillings on me that I might tell them of the future. And *you*, too, want to know something. You did not come through that gate to quote to me the wisdom of your holy book. What is it, *Baba*? Be quick, for my Snake is getting very tired. He wishes to go back to his hole in the world beneath."

"Well, then," I answered in rather a shamefaced fashion, for Mavovo had an uncanny way of seeing into one's secret motives, "I should like to know, if you can tell me, which you can't, what has become of the white man with the long beard whom you black people call Dogeetah? He should have been here to go on this journey with us; indeed, he was to be our guide and we cannot find him. Where is he and why is he not here?"

"Have you anything about you that belonged to Dogeetah, Macumazana?"

"No," I answered; "that is, yes," and from my pocket I produced the stump of pencil that Brother John had given me, which, being economical, I had saved up ever since. Mavovo took it, and after considering it carefully as he had done in the case of the feathers, swept up a pile of ashes with his horny hand from the edge of the largest of the little fires, that indeed which had represented myself. These ashes he patted flat. Then he drew on them with the point of the pencil, tracing what seemed to me to be the rough image of a man, such as children scratch upon whitewashed walls. When he had finished he sat up and contemplated his handiwork with all the satisfaction of an artist. A breeze had risen from the sea and was blowing in little gusts, so that the fine ashes were disturbed, some of the lines of the picture being filled in and others altered or enlarged.

For a while Mavovo sat with his eyes shut. Then he opened them, studied the ashes and what remained of the picture, and taking a blanket that lay near by, threw it over his own head and over the ashes. Withdrawing it again presently he cast it aside and pointed to the picture which was now quite changed. Indeed, in the moonlight, it looked more like a landscape than anything else.

"All is clear, my father," he said in a matter-of-fact voice. "The white wanderer, Dogeetah, is not dead. He lives, but he is sick. Something is the matter with one of his legs so that he cannot walk. Perhaps a bone is broken or some beast has bitten him. He lies in a hut such as Kaffirs make, only this hut has a verandah round it like your stoep, and there are drawings on the wall. The hut is a long way off, I don't know where."

"Is that all?" I asked, for he paused.

"No, not all. Dogeetah is recovering. He will join us in that country whither we journey, at a time of trouble. That is all, and the fee is half-a-crown."

"You mean one shilling," I suggested.

"No, my father Macumazana. One shilling for simple magic such as foretelling the fate of common black people. Half-a-crown for very difficult magic that has to do with white people, magic of which only great doctors, like me, Mavovo, are the masters."

I gave him the half-crown and said:

"Look here, friend Mavovo, I believe in you as a fighter and a hunter, but as a magician I think you are a humbug. Indeed, I am so sure of it that if ever Dogeetah turns up at a time of trouble in that land whither we are journeying, I will make you a present of that double- barrelled rifle of mine which you admired so much."

One of his rare smiles appeared upon Mavovo's ugly face.

"Then give it to me now, *Baba*," he said, "for it is already earned. My Snake cannot lie--especially when the fee is half-a-crown."

I shook my head and declined, politely but with firmness.

"Ah!" said Mavovo, "you white men are very clever and think that you know everything. But it is not so, for in learning so much that is new, you have forgotten more that is old. When the Snake that is in you, Macumazana, dwelt in a black savage like me a thousand thousand years ago, you could have done and did what I do. But now you can only mock and say, 'Mavovo the brave in battle, the great hunter, the loyal man, becomes a liar when he blows the burnt feather, or reads what the wind writes upon the charmed ashes.'"

"I do not say that you are a liar, Mavovo, I say that you are deceived by your own imaginings. It is not possible that man can know what is hidden from man."

"Is it indeed so, O Macumazana, Watcher by Night? Am I, Mavovo, the pupil of Zikali, the Opener of Roads, the greatest of wizards, indeed deceived by my own imaginings? And has man no other eyes but those in his head, that he cannot see what is hidden from man? Well, you say so and all we black people know that you are very clever, and why should I, a poor Zulu, be able to see what you cannot see? Yet when to-morrow one sends you a message from the ship in which we are to sail, begging you to come fast because there is trouble on the ship, then bethink you of your words and my words, and whether or no man can see what is hidden from man in the blackness of the future. Oh! that rifle of yours is mine already, though you will not give it to me now, you who think that I am a cheat. Well, my father Macumazana, because you think I am a cheat, never again will I blow the feather or read what the wind writes upon the ashes for you or any who eat your food."

Then he rose, saluted me with uplifted right hand, collected his little pile of money and bag of medicines and marched off to the sleeping hut.

On our way round the house we met my old lame caretaker, Jack.

"*Inkoosi*," he said, "the white chief Wazela bade me say that he and the cook, Sam, have gone to sleep on board the ship to look after the goods. Sam came up just now and fetched him away; he says he will show you why to-morrow."

I nodded and passed on, wondering to myself why Stephen had suddenly determined to stay the night on the *Maria*.

Hassan

I suppose it must have been two hours after dawn on the following morning that I was awakened by knocks upon the door and the voice of Jack saying that Sam, the cook, wanted to speak to me.

Wondering what he could be doing there, as I understood he was sleeping on the ship, I called out that he was to come in. Now this Sam, I should say, hailed from the Cape, and was a person of mixed blood. The original stock, I imagine, was Malay which had been crossed with Indian coolie. Also, somewhere or other, there was a dash of white and possibly, but of this I am not sure, a little Hottentot. The result was a person of few vices and many virtues. Sammy, I may say at once, was perhaps the biggest coward I ever met. He could not help it, it was congenital, though, curiously enough, this cowardice of his never prevented him from rushing into fresh danger. Thus he knew that the expedition upon which I was engaged would be most hazardous; remembering his weakness I explained this to him very clearly. Yet that knowledge did not deter him from imploring that he might be allowed to accompany me. Perhaps this was because there was some mutual attachment between us, as in the case of Hans. Once, a good many years before, I had rescued Sammy from a somewhat serious scrape by declining to give evidence against him. I need not enter into the details, but a certain sum of money over which he had control had disappeared. I will merely say, therefore, that at the time he was engaged to a coloured lady of very expensive tastes, whom in the end he never married.

After this, as it chanced, he nursed me through an illness. Hence the attachment of which I have spoken.

Sammy was the son of a native Christian preacher, and brought up upon what he called "The Word." He had received an excellent education for a person of his class, and in addition to many native dialects with which a varied career had made him acquainted, spoke English perfectly, though in the most bombastic style. Never would he use a short word if a long one came to his hand, or rather to his tongue. For several years of his life he was, I believe, a teacher in a school at Capetown where coloured persons received their education; his "department," as he called it, being "English Language and Literature."

Wearying of or being dismissed from his employment for some reason that he never specified, he had drifted up the coast to Zanzibar, where he turned his linguistic abilities to the study of Arabic and became the manager or head cook of an hotel. After a few years he lost this billet, I know not how or why, and appeared at Durban in what he called a "reversed position." Here it was that we met again, just before my expedition to Pongo-land.

In manners he was most polite, in disposition most religious; I believe he was a Baptist by faith, and in appearance a small, brown dandy of a man of uncertain age, who wore his hair parted in the middle and, whatever the circumstances, was always tidy in his garments.

I took him on because he was in great distress, an excellent cook, the best of nurses, and above all for the reason that, as I have said, we were in a way attached to each other. Also, he always amused me intensely, which goes for something on a long journey of the sort that I contemplated.

Such in brief was Sammy.

As he entered the room I saw that his clothes were very wet and asked him at once if it were raining, or whether he had got drunk and been sleeping in the damp grass.

"No, Mr. Quatermain," he answered, "the morning is extremely fine, and like the poor Hottentot, Hans, I have abjured the use of intoxicants. Though we differ on much else, in this matter we agree."

"Then what the deuce is up?" I interrupted, to cut short his flow of fine language.

"Sir, there is trouble on the ship" (remembering Mavovo I started at these words) "where I passed the night in the company of Mr. Somers at his special request." (It was the other way about really.) "This morning before the dawn, when he thought that everybody was asleep, the Portuguese captain and some of his Arabs began to weigh the anchor quite quietly; also to hoist the sails. But Mr. Somers and I, being very much awake, came out of the cabin and he sat upon the capstan with a revolver in his hand, saying--well, sir, I will not repeat what he said."

"No, don't. What happened then?"

"Then, sir, there followed much noise and confusion. The Portugee and the Arabs threatened Mr. Somers, but he, sir, continued to sit upon the capstan with the stern courage of a rock in a rushing stream, and remarked that he would see them all somewhere before they touched it. After this, sir, I do not know what occurred, since while I watched from the bulwarks someone knocked me head over heels into the sea and being fortunately, a good swimmer, I gained the shore and hurried here to advise you."

"And did you advise anyone else, you idiot?" I asked.

"Yes, sir. As I sped along I communicated to an officer of the port that there was the devil of a mess upon the *Maria* which he would do well to investigate."

By this time I was in my shirt and trousers and shouting to Mavovo and the others. Soon they arrived, for as the costume of Mavovo and his company consisted only of a moocha and a blanket, it did not take them long to dress.

"Mavovo," I began, "there is trouble on the ship----"

"O *Baba*," he interrupted with something resembling a grin, "it is very strange, but last night I dreamed that I told you----"

"Curse your dreams," I said. "Gather the men and go down--no, that won't work, there would be murder done. Either it is all over now or it is all right. Get the hunters ready; I come with them. The luggage can be fetched afterwards."

Within less than an hour we were at that wharf off which the *Maria* lay in what one day will be the splendid port of Durban, though in those times its shipping arrangements were exceedingly primitive. A strange-looking band we must have been. I, who was completely dressed, and I trust tidy, marched ahead. Next came Hans in the filthy wide- awake hat which he usually wore and greasy corduroys and after him the oleaginous Sammy arrayed in European reach-me-downs, a billy-cock and a bright blue tie striped with red, garments that would have looked very smart had it not been for his recent immersion. After him followed the fierce-looking Mavovo and his squad of hunters, all of whom wore the "ring" or *isicoco*, as the Zulus call it; that is, a circle of polished black wax sewn into their short hair. They were a grim set of fellows, but as, according to a recent law it was not allowable for them to appear armed in the town, their guns had already been shipped, while their broad stabbing spears were rolled up in their sleeping mats, the blades wrapped round with dried grass.

Each of them, however, bore in his hand a large knobkerry of red-wood, and they marched four by four in martial fashion. It is true that when we embarked on the big boat to go to the ship much of their warlike ardour evaporated, since these men, who feared nothing on the land, were terribly afraid of that unfamiliar element, the water.

We reached the *Maria*, an unimposing kind of tub, and climbed aboard. On looking aft the first thing that I saw was Stephen seated on the capstan with a pistol in his hand, as Sammy had said. Near by, leaning on the bulwark was the villainous-looking Portugee, Delgado, apparently in the worst of tempers and surrounded by a number of equally villainous-looking Arab sailors clad in dirty white.

In front was the Captain of the port, a well-known and esteemed gentleman of the name of Cato, like myself a small man who had gone through many adventures. Accompanied by some attendants, he was seated on the after-skylight, smoking, with his eyes fixed upon Stephen and the Portugee.

"Glad to see you, Quatermain," he said. "There's some row on here, but I have only just arrived and don't understand Portuguese, and the gentleman on the capstan won't leave it to explain."

"What's up, Stephen?" I asked, after shaking Mr. Cato by the hand.

"What's up?" replied Somers. "This man," and he pointed to Delgado, "wanted to sneak out to sea with all our goods, that's all, to say nothing of me and Sammy, whom, no doubt, he'd have chucked overboard, as soon as he was out of sight of land. However, Sammy, who knows Portuguese, overheard his little plans and, as you see, I objected."

Well, Delgado was asked for his version of the affair, and, as I expected, explained that he only intended to get a little nearer to the bar and there wait till we arrived. Of course he lied and knew that we were aware of the fact and that his intention had been to slip out to sea with all our valuable property, which he would sell after having murdered or marooned Stephen and the poor cook. But as nothing could be proved, and we were now in strong enough force to look after ourselves and our belongings, I did not see the use of pursuing the argument. So I accepted the explanation with a smile, and asked everybody to join in a morning nip.

Afterwards Stephen told me that while I was engaged with Mavovo on the previous night, a message had reached him from Sammy who was on board the ship in charge of our belongings, saying that he would be glad of some company. Knowing the cook's nervous nature, fortunately enough he made up his mind at once to go and sleep upon the *Maria*. In the morning trouble arose as Sammy had told me. What he did not tell me was that he was not knocked overboard, as he said, but took to the water of his own accord, when complications with Delgado appeared imminent.

"I understand the position," I said, "and all's well that ends well. But it's lucky you thought of coming on board to sleep."

After this everything went right. I sent some of the men back in the charge of Stephen for our remaining effects, which they brought safely aboard, and in the evening we sailed. Our voyage up to Kilwa was beautiful, a gentle breeze driving us forward over a sea so calm that not even Hans, who I think was one of the worst sailors in the world, or the Zulu hunters were really sick, though as Sammy put it, they "declined their food."

I think it was on the fifth night of our voyage, or it may have been the seventh, that we anchored one afternoon off the island of Kilwa, not very far from the old Portuguese fort. Delgado, with whom we had little to do during the passage, hoisted some queer sort of signal. In response a boat came off containing what he called the Port officials, a band of cut-throat, desperate-looking, black fellows in charge of a pock-marked, elderly half-breed who was introduced to us as the Bey Hassan-ben-Mohammed. That Mr. Hassan-ben-Mohammed entirely disapproved of our presence on the ship, and especially of our proposed landing at Kilwa, was evident to me from the moment that I set eyes upon his ill-favoured countenance. After a hurried conference with Delgado, he came forward and addressed me in Arabic, of which I could not understand a word. Luckily, however, Sam the cook, who, as I think I said, was a great linguist, had a fair acquaintance with this tongue, acquired, it appears, while at the Zanzibar hotel; so, not trusting Delgado, I called on him to interpret.

"What is he saying, Sammy?" I asked.

He began to talk to Hassan and replied presently:

"Sir, he makes you many compliments. He says that he has heard what a great man who are from his friend, Delgado, also that you and Mr. Somers are English, a nation which he adores."

"Does he?" I exclaimed. "I should never have thought it from his looks. Thank him for his kind remarks and tell him that we are going to land here and march up country to shoot."

Sammy obeyed, and the conversation went on somewhat as follows:

"With all humility I (i.e. Hassan) request you not to land. This country is not a fit place for such noble gentlemen. There is nothing to eat and no head of game has been seen for years. The people in the interior are savages of the worst sort, whom hunger has driven to take to cannibalism. I would not have your blood upon my head. I beg of you, therefore, to go on in this ship to Delagoa Bay, where you will find a good hotel, or to any other place you may select."

A.Q.: "Might I ask you, noble sir, what is your position at Kilwa, that you consider yourself responsible for our safety?"

H.: "Honoured English lord, I am a trader here of Portuguese nationality, but born of an Arab mother of high birth and brought up among that people. I have gardens on the mainland, tended by my native servants who are as children to me, where I grow palms and cassava and ground nuts and plantains and many other kinds of produce. All the tribes in this district look upon me as their chief and venerated father."

A.Q.: "Then, noble Hassan, you will be able to pass us through them, seeing that we are peaceful hunters who wish to harm no one."

(A long consultation between Hassan and Delgado, during which I ordered Mavovo to bring his Zulus on deck with their guns.)

H.: "Honoured English lord, I cannot allow you to land."

A.Q.: "Noble son of the Prophet, I intend to land with my friend, my followers, my donkeys and my goods early to-morrow morning. If I can do so with your leave I shall be glad. If not----" and I glanced at the fierce group of hunters behind me.

H.: "Honoured English lord, I shall be grieved to use force, but let me tell you that in my peaceful village ashore I have at least a hundred men armed with rifles, whereas here I see under twenty."

A.Q., after reflection and a few words with Stephen Somers: "Can you tell me, noble sir, if from your peaceful village you have yet sighted the English man-of-war, *Crocodile*; I mean the steamer that is engaged in watching for the dhows of wicked slavers? A letter from her captain informed me that he would be in these waters by yesterday. Perhaps, however, he has been delayed for a day or two."

If I had exploded a bomb at the feet of the excellent Hassan its effect could scarcely have been more remarkable than that of this question. He turned--not pale, but a horrible yellow, and exclaimed:

"English man-of-war! *Crocodile*! I thought she had gone to Aden to refit and would not be back at Zanzibar for four months."

A.Q.: "You have been misinformed, noble Hassan. She will not refit till October. Shall I read you the letter?" and I produced a piece of paper from my pocket. "It may be interesting since my friend, the captain, whom you remember is named Flowers, mentions you in it. He says----"

Hassan waved his hand. "It is enough. I see, honoured lord, that you are a man of mettle not easily to be turned from your purpose. In the name of God the Compassionate, land and go wheresoever you like."

A.Q.: "I think that I had almost rather wait until the *Crocodile* comes in."

H.: "Land! Land! Captain Delgado, get up the cargo and man your boat. Mine too is at the service of these lords. You, Captain, will like to get away by this night's tide. There is still light, Lord Quatermain, and such hospitality as I can offer is at your service."

A.Q.: "Ah! I knew Bey Hassan, that you were only joking with me when you said that you wished us to go elsewhere. An excellent jest, truly, from one whose hospitality is so famous. Well, to fall in with your wishes, we will come ashore this evening, and if the Captain Delgado chances to sight the Queen's ship *Crocodile* before he sails, perhaps he will be so good as to signal to us with a rocket."

"Certainly, certainly," interrupted Delgado, who up to this time had pretended that he understood no English, the tongue in which I was speaking to the interpreter, Sammy.

Then he turned and gave orders to his Arab crew to bring up our belongings from the hold and to lower the *Maria's* boat.

Never did I see goods transferred in quicker time. Within half an hour every one of our packages was off that ship, for Stephen Somers kept a count of them. Our personal baggage went into the *Maria's* boat, and the goods together with the four donkeys which were lowered on to the top of them, were rumbled pell-mell into the barge-like punt belonging to Hassan. Here also I was accommodated, with about half of our people, the rest taking their seats in the smaller boat under the charge of Stephen.

At length all was ready and we cast off.

"Farewell, Captain," I cried to Delgado. "If you should sight the *Crocodile*----"

At this point Delgado broke into such a torrent of bad language in Portuguese, Arabic and English that I fear the rest of my remarks never reached him.

As we rowed shorewards I observed that Hans, who was seated near to me under the stomach of a jackass, was engaged in sniffing at the sides and bottom of the barge, as a dog might do, and asked him what he was about.

"Very odd smell in this boat," he whispered back in Dutch. "It stinks of Kaffir man, just like the hold of the *Maria*. I think this boat is used to carry slaves."

"Be quiet," I whispered back, "and stop nosing at those planks." But to myself I thought, Hans is right, we are in a nest of slave-traders, and this Hassan is their leader.

We rowed past the island, on which I observed the ruins of an old Portuguese fort and some long grass-roofed huts, where, I reflected, the slaves were probably kept until they could be shipped away. Observing my glance fixed upon these, Hassan hastened to explain, through Sammy, that they were storehouses in which he dried fish and hides, and kept goods.

"How interesting!" I answered. "Further south we dry hides in the sun."

Crossing a narrow channel we arrived at a rough jetty where we disembarked, whence we were led by Hassan not to the village which I now saw upon our left, but to a pleasant-looking, though dilapidated house that stood a hundred yards from the shore. Something about the appearance of this house impressed me with the idea that it was never built by slavers; the whole look of the place with its verandah and garden suggested taste and civilisation. Evidently educated people had designed it and resided here. I glanced about me and saw, amidst a grove of neglected orange trees that were surrounded with palms of some age, the ruins of a church. About this there was no doubt, for there, surmounted by a stone cross, was a little pent-house in which still hung the bell that once summoned the worshippers to prayer.

"Tell the English lord," said Hassan to Sammy, "that these buildings were a mission station of the Christians, who abandoned them more than twenty years ago. When I came here I found them empty."

"Indeed," I answered, "and what were the names of those who dwelt in them?"

"I never heard," said Hassan; "they had been gone a long while when I came."

Then we went up to the house, and for the next hour and more were engaged with our baggage which was piled in a heap in what had been the garden and in unpacking and pitching two tents for the hunters which I caused to be placed immediately in front of the rooms that were assigned to us. Those rooms were remarkable in their way. Mine had evidently been a sitting chamber, as I judged from some such broken articles of furniture, that appeared to be of American make. That which Stephen occupied had once served as a sleeping-place, for the bedstead of iron still remained there. Also there were a hanging bookcase, now fallen, and some tattered remnants of books. One of these, that oddly enough was well-preserved, perhaps because the white ants or other creatures did not like the taste of its morocco binding, was a Keble's *Christian Year*, on the title-page of which was written, "To my dearest Elizabeth on her birthday, from her husband." I took the liberty to put it in my pocket. On the wall, moreover, still hung the small watercolour picture of a very pretty young woman with fair hair and blue eyes, in the corner of which picture was written in the same handwriting as that in the book, "Elizabeth, aged twenty." This also I annexed, thinking that it might come in useful as a piece of evidence.

"Looks as if the owners of this place had left it in a hurry, Quatermain," said Stephen.

"That's it, my boy. Or perhaps they didn't leave; perhaps they stopped here."

"Murdered?"

I nodded and said, "I dare say friend Hassan could tell us something about the matter. Meanwhile as supper isn't ready yet, let us have a look at that church while it is light."

We walked through the palm and orange grove to where the building stood finely placed upon a mound. It was well-constructed of a kind of coral rock, and a glance showed us that it had been gutted by fire; the discoloured walls told their own tale. The interior was now full of shrubs and creepers, and an ugly, yellowish snake glided from what had been the stone altar. Without, the graveyard was enclosed by a broken wall, only we could see no trace of graves. Near the gateway, however, was a rough mound.

"If we could dig into that," I said, "I expect we should find the bones of the people who inhabited this place. Does that suggest anything to you, Stephen?"

"Nothing, except that they were probably killed."

"You should learn to draw inferences. It is a useful art, especially in Africa. It suggests to me that, if you are right, the deed was not done by natives, who would never take the trouble to bury the dead. Arabs, on the contrary, might do so, especially if there were any bastard Portuguese among them who called themselves Christians. But whatever happened must have been a long while ago," and I pointed to a self-sown hardwood tree growing from the mound which could scarcely have been less than twenty years old.

We returned to the house to find that our meal was ready. Hassan had asked us to dine with him, but for obvious reasons I preferred that Sammy should cook our food and that he should dine with us. He appeared full of compliments, though I could see hate and suspicion in his eye, and we fell to on the kid that we had bought from him, for I did not wish to accept any gifts from this fellow. Our drink was square-face gin, mixed with water that I sent Hans to fetch with his own hands from the stream that ran by the house, lest otherwise it should be drugged.

At first Hassan, like a good Mohammedan, refused to touch any spirits, but as the meal went on he politely relented upon this point, and I poured him out a liberal tot. The appetite comes in eating, as the Frenchman said, and the same thing applies to drinking. So at least it was in Hassan's case, who probably thought that the quantity swallowed made no difference to his sin. After the third dose of square-face he grew quite amiable and talkative. Thinking the opportunity a good one, I sent for Sammy, and through him told our host that we were anxious to hire twenty porters to carry our packages. He declared that there was not such a thing as a porter within a hundred miles, whereon I gave him some more gin. The end of it was that we struck a bargain, I forget for how much, he promising to find us twenty good men who were to stay with us for as long as we wanted them.

Then I asked him about the destruction of the mission station, but although he was half-drunk, on this point he remained very close. All he would say was that he had heard that twenty years ago the people called the Mazitu, who were very fierce, had raided right down to the coast and killed those who dwelt there, except a white man and his wife who had fled inland and never been seen again.

"How many of them were buried in that mound by the church?" I asked quickly.

"Who told you they were buried there?" he replied, with a start, but seeing his mistake, went on, "I do not know what you mean. I never heard of anyone being buried. Sleep well, honoured lords, I must go and see to the loading of my goods upon the *Maria*." Then rising, he salaamed and walked, or rather rolled, away.

"So the *Maria* hasn't sailed after all," I said, and whistled in a certain fashion. Instantly Hans crept into the room out of the darkness, for this was my signal to him.

"Hans," I said, "I hear sounds upon that island. Slip down to the shore and spy out what is happening. No one will see you if you are careful."

"No, Baas," he answered with a grin, "I do not think that anyone will see Hans if he is careful, especially at night," and he slid away as quietly as he had come.

Now I went out and spoke to Mavovo, telling him to keep a good watch and to be sure that every man had his gun ready, as I thought that these people were slave-traders and might attack us in the night.

In that event, I said, they were to fall back upon the stoep, but not to fire until I gave the word.

"Good, my father," he answered. "This is a lucky journey; I never thought there would be hope of war so soon. My Snake forgot to mention it the other night. Sleep safe, Macumazana. Nothing that walks shall reach you while we live."

"Don't be so sure," I answered, and we lay down in the bedroom with our clothes on and our rifles by our sides.

The next thing I remember was someone shaking me by the shoulder. I thought it was Stephen, who had agreed to keep awake for the first part of the night and to call me at one in the morning. Indeed, he was awake, for I could see the glow from the pipe he smoked.

"Baas," whispered the voice of Hans, "I have found out everything. They are loading the *Maria* with slaves, taking them in big boats from the island."

"So," I answered. "But how did you get here? Are the hunters asleep without?"

He chuckled. "No, they are not asleep; they look with all their eyes and listen with all their ears, yet old Hans passed through them; even the Baas Somers did not hear him."

"That I didn't," said Stephen; "thought a rat was moving, no more."

I stepped through the place where the door had been on to the stoep. By the light of the fire which the hunters had lit without I could see Mavovo sitting wide awake, his gun upon his knees, and beyond him two sentries. I called him and pointed to Hans.

"See," I said, "what good watchmen you are when one can step over your heads and enter my room without your knowing it!"

Mavovo looked at the Hottentot and felt his clothes and boots to see whether they were wet with the night dew.

"*Ow!*" he exclaimed in a surly voice, "I said that nothing which walks could reach you, Macumazana, but this yellow snake has crawled between us on his belly. Look at the new mud that stains his waistcoat."

"Yet snakes can bite and kill," answered Hans with a snigger. "Oh! you Zulus think that you are very brave, and shout and flourish spears and battleaxes. One poor Hottentot dog is worth a whole impi of you after all. No, don't try to strike me, Mavovo the warrior, since we both serve the same master in our separate ways. When it comes to fighting I will leave the matter to you, but when it is a case of watching or spying, do you leave it to Hans. Look here, Mavovo," and he opened his hand in which was a horn snuff-box such as Zulus sometimes carry in their ears. "To whom does this belong?"

"It is mine," said Mavovo, "and you have stolen it."

"Yes," jeered Hans, "it is yours. Also I stole it from your ear as I passed you in the dark. Don't you remember that you thought a gnat had tickled you and hit up at your face?"

"It is true," growled Mavovo, "and you, snake of a Hottentot, are great in your own low way. Yet next time anything tickles me, I shall strike, not with my hand, but with a spear."

Then I turned them both out, remarking to Stephen that this was a good example of the eternal fight between courage and cunning. After this, as I was sure that Hassan and his friends were too busy to interfere with us that night, we went to bed and slept the sleep of the just.

When I got up the next morning I found that Stephen Somers had already risen and gone out, nor did he appear until I was half through my breakfast.

"Where on earth have you been?" I asked, noting that his clothes were torn and covered with wet moss.

"Up the tallest of those palm trees, Quatermain. Saw an Arab climbing one of them with a rope and got another Arab to teach me the trick. It isn't really difficult, though it looks alarming."

"What in the name of goodness----" I began.

"Oh!" he interrupted, "my ruling passion. Looking through the glasses I thought I caught sight of an orchid growing near the crown, so went up. It wasn't an orchid after all, only a mass of yellow pollen. But I learned something for my pains. Sitting in the top of that palm I saw the *Maria* working out from under the lee of the island. Also, far away, I noted a streak of smoke, and watching it through the glasses, made out what looked to me uncommonly like a man-of-war steaming slowly along the coast. In fact, I am sure it was, and English too. Then the mist came up and I lost sight of them."

"My word!" I said, "that will be the *Crocodile*. What I told our host, Hassan, was not altogether bunkum. Mr. Cato, the port officer at Durban, mentioned to me that the *Crocodile* was expected to call there within the next fortnight to take in stores after a slave- hunting cruise down the coast. Now it would be odd if she chanced to meet the *Maria* and asked to have a look at her cargo, wouldn't it?"

"Not at all, Quatermain, for unless one or the other of them changes her course that is just what she must do within the next hour or so, and I jolly well hope she will. I haven't forgiven that beast, Delgado, the trick he tried to play on us by slipping away with our goods, to say nothing of those poor devils of slaves. Pass the coffee, will you?"

For the next ten minutes we ate in silence, for Stephen had an excellent appetite and was hungry after his morning climb.

Just as we finished our meal Hassan appeared, looking even more villainous than he had done the previous day. I saw also that he was in a truculent mood, induced perhaps by the headache from which he was evidently suffering as a result of his potations. Or perhaps the fact that the *Maria* had got safe away with the slaves, as he imagined unobserved by us, was the cause of the change of his demeanour. A third alternative may have been that he intended to murder us during the previous night and found no safe opportunity of carrying out his amiable scheme.

We saluted him courteously, but without salaaming in reply he asked me bluntly through Sammy when we intended to be gone, as such "Christian dogs defiled his house," which he wanted for himself.

I answered, as soon as the twenty bearers whom he had promised us appeared, but not before.

"You lie," he said. "I never promised you bearers; I have none here."

"Do you mean that you shipped them all away in the *Maria* with the slaves last night?" I asked, sweetly.

My reader, have you ever taken note of the appearance and proceedings of a tom-cat of established age and morose disposition when a little dog suddenly disturbs it on the prowl? Have you observed how it contorts itself into arched but unnatural shapes, how it swells visibly to almost twice its normal size, how its hair stands up and its eyes flash, and the stream of unmentionable language that proceeds from its open mouth? If so, you will have a very good idea of the effect produced upon Hassan by this remark of mine. The fellow looked as though he were going to burst with rage. He rolled about, his bloodshot eyes seemed to protrude, he cursed us horribly, he put his hand upon the hilt of the great knife he wore, and finally he did what the tom-cat does, he spat.

Now, Stephen was standing with me, looking as cool as a cucumber and very much amused, and being, as it chanced, a little nearer to Hassan than I was, received the full benefit of this rude proceeding. My word! didn't it wake him up. He said something strong, and the next second flew at the half-breed like a tiger, landing him a beauty straight upon the nose. Back staggered Hassan, drawing his knife as he did so, but Stephen's left in the eye caused him to drop it, as he dropped himself. I pounced upon the knife, and since it was too late to interfere, for the mischief had been done, let things take their course and held back the Zulus who had rushed up at the noise.

Hassan rose and, to do him credit, came on like a man, head down. His great skull caught Stephen, who was the lighter of the two, in the chest and knocked him over, but before the Arab could follow up the advantage, he was on his feet again. Then ensued a really glorious mill. Hassan fought with head and fists and feet, Stephen with fists alone. Dodging his opponent's rushes, he gave it to him as he passed, and soon his coolness and silence began to tell. Once he was knocked over by a hooked one under the jaw, but in the next round he sent the Arab literally flying head over heels. Oh! how those Zulus cheered, and I, too, danced with delight. Up Hassan came again, spitting out several teeth and, adopting new tactics, grabbed Stephen round the middle. To and fro they swung, the Arab trying to kick the Englishman with his knees and to bite him also, till the pain reminded him of the absence of his front teeth. Once he nearly got him down--nearly, but not quite, for the collar by which he had gripped him (his object was to strangle) burst and, at that juncture, Hassan's turban fell over his face, blinding him for a moment.

Then Stephen gripped him round the middle with his left arm and with his right pommelled him unmercifully till he sank in a sitting position to the ground and held up his hand in token of surrender.

"The noble English lord has beaten me," he gasped.

"Apologise!" yelled Stephen, picking up a handful of mud, "or I shove this down your dirty throat."

He seemed to understand. At any rate, he bowed till his forehead touched the ground, and apologised very thoroughly.

"Now that is over," I said cheerfully to him, "so how about those bearers?"

"I have no bearers," he answered.

"You dirty liar," I exclaimed; "one of my people has been down to your village there and says it is full of men."

"Then go and take them for yourself," he replied, viciously, for he knew that the place was stockaded.

Now I was in a fix. It was all very well to give a slave-dealer the thrashing he deserved, but if he chose to attack us with his Arabs we should be in a poor way. Watching me with the eye that was not bunged up, Hassan guessed my perplexity.

"I have been beaten like a dog," he said, his rage returning to him with his breath, "but God is compassionate and just, He will avenge in due time."

The words had not left his lips for one second when from somewhere out at sea there floated the sullen boom of a great gun. At this moment, too, an Arab rushed up from the shore, crying:

"Where is the Bey Hassan?"

"Here," I said, pointing at him.

The Arab stared until I thought his eyes would drop out, for the Bey Hassan was indeed a sight to see. Then he gabbled in a frightened voice:

"Captain, an English man-of-war is chasing the *Maria*."

Boom went the great gun for the second time. Hassan said nothing, but his jaw dropped, and I saw that he had lost exactly three teeth.

"That is the *Crocodile*," I remarked slowly, causing Sammy to translate, and as I spoke, produced from my inner pocket a Union Jack which I had placed there after I heard that the ship was sighted. "Stephen," I went on as I shook it out, "if you have got your wind, would you mind climbing up that palm tree again and signalling with this to the *Crocodile* out at sea?"

"By George! that's a good idea," said Stephen, whose jovial face, although swollen, was now again wreathed in smiles. "Hans, bring me a long stick and a bit of string."

But Hassan did not think it at all a good idea.

"English lord," he gasped, "you shall have the bearers. I will go to fetch them."

"No, you won't," I said, "you will stop here as a hostage. Send that man."

Hassan uttered some rapid orders and the messenger sped away, this time towards the stockaded village on the right.

As he went another messenger arrived, who also stared amazedly at the condition of his chief.

"Bey--if you are the Bey," he said, in a doubtful voice, for by now the amiable face of Hassan had begun to swell and colour, "with the telescope we have seen that the English man-of-war has sent a boat and boarded the *Maria*."

"God is great!" muttered the discomfited Hassan, "and Delgado, who is a thief and a traitor from his mother's breast, will tell the truth. The English sons of Satan will land here. All is finished; nothing is left but flight. Bid the people fly into the bush and take the slaves --I mean their servants. I will join them."

"No, you won't," I interrupted, through Sammy; "at any rate, not at present. You will come with us."

The miserable Hassan reflected, then he asked:

"Lord Quatermain" (I remember the title, because it is the nearest I ever got, or am likely to get, to the peerage), "if I furnish you with the twenty bearers and accompany you for some days on your journey inland, will you promise not to signal to your countrymen on the ship and bring them ashore?"

"What do you think?" I asked of Stephen.

"Oh!" he answered, "I think I'd agree. This scoundrel has had a pretty good dusting, and if once the *Crocodile* people land, there'll be an end of our expedition. As sure as eggs are eggs they will carry us off to Zanzibar or somewhere to give evidence before a slave court. Also nothing will be gained, for by the time the sailors get here, all these rascals will have bolted, except our friend, Hassan. You see it isn't as though we were sure he would be hung. He'd probably escape after all. International law, subject of a foreign Power, no direct proof--that kind of thing, you know."

"Give me a minute or two," I said, and began to reflect very deeply.

Whilst I was thus engaged several things happened. I saw twenty natives being escorted towards us, doubtless the bearers who had been promised; also I saw many others, accompanied by other natives, flying from the village into the bush. Lastly, a third messenger arrived, who announced that the *Maria* was sailing away, apparently in charge of a prize-crew, and that the man-of-war was putting about as though to accompany her. Evidently she had no intention of effecting a landing upon what was, nominally at any rate, Portuguese territory. Therefore, if anything was to be done, we must act at once.

Well, the end of it was that, like a fool, I accepted Stephen's advice and did nothing, always the easiest course and generally that which leads to most trouble. Ten minutes afterwards I changed my mind, but then it was too late; the *Crocodile* was out of signalling distance. This was subsequent to a conversation with Hans.

"Baas," said that worthy, in his leery fashion, "I think you have made a mistake. You forget that these yellow devils in white robes who have run away will come back again, and that when you return from up country, they may be waiting for you. Now if the English man-of-war had destroyed their town, and their slave-sheds, they might have gone somewhere else. However," he added, as an afterthought, glancing at the disfigured Hassan, "we have their captain, and of course you mean to hang him, Baas. Or if you don't like to, leave it to me. I can hang men very well. Once, when I was young, I helped the executioner at Cape Town."

"Get out," I said, but, nevertheless, I knew that Hans was right.

The Slave Road

The twenty bearers having arrived, in charge of five or six Arabs armed with guns, we went to inspect them, taking Hassan with us, also the hunters. They were a likely lot of men, though rather thin and scared-looking, and evidently, as I could see from their physical appearance and varying methods of dressing the hair, members of different tribes. Having delivered them, the Arabs, or rather one of them, entered into excited conversation with Hassan. As Sammy was not at hand I do not know what was said, although I gathered that they were contemplating his rescue. If so, they gave up the idea and began to run away as their companions had done. One of them, however, a bolder fellow than the rest, turned and fired at me. He missed by some yards, as I could tell from the sing of the bullet, for these Arabs are execrable shots. Still his attempt at murder irritated me so much that I determined he should not go scot-free. I was carrying the little rifle called "Intombi," that with which, as Hans had reminded me, I shot the vultures at Dingaan's kraal many years before. Of course, I could have killed the man, but this I did not wish to do. Or I could have shot him through the leg, but then we should have had to nurse him or leave him to die! So I selected his right arm, which was outstretched as he fled, and at about fifty paces put a bullet through it just above the elbow.

"There," I said to the Zulus as I saw it double up, "that low fellow will never shoot at anyone again."

"Pretty, Macumazana, very pretty!" said Mavovo, "but as you can aim so well, why not have chosen his head? That bullet is half-wasted."

Next I set to work to get into communication with the bearers, who thought, poor devils, that they had been but sold to a new master. Here I may explain that they were slaves not meant for exportation, but men kept to cultivate Hassan's gardens. Fortunately I found that two of them belonged to the Mazitu people, who it may be remembered are of the same blood as the Zulus, although they separated from the parent stock generations ago. These men talked a dialect that I could understand, though at first not very easily. The foundation of it was Zulu, but it had become much mixed with the languages of other tribes whose women the Mazitu had taken to wife.

Also there was a man who could speak some bastard Arabic, sufficiently well for Sammy to converse with him.

I asked the Mazitus if they knew the way back to their country. They answered yes, but it was far off, a full month's journey. I told them that if they would guide us thither, they should receive their freedom and good pay, adding that if the other men served us well, they also should be set free when we had done with them. On receiving this information the poor wretches smiled in a sickly fashion and looked at Hassan-ben-Mohammed, who glowered at them and us from the box on which he was seated in charge of Mavovo.

How can we be free while that man lives, their look seemed to say. As though to confirm their doubts Hassan, who understood or guessed what was passing, asked by what right we were promising freedom to his slaves.

"By right of that," I answered, pointing to the Union Jack which Stephen still had in his hand. "Also we will pay you for them when we return, according as they have served us."

"Yes," he muttered, "you will pay me for them when you return, or perhaps before that, Englishman."

It was three o'clock in the afternoon before we were able to make a start. There was so much to be arranged that it might have been wiser to wait till the morrow, had we not determined that if we could help it nothing would induce us to spend another night in that place. Blankets were served out to each of the bearers who, poor naked creatures, seemed quite touched at the gift of them; the loads were apportioned, having already been packed at Durban in cases such as one man could carry. The pack saddles were put upon the four donkeys which proved to be none the worse for their journey, and burdens to a weight of about 100 lbs. each fixed on them in waterproof hide bags, besides cooking calabashes and sleeping mats which Hans produced from somewhere. Probably he stole them out of the deserted village, but as they were necessary to us I confess I asked no questions. Lastly, six or eight goats which were wandering about were captured to take with us for food till we could find game. For these I offered to pay Hassan, but when I handed him the money he threw it down in a rage, so I picked it up and put it in my pocket again with a clear conscience.

At length everything was more or less ready, and the question arose as to what was to be done with Hassan. The Zulus, like Hans, wished to kill him, as Sammy explained to him in his best Arabic. Then this murderous fellow showed what a coward he was at heart. He flung himself upon his knees, he wept, he invoked us in the name of the Compassionate Allah who, he explained, was after all the same God that we worshipped, till Mavovo, growing impatient of the noise, threatened him with his kerry, whereon he became silent. The easy-natured Stephen was for letting him go, a plan that seemed to have advantages, for then at least we should be rid of his abominable company. After reflection, however, I decided that we had better take him along with us, at any rate for a day or so, to hold as a hostage in case the Arabs should follow and attack us. At first he refused to stir, but the assegai of one of the Zulu hunters pressed gently against what remained of his robe, furnished an argument that he could not resist.

At length we were off. I with the two guides went ahead. Then came the bearers, then half of the hunters, then the four donkeys in charge of Hans and Sammy, then Hassan and the rest of the hunters, except Mavovo, who brought up the rear with Stephen. Needless to say, all our rifles were loaded, and generally we were prepared for any emergency. The only path, that which the guides said we must follow, ran by the seashore for a few hundred yards and then turned inland through Hassan's village where he lived, for it seemed that the old mission house was not used by him. As we marched along a little rocky cliff-- it was not more than ten feet high--where a deep-water channel perhaps fifty yards in breadth separated the mainland from the island whence the slaves had been loaded on to the *Maria*, some difficulty arose about the donkeys. One of these slipped its load and another began to buck and evinced an inclination to leap into the sea with its precious burden. The rearguard of hunters ran to get hold of it, when suddenly there was a splash.

The brute's in! I thought to myself, till a shout told me that not the ass, but Hassan had departed over the cliff's edge. Watching his opportunity and being, it was clear, a first-rate swimmer, he had flung himself backwards in the midst of the confusion and falling into deep water, promptly dived. About twenty yards from the shore he came up for a moment, then dived again heading for the island. I dare say I could have potted him through the head with a snap shot, but somehow I did not like to kill a man swimming for his life as though he were a hippopotamus or a crocodile. Moreover, the boldness of the manœuvre appealed to me. So I refrained from firing and called to the others to do likewise.

As our late host approached the shore of the island I saw Arabs running down the rocks to help him out of the water. Either they had not left the place, or had re-occupied it as soon as *H.M.S.Crocodile* had vanished with her prize. As it was clear that to recapture Hassan would involve an attack upon the garrison of the island which we were in no position to carry out, I gave orders for the march to be resumed. These, the difficulty with the donkey having been overcome, were obeyed at once.

It was fortunate that we did not delay, for scarcely had the caravan got into motion when the Arabs on the island began to fire at us. Luckily no one was hit, and we were soon round a point and under cover; also their shooting was as bad as usual. One missile, however, it was a pot-leg, struck a donkey-load and smashed a bottle of good brandy and a tin of preserved butter. This made me angry, so motioning to the others to proceed I took shelter behind a tree and waited till a torn and dirty turban, which I recognised as that of Hassan, poked up above a rock. Well, I put a bullet through that turban, for I saw the thing fly, but unfortunately, not through the head beneath it. Having left this P.P.C. card on our host, I bolted from the rock and caught up the others.

Presently we passed round the village; through it I would not go for fear of an ambuscade. It was quite a big place, enclosed with a strong fence, but hidden from the sea by a rise in the intervening land. In the centre was a large eastern-looking house, where doubtless Hassan dwelt with his harem. After we had gone a little way further, to my astonishment I saw flames breaking out from the palm-leaf roof of this house. At the time I could not imagine how this happened, but when, a day or two later, I observed Hans wearing a pair of large and very handsome gold pendants in his ears and a gold bracelet on his wrist, and found that he and one of the hunters were extremely well set up in the matter of British sovereigns--well, I had my doubts. In due course the truth came out. He and the hunter, an adventurous spirit, slipped through a gate in the fence without being observed, ran across the deserted village to the house, stole the ornaments and money from the women's apartments and as they departed, fired the place "in exchange for the bottle of good brandy," as Hans explained.

I was inclined to be angry, but after all, as we had been fired on, Hans's exploit became an act of war rather than a theft. So I made him and his companion divide the gold equally with the rest of the hunters, who no doubt had kept their eyes conveniently shut, not forgetting Sammy, and said no more. They netted £8 apiece, which pleased them very much. In addition to this I gave £1 each, or rather goods to that value, to the bearers as their share of the loot.

Hassan, I remarked, was evidently a great agriculturist, for the gardens which he worked by slave labour were beautiful, and must have brought him in a large revenue.

Passing through these gardens we came to sloping land covered with bush. Here the track was not too good, for the creepers hampered our progress. Indeed, I was very glad when towards sunset we reached the crest of a hill and emerged upon a tableland which was almost clear of trees and rose gradually till it met the horizon. In that bush we might easily have been attacked, but in this open country I was not so much afraid, since the loss to the Arabs would have been great before we were overpowered. As a matter of fact, although spies dogged us for days no assault was ever attempted.

Finding a convenient place by a stream we camped for the night, but as it was so fine, did not pitch the tents. Afterwards I was sorry that we had not gone further from the water, since the mosquitoes bred by millions in the marshes bordering the stream gave us a dreadful time. On poor Stephen, fresh from England, they fell with peculiar ferocity, with the result that in the morning what between the bruises left by Hassan and their bites, he was a spectacle for men and angels. Another thing that broke our rest was the necessity of keeping a strict watch in case the slave-traders should elect to attack us in the hours of darkness; also to guard against the possibility of our bearers running away and perhaps stealing the goods. It is true that before they went to sleep I explained to them very clearly that any of them who attempted to give us the slip would certainly be seen and shot, whereas if they remained with us they would be treated with every kindness. They answered through the two Mazitu that they had nowhere to go, and did not wish to fall again into the power of Hassan, of whom they spoke literally with shudders, pointing the while to their scarred backs and the marks of the slave yokes upon their necks. Their protestations seemed and indeed proved to be sincere, but of this of course we could not then be sure.

As I was engaged at sunrise in making certain that the donkeys had not strayed and generally that all was well, I noted through the thin mist a little white object, which at first I thought was a small bird sitting on an upright stick about fifty yards from the camp. I went towards it and discovered that it was not a bird but a folded piece of paper stuck in a cleft wand, such as natives often use for the carrying of letters. I opened the paper and with great difficulty, for the writing within was bad Portuguese, read as follows:

"English Devils.--Do not think that you have escaped me. I know where you are going, and if you live through the journey it will be but to die at my hands after all. I tell you that I have at my command three hundred brave men armed with guns who worship Allah and thirst for the blood of Christian dogs. With these I will follow, and if you fall into my hands alive, you shall learn what it is to die by fire or pinned over ant-heaps in the sun. Let us see if your English man-of-war will help you then, or your false God either. Misfortune go with you, white-skinned robbers of honest men!"

This pleasing epistle was unsigned, but its anonymous author was not hard to identify. I showed it to Stephen who was so infuriated at its contents that he managed to dab some ammonia with which he was treating his mosquito bites into his eye. When at length the pain was soothed by bathing, we concocted this answer:

"Murderer, known among men as Hassan-ben-Mohammed--Truly we sinned in not hanging you when you were in our power. Oh! wolf who grows fat upon the blood of the innocent, this is a fault that we shall not commit again. Your death is near to you and we believe at our hands. Come with all your villains whenever you will. The more there are of them the better we shall be pleased, who would rather rid the world of many fiends than of a few,

"Till we meet again, Allan Quatermain, Stephen Somers."

"Neat, if not Christian," I said when I had read the letter over.

"Yes," replied Stephen, "but perhaps just a little bombastic in tone. If that gentleman did arrive with three hundred armed men--eh?"

"Then, my boy," I answered, "in this way or in that we shall thrash him. I don't often have an inspiration, but I've got one now, and it is to the effect that Mr. Hassan has not very long to live and that we shall be intimately connected with his end. Wait till you have seen a slave caravan and you will understand my feelings. Also I know these gentry. That little prophecy of ours will get upon his nerves and give him a foretaste of things. Hans, go and set this letter in that cleft stick. The postman will call for it before long."

As it happened, within a few days we did see a slave caravan, some of the merchandise of the estimable Hassan.

We had been making good progress through a beautiful and healthy country, steering almost due west, or rather a little to the north of west. The land was undulating and rich, well-watered and only bush- clad in the neighbourhood of the streams, the higher ground being open, of a park-like character, and dotted here and there with trees. It was evident that once, and not very long ago, the population had been dense, for we came to the remains of many villages, or rather towns with large market-places. Now, however, these were burned with fire, or deserted, or occupied only by a few old bodies who got a living from the overgrown gardens. These poor people, who sat desolate and crooning in the sun, or perhaps worked feebly at the once fertile fields, would fly screaming at our approach, for to them men armed with guns must of necessity be slave-traders.

Still from time to time we contrived to catch some of them, and through one member of our party or the other to get at their stories. Really it was all one story. The slaving Arabs, on this pretext or on that, had set tribe against tribe. Then they sided with the stronger and conquered the weaker by aid of their terrible guns, killing out the old folk and taking the young men, women and children (except the infants whom they butchered) to be sold as slaves. It seemed that the business had begun about twenty years before, when Hassan-ben-Mohammed and his companions arrived at Kilwa and drove away the missionary who had built a station there.

At first this trade was extremely easy and profitable, since the raw material lay near at hand in plenty. By degrees, however, the neighbouring communities had been worked out. Countless numbers of them were killed, while the pick of the population passed under the slave yoke, and those of them who survived, vanished in ships to unknown lands. Thus it came about that the slavers were obliged to go further afield and even to conduct their raids upon the borders of the territory of the great Mazitu people, the inland race of Zulu origin of whom I have spoken. According to our informants, it was even rumoured that they proposed shortly to attack these Mazitu in force, relying on their guns to give them the victory and open to them a new and almost inexhaustible store of splendid human merchandise. Meanwhile they were cleaning out certain small tribes which hitherto had escaped them, owing to the fact that they had their residence in bush or among difficult hills.

The track we followed was the recognised slave road. Of this we soon became aware by the numbers of skeletons which we found lying in the tall grass at its side, some of them with heavy slave-sticks still upon their wrists. These, I suppose, had died from exhaustion, but others, as their split skulls showed had been disposed of by their captors.

On the eighth day of our march we struck the track of a slave caravan. It had been travelling towards the coast, but for some reason or other had turned back. This may have been because its leaders had been warned of the approach of our party. Or perhaps they had heard that another caravan, which was at work in a different district, was drawing near, bringing its slaves with it, and wished to wait for its arrival in order that they might join forces.

The spoor of these people was easy to follow. First we found the body of a boy of about ten. Then vultures revealed to us the remains of two young men, one of whom had been shot and the other killed by a blow from an axe. Their corpses were roughly hidden beneath some grass, I know not why. A mile or two further on we heard a child wailing and found it by following its cries. It was a little girl of about four who had been pretty, though now she was but a living skeleton. When she saw us she scrambled away on all fours like a monkey. Stephen followed her, while I, sick at heart, went to get a tin of preserved milk from our stores. Presently I heard him call to me in a horrified voice. Rather reluctantly, for I knew that he must have found something dreadful, I pushed my way through the bush to where he was. There, bound to the trunk of a tree, sat a young woman, evidently the mother of the child, for it clung to her leg.

Thank God she was still living, though she must have died before another day dawned. We cut her loose, and the Zulu hunters, who are kind folk enough when they are not at war, carried her to camp. In the end with much trouble we saved the lives of that mother and child. I sent for the two Mazitus, with whom I could by now talk fairly well, and asked them why the slavers did these things.

They shrugged their shoulders and one of them answered with a rather dreadful laugh:

"Because, Chief, these Arabs, being black-hearted, kill those who can walk no more, or tie them up to die. If they let them go they might recover and escape, and it makes the Arabs sad that those who have been their slaves should live to be free and happy."

"Does it? Does it indeed?" exclaimed Stephen with a snort of rage that reminded me of his father. "Well, if ever I get a chance I'll make them sad with a vengeance."

Stephen was a tender-hearted young man, and for all his soft and indolent ways, an awkward customer when roused.

Within forty-eight hours he got his chance, thus: That day we camped early for two reasons. The first was that the woman and child we had rescued wee so weak they could not walk without rest, and we had no men to spare to carry them; the second that we came to an ideal spot to pass the night. It was, as usual, a deserted village through which ran a beautiful stream of water. Here we took possession of some outlying huts with a fence round them, and as Mavovo had managed to shoot a fat eland cow and her half-grown calf, we prepared to have a regular feast. Whilst Sammy was making some broth for the rescued woman, and Stephen and I smoked our pipes and watched him, Hans slipped through the broken gate of the thorn fence, or *boma*, and announced that Arabs were coming, two lots of them with many slaves.

We ran out to look and saw that, as he had said, two caravans were approaching, or rather had reached the village, but at some distance from us, and were now camping on what had once been the market-place. One of these was that whose track we had followed, although during the last few hours of our march we had struck away from it, chiefly because we could not bear such sights as I have described. It seemed to comprise about two hundred and fifty slaves and over forty guards, all black men carrying guns, and most of them by their dress Arabs, or bastard Arabs. In the second caravan, which approached from another direction, were not more than one hundred slaves and about twenty or thirty captors.

"Now," I said, "let us eat our dinner and then, if you like, we will go to call upon those gentlemen, just to show that we are not afraid of them. Hans, get the flag and tie it to the top of that tree; it will show them to what country we belong."

Up went the Union Jack duly, and presently through our glasses we saw the slavers running about in a state of excitement; also we saw the poor slaves turn and stare at the bit of flapping bunting and then begin to talk to each other. It struck me as possible that someone among their number had seen a Union Jack in the hands of an English traveller, or had heard of it as flying upon ships or at points on the coast, and what it meant to slaves. Or they may have understood some of the remarks of the Arabs, which no doubt were pointed and explanatory. At any rate, they turned and stared till the Arabs ran among them with sjambocks, that is, whips of hippopotamus hide, and suppressed their animated conversation with many blows.

At first I thought that they would break camp and march away; indeed, they began to make preparations to do this, then abandoned the idea, probably because the slaves were exhausted and there was no other water they could reach before nightfall. In the end they settled down and lit cooking fires. Also, as I observed, they took precautions against attack by stationing sentries and forcing the slaves to construct a *boma* of thorns about their camp.

"Well," said Stephen, when we had finished our dinner, "are you ready for that call?"

"No!" I answered, "I do not think that I am. I have been considering things, and concluded that we had better leave well alone. By this time those Arabs will know all the story of our dealings with their worthy master, Hassan, for no doubt he has sent messengers to them. Therefore, if we go to their camp, they may shoot us at sight. Or, if they receive us well, they may offer hospitality and poison us, or cut our throats suddenly. Our position might be better, still it is one that I believe they would find difficult to take. So, in my opinion, we had better stop still and await developments."

Stephen grumbled something about my being over-cautious, but I took no heed of him. One thing I did do, however. Sending for Hans, I told him to take one of the Mazitu--I dared not risk them both for they were our guides--and another of the natives whom we had borrowed from Hassan, a bold fellow who knew all the local languages, and creep down to the slavers' camp as soon as it was quite dark. There I ordered him to find out what he could, and if possible to mix with the slaves and explain that we were their friends. Hans nodded, for this was exactly the kind of task that appealed to him, and went off to make his preparations.

Stephen and I also made some preparations in the way of strengthening our defences, building large watch-fires and setting sentries.

The night fell, and Hans with his companions departed stealthily as snakes. The silence was intense, save for the occasional wailings of the slaves, which now and again broke out in bursts of melancholy sound, "*La-lu-La-lua*" and then died away, to be followed by horrid screams as the Arabs laid their lashes upon some poor wretch. Once too, a shot was fired.

"They have seen Hans," said Stephen.

"I think not," I answered, "for if so there would have been more than one shot. Either it was an accident or they were murdering a slave."

After this nothing more happened for a long while, till at length Hans seemed to rise out of the ground in front of me, and behind him I saw the figures of the Mazitu and the other man.

"Tell your story," I said.

"Baas, it is this. Between us we have learned everything. The Arabs know all about you and what men you have. Hassan has sent them orders to kill you. It is well that you did not go to visit them, for certainly you would have been murdered. We crept near and overheard their talk. They purpose to attack us at dawn to-morrow morning unless we leave this place before, which they will know of as we are being watched."

"And if so, what then?" I asked.

"Then, Baas, they will attack as we are making up the caravan, or immediately afterwards as we begin to march."

"Indeed. Anything more, Hans?"

"Yes, Baas. These two men crept among the slaves and spoke with them. They are very sad, those slaves, and many of them have died of heart- pain because they have been taken from their homes and do not know where they are going. I saw one die just now; a young woman. She was talking to another woman and seemed quite well, only tired, till suddenly she said in a loud voice, 'I am going to die, that I may come back as a spirit and bewitch these devils till they are spirits too.' Then she called upon the fetish of her tribe, put her hands to her breast and fell down dead. At least," added Hans, spitting reflectively, "she did not fall quite down because the slave-stick held her head off the ground. The Arabs were very angry, both because she had cursed them and was dead. One of them came and kicked her body and afterwards shot her little boy who was sick, because the mother had cursed them. But fortunately he did not see us, because we were in the dark far from the fire."

"Anything more, Hans?"

"One thing, Baas. These two men lent the knives you gave them to two of the boldest among the slaves that they might cut the cords of the slave-sticks and the other cords with which they were tied, and then pass them down the lines, that their brothers might do the same. But perhaps the Arabs will find it out, and then the Mazitu and the other must lose their knives. That is all. Has the Baas a little tobacco?"

"Now, Stephen," I said when Hans had gone and I had explained everything, "there are two courses open to us. Either we can try to give these gentlemen the slip at once, in which case we must leave the woman and child to their fate, or we can stop where we are and wait to be attacked."

"I won't run," said Stephen sullenly; "it would be cowardly to desert that poor creature. Also we should have a worse chance marching. Remember Hans said that they are watching us."

"Then you would wait to be attacked?"

"Isn't there a third alternative, Quatermain? To attack them?"

"That's the idea," I said. "Let us send for Mavovo."

Presently he came and sat down in front of us, while I set out the case to him.

"It is the fashion of my people to attack rather than to be attacked, and yet, my father, in this case my heart is against it. Hans" (he called him *Inblatu*, a Zulu word which means Spotted Snake, that was the Hottentot's Kaffir name) "says that there are quite sixty of the yellow dogs, all armed with guns, whereas we have not more than fifteen, for we cannot trust the slave men. Also he says that they are within a strong fence and awake, with spies out, so that it will be difficult to surprise them. But here, father, we are in a strong fence and cannot be surprised. Also men who torture and kill women and children, except in war must, I think, be cowards, and will come on faintly against good shooting, if indeed they come at all. Therefore, I say, 'Wait till the buffalo shall either charge or run.' But the word is with you, Macumazana, wise Watcher-by-Night, not with me, your hunter. Speak, you who are old in war, and I will obey."

"You argue well," I answered; "also another reason comes to my mind. Those Arab brutes may get behind the slaves, of whom we should butcher a lot without hurting them. Stephen, I think we had better see the thing through here."

"All right, Quatermain. Only I hope that Mavovo is wrong in thinking that those blackguards may change their minds and run away."

"Really, young man, you are becoming very blood-thirsty--for an orchid grower," I remarked, looking at him. "Now, for my part, I devoutly hope that Mavovo is right, for let me tell you, if he isn't it may be a nasty job."

"I've always been peaceful enough up to the present," replied Stephen. "But the sight of those unhappy wretches of slaves with their heads cut open, and of the woman tied to a tree to starve----"

"Make you wish to usurp the functions of God Almighty," I said. "Well, it is a natural impulse and perhaps, in the circumstances, one that will not displease Him. And now, as we have made up our minds what we are going to do, let's get to business so that these Arab gentlemen may find their breakfast ready when they come to call."

The Rush of the Slaves

Well, we did all that we could in the way of making ready. After we had strengthened the thorn fence of our *boma* as much as possible and lit several large fires outside of it to give us light, I allotted his place to each of the hunters and saw that their rifles were in order and that they had plenty of ammunition. Then I made Stephen lie down to sleep, telling him that I would wake him to watch later on. This, however, I had no intention of doing as I wanted him to rise fresh and with a steady nerve on the occasion of his first fight.

As soon as I saw that his eyes were shut I sat down on a box to think. To tell the truth, I was not altogether happy in my mind. To begin with I did not know how the twenty bearers would behave under fire.

They might be seized with panic and rush about, in which case I determined to let them out of the *boma*. to take their chance, for panic is a catching thing.

A worse matter was our rather awkward position. There were a good many trees round the camp among which an attacking force could take cover. But what I feared much more than this, or even than the reedy banks of the stream along which they could creep out of reach of our bullets, was a sloping stretch of land behind us, covered with thick grass and scrub and rising to a crest about two hundred yards away. Now if the Arabs got round to this crest they would fire straight into our *boma*. and make it untenable. Also if the wind were in their favour, they might burn us out or attack under the clouds of smoke. As a matter of fact, by the special mercy of Providence, none of these things happened, for a reason which I will explain presently.

In the case of a night, or rather a dawn attack, I have always found that hour before the sky begins to lighten very trying indeed. As a rule everything that can be done is done, so that one must sit idle. Also it is then that both the physical and the moral qualities are at their lowest ebb, as is the mercury in the thermometer. The night is dying, the day is not yet born. All nature feels the influence of that hour. Then bad dreams come, then infants wake and call, then memories of those who are lost to us arise, then the hesitating soul often takes its plunge into the depths of the Unknown. It is not wonderful, therefore, that on this occasion the wheels of Time drave heavily for me. I knew that the morning was at hand by many signs. The sleeping bearers turned and muttered in their sleep, a distant lion ceased its roaring and departed to its own place, an alert-minded cock crew somewhere, and our donkeys rose and began to pull at their tether- ropes. As yet, however, it was quite dark. Hans crept up to me; I saw his wrinkled, yellow face in the light of the watch-fire.

"I smell the dawn," he said and vanished again.

Mavovo appeared, his massive frame silhouetted against the blackness.

"Watcher-by-Night, the night is done," he said. "If they come at all, the enemy should soon be here."

Saluting, he too passed away into the dark, and presently I heard the sounds of spear-blades striking together and of rifles being cocked.

I went to Stephen and woke him. He sat up yawning, muttered something about greenhouses; then remembering, said:

"Are those Arabs coming? We are in for a fight at last. Jolly, old fellow, isn't it?"

"You are a jolly old fool!" I answered inconsequently; and marched off in a rage.

My mind was uneasy about this inexperienced young man. If anything should happen to him, what should I say to his father? Well, in that event, it was probable that something would happen to me too. Very possibly we should both be dead in an hour. Certainly I had no intention of allowing myself to be taken alive by those slaving devils. Hassan's remarks about fires and ant-heaps and the sun were too vividly impressed upon my memory.

In another five minutes everybody was up, though it required kicks to rouse most of the bearers from their slumbers. They, poor men, were accustomed to the presence of Death and did not suffer him to disturb their sleep. Still I noted that they muttered together and seemed alarmed.

"If they show signs of treachery, you must kill them," I said to Mavovo, who nodded in his grave, silent fashion.

Only we left the rescued slave-woman and her child plunged in the stupor of exhaustion in a corner of the camp. What was the use of disturbing her?

Sammy, who seemed far from comfortable, brought two pannikins of coffee to Stephen and myself.

"This is a momentous occasion, Messrs. Quatermain and Somers," he said as he gave us the coffee, and I noted that his hand shook and his teeth chattered. "The cold is extreme," he went on in his copybook English by way of explaining these physical symptoms which he saw I had observed. "Mr. Quatermain, it is all very well for you to paw the ground and smell the battle from afar, as is written in the Book of Job. But I was not brought up to the trade and take it otherwise. Indeed I wish I was back at the Cape, yes, even within the whitewashed walls of the Place of Detention."

"So do I," I muttered, keeping my right foot on the ground with difficulty.

But Stephen laughed outright and asked:

"What will you do, Sammy, when the fighting begins?"

"Mr. Somers," he answered, "I have employed some wakeful hours in making a hole behind that tree-trunk, through which I hope bullets will not pass. There, being a man of peace, I shall pray for our success."

"And if the Arabs get in, Sammy?"

"Then, sir, under Heaven, I shall trust to the fleetness of my legs."

I could stand it no longer, my right foot flew up and caught Sammy in the place at which I had aimed. He vanished, casting a reproachful look behind him.

Just then a terrible clamour arose in the slavers' camp which hitherto had been very silent, and just then also the first light of dawn glinted on the barrels of our guns.

"Look out!" I cried, as I gulped down the last of my coffee, "there's something going on there."

The clamour grew louder and louder till it seemed to fill the skies with a concentrated noise of curses and shrieking. Distinct from it, as it were, I heard shouts of alarm and rage, and then came the sounds of gunshots, yells of agony and the thud of many running feet. By now the light was growing fast, as it does when once it comes in these latitudes. Three more minutes, and through the grey mist of the dawn we saw dozens of black figures struggling up the slope towards us. Some seemed to have logs of wood tied behind them, others crawled along on all fours, others dragged children by the hand, and all yelled at the top of their voices.

"The slaves are attacking us," said Stephen, lifting his rifle.

"Don't shoot," I cried. "I think they have broken loose and are taking refuge with us."

I was right. These unfortunates had used the two knives which our men smuggled to them to good purpose. Having cut their bonds during the night they were running to seek the protection of the Englishmen and their flag. On they surged, a hideous mob, the slave-sticks still fast to the necks of many of them, for they had not found time or opportunity to loose them all, while behind came the Arabs firing. The position was clearly very serious, for if they burst into our camp, we should be overwhelmed by their rush and fall victims to the bullets of their captors.

"Hans," I cried, "take the men who were with you last night and try to lead those slaves round behind us. Quick! Quick now before we are stamped flat."

Hans darted away, and presently I saw him and the two other men running towards the approaching crowd, Hans waving a shirt or some other white object to attract their attention. At the time the foremost of them had halted and were screaming, "Mercy, English! Save us, English!" having caught sight of the muzzles of our guns.

This was a fortunate occurrence indeed, for otherwise Hans and his companions could never have stopped them. The next thing I saw was the white shirt bearing away to the left on a line which led past the fence of our *boma*. into the scrub and high grass behind the camp. After it struggled and scrambled the crowd of slaves like a flock of sheep after the bell-wether. To them Hans's shirt was a kind of "white helmet of Navarre."

So that danger passed by. Some of the slaves had been struck by the Arab bullets or trodden down in the rush or collapsed from weakness, and at those of them who still lived the pursuers were firing. One woman, who had fallen under the weight of the great slave-stick which was fastened about her throat, was crawling forward on her hands and knees. An Arab fired at her and the bullet struck the ground under her stomach but without hurting her, for she wriggled forward more quickly. I was sure that he would shoot again, and watched. Presently, for by now the light was good, I saw him, a tall fellow in a white robe, step from behind the shelter of a banana-tree about a hundred and fifty yards away, and take a careful aim at the woman. But I too took aim and--well, I am not bad at this kind of snap-shooting when I try. That Arab's gun never went off. Only he went up two feet or more into the air and fell backwards, shot through the head which was the part of his person that I had covered.

The hunters uttered a low "*Ow!*" of approval, while Stephen, in a sort of ecstasy, exclaimed:

"Oh! what a heavenly shot!"

"Not bad, but I shouldn't have fired it," I answered, "for they haven't attacked us yet. It is a kind of declaration of war, and," I added, as Stephen's sun-helmet leapt from his head, "there's the answer. Down, all of you, and fire through the loopholes."

Then the fight began. Except for its grand finale it wasn't really much of a fight when compared with one or two we had afterwards on this expedition. But, on the other hand, its character was extremely awkward for us. The Arabs made one rush at the beginning, shouting on Allah as they came. But though they were plucky villains they did not repeat that experiment. Either by good luck or good management Stephen knocked over two of them with his double-barrelled rifle, and I also emptied my large-bore breech-loader--the first I ever owned--among them, not without results, while the hunters made a hit or two.

After this the Arabs took cover, getting behind trees and, as I had feared, hiding in the reeds on the banks of the stream. Thence they harassed us a great deal, for amongst them were some very decent shots. Indeed, had we not taken the precaution of lining the thorn fence with a thick bank of earth and sods, we should have fared badly. As it was, one of the hunters was killed, the bullet passing through the loophole and striking him in the throat as he was about to fire, while the unfortunate bearers who were on rather higher ground, suffered a good deal, two of them being dispatched outright and four wounded. After this I made the rest of them lie flat on the ground close against the fence, in such a fashion that we could fire over their bodies.

Soon it became evident that there were more of these Arabs than we had thought, for quite fifty of them were firing from different places. Moreover, by slow degrees they were advancing with the evident object of outflanking us and gaining the high ground behind. Some of them, of course, we stopped as they rushed from cover to cover, but this kind of shooting was as difficult as that at bolting rabbits across a woodland ride, and to be honest, I must say that I alone was much good at the game, for here my quick eye and long practice told.

Within an hour the position had grown very serious indeed, so much so that we found it necessary to consider what should be done. I pointed out that with our small number a charge against the scattered riflemen, who were gradually surrounding us, would be worse than useless, while it was almost hopeless to expect to hold the *boma* till nightfall. Once the Arabs got behind us, they could rake us from the higher ground. Indeed, for the last half-hour we had directed all our efforts to preventing them from passing this *boma*, which, fortunately, the stream on the one side and a stretch of quite open land on the other made it very difficult for them to do without more loss than they cared to face.

"I fear there is only one thing for it," I said at length, during a pause in the attack while the Arabs were either taking counsel or waiting for more ammunition, "to abandon the camp and everything and bolt up the hill. As those fellows must be tired and we are all good runners, we may save our lives in that way."

"How about the wounded," asked Stephen, "and the slave-woman and child?"

"I don't know," I answered, looking down.

Of course I did know very well, but here, in an acute form, arose the ancient question: Were we to perish for the sake of certain individuals in whom we had no great interest and whom we could not save by remaining with them? If we stayed where we were our end seemed fairly certain, whereas if we ran for it, we had a good chance of escape. But this involved the desertion of several injured bearers and a woman and child whom we had picked up starving, all of whom would certainly be massacred, save perhaps the woman and child.

As these reflections flitted through my brain I remembered that a drunken Frenchman named Leblanc, whom I had known in my youth and who had been a friend of Napoleon, or so he said, told me that the great emperor when he was besieging Acre in the Holy Land, was forced to retreat. Being unable to carry off his wounded men, he left them in a monastery on Mount Carmel, each with a dose of poison by his side. Apparently they did not take the poison, for according to Leblanc, who said he was present there (not as a wounded man), the Turks came and butchered them. So Napoleon chose to save his own life and that of his army at the expense of his wounded. But, after all, I reflected, he was no shining example to Christian men and I hadn't time to find any poison. In a few words I explained the situation to Mavovo, leaving out the story of Napoleon, and asked his advice.

"We must run," he answered. "Although I do not like running, life is more than stores, and he who lives may one day pay his debts."

"But the wounded, Mavovo; we cannot carry them."

"I will see to them, Macumazana; it is the fortune of war. Or if they prefer it, we can leave them--to be nursed by the Arabs," which of course was just Napoleon and his poison over again.

I confess that I was about to assent, not wishing that I and Stephen, especially Stephen, should be potted in an obscure engagement with some miserable slave-traders, when something happened.

It will be remembered that shortly after dawn Hans, using a shirt for a flag, had led the fugitive slaves past the camp up to the hill behind. There he and they had vanished, and from that moment to this we had seen nothing of him or them. Now of a sudden he reappeared still waving the shirt. After him rushed a great mob of naked men, two hundred of them perhaps, brandishing slave-sticks, stones and the boughs of trees. When they had almost reached the *boma* whence we watched them amazed, they split into two bodies, half of them passing to our left, apparently under the command of the Mazitu who had accompanied Hans to the slave-camp, and the other half to the right following the old Hottentot himself. I stared at Mavovo, for I was too thunderstruck to speak.

"Ah!" said Mavovo, "that Spotted Snake of yours" (he referred to Hans), "is great in his own way, for he has even been able to put courage into the hearts of slaves. Do you not understand, my father, that they are about to attack those Arabs, yes, and to pull them down, as wild dogs do a buffalo calf?"

It was true: this was the Hottentot's superb design. Moreover, it succeeded. Up on the hillside he had watched the progress of the fight and seen how it must end. Then, through the interpreter who was with him, he harangued those slaves, pointing out to them that we, their white friends, were about to be overwhelmed, and that they must either strike for themselves, or return to the yoke. Among them were some who had been warriors in their own tribes, and through these he stirred the others. They seized the slave-sticks from which they had been freed, pieces of rock, anything that came to their hands, and at a given signal charged, leaving only the women and children behind them.

Seeing them come the scattered Arabs began to fire at them, killing some, but thereby revealing their own hiding-places. At these the slaves rushed. They hurled themselves upon the Arabs; they tore them, they dashed out their brains in such fashion that within another five minutes quite two-thirds of them were dead; and the rest, of whom we took some toll with our rifles as they bolted from cover, were in full flight.

It was a terrible vengeance. Never did I witness a more savage scene than that of these outraged men wreaking their wrongs upon their tormentors. I remember that when most of the Arabs had been killed and a few were escaped, the slaves found one, I think it was the captain of the gang, who had hidden himself in a little patch of dead reeds washed up by the stream. Somehow they managed to fire these; I expect that Hans, who had remained discreetly in the background after the fighting began, emerged when it was over and gave them a match. In due course out came the wretched Arab. Then they flung themselves on him as marching ants do upon a caterpillar, and despite his cries for mercy, tore him to fragments, literally to fragments. Being what they were, it was hard to blame them. If we had seen our parents shot, our infants pitilessly butchered, our homes destroyed and our women and children marched off in the slave-sticks to be sold into bondage, should we not have done the same? I think so, although we are not ignorant savages.

Thus our lives were saved by those whom we had tried to save, and for once justice was done even in those dark parts of Africa, for in that time they were dark indeed. Had it not been for Hans and the courage which he managed to inspire into the hearts of these crushed blacks, I have little doubt but that before nightfall we should have been dead, for I do not think that any attempt at retreat would have proved successful. And if it had, what would have happened to us in that wild country surrounded by enemies and with only the few rounds of ammunition that we could have carried in our flight?

"Ah! Baas," said the Hottentot a little while later, squinting at me with his bead-like eyes, "after all you did well to listen to my prayer and bring me with you. Old Hans is a drunkard, yes, or at least he used to be, and old Hans gambles, yes, and perhaps old Hans will go to hell. But meanwhile old Hans can think, as he thought one day before the attack on Maraisfontein, as he thought one day on the Hill of Slaughter by Dingaan's kraal, and as he thought this morning up there among the bushes. Oh! he knew how it must end. He saw that those dogs of Arabs were cutting down a tree to make a bridge across that deep stream and get round to the high ground at the back of you, whence they would have shot you all in five minutes. And now, Baas, my stomach feels very queer. There was no breakfast on the hillside and the sun was very hot. I think that just one tot of brandy--oh! I know, I promised not to drink, but if *you* give it me the sin is yours, not mine."

Well, I gave him the tot, a stiff one, which he drank quite neat, although it was against my principles, and locked up the bottle afterwards. Also I shook the old fellow's hand and thanked him, which seemed to please him very much, for he muttered something to the effect that it was nothing, since if I had died he would have died too, and therefore he was thinking of himself, not of me. Also two big tears trickled down his snub nose, but these may have been produced by the brandy.

Well, we were the victors and elated as may be imagined, for we knew that the few slavers who had escaped would not attack us again. Our first thought was for food, for it was now past midday and we were starving. But dinner presupposed a cook, which reminded us of Sammy. Stephen, who was in such a state of jubilation that he danced rather than walked, the helmet with a bullet-hole through it stuck ludicrously upon the back of his head, started to look for him, and presently called to me in an alarmed voice. I went to the back of the camp and, staring into a hole like a small grave, that had been hollowed behind a solitary thorn tree, at the bottom of which lay a huddled heap, I found him. It was Sammy to all appearance. We got hold of him, and up he came, limp, senseless, but still holding in his hand a large, thick Bible, bound in boards. Moreover, in the exact centre of this Bible was a bullet-hole, or rather a bullet which had passed through the stout cover and buried itself in the paper behind. I remember that the point of it reached to the First Book of Samuel.

As for Sammy himself, he seemed to be quite uninjured, and indeed after we had poured some water on him--he was never fond of water--he revived quickly enough. Then we found out what had happened.

"Gentlemen," he said, "I was seated in my place of refuge, being as I have told you a man of peace, enjoying the consolation of religion"-- he was very pious in times of trouble. "At length the firing slackened, and I ventured to peep out, thinking that perhaps the foe had fled, holding the Book in front of my face in case of accidents. After that I remember no more."

"No," said Stephen, "for the bullet hit the Bible and the Bible hit your head and knocked you silly."

"Ah!" said Sammy, "how true is what I was taught that the Book shall be a shield of defence to the righteous. Now I understand why I was moved to bring the thick old Bible that belonged to my mother in heaven, and not the little thin one given to me by the Sunday school teacher, through which the ball of the enemy would have passed."

Then he went off to cook the dinner.

Certainly it was a wonderful escape, though whether this was a direct reward of his piety, as he thought, is another matter.

As soon as we had eaten, we set to work to consider our position, of which the crux was what to do with the slaves. There they sat in groups outside the fence, many of them showing traces of the recent conflict, and stared at us stupidly. Then of a sudden, as though with one voice, they began to clamour for food.

"How are we to feed several hundred people?" asked Stephen.

"The slavers must have done it somehow," I answered. "Let's go and search their camp."

So we went, followed by our hungry clients, and, in addition to many more things, to our delight found a great store of rice, mealies and other grain, some of which was ground into meal. Of this we served out an ample supply together with salt, and soon the cooking pots were full of porridge. My word! how those poor creatures did eat, nor, although it was necessary to be careful, could we find it in our hearts to stint them of the first full meal that had passed their lips after weeks of starvation. When at length they were satisfied we addressed them, thanking them for their bravery, telling them that they were free and asking what they meant to do.

Upon this point they seemed to have but one idea. They said that they would come with us who were their protectors. Then followed a great *indaba*, or consultation, which really I have not time to set out. The end of it was that we agreed that so many of them as wished should accompany us till they reached country that they knew, when they would be at liberty to depart to their own homes. Meanwhile we divided up the blankets and other stores of the Arabs, such as trade goods and beads, among them, and then left them to their own devices, after placing a guard over the foodstuffs. For my part I hoped devoutly that in the morning we should find them gone.

After this we returned to our *boma* just in time to assist at a sad ceremony, that of the burial of my hunter who had been shot through the head. His companions had dug a deep hole outside the fence and within a few yards of where he fell. In this they placed him in a sitting position with his face turned towards Zululand, setting by his side two gourds that belonged to him, one filled with water and the other with grain. Also they gave him a blanket and his two assegais, tearing the blanket and breaking the handles of the spears, to "kill" them as they said. Then quietly enough they threw in the earth about him and filled the top of the hole with large stones to prevent the hyenas from digging him up. This done, one by one, they walked past the grave, each man stopping to bid him farewell by name. Mavovo, who came last, made a little speech, telling the deceased to *namba kachle*, that is, go comfortably to the land of ghosts, as, he added, no doubt he would do who had died as a man should. He requested him, moreover, if he returned as a spirit, to bring good and not ill- fortune on us, since otherwise when he, Mavovo, became a spirit in his turn, he would have words to say to him on the matter. In conclusion, he remarked that as his, Mavovo's Snake, had foretold this event at Durban, a fact with which the deceased would now be acquainted he, the said deceased, could never complain of not having received value for the shilling he had paid as a divining fee.

"Yes," exclaimed one of the hunters with a note of anxiety in his voice, "but your Snake mentioned six of us to you, O doctor!"

"It did," replied Mavovo, drawing a pinch of snuff up his uninjured nostril, "and our brother there was the first of the six. Be not afraid, the other five will certainly join him in due course, for my Snake must speak the truth. Still, if anyone is in a hurry," and he glared round the little circle, "let him stop and talk with me alone. Perhaps I could arrange that his turn----" here he stopped, for they were all gone.

"Glad *I* didn't pay a shilling to have my fortune told by Mavovo," said Stephen, when we were back in the *boma*, "but why did they bury his pots and spears with him?"

"To be used by the spirit on its journey," I answered. "Although they do not quite know it, these Zulus believe, like all the rest of the world, that man lives on elsewhere."

The Magic Mirror

I did not sleep very well that night, for now that the danger was over I found that the long strain of it had told upon my nerves. Also there were many noises. Thus, the bearers who were shot had been handed over to their companions, who disposed of them in a simple fashion, namely by throwing them into the bush where they attracted the notice of hyenas. Then the four wounded men who lay near to me groaned a good deal, or when they were not groaning uttered loud prayers to their local gods. We had done the best we could for these unlucky fellows. Indeed, that kind-hearted little coward, Sammy, who at some time in his career served as a dresser in a hospital, had tended their wounds, none of which were mortal, very well indeed, and from time to time rose to minister to them.

But what disturbed me most was the fearful hubbub which came from the camp below. Many of the tropical African tribes are really semi- nocturnal in their habits, I suppose because there the night is cooler than the day, and on any great occasion this tendency asserts itself.

Thus every one of these freed slaves seemed to be howling his loudest to an accompaniment of clashing iron pots or stones, which, lacking their native drums, they beat with sticks.

Moreover, they had lit large fires, about which they flitted in an ominous and unpleasant fashion, that reminded me of some mediaeval pictures of hell, which I had seen in an old book.

At last I could stand it no longer, and kicking Hans who, curled up like a dog, slept at my feet, asked him what was going on. His answer caused me to regret the question.

"Plenty of those slaves cannibal men, Baas. Think they eat the Arabs and like them very much," he said with a yawn, then went to sleep again.

I did not continue the conversation.

When at length we made a start on the following morning the sun was high over us. Indeed, there was a great deal to do. The guns and ammunition of the dead Arabs had to be collected; the ivory, of which they carried a good store, must be buried, for to take it with us was impossible, and the loads apportioned.] Also it was necessary to make litters for the wounded, and to stir up the slaves from their debauch, into the nature of which I made no further inquiries, was no easy task. On mustering them I found that a good number had vanished during the night, where to I do not know. Still a mob of well over two hundred people, a considerable portion of whom were women and children, remained, whose one idea seemed to be to accompany us wherever we might wander. So with this miscellaneous following at length we started.

To describe our adventures during the next month would be too long if not impossible, for to tell the truth, after the lapse of so many years, these have become somewhat entangled in my mind. Our great difficulty was to feed such a multitude, for the store of rice and grain, upon which we were quite unable to keep a strict supervision, they soon devoured. Fortunately the country through which we passed, at this time of the year (the end of the wet season) was full of game, of which, travelling as we did very slowly, we were able to shoot a great deal. But this game killing, delightful as it may be to the sportsman, soon palled on us as a business. To say nothing of the expenditure of ammunition, it meant incessant work.

Against this the Zulu hunters soon began to murmur, for, as Stephen and I could rarely leave the camp, the burden of it fell on them. Ultimately I hit upon this scheme. Picking out thirty or forty of the likeliest men among the slaves, I served out to each of them ammunition and one of the Arab guns, in the use of which we drilled them as best we could. Then I told them that they must provide themselves and their companions with meat. Of course accidents happened. One man was accidentally shot and three others were killed by a cow elephant and a wounded buffalo. But in the end they learned to handle their rifles sufficiently well to supply the camp. Moreover, day by day little parties of the slaves disappeared, I presume to seek their own homes, so that when at last we entered the borders of the Mazitu country there were not more than fifty of them left, including seventeen of those whom we had taught to shoot.

Then it was that our real adventures began.

One evening, after three days' march through some difficult bush in which lions carried off a slave woman, killed one of the donkeys and mauled another so badly that it had to be shot, we found ourselves upon the edge of a great grassy plateau that, according to my aneroid, was 1,640 feet above sea level.

"What place is this?" I asked of the two Mazitu guides, those same men whom we had borrowed from Hassan.

"The land of our people, Chief," they answered, "which is bordered on one side by the bush and on the other by the great lake where live the Pongo wizards."

I looked about me at the bare uplands that already were beginning to turn brown, on which nothing was visible save vast herds of buck such as were common further south. A dreary prospect it was, for a slight rain was falling, accompanied by mist and a cold wind.

"I do not see your people or their kraals," I said; "I only see grass and wild game."

"Our people will come," they replied, rather nervously. "No doubt even now their spies watch us from among the tall grass or out of some hole."

"The deuce they do," I said, or something like it, and thought no more of the matter. When one is in conditions in which anything *may* happen, such as, so far as I am concerned, have prevailed through most of my life, one grows a little careless as to what *will* happen. For my part I have long been a fatalist, to a certain extent. I mean I believe that the individual, or rather the identity which animates him, came out from the Source of all life a long while, perhaps hundreds of thousands or millions of years ago, and when his career is finished, perhaps hundreds of thousands or millions of years hence, or perhaps to-morrow, will return perfected, but still as an individual, to dwell in or with that Source of Life. I believe also that his various existences, here or elsewhere, are fore-known and fore- ordained, although in a sense he may shape them by the action of his free will, and that nothing which he can do will lengthen or shorten one of them by a single hour. Therefore, so far as I am concerned, I have always acted up to the great injunction of our Master and taken no thought for the morrow.

However, in this instance, as in many others of my experience, the morrow took plenty of thought for itself. Indeed, before the dawn, Hans, who never seemed really to sleep any more than a dog does, woke me up with the ominous information that he heard a sound which he thought was caused by the tramp of hundreds of marching men.

"Where?" I asked, after listening without avail--to look was useless, for the night was dark as pitch.

He put his ear to the ground and said:

"There."

I put *my* ear to the ground, but although my senses are fairly acute, could hear nothing.

Then I sent for the sentries, but these, too, could hear nothing. After this I gave the business up and went to sleep again.

However, as it proved, Hans was quite right; in such matters he generally was right, for his senses were as keen as those of any wild beast. At dawn I was once more awakened, this time by Mavovo, who reported that we were being surrounded by a regiment, or regiments. I rose and looked out through the mist. There, sure enough, in dim and solemn outline, though still far off, I perceived rank upon rank of men, armed men, for the light glimmered faintly upon their spears.

"What is to be done, Macumazana?" asked Mavovo.

"Have breakfast, I think," I answered. "If we are going to be killed it may as well be after breakfast as before," and calling the trembling Sammy, I instructed him to make the coffee. Also I awoke Stephen and explained the situation to him.

"Capital!" he answered. "No doubt these are the Mazitu, and we have found them much more easily than we expected. People generally take such a lot of hunting for in this confounded great country."

"That's not such a bad way of looking at things," I answered, "but would you be good enough to go round the camp and make it clear that not on any account is anyone to fire without orders. Stay, collect all the guns from those slaves, for heaven knows what they will do with them if they are frightened!"

Stephen nodded and sauntered off with three or four of the hunters. While he was gone, in consultation with Mavovo, I made certain little arrangements of my own, which need not be detailed. They were designed to enable us to sell our lives as dearly as possible, should things come to the worst. One should always try to make an impression upon the enemy in Africa, for the sake of future travellers if for no other reason.

In due course Stephen and the hunters returned with the guns, or most of them, and reported that the slave people were in great state of terror, and showed a disposition to bolt.

"Let them bolt," I answered. "They would be of no use to us in a row and might even complicate matters. Call in the Zulus who are watching at once."

He nodded, and a few minutes later I heard--for the mist which hung about the bush to the east of the camp was still too dense to allow of my seeing anything--a clamour of voices, followed by the sound of scuttling feet. The slave people, including our bearers, had gone, every one of them. They even carried away the wounded. Just as the soldiers who surrounded us were completing their circle they bolted between the two ends of it and vanished into the bush out of which we had marched on the previous evening. Often since then I have wondered what became of them. Doubtless some perished, and the rest worked their way back to their homes or found new ones among other tribes. The experiences of those who escaped must be interesting to them if they still live. I can well imagine the legends in which these will be embodied two or three generations hence.

Deducting the slave people and the bearers whom we had wrung out of Hassan, we were now a party of seventeen, namely eleven Zulu hunters including Mavovo, two white men, Hans and Sammy, and the two Mazitus who had elected to remain with us, while round us was a great circle of savages which closed in slowly.

As the light grew--it was long in coming on that dull morning--and the mist lifted, I examined these people, without seeming to take any particular notice of them. They were tall, much taller than the average Zulu, and slighter in their build, also lighter in colour. Like the Zulus they carried large hide shields and one very broad- bladed spear. Throwing assegais seemed to be wanting, but in place of them I saw that they were armed with short bows, which, together with a quiver of arrows, were slung upon their backs. The officers wore a short skin cloak or kaross, and the men also had cloaks, which I found out afterwards were made from the inner bark of trees.

They advanced in the most perfect silence and very slowly. Nobody said anything, and if orders were given this must have been done by signs. I could not see that any of them had firearms.

"Now," I said to Stephen, "perhaps if we shot and killed some of those fellows, they might be frightened and run away. Or they might not; or if they did they might return."

"Whatever happened," he remarked sagely, "we should scarcely be welcome in their country afterwards, so I think we had better do nothing unless we are obliged."

I nodded, for it was obvious that we could not fight hundreds of men, and told Sammy, who was perfectly livid with fear, to bring the breakfast. No wonder he was afraid, poor fellow, for we were in great danger. These Mazitu had a bad name, and if they chose to attack us we should all be dead in a few minutes.

The coffee and some cold buck's flesh were put upon our little camp- table in front of the tent which we had pitched because of the rain, and we began to eat. The Zulu hunters also ate from a bowl of mealie porridge which they had cooked on the previous night, each of them with his loaded rifle upon his knees. Our proceedings appeared to puzzle the Mazitu very much indeed. They drew quite near to us, to within about forty yards, and halted there in a dead circle, staring at us with their great round eyes. It was like a scene in a dream; I shall never forget it.

Everything about us appeared to astonish them, our indifference, the colour of Stephen and myself (as a matter of fact at that date Brother John was the only white man they had ever seen), our tent and our two remaining donkeys. Indeed, when one of these beasts broke into a bray, they showed signs of fright, looking at each other and even retreating a few paces.

At length the position got upon my nerves, especially as I saw that some of them were beginning to fiddle with their bows, and that their General, a tall, one-eyed old fellow, was making up his mind to do something. I called to one of the two Mazitus, whom I forgot to say we had named Tom and Jerry, and gave him a pannikin of coffee.

"Take that to the captain there with my good wishes, Jerry, and ask him if he will drink with us," I said.

Jerry, who was a plucky fellow, obeyed. Advancing with the steaming coffee, he held it under the Captain's nose. Evidently he knew the man's name, for I heard him say:

"O Babemba, the white lords, Macumazana and Wazela, ask if you will share their holy drink with them?"

I could perfectly understand the words, for these people spoke a dialect so akin to Zulu that by now it had no difficulty for me.

"Their holy drink!" exclaimed the old fellow, starting back. "Man, it is hot red-water. Would these white wizards poison me with *mwavi*?"

Here I should explain that *mwavi* or *mkasa*, as it is sometimes called, is the liquor distilled from the inner bark of a sort of mimosa tree or sometimes from a root of the strychnos tribe, which is administered by the witch-doctors to persons accused of crime. If it makes them sick they are declared innocent. If they are thrown into convulsions or stupor they are clearly guilty and die, either from the effects of the poison or afterwards by other means.

"This is no *mwavi* O Babemba," said Jerry. "It is the divine liquor that makes the white ,lords shoot straight with their wonderful guns which kill at a thousand paces. See, I will swallow some of it," and he did, though it must have burnt his tongue.

Thus encouraged, old Babemba sniffed at the coffee and found it fragrant. Then he called a man, who from his peculiar dress I took to be a doctor, made him drink some, and watched the results, which were that the doctor tried to finish the pannikin. Snatching it away indignantly Babemba drank himself, and as I had half-filled the cup with sugar, found the mixture good.

"It is indeed a holy drink," he said, smacking his lips. "Have you any more of it?"

"The white lords have more," said Jerry. "They invite you to eat with them."

Babemba stuck his finger into the tin, and covering it with the sediment of sugar, sucked and reflected.

"It's all right," I whispered to Stephen. "I don't think he'll kill us after drinking our coffee, and what's more, I believe he is coming to breakfast."

"This may be a snare," said Babemba, who now began to lick the sugar out of the pannikin.

"No," answered Jerry with creditable resource; "though they could easily kill you all, the white lords do not hurt those who have partaken of their holy drink, that is unless anyone tries to harm them."

"Cannot you bring some more of the holy drink here?" he asked, giving a final polish to the pannikin with his tongue.

"No," said Jerry, "if you want it you must go there. Fear nothing. Would I, one of your own people, betray you?"

"True!" exclaimed Babemba. "By your talk and your face you are a Mazitu. How came you--well, we will speak of that afterwards. I am very thirsty. I will come. Soldiers, sit down and watch, and if any harm happens to me, avenge it and report to the king."

Now, while all this was going on, I had made Hans and Sammy open one of the boxes and extract therefrom a good-sized mirror in a wooden frame with a support at the back so that it could be stood anywhere. Fortunately it was unbroken; indeed, our packing had been so careful that none of the looking-glasses or other fragile things were injured. To this mirror I gave a hasty polish, then set it upright upon the table.

Old Babemba came along rather suspiciously, his one eye rolling over us and everything that belonged to us. When he was quite close it fell upon the mirror. He stopped, he stared, he retreated, then drawn by his overmastering curiosity, came on again and again stood still.

"What is the matter?" called his second in command from the ranks.

"The matter is," he answered, "that here is great magic. Here I see myself walking towards myself. There can be no mistake, for one eye is gone in my other self."

"Advance, O Babemba," cried the doctor who had tried to drink all the coffee, "and see what happens. Keep your spear ready, and if your witch-self attempts to harm you, kill it."

Thus encouraged, Babemba lifted his spear and dropped it again in a great hurry.

"That won't do, fool of a doctor," he shouted back. "My other self lifts a spear also, and what is more all of you who should be behind are in front of me. The holy drink has made me drunk; I am bewitched. Save me!"

Now I saw that the joke had gone too far, for the soldiers were beginning to string their bows in confusion. Luckily at this moment, the sun at length came out almost opposite to us.

"O Babemba," I said in a solemn voice, "it is true that this magic shield, which we have brought as a gift to you, gives you another self. Henceforth your labours will be halved, and your pleasures doubled, for when you look into this shield you will be not one but two. Also it has other properties--see," and lifting the mirror I used it as a heliograph, flashing the reflected sunlight into the eyes of the long half-circle of men in front of us. My word! didn't they run.

"Wonderful!" exclaimed old Babemba, "and can I learn to do that also, white lord?"

"Certainly," I answered, "come and try. Now, hold it so while I say the spell," and I muttered some hocus-pocus, then directed it towards certain of the Mazitu who were gathering again. "There! Look! Look! You have hit them in the eye. You are a master of magic. They run, they run!" and run they did indeed. "Is there anyone yonder whom you dislike?"

"Yes, plenty," answered Babemba with emphasis, "especially that witch- doctor who drank nearly all the holy drink."

"Very well; by-and-by I will show you how you can burn a hole in him with this magic. No, not now, not now. For a while this mocker of the sun is dead. Look," and dipping the glass beneath the table I produced it back first. "You cannot see anything, can you?"

"Nothing except wood," replied Babemba, staring at the deal slip with which it was lined.

Then I threw a dish-cloth over it and, to change the subject, offered him another pannikin of the "holy drink" and a stool to sit on.

The old fellow perched himself very gingerly upon the stool, which was of the folding variety, stuck the iron-tipped end of his great spear in the ground between his knees and took hold of the pannikin. Or rather he took hold of a pannikin and not the right one. So ridiculous was his appearance that the light-minded Stephen, who, forgetting the perils of the situation, had for the last minute or two been struggling with inward laughter, clapped down his coffee on the table and retired into the tent, where I heard him gurgling in unseemly merriment. It was this coffee that in the confusion of the moment Sammy gave to old Babemba. Presently Stephen reappeared, and to cover his confusion seized the pannikin meant for Babemba and drank it, or most of it. Then Sammy, seeing his mistake, said:

"Mr. Somers, I regret that there is an error. You are drinking from the cup which that stinking savage has just licked clean."

The effect was dreadful and instantaneous, for then and there Stephen was violently sick.

"Why does the white lord do that?" asked Babemba. "Now I see that you are truly deceiving me, and that what you are giving me to swallow is nothing but hot *mwavi.*, which in the innocent causes vomiting, but that in those who mean evil, death."

"Stop that foolery, you idiot," I muttered to Stephen, kicking him on the shins, "or you'll get our throats cut." Then, collecting myself with an effort, I said:

"Oh! not at all, General. This white lord is the priest of the holy drink and--what you see is a religious rite."

"Is it so," said Babemba. "Then I hope that the rite is not catching."

"Never," I replied, proffering him a biscuit. "And now, General Babemba, tell me, why do you come against us with about five hundred armed men?"

"To kill you, white lords--oh! how hot is this holy drink, yet pleasant. You said that it was not catching, did you not? For I feel----"

"Eat the cake," I answered. "And why do you wish to kill us? Be so good as to tell me the truth now, or I shall read it in the magic shield which portrays the inside as well as the out," and lifting the cloth I stared at the glass.

"If you can read my thoughts, white lord, why trouble me to tell them?" asked Babemba sensibly enough, his mouth full of biscuit. "Still, as that bright thing may lie, I will set them out. Bausi, king of our people, has sent me to kill you, because news has reached him that you are great slave dealers who come hither with guns to capture the Mazitus and take them away to the Black Water to be sold and sent across it in big canoes that move of themselves. Of this he has been warned by messengers from the Arab men. Moreover, we know that it is true, for last night you had with you many slaves who, seeing our spears, ran away not an hour ago."

Now I stared hard at the looking-glass and answered coolly:

"This magic shield tells a somewhat different story. It says that your king, Bausi, for whom by the way we have many things as presents, told you to lead us to him with honour, that we might talk over matters with him."

The shot was a good one. Babemba grew confused.

"It is true," he stammered, "that--I mean, the king left it to my judgment. I will consult the witch-doctor."

"If he left it to your judgment, the matter is settled," I said, "since certainly, being so great a noble, you would never try to murder those of whose holy drink you have just partaken. Indeed if you did so," I added in a cold voice, "you would not live long yourself. One secret word and that drink will turn to *mwavi.* of the worst sort inside of you."

"Oh! yes, white lord, it is settled," exclaimed Babemba, "it is settled. Do not trouble the secret word. I will lead you to the king and you shall talk with him. By my head and my father's spirit you are safe from me. Still, with your leave, I will call the great doctor, Imbozwi, and ratify the agreement in his presence, and also show him the magic shield."

So Imbozwi was sent for, Jerry taking the message. Presently he arrived. He was a villainous-looking person of uncertain age, humpbacked like the picture of Punch, wizened and squint-eyed. His costume was of the ordinary witch-doctor type being set off with snake skins, fish bladders, baboon's teeth and little bags of medicine. To add to his charms a broad strip of pigment, red ochre probably, ran down his forehead and the nose beneath, across the lips and chin, ending in a red mark the size of a penny where the throat joins the chest. His woolly hair also, in which was twisted a small ring of black gum, was soaked with grease and powdered blue. It was arranged in a kind of horn, coming to a sharp point about five inches above the top of the skull. Altogether he looked extremely like the devil. What was more, he was a devil in a bad temper, for the first words he said embodied a reproach to us for not having asked him to partake of our "holy drink" with Babemba.

We offered to make him some more, but he refused, saying that we should poison him.

Then Babemba set the matter out, rather nervously I thought, for evidently he was afraid of this old wizard, who listened in complete silence. When Babemba explained that without the king's direct order it would be foolish and unjustifiable to put to death such magicians as we were, Imbozwi spoke for the first time, asking why he called us magicians.

Babemba instanced the wonders of the shining shield that showed pictures.

"Pooh!" said Imbozwi, "does not calm water or polished iron show pictures?"

"But this shield will make fire," said Babemba. "The white lords say it can burn a man up."

"Then let it burn me up," replied Imbozwi with ineffable contempt, "and I will believe that these white men are magicians worthy to be kept alive, and not common slave-traders such as we have often heard of."

"Burn him, white lords, and show him that I am right," exclaimed the exasperated Babemba, after which they fell to wrangling. Evidently they were rivals, and by this time both of them had lost their tempers.

The sun was now very hot, quite sufficiently so to enable us to give Mr. Imbozwi a taste of our magic, which I determined he should have. Not being certain whether an ordinary mirror would really reflect enough heat to scorch, I drew from my pocket a very powerful burning- glass which I sometimes used for the lighting of fires in order to save matches, and holding the mirror in one hand and the burning-glass in the other, I worked myself into a suitable position for the experiment. Babemba and the witch-doctor were arguing so fiercely that neither of them seemed to notice what I was doing. Getting the focus right, I directed the concentrated spark straight on to Imbozwi's greased top-knot, where I knew he would feel nothing, my plan being to char a hole in it. But as it happened this top-knot was built up round something of a highly inflammable nature, reed or camphor-wood, I expect. At any rate, about thirty seconds later the top-knot was burning like a beautiful torch.

"*Ow*" said the Kaffirs who were watching. "My Aunt!" exclaimed Stephen. "Look, look!" shouted Babemba in tones of delight. "Now will you believe, O blown-out bladder of a man, that there are greater magicians than yourself in the world?"

"What is the matter, son of a dog, that you make a mock of me?" screeched the unfuriated Imbozwi, who alone was unaware of anything unusual.

As he spoke some suspicion rose in his mind which caused him to put his hand to his top-knot, and withdraw it with a howl. Then he sprang up and began to dance about, which of course only fanned the fire that had now got hold of the grease and gum. The Zulus applauded; Babemba clapped his hands; Stephen burst into one of his idiotic fits of laughter. For my part I grew frightened. Near at hand stood a large wooden pot such as the Kaffirs make, from which the coffee kettle had been filled, that fortunately was still half-full of water. I seized it and ran to him.

"Save me, white lord!" he howled. "You are the greatest of magicians and I am your slave."

Here I cut him short by clapping the pot bottom upwards on his burning head, into which it vanished as a candle does into an extinguisher. Smoke and a bad smell issued from beneath the pot, the water from which ran all over Imbozwi, who stood quite still. When I was sure the fire was out, I lifted the pot and revealed the discomfited wizard, but without his elaborate head-dress. Beyond a little scorching he was not in the least hurt, for I had acted in time; only he was bald, for when touched the charred hair fell off at the roots.

"It is gone," he said in an amazed voice after feeling at his scalp.

"Yes," I answered, "quite. The magic shield worked very well, did it not?"

"Can you put it back again, white lord?" he asked.

"That will depend upon how you behave," I replied.

Then without another word he turned and walked back to the soldiers, who received him with shouts of laughter. Evidently Imbozwi was not a popular character, and his discomfiture delighted them.

Babemba also was delighted. Indeed, he could not praise our magic enough, and at once began to make arrangements to escort us to the king at his head town, which was called Beza, vowing that we need fear no harm at his hands or those of his soldiers. In fact, the only person who did not appreciate our black arts was Imbozwi himself. I caught a look in his eye as he marched off which told me that he hated us bitterly, and reflected to myself that perhaps I had been foolish to use that burning-glass, although in truth I had not intended to set his head on fire.

"My father," said Mavovo to me afterwards, "it would have been better to let that snake burn to death, for then you would have killed his poison. I am something of a doctor myself, and I tell you there is nothing our brotherhood hates so much as being laughed at. You have made a fool of him before all his people and he will not forget it, Macumazana."

Bausi the King

About midday we made a start for Beza Town where King Bausi lived, which we understood we ought to reach on the following evening. For some hours the regiment marched in front, or rather round us, but as we complained to Babemba of the noise and dust, with a confidence that was quite touching, he sent it on ahead. First, however, he asked us to pass our word "by our mothers," which was the most sacred of oaths among many African peoples, that we would not attempt to escape. I confess that I hesitated before giving an answer, not being entirely enamoured of the Mazitu and of our prospects among them, especially as I had discovered through Jerry that the discomfited Imbozwi had departed from the soldiers on some business of his own. Had the matter been left to me, indeed, I should have tried to slip back into the bush over the border, and there put in a few months shooting during the dry season, while working my way southwards. This, too, was the wish of the Zulu hunters, of Hans, and I need not add of Sammy. But when I mentioned the matter to Stephen, he implored me to abandon the idea.

"Look here, Quatermain," he said, "I have come to this God-forsaken country to get that great Cypripedium, and get it I will or die in the attempt. Still," he added after surveying our rather blank faces, "I have no right to play with your lives, so if you think the thing too dangerous I will go on alone with this old boy, Babemba. Putting everything else aside, I think that one of us ought to visit Bausi's kraal in case the gentleman who you call Brother John should turn up there. In short, I have made up my mind, so it is no use talking."

I lit my pipe, and for quite a time contemplated this obstinate young man while considering the matter from every point of view. Finally, I came to the conclusion that he was right and I was wrong. It was true that by bribing Babemba, or otherwise, there was still an excellent prospect of effecting a masterly retreat and of avoiding many perils. On the other hand, we had not come to this wild place in order to retreat. Further, at whose expense had we come here? At that of Stephen Somers who wished to proceed. Lastly, to say nothing of the chance of meeting Brother John, to whom I felt no obligation since he had given us the slip at Durban, I did not like the idea of being beaten. We had started out to visit some mysterious savages who worshipped a monkey and a flower, and we might as well go on till circumstances were too much for us. After all, dangers are everywhere; those who turn back because of dangers will never succeed in any life that we can imagine.

"Mavovo," I said presently, pointing to Stephen with my pipe, "the *inkoosi* Wazela does not wish to try to escape. He wishes to go on to the country of the Pongo people if we can get there. And, Mavovo, remember that he has paid for everything; we are his hired servants. Also that he says that if we run back he will walk forward alone with these Mazitus. Still, if any of you hunters desire to slip off, he will not look your way, nor shall I. What say you?"

"I say, Macumazana, that, though young, Wazela is a chief with a great heart, and that where you and he go, I shall go also, as I think will the rest of us. I do not like these Mazitu, for if their fathers were Zulus their mothers were low people. They are bastards, and of the Pongo I hear nothing but what is evil. Still, no good ox ever turns in the yoke because of a mud-hole. Let us go on, for if we sink in the swamp what does it matter? Moreover, my Snake tells me that we shall not sink, at least not all of us."

So it was arranged that no effort should be made to return. Sammy, it is true, wished to do so, but when it came to the point and he was offered one of the remaining donkeys and as much food and ammunition as he could carry, he changed his mind.

"I think it better, Mr. Quatermain," he said, "to meet my end in the company of high-born, lofty souls than to pursue a lonely career towards the inevitable in unknown circumstances."

"Very well put, Sammy," I answered; "so while waiting for the inevitable, please go and cook the dinner."

Having laid aside our doubts, we proceeded on the journey comfortably enough, being well provided with bearers to take the place of those who had run away. Babemba, accompanied by a single orderly, travelled with us, and from him we collected much information. It seemed that the Mazitu were a large people who could muster from five to seven thousand spears. Their tradition was that they came from the south and were of the same stock as the Zulus, of whom they had heard vaguely. Indeed, many of their customs, to say nothing of their language, resembled those of that country. Their military organisation, however, was not so thorough, and in other ways they struck me as a lower race. In one particular, it is true, that of their houses, they were more advanced, for these, as we saw in the many kraals that we passed, were better built, with doorways through which one could walk upright, instead of the Kaffir bee-holes.

We slept in one of these houses on our march, and should have found it very comfortable had it not been for the innumerable fleas which at length drove us out into the courtyard. For the rest, these Mazitu much resembled the Zulus. They had kraals and were breeders of cattle; they were ruled by headmen under the command of a supreme chief or king; they believed in witchcraft and offered sacrifice to the spirits of their ancestors, also in some kind of a vague and mighty god who dominated the affairs of the world and declared his will through the doctors. Lastly, they were, and I dare say still are, a race of fighting men who loved war and raided the neighbouring peoples upon any and every pretext, killing their men and stealing their women and cattle. They had their virtues, too, being kindly and hospitable by nature, though cruel enough to their enemies. Moreover, they detested dealing in slaves and those who practised it, saying that it was better to kill a man than to deprive him of his freedom. Also they had a horror of the cannibalism which is so common in the dark regions of Africa, and for this reason, more than any other, loathed the Pongo folk who were supposed to be eaters of men.

On the evening of the second day of our march, during which we had passed through a beautiful and fertile upland country, very well watered, and except in the valleys, free from bush, we arrived at Beza. This town was situated on a wide plain surrounded by low hills and encircled by a belt of cultivated land made beautiful by the crops of maize and other cereals which were then ripe to harvest. It was fortified in a way. That is, a tall, unclimbable palisade of timber surrounded the entire town, which fence was strengthened by prickly pears and cacti planted on its either side.

Within this palisade the town was divided into quarters more or less devoted to various trades. Thus one part of it was called the Ironsmiths' Quarter; another the Soldiers' Quarter; another the Quarter of the Land-tillers; another that of the Skin-dressers, and so on. The king's dwelling and those of his women and dependents were near the North gate, and in front of these, surrounded by semi-circles of huts, was a wide space into which cattle could be driven if necessary. This, however, at the time of our visit, was used as a market and a drilling ground.

We entered the town, that must in all have contained a great number of inhabitants, by the South gate, a strong log structure facing a wooded slope through which ran a road. Just as the sun was setting we marched to the guest-huts up a central street lined with the population of the place who had gathered to stare at us. These huts were situated in the Soldiers' Quarter, not far from the king's house and surrounded by an inner fence to keep them private.

None of the people spoke as we passed them, for the Mazitu are polite by nature;

also it seemed to me that they regarded us with awe tempered by curiosity. They only stared, and occasionally those of them who were soldiers saluted us by lifting their spears. The huts into which we were introduced by Babemba, with whom we had grown very friendly, were good and clean.

Here all our belongings, including the guns which we had collected just before the slaves ran away, were placed in one of the huts over which a Mazitu mounted guard, the donkeys being tied to the fence at a little distance. Outside this fence stood another armed Mazitu, also on guard.

"Are we prisoners here?" I asked of Babemba.

"The king watches over his guests," he answered enigmatically. "Have the white lords any message for the king whom I am summoned to see this night?"

"Yes," I answered. "Tell the king that we are the brethren of him who more than a year ago cut a swelling from his body, whom we have arranged to meet here. I mean the white lord with a long beard who among you black people is called Dogeetah."

Babemba started. "You are the brethren of Dogeetah! How comes it then that you never mentioned his name before, and when is he going to meet you here? Know that Dogeetah is a great man among us, for with him alone of all men the king has made blood-brotherhood. As the king is, so is Dogeetah among the Mazitu."

"We never mentioned him because we do not talk about everything at once, Babemba. As to when Dogeetah will meet us I am not sure; I am only sure that he is coming."

"Yes, lord Macumazana, but when, when? That is what the king will want to know and that is what you must tell him. Lord," he added, dropping his voice, "you are in danger here where you have many enemies, since it is not lawful for white men to enter this land. If you would save your lives, be advised by me and be ready to tell the king to-morrow when Dogeetah, whom he loves, will appear here to vouch for you, and see that he does appear very soon and by the day you name. Since otherwise when he comes, if come he does, he may not find you able to talk to him. Now I, your friend, have spoken and the rest is with you."

Then without another word he rose, slipped through the door of the hut and out by the gateway of the fence from which the sentry moved aside to let him pass. I, too, rose from the stool on which I sat and danced about the hut in a perfect fury.

"Do you understand what that infernal (I am afraid I used a stronger word) old fool told me?" I exclaimed to Stephen. "He says that we must be prepared to state exactly when that other infernal old fool, Brother John, will turn up at Beza Town, and that if we don't we shall have our throats cut as indeed has already been arranged."

"Rather awkward," replied Stephen. "There are no express trains to Beza, and if there were we couldn't be sure that Brother John would take one of them. I suppose there *is* a Brother John?" he added reflectively. "To me he seems to be--intimately connected with Mrs. Harris."

"Oh! there is, or there was," I explained. "Why couldn't the confounded ass wait quietly for us at Durban instead of fooling off butterfly hunting to the north of Zululand and breaking his leg or his neck there if he has done anything of the sort?"

"Don't know, I am sure. It's hard enough to understand one's own motives, let alone Brother John's."

Then we sat down on our stools again and stared at each other. At this moment Hans crept into the hut and squatted down in front of us. He might have walked in as there was a doorway, but he preferred to creep on his hands and knees, I don't know why.

"What is it, you ugly little toad?" I asked viciously, for that was just what he looked like; even the skin under his jaw moved like a toad's.

"The Baas is in trouble?" remarked Hans.

"I should think he was," I answered, "and so will you be presently when you are wriggling on the point of a Mazitu spear."

"They are broad spears that would make a big hole," remarked Hans again, whereupon I rose to kick him out, for his ideas were, as usual, unpleasant.

"Baas," he went on, "I have been listening--there is a very good hole in this hut for listening if one lies against the wall and pretends to be asleep. I have heard all and understood most of your talk with that one-eyed savage and the Baas Stephen."

"Well, you little sneak, what of it?"

"Only, Baas, that if we do not want to be killed in this place from which there is no escape, it is necessary that you should find out exactly on what day and at what hour Dogeetah is going to arrive."

"Look here, you yellow idiot," I exclaimed, "if you are beginning that game too, I'll----" then I stopped, reflecting that my temper was getting the better of me and that I had better hear what Hans had to say before I vented it on him.

"Baas, Mavovo is a great doctor; it is said that his Snake is the straightest and the strongest in all Zululand save that of his master, Zikali, the old slave. He told you that Dogeetah was laid up somewhere with a hurt leg and that he was coming to meet you here; no doubt therefore he can tell you also *when* he is coming. I would ask him, but he won't set his Snake to work for me. So you must ask him, Baas, and perhaps he will forget that you laughed at his magic and that he swore you would never see it again."

"Oh! blind one," I answered, "how do I know that Mavovo's story about Dogeetah was not all nonsense?"

Hans stared at me amazed.

"Mavovo's story nonsense! Mavovo's Snake a liar! Oh! Baas, that is what comes of being too much a Christian. Now, thanks to your father the Predikant, I am a Christian too, but not so much that I have forgotten how to know good magic from bad. Mavovo's Snake a liar, and after he whom we buried yonder was the first of the hunters whom the feathers named to him at Durban!" and he began to chuckle in intense amusement, then added, "Well, Baas, there it is. You must either ask Mavovo, and very nicely, or we shall all be killed. *I* don't mind much, for I should rather like to begin again a little younger somewhere else, but just think what a noise Sammy will make!" and turning he crept out as he had crept in.

"Here's a nice position," I groaned to Stephen when he had gone. "I, a white man, who, in spite of some coincidences with which I am acquainted, know that all this Kaffir magic is bosh am to beg a savage to tell me something of which he *must* be ignorant. That is, unless we educated people have got hold of the wrong end of the stick altogether. It is humiliating; it isn't Christian, and I'm hanged if I'll do it!"

"I dare say you will be--hanged I mean--whether you do it or whether you don't," replied Stephen with his sweet smile. "But I say, old fellow, how do you know it is all bosh? We are told about lots of miracles which weren't bosh, and if miracles ever existed, why can't they exist now? But there, I know what you mean and it is no use arguing. Still, if you're proud, I ain't. I'll try to soften the stony heart of Mavovo--we are rather pals, you know--and get him to unroll the book of his occult wisdom," and he went.

A few minutes later I was called out to receive a sheep which, with milk, native beer, some corn, and other things, including green forage for the donkeys, Bausi had sent for us to eat. Here I may remark that while we were among the Mazitu we lived like fighting cocks. There was none of that starvation which is, or was, so common in East Africa where the traveller often cannot get food for love or money--generally because there is none.

When this business was settled by my sending a message of thanks to the king with an intimation that we hoped to wait upon him on the morrow with a few presents, I went to seek Sammy in order to tell him to kill and cook the sheep. After some search I found, or rather heard him beyond a reed fence which divided two of the huts. He was acting as interpreter between Stephen Somers and Mavovo.

"This Zulu man declares, Mr. Somers," he said, "that he quite understands everything you have been explaining, and that it is probable that we shall all be butchered by this savage Bausi, if we cannot tell him when the white man, Dogeetah, whom he loves, will arrive here. He says also that he thinks that by his magic he could learn when this will happen--if it is to happen at all--(which of course, Mr. Somers, for your private information only, is a mighty lie of the ignorant heathen). He adds, however, that he does not care one brass farthing--his actual expression, Mr. Somers, is 'one grain of corn on a mealie-cob'--about his or anybody else's life, which from all I have heard of his proceedings I can well believe to be true. He says in his vulgar language that there is no difference between the belly of a Mazitu-land hyena and that of any other hyena, and that the earth of Mazitu-land is as welcome to his bones as any other earth, since the earth is the wickedest of all hyenas, in that he has observed that soon or late it devours everlastingly everything which once it bore. You must forgive me for reproducing his empty and childish talk, Mr. Somers, but you bade me to render the words of this savage with exactitude. In fact, Mr. Somers, this reckless person intimates, in short that some power with which he is not acquainted-- he calls it the 'Strength that makes the Sun to shine and broiders the blanket of the night with stars' (forgive me for repeating his silly words), caused him 'to be born into this world, and, at an hour already appointed, will draw him from this world back into its dark, eternal bosom, there to be rocked in sleep, or nursed to life again, according to its unknown will'--I translate exactly, Mr. Somers, although I do not know what it all means--and that he does not care a curse when this happens. Still, he says that whereas he is growing old and has known many sorrows--he alludes here, I gather, to some nigger wives of his whom another savage knocked on the head; also to a child to whom he appears to have been attached--you are young with all your days and he, hopes, joys, before you. Therefore he would gladly do anything in his power to save your life, because although you are white and he is black he has conceived an affection for you and looks on you as his child. Yes, Mr. Somers, although I blush to repeat it, this black fellow says he looks upon you as his child. He adds, indeed, that if the opportunity arises, he will gladly give his life to save your life, and that it cuts his heart in two to refuse you anything. Still he must refuse this request of yours, that he will ask the creature he calls his Snake--what he means by that, I don't know, Mr. Somers--to declare when the white man, named Dogeetah, will arrive in this place. For this reason, that he told Mr. Quatermain when he laughed at him about his divinations that he would make no more magic for him or any of you, and that he will die rather than break his word. That's all, Mr. Somers, and I dare say you will think--quite enough, too."

"I understand," replied Stephen. "Tell the chief, Mavovo" (I observed he laid an emphasis on the word, *chief*) "that I *quite* understand, and that I thank him very much for explaining things to me so fully. Then ask him whether, as the matter is so important, there is no way out of this trouble?"

Sammy translated into Zulu, which he spoke perfectly, as I noted without interpolations or additions.

"Only one way," answered Mavovo in the intervals of taking snuff. "It is that Macumazana himself shall ask me to do this thing, Macumazana is my old chief and friend, and for his sake I will forget what in the case of others I should always remember. If he will come and ask me, without mockery, to exercise my skill on behalf of all of us, I will try to exercise it, although I know very well that he believes it to be but as an idle little whirlwind that stirs the dust, that raises the dust and lets it fall again without purpose or meaning, forgetting, as the wise white men forget, that even the wind which blows the dust is the same that breathes in our nostrils, and that to it, we also are as is the dust."

Now I, the listener, thought for a moment or two. The words of this fighting savage, Mavovo, even those of them of which I had heard only the translation, garbled and beslavered by the mean comments of the unutterable Sammy, stirred my imagination. Who was I that I should dare to judge of him and his wild, unknown gifts? Who was I that I should mock at him and by my mockery intimate that I believed him to be a fraud?

Stepping through the gateway of the fence, I confronted him.

"Mavovo," I said, "I have overheard your talk. I am sorry if I laughed at you in Durban. I do not understand what you call your magic. It is beyond me and may be true or may be false. Still, I shall be grateful to you if you will use your power to discover, if you can, whether Dogeetah is coming here, and if so, when. Now, do as it may please you; I have spoken."

"And I have heard, Macumazana, my father. To-night I will call upon my Snake. Whether it will answer or what it will answer, I cannot say."

Well, he did call upon his Snake with due and portentous ceremony and, according to Stephen, who was present, which I declined to be, that mystic reptile declared that Dogeetah, alias Brother John, would arrive in Beza Town precisely at sunset on the third day from that night. Now as he had divined on Friday, according to our almanac, this meant that we might hope to see him--hope exactly described my state of mind on the matter--on the Monday evening in time for supper.

"All right," I said briefly. "Please do not talk to me any more about this impious rubbish, for I want to go to sleep."

Next morning early we unpacked our boxes and made a handsome selection of gifts for the king, Bausi, hoping thus to soften his royal heart. It included a bale of calico, several knives, a musical box, a cheap American revolver, and a bundle of tooth-picks; also several pounds of the best and most fashionable beads for his wives. This truly noble present we sent to the king by our two Mazitu servants, Tom and Jerry, who were marched off in the charge of several sentries, for I hoped that these men would talk to their compatriots and tell them what good fellows we were. Indeed I instructed them to do so.

Imagine our horror, therefore, when about an hour later, just as we were tidying ourselves up after breakfast, there appeared through the gate, not Tom and Jerry, for they had vanished, but a long line of Mazitu soldiers each of whom carried one of the articles that we had sent. Indeed the last of them held the bundle of toothpicks on his fuzzy head as though it were a huge faggot of wood. One by one they set them down upon the lime flooring of the verandah of the largest hut. Then their captain said solemnly:

"Bausi, the Great Black One, has no need of the white men's gifts."

"Indeed," I replied, for my dander was up. "Then he won't get another chance at them."

The men turned away without more words, and presently Babemba turned up with a company of about fifty soldiers.

"The king is waiting to see you, white lords," he said in a voice of very forced jollity, "and I have come to conduct you to him."

"Why would he not accept our presents?" I asked, pointing to the row of them.

"Oh! that is because of Imbozwi's story of the magic shield. He said he wanted no gifts to burn his hair off. But, come, come. He will explain for himself. If the Elephant is kept waiting he grows angry and trumpets."

"Does he?" I said. "And how many of us are to come?"

"All, all, white lord. He wishes to see every one of you."

"Not me, I suppose?" said Sammy, who was standing close by. "I must stop to make ready the food."

"Yes, you too," replied Babemba. "The king would look on the mixer of the holy drink."

Well, there was no way out of it, so off we marched, all well armed as I need not say, and were instantly surrounded by the soldiers. To give an unusual note to the proceedings I made Hans walk first, carrying on his head the rejected musical box from which flowed the touching melody of "Home, Sweet Home." Then came Stephen bearing the Union Jack on a pole, then I in the midst of the hunters and accompanied by Babemba, then the reluctant Sammy, and last of all the two donkeys led by Mazitus, for it seemed that the king had especially ordered that these should be brought also.

It was a truly striking cavalcade, the sight of which under any other circumstances would have made me laugh. Nor did it fail in its effect, for even the silent Mazitu people through whom we wended our way, were moved to something like enthusiasm. "Home, Sweet Home" they evidently thought heavenly, though perhaps the two donkeys attracted them most, especially when these brayed.

"Where are Tom and Jerry?" I asked of Babemba.

"I don't know," he answered; "I think they have been given leave to go to see their friends."

Imbozwi is suppressing evidence in our favour, I thought to myself, and said no more.

Presently we reached the gate of the royal enclosure. Here to my dismay the soldiers insisted on disarming us, taking away our rifles, our revolvers, and even our sheath knives. In vain did I remonstrate, saying that we were not accustomed to part with these weapons. The answer was that it was not lawful for any man to appear before the king armed even with so much as a dancing-stick. Mavovo and the Zulus showed signs of resisting and for a minute I thought there was going to be a row, which of course would have ended in our massacre, for although the Mazitus feared guns very much, what could we have done against hundreds of them? I ordered him to give way, but for once he was on the point of disobeying me. Then by a happy thought I reminded him that, according to his Snake, Dogeetah was coming, and that therefore all would be well. So he submitted with an ill grace, and we saw our precious guns borne off we knew not where.

Then the Mazitu soldiers piled their spears and bows at the gate of the kraal and we proceeded with only the Union Jack and the musical box, which was now discoursing "Britannia rules the waves."

Across the open space we marched to where several broad-leaved trees grew in front of a large native house. Not far from the door of this house a fat, middle-aged and angry-looking man was seated on a stool, naked except for a moocha of catskins about his loins and a string of large blue beads round his neck.

"Bausi, the King," whispered Babemba.

At his side squatted a little hunchbacked figure, in whom I had no difficulty in recognising Imbozwi, although he had painted his scorched scalp white with vermillion spots and adorned his snub nose with a purple tip, his dress of ceremony I presume. Round and behind there were a number of silent councillors. At some signal or on reaching a given spot, all the soldiers, including old Babemba, fell upon their hands and knees and began to crawl. They wanted us to do the same, but here I drew the line, feeling that if once we crawled we must always crawl.

So at my word we advanced upright, but with slow steps, in the midst of all this wriggling humanity and at length found ourselves in the august presence of Bausi, "the Beautiful Black One," King of the Mazitu.

The Sentence

We stared at Bausi and Bausi stared at us.

"I am the Black Elephant Bausi," he exclaimed at last, worn out by our solid silence, "and I trumpet! I trumpet! I trumpet!" (It appeared that this was the ancient and hallowed formula with which a Mazitu king was wont to open a conversation with strangers.)

After a suitable pause I replied in a cold voice:

"We are the white lions, Macumazana and Wazela, and we roar! we roar! we roar!"

"I can trample," said Bausi.

"And we can bite," I said haughtily, though how we were to bite or do anything else effectual with nothing but a Union Jack, I did not in the least know.

"What is that thing?" asked Bausi, pointing to the flag.

"That which shadows the whole earth," I answered proudly, a remark that seemed to impress him, although he did not at all understand it, for he ordered a soldier to hold a palm leaf umbrella over him to prevent it from shadowing *him*.

"And that," he asked again, pointing to the music box, "which is not alive and yet makes a noise?"

"That sings the war-song of our people," I said. "We sent it to you as a present and you returned it. Why do you return our presents, O Bausi?"

Then of a sudden this potentate grew furious.

"Why do you come here, white men," he asked, "uninvited and against the law of my land, where only one white man is welcome, my brother Dogeetah, who cured me of sickness with a knife? I know who you are. You are dealers in men. You come here to steal my people and sell them into slavery. You had many slaves with you on the borders of my country, but you sent them away. You shall die, you shall die, you who call yourselves lions, and the painted rag which you say shadows the world, shall rot with your bones. As for that box which sings a war- song, I will smash it; it shall not bewitch me as your magic shield bewitched my great doctor, Imbozwi, burning off his hair."

Then springing up with wonderful agility for one so fat, he knocked the musical box from Hans' head, so that it fell to the ground and after a little whirring grew silent.

"That is right," squeaked Imbozwi. "Trample on their magic, O Elephant. Kill them, O Black One; burn them as they burned my hair."

Now things were, I felt, very serious, for already Bausi was looking about him as though to order his soldiers to make an end of us. So I said in desperation:

"O King, you mentioned a certain white man, Dogeetah, a doctor of doctors, who cured you of sickness with a knife, and called him your brother. Well, he is our brother also, and it was by his invitation that we have come to visit you here, where he will meet us presently."

"If Dogeetah is your friend, then you are my friends," answered Bausi, "for in this land he rules as I rule, he whose blood flows in my veins, as my blood flows in his veins. But you lie. Dogeetah is no brother of slave-dealers, his heart is good and yours are evil. You say that he will meet you here. When will he meet you? Tell me, and if it is soon, I will hold my hand and wait to hear his report of you before I put you to death, for if he speaks well of you, you shall not die."

Now I hesitated, as well I might, for I felt that looking at our case from his point of view, Bausi, believing us to be slave-traders, was not angry without cause. While

I was racking my brains for a reply that might be acceptable to him and would not commit us too deeply, to my astonishment Mavovo stepped forward and confronted the king.

"Who are you, fellow?" shouted Bausi.

"I am a warrior, O King, as my scars show," and he pointed to the assegai wounds upon his breast and to his cut nostril. "I am a chief of a people from whom your people sprang and my name is Mavovo, Mavovo who is ready to fight you or any man whom you may name, and to kill him or you if you will. Is there one here who wishes to be killed?"

No one answered, for the mighty-chested Zulu looked very formidable.

"I am a doctor also," went on Mavovo, "one of the greatest of doctors who can open the 'Gates of Distance' and read that which is hid in the womb of the Future. Therefore I will answer your questions which you put to the lord Macumazana, the great and wise white man whom I serve, because we have fought together in many battles. Yes, I will be his Mouth, I will answer. The white man Dogeetah, who is your blood- brother and whose word is your word among the Mazitu, will arrive here at sunset on the second day from now. I have spoken."

Bausi looked at me in question.

"Yes," I exclaimed, feeling that I must say something and that it did not much matter what I said, "Dogeetah will arrive here on the second day from now within half an hour after sunset."

Something, I know not what, prompted me to allow that extra half-hour, which in the event, saved all our lives. Now Bausi consulted a while with the execrable Imbozwi and also with the old one-eyed General Babemba while we watched, knowing that our fate hung upon the issue.

At length he spoke.

"White men," he said, "Imbozwi, the head of the witch-finders here, whose hair you burnt off by your evil magic, says that it would be better to kill you at once as your hearts are bad and you are planning mischief against my people. So I think also. But Babemba my General, with whom I am angry because he did not obey my orders and put you to death on the borders of my country when he met you there with your caravan of slaves, thinks otherwise. He prays me to hold my hand, first because you have bewitched him into liking you and secondly because if you should happen to be speaking the truth--which we do not believe--and to have come here at the invitation of my brother Dogeetah, he, Dogeetah, would be pained if he arrived and found you dead, nor could even he bring you to life again. This being so, since it matters little whether you die now or later, my command is that you be kept prisoners till sunset of the second day from this, and that then you will be led out and tied to stakes in the market-place, there to wait till the approach of darkness, by when you say Dogeetah will be here. If he arrives and owns you as his brethren, well and good; if he does not arrive, or disowns you--better still, for then you shall be shot to death with arrows as a warning to all other stealers of men not to cross the borders of the Mazitu."

I listened to this atrocious sentence with horror, then gasped out:

"We are not stealers of men, O King, we are freers of men, as Tom and Jerry of your own people could tell you."

"Who are Tom and Jerry?" he asked, indifferently. "Well, it does not matter, for doubtless they are liars like the rest of you. I have spoken. Take them away, feed them well and keep them safe till within an hour of sunset on the second day from this."

Then, without giving us any further opportunity of speaking, Bausi rose, and followed by Imbozwi and his councillors, marched off into his big hut. We too, were marched off, this time under a double guard commanded by someone whom I had not seen before. At the gate of the kraal we halted and asked for the arms that had been taken from us. No answer was given; only the soldiers put their hands upon our shoulders and thrust us along.

"This is a nice business," I whispered to Stephen.

"Oh! it doesn't matter," he answered. "There are lots more guns in the huts. I am told that these Mazitus are dreadfully afraid of bullets. So all we have to do is just to break out and shoot our way through them, for of course they will run when we begin to fire."

I looked at him but did not answer, for to tell the truth I felt in no mood for argument.

Presently we arrived at our quarters, where the soldiers left us, to camp outside. Full of his warlike plan, Stephen went at once to the hut in which the slavers' guns had been stored with our own spare rifles and all the ammunition. I saw him emerge looking very blank indeed and asked him what was the matter.

"Matter!" he answered in a voice that for once really was full of dismay. "The matter is that those Mazitu have stolen all the guns and all the ammunition. There's not enough powder left to make a blue devil."

"Well," I replied, with the kind of joke one perpetrates under such circumstances, "we shall have plenty of blue devils without making any more."

Truly ours was a dreadful situation. Let the reader imagine it. Within a little more than forty-eight hours we were to be shot to death with arrows if an erratic old gentleman who, for aught I knew might be dead, did not turn up at what was then one of the remotest and most inaccessible spots in Central Africa. Moreover, our only hope that such a thing would happen, if hope it could be called, was the prophecy of a Kaffir witch-doctor.

To rely on this in any way was so absurd that I gave up thinking of it and set my mind to considering if there were any possible means of escape. After hours of reflection I could find none. Even Hans, with all his experience and nearly superhuman cunning, could suggest none. We were unarmed and surrounded by thousands of savages, all of whom save perhaps Babemba, believed us to be slave-traders, a race that very properly they held in abhorrence, who had visited the country with the object of stealing their women and children. The king, Bausi, a very prejudiced fellow, was dead against us. Also by a piece of foolishness which I now bitterly regretted, as indeed I regretted the whole expedition, or at any rate entering on it in the absence of Brother John, we had made an implacable enemy of the head medicine- man, who to these folk was a sort of Archbishop of Canterbury. Short of a miracle, there was no hope for us. All that we could do was to say our prayers and prepare for the end.

Mavovo, it is true, remained cheerful. His faith in his "Snake" was really touching. He offered to go through that divination process again in our presence and demonstrate that there was no mistake. I declined because I had no faith in divinations, and Stephen also declined, for another reason, namely that the result might prove to be different, which, he held, would be depressing. The other Zulus oscillated between belief and scepticism, as do the unstable who set to work to study the evidences of Christianity. But Sammy did not oscillate, he literally howled, and prepared the food which poured in upon us so badly that I had to turn on Hans to do the cooking, for however little appetite we might have, it was necessary that we should keep up our strength by eating.

"What, Mr. Quatermain," asked Sammy between his tears, "is the use of dressing viands that our systems will never have time to thoroughly assimilate?"

The first night passed somehow, and so did the next day and the next night which heralded our last morning. I got up quite early and watched the sunrise. Never, I think, had I realised before what a beautiful thing the sunrise is, at least not to the extent I did now when I was saying good-bye to it for ever. Unless indeed there should prove to be still lovelier sunrises beyond the dark of death! Then I went into our hut, and as Stephen, who had the nerves of a rhinoceros, was still sleeping like a tortoise in winter, I said my prayers earnestly enough, mourned over my sins which proved to be so many that at last I gave up the job in despair, and then tried to occupy myself by reading the Old Testament, a book to which I have always been extremely attached.

As a passage that I lit on described how the prophet Samuel for whom I could not help reading "Imbozwi," hewed Agag in pieces after Bausi--I mean Saul--had relented and spared his life, I cannot say that it consoled me very much. Doubtless, I reflected, these people believe that I, like Agag, had "made women childless" by my sword, so there remained nothing save to follow the example of that unhappy king and walk "delicately" to doom.

Then, as Stephen was still sleeping--how *could* he do it, I wondered --I set to work to make up the accounts of the expedition to date. It had already cost £1,423. Just fancy expending £1,423 in order to be tied to a post and shot to death with arrows. And all to get a rare orchid! Oh! I reflected to myself, if by some marvel I should escape, or if I should live again in any land where these particular flowers flourish, I would never even look at them. And as a matter of fact I never have.

At length Stephen did wake up and, as criminals are reported to do in the papers before execution, made an excellent breakfast.

"What's the good of worrying?" he said presently. "I shouldn't if it weren't for my poor old father. It must have come to this one day, and the sooner it is over the sooner to sleep, as the song says. When one comes to think of it there are enormous advantages in sleep, for that's the only time one is quite happy. Still, I should have liked to see that Cypripedium first."

"Oh! drat the Cypripedium!" I exclaimed, and blundered from the hut to tell Sammy that if he didn't stop his groaning I would punch his head.

"Jumps! Regular jumps! Who'd have thought it of Quatermain?" I heard Stephen mutter in the intervals of lighting his pipe.

The morning went "like lightning that is greased," as Sammy remarked. Three o'clock came and Mavovo and his following sacrificed a kid to the spirits of their ancestors, which, as Sammy remarked again, was "a horrible, heathen ceremony much calculated to prejudice our cause with Powers Above."

When it was over, to my delight, Babemba appeared. He looked so pleasant that I jumped to the conclusion that he brought the best of news with him. Perhaps that the king had pardoned us, or perhaps-- blessed thought--that Brother John had really arrived before his time.

But not a bit of it! All he had to say was that he had caused inquiries to be made along the route that ran to the coast and that certainly for a hundred miles there was at present no sign of Dogeetah. So as the Black Elephant was growing more and more enraged under the stirrings up of Imbozwi, it was obvious that that evening's ceremony must be performed. Indeed, as it was part of his duty to superintend the erection of the posts to which we were to be tied and the digging of our graves at their bases, he had just come to count us again to be sure that he had not made any mistake as to the number. Also, if there were any articles that we would like buried with us, would we be so kind as to point them out and he would be sure to see to the matter. It would be soon over, and not painful, he added, as he had selected the very best archers in Beza Town who rarely missed and could, most of them, send an arrow up to the feather into a buffalo.

Then he chatted a little about other matters, as to where he should find the magic shield I had given him, which he would always value as a souvenir, etc., took a pinch of snuff with Mavovo and departed, saying that he would be sure to return again at the proper time.

It was now four o'clock, and as Sammy was quite beyond it, Stephen made himself some tea. It was very good tea, especially as we had milk to put in it, although I did not remember what it tasted like till afterwards.

Now, having abandoned hope, I went into a hut alone to compose myself to meet my end like a gentleman, and seated there in silence and semi- darkness my spirit grew much calmer. After all, I reflected, why should I cling to life? In the country whither I travelled, as the reader who has followed my adventures will know, were some whom I clearly longed to see again, notably my father and my mother, and two noble women who were even more to me. My boy, it is true, remained (he was alive then), but I knew that he would find friends, and as I was not so badly off at that time, I had been able to make a proper provision for him. Perhaps it was better that I should go, seeing that if I lived on it would only mean more troubles and more partings.

What was about to befall me of course I could not tell, but I knew then as I know now, that it was not extinction or even that sleep of which Stephen had spoken. Perhaps I was passing to some place where at length the clouds would roll away and I should understand; whence, too, I should see all the landscape of the past and future, as an eagle does watching from the skies, and be no longer like one struggling through dense bush, wild-beast and serpent haunted, beat upon by the storms of heaven and terrified with its lightnings, nor knowing whither I hewed my path. Perhaps in that place there would be no longer what St. Paul describes as another law in my members warring against the law of my mind, and bringing me into captivity to the law of sin. Perhaps there the past would be forgiven by the Power which knows whereof we are made, and I should become what I have always longed to be--good in every sense and even find open to me new and better roads of service. I take these thoughts from a note that I made in my pocket-book at the time.

Thus I reflected and then wrote a few lines of farewell in the fond and foolish hope that somehow they might find those to whom they were addressed (I have those letters still and very oddly they read to-day). This done, I tried to throw out my mind towards Brother John if he still lived, as indeed I had done for days past, so that I might inform him of our plight and, I am afraid, reproach him for having brought us to such an end by his insane carelessness or want of faith.

Whilst I was still engaged thus Babemba arrived with his soldiers to lead us off to execution. It was Hans who came to tell me that he was there. The poor old Hottentot shook me by the hand and wiped his eyes with his ragged coat-sleeve.

"Oh! Baas, this is our last journey," he said, "and you are going to be killed, Baas, and it is all my fault, Baas, because I ought to have found a way out of the trouble which is what I was hired to do. But I can't, my head grows so stupid. Oh! if only I could come even with Imbozwi I shouldn't mind, and I will, I *will*, if I have to return as a ghost to do it. Well, Baas, you know the Predikant, your father, told us that we don't go out like a fire, but burn again for always elsewhere----"

("I hope not," I thought to myself.)

"And that quite easily without anything to pay for the wood. So I hope that we shall always burn together, Baas. And meanwhile, I have brought you a little something," and he produced what looked like a peculiarly obnoxious horseball. "You swallow this now and you will never feel anything; it is a very good medicine that my grandfather's grandfather got from the Spirit of his tribe. You will just go to sleep as nicely as though you were very drunk, and wake up in the beautiful fire which burns without any wood and never goes out for ever and ever, Amen."

"No, Hans," I said, "I prefer to die with my eyes open."

"And so would I, Baas, if I thought there was any good in keeping them open, but I don't, for I can't believe any more in the Snake of that black fool, Mavovo. If it had been a good Snake, it would have told him to keep clear of Beza Town, so I will swallow one of these pills and give the other to the Baas Stephen," and he crammed the filthy mess into his mouth and with an effort got it down, as a young turkey does a ball of meal that is too big for its throat.

Then, as I heard Stephen calling me, I left him invoking a most comprehensive and polyglot curse upon the head of Imbozwi, to whom he rightly attributed all our woes.

"Our friend here says it is time to start," said Stephen, rather shakily, for the situation seemed to have got a hold of him at last, and nodding towards old Babemba, who stood there with a cheerful smile looking as though he were going to conduct us to a wedding.

"Yes, white lord," said Babemba, "it is time, and I have hurried so as not to keep you waiting. It will be a very fine show, for the 'Black Elephant' himself is going to do you the honour to be present, as will all the people of Beza Town and those for many miles round."

"Hold your tongue, you old idiot," I said, "and stop your grinning. If you had been a man and not a false friend you would have got us out of this trouble, knowing as you do very well that we are no sellers of men, but rather the enemy of those who do such things."

"Oh! white lord," said Babemba, in a changed voice, "believe me I only smile to make you happy up to the end. My lips smile, but I am crying inside. I know that you are good and have told Bausi so, but he will not believe me, who thinks that I have been bribed by you. What can I do against that evil-hearted Imbozwi, the head of the witch-doctors, who hates you because he thinks you have better magic than he has and who whispers day and night into the king's ear, telling him that if he does not kill you, all our people will be slain or sold for slaves, as you are only the scouts or a big army that is coming. Only last night Imbozwi held a great divination *indaba*, and read this and a great deal more in the enchanted water, making the king think he saw it in pictures, whereas I, looking over his shoulder, could see nothing at all, except the ugly face of Imbozwi reflected in the water. Also he swore that his spirit told me that Dogeetah, the king's blood-brother, being dead, would never come to Beza Town again. I have done my best. Keep your heart white towards me, O Macumazana, and do not haunt me, for I tell you I have done my best, and if ever I should get a chance against Imbozwi, which I am afraid I shan't, as he will poison me first, I will pay him back. Oh! he shall not die quickly as you will."

"I wish I could get a chance at him," I muttered, for even in this solemn moment I could cultivate no Christian spirit towards Imbozwi.

Feeling that he was honest after all, I shook old Babemba's hand and gave him the letters I had written, asking him to try and get them to the coast. Then we started on our last walk.

The Zulu hunters were already outside the fence, seated on the ground, chatting and taking snuff. I wondered if this was because they really believed in Mavovo's confounded Snake, or from bravado, inspired by the innate courage of their race. When they saw me they sprang to their feet and, lifting their right hands, gave me a loud and hearty salute of "Inkoosi! Baba! Inkoosi! Macumazana!" Then, at a signal from Mavovo, they broke into some Zulu war-chant, which they kept up till we reached the stakes. Sammy, too, broke into a chant, but one of quite a different nature.

"Be quiet!" I said to him. "Can't you die like a man?"

"No, indeed I cannot, Mr. Quatermain," he answered, and went on howling for pity in about twenty different languages.

Stephen and I walked together, he still carrying the Union Jack, of which no one tried to deprive him. I think the Mazitu believed it was his fetish. We didn't talk much, though once he said:

"Well, the love of orchids has brought many a man to a bad end. I wonder whether the Governor will keep my collection or sell it."

After this he relapsed into silence, and not knowing and indeed not caring what would happen to his collection, I made no answer.

We had not far to go; personally I could have preferred a longer walk. Passing with our guards down a kind of by-street, we emerged suddenly at the head of the market-place, to find that it was packed with thousands of people gathered there to see our execution. I noticed that they were arranged in orderly companies and that a broad open roadway was left between them, running to the southern gate of the market, I suppose to facilitate the movements of so large a crowd.

All this multitude received us in respectful silence, though Sammy's howls caused some of them to smile, while the Zulu war-chant appeared to excite their wonder, or admiration. At the head of the market- place, not far from the king's enclosure, fifteen stout posts had been planted on as many mounds. These mounds were provided so that everyone might see the show and, in part at any rate, were made of soil hollowed from fifteen deep graves dug almost at the foot of the mounds. Or rather there were seventeen posts, an extra large one being set at each end of the line in order to accommodate the two donkeys, which it appeared were also to be shot to death. A great number of soldiers kept a space clear in front of the posts. On this space were gathered Bausi, his councillors, some of his head wives, Imbozwi more hideously painted than usual, and perhaps fifty or sixty picked archers with strung bows and an ample supply of arrows, whose part in the ceremony it was not difficult for us to guess.

"King Bausi," I said as I was led past that potentate, "you are a murderer and Heaven Above will be avenged upon you for this crime. If our blood is shed, soon you shall die and come to meet us where *we* have power, and your people shall be destroyed."

My words seemed to frighten the man, for he answered:

"I am no murderer. I kill you because you are robbers of men. Moreover, it is not I who have passed sentence on you. It is Imbozwi here, the chief of the doctors, who has told me all about you, and whose spirit says you must die unless my brother Dogeetah appears to save you. If Dogeetah comes, which he cannot do because he is dead, and vouches for you, then I shall know that Imbozwi is a wicked liar, and as you were to die, so he shall die."

"Yes, yes," screeched Imbozwi. "If Dogeetah comes, as that false wizard prophesies," and he pointed to Mavovo, "then I shall be ready to die in your place, white slave-dealers. Yes, yes, then you may shoot *me* with arrows."

"King, take note of those words, and people, take note of those words, that they may be fulfilled if Dogeetah comes," said Mavovo in a great, deep voice.

"I take note of them," answered Bausi, "and I swear by my mother on behalf of all the people, that they shall be fulfilled--if Dogeetah comes."

"Good," exclaimed Mavovo, and stalked on to the stake which had been pointed out to him.

As he went he whispered something into Imbozwi's ear that seemed to frighten that limb of Satan, for I saw him start and shiver. However, he soon recovered, for in another minute he was engaged in superintending those whose business it was to lash us to the posts.

This was done simply and effectively by tying our wrists with a grass rope behind these posts, each of which was fitted with two projecting pieces of wood that passed under our arms and practically prevented us from moving. Stephen and I were given the places of honour in the middle, the Union Jack being fixed, by his own request, to the top of Stephen's stake. Mavovo was on my right, and the other Zulus were ranged on either side of us. Hans and Sammy occupied the end posts respectively (except those to which the poor jackasses were bound). I noted that Hans was already very sleepy and that shortly after he was fixed up, his head dropped forward on his breast. Evidently his medicine was working, and almost I regretted that I had not taken some while I had the chance.

When we were all fastened, Imbozwi came round to inspect. Moreover, with a piece of white chalk he made a round mark on the breast of each of us; a kind of bull's eye for the archers to aim at.

"Ah! white man," he said to me as he chalked away at my shooting coat, "you will never burn anyone's hair again with your magic shield. Never, never, for presently I shall be treading down the earth upon you in that hole, and your goods will belong to me."

I did not answer, for what was the use of talking to this vile brute when my time was so short. So he passed on to Stephen and began to chalk him. Stephen, however, in whom the natural man still prevailed, shouted:

"Take your filthy hands off me," and lifting his leg, which was unfettered, gave the painted witch-doctor such an awful kick in the stomach, that he vanished backwards into the grave beneath him.

"Ow! Well done, Wazela!" said the Zulus, "we hope that you have killed him."

"I hope so too," said Stephen, and the multitude of spectators gasped to see the sacred person of the head witch-doctor, of whom they evidently went in much fear, treated in such a way. Only Babemba grinned, and even the king Bausi did not seem displeased.

But Imbozwi was not to be disposed of so easily, for presently, with the help of sundry myrmidons, minor witch-doctors, he scrambled out of the grave, cursing and covered with mud, for it was wet down there. After that I took no more heed of him or of much else. Seeing that I had only half an hour to live, as may be imagined, I was otherwise engaged.

The Coming of Dogeetah

The sunset that day was like the sunrise, particularly fine, although as in the case of the tea, I remembered little of it till afterwards. In fact, thunder was about, which always produces grand cloud effects in Africa.

The sun went down like a great red eye, over which there dropped suddenly a black eyelid of cloud with a fringe of purple lashes.

There's the last I shall see of you, my old friend, thought I to myself, unless I catch you up presently.

The gloom began to gather. The king looked about him, also at the sky overhead, as though he feared rain, then whispered something to Babemba, who nodded and strolled up to my post.

"White lord," he said, "the Elephant wishes to know if you are ready, as presently the light will be very bad for shooting?"

"No," I answered with decision, "not till half an hour after sundown as was agreed."

Babemba went to the king and returned to me.

"White lord, the king says that a bargain is a bargain, and he will keep to his word. Only you must not then blame him if the shooting is bad, since of course he did not know that the night would be so cloudy, which is not usual at this time of year."

It grew darker and darker, till at length we might have been lost in a London fog. The dense masses of the people looked like banks, and the archers, flitting to and fro as they made ready, might have been shadows in Hades. Once or twice lightning flashed and was followed after a pause by the distant growling of thunder. The air, too, grew very oppressive. Dense silence reigned. In all those multitudes no one spoke or stirred; even Sammy ceased his howling, I suppose because he had become exhausted and fainted away, as people often do just before they are hanged. It was a most solemn time. Nature seemed to be adapting herself to the mood of sacrifice and making ready for us a mighty pall.

At length I heard the sound of arrows being drawn from their quivers, and then the squeaky voice of Imbozwi, saying:

"Wait a little, the cloud will lift. There is light behind it, and it will be nicer if they can see the arrows coming."

The cloud did begin to lift, very slowly, and from beneath it flowed a green light like that in a cat's eye.

"Shall we shoot, Imbozwi?" asked the voice of the captain of the archers.

"Not yet, not yet. Not till the people can watch them die."

The edge of cloud lifted a little more; the green light turned to a fiery red thrown by the sunk sun and reflected back upon the earth from the dense black cloud above. It was as though all the landscape had burst into flames, while the heaven over us remained of the hue of ink. Again the lightning flashed, showing the faces and staring eyes of the thousands who watched, and even the white teeth of a great bat that flittered past. That flash seemed to burn off an edge of the lowering cloud and the light grew stronger and stronger, and redder and redder.

Imbozwi uttered a hiss like a snake. I heard a bow-string twang, and almost at the same moment the thud of an arrow striking my post just above my head. Indeed, by lifting myself I could touch it. I shut my eyes and began to see all sorts of queer things that I had forgotten for years and years. My brain swam and seemed to melt into a kind of confusion. Through the intense silence I thought I heard the sound of some animal running heavily, much as a fat bull eland does when it is suddenly disturbed. Someone uttered a startled exclamation, which caused me to open my eyes again. The first thing I saw was the squad of savage archers lifting their bows--evidently that first arrow had been a kind of trial shot. The next, looking absolutely unearthly in that terrible and ominous light, was a tall figure seated on a white ox shambling rapidly towards us along the open roadway that ran from the southern gate of the market-place.

Of course, I knew that I dreamed, for this figure exactly resembled Brother John. There was his long, snowy beard. There in his hand was his butterfly net, with the handle of which he seemed to be prodding the ox. Only he was wound about with wreaths of flowers as were the great horns of the ox, and on either side of him and before and behind him ran girls, also wreathed with flowers. It was a vision, nothing else, and I shut my eyes again awaiting the fatal arrow.

"Shoot!" screamed Imbozwi.

"Nay, shoot not!" shouted Babemba. "*Dogeetah is come!*"

A moment's pause, during which I heard arrows falling to the ground; then from all those thousands of throats a roar that shaped itself to the words:

"Dogeetah! Dogeetah is come to save the white lords."

I must confess that after this my nerve, which is generally pretty good, gave out to such an extent that I think I fainted for a few minutes. During that faint I seemed to be carrying on a conversation with Mavovo, though whether it ever took place or I only imagined it I am not sure, since I always forgot to ask him.

He said, or I thought he said, to me:

"And now, Macumazana, my father, what have you to say? Does my Snake stand upon its tail or does it not? Answer, I am listening."

To which I replied, or seemed to reply:

"Mavovo, my child, certainly it appears as though your Snake *does* stand upon its tail. Still, I hold that all this is a phantasy; that we live in a land of dream in which nothing is real except those things which we cannot see or touch or hear. That there is no me and no you and no Snake at all, nothing but a Power in which we move, that shows us pictures and laughs when we think them real."

Whereon Mavovo said, or seemed to say:

"Ah! at last you touch the truth, O Macumazana, my father. All things are a shadow and we are shadows in a shadow. But what throws the shadow, O Macumazana, my father? Why does Dogeetah appear to come hither riding on a white ox and why do all these thousands think that my Snake stands so very stiff upon its tail?"

"I'm hanged if I know," I replied and woke up.

There, without doubt, *was* old Brother John with a wreath of flowers --I noted in disgust that they were orchids--hanging in a bacchanalian fashion from his dinted sun-helmet over his left eye. He was in a furious rage and reviling Bausi, who literally crouched before him, and I was in a furious rage and reviling him. What I said I do not remember, but he said, his white beard bristling with indignation while he threatened Bausi with the handle of the butterfly net:

"You dog! You savage, whom I saved from death and called Brother. What were you doing to these white men who are in truth my brothers, and to their followers? Were you about to kill them? Oh! if so, I will forget my vow, I will forget the bond that binds us and----"

"Don't, pray don't," said Bausi. "It is all a horrible mistake; I am not to be blamed at all. It is that witch-doctor, Imbozwi, whom by the ancient law of the land I must obey in such matters. He consulted his Spirit and declared that you were dead; also that these white lords were the most wicked of men, slave-traders with spotted hearts, who came hither to spy out the Mazitu people and to destroy them with magic and bullets."

"Then he lied," thundered Brother John, "and he knew that he lied."

"Yes, yes, it is evident that he lied," answered Bausi. "Bring him here, and with him those who serve him."

Now by the light of the moon which was shining brightly in the heavens, for the thunder-clouds had departed with the last glow of sunset, soldiers began an active search for Imbozwi and his confederates. Of these they caught eight or ten, all wicked-looking fellows hideously painted and adorned like their master, but Imbozwi himself they could not find.

I began to think that in the confusion he had given us the slip, when presently from the far end of the line, for we were still all tied to our stakes, I heard the voice of Sammy, hoarse, it is true, but quite cheerful now, saying:

"Mr. Quatermain, in the interests of justice, will you inform his Majesty that the treacherous wizard for whom he is seeking, is now peeping and muttering at the bottom of the grave which was dug to receive my mortal remains."

I did inform his Majesty, and in double-quick time our friend Imbozwi was once more fished out of a grave by the strong arms of Babemba and his soldiers, and dragged into the presence of the irate Bausi.

"Loose the white lords and their followers," said Bausi, "and let them come here."

So our bonds were undone and we walked to where the king and Brother John stood, the miserable Imbozwi and his attendant doctors huddled in a heap before them.

"Who is this?" said Bausi to him, pointing at Brother John. "Is it not he whom you vowed was dead?"

Imbozwi did not seem to think that the question required an answer, so Bausi continued:

"What was the song that you sang in our ears just now--that if Dogeetah came you would be ready to be shot to death with arrows in the place of these white lords whose lives you swore away, was it not?"

Again Imbozwi made no answer, although Babemba called his attention to the king's query with a vigorous kick. Then Bausi shouted:

"By your own mouth are you condemned, O liar, and that shall be done to you which you have yourself decreed," adding almost in the words of Elijah after he had triumphed over the priests of Baal, "Take away these false prophets. Let none of them escape. Say you not so, O people?"

"Aye," roared the multitude fiercely, "take them away."

"Not a popular character, Imbozwi," Stephen remarked to me in a reflective voice. "Well, he is going to be served hot on his own toast now, and serve the brute right."

"Who is the false doctor now?" mocked Mavovo in the silence that followed. "Who is about to sup on arrow-heads, O Painter-of-white- spots?" and he pointed to the mark that Imbozwi had so gleefully chalked over his heart as a guide to the arrows of the archers.

Now, seeing that all was lost, the little humpbacked villain with a sudden twist caught me by the legs and began to plead for mercy. So piteously did he plead, that being already softened by the fact of our wonderful escape from those black graves, my heart was melted in me. I turned to ask the king to spare his life, though with little hope that the prayer would be granted, for I saw that Bausi feared and hated the man and was only too glad of the opportunity to be rid of him. Imbozwi, however, interpreted my movement differently, since among savages the turning of the back always means that a petition is refused. Then, in his rage and despair, the venom of his wicked heart boiled over. He leapt to his feet, and drawing a big, carved knife from among his witch-doctor's trappings, sprang at me like a wild cat, shouting:

"At least you shall come too, white dog!"

Most mercifully Mavovo was watching him, for that is a good Zulu saying which declares that "Wizard is Wizard's fate." With one bound he was on him. Just as the knife touched me--it actually pricked my skin though without drawing blood, which was fortunate as probably it was poisoned--he gripped Imbozwi's arm in his grasp of iron and hurled him to the ground as though he were but a child.

After this of course all was over.

"Come away," I said to Stephen and Brother John; "this is no place for us."

So we went and gained our huts without molestation and indeed quite unobserved, for the attention of everyone in Beza Town was fully occupied elsewhere. From the market-place behind us rose so hideous a clamour that we rushed into my hut and shut the door to escape or lessen the sound. It was dark in the hut, for which I was really thankful, for the darkness seemed to soothe my nerves. Especially was this so when Brother John said:

"Friend, Allan Quatermain, and you, young gentleman, whose name I don't know, I will tell you what I think I never mentioned to you before, that, in addition to being a doctor, I am a clergyman of the American Episcopalian Church. Well, as a clergyman, I will ask your leave to return thanks for your very remarkable deliverance from a cruel death."

"By all means," I muttered for both of us, and he did so in a most earnest and beautiful prayer. Brother John may or may not have been a little touched in the head at this time of his life, but he was certainly an able and a good man.

Afterwards, as the shrieks and shouting had now died down to a confused murmur of many voices, we went and sat outside under the projecting eaves of the hut, where I introduced Stephen Somers to Brother John.

"And now," I said, "in the name of goodness, where do you come from tied up in flowers like a Roman priest at sacrifice, and riding on a bull like the lady called Europa? And what on earth do you mean by playing us such a scurvy trick down there in Durban, leaving us without a word after you had agreed to guide us to this hellish hole?"

Brother John stroked his long beard and looked at me reproachfully.

"I guess, Allan," he said in his American fashion, "there is a mistake somewhere. To answer the last part of your question first, I did not leave you without a word; I gave a letter to that lame old Griqua gardener of yours, Jack, to be handed to you when you arrived."

"Then the idiot either lost it and lied to me, as Griquas will, or he forgot all about it."

"That is likely. I ought to have thought of that, Allan, but I didn't. Well, in that letter I said that I would meet you here, where I should have been six weeks ago awaiting you. Also I sent a message to Bausi to warn him of your coming in case I should be delayed, but I suppose that something happened to it on the road."

"Why did you not wait and come with us like a sensible man?"

"Allan, as you ask me straight out, I will tell you, although the subject is one of which I do not care to speak. I knew that you were going to journey by Kilwa; indeed it was your only route with a lot of people and so much baggage, and I did not wish to visit Kilwa." He paused, then went on: "A long while ago, nearly twenty-three years to be accurate, I went to live at Kilwa as a missionary with my young wife. I built a mission station and a church there, and we were happy and fairly successful in our work. Then on one evil day the Swahili and other Arabs came in dhows to establish a slave-dealing station. I resisted them, and the end of it was that they attacked us, killed most of my people and enslaved the rest. In that attack I received a cut from a sword on the head--look, here is the mark of it," and drawing his white hair apart he showed us a long scar that was plainly visible in the moonlight.

"The blow knocked me senseless just about sunset one evening. When I came to myself again it was broad daylight and everybody was gone, except one old woman who was tending me. She was half-crazed with grief because her husband and two sons had been killed, and another son, a boy, and a daughter had been taken away. I asked her where my young wife was. She answered that she, too, had been taken away eight or ten hours before, because the Arabs had seen the lights of a ship out at sea, and thought they might be those of a British man-of-war that was known to be cruising on the coast. On seeing these they had fled inland in a hurry, leaving me for dead, but killing the wounded before they went. The old woman herself had escaped by hiding among some rocks on the seashore, and after the Arabs had gone had crept back to the house and found me still alive.

"I asked her where my wife had been taken. She said she did not know, but some others of our people told her that they had heard the Arabs say they were going to some place a hundred miles inland, to join their leader, a half-bred villain named Hassan-ben-Mohammed, to whom they were carrying my wife as a present.

"Now we knew this wretch, for after the Arabs landed at Kilwa, but before actual hostilities broke out between us, he had fallen sick of smallpox and my wife had helped to nurse him. Had it not been for her, indeed, he would have died. However, although the leader of the band, he was not present at the attack, being engaged in some slave-raiding business in the interior.

"When I learned this terrible news, the shock of it, or the loss of blood, brought on a return of insensibility, from which I only awoke two days later to find myself on board a Dutch trading vessel that was sailing for Zanzibar. It was the lights of this ship that the Arabs had seen and mistaken for those of an English man-of-war. She had put into Kilwa for water, and the sailors, finding me on the verandah of the house and still living, in the goodness of their hearts carried me on board. Of the old woman they had seen nothing; I suppose that at their approach she ran away.

"At Zanzibar, in an almost dying condition, I was handed over to a clergyman of our mission, in whose house I lay desperately ill for a long while. Indeed six months went by before I fully recovered my right mind. Some people say that I have never recovered it; perhaps you are one of them, Allan.

"At last the wound in my skull healed, after a clever English naval surgeon had removed some bits of splintered bone, and my strength came back to me. I was and still am an American subject, and in those days we had no consul at Zanzibar, if there is one there now, of which I am not sure, and of course no warship. The English made what inquiries they could for me, but could find out little or nothing, since all the country about Kilwa was in possession of Arab slave-traders who were supported by a ruffian who called himself the Sultan of Zanzibar."

Again he paused, as though overcome by the sadness of his recollections.

"Did you never hear any more of your wife?" asked Stephen.

"Yes, Mr. Somers; I heard at Zanzibar from a slave whom our mission bought and freed, that he had seen a white woman who answered to her description alive and apparently well, at some place I was unable to identify. He could only tell me that it was fifteen days' journey from the coast. She was then in charge of some black people, he did not know of what tribe, who, he believed, had found her wandering in the bush. He noted that the black people seemed to treat her with the greatest reverence, although they could not understand what she said. On the following day, whilst searching for six lost goats, he was captured by Arabs who, he heard afterwards, were out looking for this white woman. The day after the man had told me this, he was seized with inflammation of the lungs, of which, being in a weak state from his sufferings in the slave gang, he quickly died. Now you will understand why I was not particularly anxious to revisit Kilwa."

"Yes," I said, "we understand that, and a good deal more of which we will talk later. But, to change the subject, where do you come from now, and how did you happen to turn up just in the nick of time?"

"I was journeying here across country by a route I will show you on my map," he answered, "when I met with an accident to my leg" (here Stephen and I looked at each other) "which kept me laid up in a Kaffir hut for six weeks. When I got better, as I could not walk very well I rode upon oxen that I had trained. That white beast you saw is the last of them; the others died of the bite of the tsetse fly. A fear which I could not define caused me to press forward as fast as possible; for the last twenty-four hours I have scarcely stopped to eat or sleep. When I got into the Mazitu country this morning I found the kraals empty, except for some women and girls, who knew me again, and threw these flowers over me. They told me that all the men had gone to Beza Town for a great feast, but what the feast was they either did not know or would not reveal. So I hurried on and arrived in time--thank God in time! It is a long story; I will tell you the details afterwards. Now we are all too tired. What's that noise?"

I listened and recognised the triumphant song of the Zulu hunters, who were returning from the savage scene in the market-place. Presently they arrived, headed by Sammy, a very different Sammy from the wailing creature who had gone out to execution an hour or two before. Now he was the gayest of the gay, and about his neck were strung certain weird ornaments which I identified as the personal property of Imbozwi.

"Virtue is victorious and justice has been done, Mr. Quatermain. These are the spoils of war," he said, pointing to the trappings of the late witch-doctor.

"Oh! get out, you little cur! We want to know nothing more," I said. "Go, cook us some supper," and he went, not in the least abashed.

The hunters were carrying between them what appeared to be the body of Hans. At first I was frightened, thinking that he must be dead, but examination showed that he was only in a state of insensibility such as might be induced by laudanum. Brother John ordered him to be wrapped up in a blanket and laid by the fire, and this was done.

Presently Mavovo approached and squatted down in front of us.

"Macumazana, my father," he said quietly, "what words have you for me?"

"Words of thanks, Mavovo. If you had not been so quick, Imbozwi would have finished me. As it is, the knife only touched my skin without breaking it, for Dogeetah has looked to see."

Mavovo waved his hand as though to sweep this little matter aside, and asked, looking me straight in the eyes:

"And what other words, Macumazana? As to my Snake I mean."

"Only that you were right and I was wrong," I answered shamefacedly. "Things have happened as you foretold, how or why I do not understand."

"No, my father, because you white men are so vain" ("blown out was his word), "that you think you have all wisdom. Now you have learned that this is not so. I am content. The false doctors are all dead, my father, and I think that Imbozwi----"

I held up my hand, not wishing to hear details. Mavovo rose, and with a little smile, went about his business.

"What does he mean about his Snake?" inquired Brother John curiously.

I told him as briefly as I could, and asked him if he could explain the matter. He shook his head.

"The strangest example of native vision that I have ever heard of," he answered, "and the most useful. Explain! There is no explanation, except the old one that there are more things in heaven and earth, etc., and that God gives different gifts to different men."

Then we ate our supper; I think one of the most joyful meals of which I have ever partaken. It is wonderful how good food tastes when one never expected to swallow another mouthful. After it was finished the others went to bed but, with the still unconscious Hans for my only companion, I sat for a while smoking by the fire, for on this high tableland the air was chilly. I felt that as yet I could not sleep; if for no other reason because of the noise that the Mazitu were making in the town, I suppose in celebration of the execution of the terrible witch-doctors and the return of Dogeetah.

Suddenly Hans awoke, and sitting up, stared at me through the bright flame which I had recently fed with dry wood.

"Baas," he said in a hollow voice, "there you are, here I am, and there is the fire which never goes out, a very good fire. But, Baas, why are we not inside of it as your father the Predikant promised, instead of outside here in the cold?"

"Because you are still in the world, you old fool, and not where you deserve to be," I answered. "Because Mavovo's Snake was a snake with a true tongue after all, and Dogeetah came as it foretold. Because we are all alive and well, and it is Imbozwi with his spawn who are dead upon the posts. That is why, Hans, as you would have seen for yourself if you had kept awake, instead of swallowing filthy medicine like a frightened woman, just because you were afraid of death, which at your age you ought to have welcomed."

"Oh! Baas," broke in Hans, "don't tell me that things are so and that we are really alive in what your honoured father used to call this gourd full of tears. Don't tell me, Baas, that I made a coward of myself and swallowed that beastliness--if you knew what it was made of you would understand, Baas--for nothing but a bad headache. Don't tell me that Dogeetah came when my eyes were not open to see him, and worst of all, that Imbozwi and his children were tied to those poles when I was not able to help them out of the bottle of tears into the fire that burns for ever and ever. Oh! it is too much, and I swear, Baas, that however often I have to die, henceforward it shall always be with my eyes open," and holding his aching head between his hands he rocked himself to and fro in bitter grief.

Well might Hans be sad, seeing that he never heard the last of the incident. The hunters invented a new and gigantic name for him, which meant "The little-yellow-mouse-who-feeds-on-sleep-while-the-black- rats-eat-up-their-enemies." Even Sammy made a mock of him, showing him the spoils which he declared he had wrenched unaided from the mighty master of magic, Imbozwi. As indeed he had--after the said Imbozwi was stone dead at the stake.

It was very amusing until things grew so bad that I feared Hans would kill Sammy, and had to put a stop to the joke.

Brother John's Story

Although I went to bed late I was up before sunrise. Chiefly because I wished to have some private conversation with Brother John, whom I knew to be a very early riser. Indeed, he slept less than any man I ever met.

As I expected, I found him astir in his hut; he was engaged in pressing flowers by candlelight.

"John," I said, "I have brought you some property which I think you have lost," and I handed him the morocco-bound *Christian Year* and the water-colour drawing which we had found in the sacked mission house at Kilwa.

He looked first at the picture and then at the book; at least, I suppose he did, for I went outside the hut for a while--to observe the sunrise. In a few minutes he called me, and when the door was shut, said in an unsteady voice:

"How did you come by these relics, Allan?"

I told him the story from beginning to end. He listened without a word, and when I had finished said:

"I may as well tell what perhaps you have guessed, that the picture is that of my wife, and the book is her book."

"Is!" I exclaimed.

"Yes, Allan. I say *is* because I do not believe that she is dead. I cannot explain why, any more than I could explain last night how that great Zulu savage was able to prophesy my coming. But sometimes we can wring secrets from the Unknown, and I believe that I have won this truth in answer to my prayers, that my wife still lives."

"After twenty years, John?"

"Yes, after twenty years. Why do you suppose," he asked almost fiercely, "that for two-thirds of a generation I have wandered about among African savages, pretending to be crazy because these wild people revere the mad and always let them pass unharmed?"

"I thought it was to collect butterflies and botanical specimens."

"Butterflies and botanical specimens! These were the pretext. I have been and am searching for my wife. You may think it a folly, especially considering what was her condition when we separated--she was expecting a child, Allan--but I do not. I believe that she is hidden away among some of these wild peoples."

"Then perhaps it would be as well not to find her," I answered, bethinking me of the fate which had overtaken sundry white women in the old days, who had escaped from shipwrecks on the coast and become the wives of Kaffirs.

"Not so, Allan. On that point I fear nothing. If God has preserved my wife, He has also protected her from every harm. And now," he went on, "you will understand why I wish to visit these Pongo--the Pongo who worship a white goddess!"

"I understand," I said and left him, for having learned all there was to know, I thought it best not to prolong a painful conversation. To me it seemed incredible that this lady should still live, and I feared the effect upon him of the discovery that she was no more. How full of romance is this poor little world of ours! Think of Brother John (Eversley was his real name as I discovered afterwards), and what his life had been. A high-minded educated man trying to serve his Faith in the dark places of the earth, and taking his young wife with him, which for my part I have never considered a right thing to do. Neither tradition nor Holy Writ record that the Apostles dragged their wives and families into the heathen lands where they went to preach, although I believe that some of them were married. But this is by the way.

Then falls the blow; the mission house is sacked, the husband escapes by a miracle and the poor young lady is torn away to be the prey of a vile slave-trader. Lastly, according to the quite unreliable evidence of some savage already in the shadow of death, she is seen in the charge of other unknown savages. On the strength of this the husband, playing the part of a mad botanist, hunts for her for a score of years, enduring incredible hardships and yet buoyed up by a high and holy trust. To my mind it was a beautiful and pathetic story. Still, for reasons which I have suggested, I confess that I hoped that long ago she had returned into the hands of the Power which made her, for what would be the state of a young white lady who for two decades had been at the mercy of these black brutes?

And yet, and yet, after my experience of Mavovo and his Snake, I did not feel inclined to dogmatise about anything. Who and what was I, that I should venture not only to form opinions, but to thrust them down the throats of others? After all, how narrow are the limits of the knowledge upon which we base our judgments. Perhaps the great sea of intuition that surrounds us is safer to float on than are these little islets of individual experience, whereon we are so wont to take our stand.

Meanwhile my duty was not to speculate on the dreams and mental attitudes of others, but like a practical hunter and trader, to carry to a successful issue an expedition that I was well paid to manage, and to dig up a certain rare flower root, if I could find it, in the marketable value of which I had an interest. I have always prided myself upon my entire lack of imagination and all such mental phantasies, and upon an aptitude for hard business and an appreciation of the facts of life, that after all are the things with which we have to do. This is the truth; at least, I hope it is. For if I were to be *quite* honest, which no one ever has been, except a gentleman named Mr. Pepys, who, I think, lived in the reign of Charles II, and who, to judge from his memoirs, which I have read lately, did not write for publication, I should have to admit that there is another side to my nature. I sternly suppress it, however, at any rate for the present.

While we were at breakfast Hans who, still suffering from headache and remorse, was lurking outside the gateway far from the madding crowd of critics, crept in like a beaten dog and announced that Babemba was approaching followed by a number of laden soldiers. I was about to advance to receive him. Then I remembered that, owing to a queer native custom, such as that which caused Sir Theophilus Shepstone, whom I used to know very well, to be recognised as the holder of the spirit of the great Chaka and therefore as the equal of the Zulu monarchs, Brother John was the really important man in our company. So I gave way and asked him to be good enough to take my place and to live up to that station in savage life to which it had pleased God to call him.

I am bound to say he rose to the occasion very well, being by nature and appearance a dignified old man. Swallowing his coffee in a hurry, he took his place at a little distance from us, and stood there in a statuesque pose. To him entered Babemba crawling on his hands and knees, and other native gentlemen likewise crawling, also the burdened soldiers in as obsequious an attitude as their loads would allow.

"O King Dogeetah," said Babemba, "your brother king, Bausi, returns the guns and fire-goods of the white men, your children, and sends certain gifts."

"Glad to hear it, General Babemba," said Brother John, "although it would be better if he had never taken them away. Put them down and get on to your feet. I do not like to see men wriggling on their stomachs like monkeys."

The order was obeyed, and we checked the guns and ammunition; also our revolvers and the other articles that had been taken away from us. Nothing was missing or damaged; and in addition there were four fine elephant's tusks, an offering to Stephen and myself, which, as a business man, I promptly accepted; some karosses and Mazitu weapons, presents to Mavovo and the hunters, a beautiful native bedstead with ivory legs and mats of finely-woven grass, a gift to Hans in testimony to his powers of sleep under trying circumstances (the Zulus roared when they heard this, and Hans vanished cursing behind the huts), and for Sammy a weird musical instrument with a request that in future he would use it in public instead of his voice.

Sammy, I may add, did not see the joke any more than Hans had done, but the rest of us appreciated the Mazitu sense of humour very much.

"It is very well, Mr. Quatermain," he said, "for these black babes and sucklings to sit in the seat of the scornful. On such an occasion silent prayers would have been of little use, but I am certain that my loud crying to Heaven delivered you all from the bites of the heathen arrows."

"O Dogeetah and white lords," said Babemba, "the king invites your presence that he may ask your forgiveness for what has happened, and this time there will be no need for you to bring arms, since henceforward no hurt can come to you from the Mazitu people."

So presently we set out once more, taking with us the gifts that had been refused. Our march to the royal quarters was a veritable triumphal progress. The people prostrated themselves and clapped their hands slowly in salutation as we passed, while the girls and children pelted us with flowers as though we were brides going to be married. Our road ran by the place of execution where the stakes, at which I confess I looked with a shiver, were still standing, though the graves had been filled in.

On our arrival Bausi and his councillors rose and bowed to us. Indeed, the king did more, for coming forward he seized Brother John by the hand, and insisted upon rubbing his ugly black nose against that of this revered guest. This, it appeared, was the Mazitu method of embracing, an honour which Brother John did not seem at all to appreciate. Then followed long speeches, washed down with draughts of thick native beer. Bausi explained that his evil proceedings were entirely due to the wickedness of the deceased Imbozwi and his disciples, under whose tyranny the land had groaned for long, since the people believed them to speak "with the voice of 'Heaven Above.'"

Brother John, on our behalf, accepted the apology, and then read a lecture, or rather preached a sermon, that took exactly twenty-five minutes to deliver (he is rather long in the wind), in which he demonstrated the evils of superstition and pointed to a higher and a better path. Bausi replied that he would like to hear more of that path another time which, as he presumed that we were going to spend the rest of our lives in his company, could easily be found--say during the next spring when the crops had been sown and the people had leisure on their hands.

After this we presented our gifts, which now were eagerly accepted. Then I took up my parable and explained to Bausi that so far from stopping in Beza Town for the rest of our lives, we were anxious to press forward at once to Pongo-land. The king's face fell, as did those of his councillors.

"Listen, O lord Macumazana, and all of you," he said. "These Pongo are horrible wizards, a great and powerful people who live by themselves amidst the swamps and mix with none. If the Pongo catch Mazitu or folk of any other tribe, either they kill them or take them as prisoners to their own land where they enslave them, or sometimes sacrifice them to the devils they worship."

"That is so," broke in Babemba, "for when I was a lad I was a slave to the Pongo and doomed to be sacrificed to the White Devil. It was in escaping from them that I lost this eye."

Needless to say, I made a note of this remark, though I did not think the moment opportune to follow the matter up. If Babemba has once been to Pongo-land, I reflected to myself, Babemba can go again or show us the way there.

"And if we catch any of the Pongo," went on Bausi, "as sometimes we do when they come to hunt for slaves, we kill them. Ever since the Mazitu have been in this place there has been hate and war between them and the Pongo, and if I could wipe out those evil ones, then I should die happily."

"That you will never do, O King, while the White Devil lives," said Babemba. "Have you not heard the Pongo prophecy, that while the White Devil lives and the Holy Flower blooms, they will live. But when the White Devil dies and the Holy Flower ceases to bloom, then their women will become barren and their end will be upon them."

"Well, I suppose that this White Devil will die some day," I said.

"Not so, Macumazana. It will never die of itself. Like its wicked Priest, it has been there from the beginning and will always be there unless it is killed. But who is there that can kill the White Devil?"

I thought to myself that I would not mind trying, but again I did not pursue the point.

"My brother Dogeetah and lords," exclaimed Bausi, "it is not possible that you should visit these wizards except at the head of an army. But how can I send an army with you, seeing that the Mazitu are a land people and have no canoes in which to cross the great lake, and no trees whereof to make them?"

We answered that we did not know but would think the matter over, as we had come from our own place for this purpose and meant to carry it out.

Then the audience came to an end, and we returned to our huts, leaving Dogeetah to converse with his "brother Bausi" on matters connected with the latter's health. As I passed Babemba I told him that I should like to see him alone, and he said that he would visit me that evening after supper. The rest of the day passed quietly, for we had asked that people might be kept away from our encampment.

We found Hans, who had not accompanied us, being a little shy of appearing in public just then, engaged in cleaning the rifles, and this reminded me of something. Taking the double-barrelled gun of which I have spoken, I called Mavovo and handed it to him, saying:

"It is yours, O true prophet."

"Yes, my father," he answered, "it is mine for a little while, then perhaps it will be yours again."

The words struck me, but I did not care to ask their meaning. Somehow I wanted to hear no more of Mavovo's prophecies.

Then we dined, and for the rest of that afternoon slept, for all of us, including Brother John, needed rest badly. In the evening Babemba came, and we three white men saw him alone.

"Tell us about the Pongo and this white devil they worship," I said.

"Macumazana," he answered, "fifty years have gone by since I was in that land and I see things that happened to me there as through a mist. I went to fish amongst the reeds when I was a boy of twelve, and tall men robed in white came in a canoe and seized me. They led me to a town where there were many other such men, and treated me very well, giving me sweet things to eat till I grew fat and my skin shone. Then in the evening I was taken away, and we marched all night to the mouth of a great cave. In this cave sat a horrible old man about whom danced robed people, performing the rites of the White Devil.

"The old man told me that on the following morning I was to be cooked and eaten, for which reason I had been made so fat. There was a canoe at the mouth of the cave, beyond which lay water. While all were asleep I crept to the canoe. As I loosed the rope one of the priests woke up and ran at me. But I hit him on the head with the paddle, for though only a boy I was bold and strong, and he fell into the water. He came up again and gripped the edge of the canoe, but I struck his fingers with the paddle till he let go. A great wind was blowing that night, tearing off boughs from the trees which grew upon the other shore of the water. It whirled the canoe round and round and one of the boughs struck me in the eye. I scarcely felt it at the time, but afterwards the eye withered. Or perhaps it was a spear or a knife that struck me in the eye, I do not know. I paddled till I lost my senses and always that wind blew. The last thing that I remember was the sound of the canoe being driven by the gale through reeds. When I woke up again I found myself near a shore, to which I waded through the mud, scaring great crocodiles. But this must have been some days later, for now I was quite thin. I fell down upon the shore, and there some of our people found me and nursed me till I recovered. That is all."

"And quite enough too," I said. "Now answer me. How far was the town from the place where you were captured in Mazitu-land?"

"A whole day's journey in the canoe, Macumazana. I was captured in the morning early and we reached the harbour in the evening at a place where many canoes were tied up, perhaps fifty of them, some of which would hold forty men."

"And how far was the town from this harbour?"

"Quite close, Macumazana."

Now Brother John asked a question.

"Did you hear anything about the land beyond the water by the cave?"

"Yes, Dogeetah. I heard then, or afterwards--for from time to time rumours reach us concerning these Pongo--that it is an island where grows the Holy Flower, of which you know, for when last you were here you had one of its blooms. I heard, too, that this Holy Flower was tended by a priestess named Mother of the Flower, and her servants, all of whom were virgins."

"Who was the priestess?"

"I do not know, but I heave heard that she was one of those people who, although their parents are black, are born white, and that if any females among the Pongo are born white, or with pink eyes, or deaf and dumb, they are set apart to be the servants of the priestess. But this priestess must now be dead, seeing that when I was a boy she was already old, very, very old, and the Pongo were much concerned because there was no one of white skin who could be appointed to succeed her. Indeed she *is* dead, since many years ago there was a great feast in Pongo-land and numbers of slaves were eaten, because the priests had found a beautiful new princess who was white with yellow hair and had finger-nails of the right shape."

Now I bethought me that this finding of the priestess named "Mother of the Flower," who must be distinguished by certain personal peculiarities, resembled not a little that of the finding of the Apis bull-god, which also must have certain prescribed and holy markings, by the old Egyptians, as narrated by Herodotus. However, I said nothing about it at the time, because Brother John asked sharply:

"And is this priestess also dead?"

"I do not know, Dogeetah, but I think not. If she were dead I think that we should have heard some rumour of the Feast of the eating of the dead Mother."

"Eating the dead mother!" I exclaimed.

"Yes, Macumazana. It is the law among the Pongo that, for a certain sacred reason, the body of the Mother of the Flower, when she dies, must be partaken of by those who are privileged to the holy food."

"But the White Devil neither dies nor is eaten?" I said.

"No, as I have told you, he never dies. It is he who causes others to die, as if you go to Pongo-land doubtless you will find out," Babemba added grimly.

Upon my word, thought I to myself, as the meeting broke up because Babemba had nothing more to say, if I had my way I would leave Pongo- land and its white devil alone. Then I remembered how Brother John stood in reference to this matter, and with a sigh resigned myself to fate. As it proved it, I mean Fate, was quite equal to the occasion. The very next morning, early, Babemba turned up again.

"Lords, lords," he said, "a wonderful thing has happened! Last night we spoke of the Pongo and now behold! an embassy from the Pongo is here; it arrived at sunrise."

"What for?" I asked.

"To propose peace between their people and the Mazitu. Yes, they ask that Bausi should send envoys to their town to arrange a lasting peace. As if anyone would go!" he added.

"Perhaps some might dare to," I answered, for an idea occurred to me, "but let us go to see Bausi."

Half an hour later we were seated in the king's enclosure, that is, Stephen and I were, for Brother John was already in the royal hut, talking to Bausi. As we went a few words had passed between us.

"Has it occurred to you, John," I asked, "that if you really wish to visit Pongo-land here is perhaps what you would call a providential opportunity. Certainly none of these Mazitu will go, since they fear lest they should find a permanent peace--inside of the Pongo. Well, you are a blood-brother to Bausi and can offer to play the part of Envoy Extraordinary, with us as the members of your staff."

"I have already thought of it, Allan," he replied, stroking his long beard.

We sat down among a few of the leading councillors, and presently Bausi came out of his hut accompanied by Brother John, and having greeted us, ordered the Pongo envoys to be admitted. They were led in at once, tall, light-coloured men with regular and Semitic features, who were clothed in white linen like Arabs, and wore circles of gold or copper upon their necks and wrists.

In short, they were imposing persons, quite different from ordinary Central African natives, though there was something about their appearance which chilled and repelled me. I should add that their spears had been left outside, and that they saluted the king by folding their arms upon their breasts and bowing in a dignified fashion.

"Who are you?" asked Bausi, "and what do you want?"

"I am Komba," answered their spokesman, quite a young man with flashing eyes, "the Accepted-of-the-Gods, who, in a day to come that perhaps is near, will be the Kalubi of the Pongo people, and these are my servants. I have come here bearing gifts of friendship which are without, by the desire of the holy Motombo, the High Priest of the gods----"

"I thought that the Kalubi was the priest of your gods," interrupted Bausi.

"Not so. The Kalubi is the King of the Pongo as you are the King of the Mazitu. The Motombo, who is seldom seen, is King of the spirits and the Mouth of the gods."

Bausi nodded in the African fashion, that is by raising the chin, not depressing it, and Komba went on:

"I have placed myself in your power, trusting to your honour. You can kill me if you wish, though that will avail nothing, since there are others waiting to become Kalubi in my place."

"Am I a Pongo that I should wish to kill messengers and eat them?" asked Bausi, with sarcasm, a speech at which I noticed the Pongo envoys winced a little.

"King, you are mistaken. The Pongo only eat those whom the White God has chosen. It is a religious rite. Why should they who have cattle in plenty desire to devour men?"

"I don't know," grunted Bausi, "but there is one here who can tell a different story," and he looked at Babemba, who wriggled uncomfortably.

Komba also looked at him with his fierce eyes.

"It is not conceivable," he said, "that anybody should wish to eat one so old and bony, but let that pass. I thank you, King, for your promise of safety. I have come here to ask that you should send envoys to confer with the Kalubi and the Motombo, that a lasting peace may be arranged between our peoples."

"Why do not the Kalubi and the Motombo come here to confer?" asked Bausi.

"Because it is not lawful that they should leave their land, O King. Therefore they have sent me who am the Kalubi-to-come. Hearken. There has been war between us for generations. It began so long ago that only the Motombo knows of its beginning which he has from the gods. Once the Pongo people owned all this land and only had their sacred places beyond the water. Then your forefathers came and fell on them, killing many, enslaving many and taking their women to wife. Now, say the Motombo and the Kalubi, in the place of war let there be peace; where there is but barren sand, there let corn and flowers grow; let the darkness, wherein men lose their way and die, be changed to pleasant light in which they can sit in the sun holding each other's hands."

"Hear, hear!" I muttered, quite moved by this eloquence. But Bausi was not at all moved; indeed, he seemed to view these poetic proposals with the darkest suspicion.

"Give up killing our people or capturing them to be sacrificed to your White Devil, and then in a year or two we may listen to your words that are smeared with honey," he said. "As it is, we think that they are but a trap to catch flies. Still, if there are any of our councillors willing to visit your Motombo and your Kalubi and hear what they have to propose, taking the risk of whatever may happen to them there, I do not forbid it. Now, O my Councillors, speak, not altogether, but one by one, and be swift, since to the first that speaks shall be given this honour."

I think I never heard a denser silence than that which followed this invitation. Each of the *indunas* looked at his neighbour, but not one of them uttered a single word.

"What!" exclaimed Bausi, in affected surprise. "Do none speak? Well, well, you are lawyers and men of peace. What says the great general, Babemba?"

"I say, O King, that I went once to Pongo-land when I was young, taken by the hair of my head, to leave an eye there and that I do not wish to visit it again walking on the soles of my feet."

"It seems, O Komba, that since none of my people are willing to act as envoys, if there is to be talk of peace between us, the Motombo and the Kalubi must come here under safe conduct."

"I have said that cannot be, O King."

"If so, all is finished, O Komba. Rest, eat of our food and return to your own land."

Then Brother John rose and said:

"We are blood-brethren, Bausi, and therefore I can speak for you. If you and your councillors are willing, and these Pongos are willing, I and my friends do not fear to visit the Motombo and the Kalubi, to talk with them of peace on behalf of your people, since we love to see new lands and new races of mankind. Say, Komba, if the king allows, will you accept us as ambassadors?"

"It is for the king to name his own ambassadors," answered Komba. "Yet the Kalubi has heard of the presence of you white lords in Mazitu-land and bade me say that if it should be your pleasure to accompany the embassy and visit him, he would give you welcome. Only when the matter was laid before the Motombo, the oracle spoke thus:

"'Let the white men come if come they will, or let them stay away. But if they come, let them bring with them none of those iron tubes, great or small, whereof the land has heard, that vomit smoke with a noise and cause death from afar. They will not need them to kill meat, for meat shall be given to them in plenty; moreover, among the Pongo they will be safe, unless they offer insult to the god.'"

These words Komba spoke very slowly and with much emphasis, his piercing eyes fixed upon my face as though to read the thoughts it hid. As I heard them my courage sank into my boots. Well, I knew that the Kalubi was asking us to Pongo-land that we might kill this Great White Devil that threatened his life, which, I took it, was a monstrous ape. And how could we face that or some other frightful brute without firearms? My mind was made up in a minute.

"O Komba," I said, "my gun is my father, my mother, my wife and all my other relatives. I do not stir from here without it."

"Then, white lord," answered Komba, "you will do well to stop in this place in the midst of your family, since, if you try to bring it with you to Pongo-land, you will be killed as you set foot upon the shore."

Before I could find an answer Brother John spoke, saying:

"It is natural that the great hunter, Macumazana, should not wish to be parted from what which to him is as a stick to a lame man. But with me it is different. For years I have used no gun, who kill nothing that God made, except a few bright-winged insects. I am ready to visit your country with naught save this in my hand," and he pointed to the butterfly net that leaned against the fence behind him.

"Good, you are welcome," said Komba, and I thought that I saw his eyes gleam with unholy joy. There followed a pause, during which I explained everything to Stephen, showing that the thing was madness. But here, to my horror, that young man's mulish obstinacy came in.

"I say, you know, Quatermain," he said, "we can't let the old boy go alone, or at least I can't. It's another matter for you who have a son dependent on you. But putting aside the fact that I mean to get----" he was about to add, "the orchid," when I nudged him. Of course, it was ridiculous, but an uneasy fear took me lest this Komba should in some mysterious way understand what he was saying. "What's up? Oh! I see, but the beggar can't understand English. Well, putting aside everything else, it isn't the game, and there you are, you know. If Mr. Brother John goes, I'll go too, and indeed if he doesn't go, I'll go alone."

"You unutterable young ass," I muttered in a stage aside.

"What is it the young white lord says he wishes in our country?" asked the cold Komba, who with diabolical acuteness had read some of Stephen's meaning in his face.

"He says that he is a harmless traveller who would like to study the scenery and to find out if you have any gold there," I answered.

"Indeed. Well, he shall study the scenery and we have gold," and he touched the bracelets on his arm, "of which he shall be given as much as he can carry away. But perchance, white lords, you would wish to talk this matter over alone. Have we your leave to withdraw a while, O King?"

Five minutes later we were seated in the king's "great house" with Bausi himself and Babemba. Here there was a mighty argument. Bausi implored Brother John not to go, and so did I. Babemba said that to go would be madness, as he smelt witchcraft and murder in the air, he who knew the Pongo.

Brother John replied sweetly that he certainly intended to avail himself of this heaven-sent opportunity to visit one of the few remaining districts in this part of Africa through which he had not yet wandered. Stephen yawned and fanned himself with a pocket- handkerchief, for the hut was hot, and remarked that having come so far after a certain rare flower he did not mean to return empty- handed.

"I perceive, Dogeetah," said Bausi at last, "that you have some reason for this journey which you are hiding from me. Still, I am minded to hold you here by force."

"If you do, it will break our brotherhood," answered Brother John. "Seek not to know what I would hide, Bausi, but wait till the future shall declare it."

Bausi groaned and gave in. Babemba said that Dogeetah and Wazela were bewitched, and that I, Macumazana, alone retained my senses.

"Then that's settled," exclaimed Stephen. "John and I are to go as envoys to the Pongo, and you, Quatermain, will stop here to look after the hunters and the stores."

"Young man," I replied, "do you wish to insult me? After your father put you in my charge, too! If you two are going, I shall come also, if I have to do so mother-naked. But let me tell you once and for all in the most emphatic language I can command, that I consider you a brace of confounded lunatics, and that if the Pongo don't eat you, it will be more than you deserve. To think that at my age I should be dragged among a lot of cannibal savages without even a pistol, to fight some unknown brute with my bare hands! Well, we can only die once--that is, so far as we know at present."

"How true," remarked Stephen; "how strangely and profoundly true!"

Oh! I could have boxed his ears.

We went into the courtyard again, whither Komba was summoned with his attendants. This time they came bearing gifts, or having them borne for them. These consisted, I remember, of two fine tusks of ivory which suggested to me that their country could not be entirely surrounded by water, since elephants would scarcely live upon an island; gold dust in a gourd and copper bracelets, which showed that it was mineralized; white native linen, very well woven, and some really beautiful decorated pots, indicating that the people had artistic tastes. Where did they get them from, I wonder, and what was the origin of their race? I cannot answer the question, for I never found out with any certainty. Nor do I think they knew themselves.

The *indaba* was resumed. Bausi announced that we three white men with a servant apiece (I stipulated for this) would visit Pongo-land as his envoys, taking no firearms with us, there to discuss terms of peace between the two peoples, and especially the questions of trade and intermarriage. Komba was very insistent that this should be included; at the time I wondered why. He, Komba, on behalf of the Motombo and the Kalubi, the spiritual and temporal rulers of his land, guaranteed us safe conduct on the understanding that we attempted no insult or violence to the gods, a stipulation from which there was no escape, though I liked it little. He swore also that we should be delivered safe and sound in the Mazitu country within six days of our having left its shores.

Bausi said that it was good, adding that he would send five hundred armed men to escort us to the place where we were to embark, and to receive us on our return; also that if any hurt came to us he would wage war upon the Pongo people for ever until he found means to destroy them.

So we parted, it being agreed that we were to start upon our journey on the following morning.

Rica Town

As a matter of fact we did not leave Beza Town till twenty-four hours later than had been arranged, since it took some time for old Babemba, who was to be in charge of it, to collect and provision our escort of five hundred men.

Here, I may mention, that when we got back to our huts we found the two Mazitu bearers, Tom and Jerry, eating a hearty meal, but looking rather tired. It appeared that in order to get rid of their favourable evidence, the ceased witch-doctor, Imbozwi, who for some reason or other had feared to kill them, caused them to be marched off to a distant part of the land where they were imprisoned. On the arrival of the news of the fall and death of Imbozwi and his subordinates, they were set at liberty, and at once returned to us at Beza Town.

Of course it became necessary to explain to our servants what we were about to do. When they understood the nature of our proposed expedition they shook their heads, and when they learned that we had promised to leave our guns behind us, they were speechless with amazement.

"*Kransick! Kransick!*" which means "ill in the skull," or "mad," exclaimed Hans to the others as he tapped his forehead significantly. "They have caught it from Dogeetah, one who lives on insects which he entangles in a net, and carries no gun to kill game. Well, I knew they would."

The hunters nodded in assent, and Sammy lifted his arms to Heaven as though in prayer. Only Mavovo seemed indifferent. Then came the question of which of them was to accompany us.

"So far as I am concerned that is soon settled," said Mavovo. "I go with my father, Macumazana, seeing that even without a gun I am still strong and can fight as my male ancestors fought with a spear."

"And I, too, go with the Baas Quatermain," grunted Hans, "seeing that even without a gun I am cunning, as *my* female ancestors were before me."

"Except when you take medicine, Spotted Snake, and lose yourself in the mist of sleep," mocked one of the Zulus. "Does that fine bedstead which the king sent you go with you?"

"No, son of a fool!" answered Hans. "I'll lend it to you who do not understand that there is more wisdom within me when I am asleep than there is in you when you are awake."

It remained to be decided who the third man should be. As neither of Brother John's two servants, who had accompanied him on his cross- country journey, was suitable, one being ill and the other afraid, Stephen suggested Sammy as the man, chiefly because he could cook.

"No, Mr. Somers, no," said Sammy, with earnestness. "At this proposal I draw the thick rope. To ask one who can cook to visit a land where he will be cooked, is to seethe the offspring in its parent's milk."

So we gave him up, and after some discussion fixed upon Jerry, a smart and plucky fellow, who was quite willing to accompany us. The rest of that day we spent in making our preparations which, if simple, required a good deal of thought. To my annoyance, at the time I wanted to find Hans to help me, he was not forthcoming. When at length he appeared I asked him where he had been. He answered, to cut himself a stick in the forest, as he understood we should have to walk a long way. Also he showed me the stick, a long, thick staff of a hard and beautiful kind of bamboo which grows in Mazitu-land.

"What do you want that clumsy thing for," I said, "when there are plenty of sticks about?"

"New journey, new stick! Baas. Also this kind of wood is full of air and might help me to float if we are upset into the water."

"What an idea!" I exclaimed, and dismissed the matter from my mind.

At dawn, on the following day, we started, Stephen and I riding on the two donkeys, which were now fat and lusty, and Brother John upon his white ox, a most docile beast that was quite attached to him. All the hunters, fully armed, came with us to the borders of the Mazitu country, where they were to await our return in company with the Mazitu regiment. The king himself went with us to the west gate of the town, where he bade us all, and especially Brother John, an affectionate farewell. Moreover, he sent for Komba and his attendants, and again swore to him that if any harm happened to us, he would not rest till he had found a way to destroy the Pongo, root and branch.

"Have no fear," answered the cold Komba, "in our holy town of Rica we do not tie innocent guests to stakes to be shot to death with arrows."

The repartee, which was undoubtedly neat, irritated Bausi, who was not fond of allusions to this subject.

"If the white men are so safe, why do you not let them take their guns with them?" he asked, somewhat illogically.

"If we meant evil, King, would their guns help them, they being but few among so many. For instance, could we not steal them, as you did when you plotted the murder of these white lords. It is a law among the Pongo that no such magic weapon shall be allowed to enter their land."

"Why?" I asked, to change the conversation, for I saw that Bausi was growing very wrath and feared complications.

"Because, my lord Macumazana, there is a prophecy among us that when a gun is fired in Pongo-land, its gods will desert us, and the Motombo, who is their priest, will die. That saying is very old, but until a little while ago none knew what it meant, since it spoke of 'a hollow spear that smoked,' and such a weapon was not known to us."

"Indeed," I said, mourning within myself that we should not be in a position to bring about the fulfilment of that prophecy, which, as Hans said, shaking his head sadly, "was a great pity, a very great pity!"

Three days' march over country that gradually sloped downwards from the high tableland on which stood Beza Town, brought us to the lake called Kirua, a word which, I believe, means The Place of the Island. Of the lake itself we could see nothing, because of the dense brake of tall reeds which grew out into the shallow water for quite a mile from the shore and was only pierced here and there with paths made by the hippopotami when they came to the mainland at night to feed. From a high mound which looked exactly like a tumulus and, for aught I know, may have been one, however, the blue waters beyond were visible, and in the far distance what, looked at through glasses, appeared to be a tree-clad mountain top. I asked Komba what it might be, and he answered that it was the Home of the gods in Pongo-land.

"What gods?" I asked again, whereon he replied like a black Herodotus, that of these it was not lawful to speak.

I have rarely met anyone more difficult to pump than that frigid and un-African Komba.

On the top of this mound we planted the Union Jack, fixed to the tallest pole that we could find. Komba asked suspiciously why we did so, and as I was determined to show this unsympathetic person that there were others as unpumpable as himself, I replied that it was the god of our tribe, which we set up there to be worshipped, and that anyone who tried to insult or injure it, would certainly die, as the witch-doctor, Imbozwi, and his children had found out. For once Komba seemed a little impressed, and even bowed to the bunting as he passed by.

What I did not inform him was that we had set the flag there to be a sign and a beacon to us in case we should ever be forced to find our way back to this place unguided and in a hurry. As a matter of fact, this piece of forethought, which oddly enough originated with the most reckless of our party, Stephen, proved our salvation, as I shall tell later on. At the foot of the mound we set our camp for the night, the Mazitu soldiers under Babemba, who did not mind mosquitoes, making theirs nearer to the lake, just opposite to where a wide hippopotamus lane pierced the reeds, leaving a little canal of clear water.

I asked Komba when and how we were to cross the lake. He said that we must start at dawn on the following morning when, at this time of the year, the wind generally blew off shore, and that if the weather were favourable, we should reach the Pongo town of Rica by nightfall. As to how we were to do this, he would show me if I cared to follow him. I nodded, and he led me four or five hundred yards along the edge of the reeds in a southerly direction.

As we went, two things happened. The first of these was that a very large, black rhinoceros, which was sleeping in some bushes, suddenly got our wind and, after the fashion of these beasts, charged down on us from about fifty yards away. Now I was carrying a heavy, single- barrelled rifle, for as yet we and our weapons were not parted. On came the rhinoceros, and Komba, small blame to him for he only had a spear, started to run. I cocked the rifle and waited my chance.

When it was not more than fifteen paces away the rhinoceros threw up its head, at which, of course, it was useless to fire because of the horn, and I let drive at the throat. The bullet hit it fair, and I suppose penetrated to the heart. At any rate, it rolled over and over like a shot rabbit, and with a single stretch of its limbs, expired almost at my feet.

Komba was much impressed. He returned; he stared at the dead rhinoceros and at the hole in its throat; he stared at me; he stared at the still smoking rifle.

"The great beast of the plains killed with a noise!" he muttered. "Killed in an instant by this little monkey of a white man" (I thanked him for that and made a note of it) "and his magic. Oh! the Motombo was wise when he commanded----" and with an effort he stopped.

"Well, friend, what is the matter?" I asked. "You see there was no need for you to run. If you had stepped behind me you would have been as safe as you are now--after running."

"It is so, lord Macumazana, but the thing is strange to me. Forgive me if I do not understand."

"Oh! I forgive you, my lord Kalubi--that is--to be. It is clear that you have a good deal to learn in Pongo-land."

"Yes, my lord Macumazana, and so perhaps have you," he replied dryly, having by this time recovered his nerve and sarcastic powers.

Then after telling Mavovo, who appeared mysteriously at the sound of the shot--I think he was stalking us in case of accidents--to fetch men to cut up the rhinoceros, Komba and I proceeded on our walk.

A little further on, just by the edge of the reeds, I caught sight of a narrow, oblong trench dug in a patch of stony soil, and of a rusted mustard tin half-hidden by some scanty vegetation.

"What is that?" I asked, in seeming astonishment, though I knew well what it must be.

"Oh!" replied Komba, who evidently was not yet quite himself, "that is where the white lord Dogeetah, Bausi's blood-brother, set his little canvas house when he was here over twelve moons ago."

"Really!" I exclaimed, "he never told me he was here." (This was a lie, but somehow I was not afraid of lying to Komba.) "How do you know that he was here?"

"One of our people who was fishing in the reeds saw him."

"Oh! that explains it, Komba. But what an odd place for him to fish in; so far from home; and I wonder what he was fishing for. When you have time, Komba, you must explain to me what it is that you catch amidst the roots of thick reeds in such shallow water."

Komba replied that he would do so with pleasure--when he had time. Then, as though to avoid further conversation he ran forward, and thrusting the reeds apart, showed me a great canoe, big enough to hold thirty or forty men, which with infinite labour had been hollowed out of the trunk of a single, huge tree. This canoe differed from the majority of those that personally I have seen used on African lakes and rivers, in that it was fitted for a mast, now unshipped. I looked at it and said it was a fine boat, whereon Komba replied that there were a hundred such at Rica Town, though not all of them were so large.

Ah! thought I to myself as we walked back to the camp. Then, allowing an average of twenty to a canoe, the Pongo tribe number about two thousand males old enough to paddle, an estimate which turned out to be singularly correct.

Next morning at dawn we started, with some difficulty. To begin with, in the middle of the night old Babemba came to the canvas shelter under which I was sleeping, woke me up and in a long speech implored me not to go. He said he was convinced that the Pongo intended foul play of some sort and that all this talk of peace was a mere trick to entrap us white men into the country, probably in order to sacrifice us to its gods for a religious reason.

I answered that I quite agreed with him, but that as my companions insisted upon making this journey, I could not desert them. All that I could do was to beg him to keep a sharp look-out so that he might be able to help us in case we got into trouble.

"Here I will stay and watch for you, lord Macumazana," he answered, "but if you fall into a snare, am I able to swim through the water like a fish, or to fly through the air like a bird to free you?"

After he had gone one of the Zulu hunters arrived, a man named Ganza, a sort of lieutenant to Mavovo, and sang the same song. He said that it was not right that I should go without guns to die among devils and leave him and his companions wandering alone in a strange land.

I answered that I was much of the same opinion, but that Dogeetah insisted upon going and that I had no choice.

"Then let us kill Dogeetah, or at any rate tie him up, so that he can do no more mischief in his madness," Ganza suggested blandly, whereon I turned him out.

Lastly Sammy arrived and said:

"Mr. Quatermain, before you plunge into this deep well of foolishness, I beg that you will consider your responsibilities to God and man, and especially to us, your household, who are now but lost sheep far from home, and further, that you will remember that if anything disagreeable should overtake you, you are indebted to me to the extent of two months' wages which will probably prove unrecoverable."

I produced a little leather bag from a tin box and counted out to Sammy the wages due to him, also those for three months in advance.

To my astonishment he began to weep. "Sir," he said, "I do not seek filthy lucre. What I mean is that I am afraid you will be killed by these Pongo, and, alas! although I love you, sir, I am too great a coward to come and be killed with you, for God made me like that. I pray you not to go, Mr. Quatermain, because I repeat, I love you, sir."

"I believe you do, my good fellow," I answered, "and I also am afraid of being killed, who only seem to be brave because I must. However, I hope we shall come through all right. Meanwhile, I am going to give this box and all the gold in it, of which there is a great deal, into your charge, Sammy, trusting to you, if anything happens to us, to get it safe back to Durban if you can."

"Oh! Mr. Quatermain," he exclaimed, "I am indeed honoured, especially as you know that once I was in jail for--embezzlement--with extenuating circumstances, Mr.

Quatermain. I tell you that although I am a coward, I will die before anyone gets his fingers into that box."

"I am sure that you will, Sammy my boy," I said. "But I hope, although things look queer, that none of us will be called upon to die just yet."

The morning came at last, and the six of us marched down to the canoe which had been brought round to the open waterway. Here we had to undergo a kind of customs-house examination at the hands of Komba and his companions, who seemed terrified lest we should be smuggling firearms.

"You know what rifles are like," I said indignantly. "Can you see any in our hands? Moreover, I give you my word that we have none."

Komba bowed politely, but suggested that perhaps some "little guns," by which he meant pistols, remained in our baggage--by accident. Komba was a most suspicious person.

"Undo all the loads," I said to Hans, who obeyed with an enthusiasm which I confess struck me as suspicious.

Knowing his secretive and tortuous nature, this sudden zeal for openness seemed almost unnatural. He began by unrolling his own blanket, inside of which appeared a miscellaneous collection of articles. I remember among them a spare pair of very dirty trousers, a battered tin cup, a wooden spoon such as Kaffirs use to eat their *scoff* with, a bottle full of some doubtful compound, sundry roots and other native medicines, an old pipe I had given him, and last but not least, a huge head of yellow tobacco in the leaf, of a kind that the Mazitu, like the Pongos, cultivate to some extent.

"What on earth do you want so much tobacco for, Hans?" I asked.

"For us three black people to smoke, Baas, or to take as snuff, or to chew. Perhaps where we are going we may find little to eat, and then tobacco is a food on which one can live for days. Also it brings sleep at nights."

"Oh! that will do," I said, fearing lest Hans, like a second Walter Raleigh, was about to deliver a long lecture upon the virtue of tobacco.

"There is no need for the yellow man to take this weed to our land," interrupted Komba, "for there we have plenty. Why does he cumber himself with the stuff?" and he stretched out his hand idly as though to take hold of and examine it closely.

At this moment, however, Mavovo called attention to his bundle which he had undone, whether on purpose or by accident, I do not know, and forgetting the tobacco, Komba turned to attend to him. With a marvellous celerity Hans rolled up his blanket again. In less than a minute the lashings were fast and it was hanging on his back. Again suspicion took me, but an argument which had sprung up between Brother John and Komba about the former's butterfly net, which Komba suspected of being a new kind of gun or at least a magical instrument of a dangerous sort, attracted my notice. After this dispute, another arose over a common garden trowel that Stephen had thought fit to bring with him. Komba asked what it was for. Stephen replied through Brother John that it was to dig up flowers.

"Flowers!" said Komba. "One of our gods is a flower. Does the white lord wish to dig up our god?"

Of course this was exactly what Stephen did desire to do, but not unnaturally he kept the fact to himself. The squabble grew so hot that finally I announced that if our little belongings were treated with so much suspicion, it might be better that we should give up the journey altogether.

"We have passed our word that we have no firearms," I said in the most dignified manner that I could command, "and that should be enough for you, O Komba."

Then Komba, after consultation with his companions, gave way. Evidently he was anxious that we should visit Pongo-land.

So at last we started. We three white men and our servants seated ourselves in the stern of the canoe on grass cushions that had been provided. Komba went to the bows and his people, taking the broad paddles, rowed and pushed the boat along the water-way made by the hippopotami through the tall and matted reeds, from which ducks and other fowl rose in multitudes with a sound like thunder. A quarter of an hour or so of paddling through these weed-encumbered shallows brought us to the deep and open lake. Here, on the edge of the reeds a tall pole that served as a mast was shipped, and a square sail, made of closely-woven mats, run up. It filled with the morning off-land breeze and presently we were bowling along at a rate of quite eight miles the hour. The shore grew dim behind us, but for a long while above the clinging mists I could see the flag that we had planted on the mound. By degrees it dwindled till it became a mere speck and vanished. As it grew smaller my spirits sank, and when it was quite gone, I felt very low indeed.

Another of your fool's errands, Allan my boy, I said to myself. I wonder how many more you are destined to survive.

The others, too, did not seem in the best of spirits. Brother John stared at the horizon, his lips moving as though he were engaged in prayer, and even Stephen was temporarily depressed. Jerry had fallen asleep, as a native generally does when it is warm and he has nothing to do. Mavovo looked very thoughtful. I wondered whether he had been consulting his Snake again, but did not ask him. Since the episode of our escape from execution by bow and arrow I had grown somewhat afraid of that unholy reptile. Next time it might foretell our immediate doom, and if it did I knew that I should believe.

As for Hans, he looked much disturbed, and was engaged in wildly hunting for something in the flap pockets of an antique corduroy waistcoat which, from its general appearance, must, I imagine, years ago have adorned the person of a British game-keeper.

"Three," I heard him mutter. "By my great grandfather's spirit! only three left."

"Three what?" I asked in Dutch.

"Three charms, Baas, and there ought to have been quite twenty-four. The rest have fallen out through a hole that the devil himself made in this rotten stuff. Now we shall not die of hunger, and we shall not be shot, and we shall not be drowned, at least none of those things will happen to me. But there are twenty-one other things that may finish us, as I have lost the charms to ward them off. Thus----"

"Oh! stop your rubbish," I said, and fell again into the depths of my uncomfortable reflections. After this I, too, went to sleep. When I woke it was past midday and the wind was falling. However, it held while we ate some food we had brought with us, after which it died away altogether, and the Pongo people took to their paddles. At my suggestion we offered to help them, for it occurred to me that we might just as well learn how to manage these paddles. So six were given to us, and Komba, who now I noted was beginning to speak in a somewhat imperious tone, instructed us in their use. At first we made but a poor hand at the business, but three or four hours' steady practice taught us a good deal. Indeed, before our journey's end, I felt that we should be quite capable of managing a canoe, if ever it became necessary for us to do so.

By three in the afternoon the shores of the island we were approaching --if it really was an island, a point that I never cleared up--were well in sight, the mountain top that stood some miles inland having been visible for hours. In fact, through my glasses, I had been able to make out its configuration almost from the beginning of the voyage. About five we entered the mouth of a deep bay fringed on either side with forests, in which were cultivated clearings with small villages of the ordinary African stamp. I observed from the smaller size of the trees adjacent to these clearings, that much more land had once been under cultivation here, probably within the last century, and asked Komba why this was so.

He answered in an enigmatic sentence which impressed me so much that I find I entered it verbatim in my notebook.

"When man dies, corn dies. Man is corn, and corn is man."

Under this entry I see that I wrote "Compare the saying, 'Bread is the staff of life.'"

I could not get any more out of him. Evidently he referred, however, to a condition of shrinking in the population, a circumstance which he did not care to discuss.

After the first few miles the bay narrowed sharply, and at its end came to a point where a stream of no great breadth fell into it. On either side of this stream that was roughly bridged in many places stood the town of Rica. It consisted of a great number of large huts roofed with palm leaves and constructed apparently of whitewashed clay, or rather, as we discovered afterwards, of lake mud mixed with chopped straw or grass.

Reaching a kind of wharf which was protected from erosion by piles formed of small trees driven into the mud, to which were tied a fleet of canoes, we landed just as the sun was beginning to sink. Our approach had doubtless been observed, for as we drew near the wharf a horn was blown by someone on the shore, whereon a considerable number of men appeared. I suppose out of the huts, and assisted to make the canoe fast. I noted that these all resembled Komba and his companions in build and features; they were so like each other that, except for the difference of their ages, it was difficult to tell them apart. They might all have been members of one family; indeed, this was practically the case, owing to constant intermarriage carried on for generations.

There was something in the appearance of these tall, cold, sharp- featured, white-robed men that chilled my blood, something unnatural and almost inhuman. Here was nothing of the usual African jollity. No one shouted, no one laughed or chattered. No one crowded on us, trying to handle our persons or clothes. No one appeared afraid or even astonished. Except for a word or two they were silent, merely contemplating us in a chilling and distant fashion, as though the arrival of three white men in a country where before no white man had ever set foot were an everyday occurrence.

Moreover, our personal appearance did not seem to impress them, for they smiled faintly at Brother John's long beard and at my stubbly hair, pointing these out to each other with their slender fingers or with the handles of their big spears. I remarked that they never used the blade of the spear for this purpose, perhaps because they thought that we might take this for a hostile or even a warlike demonstration. It is humiliating to have to add that the only one of our company who seemed to move them to wonder or interest was Hans. His extremely ugly and wrinkled countenance, it was clear, did appeal to them to some extent, perhaps because they had never seen anything in the least like it before, or perhaps for another reason which the reader may guess in due course.

At any rate, I heard one of them, pointing to Hans, ask Komba whether the ape-man was our god or only our captain. The compliment seemed to please Hans, who hitherto had never been looked on either as a god or a captain. But the rest of us were not flattered; indeed, Mavovo was indignant, and told Hans outright that if he heard any more such talk he would beat him before these people, to show them that he was neither a captain nor a god.

"Wait till I claim to be either, O butcher of a Zulu, before you threaten to treat me thus!" ejaculated Hans, indignantly. Then he added, with his peculiar Hottentot snigger, "Still, it is true that before all the meat is eaten (i.e. before all is done) you may think me both," a dark saying which at the time we did not understand.

When we had landed and collected our belongings, Komba told us to follow him, and led us up a wide street that was very tidily kept and bordered on either side by the large huts whereof I have spoken. Each of these huts stood in a fenced garden of its own, a thing I have rarely seen elsewhere in Africa. The result of this arrangement was that although as a matter of fact it had but a comparatively small population, the area covered by Rica was very great. The town, by the way, was not surrounded with any wall or other fortification, which showed that the inhabitants feared no attack. The waters of the lake were their defence.

For the rest, the chief characteristic of this place was the silence that brooded there. Apparently they kept no dogs, for none barked, and no poultry, for I never heard a cock crow in Pongo-land. Cattle and native sheep they had in abundance, but as they did not fear any enemy, these were pastured outside the town, their milk and meat being brought in as required. A considerable number of people were gathered to observe us, not in a crowd, but in little family groups which collected separately at the gates of the gardens.

For the most part these consisted of a man and one or more wives, finely formed and handsome women. Sometimes they had children with them, but these were very few; the most I saw with any one family was three, and many seemed to possess none at all. Both the women and the children, like the men, were decently clothed in long, white garments, another peculiarity which showed that these natives were no ordinary African savages.

Oh! I can see Rica Town now after all these many years: the wide street swept and garnished, the brown-roofed, white-walled huts in their fertile, irrigated gardens, the tall, silent folk, the smoke from the cooking fires rising straight as a line in the still air, the graceful palms and other tropical trees, and at the head of the street, far away to the north, the rounded, towering shape of the forest-clad mountain that was called House of the Gods. Often that vision comes back to me in my sleep, or at times in my waking hours when some heavy odour reminds me of the overpowering scent of the great trumpet-like blooms which hung in profusion upon broad-leaved bushes that were planted in almost every garden.

On we marched till at last we reached a tall, live fence that was covered with brilliant scarlet flowers, arriving at its gate just as the last red glow of day faded from the sky and night began to fall. Komba pushed open the gate, revealing a scene that none of us are likely to forget. The fence enclosed about an acre of ground of which the back part was occupied by two large huts standing in the usual gardens.

In front of these, not more than fifteen paces from the gate, stood another building of a totally different character. It was about fifty feet in length by thirty broad and consisted only of a roof supported upon carved pillars of wood, the spaces between the pillars being filled with grass mats or blinds. Most of these blinds were pulled down, but four exactly opposite the gate were open. Inside the shed forty or fifty men, who wore white robes and peculiar caps and who were engaged in chanting a dreadful, melancholy song, were gathered on three sides of a huge fire that burned in a pit in the ground. On the fourth side, that facing the gate, a man stood alone with his arms outstretched and his back towards us.

Of a sudden he heard our footsteps and turned round, springing to the left, so that the light might fall on us. Now we saw by the glow of the great fire, that over it was an iron grid not unlike a small bedstead, and that on this grid lay some fearful object. Stephen, who was a little ahead, stared, then exclaimed in a horrified voice:

"My God! it is a woman!"

In another second the blinds fell down, hiding everything, and the singing ceased.

The Kalubi's Oath

"Be silent!" I whispered, and all understood my tone if they did not catch the words. Then steadying myself with an effort, for this hideous vision, which might have been a picture from hell, made me feel faint, I glanced at Komba, who was a pace or two in front of us. Evidently he was much disturbed--the motions of his back told me this --by the sense of some terrible mistake that he had made. For a moment he stood still, then wheeled round and asked me if we had seen anything.

"Yes," I answered indifferently, "we saw a number of men gathered round a fire, nothing more."

He tried to search our faces, but luckily the great moon, now almost at her full, was hidden behind a thick cloud, so that he could not read them well. I heard him sigh in relief as he said:

"The Kalubi and the head men are cooking a sheep; it is their custom to feast together on those nights when the moon is about to change. Follow me, white lords."

Then he led us round the end of the long shed at which we did not even look, and through the garden on its farther side to the two fine huts I have mentioned. Here he clapped his hands and a woman appeared, I know not whence. To her he whispered something. She went away and presently returned with four or five other women who carried clay lamps filled with oil in which floated a wick of palm fibre. These lamps were set down in the huts that proved to be very clean and comfortable places, furnished after a fashion with wooden stools and a kind of low table of which the legs were carved to the shape of antelope's feet. Also there was a wooden platform at the end of the hut whereon lay beds covered with mats and stuffed with some soft fibre.

"Here you may rest safe," he said, "for, white lords, are you not the honoured guests of the Pongo people? Presently food" (I shuddered at the word) "will be brought to you, and after you have eaten well, if it is your pleasure, the Kalubi and his councillors will receive you in yonder feast-house and you can talk with them before you sleep. If you need aught, strike upon that jar with a stick," and he pointed to what looked like a copper cauldron that stood in the garden of the hut near the place where the women were already lighting a fire, "and some will wait on you. Look, here are your goods; none are missing, and here comes water in which you may wash. Now I must go to make report to the Kalubi," and with a courteous bow he departed.

So after a while did the silent, handsome women--to fetch our meal, I understood one of them to say, and at length we were alone.

"My aunt!" said Stephen, fanning himself with his pocket-handkerchief, "did you see that lady toasting? I have often heard of cannibals, those slaves, for instance, but the actual business! Oh! my aunt!"

"It is no use addressing your absent aunt--if you have got one. What did you expect if you would insist on coming to a hell like this?" I asked gloomily.

"Can't say, old fellow. Don't trouble myself much with expectations as a rule. That's why I and my poor old father never could get on. I always quoted the text 'Sufficient to the day is the evil thereof' to him, until at length he sent for the family Bible and ruled it out with red ink in a rage. But I say, do you think that we shall be called upon to understudy St. Lawrence on that grid?"

"Certainly, I do," I replied, "and, as old Babemba warned you, you can't complain."

"Oh! but I will and I can. And so will you, won't you, Brother John?"

Brother John woke up from a reverie and stroked his long beard.

"Since you ask me, Mr. Somers," he said, reflectively, "if it were a case of martyrdom for the Faith, like that of the saint to whom you have alluded, I should not object--at any rate in theory. But I confess that, speaking from a secular point of view, I have the strongest dislike to being cooked and eaten by these very disagreeable savages. Still, I see no reason to suppose that we shall fall victims to their domestic customs."

I, being in a depressed mood, was about to argue to the contrary, when Hans poked his head into the hut and said:

"Dinner coming, Baas, very fine dinner!"

So we went out into the garden where the tall, impassive ladies were arranging many wooden dishes on the ground. Now the moon was clear of clouds, and by its brilliant light we examined their contents. Some were cooked meat covered with a kind of sauce that made its nature indistinguishable. As a matter of fact, I believe it was mutton, but-- who could say? Others were evidently of a vegetable nature. For instance, there was a whole platter full of roasted mealie cobs and a great boiled pumpkin, to say nothing of some bowls of curdled milk. Regarding this feast I became aware of a sudden and complete conversion to those principles of vegetarianism which Brother John was always preaching to me.

"I am sure you are quite right," I said to him, nervously, "in holding that vegetables are the best diet in a hot climate. At any rate I have made up my mind to try the experiment for a few days," and throwing manners to the winds, I grabbed four of the upper mealie cobs and the top of the pumpkin which I cut off with a knife. Somehow I did not seem to fancy that portion of it which touched the platter, for who knew what those dishes might have contained and how often they were washed.

Stephen also appeared to have found salvation on this point, for he, too, patronized the mealie cobs and the pumpkin; so did Mavovo, and so did even that inveterate meat-eater, Hans. Only the simple Jerry tackled the fleshpots of Egypt, or rather of Pongo-land, with appetite, and declared that they were good. I think that he, being the last of us through the gateway, had not realized what it was which lay upon the grid.

At length we finished our simple meal--when you are very hungry it takes a long time to fill oneself with squashy pumpkin, which is why I suppose ruminants and other grazing animals always seem to be eating-- and washed it down with water in preference to the sticky-looking milk which we left to the natives.

"Allan," said Brother John to me in a low voice as we lit our pipes, "that man who stood with his back to us in front of the gridiron was the Kalubi. Against the firelight I saw the gap in his hand where I cut away the finger."

"Well, if we want to get any further, you must cultivate him," I answered. "But the question is, shall we get further than--that grid? I believe we have been trapped here to be eaten."

Before Brother John could reply, Komba arrived, and after inquiring whether our appetites had been good, intimated that the Kalubi and head men were ready to receive us. So off we went with the exception of Jerry, whom we left to watch our things, taking with us the presents we had prepared.

Komba led us to the feast-house, where the fire in the pit was out, or had been covered over, and the grid and its horrible burden had disappeared. Also now all the mats were rolled up, so that the clear moonlight flowed into and illuminated the place. Seated in a semicircle on wooden stools with their faces towards the gateway were the Kalubi, who occupied the centre, and eight councillors, all of them grey-haired men. This Kalubi was a tall, thin individual of middle age with, I think, the most nervous countenance that I ever saw. His features twitched continually and his hands were never still. The eyes, too, as far as I could see them in that light, were full of terrors.

He rose and bowed, but the councillors remained seated, greeting us with a long-continued and soft clapping of the hands, which, it seemed, was the Pongo method of salute.

We bowed in answer, then seated ourselves on three stools that had been placed for us, Brother John occupying the middle stool. Mavovo and Hans stood behind us, the latter supporting himself with his large bamboo stick. As soon as these preliminaries were over the Kalubi called upon Komba, whom he addressed in formal language as "You-who- have-passed-the-god," and "You-the-Kalubi-to-be" (I thought I saw him wince as he said these words), to give an account of his mission and of how it came about that they had the honour of seeing the white lords there.

Komba obeyed. After addressing the Kalubi with every possible title of honour, such as "Absolute Monarch," "Master whose feet I kiss," "He whose eyes are fire and whose tongue is a sword," "He at whose nod people die," "Lord of the Sacrifice, first Taster of the Sacred meat," "Beloved of the gods" (here the Kalubi shrank as though he had been pricked with a spear), "Second to none on earth save the Motombo the most holy, the most ancient, who comes from heaven and speaks with the voice of heaven," etc., etc., he gave a clear but brief account of all that had happened in the course of his mission to Beza Town.

Especially did he narrate how, in obedience to a message which he had received from the Motombo, he had invited the white lords to Pongo- land, and even accepted them as envoys from the Mazitu when none would respond to King Bausi's invitation to fill that office. Only he had stipulated that they should bring with them none of their magic weapons which vomited out smoke and death, as the Motombo had commanded. At this information the expressive countenance of the Kalubi once more betrayed mental disturbance that I think Komba noted as much as we did. However, he said nothing, and after a pause, Komba went on to explain that no such weapons had been brought, since, not satisfied with our word that this was so, he and his companions had searched our baggage before we left Mazitu-land.

Therefore, he added, there was no cause to fear that we should bring about the fulfilment of the old prophecy that when a gun was fired among the Pongo the gods would desert the land and the people cease to be a people.

Having finished his speech, he sat down in a humble place behind us. Then the Kalubi, after formally accepting us as ambassadors from Bausi, King of the Mazitu, discoursed at length upon the advantages which would result to both peoples from a lasting peace between them. Finally he propounded the articles of such a peace. These, it was clear, had been carefully prepared, but to set them out would be useless, since they never came to anything, and I doubt whether it was intended that they should. Suffice it to say that they provided for intermarriage, free trade between the countries, blood-brotherhood, and other things that I have forgotten, all of which was to be ratified by Bausi taking a daughter of the Kalubi to wife, and the Kalubi taking a daughter of Bausi.

We listened in silence, and when he had finished, after a pretended consultation between us, I spoke as the Mouth of Brother John, who, I explained, was too grand a person to talk himself, saying that the proposals seemed fair and reasonable, and that we should be happy to submit them to Bausi and his council on our return.

The Kalubi expressed great satisfaction at this statement, but remarked incidentally that first of all the whole matter must be laid before the Motombo for his opinion, without which no State transaction had legal weight among the Pongo. He added that with our approval he proposed that we should visit his Holiness on the morrow, starting when the sun was three hours old, as he lived at a distance of a day's journey from Rica. After further consultation we replied that although we had little time to spare, as we understood that the Motombo was old and could not visit us, we, the white lords, would stretch a point and call on him. Meanwhile we were tired and wished to go to bed. Then we presented our gifts, which were gracefully accepted, with an intimation that return presents would be made to us before we left Pongo-land.

After this the Kalubi took a little stick and broke it, to intimate that the conference was at an end, and having bade him and his councillors good night we retired to our huts.

I should add, because it has a bearing on subsequent events, that on this occasion we were escorted, not by Komba, but by two of the councillors. Komba, as I noted for the first time when we rose to say good-bye, was no longer present at the council. When he left it I cannot say, since it will be remembered that his seat was behind us in the shadow, and none of us saw him go.

"What do you make of all that?" I asked the others when the door was shut.

Brother John merely shook his head and said nothing, for in those days he seemed to be living in a kind of dreamland.

Stephen answered. "Bosh! Tommy rot! All my eye and my elbow! Those man-eating Johnnies have some game up their wide sleeves, and whatever it may be, it isn't peace with the Mazitu."

"I agree," I said. "If the real object were peace they would have haggled more, stood out for better terms, or hostages, or something. Also they would have got the consent of this Motombo beforehand. Clearly he is the master of the situation, not the Kalubi, who is only his tool; if business were meant he should have spoken first, always supposing that he exists and isn't a myth. However, if we live we shall learn, and if we don't, it doesn't matter, though personally I think we should be wise to leave Motombo alone and to clear out to Mazitu-land by the first canoe to-morrow morning."

"I intend to visit this Motombo," broke in Brother John with decision.

"Ditto, ditto," exclaimed Stephen, "but it's no use arguing that all over again."

"No," I replied with irritation. "It is, as you remark, of no use arguing with lunatics. So let's go to bed, and as it will probably be our last, have a good night's sleep."

"Hear, hear!" said Stephen, taking off his coat and placing it doubled up on the bed to serve as a pillow. "I say," he added, "stand clear a minute while I shake this blanket. It's covered with bits of something," and he suited the action to the word.

"Bits of something?" I said suspiciously. "Why didn't you wait a minute to let me see them. I didn't notice any bits before."

"Rats running about the roof, I expect," said Stephen carelessly.

Not being satisfied, I began to examine this roof and the clay walls, which I forgot to mention were painted over in a kind of pattern with whorls in it, by the feeble light of the primitive lamps. While I was thus engaged there was a knock on the door. Forgetting all about the dust, I opened it and Hans appeared.

"One of these man-eating devils wants to speak to you, Baas. Mavovo keeps him without."

"Let him in," I said, since in this place fearlessness seemed our best game, "but watch well while he is with us."

Hans whispered a word over his shoulder, and next moment a tall man wrapped from head to foot in white cloth, so that he looked like a ghost, came or rather shot into the hut and closed the door behind him.

"Who are you?" I asked.

By way of answer he lifted or unwrapped the cloth from about his face, and I saw that the Kalubi himself stood before us.

"I wish to speak alone with the white lord, Dogeetah," he said in a hoarse voice, "and it must be now, since afterwards it will be impossible."

Brother John rose and looked at him.

"How are you, Kalubi, my friend?" he asked. "I see that your wound has healed well."

"Yes, yes, but I would speak with you alone."

"Not so," replied Brother John. "If you have anything to say, you must say it to all of us, or leave it unsaid, since these lords and I are one, and that which I hear, they hear."

"Can I trust them?" muttered the Kalubi.

"As you can trust me. Therefore speak, or go. Yet, first, can we be overheard in this hut?"

"No, Dogeetah. The walls are thick. There is no one on the roof, for I have looked all round, and if any strove to climb there, we should hear. Also your men who watch the door would see him. None can hear us save perhaps the gods."

"Then we will risk the gods, Kalubi. Go on; my brothers know your story."

"My lords," he began, rolling his eyes about him like a hunted creature, "I am in a terrible pass. Once, since I saw you, Dogeetah, I should have visited the White God that dwells in the forest on the mountain yonder, to scatter the sacred seed. But I feigned to be sick, and Komba, the Kalubi-to-be, 'who has passed the god,' went in my place and returned unharmed. Now to-morrow, the night of the full moon, as Kalubi, I must visit the god again and once more scatter the seed and--Dogeetah, he will kill me whom he has once bitten. He will certainly kill me unless I can kill him. Then Komba will rule as Kalubi in my stead, and he will kill you in a way you can guess, by the 'Hot death,' as a sacrifice to the gods, that the women of the Pongo may once more become the mothers of many children. Yes, yes, unless we can kill the god who dwells in the forest, we all must die," and he paused, trembling, while the sweat dropped from him to the floor.

"That's pleasant," said Brother John, "but supposing that we kill the god how would that help us or you to escape from the Motombo and these murdering people of yours? Surely they would slay us for the sacrilege."

"Not so, Dogeetah. If the god dies, the Motombo dies. It is known from of old, and therefore the Motombo watches over the god as a mother over her child. Then, until a new god is found, the Mother of the Holy Flower rules, she who is merciful and will harm none, and I rule under her and will certainly put my enemies to death, especially that wizard Komba."

Here I thought I heard a faint sound in the air like the hiss of a snake, but as it was not repeated and I could see nothing, concluded that I was mistaken.

"Moreover," he went on, "I will load you with gold dust and any gifts you may desire, and set you safe across the water among your friends, the Mazitu."

"Look here," I broke in, "let us understand matters clearly, and, John, do you translate to Stephen. Now, friend Kalubi, first of all, who and what is this god you talk of?"

"Lord Macumazana, he is a huge ape white with age, or born white, I know not which. He is twice as big as any man, and stronger than twenty men, whom he can break in his hands, as I break a reed, or whose heads he can bite off in his mouth, as he bit off my finger for a warning. For that is how he treats the Kalubis when he wearies of them. First he bites off a finger and lets them go, and next he breaks them like a reed, as also he breaks those who are doomed to sacrifice before the fire."

"Ah!" I said, "a great ape! I thought as much. Well, and how long has this brute been a god among you?"

"I do not know how long. From the beginning. He was always there, as the Motombo was always there, for they are one."

"That's a lie any way," I said in English, then went on. "And who is this Mother of the Holy Flower? Is she also always there, and does she live in the same place as the ape god?"

"Not so, lord Macumazana. She dies like other mortals, and is succeeded by one who takes her place. Thus the present Mother is a white woman of your race, now of middle age. When she dies she will be succeeded by her daughter, who also is a white woman and very beautiful. After she dies another who is white will be found, perhaps one who is of black parents but born white."

"How old is this daughter?" interrupted Brother John in a curiously intent voice, "and who is her father?"

"The daughter was born over twenty years ago, Dogeetah, after the Mother of the

Flower was captured and brought here. She says that the father was a white man to whom she was married, but who is dead."

Brother John's head dropped upon his chest, and his eyes shut as though he had gone to sleep.

"As for where the Mother lives," went on the Kalubi, "it is on the island in the lake at the top of the mountain that is surrounded by water. She has nothing to do with the White God, but those women who serve her go across the lake at times to tend the fields where grows the seed that the Kalubi sows, of which the corn is the White God's food."

"Good," I said, "now we understand--not much, but a little. Tell us next what is your plan? How are we to come into the place where this great ape lives? And if we come there, how are we to kill the beast, seeing that your successor, Komba, was careful to prevent us from bringing our firearms to your land?"

"Aye, lord Macumazana, may the teeth of the god meet in his brain for that trick; yes, may he die as I know how to make him die. That prophecy of which he told you is no prophecy from of old. It arose in the land within the last moon only, though whether it came from Komba or from the Motombo I know not. None save myself, or at least very few here, had heard of the iron tubes that throw out death, so how should there be a prophecy concerning them?"

"I am sure I don't know, Kalubi, but answer the rest of the question."

"As to your coming into the forest--for the White God lives in a forest on the slopes of the mountain, lords--that will be easy since the Motombo and the people will believe that I am trapping you there to be a sacrifice, such as they desire for sundry reasons," and he looked at the plump Stephen in a very suggestive way. "As to how you are to kill the god without your tubes of iron, that I do not know. But you are very brave and great magicians. Surely you can find a way."

Here Brother John seemed to wake up again.

"Yes," he said, "we shall find a way. Have no fear of that, O Kalubi. We are not afraid of the big ape whom you call a god. Yet it must be at a price. We will not kill this beast and try to save your life, save at a price."

"What price?" asked the Kalubi nervously. "There are wives and cattle --no, you do not want the wives, and the cattle cannot be taken across the lake. There are gold dust and ivory. I have already promised these, and there is nothing more that I can give."

"The price is, O Kalubi, that you hand over to us to be taken away the white woman who is called Mother of the Holy Flower, with her daughter----"

"And," interrupted Stephen, to whom I had been interpreting, "the Holy Flower itself, all of it dug up by the roots."

When he heard these modest requests the poor Kalubi became like one upon the verge of madness.

"Do you understand," he gasped, "do you understand that you are asking for the gods of my country?"

"Quite," replied Brother John with calmness; "for the gods of your country--nothing more nor less."

The Kalubi made as though he would fly from the hut, but I caught him by the arm and said:

"See, friend, things are thus. You ask us, at great danger to ourselves, to kill one of the gods of your country, the highest of them, in order to save your life. Well, in payment we ask you to make a present of the remaining gods of your country, and to see us and them safe across the lake. Do you accept or refuse?"

"I refuse," answered the Kalubi sullenly. "To accept would mean the last curse upon my spirit; that is too horrible to tell."

"And to refuse means the first curse upon your body; namely, that in a few hours it must be broken and chewed by a great monkey which you call a god. Yes, broken and chewed, and afterwards, I think, cooked and eaten as a sacrifice. Is it not so?"

The Kalubi nodded his head and groaned.

"Yet," I went on, "for our part we are glad that you have refused, since now we shall be rid of a troublesome and dangerous business and return in safety to Mazitu land."

"How will you return in safety, O lord Macumazana, you who are doomed to the 'Hot Death' if you escape the fangs of the god?"

"Very easily, O Kalubi, by telling Komba, the Kalubi-to-be, of your plots against this god of yours, and how we have refused to listen to your wickedness. In fact, I think this may be done at once while you are here with us, O Kalubi, where perhaps you do not expect to be found. I will go strike upon the pot without the door; doubtless though it is late, some will hear. Nay, man, stand you still; we have knives and our servants have spears," and I made as though to pass him.

"Lord," he said, "I will give you the Mother of the Holy Flower and her daughter; aye, and the Holy Flower itself dug up by the roots, and I swear that if I can, I will set you and them safe across the lake, only asking that I may come with you, since here I dare not stay. Yet the curse will come too, but if so, it is better to die of a curse in a day to be, than to-morrow at the fangs of the god. Oh! why was I born! Why was I born!" and he began to weep.

"That is a question many have asked and none have been able to answer, O friend Kalubi, though mayhap there is an answer somewhere," I replied in a kind voice.

For my heart was stirred with pity of this poor wretch mazed and lost in his hell of superstition; this potentate who could not escape from the trappings of a hateful power, save by the door of a death too horrible to contemplate; this priest whose doom it was to be slain by the very hands of his god, as those who went before him had been slain, and as those who came after him would be slain.

"Yet," I went on, "I think you have chosen wisely, and we hold you to your word. While you are faithful to us, we will say nothing. But of this be sure--that if you attempt to betray us, we who are not so helpless as we seem, will betray you, and it shall be you who die, not us. Is it a bargain?"

"It is a bargain, white lord, although blame me not if things go wrong, since the gods know all, and they are devils who delight in human woe and mock at bargains and torment those who would injure them. Yet, come what will, I swear to keep faith with you thus, by the oath that may not be broken," and drawing a knife from his girdle, he thrust out the tip of his tongue and pricked it. From the puncture a drop of blood fell to the floor.

"If I break my oath," he said, "may my flesh grow cold as that blood grows cold, and may it rot as that blood rots! Aye, and may my spirit waste and be lost in the world of ghosts as that blood wastes into the air and is lost in the dust of the world!"

It was a horrible scene and one that impressed me very much, especially as even then there fell upon me a conviction that this unfortunate man was doomed, that a fate which he could not escape was upon him.

We said nothing, and in another moment he had thrown his white wrappings over his face and slipped through the door.

"I am afraid we are playing it rather low down on that jumpy old boy," said Stephen remorsefully.

"The white woman, the white woman and her daughter," muttered Brother John.

"Yes," reflected Stephen aloud. "One is justified in doing anything to get two white women out of this hell, if they exist. So one may as well have the orchid also, for they'd be lonely without it, poor things, wouldn't they? Glad I thought of that, it's soothing to the conscience."

"I hope you'll find it so when we are all on that iron grid which I noticed is wide enough for three," I remarked sarcastically. "Now be quiet, I want to go to sleep."

I am sorry to have to add that for the most of that night Want remained my master. But if I couldn't sleep, I could, or rather was obliged to, think, and I thought very hard indeed.

First I reflected on the Pongo and their gods. What were these and why did they worship them? Soon I gave it up, remembering that the problem was one which applied equally to dozens of the dark religions of this vast African continent, to which none could give an answer, and least of all their votaries. That answer indeed must be sought in the horrible fears of the unenlightened human heart, which sees death and terror and evil around it everywhere and, in this grotesque form or in that, personifies them in gods, or rather in devils who must be propitiated. For always the fetish or the beast, or whatever it may be, is not the real object of worship. It is only the thing or creature which is inhabited by the spirit of the god or devil, the temple, as it were, that furnishes it with a home, which temple is therefore holy. And these spirits are diverse, representing sundry attributes or qualities.

Thus the great ape might be Satan, a prince of evil and blood. The Holy Flower might symbolise fertility and the growth of the food of man from the bosom of the earth. The Mother of the Flower might represent mercy and goodness, for which reason it was necessary that she should be white in colour, and dwell, not in the shadowed forest, but on a soaring mountain, a figure of light, in short, as opposed to darkness. Or she might be a kind of African Ceres, a goddess of the corn and harvest which were symbolised in the beauteous bloom she tended. Who could tell? Not I, either then or afterwards, for I never found out.

As for the Pongo themselves, their case was obvious. They were a dying tribe, the last descendants of some higher race, grown barren from intermarriage. Probably, too, they were at first only cannibals occasionally and from religious reasons. Then in some time of dearth they became very religious in that respect, and the habit overpowered them. Among cannibals, at any rate in Africa, as I knew, this dreadful food is much preferred to any other meat. I had not the slightest doubt that although the Kalubi himself had brought us here in the wild hope that we might save him from a terrible death at the hands of the Beelzebub he served, Komba and the councillors, inspired thereto by the prophet called Motombo, designed that we should be murdered and eaten as an offering to the gods. How we were to escape this fate, being unarmed, I could not imagine, unless some special protection were vouchsafed to us. Meanwhile, we must go on to the end, whatever it might be.

Brother John, or to give him his right name, the Reverend John Eversley, was convinced that the white woman imprisoned in the mountain was none other than the lost wife for whom he had searched for twenty weary years, and that the second white woman of whom we had heard that night was, strange as it might seem, her daughter and his own. Perhaps he was right and perhaps he was wrong. But even in the latter case, if two white persons were really languishing in this dreadful land, our path was clear. We must go on in faith until we saved them or until we died.

"Our life is granted, not in Pleasure's round, Or even Love's sweet dream, to lapse, content; Duty and Faith are words of solemn sound, And to their echoes must the soul be bent,"

as some one or other once wrote, very nobly I think. Well, there was but little of "Pleasure's round" about the present entertainment, and any hope of "Love's sweet dream" seemed to be limited to Brother John (here I was quite mistaken, as I so often am). Probably the "echoes" would be my share; indeed, already I seemed to hear their ominous thunder.

At last I did go to sleep and dreamed a very curious dream. It seemed to me that I was disembodied, although I retained all my powers of thought and observation; in fact, dead and yet alive. In this state I hovered over the people of the Pongo who were gathered together on a great plain under an inky sky. They were going about their business as usual, and very unpleasant business it often was. Some of them were worshipping a dim form that I knew was the devil; some were committing murders;

some were feasting--at that on which they feasted I would not look; some were labouring or engaged in barter; some were thinking. But I, who had the power of looking into them, saw within the breast of each a tiny likeness of the man or woman or child as it might be, humbly bent upon its knees with hands together in an attitude of prayer, and with imploring, tear-stained face looking upwards to the black heaven.

Then in that heaven there appeared a single star of light, and from this star flowed lines of gentle fire that spread and widened till all the immense arc was one flame of glory. And now from the pulsing heart of the Glory, which somehow reminded me of moving lips, fell countless flakes of snow, each of which followed an appointed path till it lit upon the forehead of one of the tiny, imploring figures hidden within those savage breasts, and made it white and clean.

Then the Glory shrank and faded till there remained of it only the similitude of two transparent hands stretched out as though in blessing--and I woke up wondering how on earth I found the fancy to invent such a vision, and whether it meant anything or nothing.

Afterwards I repeated it to Brother John, who was a very spiritually minded as well as a good man--the two things are often quite different --and asked him to be kind enough to explain. At the time he shook his head, but some days later he said to me:

"I think I have read your riddle, Allan; the answer came to me quite of a sudden. In all those sin-stained hearts there is a seed of good and an aspiration towards the right. For every one of them also there is at last mercy and forgiveness, since how could they learn who never had a teacher? Your dream, Allan, was one of the ultimate redemption of even the most evil of mankind, by gift of the Grace that shall one day glow through the blackness of the night in which they wander."

That is what he said, and I only hope that he was right, since at present there is something very wrong with the world, especially in Africa.

Also we blame the blind savage for many things, but on the balance are we so much better, considering our lights and opportunities? Oh! the truth is that the devil--a very convenient word that--is a good fisherman. He has a large book full of flies of different sizes and colours, and well he knows how to suit them to each particular fish. But white or black, every fish takes one fly or the other, and then comes the question--is the fish that has swallowed the big gaudy lure so much worse or more foolish than that which has fallen to the delicate white moth with the same sharp barb in its tail?

In short, are we not all miserable sinners as the Prayer Book says, and in the eye of any judge who can average up the elemental differences of those waters wherein we were bred and are called upon to swim, is there so much to choose between us? Do we not all need those outstretched Hands of Mercy which I saw in my dream?

But there, there! What right has a poor old hunter to discuss things that are too high for him?

The Motombo

After my dream I went to sleep again, till I was finally aroused by a strong ray of light hitting me straight in the eye.

Where the dickens does that come from? thought I to myself, for these huts had no windows.

Then I followed the ray to its source, which I perceived was a small hole in the mud wall some five feet above the floor. I rose and examined the said hole, and noted that it appeared to have been freshly made, for the clay at the sides of it was in no way discoloured. I reflected that if anyone wanted to eavesdrop, such an aperture would be convenient, and went outside the hut to pursue my investigations. Its wall, I found, was situated about four feet from the eastern part of the encircling reed fence, which showed no signs of disturbance, although there, in the outer face of the wall, was the hole, and beneath it on the lime flooring lay some broken fragments of plaster. I called Hans and asked him if he had kept watch round the hut when the wrapped-up man visited us during the night. He answered yes, and that he could swear that no one had come near it, since several times he had walked to the back and looked.

Somewhat comforted, though not satisfied, I went in to wake up the others, to whom I said nothing of this matter since it seemed foolish to alarm them for no good purpose. A few minutes later the tall, silent women arrived with our hot water. It seemed curious to have hot water brought to us in such a place by these very queer kind of housemaids, but so it was. The Pongo, I may add, were, like the Zulus, very clean in their persons, though whether they all used hot water, I cannot say. At any rate, it was provided for us.

Half an hour later they returned with breakfast, consisting chiefly of a roasted kid, of which, as it was whole, and therefore unmistakable, we partook thankfully. A little later the Majestic Komba appeared. After many compliments and inquiries as to our general health, he asked whether we were ready to start on our visit to the Motombo who, he added, was expecting us with much eagerness. I inquired how he knew that, since we had only arranged to call on him late on the previous night, and I understood that he lived a day's journey away. But Komba put the matter by with a smile and a wave of his hand.

So in due course off we went, taking with us all our baggage, which now that it had been lightened by the delivery of the presents, was of no great weight.

Five minutes' walk along the wide, main street led us to the northern gate of Rica Town. Here we found the Kalubi himself with an escort of thirty men armed with spears; I noted that unlike the Mazitu they had no bows and arrows. He announced in a loud voice that he proposed to do us the special honour of conducting us to the sanctuary of the Holy One, by which we understood him to mean the Motombo. When we politely begged him not to trouble, being in an irritable mood, or assuming it, he told us rudely to mind our own business. Indeed, I think this irritability was real enough, which, in the circumstances known to the reader, was not strange. At any rate, an hour or so later it declared itself in an act of great cruelty which showed us how absolute was this man's power in all temporal matters.

Passing through a little clump of bush we came to some gardens surrounded by a light fence through which a number of cattle of a small and delicate breed--they were not unlike Jerseys in appearance-- had broken to enjoy themselves by devouring the crops. This garden, it appeared, belonged to the Kalubi for the time being, who was furious at the destruction of its produce by the cattle which also belonged to him.

"Where is the herd?" he shouted.

A hunt began--and presently the poor fellow--he was no more than a lad, was discovered asleep behind a bush. When he was dragged before him the Kalubi pointed, first to the cattle, then to the broken fence and the devastated garden. The lad began to mutter excuses and pray for mercy.

"Kill him!" said the Kalubi, whereon the herd flung himself to the ground, and clutching him by the ankles, began to kiss his feet, crying out that he was afraid to die. The Kalubi tried to kick himself free, and failing in this, lifted his big spear and made an end of the poor boy's prayers and life at a single stroke.

The escort clapped their hands in salute or approval, after which four of them, at a sign, took up the body and started with it at a trot for Rica Town, where probably that night it appeared upon the grid. Brother John saw, and his big white beard bristled with indignation like the hair on the back of an angry cat, while Stephen spluttered something beginning with "You brute," and lifted his fist as though to knock the Kalubi down. This, had I not caught hold of him, I have no doubt he would have done.

"O Kalubi!" gasped Brother John, "do you not know that blood calls for blood? In the hour of your own death remember this death."

"Would you bewitch me, white man?" said the Kalubi, glaring at him angrily. "If so----" and once more he lifted the spear, but as John never stirred, held it poised irresolutely. Komba thrust himself between them, crying:

"Back, Dogeetah, who dare to meddle with our customs! Is not the Kalubi Lord of life and death?"

Brother John was about to answer, but I called to him in English:

"For Heaven's sake be silent, unless you want to follow the boy. We are in these men's power."

Then he remembered and walked away, and presently we marched forward as though nothing had happened. Only from that moment I do not think that any of us worried ourselves about the Kalubi and what might befall him. Still, looking back on the thing, I think that there was this excuse to be made for the man. He was mad with the fear of death and knew not what he did.

All that day we travelled on through a rich, flat country that, as we could tell from various indications, had once been widely cultivated. Now the fields were few and far between, and bush, for the most part a kind of bamboo scrub, was reoccupying the land. About midday we halted by a water-pool to eat and rest, for the sun was hot, and here the four men who had carried off the boy's body rejoined us and made some report. Then we went forward once more towards what seemed to be a curious and precipitous wall of black cliff, beyond which the volcanic-looking mountain towered in stately grandeur. By three o'clock we were near enough to this cliff, which ran east and west as far as the eye could reach, to see a hole in it, apparently where the road terminated, that appeared to be the mouth of a cave.

The Kalubi came up to us, and in a shy kind of way tried to make conversation. I think that the sight of this mountain, drawing ever nearer, vividly recalled his terrors and caused him to desire to efface the bad impression he knew he had made on us, to whom he looked for safety. Among other things he told us that the hole we saw was the door of the House of the Motombo.

I nodded my head, but did not answer, for the presence of this murderous king made me feel sick. So he went away again, looking at us in a humble and deprecatory manner.

Nothing further happened until we reached the remarkable wall of rock that I have mentioned, which I suppose is composed of some very hard stone that remained when the softer rock in which it lay was disintegrated by millions of years of weather or washings by the water of the lake. Or perhaps its substance was thrown out of the bowels of the volcano when this was active. I am no geologist, and cannot say, especially as I lacked time to examine the place. At any rate there it was, and there in it appeared the mouth of a great cave that I presume was natural, having once formed a kind of drain through which the lake overflowed when Pongo-land was under water.

We halted, staring dubiously at this darksome hole, which no doubt was the same that Babemba had explored in his youth. Then the Kalubi gave an order, and some of the soldiers went to huts that were built near the mouth of the cave, where I suppose guardians or attendants lived, though of these we saw nothing. Presently they returned with a number of lighted torches that were distributed among us. This done, we plunged, shivering (at least, I shivered), into the gloomy recesses of that great cavern, the Kalubi going before us with half of our escort, and Komba following behind us with the remainder.

The floor of the place was made quite smooth, doubtless by the action of water, as were the walls and roof, so far as we could see them, for it was very wide and lofty. It did not run straight, but curved about in the thickness of the cliff. At the first turn the Pongo soldiers set up a low and eerie chant which they continued during its whole length, that according to my pacings was something over three hundred yards. On we wound, the torches making stars of light in the intense blackness, till at length we rounded a last corner where a great curtain of woven grass, now drawn, was stretched across the cave. Here we saw a very strange sight.

On either side of it, near to the walls, burned a large wood fire that gave light to the place. Also more light flowed into it from its further mouth that was not more than twenty paces from the fires. Beyond the mouth was water which seemed to be about two hundred yards wide, and beyond the water rose the slopes of the mountain that was covered with huge trees. Moreover, a little bay penetrated into the cavern, the point of which bay ended between the two fires. Here the water, which was not more than six or eight feet wide, and shallow, formed the berthing place of a good-sized canoe that lay there. The walls of the cavern, from the turn to the point of the tongue of water, were pierced with four doorways, two on either side, which led, I presume, to chambers hewn in the rock. At each of these doorways stood a tall woman clothed in white, who held in her hand a burning torch. I concluded that these were attendants set there to guide and welcome us, for after I had passed, they vanished into the chambers.

But this was not all. Set across the little bay of water just above the canoe that floated there was a wooden platform, eight feet or so square, on either side of which stood an enormous elephant's tusk, bigger indeed than any I have seen in all my experience, which tusks seemed to be black with age. Between the tusks, squatted upon rugs of some kind of rich fur, was what from its shape and attitude I at first took to be a huge toad. In truth, it had all the appearance of a very bloated toad. There was the rough corrugated skin, there the prominent backbone (for its back was towards us), and there were the thin, splayed-out legs.

We stared at this strange object for quite a long while, unable to make it out in that uncertain light, for so long indeed, that I grew nervous and was about to ask the Kalubi what it might be. As my lips opened, however, it stirred, and with a slow, groping, circular movement turned itself towards us very slowly. At length it was round, and as the head came in view all the Pongo from the Kalubi down ceased their low, weird chant and flung themselves upon their faces, those who had torches still holding them up in their right hands.

Oh! what a thing appeared! It was not a toad, but a man that moved upon all fours. The large, bald head was sunk deep between the shoulders, either through deformity or from age, for this creature was undoubtedly very old. Looking at it, I wondered how old, but could form no answer in my mind. The great, broad face was sunken and withered, like to leather dried in the sun; the lower lip hung pendulously upon the prominent and bony jaw. Two yellow, tusk-like teeth projected one at each corner of the great mouth; all the rest were gone, and from time to time it licked the white gums with a red- pointed tongue as a snake might do. But the chief wonder of the Thing lay in its eyes that were large and round, perhaps because the flesh had shrunk away from them, which gave them the appearance of being set in the hollow orbits of a skull. These eyes literally shone like fire; indeed, at times they seemed positively to blaze, as I have seen a lion's eyes do in the dark. I confess that the aspect of the creature terrified and for a while paralysed me; to think that it was human was awful.

I glanced at the others and saw that they, too, were frightened. Stephen turned very white. I thought that he was going to be sick again, as he was after he drank the coffee out of the wrong bowl on the day we entered Mazitu-land. Brother John stroked his white beard and muttered some invocation to Heaven to protect him. Hans exclaimed in his abominable Dutch:

"*Oh! keek, Baas, da is je lelicher oud deel*" ("Oh! look, Baas, there is the ugly old devil himself!")

Jerry went flat on his face among the Pongo, muttering that he saw Death before him. Only Mavovo stood firm; perhaps because as a witch- doctor of repute he felt that it did not become him to show the white feather in the presence of an evil spirit.

The toad-like creature on the platform swayed its great head slowly as a tortoise does, and contemplated us with its flaming eyes. At length it spoke in a thick, guttural voice, using the tongue that seemed to be common to this part of Africa and indeed to that branch of the Bantu people to which the Zulus belong, but, as I thought, with a foreign accent.

"So *you* are the white men come back," it said slowly. "Let me count!" and lifting one skinny hand from the ground, it pointed with the forefinger and counted. "One. Tall, with a white beard. Yes, that is right. Two. Short, nimble like a monkey, with hair that wants no comb; clever, too, like a father of monkeys. Yes, that is right. Three. Smooth-faced, young and stupid, like a fat baby that laughs at the sky because he is full of milk, and thinks that the sky is laughing at him. Yes, that is right. All three of you are just the same as you used to be. Do you remember, White Beard, how, while we killed you, you said prayers to One Who sits above the world, and held up a cross of bone to which a man was tied who wore a cap of thorns? Do you remember how you kissed the man with the cap of thorns as the spear went into you? You shake your head--oh! you are a clever liar, but I will show you that you are a liar, for I have the thing yet," and snatching up a horn which lay on the kaross beneath him, he blew.

As the peculiar, wailing note that the horn made died away, a woman dashed out of one of the doorways that I have described and flung herself on her knees before him. He muttered something to her and she dashed back again to re-appear in an instant holding in her hand a yellow ivory crucifix.

"Here it is, here it is," he said. "Take it, White Beard, and kiss it once more, perhaps for the last time," and he threw the crucifix to Brother John, who caught it and stared at it amazed. "And do you remember, Fat Baby, how we caught you? You fought well, very well, but we killed you at last, and you were good, very good; we got much strength from you.

"And do you remember, Father of Monkeys, how you escaped from us by your cleverness? I wonder where you went to and how you died. I shall not forget you, for you gave me this," and he pointed to a big white scar upon his shoulder. "You would have killed me, but the stuff in that iron tube of yours burned slowly when you held the fire to it, so that I had time to jump aside and the iron ball did not strike me in the heart as you meant that it should. Yet, it is still here; oh! yes, I carry it with me to this day, and now that I have grown thin I can feel it with my finger."

I listened astonished to this harangue, which if it meant anything, meant that we had all met before, in Africa at some time when men used matchlocks that were fired with a fuse--that is to say, about the year 1700, or earlier. Reflection, however, showed me the interpretation of this nonsense. Obviously this old priest's forefather, or, if one put him at a hundred and twenty years of age, and I am sure that he was not a day less, perhaps his father, as a young man, was mixed up with some of the first Europeans who penetrated to the interior of Africa. Probably these were Portuguese, of whom one may have been a priest and the other two an elderly man and his son, or young brother, or companion. The manner of the deaths of these people and of what happened to them generally would of course be remembered by the descendants of the chief or head medicine-man of the tribe.

"Where did we meet, and when, O Motombo?" I asked.

"Not in this land, not in this land, Father of Monkeys," he replied in his low rumbling voice, "but far, far away towards the west where the sun sinks in the water; and not in this day, but long, long ago. Twenty Kalubis have ruled the Pongo since that day; some have ruled for many years and some have ruled for a few years--that depends upon the will of my brother, the god yonder," and he chuckled horribly and jerked his thumb backwards over his shoulder towards the forest on the mountain. "Yes, twenty have ruled, some for thirty years and none for less than four."

"Well, you *are* a large old liar," I thought to myself, for, taking the average rule of the Kalubis at ten years, this would mean that we met him two centuries ago at least.

"You were clothed otherwise then," he went on, "and two of you wore hats of iron on the head, but that of White Beard was shaven. I caused a picture of you to be beaten by the master-smith upon a plate of copper. I have it yet."

Again he blew upon his horn; again a woman darted out, to whom he whispered; again she went to one of the chambers and returned bearing an object which he cast to us.

We looked at it. It was a copper or bronze plaque, black, apparently with age, which once had been nailed on something for there were the holes. It represented a tall man with a long beard and a tonsured head who held a cross in his hand; and two other men, both short, who wore round metal caps and were dressed in queer-looking garments and boots with square toes. These man carried big and heavy matchlocks, and in the hand of one of them was a smoking fuse. That was all we could make out of the thing.

"Why did you leave the far country and come to this land, O Motombo?" I asked.

"Because we were afraid that other white men would follow on your steps and avenge you. The Kalubi of that day ordered it, though I said No, who knew that none can escape by flight from what must come when it must come. So we travelled and travelled till we found this place, and here we have dwelt from generation to generation. The gods came with us also; my brother that dwells in the forest came, though we never saw him on the journey, yet he was here before us. The Holy Flower came too, and the white Mother of the Flower--she was the wife of one of you, I know not which."

"Your brother the god?" I said. "If the god is an ape as we have heard, how can he be the brother of a man?"

"Oh! you white men do not understand, but we black people understand. In the beginning the ape killed my brother who was Kalubi, and his spirit entered into the ape, making him as a god, and so he kills every other Kalubi and their spirits enter also into him. Is it not so, O Kalubi of to-day, you without a finger?" and he laughed mockingly.

The Kalubi, who was lying on his stomach, groaned and trembled, but made no other answer.

"So all has come about as I foresaw," went on the toad-like creature. "You have returned, as I knew you would, and now we shall learn whether White Beard yonder spoke true words when he said that his god would be avenged upon our god. You shall go to be avenged on him if you can, and then we shall learn. But this time you have none of your iron tubes which alone we fear. For did not the god declare to us through me that when the white men came back with an iron tube, then he, the god, would die, and I, the Motombo, the god's Mouth, would die, and the Holy Flower would be torn up, and the Mother of the Flower would pass away, and the people of the Pongo would be dispersed and become wanderers and slaves? And did he not declare that if the white men came again without their iron tubes, then certain secret things would happen--oh! ask them not, in time they shall be known to you, and the people of the Pongo who were dwindling would again become fruitful and very great? And that is why we welcome you, white men, who arise again from the land of ghosts, because through you we, the Pongo, shall become fruitful and very great."

Of a sudden he ceased his rumbling talk, his head sank back between his shoulders and he sat silent for a long while, his fierce, sparkling eyes playing on us as though he would read our very thoughts. If he succeeded, I hope that mine pleased him. To tell the truth, I was filled with mixed fear, fury and loathing. Although, of course, I did not believe a word of all the rubbish he had been saying, which was akin to much that is evolved by these black-hearted African wizards, I hated the creature whom I felt to be only half- human. My whole nature sickened at his aspect and talk. And yet I was dreadfully afraid of him. I felt as a man might who wakes up to find himself alone with some peculiarly disgusting Christmas-story kind of ghost. Moreover I was quite sure that he meant us ill, fearful and imminent ill. Suddenly he spoke again:

"Who is that little yellow one," he said, "that old one with a face like a skull," and he pointed to Hans, who had kept as much out of sight as possible behind Mavovo, "that wizened, snub-nosed one who might be a child of my brother the god, if ever he had a child? And why, being so small, does he need so large a staff?" Here he pointed again to Hans's big bamboo stick. "I think he is as full of guile as a new-filled gourd with water. The big black one," and he looked at Mavovo, "I do not fear, for his magic is less than my magic," (he seemed to recognise a brother doctor in Mavovo) "but the little yellow one with the big stick and the pack upon his back, I fear him. I think he should be killed."

He paused and we trembled, for if he chose to kill the poor Hottentot, how could we prevent him? But Hans, who saw the great danger, called his cunning to his aid.

"O Motombo," he squeaked, "you must not kill me for I am the servant of an ambassador. You know well that all the gods of every land hate and will be revenged upon those who touch ambassadors or their servants, whom they, the gods, alone may harm. If you kill me I shall haunt you. Yes, I shall sit on your shoulder at night and jibber into your ear so that you cannot sleep, until you die. For though you are old you must die at last, Motombo."

"It is true," said the Motombo. "Did I not tell you that he was full of cunning? All the gods will be avenged upon those who kill ambassadors or their servants. That"--here he laughed again in his dreadful way--"is the rights of the gods alone. Let the gods of the Pongo settle it."

I uttered a sigh of relief, and he went on in a new voice, a dull, business-like voice if I may so describe it:

"Say, O Kalubi, on what matter have you brought these white men to speak with me, the Mouth of the god? Did I dream that it was a matter of a treaty with the King of the Mazitu? Rise and speak."

So the Kalubi rose and with a humble air set out briefly and clearly the reason of our visit to Pongo-land as the envoys of Bausi and the heads of the treaty that had been arranged subject to the approval of the Motombo and Bausi. We noted that the affair did not seem to interest the Motombo at all. Indeed, he appeared to go to sleep while the speech was being delivered, perhaps because he was exhausted with the invention of his outrageous falsehoods, or perhaps for other reasons. When it was finished he opened his eyes and pointed to Komba, saying:

"Arise, Kalubi-that-is-to-be."

So Komba rose, and in his cold, precise voice narrated his share in the transaction, telling how he had visited Bausi, and all that had happened in connection with the embassy. Again the Motombo appeared to go to sleep, only opening his eyes once as Komba described how we had been searched for firearms, whereon he nodded his great head in approval and licked his lips with his thin red tongue. When Komba had done, he said:

"The gods tell me that the plan is wise and good, since without new blood the people of the Pongo will die, but of the end of the matter the god knows alone, if even he can read the future."

He paused, then asked sharply:

"Have you anything more to say, O Kalubi-that-is-to-be? Now of a sudden the god puts it into my mouth to ask if you have anything more to say?"

"Something, O Motombo. Many moons ago the god bit *off* the finger of our High Lord, the Kalubi. The Kalubi, having heard that a white man skilled in medicine who could cut off limbs with knives, was in the country of the Mazitu and camped on the borders of the great lake, took a canoe and rowed to where the white man was camped, he with the beard, who is named Dogeetah, and who stands before you. I followed him in another canoe, because I wished to know what he was doing, also to see a white man. I hid my canoe and those who went with me in the reeds far from the Kalubi's canoe. I waded through the shallow water and concealed myself in some thick reeds quite near to the white man's linen house. I saw the white man cut off the Kalubi's finger and I heard the Kalubi pray the white man to come to our country with the iron tubes that smoke, and to kill the god of whom he was afraid."

Now from all the company went up a great gasp, and the Kalubi fell down upon his face again, and lay still. Only the Motombo seemed to show no surprise, perhaps because he already knew the story.

"Is that all?" he asked.

"No, O Mouth of the god. Last night, after the council of which you have heard, the Kalubi wrapped himself up like a corpse and visited the white men in their hut. I thought that he would do so, and had made ready. With a sharp spear I bored a hole in the wall of the hut, working from outside the fence. Then I thrust a reed through from the fence across the passage between the fence and the wall, and through the hole in the hut, and setting my ear to the end of the reed, I listened."

"Oh! clever, clever!" muttered Hans in involuntary admiration, "and to think that I looked and looked too low, beneath the reed. Oh! Hans, though you are old, you have much to learn."

"Among much else I heard this," went on Komba in sentences so clear and cold that they reminded me of the tinkle of falling ice, "which I think is enough, though I can tell you the rest if you wish, O Mouth. I heard," he said, in the midst of a silence that was positively awful, "our lord, the Kalubi, whose name is Child of the god, agree with the white men that they should kill the god--how I do not know, for it was not said--and that in return they should receive the persons of the Mother of the Holy Flower and of her daughter, the Mother-that-is-to-be, and should dig up the Holy Flower itself by the roots and take it away across the water, together with the Mother and the Mother-that-is-to-be. That is all, O Motombo."

Still in the midst of an intense silence, the Motombo glared at the prostrate figure of the Kalubi. For a long while he glared. Then the silence was broken, for the wretched Kalubi sprang from the floor, seized a spear and tried to kill himself. Before the blade touched him it was snatched from his hand, so that he remained standing, but weaponless.

Again there was silence and again it was broken, this time by the Motombo, who rose from his seat before which he stood, a huge, bloated object, and roared aloud in his rage. Yes, he roared like a wounded buffalo. Never would I have believed that such a vast volume of sound could have proceeded from the lungs of a single aged man. For fully a minute his furious bellowings echoed down that great cave, while all the Pongo soldiers, rising from their recumbent position, pointed their hands, in some of which torches still burned, at the miserable Kalubi on whom their wrath seemed to be concentrated, rather than on us, and hissed like snakes.

Really it might have been a scene in hell with the Motombo playing the part of Satan. Indeed, his swollen, diabolical figure supported on the thin, toad-like legs, the great fires burning on either side, the lurid lights of evening reflected from the still water beyond and glowering among the tree tops of the mountain, the white-robed forms of the tall Pongo, bending, every one of them, towards the wretched culprit and hissing like so many fierce serpents, all suggested some uttermost deep in the infernal regions as one might conceive them in a nightmare.

It went on for some time, I don't know how long, till at length the Motombo picked up his fantastically shaped horn and blew. Thereon the women darted from the various doorways, but seeing that they were not wanted, checked themselves in their stride and remained standing so, in the very attitude of runners about to start upon a race. As the blast of the horn died away the turmoil was suddenly succeeded by an utter stillness, broken only by the crackling of the fires whose flames, of all the living things in that place, alone seemed heedless of the tragedy which was being played.

"All up now, old fellow!" whispered Stephen to me in a shaky voice.

"Yes," I answered, "all up high as heaven, where I hope we are going. Now back to back, and let's make the best fight we can. We've got the spears."

While we were closing in the Motombo began to speak.

"So you plotted to kill the god, Kalubi-who-*was*," he screamed, "with these white ones whom you would pay with the Holy Flower and her who guards it. Good! You shall go, all of you, and talk with the god. And I, watching here, will learn who dies--you or the god. Away with them!"

The Gods

With a roar the Pongo soldiers leapt on us. I think that Mavovo managed to get his spear up and kill a man, for I saw one of them fall backwards and lie still. But they were too quick for the rest of us. In half a minute we were seized, the spears were wrenched from our hands and we were thrown headlong into the canoe, all six of us, or rather seven including the Kalubi. A number of the soldiers, including Komba, who acted as steersman, also sprang into the canoe that was instantly pushed out from beneath the bridge or platform on which the Motombo sat and down the little creek into the still water of the canal or estuary, or whatever it may be, that separates the wall of rock which the cave pierces from the base of the mountain.

As we floated out of the mouth of the cave the toad-like Motombo, who had wheeled round upon his stool, shouted an order to Komba.

"O Kalubi," he said, "set the Kalubi-who-*was* and the three white men and their three servants on the borders of the forest that is named House-of-the-god and leave them there. Then return and depart, for here I would watch alone. When all is finished I will summon you."

Komba bowed his handsome head and at a sign two of the men got out paddles, for more were not needed, and with slow and gentle strokes rowed us across the water. The first thing I noted about this water at the time was that its blackness was inky, owing, I suppose, to its depth and the shadows of the towering cliff on one side and of the tall trees on the other. Also I observed--for in this emergency, or perhaps because of it, I managed to keep my wits about me--that its banks on either side were the home of great numbers of crocodiles which lay there like logs. I saw, further, that a little lower down where the water seemed to narrow, jagged boughs projected from its surface as though great trees had fallen, or been thrown into it. I recalled in a numb sort of way that old Babemba had told us that when he was a boy he had escaped in a canoe down this estuary, and reflected that it would not be possible for him to do so now because of those snags. Unless, indeed, he had floated over them in a time of great flood.

A couple of minutes or so of paddling brought us to the further shore which, as I think I have said, was only about two hundred yards from the mouth of the cave. The bow of the canoe grated on the bank, disturbing a huge crocodile that vanished into the depths with an angry plunge.

"Land, white lords, land," said Komba with the utmost politeness, "and go, visit the god who doubtless is waiting for you. And now, as we shall meet no more--farewell. You are wise and I am foolish, yet hearken to my counsel. If ever you should return to the Earth again, be advised by me. Cling to your own god if you have one, and do not meddle with those of other peoples. Again farewell."

The advice was excellent, but at that moment I felt a hate for Komba which was really superhuman. To me even the Motombo seemed an angel of light as compared with him. If wishes could have killed, our farewell would indeed have been complete.

Then, admonished by the spear points of the Pongo, we landed in the slimy mud. Brother John went first with a smile upon his handsome countenance that I thought idiotic under the circumstances, though doubtless he knew best when he ought to smile, and the wretched Kalubi came last. Indeed, so great was his shrinking from that ominous shore, that I believe he was ultimately propelled from the boat by his successor in power, Komba. Once he had trodden it, however, a spark of spirit returned to him, for he wheeled round and said to Komba,

"Remember, O Kalubi, that my fate to-day will be yours also in a day to come. The god wearies of his priests. This year, next year, or the year after; he always wearies of his priests."

"Then, O Kalubi-that-was," answered Komba in a mocking voice as the canoe was pushed off, "pray to the god for me, that it may be the year after; pray it as your bones break in his embrace."

While we watched that craft depart there came into my mind the memory of a picture in an old Latin book of my father's, which represented the souls of the dead being paddled by a person named Charon across a river called the Styx. The scene before us bore a great resemblance to that picture. There was Charon's boat floating on the dreadful Styx. Yonder glowed the lights of the world, here was the gloomy, unknown shore. And we, we were the souls of the dead awaiting the last destruction at the teeth and claws of some unknown monster, such as that which haunts the recesses of the Egyptian hell. Oh! the parallel was painfully exact. And yet, what do you think was the remark of that irrepressible young man Stephen?

"Here we are at last, Allan, my boy," he said, "and after all without any trouble on our own part. I call it downright providential. Oh! isn't it jolly! Hip, hip, hooray!"

Yes, he danced about in that filthy mud, threw up his cap and cheered!

I withered, or rather tried to wither him with a look, muttering the single word: "Lunatic."

Providential! Jolly! Well, it's fortunate that some people's madness takes a cheerful turn. Then I asked the Kalubi where the god was.

"Everywhere," he replied, waving his trembling hand at the illimitable forest. "Perhaps behind this tree, perhaps behind that, perhaps a long way off. Before morning we shall know."

"What are you going to do?" I inquired savagely.

"Die," he answered.

"Look here, fool," I exclaimed, shaking him, "you can die if you like, but we don't mean to. Take us to some place where we shall be safe from this god."

"One is never safe from the god, lord, especially in his own House," and he shook his silly head and went on, "How can we be safe when there is nowhere to go and even the trees are too big to climb?"

I looked at them, it was true. They were huge and ran up for fifty or sixty feet without a bough. Moreover, it was probable that the god climbed better than we could. The Kalubi began to move inland in an indeterminate fashion, and I asked him where he was going.

"To the burying-place," he answered. "There are spears yonder with the bones."

I pricked up my ears at this--for when one has nothing but some clasp knives, spears are not to be despised--and ordered him to lead on. In another minute we were walking uphill through the awful wood where the gloom at this hour of approaching night was that of an English fog.

Three or four hundred paces brought us to a kind of clearing, where I suppose some of the monster trees had fallen down in past years and never been allowed to grow up again. Here, placed upon the ground, were a number of boxes made of imperishable ironwood, and on the top of each box sat, or rather lay, a mouldering and broken skull.

"Kalubi-that-were!" murmured our guide in explanation. "Look, Komba has made my box ready," and he pointed to a new case with the lid off.

"How thoughtful of him!" I said. "But show us the spears before it gets quite dark." He went to one of the newer coffins and intimated that we should lift off the lid as he was afraid to do so.

I shoved it aside. There within lay the bones, each of them separate and wrapped up in something, except of course the skull. With these were some pots filled apparently with gold dust, and alongside of the pots two good spears that, being made of copper, had not rusted much. We went on to other coffins and extracted from them more of these weapons that were laid there for the dead man to use upon his journey through the Shades, until we had enough. The shafts of most of them were somewhat rotten from the damp, but luckily they were furnished with copper sockets from two and a half to three feet long, into which the wood of the shaft fitted, so that they were still serviceable.

"Poor things these to fight a devil with," I said.

"Yes, Baas," said Hans in a cheerful voice, "very poor. It is lucky that I have got a better."

I stared at him; we all stared at him.

"What do you mean, Spotted Snake?" asked Mavovo.

"What do you mean, child of a hundred idiots? Is this a time to jest? Is not one joker enough among us?" I asked, and looked at Stephen.

"Mean, Baas? Don't you know that I have the little rifle with me, that which is called *Intombi*, that with which you shot the vultures at Dingaan's kraal? I never told you because I was sure you knew; also because if you didn't know it was better that you should not know, for if *you* had known, those Pongo *skellums* (that is, vicious ones) might have come to know also. And if *they* had known----"

"Mad!" interrupted Brother John, tapping his forehead, "quite mad, poor fellow! Well, in these depressing circumstances it is not wonderful."

I inspected Hans again, for I agreed with John. Yet he did not look mad, only rather more cunning than usual.

"Hans," I said, "tell us where this rifle is, or I will knock you down and Mavovo shall flog you."

"Where, Baas! Why, cannot you see it when it is before your eyes?"

"You are right, John," I said, "he's off it"; but Stephen sprang at Hans and began to shake him.

"Leave go, Baas," he said, "or you may hurt the rifle."

Stephen obeyed in sheer astonishment. Then, oh! then Hans did something to the end of his great bamboo stick, turned it gently upside down and out of it slid the barrel of a rifle neatly tied round with greased cloth and stoppered at the muzzle with a piece of tow!

I could have kissed him. Yes, such was my joy that I could have kissed that hideous, smelly old Hottentot.

"The stock?" I panted. "The barrel isn't any use without the stock, Hans."

"Oh! Baas," he answered, grinning, "do you think that I have shot with you all these years without knowing that a rifle must have a stock to hold it by?"

Then he slipped off the bundle from his back, undid the lashings of the blanket, revealing the great yellow head of tobacco that had excited my own and Komba's interest on the shores of the lake. This head he tore apart and produced the stock of the rifle nicely cleaned, a cap set ready on the nipple, on to which the hammer was let down, with a little piece of wad between to prevent the cap from being fired by any sudden jar.

"Hans," I exclaimed, "Hans, you are a hero and worth your weight in gold!"

"Yes, Baas, though you never told me so before. Oh! I made up my mind that I wouldn't go to sleep in the face of the Old Man (death). Oh! which of you ought to sleep now upon that bed that Bausi sent me?" he asked as he put the gun together. "*You*, I think, you great stupid Mavovo. *You* never brought a gun. If you were a wizard worth the name you would have sent the rifles on and had them ready to meet us here. Oh! will you laugh at me any more, you thick-head of a Zulu?"

"No," answered Mavovo candidly. "I will give you *sibonga*. Yes, I will make for you Titles of Praise, O clever Spotted Snake."

"And yet," went on Hans, "I am not all a hero; I am worth but half my weight in gold. For, Baas, although I have plenty of powder and bullets in my pocket, I lost the caps out of a hole in my waistcoat. You remember, Baas, I told you it was charms I lost. But three remain; no, four, for there is one on the nipple. There, Baas, there is *Intombi* all ready and loaded. And now when the white devil comes you can shoot him in the eye, as you how to do up to a hundred yards, and send him to the other devils down in hell. Oh! won't your holy father the Predikant be glad to see him there."

Then with a self-satisfied smirk he half-cocked the rifle and handed it to me ready for action.

"I thank God!" said Brother John solemnly, "who has taught this poor Hottentot how to save us."

"No, Baas John, God never taught me, I taught myself. But, see, it grows dark. Had we not better light a fire," and forgetting the rifle he began to look about for wood.

"Hans," called Stephen after him, "if ever we get out of this, I will give you £500, or at least my father will, which is the same thing."

"Thank you, Baas, thank you, though just now I'd rather have a drop of brandy and--I don't see any wood."

He was right. Outside of the graveyard clearing lay, it is true, some huge fallen boughs. But these were too big for us to move or cut. Moreover, they were so soaked with damp, like everything in this forest, that it would be impossible to fire them.

The darkness closed in. It was not absolute blackness, because presently the moon rose, but the sky was rainy and obscured it; moreover, the huge trees all about seemed to suck up whatever light there was. We crouched ourselves upon the ground back to back as near as possible to the centre of the place, unrolled such blankets as we had to protect us from the damp and cold, and ate some biltong or dried game flesh and parched corn, of which fortunately the boy Jerry carried a bagful that had remained upon his shoulders when he was thrown into the canoe. Luckily I had thought of bringing this food with us; also a flask of spirits.

Then it was that the first thing happened. Far away in the forest resounded a most awful roar, followed by a drumming noise, such a roar as none of us had ever heard before, for it was quite unlike that of a lion or any other beast.

"What is that?" I asked.

"The god," groaned the Kalubi, "the god praying to the moon with which he always rises."

I said nothing, for I was reflecting that four shots, which was all we had, was not many, and that nothing should tempt me to waste one of them. Oh! why had Hans put on that rotten old waistcoat instead of the new one I gave him in Durban?

Since we heard no more roars Brother John began to question the Kalubi as to where the Mother of the Flower lived.

"Lord," answered the man in a distracted way, "there, towards the East. You walk for a quarter of the sun's journey up the hill, following a path that is marked by notches cut upon the trees, till beyond the garden of the god at the top of the mountain more water is found surrounding an island. There on the banks of the water a canoe is hidden in the bushes, by which the water may be crossed to the island, where dwells the Mother of the Holy Flower."

Brother John did not seem to be quite satisfied with the information, and remarked that he, the Kalubi, would be able to show us the road on the morrow.

"I do not think that I shall ever show you the road," groaned the shivering wretch.

At that moment the god roared again much nearer. Now the Kalubi's nerve gave out altogether, and quickened by some presentiment, he began to question Brother John, whom he had learned was a priest of an unknown sort, as to the possibility of another life after death.

Brother John, who, be it remembered, was a very earnest missionary by calling, proceeded to administer some compressed religious consolations, when, quite near to us, the god began to beat upon some kind of very large and deep drum. He didn't roar this time, he only worked away at a massed-band military drum. At least that is what it sounded like, and very unpleasant it was to hear in that awful forest with skulls arranged on boxes all round us, I can assure you, my reader.

The drumming ceased, and pulling himself together, Brother John continued his pious demonstrations. Also just at that time a thick rain-cloud quite obscured the moon, so that the darkness grew dense. I heard John explaining to the Kalubi that he was not really a Kalubi, but an immortal soul (I wonder whether he understood him). Then I became aware of a horrible shadow--I cannot describe it in any other way--that was blacker than the blackness, which advanced towards us at extraordinary speed from the edge of the clearing.

Next second there was a kind of scuffle a few feet from me, followed by a stifled yell, and I saw the shadow retreating in the direction from which it had come.

"What's the matter?" I asked.

"Strike a match," answered Brother John; "I think something has happened."

I struck a match, which burnt up very well, for the air was quite still. In the light of it I saw first the anxious faces of our party-- how ghastly they looked!--and next the Kalubi who had risen and was waving his right arm in the air, a right arm that was bloody and *lacked the hand*.

"The god has visited me and taken away my hand!" he moaned in a wailing voice.

I don't think anybody spoke; the thing was beyond words, but we tried to bind the poor fellow's arm up by the light of matches. Then we sat down again and watched.

The darkness grew still denser as the thick of the cloud passed over the moon, and for a while the silence, that utter silence of the tropical forest at night, was broken only by the sound of our breathing, the buzz of a few mosquitoes, the distant splash of a plunging crocodile and the stifled groans of the mutilated man.

Again I saw, or thought I saw--this may have been half an hour later-- that black shadow dart towards us, as a pike darts at a fish in a pond. There was another scuffle, just to my left--Hans sat between me and the Kalubi--followed by a single prolonged wail.

"The king-man has gone," whispered Hans. "I felt him go as though a wind had blown him away. Where he was there is nothing but a hole."

Of a sudden the moon shone out from behind the clouds. In its sickly light about half-way between us and the edge of the clearing, say thirty yards off, I saw--oh! what did I see! The devil destroying a lost soul. At least, that is what it looked like. A huge, grey-black creature, grotesquely human in its shape, had the thin Kalubi in its grip. The Kalubi's head had vanished in its maw and its vast black arms seemed to be employed in breaking him to pieces.

Apparently he was already dead, though his feet, that were lifted off the ground, still moved feebly.

I sprang up and covered the beast with the rifle which was cocked, getting full on to its head which showed the clearest, though this was rather guesswork, since I could not see distinctly the fore-sight. I pulled, but either the cap or the powder had got a little damp on the journey and hung fire for the fraction of a second. In that infinitesimal time the devil--it is the best name I can give the thing --saw me, or perhaps it only saw the light gleaming on the barrel. At any rate it dropped the Kalubi, and as though some intelligence warned it what to expect, threw up its massive right arm--I remember how extraordinarily long the limb seemed and that it looked thick as a man's thigh--in such a fashion as to cover its head.

Then the rifle exploded and I heard the bullet strike. By the light of the flash I saw the great arm tumble down in a dead, helpless kind of way, and next instant the whole forest began to echo with peal upon peal of those awful roarings that I have described, each of which ended with a dog-like *yowp* of pain.

"You have hit him, Baas," said Hans, "and he isn't a ghost, for he doesn't like it. But he's still very lively."

"Close up," I answered, "and hold out the spears while I reload."

My fear was that the brute would rush on us. But it did not. For all that dreadful night we saw or heard it no more. Indeed, I began to hope that after all the bullet had reached some mortal part and that the great ape was dead.

At length, it seemed to be weeks afterwards, the dawn broke and revealed us sitting white and shivering in the grey mist; that is, all except Stephen, who had gone comfortably to sleep with his head resting on Mavovo's shoulder. He is a man so equably minded and so devoid of nerves, that I feel sure he will be one of the last to be disturbed by the trump of the archangel. At least, so I told him indignantly when at length we roused him from his indecent slumbers.

"You should judge things by results, Allan," he said with a yawn. "I'm as fresh as a pippin while you all look as though you had been to a ball with twelve extras. Have you retrieved the Kalubi yet?"

Shortly afterwards, when the mist lifted a little, we went out in a line to "retrieve the Kalubi," and found--well, I won't describe what we found. He was a cruel wretch, as the incident of the herd-boy had told us, but I felt sorry for him. Still, his terrors were over, or at least I hope so.

We deposited him in the box that Komba had kindly provided in preparation for this inevitable event, and Brother John said a prayer over his miscellaneous remains. Then, after consultation and in the very worst of spirits, we set out to seek the way to the home of the Mother of the Flower. The start was easy enough, for a distinct, though very faint path led from the clearing up the slope of the hill. Afterwards it became more difficult for the denser forest began. Fortunately very few creepers grew in this forest, but the flat tops of the huge trees meeting high above entirely shut out the sky, so that the gloom was great, in places almost that of night.

Oh! it was a melancholy journey as, filled with fears, we stole, a pallid throng, from trunk to trunk, searching them for the notches that indicated our road, and speaking only in whispers, lest the sound of our voices should attract the notice of the dreadful god. After a mile or two of this we became aware that its notice was attracted despite our precautions, for at times we caught glimpses of some huge grey thing slipping along parallel to us between the boles of the trees. Hans wanted me to try a shot, but I would not, knowing that the chances of hitting it were small indeed. With only three charges, or rather three caps left, it was necessary to be saving.

We halted and held a consultation, as a result of which we decided that there was no more danger in going on than in standing still or attempting to return. So we went on, keeping close together. To me, as I was the only one with a rifle, was accorded what I did not at all appreciate, the honour of heading the procession.

Another half-mile and again we heard that strange rolling sound which was produced, I believe, by the great brute beating upon its breast, but noted that it was not so continuous as on the previous night.

"Ha!" said Hans, "he can only strike his drum with one stick now. Your bullet broke the other, Baas."

A little farther and the god roared quite close, so loudly that the air seemed to tremble.

"The drum is all right, whatever may have happened to the sticks," I said.

A hundred yards or so more and the catastrophe occurred. We had reached a spot in the forest where one of the great trees had fallen down, letting in a little light. I can see it to this hour. There lay the enormous tree, its bark covered with grey mosses and clumps of a giant species of maidenhair fern. On our side of it was the open space which may have measured forty feet across, where the light fell in a perpendicular ray, as it does through the smoke-hole of a hut. Looking at this prostrate trunk, I saw first two lurid and fiery eyes that glowed red in the shadow; and then, almost in the same instant, made out what looked like the head of a fiend enclosed in a wreath of the delicate green ferns. I can't describe it, I can only repeat that it looked like the head of a very large fiend with a pallid face, huge overhanging eyebrows and great yellow tushes on either side of the mouth.

Before I had even time to get the rifle up, with one terrific roar the brute was on us. I saw its enormous grey shape on the top of the trunk, I saw it pass me like a flash, running upright as a man does, but with the head held forward, and noted that the arm nearest to me was swinging as though broken. Then as I turned I heard a scream of terror and perceived that it had gripped the poor Mazitu, Jerry, who walked last but one of our line which was ended by Mavovo. Yes, it had gripped him and was carrying him off, clasped to its breast with its sound arm. When I say that Jerry, although a full-grown man and rather inclined to stoutness, looked like a child in that fell embrace, it will give some idea of the creature's size.

Mavovo, who had the courage of a buffalo, charged at it and drove the copper spear he carried into its side. They all charged like berserkers, except myself, for even then, thank Heaven! I knew a trick worth two of that. In three seconds there was a struggling mass in the centre of the clearing. Brother John, Stephen, Mavovo and Hans were all stabbing at the enormous gorilla, for it was a gorilla, although their blows seemed to do it no more harm than pinpricks. Fortunately for them, for its part, the beast would not let go of Jerry, and having only one sound arm, could but snap at its assailants, for if it had lifted a foot to rend them, its top-heavy bulk would have caused it to tumble over.

At length it seemed to realise this, and hurled Jerry away, knocking down Brother John and Hans with his body. Then it leapt on Mavovo, who, seeing it come, placed the copper socket of the spear against his own breast, with the result that when the gorilla tried to crush him, the point of the spear was driven into its carcase. Feeling the pain, it unwound its arm from about Mavovo, knocking Stephen over with the backward sweep. Then it raised its great hand to crush Mavovo with a blow, as I believe gorillas are wont to do.

This was the chance for which I was waiting. Up till that moment I had not dared to fire, fearing lest I should kill one of my companions. Now for an instant it was clear of them all, and steadying myself, I aimed at the huge head and let drive. The smoke thinned, and through it I saw the gigantic ape standing quite still, like a creature lost in meditation.

Then it threw up its sound arm, turned its fierce eyes to the sky, and uttering one pitiful and hideous howl, sank down dead. The bullet had entered just behind the ear and buried itself in the brain.

The great silence of the forest flowed in over us, as it were; for quite a while no one did or said anything. Then from somewhere down amidst the mosses I heard a thin voice, the sound of which reminded me of air being squeezed out of an indiarubber cushion.

"Very good shot, Baas," it piped up, "as good as that which killed the king-vulture at Dingaan's kraal, and more difficult. But if the Baas could pull the god off me I should say--Thank you."

The "thank you" was almost inaudible, and no wonder, for poor Hans had fainted. There he lay under the huge bulk of the gorilla, just his nose and mouth appearing between the brute's body and its arm. Had it not been for the soft cushion of wet moss in which he reclined, I think that he would have been crushed flat.

We rolled the creature off him somehow and poured a little brandy down his throat, which had a wonderful effect, for in less than a minute he sat up, grasping like a dying fish, and asked for more.

Leaving Brother John to examine Hans to see if he was really injured, I bethought me of poor Jerry and went to look at him. One glance was enough. He was quite dead. Indeed, he seemed to be crushed out of shape like a buck that has been enveloped in the coils of a boa-constrictor. Brother John told me afterwards that both his arms and nearly all his ribs had been broken in that terrible embrace. Even his spine was dislocated.

I have often wondered why the gorilla ran down the line without touching me or the others, to vent his rage upon Jerry. I can only suggest that it was because the unlucky Mazitu had sat next to the Kalubi on the previous night, which may have caused the brute to identify him by smell with the priest whom he had learned to hate and killed. It is true that Hans had sat on the other side of the Kalubi, but perhaps the odour of the Pongo had not clung to him so much, or perhaps it meant to deal with him after it had done with Jerry.

When we knew that the Mazitu was past human help and had discovered to our joy that, save for a few bruises, no one else was really hurt, although Stephen's clothes were half-torn off him, we made an examination of the dead god. Truly it was a fearful creature.

What its exact weight or size may have been we had no means of ascertaining, but I never saw or heard of such an enormous ape, if a gorilla is really an ape. It needed the united strength of the five of us to lift the carcase with a great effort off the fainting Hans and even to roll it from side to side when subsequently we removed the skin. I would never have believed that so ancient an animal of its stature, which could not have been more than seven feet when it stood erect, could have been so heavy. For ancient undoubtedly it was. The long, yellow, canine tusks were worn half-away with use; the eyes were sunken far into the skull; the hair of the head, which I am told is generally red or brown, was quite white, and even the bare breast, which should be black, was grey in hue. Of course, it was impossible to say, but one might easily have imagined that this creature was two hundred years or more old, as the Motombo had declared it to be.

Stephen suggested that it should be skinned, and although I saw little prospect of our being able to carry away the hide, I assented and helped in the operation on the mere chance of saving so great a curiosity. Also, although Brother John was restless and murmured something about wasting time, I thought it necessary that we should have a rest after our fearful anxieties and still more fearful encounter with this consecrated monster. So we set to work, and as a result of more than an hour's toil, dragged off the hide, which was so tough and thick that, as we found, the copper spears had scarcely penetrated to the flesh. The bullet that I had put into it on the previous night struck, we discovered, upon the bone of the upper arm, which it shattered sufficiently to render that limb useless, if it did not break it altogether. This, indeed, was fortunate for us, for had the creature retained both its arms uninjured, it would certainly have killed more of us in its attack. We were saved only by the fact that when it was hugging Jerry it had no limb left with which it could strike, and luckily did not succeed in its attempts to get hold with its tremendous jaws that had nipped off the Kalubi's hand as easily as a pair of scissors severs the stalk of a flower.

When the skin was removed, except that of the hands, which we did not attempt to touch, we pegged it out, raw side uppermost, to dry in the centre of the open place where the sun struck. Then, having buried poor Jerry in the hollow trunk of the great fallen tree, we washed ourselves with the wet mosses and ate some of the food that remained to us.

After this we started forward again in much better spirits. Jerry, it was true, was dead, but so was the god, leaving us happily still alive and practically untouched. Never more would the Kalubis of Pongo-land shiver out their lives at the feet of this dreadful divinity who soon or late must become their executioner, for I believe, with the exception of two who committed suicide through fear, that no Kalubi was ever known to have died except by the hand--or teeth--of the god.

What would I not give to know that brute's history? Could it possibly, as the Motombo said, have accompanied the Pongo people from their home in Western or Central Africa, or perhaps have been brought here by them in a state of captivity? I am unable to answer the question, but it should be noted that none of the Mazitu or other natives had ever heard of the existence of more true gorillas in this part of

Africa. The creature, if it had its origin in the locality, must either have been solitary in its habits or driven away from its fellows, as sometimes happens to old elephants, which then, like this gorilla, become fearfully ferocious.

That is all I can say about the brute, though of course the Pongo had their own story. According to them it was an evil spirit in the shape of an ape, which evil spirit had once inhabited the body of an early Kalubi, and had been annexed by the ape when it killed the said Kalubi. Also they declared that the reason the creature put all the Kalubis to death, as well as a number of other people who were offered up to it, was that it needed "to refresh itself with the spirits of men," by which means it was enabled to avoid the effects of age. It will be remembered that the Motombo referred to this belief, of which afterwards I heard in more detail from Babemba. But if this god had anything supernatural about it, at least its magic was no shield against a bullet from a Purdey rifle.

Only a little way from the fallen tree we came suddenly upon a large clearing, which we guessed at once must be that "Garden of the god" where twice a year the unfortunate Kalubis were doomed to scatter the "sacred seed." It was a large garden, several acres of it, lying on a shelf, as it were, of the mountain and watered by a stream. Maize grew in it, also other sorts of corn, while all round was a thick belt of plantain trees. Of course these crops had formed the food of the god who, whenever it was hungry, came to this place and helped itself, as we could see by many signs. The garden was well kept and comparatively free from weeds. At first we wondered how this could be, till I remembered that the Kalubi, or someone, had told me that it was tended by the servants of the Mother of the Flower, who were generally albinos or mutes.

We crossed it and pushed on rapidly up the mountain, once more following an easy and well-beaten path, for now we saw that we were approaching what we thought must be the edge of a crater. Indeed, our excitement was so extreme that we did not speak, only scrambled forward, Brother John, notwithstanding his lame leg, leading at a greater pace than we could equal. He was the first to reach our goal, closely followed by Stephen. Watching, I saw him sink down as though in a swoon. Stephen also appeared astonished, for he threw up his hands.

I rushed to them, and this was what I saw. Beneath us was a steep slope quite bare of forest, which ceased at its crest. This slope stretched downwards for half a mile or more to the lip of a beautiful lake, of which the area was perhaps two hundred acres. Set in the centre of the deep blue water of this lake, which we discovered afterwards to be unfathomable, was an island not more than five and twenty or thirty acres in extent, that seemed to be cultivated, for on it we could see fields, palms and other fruit-bearing trees. In the middle of the island stood a small, near house thatched after the fashion of the country, but civilized in its appearance, for it was oblong, not round, and encircled by a verandah and a reed fence. At a distance from this house were a number of native huts, and in front of it a small enclosure surrounded by a high wall, on the top of which mats were fixed on poles as though to screen something from wind or sun.

"The Holy Flower lives there, you bet," gasped Stephen excitedly--he could think of nothing but that confounded orchid. "Look, the mats are up on the sunny side to prevent its scorching, and those palms are planted round to give it shade."

"The Mother of the Flower lives there," whispered Brother John, pointing to the house. "Who is she? Who is she? Suppose I should be mistaken after all. God, let me not be mistaken, for it would be more than I can bear."

"We had better try to find out," I remarked practically, though I am sure I sympathised with his suspense, and started down the slope at a run.

In five minutes or less we reached the foot of it, and, breathless and perspiring though we were, began to search amongst the reeds and bushes growing at the edge of the lake for the canoe of which we had been told by the Kalubi. What if there were none? How could we cross that wide stretch of deep water? Presently Hans, who, following certain indications which caught his practised eye, had cast away to the left, held up his hand and whistled. We ran to him.

"Here it is, Baas," he said, and pointed to something in a tiny bush- fringed inlet, that at first sight looked like a heap of dead reeds. We tore away at the reeds, and there, sure enough, was a canoe of sufficient size to hold twelve or fourteen people, and in it a number of paddles.

Another two minutes and we were rowing across that lake.

We came safely to the other side, where we found a little landing- stage made of poles sunk into the lake. We tied up the canoe, or rather I did, for nobody else remembered to take that precaution, and presently were on a path which led through the cultivated fields to the house. Here I insisted upon going first with the rifle, in case we should be suddenly attacked. The silence and the absence of any human beings suggested to me that this might very well happen, since it would be strange if we had not been seen crossing the lake.

Afterwards I discovered why the place seemed so deserted. It was owing to two reasons. First, it was now noontime, an hour at which these poor slaves retired to their huts to eat and sleep through the heat of the day. Secondly, although the "Watcher," as she was called, had seen the canoe on the water, she concluded that the Kalubi was visiting the Mother of the Flower and, according to practice on these occasions, withdrew herself and everybody else, since the rare meetings of the Kalubi and the Mother of the Flower partook of the nature of a religious ceremony and must be held in private.

First we came to the little enclosure that was planted about with palms and, as I have described, screened with mats. Stephen ran at it and, scrambling up the wall, peeped over the top.

Next instant he was sitting on the ground, having descended from the wall with the rapidity of one shot through the head.

"Oh! by Jingo!" he ejaculated, "oh! by Jingo!" and that was all I could get out of him, though it is true I did not try very hard at the time.

Not five paces from this enclosure stood a tall reed fence that surrounded the house. It had a gate also of reeds, which was a little ajar. Creeping up to it very cautiously, for I thought I heard a voice within, I peeped through the half-opened gate. Four or five feet away was the verandah from which a doorway led into one of the rooms of the house where stood a table on which was food.

Kneeling on mats upon this verandah were--*two white women*--clothed in garments of the purest white adorned with a purple fringe, and wearing bracelets and other ornaments of red native gold. One of these appeared to be about forty years of age. She was rather stout, fair in colouring, with blue eyes and golden hair that hung down her back. The other might have been about twenty. She also was fair, but her eyes were grey and her long hair was of a chestnut hue. I saw at once that she was tall and very beautiful. The elder woman was praying, while the other, who knelt by her side, listened and looked up vacantly at the sky.

"O God," prayed the woman, "for Christ's sake look in pity upon us two poor captives, and if it be possible, send us deliverance from this savage land. We thank Thee Who hast protected us unharmed and in health for so many years, and we put our trust in Thy mercy, for Thou alone canst help us. Grant, O God, that our dear husband and father may still live, and that in Thy good time we may be reunited to him. Or if he be dead and there is no hope for us upon the earth, grant that we, too, may die and find him in Thy Heaven."

Thus she prayed in a clear, deliberate voice, and I noticed that as she did so the tears ran down her cheeks. "Amen," she said at last, and the girl by her side, speaking with a strange little accent, echoed the "Amen."

I looked round at Brother John. He had heard something and was utterly overcome. Fortunately enough he could not move or even speak.

"Hold him," I whispered to Stephen and Mavovo, "while I go in and talk to these ladies."

Then, handing the rifle to Hans, I took off my hat, pushed the gate a little wider open, slipped through it and called attention to my presence by coughing.

The two women, who had risen from their knees, stared at me as though they saw a ghost.

"Ladies," I said, bowing, "pray do not be alarmed. You see God Almighty sometimes answers prayers. In short, I am one of--a party--of white people who, with some trouble, have succeeded in getting to this place and--and--would you allow us to call on you?"

Still they stared. At length the elder woman opened her lips.

"Here I am called the Mother of the Holy Flower, and for a stranger to speak with the Mother is death. Also if you are a man, how did you reach us alive?"

"That's a long story," I answered cheerfully. "May we come in? We will take the risks, we are accustomed to them and hope to be able to do you a service. I should explain that three of us are white men, two English and one--American."

"American!" she gasped, "American! What is he like, and how is he named?"

"Oh!" I replied, for my nerve was giving out and I grew confused, "he is oldish, with a white beard, rather like Father Christmas in short, and his Christian name (I didn't dare to give it all at once) is--er-- John, Brother John, we call him. Now I think of it," I added, "he has some resemblance to your companion there."

I thought that the lady was going to die, and cursed myself for my awkwardness. She flung her arm about the girl to save herself from falling--a poor prop, for she, too, looked as though she were going to die, having understood some, if not all, of my talk. It must be remembered that this poor young thing had never even seen a white man before.

"Madam, madam," I expostulated, "I pray you to bear up. After living through so much sorrow it would be foolish to decease of--joy. May I call in Brother John? He is a clergyman and might be able to say something appropriate, which I, who am only a hunter, cannot do."

She gathered herself together, opened her eyes and whispered:

"Send him here."

I pushed open the gate behind which the others were clustered. Catching Brother John, who by now had recovered somewhat, by the arm, I dragged him forward. The two stood staring at each other, and the young lady also looked with wide eyes and open mouth.

"Elizabeth!" said John.

She uttered a faint scream, then with a cry of "*Husband!*" flung herself upon his breast.

I slipped through the gate and shut it fast.

"I say, Allan," said Stephen, when we had retreated to a little distance, "did you see her?"

"Her? Who? Which?" I asked.

"The young lady in the white clothes. She is lovely."

"Hold your tongue, you donkey!" I answered. "Is this a time to talk of female looks?"

Then I went away behind the wall and literally wept for joy. It was one of the happiest moments of my life, for how seldom things happen as they should!

Also I wanted to put up a little prayer of my own, a prayer of thankfulness and for strength and wit to overcome the many dangers that yet awaited us.

The Home of the Holy Flower

Half an hour or so passed, during which I was engaged alternately in thinking over our position and in listening to Stephen's rhapsodies. First he dilated on the loveliness of the Holy Flower that he had caught a glimpse of when he climbed the wall, and secondly, on the beauty of the eyes of the young lady in white. Only by telling him that he might offend her did I persuade him not to attempt to break into the sacred enclosure where the orchid grew. As we were discussing the point, the gate opened and she appeared.

"Sirs," she said, with a reverential bow, speaking slowly and in the drollest halting English, "the mother and the father--yes, the father --ask, will you feed?"

We intimated that we would "feed" with much pleasure, and she led the way to the house, saying:

"Be not astonished at them, for they are very happy too, and please forgive our unleavened bread."

Then in the politest way possible she took me by the hand, and followed by Stephen, we entered the house, leaving Mavovo and Hans to watch outside.

It consisted of but two rooms, one for living and one for sleeping. In the former we found Brother John and his wife seated on a kind of couch gazing at each other in a rapt way. I noted that they both looked as though they had been crying--with happiness, I suppose.

"Elizabeth," said John as we entered, "this is Mr. Allan Quatermain, through whose resource and courage we have come together again, and this young gentleman is his companion, Mr. Stephen Somers."

She bowed, for she seemed unable to speak, and held out her hand, which we shook.

"What be 'resource and courage'?" I heard her daughter whisper to Stephen, "and why have you none, O Stephen Somers?"

"It would take a long time to explain," he said with his jolly laugh, after which I listened to no more of their nonsense.

Then we sat down to the meal, which consisted of vegetables and a large bowl of hard-boiled ducks' eggs, of which eatables an ample supply was carried out to Hans and Mavovo by Stephen and Hope. This, it seemed, was the name that her mother had given to the girl when she was born in the hour of her black despair.

It was an extraordinary story that Mrs. Eversley had to tell, and yet a short one. She *had* escaped from Hassan-ben-Mohammed and the slave-traders, as the rescued slave told her husband at Zanzibar before he died, and, after days of wandering, been captured by some of the Pongo who were scouring the country upon dark business of their own, probably in search of captives. They brought her across the lake to Pongo-land and, the former Mother of the Flower, an albino, having died at a great age, installed her in the office on this island, which from that day she had never left. Hither she was led by the Kalubi of the time and some others who had "passed the god." This brute, however, she had never seen, although once she heard him roar, for it did not molest them or even appear upon their journey.

Shortly after her arrival on the island her daughter was born, on which occasion some of the women "servants of the Flower" nursed her. From that moment both she and the child were treated with the utmost care and veneration, since the Mother of the Flower and the Flower itself being in some strange way looked upon as embodiments of the natural forces of fertility, this birth was held to be the best of omens for the dwindling Pongo race. Also it was hoped that in due course the "Child of the Flower" would succeed the Mother in her office. So here they dwelt absolutely helpless and alone, occupying themselves with superintending the agriculture of the island. Most fortunately also when she was captured, Mrs. Eversley had a small Bible in her possession which she had never lost. From this she was able to teach her child to read and all that is to be learned in the pages of Holy Writ.

Often I have thought that if I were doomed to solitary confinement for life and allowed but one book, I would choose the Bible, since, in addition to all its history and the splendour of its language, it contains the record of the hope of man, and therefore should be sufficient for him. So at least it had proved to be in this case.

Oddly enough, as she told us, like her husband, Mrs. Eversley during all those endless years had never lost some kind of belief that she would one day be saved otherwise than by death.

"I always thought that you still lived and that we should meet again, John," I heard her say to him.

Also her own and her daughter's spirits were mysteriously supported, for after the first shock and disturbance of our arrival we found them cheerful people; indeed, Miss Hope was quite a merry soul. But then she had never known any other life, and human nature is very adaptable. Further, if I may say so, she had grown up a lady in the true sense of the word. After all, why should she not, seeing that her mother, the Bible and Nature had been her only associates and sources of information, if we except the poor slaves who waited on them, most of whom were mutes.

When Mrs. Eversley's story was done, we told ours, in a compressed form. It was strange to see the wonder with which these two ladies listened to its outlines, but on that I need not dwell. When it was finished I heard Miss Hope say:

"So it would seem, O Stephen Somers, that it is you who are saviour to us."

"Certainly," answered Stephen, "but why?"

"Because you see the dry Holy Flower far away in England, and you say, 'I must be Holy Father to that Flower.' Then you pay down shekels (here her Bible reading came in) for the cost of journey and hire brave hunter to kill devil-god and bring my old white-head parent with you. Oh yes, you are saviour," and she nodded her head at him very prettily.

"Of course," replied Stephen with enthusiasm; "that is, not exactly, but it is all the same thing, as I will explain later. But, Miss Hope, meanwhile could you show us the Flower?"

"Oh! Holy Mother must do that. If you look thereon without her, you die."

"Really!" said Stephen, without alluding to his little feat of wall climbing.

Well, the end of it was that after a good deal of hesitation, the Holy Mother obliged, saying that as the god was dead she supposed nothing else mattered. First, however, she went to the back of the house and clapped her hands, whereon an old woman, a mute and a very perfect specimen of an albino native, appeared and stared at us wonderingly. To her Mrs. Eversley talked upon her fingers, so rapidly that I could scarcely follow her movements. The woman bowed till her forehead nearly touched the ground, then rose and ran towards the water.

"I have sent her to fetch the paddles from the canoe," said Mrs. Eversley, "and to put my mark upon it. Now none will dare to use it to cross the lake."

"That is very wise," I replied, "as we don't want news of our whereabouts to get to the Motombo."

Next we went to the enclosure, where Mrs. Eversley with a native knife cut a string of palm fibres that was sealed with clay on to the door and one of its uprights in such a fashion that none could enter without breaking the string. The impression was made with a rude seal that she wore round her neck as a badge of office. It was a very curious object fashioned of gold and having deeply cut upon its face a rough image of an ape holding a flower in its right paw. As it was also ancient, this seemed to show that the monkey god and the orchid had been from the beginning jointly worshipped by the Pongo.

When she had opened the door, there appeared, growing in the centre of the enclosure, the most lovely plant, I should imagine, that man ever saw. It measured some eight feet across, and the leaves were dark green, long and narrow. From its various crowns rose the scapes of bloom. And oh! those blooms, of which there were about twelve, expanded now in the flowering season. The measurements made from the dried specimen I have given already, so I need not repeat them. I may say here, however, that the Pongo augured the fertility or otherwise of each succeeding year from the number of the blooms on the Holy Flower. If these were many the season would prove very fruitful; if few, less so; while if, as sometimes happened, the plant failed to flower, draught and famine were always said to follow. Truly those were glorious blossoms, standing as high as a man, with their back sheaths of vivid white barred with black, their great pouches of burnished gold and their wide wings also of gold. Then in the centre of each pouch appeared the ink-mark that did indeed exactly resemble the head of a monkey. But if this orchid astonished me, its effect upon Stephen, with whom this class of flower was a mania, may be imagined. Really he went almost mad. For a long while he glared at the plant, and finally flung himself upon his knees, causing Miss Hope to exclaim:

"What, O Stephen Somers! do you also make sacrifice to the Holy Flower?"

"Rather," he answered; "I'd--I'd--die for it!"

"You are likely to before all is done," I remarked with energy, for I hate to see a grown man make a fool of himself. There's only one thing in the world which justifies *that*, and it isn't a flower.

Mavovo and Hans had followed us into the enclosure, and I overheard a conversation between them which amused me. The gist of it was that Hans explained to Mavovo that the white people admired this weed--he called it a weed--because it was like gold, which was the god they really worshipped, although that god was known among them by many names. Mavovo, who was not at all interested in the affair, replied with a shrug that it might be so, though for his part he believed the true reason to be that the plant produced some medicine which gave courage or strength. Zulus, I may say, do not care for flowers unless they bear a fruit that is good to eat.

When I had satisfied myself with the splendour of these magnificent blooms, I asked Mrs. Eversley what certain little mounds might be that were dotted about the enclosure, beyond the circle of cultivated peaty soil which surrounded the orchid's roots.

"They are the graves of the Mothers of the Holy Flower," she answered. "There are twelve of them, and here is the spot chosen for the thirteenth, which was to have been mine."

To change the subject I asked another question, namely: If there were more such orchids growing in the country?

"No," she replied, "or at least I never heard of any. Indeed, I have always been told that this one was brought from far away generations ago. Also, under an ancient law, it is never allowed to increase. Any shoots it sends up beyond this ring must be cut off by me and destroyed with certain ceremonies. You see that seed-pod which has been left to grow on the stalk of one of last year's blooms. It is now ripe, and on the night of the next new moon, when the Kalubi comes to visit me, I must with much ritual burn it in his presence, unless it has burst before he arrives, in which case I must burn any seedlings that may spring up with almost the same ritual."

"I don't think the Kalubi will come any more; at least, not while you are here. Indeed, I am sure of it," I said.

As we were leaving the place, acting on my general principle of making sure of anything of value when I get the chance, I broke off that ripe seed-pod, which was of the size of an orange. No one was looking at the time, and as it went straight into my pocket, no one missed it.

Then, leaving Stephen and the young lady to admire this Cypripedium-- or each other--in the enclosure, we three elders returned to the house to discuss matters.

"John and Mrs. Eversley," I said, "by Heaven's mercy you are reunited after a terrible separation of over twenty years. But what is to be done now? The god, it is true, is dead, and therefore the passage of the forest will be easy. But beyond it is the water which we have no means of crossing and beyond the water that old wizard, the Motombo, sits in the mouth of his cave watching like a spider in its web. And beyond the Motombo and his cave are Komba, the new Kalubi and his tribe of cannibals----"

"Cannibals!" interrupted Mrs. Eversley, "I never knew that they were cannibals. Indeed, I know little about the Pongo, whom I scarcely ever see."

"Then, madam, you must take my word for it that they are; also, as I believe, that they have every expectation of eating *us*. Now, as I presume that you do not wish to spend the rest of your lives, which would probably be short, upon this island, I want to ask how you propose to escape safely out of the Pongo country?"

They shook their heads, which were evidently empty of ideas. Only John stroked his white beard, and inquired mildly:

"What have you arranged, Allan? My dear wife and I are quite willing to leave the matter to you, who are so resourceful."

"Arranged!" I stuttered. "Really, John, under any other circumstances----" Then after a moment's reflection I called to Hans and Mavovo, who came and squatted down upon the verandah.

"Now," I said, after I had put the case to them, "what have *you* arranged?" Being devoid of any feasible suggestions, I wished to pass on that intolerable responsibility.

"My father makes a mock of us," said Mavovo solemnly. "Can a rat in a pit arrange how it is to get out with the dog that is waiting at the top? So far we have come in safety, as the rat does into the pit. Now I see nothing but death."

"That's cheerful," I said. "Your turn, Hans."

"Oh! Baas," replied the Hottentot, "for a while I grew clever again when I thought of putting the gun *Intombi* into the bamboo. But now my head is like a rotten egg, and when I try to shake wisdom out of it my brain melts and washes from side to side like the stuff in the rotten egg. Yet, yet, I have a thought--let us ask the Missie. Her brain is young and not tired, it may hit on something: to ask the Baas Stephen is no good, for already he is lost in other things," and Hans grinned feebly.

More to give myself time than for any other reason I called to Miss Hope, who had just emerged from the sacred enclosure with Stephen, and put the riddle to her, speaking very slowly and clearly, so that she might understand me. To my surprise she answered at once.

"What is a god, O Mr. Allen? Is it not more than man? Can a god be bound in a pit for a thousand years, like Satan in Bible? If a god want to move, see new country and so on, who can say no?"

"I don't quite understand," I said, to draw her out further, although, in fact, I had more than a glimmering of what she meant.

"O Allan, Holy Flower there a god, and my mother priestess. If Holy Flower tired of this land, and want to grow somewhere else, why priestess not carry it and go too?"

"Capital idea," I said, "but you see, Miss Hope, there are, or were, two gods, one of which cannot travel."

"Oh! that very easy, too. Put skin of god of the woods on to this man," and she pointed to Hans, "and who know difference? They like as two brothers already, only he smaller."

"She's got it! By Jingo, she's got it!" exclaimed Stephen in admiration.

"What Missie say?" asked Hans, suspiciously.

I told him.

"Oh! Baas," exclaimed Hans, "think of the smell inside of that god's skin when the sun shines on it. Also the god was a very big god, and I am small."

Then he turned and made a proposal to Mavovo, explaining that his stature was much better suited to the job.

"First will I die," answered the great Zulu. "Am I, who have high blood in my veins and who am a warrior, to defile myself by wrapping the skin of a dead brute about me and appear as an ape before men? Propose it to me again, Spotted Snake, and we shall quarrel."

"See here, Hans," I said. "Mavovo is right. He is a soldier and very strong in battle. You also are very strong in your wits, and by doing this you will make fools of all the Pongo. Also, Hans, it is better that you should wear the skin of a gorilla for a few hours than that I, your master, and all these should be killed."

"Yes, Baas, it is true, Baas; though for myself I almost think that, like Mavovo, I would rather die. Yet it would be sweet to deceive those Pongo once again, and, Baas, I won't see you killed just to save myself another bad smell or two. So, if you wish it, I will become a god."

Thus through the self-sacrifice of that good fellow, Hans, who is the real hero of this history, that matter was settled, if anything could be looked on as settled in our circumstances. Then we arranged that we would start upon our desperate adventure at dawn on the following morning.

Meanwhile, much remained to be done. First, Mrs. Eversley summoned her attendants, who, to the number of twelve, soon appeared in front of the verandah. It was very sad to see these poor women, all of whom were albinos and unpleasant to look on, while quite half appeared to be deaf and dumb. To these, speaking as a priestess, she explained that the god who dwelt in the woods was dead, and that therefore she must take the Holy Flower, which was called "Wife of the god" and make report to the Motombo of this dreadful catastrophe. Meanwhile, they must remain on the island and continue to cultivate the fields.

This order threw the poor creatures, who were evidently much attached to their mistress and her daughter, into a great state of consternation. The eldest of them all, a tall, thin old lady with white wool and pink eyes who looked, as Stephen said, like an Angora rabbit, prostrated herself and kissing the Mother's foot, asked when she would return, since she and the "Daughter of the Flower" were all they had to love, and without them they would die of grief.

Suppressing her evident emotion as best she could, the Mother replied that she did not know; it depended on the will of Heaven and the Motombo. Then to prevent further argument she bade them bring their picks with which they worked the land; also poles, mats, and palmstring, and help to dig up the Holy Flower. This was done under the superintendence of Stephen, who here was thoroughly in his element, although the job proved far from easy. Also it was sad, for all these women wept as they worked, while some of them who were not dumb, wailed aloud.

Even Miss Hope cried, and I could see that her mother was affected with a kind of awe. For twenty years she had been guardian of this plant, which I think she had at last not unnaturally come to look upon with some of the same veneration that was felt for it by the whole Pongo people.

"I fear," she said, "lest this sacrilege should bring misfortune upon us."

But Brother John, who held very definite views upon African superstitions, quoted the second commandment to her, and she became silent.

We got the thing up at last, or most of it, with a sufficiency of earth to keep it alive, injuring the roots as little as possible in the process. Underneath it, at a depth of about three feet, we found several things. One of these was an ancient stone fetish that was rudely shaped to the likeness of a monkey and wore a gold crown. This object, which was small, I still have. Another was a bed of charcoal, and amongst the charcoal were some partially burnt bones, including a skull that was very little injured. This may have belonged to a woman of a low type, perhaps the first Mother of the Flower, but its general appearance reminded me of that of a gorilla. I regret that there was neither time nor light to enable me to make a proper examination of these remains, which we found it impossible to bring away.

Mrs. Eversley told me afterwards, however, that the Kalubis had a tradition that the god once possessed a wife which died before the Pongo migrated to their present home. If so, these may have been the bones of that wife. When it was finally clear of the ground on which it had grown for so many generations, the great plant was lifted on to a large mat, and after it had been packed with wet moss by Stephen in a most skilful way, for he was a perfect artist at this kind of work, the mat was bound round the roots in such a fashion that none of the contents could escape. Also each flower scape was lashed to a thin bamboo so as to prevent it from breaking on the journey. Then the whole bundle was lifted on to a kind of bamboo stretcher that we made and firmly secured to it with palm-fibre ropes.

By this time it was growing dark and all of us were tired.

"Baas," said Hans to me, as we were returning to the house, "would it not be well that Mavovo and I should take some food and go sleep in the canoe? These women will not hurt us there, but if we do not, I, who have been watching them, fear lest in the night they should make paddles of sticks and row across the lake to warn the Pongo."

Although I did not like separating our small party, I thought the idea so good that I consented to it, and presently Hans and Mavovo, armed with spears and carrying an ample supply of food, departed to the lake side.

One more incident has impressed itself upon my memory in connection with that night. It was the formal baptism of Hope by her father. I never saw a more touching ceremony, but it is one that I need not describe.

Stephen and I slept in the enclosure by the packed flower, which he would not leave out of his sight. It was as well that we did so, since about twelve o'clock by the light of the moon I saw the door in the wall open gently and the heads of some of the albino women appear through the aperture. Doubtless, they had come to steal away the holy plant they worshipped. I sat up, coughed, and lifted the rifle, whereon they fled and returned no more.

Long before dawn Brother John, his wife and daughter were up and making preparations for the march, packing a supply of food and so forth. Indeed, we breakfasted by moonlight, and at the first break of day, after Brother John had first offered up a prayer for protection, departed on our journey.

It was a strange out-setting, and I noted that both Mrs. Eversley and her daughter seemed sad at bidding good-bye to the spot where they had dwelt in utter solitude and peace for so many years; where one of them, indeed, had been born and grown up to womanhood. However, I kept on talking to distract their thoughts, and at last we were off.

I arranged that, although it was heavy for them, the two ladies, whose white robes were covered with curious cloaks made of soft prepared bark, should carry the plant as far as the canoe, thinking it was better that the Holy Flower should appear to depart in charge of its consecrated guardians. I went ahead with the rifle, then came the stretcher and the flower, while Brother John and Stephen, carrying the paddles, brought up the rear. We reached the canoe without accident, and to our great relief found Mavovo and Hans awaiting us. I learned, however, that it was fortunate they had slept in the boat, since during the night the albino women arrived with the evident object of possessing themselves of it, and only ran away when they saw that it was guarded. As we were making ready the canoe those unhappy slaves appeared in a body and throwing themselves upon their faces with piteous words, or those of them who could not speak, by signs, implored the Mother not to desert them, till both she and Hope began to cry. But there was no help for it, so we pushed off as quickly as we could, leaving the albinos weeping and wailing upon the bank.

I confess that I, too, felt compunction at abandoning them thus, but what could we do? I only trust that no harm came to them, but of course we never heard anything as to their fate.

On the further side of the lake we hid away the canoe in the bushes where we had found it, and began our march. Stephen and Mavovo, being the two strongest among us, now carried the plant, and although Stephen never murmured at its weight, how the Zulu did swear after the first few hours! I could fill a page with his objurgations at what he considered an act of insanity, and if I had space, should like to do so, for really some of them were most amusing. Had it not been for his friendship for Stephen I think that he would have thrown it down.

We crossed the Garden of the god, where Mrs. Eversley told me the Kalubi must scatter the sacred seed twice a year, thus confirming the story that we had heard. It seems that it was then, as he made his long journey through the forest, that the treacherous and horrid brute which we had killed, would attack the priest of whom it had grown weary. But, and this shows the animal's cunning, the onslaught always took place *after* he had sown the seed which would in due season produce the food it ate. Our Kalubi, it is true, was killed before we had reached the Garden, which seems an exception to the rule. Perhaps, however, the gorilla knew that his object in visiting it was not to provide for its needs. Or perhaps our presence excited it to immediate action.

Who can analyse the motives of a gorilla?

These attacks were generally spread over a year and a half. On the first occasion the god which always accompanied the priest to the garden and back again, would show animosity by roaring at him. On the second he would seize his hand and bite off one of the fingers, as happened to our Kalubi, a wound that generally caused death from blood poisoning. If, however, the priest survived, on the third visit it killed him, for the most part by crushing his head in its mighty jaws. When making these visits the Kalubi was accompanied by certain dedicated youths, some of whom the god always put to death. Those who had made the journey six times without molestation were selected for further special trials, until at last only two remained who were declared to have "passed" or "been accepted by" the god. These youths were treated with great honour, as in the instance of Komba and on the destruction of the Kalubi, one of them took his office, which he generally filled without much accident, for a minimum of ten years, and perhaps much longer.

Mrs. Eversley knew nothing of the sacramental eating of the remains of the Kalubi, or of the final burial of his bones in the wooden coffins that we had seen, for such things, although they undoubtedly happened, were kept from her. She added, that each of the three Kalubis whom she had known, ultimately went almost mad through terror at his approaching end, especially after the preliminary roarings and the biting off of the finger. In truth uneasy lay the head that wore a crown in Pongo-land, a crown that, mind you, might not be refused upon pain of death by torture. Personally, I can imagine nothing more terrible than the haunted existence of these poor kings whose pomp and power must terminate in such a fashion.

I asked her whether the Motombo ever visited the god. She answered, Yes, once in every five years. Then after many mystic ceremonies he spent a week in the forest at a time of full moon. One of the Kalubis had told her that on this occasion he had seen the Motombo and the god sitting together under a tree, each with his arm round the other's neck and apparently talking "like brothers." With the exception of certain tales of its almost supernatural cunning, this was all that I could learn about the god of the Pongos which I have sometimes been tempted to believe was really a devil hid in the body of a huge and ancient ape.

No, there was one more thing which I quote because it bears out Babemba's story. It seems that captives from other tribes were sometimes turned into the forest that the god might amuse itself by killing them. This, indeed, was the fate to which we ourselves had been doomed in accordance with the hateful Pongo custom.

Certainly, thought I to myself when she had done, I did a good deed in sending that monster to whatever dim region it was destined to inhabit, where I sincerely trust it found all the dead Kalubis and its other victims ready to give it an appropriate welcome.

After crossing the god's garden, we came to the clearing of the Fallen Tree, and found the brute's skin pegged out as we had left it, though shrunken in size. Only it had evidently been visited by a horde of the forest ants which, fortunately for Hans, had eaten away every particle of flesh, while leaving the hide itself absolutely untouched, I suppose because it was too tough for them. I never saw a neater job. Moreover, these industrious little creatures had devoured the beast itself. Nothing remained of it except the clean, white bones lying in the exact position in which we had left the carcase. Atom by atom that marching myriad army had eaten all and departed on its way into the depths of the forest, leaving this sign of their passage.

How I wished that we could carry off the huge skeleton to add to my collection of trophies, but this was impossible. As Brother John said, any museum would have been glad to purchase it for hundreds of pounds, for I do not suppose that its like exists in the world. But it was too heavy; all I could do was to impress its peculiarities upon my mind by a close study of the mighty bones. Also I picked out of the upper right arm, and kept the bullet I had fired when it carried off the Kalubi. This I found had sunk into and shattered the bone, but without absolutely breaking it.

On we went again bearing with us the god's skin, having first stuffed the head, hands and feet (these, I mean the hands and feet, had been cleaned out by the ants) with wet moss in order to preserve their shape. It was no light burden, at least so declared Brother John and Hans, who bore it between them upon a dead bough from the fallen tree.

Of the rest of our journey to the water's edge there is nothing to tell, except that notwithstanding our loads, we found it easier to walk down that steep mountain side than it had been to ascend the same. Still our progress was but slow, and when at length we reached the burying-place only about an hour remained to sunset. There we sat down to rest and eat, also to discuss the situation.

What was to be done? The arm of stagnant water lay near to us, but we had no boat with which to cross to the further shore. And what was that shore? A cave where a creature who seemed to be but half-human, sat watching like a spider in its web. Do not let it be supposed that this question of escape had been absent from our minds. On the contrary, we had even thought of trying to drag the canoe in which we crossed to and from the island of the Flower through the forest. The idea was abandoned, however, because we found that being hollowed from a single log with a bottom four or five inches thick, it was impossible for us to carry it so much as fifty yards. What then could we do without a boat? Swimming seemed to be out of the question because of the crocodiles. Also on inquiry I discovered that of the whole party Stephen and I alone could swim. Further there was no wood of which to make a raft.

I called to Hans and leaving the rest in the graveyard where we knew that they were safe, we went down to the edge of the water to study the situation, being careful to keep ourselves hidden behind the reeds and bushes of the mangrove tribe with which it was fringed. Not that there was much fear of our being seen, for the day, which had been very hot, was closing in and a great storm, heralded by black and bellying clouds, was gathering fast, conditions which must render us practically invisible at a distance.

We looked at the dark, slimy water--also at the crocodiles which sat upon its edge in dozens waiting, eternally waiting, for what, I wondered. We looked at the sheer opposing cliff, but save where a black hole marked the cave mouth, far as the eye could see, the water came up against it, as that of a moat does against the wall of a castle. Obviously, therefore, the only line of escape ran through this cave, for, as I have explained, the channel by which I presume Babemba reached the open lake, was now impracticable. Lastly, we searched to see if there was any fallen log upon which we could possibly propel ourselves to the other side, and found--nothing that could be made to serve, no, nor, as I have said, any dry reeds or brushwood out of which we might fashion a raft.

"Unless we can get a boat, here we must stay," I remarked to Hans, who was seated with me behind a screen of rushes at the water's edge.

He made no answer, and as I thought, in a sort of subconscious way, I engaged myself in watching a certain tragedy of the insect world. Between two stout reeds a forest spider of the very largest sort had spun a web as big as a lady's open parasol. There in the midst of this web of which the bottom strands almost touched the water, sat the spider waiting for its prey, as the crocodiles were waiting on the banks, as the great ape had waited for the Kalubis, as Death waits for Life, as the Motombo was waiting for God knows what.

It rather resembled the Motombo in his cave, did that huge, black spider with just a little patch of white upon its head, or so I thought fancifully enough. Then came the tragedy. A great, white moth of the Hawk species began to dart to and fro between the reeds, and presently struck the web on its lower side some three inches above the water. Like a flash that spider was upon it. It embraced the victim with its long legs to still its tremendous battlings. Next, descending below, it began to make the body fast, when something happened. From the still surface of the water beneath poked up the mouth of a very large fish which quite quietly closed upon the spider and sank again into the depths, taking with it a portion of the web and thereby setting the big moth free. With a struggle it loosed itself, fell on to a piece of wood and floated away, apparently little the worse for the encounter.

"Did you see that, Baas?" said Hans, pointing to the broken and empty web. "While you were thinking, I was praying to your reverend father the Predikant, who taught me how to do it, and he has sent us a sign from the Place of Fire."

Even then I could not help laughing to myself as I pictured what my dear father's face would be like if he were able to hear his convert's remarks. An analysis of Hans's religious views would be really interesting, and I only regret that I never made one. But sticking to business I merely asked:

"What sign?"

"Baas, this sign: That web is the Motombo's cave. The big spider is the Motombo. The white moth is us, Baas, who are caught in the web and going to be eaten."

"Very pretty, Hans," I said, "but what is the fish that came up and swallowed the spider so that the moth fell on the wood and floated away?"

"Baas, *you* are the fish, who come up softly, softly out of the water in the dark, and shoot the Motombo with the little rifle, and then the rest of us, who are the moth, fall into the canoe and float away. There is a storm about to break, Baas, and who will see you swim the stream in the storm and the night?"

"The crocodiles," I suggested.

"Baas, I didn't see a crocodile eat the fish. I think the fish is laughing down there with the fat spider in its stomach. Also when there is a storm crocodiles go to bed because they are afraid lest the lightning should kill them for their sins."

Now I remembered that I had often heard, and indeed to some extent noted, that these great reptiles do vanish in disturbed weather, probably because their food hides away. However that might be, in an instant I made up my mind.

As soon as it was quite dark I would swim the water, holding the little rifle, *Intombi*, above my head, and try to steal the canoe. If the old wizard was watching, which I hoped might not be the case, well, I must deal with him as best I could. I knew the desperate nature of the expedient, but there was no other way. If we could not get a boat we must remain in that foodless forest until we starved. Or if we returned to the island of the Flower, there ere long we should certainly be attacked and destroyed by Komba and the Pongos when they came to look for our bodies.

"I'll try it, Hans," I said.

"Yes, Baas, I thought you would. I'd come, too, only I can't swim and when I was drowning I might make a noise, because one forgets oneself then, Baas. But it will be all right, for if it were otherwise I am sure that your reverend father would have shown us so in the sign. The moth floated off quite comfortably on the wood, and just now I saw it spread its wings and fly away. And the fish, ah! how he laughs with that fat old spider in his stomach!"

Fate Stabs

We went back to the others whom we found crouched on the ground among the coffins, looking distinctly depressed. No wonder; night was closing in, the thunder was beginning to growl and echo through the forest and rain to fall in big drops. In short, although Stephen remarked that every cloud has a silver lining, a proverb which, as I told him, I seemed to have heard before, in no sense could the outlook be considered bright.

"Well, Allan, what have you arranged?" asked Brother John, with a faint attempt at cheerfulness as he let go of his wife's hand. In those days he always seemed to be holding his wife's hand.

"Oh!" I answered, "I am going to get the canoe so that we can all row over comfortably."

They stared at me, and Miss Hope, who was seated by Stephen, asked in her usual Biblical language:

"Have you the wings of a dove that you can fly, O Mr. Allan?"

"No," I answered, "but I have the fins of a fish, or something like them, and I can swim."

Now there arose a chorus of expostulation.

"You shan't risk it," said Stephen, "I can swim as well as you and I'm younger. I'll go, I want a bath."

"That you will have, O Stephen," interrupted Miss Hope, as I thought in some alarm. "The latter rain from heaven will make you clean." (By now it was pouring.)

"Yes, Stephen, you can swim," I said, "but you will forgive me for saying that you are not particularly deadly with a rifle, and clean shooting may be the essence of this business. Now listen to me, all of you. I am going. I hope that I shall succeed, but if I fail it does not so very much matter, for you will be no worse off than you were before. There are three pairs of you. John and his wife; Stephen and Miss Hope; Mavovo and Hans. If the odd man of the party comes to grief, you will have to choose a new captain, that is all, but while I lead I mean to be obeyed."

Then Mavovo, to whom Hans had been talking, spoke.

"My father Macumazana is a brave man. If he lives he will have done his duty. If he dies he will have done his duty still better, and, on the earth or in the under-world among the spirits of our fathers, his name shall be great for ever; yes, his name shall be a song."

When Brother John had translated these words, which I thought fine, there was silence.

"Now," I said, "come with me to the water's edge, all of you. You will be in less danger from the lightning there, where are no tall trees. And while I am gone, do you ladies dress up Hans in that gorilla-skin as best you can, lacing it on to him with some of that palm-fibre string which we brought with us, and filling out the hollows and the head with leaves or reeds. I want him to be ready when I come back with the canoe."

Hans groaned audibly, but made no objection and we started with our impedimenta down to the edge of the estuary where we hid behind a clump of mangrove bushes and tall, feathery reeds. Then I took off some of my clothes, stripping in fact to my flannel shirt and the cotton pants I wore, both of which were grey in colour and therefore almost invisible at night.

Now I was ready and Hans handed me the little rifle.

"It is at full cock, Baas, with the catch on," he said, "and carefully loaded. Also I have wrapped the lining of my hat, which is very full of grease, for the hair makes grease especially in hot weather, Baas, round the lock to keep away the wet from the cap and powder. It is not tied, Baas, only twisted. Give the rifle a shake and it will fall off."

"I understand," I said, and gripped the gun with my left hand by the tongue just forward of the hammer, in such a fashion that the horrid greased rag from Hans's hat was held tight over the lock and cap. Then I shook hands with the others and when I came to Miss Hope I am proud to add that she spontaneously and of her own accord imprinted a kiss upon my mediaeval brow. I felt inclined to return it, but did not.

"It is the kiss of peace, O Allan," she said. "May you go and return in peace."

"Thank you," I said, "but get on with dressing Hans in his new clothes."

Stephen muttered something about feeling ashamed of himself. Brother John put up a vigorous and well-directed prayer. Mavovo saluted with the copper assegai and began to give me *sibonga* or Zulu titles of praise beneath his breath, and Mrs. Eversley said:

"Oh! I thank God that I have lived to see a brave English gentleman again," which I thought a great compliment to my nation and myself, though when I afterwards discovered that she herself was English by birth, it took off some of the polish.

Next, just after a vivid flash of lightning, for the storm had broken in earnest now, I ran swiftly to the water's edge, accompanied by Hans, who was determined to see the last of me.

"Get back, Hans, before the lightning shows you," I said, as I slid gently from a mangrove-root into that filthy stream, "and tell them to keep my coat and trousers dry if they can."

"Good-bye, Baas," he murmured, and I heard that he was sobbing. "Keep a good heart, O Baas of Baases. After all, this is nothing to the vultures of the Hill of Slaughter. *Intombi* pulled us through then, and so she will again, for she knows who can hold her straight!"

That was the last I heard of Hans, for if he said any more, the hiss of the torrential rain smothered his words.

Oh! I had tried to "keep a good heart" before the others, but it is beyond my powers to describe the deadly fright I felt, perhaps the worst of all my life, which is saying a great deal. Here I was starting on one of the maddest ventures that was ever undertaken by man. I needn't put its points again, but that which appealed to me most at the moment was the crocodiles. I have always hated crocodiles since--well, never mind--and the place was as full of them as the ponds at Ascension are of turtles.

Still I swam on. The estuary was perhaps two hundred yards wide, not more, no great distance for a good swimmer as I was in those days. But then I had to hold the rifle above the water with my left hand at all cost, for if once it went beneath it would be useless. Also I was desperately afraid of being seen in the lightning flashes, although to minimise this risk I had kept my dark-coloured cloth hat upon my head. Lastly there was the lightning itself to fear, for it was fearful and continuous and seemed to be striking along the water. It was a fact that a fire-ball or something of the sort hit the surface within a few yards of me, as though it had aimed at the rifle-barrel and just missed. Or so I thought, though it may have been a crocodile rising at the moment.

In one way, or rather, in two, however, I was lucky. The first was the complete absence of wind which must have raised waves that might have swamped me and would at any rate have wetted the rifle. The second was that there was no fear of my losing my path for in the mouth of the cave I could see the glow of the fires which burned on either side of the Motombo's seat. They served the same purpose to me as did the lamp of the lady called Hero to her lover Leander when he swam the Hellespont to pay her clandestine visits at night. But he had something pleasant to look forward to, whereas I----! Still, there was another point in common between us. Hero, if I remember right, was a priestess of the Greek goddess of love, whereas the party who waited me was also in a religious line of business. Only, as I firmly believe, he was a priest of the devil.

I suppose that swim took me about a quarter-of-an-hour, for I went slowly to save my strength, although the crocodiles suggested haste. But thank Heaven they never appeared to complicate matters. Now I was quite near the cave, and now I was beneath the overhanging roof and in the shallow water of the little bay that formed a harbour for the canoe. I stood upon my feet on the rock bottom, the water coming up to my breast, and peered about me, while I rested and worked my left arm, stiff with the up-holding of the gun, to and fro. The fires had burnt somewhat low and until my eyes were freed from the raindrops and grew accustomed to the light of the place I could not see clearly.

I took the rag from round the lock of the rifle, wiped the wet off the barrel with it and let it fall. Then I loosed the catch and by touching a certain mechanism, made the rifle hair-triggered. Now I looked again and began to make out things. There was the platform and there, alas! on it sat the toad-like Motombo. But his back was to me; he was gazing not towards the water, but down the cave. I hesitated for one fateful moment. Perhaps the priest was asleep, perhaps I could get the canoe away without shooting. I did not like the job; moreover, his head was held forward and invisible, and how was I to make certain of killing him with a shot in the back? Lastly, if possible, I wished to avoid firing because of the report.

At that instant the Motombo wheeled round. Some instinct must have warned him of my presence, for the silence was gravelike save for the soft splash of the rain without. As he turned the lightning blazed and he saw me.

"It is the white man," he muttered to himself in his hissing whisper, while I waited through the following darkness with the rifle at my shoulder, "the white man who shot me long, long ago, and again he has a gun! Oh! Fate stabs, doubtless the god is dead and I too must die!"

Then as if some doubt struck him he lifted the horn to summon help.

Again the lightning flashed and was accompanied by a fearful crack of thunder. With a prayer for skill, I covered his head and fired by the glare of it just as the trumpet touched his lips. It fell from his hand. He seemed to shrink together, and moved no more.

Oh! thank God, thank God! in this supreme moment of trial the art of which I am a master had not failed me. If my hand had shaken ever so little, if my nerves, strained to breaking point, had played me false in the least degree, if the rag from Hans's hat had not sufficed to keep away the damp from the cap and powder! Well, this history would never have been written and there would have been some more bones in the graveyard of the Kalubis, that is all!

For a moment I waited, expecting to see the women attendants dart from the doorways in the sides of the cave, and to hear them sound a shrill alarm. None appeared, and I guessed that the rattle of the thunder had swallowed up the crack of the rifle, a noise, be it remembered, that none of them had ever heard. For an unknown number of years this ancient creature, I suppose, had squatted day and night upon that platform, whence, I daresay, it was difficult for him to move. So after they had wrapped his furs round him at sunset and made up the fires to keep him warm, why should his women come to disturb him unless he called them with his horn? Probably it was not even lawful that they should do so.

Somewhat reassured I waded forward a few paces and loosed the canoe which was tied by the prow. Then I scrambled into it, and laying down the rifle, took one of the paddles and began to push out of the creek. Just then the lightning flared once more, and by it I caught sight of the Motombo's face that was now within a few feet of my own. It seemed to be resting almost on his knees, and its appearance was dreadful. In the centre of the forehead was a blue mark where the bullet had entered, for I had made no mistake in that matter. The deep-set round eyes were open and, all their fire gone, seemed to stare at me from beneath the overhanging brows. The massive jaw had fallen and the red tongue hung out upon the pendulous lip. The leather-like skin of the bloated cheeks had assumed an ashen hue still streaked and mottled with brown.

Oh! the thing was horrible, and sometimes when I am out of sorts, it haunts me to this day. Yet that creature's blood does not lie heavy on my mind, of it my conscience is not afraid. His end was necessary to save the innocent and I am sure that it was well deserved. For he was a devil, akin to the great god ape I had slain in the forest, to whom, by the way, he bore a most remarkable resemblance in death. Indeed if their heads had been laid side by side at a little distance, it would not have been too easy to tell them apart with their projecting brows, beardless, retreating chins and yellow tushes at the corners of the mouth.

Presently I was clear of the cave. Still for a while I lay to at one side of it against the towering cliff, both to listen in case what I had done should be discovered, and for fear lest the lightning which was still bright, although the storm centre was rapidly passing away, should reveal me to any watchers.

For quite ten minutes I hid thus, and then, determining to risk it, paddled softly towards the opposite bank keeping, however, a little to the west of the cave and taking my line by a certain very tall tree which, as I had noted, towered up against the sky at the back of the graveyard.

As it happened my calculations were accurate and in the end I directed the bow of the canoe into the rushes behind which I had left my companions. Just then the moon began to struggle out through the thinning rain-clouds, and by its light they saw me, and I saw what for a moment I took to be the gorilla-god himself waddling forward to seize the boat. There was the dreadful brute exactly as he had appeared in the forest, except that it seemed a little smaller.

Then I remembered and laughed and that laugh did me a world of good.

"Is that you, Baas?" said a muffled voice, speaking apparently from the middle of the gorilla. "Are you safe, Baas?"

"Of course," I answered, "or how should I be here?" adding cheerfully, "Are you comfortable in that nice warm skin on this wet night, Hans?"

"Oh! Baas," answered the voice, "tell me what happened. Even in this stink I burn to know."

"Death happened to the Motombo, Hans. Here, Stephen, give me your hand and my clothes, and, Mavovo, hold the rifle and the canoe while I put them on."

Then I landed and stepping into the reeds, pulled off my wet shirt and pants, which I stuffed away into the big pockets of my shooting coat, for I did not want to lose them, and put on the dry things that, although scratchy, were quite good enough clothing in that warm climate. After this I treated myself to a good sup of brandy from the flask, and ate some food which I seemed to require. Then I told them the story, and cutting short their demonstrations of wonder and admiration, bade them place the Holy Flower in the canoe and get in themselves. Next with the help of Hans who poked out his fingers through the skin of the gorilla's arms, I carefully re-loaded the rifle, setting the last cap on the nipple. This done, I joined them in the canoe, taking my seat in the prow and bidding Brother John and Stephen paddle.

Making a circuit to avoid observation as before, in a very short time we reached the mouth of the cave. I leant forward and peeped round the western wall of rock. Nobody seemed to be stirring. There the fires burned dimly, there the huddled shape of the Motombo still crouched upon the platform. Silently, silently we disembarked, and I formed our procession while the others looked askance at the horrible face of the dead Motombo.

I headed it, then came the Mother of the Flower, followed by Hans, playing his part of the god of the forest; then Brother John and Stephen carrying the Holy Flower. After it walked Hope, while Mavovo brought up the rear. Near to one of the fires, as I had noted on our first passage of the cave, lay a pile of the torches which I have already mentioned. We lit some of them, and at a sign from me, Mavovo dragged the canoe back into its little dock and tied the cord to its post. Its appearance there, apparently undisturbed, might, I thought, make our crossing of the water seem even more mysterious. All this while I watched the doors in the sides of the cave, expecting every moment to see the women rush out. But none came. Perhaps they slept, or perhaps they were absent; I do not know to this day.

We started, and in solemn silence threaded our way down the windings of the cave, extinguishing our torches as soon as we saw light at its inland outlet. At a few paces from its mouth stood a sentry. His back was towards the cave, and in the uncertain gleams of the moon, struggling with the clouds, for a thin rain still fell, he never noted us till we were right on to him. Then he turned and saw, and at the awful sight of this procession of the gods of his land, threw up his arms, and without a word fell senseless. Although I never asked, I think that Mavovo took measures to prevent his awakening. At any rate when I looked back later on, I observed that he was carrying a big Pongo spear with a long shaft, instead of the copper weapon which he had taken from one of the coffins.

On we marched towards Rica Town, following the easy path by which we had come. As I have said, the country was very deserted and the inhabitants of such huts as we passed were evidently fast asleep. Also there were no dogs in this land to awake them with their barking. Between the cave and Rica we were not, I think, seen by a single soul.

Through that long night we pushed on as fast was we could travel, only stopping now and again for a few minutes to rest the bearers of the Holy Flower. Indeed at times Mrs. Eversley relieved her husband at this task, but Stephen, being very strong, carried his end of the stretcher throughout the whole journey.

Hans, of course, was much oppressed by the great weight of the gorilla skin, which, although it had shrunk a good deal, remained as heavy as ever. But he was a tough old fellow, and on the whole got on better than might have been expected, though by the time we reached the town he was sometimes obliged to follow the example of the god itself and help himself forward with his hands, going on all fours, as a gorilla generally does.

We reached the broad, long street of Rica about half an hour before dawn, and proceeded down it till we were past the Feast-house still quite unobserved, for as yet none were stirring on that wet morning. Indeed it was not until we were within a hundred yards of the harbour that a woman possessed of the virtue, or vice, of early rising, who had come from a hut to work in her garden, saw us and raised an awful, piercing scream.

"The gods!" she screamed. "The gods are leaving the land and taking the white men with them."

Instantly there arose a hubbub in the houses. Heads were thrust out of the doors and people ran into the gardens, every one of whom began to yell till one might have thought that a massacre was in progress. But as yet no one came near us, for they were afraid.

"Push on," I cried, "or all is lost."

They answered nobly. Hans struggled forward on all fours, for he was nearly done and his hideous garment was choking him, while Stephen and Brother John, exhausted though they were with the weight of the great plant, actually broke into a feeble trot. We came to the harbour and there, tied to the wharf, was the same canoe in which we had crossed to Pongo-land. We sprang into it and cut the fastenings with my knife, having no time to untie them, and pushed off from the wharf.

By now hundreds of people, among them many soldiers were hard upon and indeed around us, but still they seemed too frightened to do anything. So far the inspiration of Hans' disguise had saved us. In the midst of them, by the light of the rising sun, I recognised Komba, who ran up, a great spear in his hand, and for a moment halted amazed.

Then it was that the catastrophe happened which nearly cost us all our lives.

Hans, who was in the stern of the canoe, began to faint from exhaustion, and in his efforts to obtain air, for the heat and stench of the skin were overpowering him, thrust his head out through the lacings of the hide beneath the reed-stuffed mask of the gorilla, which fell over languidly upon his shoulder. Komba saw his ugly little face and knew it again.

"It is a trick!" he roared. "These white devils have killed the god and stolen the Holy Flower and its priestess. The yellow man is wrapped in the skin of the god. To the boats! To the boats!"

"Paddle," I shouted to Brother John and Stephen, "paddle for your lives! Mavovo, help me get up the sail."

As it chanced on that stormy morning the wind was blowing strongly towards the mainland.

We laboured at the mast, shipped it and hauled up the mat sail, but slowly for we were awkward at the business. By the time that it began to draw the paddles had propelled us about four hundred yards from the wharf, whence many canoes, with their sails already set, were starting in pursuit. Standing in the prow of the first of these, and roaring curses and vengeance at us, was Komba, the new Kalubi, who shook a great spear above his head.

An idea occurred to me, who knew that unless something were done we must be overtaken and killed by these skilled boatmen. Leaving Mavovo to attend to the sail, I scrambled aft, and thrusting aside the fainting Hans, knelt down in the stern of the canoe. There was still one charge, or rather one cap, left, and I meant to use it. I put up the largest flapsight, lifted the little rifle and covered Komba, aiming at the point of his chin. *Intombi* was not sighted for or meant to use at this great distance, and only by this means of allowing for the drop of the bullet, could I hope to hit the man in the body.

The sail was drawing well now and steadied the boat, also, being still under the shelter of the land, the water was smooth as that of a pond, so really I had a very good firing platform. Moreover, weary though I was, my vital forces rose to the emergency and I felt myself grow rigid as a statue. Lastly, the light was good, for the sun rose behind me, its level rays shining full on to my mark. I held my breath and touched the trigger. The charge exploded sweetly and almost at the instant; as the smoke drifted to one side, I saw Komba throw up his arms and fall backwards into the canoe. Then, quite a long while afterwards, or so it seemed, the breeze brought the faint sound of the thud of that fateful bullet to our ears.

Though perhaps I ought not to say so, it was really a wonderful shot in all the circumstances, for, as I learned afterwards, the ball struck just where I hoped that it might, in the centre of the breast, piercing the heart. Indeed, taking everything into consideration, I think that those four shots which I fired in Pongo-land are the real record of my career as a marksman. The first at night broke the arm of the gorilla god and would have killed him had not the charge hung fire and given him time to protect his head. The second did kill him in the midst of a great scrimmage when everything was moving. The third, fired by the glare of lightning after a long swim, slew the Motombo, and the fourth, loosed at this great distance from a moving boat, was the bane of that cold-blooded and treacherous man, Komba, who thought that he had trapped us to Pongo-land to be murdered and eaten as a sacrifice. Lastly there was always the consciousness that no mistake must be made, since with but four percussion caps it could not be retrieved.

I am sure that I could not have done so well with any other rifle, however modern and accurate it might be. But to this little Purdey weapon I had been accustomed from my youth, and that, as any marksman will know, means a great deal. I seemed to know it and it seemed to know me. It hangs on my wall to this day, although of course I never use it now in our breech-loading era. Unfortunately, however, a local gunsmith to whom I sent it to have the lock cleaned, re-browned it and scraped and varnished the stock, etc., without authority, making it look almost new again. I preferred it in its worn and scratched condition.

To return: the sound of the shot, like that of John Peel's horn, aroused Hans from his sleep. He thrust his head between my legs and saw Komba fall.

"Oh! beautiful, Baas, beautiful!" he said faintly. "I am sure that the ghost of your reverend father cannot kill his enemies more nicely down there among the Fires. Beautiful!" and the silly old fellow fell to kissing my boots, or what remained of them, after which I gave him the last of the brandy.

This quite brought him to himself again, especially when he was free from that filthy skin and had washed his head and hands.

The effect of the death of Komba upon the Pongos was very strange. All the other canoes clustered round that in which he lay. Then, after a hurried consultation, they hauled down their sails and paddled back to the wharf. Why they did this I cannot tell. Perhaps they thought that he was bewitched, or only wounded and required the attentions of a medicine-man. Perhaps it was not lawful for them to proceed except under the guidance of some reserve Kalubi who had "passed the god" and who was on shore. Perhaps it was necessary, according to their rites, that the body of their chief should be landed with certain ceremonies. I do not know. It is impossible to be sure as to the mysterious motives that actuate many of these remote African tribes.

At any rate the result was that it gave us a great start and a chance of life, who must otherwise have died upon the spot. Outside the bay the breeze blew merrily, taking us across the lake at a spanking pace, until about midday when it began to fall. Fortunately, however, it did not altogether drop till three o'clock by which time the coast of Mazitu-land was comparatively near; we could even distinguish a speck against the skyline which we knew was the Union Jack that Stephen had set upon the crest of a little hill.

During those hours of peace we ate the food that remained to us, washed ourselves as thoroughly as we could and rested. Well was it, in view of what followed, that we had this time of repose. For just as the breeze was failing I looked aft and there, coming up behind us, still holding the wind, was the whole fleet of Pongo canoes, thirty or forty of them perhaps, each carrying an average of about twenty men. We sailed on for as long as we could, for though our progress was but slow, it was quicker than what we could have made by paddling. Also it was necessary that we should save our strength for the last trial.

I remember that hour very well, for in the nervous excitement of it every little thing impressed itself upon my mind. I remember even the shape of the clouds that floated over us, remnants of the storm of the previous night. One was like a castle with a broken-down turret showing a staircase within; another had a fantastic resemblance to a wrecked ship with a hole in her starboard bow, two of her masts broken and one standing with some fragments of sails flapping from it, and so forth.

Then there was the general aspect of the great lake, especially at a spot where two currents met, causing little waves which seemed to fight with each other and fall backwards in curious curves. Also there were shoals of small fish, something like chub in shape, with round mouths and very white stomachs, which suddenly appeared upon the surface, jumping at invisible flies. These attracted a number of birds that resembled gulls of a light build. They had coal-black heads, white backs, greyish wings, and slightly webbed feet, pink as coral, with which they seized the small fish, uttering as they did so, a peculiar and plaintive cry that ended in a long-drawn *e-e-é*. The father of the flock, whose head seemed to be white like his back, perhaps from age, hung above them, not troubling to fish himself, but from time to time forcing one of the company to drop what he had caught, which he retrieved before it reached the water. Such are some of the small things that come back to me, though there were others too numerous and trivial to mention.

When the breeze failed us at last we were perhaps something over three miles from the shore, or rather from the great bed of reeds which at this spot grow in the shallows off the Mazitu coast to a breadth of seven or eight hundred yards, where the water becomes too deep for them. The Pongos were then about a mile and a half behind. But as the wind favoured them for a few minutes more and, having plenty of hands, they could help themselves on by paddling, when at last it died to a complete calm, the distance between us was not more than one mile. This meant that they must cover four miles of water, while we covered three.

Letting down our now useless sail and throwing it and the mast overboard to lighten the canoe, since the sky showed us that there was no more hope of wind, we began to paddle as hard as we could. Fortunately the two ladies were able to take their share in this exercise, since they had learned it upon the Lake of the Flower, where it seemed they kept a private canoe upon the other side of the island which was used for fishing. Hans, who was still weak, we set to steer with a paddle aft, which he did in a somewhat erratic fashion.

A stern chase is proverbially a long chase, but still the enemy with their skilled rowers came up fast. When we were a mile from the reeds they were within half a mile of us, and as we tired the proportion of distance lessened. When we were two hundred yards from the reeds they were not more than fifty or sixty yards behind, and then the real struggle began.

It was short but terrible. We threw everything we could overboard, including the ballast stones at the bottom of the canoe and the heavy hide of the gorilla. This, as it proved, was fortunate, since the thing sank but slowly and the foremost Pongo boats halted a minute to recover so precious a relic, checking the others behind them, a circumstance that helped us by twenty or thirty yards.

"Over with the plant!" I said.

But Stephen, looking quite old from exhaustion and with the sweat streaming from him as he laboured at his unaccustomed paddle, gasped:

"For Heaven's sake, no, after all we have gone through to get it."

So I didn't insist; indeed there was neither time nor breath for argument.

Now we were in the reeds, for thanks to the flag which guided us, we had struck the big hippopotamus lane exactly, and the Pongos, paddling like demons, were about thirty yards behind. Thankful was I that those interesting people had never learned the use of bows and arrows, and that their spears were too heavy to throw. By now, or rather some time before, old Babemba and the Mazitu had seen us, as had our Zulu hunters. Crowds of them were wading through the shallows towards us, yelling encouragements as they came. The Zulus, too, opened a rather wild fire, with the result that one of the bullets struck our canoe and another touched the brim of my hat. A third, however, killed a Pongo, which caused some confusion in the ranks of Tusculum.

But we were done and they came on remorselessly. When their leading boat was not more than ten yards from us and we were perhaps two hundred from the shore, I drove my paddle downwards and finding that the water was less than four feet deep, shouted:

"Overboard, all, and wade. It's our last chance!"

We scrambled out of that canoe the prow of which, as I left it the last, I pushed round across the water-lane to obstruct those of the Pongo. Now I think all would have gone well had it not been for Stephen, who after he had floundered forward a few paces in the mud, bethought him of his beloved orchid. Not only did he return to try to rescue it, he also actually persuaded his friend Mavovo to accompany him. They got back to the boat and began to lift the plant out when the Pongo fell upon them, striking at them with their spears over the width of our canoe. Mavovo struck back with the weapon he had taken from the Pongo sentry at the cave mouth, and killed or wounded one of them. Then some one hurled a ballast stone at him which caught him on the side of the head and knocked him down into the water, whence he rose and reeled back, almost senseless, till some of our people got hold of him and dragged him to the shore.

So Stephen was left alone, dragging at the great orchid, till a Pongo reaching over the canoe drove a spear through his shoulder. He let go of the orchid because he must and tried to retreat. Too late! Half a dozen or more of the Pongo pushed themselves between the stern or bow of our canoe and the reeds, and waded forward to kill him. I could not help, for to tell the truth at the moment I was stuck in a mud-hole made by the hoof of a hippopotamus, while the Zulu hunters and the Mazitu were as yet too far off. Surely he must have died had it not been for the courage of the girl Hope, who, while wading shorewards a little in front of me, had turned and seen his plight. Back she came, literally bounding through the water like a leopard whose cubs are in danger.

Reaching Stephen before the Pongo she thrust herself between him and them and proceeded to address them with the utmost vigour in their own language, which of course she had learned from those of the albinos who were not mutes.

What she said I could not exactly catch because of the shouts of the advancing Mazitu. I gathered, however, that she was anathematizing them in the words of some old and potent curse that was only used by the guardians of the Holy Flower, which consigned them, body and spirit, to a dreadful doom. The effect of this malediction, which by the way neither the young lady nor her mother would repeat to me afterwards, was certainly remarkable. Those men who heard it, among them the would-be slayers of Stephen, stayed their hands and even inclined their heads towards the young priestess, as though in reverence or deprecation, and thus remained for sufficient time for her to lead the wounded Stephen out of danger. This she did wading backwards by his side and keeping her eyes fixed full upon the Pongo. It was perhaps the most curious rescue that I ever saw.

The Holy Flower, I should add, they recaptured and carried off, for I saw it departing in one of their canoes. That was the end of my orchid hunt and of the money which I hoped to make by the sale of this floral treasure. I wonder what became of it. I have good reason to believe that it was never replanted on the Island of the Flower, so perhaps it was borne back to the dim and unknown land in the depths of Africa whence the Pongo are supposed to have brought it when they migrated.

After this incident of the wounding and the rescue of Stephen by the intrepid Miss Hope, whose interest in him was already strong enough to induce her to risk her life upon his behalf, all we fugitives were dragged ashore somehow by our friends. Here, Hans, I and the ladies collapsed exhausted, though Brother John still found sufficient strength to do what he could for the injured Stephen and Mavovo.

Then the Battle of the Reeds began, and a fierce fray it was. The Pongos who were about equal in numbers to our people, came on furiously, for they were mad at the death of their god with his priest, the Motombo, of which I think news had reached them and at the carrying off of the Mother of the Flower. Springing from their canoes because the waterway was too narrow for more than one of these to travel at a time, they plunged into the reeds with the intention of wading ashore. Here their hereditary enemies, the Mazitu, attacked them under the command of old Babemba. The struggle that ensued partook more of the nature of a series of hand-to-hand fights than of a set battle. It was extraordinary to see the heads of the combatants moving among the reeds as they stabbed at each other with the great spears, till one went down. There were few wounded in that fray, for those who fell sank in the mud and water and were drowned.

On the whole the Pongo, who were operating in what was almost their native element, were getting the best of it, and driving the Mazitu back. But what decided the day against them were the guns of our Zulu hunters. Although I could not lift a rifle myself I managed to collect these men round me and to direct their fire, which proved so terrifying to the Pongos that after ten or a dozen of them had been knocked over, they began to give back sullenly and were helped into their canoes by those men who were left in charge of them.

Then at length at a signal they got out their paddles, and, still shouting curses and defiance at us, rowed away till they became but specks upon the bosom of the great lake and vanished.

Two of the canoes we captured, however, and with them six or seven Pongos. These the Mazitu wished to put to death, but at the bidding of Brother John, whose orders, it will be remembered, had the same authority in Mazitu-land as those of the king, they bound their arms and made them prisoners instead.

In about half an hour it was all over, but of the rest of that day I cannot write, as I think I fainted from utter exhaustion, which was not, perhaps, wonderful, considering all that we had undergone in the four and a half days that had elapsed since we first embarked upon the Great Lake. For constant strain, physical and mental, I recall no such four days during the whole of my adventurous life. It was indeed wonderful that we came through them alive.

The last thing I remember was the appearance of Sammy, looking very smart, in his blue cotton smock, who, now that the fighting was over, emerged like a butterfly when the sun shines after rain.

"Oh! Mr. Quatermain," he said, "I welcome you home again after arduous exertions and looking into the eyes of bloody war. All the days of absence, and a good part of the nights, too, while the mosquitoes hunted slumber, I prayed for your safety like one o'clock, and perhaps, Mr. Quatermain, that helped to do the trick, for what says poet? Those who serve and wait are almost as good as those who cook dinner."

Such were the words which reached and, oddly enough, impressed themselves upon my darkening brain. Or rather they were part of the words, excerpts from a long speech that there is no doubt Sammy had carefully prepared during our absence.

The True Holy Flower

When I came to myself again it was to find that I had slept fifteen or sixteen hours, for the sun of a new day was high in the heavens. I was lying in a little shelter of boughs at the foot of that mound on which we flew the flag that guided us back over the waters of the Lake Kirua. Near by was Hans consuming a gigantic meal of meat which he had cooked over a neighbouring fire. With him, to my delight, I saw Mavovo, his head bound up, though otherwise but little the worse. The stone, which probably would have killed a thin-skulled white man, had done no more than knock him stupid and break the skin of his scalp, perhaps because the force of it was lessened by the gum man's-ring which, like most Zulus of a certain age or dignity, he wore woven in his hair.

The two tents we had brought with us to the lake were pitched not far away and looked quite pretty and peaceful there in the sunlight.

Hans, who was watching me out of the corner of his eye, ran to me with a large pannikin of hot coffee which Sammy had made ready against my awakening; for they knew that my sleep was, or had become of a natural order. I drank it to the last drop, and in all my life never did I enjoy anything more. Then while I began upon some pieces of the toasted meat, I asked him what had happened.

"Not much, Baas," he answered, "except that we are alive, who should be dead. The Maam and the Missie are still asleep in that tent, or at least the Maam is, for the Missie is helping Dogeetah, her father, to nurse Baas Stephen, who has an ugly wound. The Pongos have gone and I think will not return, for they have had enough of the white man's guns. The Mazitu have buried those of their dead whom they could recover, and have sent their wounded, of whom there were only six, back to Beza Town on litters. That is all, Baas."

Then while I washed, and never did I need a bath more, and put on my underclothes, in which I had swum on the night of the killing of the Motombo, that Hans had wrung out and dried in the sun, I asked that worthy how he was after his adventures.

"Oh! well enough, Baas," he answered, "now that my stomach is full, except that my hands and wrists are sore with crawling along the ground like a babyan (baboon), and that I cannot get the stink of that god's skin out of my nose. Oh! you don't know what it was: if I had been a white man it would have killed me. But, Baas, perhaps you did well to take drunken old Hans with you on this journey after all, for I was clever about the little gun, wasn't I? Also about your swimming of the Crocodile Water, though it is true that the sign of the spider and the moth which your reverend father sent, taught me that. And now we have got back safe, except for the Mazitu, Jerry, who doesn't matter, for there are plenty more like him, and the wound in Baas Stephen's shoulder, and that heavy flower which he thought better than brandy."

"Yes, Hans," I said, "I did well to take you and you are clever, for had it not been for you, we should now be cooked and eaten in Pongo-land. I thank you for your help, old friend. But, Hans, another time please sew up the holes in your waistcoat pocket. Four caps wasn't much, Hans."

"No, Baas, but it was enough; as they were all good ones. If there had been forty you could not have done much more. Oh! your reverend father knew all that" (my departed parent had become a kind of patron saint to Hans) "and did not wish this poor old Hottentot to have more to carry than was needed. He knew you wouldn't miss, Baas, and that there were only one god, one devil, and one man waiting to be killed."

I laughed, for Hans's way of putting things was certainly original, and having got on my coat, went to see Stephen. At the door of the tent I met Brother John, whose shoulder was dreadfully sore from the rubbing of the orchid stretcher, as were his hands with paddling, but who otherwise was well enough and of course supremely happy.

He told me that he had cleansed and sewn up Stephen's wound, which appeared to be doing well, although the spear had pierced right through the shoulder, luckily without cutting any artery. So I went in to see the patient and found him cheerful enough, though weak from weariness and loss of blood, with Miss Hope feeding him with broth from a wooden native spoon. I didn't stop very long, especially after he got on to the subject of the lost orchid, about which he began to show signs of excitement. This I allayed as well as I could by telling him that I had preserved a pod of the seed, news at which he was delighted.

"There!" he said. "To think that you, Allan, should have remembered to take that precaution when I, an orchidist, forgot all about it!"

"Ah! my boy," I answered, "I have lived long enough to learn never to leave anything behind that I can possibly carry away. Also, although not an orchidist, it occurred to me that there are more ways of propagating a plant than from the original root, which generally won't go into one's pocket."

Then he began to give me elaborate instructions as to the preservation of the seed-pod in a perfectly dry and air-tight tin box, etc., at which point Miss Hope unceremoniously bundled me out of the tent.

That afternoon we held a conference at which it was agreed that we should begin our return journey to Beza Town at once, as the place where we were camped was very malarious and there was always a risk of the Pongo paying us another visit.

So a litter was made with a mat stretched over it in which Stephen could be carried, since fortunately there were plenty of bearers, and our other simple preparations were quickly completed. Mrs. Eversley and Hope were mounted on the two donkeys; Brother John, whose hurt leg showed signs of renewed weakness, rode his white ox, which was now quite fat again; the wounded hero, Stephen, as I have said, was carried; and I walked, comparing notes with old Babemba on the Pongo, their manners, which I am bound to say were good, and their customs, that, as the saying goes, were "simply beastly."

How delighted that ancient warrior was to hear again about the sacred cave, the Crocodile Water, the Mountain Forest and its terrible god, of the death of which and of the Motombo he made me tell him the story three times over. At the conclusion of the third recital he said quietly:

"My lord Macumazana, you are a great man, and I am glad to have lived if only to know you. No one else could have done these deeds."

Of course I was complimented, but felt bound to point out Hans's share in our joint achievement.

"Yes, yes," he answered, "the Spotted Snake, Inhlatu, has the cunning to scheme, but you have the power to do, and what is the use of a brain to plot without the arm to strike? The two do not go together because the plotter is not a striker. His mind is different. If the snake had the strength and brain of the elephant, and the fierce courage of the buffalo, soon there would be but one creature left in the world. But the Maker of all things knew this and kept them separate, my lord Macumazana."

I thought, and still think, that there was a great deal of wisdom in this remark, simple as it seems. Oh! surely many of these savages whom we white men despise, are no fools.

After about an hour's march we camped till the moon rose which it did at ten o'clock, when we went on again till near dawn, as it was thought better that Stephen should travel in the cool of the night. I remember that our cavalcade, escorted before, behind and on either flank by the Mazitu troops with their tall spears, looked picturesque and even imposing as it wound over those wide downs in the lovely and peaceful light of the moon.

There is no need for me to set out the details of the rest of our journey, which was not marked by any incident of importance.

Stephen bore it very well, and Brother John, who was one of the best doctors I ever met, gave good reports of him, but I noted that he did not seem to get any stronger, although he ate plenty of food. Also, Miss Hope, who nursed him, for her mother seemed to have no taste that way, informed me that he slept but little, as indeed I found out for myself.

"O Allan," she said, just before we reached Beza Town, "Stephen, your son" (she used to call him my son, I don't know why) "is sick. The father says it is only the spear-hurt, but I tell you it is more than the spear-hurt. He is sick in himself," and the tears that filled her grey eyes showed me that she spoke what she believed. As a matter of fact she was right, for on the night after we reached the town, Stephen was seized with an attack of some bad form of African fever, which in his weak state nearly cost him his life, contracted, no doubt, at that unhealthy Crocodile Water.

Our reception at Beza was most imposing, for the whole population, headed by old Bausi himself, came out to meet us with loud shouts of welcome, from which we had to ask them to desist for Stephen's sake.

So in the end we got back to our huts with gratitude of heart. Indeed, we should have been very happy there for a while, had it not been for our anxiety about Stephen. But it is always thus in the world; who was ever allowed to eat his pot of honey without finding a fly or perhaps a cockroach in his mouth?

In all, Stephen was really ill for about a month. On the tenth day after our arrival at Beza, according to my diary, which, having little else to do, I entered up fully at this time, we thought that he would surely die. Even Brother John, who attended him with the most constant skill, and who had ample quinine and other drugs at his command, for these we had brought with us from Durban in plenty, gave up the case. Day and night the poor fellow raved and always about that confounded orchid, the loss of which seemed to weigh upon his mind as though it were a whole sackful of unrepented crimes.

I really think that he owed his life to a subterfuge, or rather to a bold invention of Hope's. One evening, when he was at his very worst and going on like a mad creature about the lost plant--I was present in the hut at the time alone with him and her--she took his hand and pointing to a perfectly open space on the floor, said:

"Look, O Stephen, the flower has been brought back."

He stared and stared, and then to my amazement answered:

"By Jove, so it has! But those beggars have broken off all the blooms except one."

"Yes," she echoed, "but one remains and it is the finest of them all."

After this he went quietly to sleep and slept for twelve hours, then took some food and slept again and, what is more, his temperature went down to, or a little below, normal. When he finally woke up, as it chanced, I was again present in the hut with Hope, who was standing on the spot which she had persuaded him was occupied by the orchid. He stared at this spot and he stared at her--me he could not see, for I was behind him--then said in a weak voice:

"Didn't you tell me, Miss Hope, that the plant was where you are and that the most beautiful of the flowers was left?"

I wondered what on earth her answer would be. However, she rose to the occasion.

"O Stephen," she replied, in her soft voice and speaking in a way so natural that it freed her words from any boldness, "it is here, for am I not its child"--her native appellation, it will be remembered, was "Child of the Flower." "And the fairest of the flowers is here, too, for I am that Flower which you found in the island of the lake. O Stephen, I pray you to trouble no more about a lost plant of which you have seed in plenty, but make thanks that you still live and that through you my mother and I still live, who, if you had died, would weep our eyes away."

"Through me," he answered. "You mean through Allan and Hans. Also it was you who saved my life there in the water. Oh! I remember it all now. You are right, Hope; although I didn't know it, you are the true Holy Flower that I saw."

She ran to him and kneeling by his side, gave him her hand, which he pressed to his pale lips.

Then I sneaked out of that hut and left them to discuss the lost flower that was found again. It was a pretty scene, and one that to my mind gave a sort of spiritual meaning to the whole of an otherwise rather insane quest. He sought an ideal flower, he found--the love of his life.

After this, Stephen recovered rapidly, for such love is the best of medicines--if it be returned.

I don't know what passed between the pair and Brother John and his wife, for I never asked. But I noted that from this day forward they began to treat him as a son. The new relationship between Stephen and Hope seemed to be tacitly accepted without discussion. Even the natives accepted it, for old Mavovo asked me when they were going to be married and how many cows Stephen had promised to pay Brother John for such a beautiful wife. "It ought to be a large herd," he said, "and of a big breed of cattle."

Sammy, too, alluded to the young lady in conversation with me, as "Mr. Somers's affianced spouse." Only Hans said nothing. Such a trivial matter as marrying and giving in marriage did not interest him. Or, perhaps, he looked upon the affair as a foregone conclusion and therefore unworthy of comment.

We stayed at Bausi's kraal for a full month longer whilst Stephen recovered his strength. I grew thoroughly bored with the place and so did Mavovo and the Zulus, but Brother John and his wife did not seem to mind. Mrs. Eversley was a passive creature, quite content to take things as they came and after so long an absence from civilization, to bide a little longer among savages. Also she had her beloved John, at whom she would sit and gaze by the hour like a cat sometimes does at a person to whom it is attached. Indeed, when she spoke to him, her voice seemed to me to resemble a kind of blissful purr. I think it made the old boy rather fidgety sometimes, for after an hour or two of it he would rise and go to hunt for butterflies.

To tell the truth, the situation got a little on my nerves at last, for wherever I looked I seemed to see there Stephen and Hope making love to each other, or Brother John and his wife admiring each other, which didn't leave me much spare conversation. Evidently they thought that Mavovo, Hans, Sammy, Bausi, Babemba and Co. were enough for me-- that is, if they reflected on the matter at all. So they were, in a sense, for the Zulu hunters began to get out of hand in the midst of this idleness and plenty, eating too much, drinking too much native beer, smoking too much of the intoxicating *dakka*, a mischievous kind of help, and making too much love to the Mazitu women, which of course resulted in the usual rows that I had to settle.

At last I struck and said that we must move on as Stephen was now fit to travel.

"Quite so," said Brother John, mildly. "What have you arranged, Allan?"

With some irritation, for I hated that sentence of Brother John's, I replied that I had arranged nothing, but that as none of them seemed to have any suggestions to make, I would go out and talk the matter over with Hans and Mavovo, which I did.

I need not chronicle the results of our conference since other arrangements were being made for us at which I little guessed.

It all came very suddenly, as great things in the lives of men and nations sometimes do. Although the Mazitu were of the Zulu family, their military organization had none of the Zulu thoroughness. For instance, when I remonstrated with Bausi and old Babemba as to their not keeping up a proper system of outposts and intelligence, they laughed at me and answered that they never had been attacked and now that the Pongo had learnt a lesson, were never likely to be.

By the way, I see that I have not yet mentioned that at Brother John's request those Pongos who had been taken prisoners at the Battle of the Reeds were conducted to the shores of the lake, given one of the captured canoes and told that they might return to their own happy land. To our astonishment about three weeks later they reappeared at Beza Town with this story.

They said that they had crossed the lake and found Rica still standing, but utterly deserted. They then wandered through the country and even explored the Motombo's cave. There they discovered the remains of the Motombo, still crouched upon his platform, but nothing more. In one hut of a distant village, however, they came across an old and dying woman who informed them with her last breath that the Pongos, frightened by the iron tubes that vomited death and in obedience to some prophecy, "had all gone back whence they came in the beginning," taking with them the recaptured "Holy Flower." She had been left with a supply of food because she was too weak to travel. So, perhaps, that flower grows again in some unknown place in Africa, but its worshippers will have to provide themselves with another god of the forest, another Mother of the Flower, and another high-priest to fill the office of the late Motombo.

These Pongo prisoners, having now no home, and not knowing where their people had gone except that it was "towards the north," asked for leave to settle among the Mazitu, which was granted them. Their story confirmed me in my opinion that Pongo-land is not really an island, but is connected on the further side with the continent by some ridge or swamp. If we had been obliged to stop much longer among the Mazitu, I would have satisfied myself as to this matter by going to look. But that chance never came to me until some years later when, under curious circumstances, I was again destined to visit this part of Africa.

To return to my story. On the day following this discussion as to our departure we all breakfasted very early as there was a great deal to be done. There was a dense mist that morning such as in these Mazitu uplands often precedes high, hot wind from the north at this season of the year, so dense indeed that it was impossible to see for more than a few yards. I suppose that this mist comes up from the great lake in certain conditions of the weather. We had just finished our breakfast and rather languidly, for the thick, sultry air left me unenergetic, I told one of the Zulus to see that the two donkeys and the white ox which I had caused to be brought into the town in view of our near departure and tied up by our huts, were properly fed. Then I went to inspect all the rifles and ammunition, which Hans had got out to be checked and overhauled. It was at this moment that I heard a far-away and unaccustomed sound, and asked Hans what he thought it was.

"A gun, Baas," he answered anxiously.

Well might he be anxious, for as we both knew, no one in the neighbourhood had guns except ourselves, and all ours were accounted for. It is true that we had promised to give the majority of those we had taken from the slavers to Bausi when we went away, and that I had been instructing some of his best soldiers in the use of them, but not one of these had as yet been left in their possession.

I stepped to a gate in the fence and ordered the sentry there to run to Bausi and Babemba and make report and inquiries, also to pray them to summon all the soldiers, of whom, as it happened, there were at the time not more than three hundred in the town. As perfect peace prevailed, the rest, according to their custom, had been allowed to go to their villages and attend to their crops. Then, possessed by a rather undefined nervousness, at which the others were inclined to laugh, I caused the Zulus to arm and generally make a few arrangements to meet any unforeseen crisis. This done I sat down to reflect what would be the best course to take if we should happen to be attacked by a large force in that straggling native town, of which

I had often studied all the strategic possibilities. When I had come to my own conclusion I asked Hans and Mavovo what they thought, and found that they agreed with me that the only defensible place was outside the town where the road to the south gate ran down to a rocky wooded ridge with somewhat steep flanks. It may be remembered that it was by this road and over this ridge that Brother John had appeared on his white ox when we were about to be shot to death with arrows at the posts in the market-place.

Whilst we were still talking two of the Mazitu captains appeared, running hard and dragging between them a wounded herdsman, who had evidently been hit in the arm by a bullet.

This was his story. That he and two other boys were out herding the king's cattle about half a mile to the north of the town, when suddenly there appeared a great number of men dressed in white robes, all of whom were armed with guns. These men, of whom he thought there must be three or four hundred, began to take the cattle and seeing the three herds, fired on them, wounding him and killing his two companions. He then ran for his life and brought the news. He added that one of the men had called after him to tell the white people that they had come to kill them and the Mazitu who were their friends and to take away the white women.

"Hassan-ben-Mohammed and his slavers!" I said, as Babemba appeared at the head of a number of soldiers, crying out:

"The slave-dealing Arabs are here, lord Macumazana. They have crept on us through the mist. A herald of theirs has come to the north gate demanding that we should give up you white people and your servants, and with you a hundred young men and a hundred young women to be sold as slaves. If we do not do this they say that they will kill all of us save the unmarried boys and girls, and that you white people they will take and put to death by burning, keeping only the two women alive. One Hassan sends this message."

"Indeed," I answered quietly, for in this fix I grew quite cool as was usual with me. "And does Bausi mean to give us up?"

"How can Bausi give up Dogeetah who is his blood brother, and you, his friend?" exclaimed the old general, indignantly. "Bausi sends me to his brother Dogeetah that he may receive the orders of the white man's wisdom, spoken through your mouth, lord Macumazana."

"Then there's a good spirit in Bausi," I replied, "and these are Dogeetah's orders spoken through my mouth. Go to Hassan's messengers and ask him whether he remembers a certain letter which two white men left for him outside their camp in a cleft stick. Tell him that the time has now come for those white men to fulfil the promise they made in that letter and that before to-morrow he will be hanging on a tree. Then, Babemba, gather your soldiers and hold the north gate of the town for as long as you can, defending it with bows and arrows. Afterwards retreat through the town, joining us among the trees on the rocky slope that is opposite the south gate. Bid some of your men clear the town of all the aged and women and children and let them pass though the south gate and take refuge in the wooded country beyond the slope. Let them not tarry. Let them go at once. Do you understand?"

"I understand everything, lord Macumazana. The words of Dogeetah shall be obeyed. Oh! would that we had listened to you and kept a better watch!"

He rushed off, running like a young man and shouting orders as he went.

"Now," I said, "we must be moving."

We collected all the rifles and ammunition, with some other things, I am sure I forget what they were, and with the help of a few guards whom Babemba had left outside our gate started through the town, leading with us the two donkeys and the white ox. I remember by an afterthought, telling Sammy, who was looking very uncomfortable, to return to the huts and fetch some blankets and a couple of iron cooking-pots which might become necessities to us.

"Oh! Mr. Quatermain," he answered, "I will obey you, though with fear and trembling."

He went and when a few hours afterwards I noted that he had never reappeared, I came to the conclusion, with a sigh, for I was very fond of Sammy in a way, that he had fallen into trouble and been killed. Probably, I thought, "his fear and trembling" had overcome his reason and caused him to run in the wrong direction with the cooking-pots.

The first part of our march through the town was easy enough, but after we had crossed the market-place and emerged into the narrow way that ran between many lines of huts to the south gate it became more difficult, since this path was already crowded with hundreds of terrified fugitives, old people, sick being carried, little boys, girls, and women with infants at the breast. It was impossible to control these poor folk; all we could do was to fight our way through them. However, we got out at last and climbing the slope, took up the best position we could on and just beneath its crest where the trees and scattered boulders gave us very fair cover, which we improved upon in every way feasible in the time at our disposal, by building little breastworks of stone and so forth. The fugitives who had accompanied us, and those who followed, a multitude in all, did not stop here, but flowed on along the road and vanished into the wooded country behind.

I suggested to Brother John that he should take his wife and daughter and the three beasts and go with them. He seemed inclined to accept the idea, needless to say for their sakes, not for his own, for he was a very fearless old fellow. But the two ladies utterly refused to budge. Hope said that she would stop with Stephen, and her mother declared that she had every confidence in me and preferred to remain where she was. Then I suggested that Stephen should go too, but at this he grew so angry that I dropped the subject.

So in the end we established them in a pleasant little hollow by a spring just over the crest of the rise, where unless our flank were turned or we were rushed, they would be out of the reach of bullets. Moreover, without saying anything more we gave to each of them a double-barrelled and loaded pistol.

The Battle of the Gate

By now heavy firing had begun at the north gate of the town, accompanied by much shouting. The mist was still too thick to enable us to see anything at first. But shortly after the commencement of the firing a strong, hot wind, which always followed these mists, got up and gradually gathered to a gale, blowing away the vapours. Then from the top of the crest, Hans, who had climbed a tree there, reported that the Arabs were advancing on the north gate, firing as they came, and that the Mazitu were replying with their bows and arrows from behind the palisade that surrounded the town. This palisade, I should state, consisted of an earthen bank on the top of which tree trunks were set close together. Many of these had struck in that fertile soil, so that in general appearance this protective work resembled a huge live fence, on the outer and inner side of which grew great masses of prickly pear and tall, finger-like cacti. A while afterwards Hans reported that the Mazitu were retreating and a few minutes later they began to arrive through the south gate, bringing several wounded with them. Their captain said that they could not stand against the fire of the guns and had determined to abandon the town and make the best fight they could upon the ridge.

A little later the rest of the Mazitu came, driving before them all the non-combatants who remained in the town. With these was King Bausi, in a terrible state of excitement.

"Was I not wise, Macumazana," he shouted, "to fear the slave-traders and their guns? Now they have come to kill those who are old and to take the young away in their gangs to sell them."

"Yes, King," I could not help answering, "you were wise. But if you had done what I said and kept a better look-out Hassan could not have crept on you like a leopard on a goat."

"It is true," he groaned; "but who knows the taste of a fruit till he has bitten it?"

Then he went to see to the disposal of his soldiers along the ridge, placing, by my advice, the most of them at each end of the line to frustrate any attempt to out-flank us. We, for our part, busied ourselves in serving out those guns which we had taken in the first fight with the slavers to the thirty or forty picked men whom I had been instructing in the use of firearms. If they did not do much damage, at least, I thought, they could make a noise and impress the enemy with the idea that we were well armed.

Ten minutes or so later Babemba arrived with about fifty men, all the Mazitu soldiers who were left in the town. He reported that he had held the north gate as long as he could in order to gain time, and that the Arabs were breaking it in. I begged him to order the soldiers to pile up stones as a defence against the bullets and to lie down behind them. This he went to do.

Then, after a pause, we saw a large body of the Arabs who had effected an entry, advancing down the central street towards us. Some of them had spears as well as guns, on which they carried a dozen or so of human heads cut from the Mazitus who had been killed, waving them aloft and shouting in triumph. It was a sickening sight, and one that made me grind my teeth with rage. Also I could not help reflecting that ere long our heads might be upon those spears. Well, if the worst came to the worst I was determined that I would not be taken alive to be burned in a slow fire or pinned over an ant-heap, a point upon which the others agreed with me, though poor Brother John had scruples as to suicide, even in despair.

It was just then that I missed Hans and asked where he had gone. Somebody said that he thought he had seen him running away, whereon Mavovo, who was growing excited, called out:

"Ah! Spotted Snake has sought his hole. Snakes hiss, but they do not charge."

"No, but sometimes they bite," I answered, for I could not believe that Hans had showed the white feather. However, he was gone and clearly we were in no state to send to look for him.

Now our hope was that the slavers, flushed with victory, would advance across the open ground of the market-place, which we could sweep with our fire from our position on the ridge. This, indeed, they began to do, whereon, without orders, the Mazitu to whom we had given the guns, to my fury and dismay, commenced to blaze away at a range of about four hundred yards, and after a good deal of firing managed to kill or wound two or three men. Then the Arabs, seeing their danger, retreated and, after a pause, renewed their advance in two bodies. This time, however, they followed the streets of huts that were built thickly between the outer palisade of the town and the market-place, which, as it had been designed to hold cattle in time of need, was also surrounded with a wooden fence strong enough to resist the rush of horned beasts. On that day, I should add, as the Mazitu never dreamed of being attacked, all their stock were grazing on some distant veldt. In this space between the two fences were many hundreds of huts, wattle and grass built, but for the most part roofed with palm leaves, for here, in their separate quarters, dwelt the great majority of the inhabitants of Beza Town, of which the northern part was occupied by the king, the nobles and the captains. This ring of huts, which entirely surrounded the market-place except at the two gateways, may have been about a hundred and twenty yards in width.

Down the paths between these huts, both on the eastern and the western side, advanced the Arabs and half-breeds, of whom there appeared to be about four hundred, all armed with guns and doubtless trained to fighting. It was a terrible force for us to face, seeing that although we may have had nearly as many men, our guns did not total more than fifty, and most of those who held them were quite unused to the management of firearms.

Soon the Arabs began to open fire on us from behind the huts, and a very accurate fire it was, as our casualties quickly showed, notwithstanding the stone *schanzes* we had constructed. The worst feature of the thing also was that we could not reply with any effect, as our assailants, who gradually worked nearer, were effectively screened by the huts, and we had not enough guns to attempt organised volley firing. Although I tried to keep a cheerful countenance I confess that I began to fear the worst and even to wonder if we could possibly attempt to retreat. This idea was abandoned, however, since the Arabs would certainly overtake and shoot us down.

One thing I did. I persuaded Babemba to send about fifty men to build up the southern gate, which was made of trunks of trees and opened outwards, with earth and the big stones that lay about in plenty. While this was being done quickly, for the Mazitu soldiers worked at the task like demons and, being sheltered by the palisade, could not be shot, all of a sudden I caught sight of four or five wisps of smoke that arose in quick succession at the north end of the town and were instantly followed by as many bursts of flame which leapt towards us in the strong wind.

Someone was firing Beza Town! In less than an hour the flames, driven by the gale through hundreds of huts made dry as tinder by the heat, would reduce Beza to a heap of ashes. It was inevitable, nothing could save the place! For an instant I thought that the Arabs must have done this thing. Then, seeing that new fires continually arose in different places, I understood that no Arabs, but a friend or friends were at work, who had conceived the idea of *destroying the Arabs with fire*.

My mind flew to Sammy. Without doubt Sammy had stayed behind to carry out this terrible and masterly scheme, of which I am sure none of the Mazitu would have thought, since it involved the absolute destruction of their homes and property.

Sammy, at whom we had always mocked, was, after all, a great man, prepared to perish in the flames in order to save his friends!

Babemba rushed up, pointing with a spear to the rising fire. Now my inspiration came.

"Take all your men," I said, "except those who are armed with guns. Divide them, encircle the town, guard the north gate, though I think none can win back through the flames, and if any of the Arabs succeed in breaking through the palisade, kill them."

"It shall be done," shouted Babemba, "but oh! for the town of Beza where I was born! Oh! for the town of Beza!"

"Drat the town of Beza!" I holloaed after him, or rather its native equivalent. "It is of all our lives that I'm thinking."

Three minutes later the Mazitu, divided into two bodies, were running like hares to encircle the town, and though a few were shot as they descended the slope, the most of them gained the shelter of the palisade in safety, and there at intervals halted by sections, for Babemba managed the matter very well.

Now only we white people, with the Zulu hunters under Mavovo, of whom there were twelve in all, and the Mazitu armed with guns, numbering about thirty, were left upon the slope.

For a little while the Arabs did not seem to realise what had happened, but engaged themselves in peppering at the Mazitu, who, I think, they concluded were in full flight. Presently, however, they either heard or saw.

Oh! what a hubbub ensued. All the four hundred of them began to shout at once. Some of them ran to the palisade and began to climb it, but as they reached the top of the fence were pinned by the Mazitu arrows and fell backwards, while a few who got over became entangled in the prickly pears on the further side and were promptly speared. Giving up this attempt, they rushed back along the lane with the intention of escaping at the north-gate. But before ever they reached the head of the market-place the roaring, wind-swept flames, leaping from hut to hut, had barred their path. They could not face that awful furnace.

Now they took another counsel and in a great confused body charged down the market-place to break out at the south gate, and our turn came. How we raked them as they sped across the open, an easy mark! I know that I fired as fast as I could using two rifles, swearing the while at Hans because he was not there to load for me. Stephen was better off in this respect, for, looking round, to my astonishment I saw Hope, who had left her mother on the other side of the hill, in the act of capping his second gun. I should explain that during our stay in Beza Town we had taught her how to use a rifle.

I called to him to send her away, but again she would not go, even after a bullet had pierced her dress.

Still, all our shooting could not stop that rush of men, made desperate by the fear of a fiery death. Leaving many stretched out behind them, the first of the Arabs drew near to the south gate.

"My father," said Mavovo in my ear, "now the real fighting is going to begin. The gate will soon be down. We must be the gate."

I nodded, for if the Arabs once got through, there were enough of them left to wipe us out five times over. Indeed, I do not suppose that up to this time they had actually lost more than forty men. A few words explained the situation to Stephen and Brother John, whom I told to take his daughter to her mother and wait there with them. The Mazitu I ordered to throw down their guns, for if they kept these I was sure they would shoot some of us, and to accompany us, bringing their spears only.

Then we rushed down the slope and took up our position in a little open space in front of the gate, that now was tottering to its fall beneath the blows and draggings of the Arabs. At this time the sight was terrible and magnificent, for the flames had got hold of the two half-circles of huts that embraced the market-place, and, fanned by the blast, were rushing towards us like a thing alive. Above us swept a great pall of smoke in which floated flakes of fire, so thick that it hid the sky, though fortunately the wind did not suffer it to sink and choke us. The sounds also were almost inconceivable, for to the crackling roar of the conflagration as it devoured hut after hut, were added the coarse, yelling voices of the half-bred Arabs, as in mingled rage and terror they tore at the gateway or each other, and the reports of the guns which many of them were still firing, half at hazard.

We formed up before the gate, the Zulus with Stephen and myself in front and the thirty picked Mazitu, commanded by no less a person than Bausi, the king, behind. We had not long to wait, for presently down the thing came and over it and the mound of earth and stones we had built beyond, began to pour a mob of white-robed and turbaned men whose mixed and tumultuous exit somehow reminded me of the pips and pulp being squeezed out of a grenadilla fruit.

I gave the word, and we fired into that packed mass with terrible effect. Really I think that each bullet must have brought down two or three of them. Then, at a command from Mavovo, the Zulus threw down their guns and charged with their broad spears. Stephen, who had got hold of an assegai somehow, went with them, firing a Colt's revolver as he ran, while at their backs came Bausi and his thirty tall Mazitu.

I will confess at once that I did not join in this terrific onslaught. I felt that I had not weight enough for a scrimmage of the sort, also that I should perhaps be better employed using my wits outside and watching for a chance to be of service, like a half-back in a football field, than in getting my brains knocked out in a general row. Or mayhap my heart failed me and I was afraid. I dare say, for I have never pretended to great courage. At any rate, I stopped outside and shot whenever I got the chance, not without effect, filling a humble but perhaps a useful part.

It was really magnificent, that fray. How those Zulus did go in. For quite a long while they held the narrow gateway and the mound against all the howling, thrusting mob, much as the Roman called Horatius and his two friends held the entrance to some bridge or other long ago at Rome against a great force of I forget whom. They shouted their Zulu battle-cry of *Laba! Laba* that of their regiment, I suppose, for most of them were men of about the same age, and stabbed and fought and struggled and went down one by one.

Back the rest of them were swept; then, led by Mavovo, Stephen and Bausi, charged again, reinforced with the thirty Mazitu. Now the tongues of flame met almost over them, the growing fence of prickly pear and cacti withered and crackled, and still they fought on beneath that arch of fire.

Back they were driven again by the mere weight of numbers. I saw Mavovo stab a man and go down. He rose and stabbed another, then fell again for he was hard hit.

Two Arabs rushed to kill him. I shot them both with a right and left, for fortunately my rifle was just reloaded. He rose once more and killed a third man. Stephen came to his support and grappling with an Arab, dashed his head against the gate-post so that he fell. Old Bausi, panting like a grampus, plunged in with his remaining Mazitu and the combatants became so confused in the dark gloom of the overhanging smoke that I could scarcely tell one from the other. Yet the maddened Arabs were winning, as they must, for how could our small and ever-lessening company stand against their rush?

We were in a little circle now of which somehow I found myself the centre, and they were attacking us on all sides. Stephen got a knock on the head from the butt end of a gun, and tumbled against me, nearly upsetting me. As I recovered myself I looked round in despair.

Now it was that I saw a very welcome sight, namely Hans, yes, the lost Hans himself, with his filthy hat whereof I noticed even then the frayed ostrich feathers were smouldering, hanging by a leather strap at the back of his head. He was shambling along in a sly and silent sort of way, but at a great rate with his mouth open, beckoning over his shoulder, and behind him came about one hundred and fifty Mazitu.

Those Mazitu soon put another complexion upon the affair, for charging with a roar, they drove back the Arabs, who had no space to develop their line, straight into the jaws of that burning hell. A little later the rest of the Mazitu returned with Babemba and finished the job. Only quite a few of the Arabs got out and were captured after they had thrown down their guns. The rest retreated into the centre of the market-place, whither our people followed them. In this crisis the blood of these Mazitu told, and they stuck to the enemy as Zulus themselves would certainly have done.

It was over! Great Heaven! it was over, and we began to count our losses. Four of the Zulus were dead and two others were badly wounded --no, three, including Mavovo. They brought him to me leaning on the shoulder of Babemba and another Mazitu captain. He was a shocking sight, for he was shot in three places, and badly cut and battered as well. He looked at me a little while, breathing heavily, then spoke.

"It was a very good fight, my father," he said. "Of all that I have fought I can remember none better, although I have been in far greater battles, which is well as it is my last. I foreknew it, my father, for though I never told it you, the first death lot that I drew down yonder in Durban was my own. Take back the gun you gave me, my father. You did but lend it me for a little while, as I said to you. Now I go to the Underworld to join the spirits of my ancestors and of those who have fallen at my side in many wars, and of those women who bore my children. I shall have a tale to tell them there, my father, and together we will wait for you--till you, too, die in war!"

Then he lifted up his arm from the neck of Babemba, and saluted me with a loud cry of *Baba! Inkosi*! giving me certain great titles which I will not set down, and having done so sank to the earth.

I sent one of the Mazitu to fetch Brother John, who arrived presently with his wife and daughter. He examined Mavovo and told him straight out that nothing could help him except prayer.

"Make no prayers for me, Dogeetah," said the old heathen; "I have followed my star," (i.e. lived according to my lights) "and am ready to eat the fruit that I have planted. Or if the tree prove barren, then to drink of its sap and sleep."

Waving Brother John aside he beckoned to Stephen.

"O Wazela!" he said, "you fought very well in that fight; if you go on as you have begun in time you will make a warrior of whom the Daughter of the Flower and her children will sing songs after you have come to join me, your friend. Meanwhile, farewell! Take this assegai of mine and clean it not, that the red rust thereon may put you in mind of Mavovo, the old Zulu doctor and captain with whom you stood side by side in the Battle of the Gate, when, as though they were winter grass, the fire burnt up the white-robed thieves of men who could not pass our spears."

Then he waved his hand again, and Stephen stepped aside muttering something, for he and Mavovo had been very intimate and his voice choked in his throat with grief. Now the old Zulu's glazing eye fell upon Hans, who was sneaking about, I think with a view of finding an opportunity of bidding him a last good-bye.

"Ah! Spotted Snake," he cried, "so you have come out of your hole now that the fire has passed it, to eat the burnt frogs in the cinders. It is a pity that you who are so clever should be a coward, since our lord Macumazana needed one to load for him on the hill and would have killed more of the hyenas had you been there."

"Yes, Spotted Snake, it is so," echoed an indignant chorus of the other Zulus, while Stephen and I and even the mild Brother John looked at him reproachfully.

Now Hans, who generally was as patient under affront as a Jew, for once lost his temper. He dashed his hat upon the ground, and danced on it; he spat towards the surviving Zulu hunters; he even vituperated the dying Mavovo.

"O son of a fool!" he said, "you pretend that you can see what is hid from other men, but I tell you that there is a lying spirit in your lips. You called me a coward because I am not big and strong as you were, and cannot hold an ox by the horns, but at least there is more brain in my stomach than in all your head. Where would all of you be now had it not been for poor Spotted Snake the 'coward,' who twice this day has saved every one of you, except those whom the Baas's father, the reverend Predikant, has marked upon the forehead to come and join him in a place that is even hotter and brighter than that burning town?"

Now we looked at Hans, wondering what he meant about saving us twice, and Mavovo said:

"Speak on quickly, O Spotted Snake, for I would hear the end of your story. How did you help us in your hole?"

Hans began to grub about in his pockets, from which finally he produced a match-box wherein there remained but one match.

"With this," he said. "Oh! could none of you see that the men of Hassan had all walked into a trap? Did none of you know that fire burns thatched houses, and that a strong wind drives it fast and far? While you sat there upon the hill with your heads together, like sheep waiting to be killed, I crept away among the bushes and went about my business. I said nothing to any of you, not even to the Baas, lest he should answer me, 'No, Hans, there may be an old woman sick in one of those huts and therefore you must not fire them.' In such matters who does not know that white people are fools, even the best of them, and in fact there were several old women, for I saw them running for the gateway. Well, I crept up by the green fence which I knew would not burn and I came to the north gate. There was an Arab sentry left there to watch.

"He fired at me, look! Well for Hans his mother bore him short"; and he pointed to a hole in the filthy hat. "Then before that Arab could load again, poor coward Hans got his knife into him from behind. Look!" and he produced a big blade, which was such as butchers use, from his belt and showed it to us. "After that it was easy, since fire is a wonderful thing. You make it small and it grows big of itself, like a child, and never gets tired, and is always hungry, and runs fast as a horse. I lit six of them where they would burn quickest. Then I saved the last match, since we have few left, and came through the gate before the fire ate me up; me, its father, me the Sower of the Red Seed!"

We stared at the old Hottentot in admiration, even Mavovo lifted his dying head and stared. But Hans, whose annoyance had now evaporated, went on in a jog-trot mechanical voice:

"As I was returning to find the Baas, if he still lived, the heat of the fire forced me to the high ground to the west of the fence, so that I saw what was happening at the south gate, and that the Arab men must break through there because you who held it were so few. So I ran down to Babemba and the other captains very quickly, telling them there was no need to guard the fence any more, and that they must get to the south gate and help you, since otherwise you would all be killed, and they, too, would be killed afterwards. Babemba listened to me and started sending out messengers to collect the others and we got here just in time. Such is the hole I hid in during the Battle of the Gate, O Mavovo. That is all the story which I pray that you will tell to the Baas's reverend father, the Predikant, presently, for I am sure that it will please him to learn that he did not teach me to be wise and help all men and always to look after the Baas Allan, to no purpose. Still, I am sorry that I wasted so many matches, for where shall we get any more now that the camp is burnt?" and he gazed ruefully at the all but empty box.

Mavovo spoke once more in a slow, gasping voice.

"Never again," he said, addressing Hans, "shall you be called Spotted Snake, O little yellow man who are so great and white of heart. Behold! I give you a new name, by which you shall be known with honour from generation to generation. It is 'Light in Darkness.' It is 'Lord of the Fire.'"

Then he closed his eyes and fell back insensible. Within a few minutes he was dead. But those high names with which he christened Hans with his dying breath, clung to the old Hottentot for all his days. Indeed from that day forward no native would ever have ventured to call him by any other. Among them, far and wide, they became his titles of honour.

The roar of the flames grew less and the tumult within their fiery circle died away. For now the Mazitu were returning from the last fight in the market-place, if fight it could be called, bearing in their arms great bundles of the guns which they had collected from the dead Arabs, most of whom had thrown down their weapons in a last wild effort to escape. But between the spears of the infuriated savages on the one hand and the devouring fire on the other what escape was there for them? The blood-stained wretches who remained in the camps and towns of the slave-traders, along the eastern coast of Africa, or in the Isle of Madagascar, alone could tell how many were lost, since of those who went out from them to make war upon the Mazitu and their white friends, none returned again with the long lines of expected captives. They had gone to their own place, of which sometimes that flaming African city has seemed to me a symbol. They were wicked men indeed, devils stalking the earth in human form, without pity, without shame. Yet I could not help feeling sorry for them at the last, for truly their end was awful.

They brought the prisoners up to us, and among them, his white robe half-burnt off him, I recognised the hideous pock-marked Hassan-ben- Mohammed.

"I received your letter, written a while ago, in which you promised to make us die by fire, and, this morning, I received your message, Hassan," I said, "brought by the wounded lad who escaped from you when you murdered his companions, and to both I sent you an answer. If none reached you, look around, for there is one written large in a tongue that all can read."

The monster, for he was no less, flung himself upon the ground, praying for mercy. Indeed, seeing Mrs. Eversley, he crawled to her and catching hold of her white robe, begged her to intercede for him.

"You made a slave of me after I had nursed you in the spotted sickness," she answered, "and tried to kill my husband for no fault. Through you, Hassan, I have spent all the best years of my life among savages, alone and in despair. Still, for my part, I forgive you, but oh! may I never see your face again."

Then she wrenched herself free from his grasp and went away with her daughter.

"I, too, forgive you, although you murdered my people and for twenty years made my time a torment," said Brother John, who was one of the truest Christians I have ever known. "May God forgive you also"; and he followed his wife and daughter.

Then the old king, Bausi, who had come through that battle with a slight wound, spoke, saying:

"I am glad, Red Thief, that these white people have granted you what you asked--namely, their forgiveness--since the deed is greatly to their honour and causes me and my people to think them even nobler than we did before. But, O murderer of men and woman and trafficker in children, I am judge here, not the white people. Look on your work!" and he pointed first to the lines of Zulu and Mazitu dead, and then to his burning town. "Look and remember the fate you promised to us who have never harmed you. Look! Look! Look! O Hyena of a man!"

At this point I too went away, nor did I ever ask what became of Hassan and his fellow-captives. Moreover, whenever any of the natives or Hans tried to inform me, I bade them hold their tongues.

Epilogue

I have little more to add to this record, which I fear has grown into quite a long book. Or, at any rate, although the setting of it down has amused me during the afternoons and evenings of this endless English winter, now that the spring is come again I seem to have grown weary of writing. Therefore I shall leave what remains untold to the imagination of anyone who chances to read these pages.

We were victorious, and had indeed much cause for gratitude who still lived to look upon the sun. Yet the night that followed the Battle of the Gate was a sad one, at least for me, who felt the death of my friend the foresighted hero, Mavovo, of the bombastic but faithful Sammy, and of my brave hunters more than I can say. Also the old Zulu's prophecy concerning me, that I too should die in battle, weighed upon me, who seemed to have seen enough of such ends in recent days and to desire one more tranquil.

Living here in peaceful England as I do now, with no present prospect of leaving it, it does not appear likely that it will be fulfilled. Yet, after my experience of the divining powers of Mavovo's "Snake"-- well, those words of his make me feel uncomfortable. For when all is said and done, who can know the future? Moreover, it is the improbable that generally happens.

Further, the climatic conditions were not conducive to cheerfulness, for shortly after sunset it began to rain and poured for most of the night, which, as we had little shelter, was inconvenient both to us and to all the hundreds of the homeless Mazitu.

However, the rain ceased in due time, and on the following morning the welcome sun shone out of a clear sky. When we had dried and warmed ourselves a little in its rays, someone suggested that we should visit the burned-out town where, except for some smouldering heaps that had been huts, the fire was extinguished by the heavy rain. More from curiosity than for any other reason I consented and accompanied by Bausi, Babemba and many of the Mazitu, all of us, except Brother John, who remained behind to attend to the wounded, climbed over the debris of the south gate and walked through the black ruins of the huts, across the market-place that was strewn with dead, to what had been our own quarters.

These were a melancholy sight, a mere heap of sodden and still smoking ashes. I could have wept when I looked at them, thinking of all the trade goods and stores that were consumed beneath, necessities for the most part, the destruction of which must make our return journey one of great hardship.

Well, there was nothing to be said or done, so after a few minutes of contemplation we turned to continue our walk through what had been the royal quarters to the north gate. Hans, who, I noted, had been ferreting about in his furtive way as though he were looking for something, and I were the last to leave. Suddenly he laid his hand upon my arm and said:

"Baas, listen! I hear a ghost. I think it is the ghost of Sammy asking us to bury him."

"Bosh!" I answered, and then listened as hard as I could.

Now I also seemed to hear something coming from I knew not where, words which were frequently repeated and which seemed to be:

"O Mr. Quatermain, I beg you to be so good as to open the door of this oven"

For a while I thought I must be cracked. However, I called back the others and we all listened. Of a sudden Hans made a pounce, like a terrier does at the run of a mole that he hears working underground, and began to drag, or rather to shovel, at a heap of ashes in front of us, using a bit of wood as they were still too hot for his hands. Then we listened again and this time heard the voice quite clearly coming from the ground.

"Baas," said Hans, "it is Sammy in the corn-pit!"

Now I remembered that such a pit existed in front of the huts which, although empty at the time, was, as is common among the Bantu natives, used to preserve corn that would not immediately be needed. Once I myself went through a very tragic experience in one of these pits, as any who may read the history of my first wife, that I have called *Marie*, can see for themselves.

Soon we cleared the place and had lifted the stone, with ventilating holes in it--well was it for Sammy that those ventilating holes existed; also that the stone did not fit tight. Beneath was a bottle-shaped and cemented structure about ten feet deep by, say, eight wide. Instantly through the mouth of this structure appeared the head of Sammy with his mouth wide open like that of a fish gasping for air. We pulled him out, a process that caused him to howl, for the heat had made his skin very tender, and gave him water which one of the Mazitu fetched from a spring. Then I asked him indignantly what he was doing in that hole, while we wasted our tears, thinking that he was dead.

"Oh! Mr. Quatermain," he said, "I am a victim of too faithful service. To abandon all these valuable possessions of yours to a rapacious enemy was more than I could bear. So I put every one of them in the pit, and then, as I thought I heard someone coming, got in myself and pulled down the stone. But, Mr. Quatermain, soon afterwards the enemy added arson to murder and pillage, and the whole place began to blaze. I could hear the fire roaring above and a little later the ashes covered the exit so that I could no longer lift the stone, which indeed grew too hot to touch. Here, then, I sat all night in the most suffocating heat, very much afraid, Mr. Quatermain, lest the two kegs of gunpowder that were with me should explode, till at last, just as I had abandoned hope and prepared to die like a tortoise baked alive by a bushman, I heard your welcome voice. And Mr. Quatermain, if there is any soothing ointment to spare, I shall be much obliged, for I am scorched all over."

"Ah! Sammy, Sammy," I said, "you see what comes of cowardice? On the hill with us you would not have been scorched, and it is only by the merest chance of owing to Hans's quick hearing that you were not left to perish miserably in that hole."

"That is so, Mr. Quatermain. I plead guilty to the hot impeachment. But on the hill I might have been shot, which is worse than being scorched. Also you gave me charge of your goods and I determined to preserve them even at the risk of personal comfort. Lastly, the angel who watches me brought you here in time before I was quite cooked through. So all's well that ends well, Mr. Quatermain, though it is true that for my part I have had enough of bloody war, and if I live to regain civilized regions I propose henceforth to follow the art of food-dressing in the safe kitchen of an hotel; that is, if I cannot obtain a berth as an instructor in the English tongue!"

"Yes," I answered, "all's well that ends well, Sammy my boy, and at any rate you have saved the stores, for which we should be thankful to you. So go along with Mr. Stephen and get doctored while we haul them out of that grain-pit."

Three days later we bid farewell to old Bausi, who almost wept at parting with us, and the Mazitu, who were already engaged in the re-building of their town. Mavovo and the other Zulus who died in the Battle of the Gate, we buried on the ridge opposite to it, raising a mound of earth over them that thereby they might be remembered in generations to come, and laying around them the Mazitu who had fallen in the fight. As we passed that mound on our homeward journey, the Zulus who remained alive, including two wounded men who were carried in litters, stopped and saluted solemnly, praising the dead with loud songs. We white people too saluted, but in silence, by raising our hats.

By the why, I should add that in this matter also Mavovo's "Snake" did not lie. He had said that six of his company would be killed upon our expedition, and six were killed, neither more nor less.

After much consulting we determined to take the overland route back to Natal, first because it was always possible that the slave-trading fraternity, hearing of their terrible losses, might try to attack us again on the coast, and secondly for the reason that even if they did not, months or perhaps years might pass before we found a ship at Kilwa, then a port of ill repute, to carry us to any civilized place. Moreover, Brother John, who had travelled it, knew the inland road well and had established friendly relations with the tribes through whose country we must pass, till we reached the brothers of Zululand, where I was always welcome. So as the Mazitu furnished us with an escort and plenty of bearers for the first part of the road and, thanks to Sammy's stewardship in the corn-pit, we had ample trade goods left to hire others later on, we made up our minds to risk the longer journey.

As it turned out this was a wise conclusion, since although it took four weary months, in the end we accomplished it without any accident whatsoever, if I except a slight attack of fever from which both Miss Hope and I suffered for a while. Also we got some good shooting on the road. My only regret was that this change of plan obliged us to abandon the tusks of ivory we had captured from the slavers and buried where we alone could find them.

Still, it was a dull time for me, who, for obvious reasons, of which I have already spoken, was literally a fifth wheel to the coach. Hans was an excellent fellow, and, as the reader knows, quite a genius in his own way, but night after night in Hans's society began to pall on me at last, while even his conversation about my "reverend father," who seemed positively to haunt him, acquired a certain sameness. Of course, we had other subjects in common, especially those connected with Retief's massacre, whereof we were the only two survivors, but of these I seldom cared to speak. They were and still remain too painful.

Therefore, for my part I was thankful when at last, in Zululand, we fell in with some traders whom I knew, who hired us one of their wagons. In this vehicle, abandoning the worn-out donkeys and the white ox, which we presented to a chief of my acquaintance, Brother John and the ladies proceeded to Durban, Stephen attending them on a horse that we had bought, while I, with Hans, attached myself to the traders.

At Durban a surprise awaited us since, as we trekked into the town, which at that time was still a small place, whom should we meet but Sir Alexander Somers, who, hearing that wagons were coming from Zululand, had ridden out in the hope of obtaining news of us. It seemed that the choleric old gentleman's anxiety concerning his son had so weighed on his mind that at length he made up his mind to proceed to Africa to hunt for him. So there he was. The meeting between the two was affectionate but peculiar.

"Hullo, dad!" said Stephen. "Whoever would have thought of seeing you here?"

"Hullo, Stephen," said his father. "Whoever would have expected to find you alive and looking well--yes, very well? It is more than you deserve, you young ass, and I hope you won't do it again."

Having delivered himself thus, the old boy seized Stephen by the hair and solemnly kissed him on the brow.

"No, dad," answered his son, "I don't mean to do it again, but thanks to Allan there we've come through all right. And, by the way, let me introduce you to the lady I am going to marry, also to her father and mother."

Well, all the rest may be imagined. They were married a fortnight later in Durban and a very pleasant affair it was, since Sir Alexander, who by the way, treated me most handsomely from a business point of view, literally entertained the whole town on that festive occasion. Immediately afterwards Stephen, accompanied by Mr. and Mrs. Eversley and his father, took his wife home "to be educated," though what that process consisted of I never heard. Hans and I saw them off at the Point and our parting was rather sad, although Hans went back the richer by the £500 which Stephen had promised him. He bought a farm with the money, and on the strength of his exploits, established himself as a kind of little chief. Of whom more later--as they say in the pedigree books.

Sammy, too, was set up as the proprietor of a small hotel, where he spent most of his time in the bar dilating to the customers in magnificent sentences that reminded me of the style of a poem called "The Essay on Man" (which I once tried to read and couldn't), about his feats as a warrior among the wild Mazitu and the man-eating, devil-worshipping Pongo tribes.

Two years or less afterwards I received a letter, from which I must quote a passage:

"As I told you, my father has given a living which he owns to Mr. Eversley, a pretty little place where there isn't much for a parson to do. I think it rather bores my respected parents-in-law. At any rate, 'Dogeetah' spends a lot of his time wandering about the New Forest, which is near by, with a butterfly-net and trying to imagine that he is back in Africa. The 'Mother of the Flower' (who, after a long course of boot-kissing mutes, doesn't get on with English servants) has another amusement. There is a small lake in the Rectory grounds in which is a little island. Here she has put up a reed fence round a laurustinus bush which flowers at the same time of year as did the Holy Flower, and within this reed fence she sits whenever the weather will allow, as I believe going through 'the rites of the Flower.' At least when I called upon her there one day, in a boat, I found her wearing a white robe and singing some mystical native song."

Many years have gone by since then. Both Brother John and his wife have departed to their rest and their strange story, the strangest almost of all stories, is practically forgotten. Stephen, whose father has also departed, is a prosperous baronet and rather heavy member of Parliament and magistrate, the father of many fine children, for the Miss Hope of old days has proved as fruitful as a daughter of the Goddess of Fertility, for that was the "Mother's" real office, ought to be.

"Sometimes," she said to me one day with a laugh, as she surveyed a large (and noisy) selection of her numerous offspring, "sometimes, O Allan"--she still retains that trick of speech--"I wish that I were back in the peace of the Home of the Flower. Ah!" she added with something of a thrill in her voice, "never can I forget the blue of the sacred lake or the sight of those skies at dawn. Do you think that I shall see them again when I die, O Allan?"

At the time I thought it rather ungrateful of her to speak thus, but after all human nature is a queer thing and we are all of us attached to the scenes of our childhood and long at times again to breathe our natal air.

I went to see Sir Stephen the other day, and in his splendid greenhouses the head gardener, Woodden, an old man now, showed me three noble, long-leaved plants which sprang from the seed of the Holy Flower that I had saved in my pocket.

But they have not yet bloomed.

Somehow I wonder what will happen when they do. It seems to me as though when once more the glory of that golden bloom is seen of the eyes of men, the ghosts of the terrible god of the Forest, of the hellish and mysterious Motombo, and perhaps of the Mother of the Flower herself, will be there to do it reverence. If so, what gifts will they bring to those who stole and reared the sacred seed?

P.S.--I shall know ere long, for just as I laid down my pen a triumphant epistle from Stephen was handed to me in which he writes excitedly that at length two of the three plants are *showing for flower*.

Allan Quatermain.

Finished

Dedication

Ditchingham House, Norfolk, May, 1917.

My dear Roosevelt,—

You are, I know, a lover of old Allan Quatermain, one who understands and appreciates the views of life and the aspirations that underlie and inform his manifold adventures.

Therefore, since such is your kind wish, in memory of certain hours wherein both of us found true refreshment and companionship amidst the terrible anxieties of the World's journey along that bloodstained road by which alone, so it is decreed, the pure Peak of Freedom must be scaled, I dedicate to you this tale telling of the events and experiences of my youth.

Your sincere friend,

H. Rider Haggard.

To Colonel Theodore Roosevelt, Sagamore Hill, U.s.a.

Table of Contents:

Introduction

This book, although it can be read as a separate story, is the third of the trilogy of which *Marie* and *Child of Storm* are the first two parts. It narrates, through the mouth of Allan Quatermain, the consummation of the vengeance of the wizard Zikali, alias The Opener of Roads, or "The-Thing-that-should-never-have-been-born," upon the royal Zulu House of which Senzangacona was the founder and Cetewayo, our enemy in the war of 1879, the last representative who ruled as a king. Although, of course, much is added for the purposes of romance, the main facts of history have been adhered to with some faithfulness.

With these the author became acquainted a full generation ago, Fortune having given him a part in the events that preceded the Zulu War. Indeed he believes that with the exception of Colonel Phillips, who, as a lieutenant, commanded the famous escort of twenty-five policemen, he is now the last survivor of the party who, under the leadership of Sir Theophilus Shepstone, or Sompesu as the natives called him from the Zambesi to the Cape, were concerned in the annexation of the Transvaal in 1877. Recently also he has been called upon as a public servant to revisit South Africa and took the opportunity to travel through Zululand, in order to refresh his knowledge of its people, their customs, their mysteries, and better to prepare himself for the writing of this book. Here he stood by the fatal Mount of Isandhlwana which, with some details of the battle, is described in these pages, among the graves of many whom once he knew, Colonels Durnford, Pulleine and others. Also he saw Ulundi's plain where the traces of war still lie thick, and talked with an old Zulu who fought in the attacking Impi until it crumbled away before the fire of the Martinis and shells from the heavy guns. The battle of the Wall of Sheet Iron, he called it, perhaps because of the flashing fence of bayonets.

Lastly, in a mealie patch, he found the spot on which the corn grows thin, where King Cetewayo breathed his last, poisoned without a doubt, as he has known for many years. It is to be seen at the Kraal, ominously named Jazi or, translated into English, "Finished." The tragedy happened long ago, but even now the quiet-faced Zulu who told the tale, looking about him as he spoke, would not tell it all. "Yes, as a young man, I was there at the time, but I do not remember, I do not know—the Inkoosi Lundanda (i.e. this Chronicler, so named in past years by the Zulus) stands on the very place where the king died—His bed was on the left of the door-hole of the hut," and so forth, but no certain word as to the exact reason of this sudden and violent death or by whom it was caused. The name of that destroyer of a king is for ever hid.

In this story the actual and immediate cause of the declaration of war against the British Power is represented as the appearance of the white goddess, or spirit of the Zulus, who is, or was, called Nomkubulwana or Inkosazana-y-Zulu, i.e. the Princess of Heaven. The exact circumstances which led to this decision are not now ascertainable, though it is known that there was much difference of opinion among the Zulu Indunas or great captains, and like the writer, many believe that King Cetewayo was personally averse to war against his old allies, the English.

The author's friend, Mr. J. Y. Gibson, at present the representative of the Union in Zululand, writes in his admirable history: "There was a good deal of discussion amongst the assembled Zulu notables at Ulundi, but of how counsel was swayed it is not possible now to obtain a reliable account."

The late Mr. F. B. Fynney, F.R.G.S., who also was his friend in days bygone, and, with the exception of Sir Theophilus Shepstone, who perhaps knew the Zulus and their language better than any other official of his day, speaking of this fabled goddess wrote: "I remember that just before the Zulu War Nomkubulwana appeared revealing something or other which had a great effect throughout the land."

The use made of this strange traditional Guardian Angel in the following tale is not therefore an unsupported flight of fancy, and the same may be said of many other incidents, such as the account of the reading of the proclamation annexing the Transvaal at Pretoria in 1877, which have been introduced to serve the purposes of the romance.

Mameena, who haunts its pages, in a literal as well as figurative sense, is the heroine of *Child of Storm*, a book to which she gave her own poetic title.

1916. The Author.

Allan Quatermain Meets Anscombe

You, my friend, into whose hand, if you live, I hope these scribblings of mine will pass one day, must well remember the 12th of April of the year 1877 at Pretoria. Sir Theophilus Shepstone, or Sompesu, for I prefer to call him by his native name, having investigated the affairs of the Transvaal for a couple of months or so, had made up his mind to annex that country to the British Crown. It so happened that I, Allan Quatermain, had been on a shooting and trading expedition at the back of the Lydenburg district where there was plenty of game to be killed in those times. Hearing that great events were toward I made up my mind, curiosity being one of my weaknesses, to come round by Pretoria, which after all was not very far out of my way, instead of striking straight back to Natal. As it chanced I reached the town about eleven o'clock on this very morning of the 12th of April and, trekking to the Church Square, proceeded to outspan there, as was usual in the Seventies. The place was full of people, English and Dutch together, and I noted that the former seemed very elated and were talking excitedly, while the latter for the most part appeared to be sullen and depressed.

Presently I saw a man I knew, a tall, dark man, a very good fellow and an excellent shot, named Robinson. By the way you knew him also, for afterwards he was an officer in the Pretoria Horse at the time of the Zulu war, the corps in which you held a commission. I called to him and asked what was up.

"A good deal, Allan," he said as he shook my hand. "Indeed we shall be lucky if all isn't up, or something like it, before the day is over. Shepstone's Proclamation annexing the Transvaal is going to be read presently."

I whistled and asked,

"How will our Boer friends take it? They don't look very pleased."

"That's just what no one knows, Allan. Burgers the President is squared, they say. He is to have a pension; also he thinks it the only thing to be done. Most of the Hollanders up here don't like it, but I doubt whether they will put out their hands further than they can draw them back. The question is—what will be the line of the Boers themselves? There are a lot of them about, all armed, you see, and more outside the town."

"What do you think?"

"Can't tell you. Anything may happen. They may shoot Shepstone and his staff and the twenty-five policemen, or they may just grumble and go home. Probably they have no fixed plan."

"How about the English?"

"Oh! we are all crazy with joy, but of course there is no organization and many have no arms. Also there are only a few of us."

"Well," I answered, "I came here to look for excitement, life having been dull for me of late, and it seems that I have found it. Still I bet you those Dutchmen do nothing, except protest. They are slim and know that the shooting of an unarmed mission would bring England on their heads."

"Can't say, I am sure. They like Shepstone who understands them, and the move is so bold that it takes their breath away. But as the Kaffirs say, when a strong wind blows a small spark will make the whole veld burn. It just depends upon whether the spark is there. If an Englishman and a Boer began to fight for instance, anything might happen. Goodbye, I have got a message to deliver. If things go right we might dine at the European tonight, and if they don't, goodness knows where we shall dine."

I nodded sagely and he departed. Then I went to my wagon to tell the boys not to send the oxen off to graze at present, for I feared lest they should be stolen if there were trouble, but to keep them tied to the trek-tow. After this I put on the best coat and hat I had, feeling that as an Englishman it was my duty to look decent on such an occasion, washed, brushed my hair—with me a ceremony without meaning, for it always sticks up—and slipped a loaded Smith & Wesson revolver into my inner poacher pocket. Then I started out to see the fun, and avoiding the groups of surly-looking Boers, mingled with the crowd that I saw was gathering in front of a long, low building with a broad stoep, which I supposed, rightly, to be one of the Government offices.

Presently I found myself standing by a tall, rather loosely-built man whose face attracted me. It was clean-shaven and much bronzed by the sun, but not in any way good-looking; the features were too irregular and the nose was a trifle too long for good looks. Still the impression it gave was pleasant and the steady blue eyes had that twinkle in them which suggests humour. He might have been thirty or thirty-five years of age, and notwithstanding his rough dress that consisted mainly of a pair of trousers held up by a belt to which hung a pistol, and a common flannel shirt, for he wore no coat, I guessed at once that he was English-born.

For a while neither of us said anything after the taciturn habit of our people even on the veld, and indeed I was fully occupied in listening to the truculent talk of a little party of mounted Boers behind us. I put my pipe into my mouth and began to hunt for my tobacco, taking the opportunity to show the hilt of my revolver, so that these men might see that I was armed. It was not to be found, I had left it in the wagon.

"If you smoke Boer tobacco," said the stranger, "I can help you," and I noted that the voice was as pleasant as the face, and knew at once that the owner of it was a gentleman.

"Thank you, Sir. I never smoke anything else," I answered, whereon he produced from his trousers pocket a pouch made of lion skin of unusually dark colour.

"I never saw a lion as black as this, except once beyond Buluwayo on the borders of Lobengula's country," I said by way of making conversation.

"Curious," answered the stranger, "for that's where I shot the brute a few months ago. I tried to keep the whole skin but the white ants got at it."

"Been trading up there?" I asked.

"Nothing so useful," he said. "Just idling and shooting. Came to this country because it was one of the very few I had never seen, and have only been here a year. I think I have had about enough of it, though. Can you tell me of any boats running from Durban to India? I should like to see those wild sheep in Kashmir."

I told him that I did not know for certain as I had never taken any interest in India, being an African elephant-hunter and trader, but I thought they did occasionally. Just then Robinson passed by and called to me—

"They'll be here presently, Quatermain, but Sompesu isn't coming himself."

"Does your name happen to be Allan Quatermain?" asked the stranger. "If so I have heard plenty about you up in Lobengula's country, and of your wonderful shooting."

"Yes," I replied, "but as for the shooting, natives always exaggerate."

"They never exaggerated about mine," he said with a twinkle in his eye. "Anyhow I am very glad to see you in the flesh, though in the spirit you rather bored me because I heard too much of you. Whenever I made a particularly, bad miss, my gun-bearer, who at some time seems to have been yours, would say, 'Ah! if only it had been the Inkosi Macumazahn, how different would have been the end!' My name is Anscombe, Maurice Anscombe," he added rather shyly. (Afterwards I discovered from a book of reference that he was a younger son of Lord Mountford, one of the richest peers in England.)

Then we both laughed and he said—

"Tell me, Mr. Quatermain, if you will, what those Boers are saying behind us. I am sure it is something unpleasant, but as the only Dutch I know is 'Guten Tag' and 'Vootsack' (Good-day and Get out) that takes me no forwarder."

"It ought to," I answered, "for the substance of their talk is that they object to be 'vootsacked' by the British Government as represented by Sir Theophilus Shepstone. They are declaring that they won the land 'with their blood' and want to keep their own flag flying over it."

"A very natural sentiment," broke in Anscombe.

"They say that they wish to shoot all damned Englishmen, especially Shepstone and his people, and that they would make a beginning now were they not afraid that the damned English Government, being angered, would send thousands of damned English rooibatjes, that is, red-coats, and shoot *them* out of evil revenge."

"A very natural conclusion," laughed Anscombe again, "which I should advise them to leave untested. Hush! Here comes the show."

I looked and saw a body of blackcoated gentlemen with one officer in the uniform of a Colonel of Engineers, advancing slowly. I remember that it reminded me of a funeral procession following the corpse of the Republic that had gone on ahead out of sight. The procession arrived upon the stoep opposite to us and began to sort itself out, whereon the English present raised a cheer and the Boers behind us cursed audibly. In the middle appeared an elderly gentleman with whiskers and a stoop, in whom I recognized Mr. Osborn, known by the Kaffirs as Malimati, the Chief of the Staff. By his side was a tall young fellow, yourself, my friend, scarcely more than a lad then, carrying papers. The rest stood to right and left in a formal line. *You* gave a printed document to Mr. Osborn who put on his glasses and began to read in a low voice which few could hear, and I noticed that his hand trembled. Presently he grew confused, lost his place, found it, lost it again and came to a full stop.

"A nervous-natured man," remarked Mr. Anscombe. "Perhaps he thinks that those gentlemen are going to shoot."

"That wouldn't trouble him," I answered, who knew him well. "His fears are purely mental."

That was true since I know that this same Sir Melmoth Osborn as he is now, as I have told in the book I called *Child of Storm*, swam the Tugela alone to watch the battle of Indondakasuka raging round him, and on another occasion killed two Kaffirs rushing at him with a right and left shot without turning a hair. It was reading this paper that paralyzed him, not any fear of what might happen.

There followed a very awkward pause such as occurs when a man breaks down in a speech. The members of the Staff looked at him and at each other, then behold! you, my friend, grabbed the paper from his hand and went on reading it in a loud clear voice.

"That young man has plenty of nerve," said Mr. Anscombe.

"Yes," I replied in a whisper. "Quite right though. Would have been a bad omen if the thing had come to a stop."

Well, there were no more breakdowns, and at last the long document was finished and the Transvaal annexed. The Britishers began to cheer but stopped to listen to the formal protest of the Boer Government, if it could be called a government when everything had collapsed and the officials were being paid in postage stamps. I can't remember whether this was read by President Burgers himself or by the officer who was called State Secretary. Anyway, it was read, after which there came an awkward pause as though people were waiting to see something happen. I looked round at the Boers who were muttering and handling their rifles uneasily. Had they found a leader I really think that some of the wilder spirits among them would have begun to shoot, but none appeared and the crisis passed.

The crowd began to disperse, the English among them cheering and throwing up their hats, the Dutch with very sullen faces. The Commissioner's staff went away as it had come, back to the building with blue gums in front of it, which afterwards became Government House, that is all except you. You started across the square alone with a bundle of printed proclamations in your hand which evidently you had been charged to leave at the various public offices.

"Let us follow him," I said to Mr. Anscombe. "He might get into trouble and want a friend."

He nodded and we strolled after you unostentatiously. Sure enough you nearly did get into trouble. In front of the first office door to which you came, stood a group of Boers, two of whom, big fellows, drew together with the evident intention of barring your way.

"Mynheeren," you said, "I pray you to let me pass on the Queen's business."

They took no heed except to draw closer together and laugh insolently. Again you made your request and again they laughed. Then I saw you lift your leg and deliberately stamp upon the foot of one of the Boers. He drew back with an exclamation, and for a moment I believed that he or his fellow was going to do something violent. Perhaps they thought better of it, or perhaps they saw us two Englishmen behind and noticed Anscombe's pistol. At any rate you marched into the office triumphant and delivered your document.

"Neatly done," said Mr. Anscombe.

"Rash," I said, shaking my head, "very rash. Well, he's young and must be excused."

But from that moment I took a great liking to you, my friend, perhaps because I wondered whether in your place I should have been daredevil enough to act in the same way. For you see I am English, and I like to see an Englishman hold his own against odds and keep up the credit of the country. Although, of course, I sympathized with the Boers who, through their own fault, were losing their land without a blow struck. As you know well, for you were living near Majuba at the time, plenty of blows were struck afterwards, but of that business I cannot bear to write. I wonder how it will all work out after I am dead and if I shall ever learn what happens in the end.

Now I have only mentioned this business of the Annexation and the part you played in it, because it was on that occasion that I became acquainted with Anscombe. For you have nothing to do with this story which is about the destruction of the Zulus, the accomplishment of the vengeance of Zikali the wizard at the kraal named Finished, and incidentally, the love affairs of two people in which that old wizard took a hand, as I did to my sorrow.

It happened that Mr. Anscombe had ridden on ahead of his wagons which could not arrive at Pretoria for a day or two, and as he found it impossible to get accommodation at the European or elsewhere, I offered to let him sleep in mine, or rather alongside in a tent I had. He accepted and soon we became very good friends. Before the day was as out I discovered that he had served in a crack cavalry regiment, but resigned his commission some years before. I asked him why.

"Well," he said, "I came into a good lot of money on my mother's death and could not see a prospect of any active service. While the regiment was abroad I liked the life well enough, but at home it bored me. Too much society for my taste, and that sort of thing. Also I wanted to travel; nothing else really amuses me."

"You will soon get tired of it," I answered, "and as you are well off, marry some fine lady and settle down at home."

"Don't think so. I doubt if I should ever be happily married, I want too much. One doesn't pick up an earthly angel with a cast-iron constitution who adores you, which are the bare necessities of marriage, under every bush." Here I laughed. "Also," he added, the laughter going out of his eyes, "I have had enough of fine ladies and their ways."

"Marriage is better than scrapes," I remarked sententiously.

"Quite so, but one might get them both together. No, I shall never marry, although I suppose I ought as my brothers have no children."

"Won't you, my friend," thought I to myself, "when the skin grows again on your burnt fingers."

For I was sure they had been burnt, perhaps more than once. How, I never learned, for which I am rather sorry for it interests me to study burnt fingers, if they do not happen to be my own. Then we changed the subject.

Anscombe's wagons were delayed for a day or two by a broken axle or a bog hole, I forget which. So, as I had nothing particular to do until the Natal post-cart left, we spent the time in wandering about Pretoria, which did not take us long as it was but a little dorp in those days, and chatting with all and sundry. Also we went up to Government House as it was now called, and left cards, or rather wrote our names in a book for we had no cards, being told by one of the Staff whom we met that we should do so. An hour later a note arrived asking us both to dinner that night and telling us very nicely not to mind if we had no dress things. Of course we had to go, Anscombe rigged up in my second best clothes that did not fit him in the least, as he was a much taller man than I am, and a black satin bow that he had bought at Becket's Store together with a pair of shiny pumps.

I actually met you, my friend, for the first time that evening, and in trouble too, though you may have forgotten the incident. We had made a mistake about the time of dinner, and arriving half an hour too soon, were shown into a long room that opened on to the verandah. You were working there, being I believe a private secretary at the time, copying some despatch; I think you said that which gave an account of the Annexation. The room was lit by a paraffin lamp behind you, for it was quite dark and the window was open, or at any rate unshuttered. The gentleman who showed us in, seeing that you were very busy, took us to the far end of the room, where we stood talking in the shadow. Just then a door opened opposite to that which led to the verandah, and through it came His Excellency the Administrator, Sir Theophilus Shepstone, a stout man of medium height with a very clever, thoughtful face, as I have always thought, one of the greatest of African statesmen. He did not see us, but he caught sight of you and said testily—

"Are you mad?" To which you answered with a laugh—

"I hope not more than usual, Sir, but why?"

"Have I not told you always to let down the blinds after dark? Yet there you sit with your head against the light, about the best target for a bullet that could be imagined."

"I don't think the Boers would trouble to shoot me, Sir. If you had been here I would have drawn the blinds and shut the shutters too," you answered, laughing again.

"Go to dress or you will be late for dinner," he said still rather sternly, and you went. But when you had gone and after we had been announced to him, he smiled and added something which I will not repeat to you even now. I think it was about what you did on the Annexation day of which the story had come to him.

I mention this incident because whenever I think of Shepstone, whom I had known off and on for years in the way that a hunter knows a prominent Government official, it always recurs to my mind, embodying as it does his caution and appreciation of danger derived from long experience of the country, and the sternness he sometimes affected which could never conceal his love towards his friends. Oh! there was greatness in this man, although they did call him an "African Talleyrand." If it had not been so would every native from the Cape to the Zambesi have known and revered his name, as perhaps that of no other white man has been revered? But I must get on with my tale and leave historical discussions to others more fitted to deal with them.

We had a very pleasant dinner that night, although I was so ashamed of my clothes with smart uniforms and white ties all about me, and Anscombe kept fidgeting his feet because he was suffering agony from his new pumps which were a size too small. Everybody was in the best of spirits, for from all directions came the news that the Annexation was well received and that the danger of any trouble had passed away. Ah! if we had only known what the end of it would be!

It was on our way back to the wagon that I chanced to mention to Anscombe that there was still a herd of buffalo within a few days' trek of Lydenburg, of which I had shot two not a month before.

"Are there, by Jove!" he said. "As it happens I never got a buffalo; always I just missed them in one sense or another, and I can't leave Africa with a pair of bought horns. Let's go there and shoot some."

I shook my head and replied that I had been idling long enough and must try to make some money, news at which he seemed very disappointed.

"Look here," he said, "forgive me for mentioning it, but business is business. If you'll come you shan't be a loser."

Again I shook my head, whereat he looked more disappointed than before.

"Very well," he exclaimed, "then I must go alone. For kill a buffalo I will; that is unless the buffalo kills me, in which case my blood will be on your hands."

I don't know why, but at that moment there came into my mind a conviction that if he did go alone a buffalo or something would kill him and that then I should be sorry all my life.

"They are dangerous brutes, much worse than lions," I said.

"And yet you, who pretend to have a conscience, would expose me to their rage unprotected and alone," he replied with a twinkle in his eye which I could see even by moonlight." Oh! Quatermain, how I have been mistaken in your character.

"Look here, Mr. Anscombe," I said, "it's no use. I cannot possibly go on a shooting expedition with you just now. Only to-day I have heard from Natal that my boy is not well and must undergo an operation which will lay him up for quite six weeks, and may be dangerous. So I must get down to Durban before it takes place. After that I have a contract in Matabeleland whence you have just come, to take charge of a trading store there for a year; also perhaps to try to shoot a little ivory for myself. So I am fully booked up till, let us say, October, 1878, that is for about eighteen months, by which time I daresay I shall be dead."

"Eighteen months," replied this cool young man. "That will suit me very well. I will go on to India as I intended, then home for a bit and will meet you on the 1st of October, 1878, after which we will proceed to the Lydenburg district and shoot those buffalo, or if they have departed, other buffalo. Is it a bargain?"

I stared at him, thinking that the Administrator's champagne had got into his head.

"Nonsense," I exclaimed. "Who knows where you will be in eighteen months? Why, by that time you will have forgotten all about me."

"If I am alive and well, on the 1st of October, I878, I shall be exactly where I am now, upon this very square in Pretoria, with a wagon, or wagons, prepared for a hunting trip. But as not unnaturally you have doubts upon that point, I am prepared to pay forfeit if I fail, or even if circumstances cause you to fail."

Here he took a cheque-book from his letter-case and spread it out on the little table in the tent, on which there were ink and a pen, adding—

"Now, Mr. Quatermain, will it meet your views if I fill this up for £250?"

"No," I answered; "taking everything into consideration the sum is excessive. But if you do not mind facing the risks of my non-appearance, to say nothing of your own, you may make it £50."

"You are very moderate in your demands," he said as he handed me the cheque which I put in my pocket, reflecting that it would just pay for my son's operation.

"And you are very foolish in your offers," I replied. "Tell me, why do you make such crack-brained arrangements?"

"I don't quite know. Something in me seems to say that we *shall* make this expedition and that it will have a very important effect upon my life. Mind you, it is to be to the Lydenburg district and nowhere else. And now I am tired, so let's turn in."

Next morning we parted and went our separate ways.

Mr. Marnham

So much for preliminaries, now for the story.

The eighteen months had gone by, bringing with them to me their share of adventure, weal and woe, with all of which at present I have no concern. Behold me arriving very hot and tired in the post-cart from Kimberley, whither I had gone to invest what I had saved out of my Matabeleland contract in a very promising speculation whereof, today, the promise remains and no more. I had been obliged to leave Kimberly in a great hurry, before I ought indeed, because of the silly bargain which I have just recorded. Of course I was sure that I should never see Mr. Anscombe again, especially as I had heard nothing of him during all this while, and had no reason to suppose that he was in Africa. Still I had taken his £50 and he *might* come. Also I have always prided myself upon keeping an appointment.

The post-cart halted with a jerk in front of the European Hotel, and I crawled, dusty and tired, from its interior, to find myself face to face with Anscombe, who was smoking a pipe upon the stoep!

"Hullo, Quatermain," he said in his pleasant, drawling voice, "here you are, up to time. I have been making bets with these five gentlemen," and he nodded at a group of loungers on the stoep," as to whether you would or would not appear, I putting ten to one on you in drinks. Therefore you must now consume five whiskies and sodas, which will save them from consuming fifty and a subsequent appearance at the Police Court."

I laughed and said I would be their debtor to the extent of one, which was duly produced.

After it was drunk Anscombe and I had a chat. He said that he had been to India, shot, or shot at whatever game he meant to kill there, visited his relations in England and thence proceeded to keep his appointment with me in Africa. At Durban he had fitted himself out in a regal way with two wagons, full teams, and some spare oxen, and trekked to Pretoria where he had arrived a few days before. Now he was ready to start for the Lydenburg district and look for those buffalo.

"But," I said, "the buffalo probably long ago departed. Also there has been a war with Sekukuni, the Basuto chief who rules all that country, which remains undecided, although I believe some kind of a peace has been patched up. This may make hunting in this neighborhood dangerous. Why not try some other ground, to the north of the Transvaal, for instance?"

"Quatermain," he answered, "I have come all the way from England, I will not say to kill, but to try to kill buffalo in the Lydenburg district, with you if possible, if not, without you, and thither I am going. If you think it unsafe to accompany me, don't come; I will get on as best I can alone, or with some other skilled person if I can find one."

"If you put it like that I shall certainly come," I replied, "with the proviso that should the buffalo prove to be non-existent or the pursuit of them impossible, we either give up the trip, or go somewhere else, perhaps to the country at the back of Delagoa Bay."

"Agreed," he said; after which we discussed terms, he paying me my salary in advance.

On further consideration we determined, as two were quite unnecessary for a trip of the sort, to leave one of my wagons and half the cattle in charge of a very respectable man, a farmer who lived about five miles from Pretoria just over the pass near to the famous Wonder-boom tree which is one of the sights of the place. Should we need this wagon it could always be sent for; or, if we found the Lydenburg hunting-ground, which he was so set upon visiting, unproductive or impossible, we could return to Pretoria over the high-veld and pick it up before proceeding elsewhere.

These arrangements took us a couple of days or so. On the third we started, without seeing you, my friend, or any one else that I knew, since just at that time every one seemed to be away from Pretoria. You, I remember, had by now become the Master of the High Court and were, they informed me at your office, absent on circuit.

The morning of our departure was particularly lovely and we trekked away in the best of spirits, as so often happens to people who are marching into trouble. Of our journey there is little to say as everything went smoothly, so that we arrived at the edge of the high-veld feeling as happy as the country which has no history is reported to do. Our road led us past the little mining settlement of Pilgrim's Rest where a number of adventurous spirits, most of them English, were engaged in washing for gold, a job at which I once took a turn near this very place without any startling success. Of the locality I need only say that the mountainous scenery is among the most beautiful, the hills are the steepest and the roads are, or were, the worst that I have ever travelled over in a wagon.

However, "going softly" as the natives say, we negotiated them without accident and, leaving Pilgrim's Rest behind us, began to descend towards the low-veld where I was informed a herd of buffalo could still be found, since, owing to the war with Sekukuni, no one had shot at them of late. This war had been suspended for a while, and the Land-drost at Pilgrim's Rest told me he thought it would be safe to hunt on the borders of that Chief's country, though he should not care to do so himself.

Game of the smaller sort began to be plentiful about here, so not more than a dozen miles from Pilgrim's Rest we outspanned early in the afternoon to try to get a blue wildebeeste or two, for I had seen the spoor of these creatures in a patch of soft ground, or failing them some other buck. Accordingly, leaving the wagon by a charming stream that wound and gurgled over a bed of granite, we mounted our salted horses, which were part of Anscombe's outfit, and set forth rejoicing. Riding through the scattered thorns and following the spoor where I could, within half an hour we came to a little glade. There, not fifty yards away, I caught of a single blue wildebeeste bull standing in the shadow of the trees on the further side of the glade, and pointed out the ugly beast, for it is the most grotesque of all the antelopes, to Anscombe.

"Off you get," I whispered. "It's a lovely shot, you can't miss it."

"Oh, can't I!" replied Anscombe. "Do you shoot."

I refused, so he dismounted, giving me his horse to hold, and kneeling down solemnly and slowly covered the bull. Bang went his rifle, and I saw a bough about a yard above the wildebeeste fall on to its back. Off it went like lightning, whereon Anscombe let drive with the left barrel of the Express, almost at hazard as it seemed to me, and by some chance hit it above the near fore-knee, breaking its leg.

"That was a good shot," he cried, jumping on to his horse.

"Excellent," I answered. "But what are you going to do?"

"Catch it. It is cruel to leave a wounded animal," and off he started.

Of course I had to follow, but the ensuing ride remains among the more painful of my hunting memories. We tore through thorn trees that scratched my face and damaged my clothes; we struck a patch of antbear holes, into one of which my horse fell so that my stomach bumped against its head; we slithered down granite koppies, and this was the worst of it, at the end of each chapter, so to speak, always caught sight of that accursed bull which I fondly hoped would have vanished into space. At length after half an hour or so of this game we reached a stretch of open, rolling ground, and there not fifty yards ahead of us was the animal still going like a hare, though how it could do so on three legs I am sure I do not know. We coursed it like greyhounds, till at last Anscombe, whose horse was the faster, came alongside of the exhausted creature, whereon it turned suddenly and charged.

Anscombe held out his rifle in his right hand and pulled the trigger, which, as he had forgotten to reload it, was a mere theatrical performance. Next second there was such a mix-up that for a while I could not distinguish which was Anscombe, which was the wildebeeste, and which the horse. They all seemed to be going round and round in a cloud of dust. When things settled themselves a little I discovered the horse rolling on the ground, Anscombe on his back with his hands up in an attitude of prayer and the wildebeeste trying to make up its mind which of them it should finish first. I settled the poor thing's doubts by shooting it through the heart, which I flatter myself was rather clever of me under the circumstances. Then I dismounted to examine Anscombe, who, I presumed, was done for. Not a bit of it. There he sat upon the ground blowing like a blacksmith's bellows and panting out—

"What a glorious gallop. I finished it very well, didn't I? You couldn't have made a better shot yourself."

"Yes," I answered, "you finished it very well as you will find out if you will take the trouble to open your rifle and count your cartridges. I may add that if we are going to hunt together I hope you will never lead me such a fool's chase again."

He rose, opened the rifle and saw that it was empty, for although he had never re-loaded he had thrown out the two cartridges which he had discharged in the glen.

"By Jingo," he said, "you must have shot it, though I could have sworn that it was I. Quatermain, has it ever struck you what a strange thing is the human imagination?"

"Drat the human imagination," I answered, wiping away the blood that was trickling into my eye from a thorn scratch. "Let's look at your horse. If it is lamed you will have to ride Imagination back to the wagon which must be six miles away, that is if we can find it before dark."

Sighing out something about a painfully practical mind, he obeyed, and when the beast was proved to be nothing more than blown and a little bruised, made remarks as to the inadvisability of dwelling on future evil events, which I reminded him had already been better summed up in the New Testament.

After this we contemplated the carcasse of the wildebeeste which it seemed a pity to leave to rot. Just then Anscombe, who had moved a few yards to the right out of the shadow of an obstructing tree, exclaimed—

"I say, Quatermain, come here and tell me if I have been knocked silly, or if I really see a quite uncommon kind of house built in ancient Greek style set in a divine landscape."

"Temple to Diana, I expect," I remarked as I joined him on the further side of the tree.

I looked and rubbed my eyes. There, about half a mile away, situated in a bay of the sweeping hills and overlooking the measureless expanse of bush-veld beneath, was a remarkable house, at least for those days and that part of Africa. To begin with the situation was superb. It stood on a green and swelling mound behind which was a wooded kloof where ran a stream that at last precipitated itself in a waterfall over a great cliff. Then in front was that glorious view of the bush-veld, at which a man might look for a lifetime and not grow tired, stretching away to the Oliphant's river and melting at last into the dim line of the horizon.

The house itself also, although not large, was of a kind new to me. It was deep, but narrow fronted, and before it were four columns that carried the roof which projected so as to form a wide verandah. Moreover it seemed to be built of marble which glistened like snow in the setting sun. In short in that lonely wilderness, at any rate from this distance, it did look like the deserted shrine of some forgotten god.

"Well, I'm bothered!" I said.

"So am I," answered Anscombe, "to know the name of the Lydenburg district architect whom I should like to employ; though I suspect it is the surroundings that make the place look so beautiful. Hullo! here comes somebody, but he doesn't look like an architect; he looks like a wicked baronet disguised as a Boer."

True enough, round a clump of bush appeared an unusual looking person, mounted on a very good horse. He was tall, thin and old, at least he had a long white beard which suggested age, although his figure, so far as it could be seen beneath his rough clothes, seemed vigorous. His face was clean cut and handsome, with a rather hooked nose, and his eyes were grey, but as I saw when he came up to us, somewhat bloodshot at the corners. His general aspect was refined and benevolent, and as soon as he opened his mouth I perceived that he was a person of gentle breeding.

And yet there was something about him, something in his atmosphere, so to speak, that I did not like. Before we parted that evening I felt sure that in one way or another he was a wrong-doer, not straight; also that he had a violent temper.

He rode up to us and asked in a pleasant voice, although the manner of his question, which was put in bad Dutch, was not pleasant,

"Who gave you leave to shoot on our land?"

"I did not know that any leave was required; it is not customary in these parts," I answered politely in English. "Moreover, this buck was wounded miles away."

"Oh!" he exclaimed in the same tongue, "that makes a difference, though I expect it was still on our land, for we have a lot; it is cheap about here." Then after studying a little, he added apologetically, "You mustn't think me strange, but the fact is my daughter hates things to be killed near the house, which is why there's so much game about."

"Then pray make her our apologies," said Anscombe, "and say that it shall not happen again."

He stroked his long beard and looked at us, for by now he had dismounted, then said—

"Might I ask you gentlemen your names?"

"Certainly," I replied. "I am Allan Quatermain and my friend is the Hon. Maurice Anscombe."

He started and said—

"Of Allan Quatermain of course I have heard. The natives told me that you were trekking to those parts; and if you, sir, are one of Lord Mountford's sons, oddly enough I think I must have known your father in my youth. Indeed I served with him in the Guards."

"How very strange," said Anscombe. "He's dead now and my brother is Lord Mountford. Do you like life here better than that in the Guards? I am sure I should."

"Both of them have their advantages," he answered evasively, "of which, if, as I think, you are also a soldier, you can judge for yourself. But won't you come up to the house? My daughter Heda is away, and my partner Mr. Rodd" (as he mentioned this name I saw a blue vein, which showed above his cheek bone, swell as though under pressure of some secret emotion) "is a retiring sort of a man—indeed some might think him sulky until they came to know him. Still, we can make you comfortable and even give you a decent bottle of wine."

"No, thank you very much," I answered, "we must get back to the wagon or our servants will think that we have come to grief. Perhaps you will accept the wildebeeste if it is of any use to you."

"Very well," he said in a voice that suggested regret struggling with relief. To the buck he made no allusion, perhaps because he considered that it was already his own property. "Do you know your way? I believe your wagon is camped out there to the east by what we call the Granite stream. If you follow this Kaffir path," and he pointed to a track near by, "it will take quite close."

"Where does the path run to?" I asked. "There are no kraals about, are there?"

"Oh! to the Temple, as my daughter calls our house. My partner and I are labour agents, we recruit natives for the Kimberley Mines," he said in explanation, adding,

"Where do you propose to shoot?"

I told him.

"Isn't that rather a risky district?" he said. "I think that Sekukuni will soon be giving more trouble, although there is a truce between him and the English. Still he might send a regiment to raid that way."

I wondered how our friend knew so much of Sekukuni's possible intentions, but only answered that I was accustomed to deal with natives and did not fear them.

"Ah!" he said, "well, you know your own business best. But if you should get into any difficulty, make straight for this place. The Basutos will not interfere with you here."

Again I wondered why the Basutos should look upon this particular spot as sacred, but thinking it wisest to ask no questions, I only answered—

"Thank you very much. We'll bear your invitation in mind, Mr.—"

"Marnham."

"Marnham," I repeated after him. "Good-bye and many thanks for your kindness."

"One question," broke in Anscombe, "if you will not think me rude. What is the name of the architect who designed that most romantic-looking house of yours which seems to be built of marble?"

My daughter designed it, or at least I think she copied it from some old drawing of a ruin. Also it *is* marble; there's a whole hill of the stuff not a hundred yards from the door, so it was cheaper to use than anything else. I hope you will come and see it on your way back, though it is not as fine as it appears from a distance. It would be very pleasant after all these years to talk to an English gentleman again."

Then we parted, I rather offended because he did not seem to include me in the description, he calling after us—

"Stick close to the path through the patch of big trees, for the ground is rather swampy there and it's getting dark."

Presently we came to the place he mentioned where the timber, although scattered, was quite large for South Africa, of the yellow-wood species, and interspersed wherever the ground was dry with huge euphorbias, of which the tall finger-like growths and sad grey colouring looked unreal and ghostlike in the waning light. Following the advice given to us, we rode in single file along the narrow path, fearing lest otherwise we should tumble into some bog hole, until we came to higher land covered with the scattered thorns of the country.

"Did that bush give you any particular impression?" asked Anscombe a minute or two later.

"Yes," I answered, "it gave me the impression that we might catch fever there. See the mist that lies over it," and turning in my saddle I pointed with the rifle in my hand to what looked like a mass of cotton wool over which, without permeating it, hung the last red glow of sunset, producing a curious and indeed rather unearthly effect. "I expect that thousands of years ago there was a lake yonder, which is why trees grow so big in the rich soil."

"You are curiously mundane, Quatermain," he answered. "I ask you of spiritual impressions and you dilate to me of geological formations and the growth of timber. You felt nothing in the spiritual line?"

"I felt nothing except a chill," I answered, for I was tired and hungry. "What the devil are you driving at?"

"Have you got that flask of Hollands about you, Quatermain?"

"Oh! those are the spirits you are referring to," I remarked with sarcasm as I handed it to him.

He took a good pull and replied—

"Not at all, except in the sense that bad spirits require good spirits to correct them, as the Bible teaches. To come to facts," he added in a changed voice, "I have never been in a place that depressed me more than that thrice accursed patch of bush."

"Why did it depress you?" I asked, studying him as well as I could in the fading light. To tell the truth I feared lest he had knocked his head when the wildebeeste upset him, and was suffering from delayed concussion.

"Can't tell you, Quatermain. I don't look like a criminal, do I? Well, I entered those trees feeling a fairly honest man, and I came out of them feeling like a murderer. It was as though something terrible had happened to me there; it was as though I had killed someone there. Ugh!" and he shivered and took another pull at the Hollands.

"What bosh!" I said. "Besides, even if it were to come true, I am sorry to say I've killed lots of men in the way of business and they don't bother me overmuch."

"Did you ever kill one to win a woman?"

"Certainly not. Why, that would be murder. How can you ask me such a thing? But I have killed several to win cattle," I reflected aloud, remembering my expedition with Saduko against the chief Bangu, and some other incidents in my career.

"I appreciate the difference, Quatermain. If you kill for cows, it is justifiable homicide; if you kill for women, it is murder."

"Yes," I replied, "that is how it seems to work out in Africa. You see, women are higher in the scale of creation than cows, therefore crimes committed for their sake are enormously greater than those committed for cows, which just makes the difference between justifiable homicide and murder."

"Good lord! what an argument," he exclaimed and relapsed into silence. Had he been accustomed to natives and their ways he would have understood the point much better than he did, though I admit it is difficult to explain.

In due course we reached the wagon without further trouble. While we were shielding our pipes after an excellent supper I asked Anscombe his impressions of Mr. Marnham.

"Queer cove, I think," he answered. "Been a gentleman, too, and still keeps the manners, which isn't strange if he is one of the Marnhams, for they are a good family. I wonder he mentioned having served with my father."

"It slipped out of him. Men who live a lot alone are apt to be surprised into saying things they regret afterwards, as I noticed he did. But why do you wonder?"

"Because is it happens, although I have only just recalled it, my father used to tell some story about a man named Marnham in his regiment. I can't remember the details, but it had to do with cards when high stakes were being played for, and with the striking of a superior officer in the quarrel that ensued, as a result of which the striker was requested to send in his papers."

"It may not have been the same man."

"Perhaps not, for I believe that more than one Marnham served in that regiment. But I remember my father saying, by way of excuse for the person concerned, that he had a most ungovernable temper. I think he added, that he left the country and took service in some army on the Continent. I should rather like to clear the thing up."

"It isn't probable that you will, for even if you should ever meet this Marnham again, I fancy you would find he held his tongue about his acquaintance with your father."

"I wonder what Miss Heda is like," went on Anscombe after a pause. "I am curious to see a girl who designs a house on the model of an ancient ruin."

"Well, you won't, for she's away somewhere. Besides we are looking for buffalo, not girls, which is a good thing as they are less dangerous."

I spoke thus decisively because I had taken a dislike to Mr. Marnham and everything to do with him, and did not wish to encourage the idea of further meetings.

"No, never, I suppose. And yet I feel as though I were certainly destined to see that accursed yellow-wood swamp again."

"Nonsense," I replied as I rose to turn in. Ah! if I had but known!

The Hunters Hunted

While I was taking off my boots I heard a noise of jabbering in some native tongue which I took to be Sisutu, and not wishing to go to the trouble of putting them on again, called to the driver of the wagon to find out what it was. This man was a Cape Colony Kaffir, a Fingo I think, with a touch of Hottentot in him. He was an excellent driver, indeed I do not think I have ever seen a better, and by no means a bad shot. Among Europeans he rejoiced in the name of Footsack, a Boer Dutch term which is generally addressed to troublesome dogs and means "Get out." To tell the truth, had I been his master he would have got out, as I suspected him of drinking, and generally did not altogether trust him. Anscombe, however, was fond of him because he had shown courage in some hunting adventure in Matabeleland, I think it was at the shooting of that very dark-coloured lion whose skin had been the means of making us acquainted nearly two years before. Indeed he said that on this occasion Footsack had saved his life, though from all that I could gather I do not think this was quite the case. Also the man, who had been on many hunting trips with sportsmen, could talk Dutch well and English enough to make himself understood, and therefore was useful.

He went as I bade him, and coming back presently, told me that a party of Basutos, about thirty in number, who were returning from Kimberley, where they had been at work in the mines, under the leadership of a Bastard named Karl, asked leave to camp by the wagon for the night, as they were afraid to go on to "Tampel" in the dark.

At first I could not make out what "Tampel" was, as it did not sound like a native name. Then I remembered that Mr. Marnham had spoken of his house as being called the Temple, of which, of course, Tampel was a corruption; also that he said he and his partner were labour agents.

"Why are they afraid?" I asked.

"Because, Baas, they say that they must go through a wood in a swamp, which they think is haunted by spooks, and they much afraid of spooks;" that is of ghosts.

"What spooks?" I asked.

"Don't know, Baas. They say spook of some one who has been killed."

"Rubbish," I replied. "Tell them to go and catch the spook; we don't want a lot of noisy fellows howling chanties here all night."

Then it was that Anscombe broke in in his humorous, rather drawling voice.

"How can you be so hard-hearted, Quatermain? After the supernatural terror which, as I told you, I experienced in that very place, I wouldn't condemn a kicking mule to go through it in this darkness. Let the poor devils stay; I daresay they are tired."

So I gave in, and presently saw their fires beginning to burn through the end canvas of the wagon which was unlaced because the night was hot. Also later on I woke up, about midnight I think, and heard voices talking, one of which I reflected sleepily, sounded very like that of Footsack.

Waking very early, as is my habit, I peeped out of the wagon, and through the morning mist perceived Footsack in converse with a particularly villainous-looking person. I at once concluded this must be Karl, evidently a Bastard compounded of about fifteen parts of various native bloods to one of white, who, to add to his attractions, was deeply scarred with smallpox and possessed a really alarming squint. It seemed to me that Footsack handed to this man something that looked suspiciously like a bottle of squareface gin wrapped up in dried grass, and that the man handed back to Footsack some small object which he put in his mouth.

Now, I wondered to myself, what is there of value that one who does not eat sweets would stow away in his mouth. Gold coin perhaps, or a quid of tobacco, or a stone. Gold was too much to pay for a bottle of gin, tobacco was too little, but how about the stone? What stone? Who wanted stones? Then suddenly I remembered that these people were said to come from Kimberley, and whistled to myself. Still I did nothing, principally because the mist was still so dense that although I could see the men's faces, I could not clearly see the articles which they passed to each other about two feet lower, where it still lay very thickly, and to bring any accusation against a native which he can prove to be false is apt to destroy authority. So I held my tongue and waited my chance. It did not come at once, for before I was dressed those Basutos had departed together with their leader Karl, for now that the sun was up they no longer feared the haunted bush.

It came later, thus: We were trekking along between the thorns upon a level and easy track which enabled the driver Footsack to sit upon the "voorkisse" or driving box of the wagon, leaving the lad who is called the voorlooper to lead the oxen. Anscombe was riding parallel to the wagon in the hope of killing some guineafowl for the pot (though a very poor shot with a rifle he was good with a shot-gun). I, who did not care for this small game, was seated smoking by the side of Footsack who, I noted, smelt of gin and generally showed signs of dissipation. Suddenly I said to him—

"Show me that diamond which the Bastard Karl gave you this morning in payment for the bottle of your master's drink."

It was a bow drawn at a venture, but the effect of the shot was remarkable. Had I not caught it, the long bamboo whip Footsack held would have fallen to the ground, while he collapsed in his seat like a man who has received a bullet in his stomach.

"Baas," he gasped, "Baas, how did you know?"

"I knew," I replied grandly, "in the same way that I know everything. Show me the diamond."

"Baas," he said, "it was not the Baas Anscombe's gin, it was some I bought in Pilgrim's Rest."

"I have counted the bottles in the case and know very well whose gin it was," I replied ambiguously, for the reason that I had done nothing of the sort. "Show me the diamond."

Footsack fumbled about his person, his hair, his waistcoat pockets and even his moocha, and ultimately from somewhere produced a stone which he handed to me. I looked at it, and from the purity of colour and size, judged it to be a diamond worth £200, or possibly more. After careful examination I put it into my pocket, saying,

"This is the price of your master's gin and therefore belongs to him as much as it does to anybody. Now if you want to keep out of trouble, tell me—whence came it into the hands of that man, Karl?"

"Baas," replied Footsack, trembling all over, "how do I know? He and the rest have been working at the mines; I suppose he found it there."

"Indeed! And did he find others of the same sort?"

"I think so, Baas. At least he said that he had been buying bottles of gin with such stones all the way down from Kimberley. Karl is a great drunkard, Baas, as I am sure, who have known him for years."

"That is not all," I remarked, keeping my eyes fixed on him. "What else did he say?"

"He said, Baas, that he was very much afraid of returning to the Baas Marnham whom the Kaffirs call White-beard, with only a few stones left."

"Why was he afraid?"

"Because the Baas Whitebeard, he who dwells at Tampel, is, he says, a very angry man if he thinks himself cheated, and Karl is afraid lest he should kill him as another was killed, he whose spook haunts the wood through which those silly people feared to pass last night."

"Who was killed and who killed him?" I asked.

"Baas, I don't know," replied Footsack, collapsing into sullen silence in a way that Kaffirs have when suddenly they realize that they have said too much. Nor did I press the matter further, having learned enough.

What had I learned? This: that Messrs. Marnham & Rodd were illicit diamond buyers, I.D.B.'s as they are called, who had cunningly situated themselves at a great distance from the scene of operations practically beyond the reach of civilized law. Probably they were engaged also in other nefarious dealings with Kaffirs, such as supplying them with guns wherewith to make war upon the Whites. Sekukuni had been fighting us recently, so that there would be a very brisk market for rifles. This, too, would account for Marnham's apparent knowledge of that Chief's plans. Possibly, however, he had no knowledge and only made a pretence of it to keep us out of the country.

Later on I confided the whole story and my suspicions to Anscombe, who was much interested.

"What picturesque scoundrels!" he exclaimed, "We really ought to go back to the Temple. I have always longed to meet some real live I.D.B.'s."

"It is probable that you have done that already without knowing it. For the rest, if you wish to visit that den of iniquity, you must do so alone."

"Wouldn't whited sepulchre be a better term, especially as it seems to cover dead men's bones?" he replied in his frivolous manner.

Then I asked him what he was going to do about Footsack and the bottle of gin, which he countered by asking me what I was going to do with that diamond.

"Give it to you as Footsack's master," I said, suiting the action to the word. "I don't wish to be mixed up in doubtful transactions."

Then followed a long argument as to who was the real owner of the stone, which ended in its being hidden away be produced if called for, and in Footsack, who ought have had a round dozen, receiving a scolding from his master, coupled with the threat that if he stole more gin he would be handed over to a magistrate—when we met one.

On the following day we reached the hot, low-lying veld which the herd of buffalo was said to inhabit. Next morning, however, when we were making ready to begin hunting, a Basuto Kaffir appeared who, on being questioned, said that he was one of Sekukuni's people sent to this district to look for two lost oxen. I did not believe this story, thinking it more probable that he was a spy, but asked him whether in his hunt for oxen he had come across buffalo.

He replied that he had, a herd of thirty-two of them, counting the calves, but that they were over the Oliphant's River about five-and-twenty miles away, in a valley between some outlying hills and the rugged range of mountains, beyond which was situated Sekukuni's town. Moreover, in proof of his story he showed me spoor of the beasts heading in that direction which was quite a week old.

Now for my part, as I did not think it wise to get too near to Sekukuni, I should have given them up and gone to hunt something else. Anscombe, however, was of a different opinion and pleaded hard that we should follow them. They were the only herd within a hundred miles, he said, if indeed there were any others this side of the Lebombo Mountains. As I still demurred, he suggested, in the nicest possible manner, that if I thought the business risky, I should camp somewhere with the wagon, while he went on with Footsack to look for the buffalo. I answered that I was well used to risks, which in a sense were my trade, and that as he was more or less in my charge I was thinking of him, not of myself, who was quite prepared to follow the buffalo, not only to Sekukuni's Mountains but over them. Then fearing that he had hurt my feelings, he apologized, and offered to go elsewhere if I liked. The upshot was that we decided to trek to the Oliphant's River, camp there and explore the bush on the other side on horseback, never going so far from the wagon that we could not reach it again before nightfall.

This, then, we did, outspanning that evening by the hot but beautiful river which was still haunted by a few hippopotamus and many crocodiles, one of which we shot before turning in. Next morning, having breakfasted off cold guineafowl, we mounted, crossed the river by a ford that was quite as deep as I liked, to which the Kaffir path led us, and, leaving Footsack with the two other boys in charge of the wagon, began to hunt for the buffalo in the rather swampy bush that stretched from the further bank to the slope of the first hills, eight or ten miles away. I did not much expect to find them, as the Basuto had said that they had gone over these hills, but either he lied or they had moved back again.

Not half a mile from the river bank, just as I was about to dismount to stalk a fine waterbuck of which I caught sight standing among some coarse grass and bushes, my eye fell upon buffalo spoor that from its appearance I knew could not be more than a few hours old. Evidently the beasts had been feeding here during the night and at dawn had moved away to sleep in the dry bush nearer the hills. Beckoning to Anscombe, who fortunately had not seen the waterbuck, at which he would certainly have fired, thereby perhaps frightening the buffalo, I showed him the spoor that we at once started to follow.

Soon it led us into other spoor, that of a whole herd of thirty or forty beasts indeed, which made our task quite easy, at least till we came to harder ground, for the animals had gone a long way. An hour or more later, when we were about seven miles from the river, I perceived ahead of us, for we were now almost at the foot of the hills, a cool and densely-wooded kloof.

"That is where they will be," I said. "Now come on carefully and make no noise."

We rode to the wide mouth of the kloof where the signs of the buffalo were numerous and fresh, dismounted and tied our horses to a thorn, so as to approach them silently on foot. We had not gone two hundred yards through the bush when suddenly about fifty paces away, standing broadside on in the shadow between two trees, I saw a splendid old bull with a tremendous pair of horns.

"Shoot," I whispered to Anscombe, "you will never get a better chance. It is the sentinel of the herd."

He knelt down, his face quite white with excitement, and covered the bull with his Express.

"Keep cool," I whispered again, "and aim behind the shoulder, half-way down."

I don't think he understood me, for at that moment off went the rifle. He hit the beast somewhere, as I heard the bullet clap, but not fatally, for it turned and lumbered off up the kloof, apparently unhurt, whereon he sent the second barrel after it, a clean miss this time. Then of a sudden all about us appeared buffaloes that had, I suppose, been sleeping invisible to us. These, with snorts and bellows, rushed off towards the river, for having their senses about them, they had no mind to be trapped in the kloof. I could only manage a shot at one of them, a large and long-horned cow which I knocked over quite dead. If I had fired again it would have been but to wound, a thing I hate. The whole business was over in a minute. We went and looked at my dead cow which I had caught through the heart.

"It's cruel to kill these things," I said, "for I don't know what use we are going to make of them, and they must love life as much as we do."

"We'll cut the horns off," said Anscombe.

"You may if you like," I answered, "but you will find it a tough job with a sheath knife."

"Yes, I think that shall be the task of the worthy Footsack to-morrow," he replied. "Meanwhile let us go and finish off my bull, as Footsack & Co. may as well bring home two pair of horns as one."

I looked at the dense bush, and knowing something of the habits of wounded buffaloes, reflected that it would be a nasty job. Still I said nothing, because if I hesitated, I knew he would want to go alone. So we started. Evidently the beast had been badly hit, for the blood spoor was easy to follow. Yet it had been able to retreat up to the end of the kloof that terminated in a cliff over which trickled a stream of water. Here it was not more than a hundred paces wide, and on either side of it were other precipitous cliffs. As we went from one of these a war-horn, such as the Basutos use, was blown. Although I heard it, oddly enough, I paid no attention to it at the time, being utterly intent upon the business in hand.

Following a wounded buffalo bull up a tree-clad and stony kloof is no game for children, as these beasts have a habit of returning on their tracks and then rushing out to gore you. So I went on with every sense alert, keeping Anscombe well behind me. As it happened our bull had either been knocked silly or inherited no guile from his parents. When he found he could go no further he stopped, waited behind a bush, and when he saw us he charged in a simple and primitive fashion. I let Anscombe fire, as I wished him to have the credit of killing it all to himself, but somehow or other he managed to miss both barrels. Then, trouble being imminent, I let drive as the beast lowered its head, and was lucky enough to break its spine (to shoot at the head of a buffalo is useless), so that it rolled over quite dead at our feet.

"You have got a magnificent pair of horns," I said, contemplating the fallen giant.

"Yes," answered Anscombe, with a twinkle of his humorous eyes, "and if it hadn't been for you I think that I should have got them in more senses than one."

As the words passed his lips some missile, from its peculiar sound I judged it was the leg off an iron pot, hurtled past my head, fired evidently from a smoothbore gun with a large charge of bad powder. Then I remembered the war-horn and all that it meant.

"Off you go," I said, "we are ambushed by Kaffirs."

We were indeed, for as we tailed down that kloof, from the top of both cliffs above us came a continuous but luckily ill-directed fire. Lead-coated stones, pot legs and bullets whirred and whistled all round us, yet until the last, just when we were reaching the tree to which we had tied our horses, quite harmlessly. Then suddenly I saw Anscombe begin to limp. Still he managed to run on and mount, though I observed that he did not put his right foot into the stirrup.

"What's the matter?" I asked as we galloped off."

"Shot through the instep, I think," he answered with a laugh, " but it doesn't hurt a bit."

"I expect it will later," I replied. "Meanwhile, thank God it wasn't at the top of the kloof. They won't catch us on the horses, which they never thought of killing first."

"They are going to try though. Look behind you."

I looked and saw twenty or thirty men emerging from the mouth of the kloof in pursuit.

"No time to stop to get those horns," he said with a sigh.

"No," I answered, "unless you are particularly anxious to say good-bye to the world pinned over a broken ant-heap in the sun, or something pleasant of the sort."

Then we rode on in silence, I thinking what a fool I had been first to allow myself to be overruled by Anscombe and cross the river, and secondly not to have taken warning from that war-horn. We could not go very fast because of the difficult and swampy nature of the ground; also the great heat of the day told on the horses. Thus it came about that when we reached the ford we were not more than ten minutes ahead of our active pursuers, good runners every one of them, and accustomed to the country. I suppose that they had orders to kill or capture us at any cost, for instead of giving up the chase, as I hoped they would, they stuck to us in surprising fashion.

We splashed through the river, and luckily on the further bank were met by Footsack who had seen us coming and guessed that something was wrong.

"Inspan!" I shouted to him, "and be quick about it if you want to see tomorrow's light. The Basutos are after us."

Off he went like a shot, his face quite green with fear.

"Now," I said to Anscombe, as we let our horses take a drink for which they were mad, "we have got to hold this ford until the wagon is ready, or those devils will get us after all. Dismount and I'll tie up the horses."

He did so with some difficulty, and at my suggestion, while I made the beasts fast, cut the lace of his boot which was full of blood, and soaked his wounded foot, that I had no time to examine, in the cool water. These things done, I helped him to the rear of a thorn tree which was thick enough to shield most of his body, and took my own stand behind a similar thorn at a distance of a few paces.

Presently the Basutos appeared, trotting along close together whereon Anscombe, who was seated behind the tree, fired both barrels of his Express at them at a range of about two hundred yards. It was a foolish thing to do, first because he missed them clean, for he had over-estimated the range and the bullets went above their heads, and secondly because it caused them to scatter and made them careful, whereas had they come on in a lump we could have taught them a lesson. However I said nothing, as I knew that reproaches would only make him nervous. Down went those scoundrels on to their hands and knees and, taking cover behind stones and bushes on the further bank, began to fire at us, for they were all armed with guns of one sort and another, and there was only about a hundred yards of water between us. As they effected this manoeuvre I am glad to say I was able to get two of them, while Anscombe, I think, wounded another.

After this our position grew quite warm, for as I have said the thorn trunks were not very broad, and three or four of the natives, who had probably been hunters, were by no means bad shots, though the rest of them fired wildly. Anscombe, in poking his head round the tree to shoot, had his hat knocked off by a bullet, while a slug went through the lappet of my coat. Then a worse thing happened. Either by chance or design Anscombe's horse was struck in the neck and fell struggling, whereon my beast, growing frightened, broke its riem and galloped to the wagon. That is where I ought to have left them at first, only I thought that we might need them to make a bolt on, or to carry Anscombe if he could not walk.

Quite a long while went by before, glancing behind me, I saw that the oxen that had been grazing at a little distance had at length arrived and were being inspanned in furious haste. The Basutos saw it also, and fearing lest we should escape, determined to try to end the business. Suddenly they leapt from their cover, and with more courage than I should have expected of them, rushed into the river, proposing to storm us, which, to speak truth, I think they would have done had I not been a fairly quick shot.

As it was, finding that they were losing too heavily from our fire, they retreated in a hurry, leaving their dead behind them, and even a wounded man who was clinging to a rock. He, poor wretch, was in mortal terror lest we should shoot him again, which I had not the heart to do, although as his leg was shattered above the knee by an Express bullet, it might have been true kindness. Again and again he called out for mercy, saying that he only attacked us because his chief, who had been warned of our coming "by the White Man," ordered him to take our guns and cattle.

"What white man?" I shouted. "Speak or I shoot."

There was no answer, for at this moment he fainted from loss of blood and vanished beneath the water. Then another Basuto, I suppose he was their captain, but do not know for he was hidden in some bushes, called out—

"Do not think that you shall escape, White Men. There are many more of our people coming, and we will kill you in the night when you cannot see to shoot us."

At this moment, too, Footsack shouted that the wagon was inspanned and ready. Now I hesitated what to do. If we made for the wagon, which must be very slowly because of Anscombe's wounded foot, we had to cross seventy or eighty yards of rising ground almost devoid of cover. If, on the other hand, we stayed where we were till nightfall a shot might catch one of us, or other Basutos might arrive and rush us. There was also a third possibility, that our terrified servants might trek off and leave us in order to save their own lives, which verily I believe they would have done, not being of Zulu blood. I put the problem to Anscombe, who shook his head and looked at his foot. Then he produced a lucky penny which he carried in his pocket and said—

"Let us invoke the Fates. Heads we run like heroes; tails we stay here like heroes," and he spun the penny, while I stared at him open-mouthed and not without admiration.

Never, I thought to myself, had this primitive method of cutting a gordian knot been resorted to in such strange and urgent circumstances.

"Heads it is!" he said coolly. "Now, my boy, do you run and I'll crawl after you. If I don't arrive, you know my people's address, and I bequeath to you all my African belongings in memory of a most pleasant trip."

"Don't play the fool," I replied sternly. "Come, put your right arm round my neck and hop on your left leg as you never hopped before."

Then we started, and really our transit was quite lively., for all those Basutos began what for them was rapid firing. I think, however, that their best shots must have fallen, for not a bullet touched us, although before we got out of their range one or two went very near.

"There," said Anscombe, as a last amazing hop brought him to the wagon rail, "there, you see how wise it is give Providence a chance sometimes."

"In the shape of a lucky penny," I grumbled as I hoisted him up.

"Certainly, for why should not Providence inhabit a penny as much as it does any other mundane thing? Oh, my dear Quatermain, have you never been taught to look to the pence and let the rest take care of itself?"

"Stop talking rubbish and look to your foot, for the wagon is starting," I replied.

Then off we went at a good round trot, for never have I seen oxen more scientifically driven than they were by Footsack and his friends on this occasion, or a greater pace got out of them. As soon as we reached a fairly level piece of ground I made Anscombe lie down on the cartel of the wagon and examined his wound as well as circumstances would allow. I found that the bullet or whatever the missile may have been, had gone through his right instep just beneath the big sinew, but so far as I could judge without injuring any bone. There was nothing to be done except rub in some carbolic ointment, which fortunately he had in his medicine chest, and bind up the wound as best I could with a clean handkerchief, after which I tied a towel, that was *not* clean, over the whole foot.

By this time evening was coming on, so we ate of such as we had with us, which we needed badly enough, without stopping the wagon. I remember that it consisted of cheese and hard biscuits. At dark we were obliged to halt a little by a stream until the moon rose, which fortunately she did very soon, as she was only just past her full. As soon as she was up we started again, and with a breathing space or two, trekked all that night, which I spent seated on the after part of the wagon and keeping a sharp look out, while, notwithstanding the roughness of the road and his hurt, Anscombe slept like a child upon the cartel inside.

I was very tired, so tired that the fear of surprise was the only thing that kept me awake, and I recall reflecting in a stupid kind of way, that it seemed always to have been my lot in life to watch thus, in one sense or another, while others slept.

The night passed somehow without anything happening, and at dawn we halted for a while to water the oxen, which we did with buckets, and let them eat what grass they could reach from their yokes, since we did not dare to outspan them. Just as we were starting on again the voortrekker, whom I had set to watch at a little distance, ran up with his eyes bulging out of his head, and reported that he had seen a Basuto with an assegai hanging about in the bush, as though to keep touch with us, after which we delayed no more.

All that day we blundered on, thrashing the weary cattle that at every halt tried to lie down, and by nightfall came to the outspan near to the house called the Temple, where we had met the Kaffirs returning from the diamond fields. This journey we had accomplished in exactly half the time it had taken on the outward trip. Here we were obliged to stop, as our team must have rest and food. So we outspanned and slept that night without much fear, since I thought it most improbable that the Basutos would attempt to follow us so far, as we were now within a day's trek of Pilgrim's Rest, whither we proposed to proceed on the morrow. But that is just where I made a mistake.

Doctor Rodd

I did get a little sleep that night, with one eye open, but before dawn I was up again seeing to the feeding of our remaining horse with some mealies that we carried, and other matters. The oxen we had been obliged to unyoke that they might fill themselves with grass and water, since otherwise I feared that we should never get them on to their feet again. As it was, the poor brutes were so tired that some of them could scarcely eat, and all lay down at the first opportunity.

Having awakened Footsack and the other boys that they might be ready to take advantage of the light when it came, for I was anxious to be away, I drank a nip of Hollands and water and ate a biscuit, making Anscombe do the same. Coffee would have been more acceptable, but I thought it wiser not to light a fire for fear of showing our whereabouts.

Now a faint glimmer in the east told me that the dawn was coming. Just by the wagon grew a fair-sized, green-leaved tree, and as it was quite easy to climb even by starlight, up it I went so as to get above the ground mist and take a look round before we trekked. Presently the sky grew pearly and light began to gather; then the edge of the sun appeared, throwing long level rays across the world. Everywhere the mist lay dense as cotton wool, except at one spot about a mile behind us where there was a little hill or rather a wave of the ground, over which we had trekked upon the preceding evening. The top of this rise was above mist level, and on it no trees grew because the granite came to the surface. Having discovered nothing, I called to the boys to drive up the oxen, some of which had risen and were eating again, and prepared to descend from my tree.

As I did so, out of the corner of my eye I caught sight of something that glittered far away, so far that it would only have attracted the notice of a trained hunter. Yes, something was shining on the brow of the rise of which I have spoken. I stared at it through my glasses and saw what I had feared to see. A body of natives was crossing the rise and the glitter was caused by the rays of dawn striking on their spears and gun-barrels.

I came down out of that tree like a frightened wild cat and ran to the wagon, thinking hard as I went. The Basutos were after us, meaning to attack as soon as there was sufficient light. In ten minutes or less they would be here. There was no time to inspan the oxen, and even if there had been, stiff and weary as the beasts were, we should be overtaken before we had gone a hundred yards on that bad road. What then was to be done? Run for it? It was impossible, Anscombe could not run. My eye fell upon the horse munching the last of his mealies.

"Footsack," I said as quietly as I could, "never mind about inspanning yet, but saddle up the horse. Be quick now."

He looked at me doubtfully, but obeyed, having seen nothing. If he had seen I knew that he would have been off. I nipped round to the end of the wagon, calling to the other two boys to let the oxen be a while and come to me.

"Now, Anscombe," I said, "hand out the rifles and cartridges. Don't stop to ask questions, but do what I tell you. They are on the rack by your side. So. Now put on your revolver and let me help you down. Man, don't forget your hat."

He obeyed quickly enough, and presently was standing on one leg by my side, looking cramped and tottery.

"The Basutos are on us," I said.

He whistled and remarked something about Chapter No. 2.

"Footsack," I called, "bring the horse here; the Baas wishes to ride a little to ease his leg."

He did so, stopping a moment to pull the second girth tight. Then we helped Anscombe into the saddle.

"Which way?" he asked.

I looked at the long slope in front of us. It was steep and bad going. Anscombe might get up it on the horse before the Kaffirs overtook us, but it was extremely problematical if we could do so. I might perhaps if I mounted behind him and the horse could bear us both, which was doubtful, but how about our poor servants? He saw the doubt upon my face and said in his quiet way,

"You may remember that our white-bearded friend told us to make straight for his place in case of any difficulty with the Basutos. It seems to have arisen."

"I know he did," I answered, "but I cannot make up my mind which is the more dangerous, Marnham or the Basutos. I rather think that he set them on to us."

"It is impossible to solve problems at this hour of the morning, Quatermain, and there is no time to toss. So I vote for the Temple."

"It seems our best chance. At any rate that's your choice, so let's go."

Then I sang out to the Kaffirs, "The Basutos are on us. We go to Tampel for refuge. Run!"

My word! they did run. I never saw athletes make better time over the first quarter of a mile. We ran, too, or at least the horse did, I hanging on to the stirrup and Anscombe holding both the rifles beneath his arm. But the beast was tired, also blown out with that morning feed of mealies, so our progress was not very fast. When we were about two hundred yards from the wagon I looked back and saw the Basutos beginning to arrive. They saw us also, and uttering a sort of whistling war cry, started in pursuit.

After this we had quite an interesting time. I scrambled on to the horse behind Anscombe, whereon that intelligent animal, feeling the double weight, reduced its pace proportionately, to a slow tripple, indeed, out of which it could not be persuaded to move. So I slipped off again over its tail and we went on as before. Meanwhile the Basutos, very active fellows, were coming up. By this time the yellow-wood grove in the swamp, of which I have already written, was close to us, and it became quite a question which of us would get there first (I may mention that Footsack & Co. had already attained its friendly shelter). Anscombe kicked the horse with his sound heel and I thumped it with my fist, thereby persuading it to a hand gallop.

As we reached the outlying trees of the wood the first Basuto, a lank fellow with a mouth like a rat trap, arrived and threw an assegai at us which passed between Anscombe's back and my nose. Then he closed and tried to stab with another assegai. I could do nothing, but Anscombe showed himself cleverer than I expected. Dropping the reins, he drew his pistol and managed to send a bullet through that child of nature's head, so that he went down like a stone.

"And you tell me I am a bad shot," he drawled.

"It was a fluke," I gasped, for even in these circumstances truth would prevail.

"Wait and you'll see," he replied, re-cocking the revolver.

As a matter of fact there was no need for more shooting, since at the verge of the swamp the Basutos pulled up. I do not think that the death of their companion caused them to do this, for they seemed to take no notice of him. It was as though they had reached some boundary which they knew it would not be lawful for them to pass. They simply stopped, took the dead man's assegai and shield from the body and walked quietly back towards the wagon, leaving him where he lay. The horse stopped also, or rather proceeded at a walk.

"There!" exclaimed Anscombe. "Did I not tell you I had a presentiment that I should kill a man in this accursed wood?"

"Yes," I said as soon as I had recovered my breath, "but you mixed up a woman with the matter and I don't see one."

"That's true," he replied, "I hope we shan't meet her later."

Then we went on as quickly as we could, which was not very fast, for I feared lest the Basutos should change their minds and follow us. As the risk of this became less our spirits rose, since if we had lost the wagon and the oxen, at least we had saved our lives, which was almost more than we could have expected in the circumstances. At last we came to that glade where we had killed the wildebeeste not a week before. There lay its skeleton picked clean by the great brown kites that frequent the bush-veld, some of which still sat about in the trees.

"Well, I suppose we must go on to Tampel," said Anscombe rather faintly, for I could see that his wound was giving him a good deal of pain.

As he spoke from round the tree whence he had first emerged, appeared Mr. Marnham, riding the same horse and wearing the same clothes. The only difference between his two entries was that the first took place in the late evening and the second in the early morning.

"So here you are again," he said cheerfully.

"Yes," I answered, "and it is strange to meet you at the same spot. Were you expecting us?"

"Not more than I expect many things," he replied with a shrewd glance at me, adding, "I always rise with the sun, and thinking that I heard a shot fired in the distance, came to see what was happening. The Basutos attacked you at daybreak, did they not?"

"They did, but how did you know that, Mr. Marnham?"

"Your servants told me. I met them running to the house looking very frightened. You are wounded, Mr. Anscombe?"

"Yes, a couple of days ago on the border of Sekukuni's country where the natives tried to murder us."

"Ah!" he replied without surprise. "I warned you the trip was dangerous, did I not? Well, come on home where my partner, Rodd, who luckily has had medical experience, will attend to you. Mr. Quatermain can tell me the story as we go."

So we went on up the long slope, I relating our adventures, to which Mr. Marnham listened without comment.

"I expect that the Kaffirs will have looted the wagon and be on the way home with your oxen by now," he said when I had finished.

"Are you not afraid that they will follow us here?" I asked.

"Oh no, Mr. Quatermain. We do business with these people, also they sometimes come to be doctored by Rodd when they are sick, so this place is sacred ground to them. They stopped hunting you when they got to the Yellow-wood swamp where our land begins, did they not?"

"Yes, but now I want to hunt them. Can you give me any help? Those oxen are tired out and footsore, so we might be able to catch them up."

He shook his head. "We have very few people here, and by the time that you could get assistance from the Camp at Barberton, if the Commandant is able and willing to give you any, which I rather doubt, they will be far away. Moreover," he added, dropping his voice, "let us come to an understanding. You are most welcome to any help or hospitality that I can offer, but if you wish to do more fighting I must ask you to go elsewhere. As I have told you, we are peaceful men who trade with these people, and do not wish to be involved in a quarrel with them, which might expose us to attack or bring us into trouble with the British Government which has annexed but not conquered their country. Do I make myself clear?"

"Perfectly. While we are with you we will do nothing, but afterwards we hold ourselves at liberty to act as we think best."

"Quite so. Meanwhile I hope that you and Mr. Anscombe will make yourselves comfortable with us for as long as you like."

In my own mind I came to the conclusion that this would be for the shortest time possible, but I only said—

"It is most kind of you to take in complete strangers thus. No, not complete," I added, looking towards Anscombe who was following on the tired horse a few paces behind, "for you knew his father, did you not?"

"His father?" he said, lifting his eyebrows. "No. Oh! I remember, I said something to that effect the other night, but it was a mistake. I mixed up two names, as one often does after a lapse of many years."

"I understand," I answered, but remembering Anscombe's story I reflected to myself that our venerable host was an excellent liar. Or more probably he meant to convey that he wished the subject of his youthful reminiscences to be taboo.

Just then we reached the house which had a pretty patch of well-kept flower-garden in front of it, surrounded by a fence covered with wire netting to keep out buck. By the gate squatted our three retainers, looking very blown and rather ashamed of themselves.

"Your master wishes to thank you for your help in a dark hour, Footsack, and I wish to congratulate you all upon the swiftness of your feet," I said in Dutch.

"Oh! Baas, the Basutos were many and their spears are sharp," he began apologetically.

"Be silent, you running dog," I said, "and go help your master to dismount."

Then we went through the gate, Anscombe leaning on my shoulder and on that of Mr. Marnham, and up the path which was bordered with fences of the monthly rose, towards the house. Really this was almost as charming to look at near at hand as it had been from far away. Of course the whole thing was crude in detail. Rough, half-shaped blocks of marble from the neighbouring quarry had been built into walls and columns. Nothing was finished, and considered bit by bit all was coarse and ugly. Yet the general effect was beautiful because it was an effect of design, the picture of an artist who did not fully understand the technicalities of painting, the work of a great writer who had as yet no proper skill in words. Never did I see a small building that struck me more. But then what experience have I of buildings, and, as Anscombe reminded me afterwards, it was but a copy of something designed when the world was young, or rather when civilization was young, and man new risen from the infinite ages of savagery, saw beauty in his dreams and tried to symbolize it in shapes of stone.

We came to the broad stoep, to which several rough blocks of marble served as steps. On it in a long chair made of native wood and seated with hide rimpis, sat or rather lolled a man in a dressing-gown who was reading a book. He raised himself as we came and the light of the sun, for the verandah faced to the east, shone full upon his face, so that I saw him well. It was that of a man of something under forty years of age, dark, powerful, and weary—not a good face, I thought. Indeed, it gave me the impression of one who had allowed the evil which exists in the nature of all of us to become his master, or had even encouraged it to do so.

In the Psalms and elsewhere we are always reading of the righteous and the unrighteous until those terms grow wearisome. It is only of late years that I have discovered, or think that I have discovered, what they mean. Our lives cannot be judged by our deeds; they must be judged by our desires or rather by our moral attitude. It is not what we do so much as what we try to do that counts in the formation of character. All fall short, all fail, but in the end those who seek to climb out of the pit, those who strive, however vainly, to fashion failure to success, are, by comparison, the righteous, while those who are content to wallow in our native mire and to glut themselves with the daily bread of vice, are the unrighteous. To turn our backs thereon wilfully and without cause, is the real unforgiveable sin against the Spirit. At least that is the best definition of the problem at which I in my simplicity can arrive.

Such thoughts have often occurred to me in considering the character of Dr. Rodd and some others whom I have known; indeed the germ of them arose in my mind which, being wearied at the time and therefore somewhat vacant, was perhaps the more open to external impressions, as I looked upon the face of this stranger on the stoep. Moreover, as I am proud to record, I did not judge him altogether wrongly. He was a blackguard who, under other influences or with a few added grains of self-restraint and of the power of recovery, might have become a good or even a saintly man. But by some malice of Fate or some evil inheritance from an unknown past, those grains were lacking, and therefore he went not up but down the hill.

"Case for you, Rodd," called out Marnham.

"Indeed," he answered, getting to his feet and speaking in a full voice, which, like his partner's, was that of an educated Englishman. "What's the matter. Horse accident?"

Then we were introduced, and Anscombe began to explain his injury.

"Um!" said the doctor, studying him with dark eyes. "Kaffir bullet through the foot some days ago. Ought to be attended to at once. Also you look pretty done, so don't tire yourself with the story, which I can get from Mr. Quatermain. Come and lie down and I'll have a look at you while they are cooking breakfast."

Then he guided us to a room of which the double French windows opened on to the stoep, a very pretty room with two beds in it. Making Anscombe lie down on one of these he turned up his trouser, undid my rough bandage and examined the wound.

"Painful?" he asked.

"Very," answered Anscombe, "right up to the thigh."

After this he drew off the nether garments and made a further examination.

"Um," he said again, "I must syringe this out. Stay still while I get some stuff."

I followed him from the room, and when we were out of hearing on the stoep inquired what he thought. I did not like the look of that leg.

"It is very bad," he answered, "so bad that I am wondering If it wouldn't be best to remove the limb below the knee and make it a job. You can see for yourself that it is septic and the inflammation is spreading up rapidly."

"Good Heavens!" I exclaimed, "do you fear mortification?"

He nodded. "Can't say what was on that slug or bit of old iron and he hasn't had the best chance since. Mortification, or tetanus, or both, are more than possible. Is he a temperate man?"

"So far as I know," I answered, and stared at him while he thought. Then he said with decision,

"That makes a difference. To lose a foot is a serious thing; some might think almost as bad as death. I'll give him a chance, but if those symptoms do not abate in twenty-four hours, I must operate. You needn't be afraid, I was house surgeon at a London Hospital—once, and I keep my hand in. Lucky you came straight here."

Having made his preparations and washed his hands, he returned, syringed the wound with some antiseptic stuff, and dressed and bandaged the leg up to the knee. After this he gave Anscombe hot milk to drink, with two eggs broken into it, and told him to rest a while as he must not eat anything solid at present. Then he threw a blanket over him, and, signing to me to come away, let down a mat over the window.

"I put a little something into that milk," he said outside, "which will send him to sleep for a few hours. So we will leave him quiet. Now you'll want a wash."

"Where are you going to take Mr. Quatermain?" asked Marnham who was seated on the stoep.

"Into my room," he answered.

"Why? There's Heda's ready."

"Heda might return at any moment," replied the doctor. "Also Mr. Quatermain had better sleep in Mr. Anscombe's room. He will very likely want some one to look after him at night."

Marnham opened his mouth to speak again, then changed his mind and was silent, as a servant is silent under rebuke. The incident was quite trifling, yet it revealed to me the relative attitude of these two men. Without a doubt Rodd was the master of his partner, who did not even care to dispute with him about the matter of the use of his daughter's bedroom. They were a queer couple who, had it not been for my anxiety as to Anscombe's illness, would have interested me very much, as indeed they were destined to do.

Well, I went to tidy up in the doctor's room, and as he left me alone while I washed, had the opportunity of studying it a little. Like the rest of the house it was lined with native wood which was made to serve as the backs of bookshelves and of cupboards filled with medicines and instruments. The books formed a queer collection. There were medical works, philosophical works, histories, novels, most of them French, and other volumes of a sort that I imagine are generally kept under lock and key; also some that had to do with occult matters. There was even a Bible. I opened it thoughtlessly, half in idle curiosity, to see whether it was ever used, only to replace it in haste. For at the very page that my eye fell on, I remember it was one of my favourite chapters in Isaiah, was a stamp in violet ink marked H. M.'s Prison—well, I won't say where.

I may state, however, that the clue enabled me in after years to learn an episode in this man's life which had brought about his ruin. There is no need to repeat it or to say more than that gambling and an evil use of his medical knowledge to provide the money to pay his debts, were the cause of his fall. The strange thing is that he should have kept the book which had probably been given to by the prison chaplain. Still everybody makes mistakes sometimes. Or it may have had associations for him, and of course he had never seen this stamp upon an unread page, which happened to leap to my eye.

Now I was able to make a shrewd guess at his later career. After his trouble he had emigrated and began to practise in South Africa. Somehow his identity had been discovered; his past was dragged up against him, possibly by rivals jealous of his skill; his business went and he found it advisable to retire to the Transvaal before the Annexation, at that time the home of sundry people of broken repute. Even there he did not stop in a town, but hid himself upon the edge of savagery. Here he foregathered with another man of queer character, Marnham, and in his company entered upon some doubtful but lucrative form of trade while still indulging his love of medicine by doctoring and operating upon natives, over whom he would in this way acquire great influence. Indeed, as I discovered before the day was over, he had quite a little hospital at the back of the house in which were four or five beds occupied by Kaffirs and served by two male native nurses whom he had trained. Also numbers of out-patients visited him, some of whom travelled from great distances, and occasionally, but not often, he attended white people who chanced to be in the neighbourhood.

The three of us breakfasted in a really charming room from the window of which could be studied a view as beautiful as any I know. The Kaffirs who waited were well trained and dressed in neat linen uniforms. The cooking was good; there was real silver on the table, then a strange sight in that part of Africa, and amongst engravings and other pictures upon the walls, hung an oil portrait of a very beautiful young woman with dark hair and eyes.

"Is that your daughter, Mr. Marnham?" I asked.

"No," he replied rather shortly, "it is her mother."

Immediately afterwards he was called from the room to speak to some one, whereon the doctor said—

"A foreigner as you see, a Hungarian; the Hungarian women are very good looking and very charming."

"So I have understood," I answered, "but does this lady live here?"

"Oh, no. She is dead, or I believe that she is dead. I am not sure, because I make it a rule never to pry into people's private affairs. All l know about her is that she was a beauty whom Marnham married late in life upon the Continent when she was but eighteen. As is common in such cases he was very jealous of her, but it didn't last long, as she died, or I understand that she died, within a year of her daughter's birth. The loss affected him so much that he emigrated to South Africa with the child and began life anew. I do not think that they correspond with Hungary, and he never speaks of her even to his daughter, which suggests that she is dead."

I reflected that all these circumstances might equally well suggest several other things, but said nothing, thinking it wisest not to pursue the subject. Presently Marnham returned and informed me that a native had just brought him word that the Basutos had made off homeward with our cattle, but had left the wagon and its contents quite untouched, not even stealing the spare guns and ammunition.

"That's luck," I said, astonished, "but extremely strange. How do you explain it, Mr. Marnham?"

He shrugged his shoulders and answered—

"As every one knows, you are a much greater expert in native habits and customs than I am, Mr. Quatermain.

"There are only two things that I can think of," I said. "One is that for some reason or other they thought the wagon tagati, bewitched you know, and that it would bring evil on them to touch it, though this did not apply to the oxen. The other is that they supposed it, but not the oxen, to belong to some friend of their own whose property they did not wish to injure."

He looked at me sharply but said nothing, and I went on to tell them the details of the attack that had been made upon us, adding—

"The odd part of the affair is that one of those Basutos called out to us that some infernal scoundrel of a white had warned Sekukuni of our coming and that he had ordered them to take our guns and cattle. This Basuto, who was wounded and praying for mercy, was drowned before he could tell me who the white man was."

"A Boer, I expect," said Marnham quietly. "As you know they are not particularly well affected towards us English just now. Also I happen to be aware that some of them are intriguing with Sekukuni against the British through Makurupiji, his 'Mouth' or prime-minister, a very clever old scamp who likes to have two stools to sit on."

"And doubtless will end by falling between them. Well, you see, now that I think of it, the wounded Kaffir only said that they were ordered to take our guns and oxen, and incidentally our lives. The wagon was not mentioned."

"Quite so, Mr. Quatermain. I will send some of our boys to help your servants to bring everything it contains up here."

"Can't you lend me a team of oxen," I asked, "to drag it to the house?"

"No, we have nothing but young cattle left. Both red-water and lung-sickness have been so bad this season that all the horned stock have been swept out of the country. I doubt whether you could beg, borrow or steal a team of oxen this side of Pretoria, except from some of the Dutchmen who won't part."

"That's awkward. I hoped to be able to trek in a day or two."

"Your friend won't be able to trek for a good many days at the best," broke in the doctor, who had been listening unconcernedly, "but of course you could get away on the horse after it has rested."

"You told me you left a span of oxen at Pretoria," said Marnham. "Why not go and fetch them here, or if you don't like to leave Mr. Anscombe, send your driver and the boys."

"Thanks for the idea. I will think it over," I answered.

That morning after Footsack and the voorlooper had been sent with some of the servants from the Temple to fetch up the contents of the wagon, for I was too tired to accompany them, having found that Anscombe was still asleep, I determined to follow his example. Finding a long chair on the stoep, I sat down and slumbered in it sweetly for hours. I dreamt of all sorts of things, then through my dreams it seemed to me that I heard two voices talking, those of our Marnham and Rodd, not on the stoep, but at a distance from it. As a matter of fact they were talking, but so far away that in my ordinary waking state I could never have heard them. My own belief is that the senses, and I may add the semi-spiritual part of us, are much more acute when we lie half bound in the bonds of sleep, than when we are what is called wide awake. Doubtless when we are quite bound they attain the limits of their power and, I think, sail at times to the uttermost ends of being. But unhappily of their experiences we remember nothing when we awake. In half sleep it is different; then we do retain some recollection.

In this curious condition of mind it seemed to me that Rodd said to Marnham—

"Why have you brought these men here?"

"I did not bring them here," he answered. "Luck, Fate, Fortune, God or the Devil, call it what you will, brought them here, though if you had your wish, it is true they would never have come. Still, as they have come, I am glad. It is something to me, living in this hell, to get a chance of talking to English gentlemen again before I die."

"English gentlemen," remarked Rodd reflectively, "Well, Anscombe is of course, but how about that other hunter? After all, in what way is he better than the scores of other hunters and Kaffir traders and wanderers whom one meets in this strange land?"

"In what way indeed?" thought I to myself, in my dream.

"If you can't see, I can't explain to you. But as I happen to know, the man is of blood as good as mine—and a great deal better than yours," he added with a touch of insolence. "Moreover, he has an honest name among white and black, which is much in this country."

"Yes," replied the doctor in the same reflective voice, "I agree with you, I let him pass as a gentleman. But I repeat, Why did you bring them here when with one more word it would have been so easy—" and he stopped.

"I have told you, it was not I. What are you driving at?"

"Do you think it is exactly convenient, especially when we are under the British flag again, to have two people who, we both admit, are English gentlemen, that is, clean, clear-eyed men, considering us and our affairs for an indefinite period, just because you wish for the pleasure of their society? Would it not have been better to tell those Basutos to let them trek on to Pretoria?"

"I don't know what would have been better. I repeat, what are you driving at?

"Heda is coming home in a day or two; she might be here any time," remarked Rodd as he knocked the ashes out of his pipe.

"Yes, because you made me write and say that I wanted her. But what of that?"

"Nothing in particular, except that I am not sure that I wish her to associate with 'an English gentleman' like this Anscombe."

Marnham laughed scornfully. "Ah! I understand," he said. "Too clean and straight. Complications might ensue and the rest of it. Well, I wish to God they would, for I know the Anscombes, or used to, and I know the genus called Rodd."

"Don't be insulting; you may carry the thing too far one day, and whatever I have done I have paid for. But you've not paid—yet."

"The man is very ill. You are a skilled doctor. If you're afraid of him, why don't you kill him?" asked Marnham with bitter scorn.

"There you have me," replied Rodd. "Men may shed much, but most of them never shed their professional honour. I shall do my honest best to cure Mr. Anscombe, and I tell you that he will take some curing."

Then I woke up, and as no one was in sight, wondered whether or no I had been dreaming. The upshot of it was that I made up my mind to send Footsack to Pretoria for the oxen, not to go myself.

A Game of Cards

I slept in Anscombe's room that night and looked after him. He was very feverish and the pain in his leg kept him awake a good deal. He told me that he could not bear Dr. Rodd and wished to get away at once. I had to explain to him that this was impossible until his spare oxen arrived which I was going to send for to Pretoria, but of other matters, including that of the dangerous state of his foot, I said nothing. I was thankful when towards two in the morning, he fell into a sound sleep and allowed me to do the same.

Before breakfast time, just as I had finished dressing myself in some of the clean things which had been brought from the wagon, Rodd came and made a thorough and business-like examination of his patient, while I awaited the result with anxiety on the stoep. At length he appeared and said—

"Well, I think that we shall be able to save the foot, though I can't be quite sure for another twenty-four hours. The worst symptoms have abated and his temperature is down by two degrees. Anyway he will have to stay in bed and live on light food till it is normal, after which he might lie in a long chair on the stoep. On no account must he attempt to stand."

I thanked him for his information heartily enough and asked him if he knew where Marnham was, as I wanted to speak to him with reference to the despatch of Footsack to fetch the oxen from Pretoria.

"Not up yet, I think," he answered. "I fancy that yesterday was one of his 'wet' nights, excitement of meeting strangers and so on."

"Wet nights?" I queried, wishing for a clearer explanation.

"Yes, he is a grand old fellow, one of the best, but like most other people he has his little weaknesses, and when the fit is on him he can put away a surprising amount of liquor. I tell you so that you should not be astonished if you notice anything, or try to argue with him when he is in that state, as then his temper is apt to be—well, lively. Now I must go and give him a pint of warm milk; that is his favourite antidote, and in fact the best there is."

I thought to myself that we had struck a nice establishment in which to be tied, literally by the leg, for an indefinite period. I was not particularly flush at the time, but I know I would have paid a £100 to be out of it; before the end I should have been glad to throw in everything that I had. But mercifully that was hidden from me.

Rodd and I breakfasted together and discoursed of Kaffir customs, as to which he was singularly well informed. Then I accompanied him to see his native patients in the little hospital of which I have spoken. Believing the man to be a thorough scamp as I did, it was astonishing to me to note how gentle and forbearing he was to these people. Of his skill I need say nothing, as that was evident. He was going to perform an internal operation upon a burly old savage, rather a serious one I believe; at any rate it necessitated chloroform. He asked me if I would like to assist, but I declined respectfully, having no taste for such things. So I left him boiling his instruments and putting on what looked like a clean nightgown over his clothes, and returned to the stoep.

Here I found Marnham, whose eyes were rather bloodshot, though otherwise, except for a shaky hand, he seemed right enough. He murmured something about having overslept himself and inquired very politely, for his manners were beautiful, after Anscombe and as to whether we were quite comfortable and so forth. After this I consulted him as to the best road for our servants to travel by to Pretoria, and later on despatched them, giving Footsack various notes to ensure the delivery of the oxen to him. Also I gave him some money to pay for their keep and told him with many threats to get back with the beasts as quick as he could travel. Then I sent him and the two other boys off, not without misgivings, although he was an experienced man in his way and promised faithfully to fulfil every injunction to the letter. To me he seemed so curiously glad to go that I inquired the reason, since after a journey like ours, it would have been more natural if he had wished to rest.

"Oh! Baas," he said, "I don't think this Tampel very healthy for coloured people. I am told of some who have died here. That man Karl who gave me the diamond, I think he must have died also, at least I saw his spook last night standing over me and shaking his head, and the boys saw it too."

"Oh! be off with your talk of spooks," I said, "and come back quickly with those oxen, or I promise you that you will die and be a spook yourself."

"I will, Baas, I will!" he ejaculated and departed almost at a run, leaving me rather uncomfortable.

I believed nothing of the tale of the spook of Karl, but I saw that Footsack believed in it, and was afraid lest he might be thereby prevented from returning. I would much rather have gone myself, but it was impossible for me to leave Anscombe so ill in the hands of our strange hosts. And there was no one else whom I could send. I might perhaps have ridden to Pilgrim's Rest and tried to find a white messenger there; indeed afterwards I regretted not having done so, although it would have involved at least a day's absence at a very critical time. But the truth is I never thought of it until too late, and probably if I had, I should not have been able to discover anyone whom I could trust.

As I walked back to the house, having parted from Footsack on the top of a neighbouring ridge whence I could point out his path to him, I met Marnham riding away. He pulled up and said that he was going down to the Granite stream to arrange about setting some one up to watch the wagon. I expressed sorrow that he should have the trouble, which should have been mine if I could have got away, whereon he answered that he was glad of the opportunity for a ride, as it was something to do.

"How do you fill in your time here," I asked carelessly, "as you don't farm?"

"Oh! by trading," he replied, and with a nod set his horse to a canter.

A queer sort of trading, thought I to myself, where there is no store. Now what exactly does he trade in, I wonder?

As it happened I was destined to find out before I was an hour older. Having given Anscombe a look and found that he was comfortable, I thought that I would inspect the quarry whence the marble came of which the house was built, as it had occurred to me that if there was plenty of it, it might be worth exploiting some time in the future. It had been pointed out to me in the midst of some thorns in a gully that ran at right angles to the main kloof not more than a few hundred yards from the house. Following a path over which the stones had been dragged originally, I came to the spot and discovered that a little cavity had been quarried in what seemed to me to be a positive mountain of pure white marble. I examined the place as thoroughly as I could, climbing among some bushes that grew in surface earth which had been washed down from the top, in order to do so.

At the back of these bushes there was a hole large enough for a man to creep through. I crept through with the object of ascertaining whether the marble veins continued. To my surprise I found a stout yellow-wood door within feet of the mouth of the hole. Reflecting that no doubt it was here that the quarrymen kept, or had kept tools and explosives, I gave it a push. I suppose it had been left unfastened accidentally, or that something had gone wrong with the lock; at any rate it swung open. Pursuing my researches as to the depth of the marble I advanced boldly and, the place being dark, struck a match. Evidently the marble did continue, as I could see by the glittering roof of a cavern, for such it was. But the floor attracted my attention as well as the roof, for on it were numerous cases not unlike coffins, bearing the stamp of a well-known Birmingham firm, labelled "fencing iron" and addressed to Messrs. Marnham & Rodd, Transvaal, *via* Delagoa Bay.

I knew at once what they were, having seen the like before, but if any doubt remained in my mind it was easy to solve, for as it chanced one of the cases was open and half emptied. I slipped my hand into it. As I thought it contained the ordinary Kaffir gun of commerce, cost delivered in Africa, say 35s.; cost delivered to native chief in cash or cattle, say £10, which, when the market is eager, allows for a decent profit. Contemplating those cases, survivors probably of a much larger stock, I understood how it came about that Sekukuni had dared to show fight against the Government. Doubtless it was hence that the guns had come which sent a bullet through Anscombe's foot and nearly polished off both of us.

Moreover, as further matches showed me, that cave contained other stores—item, kegs of gunpowder; item, casks of cheap spirit; item, bars of lead, also a box marked "bullet moulds" and another marked "Percussion caps." I think, too, there were some innocent bags full of beads and a few packages of Birmingham-made assegai blades. There may have been other things, but if so I did not wait to investigate them. Gathering up the ends of my matches and, in case there should be any dust in the place that would show footmarks, flapping the stone floor behind me with my pocket handkerchief, I retired and continued my investigations of that wonderful marble deposit from the bottom of the quarry, to which, having re-arranged the bushes, I descended by another route, leaping like a buck from stone to stone.

It was just as well that I did so, for a few minutes later Dr. Rodd appeared.

"Made a good job of your operation?" I asked cheerfully.

"Pretty fair, thanks," he answered, "although that Kaffir tried to brain the nurse-man when he was coming out of the anesthetic. But are you interested in geology?"

"A little," I replied, "that is if there is any chance of making money out of it, which there ought to be here, as this marble looks almost as good as that of Carrara. But flint instruments are more my line, that is in an ignorant and amateur way, as I think they are in yours, for I saw some in your room. Tell me, what do you think of this. Is it a scraper?" and I produced a stone out of my pocket which I had found a week before in the bush-veld.

At once he forgot his suspicions, of which I could see he arrived very full indeed. This curious man, as it happened, was really fond of flint instruments, of which he knew a great deal.

"Did you find this here?" he asked.

I led him several yards further from the mouth of the cave and pointed out the exact spot where I said I had picked it up amongst some quarry debris. Then followed a most learned discussion, for it appeared that this was a flint instrument of the rarest and most valuable type, one that Noah might have used, or Job might have scraped himself with, and the question was how the dickens had it come among that quarry debris. In the end we left the problem undecided, and having presented the article to Dr. Rodd, a gift for which he thanked me with real warmth, I returned to the house filled with the glow that rewards one who has made a valuable discovery.

Of the following three days I have nothing particular to say, except that during them I was perhaps more acutely bored than ever I had been in my life before. The house was beautiful in its own fashion; the food was excellent; there was everything I could want to drink, and Rodd announced that he no longer feared the necessity of operation upon Anscombe's leg. His recovery was now a mere matter of time, and meanwhile he must not use his foot or let the blood run into it more than could be helped, which meant that he must keep himself in a recumbent position. The trouble was that I had nothing on earth do except study the characters of our hosts, which I found disagreeable and depressing. I might have gone out shooting, but nothing of the sort was allowed upon the property in obedience to the wish of Miss Heda, a mysterious young person who was always expected and never appeared, and beyond it I was afraid to travel for fear of Basutos. I might have gone to Pilgrim's Rest or Lydenburg to make report of the nefarious deeds of the said Basutos, but at best it would have taken one or two days, and possibly I should have been detained by officials who never consider any one's time except their own.

This meant that I should have been obliged to leave Anscombe alone, which I did not wish to do, so I just sat still and, as I have said, was intensely bored, hanging about the place and smoking more than was good for me.

In due course Anscombe emerged on to the stoep, where he lay with his leg up, and was also bored, especially after he had tried to pump old Marnham about his past in the Guards and completely failed. It was in this mood of utter dejection that we agreed to play a game of cards one evening. Not that either of us cared for cards; indeed, personally, I have always detested them because, with various-coloured counters to represent money which never passed, they had formed one of the afflictions of my youth.

It was so annoying if you won, to be handed a number of green counters and be informed that they represented so many hundreds or thousands of pounds, or vice-versa if you lost, for as it cost no one anything, my dear father insisted upon playing for enormous stakes. Never in any aspect of life have I cared for fooling. Anscombe also disliked cards, I think because his ancestors too had played with counters, such as some that I have seen belonging to the Cocoa-Tree Club and other gambling places of a past generation, marked as high as a thousand guineas, which counters must next morning be redeemed in hard cash, whereby his family had been not a little impoverished.

"I fancy you will find they are high-fliers," he said when the pair had left to fetch a suitable table, for the night being very hot we were going to play on the stoep by the light of the hanging paraffin lamp and some candles. I replied to the effect that I could not afford to lose large sums of money, especially to men who for aught I knew might then be engaged in marking the cards.

"I understand," he answered. "Don't you bother about that, old fellow. This is my affair, arranged for my special amusement. I shan't grumble if the fun costs something, for I am sure there will be fun."

"All right," I said, "only if we should happen to win money, it's yours, not mine."

To myself I reflected, however, that with these two opponents we had about as much chance of winning as a snowflake has of resisting the atmosphere of the lower regions.

Presently they returned with the table, which had a green cloth over it that hung down half-way to the ground. Also one of the native boys brought a tray with spirits, from which I judged by various signs, old Marnham, who had already drunk his share at dinner, had helped himself freely on the way. Soon we were arranged, Anscombe, who was to be my partner, opposite to me in his long chair, and the game began.

I forget what particular variant of cards it was we played, though I know it admitted of high and progressive stakes. At first, however, these were quite moderate and we won, as I suppose we were meant to do. After half an hour or so Marnham rose to help himself to brandy and water, a great deal of brandy and very little water, while I took a nip of Hollands, and Anscombe and Rodd filled their pipes.

"I think this is getting rather slow," said Rodd to Anscombe. "I vote we put a bit more on."

"As much as you like," answered Anscombe with a little drawl and twinkle of the eye, which always showed that he was amused. "Both Quatermain and I are born gamblers. Don't look angry, Quatermain, you know you are. Only if we lose you will have to take a cheque, for I have precious little cash."

"I think that will be good enough," replied the doctor quietly—"if you lose."

So the stakes were increased to an amount that made my hair stand up stiffer even than usual, and the game went on. Behold! a marvel came to pass. How it happened I do not know, unless Marnham had brought the wrong cards by mistake or had grown too fuddled to understand his partner's telegraphic signals, which I, being accustomed to observe, saw him make, not once but often, still we won! What is more, with a few set-backs, we went on winning, till presently the sums written down to our credit, for no actual cash passed, were considerable. And all the while, at the end of each bout Marnham helped himself to more brandy, while the doctor grew more mad in a suppressed-thunder kind of a way. For my part I became alarmed, especially as I perceived that Anscombe was on the verge of breaking into open merriment, and his legs being up I could not kick him under the table.

"My partner ought to go to bed. Don't you think we should stop?" I said.

"On the whole I do," replied Rodd, glowering at Marnham, who, somewhat unsteadily, was engaged in wiping drops of brandy from his long beard.

"D——d if I do," exclaimed that worthy. "When I was young and played with gentlemen they always gave losers an opportunity of revenge."

"Then," replied Anscombe with a flash of his eyes, "let us try to follow in the footsteps of the gentlemen with whom you played in your youth. I suggest that we double the stakes."

"That's right! That's the old form!" said Marnham.

The doctor half rose from his chair, then sat down again. Watching him, I concluded that he believed his partner, a seasoned vessel, was not so drunk as he pretended to be, and either in an actual or a figurative sense, had a card up his sleeve. If so, it remained there, for again we won; all the luck was with us.

"I am getting tired," drawled Anscombe. "Lemon and water are not sustaining. Shall we stop?"

"By Heaven! no," shouted Marnham, to which Anscombe replied that if it was wished, he would play another hand, but no more.

"All right," said Marnham, "but let it be for double or quits."

He spoke quite quietly and seemed suddenly to have grown sober. Now I think that Rodd made up his mind that he really was acting and that he really had that card up his sleeve. At any rate he did not object. I, however, was of a different opinion, having often seen drunken men succumb to an acces of sobriety under the stress of excitement and remarked that it did not last long.

"Do you really mean that?" I said, speaking for the first time and addressing myself to the doctor. "I don't quite know what the sum involved is, but it must be large."

"Of course," he answered.

Then remembering that at the worst Anscombe stood to lose nothing, I shrugged my shoulders and held my tongue. It was Marnham's deal, and although he was somewhat in the shadow of the hanging lamp and the candles had guttered out, I distinctly saw him play some hocus-pocus with the cards, but in the circumstances made no protest. As it chanced he must have hocus-pocused them wrong, for though *his* hand was full of trumps, Rodd held nothing at all. The battle that ensued was quite exciting, but the end of it was that an ace in the hand of Anscombe, who really was quite a good player, did the business, and we won again.

In the rather awful silence that followed Anscombe remarked in his cheerful drawl—

"I'm not sure that my addition is quite right; we'll check that in the morning, but I make out that you two gentlemen owe Quatermain and myself £749 10s."

Then the doctor broke out.

"You accursed old fool," he hissed—there is no other word for it—at Marnham. "How are you going to pay all this money that you have gambled away, drunken beast that you are!"

"Easily enough, you felon," shouted Marnham. "So," and thrusting his hand into his pocket he pulled out a number of diamonds which he threw upon the table, adding, "there's what will cover it twice over, and there are more where they came from, as you know well enough, my medical jailbird."

"You dare to call me that," gasped the doctor in a voice laden with fury, so intense that it had deprived him of his reason, "you—you—murderer! Oh! why don't I kill you as I shall some day?" and lifting his glass, which was half full, he threw the contents into Marnham's face.

"That's a nice man for a prospective, son-in-law, isn't he?" exclaimed the old scamp, as, seizing the brandy decanter, he hurled it straight at Rodd's head, only missing him by an inch.

"Don't you think you had both better go to bed, gentlemen?" I inquired. "You are saying things you might regret in the morning."

Apparently they did think it, for without another word they rose and marched off in different directions to their respective rooms, which I heard both of them lock. For my part I collected the I.O.U.'s; also the diamonds which still lay upon the table, while Anscombe examined the cards.

"Marked, by Jove! he said. "Oh! my dear Quatermain, never have I had such an amusing evening in all my life."

"Shut up, you silly idiot," I answered. "There'll be murder done over this business, and I only hope it won't be on us."

Miss Heda

It might be thought that after all this there would have been a painful explanation on the following morning, but nothing of the sort happened. After all the greatest art is the art of ignoring things, without which the world could scarcely go on, even among the savage races. Thus on this occasion the two chief actors in the scene of the previous night pretended that they had forgotten what took place, as I believe, to a large extent truly. The fierce flame of drink in the one and of passion in the other had burnt the web of remembrance to ashes. They knew that something unpleasant had occurred and its main outlines; the rest had vanished away; perhaps because they knew also that they were not responsible for what they said and did, and therefore that what occurred had no right to a permanent niche in their memories. It was, as it were, something outside of their normal selves. At least so I conjectured, and their conduct seemed to give colour to my guess.

The doctor spoke to me of the matter first.

"I fear there was a row last night," he said; "it has happened here before over cards, and will no doubt happen again until matters clear themselves up somehow. Marnham, as you see, drinks, and when drunk is the biggest liar in the world, and I, I am sorry to say, am cursed with a violent temper. Don't judge either of us too harshly. If you were a doctor you would know that all these things come to us with our blood, and we didn't fashion our own clay, did we? Have some coffee, won't you?"

Subsequently when Rodd wasn't there, Marnham spoke also and with that fine air of courtesy which was peculiar to him.

"I owe a deep apology," he said, "to yourself and Mr. Anscombe. I do not recall much about it, but I know there was a scene last night over those cursed cards. A weakness overtakes me sometimes. I will say no more, except that you, who are also a man who perhaps have felt weaknesses of one sort or another, will, I hope, make allowances for me and pay no attention to anything that I may have said or done in the presence of guests; yes, that is what pains me—in the presence of guests."

Something in his distinguished manner caused me to reflect upon every peccadillo that I had ever committed, setting it in its very worst light.

"Quite so," I answered, "quite so. Pray do not mention the matter any more, although—" These words seemed to jerk themselves out of my throat, "you did call each other by such very hard names."

"I daresay," he answered with a vacant smile, "but if so they meant nothing."

"No, I understand, just like a lovers' quarrel. But look here, you left some diamonds on the table which I took to keep the Kaffirs out of temptation. I will fetch them."

"Did I? Well, probably I left some I.O.U.'s also which might serve for pipelights. So suppose we set the one against the other. I don't know the value of either the diamonds or the pipelights, it may be less or more, but for God's sake don't let me see the beastly things again. There's no need, I have plenty."

"I must speak to Anscombe," I answered. "The money at stake was his, not mine."

"Speak to whom you will," he replied, and I noted that the throbbing vein upon his forehead indicated a rising temper. "But never let me see those diamonds again. Throw them into the gutter if you wish, but never let me see them again, or there will be trouble."

Then he flung out of the room, leaving his breakfast almost untasted.

Reflecting that this queer old bird probably did not wish to be cross-questioned as to his possession of so many uncut diamonds, or that they were worth much less than the sum he had lost, or possibly that they were not diamonds at all but glass, I went to report the matter to Anscombe. He only laughed and said that as I had got the things I had better keep them until something happened, for we had both got it into our heads that something would happen before we had done with that establishment.

So I went to put the stones away as safely as I could. While I was doing so I heard the rumble of wheels, and came out just in time to see a Cape cart, drawn by four very good horses and driven by a Hottentot in a smart hat and a red waistband, pull up at the garden gate. Out of this cart presently emerged a neatly dressed lady, of whom all I could see was that she was young, slender and rather tall; also, as her back was towards me, that she had a great deal of auburn hair.

"There!" said Anscombe. "I knew that something would happen. Heda has happened. Quatermain, as neither her venerated parent nor her loving fiancé, for such I gather he is, seems to be about, you had better go and give her a hand."

I obeyed with a groan, heartily wishing that Heda hadn't happened, since some sense warned me that she would only add to the present complications. At the gate, having given some instructions to a very stout young coloured woman who, I took it, was her maid, about a basket of flower roots in the cart, she turned round suddenly and we came face to face with the gate between us. For a moment we stared at each other, I reflecting that she really was very pretty with her delicately-shaped features, her fresh, healthy-looking complexion, her long dark eyelashes and her lithe and charming figure. What she reflected about me I don't know, probably nothing half so complimentary. Suddenly, however, her large greyish eyes grew troubled and a look of alarm appeared upon her face.

"Is anything wrong with my father?" she asked. "I don't see him."

"If you mean Mr. Marnham," I replied, lifting my hat, "I believe that Dr. Rodd and he—"

"Never mind about Dr. Rodd," she broke in with a contemptuous little jerk of her chin," how is my father?"

"I imagine much as usual. He and Dr. Rodd were here a little while ago, I suppose that they have gone out" (as a matter of fact they had, but in different directions).

"Then that's all right," she said with a sigh of relief. "You see, I heard that he was very ill, which is why I have come back."

So, thought I to myself, she loves that old scamp and she—doesn't love the doctor. There will be more trouble as sure as five and two are seven. All we wanted was a woman to make the pot boil over.

Then I opened the gate and took a travelling bag from her hand with my politest bow.

"My name is Quatermain and that of my friend Anscombe. We are staying here, you know," I said rather awkwardly.

"Indeed," she answered with a delightful smile, "what a very strange place to choose to stay in."

"It is a beautiful house," I remarked.

"Not bad, although I designed it, more or less. But I was alluding to its inhabitants."

This finished me, and I am sure she felt that I could think of nothing nice to say about those inhabitants, for I heard her sigh. We walked side by side up the rose-fringed path and presently arrived at the stoep, where Anscombe, whose hair I had cut very nicely on the previous day, was watching us from his long chair. They looked at each other, and I saw both of them colour a little, out of mere foolishness, I suppose.

"Anscombe," I said, "this is—" and I paused, not being quite certain whether she also was called Marnham. "Heda Marnham," she interrupted.

"Yes—Miss Heda Marnham, and this is the Honourable Maurice Anscombe."

"Forgive me for not rising, Miss Marnham," said Anscombe in his pleasant voice (by the way hers was pleasant too, full and rather low, with just a suggestion of something foreign about it). "A shot through the foot prevents me at present."

"Who shot you?" she asked quickly.

"Oh! only a Kaffir."

"I am so sorry, I hope you will get well soon. Forgive me now, I must go to look for my father."

"She is uncommonly pretty," remarked Anscombe, "and a lady into the bargain. In reflecting on old Marnham's sins we must put it to his credit that he has produced a charming daughter."

"Too pretty and charming by half," I grunted.

"Perhaps Dr. Rodd is of the same way of thinking. Great shame that such a girl should be handed over to a medical scoundrel like Dr. Rodd. I wonder if she cares for him?"

"Just about as much as a canary cares for a tom-cat. I have found that out already."

"Really, Quatermain, you are admirable. I never knew anyone who could make a better use of the briefest opportunity."

Then we were silent, waiting, not without a certain impatience, for the return of Miss Heda. She did return with surprising quickness considering that she had found time to search for her parent, to change into a clean white dress, and to pin a single hibiscus flower on to her bodice which gave just the touch of colour that was necessary to complete her costume.

"I can't find my father," she said, "but the boys say he has gone out riding. I can't find anybody. When you have been summoned from a long way off and travelled post-haste, rather to your own inconvenience, it is amusing, isn't it?"

"Wagons and carts in South Africa don't arrive like express trains, Miss Marnham," said Anscombe, "so you shouldn't be offended."

"I am not at all offended, Mr. Anscombe. Now that I know there is nothing the matter with my father I'm—But, tell me, how did you get your wound?"

So he told her with much amusing detail after his fashion. She listened quietly with a puckered up brow and only made one comment. It was,—

"I wonder what white man told those Sekukuni Kaffirs that you were coming."

"I don't know," he answered, "but he deserves a bullet through him somewhere above the ankle."

"Yes, though few people get what they deserve in this wicked world."

"So I have often thought. Had it been otherwise, for example, I should have been—"

"What would you have been?" she asked, considering him curiously.

"Oh! a better shot than Mr. Allan Quatermain, and as beautiful as a lady I once saw in my youth."

"Don't talk rubbish before luncheon," I remarked sternly, and we all laughed, the first wholesome laughter that I had heard at the Temple. For this young lady seemed to bring happiness and merriment with her. I remember wondering what it was of which her coming reminded me, and concluding that it was like the sight and smell of a peach orchard in full bloom stumbled on suddenly in the black desert of the burnt winter veld.

After this we became quite friendly. She dilated on her skill in having produced the Temple from an old engraving, which she fetched and showed to us, at no greater an expense than it would have cost to build an ordinary house.

"That is because the marble was at hand," said Anscombe.

"Quite so," she replied demurely. "Speaking in a general sense one can do many things in life—if the marble is at hand. Only most of us when we look for marble find sandstone or mud."

"Bravo!" said Anscombe, "I have generally lit upon the sandstone."

"And I on the mud," she mused.

"And I on all three, for the earth contains marble and mud and sandstone, to say nothing of gold and jewels," I broke in, being tired of silence.

But neither of them paid much attention to me. Anscombe did say, out of politeness, I suppose, that pitch and subterranean fires should be added, or some such nonsense.

Then she began to tell him of her infantile memories of Hungary, which were extremely faint; of how they came this place and lived first of all in two large Kaffir huts, until suddenly they began to grow rich; of her school days at Maritzburg; of the friends with whom she had been staying, and I know not what, until at last I got up and went out for a walk.

When I returned an hour or so later they were still talking, and so continued to do until Dr. Rodd arrived upon the scene. At first they did not see him, for he stood at an angle to them, but I saw him and watched his face with a great deal of interest. It, or rather its expression, was not pleasant; before now I have seen something like it on that of a wild beast which thinks that it is about to be robbed of its prey by a stronger wild beast, in short, a mixture of hate, fear and jealousy—especially jealousy. At the last I did not wonder, for these two seemed to be getting on uncommonly well.

They were, so to speak, well matched. She, of course, was the better looking of the two, a really pretty and attractive young woman indeed, but the vivacity of Anscombe's face, the twinkle of his merry blue eyes and its general refinement made up for what he lacked—regularity of feature. I think he had just told her one of his good stories which he always managed to make so humorous by a trick of pleasing and harmless exaggeration, and they were both laughing merrily. Then she caught sight of the doctor and her merriment evaporated like a drop of water on a hot shovel. Distinctly I saw her pull herself together and prepare for something.

"How do you do?" she said rapidly, rising and holding out her slim sun-browned hand. "But I need not ask, you look so well."

"How do you do, my dear," with a heavy emphasis on the "dear" he answered slowly. "But I needn't ask, for I see that you are in perfect health and spirits," and he bent forward as though to kiss her.

Somehow or other she avoided that endearment or seal of possession. I don't quite know how, as I turned my head away, not wishing to witness what I felt to be unpleasant. When I looked up again, however, I saw that she had avoided it, the scowl on his face the demureness of hers and Anscombe's evident amusement assured me of this. She was asking about her father; he answered that he also seemed quite well.

"Then why did you write to tell me that I ought to come as he was not at all well?" she inquired, with a lifting of her delicate eyebrows.

The question was never answered, for at that moment Marnham himself appeared.

"Oh! father," she said, and rushed into his arms, while he kissed her tenderly on both cheeks.

So I was not mistaken, thought I to myself, she does really love this moral wreck, and what is more, he loves her, which shows that there must be good in him. Is anyone truly bad, I wondered, or for the matter of that, truly good either? Is it not all a question of circumstance and blood?

Neither then or at any other time have I found an answer to the problem. At any rate to me there seemed something beautiful about the meeting of these two.

The influence of Miss Heda in the house was felt at once. The boys became smarter and put on clean clothes. Vases of flowers appeared in the various rooms; ours was turned out and cleaned, a disagreeable process so far as we were concerned. Moreover, at dinner both Marnham and Rodd wore dress clothes with short jackets, a circumstance that put Anscombe and myself to shame since we had none. It was curious to see how with those dress clothes, which doubtless awoke old associations within him, Marnham changed his colour like a chameleon. Really he might have been the colonel of a cavalry regiment rising to toast the Queen after he had sent round the wine, so polite and polished was his talk. Who could have identified the man with the dry old ruffian of twenty-four hours before, he who was drinking claret (and very good claret too) mixed with water and listening with a polite interest to all the details of his daughter's journey? Even the doctor looked a gentleman, which doubtless he was once upon a time, in evening dress. Moreover, some kind of truce had been arranged. He no longer called Miss Heda "My dear" or attempted any familiarities, while she on more than one occasion very distinctly called him Dr. Rodd.

So much for that night and for several others that followed. As for the days they went by pleasantly and idly. Heda walked about on her father's arm, conversed in friendly fashion with the doctor, always watching him, I noticed, as a cat watches a dog that she knows is waiting an opportunity to spring, and for the rest associated with us as much as she could. Particularly did she seem to take refuge behind my own insignificance, having, I suppose, come to the conclusion that I was a harmless person who might possibly prove useful. But all the while I felt that the storm was banking up. Indeed Marnham himself, at any rate to a great extent, played the part of the cloud-compelling Jove, for soon it became evident to me, and without doubt to Dr. Rodd also, that he was encouraging the intimacy between his daughter and Anscombe by every means in his power.

In one way and another he had fully informed himself as to Anscombe's prospects in life, which were brilliant enough. Moreover he liked the man who, as the remnant of the better perceptions of his youth told him, was one of the best class of Englishmen, and what is more, he saw that Heda liked him also, as much indeed as she disliked Rodd. He even spoke to me of the matter in a round-about kind of fashion, saying that the young woman who married Anscombe would be lucky and that the father who had him for a son-in-law might go to his grave confident of his child's happiness. I answered that I agreed with him, unless the lady's affections had already caused her to form other ties.

"Affections!" he exclaimed, dropping all pretence, "there are none involved in this accursed business, as you are quite sharp enough to have seen for yourself."

"I understood that an engagement was involved," I remarked.

"On my part, perhaps, not on hers," he answered. "Oh! can't you understand, Quatermain, that sometimes men find themselves forced into strange situations against their will?"

Remembering the very ugly name that I had heard Rodd call Marnham on the night of the card party, I reflected that I could understand well enough, but I only said—

"After all marriage is a matter that concerns a woman even more than it does her father, one, in short, of which she must be the judge."

"Quite so, Quatermain, but there are some daughters who are prepared to make great sacrifices for their fathers. Well, she will be of age ere long, if only I can stave it off till then. But how, how?" and with a groan he turned and left me.

That old gentleman's neck is in some kind of a noose, thought I to myself, and his difficulty is to prevent the rope from being drawn tight. Meanwhile this poor girl's happiness and future are at stake.

"Allan," said Anscombe to me a little later, for by now he called me by my Christian name, "I suppose you haven't heard anything about those oxen, have you?"

"No, I could scarcely expect to yet, but why do you ask?"

He smiled in his droll fashion and replied, "Because, interesting as this household is in sundry ways, I think it is about time that we, or at any rate that I, got out of it."

"Your leg isn't fit to travel yet, Anscombe, although Rodd says that all the symptoms are very satisfactory."

"Yes, but to tell you the truth I am experiencing other symptoms quite unknown to that beloved physician and so unfamiliar to myself that I attribute them to the influences of the locality. Altitude affects the heart, does it not, and this house stands high."

"Don't play off your jokes on me," I said sternly. "What do you mean?"

"I wonder if you find Miss Heda attractive, Allan, or if you are too old. I believe there comes an age when the only beauties that can move a man are those of architecture, or scenery, or properly cooked food."

"Hang it all! I am not Methusaleh," I replied; "but if you mean that you are falling in love with Heda, why the deuce don't you say so, instead of wasting my time and your own?"

"Because time was given to us to waste. Properly considered it is the best use to which it can be put, or at any rate the one that does least mischief. Also because I wished to make you say it for me that I might judge from the effect of your words whether it is or is not true. I may add that I fear the former to be the case."

"Well, if you are in love with the girl you can't expect one so ancient as myself, who is quite out of touch with such follies, to teach you how to act."

"No, Allan. Unfortunately there are occasions when one must rely upon one's own wisdom, and mine, what there is of it, tells me I had better get out of this. But I can't ride even if I took the horse and you ran behind, and the oxen haven't come."

"Perhaps you could borrow Miss Marnham's cart in which to run away from her," I suggested sarcastically.

"Perhaps, though I believe it would be fatal to my foot to sit up in a cart for the next few days, and the horses seem to have been sent off somewhere. Look here, old fellow," he went on, dropping his bantering tone, "it's rather awkward to make a fool of oneself over a lady who is engaged to some one else, especially if one suspects that with a little encouragement she might begin to walk the same road. The truth is I have taken the fever pretty bad, worse than ever I did before, and if it isn't stopped soon it will become chronic."

"Oh no, Anscombe, only intermittent at the worst, and African malaria nearly always yields to a change of climate."

"How can I expect a cynic and a misogynist to understand the simple fervour of an inexperienced soul—Oh! drat it all, Quatermain, stop your acid chaff and tell me what is to be done. Really I am in a tight place."

"Very; so tight that I rejoice to think, as you were kind enough to point out, that my years protect me from anything of the sort. I have no advice to give; I think you had better ask it of the lady."

"Well, we did have a little conversation, hypothetical of course, about some friends of ours who found themselves similarly situated, and I regret to say without result."

"Indeed. I did not know you had any mutual acquaintances. What did she say and do?"

"She said nothing, only sighed and looked as though she were going to burst into tears, and all she did was to walk away. I'd have followed her if I could, but as my crutch wasn't there it was impossible. It seemed to me that suddenly I had come up against a brick wall, that there was something on her mind which she could not or would not let out.

"Yes, and if you want to know, I will tell you what it is. Rodd has got a hold over Marnham of a sort that would bring him somewhere near the gallows. As the price of his silence Marnham has promised him his daughter. The daughter knows that her father is in this man's power, though I think she does not know in what way, and being a good girl—"

"An angel you mean—do call her by her right name, especially in a place where angels are so much wanted."

"Well, an angel if you like—she has promised on her part to marry a man she loathes in order to save her parent's bacon."

"Just what I concluded, from what we heard in the row. I wonder which of that pair is the bigger blackguard. Well, Allan, that settles it. You and I are on the side of the angel. You will have to get her out of this scrape and—if she'll have me, I'll marry her; and if she won't, why it can't be helped. Now that's a fair division of labour. How are you going to do it? I haven't an idea, and if I had, I should not presume to interfere with one so much older and wiser than myself."

"I suppose that by the time you appeared in it, the game of heads I win and tails you lose had died out of the world," I replied with an indignant snort. "I think the best thing I can do will be to take the horse and look for those oxen. Meanwhile you can settle your business by the light of your native genius, and I only hope you'll finish it without murder and sudden death."

"I say, old fellow," said Anscombe earnestly, "you don't really mean to go off and leave me in this hideousness? I haven't bothered much up to the present because I was sure that you would find a way out, which would be nothing to a man of your intellect and experience. I mean it honestly, I do indeed."

"Do you? Well, I can only say that my mind is a perfect blank, but if you will stop talking I will try to think the matter over. There's Miss Heda in the garden cutting flowers. I will go to help her, which will be a very pleasant change."

And I went, leaving him to stare after me jealously.

The Stoep

When I reached Miss Heda she was collecting half-opened monthly roses from the hedge, and not quite knowing what to say I made the appropriate quotation. At least it was appropriate to my thought, and, from her answer, to hers also.

"Yes," she said, "I am gathering them while I may," and she sighed and, as I thought, glanced towards the verandah, though of this I could not be sure because of the wide brim of the hat she was wearing.

Then we talked a little on indifferent matters, while I pricked my fingers helping to pluck the roses. She asked me if I thought that Anscombe was getting on well, and how long it would be before he could travel. I replied that Dr. Rodd could tell her better than myself, but that I hoped in about a week.

"In a week!" she said, and although she tried to speak lightly there was dismay in her voice.

"I hope you don't think it too long," I answered; "but even if he is fit to go, the oxen have not come yet, and I don't quite know when they will."

"Too long!" she exclaimed. "Too long! Oh! if you only knew what it is to me to have such guests as you are in this place," and her dark eyes filled with tears.

By now we had passed to the side of the house in search of some other flower that grew in the shade, I think it was mignonette, and were out of sight of the verandah and quite alone.

"Mr. Quatermain," she said hurriedly, "I am wondering whether to ask your advice about something, if you would give it. I have no one to consult here," she added rather piteously.

"That is for you to decide. If you wish to do so I am old enough to be your father, and will do my best to help."

We walked on to an orange grove that stood about forty yards away, ostensibly to pick some fruit, but really because we knew that there we should be out of hearing and could see any one who approached.

"Mr. Quatermain," she said presently in a low voice, I am in great trouble, almost the greatest a woman can have. I am engaged to be married to a man whom I do not care for.

"Then why not break it off? It may be unpleasant, but it is generally best to face unpleasant things, and nothing can be so bad as marrying a man whom you do not—care for.

"Because I cannot—I dare not. I have to obey."

"How old are you, Miss Marnham?"

"I shall be of age in three months' time. You may guess that I did not intend to return here until they were over, but I was, well—trapped. He wrote to me that my father was ill and I came."

"At any rate when they are over you will not have to obey any one. It is not long to wait."

"It is an eternity. Besides this is not so much a question of obedience as of duty and of love. I love my father who, whatever his faults, has always been very kind to me."

"And I am sure he loves you. Why not go to him and tell him your trouble?"

"He knows it already, Mr. Quatermain, and hates this marriage even more than I do, if that is possible. But he is driven to it, as I am. Oh! I must tell the truth. The doctor has some hold over him. My father has done something dreadful; I don't know what and I don't want to know, but if it came out it would ruin my father, or worse,

worse. I am the price of his silence. On the day of our marriage he will destroy the proofs. If I refuse to marry him, they will be produced and then—"

"It is difficult," I said.

"It is more than difficult, it is terrible. If you could see all there is in my heart, you would know how terrible."

"I think I can see, Miss Heda. Don't say any more now. Give me time to consider. In case of necessity come to me again, and be sure that I will protect you."

"But you are going in a week."

"Many things happen in a week. Sufficient to the day is its evil. At the end of the week we will come to some decision unless everything is already decided."

For the next twenty-four hours I reflected on this pretty problem as hard as ever I did on anything in all my life. Here was a young woman who must somehow protected from a scoundrel, but who could not be protected because she herself had to protect another scoundrel—to wit, her own father. Could the thing be faced out? Impossible, for I was sure that Marnham had committed a murder, or murders, of which Rodd possessed evidence that would hang him. Could Heda be married to Anscombe at once? Yes, if both were willing, but then Marnham would still be hung. Could they elope? Possibly, but with the same result. Could I take her away and put her under the protection of the Court at Pretoria? Yes, but with the same result. I wondered what my Hottentot retainer, Hans, would have advised, he who was named Light-in-Darkness, and in his own savage way was the cleverest and most cunning man that I have met. Alas! I could not raise him from the grave to tell me, and yet I knew well what he would have answered.

"Baas," he would have said, "this is a rope which only the pale old man (i.e. death) can cut. Let this doctor die or let the father die, and the maiden will be free. Surely heaven is longing for one or both of them, and if necessary, Baas, I believe that I can point out a path to heaven!"

I laughed to myself at the thought, which was one that a white man could not entertain even as a thought. And I felt that the hypothetical Hans was right, death alone could cut this knot, and the reflection made me shiver.

That night I slept uneasily and dreamed. I dreamed that once more I was in the Black Kloof in Zululand, seated in front of the huts at the end of the kloof. Before me squatted the old wizard, Zikali, wrapped up in his kaross—Zikali, the "Thing-that-should-never-have-been-born," whom I had not seen for years. Near him were the ashes of a fire, by the help of which I knew he had been practising divination. He looked up and laughed one of his terrible laughs.

"So you are here again, Macumazahn," he said, "grown older, but still the same; here at the appointed hour. What do you come to seek from the Opener of Roads? Not Mameena as I think this time. No, no, it is she who seeks you this time, Macumazahn. She found you once, did she not? Far away to the north among a strange people who worshipped an Ivory Child, a people of whom I knew in my youth, and afterwards, for was not their prophet, Harut, a friend of mine and one of our brotherhood? She found you beneath the tusks of the elephant, Jana, whom Macumazahn the skilful could not hit. Oh! do not look astonished."

"How do you know?" I asked in my dream.

"Very simply, Macumazahn. A little yellow man named Hans has been with me and told me all the story not an hour ago, after which I sent for Mameena to learn if it were true. She will be glad to meet you, Macumazahn, she who has a hungry heart that does not forget. Oh! don't be afraid. I mean here beneath the sun, in the land beyond there will be no need for her to meet you since she will dwell ever at your side."

"Why do you lie to me, Zikali?" I seemed to ask. "How can a dead man speak to you and how can I meet a woman who is dead?"

"Seek the answer to that question in the hour of the battle when the white men, your brothers, fall beneath assegai as weeds fall before the hoe—or perhaps before it. But have done with Mameena, since she who never grows more old can well afford to wait. It is not of Mameena that you came to speak to me; it is of a fair white woman named Heddana you would speak, and of the man she loves, you, who will ever be mixing yourself up in affairs of others, and therefore must bear their burdens with no pay save that of honour. Hearken, for the time is short. When the storm bursts upon them bring hither the fair maiden, Heddana, and the white lord, Mauriti, and I will shelter them for your sake. Take them nowhere else. Bring them hither if they would escape trouble. I shall be glad to see you, Macumazahn, for at last I am about to smite the Zulu House of Senzangacona, my foes, with a bladder full of blood, and oh! it stains their doorposts red."

Then I woke up, feeling afraid, as one does after a nightmare, and was comforted to hear Anscombe sleeping quietly on the other side of the room.

"Mauriti. Why did Zikali call him Mauriti?" I wondered drowsily to myself. "Oh! of course his name is Maurice, and it was a Zulu corruption of a common sort as was Heddana of Heda." Then I dozed off again, and by the morning had forgotten all about my dream until it was brought back to me by subsequent events. Still it was this and nothing else that put it into my head to fly to Zululand on an emergency that was to arise ere long.

That evening Rodd was absent from dinner, and on inquiring where he might be, I was informed that he had ridden to visit a Kaffir headman, a patient of his who lived at a distance, and would very probably sleep at the kraal, returning early next day. One of the topics of conversation during dinner was as to where the exact boundary line used to run between the Transvaal and the country over which the Basuto chief, Sekukuni, claimed ownership and jurisdiction. Marnham said that it passed within a couple of miles of his house, and when we rose, the moon being very bright, offered to show me where the beacons had been placed years before by a Boer Commission. I accepted, as the night was lovely for a stroll after the hot day. Also I was half conscious of another undefined purpose in my mind, which perhaps may have spread to that of Marnham. Those two young people looked very happy together there on the stoep, and as they must part so soon it would, I thought, be kind to give them the opportunity of a quiet chat.

So off we went to the brow of the hill on which the Temple stood, whence old Marnham pointed out to me a beacon, which I could not see in the dim, silvery bush-veld below, and how the line ran from it to another beacon somewhere else.

"You know the Yellow-wood swamp," he said. "It passes straight through that. That is why those Basutos who were following you pulled up upon the edge of the swamp, though as a matter of fact, according to their ideas, they had a perfect right to kill you on their side of the line which cuts through the middle."

I made some remark to the effect that I presumed that the line had in fact ceased to exist at all, as the Basuto territory had practically become British; after which we strolled back to the house. Walking quietly between the tall rose hedges and without speaking, for each of us was preoccupied with his own thoughts, suddenly we came upon a very pretty scene.

We had left Anscombe and Heda seated side by side on the stoep. They were still there, but much closer together. In fact his arms were round her, and they were kissing each other in a remarkably whole-hearted way. About this there could be no mistake, since the rimpi-strung couch on which they sat was immediately under the hanging lamp—a somewhat unfortunate situation for such endearments. But what did they think of hanging lamps or any other lights, save those of their own eyes, they who were content to kiss and murmur words of passion as though they were as much alone as Adam and Eve in Eden? What did they think either of the serpent coiled about the bole of this tree of knowledge whereof they had just plucked the ripe and maddening fruit?

By a mutual instinct Marnham and I withdrew ourselves, very gently indeed, purposing to skirt round the house and enter it from behind, or to be seized with a fit of coughing at the gate, or to do something to announce our presence at a convenient distance. When we had gone a little way we heard a crash in the bushes.

"Another of those cursed baboons robbing the garden," remarked Marnham reflectively.

"I think he is going to rob the house also," I replied, turning to point to something dark that seemed to be leaping up on to the verandah.

Next moment we heard Heda utter a little cry of alarm, and a man say in a low fierce voice-

"So I have caught you at last, have I!"

"The doctor has returned from his business rounds sooner than was expected, and I think that we had better join the party," I remarked, and made a bee line for the stoep, Marnham following me.

I think that I arrived just in time to prevent mischief. There, with a revolver in his hand, stood Rodd, tall and formidable, his dark face looking like that of Satan himself, a very monument of rage and jealousy. There in front of him on the couch sat Heda, grasping its edge with her fingers, her cheeks as pale as a sheet and her eyes shining. By her side was Anscombe, cool and collected as usual, I noticed, but evidently perplexed.

"If there is any shooting to be done," he was saying, "I think you had better begin with me."

His calmness seemed to exasperate Rodd, who lifted the revolver. But I too was prepared, for in that house I always went armed. There was no time to get at the man, who was perhaps fifteen feet away, and I did not want to hurt him. So I did the best I could; that is, I fired at the pistol in his hand, and the light being good, struck it near the hilt and knocked it off the barrel before the he could press the trigger, if he really meant to shoot.

"That's a good shot," remarked Anscombe who had seen me, while Rodd stared at the hilt which he still held.

"A lucky one," I answered, walking forward. "And now, Dr. Rodd, will you be so good as to tell me what you mean by flourishing a revolver, presumably loaded, in the faces of a lady and an unarmed man?"

"What the devil is that to you," he asked furiously, "and what do you mean by firing at me?"

"A great deal," I answered, "seeing that a young woman and my friend are concerned. As for firing at you, had I done so you would not be asking questions now. I fired at the pistol in your hand, but if there is more trouble next time it shall be at the holder," and I glanced at my revolver.

Seeing that I meant business he made no reply, but turned upon Marnham who had followed me.

"This is your work, you old villain," he said in a low voice that was heavy with hate. "You promised your daughter to me. She is engaged to me, and now I find her in this wanderer's arms."

"What have I to do with it?" said Marnham. "Perhaps she has changed her mind. You had better ask her."

"There is no need to ask me," interrupted Heda, who now seemed to have got her nerve again. "I *have* changed my mind. I never loved you, Dr. Rodd, and I will not marry you. I love Mr. Anscombe here, and as he has asked me to be his wife I mean to marry him."

"I see," he sneered, "you want to be a peeress one day, no doubt. Well, you never shall if I can help it. Perhaps, too, this fine gentleman of yours will not be so particularly anxious to marry you when he learns that you are the daughter of a murderer."

That word was like a bombshell bursting among us. We looked at each other as people, yet dazed with the shock, might on a battlefield when the noise of the explosion has died and the smoke cleared away, to see who is still alive. Anscombe spoke the first.

"I don't know what you mean or to what you refer," he said quietly. "But at any rate this lady who has promised to marry me is innocent, and therefore if all her ancestors had been murderers it would not in the slightest turn me from my purpose of marrying her."

She looked at him, and all the gratitude in the world shone in her frightened eyes. Marnham stepped, or rather staggered forward, the blue vein throbbing on forehead.

"He lies," he said hoarsely, tugging at his long beard. "Listen now and I will tell you the truth. Once, more than a year ago, I was drunk and in a rage. In this state I fired at a Kaffir to frighten him, and by some devil's chance shot him dead. That's what he calls being a murderer."

"I have another tale," said Rodd, "with which I will not trouble this company just now. Look here, Heda, either you fulfil your promise and marry me, or your father swings."

She gasped and sank together on the seat as though she had been shot. Then I took up my parable.

"Are you the man," I asked, "to accuse others of crime? Let us see. You have spent several months in an English prison (I gave the name) for a crime I won't mention."

"How do you know—" he began.

"Never mind, I do know and the prison books will show it. Further, your business is that of selling guns and ammunition to the Basutos of Sekukuni's tribe, who, although the expedition against them has been temporarily recalled, are still the Queen's enemies. Don't deny it, for I have the proofs. Further, it was you who advised Sekukuni to kill us when we went down to his country to shoot the other day, because you were afraid that we should discover whence he got his guns." (This was a bow drawn at a venture, but the arrow went home, for I saw his jaw drop.) "Further, I believe you to be an illicit diamond buyer, and I believe also that you have again been arranging with the Basutos to make an end of us, though of these last two items at present I lack positive proof. Now, Dr. Rodd, I ask you for the second time whether you are a person to accuse others of crimes and whether, should you do so, you will be considered a credible witness when your own are brought to light?"

"If had been guilty of any of these things, which I am not, it is obvious that my partner must have shared in all of them, except the first. So if you inform against me, you inform against him, and the father of Heda, whom your friend wishes to marry, will, according to your showing, be proved a gun-runner, a thief and a would-be murderer of his guests. I should advise you to leave that business alone, Mr. Quatermain."

The reply was bold and clever, so much so that I regarded this blackguard with a certain amount of admiration, as I answered—

"I shall take your advice if you take mine to leave another business alone, that of this young lady and her father, but not otherwise."

"Then spare your breath and do your worst; only careful, sharp as you think yourself, that your meddling does not recoil on your own head. Listen, Heda, either you make up your mind to marry me at once and arrange that this young gentleman, who as a doctor I assure you is now quite fit to travel without injury to his health, leaves this house to-morrow with the spy Quatermain—you might lend him the Cape cart to go in—or I start with the proofs to lay a charge of murder against your father. I give you till to-morrow morning to have a family council to think it over. Good-night."

"Good-night," I answered as he passed me, "and please be careful that none of us see your face again before to-morrow morning. As you may happen to have heard, my native name means Watcher-by-Night," and I looked at the revolver in my hand.

When he had vanished I remarked in as cheerful voice as I could command, that I thought it was bedtime, and as nobody stirred, added, "Don't be afraid, young lady. If you feel lonely, you must tell that stout maid of yours to sleep in your room. Also, as the night is so hot I shall take my nap on the stoep, there, just opposite your window. No, don't let us talk any more now. There will be plenty of time for that to-morrow."

She rose, looked at Anscombe, looked at me, looked at her father very pitifully; then with a little exclamation of despair passed into her room by the French window, where presently I heard her call the native maid and tell her that she was to sleep with her.

Marnham watched her depart. Then he too went with his head bowed and staggering a little in his walk. Next Anscombe rose and limped off into his room, I following him.

"Well, young man," I said, "you have put us all in the soup now and no mistake."

"Yes, Allan, I am afraid I have. But on the whole don't you think it rather interesting soup—so many unexpected ingredients, you see!"

"Interesting soup! Unexpected ingredients!" I repeated after him, adding, "Why not call it hell's broth at once?"

Then he became serious, dreadfully serious.

"Look here," he said, "I love Heda, and whatever her family history may be I mean to marry her and face the row at home."

"You could scarcely do less in all the circumstances, and as for rows, that young lady would soon fit herself into any place that you can give her. But the question is, how can you marry her?"

"Oh! something will happen," he replied optimistically.

"You are quite right there. Something will certainly happen, but the point is—what? Something was very near happening when I turned up on that stoep, so near that I think it was lucky for you, or for Miss Heda, or both, that I have learned how to handle a pistol. Now let me see your foot, and don't speak another word to me about all this business to-night. I'd rather tackle it when I am clear-headed in the morning."

"Well, I examined his instep and leg very carefully and found that Rodd was right. Although it still hurt him to walk, the wound was quite healed and all inflammation had gone from the limb. Now it was only a question of time for the sinews to right themselves. While I was thus engaged he held forth on the virtues and charms of Heda, I making no comment.

"Lie down and get to sleep, if you can," I said when I had finished. "The door is locked and I am going on to the stoep, so you needn't be afraid of the windows. Good-night."

I went out and sat myself down in such a position that by the light of the hanging lamp, which still burned, I could make sure that no one could approach either Heda's or my room without my seeing him. For the rest, all my life I have been accustomed to night vigils, and the loaded revolver hung from my wrist by a loop of hide. Moreover, never had I felt less sleepy. There I sat hour after hour, thinking.

The substance of my thoughts does not matter, since the events that followed make them superfluous to the story. I will merely record, therefore, that towards dawn a great horror took hold of me. I did not know of what I was afraid, but I was much afraid of something. Nothing was passing in either Heda's or our room, of that I made sure by personal examination. Therefore it would seem that my terrors were unnecessary, and yet they grew and grew. I felt sure that something was happening somewhere, a dread occurrence which it was beyond my power to prevent, though whether it were in this house or at the other end of Africa I did not know.

The mental depression increased and culminated. Then of a sudden it passed completely away, and as I mopped the sweat from off my brow I noticed that dawn was breaking. It was a tender and beautiful dawn, and in a dim way I took it as a good omen. Of course it was nothing but the daily resurrection of the sun, and yet it brought to me comfort and hope. The night was past with all its fears; the light had come with all its joys. From that moment I was certain that we should triumph over these difficulties and that the end of them would be peace.

So sure was I that I ventured to take a nap, knowing that the slightest movement or sound would wake me. I suppose I slept until six o'clock, when I was aroused by a footfall. I sprang up, and saw before me one of our native servants. He was trembling and his face was ashen beneath the black. Moreover he could not speak. All he did was to put his head on one side, like a dead man, and keep on pointing downwards. Then with his mouth open and starting eyes he beckoned to me to follow him.

I followed.

Rodd's Last Card

The man led me to Marnham's room, which I had never entered before. All I could see at first, for the shutters were closed, was that the place seemed large, as bedchambers go in South Africa. When my eyes grew accustomed to the light, I made out the figure of a man seated in a chair with his head bent forward over a table that was placed at the foot of the bed almost in the centre of the room. I threw open the shutters and the morning light poured in. The man was Marnham. On the table were writing materials, also a brandy bottle with only a dreg of spirit in it. I looked for the glass and found it by his side on the floor, shattered, not merely broken.

"Drunk," I said aloud, whereon the servant, who understood me, spoke for the first time, saying in a frightened voice in Dutch—

"No, Baas, dead, half cold. I found him so just now."

I bent down and examined Marnham, also felt his face. Sure enough, he was dead, for his jaw had fallen; also his flesh was chill, and from him came a horrible smell of brandy. I thought for a moment, then bade the boy fetch Dr. Rodd and say nothing to any one else, He went, and now for the first time I noticed a large envelope addressed "Allan Quatermain, Esq." in a somewhat shaky hand. This I picked up and slipped into my pocket.

Rodd arrived half dressed.

"What's the matter now?" he growled.

I pointed to Marnham, saying—

"That is a question for you to answer.

"Oh! drunk again, I suppose," he said. Then he did as I had done, bent down and examined him. A few seconds later he stepped or reeled back, looking as frightened as a man could be, and exclaiming—

"Dead as a stone, by God! Dead these three hours or more."

"Quite so," I answered, "but what killed him?"

"How should I know?" he asked savagely. "Do you suspect me of poisoning him?"

"My mind is open," I replied; "but as you quarrelled so bitterly last night, others might."

The bolt went home; he saw his danger.

"Probably the old sot died in a fit, or of too much brandy. How can one know without a post-mortem? But that mustn't be made by me. I'm off to inform the magistrate and get hold of another doctor. Let the body remain as it is until I return.

I reflected quickly. Ought I to let him go or not? If he had any hand in this business, doubtless he intended to escape. Well, supposing this were so and he did escapee, that would be a good thing for Heda, and really it was no affair of mine to bring the fellow to justice. Moreover there was nothing to show that he was guilty; his whole manner seemed to point another way, though of course he might be acting.

"Very well," I replied, "but return as quickly as possible."

He stood for a few seconds like a man who is dazed. It occurred to me that it might have come into his mind with Marnham's death that he had lost his hold over Heda. But if so he said nothing of it, but only asked—

"Will you go instead of me?"

"On the whole I think not," I replied, "and if I did, the story I should have to tell might not tend to your advantage.

"That's true, damn you!" he exclaimed and left the room.

Ten minutes later he was galloping towards Pilgrim's Rest. Before I departed from the death chamber I examined the place carefully to see if I could find any poison or other deadly thing, but without success. One thing I did discover, however. Turning the leaf of a blotting-book that was by Marnham's elbow, I came upon a sheet of paper on which were written these words in his hand, "Greater love hath no man than this—" that was all.

Either he had forgotten the end of the quotation or changed his mind, or was unable through weakness to finish the sentence. This paper also I put in my pocket. Bolting the shutters and locking the door I returned to the stoep, where I was alone, for as yet no one else was stirring. Then I remembered the letter in my pocket and opened it. It ran—

"Dear Mr. Quatermain,—

"I have remembered that those who quarrel with Dr. Rodd are apt to die soon and suddenly; at any rate life at my age is always uncertain. Therefore, as I know you to be an honest man, I am enclosing my will that it may be in safe keeping and purpose to send it to your room to-morrow morning. Perhaps when you return to Pretoria you will deposit it in the Standard Bank there, and if I am still alive, forward me the receipt. You will see that I leave everything to my daughter whom I dearly love, and that there is enough to keep the wolf from her door, besides my share in this property, if it is ever realized.

"After all that has passed to-night I do not feel up to writing a long letter, so

"Remain sincerely yours,

"H. A. Marnham."

"PS.—I should like to state clearly upon paper that my earnest hope and wish are that Heda may get clear of that black-hearted, murderous, scoundrel Rodd and marry Mr. Anscombe, whom I like and who, I am sure, would make her a good husband."

Thinking to myself this did not look very like the letter of a suicide, I glanced through the will, as the testator seemed to have wished that I should do so. It was short, but properly drawn, signed, and witnessed, and bequeathed a sum of £9,000, which was on deposit at the Standard Bank, together with all his other property, real and personal, to Heda for her own sole use, free from the debts and engagements of her husband, should she marry. Also she was forbidden to spend more than £1,000 of the capital. In short the money was strictly tied up. With the will were some other papers that apparently referred to certain property in Hungary to which Heda might become entitled, but about these I did not trouble.

Replacing these documents in a safe inner pocket in the lining of my waistcoat, I went into our room and woke up Anscombe who was sleeping soundly, a fact that caused an unreasonable irritation in my mind. When at length he was thoroughly aroused I said to him—

"You are in luck's way, my friend. Marnham is dead."

"Oh! poor Heda," he exclaimed, "she loved him. It will half break her heart."

"If it breaks half of her heart," I replied, "it will mend the other half, for now her filial affection can't force her to marry Rodd, and that is where you are in luck's way."

Then I told him all the story.

"Was he murdered or did he commit suicide?" he asked when I had finished.

"I don't know, and to tell you the truth I don't want to know; nor will you if you are wise, unless knowledge is forced upon you. It is enough that he is dead, and for his daughter's sake the less the circumstances of his end are examined into the better."

"Poor Heda!" he said again, "who will tell her? I can't. *You* found him, Allan."

"I expected that job would be my share of the business, Anscombe. Well, the sooner it is over the better. Now dress yourself and come on to the stoep."

Then I left him and next minute met Heda's fat, half-breed maid, a stupid but good sort of a woman who was called Kaatje, emerging from her mistress's room with a jug, to fetch hot water, I suppose.

"Kaatje," I said, "go back and tell the Missie Heda that I want to speak to her as soon as I can. Never mind the hot water, but stop and help her to dress."

She began to grumble a little in a good-natured way, but something in my eye stopped her and she went back into the room. Ten minutes later Heda was by my side.

"What is it, Mr. Quatermain?" she asked. "I feel sure that something dreadful has happened."

"It has, my dear," I answered, "that is, if death is dreadful. Your father died last night."

"Oh!" she said, "oh!" and sank back on to the seat.

"Bear up," I went on, "we must all die one day, and he had reached the full age of man."

"But I loved him," she moaned. "He had many faults I know, still I loved him."

"It is the lot of life, Heda, that we should lose what we love. Be thankful, therefore, that you have some one left to love."

"Yes, thank God! that's true. If it had been him—no, it's wicked to say that."

Then I told her the story, and while I was doing so, Anscombe joined us, walking by aid of his stick. Also I showed them both Marnham's letter to me and the will, but the other bit of paper I did not speak of or show.

She sat very pale and quiet and listened till I had done. Then she said—

"I should like to see him."

"Perhaps it is as well," I answered. "If you can bear it, come at once, and do you come also, Anscombe."

We went to the room, Anscombe and Heda holding each other by the hand. I unlocked the door and, entering, threw open a shutter. There sat the dead man as I had left him, only his head had fallen over a little. She gazed at him, trembling, then advanced and kissed his cold forehead, muttering,

"Good-bye, father. Oh! good-bye, father."

A thought struck me, and I asked—

"Is there any place here where your father locked up things? As I have shown you, you are his heiress, and if so it might be as well in this house that you should possess yourself of his property."

"There is a safe in the corner," she answered, "of which he always kept the key in his trouser pocket."

"Then with your leave I will open it in your presence."

Going to the dead man I searched his pocket and found in it a bunch of keys. These I withdrew and went to the safe over which a skin rug was thrown. I unlocked it easily enough. Within were two bags of gold, each marked £100; also another larger bag marked "My wife's jewelry. For Heda"; also some papers and a miniature of the lady whose portrait hung in the sitting-room; also some loose gold.

"Now who will take charge of these?" I asked. "I do not think it safe to leave them here."

"You, of course," said Anscombe, while Heda nodded.

So with a groan I consigned all these valuables to my capacious pockets. Then I locked up the empty safe, replaced the keys where I had found them on Marnham, fastened the shutter and left the room with Anscombe, waiting for a while outside till Heda joined us, sobbing a little. After this we got something to eat, insisting on Heda doing the same.

On leaving the table I saw a curious sight, namely, the patients whom Rodd was attending in the little hospital of which I have spoken, departing towards the bush-veld, those of them who could walk well and the attendants assisting the others. They were already some distance away, too far indeed for me to follow, as I did not wish to leave the house. The incident filled me with suspicion, and I went round to the back to make inquiries, but could find no one. As I passed the hospital door, however, I heard a voice calling in Sisutu—

"Do not leave me behind, my brothers."

I entered and saw the man on whom Rodd had operated the day of our arrival, lying in bed and quite alone. I asked him where the others had gone. At first he would not answer, but when I pretended to leave him, called out that it was back to their own country. Finally, to cut the story short, I extracted from him that they had left because they had news that the Temple was going to be attacked by Sekukuni and did not wish to be here when I and Anscombe were killed. How the news reached him he refused, or could not, say; nor did he seem to know anything of the death of Marnham. When I pressed him on the former point, he only groaned and cried for water, for he was in pain and thirsty. I asked him who had told Sekukuni's people to kill us, but he refused to speak.

"Very well," I said, "then you shall lie here alone and die of thirst," and again I turned towards the door.

At this he cried out—

"I will tell you. It was the white medicine-man who lives here; he who cut me open. He arranged it all a few days ago because he hates you. Last night he rode to tell the impi when to come."

"When is it to come?" I asked, holding the jug of water towards him.

"To-night at the rising of the moon, so that it may get far away before the dawn. My people are thirsty for your blood and for that of the other white chief, because you killed so many of them by the river. The others they will not harm."

"How did you learn all this?" I asked him again, but without result, for he became incoherent and only muttered something about being left alone because the others could not carry him. So I gave him some water, after which he fell asleep, or pretended to do so, and I left him, wondering whether he was delirious, or spoke truth. As I passed the stables I saw that my own horse was there, for in this district horses are always shut up at night to keep them from catching sickness, but that the four beasts that had brought Heda from Natal in the Cape cart were gone, though it was evident that they had been kraaled here till within an hour or two. I threw my horse a bundle of forage and returned to the house by the back entrance. The kitchen was empty, but crouched by the door of Marnham's room sat the boy who had found him dead. He had been attached to his master and seemed half dazed. I asked him where the other servants were, to which he replied that they had all run away. Then I asked him where the horses were. He answered that the Baas Rodd had ordered them to be turned out before he rode off that morning. I bade him accompany me to the stoep, as I dared not let him out of my sight, which he did unwillingly enough.

There I found Anscombe and Heda. They were seated side by side upon the couch. Tears were running down her face and he, looking very troubled, held her by the hand. Somehow that picture of Heda has always remained fixed in my mind. Sorrow becomes some women and she was one of them. Her beautiful dark grey eyes did not grow red with weeping; the tears just welled up in them and fell like dewdrops from the heart of a flower.

She sat very upright and very still, as he did, looking straight in front of her, while a ray of sunshine, falling on her head, showed the chestnut-hued lights in her waving hair, of which she had a great abundance.

Indeed the pair of them, thus seated side by side, reminded me of an engraving I had seen somewhere of the statues of a husband and wife in an old Egyptian tomb. With just such a look did the woman of thousands of years ago sit gazing in patient hope into the darkness of the future. Death had made her sad, but it was gone by, and the little wistful smile about her lips seemed to suggest that in this darkness her sorrowful eyes already saw the stirring of the new life to be. Moreover, was not the man she loved the companion of her hopes as he had been of her woes. Such was the fanciful thought that sprang up in my mind, even in the midst of those great anxieties, like a single flower in a stony wilderness of thorns or one star on the blackness of the night.

In a moment it had gone and I was telling them of what I had learned. They listened till I had finished. Then Anscombe said slowly—

"Two of us can't hold this house against an impi. We must get out of it."

"Both your conclusions seem quite sound," I remarked, "that is if yonder old Kaffir is telling the truth. But the question is—how? We can't all three of us ride on one nag, as you are still a cripple."

"There is the Cape cart," suggested Heda.

"Yes, but the horses have been turned out, and I don't know where to look for them. Nor dare I send that boy alone, for probably he would bolt like the others. I think that you had better get on my horse and ride for it, leaving us to take our chance. I daresay the whole thing is a lie and that we shall be in no danger," I added by way of softening the suggestion.

"That I will never do," she replied with so much quiet conviction that I saw it was useless to pursue the argument.

I thought for a moment, as the position was very difficult. The boy was not to be trusted, and if I went with him I should be leaving these two alone and, in Anscombe's state, almost defenceless. Still it seemed as though I must. Just then I looked up, and there at the garden gate saw Anscombe's driver, Footsack, the man whom I had despatched to Pretoria to fetch his oxen. I noted that he looked frightened and was breathless, for his eyes started out of his head. Also his hat was gone and he bled a little from his face.

Seeing us he ran up the path and sat down as though he were tired.

"Where are the oxen?" I asked.

"Oh! Baas," he answered, "the Basutos have got them. We heard from an old black woman that Sekukuni had an impi out, so we waited on the top of that hill about an hour's ride away to see if it was true. Then suddenly the doctor Baas appeared riding, and I ran out and asked him if it were safe to go on. He knew me again and answered—

"'Yes, quite safe, for have I not just ridden this road without meeting so much as a black child. Go on, man; your masters will be glad to have their oxen, as they wish to trek, or will by nightfall.' Then he laughed and rode away.

"So we went on, driving the oxen. But when we came to the belt of thorns at the bottom of the hill, we found that the doctor Baas had either lied to us or he had not seen. For there suddenly the tall grass on either side of the path grew spears; yes, everywhere were spears. In a minute the two voorloopers were assegaied. As for me, I ran forward, not back, since the Kaffirs were behind me, across the path, Baas, driving off the oxen. They sprang at me, but I jumped this way and that way and avoided them. Then they threw assegais—see, one of them cut my cheek, but the rest missed. They had guns in their hands also, but none shot. I think they did not wish to make a noise. Only one of them shouted after me—

"'Tell Macumazahn that we are going to call on him tonight when he cannot see to shoot. We have a message for him from our brothers whom he killed at the drift of the Oliphant's River.'

"Then I ran on here without stopping, but I saw no more Kaffirs. That is all, Baas."

Now I did not delay to cross-examine the man or to sift the true from the false in his story, since it was clear to me that he had run into a company of Basutos, or rather been beguiled thereto by Rodd, and lost our cattle, also his companions, who were either killed as he said, or had escaped some other way.

"Listen, man," I said. "I am going to fetch some horses. Do you stay here and help the Missie to pack the cart and make the harness ready. If you disobey me or run away, then I will find you and you will never run again. Do you understand?"

He vowed that he did and went to get some water, while I explained everything to Anscombe and Heda, pointing out that all the information we could gather seemed to show that no attack was to be made upon the house before nightfall, and that therefore we had the day before us. As this was so I proposed to go to look for the horses myself, since otherwise I was sure we should never find them. Meanwhile Heda must pack and make ready the cart with the help of Footsack, Anscombe superintending everything, as he could very well do since he was now able to walk leaning on a stick.

Of course neither of them liked my leaving them, but in view of our necessities they raised no objection. So off I went, taking the boy with me. He did not want to go, being, as I have said, half dazed with grief or fear, or both, but when I had pointed out to him clearly that I was quite prepared to shoot him if he played tricks, he changed his mind. Having saddled my mare that was now fresh and fat, we started, the boy guiding me to a certain kloof at the foot of which there was a small plain of good grass where he said the horses were accustomed to graze.

Here sure enough we found two of them, and as they had been turned out with their headstalls on, were able to tie them to trees with the riems which were attached to the headstalls. But the others were not there, and as two horses could not drag a heavy Cape cart, I was obliged to continue the search. Oh! what a hunt those beasts gave me. Finding themselves free, for as Rodd's object was that they should stray, he had ordered the stable-boy not to kneel-halter them, after filling themselves with grass they had started off for the farm where they were bred, which, it seemed, was about fifty miles away, grazing as they went. Of course I did not know this at the time, so for several hours I rode up and down the neighbouring kloofs, as the ground was too hard for me to hope to follow them by their spoor.

It occurred to me to ask the boy where the horses came from, a question that he happened to be able to answer, as he had brought them home when they were bought the year before. Having learned in what direction the place lay I rode for it at an angle, or rather for the path that led to it, making the boy run alongside, holding to my stirrup leather. About three o'clock in the afternoon I struck this path, or rather track, at a point ten or twelve miles away from the Temple, and there, just mounting a rise, met the two horses quietly walking towards me. Had I been a quarter of an hour later they would have passed and vanished into a sea of thorn-veld. We caught them without trouble and once more headed homewards, leading them by their riems.

Reaching the glade where the other two were tied up, we collected them also and returned to the house, where we arrived at five o'clock. As everything seemed quiet I put my mare into the stable, slipped its bit and gave it some forage. Then I went round the house, and to my great joy found Anscombe and Heda waiting anxiously, but with nothing to report, and with them Footsack. Very hastily I swallowed some food, while Footsack inspanned the horses. In a quarter of an hour all was ready. Then suddenly, in an inconsequent female fashion, Heda developed a dislike to leaving her father unburied.

"My dear young lady," I said, "it seems that you must choose between that and our all stopping to be buried with him."

She saw the point and compromised upon paying him a visit of farewell, which I left her to do in Anscombe's company, while I fetched my mare. To tell the truth I felt as though I had seen enough of the unhappy Marnham, and not for £50 would I have entered that room again. As l passed the door of the hospital, leading my horse, I heard the old Kaffir screaming within and sent the boy who was with me to find out what was the matter with him. That was the last I saw of either of them, or ever shall see this side of kingdom come. I wonder what became of them?

When I got back to the front of the house I found the cart standing ready at the gate, Footsack at the head of the horses and Heda with Anscombe at her side. It had been neatly packed during the day by Heda with such of her and our belongings as it would hold, including our arms and ammunition. The rest, of course, we were obliged to abandon. Also there were two baskets full of food, some bottles of brandy and a good supply of overcoats and wraps. I told Footsack to take the reins, as I knew him to be a good driver, and helped Anscombe to a seat at his side, while Heda and the maid Kaatje got in behind in order to balance the vehicle. I determined to ride, at any rate for the present.

"Which way, Baas?" asked Footsack.

"Down to the Granite Stream where the wagon stands," I answered.

"That will be through the Yellow-wood Swamp. Can't we take the other road to Pilgrim's Rest and Lydenburg, or to Barberton?" asked Anscombe in a vague way, and as I thought, rather nervously.

"No," I answered, "that is unless you wish to meet those Basutos who stole the oxen and Dr. Rodd returning, if he means to return."

"Oh! let us go through the Yellow-wood," exclaimed Heda, who, I think, would rather have met the devil than Dr. Rodd.

"Ah! if I had but known that we were heading straight for that person, sooner would I have faced the Basutos twice over. But I did what seemed wisest, thinking that he would be sure to return with another doctor or a magistrate by the shorter and easier path which he had followed in the morning. It just shows once more how useless are all our care and foresight, or how strong is Fate, have it which way you will.

So we started down the slope, and I, riding behind, noted poor Heda staring at the marble house, which grew ever more beautiful as it receded and the roughness of its building disappeared, especially at that part of it which hid the body of her old scamp of a father whom still she loved. We came down to the glen and once more saw the bones of the blue wildebeeste that we had shot—oh! years and years ago, or so it seemed. Then we struck out for the Granite Stream.

Before we reached the patch of Yellow-wood forest where I knew that the cart must travel very slowly because of the trees and the swampy nature of the ground, I pushed on ahead to reconnoitre, fearing lest there might be Basutos hidden in this cover. Riding straight through it I went as far as the deserted wagon at a sharp canter, seeing nothing one. Once indeed, towards the end of the wood where it was more dense, I thought that I heard a man cough and peered about me through the gloom, for here the rays of the sun, which was getting low in the heavens, scarcely penetrated. As I could perceive no one I came to the conclusion that I must have been deceived by my fancy. Or perhaps it was some baboon that coughed, though it was strange that a baboon should have come to such a low-lying spot where there was nothing for it to eat.

The place was eerie, so much so that I bethought me of tales of the ghosts whereby it was supposed to be haunted. Also, oddly enough, of Anscombe's presentiment which he had fulfilled by killing a Basuto. Look! There lay his grinning skull with some patches of hair still on it, dragged away from the rest of the bones by a hyena. I cantered on down the slope beyond the wood and through the scattered thorns to the stream on the banks of which the wagon should be. It had gone, and by the freshness of the trail, within an hour or two. A moment's reflection told me what had happened. Having stolen our oxen the Basutos drove them to the wagon, inspanned them and departed with their loot. On the whole I was glad to see this, since it suggested that they had retired towards their own country, leaving our road open.

Turning my horse I rode back again to meet the cart. As I reached the edge of the wood at the top of the slope I heard a whistle blown, a very shrill whistle, of which the sound would travel for a mile or two on that still air. Also I heard the sound of men's voices in altercation and caught words, such as—"Let go, or by Heaven—!" then a furious laugh and other words which seemed to be—"In five minutes the Kaffirs will be here. In ten you will be dead. Can I help it if they kill you after I have warned you to turn back?" Then a woman's scream.

Rodd's voice, Anscombe's voice and Kaatje's scream—not Heda's but Kaatje's!

Then as I rode furiously round the last patch of intervening trees the sound of a pistol shot. I was out of them now and saw everything. There was the cart on the further side of a swamp. The horses were standing still and snorting. Holding the rein of one of the leaders was Rodd, whose horse also stood close by. He was rocking on his feet and as I leapt from my mare and ran up, I saw his face. it was horrible, full of pain and devilish rage. With his disengaged hand he pointed to Anscombe sitting in the cart and grasping a pistol that still smoked.

"You've killed me," he said in a hoarse, choking voice, for he was shot through the lung, "to get her," and he waved his hand towards Heda who was peering at him between the heads of the two men. "You are a murderer, as her father was, and as David was before you. Well, I hope you won't keep her long. I hope you'll die as I do and break her false heart, you damned thief."

All of this he said in a slow voice, pausing between the words and speaking ever more thickly as the blood from his wound choked him. Then of a sudden it burst in a stream from his lips, and still pointing with an accusing finger at Anscombe, he fell backwards into the slimy pool behind him and there vanished without a struggle.

So horrible was the sight that the driver, Footsack, leapt from the cart, uttering a kind of low howl, ran to Rodd's horse, scrambled into the saddle and galloped off, striking it with his fist, where to I do not know. Anscombe put his hand before his eyes, Heda sank down on the seat in a heap, and the coloured woman, Kaatje, beat her breast and said something in Dutch about being accursed or bewitched. Luckily I kept my wits and went to the horses' heads, fearing lest they should start and drag the trap into the pool. "Wake up," I said. "That fellow has only got what he deserved, and you were quite right to shoot him."

"I am glad you think so," answered Anscombe absently. "It was so like murder. Don't you remember I told you I should kill a man in this place and about a woman?"

"I remember nothing," I answered boldly, "except that if we stop here much longer we shall have those Basutos on us. That brute was whistling to them and holding the horses till they came to kill us. Pull yourself together, take the reins and follow me."

He obeyed, being a skilful whip enough who, as he informed me afterwards, had been accustomed to drive a four-in-hand at home. Mounting my horse, which stood by, I guided the cart out of the wood and down the slope beyond, till at length we came to our old outspan where I proposed to turn on to the wagon track which ran to Pilgrim's Rest. I say proposed, for when I looked up it I perceived about five hundred yards away a number of armed Basutos running towards us, the red light of the sunset shining on their spears. Evidently the scout or spy to whom Rodd whistled, had called them out of their ambush which they had set for us on the Pilgrim's Rest road in order that they might catch us if we tried to escape that way.

Now there was only one thing to be done. At this spot a native track ran across the little stream and up a steepish slope beyond. On the first occasion of our outspanning here I had the curiosity to mount this slope, reflecting as I did so that although rough it would be quite practicable for a wagon. At the top of it I found a wide flat plain, almost high-veld, for the bushes were very few, across which the track ran on. On subsequent inquiry I discovered that it was one used by the Swazis and other natives when they made their raids upon the Basutos, or when bodies of them went to work in the mines.

"Follow me," I shouted and crossed the stream which was shallow between the little pools, then led the way up the stony slope. The four horses negotiated it very well and the Cape cart, being splendidly built, took no harm. At the top I looked back and saw that the Basutos were following us.

"Flog the horses!" I cried to Anscombe, and off we went at a hand gallop along the native track, the cart swaying and bumping upon the rough veld. The sun was setting now, in half an hour it would be quite dark.

Could we keep ahead of them for that half hour?

Flight

The sun sank in a blaze of glory. Looking back by the light of its last rays I saw a single native silhouetted against the red sky. He was standing on a mound that we had passed a mile or more behind us, doubtless waiting for his companions whom he had outrun. So they had not given up the chase. What was to be done? Once it was completely dark we could not go on. We should lose our way; the horses would get into ant-bear holes and break their legs. Perhaps we might become bogged in some hollow, therefore we must wait till the moon rose, which would not be for a couple of hours.

Meanwhile those accursed Basutos would be following us even in the dark. This would hamper them, no doubt, but they would keep the path, with which they were probably familiar, beneath their feet, and what is more, the ground being soft with recent rain, they could feel the wheel spoor with their fingers. I looked about me. Just here another track started off in a nor'-westerly direction from that which we were following. Perhaps it ran to Lydenburg; I do not know. To our left, not more than a hundred yards or so away, the higher veld came to an end and sloped in an easterly direction down to bush-land below.

Should I take the westerly road which ran over a great plain? No, for then we might be seen for miles and cut off. Moreover, even if we escaped the natives, was it desirable should plunge into civilization just now and tell all our story, as in that case we must do. Rodd's death was quite justified, but it had happened on Transvaal territory and would require a deal of explanation. Fortunately there was no witness of it, except ourselves. Yes, there was though—the driver Footsack, if he had got away, which, being mounted, would seem probable, a man who, for my part, I would not trust for a moment. It would be an ugly thing to see Anscombe in the dock charged with murder and possibly myself, with Footsack giving evidence against us before a Boer jury who might be hard on Englishmen. Also there was the body with a bullet in it.

Suddenly there came into my mind a recollection of the very vivid dream of Zikali which had visited me, and I reflected that in Zululand there would be little need to trouble about the death of Rodd. But Zululand was a long way off, and if we were to avoid the Transvaal, there was only one way of going there, namely through Swaziland. Well, among the Swazis we should be quite safe from the Basutos, since the two peoples were at fierce enmity. Moreover I knew the Swazi chiefs and king very well, having traded there, and could explain that I came to collect debts owing to me.

There was another difficulty. I had heard that the trouble between the English Government and Cetewayo, the Zulu king, was coming to a head, and that the High Commissioner, Sir Bartle Frere, talked of presenting him with an ultimatum. It would be awkward if this arrived while we were in the country, though even so, being on such friendly terms with the Zulus of all classes, I did not think that I, or any with me, would run great risks.

All these thoughts rushed through my brain while I considered what to do. At the moment it was useless to ask the opinion of the others who were but children in native matters. I and I alone must take the responsibility and act, praying that I might do so aright. Another moment and I had made up my mind.

Signing to Anscombe to follow me, I rode about a hundred yards or more down the nor'-westerly path. Then I turned sharply along a rather stony ridge of ground, the cart following me all the time, and came back across our own track, our my object being of course to puzzle any Kaffirs who might spoor us. Now we were on the edge of the gentle slope that led down to the bush-veld. Over this I rode towards a deserted cattle kraal built of stones, in the rich soil of which grew sundry trees; doubtless one of those which had been abandoned when Mosilikatze swept all this country on his way north about the year 1838. The way to it was easy, since the surrounding stones had been collected to build the kraal generations before. As we passed over the edge of the slope in the gathering gloom, Heda cried—

"Look!" and pointed in the direction whence we came. Far away a sheet of flame shot upwards.

"The house is burning," she exclaimed.

"Yes," I said, "it can be nothing else;" adding to myself, "a good job too, for now there will be no postmortem on old Marnham."

Who fired the place I never learnt. It may have been the Basutos, or Marnham's body-servant, or Footsack, or a spark from the kitchen fire. At any rate it blazed merrily enough notwithstanding the marble walls, as a wood-lined and thatched building of course would do. On the whole I suspected the boy, who may very well have feared lest he should be accused of having had a hand in his master's death. At least it was gone, and watching the distant flames I bethought me that with it went all Heda's past. Twenty-four hours before her father was alive, the bondservant of Rodd and a criminal. Now he was ashes and Rodd was dead, while she and the man she loved were free, with all the world before them. I wished that I could have added that they were safe. Afterwards she told me that much the same ideas passed through her own mind.

Dismounting I led the horses into the old kraal through the gap in the wall which once had been the gateway. It was a large kraal that probably in bygone days had held the cattle of some forgotten head chief whose town would have stood on the brow of the rise; so large that notwithstanding the trees I have mentioned, there was plenty of room for the cart and horses in its centre. Moreover, on such soil the grass grew so richly that after we had slipped their bits, the horses were able to fill themselves without being unharnessed. Also a little stream from a spring on the brow ran within a few yards whence, with the help of Kaatje, a strong woman, I watered them with the bucket which hung underneath the cart. Next we drank ourselves and ate some food in the darkness that was now complete. Then leaving Kaatje to stand at the head of the horses in case they should attempt any sudden movement, I climbed into the cart, and we discussed things in low whispers.

It was a curious debate in that intense gloom which, close as our faces were together, prevented us from seeing anything of each other, except once when a sudden flare of summer lightning revealed them, white and unnatural as those of ghosts. On our present dangers I did not dwell, putting them aside lightly, though I knew they were not light. But of the alternative as to whether we should try to escape to Lydenburg and civilization, or to Zululand and savagery, I felt it to be my duty to speak.

"To put it plainly," said Anscombe in his slow way when I had finished, "you mean that in the Transvaal I might be tried as a murderer and perhaps convicted, whereas if we vanish into Zululand the probability is that this would not happen."

"I mean," I whispered back, "that we might both be tried and, if Footsack should chance to appear and give evidence, find ourselves in an awkward position. Also there is another witness—Kaatje, and for the matter of that, Heda herself. Of course her evidence would be in our favour, but to make it understood by a jury she would have to explain a great deal of which she might prefer not to speak. Further, at the best, the whole business would get into the English papers, which you and your relatives might think disagreeable, especially in view of the fact that, as I understand, you and Heda intend to marry."

"Still I think that I would rather face it out," he said in his outspoken way, "even if it should mean that I could never return to England. After all, of what have I to be afraid? I shot this scoundrel because I was obliged to do so."

"Yes, but it is of this that you may have to convince a jury who might possibly find a motive in Rodd's past, and your present, relationship to the same lady. But what has she to say?"

"I have to say," whispered Heda, "that for myself I care nothing, but that I could never bear to see all these stories about my poor father raked up. Also there is Maurice to be considered. It would be terrible if they put him in prison—or worse. Let us go to Zululand, Mr. Quatermain, and afterwards get out of Africa. Don't you agree, Maurice?"

"What does Mr. Quatermain think himself?" he answered. "He is the oldest and by far the wisest of us and I will be guided by him."

Now I considered and said—

"There is such a thing as flying from present troubles to others that may be worse, the 'ills we know not of.' Zululand is disturbed. If war broke out there we might all be killed. On the other hand we might not, and it ought to be possible for you to work up to Delagoa Bay and there get some ship home, that is if you wish to keep clear of British law. I cannot do so, as I must stay in Africa. Nor can I take the responsibility of settling what you are to do, since if things went wrong, it would be on my head. However, if you decide for the Transvaal or Natal and we escape, I must tell you that I shall go to the first magistrate we find and make a full deposition of all that has happened. It is not possible for me to live with the charge of having been concerned in the shooting of a white man hanging over me that might be brought up at any time, perhaps when no one was left in the country to give evidence on my behalf, for then, even if I were acquitted my name would always be tarnished. In Zululand, on the other hand, there are no magistrates before whom I could depose, and if this business should come out, I can always say that we went there to escape from the Basutos. Now I am going to get down to see if the horses are all right. Do you two talk the thing over and make up your minds. Whatever you agree on, I shall accept and do my best to carry through." Then, without waiting for an answer, I slipped from the cart.

Having examined the horses, who were cropping all the grass within reach of them, I crept to the wall of the kraal so as to be quite out of earshot. The night was now pitch dark, dark as it only knows how to be in Africa. More, a thunderstorm was coming up of which that flash of sheet lightning had been a presage. The air was electric. From the vast bush-clad valley beneath us came a wild, moaning sound caused, I suppose, by wind among the trees, though here I felt none; far away a sudden spear of lightning stabbed the sky. The brooding trouble of nature spread to my own heart. I was afraid, and not of our present dangers, though these were real enough, so real that in a few hours we might all be dead.

To dangers I was accustomed; for years they had been my daily food by day and by night, and, as I think I have said elsewhere, I am a fatalist, one who knows full well that when God wants me He will take me; that is if He can want such a poor, erring creature. Nothing that I did or left undone could postpone or hasten His summons for a moment, though of course I knew it to be my duty to fight against death and to avoid it for as long as I might, because that I should do so was a portion of His plan. For we are all part of a great pattern, and the continuance or cessation of our lives re-acts upon other lives, and therefore life is a trust.

No, it was of greater things that I felt afraid, things terrible and imminent which I could not grasp and much less understand. I understand them now, but who would have guessed that on the issue of that whispered colloquy in the cart behind me, depended the fate of a people and many thousands of lives? As I was to learn in days to come, if Anscombe and Heda had determined upon heading for the Transvaal, there would, as I believe, have been no Zulu war, which in its turn meant that there would have been no Boer Rebellion and that the mysterious course of history would have been changed.

I shook myself together and returned to the cart.

"Well," I whispered, but there was no answer. A moment later there came another flash of lightning.

"There," said Heda, "how many do you make it?

"Ninety-eight," he answered.

"I counted ninety-nine," she said, "but anyway it was within the hundred. Mr. Quatermain, we will go to Zululand, if you please, if you will show us the way there."

"Right," I answered, "but might I ask what that has to do with your both counting a hundred?"

"Only this," she said, "we could not make up our minds. Maurice was for the Transvaal, I was for Zululand. So you see we agreed that if another flash came before we counted a hundred, we would go to Zululand, and if it didn't, to Pretoria. A very good way of settling, wasn't it?"

"Excellent!" I replied, "quite excellent for those who could think of such a thing."

As a matter of fact I don't know which of them thought of it because I never inquired. But I did remember afterwards how Anscombe had tossed with a lucky penny when it was a question whether we should or should not run for the wagon during our difficulty by the Oliphant's River; also when I asked him the reason for this strange proceeding he answered that Providence might inhabit a penny as well as anything else, and that he wished to give it—I mean Providence—a chance. How much more then, he may have argued, could it inhabit a flash of lightning which has always been considered a divine manifestation from the time of the Roman Jove, and no doubt far before him.

Forty or fifty generations ago, which is not long, our ancestors set great store by the behaviour of lightning and thunder, and doubtless the instinct is still in our blood, in the same way that all our existing superstitions about the moon come down to us from the time when our forefathers worshipped her. They did this for tens of hundreds or thousands of years, and can we expect a few coatings of the veneer that we politely call civilization, which after all is only one of our conventions that vanish in any human stress such as war, to kill out the human impulse it seems to hide? I do not know, though I have my own opinion, and probably these young people never reasoned the matter out. They just acted on an intuition as ancient as that which had attracted them to each other, namely a desire to consult the ruling fates by omens or symbols. Or perhaps Anscombe thought that as his experience with the penny had proved so successful, he would give Providence another "chance." If so it took it and no mistake. Confound it! I don't know what he thought; I only dwell on the matter because of the great results which followed this consultation of the Sybilline books of heaven.

As it happened my speculations, if I really indulged in any at that time, were suddenly extinguished by the bursting of the storm. It was of the usual character, short but very violent. Of a sudden the sky became alive with lightnings and the atmosphere with the roar of winds. One flash struck a tree quite near the kraal, and I saw that tree seem to melt in its fiery embrace, while about where it had been, rose a column of dust from the ground beneath. The horses were so frightened that luckily they stood quite quiet, as I have often known animals to do in such circumstances. Then came the rain, a torrential rain as I, who was out in it holding the horses, became painfully aware. It thinned after a while, however, as the storm rolled away.

Suddenly in a silence between the tremendous echoes of the passing thunder I thought that I heard voices somewhere on the brow of the slope, and as the horses were now quite calm, I crept through the trees to that part of the enclosure which I judged to be nearest to them.

Voices they were sure enough, and of the Basutos who were pursuing us. What was more, they were coming down the slope. The top of the old wall reached almost to my chin. Taking off my hat I thrust my head forward between two loose stones, that I might hear the better.

The men were talking together in Sisutu. One, whom I took to be their captain, said to the others—

"That white-headed old jackal, Macumazahn, has given us the slip again. He doubled on his tracks and drove the horses down the hillside to the lower path in the valley. I could feel where the wheels went over the edge."

"It is so, Father," answered another voice, "but we shall catch him and the others at the bottom if we get there before the moon rises, since they cannot have moved far in this rain and darkness. Let me go first and guide you who know every tree and stone upon this slope where I used to herd cattle when I was a child."

"Do so," said the captain. "I can see nothing now the lightning has gone, and were it not that I have sworn to dip my spear in the blood of Macumazahn who has fooled us again, I would give up the hunt."

"I think it would be better to give it up in any case," said a third voice, "since it is known throughout the land that no luck has ever come to those who tried to trap the Watcher-by-Night. Oh! he is a leopard who springs and is gone again. How many are the throats in which his fangs have met. Leave him alone, I say, lest our fate should be that of the white doctor in the Yellow-wood Swamp, he who set us on this hunt. We have his wagon and his cattle; let us be satisfied."

"I will leave him alone when he sleeps for the last time, and not before," answered the captain, "he who shot my brother in the drift the other day. What would Sekukuni say if we let him escape to bring the Swazis on us? Moreover, we want that white maiden for a hostage in case the English should attack us again. Come, you who know the road, and lead us."

There was some disturbance as this man passed to the front. Then I heard the line move forward. Presently they were going by the wall within a foot or two of me. Indeed by ill-luck just as we were opposite to each other the captain stumbled and fell against the wall.

"There is an old cattle kraal here," he said. "What if those white rats have hidden in it?"

I trembled as I heard the words. If a horse should neigh or make any noise that could be heard above the hiss of the rain! I did not dare to move for fear lest I should betray myself. There I stood so close to the Kaffirs that I could smell them and hear the rain pattering on their bodies. Only very stealthily I drew my hunting knife with my right hand. At that moment the lightning, which I thought had quite gone by, flashed again for the last time, revealing the fat face of the Basuto captain within a foot of my own, for he was turned towards the wall on which one of his hands rested. Moreover, the blue and ghastly light revealed mine to him thrust forward between the two stones, my eyes glaring at him.

"The head of a dead man is set upon the wall!" he cried in terror. "It is the ghost of—"

He got no further, for as the last word passed his lips I drove the knife at him with all my strength deep into his throat. He fell back into the arms of his followers, and next instant I heard the sound of many feet rushing in terror down the hill. What became of him I do not know, but if he still lives, probably he agrees with his tribesman that Macumazahn—Watcher-by-Night, or his ghost "is a leopard who springs and kills and is gone again"; also, that those who try to trap him meet with no luck. I say, or his ghost—because I am sure he thought that I was a spirit of the dead; doubtless I must have looked like one with my white, rain-drowned face appearing there between the stones and made ghastly and livid by the lightning.

Well, they had gone, the whole band of them, not less than thirty or forty men, so I went also, back to the cart where I found the others very comfortable indeed beneath the rainproof tilt. Saying nothing of what had happened, of which they were as innocent as babes, I took a stiff tot of brandy, for I was chilled through by the wet, and while waiting for the moon to rise, busied myself with getting the bits back into the horses' mouths—an awkward job in the dark. At length it appeared in a clear sky, for the storm had quite departed and the rain ceased. As soon as there was light enough I took the near leader by the bridle and led the cart to the brow of the hill, which was not easy under the conditions, making Kaatje follow with my horse.

Then, as there were no signs of any Basutos, we started on again, I riding about a hundred yards ahead, keeping a sharp look-out for a possible ambush. Fortunately, however, the veld was bare and open, consisting of long waves of ground. One start I did get, thinking that I saw men's heads just on the crest of a wave, which turned out to be only a herd of springbuck feeding among the tussocks of grass. I was very glad to see them, since their presence assured me that no human being had recently passed that way.

All night long we trekked, following the Kaffir path for as could see it, and after that going by my compass. I knew whereabouts the drift of the Crocodile River should be, as I had crossed it twice before in my life, and kept my eyes open for a certain tall koppie which stood within half a mile it on the Swazi side of the river. Ultimately to my joy I caught sight of this hill faintly outlined against the sky and headed for it. Half a mile further on I struck a wagon-track made by Boers trekking into Swazi-Land to trade or shoot. Then I knew that the drift was straight ahead of us, and called to Anscombe to flog up the weary horses.

We reached the river just before the dawn. To my horror it was very full, so full that the drift looked dangerous, for it had been swollen by the thunder-rain of the previous night. Indeed some wandering Swazis on the further bank shouted to us that we should be drowned if we tried to cross.

"Which means that the only thing to do is to stay until the water runs down," I said to Anscombe, for the two women, tired out, were asleep.

"I suppose so," he answered, "unless those Basutos—"

I looked back up the long slope down which we had come and saw no one. Then I raised myself in my stirrups and looked along another track that joined the road just here, leading from the bush-veld, as ours led from the high-veld. The sun was rising now, dispersing the mist that hung about the trees after the wet. Searching among these with my eyes, presently I perceived the light gleaming upon what I knew must be the points of spears projecting above the level of the ground vapour.

"Those devils are after us by the lower road," I said to Anscombe, adding, "I heard them pass the old cattle kraal last night. They followed our spoor over the edge of the hill, but in the dark lost it among the stones."

He whistled and asked what was to be done.

"That is for you to decide," I answered. "For my part I'd rather risk the river than the Basutos," and I looked at the slumbering Heda.

"Can we bolt back the way we came, Allan?"

"The horses are very spent and we might meet more Basutos," and again I looked at Heda.

"A hard choice, Allan. It is wonderful how women complicate everything in life, because they are life, I suppose." He thought a moment and went on, "Let's try the river. If we fail, it will be soon over, and it is better to drown than be speared."

"Or be kept alive by savages who hate us," I exclaimed, with my eyes still fixed upon Heda.

Then I got to business. There were hide riems on the bridles of the leaders. I undid these and knotted their loose ends firmly together. To them I made fast the riem of my own mare, slipping a loop I tied in it, over my right hand and saying—

"Now I will go first, leading the horses. Do you drive after me for all you are worth, even if they are swept off their feet. I can trust my beast to swim straight, and being a mare, I hope that the horses will follow her as they have done all night. Wake up Heda and Kaatje."

He nodded, and looking very pale, said—

"Heda my dear, I am sorry to disturb you, but we have to get over a river with a rough bottom, so you and Kaatje must hang on and sit tight. Don't be frightened, you are as safe as a church."

"God forgive him for that lie," thought I to myself as, having tightened the girths, I mounted my mare. Then gripping the riem I kicked the beast to a canter, Anscombe flogging up the team as we swung down the bank to the edge of the foaming torrent, on the further side of which the Swazis shouted and gesticulated to us to go back.

We were in it now, for, as I had hoped, the horses followed the mare without hesitation. For the first twenty yards or so all went well, I heading up the stream. Then suddenly I felt that the mare was swimming.

"Flog the horses and don't let them turn," I shouted to Anscombe.

Ten more yards and I glanced over my shoulder. The team was swimming also, and behind them the cart rocked and bobbed like a boat swinging in a heavy sea. There came a strain on the riem; the leaders were trying to turn! I pulled hard and encouraged them with my voice, while Anscombe, who drove splendidly, kept their heads as straight as he could. Mercifully they came round again and struck out for the further shore, the water-logged cart floating after them. Would it turn over? That was the question in my mind. Five seconds; ten seconds and it was still upright. Oh! it was going. No, a fierce back eddy caught it and set it straight again. My mare touched bottom and there was hope. It struggled forward, being swept down the stream all the time. Now the horses in the cart also found their footing and we were saved.

No, the wet had caused the knot of one of the riems to slip beneath the strain, or perhaps it broke—I don't know. Feeling the pull slacken the leaders whipped round on to the wheelers. There they all stood in a heap, their heads and part of their necks above water, while the cart floated behind them on its side. Kaatje screamed and Anscombe flogged. I leapt from my mare and struggled to the leaders, the water up to my chin. Grasping their bits I managed to keep them from turning further. But I could do no more and death came very near to us. Had it not been for some of those brave Swazis on the bank it would have found us, every one. But they plunged in, eight of them, holding each other's hands, and half-swimming, half-wading, reached us. They got the horses by the head and straightened them out, while Anscombe plied his whip. A dash forward and the wheels were on the bottom again.

Three minutes later we were safe on the further bank, which my mare had already reached, where I lay gasping on my face, ejaculating prayers of thankfulness and spitting out muddy water.

Nombe

The Swazis, shivering, for all these people hate cold, and shaking themselves like a dog when he comes to shore, gathered round, examining me.

"Why!" said one of them, an elderly man who seemed to be their leader, "this is none other than Macumazahn, Watcher-by-Night, the old friend of all us black people. Surely the spirits of our fathers have been with us who might have risked our lives to save a Boer or a half-breed." (The Swazis, I may explain, did not like the Boers for reasons they considered sound.)

"Yes," I said, sitting up, "it is I, Macumazahn."

"Then why," asked the man, "did you, whom all know to be wise, show yourself to have suddenly become a fool?" and he pointed to the raging river.

"And why," I asked, "do you show yourself a fool by supposing that I, whom you know to be none, am a fool? Look across the water for your answer."

He looked and saw the Basutos, fifty or more of them, arriving, just too late.

"Who are these?" he asked.

"They are the people of Sekukuni whom you should know well enough. They have hunted us all night, yes, and before, seeking to murder us; also they have stolen our oxen, thirty-two fine oxen which I give to your king if he can take them back. Now perhaps you understand why we dared the Crocodile River in its rage."

At the name of Sekukuni the man, who it seemed was the captain of some border guards, stiffened all over like a terrier which perceives a rat. "What!" he exclaimed, "do these dirty Basuto dogs dare to carry spears so near our country? Have they not yet learned their lesson?"

Then he rushed into the water, shaking an assegai he had snatched up, and shouted,

"Bide a while, you fleas from the kaross of Sekukuni, till I can come across and crack you between my thumb and finger. Or at the least wait until Macumazahn has time to get his rifle. No, put down those guns of yours; for every shot you fire I swear that I will cut ten Basuto throats when we come to storm your koppies, as we shall do ere long."

"Be silent," I said, "and let me speak."

Then I, too, called across the river, asking where was that fat captain of theirs, as I would talk with him. One of the men shouted back that he had stopped behind, very sick, because of a ghost that he had seen.

"Ah!" I answered, "a ghost who pricked him in the throat. Well, I was that ghost, and such are the things that happen to those who would harm Macumazahn and his friends. Did you not say last night that he is a leopard who leaps out in the dark, bites and is gone again?"

"Yes," the man shouted back, "and it is true, though had we known, O Macumazahn, that you were the ghost hiding in those stones, you should never have leapt again. Oh! that white medicine-man who is dead has sent us on a mad errand."

"So you will think when I come to visit you among your koppies. Go home and take a message from Macumazahn to Sekukuni, who believes that the English have run away from him. Tell him that they will return again and these Swazis with them, and that then he will cease to live and his town will be burnt and his tribe will no more be a tribe. Away now, more swiftly than you came, since the water by which you thought to trap us is falling, and a Swazi impi gathers to make an end of every one of you."

The man attempted no answer, nor did his people so much as fire on us. They turned tail and crept off like a pack of frightened jackals—pursued by the mocking of the Swazis.

Still in a way they had the laugh of us, seeing that they gave us a terrible fright and stole our wagon and thirty-two oxen. Well, a year or two later I helped to pay them back for that fright and even recovered some of the oxen.

When they had gone the Swazis led us to a kraal about two miles from the river, sending on a runner with orders to make huts and food ready for us. It was just as much as we could do to reach it, for we were all utterly worn out, as were the horses. Still we did get there at last, the hot sun warming us as we went. Arrived at the kraal I helped Heda and Kaatje from the cart—the former could scarcely walk, poor dear—and into the guest hut which seemed clean, where food of a sort and fur karosses were brought to them in which to wrap themselves while their clothes dried.

Leaving them in charge of two old women, I went to see to Anscombe, who as yet could not do much for himself, also to the outspanning of the horses which were put into a cattle kraal, where they lay down at once without attempting to eat the green forage which was given to them. After this I gave our goods into the charge of the kraal-head, a nice old fellow whom I had never met before, and he led Anscombe to another hut close to that where the women were. Here we drank some maas, that is curdled milk, ate a little mutton, though we were too fatigued to be very hungry, and stripping off our wet clothes, threw them out into the sun to dry.

"That was a close shave," said Anscombe as he wrapped up in the kaross.

"Very," I answered. "So close that I think you must have been started in life with an extra strong guardian angel well accustomed to native ways."

"Yes," he replied, "and, old fellow, I believe that on earth he goes by the name of Allan Quatermain."

After this I remember no more, for I went to sleep, and so remained for about twenty-four hours. This was not wonderful, seeing that for two days and nights practically I had not rested, during which time I went through much fatigue and many emotions.

When at length I did wake up, the first thing I saw was Anscombe already dressed, engaged in cleaning my clothes with a brush from his toilet case. I remember thinking how smart and incongruous that dressing-bag, made appropriately enough of crocodile hide, looked in this Kaffir hut with its silver-topped bottles and its ivory-handled razors.

"Time to get up, Sir. Bath ready, Sir," he said in his jolly, drawling voice, pointing to a calabash full of hot water. "Hope you slept as well as I did, Sir."

"You appear to have recovered your spirits," I remarked as I rose and began to wash myself.

"Yes, Sir, and why not? Heda is quite well, for I have seen her. These Swazis are very good people, and as Kaatje understands their language, bring us all we want. Our troubles seem to be done with. Old Marnham is dead, and doubtless cremated; Rodd is dead and, let us hope, in heaven; the Basutos have melted away, the morning is fine and warm and a whole kid is cooking for breakfast."

"I wish there were two, for I am ravenous," I remarked.

"The horses are getting rested and feeding well, though some of their legs have filled, and the trap is little the worse, for I have walked to look at them, or rather hopped, leaning on the shoulder of a very sniffy Swazi boy. Do you know, old fellow, I believe there never were any Basutos; also that the venerable Marnham and the lurid Todd had no real existence, that they were but illusions, a prolonged nightmare—no more. Here is your shirt. I am sorry that I have not had time to wash it, but it has cooked well in the sun, which, being flannel, is almost as good."

"At any rate Heda remains," I remarked, cutting his nonsense short, "and I suppose she is not a nightmare or a delusion."

"Yes, thank God! she remains," he replied with earnestness. "Oh! Allan, I thought she must drown in that river, and if I had lost her, I think I should have gone mad. Indeed, at the moment I felt myself going mad while I dragged and flogged at those horses."

"Well, you didn't lose her, and if she had drowned, you would have drowned also. So don't talk any more about it. She is safe, and now we have got to keep her so, for you are not married yet, my boy, and there are generally more trees in a wood than one can see. Still we are alive and well, which is more than we had any right to expect, and, as you say, let us thank God for that."

Then I put on my coat and my boots which Anscombe had greased as he had no blacking, and crept from the hut.

There, only a few yards away, engaged in setting the breakfast in the shadow of another hut on a tanned hide that served for a tablecloth while Kaatje saw to the cooking close by, I found Heda, still a little pale and sorrowful but otherwise quite well and rested. Moreover, she had managed to dress herself very nicely, I suppose by help of spare clothes in the cart, and therefore looked as charming as she always did. I think that her perfect manners were one of her greatest attractions. Thus on this morning her first thought was to thank me very sweetly for all she was good enough to say I had done for her and Anscombe, thereby, as she put it, saving their lives several times over.

"My dear young lady," I answered as roughly as I could, "don't flatter yourself on that point; it was my own life of which I was thinking."

But she only smiled and, shaking her head in a fascinating way that was peculiar to her, remarked that I could not deceive her as I did the Kaffirs. After this the solid Kaatje brought the food and we breakfasted very heartily, or at least I did.

Now I am not going to set out all the details of our journey through Swazi-Land, for though in some ways it was interesting enough, also as comfortable as a stay among savages can be, for everywhere we were kindly received, to do so would be too long, and I must get on with my story. At the king's kraal, which we did not reach for some days as the absence of roads and the flooded state of the rivers, also the need of sparing our horses, caused us to travel very slowly, I met a Boer who I think was concession hunting.

He told me that things were really serious in Zululand, so serious that he thought there was a probability of immediate war between the English and the Zulus. He said also that Cetewayo, the Zulu king, had sent messengers to stir up the Basutos and other tribes against the white men, with the result that Sekukuni had already made a raid towards Pilgrim's Rest and Lydenburg.

I expressed surprise and asked innocently if he had done any harm. The Boer replied he understood that they had stolen some cattle, killed two white men, if not more, and burnt their house. He added, however, that he was not sure whether the white men had been killed by the Kaffirs or by other white men with whom they had quarrelled. There was a rumour to this effect, and he understood that the magistrate of Barberton had gone with some mounted police and armed natives to investigate the matter.

Then we parted, as, having got his concession to which the king Umbandine had put his mark when he was drunk on brandy that the Boer himself had brought with him as a present, he was anxious to be gone before he grew sober and revoked it. Indeed, he was in so great a hurry that he never stopped to inquire what I was doing in Swazi-Land, nor do I think he realized that I was not alone. Certainly he was quite unaware that I had been mixed up in these Basuto troubles. Still his story as to the investigation concerning the deaths of Marnham and Rodd made me uneasy, since I feared lest he should hear something on his journey and put two and two together, though as a matter of fact I don't think he ever did either of these things.

The Swazis told me much the same story as to the brewing Zulu storm. In fact an old Induna or councillor, whom I knew, informed me that Cetewayo had sent messengers to them, asking for their help if it should come to fighting with the white men, but that the king and councillors answered that they had always been the Queen's children (which was not strictly true, as they were never under English rule) and did not wish to "bite her feet if she should have to fight with her hands." I replied that I hoped they would always act up to these fine words, and changed the subject.

Now once more the question arose as to whether we should make for Natal or press on to Zululand. The rumour of coming war suggested that the first would be our better course, while the Boer's story as to the investigation of Rodd's death pointed the other way. Really I did not know which to do, and as usual Anscombe and Heda seemed inclined to leave the decision to me. I think that after all Natal would have gained the day had it not been for a singular circumstance, not a flash of lightning this time. Indeed, I had almost made up my mind to risk trouble and inquiry as to Rodd's death, remembering that in Natal these two young people could get married, which, being in loco parentis, I thought it desirable they should do as soon as possible, if only to ease me of my responsibilities. Also thence I could attend to the matter of Heda's inheritance and rid myself of her father's will that already had been somewhat damaged in the Crocodile River, though not as much as it might have been since I had taken the precaution to enclose it in Anscombe's sponge bag before we left the house.

The circumstance was this: On emerging from the cart one morning, where I slept to keep an eye upon the valuables, for it will be remembered that we had a considerable sum in gold with us, also Heda's jewels, a Swazi informed me that a messenger wished to see me. I asked what messenger and whence did he come. He replied that the messenger was a witch-doctoress named Nombe, and that she came from Zululand and said that I knew her father.

I bade the man bring her to me, wondering who on earth she could be, for it is not usual for the Zulus to send women as messengers, and from whom it came. However, I knew exactly what she would be like, some hideous old hag smelling horribly of grease and other abominations, with a worn snake skin and some human bones tied about her.

Presently she came, escorted by the Swazi who was grinning, for I think he guessed what I expected to see. I stared and rubbed my eyes, thinking that I must still be asleep, for instead of a fat old Isanusi there appeared a tall and graceful young woman, rather light-coloured, with deep and quiet eyes and a by no means ill-favoured face, remarkable for a fixed and somewhat mysterious smile. She was a witch-doctoress sure enough, for she wore in her hair the regulation bladders and about her neck the circlet of baboon's teeth, also round her middle a girdle from which hung little bags of medicines.

She contemplated me gravely and I contemplated her, waiting till she should choose to speak. At length, having examined me inch by inch, she saluted by raising her rounded arm and tapering hand, and remarked in a soft, full voice—

"All is as the picture told. I perceive before me the lord Macumazahn."

I thought this a strange saying, seeing that I could not recollect having given my photograph to any one in Zululand.

"You need no magic to tell you that, doctoress," I remarked, "but where did you see my picture?"

"In the dust far away," she replied.

"And who showed it to you?"

"One who knew you, O Macumazahn, in the years before I came out of the Darkness, one named Opener of Roads, and with him another who also knew you in those years, one who has gone down to the Darkness."

Now for some occult reason I shrank from asking the name of this "one who had gone down to the Darkness,' although I was sure that she was waiting for the question. So I merely remarked, without showing surprise—

"So Zikali still lives, does he? He should have been dead long ago."

"You know well that he lives, Macumazahn, for how could he die till his work was accomplished? Moreover, you will remember that he spoke to you when last moon was but just past her full—in a dream, Macumazahn. I brought that dream, although you did not see me."

"Pish!" I exclaimed. "Have done with your talk of dreams. Who thinks anything of dreams?"

"You do," she replied even more placidly than before, "you whom that dream has brought hither—with others."

"You lie," I said rudely. "The Basutos brought me here."

"The Watcher-by-Night is pleased to say that I lie, so doubtless I do lie," she answered, her fixed smile deepening a little. Then she folded her arms across her breast and remained silent.

"You are a messenger, O seer of pictures in the dust and bearer of the cup of dreams," I said with sarcasm. "Who sends a message by your lips for me, and what are the words of the message?"

"My Lords the Spirits spoke the message by the mouth of the master Zikali. He sends it on to you by the lips of your servant, the doctoress Nombe."

"Are you indeed a doctoress, being so young?" I asked, for somehow I wished to postpone the hearing of that message.

"O Macumazahn, I have heard the call, I have felt the pain in my back, I have drunk of the black medicine and of the white medicine, yes, for a whole year. I have been visited by the multitude of Spirits and seen the shades of those who live and of those who are dead. I have dived into the river and drawn my snake from its mud; see, its skin is about me now," and opening the mantle she wore she showed what looked like the skin of a black mamba, fastened round her slender body. "I have dwelt in the wilderness alone and listened to its voices. I have sat at the feet of my master, the Opener of Roads, and looked down the road and drunk of his wisdom. Yes, I am in truth a doctoress."

"Well, after all this, you should be as wise as you are pretty."

"Once before, Macumazahn, you told a maid of my people that she was pretty and she came to no good end; though to one that was great. Therefore do not say to me that I am pretty, though I am glad that you should think so who can compare me with so many whom you have known," and she dropped her eyes, looking a little shy.

It was the first human touch I had seen about her, and I was glad to have found a weak spot in her armour. Moreover, from that moment she was always my friend.

"As you will, Nombe. Now for your message."

"My Lords the Spirits, speaking through Zikali as one who makes music speak through a pipe of reeds, say—"

"Never mind what the spirits say. Tell me what Zikali says," I interrupted.

"So be it, Macumazahn. These are the words of Zikali: 'O Watcher-by-Night, the time draws on when the Thing-who-should-never-have-been-born will be as though he never had been born, whereat he rejoices. But first there is much for him to do, and as he told you nearly three hundred moons ago, in what must be done you will have your part. Of that he will speak to you afterwards. Macumazahn, you dreamed a dream, did you not, lying asleep in the house that was built of white stone which now is black with fire? I, Zikali, sent you that dream through the arts of a child of mine who is named Nombe, she to whom I have given a Spirit to guide her feet. You did well to follow it, Macumazahn, for had you tried the other path, which would have led you back to the towns of the white men, you and those with you must have been killed, how it does not matter. Now by the mouth of Nombe I say to you, do not follow the thought that is in your mind as she speaks to you and go to Natal, since if you do so, you and those with you will come to much shame and trouble that to you would be worse than death, over the matter of the killing of a certain white doctor in a swamp where grow yellow-wood trees. For there in Natal you will be taken, all of you, and sent back to the Transvaal to be tried before a man who wears upon his head horse's hair stained white. But if you come to Zululand this shadow shall pass away from you, since great things are about to happen which will cause so small a matter to be forgot. Moreover, I Zikali, who do not lie, promise this: That however great may be their dangers here in Zululand, those half-fledged ones whom you, the old night-hawk, cover with your wings, shall in the end suffer no harm; those of whom I spoke to you in your dream, the white lord, Mauriti, and the white lady, Heddana, who stretch out their arms one to another. I wait to welcome you, here at the Black Kloof, whither my daughter Nombe will guide you. Cetewayo, the king, also will welcome you, and so will another whose name I do not utter. Now choose. I have spoken.'"

Having delivered her message Nombe stood quite still, smiling as before, and apparently indifferent as to its effect.

"How do I know that you come from Zikali?" I asked. "You may be but the bait set upon a trap."

From somewhere within her robe she produced a knife and handed it to me, remarking—

"The Master says you will remember this, and by it know that the message comes from him. He bade me add that with it was carved a certain image that once he gave to you at Panda's kraal, wrapped round with a woman's hair, which image you still have."

I looked at the knife and did remember it, for it was one of those of Swedish make with a wooden handle, the first that I had ever seen in Africa. I had made a present of it to Zikali when I returned to Zululand before the war between the Princes. The image, too, I still possessed. It was that of the woman called Mameena who brought about the war, and the wrapping which covered it was of the hair that once grew upon her head.

"The words are Zikali's," I said, returning her the knife, "but why do you call yourself the child of one who is too old to be a father?"

"The Master says that my great-grandmother was his daughter and that therefore I am his child. Now, Macumazahn, I go to eat with my people, for I have servants with me. Then I must speak with the Swazi king, for whom I also have a message, which I cannot do at present because he is still drunk with the white man's liquor. After that I shall be ready to return with you to Zululand."

"I never said that I was going to Zululand, Nombe."

"Yet your heart has gone there already, Macumazahn, and you must follow your heart. Does not the image which was carved with the knife you gave, hold a white heart in its hand, and although it seems to be but a bit of Umzimbeete wood, is it not alive and bewitched, which perhaps is why you could never make up your mind to burn it, Macumazahn?"

"I wish I had," I replied angrily; but having thrown this last spear, with a flash of her unholy eyes Nombe had turned and gone.

A clever woman and thoroughly coached, thought I. Well, Zikali was never one to suffer fools, and doubtless she is another of the pawns whom he uses on his board of policy. Oh! she, or rather he was right; my heart was in Zululand, though not in the way he thought, and I longed to see the end of that great game played by a wizard against a despot and his hosts.

So we went to Zululand because after talking it over we all came to the conclusion that this was the best thing to do, especially as there we seemed to be sure of a welcome. For later in the day Nombe repeated to Anscombe and Heda the invitation which she had delivered to me, assuring them also that in Zululand they would come to no harm.

It was curious to watch the meeting between Heda and Nombe. The doctoress appeared just as we had risen from breakfast, and Heda, turning round, came face to face with her.

Is this your witch, Mr. Quatermain?" she asked me in her vivacious way. "Why, she is different from what I expected, quite good-looking and, yes, impressive. I am not sure that she does not frighten me a little."

"What does the Inkosikaasi (i.e., the chieftainess) say concerning me, Macumazahn?" asked Nombe.

"Only what I said, that you are young who she thought would be old, and pretty who she thought would be ugly."

"To grow old we must first be young, Macumazahn, and in due season all of us will become ugly, even the Inkosikaasi. But I thought she said also that she feared me."

"Do you know English, Nombe?"

"Nay, but I know how to read eyes, and the Inkosikaasi has eyes that talk. Tell her that she has no reason to fear me who would be her friend, though I think that she will bring me little luck."

It was scarcely necessary, so far as Heda was concerned, but I translated, leaving out the last sentence.

"Say to her that I am grateful who have few friends, and that I will fear her no more," said Heda.

Again I translated, whereon Nombe stretched out her hand, saying—

"Let her not scorn to take it, it is clean. It has brought no man to his death—" Here she looked at Heda meaningly. "Moreover, though she is white and I am black, I like herself am of high blood and come of a race of warriors who did nothing small, and lastly, we are of an age, and if she is beautiful, I am wise and have gifts great as her own."

Once more I interpreted for the benefit of Anscombe, for Heda understood Zulu well enough, although she had pretended not to do so, after which the two shook hands, to Anscombe's amusement and my wonder. For I felt this scene to be strained and one that hid, or presaged, something I did not comprehend.

"This is the Chief she loves?" said Nombe to me, studying Anscombe with her steady eyes after Heda had gone. "Well, he is no common man and brave, if idle; one, too, who may grow tall in the world, should he live, when he has learned to think. But, Macumazahn, if she met you both at the same time why did she not choose you?"

"Just now you said you were wise, Nombe," I replied laughing, "but now I see that, like most of your trade, you are but a vain boaster. Is there a hat upon my head that you cannot see the colour of my hair, and is it natural that youth should turn to age?"

"Sometimes if the mind is old, Macumazahn, which is why I love the Spirits only who are more ancient than the mountains, and with them Zikali their servant, who was young before the Zulus were a people, or so he says, and still year by year gathers wisdom as the bee gathers honey. Inspan your horses, Macumazahn, for I have done my business and am ready to start."

Zikali

Ten days had gone by when once more I found myself drawing near to the mouth of the Black Kloof where dwelt Zikali the Wizard. Our journey in Zululand had been tedious and uneventful. It seemed to me that we met extraordinarily few people; it was as though the place had suddenly become depopulated, and I even passed great kraals where there was no one to be seen. I asked Nombe what was the meaning of this, for she and three silent men she had with her were acting as our guides. Once she answered that the people had moved because of lack of food, as the season had been one of great scarcity owing to drought, and once that they had been summoned to a gathering at the king's kraal near Ulundi. At any rate they were not there, and the few who did appear stared at us strangely.

Moreover, I noticed that they were not allowed to speak to us. Also Heda was kept in the cart and Nombe insisted that the rear canvas curtain should be closed and a blanket fastened behind Anscombe who drove, evidently with the object that she should not be seen. Further, on the plea of weariness, from the time that we entered Zulu territory Nombe asked to be allowed to ride in the cart with Kaatje and Heda, her real reason, as I was sure, being that she might keep a watch on them. Lastly we travelled by little-frequented tracks, halting at night in out-of-the-way places, where, however, we always found food awaiting us, doubtless by arrangement.

With one man whom I had known in past days and who recognized me, I did manage to have a short talk. He asked me what I was doing in Zululand at that time. I replied that I was on a visit to Zikali, whereon he said I should be safer with him than with any one else.

Our conversation went no further, for just then one of Nombe's servants appeared and made some remark to the man of which I could not catch the meaning, whereon he promptly turned and deported, leaving me wondering and uneasy.

Evidently we were being isolated, but when I remonstrated with Nombe she only answered with her most unfathomable smile—

"O Macumazahn, you must ask Zikali of all these things. I am no one and know nothing, who only do what the Master tells me is for your good."

"I am minded to turn and depart from Zululand," I said angrily, "for in this low veld whither you have led us there is fever and the horses will catch sickness or be bitten by the tsetse fly and perish."

"I cannot say, Macumazahn, who only travel by the road the Master pointed out. Yet if you will be guided by me, you will not try to leave Zululand."

"You mean that I am in a trap, Nombe."

"I mean that the country is full of soldiers and that all white men have fled from it. Therefore, even if you were allowed to pass because the Zulus love you, Macumazahn, it might well happen that those with you would stay behind, sound asleep, Macumazahn, for which, like you, I should be sorry."

After this I said no more, for I knew that she meant to warn me. We had entered on this business and must see it through to its end, sweet or bitter.

As for Anscombe and Heda their happiness seemed to be complete. The novelty of the life charmed them, and of its dangers they took no thought, being content to leave me, in whom they had a blind faith, to manage everything. Moreover, Heda, who in the joy of her love was beginning to forget the sorrow of her father's death and the other tragic events through which she had just passed, took a great fancy to the young witch-doctoress who conversed with her in Zulu, a language of which, having lived so long in Natal, Heda knew much already. Indeed, when I suggested to her that to be over-trusting was not wise, she fired up and replied that she had been accustomed to natives all her life and could judge them, adding that she had every confidence in Nombe.

After this I held my tongue and said no more of my doubts. What was the use since Heda would not listen to them, and at that time Anscombe was nothing but her echo?

So this, for me, very dull journey continued, till at length, after being held up for a couple of days by a flooded river where there was nothing to do but sit and smoke, as Nombe requested me not to make a noise by shooting at the big game that abounded, we began to emerge from the bush-veld on to the lovely uplands in the neighbourhood of Nongoma. Leaving these on our right we headed for a place called Ceza, a natural stronghold consisting of a flat plain on the top of a mountain, which plain is surrounded by bush. It is at the foot of this stronghold that the Black Kloof lies, being one of the ravines that run up into the mountain.

So thither we came at last. It was drawing towards sunset, a tremendous and stormy sunset, as we approached the place, and lo! it looked exactly as it had done when first I saw it more than a score of years before, forbidding as the mouth of hell, vast and lonesome. There stood the columns of boulders fantastically piled one upon another; there grew the sparse trees upon its steep sides, mingled with aloes that looked like the shapes of men; there was the granite bottom swept almost clean by floods in some dim age, and the little stream that flowed along it. There, too, was the spot where once I had outspanned my wagons on the night when my servants swore that they saw the Imikovu, or wizard-raised spectres, floating past them on the air in the shapes of the Princes and others who were soon to fall at the battle of the Tugela. Up it we went, I riding and Nombe, who had descended from the cart that followed, walking by my side and watching me.

"You seem sad, Macumazahn," she said at length.

"Yes, Nombe, I am sad. This place makes me so."

"Is it the place, Macumazahn, or is it the thought of one whom once you met in the place, one who is dead?"

I looked at her, pretending not to understand, and she went on—

"I have the gift of vision, Macumazahn, which comes at times to those of my trade, and now and again, amongst others, I have seemed to see the spirit of a certain woman haunting this kloof as though she were waiting for some one."

"Indeed, and what may that woman be like?" I inquired carelessly.

As it chances I can see her now gliding backwards in front of you just there, and therefore am able to answer your question, Macumazahn. She is tall and slender, beautifully made, and light-coloured for one of us black people. She has large eyes like a buck, and those eyes are full of fire that does not come from the sun but from within. Her face is tender yet proud, oh! so proud that she makes me afraid. She wears a cloak of grey fur, and about her neck there is a circlet of big blue beads with which her fingers play. A thought comes from her to me. These are the words of the thought: 'I have waited long in this dark place, watching by day and night till you, the Watcher-by-Night, return to meet me here. At length you have come, and in this enchanted place my hungry spirit can feed upon your spirit for a while. I thank you for coming, who now am no more lonely. Fear nothing, Macumazahn, for by a certain kiss I swear to you that till the appointed hour when you become as I am, I will be a shield upon your arm and a spear in your hand.' Such are the words of her thought, Macumazahn, but she has gone away and I hear no more. It was as though your horse rode over her and she passed through you."

Then, like one who wished to answer no questions, Nombe turned and went back to the cart, where she began to talk indifferently with Heda, for as soon as we entered the kloof her servants had drawn back the curtains and let fall the blanket. As for me, I groaned, for of course I knew that Zikali, who was well acquainted with the appearance of Mameena, had instructed Nombe to say all this to me in order to impress my mind for some reason of his own. Yet he had done it cleverly, for such words as those Mameena might well have uttered could her great spirit have need to walk the earth again. Was such a thing possible, I wondered? No, it was not possible, yet it was true that her atmosphere seemed to cling about this place and that my imagination, excited by memory and Nombe's suggestions, seemed to apprehend her presence.

As I reflected the horse advanced round the little bend in the ever-narrowing cliffs, and there in front of me, under the gigantic mass of overhanging rock, appeared the kraal of Zikali surrounded by its reed fence, The gate of the fence was open, and beyond it, on his stool in front of the large hut, sat Zikali. Even at that distance it was impossible to mistake his figure, which was like no other that I had known in the world. A broad-shouldered dwarf with a huge head, deep, sunken eyes and snowy hair that hung upon his shoulders; the whole frame and face pervaded with an air of great antiquity, and yet owing to the plumpness of the flesh and that freshness of skin which is sometimes seen in the aged, comparatively young-looking.

Such was the great wizard Zikali, known throughout the land for longer than any living man could remember as "Opener of Roads," a title that referred to his powers of spiritual vision, also as the "Thing-that-should-never-have-been-born," a name given to him by Chaka, the first and greatest of the Zulu kings, because of his deformity.

There he sat silent, impassive, staring open-eyed at the red ball of the setting sun, looking more like some unshapely statue than a man. His silent, fierce-faced servants appeared. To me they looked like the same men whom I had seen here three and twenty years before, only grown older. Indeed, I think they were, for they greeted me by name and saluted by raising their broad spears. I dismounted and waited while Anscombe, whose foot was now quite well again, helped Heda from the cart which was led away by the servants. Anscombe, who seemed a little oppressed, remarked that this was a strange place.

"Yes," said Heda, "but it is magnificent. I like it."

Then her eye fell upon Zikali seated before the hut and she turned pale.

"Oh! what a terrible-looking man," she murmured, "if he is a man."

The maid Kaatje saw him also and uttered a little cry.

"Don't be frightened, dear," said Anscombe, "he is only an old dwarf."

"I suppose so," she exclaimed doubtfully, "but to me he is like the devil."

Nombe slid past us. She threw off the kaross she wore and for the first time appeared naked except for the mucha about her middle and her ornaments. Down she went on her hands and knees and in this humble posture crept towards Zikali. Arriving in front of him she touched the ground with her forehead, then lifting her right arm, gave the salute of Makosi, to which as a great wizard he was entitled, being supposed to be the home of many spirits. So far as I could see he took no notice of her. Presently she moved and squatted herself down on his right hand, while two of his attendants appeared from behind the hut and took their stand between him and its doorway, holding their spears raised. About a minute later Nombe beckoned to us to approach, and we went forward across the courtyard, I a little ahead of the others. As we drew near Zikali opened his mouth and uttered a loud and terrifying laugh. How well I remembered that laugh which I had first heard at Dingaan's kraal as a boy after the murder of Retief and the Boers.

"I begin to think that you are right and that this old gentleman must be the devil," said Anscombe to Heda, then lapsed into silence.

As I was determined not to speak first I took the opportunity to fill my pipe. Zikali, who was watching me, although all the while he seemed to be staring at the setting sun, made a sign. One of the servants dashed away and immediately returned, bearing a flaming brand which proffered to me as a pipe-lighter. Then he departed again to bring three carved stools of red wood which he placed for us. I looked at mine and knew it again by the carvings. It was the same on which I had sat when first I met Zikali. At length he spoke in his deep, slow voice.

"Many years have gone by, Macumazahn, since you made use of that stool. They are cut in notches upon the leg you hold and you may count them if you will."

I examined the leg. There were the notches, twenty-two or three of them. On the other legs were more notches too numerous to reckon.

"Do not look at those, Macumazahn, for they have nothing to do with you. They tell the years since the first of the House of Senzangacona sat upon that stool, since Chaka sat upon it, since Dingaan and others sat upon it, one Mameena among them. Well, much has happened since it served you for a rest. You have wandered far and seen strange things and lived where others would have died because it was your lot to live, of all of which we will talk afterwards. And now when you are grey you have come back here, as the Opener of Roads told you you would do, bringing with you new companions, you who have the art of making friends even when you are old, which is one given to few men. Where are those with whom you used to company, Macumazahn? Where are Saduko and Mameena and the rest? All gone except the Thing-who-should-never-have-been-born," and again he laughed loudly.

"And who it seems has never learned when to die," I remarked, speaking for the first time.

"Just so, Macumazahn, because I cannot die until my work is finished. But thanks be to the spirits of my fathers and to my own that I live on to glut with vengeance, the end draws near at last, and as I promised you in the dead days, you shall have your share in it, Macumazahn."

He paused, then continued, still staring at the sinking sun, which made his remarks about us, whom he did not seem to see, uncanny—

"That white man with you is brave and well-born, one who loves fighting, I think, and the maiden is fair and sweet, with a high spirit. She is thinking to herself that I am an old wizard whom, if she were not afraid of me, she would ask to tell her her fortune. See, she understands and starts. Well, perhaps I will one day. Meanwhile, here is a little bit of it. She will have five children, of whom two will die and one will give her so much trouble that she will wish it had died also. But who their father will be I do not say. Nombe my child, lead away this White One and her woman to the hut that has been made ready for her, for she is weary and would rest. See, too, that she lacks for nothing which we can give her who is our guest. Let the white lord, Mauriti, accompany her to the hut and be shown that next to it in which he and Macumazahn will sleep, so that he may be sure that she is safe, and attend to the horses if he wills. There is a place to tether them behind the huts, and the men who travelled with you will help him. Afterwards, when I have spoken with him, Macumazahn can join them that they may eat before they sleep."

These directions I translated to Anscombe, who went gladly enough with Heda, for I think they were both afraid of the terrible old dwarf and did not desire his company in the gathering gloom.

"The sun sinks once more, Macumazahn," he said when they were gone, "and the air grows chill. Come with me now into my hut where the fire burns, for I am aged and the cold strikes through me. Also there we can be alone."

So speaking he turned and crawled into the hut, looking like a gigantic white-headed beetle as he did so, a creature, I remembered, to which I had once compared him in the past. I followed, carrying the historic stool, and when he had seated himself on his kaross on the further side of the fire, took up my position opposite to him. This fire was fed with some kind of root or wood that gave a thin clear flame with little or no smoke. Over it he crouched, so closely that his great head seemed to be almost in the flame at which he stared with unblinking eyes as he had done at the sun, circumstances which added to his terrifying appearance and made me think of a certain region and its inhabitants.

"Why do you come here, Macumazahn?" he asked after studying me for a while through that window of fire.

"Because you brought me, Zikali, partly through your messenger, Nombe, and partly by means of a dream which she says you sent."

"Did I, Macumazahn? If so, I have forgotten it. Dreams are as many as gnats by the water; they bite us while we sleep, but when we wake up we forget them. Also it is foolishness to say that one man can send a dream to another."

"Then your messenger lied, Zikali, especially as she added that she brought it."

"Of course she lied, Macumazahn. Is she not my pupil whom I have trained from a child? Moreover, she lied well, it would seem, who guessed what sort of a dream you would have when you thought of turning your steps to Zululand."

"Why do you play at sticks (i.e. fence) with me, Zikali, seeing that neither of us are children?"

"O Macumazahn, that is where you are mistaken, seeing that both of us, old though we be and cunning though we think ourselves, are nothing but babes in the arms of Fate. Well, well, I will tell you the truth, since it would be foolish to try to throw dust into such eyes as yours. I knew that you were down in Sekukuni's country and I was watching you—through my spies. You have been nowhere during all these years that I was not watching you—through my spies. For instance, that Arab-looking man named Harut, whom first you met at a big kraal in a far country, was a spy of mine. He has visited me lately and told me much of your doings. No, don't ask me of him now who would talk to you of other matters—"

"Does Harut still live then, and has he found a new god in place of the Ivory Child?" I interrupted.

"Macumazahn, if he did not live, how could he visit and speak with me? Well, I watched you there by the Oliphant's River where you fought Sekukuni's people, and afterwards in the marble hut where you found the old white man dead in his chair and got the writings that you have in your pocket which concern the maiden Heddana; also afterwards when the white man, your friend, killed the doctor who fell into a mud hole and the Basutos stole his cattle and wagon."

"How do you know all these things, Zikali?"

"Have I not told you—through my spies. Was there not a half-breed driver called Footsack, and do not the Basutos come and go between the Black Kloof and Sekukuni's town, bearing me tidings?"

"Yes, Zikali, and so does the wind and so do the birds."

"True! O Macumazahn, I see that you are one who has watched Nature and its ways as closely as my spies watch you. So I learned these matters and knew that you were in trouble over the death of these white men, and your friends likewise, and as you were always dear to me, I sent that child Nombe to bring you to me, thinking from what I knew of you that you would be more likely to follow a woman who is both wise and good to look at, than a man who might be neither. I told her to say to you that you and the others would be safer here than in Natal at present. It seems that you hearkened and came. That is all."

"Yes, I hearkened and came. But, Zikali, that is not all, for you know well that you sent for me for your own sake, not for mine."

"O Macumazahn, who can prevent a needle from piercing cloth when it is pushed by a finger like yours? Your wits are too sharp for me, Macumazahn; your eyes read through the blanket of cunning with which I would hide my thought. You speak truly. I did send for you for my own sake as well as for yours. I sent for you because I wanted your counsel, Macumazahn, and because Cetewayo the king also wants your counsel, and I wished to see you before you saw Cetewayo. Now you have the whole truth."

"What do you want my counsel about, Zikali?"

He leaned forward till his white locks almost seemed to mingle with the thin flame, through which he glared at me with eyes that were fiercer than the fire.

"Macumazahn, you remember the story that I told you long ago, do you not?"

"Very well, Zikali. It was that you hate the House of Senzangacona which has given all its kings to Zululand. First, because you are one of the Dwandwe tribe whom the Zulus crushed and mocked at. Secondly, because Chaka the Lion named you the "Thing-that-should-never-have-been-born" and killed your wives, for which crime you brought about the death of Chaka. Thirdly, because you have matched your single wit for many years against all the power of the royal House and yet kept your life in you, notably when Panda threatened you in my presence at the trial of one who has 'gone down,' and you told him to kill you if he dared. Now you would prove that you were right by causing your cunning to triumph over the royal House."

"True, quite true, O Macumazahn. You have a good memory, Macumazahn, especially for anything that has to do with that woman who has 'gone down.' I sent her down, but how was she named, Macumazahn? I forget, I forget, whose mind being old, falls suddenly into black pits of darkness—like her who went down."

He paused and we stared at each other through the veil of fire. Then as I made no answer, he went on—

"Oh! I remember now, she was called Mameena, was she not, a name taken from the wailing of the wind? Hark! It is wailing now."

I listened; it was, and I shivered to hear it, since but a minute before the night had been quite still. Yes, the wind moaned and wailed about the rocks of the Black Kloof.

"Well, enough of her. Why trouble about the dead when there are so many to be sent to join them? Macumazahn, the hour is at hand. The fool Cetewayo has quarrelled with your people, the English, and on my counsel. He has sent and killed women, or allowed others to do so, across the river in Natal. His messengers came to me asking what he should do. I answered, 'Shall a king of the blood of Chaka fear to allow his own wicked ones to be slain because they have stepped across a strip of water, and still call himself king of the Zulus?' So those women were dragged back across the water and killed; and now the Queen's man from the Cape asks many things, great fines of cattle, the giving up of the slayers, and that an end should be made of the Zulu army, which is to lay down its spears and set to hoeing like the old women in the kraals."

"And if the king refuses, what then, Zikali?"

"Then, Macumazahn, the Queen's man will declare war on the Zulus; already he gathers his soldiers for the war."

"Will Cetewayo refuse, Zikali?"

"I do not know. His mind swings this way and that, like a pole balanced on a rock. The ends of the pole are weighted with much counsel, and it hangs so even that if a grasshopper lit on one end or the other, it would turn the scale."

"And do you wish me to be that grasshopper, Zikali?"

"Who else? That is why I brought you to Zululand."

"So you wish me to counsel Cetewayo to lie down in the bed that the English have made for him. If he seeks my advice I will do so gladly, for so I am sure he will sleep well."

"Why do you mock me, Macumazahn? I wish you to counsel Cetewayo to throw back his word into the teeth of the Queen's man and to fight the English."

"And thus bring destruction on the Zulus and death to thousands of them and of my own people, and in return gain nothing but remorse. Do you think me mad or wicked, or both, that I should do this thing?"

"Nay, Macumazahn, you would gain much. I could show you where the king's cattle are hidden. The English will never find them, and after the war you might take as many as you chose. But it would be useless, for knowing you well, I am sure that you would only hand them over to the British Government, as once you handed over the cattle of Bangu, being fashioned that way by the Great-Great, Macumazahn."

"Perhaps I might, but then what should I gain, Zikali?"

"This: you would so bring things about that, being broken by war, the Zulu power could never again menace the white men, which would be a great and good deed, Macumazahn."

"Mayhap—I am not sure. But of this I am sure, that I will nor thrust my face into your nest of wasps, that the English hornets may steal the honey when they are disturbed. I leave such matters to the Queen and those who rule under her. So have done with such talk, for you do but waste your breath, Zikali."

"It is as I guessed it would be," he answered, shaking his great head. "You are too honest to prosper in the world, Macumazahn. Well, I must find other means to bring the House of Cetewayo to the end that he deserves, who has been an evil and a cruel king."

All this he said, showing neither surprise nor resentment, which convinced me of what I had suspected throughout, that never for an instant did he believe that I should fall in with his suggestions and try to influence the Zulus to declare war. No, this talk of his was but a blind; there was some deeper scheme at work in his cunning old brain which he was hiding from me. Why exactly had he beguiled me to Zululand? I could not divine, and to ask him would be worse than useless, but then and there I made up my mind that I would get away from the Black Kloof early on the following morning, if that were possible.

He began to speak of other matters in a low, droning voice, like a man who converses with himself. Sad, all of them, such as the haunted death of Saduko who had betrayed his lord, the Prince Umbelazi, because of a woman, every circumstance of which seemed to be familiar to him.

I made no answer, who was waiting for an opportunity to leave the hut, and did not care to dwell on these events. He ceased and brooded for a while, then said suddenly—

"You are hungry and would eat, Macumazahn, and I who eat little would sleep, for in sleep the multitudes of Spirits visit me, bringing tidings from afar. Well, we have spoken together and of that I am glad, for who knows when the chance will come again, though I think that soon we shall meet at Ulundi, Ulundi where Fate spreads its net. What was it I had to say to you? Ah! I remember. There is one who is always in your thoughts and whom you wish to see, one too who wishes to see you. You shall, you shall in payment for the trouble you have taken in coming so far to visit a poor old Zulu doctor whom, as you told me long ago, you know to be nothing but a cheat."

He paused and, why I could not tell, I grew weak with fear of I knew not what, and bethought me of flight.

"It is cold in this hut, is it not?" he went on. "Burn up, fire, burn up!" and plunging his hand into a catskin bag of medicines which he wore, he drew out some powder which he threw upon the embers that instantly burst into bright flame.

"Look now, Macumazahn," he said, "look to your right."

I looked and oh Heaven! there before me with outstretched arms and infinite yearning on her face, stood Mameena, Mameena as I had last seen her after I gave her the promised kiss that she used to cover her taking of the poison. For five seconds, mayhap, she stood thus, living, wonderful, but still as death, the fierce light showing all. Then the flame died down again and she was gone.

I turned and next instant was out of the hut, pursued by the terrible laughter of Zikali.

Trapped

Outside in the cool night air I recovered myself, sufficiently at any rate to be able to think, and saw at once that the thing was an illusion for which Zikali had prepared my mind very carefully by means of the young witch-doctoress, Nombe. He knew well enough that this remarkable woman, Mameena, had made a deep impression on me nearly a quarter of a century before, as she had done upon other men with whom she had been associated. Therefore it was probable that she would always be present to my thought, since whatever a man forgets, he remembers the women who have shown him favour, true or false, for Nature has decreed it thus.

Moreover, this was one to be remembered for herself, since she was beautiful and most attractive in her wild way. Also she had brought about a great war, causing the death of thousands, and lastly her end might fairly be called majestic. All these impressions Zikali had instructed Nombe to revivify by her continual allusions to Mameena, and lastly by her pretence that she saw her walking in front of me. Then when I was tired and hungry, in that place which for me was so closely connected with this woman, and in his own uncanny company, either by mesmerism or through the action of the drug he threw upon the fire, he had succeeded in calling up the illusion of her presence to my charmed sight. All this was clear enough, what remained obscure was his object.

Possibly he had none beyond an impish desire to frighten me, which is common enough among practitioners of magic in all lands. Well, for a little while he had succeeded, although to speak truth I remained uncertain whether in a sense I was not more thrilled and rejoiced than frightened. Mameena had never been so ill to look upon, and I knew that dead or living I had nothing to fear from her who would have walked through hell fire for my sake, would have done anything, except perhaps sacrifice her ambition. No, even if this were her ghost I should have been glad to see her again.

But it was not a ghost; it was only a fancy reproduced exactly as my mind had photographed her, almost as my eyes last saw her, when her kiss was still warm upon my lips.

Such were my thoughts as I stood outside that hut with the cold perspiration running down my face, for to tell the truth my nerves were upset, although without reason. So upset were they that when suddenly a silent-footed man appeared out of the darkness I jumped as high as though I had set my foot on a puff-adder, and until I recognized him by his voice as one of Nombe's servants who had accompanied us from Swazi-Land, felt quite alarmed. As a matter of fact he had only come to tell me that our meal was ready and that the other "high White Ones" were waiting for me.

He led me round the fence that encircled Zikali's dwelling-place, to two huts that stood nearly behind it, almost against the face of the rock which, overhanging in a curve, formed a kind of natural roof above them. I thought they must have been built since I visited the place, as I, who have a good memory for such things, did not remember them. Indeed, on subsequent examination I found that they were quite new, for the poles that formed their uprights were still green and the grass of the thatch was scarcely dry. It looked to me as if they had been specially constructed for our accommodation.

In one of these huts, that to the right which was allotted to Anscombe and myself, I found the others waiting for me, also the food. It was good of its sort and well cooked, and we ate it by the light of some candles that we had with us, Kaatje serving us. Yet, although a little while before I had been desperately hungry, now my appetite seemed to have left me and I made but a poor meal. Heda and Anscombe also seemed oppressed and ate sparingly. We did not talk much until Kaatje had taken away the tin plates and gone to eat her own supper by a fire that burned outside the hut. Then Heda broke out, saying that she was terrified of this place and especially of its master, the old dwarf, and felt sure that something terrible was going to happen to her. Anscombe did his best to calm her, and I also told her she had nothing to fear.

"If there is nothing to fear, Mr. Quatermain," she answered, turning on me, "why do you look so frightened yourself? By your face you might have seen a ghost."

This sudden and singularly accurate thrust, for after all I had seen something that looked very like a ghost, startled me, and before I could invent any soothing and appropriate fib, Nombe appeared, saying that she had come to lead Heda to her sleeping-place. After this further conversation was impossible since, although Nombe knew but few words of English, she was a great thought-reader and I feared to speak of anything secret in her presence. So we all went out of the hut, Nombe and I drawing back a little to the fire while the lovers said good-night to each other.

"Nombe," I said, "the Inkosikazi Heddana is afraid. The rocks of this kloof lie heavy on her heart; the face of the Opener of Roads is fearful to her and his laughter grates upon her ears. Do you understand?"

"I understand, Macumazahn, and it is as I expected. When you yourself are frightened it is natural that she, an untried maiden, should be frightened also in this home of spirits."

"It is men we fear, not spirits, now when all Zululand is boiling like a pot," I replied angrily.

"Have it as you will, Macumazahn," she said, and at that moment her quiet, searching eyes and fixed smile were hateful to me. "At least you admit that you do fear. Well, for the lady Heddana fear nothing. I sleep across the door of her hut, and while I who have learned to love her, live, I say—for her fear nothing, whatever may chance or whatever you may see or hear."

"I believe you, but, Nombe, you might die."

"Yes, I may die, but be sure of this, that when I die she will be safe, and he who loves her also. Sleep well, Macumazahn, and do not dream too much of what you heard and saw in Zikali's house."

Then before I could speak she turned and left me.

I did *not* sleep well; I slept very badly. To begin with, Maurice Anscombe, generally the most cheerful and nonchalant of mortals with a jest for every woe, was in a most depressed condition, and informed me of it several times, while I was getting ready to turn in. He said he thought the place hateful and felt as if people he could not see were looking at him (I had the same sensation but did not mention the fact to him). When I told him he was talking stuff, he only replied that he could not help it, and pointed out that it was not his general habit to be downcast in any danger, which was quite true. Now, he added, he was enjoying much the same sensations as he did when first he saw

the Yellow-wood Swamp and got the idea into his head that he would kill some one there, which happened in due course.

"Do you mean that you think you are going to kill somebody else?" I asked anxiously.

"No," he answered, "I think I am going to be killed, or something like it, probably by that accursed old villain of a witch-doctor, who I don't believe is altogether human."

"Others have thought that before now, Anscombe, and to be plain, I don't know that he is. He lives too much with the dead to be like other people."

"And with Satan, to whom I expect he makes sacrifices. The truth is I'm afraid of his playing some of his tricks with Heda. It is for her I fear, not for myself, Allan. Oh! why on earth did you come here?"

"Because you wished it and it seemed the safest thing to do. Look here, my boy, as usual the trouble comes through a woman. When a man's single—you know the rest. You used to be able to laugh at anything, but now that you are practically double you can't laugh any more. Well, that's the common lot of man and you've got to put up with it. Adam was pretty jolly in his garden until Eve was started, but you know what happened afterwards. The rest of his life was a compound of temptation, anxiety, family troubles, remorse, hard labour with primitive instruments, and a flaming sword behind him. If you had left your Eve alone you would have escaped all this. But you see you didn't, and as a matter of fact, nobody ever does who is worth his salt, for Nature has arranged it so."

"You appear to talk with experience, Allan," he retorted blandly. "By the way, that girl Nombe, when she isn't star-gazing or muttering incantations, is always trying to explain to Heda some tale about you and a lady called Mameena. I gather that you were introduced to her in this neighbourhood where, Nombe says, you were in the habit of kissing her in public, which sounds an odd kind of a thing to do; all of which happened before she, Nombe, was born. She adds, according to Kaatje's interpretation, that you met her again this afternoon, which, as I understand the young woman has been long dead, seems so incomprehensible that I wish you would explain."

"With reference to Heda," I said, ignoring the rest as unworthy of notice, "I think you may make your mind easy. Zikali knows that she is in my charge and I don't believe that he wants to quarrel with me. Still, as you are uncomfortable here, the best thing to do will be to get away as early as possible to-morrow morning, where to we can decide afterwards. And now I am going to sleep, so please stop arguing."

As I have already hinted, my attempts in the sleep line proved a failure, for whenever I did drop off I was pursued by bad dreams, which resulted from lying down so soon after supper. I heard the cries of desperate men in their mortal agony. I saw a rain-swollen river; its waters were red with blood. I beheld a vision of one who I knew by his dress to be a Zulu king, although I could not see his face. He was flying and staggering with weariness as he fled. A great hound followed him. It lifted its head from the spoor; it was that of Zikali set upon the hound's body, Zikali who laughed instead of baying. Then one whose copper ornaments tinkled as she walked, entered beside me, whispering into my ear. "A quarter of a hundred years have gone by since we talked together in this haunted kloof," she seemed to whisper, "and before we talk again face to face there remain to pass of years"—

Here she ceased, though naturally I should have liked to hear the number. But that is just where dreams break down. They tell us only of what we know, or can evolve therefrom. Of what it is impossible for us to know they tell us nothing—at least as a general rule.

I woke up with a start, and feeling stifled in that hot place and aggravated by the sound of Anscombe's peaceful breathing, threw a coat about me and, removing the door-board, crept into the air. The night was still, the stars shone, and at a little distance the embers of the fire still glowed. By it was seated a figure wrapped in a kaross. The end of a piece of wood that the fire had eaten through fell on to the red ashes and flamed up brightly. By its light I saw that the figure was Nombe's. The eternal smile was still upon her face, the smile which suggested a knowledge of hidden things that from moment to moment amused her soul. Her lips moved as though she were talking to an invisible companion, and from time to time, like one who acts upon directions, she took a pinch of ashes and blew them, either towards Heda's hut or ours. Yes, she did this when all decent young women should have been asleep, like one who keeps some unholy, midnight assignation.

Talking with her master, Zikali, or trying to cast spells upon us, confound her, I thought I to myself, and very silently crept back into the hut. Afterwards it occurred to me that she might have had another motive, namely of watching to see that none of us left the huts.

The rest of the night went by somehow. Once, listening with all my ears, I thought that I caught the sound of a number of men tramping and of some low word of command, but as I heard no more, concluded that fancy had deceived me. There I lay, puzzling over the situation till my head ached, and wondering how we were to get clear of the Black Kloof and Zikali, and out of Zululand which I gathered was no place for white people at the moment

It seemed to me that the only thing was to make start for Dundee on the Natal border, and for the rest to trust to fortune. If we got into trouble over the death of Rodd, unpleasant as this would be, the matter must be faced out, that was all. For even if any witness appeared against us, the man had been killed in self-defence whilst trying to bring about our deaths at the hands of Basutos. I could see now that I was foolish not to have taken this line from the first, but as I think I have already explained, what weighed with me was the terror of involving these young people in a scandal which might shadow all their future lives. Also some fate inch by inch had dragged me into Zululand. Fortunately in life there are few mistakes, and even worse than mistakes that cannot be repaired, if the wish towards reparation is real and earnest. Were it otherwise not many of us would escape destruction in one form or another.

Thus I reflected until at length light flowing faintly through the smoke-hole of the hut told me that dawn was at hand. Seeing it I rose quietly, for I did not wish to wake Anscombe, dressed and left the hut. My object was to find Nombe, who I hoped would be still sitting by the fire, and send her to Zikali with a message that I wished to speak with him at once. Glancing round me in the grey dawn I saw that she was gone and that as yet no one seemed to be stirring. Hearing a horse snort at a little distance, I made my way towards the sound and in a little bay of the overhanging cliff discovered the cart and near by our beasts tied up with a plentiful supply of forage. Since so far as I could judge in that uncertain light, nothing seemed to be wrong with them except weariness, for three of them were still lying down, I walked on to the gate of the fence which surrounded Zikali's big hut, proposing to wait there until some one appeared by whom I could send my message.

I reached the gate which I tried and found to be fastened on its inner side. Then I sat down, lit my pipe and waited. It was extraordinarily lonesome in that place; at least this was the feeling that came over me. No doubt the sun was up behind the Ceza Stronghold that I have mentioned, which towered high behind me, for the sky above grew light with the red rays of its rising. But all the vast Black Kloof with its huge fantastic rocks was still plunged in gloom, whereof the shadows seemed to oppress my heart, weary as I was with my wakeful night and many anxieties. I was horribly nervous also and, as it proved, not without reason. Presently I heard rustlings on the further side of the fence as of people creeping about cautiously, and the sound of whispering. Then of a sudden the gate was thrown open and through it emerged about a dozen Zulu warriors, all of them ringed men, who instantly surrounded me, seated there upon the ground.

I looked at them and they looked at me for quite a long while, since following my usual rule, I determined not to be the first to speak. Moreover, if they meant to kill me there was no use in speaking. At length their leader, an elderly man with thin legs, a large stomach and a rather pleasant countenance, saluted politely, saying—

"Good morning, O Macumazahn."

"Good morning, O Captain, whose name and business I do not know," I answered.

The winds know the mountain on which they blow, but the mountain does not know the winds which it cannot see," he remarked with poetical courtesy; a Zulu way of saying that more people are acquainted with Tom Fool than Tom Fool is aware of.

"Perhaps, Captain; yet the mountain can feel the winds," and I might have added, smell them, for the Kloof was close and these Kaffirs had not recently bathed.

"I am named Goza and come on an errand from the king, O Macumazahn."

"Indeed, Goza, and is your errand to cut my throat?"

"Not at present, Macumazahn, that is, unless you refuse to do what the king wishes."

"And what does the king wish, Goza?"

"He wishes, Macumazahn, that you, his friend, should visit him."

"Which is just what I was on my way to do, Goza." (This was not true, but it didn't matter, for, if a lie, in the words of the schoolgirl's definition, is an abomination to the Lord, it is a very present help in time of trouble.) "After we have eaten I and my friends will accompany you to the king's kraal at Ulundi."

"Not so, Macumazahn. The king said nothing about your friends, of whom I do not think he has heard any more than we have. Moreover, if your friends are white, you will do well not to mention them, since the order is that all white people in Zululand who have not come here by the king's desire, are to be killed at once, except yourself, Macumazahn."

"Is it so, Goza? Well, as you will have understood, I am quite alone here and have no friends. Only I did not wish to travel so early."

"Of course we understand that you are quite alone and have no friends, is it not so, my brothers?"

"Yes, yes, we understand," they exclaimed in chorus, one of them adding, "and shall so report to the King."

"What kind of blankets do you like; the plain grey ones or the white ones with the blue stripes?" I asked, desiring to confirm them in this determination.

"The grey ones are warmer, Macumazahn, and do not show dirt so much," answered Goza thoughtfully.

"Good, I will remember when I have the chance."

"The promise of Macumazahn is known from of old to be as a tree that elephants cannot pull down and white ants will not eat," said the sententious Goza, thereby intimating his belief that some time or other they would receive those blankets. As a matter of fact the survivors of the party and the families of the others did receive them after the war, for in dealing with natives I have always made a point of trying to fulfil any promise or engagement made for value received.

"And now," went on Goza, "will the Inkosi be pleased to start, as we have to travel far to-day?"

"Impossible," I replied. "Before I leave I must eat, for who can journey upon yesterday's food? Also I must saddle my horse, collect what belongs to me, and bid farewell to my host, Zikali."

"Of meat we have plenty with us, Macumazahn, and therefore you will not hunger on the way. Your horse and everything that is yours shall be brought after you; since were you mounted on that swift beast and minded to escape, how could we catch you with our feet, and did you please to shoot us with your rifle, how could we who have only spears, save ourselves from dying? As for the Opener of Roads, his servants have told us that he means to sleep all to-day that he may talk with spirits in his dreams, and therefore it is useless for you to wait to bid him farewell. Moreover, the orders of the king are that we should bring you to him at once."

After this for a time there was silence, while I sat immovable revolving the situation, and the Zulus regarded me with a benignant interest. Goza took his snuff-box from his ear, shook out some into the palm of his hand and, after offering it to me in vain, inhaled it himself.

"The orders of the king are (sneeze) that we should bring you to him alive if possible, and if not (sneeze) dead. Choose which you will, Macumazahn. Perhaps you may prefer to go to Ulundi dead, which would—ah! how strong is this snuff, it makes me weep like a woman—save you the trouble of walking. But if you prefer that we should carry you, be so good, Macumazahn, first to write the words which will cause the grey blankets to be delivered to us, for we know well that even your bones would desire to keep your promise. Is it not a proverb in the land from the time of the slaying of Bangu when you gave the cattle you had earned to Saduko's wanderers?"

I listened and an idea occurred to me, as perhaps it had to Goza.

"I hear you, Goza," I said, "and I will start for Ulundi on my feet—to save *you* the trouble of carrying me. But as the times are rough and accidents may always happen; as, too, I wish to make sure that you should get those blankets, and it may chance that I shall arrive there on my back, first I will write words which, if they are delivered to the witch-doctoress Nombe, will, sooner or later, turn into blankets."

"Write the words quickly, Macumazahn, and they will be delivered," said Goza.

So I drew out my pocket-book and wrote—

"DEAR ANSCOMBE,—

"There is treachery afoot and I think that Zikali is at the bottom of it. I am being carried off to Cetewayo at Ulundi, by a party of armed Zulus who will not allow me to communicate with you, probably by Zikali's orders. You must do the best you can for Heda and yourself. Escape to Natal if you are able. Of course I will help if I get the chance, but if war is about to break out Cetewayo may kill me. I think that you can trust Nombe; also that Zikali does not wish to work you any ill unless he is obliged, though I have no doubt that he has trapped us here for some dark purpose of his own. Tell him through Nombe that if harm comes to you I will kill him if I live, and that if I die, I will settle the score with him afterwards. God save and bless you both. Keep up your courage and use your wits.

"Your friend,

"A. Q."

I tore out the sheet, folded, addressed it and presented it to Goza, remarking that although it seemed to be but paper, it really was fourteen blankets—if given at once to Nombe.

He nodded and handed it to one of his men, who departed in the direction of our huts. So, thought I to myself, Nombe knows all about this business, which means that it is being worked by Zikali. That is why she spoke to me as she did last night.

"It is time to start, Macumazahn, and I think you told us that you would prefer to do so on your feet," said Goza, looking suggestively at his spear.

"I am ready," I said, rising because I must. For a moment I contemplated the door in the kraal fence, wondering whether it would be safe to bolt through it and take refuge with Zikali. No, it was not safe, since Zikali sat there in his hut pulling the strings and probably might refuse to see me. Moreover, it was likely enough that before I could find him one of those broad spears would find my heart. There was nothing to be done except submit. Still I did call out in a loud voice—

"Farewell, Zikali. I leave you without a present against my will who am being taken by soldiers to visit the king at Ulundi. When we meet again I will talk all this matter over with you."

There was no answer, and as Goza took the opportunity to say that he disliked the noise of shouting extremely, which sometimes made him do things that he afterwards regretted, I became silent. Then we departed, I in the exact centre of that guard of Zulus, heavy-hearted and filled with fears both for myself and those I left behind me.

Down the Black Kloof we tramped, emerging on the sunlit plain beyond without meeting any one. A couple of miles further on we came to a small stream where Goza announced we would halt to eat. So we ate of cold toasted meat which one of the men produced from a basket he carried, unpalatable food but better than nothing. Just as we had finished I looked up and saw the soldier to whom my note had been given. He was leading my mare that had been saddled. On it were my large saddle-bags packed with my belongings, also my thick overcoat, mackintosh, waterbottle, and other articles down to a bag of tobacco, a spare pipe and a box of wax matches. Moreover, the man carried my double-barrelled Express rifle and a shot-gun that could be used for ball, together with two bags of cartridges. Practically nothing belonging to me had been forgotten.

I asked him who had collected the things. He replied the doctress Nombe had done so and had brought him the horse saddled to carry them. He did not know who saddled the horse as he had seen no one but Nombe to whom he had given the writing which she hid away. In answer to further questions, he said that Nombe had sent me a message. It was—

"I bid farewell to Macumazahn for a little while and wish him good fortune till we meet again. Let him not be afraid in the battle, for even if he is hurt it will not be to death, since those go with him whom he cannot see, and protect him with their shields. Say to Macumazahn that I, Nombe, remember in the morning what I said in the night and that what seems to be quite lost is ofttimes found again. Wish him good fortune and tell him I am sorry that I had not time to cause his spare garments to be cleansed with water, but that I have been careful to find his little box with the white man's medicines."

I could extract nothing more from this soldier, who was either very stupid, or chose to appear so; nor indeed did I dare to put direct questions about the cart and those who travelled in it.

Soon we marched again, for Goza would not allow me to ride the horse, fearing that I should escape on it. Nor would he let me carry either of the guns lest I should make use of them. All day we travelled, reaching the Nongoma heights in the late afternoon. On this beautiful spot we found a kraal situated where afterwards a magistracy was built when we conquered the country, whence there is one of the finest views in Zululand. There was no one in the kraal except two old women who appeared to be deaf and dumb for all I could get out of them. These aged dames, however, or others who were hidden, had made ready for our arrival, since a calf lay skinned and prepared for cooking, and by it big gourds filled with Kaffir beer and "maas" or curdled milk.

In due course we ate of these provisions, and after we had finished I gave Goza a stiff tot of brandy, of which Nombe, or perhaps Anscombe, had thoughtfully sent a bottle with my other baggage. The strong liquor made the old fellow talkative and enabled me to get a good deal of information out of him. Thus I learned that certain demands, as to which he was rather vague, had been made upon Cetewayo by the English Government, and that the King was now considering whether he should accede to them or fight. The Great Council of the nation was summoned to attend at Ulundi within a few days, when the matter would be decided. Meanwhile all the regiments were being gathered, or, as we should say, mobilized; an army, said Goza, greater than any that Chaka had ever led.

I asked him what I had to do with this business, that I, a peaceful traveller and an old friend of the Zulus, should be made prisoner and dragged off to Ulundi. He replied he did not know who was not in the council of the High Ones, but he thought that Cetewayo the king wished to see me because I was their friend, perhaps that he might send me as a messenger to the white people. I asked him how the king knew that I was in the country, to which he replied that Zikali had told him I was coming, he did not know how, whereon he, Goza, was sent at once to fetch me. I could get no more out of him.

I wondered if it would be worth while to make him quite drunk and then attempt to escape on the horse, but gave up the idea. To begin with, his men were at hand and there was not enough brandy to make them all drunk. Also even if I succeeded in winning away here in the heart of Zululand, it would not help Anscombe or Heda and I should probably be cut off and killed before I could get out of the country. So I abandoned the plan and went to sleep instead.

Next morning we left Nongoma early in the hope of reaching Ulundi that evening if the Ivuna and Black Umfolozi Rivers proved fordable. As it chanced, although they were high, we were able to cross them, I seated on the horse which two of the Zulus led. Next we tramped for miles through the terrible Bekameezi Valley, a hot and desolate place which the Zulus swear is haunted. So unhealthy is this valley, which is the home of large game, that whole kraals full of people who have tried to cultivate the rich land, have died in it of fever, or fled away leaving their crops unreaped. Now no man dwells there. After this we climbed a terrible mount to the high land of Mahlabatini, and having eaten, pushed on once more.

At length we sighted the great hill-encircled plain of Ulundi which may be called the cradle of the Zulu race as, politically speaking, it was destined to be its coffin. On the ridge to the west once stood the Nobamba kraal where dwelt Senzangacona, the father of Chaka the Lion. Nearer to the White Umfolozi was Panda's dwelling-place, Nodwengu, which once I knew so well, while on the slope of the hills of the north-east stood the town of Ulundi in which Cetewayo dwelt, bathed in the lights of sunset.

Indeed it and all the vast plain were red as though with blood, red as they were destined to be on the coming day of the last battle of the Zulus.

Cetewayo

It was dark when at last we reached the Ulundi kraal, for the growing moon was obscured by clouds. Therefore I could see nothing and was only aware, by the sound of voices and the continual challenging, that we were passing through great numbers of men. At length we were admitted at the eastern gate and I was taken to a hut where I at once flung myself down to sleep, being so weary that I could not attempt to eat. Next morning as I was finishing my breakfast in the little fenced courtyard of this guest-hut, Goza appeared and said that the king commanded me to be brought to him at once, adding that I must "speak softly" to him, as he was "very angry."

So off we went across the great cattle kraal where a regiment of young men, two thousand strong or so, were drilling with a fierce intensity which showed they knew that they were out for more than exercise. About the sides of the kraal also stood hundreds of soldiers, all of them talking and, it seemed to me, excited, for they stamped upon the ground and even jumped into the air to give point to their arguments. Suddenly some of them caught sight of me, whereon a tall, truculent fellow called out—

"What does a white man at Ulundi at such a time, when even John Dunn dare not come? Let us kill him and send his head as a present to the English general across the Tugela. That will settle this long talk about peace or war."

Others of a like mind echoed this kind proposal, with the result that presently a score or so of them made a rush at me, brandishing their sticks, since they might not carry arms in the royal kraal. Goza did his best to keep them off, but was swept aside like a feather, or rather knocked over, for I saw him on his back with his thin legs in the air.

"You must climb out of this pit by yourself," he began, addressing me in his pompous and figurative way. Then somebody stamped on his face, and fixing his teeth in his assailant's heel, he grew silent for a while.

The truculent blackguard, who was about six feet three high and had a mouth like a wolf's throat, arrived in front, of me and, bending down, roared out—

"We are going to kill you, White Man."

I had a pistol in my pocket and could perfectly well have killed him, as I was much tempted to do. A second's reflection showed me, however, that this would be useless, and in a sense put me in the wrong, though when the matter came on for argument it would interest me no more. So I just folded my arms and, looking up at him, said—

"Why, Black Man?"

"Because your face is white," he roared.

"No," I answered, "because your heart is black and your eyes are so full of blood that you do not know Macumazahn when you see him."

"Wow!" said one, "it is Watcher-by-Night whom our fathers knew before us. Leave him alone."

"No," shouted the great fellow, "I will send him to watch where it is always night, I who keep a club for white rats," and he brandished his stick over me.

Now my temper rose. Watching my opportunity, I stretched out my right foot and hooked him round the ankle, at the same time striking up with all my force. My fist caught him beneath the chin and over he went backwards sprawling on the ground.

"Son of a dog!" I said, "if a single stick touches me, at least you shall go first," and whipping out my revolver, I pointed it at him.

He lay quiet enough, but how the matter would have ended I do not know, for passion was running high, had not Goza at this moment risen with a bleeding nose and called out—

"O Fools, would you kill the king's guest to whom the king himself has given safe-conduct. Surely you are pots full of beer, not men."

"Why not?" answered one. "This is the Place of Soldiers. The king's house is yonder. Give the old jackal a start of a length of ten assegais. If he reaches it first, he can shake hands with his friend, the king. If not we will make him into medicine."

"Yes, yes, run for it, Jackal," clamoured the others, knocking their shields with their sticks, as men do who would frighten a buck, and opening out to make a road for me.

Now while all this was going on, with some kind of sixth sense I had noted a big man whose face was shrouded by a blanket thrown over his head, who very quietly had joined these drunken rioters, and vaguely wondered who he might be.

"I will not run," I said slowly, "that I may be saved by the king. Nay, I will die here, though some of you shall die first. Go to the king, Goza, and tell him how his servants have served his guest," and I lifted my pistol, waiting till the first stick touched me to put a bullet through the bully on the ground.

"There is no need," said a deep voice that proceeded from the draped man of whom I have spoken, "for the king has come to see for himself."

Then the blanket was thrown back, revealing Cetewayo grown fat and much aged since last I saw him, but undoubtedly Cetewayo.

"Bayete!" roared the mob in salute, while some of those who had been most active in the tumult tried to slip away.

"Let no man stir," said Cetewayo, and they stood as though they were rooted to the ground, while I slipped my pistol back into my pocket.

"Who are you, White Man?" he asked, looking at me, "and what do you here?"

"The King should know Macumazahn," I answered, lifting my hat, "whom Dingaan knew, whom Panda knew well, and whom the King knew before he was a king."

"Yes, I know you," he answered, "although since we spoke together you have shrunk like an oxhide in the sun, and time has stained your heard white."

"And the King has grown fat like the ox on summer grass. As for what I do here, did not the King send for me by Goza, and was I not brought like a baby in a blanket."

"The last time we met," he went on, taking no heed of my words, "was yonder at Nodwengu when the witch Mameena was tried for sorcery, she who made my brother mad and brought about the great battle, in which you fought for him with the Amawombe regiment. Do you not remember how she kissed you, Macumazahn, and took poison between the kisses, and how before she grew silent she spoke evil words to me, saying that I was doomed to pull down my own House and to die as she died, words that have haunted me ever since and now haunt me most of all? I wish to speak to you concerning them, Macumazahn, for it is said in the land that this beautiful witch loved you alone and that you only knew her mind."

I made no reply, who was heartily tired of this subject of Mameena whom no one seemed able to forget.

"Well," he went on, "we will talk of that matter alone, since it is not natural that you should wish to speak of your dead darlings before the world," and with a wave of the hand he put the matter aside. Then suddenly his attitude changed. His face, that had been thoughtful and almost soft, became fierce, his form seemed to swell and he grew terrible.

"What was that dog doing?" he asked of Goza, pointing to the brute whom I had knocked down and who still lay prostrate on his back, afraid to stir.

"O King," answered Goza, "he was trying to kill Macumazahn because he is a white man, although I told him that he was your guest, being brought to you by the royal command. He was trying to kill him by giving him a start of ten spears' length and making him run to the isigodhlo (the king's house) and beating him to death with the sticks of these men if they caught him, which, as he is old and they are young, they must have done. Only the Watcher-by-Night would not run; no, although he is so small he knocked him to the earth with his fist, and there he lies. That is all, O King."

"Rise, dog," said Cetewayo, and the man rose trembling with fear, and, being bidden, gave his name, which I forget.

"Listen, dog," went on the king in the same cold voice. "What Goza says is true, for I saw and heard it all with my eyes and ears. You would have made yourself as the king. You dared to try to kill the king's guest to whom he had given safe-conduct, and to stain the king's doorposts with his blood, thereby defiling his house and showing him to the white people as a murderer of one of them whom he had promised to protect. Macumazahn, do *you* say how he shall die, and I will have it done."

"I do not wish him to die," I answered, "I think that he and those with him were drunk. Let him go, O King."

"Aye, Macumazahn, I will let him go. See now, we are in the centre of the cattle-kraal, and to the eastern gate is as far as to the isigodhlo. Let this man have a start of ten spears' length and run to the eastern gate, as he would have made Macumazahn run to the king's house, and let his companions, those who would have hunted Macumazahn, hunt him.

"If he wins through to the gate he can go on to the Government in Natal and tell them of the cruelty of the Zulus. Only then, let those who hunted him be brought before me for trial and perhaps we shall see how *they* can run."

Now the poor wretch caught hold of my hand, begging me to intercede for him, but soldiers who had come up dragged him away and, having measured the distance allowed him, set him on a mark made upon the ground. Presently at a word off he sped like an arrow, and after him went his friends, ten or more of them. I think they caught him just by the gate doubling like a hare, or so the shouts of laughter from the watching regiment told me, for myself I would not look.

"That dog ate his own stomach," said Cetewayo grimly, thereby indicating in native fashion that the biter had been bit or the engineer hoist with his petard. "It is long since there has been a war in the land, and some of these young soldiers who have never used an assegai save to skin an ox or cut the head from a chicken, shout too loud and leap too high. Now they will be quieter, and while you stay here you may walk where you will in safety, Macumazahn," he added thoughtfully.

Then dismissing the matter from his mind, as we white people dismiss any trivial incident in a morning stroll, he talked for a few minutes to the commanding officer of the regiment that was drilling, who ran up to make some report to him, and walked back towards the isigodhlo, beckoning me to follow with Goza.

After waiting for a little while outside the gate in the surrounding fence, a body-servant ordered us to enter, which we did to find the king seated on the shady side of his big hut quite alone. At a sign I also sat myself down upon a stool that had been set for me, while Goza, whose nose was still bleeding, squatted at my side.

"Your manners are not so good as they were once, Macumazahn," said Cetewayo presently, "or perhaps you have been so long away from the royal kraal that you have forgotten its customs."

I stared at him, wondering what he could mean, whereon he added with a laugh—

"What is that in your pocket? Is it not a loaded pistol, and do you not remember that it is death to appear before the king armed? Now I might kill you and have no blame, although you are my guest, for who knows that you are not sent by the English Queen to shoot me?"

"I ask the King's pardon," I said humbly enough. "I did not think about the pistol. Let your servants take it away."

"Perhaps it is safer in your pocket, where I saw you place it in the cattle-kraal, Macumazahn, than in their hands, which do not know how to hold such things. Moreover, I know that you are not one who stabs in the dark, even when our peoples growl round each other like two dogs about to fight, and if you were, in this place your life would have to pay for mine. There is beer by your side; drink and fear nothing. Did you see the Opener of Roads, Goza, and if so, what is his answer to my message?"

"O King, I saw him," answered Goza. "The Father of the doctors, the friend and master of the Spirits, says he has heard the King's word, yes, that he heard it as it passed the King's lips, and that although he is very old, he will travel to Ulundi and be present at the Great Council of the nation which is to be summoned on the eighth day from this, that of the full moon. Yet he makes a prayer of the King. It is that a place may be prepared for him, for his people and for his servants who carry him, away from this town of Ulundi, where he may sojourn quite alone, a decree of death being pronounced against any who attempt to break in upon his privacy, either where he dwells or upon his journey. These are his very words, O King:

"'I, who am the most ancient man in Zululand, dwell with the spirits of my fathers, who will not suffer strangers to come nigh them and who, if they are offended, will bring great woes upon the land. Moreover, I have sworn that while there is a king in Zululand and I draw the breath of life, never again will I set foot in a royal kraal, because when last I did so at the slaying of the witch, Mameena, the king who is dead thought it well to utter threats against me, and never more will I, the Opener of Roads, be threatened by a mortal. Therefore if the King and his Council seek to drink of the water of my wisdom, it must be in the place and hour of my own choosing. If this cannot be, let me abide here in my house and let the King seek light from other doctors, since mine shall remain as a lamp to my own heart.'"

Now I saw that these words greatly disturbed Cetewayo who feared Zikali, as indeed did all the land.

"What does the old wizard mean?" he asked angrily. "He lives alone like a bat in a cave and for years has been seen of none. Yet as a bat flies forth at night, ranging far and wide in search of prey, so does his spirit seem to fly through Zululand. Everywhere I hear the same word. It is—'What says the Opener of Roads?' It is—'How can aught be done unless the Opener of Roads has declared that it shall be done, he who was here before the Black One (Chaka) was born, he who it is said was the friend of Inkosi Umkulu, the father of the Zulus who died before our great-grandfathers could remember; he who has all knowledge and is almost a spirit, if indeed he be not a spirit?' I ask you, Macumazahn, who are his friend, what does he mean, and why should I not kill him and be done?"

"O King," I answered, "in the days of your uncle Dingaan, when Dingaan slew the Boers who were his guests, and thus began the war between the White and the Black, I, who was a lad, heard the laughter of Zikali for the first time yonder at the kraal Ungungundhlovu, I who rode with Retief and escaped the slaughter, but his face I did not see. Many years later, in the days of Panda your father, I saw his face and therefore you name me his friend. Yet this friend who drew me to visit him, perhaps by your will, O King, has now caused me to be brought here to Ulundi doubtless by your will, O King, but against my own, for who wishes to come to a town where he is well-nigh slain by the first brawler he meets in the cattle kraal?"

"Yet you were not slain, Macumazahn, and perhaps you do not know all the story of that brawler," replied Cetewayo almost humbly, like one who begs pardon, though the rest of what l had said he ignored. "But still you are Zikali's friend, for between you and him there is a rope which enabled him to draw you to Zululand, which rope I have heard called by a woman's name. Therefore by the spirit of that woman, which still can draw you like a rope, I charge you, tell me—what does this old wizard mean, and why should I not kill him and be rid of one who haunts my heart like an evil vision of the night and, as I sometimes think, is an, umtakati, an evil-doer, who would work ill to me and all my House, yes, and to all my people?"

"How should I know what he means, O King?" I answered with indignation, though in fact I could guess well enough. "As for killing him, cannot the King kill whom he will? Yet I remember that once I heard you father ask much the same question and of Zikali himself, saying that he was minded to find out whether or no he were mortal like other men. I remember also Zikali answered that there was a saying that when the Opener of Roads came to the end of his road, there would be no more a king of Zululand, as there was none when first he set foot upon his road. Now I have spoken, who am a white man and do not understand your sayings."

"I remember it also, Macumazahn, who was present at the time," he replied heavily. "My father feared this Zikali and his father feared him, and I have heard that the Black One himself, who feared nothing, feared him also. And I, too, fear him, so much that I dare not make up my mind upon a great matter without Ws counsel, lest he should bewitch me and the nation and bring us to nothing."

He paused, then turning to Goza, asked, "Did the Opener of Roads tell you where he wished to dwell when he comes to visit me here at Ulundi?"

"O King," answered Goza, "yonder in the hills, not further away than an aged man can walk in the half of an hour, is a place called the Valley of Bones, because there in the days of those who went before the King, and even in the King's day, many evildoers have been led to die. Zikali would dwell in this Valley of Bones, and there and nowhere else would meet the King and the Great Council, not in the daylight but after sunset when the moon has risen."

"Why," said Cetewayo, starting, "the place is ill-omened and, they say, haunted, one that no man dares to approach after the fall of darkness for fear lest the ghosts of the dead should leap upon him gibbering."

"Such were the words of the Opener of Roads, O King," replied Goza. "There and nowhere else will he meet the King, and there he demands that three huts should be built to shelter him and his folk and stored with all things needful. If this be not granted to him, then he refuses to visit the King or to give counsel to the nation."

"So be it then," said Cetewayo. "Send messengers to the Opener of Roads, Goza, saying that what he desires shall be done. Let my command go out that under pain of death none spy upon him while he journeys hither or returns. Let the huts be built forthwith, and when it is known that he is coming, let food in plenty be placed in them and afterwards morning by morning taken to the mouth of the valley. Bid him announce his arrival and the hour he chooses for our meeting by messenger. Begone."

Goza leapt up, gave the royal salute, and retreated backwards from the presence of the king, leaving us alone. I also rose to depart, but Cetewayo motioned to me to be seated.

"Macumazahn," he said, "the Great Queen's man who has come to Natal (Sir Bartle Frere) threatens me with war because two evil-doing women were taken on the Natal side of the Tugela and brought back to Zululand and killed by Mehlokazulu, being the wives of his father, Sirayo, which was done without my knowledge. Also two white men were driven away from an island in the Tugela River by some of my soldiers."

"Is that all, O King?" I asked.

"No. The Queen's man says I kill my people without trial, which is a lie told him by the missionaries, and that girls have been killed also who refused to marry those to whom they were given and ran away with other men. Also that wizards are smelt out and slain, which happens but rarely now; all of this contrary to the promises I made to Sompseu when he came to recognize me as king upon my father's death, and some other such small matters."

"What is demanded if you would avoid war, O King?"

"Nothing less than this, Macumazahn: That the Zulu army should be abolished and the soldiers allowed to marry whom and when they please, because, says the

Queen's man, he fears lest it should be used to attack the English, as though I who love the English, as those have done who went before me, desire to lay a finger on them. Also that another Queen's man should be sent to dwell here in my country, to be the eyes and ears of the English Government and have power with me in the land; yes, and more demands which would destroy the Zulus as a people and make me, their king, but a petty kraal-head."

"And what will the King answer?" I asked.

"I know not what to answer. The fine of two thousand cattle I will pay for the killing of the women. If it may be, I wish no quarrel with the English, though gladly I would have fought the Dutch had not Sompseu stretched out his arm over their land. But how can I disband the army and make an end of the regiments that have conquered in so many wars? Macumazahn, I tell you that if I did this, in a moon I should be dead. Oh! you white people think there is but one will in Zululand, that of the king. But it is not so, for he is but a single man among ten thousand thousand, who lives to work the people's wish. If he beats them with too thick a stick, or if he brings them to shame or does what the most of them do not wish, then where is the king? Then, I say, he goes a road that was trodden by Chaka and Dingaan who were before me, yes, the red road of the assegai. Therefore today, I stand like a man between two falling cliffs. If I run towards the English the Zulu cliff falls upon me. If I run towards my own people, the English cliff falls upon me, and in either case I am crushed and no more seen. Tell me then, Macumazahn, you whose heart is honest, what must I do?"

So he spoke, wringing his hands, with tears starting to his eyes, and upon my word, although I never liked Cetewayo as I had liked his father, Panda, perhaps because I loved his brother, Umbelazi, whom he killed, and had known him do many cruel deeds, my heart bled for him.

"I cannot tell you, King," I answered, thinking that I must say something, "but I pray you do not make war against the queen, for she is the most mighty One in the whole earth, and though her foot, of which you see but the little toe here in Africa, seems small to you, yet if she is angered, it will stamp the Zulus flat, so that they cease to be."

"Many have told me this, Macumazahn. Yes, even Uhamu, the son of my uncle Unzibe, or, as some say, the son of his spirit, to which his mother was married after Unzibe was dead, and others throughout the land, and in truth I think it myself. But who can hold the army which shouts for war? Ow! the Council must decide, which, means perhaps that Zikali will decide, for now all hang upon his lips."

"Then I am sorry," I exclaimed.

He looked at me shrewdly.

"Are you? So am I. Yet his counsel must be asked, and better that it should be here in my presence than yonder secretly at the Black Kloof. I would kill him if I dared, but I dare not, who am sure—why I may not say—that the same sun will see his death and mine."

He waved his hand to show that the talk on this matter was ended, then added—

"Macumazahn, you are my prisoner for a while, but give me your word that you will not try to escape and you may go where you will within an hour's ride of Ulundi. I would pay you well to stop here with me, but this I know you would never do should there be trouble between us and your people. Therefore I promise you that if war breaks out I will send you safely to Natal, or perhaps sooner, as my messenger, whence doubtless you will return to fight against me. Know that I have given orders that every other white man or woman who is found in Zululand shall be killed as a spy. Even John Dunn has fled or is flying, or so I hear, John Dunn who has fed out of my hand and grown rich on my gifts. You yourself would have been killed as you came from Swazi-Land in your cart, had not command been sent to those chiefs through whose lands you passed that neither they nor their people were so much as to look at you."

Now for one intense moment I thought, as hard as ever I had done in my life. It was evident—unless he dealing very cunningly with me, which I did not believe—that Cetewayo knew nothing of Anscombe and Heda, but thought that I had come into Zululand alone. Should I or should I not tell him and beg his protection for them? If I did so he might refuse or be unable to give it to them far away in the midst of a savage population aflame with the lust of war. As the incident of the morning showed, it war as much as he could do to protect myself, although the Zulus knew me for their friend. On the other hand no one who dwelt under Zikali's blanket, to use the Kaffir idiom, would be touched, because he was looked on as half divine and therefore everything under it down to the rat in his thatch was sacred. Now Zikali by implication and Nombe with emphasis, had promised to safeguard these two. Surely, therefore, they would run less risk in the Black Kloof than here at Ulundi, if ever they got so far.

All this went through my brain in an instant, with the result that I made up my mind to say nothing. As the issue proved, this was a terrible mistake, but who can always judge rightly? Had I spoken out it seems to me probable that Cetewayo would have granted my prayer and ordered that these two should be escorted out of Zululand before hostilities began, although of course they might have been murdered on the way. Also, for a reason that will become evident later, it is possible that there would never have been any hostilities. All I can plead is, that I acted for the best and Fate would have it so. Another moment and the chance was gone.

The gate opened and a body-servant appeared announcing that one of the great captains with some of his officers waited to see the king. Cetewayo made a sign, whereon the servant called out something, and they entered, three or four of them, saluting loudly. Seeing me they stopped and stared, whereon Cetewayo shortly, but with much clearness, repeated to them and to an induna who accompanied them, what he had already said to me, namely that I was his guest, sent for by him that he might use me as a messenger if he thought fit. He added that the man who dared to speak a word against me, or even to look at me askance, should pay the price with his life, however high his station, and he commanded that the heralds should proclaim this his decree throughout Ulundi and the neighbouring kraals. Then he held out his hand to me in token of friendship, bidding me to "go softly" and come to see him whenever I wished, and dismissed me in charge of the induna, one of the captains and some soldiers.

Within five minutes of reaching my hut I heard a loud-voiced crier proclaiming the order of the king and knew that I had no more to fear.

The Valley of Bones

The week that followed my interview with Cetewayo was indeed a miserable time for me. For myself, as I have said, I had no fear, for the king's orders were strictly obeyed. Moreover, the tale of what had happened to the brute who wished to hunt me down in the cattle-kraal had travelled far and wide and none sought to share his fate. My hut was inviolate and well supplied with necessary food, as was my mare, and I could wander where I liked and talk with whom I would. I could even ride to exercise the horse, though this I did very sparingly and only in the immediate neighbourhood of the town for fear of exciting suspicion or meeting Zulus whom the king's word had not reached. Indeed on these occasions I was always accompanied by a guard of swift-footed and armed soldiers sent "to protect me," or more probably to kill me if I did anything that seemed suspicious.

In the course of my rambles I met sundry natives whom I had known in the old days, some of them a long while ago. They all seemed glad to see me and were quite ready to talk of past times, but of the present they would say little or nothing, except that they were certain there would be war. Of Anscombe and Heda I could hear nothing, and indeed did not dare to make any direct inquiries concerning them, but several reliable men assured me that the last missionaries and traders having departed, there was not a white man, woman or child left in Zululand except myself. It was "all black" they said, referring to the colour of their people, as it had been before the time of Chaka. So I was forced to eat out my heart with anxiety in silence, hoping and praying that Zikali had played an honest part and sent them away safely.

Why should he not have done so, seeing that it was my presence he had desired, not theirs? They were only taken, or rather snared, because they were with me and could not be separated, or so I believed at the time.

One ray of comfort I did get. About the fifth day after my interview I saw Goza, who told me that the king's messengers were back from the Black Kloof and had brought "a word" for me from Zikali himself. The word was—

"Bid Goza say to Macumazahn that I was sorry not to see him to say good-bye, because that morning I slept heavily. Bid him say that I am glad he has seen the king, since for this purpose I sought his presence in Zululand. Bid him say that he is to fear nothing, and that if his heart is heavy about others whom he loves, he should make it light again, since the Spirits have them in their keeping as they have him, and never were they or he more safe than they are to-day."

Now I looked at Goza and asked if I could see this messenger. He replied, No, as he had already been despatched upon another errand. Then I asked him if the messenger had said anything else. He answered, Yes, one thing that he had forgotten, namely that the writing about blankets should now be in Natal. Then suddenly he changed the subject and asked me if I would like to accompany him to the Valley of Bones where he was ordered to inspect the huts which were being built for Zikali and his people. Of course I said I should, hoping, quite without result, that I might get something more out of him on the road.

Now this town of Cetewayo's stands, or rather stood, for it has long been burnt, on the slope of the hills to the north-east of the plains of Ulundi. Above it these hills grow steeper, and deep in the recesses of one of them is the Valley of Bones. There is nothing particularly imposing about the place; no towering cliffs or pillars of piled granite, as at the Black Kloof. It is just a vale cut out by water, bordered by steep slopes on either side, and a still steeper slope strown with large rocks at its end. Dotted here and there on these slopes grew tall aloes that from a little distance looked like scattered men, whereof the lower leaves were shrivelled and blackened by veld fires. Also there were a few euphorbias, grey, naked-looking things that end in points like fingers on a hand, and among them some sparse thorn trees, struggling to live in an inhospitable soil.

The place has one peculiarity. Jutting into it from the hillside is a ridge or spur, sixty or seventy yards in length by perhaps twenty broad, that ends in a flat point of rock which stands about forty feet above the level of the rest of the little valley. On this ridge also grew tall aloes until near its extremity the soil ceased, or had been washed away from the water-worn core of rock.

It was, and no doubt still is, a desolate-looking spot, at any rate for most of the day when owing to the shadow of the surrounding hills, it receives but little sun. Everything about it, especially when I was there in a time of rain, seemed dank and miserable, although the flat floor of the kloof was clothed with a growth of tall, coarse grass, and weeds that bore an evil-smelling flower. Perhaps some sense of appropriateness had caused the Zulu kings to choose this lonesome, deathly-looking gorge as one of their execution grounds. At any rate many had been slain here, for skulls and the larger human bones, some of them black with age, lay all about among the grass, as they had been scattered by hyenas and jackals. They were particularly thick beneath and around the table-like rock that I have mentioned.

Goza told me that this was because the King's Slayers made a custom of dragging the victim along the projecting tongue to the edge of this rock and hurling him, either dead or living, to the ground beneath; or, in the case of witches; driving them over after they had been blinded.

Such was the spot that Zikali had selected to abide in during his visit to Ulundi. Certainly where privacy was an object it was well chosen, for, as Cetewayo had said and as Goza emphasized to me, it had the repute of being the most thoroughly haunted place in all Zululand, with the sole exception, perhaps, of the ridge opposite to Dingaan's old kraal where once I shot the vultures for my life and those of my companions. Even in the daytime people gave it a wide berth, and at night nothing would induce them to approach it, at any rate alone.

Here to one side of and near the root of the tongue of land of which I have spoken, the huts that Zikali had demanded for himself and his company were being rapidly built, close to a spring of water, by a large body of men who laboured as though they wished to be done with their task. Also about half way up the donga, for really it was nothing more, at a distance of perhaps five and twenty paces from its flat point whence the condemned were hurled, a circular space of ground had been cleared and levelled which was large enough to accommodate fifty or sixty men. On this space, Goza told me, the King and the Council were to sit when they came to seek light from Zikali.

In my heart I reflected that the light they were likely to get from him would be such as may be supposed to be thrown by hell fire. For be it remembered I knew what these people never seemed to understand, that Zikali was the most bitter of their enemies. To begin with, he was of Undwandwe blood, one of the people whom the great king Chaka had destroyed. Then this same Chaka had robbed him of his wives and murdered his children, in revenge for which he had plotted the slaying of Chaka, as he did that of his brothers, Umhlangana and Dingaan, the latter of whom he involved in a quarrel with the Boers. Subsequently he brought about the war between the princes Cetewayo and Umbelazi, in which I played a part.

Now I was certain that he intended to bring about another war between the English and the Zulus, knowing well that in the end the latter would be destroyed, and with them the royal House of Senzangacona which he had sworn to level with the dust. Had he not told me as much years ago, and was he one to go back upon his word? Had he not used Mameena with her beauty and ambitions as his tool, and when she was of no further service to him, given her to death, as he had used scores of others and in due season given them to death? Was I not myself perhaps one of those tools destined to be thrown into the pit of doom when my turn came, though in what way I could help his plots was more than I could see, since he knew well that I should do my best to oppose him? Oh! I had half a mind to go to Cetewayo and tell him all I knew about Zikali, even if it involved the breaking of confidences.

But stay! Even if I were believed, this far-seeing wizard held hostages for my good behaviour, and if I betrayed him what would happen to those hostages? He sent me messages saying that they were safe, suggesting that they had escaped to Natal. How was I to know that these were true? I was utterly bewildered; I could not guess why I had been beguiled into Zululand, and I dared not step either this way or that for fear lest I should fall into some pit dug by his cunning hands and, what was worse, drag down others with me.

Moreover, was this man quite human, or perhaps an emissary of Satan upon earth who had knowledge denied to other men and a certain mastery over the Powers of Ill? Again I could not say. His term of life seemed to be extraordinarily prolonged, though none knew how old exactly he might be. Also he had a wonderful knowledge of what was passing in the minds of others, and by his arts, as I had experienced only the other day, could summon up apparitions or illusions before their eyes. Further, he was aware of events which had happened at a distance and could send or read dreams, since otherwise how did Nombe know what I had dreamt at Marnham's house? Lastly he could foretell the future, as once he had done in my own case, prophecying that I should be injured by a buffalo with a split horn.

Yet all of this might be nothing more than a mixture of keen observation, clever spying, trickery and mesmerism. I could not say which it was, nor can I with certainty to this hour.

Such were the thoughts that passed through my mind as I walked back from the Vale of Bones by the side of the big-paunched Goza, whom I caught eyeing me from time to time as a curious crow eyes any object that has attracted his attention.

"Goza," I said at last, "do the Zulus really mean to fight the English?"

He turned and pointed to a spot where the hills ran down into the great plain. Here two regiments were manoeuvring. One of these held the slopes of the hill and the other was attacking them from the plain, so fiercely that at a distance their onslaught looked like that of actual warfare.

"That looks like fighting, does it not, Macumazahn?" he replied.

"Yes, Goza, yet it may be but play."

"Quite so, Macumazahn. It may be fighting or it may be but play. Am I a prophet that I should be able to say which it is? Of that there is but one man in Zululand who knows the truth. It is he for whom the new huts are being built up yonder."

"You think he really knows, Goza?"

"No, Macumazahn, I do not think, I am sure. He is the greatest of all wizards, as he was when my father held on to his mother's apron. He pulls the strings and the Great-ones of the country dance. If he wishes war, there will be war. If he wishes peace, there will be peace."

"And which does he wish, Goza?"

"I thought perhaps you could tell me that, Macumazahn, who, he says, are such an old friend of his; also why he chooses to sojourn in a dark hole among the dead instead of in the sunshine among the living, here at Ulundi."

"Well, I cannot, Goza, since the Opener of Roads does not open his heart to me but keeps his secrets to himself. For the rest, those who talk with the dead may prefer to dwell among the dead."

"Now as always you speak truth, Macumazahn," said Goza, looking at me in a way which suggested to me that he believed I spoke anything but the truth.

Indeed I am convinced he thought that I was in the council of Zikali and acquainted with his plans. Also I am sure he knew that I had not come to Zululand alone, the incident of the blankets, which I had promised to him a bribe to keep silence, showed it, and suspected that my companions were parties to some plot together with myself. And yet at the time I could not be quite sure, and therefore dared not ask anything concerning them lest thus I should reveal their existence and bring them to death.

As a matter of fact I need not have been anxious on this point, since if Goza, who I may state, was a kind of secret service officer as well as a head messenger, knew, as I think probable, he had been commanded by Zikali to hold his tongue under penalty of a curse. Perhaps the same was true of the soldiers who had come with him to take me to Ulundi. The hint of Zikali was as powerful as the word of the king, since they, like thousands of others, believed that whereas Cetewayo could kill them, Zikali, like Satan, could blast their spirits as well as their bodies. But how was I to guess all these things at that time?

During the next two days nothing happened, though I heard that there had been one if not two meetings of the Council at the King's House during which the position of affairs was discussed. Cetewayo I did not see, although twice he sent messengers to me bringing gifts of food, who were charged to inquire whether I was well and happy and if any had offered me hurt or insult. To these I answered that I was well and unmolested but not happy, who grew lonesome, being but a solitary white man among so many thousands of the Zulus.

On the third morning, that of the day of the full moon, Goza came and informed me that Zikali had arrived at the Valley of Bones before dawn. I asked him how he, who was so old and feeble, had walked so far. He answered that he had not walked, or so he understood, but had been carried in a litter, or rather in two litters, one for himself and one for his "spirit." This staggered me even where Zikali was concerned, and I inquired what on earth Goza meant.

"Macumazahn, how can I tell you who only know what I myself am told?" he exclaimed. "Such is the report that the Opener of Roads has made himself by messengers to the king. None have seen him, for he journeys only in the night. Moreover, when Zikali passes all men are blind and even women's tongues grow dumb. Perchance by 'his spirit' he means his medicine or the witch-doctoress, Nombe, whom folks say he created, since none have seen her father or her mother, or heard who begat her; or perchance his snake is hid behind the mats of the second litter, if in truth there was one."

"It may be so," I said, feeling that it was useless to pursue the matter. "Now, Goza, I would see Zikali and at once."

"That cannot be, Macumazahn, since he has given out that he will see no one, who rests after his journey, and the king has issued orders that any who attempt to approach the Valley of Bones shall die, even if they be of the royal blood. Yes, if so much as a dog dares to draw near that place, it must die. The soldiers who ring it round have killed one already, so strict are the orders, also a boy who went towards it searching for a calf, which I think a bad omen."

"Then I will send a message to him," I persisted.

"Do so," mocked Goza. "Look, yonder sails a vulture. Ask it to take your message, for nothing else will. Be not foolish, Macumazahn, but have patience, for to-night you shall see the Opener of Roads when he attends the Council of the king in the Valley of Bones. This is the order of the king—that at the rising of the moon I lead you thither, so that you may be present at the Council in case he wishes to ask you any questions about the White People or to give you any message to the Government in Natal. Therefore at sunset I will come for you. Till then, farewell. I have business that cannot wait."

"Can I see the king?" I cried.

"Not so, Macumazahn. All to-day he makes sacrifice to the spirits of his ancestors and must not be approached," Goza called back as he departed.

Availing myself of the permission of the king to go where I would, a little later in the day I walked out of the town towards the Valley of Bones in order to ascertain for myself whether what Goza had told me was true. So it proved, for about three hundred yards from the mouth of the valley, which at that distance looked like a black hole in the hills, I found soldiers stationed about ten paces apart in a great circle which ran right up the hillside and vanished over the crest. Strolling up to one of these, whose face I thought I knew, I asked him if he would let me pass to see my friend, the Opener of Roads.

The man, who was something of a humourist replied—

"Certainly if you wish, Macumazahn. That is to say, I will let your spirit pass, but to do this, if you come one step nearer I must first make a hole in you with my spear out of which it can fly."

I thanked him for his information and gave him some snuff, which he took gratefully, being bored by his long vigil. Then I asked him how many people the great witch-doctor had with him. He said he did not know, but he had seen a number of tall men come to the mouth of the donga to fetch food that had been placed there. Again I inquired if he had seen any women, whereon he replied none, Zikali being, he understood, too old to trouble himself about the other sex. Just then an officer, making his rounds, came up and looked at me so sternly that I thought it well to retreat. Evidently there was no chance of getting through that line.

On my way back I walked as near the fence of the King's House as I dared, and saw witch-doctors passing in and out in their hideous official panoply. This told me that here also Goza had spoken the truth—the king was performing magical ceremonies, which meant that it would be impossible to approach him. In every direction I met with failure. The Fates were against me; it lay over me like a spell. Indeed I grew superstitious and began to think that Zikali had bewitched me, as he was said to have the power to do. Well, perhaps he had, for the mere fact of finding myself opposed by this persistent wall of difficulties and silence convinced me that there was something behind it to be learned.

I went back very dejected to my hut and talked to my mare which whinnied and rubbed its nose against me, for although it was well fed and looked after, the poor beast seemed as lonely as I was myself. No wonder, since like myself it was separated from all its kind and weary of inaction. After this I ate and smoked and finally dozed, no more, for whenever I tried to go to sleep I thought that I heard Zikali laughing at me, as mayhap he was doing yonder in his hut.

At length that wearisome day drew towards its end. The sun began to sink, a huge red ball of fire, now and again veiled by clouds, for the sky was stormy. Its fierce rays, striking upon other clouds, peopled the enormous heavens with fantastic shapes of light which were thickest over the hills wherein was the Valley of Bones. To my strained mind these clouds looked like battling armies, figures of flame warring against figures of darkness. The darkness won; no, the light broke out again and conquered it. And see, there above them both squatted a strange black presence crowned with fire. It might have been that of Zikali magnified ten thousand times, and hark! it laughed with the low reverberating voice of distant thunder.

Suddenly I felt that I was no longer alone and looking round, saw Goza at my side.

"What do you see up there, Macumazahn, that you stare so hard?" he asked, pointing at the sky with his stick.

"Impis fighting," I answered briefly.

"Then you must be a 'heaven-doctor,' Macumazahn, for I only see black and red clouds. Well, it is time to go to learn whether or no the impis will fight, for Zikali awaits us and the Council has started already. By the way, the king says that you will do well to put your pistol in your pocket in case any should seek to harm you in the dark."

"It is there. But, Goza, I pray you to protect me, since in the dark bullets fly wide, and if I began to shoot, one might hit you, Goza."

He smiled, making no answer, but I noticed that during the rest of that night he was careful to keep behind me as much as possible.

Our way led us through the town where everybody seemed to be standing about doing nothing and speaking very little. There was a curious air of expectancy upon their faces. They knew that the crisis was at hand, that their nation's fate hung upon the scales, and they watched my every look and movement as though in them they expected to read an omen. I too watched them out of the corners of my eyes, wondering whether I should escape from their savage company alive. If once the blood lust broke out among them, it seemed to me that I should have about as much chance as a chopped fox among a pack of hungry hounds.

Once out of the town we saw no one until we came to the circle of guards which I have already mentioned, who stood there like an endless line of black statues. In answer to their challenge Goza gave some complicated password in which my name occurred, whereon they opened out and let us through. Then we marched on to the mouth of the kloof. The place was very dark, for now the sun was down in the west and the moon in the east was cut off from us by the hills and would not be visible here for half an hour or more. Presently I saw a spot of light. It was a small fire burning near the tongue of rock which I have described.

At a distance, in front of the fire on the patch of prepared ground, squatted a number of men, between twenty and thirty of them, in a semicircle. They were wrapped up in karosses and blankets, and in their centre sat a large figure on a chair of wood.

"The King and the Great Council," whispered Goza.

One of them looked round and saw us. At some sign from the king he rose, and against the fire I saw that he was the Prime Minister, Umnyamana. He came to me and, with a nod of recognition, conducted me some paces to the right where a euphorbia tree grew among the rank herbage. Here I found a stool placed ready on which I sat down, Goza, who of course was not of the Council, squatting at my side in the grass.

Now I found that I was so situated that I could not well be seen from the fire, or even from the rock above it, while I, by moving my head a little, could see both quite clearly. After this as the last reflection from the sunk sun faded, the darkness increased until nothing remained visible except the fire and the massive outline of the rock behind. The silence was complete, for none of the Council spoke. They were so still that they might have been dead, so still that a beetle suddenly booming past me made me start as though it had been a bullet. The general impression was almost mesmeric. I felt as though I were going to sleep and yet my mind remained painfully awake, so that I was able to think things out.

I understood clearly that the body of men to my left had come together to decide whether there should be peace or war; that there were divisions of opinion among them; that the king was ready to follow the party which should prove itself the strongest, but that the real voice of decision would speak from behind that fire. It was the case of the Delphic Oracle over again with a priest instead of a priestess, and what a priest!

It was evident to me also that Zikali, who knew human nature, and especially savage human nature, had arranged all this with a view to scenic and indeed supernatural effect. Moreover, he had done it very well, since I knew myself that in this place and hour words and occurrences would affect me deeply at which I should have laughed in the sunlight and open plain. Already the Zulus were affected, for I could hear the teeth of some of them chattering, and Goza began to shiver at my side. He muttered that it was cold, and lied for the donga was extremely hot and stuffy.

At length the silver radiance of the moon spread itself on the high curtain of the dark. Then the edge of her orb appeared above the hill and an arrow of white light fell into the little valley. It struck upon and about the jutting rock, revealing a misshapen, white-headed figure squatted between its base and the fire, the figure of Zikali.

The Great Council

None had seen or heard him come, and though doubtless he had but crept round the rock and taken his place in the darkness, there appeared to be something mysterious about this sudden appearance of Zikali. So the Zulu nobles thought at any rate, for they uttered a low "Ow!" of fear and wonder.

There he sat like a huge ape staring at the sky, for the firelight shone on his deep and burning eyes. The moonlight increased, but now and again it was broken by little clouds which caused strange shadows to appear about the rock. Some of these shadows looked as though veiled figures were approaching the wizard, bending over him and departing again, after giving him their message or counsel.

"His Spirits visit him," whispered Goza, but I made no answer.

This went on for quite a long time, until the full round of the moon appeared above the hill indeed, and, for the while, the clouds had cleared away. Still Zikali sat silent and I, who was acquainted with the habits of this people, knew that I was witnessing a conflict between two they considered to be respectively a spiritual and an earthly king. It is my belief that unless he were first addressed, Zikali would have sat all night without opening his lips. Possibly Cetewayo would have done the same if the impatience of public opinion had allowed him. At any was rate it was he who gave way.

"Makosi, master of many Spirits, on behalf of the Council and the People of the Zulus I, the King, greet you here in the place that you have chosen," said Cetewayo.

Zikali made no answer.

The silence went on as before, till at length, after a pause and some whispering, Cetewayo repeated his salutation, adding—

"Has age made you deaf, O Opener of Roads, that you cannot hear the voice of the King?"

Then at last Zikali answered in his low voice that yet seemed to fill all the kloof—

"Nay, Child of Senzangacona, age has not made me deaf, but my spirit in these latter days floats far from my body. It is like a bladder filled with air that a child holds by a string, and before I can speak I must draw it from the heavens to earth again. What did you say about the place that I have chosen? Well, what better place could I choose, seeing that it was here in this very Vale of Bones that I met the first king of the Zulus, Chaka the Wild Beast, who was your uncle? Why then should I not choose it to meet the last king of the Zulus?"

Now I, listening, knew at once that this saying might be understood in two ways, namely that Cetewayo was the reigning king, or that he was the last king who would ever reign. But the Council interpreted it in the latter and worse sense, for I saw a quiver of fear go through them.

"Why should I not choose it," went on Zikali, "seeing also that this place is holy to me? Here it was, O Son of Panda, that Chaka brought my children to be killed and forced me, sitting where you sit, to watch their deaths. There on the rock above me they were killed, four of them, three sons and a daughter, and the slayers—they came to an evil end, those slayers, as did Chaka—laughed and cast them down from the rock before me. Yes, and Chaka laughed, and I too laughed, for had not the king the right to kill my children and to steal their mothers, and was I not glad that they should be taken from the world and gathered to that of Spirits whence they always talk to me, yes, even now? That is why I did not hear you at first, King, because they were talking to me."

He paused, turning one ear upwards, then continued in a new and tender voice,

"What is it you say to me, Noma, my dear little Noma? Oh! I hear you, I hear you."

Now he shifted himself along the ground on his haunches some paces to the right, and began to search about, groping with his long fingers. "Where, where?" he muttered. "Oh, I understand, further under the root, a jackal buried it, did it? Pah! how hard is this soil. Ah! I have it, but look, Noma, a stone has cut my finger. I have it, I have it," and from beneath the root of some fallen tree he drew out the skull of a child and, holding it in his right hand, softly rubbed the mould off it with his left.

"Yes, Noma, it might be yours, it is of the right size, but how can I be sure? What is it you say? The teeth? Ah! now I remember. Only the day before you were taken I pulled out that front tooth, did I not, and beneath it was another that was strangely split in two. If this skull was yours, it will be there. Come to the fire, Noma, and let us look; the moonlight is faint, is it not?"

Back to the fire he shifted himself, and bending towards the blaze, made an examination.

"True, Noma, true! Here is the split tooth, white as when I saw it all those years ago. Oh! dear child of my body, dear child of my spirit, for we do not beget with the body alone, Noma, as you know better than I do to-day, I greet you," and pressing the skull to his lips, he kissed it, then set it down in front of him between himself and the fire with the face part pointing to the king, and burst into one of his eerie and terrible laughs.

A low moan went up from his audience, and I felt the skin of Goza, who had shrunk against me, break into a profuse sweat. Then suddenly Zikali's voice changed one more and became hard and businesslike, if I may call it so, similar to that of other professional doctors.

"You have sent for me, O King, as those who went before you have sent when great things were about to happen. What is the matter on which you would speak to me?"

"You know well, Opener of Roads," answered Cetewayo, rather shakily I thought. "The matter is one of peace or war. The English threaten me and my people and make great demands on me; amongst others that the army should be disbanded. I can set them all out if you will. If I refuse to do as they bid me, then within a few days they will invade Zululand; indeed their soldiers are already gathered at the drifts."

"It is not needful, King," answered Zikali, "since I know what all know, neither more nor less. The winds whisper the demands of the white men, the birds sing them, the hyenas howl them at night. Let us see how the matter stands. When your father died Sompseu (Sir T. Shepstone), the great white chief, came from the English Government to name you king. This he could not do according to our law, since how can a stranger name the King of the Zulus? Therefore the Council of the Nation and the doctors—I was not among them, King—moved the spirit of Chaka the Lion into the body of Sompseu and made him as Chaka was and gave him power to name you to rule over the Zulus. So it came about that to the English Queen through the spirit of Chaka you swore certain things; that slaying for witchcraft should be abolished; that no man should die without fair and open trial, and other matters."

He paused a while, then went on, "These oaths you have broken, O King, as being of the blood you are and what you are, you must do."

Here there was disturbance among the Council and Cetewayo half rose from his seat, then sat down again. Zikali, gazing at the sky, waited till it had died away, then went on—

"Do any question my words? If so, then let them ask of the white men whether they be true or no. Let them ask also of the spirits of those who have died for witchcraft, and of the spirits of the women who have been slain and whose bodies were laid at the cross-roads because they married the men they chose and not the soldiers to whom the king gave them."

"How can I ask the white men who are far away?" broke out Cetewayo, ignoring the rest.

"Are the white men so far away, King? It is true that I see none and hear none, yet I seem to smell one of them close at hand." Here he took up the skull which he had laid down and whispered to it. "Ah! I thank you, my child. It seems, King, that there is a white man here hidden in this kloof, he who is named Macumazahn, a good man and a truthful, known to many of us from of old, who can tell you what his people think, though he is not one of their indunas. If you question my words, ask him."

"We know what the white men think," said Cetewayo, "so there is no need to ask Macumazahn to sing us an old song. The question is—what must the Zulus do? Must they swallow their spears and, ceasing to be a nation, become servants, or must they strike with them and drive the English into the sea, and after them the Boers?"

"Tell me first, King, who dwell far away and alone, knowing little of what passes in the land of Life, what the Zulus desire to do. Before me sits the Great Council of the Nation. Let it speak."

Then one by one the members of the Council uttered their opinions in order of rank or seniority. I do not remember the names of all who were present, or what each of them said. I recall, however, that Sigananda, a very old chief—he must have been over ninety—spoke the first. He told them that he had been friend of Chaka and one of his captains, and had fought in most of his battles. That afterwards he had been a general of Dingaan's until that king killed the Boers under Retief, when he left him and finally sided with Panda in the civil war in which Dingaan was killed with the help of the Boers. That he had been present at the battle of the Tugela, though he took no actual part in the fighting, and afterwards became a councillor of Panda's and then of Cetewayo his son. It was a long and interesting historical recital covering the whole period of the Zulu monarchy which ended suddenly with these words—

"I have noted, O King and Councillors, that whenever the black vulture of the Zulus was content to attack birds of his own feather, he has conquered. But when it has met the grey eagles of the white men, which come from over the sea, he has been conquered, and my heart tells me that as it was in the past, so it shall be in the future. Chaka was a friend of the English, so was Panda, and so has Cetewayo been until this hour. I say, therefore, let not the King tear the hand which fed him because it seems weak, lest it should grow strong and clutch him by the throat and choke him."

Next spoke Undabuko, Dabulamanzi and Magwenga, brothers of the king, who all favoured war, though the two last were guarded in their speech. After these came Uhamu, the king's uncle—he who was said to be the son of a Spirit—who was strong for peace, urging that the king should submit to the demands of the English, making the best terms he could, that he "should bend like a reed before the storm, so that after the storm had swept by, he might stand up straight again, and with him all the other reeds of the people of the Zulus."

So, too, said Seketwayo, chief of the Umdhlalosi, and more whom I cannot recall, six or seven of them. But Usibebu and the induna Untshingwayo, who afterwards commanded at Isandhlwana, were for fighting, as were Sirayo, the husband of the two women who had been taken on English territory and killed, and Umbilini, the chief of Swazi blood whose surrender was demanded by Sir Bartle Frere and who afterwards commanded the Zulus in the battle at Ihlobane. Last of all spoke the Prime Minister, Umnyamana, who declared fiercely that if the Zulu buffalo hid itself in the swamp like a timid calf when the white bull challenged it on the hills, the spirits of Chaka and all his forefathers would thrust its head into the mud and choke it.

When all had finished Cetewayo spoke, saying—

"That is a bad council which has two voices, for to which of them must the Captain listen when the impis of the foe gather in front of him? Here I have sat while the moon climbs high and counted, and what do I find? That one half of you, men of wisdom and renown, say Yes, and that the other half of you, men of wisdom and renown, say No. Which then is it to be, Yes or No? Are we to fight the English, or are we to sit still?"

"That is for the king to decide," said a voice.

"See what it is to be a king," went on Cetewayo with passion. "If I declare for war and we win, shall I be greater than I am? If victory gives me more land, more subjects, more wives and more cattle, what is the use of these things to me who already have enough of all of them? And if defeat should take everything from me, even my life perhaps, then what shall I have gained? I will tell you—the curse of the Zulus upon my name from father to son for ever. They will say, 'Cetewayo, son of Panda, pulled down a House that once was great. Because of some small matter he quarrelled with the English who were always the friends of our people, and brought the Zulus to the dust.' Sintwangu, my messenger, who brought heavy words from the Queen's induna which we must answer with other words or with spears, says that the English soldiers in Natal are few, so few that we Zulus can swallow them like bits of meat and still be hungry. But are these all the soldiers of the English? I am not sure. You are one of that people, Macumazahn," he added, turning his massive shape towards me, "tell us now, how many soldiers has your Queen?"

"King," I answered, "I do not know for certain. But if the Zulus can muster fifty thousand spears, the Queen, if there be need, can send against them ten times fifty thousand, and if she grows angry, another ten times fifty, every one armed with a rifle that will fire five bullets a minute, and to accompany the soldiers, hundreds of cannon whereof a single shot would give Ulundi to the flames. Out of the sea they will come, shipload after shipload, white men from where the sun sets and black men from where the sun rises, so many that Zululand would not hold them."

Now at these words, which I delivered as grandly as I could, something like a groan burst from the Council, though one man cried—

"Do not listen to the white traitor, O King, who is sent here to turn our hearts to water with his lies."

"Macumazahn may lie to us," went on Cetewayo, "though in the past none in the land have ever known him to lie, but he was not sent to do so, for I brought him here. For my part I do not believe that he lies. I believe that these English are as many as the pebbles in a river bed, and that to them Natal, yes, and all the Cape is but as a single, outlying cattle kraal, one cattle kraal out of a hundred. Did not Sompseu once tell us that they were countless, on that day when he came many years ago after the battle of the Tugela to name me to succeed my father Panda, the day when my faction, the Usutu, roared round him for hours like a river in flood, and he sat still like a rock in the centre of a river? Also I am minded of the words that Chaka said when Dingaan and Umbopa had stabbed him and he lay dying at the kraal Duguza, that although the dogs of his own House whom his hand fed, had eaten him up, he heard the sound of the running of the feet of a great white people that should stamp them and the Zulus flat."

He paused; and the silence was so intense that the crackling of Zikali's fire, which kept on burning brightly although I saw no fuel added to it, sounded quite loud. Presently it was broken, first by a dog near at hand, howling horribly at the moon, and next by the hooting of a great owl that flitted across the donga, the shadow of its wide wings falling for a moment on the king.

"Listen!" exclaimed Cetewayo, "a dog that howls! Methinks that it stands upon the roof of the House of Senzangacona. And an owl that hoots. Methinks that owl has its nest in the world of Spirits! Are these good omens, Councillors? I trow not. I say that I will not decide this matter of peace or war. If there is one of my own blood here who will do so, come, let him take my place and let me go away to my own lordship of Gikazi that I had when I was a prince before the witch Mameena who played with all men and loved but one"—here everybody turned and stared towards me, yes, even Zikali whom nothing else had seemed to move, till I wished that the ground would swallow me up—"caused the war between me and my brother Umbelazi whose blood earth will not swallow nor suns dry—"

"How can that be, O King?" broke in Umnyamana the Prime Minister. "How can any of your race sit in your seat while you still live? Then indeed there would be war, war between tribe and tribe and Zulu and Zulu till none were left, and the white hyenas from Natal would come and chew our bones and with them the Boers that have passed the Vaal. See now. Why is this Nyanga (i.e. witch-doctor) here?" and he pointed to Zikali beyond the fire. "Why has the Opener of Roads been brought from the Black Kloof which he has not left for years? Is it not that he may give us counsel in our need and show us a sign that his counsel is good, whether it be for war or peace? Then when he has made divination and given the counsel and shown the sign, then, O King, do you speak the word of war or peace, and send it to the Queen by yonder white man, and by that word we, the people, will abide."

At this suggestion, which I had no doubt was made by some secret agreement between Umnyamana and Zikali, Cetewayo seemed to grasp. Perhaps this was because it postponed for a little while the dreadful moment of decision, or perhaps because he hoped that in the eyes of the nation it would shift the responsibility from his shoulders to those of the Spirits speaking through the lips of their prophet. At any rate he nodded and answered—

"It is so. Let the Opener of Roads open us a road through the forests and the swamps and the rocks of doubt, danger and fear. Let him give us a sign that it is a good road on which we may safely travel, and let him tell us whether I shall live to walk that road and what I shall meet thereon. I promise him in return the greatest fee that ever yet was paid to a doctor in Zululand."

Now Zikali lifted his big head, shook his grey locks, and opening his wide mouth as though he expected manna to fall into it from the sky, he laughed out loud.

"O-ho-ho," he laughed, "Oho-ho-ho-o, it is worth while to have lived so long when life has brought me to such an hour as this. What is it that my ears hear? That I, the Indwande dwarf, I whom Chaka named 'The-Thing-that-never-should-have-been-born,' I, one of the race conquered and despised by the Zulus, am here to speak a word which the Zulus dare not utter, which the King of the Zulus dares not utter. O-ho-ho-ho! And what does the King offer to me? A fee, a great fee for the word that shall paint the Zulus red with blood or white with the slime of shame. Nay, I take no fee that is the price of blood or shame. Before I speak that word unknown—for as yet my heart has not heard it, and what the heart has not heard the lips cannot shape—I ask but one thing. It is an oath that whatever follows on the word, while there is a Zulu left living in the world, I, the Voice of the Spirits, shall be safe from hurt or from reproach, I and those of my House and those over whom I throw my blanket, be they black or be they white. That is my fee, without which I am silent."

"Izwa! We hear you. We swear it on behalf of the people," said every councillor in the semi-circle in front of him; yes, and the king said it also, stretching out his hand.

"Good," said Zikali, "it is an oath, it is an oath, sworn here upon the bones of the dead. Evil-doers you call them, but I say to you that many of those who sit before me have more evil in their hearts than had those dead. Well, let it be proclaimed, O King, and with it this—that ill shall it go with him who breaks the oath, with his family, with his kraal and all with whom he has to do.

"Now what is it you ask of me? First of all, counsel as to whether you should fight the English Queen, a matter on which you, the Great Ones, are evenly divided in opinion, as is the nation behind you. O King, Indunas, and Captains, who am I that I should judge of such a matter which is beyond my trade, a matter of the world above and of men's bodies, not of the world below and of men's spirits? Yet there was one who made the Zulu people out of nothing, as a potter fashions a vessel from clay, as a smith fashions an assegai out of the ore of the hills, yes, and tempers it with human blood. Chaka the Lion, the Wild Beast, the King among Kings, the Conqueror. I knew

Chaka as I knew his father, yes, and *his* father. Others still living knew him also, say you, Siganauda there for instance," and he pointed to the old chief who had spoken first. "Yes, Sigananda knew him as a boy knows a great man, as a soldier knows a general. But I knew his heart, aye, I shaped his heart, I was its thought. Had it not been for me he would never have been great. Then he wronged me"—here Zikali took up the skull which he said was that of his daughter, and stroked it—"and I left him.

"He was not wise, he should have killed one whom he had wronged, but perhaps he knew that I could not be killed; perhaps he had tried and found that he was but throwing spears at the moon which fell back on his own head. I forget. It is so long ago, and what does it matter? At least I took away from him the prop of my wisdom, and he fell—to rise no more. And so it has been with others. So it has been with others. Yet while he was great I knew his heart who lived in his heart, and therefore I ask myself, had he been sitting where the King sits to-day, what would Chaka have done? I will tell you. If not only the English but the Boers also and with them the Pondos, the Basutos and all the tribes of Africa had threatened him, he would have fought them—yes, and set his heel upon their necks. Therefore, although I give no counsel upon such a matter, I say to you that the counsel of Chaka is—fight—and conquer. Hearken to it or pass it by—I care not which."

He paused and a loud "Ow" of wonder and admiration rose from his audience. Myself I nearly joined in it, for I thought this one of the cleverest bits of statecraft that ever I had heard of or seen. The old wizard had taken no responsibility and given no answer to the demand for advice. All this he had thrust on to the shoulders of a dead man, and that man one whose name was magical to every Zulu, the king whose memory they adored, the great General who had gorged them with victory and power. Speaking as Chaka, after a long period of peace, he urged them once more to lift their spears and know the joys of triumph, thereby making themselves the greatest nation in Southern Africa. From the moment I heard this cunning appeal, I know what the end would be; all the rest was but of minor and semi-personal interest. I knew also for the first time how truly great was Zikali and wondered what he might have become had Fortune set him in different circumstances among a civilized people.

Now he was speaking again, and quickly before the impression died away.

"Such is the word of Chaka spoken by me who was his secret councillor, the Councillor who was seldom seen, and never heard. Does not Sigananda yonder know the voice which amongst all those present echoes in his ears alone?"

"I know it," cried the old chief. Then with his eyes starting almost from his head, Sigananda leapt up and raising his hand, gave the royal salute, the Bayete, to the spirit of Chaka, as though the dead king stood before him.

I think that most of those there thought that it did stand before him, for some of them also gave the Bayete and even Cetewayo raised his arm.

Sigananda squatted down again and Zikali went on.

"You have heard. This captain of the Lion knows his voice. So, that is done with. Now you ask of me something else—that I who am a doctor, the oldest of all the doctors and, it is thought—I know not—the wisest, should be able to answer. You ask of me—How shall this war prosper, if it is made—and what shall chance to the King during and after the war, and lastly you ask of me a sign. What I tell to you is true, is it not so?"

"It is true," answered the Council.

"Asking is easy," continued Zikali in a grumbling voice, "but answering is another matter. How can I answer without preparation, without the needful medicines also that I have not with me, who did not know what would be sought of me, who thought that my opinion was desired and no more? Go away now and return on the sixth night and I will tell you what I can do."

"Not so," cried the king. "We refuse to go, for the matter is immediate. Speak at once, Opener of Roads, lest it should be said in the land that after all you are but an ancient cheat, a stick that snaps in two when it is leant on."

"Ancient cheat! I remember that is what Macumazahn yonder once told me I am, though afterwards—Perhaps he was right, for who in his heart knows whether or not he be a cheat, a cheat who deceives himself and through himself others. A stick that snaps in two when it is leant on! Some have thought me so and some have thought otherwise. Well, you would have answers which I know not how to give, being without medicine and in face of those who are quite ignorant and therefore cannot lend me their thoughts, as it sometimes happens that men do when workers of evil are sought out in the common fashion. For then, as you may have guessed, it is the evil-doer who himself tells the doctor of his crime, though he may not know that he is telling it. Yet there is another stone that I alone can throw, another plan that I alone can practise, and that not always. But of this I would not make use since it is terrible and might frighten you or even send you back to your huts raving so that your wives, yes, and the very dogs fled, from you."

He stopped and for the first time did something to his fire, for I saw his hands going backwards and forwards, as though he warmed them at the flames.

At length an awed voice, I think it was that of Dabulamanzi, asked—

"What is this plan, Inyanga? Let us hear that we may judge."

"The plan of calling one from the dead and hearkening to the voice of the dead. Is it your desire that I should draw water from this fount of wisdom, O King and Councillors?"

War

Now men began to whisper together and Goza groaned at my side.

"Rather would I look down a live lion's throat than see the dead," he murmured. But I, who was anxious to learn how far Zikali would carry his tricks, contemptuously told him to be silent.

Presently the king called me to him and said—

"Macumazahn, you white men are reported to know all things. Tell me now, is it possible for the dead to appear?"

"I am not sure," I answered doubtfully; "some say that it is and some say that it is not possible."

"Well," said the king. "Have you ever seen one you knew in life after death?"

"No," I replied, "that is—yes. That is—I do not know. When you will tell me, King, where waking ends and sleep begins, then I will answer."

"Macumazahn," he exclaimed, "just now I announced that you were no liar, who perceive that after all you are a liar, for how can you both have seen, and not seen, the dead? Indeed I remember that you lied long ago, when you gave it out that the witch Mameena was not your lover, and afterwards showed that she was by kissing her before all men, for who kisses a woman who is not his lover, or his mother? Return, since you will not tell me the truth."

So I went back to my stool, feeling very small and yet indignant, for how was it possible to be definite about ghosts, or to explain the exact facts of the Mameena myth which clung to me like a Wait-a-bit thorn.

Then after a little consultation Cetewayo said—

"It is our desire, O Opener of Roads, that you should draw wisdom from the fount of Death, if indeed you can do so. Now let any who are afraid depart and wait for us who are not afraid, alone and in silence at the mouth of the kloof."

At this some of the audience rose, but after hesitating a little, sat down again. Only Goza actually took a step forward, but on my remarking that he would probably meet the dead coming up that way, collapsed, muttering something about my pistol, for the fool seemed to think I could shoot a spirit.

"If indeed I can do so," repeated Zikali in a careless fashion. "That is to be proved, is it not? Perhaps, too, it may be better for every one of you if I fail than if I succeed. Of one thing I warn you, should the dead appear stir not, and above all touch not, for he who does either of these things will, I think, never live to look upon the sun again. But first let me try an easier fashion."

Then once again he took up the skull that he said had been his daughter's, and whispered to it, only to lay it down presently.

"It will not serve," he said with a sigh and shaking his locks. "Noma tells me that she died a child, one who had no knowledge of war or matters of policy, and that in all these things of the world she still remains a child. She says that I must seek some one who thought much of them; one, too who still lives in the heart of a man who is present here, if that be possible, since from such a heart alone can the strength be drawn to enable the dead to appear and speak. Now let there be silence—Let there be silence, and woe to him that breaks it."

Silence there was indeed, and in it Zikali crouched himself down till his head almost rested on his knee, and seemed to go to sleep. He awoke again and chanted for half a minute or so in some language I could not understand. Then voices began to answer him, as it seemed to me from all over the kloof, also from the sky or rock above. Whether the effect was produced by ventriloquism or whether he had confederates posted at various points, I do not know.

At any rate this lord of "multitudes of spirits" seemed to be engaged in conversation with some of them. What is more, the thing was extremely well done, since each voice differed from the other; also I seemed to recognize some of them, Dingaan's for instance, and Panda's, yes, and that of Umbelazi the Handsome, the brother of the king whose death I witnessed down by the Tugela.

You will ask me what they said. I do not know. Either the words were confused or the events that followed have blotted them from my brain. All I remember is that each of them seemed to be speaking of the Zulus and their fate and to be very anxious to refer further discussion of the matter to some one else. In short they seemed to talk under protest, or that was my impression, although Goza, the only person with whom I had any subsequent debate upon the subject, appeared to have gathered one that was different, though what it was I do not recall. The only words that remained clear to me must, I thought, have come from the spirit of Chaka, or rather from Zikali or one of his myrmidons assuming that character. They were uttered in a deep full voice, spiced with mockery, and received by the wizard with "Sibonga," or titles of praise, which I who am versed in Zulu history and idiom knew had only been given to the great king, and indeed since his death had become unlawful, not to be used. The words were—

"What, Thing-that-should-never-have-been-born, do you think yourself a Thing-that-should-never-die, that you still sit beneath the moon and weave witchcrafts as of old? Often have I hunted for you in the Under-world who have an account to settle with you, as you have an account to settle with me. So, so, what does it matter since we must meet at last, even if you hide yourself at the back of the furthest star? Why do you bring me up to this place where I see some whom I would forget? Yes, they build bone on bone and taking the red earth, mould it into flesh and stand before me as last I saw them newly dead. Oh! your magic is good, Spell-weaver, and your hate is deep and your vengeance is keen. No, I have nothing to tell you to-day, who rule a greater people than the Zulus in another land. Who are these little men who sit before you? One of them has a look of Dingaan, my brother who slew me, yes, and wears his armlet. Is he the king? Answer not, for I do not care to know. Surely yonder withered thing is Sigananda. I know his eye and the Iziqu on his breast. Yes, I gave it to him after the great battle with Zweede in which he killed five men. Does he remember it, I wonder? Greeting, Sigananda; old as you are you have still twenty and one years to live, and than we will talk of the battle with Zweede. Let me begone, this place burns my spirit, and in it there is a stench of mortal blood. Farewell, O Conqueror!"

These were the words that I thought I heard Chaka say, though I daresay that I dreamt them. Indeed had it been otherwise, I mean had they really been spoken by Zikali, there would surely have been more in them, something that might have served his purpose, not mere talk which had all the inconsequence of a dream. Also no one else seemed to pay any particular attention to them, though this may have been because so many voices were sounding from different places at once, for as I have said, Zikali arranged his performance very well, as well as any medium could have done on a prepared stage in London.

In a moment, as though at a signal, the voices died away. Then other things happened. To begin with I felt very faint, as though all the strength were being taken out of me. Some queer fancy got a hold of me. I don't quite know what it was, but it had to do with the Bible story of Adam when he fell asleep and a rib was removed from him and made into a woman. I reflected that I felt as Adam must have done when he came out of his trance after this terrific operation, very weak and empty. Also, as it chanced, presently I saw Eve—or rather a woman. Looking at the fire in a kind of disembodied way, I perceived that dense smoke was rising from it, which smoke spread itself out like a fan. It thinned by degrees, and through the veil of smoke I perceived something else, namely, a woman very like one whom once I had known. There she stood, lightly clad enough, her fingers playing with the blue beads of her necklace, an inscrutable smile upon her face and her large eyes fixed on nothingness.

Oh! Heaven, I knew her, or rather thought I did at the moment, for now I am almost sure that it was Nombe dressed, or undressed, for the part. That knowledge came with reflection, but then I could have sworn, being deceived by the uncertain light, that the long dead Mameena stood before us as she had seemed to stand before me in the hut of Zikali, radiating a kind of supernatural life and beauty.

A little wind arose, shaking the dry leaves of the aloes in the kloof; 1 thought it whispered—*Hail, Mameena!* Some of the older men, too, among them a few who had seen her die, in trembling voices murmured, "It is Mameena!" whereon Zikali scowled at them and they grew silent.

As for the figure it stood there patient and unmoved, like one who has all time at its disposal, playing with the blue beads. I heard them tinkle against each other, which proves that it was human, for how could a wraith cause beads to tinkle, although it is true that Christmas-story ghosts are said to clank their chains. Her eyes roved idly and without interest over the semi-circle of terrified men before her. Then by degrees they fixed themselves upon the tree behind which I was crouching, whereon Goza sank paralyzed to the ground. She contemplated this tree for a while that seemed to me interminable; it reminded me of a setter pointing game it winded but could not see, for her whole frame grew intent and alert. She ceased playing with the beads and stretched out her slender hand towards me. Her lips moved. She spoke in a sweet, slow voice, saying—

"O Watcher-by-Night, is it thus you greet her to whom you have given strength to stand once more beneath the moon? Come hither and tell me, have you no kiss for one from whom you parted with a kiss?"

I heard. Without doubt the voice was the very voice of Mameena (so well had Nombe been instructed). Still I determined not to obey it, who would not be made a public laughing-stock for a second time in my life. Also I confess this jesting with the dead seemed to me somewhat unholy, and not on any account would I take a part in it.

All the company turned and stared at me, even Goza lifted his head and stared, but I sat still and contemplated the beauties of the night.

"If it is the spirit of Mameena, he will come," whispered Cetewayo to Umnyamana.

"Yes, yes," answered the Prime Minister, "for the rope of his love will draw him. He who has once kissed Mameena, *must* kiss her again when she asks."

Hearing this I grew furiously indignant and was about to break into explanations, when to my horror I found myself rising from that stool. I tried to cling to it, but, as it only came into the air with me, let it go.

"Hold me, Goza," I muttered, and he like a good fellow clutched me by the ankle, whereon I promptly kicked him in the mouth, at least my foot kicked him, not my will. Now I was walking towards that Shape—shadow or woman—like a man in his sleep, and as I came she stretched out her arms and smiled oh! as sweetly as an angel, though I felt quite sure that she was nothing of the sort.

Now I stood opposite to her alongside the fire of which the smoke smelt like roses at the dawn, and she seemed to bend towards me. With shame and humiliation I perceived that in another moment those arms would be about me. But somehow they never touched me; I lost sight of them in the rose-scented smoke, only the sweet, slow voice which I could have sworn was that of Mameena, murmured in my ear—well, words known to her and me alone that I had never breathed to any living being, though of course I am aware now that they must also have been known to somebody else.

"Do you doubt me any longer?" went on the murmuring. "Say, am I Nombe now? Or—or am I in truth that Mameena, whose kiss thrills your lips and soul? Hearken, Macumazahn, for the time is short. In the rout of the great battle that shall be, do not fly with the white men, but set your face towards Ulundi. One who was your friend will guard you, and whoever dies, no harm shall come to you now that the fire which burns in my heart has set all Zululand aflame. Hearken once more. Hans, the little yellow man who was named Light-in-Darkness, he who died among the Kendah people, sends you salutations and gives you praise. He bids me tell you that now of his own accord he renders to me, Mameena, the royal salute, because royal I must ever be; because also he and I who are so far apart are yet one in the love that is our life."

The smoke blew into my face, causing me to reel back. Cetewayo caught me by the arm, saying—

"Tell us, are the lips of the dead witch warm or cold?"

"I do not know," I groaned, "for I never touched her."

"How he lies! Oh! how he lies even about what our eyes saw," said Cetewayo reflectively as I blundered past him back to my seat, on which I sank half swooning. When I got my wits again the figure that pretended to be Mameena was speaking, I suppose in answer to some question of Zikali's which I had not heard. It said—

"O Lord of the Spirits, you have called me from the land of Spirits to make reply as to two matters which have not yet happened upon the earth. These replies I will give but no others, since the mortal strength that I have borrowed returns whence it came. The first matter is, if there be war between the White and Black, what will happen in that war? I see a plain ringed round with hills and on it a strange-shaped mount. I see a great battle; I see the white men go down like corn before a tempest; I see the spears of the impis redden; I see the white soldiers lie like leaves cut from a tree by frost. They are dead, all dead, save a handful that have fled away. I hear the ingoma of victory sung here at Ulundi. It is finished.

"The second matter is—what shall chance to the king? I see him tossed on the Black Water; I see him in a land full of houses, talking with a royal woman and her councillors. There, too, he conquers, for they offer him tribute of many gifts. I see him here, back here in Zululand, and hear him greeted with the royal salute. Last of all I see him dead, as men must die, and hear the voice of Zikali and the mourning of the women of his house. It is finished. Farewell, King Cetewayo, I pass to tell Panda, your father, how it fares with you. When last we parted did I not prophesy to you that we should meet again at the bottom of a gulf? Was it this gulf, think you, or another? One day you shall learn. Farewell, or fare ill, as it may happen!"

Once more the smoke spread out like a fan. When it thinned and drew together again, the Shape was gone.

Now I thought that the Zulus would be so impressed by this very queer exhibition, that they would seek no more supernatural guidance, but make up their minds for war at once. This, however, was just what they did not do. As it happened, among the assembled chiefs, was one who himself had a great repute as a witch-doctor, and therefore burned with jealousy of Zikali who appeared to be able to do things that he had never even attempted. This man leapt up and declared that all which they had seemed to hear and see was but cunning trickery, carried out after long preparation by Zikali and his confederates. The voices, he said, came from persons placed in certain spots, or sometimes were produced by Zikali himself. As for the vision, it was not that of a spirit but of a real woman, in proof of which he called attention to certain anatomical details of the figure. Finally, with much sense, he pointed out that the Council would be mad to come to any decision upon such evidence, or to give faith to prophecies, whereof the truth or falsity could only be known in the future.

Now a fierce debate broke out, the war party maintaining that the manifestations were genuine, the peace party that they were a fraud. In the end, as neither side would give way and as Zikali, when appealed to, sat silent as a stone, refusing any explanation, the king said—

"Must we sit here talking, talking, till daylight? There is but one man who can know the truth, that is Macumazahn. Let him deny it as he will, he was the lover of this Mameena while she was alive, for with my own eyes I saw him kiss her before she killed herself. It is certain, therefore, that he knows if the woman we seemed to see was Mameena or another, since there are things which a man never forgets. I propose, therefore, that we should question him and form our own judgment of his answer."

This advice, which seemed to promise a road out of a blind ally, met with instant acceptance.

"Let it be so," they cried with one voice, and in another minute I was once more conducted from behind my tree and set down upon the stool in front of the Council, with my back to the fire and Zikali, "that his eyes might not charm me."

"Now, Watcher-by-Night," said Cetewayo, "although you have lied to us in a certain matter, of this we do not think much, since it is one upon which both men and women always lie, as every judge will know. Therefore we still believe you to be an honest man, as your dealings have proved for many years. As an honest man, therefore, we beg you to give us a true answer to a plain question. Was the Shape we saw before us just now a woman or a spirit, and if a spirit, was it the ghost of Mameena, the beautiful witch who died near this place nearly the quarter of a hundred years ago, she whom you loved, or who loved you, which is just the same thing, since a man always loves a woman who loves him, or thinks that he does?"

Now after reflection I replied in these words and as conscientiously as I could—

"King and Councillors, I do not know if what we all saw was a ghost or a living person, but, as I do not believe in ghosts, or at any rate that they come back to the world on such errands, I conclude that it was a living person. Still it may have been neither, but only a mere picture produced before us by the arts of Zikali. So much for the first question. Your second is—was this spirit or woman or shadow, that of her whom I remember meeting in Zululand many years ago? King and Councillors, I can only say that it was very like her. Still one handsome young woman often greatly resembles another of the same age and colouring. Further, the moon gives an uncertain light, especially when it is tempered by smoke from a fire. Lastly, memory plays strange tricks with all of us, as you will know if you try to think of the face of any one who has been dead for more than twenty years. For the rest, the voice seemed similar, the beads and ornaments seemed similar, and the figure repeated to me certain words which I thought I alone had heard come from the lips of her who is dead. Also she gave me a strange message from another who is dead, referring to a matter which I believed was known only to me and that other. Yet Zikali is very clever and may have learned these things in some way unguessed by me, and what he has learned, others may have learned also. King and Councillors, I do not think that what we saw was the spirit of Mameena. I think it a woman not unlike to her who had been taught her lesson. I have nothing more to say, and therefore I pray you not to ask me any further questions about Mameena of whose name I grow weary."

At this point Zikali seemed to wake out of his indifference, or his torpor, for he looked up and said darkly—

"It is strange that the cleverest are always those who first fall into the trap. They go along, gazing at the stars at night, and forget the pit which they themselves have dug in the morning. O-ho-ho! Oho-ho!"

Now the wrangling broke out afresh. The peace party pointed triumphantly to the fact that I, the white man who ought to know, put no faith in this apparition, which was therefore without doubt a fraud. The war party on the other hand declared that I was deceiving them for reasons of my own, one of which would be that I did not wish to see the Zulus eat up my people. So fierce grew the debate that I thought it would end in blows and perhaps in an attack on myself or Zikali who all the while sat quite careless and unmoved, staring at the moon. At length Cetewayo shouted for silence, spitting, as was his habit when angry.

"Make an end," he cried, "lest I cause some of you to grow quiet for ever," whereon the recriminations ceased. "Opener of Roads," he went on, "many of those who are present think like Macumazahn here, that you are but an old cheat, though whether or no I be one of these I will not say. They demand a sign of you that none can dispute, and I demand it also before I speak the word of peace or war. Give us then that sign or begone to whence you came and show your face no more at Ulundi."

"What sign does the Council require, Son of Panda?" asked Zikali quietly. "Let them agree on one together and tell me now at once, for I who am old grow weary and would sleep. Then if it can be given I will give it; and if I cannot give it, I will get me back to my own house and show my face no more at Ulundi, who do not desire to listen again to fools who babble like contending waters round a stone and yet never stir the stone because they run two ways at once."

Now the Councillors stared at each other, for none knew what sign to ask. At length old Sigananda said—

"O King, it is well known that the Black One who went before you had a certain little assegai handled with the royal red wood, which drank the blood of many. It was with this assegai that Mopo his servant, who vanished from the land after the death of Dingaan, let out the life of the Black One at the kraal Duguza, but what became of it afterwards none have heard for certain. Some say that it was buried with the Black One, some that Mopo stole it. Others that Dingaan and Umhlagana burned it. Still a saying rose like a wind in the land that when that spear shall fall from heaven at the feet of the king who reigns in the place of the Black One, then the Zulus shall make their last great war and win a victory of which all the world shall hear. Now let the Opener of Roads give us this sign of the falling of the Black One's spear and I shall be content."

"Would you know the spear if it fell?" asked Cetewayo.

"I should know it, O King, who have often held it in my hand. The end of the haft is gnawed, for when he was angry the Black One used to bite it. Also a thumb's length from the blade is a black mark made with hot iron. Once the Black One made a bet with one of his captains that at a distance of ten paces he would throw the spear deeper into the body of a chief whom he wished to kill, than the captain could. The captain threw first, for I saw him with my eyes, and the spear sank to that place on the shaft where the mark is, for the Black One burned it there. Then the Black One threw and the spear went through the body of the chief who, as he died, called to him that he too should know the feel of it in his heart, as indeed he did."

I think that Cetewayo was about to assent to this suggestion, since he who desired peace believed it impossible that Zikali should suddenly cause this identical spear to fall from heaven. But Umnyamana, the Prime Induna, interposed hurriedly—

"It is not enough, O King. Zikali may have stolen the spear, for he was living and at the kraal Duguza at that time. Also he may have put about the prophecy whereof Sigananda speaks, or at least so men would say. Let him give us a greater sign than this that all may be content, so that whether we make war or peace it may be with a single mind. Now it is known that we Zulus have a guardian spirit who watches over us from the skies, she who is called Nomkubulwana, or by some the Inkosazana-y-Zulu, the Princess of Heaven. It is known also that this Princess, who is white of skin and ruddy-haired, appears always before great things happen in our land. Thus she appeared before the Black One died. Also she appeared to a number of children before the battle of the Tugela. It is said, too, that but lately she appeared to a woman near the coast and warned her to cross the Tugela because there would be war, though this woman cannot now be found. Let the Opener of Roads call down Nomkubulwana before our eyes from heaven and we will admit, every man of us, that this is a sign which cannot be questioned."

"And if he does this thing, which I hold no doctor in the world can do, what shall it signify?" asked Cetewayo.

"O King," answered Umnyamana, "if he does so, it shall signify war and victory. If he does not do so, it shall signify peace, and we will bow our heads before the Amalungwana basi bodwe" (i.e. "the little English," used as a term of derision).

"Do all agree?" asked Cetewayo.

"We agree," answered every man, stretching out his hand.

"Then, Opener of Roads, it stands thus: If you can call Nomkubulwana, should there be such a spirit, to appear before our eyes, the Council will take it as a sign that the Heavens direct us to fight the English."

So spoke Cetewayo, and I noted a tone of triumph in his voice, for his heart shrank from this war, and he was certain that Zikali could do nothing of the sort. Still the opinion of the nation, or rather of the army, was so strong in favour of it that he feared lest his refusal might bring about his deposition, if not his death. From this dilemma the supernatural test suggested by the Prime Minister and approved by the Council that represented the various tribes of people, seemed to offer a path of escape. So I read the situation, as I think rightly.

Upon hearing these words for the first time that night Zikali seemed to grow disturbed.

"What do my ears hear?" he exclaimed excitedly. "Am I the Umkulukulu, the Great-Great (i.e. God) himself, that it should be asked of me to draw the Princess of Heaven from beyond the stars, she who comes and goes like the wind, but like the wind cannot be commanded? Do they hear that if she will not come to my beckoning, then the great Zulu people must put a yoke upon their shoulders and be as slaves? Surely the King must have been listening to the doctrines of those English teachers who wear a white ribbon tied about their necks, and tell us of a god who suffered himself to be nailed to a cross of wood, rather than make war upon his foes, one whom they call the Prince of Peace. Times have changed indeed since the days of the Black One. Yes, generals have become like women; the captains of the impis are set to milk the cows. Well, what have I to do with all this? What does it matter to me who am so very old that only my head remains above the level of the earth, the rest of me being buried in the grave, who am not even a Zulu to boot, but a Dwandwe, one of the despised Dwandwe whom the Zulus mocked and conquered?

"Hearken to me, Spirits of the House of Senzangacona"—here he addressed about a dozen of Cetewayo's ancestors by name, going back for many generations. "Hearken to me, O Princess of Heaven, appointed by the Great-Great to be the guardian of the Zulu race. It is asked that you should appear, should it be your wish to signify to these your children that they must stand upon their feet and resist the white men who already gather upon their borders. And should it be your wish that they should lay down their spears and go home to sleep with their wives and hoe the gardens while the white men count the cattle and set each to his work upon the roads, then that you should not appear. Do what you will, O Spirits of the House of Senzangacona, do what you will, O Princess of Heaven. What does it matter to the Thing-that-never-should-have-been-born, who soon will be as though he never had been born, whether the House of Senzangacona and the Zulu people stand or fall?

"I, the old doctor, was summoned here to give counsel. I gave counsel, but it passed over the heads of these wise ones like a shadow of which none took note. I was asked to prophesy of what would chance if war came. I called the dead from their graves; they came in voices, and one of them put on the flesh again and spoke from the lips of flesh. The white man to whom she spoke denied her who had been his love, and the wise ones said that she was a cheat, yes, a doll that I had dressed up to deceive them. This spirit that had put on flesh, told of what would chance in the war, if war there were, and what would chance to the King, but they mock at the prophecy and now they demand a sign. Come then, Nomkubulwana, and give them the sign if you will and let there be war. Or stay away and give them no sign if you will, and let there be peace. It is nought to me, nought to the Thing-that-should-never-have-been-born."

Thus he rambled on, as it occurred to me who watched and listened, talking against time. For I observed that while he spoke a cloud was passing over the face of the moon, and that when he ceased speaking it was quite obscured by this cloud, so that the Vale of Bones was plunged in a deep twilight that was almost darkness. Further, in a nervous kind of way, he did something more to his wizard's fire which again caused it to throw out a fan of smoke that hid him and the execution rock in front of which he sat.

The cloud floated by and the moon came out as though from an eclipse; the smoke of the fire, too, thinned by degrees. As it melted and the light grew again, I became aware that something was materializing, or had appeared on the point of the rock above us. A few seconds later, to my wonder and amazement, I perceived that this something was the spirit-like form of a white woman which stood quite still upon the very point of the rock. She was clad in some garment of gleaming white cut low upon her breast, that may have been of linen, but from the way it shone, suggested that it was of glittering feathers, egrets' for instance. Her ruddy hair was outspread, and in it, too, something glittered, like mica or jewels. Her feet and milk-hued arms were bare and poised in her right hand was a little spear.

Nor did I see alone, since a moan of fear and worship went up from the Councillors. Then they grew silent stared and stared.

Suddenly Zikali lifted his head and looked at them through the thin flame of the fire which made his eyes shine like those of a tiger or of a cornered baboon.

"At what do you gaze so hard, King and Councillors?" he asked. "I see nothing. At what then do you gaze so hard?"

"On the rock above you stands a white spirit in her glory. It is the Inkosazana herself," muttered Cetewayo.

"Has she come then?" mocked the old wizard. "Nay, surely it is but a dream, or another of my tricks; some black woman painted white that I have smuggled here in my medicine bag, or rolled up in the blanket on my back. How can I prove to you that this is not another cheat like to that of the spirit of Mameena whom the white man, her lover, did not know again? Go near to her you must not, even if you could, seeing that if by chance she should *not* be a cheat, you would die, every man of you, for woe to him whom Nomkubulwana touches. How then, how? Ah! I have it. Doubtless in his pocket Macumazahn yonder hides a little gun, Macumazahn who with such a gun can cut a reed in two at thirty paces, or shave the hair from the chin of a man, as is well known in the land. Let him then take his little gun and shoot at that which you say stands upon the rock. If it be a black woman painted white, doubtless she will fall down dead, as so many have fallen from that rock. But if it be the Princess of Heaven, then the bullet will pass through her or turn aside and she will take no harm, though whether Macumazahn will take any harm is more than I can say."

Now when they heard this many remained silent, but some of the peace party began to clamour that I should be ordered to shoot at the apparition. At length Cetewayo seemed to give way to this pressure. I say seemed, because I think he wished to give way. Whether or not a spirit stood before him, he knew no more than the rest, but he did know that unless the vision were proved to be mortal he would be driven into war with the English. Therefore he took the only chance that remained to him.

"Macumazahn," he said, "I know you have your pistol on you, for only the other day you brought it into my presence, and through light and darkness you nurse it as a mother does her firstborn. Now since the Opener of Roads desires it, I command you to fire at that which seems to stand above us. If it be a mortal woman, she is a cheat and deserves to die. If it be a spirit from heaven it can take no harm. Nor can you take harm who only do that which you must."

"Woman or spirit, I will not shoot, King," I answered.

"Is it so? What! do you defy me, White Man? Do so if you will, but learn that then your bones shall whiten here in this Vale of Bones. Yes, you shall be the first of the English to go below," and turning, he whispered something to two of the Councillors.

Now I saw that I must either obey or die. For a moment my mind grew confused in face of this awful alternative. I did not believe that I saw a spirit. I believed that what stood above me was Nombe cunningly tricked out with some native pigments which at that distance and in that light made her look like a white woman. For oddly enough at that time the truth did not occur to me, perhaps because I was too surprised. Well, if it were Nombe, she deserved to be shot for playing such a trick, and what is more her death, by revealing the fraud of Zikali, would perhaps avert a great war. But then why did he make the suggestion that I should be commanded to fire at this figure? Slowly I drew out my pistol and brought it to the full cock, for it was loaded.

"I will obey, King," I said, "to save myself from being murdered. But on your head be all that may follow from this deed."

Then it was for the first time that a new idea struck me so clearly that I believe it was conveyed direct from Zikali's brain to my own. *I might shoot, but there was no need for me to hit.* After that everything grew plain.

"King," I said, "if yonder be a mortal, she is about die. Only a spirit can escape my aim. Watch now the centre of her forehead, for there the bullet will strike!"

I lifted the pistol and appeared to cover the figure with much care. As I did so, even from that distance I thought I saw a look of terror in its eyes. Then I fired, with a little jerk of the wrist sending the ball a good yard above her head.

"She is unharmed," cried a voice. "Macumazahn missed her."

"Macumazahn does not miss," I replied loftily. "If that at which he aimed is unharmed, it is because it cannot be hit."

"O-ho-o!" laughed Zikali, "the White Man who does not know the taste of his own love's lips, says that he has fired at that which cannot be hit. Let him try again. No, let him choose another target. The Spirit is the Spirit, but he who summoned her may still be a cheat. There is another bullet in your little gun, White Man; see if it can pierce the heart of Zikali, that the King and Council may learn whether he be a true prophet, the greatest of all the prophets that ever was, or whether he be but a common cheat."

Now a sudden rage filled me against this old rascal. I remembered how he had brought Mameena to her death, when he thought that it would serve him, and since then filled the land with stories concerning her and me, which met me whatever way I turned. I remembered that for years he had plotted to bring about the destruction of the Zulus, and to further his dark ends, was now engaged in causing a fearful war which would cost the lives of thousands. I remembered that he had trapped me into Zululand and then handed me over to Cetewayo, separating me from my friends who were in my charge, and for aught I knew, giving them to death. Surely the world would be well rid of him.

"Have your will," I shouted and covered him with the pistol.

Then there came into my mind a certain saying—"Judge not that ye be not judged." Who and what was I that I should dare to arraign and pass sentence upon this man who after all had suffered many wrongs? As I was about to fire I caught sight of some bright object flashing towards the king from above, and instantaneously shifted my aim and pressed the trigger. The thing, whatever it might be, flew in two. One part of it fell upon Zikali, the other part travelled on and struck Cetewayo upon the knee.

There followed a great confusion and a cry of "The king is stabbed!" I ran forward to look and saw the blade of a little assegai lying on the ground and on Cetewayo's knee a slight cut from which blood trickled.

"It is nothing," I said, "a scratch, no more, though had not the spear been stopped in its course it might have been otherwise."

"Yes," cried Zikali, "but what was it that caused the cut? Take this, Sigananda, and tell me what it may be," and he threw towards him a piece of red wood.

Sigananda looked at it. "It is the haft of the Black One's spear," he exclaimed, "which the bullet of Macumazahn has severed from the blade."

"Aye," said Zikali, "and the blade has drawn the blood of the Black One's child. Read me this omen, Sigananda; or ask it of her who stands above you."

Now all looked to the rock, but it was empty. The figure had vanished.

"Your word, King," said Zikali. "Is it for peace or war?"

Cetewayo looked at the assegai, looked at the blood trickling from his knee, looked at the faces of the councillors.

"Blood calls for blood," he moaned. "My word is—*War!*"

Kaatje Brings News

Zikali burst into one of his peals of laughter, so unholy that it caused the blood in me to run cold.

"The King's word is *war*," he cried. "Let Nomkubulwana take that word back to heaven. Let Macumazahn take it to the White Men. Let the captains cry it to the regiments and let the world grow red. The King has chosen, though mayhap, had I been he, I should have chosen otherwise; yet what am I but a hollow reed stuck in the ground up which the spirits speak to men? It is finished, and I, too, am finished for a while. Farewell, O King! Where shall we meet again, I wonder? On the earth or under it? Farewell, Macumazahn, I know where we shall meet, though you do not. O King, I return to my own place, I pray you to command that none come near me or trouble me with words, for I am spent."

"It is commanded," said Cetewayo.

As he spoke the fire went out mysteriously, and the wizard rose and hobbled off at a surprising pace round the corner of the projecting rock.

"Stay!" I called, "I would speak with you;" but although I am sure he heard me, he did not stop or look round.

I sprang up to follow him, but at some sign from Cetewayo two indunas barred my way.

"Did you not hear the King's command, White Man?" one of them asked coldly, and the tone of his question told me that war having been declared, I was now looked upon as a foe. I was about to answer sharply when Cetewayo himself addressed me.

"Macumazahn," he said, "you are now my enemy, like all your people, and from sunrise to-morrow morning your safe-conduct here ends, for if you are found at Ulundi two hours after that time, it will be lawful for any man to kill you. Yet as you are still my guest, I will give you an escort to the borders of the land. Moreover, you shall take a message from me to the Queen's officers and captains. It is—that I will send an answer to their demands upon the point of an assegai. Yet add this, that not I but the English, to whom I have always been a friend, sought this war. If Sompseu had suffered me to fight the Boers as I wished to do, it would never have come about. But he threw the Queen's blanket over the Transvaal and stood upon it, and now he declares that lands which were always the property of the Zulus, belong to the Boers. Therefore I take back all the promises which I made to him when he came hither to call me King in the Queen's name, and no more do I call him my father. As for the disbanding of my impis, let the English disband them if they can. I have spoken."

"And I have heard," I answered, "and will deliver your words faithfully, though I hold, King, that they come from the lips of one whom the Heavens have made mad."

At this bold speech some of the Councillors started up with threatening gestures. Cetewayo waved them back and answered quietly, "Perhaps it was the Queen of Heaven who stood on yonder rock who made me mad. Or perhaps she made me wise, as being the Spirit of our people she should surely do. That is a question which the future will decide, and if ever we should meet after it is decided, we will talk it over. Now, hamba gachle! (go in peace)."

"I hear the king and I will go, but first I would speak with Zikali."

"Then, White Man, you must wait till this war is finished or till you meet him in the Land of Spirits. Goza, lead Macumazahn back to his hut and set a guard about it. At the dawn a company of soldiers will be waiting with orders to take him to the border. You will go with him and answer for his safety with your life. Let him be well treated on the road as my messenger."

Then Cetewayo rose and stood while all present gave him the royal salute, after which he walked away down the kloof. I remained for a moment, making pretence to examine the blade of the little assegai that had been thrown by the figure on the rock, which I had picked from the ground. This historical piece of iron which I have no doubt is the same that Chaka always carried, wherewith, too, he is said to have killed his mother, Nandie, by the way I still possess, for I slipped it into my pocket and none tried to take it from me.

Really, however, I was wondering whether I could in any way gain access to Zikali, a problem that was settled for me by a sharp request to move on, uttered in a tone which admitted of no further argument.

Well, I trudged back to my hut in the company of Goza, who was so overcome by all the wonders he had seen that he could scarcely speak. Indeed, when I asked him what he thought of the figure that had appeared upon the rock, he replied petulantly that it was not given to him to know whence spirits came or of what stuff they were made, which showed me that he at any rate believed in its supernatural origin and that it had appeared to direct the Zulus to make war. This was all I wanted to find out, so I said nothing more, but gave up my mind to thought of my own position and difficulties.

Here I was, ordered on pain of death to depart from Ulundi at the dawn. And yet how could I obey without seeing Zikali and learning from him what had happened to Anscombe and Heda, or at any rate without communicating with him? Once more only did I break silence, offering to give Goza a gun if he would take a message from me to the great wizard. But with a shake of his big head, he answered that to do so would mean death, and guns were of no good to a dead man since, as I had shown myself that night, they had no power to shoot a spirit.

This closed the business on which I need not have troubled to enter, since an answer to all my questionings was at hand.

We reached the hut where Goza gave me over to the guard of soldiers, telling their officer that none were to be permitted to enter it save myself and that I was not to be to permitted to come out of it until he, Goza, came to fetch me a little before the dawn.

The officer asked if any one else was to be permitted to come out, a question that surprised me, though vaguely, for I was thinking of other things. Then Goza departed, remarking that he hoped I should sleep better than he would, who "felt spirits in his bones and did not wish to kiss them as I seemed to like to do." I replied facetiously, thinking of the bottle of brandy, that ere long I meant to feel them in my stomach, whereat he shook his head again with the air of one whom nothing connected with me could surprise, and vanished.

I crawled into the hut and put the board over the bee-hole-like entrance behind me. Then I began to hunt for the matches in my pocket and pricked my finger with the point of Chaka's historical assegai. While I was sucking it to my amazement I heard the sound of some one breathing on the further side of the hut. At first I thought of calling the guard, but on reflection found the matches and lit the candle, which stood by the blankets that served me as a bed. As soon as it burned up I looked towards the sound, and to my horror perceived the figure of a sleeping woman, which frightened me so much that I nearly dropped the candle.

To tell the truth, so obsessed was I with Zikali and his ghosts that for a few moments it occurred to me that this might be the Shape with which I had talked an hour or two before. I mean that which had seemed to resemble the long-dead lady Mameena, or rather the person made up to her likeness, come here to continue our conversation. At any rate I was sure, and rightly, that here was more of the handiwork of Zikali who wished to put me in some dreadful position for reasons of his own.

Pulling myself together I advanced upon the lady, only to find myself no wiser, since she was totally covered by a kaross. Now what was to be done? To escape, of which of course I had thought at once, was impossible since it meant an assegai in my ribs. To call to the guard for help seemed indiscreet, for who knew what those fools might say? To kick or shake her would undoubtedly be rude and, if it chanced to be the person who had played Mameena, would certainly provoke remarks that I should not care to face. There seemed to be only one resource, to sit down and wait till she woke up.

This I did for quite a long time, till at last the absurdity of the position and, I will admit, my own curiosity overcame me, especially as I was very tired and wanted to go to sleep. So advancing most gingerly, I turned down the kaross from over the head of the sleeping woman, much wondering whom I should see, for what man is there that a veiled woman does not interest? Indeed, does not half the interest of woman lie in the fact that her nature is veiled from man, in short a mystery which he is always seeking to solve at his peril, and I might add, never succeeds in solving?

Well, I turned down that kaross and next instant stepped back amazed and, to tell the truth, somewhat disappointed, for there, with her mouth open, lay no wondrous and spiritual Mameena, but the stout, earthly and most prosaic—Kaatje!

"Confound the woman!" thought I to myself. "What is she doing here?"

Then I remembered how wrong it was to give way to a sense of romantic disappointment at such a time, though as a matter of fact it is always in a moment of crisis or of strained nerves that we are most open to the insidious advances of romance. Also that there was no one on earth, or beyond it, whom I ought more greatly to have rejoiced to see. I had left Kaatje with Anscombe and Heda; therefore Kaatje could tell me what had become of them. And at this thought my heart sank—why was she here in this most inappropriate meeting-place, alone? Feeling that these were questions which must be answered at once, I prodded Kaatje in the ribs with my toe until, after a good deal of prodding, she awoke, sat up and yawned, revealing an excellent set of teeth in her cavernous, quarter-cast mouth. Then perceiving a man she opened that mouth even wider, as I thought with the idea of screaming for help. But here I was first with her, for before a sound could issue I had filled it full with the corner of the kaross, exclaiming in Dutch as I did so—

"Idiot of a woman, do you not know the Heer Quatermain when you see him?"

"Oh! Baas," she answered, "I thought you were some wicked Zulu come to do me a mischief." Then she burst into tears and sobs which I could not stop for at least three minutes.

"Be quiet, you fat fool!" I cried exasperated, "and tell me, where are your mistress and the Heer Anscombe?"

"I don't know, Baas, but I hope in heaven" (Kaatje was some kind of a Christian), she replied between her sobs.

"In heaven! What do you mean?" I asked, horrified.

"I mean, Baas, that I hope they are in heaven, because when last I saw them they were both dead, and dead people must be either in heaven or hell, and heaven, they say, is better than hell."

"*Dead!* Where did you see them dead?"

"In that Black Kloof, Baas, some days after you left us and went away. The old baboon man who is called Zikali gave us leave through the witch-girl, Nombe, to go also. So the Baas Anscombe set to work to inspan the horses, the Missie Heda helping him, while I packed the things. When I had nearly finished Nombe came, smiling like a cat that has caught two mice, and beckoned to me to follow her. I went and saw the cart inspanned with the four horses all looking as though they were asleep, for their heads hung down. Then after she had stared at me for a long while Nombe led me past the horses into the shadow of the overhanging cliff. There I saw my mistress and the Baas Anscombe lying side by side quite dead."

"How do you know that they were dead?" I gasped. "What had killed them?"

"I know that they were dead because they *were* dead, Baas. Their mouths and eyes were open and they lay upon their backs with their arms stretched out. The witch-girl, Nombe, said some Kaffirs had come and strangled them and then gone away again, or so I understood who cannot speak Zulu so very well. Who the Kaffirs were or why they came she did not say."

"Then what did you do?" I asked.

I ran back to the hut, Baas, fearing lest I should be strangled also, and wept there till I grew hungry. When I came out of it again they were gone. Nombe showed me a place under a tree where the earth was disturbed. She said that they were buried there by order of her master, Zikali. I don't know what became of the horses or the cart."

"And what happened to you afterwards?"

"Baas, I was kept for several days, I cannot remember how many, and only allowed out within the fence round the huts. Nombe came to see me once, bringing this," and she produced a package sewn up in a skin. "She said that I was to give it to you with a message that those whom you loved were quite safe with One who is greater than any in the land, and therefore that you must not grieve for them whose troubles were over. I think it was two nights after this that four Zulus came, two men and two women, and led me away, as I thought to kill me. But they did not kill me; indeed they were very kind to me, although when I spoke to them they pretended not to understand. They took me a long journey, travelling for the most part in the dark and sleeping in the day. This evening when the sun set they brought me through a Kaffir town and thrust me into the hut where I am without speaking to any one. Here, being very tired, I went to sleep, and that is all."

And quite enough too, thought I to myself. Then I put her through a cross-examination, but Kaatje was a stupid woman although a good and faithful servant, and all her terrible experiences had not sharpened her intelligence. Indeed, when I pressed her she grew utterly confused, began to cry, thereby taking refuge in the last impregnable female fortification, and snivelled out that she could not bear to talk of her dear mistress any more. So I gave it up, and two minutes later she was literally snoring, being very tired, poor thing.

Now I tried to think matters out as well as this disturbance would allow, for nothing hinders thought so much as snores. But what was the use of thinking? There was her story to take or to leave, and evidently the honest creature believed what she said. Further, how could she be deceived on such a point? She swore that she had seen Anscombe and Heda dead and afterwards had seen their graves.

Moreover, there was confirmation in Nombe's message which could not well have been invented, that spoke of their being well in the charge of a "Great One," a term by which the Zulus designate God, with all their troubles finished. The reason and manner of their end were left unrevealed. Zikali might have murdered them for his own purposes, or the Zulus might have killed them in obedience to the king's order that no white people in the land were to be allowed to live. Or perhaps the Basutos from Sekukuni's country, with whom the Zulus had some understanding, had followed and done them to death; indeed the strangling sounded more Basuto than Zulu—if they were really strangled.

Almost overcome though I was, I bethought me of the package and opened it, only to find another apparent proof of their end, for it contained Heda's jewels as I had found them in the bag in the safe; also a spare gold watch belonging to Anscombe with his coat-of-arms engraved upon it. That which he wore was of silver and no doubt was buried with him, since for superstitious reasons the natives would not have touched anything on his person after death. This seemed to me to settle the matter, presumptively at any rate, since to show that robbery was not the cause of their murder, their most valuable possessions which were not upon their persons had been sent to me, their friend.

So this was the end of all my efforts to secure the safety and well-being of that most unlucky pair. I wept when I thought of it there in the darkness of the hut, for the candle had burned out, and going on to my knees, put up an earnest prayer for the welfare of their souls; also that I might be forgiven my folly in leading them into such danger. And yet I did it for the best, trying to judge wisely in the light of such experience of the world as I possessed.

Now alas! when I am old I have come to the conclusion that those things which one tries to do for the best one generally does wrong, because nearly always there is some tricky fate at hand to mar them, which in this instance was named Zikali. The fact is, I suppose, that man who thinks himself a free agent, can scarcely be thus called, at any rate so far as immediate results are concerned. But that is a dangerous doctrine about which I will say no more, for I daresay that he is engaged in weaving a great life-pattern of which he only sees the tiniest piece.

One thing comforted me a little. If these two were dead I could now leave Zululand without qualms. Of course I was obliged to leave in any case, or die, but somehow that fact would not have eased my conscience. Indeed I think that had I believed they still lived, in this way or in that I should have tried not to leave, because I should have thought it for the best to stay to help them, whereby in all human probability I should have brought about my own death without helping them at all. Well, it had fallen out otherwise and there was an end. Now I could only hope that they had gone to some place where there are no more troubles, even if, at the worst, it were a place of rest too deep for dreams.

Musing thus at last I dozed off, for I was so tired that I think I should have slept although execution awaited me at the dawn instead of another journey. I did not sleep well because of that snoring female on the other side of the hut whose presence outraged my sense of propriety and caused me to be invaded by prophetic dreams of the talk that would ensue among those scandalmongering Zulus. Yes, it was of this I dreamed, not of the great dangers that threatened me or of the terrible loss of my friends, perhaps because to many men, of whom I suppose I am one, the fear of scandal or of being the object of public notice, is more than the fear of danger or the smart of sorrow.

So the night wore away, till at length I woke to see the gleam of dawn penetrating the smoke-hole and dimly illuminating the recumbent form of Kaatje, which to me looked most unattractive. Presently I heard a discreet tapping on the doorboard of the hut which I at once removed, wriggling swiftly through the hole, careless in my misery as to whether I met an assegai the other side of it or not. Without a guard of eight soldiers was standing, and with them Goza, who asked me if I were ready to start.

"Quite," I answered, "as soon as I have saddled my horse," which by the way had been led up to the hut.

Very soon this was done, for I brought out most of my few belongings with me and the bag of jewels was in my pocket. Then it was that the officer of the guard, a thin and melancholy-looking person, said in a hollow voice, addressing himself to Goza—

"The orders are that the White Man's wife is to go with him. Where is she?"

"Where a man's wife should be, in his hut I suppose," answered Goza sleepily.

Rage filled me at the words. Seldom do I remember being so angry.

"Yes," I said, "if you mean that Half-cast whom someone has thrust upon me, she is in there. So if she is to come with us, perhaps you will get her out."

Thus adjured the melancholy-looking captain, who was named Indudu, perhaps because he or his father had longed to the Dudu regiment, crawled into the hut, whence presently emerged sounds not unlike those which once I heard when a ringhals cobra followed a hare that I had wounded into a hole, a muffled sound of struggling and terror. These ended in the sudden and violent appearance of Kaatje's fat and dishevelled form, followed by that of the snakelike Indudu.

Seeing me standing there before a bevy of armed Zulus, she promptly fell upon my neck with a cry for help, for the silly woman thought she was going to be killed by them. Gripping me as an octopus grips its prey, she proceeded to faint, dragging me to my knees beneath the weight of eleven stone of solid flesh.

"Ah!" said one of the Zulus not unkindly, "she is much afraid for her husband whom she loves."

Well, I disentangled myself somehow, and seizing what I took to be a gourd of water in that dim light, poured it over her head, only to discover too late that it was not water but clotted milk. However the result was the same, for presently she sat up, made a dreadful-looking object by this liberal application of curds and whey, whereon I explained matters to her to the best of my power. The end of it was that after Indudu and Goza had wiped her down with tufts of thatch dragged from the hut and I had collected her gear with the rest of my own, we set her on the horse straddlewise, and started, the objects of much interest among such Zulus as were already abroad.

At the gate of the town there was a delay which made me nervous, since in such a case as mine delay might always mean a death-warrant. I knew that it was quite possible Cetewayo had changed, or been persuaded to change his mind and issue a command that I should be killed as one who had seen and knew too much. Indeed this fear was my constant companion during all the long journey to the Drift of the Tugela, causing me to look askance at every man we met or who overtook us, lest he should prove to be a messenger of doom.

Nor were these doubts groundless, for as I learned in the after days, the Prime Minister, Umnyamana, and others had urged Cetewayo strongly to kill me, and what we were waiting for at the gate were his final orders on the subject. However, in this matter, as in more that I could mention, the king played the part of a man of honour, and although he seemed to hesitate for reasons of policy, never had any intention of allowing me to be harmed. On the contrary the command brought was that any one who harmed Macumazahn, the king's guest and messenger, should die with all his House.

Whilst we tarried a number of women gathered round us whose conversation I could not help overhearing. One of them said to another—

"Look at the white man, Watcher-by-Night, who can knock a fly off an ox's horn with a bullet from further away than we could see it. He it was who loved and was loved by the witch Mameena, whose beauty is still famous in the land. They say she killed herself for his sake, because she declared that she would never live to grow old and ugly, so that he turned away from her. My mother told me all about it only last night."

Then you have a liar for a mother, thought I to myself, for to contradict such a one openly would have been undignified.

"Is it so?" asked one of her friends, deeply interested. "Then the lady Mameena must have had a strange taste in men, for this one is an ugly little fellow with hair like the grey ash of stubble and a wrinkled face of the colour of a flayed skin that has lain unstretched in the sun. However, I have been told that witches always love those who look unnatural."

"Yes," said Number one," but you see now that he is old he has to be satisfied with a different sort of wife. She is not beautiful, is she, although she has dipped her head in milk to make herself look white?"

So it went on till at length a runner arrived and whispered something to Indudu who saluted, showing me that it was a royal message, and ordered us to move. Of this I was glad, for had I stopped there much longer, I think I should have personally assaulted those gossiping female idiots.

Of our journey through Zululand there is nothing particular to say. We saw but few people, since most of the men had been called up to the army, and many of the kraals seemed to be deserted by the women and children who perhaps were hidden away with the cattle. Once, however, we met an impi about five thousand strong, that seemed to cover the hillside like a herd of game. It consisted of the Nodwengu and the Nokenke regiments, both of which afterwards fought at Isandhlwana. Some of their captains with a small guard came to see who we were, fine, fierce-looking men. They stared at me curiously, and with one of them, whom I knew, I had a little talk. He said that I was the last white man in Zululand and that I was lucky to be alive, for soon these, and he pointed to the hordes of warriors who were streaming past, would eat up the English to "the last bone." I answered that this remained to be seen, as the English were also great eaters, whereat he laughed, replying, that it was true that the white men had already taken the first bite—a very little one, from which I gathered that some small engagement had happened.

"Well, farewell, Macumazahn," he said, as he turned to go, "I hope that we shall meet in the battle, for I want to see if you can run as well as you can shoot."

This roused my temper and I answered him—

"I hope for your sake that we shall not meet, for if we do I promise that before I run I will show you what you never saw before, the gateway of the world of Spirits."

I mention this conversation because by some strange chance it happened at Isandhlwana that I killed this man, who was named Simpofu.

During all those days of trudging through hot suns and thunderstorms, for I had to give up the mare to Kaatje who was too fat to walk, or said she was, I was literally haunted by thoughts of my murdered friends. Heaven knows how bitterly I reproached myself for having brought them into Zululand. It seemed so terribly sad that these young people who loved each other and had so bright a future before them, should have escaped from a tragic past merely to be overwhelmed by such a fate. Again and again I questioned that lump Kaatje as to the details of their end and of all that went before and followed after the murder.

But it was quite useless; indeed, as time went on she seemed to become more nebulous on the point as though a picture were fading from her mind. But as to one thing she was always quite clear, that she had seen them dead and had seen their new-made grave. This she swore "by God in Heaven," completing the oath with an outburst of tears in a way that would have carried conviction to any jury, as it did to me.

And after all, what was more likely in the circumstances? Zikali had killed them, or caused them to be killed; or possibly they were killed in spite of him in obedience to the express, or general, order of the king, if the deed was not done by the Basutos. And yet an idea occurred to me. How about the woman on the rock that the Zulus thought was their Princess of the Heavens? Obviously this must be nonsense, since no such deity existed, therefore the person must either have been a white woman or one painted up to resemble a white woman; seen from a distance in moonlight it was impossible to say which. Now, if it were a white woman, she might, from her shape and height and the colour of her hair, be Heda herself. Yet it seemed incredible that Heda, whom Kaatje had seen dead some days before, could be masquerading in such a part and make no sign of recognition to me, even when I covered her with my pistol, whereas that Nombe would play it was likely enough.

Only then Nombe must be something of a quick-change artist since but a little while before she was beyond doubt personating the dead Mameena. If it were not so I must have been suffering from illusions, for certainly I seemed to see some one who looked like Mameena, and only Zikali, and through him Nombe, had sufficient knowledge to enable her to fill that role with such success. Perhaps the whole business was an illusion, though if so Zikali's powers must be great indeed. But then how about the assegai that Nomkubulwana, or rather her effigy, had seemed to hold and throw, whereof the blade was at present in my saddle-bag. That at any rate was tangible and real, though of course there was nothing to prove that it had really been Chaka's famous weapon.

Another thing that tormented me was my failure to see Zikali. I felt as though I had committed a crime in leaving Zululand without doing this and hearing from his own lips—well, whatever he chose to tell me. I forget if I said that while we were waiting at the gate where those silly women talked so much nonsense about Mameena and Kaatje, that I made another effort through Goza to get into touch with the wizard, but quite without avail. Goza only answered what he said before, that if I wished to die at once I had better take ten steps towards the Valley of Bones, whence, he added parenthetically, the Opener of Roads had already departed on his homeward journey. This might or might not be true; at any rate I could find no possible way of coming face to face with him, or even of getting a message to his ear. No, I was not to blame; I had done all I could, and yet in my heart I felt guilty. But then, as cynics would, say, failure is guilt.

At length we came to the ford of the Tugela, and as fortunately the water was just low enough, bade farewell to our escort before crossing to the Natal side. My parting with Goza was quite touching, for we felt that it partook of the nature of a deathbed adieu, which indeed it did. I told him and the others that I hoped their ends be easy, and that whether they met them by bullets or by bayonet thrusts, the wounds would prove quickly mortal so that they might not linger in discomfort or pain. Recognizing my kind thought for their true welfare they thanked me for it, though with no enthusiasm. Indudu, however, filled with the spirit of repartee, or rather of "tu quoque", said in his melancholy fashion that if he and I came face to face in war, he would be sure to remember my words and to cut me up in the best style, since he could not bear to think of me languishing on a bed of sickness without my wife Kaatje to nurse me (they knew I was touchy about Kaatje). Then we shook hands and parted. Kaatje, hung round with paraphernalia like the White Knight in "Alice through the Looking-glass," clinging to a cooking-pot and weeping tears of terror, faced the foaming flood upon the mare, while I grasped its tail.

When we were as I judged out of assegai shot, I turned, with the water up to my armpits, and shouted some valedictory words.

"Tell your king," I said, "that he is the greatest fool in the world to fight the English, since it will bring his country to destruction and himself to disgrace and death, as at last, in the words of your proverb, 'the swimmer goes down with the stream.'"

Here, as it happened, I slipped off the stone on which I was standing and nearly went down with the stream myself.

Emerging with my mouth full of muddy water I waited till they had done laughing and continued—

"Tell that old rogue, Zikali, that I know he has murdered my friends and that when we meet again he and all who were in the plot shall pay for it with their lives."

Now an irritated Zulu flung an assegai, and as the range proved to be shorter than I thought, for it went through Kaatje's dress, causing her to scream with alarm, I ceased from eloquence, and we struggled on to the further bank, where at length we were safe.

Thus ended this unlucky trip of mine to Zululand.

Isandhlwana

We had crossed the Tugela by what is known as the Middle Drift. A mile or so on the further side of it I was challenged by a young fellow in charge of some mounted natives, and found that I had stumbled into what was known as No. 2 Column, which consisted of a rocket battery, three battalions of the Native Contingent and some troops of mounted natives, all under the command of Colonel Durnford, R.E..

After explanations I was taken to this officer's head-quarter tent. He was a tall, nervous-looking man with a fair, handsome face and long side-whiskers. One of his arms, I remember, was supported by a sling, I think it had been injured in some Kaffir fighting. When I was introduced to him he was very busy, having, I understood from some one on his staff, just received orders to "operate against Matshana."

Learning that I had come from Zululand and was acquainted with the Zulus, he at once began to cross-examine me about Matshana, a chief of whom he seemed to know very little indeed. I told him what I could, which was not much, and before I could give him any information of real importance, was shown out and most hospitably entertained at luncheon, a meal of which I partook with gratitude in some garments that I had borrowed from one of the officers, while my own were set in the sun to dry. Well can I recall how much I enjoyed the first whisky and soda that I had tasted since I left "the Temple," and the good English food by which it was accompanied.

Presently I remembered Kaatje, whom I had left outside with some native women, and went to see what had happened to her. I found her finishing a hearty meal and engaged in conversation with a young gentleman who was writing in a notebook. Afterwards I discovered that he was a newspaper correspondent. What she told him and what he imagined, I do not know, but I may as well state the results at once. Within a few days there appeared in one of the Natal papers and, for aught I know, all over the earth, an announcement that Mr. Allan Quatermain, a well-known hunter in Zululand, after many adventures, had escaped from that country, "together with his favourite native wife, the only survivor of his extensive domestic establishment." Then followed some wild details as to the murder of my other wives by a Zulu wizard called "Road Mender, or Sick Ass" (i.e. Opener of Roads, or Zikali), and so on.

I was furious and interviewed the editor, a mild and apologetic little man, who assured me that the despatch was printed exactly as it had been received, as though that bettered the case. After this I commenced an action for libel, but as I was absent through circumstances over which I had no control when it came on for trial, the case was dismissed. I suppose the truth was that they mixed me up with a certain well-known white man in Zululand, who had a large "domestic establishment," but however this may be, it was a long while before I heard the last of that "favourite native wife."

Later in the day I and Kaatje, who stuck to me like a burr, departed from the camp.

The rest of our journey was uneventful, except for more misunderstandings about Kaatje, one of which, wherein a clergyman was concerned, was too painful to relate. At last we reached Maritzburg, where I deposited Kaatje in a boarding-house kept by another half-cast, and with a sigh of relief betook myself to the Plough Hotel, which was a long way off her.

Subsequently she obtained a place as a cook at Howick, and for a while I saw her no more.

At Maritzburg, as in duty bound, I called upon various persons in authority and delivered Cetewayo's message, leaving out all Zikali's witchcraft which would have sounded absurd. It did not produce much impression as, hostilities having already occurred, it was superfluous. Also no one was inclined to pay attention to the words of one who was neither an official nor a military officer, but a mere hunter supposed to have brought a native wife out of Zululand.

I did, however, report the murder of Anscombe and Heda, though in such times this caused no excitement, especially as they were not known to the officials concerned with such matters. Indeed the occurrence never so much as got into the papers, any more than did the deaths of Rodd and Marnham on the borders of Sekukuni's country. When people are expecting to be massacred themselves, they do not trouble about the past killing of others far away. Lastly, I posted Marnham's will to the Pretoria bank, advising them that they had better keep it safely until some claim arose, and deposited Heda's jewels and valuables in another branch of the same bank in Maritzburg with a sealed statement as to how they came into my possession.

These things done, I found it necessary to turn myself to the eternal problem of earning my living. I am a very rich man now as I write these reminiscences here in Yorkshire—King Solomon's mines made me that—but up to the time of my journey to Kukuana Land with my friends, Curtis and Good, although plenty of money passed through my hands on one occasion and another, little of it ever seemed to stick. In this way or that it was lost or melted; also I was not born one to make the best of his opportunities in the way of acquiring wealth. Perhaps this was good for me, since if I had gained the cash early I should not have met with the experiences, and during our few transitory years, experience is of more real value than cash. It may prepare us for other things beyond, whereas the mere possession of a bank balance can prepare us for nothing in a land where gold ceases to be an object of worship as it is here. Yet wealth is our god, not knowledge or wisdom, a fact which shows that the real essence of Christianity has not yet permeated human morals. It just runs over their surface, no more, and for every eye that is turned towards the divine Vision, a thousand are fixed night and day upon Mammon's glittering image.

Now I owned certain wagons and oxen, and just then the demand for these was keen. So I hired them out to the military authorities for service in the war, and incidentally myself with them. I drove what I considered a splendid bargain with an officer who wrote as many letters after his name as a Governor-General, but was really something quite humble. At least I thought it splendid until outside his tent I met a certain transport rider of my acquaintance whom I had always looked upon as a perfect fool, who told me that not half an hour before he had got twenty per cent. more for unsalted oxen and very rickety wagons. However, it did not matter much in the end as the whole outfit was lost at Isandhlwana, and owing to the lack of some formality which I had overlooked, I never recovered more than a tithe of their value. I think it was that I neglected to claim within a certain specified time.

At last my wagons were laden with ammunition and other Government goods and I trekked over awful roads to Helpmakaar, a place on the Highlands not far from Rorke's Drift where No. 3 Column was stationed. Here we were delayed awhile, I and my wagons having moved to a ford of the Buffalo, together with many others. It was during this time that I ventured to make very urgent representations to certain highly placed officers, I will not mention which, as to the necessity of laagering, that is, forming fortified camps, as soon as Zululand was entered, since from my intimate knowledge of its people I was sure that they would attack in force. These warnings of mine were received with the most perfect politeness and offers of gin to drink, which all transport riders were supposed to love, but in effect were treated with the contempt that they were held to deserve. The subject is painful and one on which I will not dwell. Why should I complain when I know that cautions from notable persons such as Sir Melmoth Osborn, and J. J. Uys, a member of one the old Dutch fighting families, met with a like fate.

By the way it was while I was waiting on the banks of the river that I came across an old friend of mine, a Zulu named Magepa, with whom I had fought at the battle of the Tugela. A few days later this man performed an extraordinary feat in saving his grandchild from death by his great swiftness in running, whereof I have preserved a note somewhere or other.

Ultimately on January 11 we received our marching orders and crossed the river by the drift, the general scheme of the campaign being that the various columns were to converge upon Ulundi. The roads, if so they can be called, were in such a fearful state that it took us ten days to cover as many miles. At length we trekked over a stony nek about five hundred yards in width. To the right of us was a stony eminence and to our left, its sheer brown cliffs of rock rising like the walls of some cyclopean fortress, the strange, abrupt mount of Isandhlwana, which reminded me of a huge lion crouching above the hill-encircled plain beyond. At the foot of this isolated mount, whereof the aspect somehow filled me with alarm, we camped on the night of January 21, taking no precautions against attack by way of laagering the wagons. Indeed the last thing that seemed to occur to those in command was that there would be serious fighting; men marched forward to their deaths as though they were going on a shooting-party, or to a picnic. I even saw cricketing bats and wickets occupying some of the scanty space upon the wagons.

Now I am not going to set out all the military details that preceded the massacre of Isandhlwana, for these are written in history. It is enough to say that on the night of January 21, Major Dartnell, who was in command of the Natal Mounted Police and had been sent out to reconnoitre the country beyond Isandhlwana, reported a strong force of Zulus in front of us. Thereon Lord Chelmsford, the General-in-Chief, moved out from the camp at dawn to his support, taking with him six companies of the 24th regiment, together with four guns and the mounted infantry. There were left in the camp two guns and about eight hundred white and nine hundred native troops, also some transport riders such as myself and a number of miscellaneous camp-followers. I saw him go from between the curtains of one of my wagons where I had made my bed on the top of a pile of baggage. Indeed I had already dressed myself at the time, for that night I slept very ill because I knew our danger, and my heart was heavy with fear.

About ten o'clock in the morning Colonel Durnford, whom I have mentioned already, rode up with five hundred Natal Zulus, about half of whom were mounted, and two rocket tubes which, of course, were worked by white men. This was after a patrol had reported that they had come into touch with some Zulus on the left front, who retired before them. As a matter of fact these Zulus were foraging in the mealie fields, since owing to the drought food was very scarce in Zululand that year and the regiments were hungry. I happened to see the meeting between Colonel Pulleine, a short, stout man who was then in command of the camp, and Colonel Durnford who, as his senior officer, took it over from him, and heard Colonel Pulleine say that his orders were "to defend the camp," but what else passed between them I do not know.

Presently Colonel Durnford saw and recognized me.

"Do you think the Zulus will attack us, Mr. Quatermain?" he said.

"I don't think so, Sir," I answered, "as it is the day of the new moon which they hold unlucky. But to-morrow it may be different."

Then he gave certain orders, dispatching Captain George Shepstone with a body of mounted natives along the ridge to the left, where presently they came in contact with the Zulus about three miles away, and making other dispositions. A little later he moved out to the front with a strong escort, followed by the rocket battery, which ultimately advanced to a small conical hill on the left front, round which it passed, never to return again.

Just before he started Colonel Durnford, seeing me still standing there, asked me if I would like to accompany him, adding that as I knew the Zulus so well I might be useful. I answered, Certainly, and called to my head driver, a man named Jan, to bring me my mare, the same that I had ridden out of Zululand, while I slipped into the wagon and, in addition to the beltful that I wore, filled all my available pockets with cartridges for my double-barrelled Express rifle.

As I mounted I gave Jan certain directions about the wagon and oxen, to which he listened, and then to my astonishment held out his hand to me, saying—

"Good-bye, Baas. You have been a kind master to me and I thank you."

"Why do you say that?" I asked.

"Because, Baas, all the Kaffirs declare that the great Zulu impi will be on to us in an hour or two and eat up every man. I can't tell how they know it, but so they swear."

"Nonsense," I answered, "it is the day of new moon when the Zulus don't fight. Still if anything of the sort should happen, you and the other boys had better slip away to Natal, since the Government must pay for the wagons and oxen."

This I said half joking, but it was a lucky jest for Jan and the rest of my servants, since they interpreted it in earnest and with the exception of one of them who went back to get a gun, got off before the Zulu horn closed round the camp, and crossed the river in safety.

Next moment I was cantering away after Colonel Durnford, whom I caught up about a quarter of a mile from the camp.

Now of course I did not see all of the terrible battle that followed and can only tell of that part of it in which I had a share. Colonel Durnford rode out about three and a half miles to the left front, I really don't quite know why, for already we were hearing firing on the top of the Nqutu Hills almost behind us, where Captain Shepstone was engaging the Zulus, or so I believe. Suddenly we met a trooper of the Natal Carabineers whose name was Whitelaw, who had been out scouting. He reported that an enormous impi was just ahead of us seated in an umkumbi, or semi-circle, as is the fashion of the Zulus before they charge. At least some of them, he said, were so seated, but others were already advancing.

Presently these appeared over the crest of the hill, ten thousand of them I should say, and amongst them I recognized the shields of the Nodwengu, the Dududu, the Nokenke and the Ingoba-makosi regiments. Now there was nothing to be done except retreat, for the impi was attacking in earnest. The General Untshingwayo, together with Undabuko, Cetewayo's brother, and the chief Usibebu who commanded the scouts, had agreed not to fight this day for the reason I have given, because it was that of the new moon, but circumstances had forced their hand and the regiments could no longer be restrained. So to the number of twenty thousand or more, say one-third of the total Zulu army, they hurled themselves upon the little English force that, owing to lack of generalship, was scattered here and there over a wide front and had no fortified base upon which to withdraw.

We fell back to a donga which we held for a little while, and then as we saw that there we should presently be overwhelmed, withdrew gradually for another two miles or so, keeping off the Zulus by our fire. In so doing we came upon the remains of the rocket battery near the foot of the conical hill I have mentioned, which had been destroyed by some regiment that passed behind us in its rush on the camp. There lay all the soldiers dead, assegaied through and through, and I noticed that one young fellow who had been shot through the head, still held a rocket in his hands.

Now somewhat behind and perhaps half a mile to the right of this hill a long, shallow donga runs across the Isandhlwana plain. This we gained, and being there reinforced by about fifty of the Natal Carabineers under Captain Bradstreet, held it for a long while, keeping off the Zulus by our terrible fire which cut down scores of them every time they attempted to advance. At this spot I alone killed from twelve to fifteen of them, for if the big bullet from my Express rifle struck a man, he did not live.

Messengers were sent back to the camp for more ammunition, but none arrived, Heaven knows why. My own belief is that the reserve cartridges were packed away in boxes and could not be got at. At last our supply began to run short, so there was nothing to be done except retreat upon the camp which was perhaps half a mile behind us.

Taking advantage of a pause in the Zulu advance which had lain down while waiting for reserves, Colonel Durnford ordered a retirement that was carried out very well. Up to that time we had lost only quite a few men, for the Zulu fire was wild and high and they had not been able to get at us with the assegai. As we rode towards the mount I observed that firing was going on in all directions, especially on the nek that connected it with the Nqutu range where Captain Shepstone and his mounted Basutos were wiped out while trying to hold back the Zulu right horn. The guns, too, were firing heavily and doing great execution.

After this all grew confused. Colonel Durnford gave orders to certain officers who came up to him, Captain Essex was one and Lieutenant Cochrane another. Then his force made for their wagons to get more ammunition. I kept near to the Colonel and a while later found myself with him and a large, mixed body of men a little to the right of the nek which we had crossed in our advance from the river. Not long afterwards there was a cry of "The Zulus are getting round us!" and looking to the left I saw them pouring in hundreds across the ridge that joins Isandhlwana Mountain to the Nqutu Range. Also they were advancing straight on to the camp.

Then the rout began. Already the native auxiliaries were slipping away and now the others followed. Of course this battle was but a small affair, yet I think that few have been more terrible, at any rate in modern times. The aspect of those plumed and shielded Zulus as they charged, shouting their war-cries and waving their spears, was awesome. They were mown down in hundreds by the Martini fire, but still they came on, and I knew that the game was up. A maddened horde of fugitives, mostly natives, began to flow past us over the nek, making for what was afterwards called Fugitives' Drift, nine miles away, and with them went white soldiers, some mounted, some on foot. Mingled with all these people, following them, on either side of them, rushed Zulus, stabbing as they ran. Other groups of soldiers formed themselves into rough squares, on which the savage warriors broke like water on a rock, By degrees ammunition ran out; only the bayonet remained. Still the Zulus could not break those squares. So they took another counsel. Withdrawing a few paces beyond the reach of the bayonets, they overwhelmed the soldiers by throwing assegais, then rushed in and finished them.

This was what happened to us, among whom were men of the 24th, Natal Carabineers and Mounted Police. Some had dismounted, but I sat on my horse, which stood quite still, I think from fright, and fired away so long as I had any ammunition. With my very last cartridge I killed the Captain Indudu who had been in charge of the escort that conducted me to the Tugela. He had caught sight of me and called out—

"Now, Macumazahn, I will cut you up nicely as I promised."

He got no further in his speech, for at that moment I sent an Express bullet through him and his tall, melancholy figure doubled up and collapsed.

All this while Colonel Durnford had been behaving as a British officer should do. Scorning to attempt flight, whenever I looked round I caught sight of his tall form, easy to recognize by the long fair moustaches and his arm in a sling, moving to and fro encouraging us to stand firm and die like men. Then suddenly I saw a Kaffir, who carried a big old smooth-bore gun, aim at him from a distance of about twenty yards, and fire. He went down, as I believe dead, and that was the end of a very gallant officer and gentleman whose military memory has in my opinion been most unjustly attacked. The real blame for that disaster does not rest upon the shoulders of either Colonel Durnford or Colonel Pulleine.

After this things grew very awful. Some fled, but the most stood and died where they were. Oddly enough during all this time I was never touched. Men fell to my right and left and in front of me; bullets and assegais whizzed past me, yet I remained quite unhurt. It was as though some Power protected me, which no doubt it did.

At length when nearly all had fallen and I had nothing left to defend myself with except my revolver, I made up my mind that it was time to go. My first impulse was to ride for the river nine miles away. Looking behind me I saw that the rough road was full of Zulus hunting down those who tried to escape. Still I thought I would try it, when suddenly there flashed across my brain the saying of whoever it was that personated Mameena in the Valley of Bones, to the effect that in the great rout of the battle I was not to join the flying but to set my face towards Ulundi and that if I did so I should be protected and no harm would come to me. I knew that all this prophecy was but a vain thing fondly imagined, although it was true that the battle and the rout had come. And yet I acted on it—why Heaven knows alone.

Setting the spurs to my horse I galloped off past Isandhlwana Mount, on the southern slopes of which a body of the 24th were still fighting their last fight, and heading for the Nqutu Range. The plain was full of Zulus, reserves running up; also to the right of me the Ulundi and Gikazi divisions were streaming forward. These, or some of them, formed the left horn of the impi, but owing to the unprepared nature of the Zulu battle, for it must always be remembered that they did not mean to fight that day, their advance had been delayed until it was too late for them entirely to enclose the camp. Thus the road, if it can so be called, to Fugitives' Drift was left open for a while, and by it some effected their escape. It was this horn, or part of it, that afterwards moved on and attacked Rorke's Drift, with results disastrous to itself.

For some hundreds of yards I rode on thus recklessly, because recklessness seemed my only chance. Thrice I met bodies of Zulus, but on each occasion they scattered before me, calling out words that I could not catch. It was as though they were frightened of something they saw about me. Perhaps they thought that I was mad to ride thus among them. Indeed I must have looked mad, or perhaps there was something else. At any rate I believed that I was going to win right through them when an accident happened.

A bullet struck my mare somewhere in the back. I don't know where it came from, but as I saw no Zulu shoot, I think it must have been one fired by a soldier who was still fighting on the slopes of the mount. The effect of it was to make the poor beast quite ungovernable. Round she wheeled and galloped at headlong speed back towards the peak, leaping over dead and dying and breaking through the living as she went. In two minutes we were rushing up its northern flank, which seemed to be quite untenanted, towards the sheer brown cliff which rose above it, for the fighting was in progress on the other side. Suddenly at the foot of this cliff the mare stopped, shivered and sank down dead, probably from internal bleeding.

I looked about me desperately. To attempt the plain on foot meant death. What then was I to do? Glancing at the cliff I saw that there was a gully in it worn by thousands of years of rainfall, in which grew scanty bushes. Into this I ran, and finding it practicable though difficult, began to climb upwards, quite unnoticed by the Zulus who were all employed upon the further side. The end of it was that I reached the very crest of the mount, a patch of bare, brown rock, except at one spot on its southern front where there was a little hollow in which at this rainy season of the year herbage and ferns grew in the accumulated soil, also a few stunted, aloe-like plants.

Into this patch I crept, having first slaked my thirst from a little pool of rain water that lay in a cup-like depression of the rock, which tasted more delicious than any nectar, and seemed to give me new life. Then covering myself as well as I could with grasses and dried leaves from the aloe plants, I lay still.

Now I was right on the brink of the cliff and had the best view of the Isandhlwana plain and the surrounding country that can be imagined. From my lofty eyrie some hundreds of feet in the air, I could see everything that happened beneath. Thus I witnessed the destruction of the last of the soldiers on the slopes below. They made a gallant end, so gallant that I was proud to be of the same blood with them. One fine young fellow escaped up the peak and reached a plateau about fifty feet beneath me. He was followed by a number of Zulus, but took refuge in a little cave whence he shot three or four of them; then his cartridges were exhausted and I heard the savages speaking in praise of him—dead. I think he was the last to die on the field of Isandhlwana.

The looting of the camp began; it was a terrible scene. The oxen and those of the horses that could be caught were driven away, except certain of the former which were harnessed to the guns and some of the wagons and, as I afterwards learned, taken to Ulundi in proof of victory. Then the slain were stripped and Kaffirs appeared wearing the red coats of the soldiers and carrying their rifles. The stores were broken into and all the spirits drunk. Even the medical drugs were swallowed by these ignorant men, with the result that I saw some of them reeling about in agony and others fall down and go to sleep.

An hour or two later an officer who came from the direction in which the General had marched, cantered right into the camp where the tents were still standing and even the flag was flying. I longed to be able to warn him, but could not. He rode up to the headquarters marquee, whence suddenly issued a Zulu waving a great spear. I saw the officer pull up his horse, remain for a moment as though indecisive, then turn and gallop madly away, quite unharmed, though one or two assegais were thrown and many shots fired at him. After this considerable movements of the Zulus went on, of which the net result was, that they evacuated the place.

Now I hoped that I might escape, but it was not to be, since on every side numbers of them crept up Isandhlwana Mountain and hid behind rocks or among the tall grasses, evidently for purposes of observation. Moreover some captains arrived on the little plateau where was the cave in which the soldier had been killed, and camped there. At least at sundown they unrolled their mats and ate, though they lighted no fire.

The darkness fell and in it escape for me from that guarded place was impossible, since I could not see where to set my feet and one false step on the steep rock would have meant my death. From the direction of Rorke's Drift I could hear continuous firing; evidently some great fight was going on there, I wondered vaguely—with what result. A little later also I heard the distant tramp of horses and the roll of gun wheels. The captains below heard it too and said one to another that it was the English soldiers returning, who had marched out of the camp at dawn. They debated one with another whether it would be possible to collect a force to fall upon them, but abandoned the idea because the regiments who had fought that day were now at a distance and too tired, and the others had rushed forward with orders to attack the white men on and beyond the river.

So they lay still and listened, and I too lay still and listened, for on that cloudy, moonless night I could see nothing. I heard smothered words of command. I heard the force halt because it could not travel further in the gloom. Then they lay down, the living among the dead, wondering doubtless if they themselves would not soon be dead, as of course must have happened had the Zulu generalship been better, for if even five thousand men had been available to attack at dawn not one of them could have escaped. But Providence ordained it otherwise. Some were taken and the others left.

About an hour before daylight 1 heard them stirring again, and when its first gleams came all of them had vanished over the nek of slaughter, with what thoughts in their hearts, I wondered, and to what fate. The captains on the plateau beneath had gone also, and so had the circle of guards upon the slopes of the mount, for I saw these depart through the grey mist. As the light gathered, however, I observed bodies of men collecting on the nek, or rather on both neks, which made it impossible for me to do what I had hoped, and run to overtake the English troops. From these I was utterly cut off. Nor could I remain longer without food on my point of rock, especially as I was sure that soon some Zulus would climb there to use it as an outlook post. So while I was still more or less hidden by the mist and morning shadows, I climbed down it by the same road that I had climbed up, and thus reached the plain. Not a living man, white or black, was to be seen, only the dead, only the dead. I was the last Englishman to stand upon the plain of Isandhlwana for weeks or rather months to come.

Of all my experiences this was, I think, the strangest, after that night of hell, to find myself alone upon this field of death, staring everywhere at the distorted faces which on the previous morn I had seen so full of life. Yet my physical needs asserted themselves. I was very hungry, who for twenty-four hours had eaten nothing, faint with hunger indeed. I passed a provision wagon that had been looted by the Zulus. Tins of bully beef lay about, also, among a wreck of broken glass, some bottles of Bass's beer which had escaped their notice. I found an assegai, cleaned it in the ground which it needed, and opening one of the tins, lay down in a tuft of grass by a dead man, or rather between him and some Zulus whom he had killed, and devoured its contents. Also I knocked the tops off a couple of the beer bottles and drank my fill. While I was doing this a large rough dog with a silver-mounted collar on its neck, I think of the sort that is called an Airedale terrier, came up to me whining. At first I thought it was an hyena, but discovering my mistake, threw it some bits of meat which it ate greedily. Doubtless it had belonged to some dead officer, though there was no name on the collar. The poor beast, which I named Lost, at once attached itself to me, and here I may say that I kept it till its death, which occurred of jaundice at Durban not long before I started on my journey to King Solomon's Mines. No man ever had a more faithful friend and companion.

When I had eaten and drunk I looked about me, wondering what I should do. Fifty yards away I saw a stout Basuto pony still saddled and bridled, although the saddle was twisted out of its proper position, which was cropping the grass as well as it could with the bit in its mouth. Advancing gently I caught it without trouble, and led it back to the plundered wagon. Evidently from the marks upon the saddlery it had belonged to Captain Shepstone's force of mounted natives.

Here I filled the large saddlebags made of buckskin with tins of beef, a couple more bottles of beer and a packet of tandstickor matches which I was fortunate enough to find. Also I took the Martini rifle from a dead soldier, together with a score or so of cartridges that remained in his belt, for apparently he must have been killed rather early in the fight.

Thus equipped I mounted the pony and once more bethought me of escaping to Natal. A look towards the nek cured me of that idea, for coming over it I saw the plumed heads of a whole horde of warriors. Doubtless these were returning from the unsuccessful attack on Rorke's Drift, though of that I knew nothing at the time. So whistling to the dog I bore to the left for the Nqutu Hills, riding as fast as the rough ground would allow, and in half an hour was out of sight of that accursed plain.

One more thing too I did. On its confines I came across a group of dead Zulus who appeared to have been killed by a shell. Dismounting I took the headdress of one of them and put it on, for I forgot to say that I had lost my hat. It was made of a band of otterskin from which rose large tufts of the black feathers of the finch which the natives call "sakabula." Also I tied his kilt of white oxtails about my middle, precautions to which I have little doubt I owe my life, since from a distance they made me look like a Kaffir mounted on a captured pony.

Then I started on again, whither I knew not.

Allan Awakes

Now I have no intention of setting down all the details of that dreadful journey through Zululand, even if I could recall them, which, for a reason to be stated, I cannot do. I remember that at first I thought of proceeding to Ulundi with some wild idea of throwing myself on the mercy of Cetewayo under pretence that I brought him a message from Natal. Within a couple of hours, however, from the top of a hill I saw ahead of me an impi and with it captured wagons, which was evidently heading for the king's kraal. So as I knew what kind of a greeting these warriors would give me, I bore away in another direction with the hope of reaching the border by a circuitous route. In this too I had no luck, since presently I caught sight of outposts stationed upon rocks, which doubtless belonged to another impi or regiment. Indeed one soldier, thinking from my dress that I also was a Zulu, called to me for news from about half a mile away, in that peculiar carrying voice which Kaffirs can command. I shouted back something about victory and that the white men were wiped out, then put an end to the conversation by vanishing into a patch of dense bush.

It is a fact that after this I have only the dimmest recollection of what happened. I remember off-saddling at night on several occasions. I remember being very hungry because all the food was eaten and the dog, Lost, catching a bush buck fawn, some of which I partially cooked on a fire of dead wood, and devoured. Next I remember—I suppose this was a day or two later—riding at night in a thunderstorm and a particularly brilliant flash of lightning which revealed scenery that seemed to be familiar to me, after which came a shock and total unconsciousness.

At length my mind returned to me. It was reborn very slowly and with horrible convulsions, out of the womb of death and terror. I saw blood flowing round me in rivers, I heard the cries of triumph and of agony. I saw myself standing, the sole survivor, on a grey field of death, and the utter loneliness of it ate into my soul, so that with all its strength it prayed that it might be numbered in this harvest. But oh! it was so strong, that soul which could not, would not die or fly away. So strong, that then, for the first time, I understood its immortality and that it could *never* die. This everlasting thing still clung for a while to the body of its humiliation, the mass of clay and nerves and appetites which it was doomed to animate, and yet knew its own separateness and eternal individuality. Striving to be free of earth, still it seemed to walk the earth, a spirit and a shadow, aware of the hatefulness of that to which it was chained, as we might imagine some lovely butterfly to be that is fated by nature to suck its strength from carrion, and remains unable to soar away into the clean air of heaven.

Something touched my hand and I reflected dreamily that if I had been still alive, for in a way I believed that I was dead, I should have thought it was a dog's tongue. With a great effort I lifted my arm, opened my eyes and looked at the hand against the light, for there was light, to see it was so thin that this light shone through between the bones. Then I let it fall again, and lo! it rested on the head of a dog which went on licking it.

A dog! What dog? Now I remembered; one that I had found on the field of Isandhlwana. Then I must be still alive. The thought made me cry, for I could feel the tears run down my cheeks, not with joy but with sorrow. I did not wish to go on living. Life was too full of struggle and of bloodshed and bereavement and fear and all horrible things. I was prepared to exchange my part in it just for rest, for the blessing of deep, unending sleep in which no more dreams could come, no more cups of joy could be held to thirsting lips, only to be snatched away.

I heard something shuffling towards me at which the dog growled, then seemed to slink away as though it were afraid. I opened my eyes again, looked, and closed them once more in terror, for what I saw suggested that perhaps I was dead after all and had reached that hell which a certain class of earnest Christian promises to us as the reward of the failings that Nature and those who begat us have handed on to us as a birth doom. It was something unnatural, grey-headed, terrific—doubtless a devil come to torment me in the inquisition vaults of Hades. Yet I had known the like when I was alive. How had it been called? I remembered, "The-thing-that-never-should-have-been-born." Hark! It was speaking in that full deep voice which was unlike to any other.

"Greeting, Macumazahn," it said. "I see that you have come back from among the dead with whom you have been dwelling for a moon and more. It is not wise of you, Macumazahn, yet I am glad who have matched my skill against Death and won, for now you will have much to tell me about his kingdom."

So it was Zikali—Zikali who had butchered my friends.

"Away from me, murderer!" I said faintly, "and let me die, or kill me as you did the others."

He laughed, but very softly, not in his usual terrific fashion, repeating the word "murderer" two or three times. Then with his great hand he lifted my head gently as a woman might, saying—

"Look before you, Macumazahn."

I looked and saw that I was in some kind of a cave. Outside the sun was setting and against its brightness I perceived two figures, a white man and a white woman who were walking hand in hand and gazing into each other's eyes. They were Anscombe and Heda passing the mouth of the cave.

"Behold the murdered, O Macumazahn, dealer of hard words."

"It is only a trick," I murmured. "Kaatje saw them dead and buried."

"Yes, yes, I forgot. The fat fool-woman saw them dead and buried. Well, sometimes the dead come to life again and for good purpose, as you should know, Macumazahn, who followed the counsel of a certain Mameena and wandered here instead of rushing onto the Zulu spears."

I tried to think the thing out and could not, so only asked—

"How did I come? What happened to me?"

"I think the sun smote you first who had no covering on your head and the lightning smote you afterwards. Yet all the while that reason had left you, One led your horse and after the Heavens had tried to kill you and failed, perhaps because my magic was too strong for them, One sent that beast which you found, yes, sent it here to lead us to where you lay. There you were discovered and brought hither. Now sleep lest you should go further than even I can fetch you back again."

He held his hands above my head, seeming to grow in stature till his white hair touched the roof of the cave, and in an instant I fancied that I was falling away, deep, deep into a gulf of nothingness.

There followed another period of dreaming, in which dreams I seemed to meet all sorts of people, dead and living, especially Lady Ragnall, a friend of mine with whom I had been concerned in a very strange adventure among the Kendah people and with whom in days to come I was destined to be concerned again, although of course I knew nothing of this, in a still stranger adventure of what I may call a spiritual order, which I may or may not try to reduce to writing. It seemed to me that I was constantly dining with her tete-a-tete and that she told me all sorts of queer things between the courses. Doubtless these illusions occurred when I was fed.

At length I woke up again, feeling much stronger, and saw the dog, Lost, watching me with its great tender eyes—oh! they talk of the eyes of women, but are they ever as beautiful as those of a loving dog? It lay by my low bed-stead, a rough affair fashioned of poles and strung with rimpis or strings of raw hide, and by it, stroking its head, sat the witch-doctoress, Nombe. I remember how pleasing she looked, a perfect type of the eternal feminine with her graceful, rounded shape and her continual, mysterious smile which suggested so much more than any mortal woman has to give.

"Good-day to you, Macumazahn," she said in her gentle voice, "you have gone through much since last we met on the night before Goza took you away to Ulundi."

Now remembering all, I was filled with indignation against this little humbug.

"The last time we met, Nombe," I said, "was when you played the part of a woman who is dead in the Vale of Bones by the king's kraal."

She regarded me with a kindly commiseration, and answered, shaking her head—

"You have been very ill, Macumazahn, and your spirit still tricks you. I played the part of no woman in any valley by the king's kraal, nor were my eyes rejoiced with the sight of you there or elsewhere till they brought you to this place, so changed that I should scarcely have known you."

"You little liar!" I said rudely.

"Do the white people always name those liars who tell them true things they cannot understand?" she inquired with a sweet innocence. Then without waiting for an answer, she patted my hand as though I were a fretful child and gave me some soup in a gourd, saying, "Drink it, it is good. The lady Heddana made it herself in the white man's fashion."

I drank the soup, which was very good, and as I handed back the gourd, answered—

"Kaatje has told me that the lady Heddana is dead. Can the dead make soup?"

She considered the point while she threw some bits of meat out of the bottom of the gourd to the dog, Lost, then replied—

"I do not know, Macumazahn, or indeed whether the dead eat as we do. Next time my Spirit visits me I will make inquiry and tell you the answer. But I do know that it is very strange that you, who always turn your back upon the truth, are so ready to accept falsehoods. Why should you believe that the lady Heddana is dead just because Kaatje told you so, when I who am still alive had sworn to you that I would protect her with my life? Nay, speak no more now. To-morrow if you are well enough you shall see and judge for yourself."

She drew up the kaross over me, again patted my hand in her motherly fashion and departed, still smiling, after which I went to sleep again, so dreamlessly that I think there was some native soporific in that soup.

On the following day two of Zikali's servants who did the rougher work of my sick room, if I may so call it, arrived and said that they were going to carry me out of the cave for a while, if that were my will. I who longed to breathe the fresh air again, said that it was very much my will, whereon they grasped the rough bedstead which I have described by either end and very carefully bore me down the cave and through its narrow entrance, where they set the bedstead in the shadow of the overhanging rock without. When I had recovered a little, for even that short journey tired me, I looked about me and perceived that as I had expected, I was in the Black Kloof, for there in front of me were the very huts which we had occupied on our arrival from Swazi-Land.

I lay a while drawing in the sweet air which to me was like a draught of nectar, and wondering whether I were not still in a dream. For instance, I wondered if I had truly seen the figures of Anscombe and Heda pass the mouth of the cave, on that day when I awoke, or if these were but another of Zikali's illusions imprinted on my weakened mind by his will power. For of what he and Nombe told me I believed nothing. Thus marvelling I fell into a doze and in my doze heard whisperings. I opened my eyes and lo! there before me stood Anscombe and Heda. It was she who spoke the first, for I was tongue-tied; I could not open my lips.

"Dear Mr. Quatermain, dear Mr. Quatermain!" she murmured in her sweet voice, then paused.

Now at last words came to me. "I thought you were both dead," I said. "Tell me, are you really alive?"

She bent down and kissed my brow, while Anscombe took my hand.

"Now you know," she answered. "We are both of us alive and well."

"Thank God!" I exclaimed. "Kaatje swore that she saw you dead and buried."

"One sees strange things in the Black Kloof," replied Anscombe speaking for the first time, "and much has happened to us since we were parted, to which you are not strong enough to listen now. When you are better, then we will tell you all. So grow well as soon as you can."

After this I think I fainted, for when I came to myself again I was back in the cave.

Another ten days or so went by before I could even leave my bed, for my recovery was very slow. Indeed for weeks I could scarcely walk at all, and six whole months passed before I really got my strength again and became as I used to be. During those days I often saw Anscombe and Heda, but only for a few minutes at a time. Also occasionally Zikali would visit me, speaking a little, generally about past history, or something of the sort, but never of the war, and go away. At length one day he said to me—

"Macumazahn, now I am sure you are going to live, a matter as to which I was doubtful, even after you seemed to recover. For, Macumazahn, you have endured three shocks, of which to-day I am not afraid to talk to you. First there was that of the battle of Isandhlwana where you were the last white man left alive."

"How do you know that, Zikali?" I asked.

"It does not matter. I do know. Did you not ride through the Zulus who parted this way and that before you, shouting what you could not understand? One of them you may remember even saluted with his spear."

"I did, Zikali. Tell me, why did they behave thus, and what did they shout?"

"I shall not tell you, Macumazahn. Think over it for the rest of your life and conclude what you choose; it will not be so wonderful as the truth. At least they did so, as a certain doll I dressed up yonder in the Vale of Bones told you they would, she whose advice you followed in riding towards Ulundi instead of back to the river where you would have met your death, like so many others of the white people."

"Who was that doll, Zikali?"

"Nay, ask me not. Perhaps it was Nombe, perhaps another. I have forgotten. I am very old and my memory begins to play me strange tricks. Still I recollect that she was a good doll, so like a dead woman called Mameena that I could scarcely have known them apart. Ah! that was a great game I played in the Vale of Bones, was it not, Macumazahn?"

"Yes, Zikali, yet I do not understand why it was played."

"Being so young you still have the impatience of youth, Macumazahn, although your hair grows white. Wait a while and you will understand all. Well, you lay that night on the topmost rock of Isandhlwana, and there you saw and heard strange things. You heard the rest of the white soldiers come and lie down to rest among their dead brothers, and depart again unharmed. Oh! what fools are these Zulu generals nowadays. They send out an impi to attack men behind walls, spears against rifles, and are defeated. Had they kept that impi to fall on the rest of the English when they walked into the trap, not a man of your people would have been left alive. Would that have happened in the time of Chaka?"

"I think not, Zikali. Still I am glad that it did happen."

"I think not too, Macumazahn, but small men, small wit. Also like you I am glad that it did not happen, since it is the Zulus I hate, not the English who have now learned a lesson and will not be caught again. Oh! many a captain in Zululand is to-day flat as a pricked bladder, and even their victory, as they call it, cost them dear.

For, mind you, Macumazahn, for every white man they killed two of them died. So, so! In the morning you left the hill—do not look astonished, Macumazahn. Perhaps those captains on the rock beneath you let you go for their own purposes, or because they were commanded, for though weak I can still lift a stone or two, Macumazahn, and afterwards told me all about it. Then you found yourself alone among the dead, like the last man in the world, Macumazahn, and that dog at your side, also a horse came to you. Perhaps I sent them, perhaps it was a chance. Who knows? Not I myself, for as I have said, my memory has grown so bad. That was your first shock, Macumazahn, the shock of standing alone among the dead like the last man in the world. You felt it, did you not?"

"As I hope I shall never feel anything again. It nearly drove me mad," I answered.

"Very nearly indeed, though I have felt worse things and only laughed, as I would tell you, had I the time. Well, then the sun struck you, for at this season of the year it is very hot in those valleys for a white man with no covering to his head, and you went quite mad, though fortunately the dog and the horse remained as Heaven had made them. That was the second shock. Then the storm burst and the lightning fell. It ran down the rifle that you still carried, Macumazahn. I will show it to you and you will see that its stock is shattered. Perhaps I turned the flash aside, for I am a great thunder-herd, or perhaps it was One mightier than I. That was the third shock, Macumazahn. Then yon were found, still living—how, the white man, your friend, will tell you. But you should cherish that dog of yours, Macumazahn, for many a man might have served you worse. And being strong, though small, or perhaps because you still have work left to do in the world before you leave it for a while, you have lived through all these things and will in time recover, though not yet."

"I hope so, Zikali, though on the whole I am not sure that I wish to recover."

"Yes, you do, Macumazahn, because the religion of you white men makes you fear death and what may come after it. You think of what you call your sins and are afraid lest you should be tortured because of them, not understanding that the spirit must be judged not by what the flesh has done but by what the spirit desired to do, by *will* not by *deed,* Macumazahn. The evil man is he who wishes to do evil, not he who wishes to do good and falls now and again into evil. Oh! I have hearkened to your white teachers and I know, I know."

"Then by your own standard you are evil, Zikali, since you wished to bring about war, and not in vain."

"Oho! Macumazahn, you think that, do you, who cannot understand that what seems to be evil is often good. I wished to bring about war and brought it about, and maybe what bred the wish was all that I have suffered in the past. But say you, who have seen what the Zulu Power means, who have seen men, women and children killed by the thousand to feed that Power, and who have seen, too, what the English Power means, is it evil that I should wish to destroy the House of the Zulu kings that the English House may take its place and that in a time to come the Black people may be free?"

"You are clever, Zikali, but it is of your own wrongs that you think. How about that skull which you kissed in the Vale of Bones?"

"Mayhap, Macumazahn, but my wrongs are the wrongs of a nation, therefore I think of the nation, and at least I do not fear death like you white men. Now hearken. Presently your friends will tell you a story. The lady Heddana will tell you how I made use of her for a certain purpose, for which purpose indeed I drew the three of you into Zululand, because without her I could not have brought about this war into which Cetewayo did not wish to enter. When you have heard that story, do not judge me too hardly, Macumazahn, who had a great end to gain."

"Yet whatever the story may be, I do judge you hardly, Zikali, who tormented me with a false tale, causing the woman Kaatje to lie to me and swear that she saw these two dead before her—how I know not."

"She did not lie to you, Macumazahn. Has not such a one as I the power to make a fat fool think that she saw what she did not see? As to how! How did I make you think in yonder hut of mine that you saw what you did not see—perhaps."

"But why did you mock me in this fashion, Zikali?"

"Truly, Macumazahn, you are blind as a bat in sunlight. When your friends have told you the story, you will understand why. Yet I admit to you that things went wrong. You should have heard that tale *before* Cetewayo brought you to the Vale of Bones. But the fool-woman delayed and blundered, and when she reached Ulundi the gates were shut against her as a spy, and not opened till too late, so that you only found her when you returned from the Council. I knew this, and that was why I dared to bid you fire at that which stood upon the rock. Had you heard Kaatje's tale you might have aimed straight, as also you would have certainly shot straight at me, out of revenge for the deaths of those you loved, Macumazahn, though whether you could have killed me before all the game is played is another matter. As it was, I was sure that you would not pierce the heart of one who *might* be a certain white woman, sure also that you would not pierce my heart whose death *might* bring about her death and that of another."

"You are very subtle, Zikali," I said in astonishment.

"So you hold because I am very simple, who understand the spirit of man—and some other things. For the rest, had you not believed that these two were dead, you would never have left Zululand. You would have tried to escape to get to them and have been killed. Is it not so?"

"Yes, I think I should have tried, Zikali. But why did you keep them prisoner?"

"For the same reason that I still keep them—and you—to hold them back a while from the world of ghosts. Had I sent them away after that night of the declaration of war, they would have been killed before they had gone an hour's journey. Oh! I am not so bad as you think, Macumazahn, and I never break my word. Now I have done."

"How goes the war?" I asked as he shuffled to his feet.

"As it must go, very ill for the Zulus. They have driven back the white men who gather strength from over the Black Water and will come on presently and wipe them out. Umnyamana would have had Cetewayo invade Natal and sweep it clean, as of course he should have done. But I sent him word that if he did so Nomkubulwana, yes, she and no other, had told me that all the spirits would be against him, and he hearkened. When next you think me wicked, remember that, Macumazahn. Now it is but a matter of time, and here you must bide till all is finished. That will be good for you who need rest, though the other two find it wearisome. Still for them it is good also to watch the fruit ripen on their tree of love. It will be the sweeter when they eat it, Macumazahn, and teach them how to live together. Oho! Oho-ho!" and he shambled off.

Heda's Tale

That evening when I was lying on my bed outside the cave, I heard the tale of Anscombe and Heda. Up to a certain point he told it, then she went on with the story.

"On the morning after our arrival at this place, Allan," said Anscombe, "I woke up to find you gone from the hut. As you did not come back I concluded that you were with Zikali, and walked about looking for you. Then food was brought to us and Heda and I breakfasted together, after which we went to where we heard the horses neighing and found that yours was gone. Returning, much frightened, we met Nombe, who gave me your note which explained everything, and we inquired of her why this had been done and what was to become of us. She smiled and answered that we had better ask the first question of the king and the second of her master Zikali, and in the meanwhile be at peace since we were quite safe.

"I tried to see Zikali but could not. Then I went to inspan the horses with the idea of following you, only to find that they were gone. Indeed I have not seen them from that day to this. Next we thought of starting on foot, for we were quite desperate. But Nombe intervened and told us that if we ventured out of the Black Kloof we should be killed. In short we were prisoners.

"This went on for some days, during which we were well treated but could not succeed in seeing Zikali. At length one morning he sent for us and we were taken to the enclosure in front of his hut, Kaatje coming with us as interpreter. For a while he sat still, looking very grim and terrible. Then he said—

"'White Chief and Lady, you think ill of me because Macumazahn has gone and you are kept prisoners here, and before all is done you will think worse. Yet I counsel you to trust me since everything that happens is for your good.'

"At this point Heda, who, as you know, talked Zulu fairly well, though not so well as she does now, broke in, and said some very angry things to him."

"Yes," interrupted Heda. "I told him that he was a liar and I believed that he had murdered you and meant to murder us."

"He listened stonily," continued Anscombe, "and answered, 'I perceive, Lady Heddana, that you understand enough of our tongue to enable me to talk to you; therefore I will send away this half-breed woman, since what I have to say is secret.'

"Then he called servants by clapping his hands and ordered them to remove Kaatje, which was done.

"'Now, Lady Heddana,' he said, speaking very slowly so that Heda might interpret to me and repeating his words whenever she did not understand, 'I have a proposal to make to you. For my own ends it is necessary that you should play a part and appear before the king and the Council as the goddess of this land who is called the Chieftainess of Heaven, which goddess is always seen as a white woman. Therefore you must travel with me to Ulundi and there do those things which I shall tell you.'

"'And if I refuse to play this trick,' said Heda, 'what then?'

"'Then, Lady Heddana, this white lord whom you love and who is to be your husband will—die—and after he is dead you must still do what I desire of you, or—die also.'

"'Would he come with me to Ulundi?' asked Heda.

"'Not so, Lady. He would stay here under guard, but quite safe, and you will be brought back to him, safe. Choose now, with death on the one hand and safety on the other. I would sleep a little. Talk the matter over in your own tongue and when it is settled awaken me again,' and he shut his eyes and appeared to go to sleep.

"So we discussed the situation, if you can call it discussion when we were both nearly mad. Heda wished to go. I begged her to let me be killed rather than trust herself into the hands of this old villain. She pointed out that even if I were killed, which she admitted might not happen, she would still be in his hands whence she could only escape by her own death, whereas if she went there was a chance that we might both continue to live, and that after all death was easy to find. So in the end I gave way and we woke up Zikali and told him so.

"He seemed pleased and spoke to us gently, saying, 'I was sure that wisdom dwelt behind those bright eyes of yours, Lady, and again I promise you that neither you nor the lord your lover shall come to any harm. Also that in payment I and my child, Nombe, will protect you even with our lives, and further, that I will bring back your friend, Macumazahn, to you, though not yet. Now go and be happy together. Nombe will tell the lady Heddana when she is to start. Of all this say nothing on your peril to the woman Kaatje, since if you do, it will be necessary that she should be made silent. Indeed, lest she should learn something, to-morrow I shall send her on to await you at Ulundi, therefore be not surprised if you see her go, and take no heed of aught she may say in going. Nombe, my child, will fill her place as servant to the lady Heddana and sleep with her at night that she may not be lonely or afraid.'

"Then he clapped his hands again and servants came and conducted us back to the huts. And now, Allan, Heda will go on with the story."

"Well, Mr. Quatermain," she said, "nothing more happened that day which we spent with bursting hearts. Kaatje did not question us as to what the witch-doctor had said after she was sent away. Indeed I noticed that she was growing very stupid and drowsy, like a person who has been drugged, as I daresay she was, and would insist upon beginning to pack up the things in a foolish kind of way, muttering something about our trekking on the following day. The night passed as usual, Kaatje sleeping very heavily by my side and snoring so much" (here I groaned sympathetically) "that I could get little rest. On the next morning after breakfast as the huts were very hot, Nombe suggested that we should sit under the shadow of the overhanging rock, just where we are now. Accordingly we went, and being tired out with all our troubles and bad nights, I fell into a doze, and so, I think, did Maurice, Nombe sitting near to us and singing all the while, a very queer kind of song.

"Presently, through my doze as it were, I saw Kaatje approaching. Nombe went to meet her, still singing, and taking her hand, led her to the cart, where they seemed to talk to the horses, which surprised me as there were no horses. Then she brought her round the cart and pointed to us, still singing. Now Kaatje began to weep and throw her hands about, while Nombe patted her on the shoulder. I tried to speak to her but could not. My tongue was tied, why I don't know, but I suppose because I was really asleep, and Maurice also was asleep and did not wake at all."

"Yes," said Anscombe, "I remember nothing of all this business."

"After a while Kaatje went away, still weeping, and then I fell asleep in earnest and did not wake until the sun was going down, when I roused Maurice and we both went back to the hut, where I found that Nombe had cooked our evening meal. I looked for Kaatje, but could not find her. Also in searching through my things I missed the bag of jewels. I called to Nombe and asked where Kaatje was, whereon she smiled and said that she had gone away, taking the bag with her. This pained me, for I had always found Kaatje quite honest—"

"Which she is," I remarked, "for those jewels are now in a bank at Maritzburg."

Heda nodded and went on, "I am glad to hear it; indeed, remembering what Zikali had said, I never really suspected her of being a thief, but thought it was all part of some plan. After this things went on as before, except that Nombe took Kaatje's place and was with me day and night. Of Kaatje's disappearance she would say nothing. Zikali we did not see.

"On the third evening after the vanishing of Kaatje, Nombe came and said that I must make ready for a journey, and while she spoke men arrived with a litter that had grass mats hung round it. Nombe brought out my long cape and put it over me, also a kind of veil of white stuff which she threw over my head, so as to hide my face. I think it was made out of one of our travelling mosquito nets. Then she said I must say good-bye to Maurice for a while. There was a scene as you may imagine. He grew angry and said that he would come with me, whereon armed men appeared, six of them, and pushed him away with the handles of their spears. In another minute I was lifted into the litter which Nombe entered with me, and so we were parted, wondering if we should ever see each other more. At the mouth of the kloof I saw another litter surrounded by a number of Zulus, which Nombe said contained Zikali.

"We travelled all that night and two succeeding nights, resting during the day in deserted kraals that appeared to have been made ready for us. It was a strange journey, for although the armed men flitted about us, neither they nor the bearers ever spoke, nor did I see Zikali, or indeed any one else. Only Nombe comforted me from time to time, telling me there was nothing to fear. Towards dawn on the third night we travelled over some hills and I was put into a new hut and told that my journey was done as we had reached a place near Ulundi.

"I slept most of the following day, but after I had eaten towards evening, Zikali crept into the hut, just as a great toad might do, and squatted down in front of me.

"'Lady,' he said, 'listen. To-night, perhaps one hour after sundown, perhaps two, perhaps three, Nombe will lead you, dressed in a certain fashion, from this hut. See now, outside of it there is a tongue of rock up which you may climb unnoted by the little path that runs between those big stones. Look,' and he showed me the place through the door-hole. 'The path ends on a flat boulder at the end of the rock. There you will take your stand, holding in your right hand a little assegai which will be given to you. Nombe will not accompany you to the rock, but she will crouch between the stones at the head of the path and perhaps from time to time whisper to you what to do. Thus when she tells you, you must throw the little spear into the air, so that it falls among a number of men gathered in debate who will be seated about twenty paces from the rock. For the rest you are to stand quite still, saying nothing and showing no alarm whatever you may hear or see. Among the men before you may be your friend, Macumazahn, but you must not appear to recognize him, and if he speaks to you, you must make no answer. Even if he should seem to shoot at you, do not be afraid. Do you understand? If so, repeat what I have told you.' I obeyed him and asked what would happen if I did not do these things, or some of them.

"He answered, 'You will be killed, Nombe will be killed, the lord Mauriti your lover will be killed, and your friend Macumazahn will be killed. Perhaps even I shall be killed and we will talk the matter over in the land of ghosts.'

"On hearing this I said I would do my best to carry out his orders, and after making me repeat them once more, he went away. Later, Nombe dressed me up as you saw me, Mr. Quatermain, put some glittering powder into my hair and touched me beneath the eyes with a dark kind of pigment. Also she gave me the little spear and made me practise standing quite still with it raised in my right hand, telling me that when I heard her say the word 'Throw,' I was to cast it into the air. Then the moon rose and we heard men talking at a distance. At last some one came to the hut and whispered to Nombe, who led me out to the little path between the rocks.

"This must have been nearly two hours after I heard the men begin to talk—"

"Excuse me," I interrupted, "but where was Nombe all those two hours?"

"With me. She never left my side, Mr. Quatermain, and while I was on the rock she was crouched within three paces of me between two big stones at the mouth of the path."

"Indeed," I replied faintly, "this is very interesting. Please continue—but one word, how was Nombe dressed? Did she wear a necklace of blue beads?"

"Just as she always is, or rather less so, for she had nothing on except her moocha, and certainly no blue beads. But why do you ask?"

"From curiosity merely. I mean, I will tell you afterwards, pray go on."

"Well, I stepped forward on to the rock and at first saw nothing, because at that moment the moon was hid by a cloud; indeed Nombe had waited for the cloud to pass over its face, before she thrust me forward. Also some smoke from a fire below was rising straight in front of me. Presently the cloud passed, the smoke thinned, and I saw the circle of those savage men seated beneath, and in their centre a great chief wearing a leopard's skin cloak who I guessed was the king. You I did not see, Mr. Quatermain, because you were behind a tree, yet I felt that you were there, a friend among all those foes. I stood still, as I had been taught to do, and heard the murmur of astonishment and caught the gleam of the moonlight from the white feathers that were sewn upon my robe.

"Then I heard also the voice of Zikali speaking from beneath. He called on you to come out to shoot at me, and the man whom I took to be the king, ordered you to obey. You appeared from behind the tree, and I was certain from the look upon your face that at that distance you did not know who I was in my strange and glittering raiment. You lifted the pistol and I was terribly afraid, for I had seen you shoot with it before on the verandah of the Temple and knew well that you do not miss. Very nearly I screamed out to you, but remembered and was silent, thinking that after all it did not much matter if I died, except for the sake of Maurice here. Also by now I guessed that I was being used to deceive those men before me into some terrible act, and that if I died, at least they would be undeceived.

"I thought that an age passed between the time you pointed the pistol and I saw the flash for which I was waiting."

"You need not have waited, Heda," I interposed, "for if I had really aimed at you you would never have seen that flash, at least so it is said. I too guessed enough to shoot above you, although at the time I did not know that it was you on the rock; indeed I thought it was Nombe painted up."

"Yes, I heard the bullet sing over me. Then I heard the voice of Zikali challenging you to shoot him, and to tell the truth, hoped that you would do so. Just before you fired for the second time, Nombe whispered to me—'Throw' and I threw the little red-handled spear into the air. Then as the pistol went off Nombe whispered—'Come.' I slipped away down the path and back with her into the hut, where she kissed me and said that I had done well indeed, after which she took off my strange robe and helped me to put on my own dress.

"That is all I know, except that some hours later I was awakened from sleep and put into the litter where I went to sleep again, for what I had gone through tired me very much. I need not trouble you with the rest, for we journeyed here in the same way that we had journeyed to Ulundi—by night. I did not see Zikali, but in answer to my questions, Nombe told me that the Zulus had declared war against the English. What part in the business I had played, she would not tell me, and I do not know to this hour, but I am sure that it was a great one.

"So we came back to the Black Kloof, where I found Maurice quite well, and now he had better go on with the tale, for if I begin to tell you of our meeting I shall become foolish."

"There isn't much more to tell," said Anscombe, "except about yourself. While Heda was away I was kept a prisoner and watched day and night by Zikali's people who would not let me stir a yard, but otherwise treated me kindly. Then one day at sunrise, or shortly after it, Heda re-appeared and told me all this story, for the end of which, as you may imagine, I thanked God.

"After that we just lived on here, happily enough since we were together, until one day Nombe told us that there had been a great battle in which the Zulus had wiped out the English, killing hundreds and hundreds of them, although for every soldier that they killed, they had lost two. Of course this made us very sad, especially as we were afraid you might be with our troops. We asked Nombe if you were present at the battle. She answered that she would inquire of her Spirit and went through some very strange performances with ashes and knuckle bones, after which she announced that you had been in the battle but were alive and coming this way with a dog that had silver on it. We laughed at her, saying that she could not possibly know anything of the sort, also that dogs as a rule did not carry silver. Whereon she only smiled and said—'Wait.'

"I think it was three days later that one night towards dawn I was awakened by hearing a dog barking outside my hut, as though it wished to call attention to its presence. It barked so persistently and in a way so unlike a Kaffir dog, that at length about dawn I went out of the hut to see what was the matter. There, standing a few yards away surrounded by some of Zikali's people, I saw Lost and knew at once that it was an English Airedale, for I have had several of the breed. It looked very tired and frightened, and while I was wondering whence on earth it could have come, I noticed that it had a silver-mounted collar and remembered Nombe and her talk about you and a dog that carried silver on it. From that moment, Allan, I was certain that you were somewhere near, especially as the beast ran up to me—it would take no notice of the Kaffirs—and kept looking towards the mouth of the kloof, as though it wished me to follow it. Just then Nombe arrived, and on seeing the dog looked at me oddly.

"'I have a message for you from my master, Mauriti,' she said to me through Heda, who by now had arrived upon the scene, having also been aroused by Lost's barking. 'It is that if you wish to take a walk with a strange dog you can do so, and bring back anything you may find.'"

"The end of it was that after we had fed Lost with milk and meat, I and six of Zikali's men started down the kloof, Lost going ahead of us and now and again running back and whining. At the mouth of the kloof it led us over a hill and down into a bush-veld valley where the thorns grew very thick. When we had gone along the valley for about two miles, one of the Kaffirs saw a Basuto pony still saddled, and caught it. The dog went on past the pony to a tree that had been shattered by lightning, and there within a few yards of the tree we found you lying senseless, Allan, or, as I thought at first, dead, and by your side a Martini rifle of which the stock also seemed to have been broken by lightning.

"Well, we put you on a shield and carried you here, meeting no one, and that is all the story, Allan."

He stopped and we stared at each other. Then I called Lost and patted its head, and the dear beast licked my hand as though it understood that it was being thanked.

"A strange tale," I said, "but God Almighty has put much wisdom into His creatures of which we know nothing. Let us thank Him," and in our hearts we did.

Thus was I rescued from death by the intelligence and fidelity of a four-footed creature. Doubtless in my semi-conscious state that resulted from shock, weariness and sun-stroke, I had all the while headed sub-consciously and without any definite object for the Black Kloof. When I was within a few miles of it I was stunned by the lightning which ran down the rifle to the ground, though not actually struck. Then the dog, which had escaped, played its part, wandering about the country to find help for me, and so I was saved.

Now of the long months that followed I have little to tell. They were not unhappy in their way, for week by week I felt myself growing stronger, though very slowly. There was a path, steep, difficult and secret, which could be gained through one of the caves in the precipice, not that in which I slept. This path ran up a water-cut kloof through a patch of thorns to a flat tableland that was part of the Ceza stronghold. By it, when I had gained sufficient strength, sometimes we used to climb to the plateau, and there take exercise, It was an agreeable change from the stifling atmosphere of the Black Kloof. The days were very dull, for we were as much out of the world as though we had been marooned on a desert island. Still from time to time we heard of the progress of the war through Nombe, for Zikali I saw but seldom.

She told of disasters to the English, of the death of a great young Chief who was deserted by his companions and died fighting bravely—afterwards I discovered that this was the Prince Imperial of France—of the advance of our armies, of defeats inflicted upon Cetewayo's impis, and finally of the destruction of the Zulus on the battlefield of Ulundi, where they hurled themselves by thousands upon the British square, to be swept away by case-shot and the hail of bullets. This battle, by the way, the Zulus call, not Ulundi or Nodwengu, for it was fought in front of Panda's old kraal of that name, but Ocwecweni, which means—"the fight of the sheet-iron fortress." I suppose they give it this name because the hedge of bayonets, flashing in the sunlight, reminded them of sheet-iron. Or it may be because these proved as impenetrable as would have done walls of iron. At any rate they dashed their naked bodies against the storm of lead and fell in heaps, only about a dozen of our men being killed, as the little graveyard in the centre of the square entrenchment, about which still lie the empty cartridge cases, records to-day.

There, then, on that plain perished the Zulu kingdom which was built up by Chaka.

Now it was after this event that I saw Zikali and begged him to let us go. I found him triumphant and yet strangely disturbed and, as I thought, more apprehensive than I had ever seen him.

"So, Zikali," I said, "if what I hear is true, you have had your way and destroyed the Zulu people. Now you should be happy."

"Is man ever happy, Macumazahn, when he has gained that which he sought for years? The two out there sigh and are sad because they cannot be married after their own white fashion, though what there is to keep them apart I do not know. Well, in time they will be married, only to find that they are not so happy as they thought they would be. Oh! a day will come when they will talk to each other and say—'Those moons which we spent waiting together in the Black Kloof were the true moons of sweetness, for then we had something to gain; now we have gained all—and what is it?'

"So it is with me, Macumazahn. Since the Zulus under Chaka killed out my people, the Ndwandwe, year by year I have plotted and waited to see them wedded to the assegai. Now it has come about. You white men have stamped them flat upon the plain of Ulundi; they are no more a nation. And yet I am not happy, for after all it was the House of Senzangacona and not the people of the Zulus, that harmed me and mine, and Cetewayo still lives. While the queen bee remains there may be a hive again. While an ember still glows in the dead ashes, the forest may yet be fired. Perhaps when Cetewayo is dead, then I shall be happy. Only his death and mine are set by Fate as close together as two sister grains of corn upon the cob."

I turned the subject, again asking his leave to depart to Natal or to join the English army.

"You cannot go yet," he answered sternly, "so trouble me no more. The land is full of wandering bands of Zulus who would kill you and your blood would be on my head. Moreover, if they saw a white woman who had sheltered with me, might they not guess something? To dress a doll for the part of the Inkosazana-y-Zulu is the greatest crime in the world, Macumazahn, and what would happen to the Opener of Roads and all his House if it were even breathed that he had dressed that doll and thus brought about the war which ruined them? When Cetewayo is killed and the dead are buried and peace falls upon the land, the peace of death, then you shall go, Macumazahn, and not before."

"At least, Zikali, send a message to the captains of the English army and tell them that we are here."

"Send a message to the hyenas and tell them where the carcase is; send a message to the hunters and tell them where the buck Zikali crouches on its form!

Hearken, Macumazahn, if you do this, or even urge me again to do it, neither you nor your friends shall ever leave the Black Kloof. I have spoken."

Then understanding that the case was hopeless, I left him and he glowered after me, for fear had made him cruel. He had won the long game and success had turned to ashes in his mouth. Or rather, he had not won—yet—since his war was against the House of Senzangacona from which he and his tribe had suffered cruel wrong. To pull it down he must pull down the Zulu nation; it was like burning a city to destroy a compromising letter. He had burnt the city, but the letter still remained intact and might be produced in evidence against him. In other words Cetewayo yet lived. Therefore his vengeance remained quite unslaked and his danger was as great, or perhaps greater than it had ever been before. For was he not the prophet who by producing the Princess of Heaven, the traditional goddess of the Zulus, before the eyes of the king and Council, had caused them to decide for war? And supposing it were so much as breathed that this spirit which they seemed to see, had been but a trick and a fraud, what then? He would be tortured to death if his dupes had time, or torn limb from limb if they had not, that is if he could die like other men—a matter as to which personally I had no doubts.

Shortly after I left Zikali Heda and I ate our evening meal together. Anscombe, as it chanced, had gone by the secret path to the tableland of which I have spoken, where he amused himself, as of course we were not allowed to fire a gun, by catching partridges, with the help of an ingenious system of grass nets which he had invented. There were springs on this tableland that formed little pools of water, at which the partridges, also occasionally guineafowl and bush pheasants, came to drink at sunrise and sunset. Here it was that he set his nets and retired to work them at those hours by means of strings that he pulled from hiding-places. So Heda and I were alone.

I told her of my ill success with Zikali, at which she was much disappointed. Then by an afterthought I suggested that perhaps she might try to do something in the way of getting a message through to the English camp at Ulundi, or elsewhere, by help of the witch-doctoress, Nombe, adding that I would speak to her myself had I not observe that I seemed to be out of favour with her of late. Heda shook her head and answered that she thought it would be useless to try, also too dangerous. Remembering Zikali's threat, on reflection I agreed with her.

"Tell me, Mr. Quatermain," she added, "is it possible for one woman to be in love with another?"

I stared at her and replied that I did not understand what she meant, since women, so far as I had observed them, were generally in love either with a man or with themselves, perhaps more often with the latter than the former. Rather a cheap joke I admit, with just enough truth in it to make it acceptable—in the Black Kloof.

"So I thought," she answered, "but really Nombe behaves in a most peculiar way. As you know she took a fancy to me from the beginning, perhaps because she had never had any other woman with whom to associate, having, so far as I can make out, been brought up here among men from a child. Indeed, her story is that she was one of twins and therefore as the younger, was exposed to die according to the Zulu superstition. Zikali, however, or a servant of his who knew what was happening, rescued and reared her, so practically I am the only female with whom she has ever been intimate. At any rate her affection for me has grown and grown until, although it seems ungrateful to say so, it has become something of a nuisance. She has told me again and again that she would die to protect me, and that if by chance anything happened to me, she would kill herself and follow me into another world. She is continually making divinations about my future, and as these, in which she entirely believes, always show me as living without her, she is much distressed and at times bursts into tears."

"Hysteria! It is very common among the Zulu women, and especially those of them who practise magic arts," I answered.

"Perhaps, but as it results in the most intense jealousy, Nombe's hysteria is awkward. For instance, she is horribly jealous of Maurice."

"The instincts of a chaperone developed early," I suggested again.

"That won't quite do, Mr. Quatermain," answered Heda with a laugh, "since she is even more jealous of you. With reference to Maurice, she explains frankly that if we marry she might, as she puts it, 'continue to sit outside the hut,' but that in your case you live 'in my head,' where she cannot come between you and me."

"Mad," I remarked, "quite mad. Still madness has to be dealt with in this world like other things, and Nombe, being an abnormal person, may suffer from abnormal ideas. It just amounts to this; she has conceived a passionate devotion to you, at which I am sure neither Maurice nor I can wonder."

"Are those the kind of compliments you used to pay in your youth, Mr. Quatermain? I expect so, and now that you are old you cannot stop them. Well, I thank you all the same, because perhaps you mean what you say. But what is to be done about Nombe? Hush! here she comes. I will leave you to reason with her, if you get the chance," and she departed in a hurry.

Nombe arrived, and something in her aspect told me that I was going to get the chance. Her eternal smile was almost gone and her dark, beautiful eyes flashed ominously. Still she began by asking in a mild voice whether the lady Heddana had eaten her supper with appetite. It will be observed that she was not interested in my appetite or whether enough was left for Anscombe when he returned. I replied that so far as I noted she had consumed about half a partridge, with other things.

"I am glad," said Nombe, "since I was not here to attend upon her, having been summoned to speak with the Master."

Then she sat down and looked at me like a thunder storm.

"I nursed you when you, were so ill, Macumazahn," she began, "but now I learn that for the milk with which I fed you, you would force me to drink bitter water that will poison me."

I replied I was well aware that without her nursing I should long ago have been dead, which was what caused me to love her like my own daughter. But would she kindly explain? This she did at once.

"You have been plotting to take away from me the lady Heddana who to me is as mother and sister and child. It is useless to lie to me, for the Master has told me all; moreover, I knew it for myself, both through my Spirit and because I had watched you."

"I have no intention of lying to you, Nombe, about this or any other matter, though I think that sometimes in the past you have lied to me. Tell me, do you expect the Inkosi Mauriti, the lady Heddana and myself to pass the rest of our lives in the Black Kloof, when they wish to get married and go across the Black Water to where their home will be, and I wish to attend to my affairs?"

"I do not know what I expect, Macumazahn, but I do know that never while I live will I be parted from the lady Heddana. At last I have found some one to love, and you and the other would steal her away from me."

I studied her for a while, then asked—

"Why do you not marry, Nombe, and have a husband, and children to love?"

"Marry?" she replied. "I am married to my Spirit which does not dwell beneath the sun, and my children are not of earth; moreover, all men are hateful to me," and her eyes added, "especially you."

"That is a calf with a dog's head," I replied in the words of the native proverb, meaning that she said what was not natural. "Well, Nombe, if you are so fond of the lady Heddana, you had better arrange with her and the Inkosi Mauriti to go away with them."

"You know well I cannot, Macumazahn. I am tied to my Master by ropes that are stronger than iron, and if I attempted to break them my Spirit would wither and I should wither with it."

"Dear me! what a dreadful business. That is what comes of taking to magic. Well, Nombe, I am afraid I have nothing to suggest, nor, to tell you the truth, can I see what I have to do with the matter."

Then she sprang up in a rage, saying—

"I understand that not only will you give me no help, but that you also mock at me, Macumazahn. Moreover, as it is with you, so it is with Mauriti, who pretends to love my lady so much, though I love her more with my little finger than he does with all his body and what he calls his soul. Yes, he too mocks at me. Now if you were both dead," she added with sudden venom, "my lady would not wish to go away. Be careful lest a spell should fall upon you, Macumazahn," and without more words she turned and went.

At first I was inclined to laugh; the whole thing seemed so absurd. On reflection, however, I perceived that in reality it was very serious to people situated as we were. This woman was a savage; more, a mystic savage of considerable powers of mind—a formidable combination. Also there were no restraints upon her, since public opinion had as little authority in the Black Kloof as the Queen's Writ. Lastly, it was not unknown for women to conceive these violent affections which, if thwarted, filled them with something like madness. Thus I remembered a very terrible occurrence of my youth which resulted in the death of one who was most dear to me. I will not dwell on it, but this, too, was the work of a passionate creature, woman I can scarcely call her, who thought she was being robbed of one whom she adored.

The end of it was that I did not enjoy my pipe that night, though luckily Anscombe returned after a successful evening's netting, about which he was so full of talk that there was no need for me to say much. So I put off any discussion of the problem until the morrow.

The King Visits Zikali

Next morning, as a result of my cogitations, I went to see Zikali. I was admitted after a good deal of trouble and delay, for although his retinue was limited and, with the exception of Nombe, entirely male, this old prophet kept a kind of semi-state and was about as difficult to approach as a European monarch. I found him crouching over a fire in his hut, since at this season of the year even in that hot place the air was chilly until midday.

"What is it, Macumazahn?" he asked. "As to your going away, have patience. I learn that he who was King of the Zulus is in full flight, with the white men tracking him like a wounded buck. When the buck is caught and killed, then you can go."

"It is about Nombe," I answered, and told him all the story, which did not seem to surprise him at all.

"Now see, Macumazahn," he said, taking some snuff, "how hard it is to dam up the stream of nature. This child, Nombe, is of my blood, one whom I saved from death in a strange way, not because she was of my blood but that I might make an experiment with her. Women, as you who are wise and have seen much will know, are in truth superior to men, though, because they are weaker in body, men have the upper hand of them and think themselves their masters, a state they are forced to accept because they must live and cannot defend themselves. Yet their brains are keener, as an assegai is keener than a hoe; they are more in touch with the hidden things that shape out fate for people and for nations; they are more faithful and more patient, and by instinct if not by reason, more far-seeing, or at least the best of them are so, and by their best, like men, they should be judged. Yet this is the hole in their shield. When they love they become the slaves of love, and for love's sake all else is brought to naught, and for this reason they cannot be trusted. With men, as you know, this is otherwise. They, too, love, by Nature's law, but always behind there is something greater than love, although often they do not understand what that may be. To be powerful, therefore, a woman must be one who does not love too much. If she cannot love at all, then she is hated and has no power, but she must not love too much.

Once I thought that I had found such a woman; she was named Mameena, whom all men worshipped and who played with all men, as I played with her. But what was the end of it? Just as things were going very well she learned to love too much some man of strange notions, who would have thwarted me and brought everything to nothing, and therefore I had to kill her, for which I was sorry."

Here he paused to take some more snuff, watching me over the spoon as he drew it up his great nostrils, but as I said nothing, went on—

"Now after Mameena was dead I bethought me that I would rear up a woman who could still love but should never love a man and therefore never become mad or foolish, because I believed that it was only man who in taking her heart from woman, would take her wits also. This child, Nombe, came to my hand, and as I thought, so I did. Never mind how I did it, by medicine perhaps, by magic perhaps, by watering her pride and making it grow tall perhaps, or by all three. At least it was done, and this I know of Nombe, she will never care for any man except as a woman may care for a brother.

"But now see what happens. She, the wise, the instructed, the man-despiser, meets a woman of another race who is sweet and good, and learns to love her, not as maids and mothers love, but as one loves the Spirit that she worships. Yes, yes, to her she is a goddess to be worshipped, one whom she desires to serve with all her heart and strength, to bow down before, making offerings, and at the end to follow into death. So it comes about that this Nombe, whose mind I thought to make as the wings of a bird floating on the air while it searches for its prey, has become even madder than other women. It is a disappointment to me, Macumazahn."

"It may be a disappointment to you, Zikali, and all that you say is very interesting. But to us it is a danger. Tell me, will you command Nombe to cease from her folly?"

"Will I forbid the mist to rise, or the wind to blow, or the lightning to strike? As she is, she is. Her heart is filled with black jealousy of Mauriti and of you, as a butcher's gourd is filled with blood, for she is not one who desires that her goddess should have other worshippers; she would keep her for herself alone."

"Then in this way or in that the gourd must be emptied, Zikali, lest we should be forced to drink from it and that black blood should poison us."

"How, unless it be broken, Macumazahn? If Heddana departs and leaves her, she will go mad, and accompany her she cannot, for her Spirit dwells here," and he tapped his own breast. "It would pull her back again and she would become a great trouble to me, for then that Spirit of hers would not suffer me to sleep, with its continual startings in search of what it had lost, and its returnings empty-handed. Well, have no fear, for at the worst the bowl can be broken and the blood poured upon the earth, as I have broken finer bowls than this before; had I all the bits of them they would make a heap so high, Macumazahn!" and he held out his hand on a level with his head, a gesture that made my back creep. "I will tell her this and it may keep her quiet for a while. Of poison you need not be afraid, since unlike mine, her Spirit hates it. Poison is not one of its weapons as it is with mine. But of spells, beware, for her Spirit has some which are very powerful."

Now I jumped up, filled with indignation, saying—

"I do not believe in Nombe's spells, and in any case how am I to guard against them?"

"If you do not believe there is no need to guard, and if you do believe, then it is for you to find out how to guard, Macumazahn. Oh! I could tell you the story of a white teacher who did not believe and would not guard—but never mind, never mind. Good-bye, Macumazahn, I will speak with Nombe. Ask her for a lock of her hair to wear upon your heart after she has enchanted it. The charm is good against spells. O-ho—Oho-o! What fools we are, white and black together! That is what Cetewayo is thinking to-day."

After this Nombe became much more agreeable. That is to say she was very polite, her smile was more fixed and her eyes more unfathomable than ever. Evidently Zikali had spoken to her and she had listened. Yet to tell the truth my distrust of this handsome young woman grew deeper day by day. I recognized that there was a great gulf between her and the normal, that she was a creature fashioned by Zikali who had trained her as a gardener trains a tree, nay, who had done more, who had grafted some foreign growth of exotic and unnatural spiritualism on to her primitive nature. The nature remained the same, but the graft or grafts bore strange flowers and fruit, unholy flowers and poisonous fruit. Therefore she was not to blame—sometimes I wonder whether in this curious world, could one see their past and their future, anybody is to blame for anything—but this did not make her the less dangerous.

Some talks I had with her only increased my apprehensions, for I found that in a way she had no conscience. Life, she told me, was but a dream, and all its laws as evolved by man were but illusions. The real life was elsewhere. There was the distant lake on which the flower of our true existence floated. Without this unseen lake of supernatural water the flower could not float; indeed there would be no flower. Moreover, the flower did not matter; sometimes it would have this shape and colour, sometimes that. It was but a thing destined to grow and bloom and rot, and during its day to be ugly or to be beautiful, to smell sweet or ill, as it might chance, and ultimately to be absorbed back into the general water of Life.

I pointed out to her that all flowers had roots which grew in soil. Looking at an orchid-like plant that crept along the bough of a tree, she answered that this was not true as some grew upon air. But however this might be, the soil, or the moisture in the air, was distilled from thousands of other flower lives that had flourished in their day and been forgotten. It did not matter when they died or how many other flowers they choked that they might live. Yet each flower had its own spirit which always had been and always would be.

I asked her of the end and the object of that spirit. She answered darkly that she did not know and if she did, would not say, but that these were very dreadful.

Such were some of her vague and figurative assertions which I only record to indicate their uncomfortable and indeed but half human nature. I forgot to add that she declared that every flower or life had a twin flower or life, which in each successive growth it was bound to find and bloom beside, or wither to the root and spring again and that ultimately these two would become one, and as one flourish eternally. Of all of which I understood and understand little, except that she had grasped the elements of some truth which she could not express in clear and definite language.

One day I was seated in Zikali's hut whither by permission I had come to ask the latest news, when suddenly Nombe appeared and crouched down before him.

"Who gave you leave to enter here, and what is your business?" he asked angrily.

"Home of Spirits," she replied in a humble voice, "be not angry with your servant. Necessity gave me leave, and my business is to tell you that strangers approach."

"Who are they that dare to enter the Black Kloof unannounced?"

"Cetewayo the King is one of them, the others I do not know, but they are many, armed all of them. They approach your gate; before a man can count two hundred they will be here."

"Where are the white chief and the lady Heddana?" asked Zikali.

"By good fortune they have gone by the secret path to the tableland and will not be back till sunset. They wished to be alone, so I did not accompany them, and Macumazahn here said that he was too weary to do so." (This was true. Also like Nombe I thought that they wished to be alone.)

"Good. Go, tell the king that I knew of his coming and am awaiting him. Bid my servants kill the ox which is in the kraal, the fat ox that they thought is sick and therefore fit food for a sick king," he added bitterly.

She glided away like a startled snake. Then Zikali turned to me and said swiftly—

"Macumazahn, you are in great danger. If you are found here you will be killed, and so will the others whom I will send to warn not to return till this king has gone away. Go at once to join them. No, it is too late, I hear the Zulus come. Take that kaross, cover yourself with it and lie among the baskets and beerpots here near the entrance of the hut in the deepest of the shadows, so that if any enter, perchance you will not be found. I too am in danger who shall be held to account for all that has happened. Perhaps they will kill me, if I can be killed. If so, get away with the others as best you can. Nombe will tell you where your horses are hidden. In that case let Heddana take Nombe with her, for when I am dead she will go, and shake her off in Natal if she troubles her. Whatever chances, remember, Macumazahn, that I have done my best to keep my word to you and to protect you and your friends. Now I go to look on this pricked bladder who was once a king."

He scrambled from the hut with slow, toad-like motions, while I with motions that were anything but slow, grabbed the grey catskin kaross and ensconced myself among the beerpots and mats in such a position that my head, over which I set a three-legged carved stool of Zikali's own cutting, was but a few inches to the left of the door-hole and therefore in the deepest of the shadows. Thence by stretching out my neck a little, I could see through the hole, also hear all that passed outside. Unless a deliberate search of the hut should be made I was fairly safe from observation, even if it were entered by strangers. One fear I had, however, it was lest the dog Lost should get into the place and smell me out. I had left him tied to the centre pole in my own hut, because he hated Zikali and always growled at him. But suppose he gnawed through the cord, or any one let him loose!

Scarcely had Zikali seated himself in his accustomed place before the hut, than the gate of the outer fence opened and approaching through it I saw forty or fifty fierce and way-worn men. In front of them, riding on a tired horse that was led by a servant, was Cetewayo himself. He was assisted to dismount, or rather threw his great bulk into the arms that were waiting to receive him.

Then after some words with his following and with one of Zikali's people, followed by three or four indunas and leaning on the arm of Umnyamana, the Prime Minister, he entered the enclosure, the rest remaining without. Zikali, who sat as though asleep, suddenly appeared to wake up and perceive him. Struggling to his feet he lifted his right arm and gave the royal salute of Bayete, and with it titles of praise, such as "Black One!" "Elephant!" "Earth-Shaker!" "Conqueror!" "Eater-up of the White men!" "Child of the Wild Beast (Chaka) whose teeth are sharper than the Wild Beast's ever were!" and so on, until Cetewayo, growing impatient, cried out—

"Be silent, Wizard. Is this a time for fine words? Do you not know my case that you offend my ears with them? Give us food to eat if you have it, after which I would speak with you alone. Be swift also; here I may not stay for long, since the white dogs are at my heels."

"I knew that you were coming, O King, to honour my poor house with a visit," said Zikali slowly, "and therefore the ox is already killed and the meat will soon be on the fire. Meanwhile drink a sup of beer, and rest."

He clapped his hands, whereon Nombe and some servants appeared with pots of beer, of which, after Zikali had tasted it to show that it was not poisoned, the king and his people drank thirstily. Then it was taken to those outside.

"What is this that my ears hear?" asked Zikali when Nombe and the others had gone, "that the White Dogs are on the spoor of the Black Bull?"

Cetewayo nodded heavily, and answered—

"My impis were broken to pieces on the plain of Ulundi; the cowards ran from the bullets as children run from bees. My kraals are burnt and I, the King, with but a faithful remnant fly for my life. The prophecy of the Black One has come true. The people of the Zulus are stamped flat beneath the feet of the great White People."

"I remember that prophecy, O King. Mopo told it to me within an hour of the death of the Black One when he gave me the little red-handled assegai that he snatched from the Black One's hand to do the deed. It makes me almost young again to think of it, although even then I was old," replied Zikali in a dreamy voice like one who speaks to himself.

Hearing him from under my kaross I bethought me that he had really grown old at last, who for the moment evidently forgot the part which this very assegai had played a few months before in the Vale of Bones. Well, even the greatest masters make such slips at times when their minds are full of other things. But if Zikali forgot, Cetewayo and his councillors remembered, as I could see by the look of quick intelligence that flashed from face to face.

"So! Mopo the murderer, he who vanished from the land after the death of my uncle Dingaan, gave you the little red assegai, did he, Opener of Roads! And but a few months ago that assegai, which old Sigananda knew again, thrown by the hand of the Inkosazana-y-Zulu, drew blood from my body after the white man, Macumazahn, had severed its shaft with his bullet. Now tell me, Opener of Roads, how did it pass from your keeping into that of the spirit Nomkubulwana?"

At this question I distinctly saw a shiver shake the frame of Zikali who realized too late the terrible mistake he had made. Yet as only the great can do, he retrieved and even triumphed over his error.

"Oho-ho!" he laughed, "who am I that I can tell how such things happen? Do you not know, O King, that the Spirits leave what they will and take what they will, whether it be but a blade of grass, or the life of a man"—here he looked at Cetewayo—"or even of a people? Sometimes they take the shadow and sometimes the substance, since spirit or matter, all is theirs. As for the little assegai, I lost it years ago. I remember that the last time I saw it was in the hands of a woman named Mameena to whom I showed it as a strange and bloody thing. After her death I found that it was gone, so doubtless she took it with her to the Under-world and there gave it to the Queen Nomkubulwana, with whom you may remember this Mameena returned from that Under-world yonder in the Bones."

"It may be so," said Cetewayo sullenly, "yet it was no spirit iron that cut my thigh, but what do I know of the ways of Spirits? Wizard, I would speak with you in your hut alone where no ear can hear us."

"My hut is the King's," answered Zikali, "yet let the King remember that those Spirits of which he does not know the ways, can always hear, yes, even the thoughts of men, and on them do judgment."

"Fear not," said Cetewayo, "amongst many other things I remember this also."

Then Zikali turned and crept into the hut, whispering as he passed me—

"Lie silent for your life." And Cetewayo having bidden his retinue to depart outside the fence and await him there, followed after him.

They sat them down on either side of the smouldering fire and stared at each other through the thin smoke there in the gloom of the hut. By turning my head that the foot of the king had brushed as he passed, I could watch them both. Cetewayo spoke the first in a hoarse, slow voice, saying—

"Wizard, I am in danger of my life and I have come to you who know all the secrets of this land, that you may tell me in what place I may hide where the white men cannot find me. It must be told into my ear alone, since I dare not trust the matter to any other, at any rate until I must. They are traitors every man of them, yes, even those who seem to be most faithful. The fallen man has no friends, least of all if he chances to be a king. Only the dead will keep his counsel. Tell me of the place I need."

"Dingaan, who was before you, once asked this same thing of me, O King, when he was flying from Panda your father, and the Boers. I gave him advice that he did not take, but sought a refuge of his own upon a certain Ghost-mountain. What happened to him there that Mopo, of whom you spoke a while ago, can tell you if he still lives."

"Surely you are an ill-omened night-bird who thus croak to me continually of the death of kings," broke in Cetewayo with suppressed rage. Then calming himself with an effort added, "Tell me now, where shall I hide?"

"Would you know, King? Then hearken. On the south slope of the Ingome Range west of the Ibululwana River, on the outskirts of the great forest, there is a kloof whereof the entrance, which only one man can pass at a time, is covered by a thicket of thorns and marked by a black rock shaped like a great toad with an open mouth, or, as some say, like myself, "The-Thing-that-should-never-have-been-born." Near to this rock dwells an old woman, blind of one eye and lacking a hand, which the Black One cut off shortly before his death, because when he killed her father, she saw the future and prophesied a like death to him, although then she was but a child. This woman is of our company, being a witch-doctoress. I will send a Spirit to her, if you so will it, to warn her to watch for you and your company, O King, and show you the mouth of the kloof, where are some old huts and water. There you will never be found unless you are betrayed."

"Who can betray me when none know whither I am going?" asked Cetewayo. "Send the Spirit, send it at once, that this one-armed witch may make ready."

"What is the hurry, King, seeing that the forest is far away? Yet be it as you will. Keep silence now, lest evil should befall you."

Then of a sudden Zikali seemed to go off into one of his trances. His form grew rigid, his eyes closed, his face became fixed as though in death, and foam appeared upon his lips. He was a dreadful sight to look on, there in the gloomy hut.

Cetewayo watched him and shivered. Then he opened his blanket and I perceived that fastened about him by a loop of hide in such a fashion that it could be drawn out in a moment, was the blade of a broad assegai, the shaft of which was shortened to about six inches. His hand grasped this shaft, and I understood that he was contemplating the murder of Zikali. Then it seemed to me that he changed his mind and that his lips shaped the words—"Not yet," though whether he really spoke them I do not know. At least he withdrew his hand and closed the blanket.

Slowly Zikali opened his eyes, staring at the roof of the hut, whence came a curious sound as of squeaking bats. He looked like a dead man coming to life again. For a few moments he turned up his ear as though he listened to the squealing, then said—

"It is well. The Spirit that I summoned has visited her of our company who is named One-hand and returned with the answer. Did you not hear it speaking in the thatch, O King?"

"I heard something, Wizard," answered Cetewayo in an awed voice. "I thought it was a bat."

"A bat it is, O King, one with wide wings and swift. This bat says that my sister, One-hand, will meet you on the third day from now at this hour on the further side of the ford of the Ibululwana, where three milk-trees grow together on a knoll. She will be sitting under the centre milk-tree and will wait for two hours, no more, to show you the secret entrance to the kloof."

"The road is rough and long, I shall have to hurry when worn out with travelling," said Cetewayo.

"That is so, O King. Therefore my counsel is that you begin the journey as soon as possible, especially as I seem to hear the baying of the white dogs not far away."

"By Chaka's head! I will not," growled Cetewayo, "who thought to sleep here in peace this night."

"As the King wills. All that I have is the King's. Only then One-hand will not be waiting and some other place of hiding must be found, since this is known to me only and to her; also that Spirit which I sent will make no second journey, nor can I travel to show it to the King."

"Yes, Wizard, it is known to you and to myself. Methinks it would be better were it known to me alone. I have a spoonful of snuff to share (i.e. a bone to pick) with you, Wizard. It would seem that you set my feet and those of the Zulu people upon a false road, yonder in the Vale of Bones, causing me to declare war upon the white men and thereby bringing us all to ruin."

"Mayhap my memory grows bad, O King, for I do not remember that I did these things. I remember that the spirit of a certain Mameena whom I called up from the dead, prophesied victory to the King, which victory has been his. Also it prophesied other victories to the King in a far land across the water, which victories doubtless shall be his in due season; for myself I gave no 'counsel to the King or to his indunas and generals.'"

"You lie, Wizard," exclaimed Cetewayo hoarsely. "Did you not summon the shape of the Princess of Heaven to be the sign of war, and did she not hold in her hand that assegai of the Black One which you have told me was in your keeping? How did it pass from your keeping into the hand of a spirit?"

"As to that matter I have spoken, O King. For the rest, is Nomkubulwana my servant to come and go at my bidding?"

"I think so," said Cetewayo coldly. "I think also that you who know the place where I purpose to hide, would do well to forget it. Surely you have lived too long, O Opener of Roads, and done enough evil to the House of Senzangacona, which you ever hated."

So he spoke, and once more I saw his hand steal towards the spearhead which was hidden beneath the blanket that he wore.

Zikali saw it also and laughed. "Oho!" he laughed, "forgetting all my warnings, and that the day of my death will be his own, the King thinks to kill me because I am old and feeble and alone and unarmed. He thinks to kill me as the Black One thought, as Dingaan thought, as even Panda thought, yet I live on to this day. Well, I bear no malice since it is natural that the King should wish to kill one who knows the secret of where he would hide himself for his own life's sake. That spearhead which the King is fingering is sharp, so sharp that my bare breast cannot turn its edge. I must find me a shield! I must find me a shield! Fire, you are not yet dead. Awake, make smoke to be my shield!" and he waved his long, monkey-like arms over the embers, from which instantly there sprang up a reek of thin white smoke that appeared to take a vague and indefinite shape which suggested the shadow of a man; for to me it seemed a nebulous and wavering shadow, no more.

"What are you staring at, O King?" went on Zikali in a fierce and thrilling voice. "Who is it that you see? Who has the fire sent to be my shield? Ghosts are so thick here that I do not know. I cannot tell one of them from the other. Who is it? Who, who of all that you have slain and who therefore are your foes?"

"Umbelazi, my brother," groaned Cetewayo. "My brother Umbelazi stands before me with spear raised; he whom I brought to his death at the battle of the Tugela. His eyes flame upon me, his spear is raised to strike. He speaks words I cannot understand. Protect me, O Wizard! Lord of Spirits, protect me from the spirit of Umbelazi."

Zikali laughed wildly and continued to wave his arms above the fire from which smoke poured ever more densely, till the hut was full of it.

When it cleared away again Cetewayo was gone!

"Saw you ever the like of that?" said Zikali, addressing the kaross under which I was sweltering. "Tell me, Macumazahn."

"Yes," I answered, thrusting out my head as a tortoise does, "when in this very hut you seemed to produce the shape, also out of smoke, I think, of one whom I used to know. Say, how do you do it, Zikali?"

"Do it. Who knows? Perchance I do nothing. Perchance I think and you fools see, no more. Or perchance the spirits of the dead who are so near to us, come at my call and take themselves bodies out of the charmed smoke of my fire. You white men are wise, answer your own question, Macumazahn. At least that smoke or that ghost saved me from a spear thrust in the heart, wherewith Cetewayo was minded to pay me for showing him a hiding-place which he desired should be secret to himself alone. Well, well, I can pay as well as Cetewayo and my count is longer. Now lie you still, Macumazahn, for I go out to watch. He will not bide long in this place which he deems haunted and ill-omened. He will be gone ere sunset, that is within an hour, and sleep elsewhere."

Then he crept from the hut and presently, though I could see nothing, for now the gate of the fence was shut, I heard voices debating and finally that of Cetewayo say angrily—

"Have done! It is my will. You can eat your food outside of this place which is bewitched; the girl will show us where are the huts of which the wizard speaks."

A few minutes later Zikali crept back into the hut, laughing to himself.

"All is safe," he said, "and you can come out of your hole, old jackal. He who calls himself a king is gone, taking with him those whom he thinks faithful, most of whom are but waiting a chance to betray him. What did I say, a king? Nay, in all Africa there is no slave so humble or so wretched as this broken man. Oh! feather by feather

I have plucked my fowl and by and by I shall cut his throat. You will be there, Macumazahn, you will be there."

"I trust not," I answered as I mopped my brow. "We have been near enough to throat-cutting this afternoon to last me a long while. Where has the king gone?"

"Not far, Macumazahn. I have sent Nombe to guide him to the huts in the little dip five spear throws to the right of the mouth of the kloof where live the old herdsman and his people who guard my cattle. He and all the rest are away with the cattle that are hidden in the Ceza Forest out of reach of the white men, so the huts are empty. Oh! now I read what you are thinking. I do not mean that he should be taken there. It is too near my house and the king still has friends."

"Why did you send Nombe?" I asked.

"Because he would have no other guide, who does not trust my men. He means to keep her with him for some days and then let her go, and thus she will be out of mischief. Meanwhile you and your friends can depart untroubled by her fancies, and join the white men who are near. Tomorrow you shall start."

"That is good," I said with a sigh of relief. Then an idea struck me and I added, "I suppose no harm will come to Nombe, who might be thought to know too much?"

"I hope not," he replied indifferently, "but that is a matter for her Spirit to decide. Now go, Macumazahn, for I am weary."

I also was weary after my prolonged seclusion under that very hot skin rug. For be it remembered I was not yet strong again, and although this was not the real reason why I had stopped behind when the others went to the plateau, I still grew easily tired. My real reason was that of Nombe—that I thought they preferred to be alone. I looked about me and saw with relief that Cetewayo and every man of his retinue were really gone. They had not even waited to eat the ox that had been killed for them, but had carried off the meat with other provisions to their sleeping-place outside the kloof. Having made sure of this I went to my hut and loosed Lost that fortunately enough had been unable to gnaw through the thick buffalo-hide rien with which I had fastened him to the pole.

He greeted me with rapture as though we had been parted for years. Had he belonged to Ulysses himself he could not have been more joyful. When one is despondent and lonesome, how grateful is the whole-hearted welcome of a dog which, we are sometimes tempted to think, is the only creature that really cares for us in the world. Every other living thing has side interests of its own, but that of a dog is centred in its master, though it is true that it also dreams affectionately of dinner and rabbits.

Then with Lost at my feet I sat outside the hut smoking and waiting for the return of Anscombe and Heda. Presently I caught sight of them in the gloaming. Their arms were around one another, and in some remarkable way they had managed to dispose their heads, forgetting that the sky was still light behind them, in such fashion that it was difficult to tell one from the other. I reflected that it was a good thing that at last we were escaping from this confounded kloof and country for one where they could marry and make an end, and became afflicted with a sneezing fit.

Heda asked where Nombe was and why supper was not ready, for Nombe played the part of cook and parlourmaid combined. I told her something of what had happened, whereon Heda, who did not appreciate its importance in the least, remarked that she, Nombe, might as well have put on the pot before she went and done sundry other things which I forget. Ultimately we got something to eat and turned in, Heda grumbling a little because she must sleep alone, for she had grown used to the company of the ever-watchful Nombe, who made her bed across the door-hole of the hut.

Anscombe was soon lost in dreams, if he did dream, but I could not sleep well that night. I was fearful of I knew not what, and so, I think, was Lost, for he fidgeted and kept poking me with his nose. At last, I think it must have been about two hours after midnight, he began to growl. I could hear nothing, although my ears are sharp, but as he went on growling I crept to the door-hole and drew aside the board. Lost slipped out and vanished, while I waited, listening. Presently I thought I heard a soft foot-fall and a whisper, also that I saw the shape of a woman which reminded me of Nombe, shown faintly by the starlight. It vanished in a moment and Lost returned wagging his tail, as he might well have done if it were Nombe who was attached to the dog. As nothing further happened I went back to bed, reflecting that I was probably mistaken, since Nombe had been sent away for some days by Zikali and would scarcely dare to return at once, even if she could do so.

Shortly before daylight Lost began to growl again in a subdued and thunderous fashion. This time I got up and dressed myself more or less. Then I went out. The dawn was just breaking and by its light I saw a strange scene. About fifty yards away in the narrow nek that ran over some boulders to the site of our huts, stood what seemed to be the goddess Nomkubulwana as I had seen her on the point of rock in the Vale of Bones. She wore the same radiant dress and in the dim glow had all the appearance of a white woman. I stood amazed, thinking that I dreamt, when from round the bend emerged a number of Zulus, creeping forward stealthily with raised spears.

They caught sight of the supernatural figure which barred their road, halted and whispered to each other. Then they turned to fly, but before they went one of them, as it seemed to me through sheer terror, hurled his assegai at the figure which remained still and unmoved.

In thirty seconds they were gone; in sixty their footsteps had died away. Then the figure wheeled slowly round and by the strengthening light I perceived that a spear transfixed its breast.

As it sank to the ground I ran up to it. It was Nombe with her face and arms whitened and her life-blood running down the glittering feather robe.

The Madness of Nombe

The dog reached Nombe first and began to lick her face, its tongue removing patches of the white which had not had time to dry. She was lying, her back supported by one of the boulders. With her left hand she patted the dog's head feebly and with her right drew out the assegai from her body, letting it fall upon the ground. Recognizing me she smiled in her usual mysterious fashion and said—

"All is well, Macumazahn, all is very well. I have deserved to die and I do not die in vain."

"Don't talk, let me see your wound," I exclaimed.

She opened her robe and pointed; it was quite a small gash beneath the breast from which blood ebbed slowly.

"Let it be, Macumazahn," she said. "I am bleeding inside and it is mortal. But I shall not die yet. Listen to me while I have my mind. Yesterday when Mauriti and Heddana went up to the plain I wished to go with them because I had news that Zulus were wandering everywhere and thought that I might be able to protect my mistress from danger. Mauriti spoke to me roughly, telling me that I was not wanted. Of that I thought little, for to such words I am accustomed from him; moreover, they are to be forgiven to a man in love. But it did not end there, for my lady Heddana also pierced me with her tongue, which hurt more than this spear thrust does, Macumazahn, for I could see that her speech had been prepared and that she took this chance to throw it at me. She said that I did not know where I should sit; that I was a thorn beneath her nail, and that whenever she wished to talk with Mauriti, or with you, Macumazahn, I was ever there with my ear open like the mouth of a gourd. She commanded me in future to come only when I was called; all of which things I am sure Mauriti had taught her, who in herself is too gentle even to think them—unless you taught her, Macumazahn."

I shook my head and she went on—

"No, it was not you who also are too gentle, and having suffered yourself, can feel for those who suffer, which Mauriti who has never suffered cannot do. Still, you too thought me a trouble, one that sticks in the flesh like a hooked thorn, or a tick from the grass, and cannot be unfastened. You spoke to the Master about it and he spoke to me."

This time I nodded in assent.

"I do not blame you, Macumazahn; indeed now I see that you were wise, for what right has a poor black doctoress to seek the love, or even to look upon the face of the great white lady whom for a little while Fate has caused to walk upon the same path with her? But yesterday I forgot that, Macumazahn, for you see we are all of us, not one self, but many selves, and each self has its times of rule. Nombe alive and well was one woman, Nombe dying is another, and doubtless Nombe dead will be a third, unless, as she prays, she should sleep for ever.

"Macumazahn, those words of Heddana's were to me what gall is to sweet milk. My blood clotted and my heart turned sour. It was not against her that I was angry, because that can never happen, but against Mauriti and against you. My Spirit whispered in my ear. It said, 'If Mauriti and Macumazahn were dead the lady Heddana would be left alone in a strange land. Then she would learn to rest upon you as upon a stick, and learn to love the stick on which she rested, though it be so rough and homely.' But how can I kill them, I asked of my Spirit, and myself escape death?

"'Poison is forbidden to you by the pact between us,' answered my Spirit, 'yet I will show you a way, who am bound to serve you in all things good or ill.'

"Then we nodded to each other in my breast, Macumazahn, and I waited for what should happen who knew that my Spirit would not lie. Yes, I waited for a chance to kill you both, forgetting, as the wicked forget in their madness, that even if I were not found out, soon or late Heddana would guess the truth and then, even if she had learned to love me a thousand times more than she ever could, would come to hate me as a mother hates a snake that has slain her child. Or even if she never learned or guessed in life, after death she would learn and hunt me and spit on me from world to world as a traitoress and a murderer, one who has sinned past pardon."

Here she seemed to grow faint and I turned to seek for help. But she caught hold of my coat and said—

"Hear me out, Macumazahn, or I will run after you till I fall and die."

So thinking it best, I stayed and she went on—

"My Spirit, which must be an evil one since Zikali gave it me when I was made a doctoress, dealt truly with me, for presently the king and his people came. Moreover, my Spirit brought it about that the king would have no other guide but me to lead him to the kraal where he slept last night, and I went as though unwillingly. At the kraal the king sent for me and questioned me in a dark hut, pretending to be alone, but I who am a doctoress knew that two other men were in that hut, taking note of all my words. He asked me of the Inkosazana-y-Zulu who appeared in the Vale of Bones and of the little assegai she held in her hand, and of the magic of the Opener of Roads, and many other things. I said that I knew nothing of the Inkosazana, but that without doubt my Master was a great magician. He did not believe me. He threatened that I should be tortured very horribly and was about to call his servants to torment me till I told the truth. Then my Spirit spoke in my heart saying, 'Now the door is open to you, as, I promised. Tell the king of the two white men whom the Master hides, and he will send to kill them, leaving the lady Heddana and you alone together.' So I pretended to be afraid and told him, whereon he laughed and answered—

"'For your sake I am glad, girl, that you have spoken the truth; besides it is useless to torture a witch, since then the spirit in her only vomits lies.'

"Next he called aloud and a man came, who it was I could not see in the dark. The king commanded him to take me to one of the other huts and tie me up there to the roof-pole. The man obeyed, but he did not tie me up; he only blocked the hut with the door-board, and sat with me there in the dark alone.

"Now I grew cunning and began to talk with him, spreading a net of sweet words, as the fowler spreads a net for cranes from which he would tear the crests. Soon by his talk I found out that the king and his people knew more than I guessed. Macumazahn, they had seen the cart which still stands under the overhanging rock by the mouth of the cave. I asked him if that were all, pretending that the cart belonged to my Master, to whom it had been brought from the field of Isandhlwana, that he might be drawn about in it, who was too weak to walk.

"The man said that if I would kiss him he would tell me everything. I bade him tell me first, swearing that then I would kiss him. Yes, Macumazahn, I, whom no man's lips have ever touched, fell as low as this. So he grew foolish and told me. He told me that they had also seen a kappje such as white women wear, hanging on the hut fence, and I remembered that after washing the headdress of my mistress I had set it there to dry in the sun. He told me also that the King suspected that she who wore that kappje was she who had played the part of the Inkosazana in the Vale of Bones. I asked him what the king would do about the matter, at the same time denying that there was any white woman in the Black Kloof. He said that at dawn the king would send and kill these foreign rats, whom the Opener of Roads kept in the thatch of his hut. Now he drew near and asked his pay. I gave it to him—with a knife-point, Macumazahn. Oh! that was a good thrust. He never spoke again. Then I slipped away, for all the others were asleep, and was here a little after midnight."

"I thought I saw you, Nombe," I said, "but was not sure, so I did nothing."

She smiled and answered—

"Ah! I was afraid that the Watcher-by-Night would be watching by night; also the dog ran up to me, but he knew me and I sent him back again. Now while I was coming home, thoughts entered my heart. I saw, as one sees by a lightning flash, all that I had done. The king and his people were not sure that the Master was hiding white folk here and would never have sent back to kill them on the chance. I had made them sure, as indeed, being mad, I meant to do. Moreover, in throwing spears at the kites I had killed my own dove, since it was on the false Inkosazana who had caused them to declare war and brought the land to ruin, that they wished to be avenged, and perchance on him who taught her her part, not on one or two wandering white men. I saw that when Cetewayo's people came, and there were many more of them outside, several hundreds I think, they would shave the whole head and burn the whole tree. Every one in the kloof would be killed.

"How could I undo the knot that I had tied and stamp out the fire that I had lit? That was the question. I bethought me of coming to you, but without arms how could you help? I bethought me of going to the Master, but I was ashamed. Also, what could he do with but a few servants, for the most of his people are away with the cattle? He is too weak to climb the steep path to the plain above, nor was there time to gather folk to carry him. Lastly, even if there were time which there was not, and we went thither they would track us out and kill us. For the rest I did not care, nor for myself, but that the lady Heddana should be butchered who was more to me than a hundred lives, and through my treachery—ah! for that I cared.

"I called on my Spirit to help me, but it would not come. My Spirit was dead in me because now I would do good and not ill. Yet another Spirit came, that of one Mameena whom once you knew. She came angrily, like a storm, and I shrank before her. She said, 'Vile witch, you have plotted to murder Macumazahn, and for that you shall answer to me before another sun has set over this earth of yours. Now you seek a way of escape from your own wickedness. Well, it can be had, but at a price.'

"'What price, O Lady of Death?' I asked.

"'The price of your own life, Witch.'

"I laughed into that ghost face of hers and said—

"'Is this all? Be swift and show me the way, O Lady of Death, and afterwards we will balance our account.'

"Then she whispered into the ear of my heart and was gone. I ran on, for the dawn was near. I whitened myself with lime, I put on the glittering cloak and powdered my hair with the sparkling earth. I took a little stick in my hand since I could find no spear and had no time to search, and just as day began to break, I crept out and stood in the bend of the path. The slayers came, twelve or so of them, but behind were many more. They saw the Inkosazana-y-Zulu barring their way and were much afraid. They fled, but out of his fright one of them threw a spear which went home, as I knew it would. He watched to see if I should fall, but I would not fall. Then he fled faster than the rest, knowing himself accursed who had lifted steel against the Queen of Heaven, and oh! I am glad, I am glad!"

She ceased, exhausted, yet with a great exultation in her beautiful eyes; indeed at that moment she looked a most triumphant creature. I stared at her, thrilled through and through. She had been wicked, no doubt, but how splendid was her end; and, thank Heaven! she was troubled with no thought of what might befall her after that end, although I was sure she believed that she would live again to face Mameena.

I knew not what to do. I did not like to leave her, especially as no earthly power could help her case, since slowly but quite surely she was bleeding to death from an internal wound. By now the sun was up and Zikali's people were about. One of them appeared suddenly and saw, then with a howl of terror turned to fly away.

"Fool! Fool!" I cried, "go summon the lady Heddana and the Inkosi Mauriti. Bid them come swiftly if they would see the doctoress Nombe before she dies."

The man leapt off like a buck, and within a few minutes I saw Heda and Anscombe running towards us, half dressed, and went to meet them.

"What is it?" she gasped.

"I have only time to tell you this," I answered. "Nombe is dying. She gave her life to save you, how I will explain afterwards. The assegai that pierced her was meant for your heart. Go, thank her, and bid her farewell. Anscombe, stop back with me."

We stood still and watched from a little distance. Heda knelt down and put her arms about Nombe. They whispered together into each other's ears. Then they kissed.

It was at this moment that Zikali appeared, leaning on two of his servants. By some occult art or instinct he seemed to know all that had happened, and oh! he looked terrible. He crouched down in front of the dying woman and, toadlike, spat his venom at her.

"You lost your Spirit, did you?" he said. "Well, it came back to me laden with the black honey of your treachery, to me, its home, as a bee comes to its hive. It has told me everything, and well for you, Witch, it is that you are dying. But think not that you shall escape me there in the world below, for thither I will follow you. Curses on you, traitress, who would have betrayed me and brought all my plans to naught. Ow! in a day to come I will pay you back a full harvest for this seed of shame that you have sown."

She opened her eyes and looked at him, then answered quite softly—

"I think your chain is broken, O Zikali, no more, my master. I think that love has cut your chain in two and I fear you never more. Keep the spirit you lent to me; it is yours, but the rest of me is my own, and in the house of my heart another comes to dwell."

Then once more she stretched out her arms towards Heda and murmuring, "Sister, forget me not, Sister, who will await you for a thousand years," she passed away.

It was a good ending to a bad business, and I confess I felt glad when it was finished. Only afterwards I regretted very much that I had not found an opportunity to ask her whether or no she had masqueraded as Mameena in the Valley of Bones. Now it is too late.

We buried poor Nombe decently in her own little hut where she used to practise her incantations. Zikali and his people wished apparently to throw her to the vultures for some secret reason that had to do with their superstitions. But Heda, who, now that Nombe was dead, developed a great affection for her not unmixed with a certain amount of compunction for which really she had no cause, withstood him to his face and insisted upon a decent interment. So she was laid to earth still plastered with the white pigment and wrapped in the bloodstained feather robe. I may add that on the following morning one of Zikali's servants informed me solemnly that because of this she had been seen during the night riding up and down the rocks on a baboon as Zulu umtagati are supposed to do. I have small doubt that as soon as we were gone they dug her up again and threw her to the vultures and the jackals according to their first intention.

On this day we at length escaped from the Black Kloof, and in our own cart, for during the night our horses arrived mysteriously from somewhere, in good condition though rather wild. I went to say good-bye to Zikali, who said little, except that we should meet once more after many moons. Anscombe and Heda he would not see at all, but only sent them a message, to the effect that he hoped they would think kindly of him through the long years to come, since he had kept his promise and preserved them safe through many dangers. I might have answered that he had first of all put them into the dangers, but considered it wise to hold my tongue. I think, however, that he guessed my thought, if one can talk of guessing in connection with Zikali, for he said that they had no reason to thank him, since if he had served their turn they had served his, adding—

"It will be strange in the times to be for the lady Heddana to remember that it was she and no other who crumpled up the Zulus like a frostbitten winter reed, since had she not appeared upon the rock in the Valley of Bones, there would have been no war."

"She did not do this, you did it, Zikali," I said, "making her your tool through love and fear."

"Nay, Macumazahn, I did not do it; it was done by what you call God and I call Fate in whose hand I am the tool. Well, say to the lady Heddana that in payment I will hold back the ghost of Nombe from haunting her, if I can. Say also that if I had not brought her and her lover to Zululand they would have been killed."

So we went from that hateful kloof which I have never seen since and hope I shall never see again, two of Zikali's men escorting us until we got into touch with white people. To these we said as little as possible. I think they believed that we were only premature tourists who had made a dash into Zululand to visit some of the battlefields. Indeed none of us ever reported our strange adventures, and after my experience with Kaatje we were particularly careful to say nothing in the hearing of any gentleman connected with the Press. But as a matter of fact there were so many people moving about and such a continual coming and going of soldiers and their belongings, that after we had managed to buy some decent clothes, which we did at the little town of Newcastle, nobody paid any attention to us.

On our way to Maritzburg one amusing thing did happen. We met Kaatje! It was about sunset that we were driving up a steep hill not far from Howick. At least I was driving, but Anscombe and Heda were walking about a hundred yards ahead of the cart, when suddenly Kaatje appeared over a rise and came face to face with them while taking an evening stroll, or as I concluded afterwards, making some journey. She saw, she stared, she uttered one wild yell, and suddenly bundled over the edge of the road. Never would I have believed that such a fat woman could have run so fast. In a minute she was down the slope and had vanished into a dense kloof where, as night was closing in and we were very tired, it was impossible for us to follow her. Nor did subsequent inquiry in Howick tell us where she was living or whence she came, for some months before she had left the place she had taken there as a cook.

Such was the end of Kaatje so far as we were concerned. Doubtless to her dying day she remained, or will remain, a firm believer in ghosts.

Anscombe and Heda were married at Maritzburg as soon as the necessary formalities had been completed. I could not attend the ceremony, which was a disappointment to me and I hope to them, but unfortunately I had a return of my illness and was laid up for a week. Perhaps this was owing to the hot sun that struck me on the neck one afternoon coming down the Town Hill where I was obliged to hang on to the rear of the cart because the brakes had given out. However I was able to send Heda a wedding gift in the shape of her jewels and money that I recovered from the bank, which she had never expected to see again; also to arrange everything about her property.

They went down to Durban for their honeymoon and, some convenient opportunity arising, sailed thence for England. I received an affectionate letter from them both, which I still treasure, thanking me very much for all I had done for them, that after all was little enough. Also Anscombe enclosed a blank cheque, begging me to fill it in for whatever sum I considered he was indebted to me on the balance of account. I thought this very kind of him and a great mark of confidence, but the cheque remained blank.

I never saw either of them again, and though I believe that they are both living, for the most part abroad—in Hungary I think—I do not suppose that I ever shall. When I came to England some years later after King Solomon's mines had made me rich, I wrote Anscombe a letter. He never answered it, which hurt me at the time. Afterwards I remembered that in their fine position it was very natural that they should not wish to renew acquaintance with an individual who had so intimate a knowledge of certain incidents that they probably regarded as hateful, such as the deaths of Marnham and Dr. Rodd, and all the surrounding circumstances. If so, I daresay that they were wise, but of course it may have been only carelessness. it is so easy for busy and fashionable folk not to answer a rather troublesome letter, or to forget to put that answer in the post. Or, indeed, the letter may never have reached them—such things often go astray, especially when people live abroad. At any rate, perhaps through my own fault, we have drifted apart. I daresay they believe that I am dead, or not to be found somewhere in Africa. However, I always think of them with affection, for Anscombe was one of the best travelling companions I ever had, and his wife a most charming girl, and wonder whether Zikali's prophecy about their children will come true. Good luck go with them!

As it chances, since then I passed the place where the Temple stood, though at a little distance. I had the curiosity, however, at some inconvenience, to ride round and examine the spot. I suppose that Heda had sold the property, for a back-veld Boer, who was absent at the time, had turned what used to be Rodd's hospital into his house. Close by, grim and gaunt, stood the burnt-out marble walls of the Temple. The verandah was still roofed over, and standing on the spot whence I had shot the pistol out of Rodd's hand, I was filled with many memories.

I could trace the whole plan of the building and visited that part of it which had been Marnham's room. The iron safe that stood in the corner had been taken away, but the legs of the bedstead remained. Also not far from it, over grown with running plants, was a little heap which I took to be the ashes of his desk, for bits of burnt wood protruded. I grubbed among them with my foot and riding crop and presently came across the remains of a charred human skull. Then I departed in a hurry.

My way took me through the Yellow-wood grove, past the horns of the blue wildebeeste which still lay there, past that mud-hole also into which Rodd had fallen dead. Here, however, I made no more search, who had seen enough of bones. To this day I do not know whether he still lies beneath the slimy ooze, or was removed and buried.

Also I saw the site of our wagon camp where the Basutos attacked us. But I will have done with these reminiscences which induce melancholy, though really there is no reason why they should.

Tout lasse, tout casse, tout passe—everything wears out, everything crumbles, everything vanishes—in the words of the French proverb that my friend Sir Henry Curtis is so fond of quoting, that at last I wrote it down in my pocket-book, only to remember afterwards that when I was a boy I had heard it from the lips of an old scamp of a Frenchman, of the name of Leblanc, who once gave me and another lessons in the Gallic tongue. But of him I have already written in *Marie* which is the first chapter in the Book of the fall of the Zulus. That headed *Child of Storm* is the second. These pages form the third and last.

Ah! indeed, tout lasse, tout casse, tout passe!

The Kraal Jazi

Now I shall pass over all the Zulu record of the next four years, since after all it has nothing to do with my tale and I do not pretend to be writing a history.

Sir Garnet Wolseley set up his Kilkenny cat Government in Zululand, or the Home Government did it for him, I do not know which. In place of one king, thirteen chiefs were erected who got to work to cut the throats of each other and of the people.

As I expected would be the case, Zikali informed the military authorities of the secret hiding-place in the Ingome Forest where he suggested to Cetewayo that he should refuge. The ex-king was duly captured there and taken first to the Cape and then to England, where, after the disgrace of poor Sir Bartle Frere, an agitation had been set on foot on his behalf. Here he saw the Queen and her ministers, once more conquering, as it had been prophesied that he would by her who wore the shape of Mameena at the memorable scene in the Valley of Bones when I was present. Often I have thought of him dressed in a black coat and seated in that villa in Melbury Road in the suburb of London which I understand is populated by artists. A strange contrast truly to the savage prince receiving the salute of triumph after the Battle of the Tugela in which he won the kingship, or to the royal monarch to whose presence I had been summoned at Ulundi. However, he was brought back to Zululand again by a British man-of-war, re-installed to a limited chieftainship by Sir Theophilus Shepstone, and freed from the strangling embrace of the black coat.

Then of course there was more fighting, as every one knew would happen, except the British Colonial Office; indeed all Zululand ran with blood. For in England Cetewayo and his rights, or wrongs, had, like the Boers and their rights, or wrongs, become a matter of Party politics to which everything else must give way. Often I wonder whether Party politics will not in the end prove the ruin of the British Empire. Well, thank Heaven, I shall not live to learn.

So Cetewayo came back and fought and was defeated by those who once had been his subjects. Now for the last scene, that is all with which I need concern myself.

At the beginning of February, 1884, business took me to Zululand; it had to do with a deal in cattle and blankets. As I was returning towards the Tugela who should I meet but friend Goza, he who had escorted me from the Black Kloof to Ulundi before the outbreak of war, and who afterwards escorted me and that unutterable nuisance, Kaatje, out of the country. At first I thought that we came together by accident, or perhaps that he had journeyed a little way to thank me for the blankets which I had sent to him, remembering my ancient promise, but afterwards I changed my opinion on this point.

Well, we talked over many matters, the war, the disasters that had befallen Zululand, and so forth. Especially did we talk of that night in the Valley of Bones and the things we had seen there side by side. I asked him if the people still believed in the Inkosazana-y-Zulu who then appeared in the moonlight on the rock. He answered that some did and some did not. For his part, he added, looking at me fixedly, he did not, since it was rumoured that Zikali had dressed up a white woman to play the part of the Spirit. Yet he could not be sure of the matter, since it was also said that when some of Cetewayo's people went to kill this white woman in the Black Kloof, Nomkubulwana, the Princess of Heaven herself, rose before them and frightened them away.

I remarked that this was very strange, and then quite casually asked him whom Zikali had dressed up to play the part of the dead Mameena upon that same occasion, since this was a point upon which I always thirsted for definite intelligence. He stared at me and replied that I ought to be able to answer my own question, since I had been much nearer to her who looked like Mameena than any one else, so near indeed that all present distinctly saw her kiss me, as it was well known she had liked to do while still alive. I replied indignantly that they saw wrong and repeated my question. Then he answered straight out—

"O Macumazahn, we Zulus believe that what we saw on that night was not Nombe or another dressed up, but the spirit of the witch Mameena itself. We believe it because we could see the light of Zikali's fire through her, not always, but sometimes; also because all that she said has come true, though everything is not yet finished."

I could get no more out of him about the matter, for when I tried to speak of it again, he turned the subject, telling me of his wonderful escapes during the war. Presently he rose to go and said casually—

"Surely I grow old in these times of trouble, Macumazahn, for thoughts slip through my head like water through the fingers. Almost I had forgotten what I wished to say to you. The other day I met Zikali, the Opener of Roads. He told me that you were in Zululand and that I should meet you—he did not say where, only that when I did meet you, I was to give you a message. This was the message—that when on your way to Natal you came to the kraal Jazi, you would find him there; also another whom you used to know, and must be sure not to go away without seeing him, since that was about to happen in which you must take your part."

"Zikali!" I exclaimed. "I have heard nothing of him since the war. I thought that by now he was certainly dead."

"Oh! no, Macumazahn, he is certainly not dead, but just the same as ever. Indeed it is believed that he and no other has kept all this broth of trouble on the boil, some say for Cetewayo's sake, and some say because he wishes to destroy Cetewayo. But what do I know of such matters who only desire to live in peace under whatever chief the English Queen sends to us, as she has a right to do having conquered us in war? When you meet the Opener of Roads at the kraal Jazi, ask him, Macumazahn."

"Where the devil is the kraal Jazi?" I inquired with irritation. "I never heard of such a place."

"Nor did I, therefore I cannot tell you, Macumazahn. For aught I can say it may be down beneath where dead men go. But wherever it is there certainly you will meet the Opener of Roads. Now farewell, Macumazahn. If it should chance that we never look into each other's eyes again, I am sure you will think of me sometimes, as I shall of you, and of all that we have seen together, especially on that night in the Vale of Bones when the ghost of the witch Mameena prophesied to us and kissed you before us all. She must have been very beautiful, Macumazahn, as indeed I have heard from those who remember her, and I don't wonder that you loved her so much. Still for my part l had rather be kissed by a living woman than by one who is dead, though doubtless it is best to be kissed by none at all. Again, farewell, and be sure to tell the Opener of Roads that I gave you his message, lest he should lay some evil charm upon me, who have seen enough evil of late."

Thus talking Goza departed. I never saw him again, and do not know if he is dead or alive. Well, he was a kindly old fellow, if no hero.

I had almost forgotten the incident of this meeting when a while later I found myself in the neighbourhood of the beautiful but semi-tropical place called Eshowe, which since those days has become the official home of the British Resident in Zululand. Indeed, although the house was not then finished, if it had been begun, Sir Melmoth Osborn already had an office there. I wished to see him in order to give him some rather important information, but when I reached a kraal of about fifty huts some five hundred yards from the site of the present Residency, my wagon stuck fast in the boggy ground. While l was trying to get it out a quiet-faced Zulu, whose name, I remember, was Umnikwa, informed me that Malimati, that is Sir Melmoth Osborn's native name, was somewhere at a little distance from Eshowe, too far away for me to get to him that night. I answered, Very well, I would sleep where I was, and asked the name of the kraal.

He replied, Jazi, at which I started, but only said that it was a strange name, seeing that it meant "Finished," or "Finished with joy." Umnikwa answered, Yes, but that it had been so called because the chief Umfokaki, or The Stranger, who married a sister of the king, was killed at this kraal by his brother, Gundane, or the Bat. I remarked that it was an ill-omened kind of name, to which the man replied, Yes, and likely to become more so, since the King Cetewayo who had been sheltering there "beneath the armpit" of Malimati, the white lord, for some months, lay in it dying. I asked him of what he was dying, and he replied that he did not know, but that doubtless the father of the witch-doctors, named Zikali, the Opener of Roads, would be able to tell me, as he was attending on Cetewayo.

"He has sent me to bid you to come at once, O Macumazahn," he added casually, "having had news that you were arriving here."

Showing no surprise, I answered that I would come, although goodness knows I was surprised enough, and leaving my servants to get my wagon out of the bog, I walked into the kraal with the messenger. He took me to a large hut placed within a fence about the gate of which some women were gathered, who all looked very anxious and disturbed. Among them I saw Dabuko the king's brother, whom I knew slightly. He greeted me and told me that Cetewayo was at the point of death within the hut, but like Umnikwa, professed ignorance of the cause of his illness.

For a long while, over an hour I should think, I sat there outside the hut, or walked to and fro. Until darkness came I could occupy myself with contemplating the scenery of the encircling hills, which is among the most beautiful in Zululand with its swelling contours and rich colouring. But after it had set in only my thoughts remained, and these I found depressing.

At length I made up my mind that I would go away, for after all what had I to do with this business of the death of Cetewayo, if in truth he was dying? I wished to see no more of Cetewayo of whom all my recollections were terrific or sorrowful. I rose to depart, when suddenly a woman emerged from the hut. I could not see who she was or even what she was like, because of the gloom; also for the reason that she had the corner of her blanket thrown over her face as though she wished to keep it hidden. For a moment she stopped opposite to me and said—

"The king who is sick desires to see you, Macumazahn." Then she pointed to the door-hole of the hut and vanished, shutting the gate of the fence behind her. Curiosity overcame me and I crawled into the hut, pushing aside the door-board in order to do so and setting it up again when I was through.

Inside burned a single candle fixed in the neck of a bottle, faintly illuminating that big and gloomy place. By its feeble light I saw a low bedstead on the left of the entrance and lying on it a man half covered by a blanket in whom I recognized Cetewayo. His face was shrunken and distorted with pain, and his great bulk seemed less, but still without doubt it was Cetewayo.

"Greeting, Macumazahn," he said feebly, "you find me in evil case, but I heard that you were here and thought that I should like to see you before I die, because I know that you are honest and will report my words faithfully. I wish you to tell the white men that my heart never really was against them; they have always been the friends of my heart, but others forced me down a road I did not wish to travel, of which now I have come to the end."

"What is the matter with you, King?" I asked.

"I do not know, Macumazahn, but I have been sick for some days. The Opener of Roads who came to doctor me, because my wives believed those white medicine-men wished me dead, says that I have been poisoned and must die. If you had been here at first you might perhaps have given me some medicine. But now it is too late," he added with a groan.

"Who then poisoned you, King?"

"I cannot tell you, Macumazahn. Perhaps my enemies, perhaps my brothers, perhaps my wives. All wish to have done with me, and the Great One, who is no longer wanted, is soon dead. Be thankful, Macumazahn, that you never were a king, for sad is the lot of kings."

"Where, then, is the Opener of Roads? "I asked.

"He was here a little while ago. Perhaps he has gone out to take the King's head" (i.e., to announce his death) "to Malimati and the white men," he answered in a faint voice.

Just then I heard a shuffling noise proceeding from that part of the hut where the shadow was deepest, and looking, saw an emaciated arm projected into the circle of the light. It was followed by another arm, then by a vast head covered with long white hair that trailed upon the ground, then by a big, mishapen body, so wasted that it looked like a skeleton covered with corrugated black skin. Slowly, like a chameleon climbing a bough, the thing crept forward, and I knew it for Zikali. He reached the side of the bed and squatted down in his toad-like fashion, then, again like a chameleon, without moving his head turned his deep and glowing eyes towards me.

"Hail, O Macumazahn," he said in his low voice. "Did l not promise you long ago that you should be with me at the last, and are you not with me and another?"

"It seems so, Zikali," I answered. "But why do you not send for the white doctors to cure the king?"

"All the doctors, white and black, in the whole world cannot cure him, Macumazahn. The Spirits call him and he dies. At his call I came fast and far, but even I cannot cure him—although because of him I myself must die."

"Why?" I asked.

"Look at me, Macumazahn, and say if I am one who should travel. Well, all come to their end at last, even the 'Thing-that-should-never-have-been-born.'"

Cetewayo lifted his head and looked at him, then said heavily—

"Perchance it would have been better for our House if that end had been sooner. Now that I lie dying many sayings concerning you come into my mind that I had forgotten. Moreover, Opener of Roads, I never sent for you, whoever may have done so, and it was not until after you came here that the great pain seized me. How did it happen," he went on with gathering force, "that the white men caught me in the secret place where you told me I should hide? Who pointed out that hidden hole to the white men? But what does it matter now?"

"Nothing at all, O Son of Panda," answered Zikali, "even less than it matters how I escaped the spear-head hidden in your robe, yonder in my hut in the Black Kloof where, had it not been for a certain spirit that stood between you and me, you would have murdered me. Tell me, Son of Panda, during these last three days have you thought at all of your brother Umbelazi, and of certain other brethren of yours whom you killed at the battle of the Tugela, when the white man here led the charge of the Amawombe against your regiments and ate up three of them?"

Cetewayo groaned but said nothing. I think he had become too faint to speak.

"Listen, Son of Panda," went on Zikali in an intense and hissing voice. "Many, many years ago, before Senzangacona, your grandfather, saw the light—who knows how long before—a man was born of high blood in the Dwandwe tribe, which man was a dwarf. Chaka the Black One conquered the Dwandwe, but this man of high blood was spared because he was a dwarf, an abortion, to whom Chaka gave the name of the 'Thing-that-never-should-have-been-born,' keeping him about him to be a mock in times of peace and safety, and because he was wise and learned in magic, to be a counsellor in times of trouble. Moreover, Chaka killed this man's wives and children for his sport, save one whom he kept to be his 'sister.'

"Therefore for the sake of his people and his butchered wives and children, this wizard swore an oath of vengeance against Chaka and all his House. Working beneath the ground like a rat, he undermined the throne of Chaka and brought him to his death by the spears of his brethren and of Mopo his servant, whom Chaka had wronged. Still working in the dark like a rat, he caused Dingaan, who stabbed Chaka, to murder the Boer Retief and his people, and thus called down upon his head the vengeance of the Whites, and afterwards brought Dingaan to his death. Then Panda, your father, arose, and his life this 'Thing-that-never-should-have-been-born' spared because once Panda had done him a kindness. Only through the witch Mameena he brought sorrow on him, causing war to arise between his children, one of whom was named Cetewayo.

"Then this Cetewayo ruled, first with his father Panda and afterwards in his place, and trouble arose between him and the English. Son of Panda, you will remember that this Cetewayo was in doubt whether to fight the English and demanded a sign of the Thing-that-never-should-have-been-born. He gave the sign, causing the Inkosazana-y-Zulu, the Princess of Heaven, to appear before him and thereby lifting the spear of War. Son of Panda, you know how that war went, how this Cetewayo was defeated and came to the 'Thing-that-never-should-have-been-born' like a hunted hyena, to learn of a hole where he might hide. You know, too, how he strove to murder the poor old doctor who showed him such a hole; how he was taken prisoner and sent across the water and afterwards set up again in the land that had learned to hate him, to bring its children to death by thousands. And you know how at last he took refuge beneath the wing of the white chief, here in the kraal Jazi, and lived, spat upon, an outcast, until at length he fell sick, as such men are apt to do, and the Thing-that-never-should-have-been-born was sent for to doctor him. And you know also how he lies dying, within him an agony as though he had swallowed a red hot spear, and before him a great blackness peopled by the ghosts of those whom he has slain, and of his forefathers whose House he has pulled down and burned."

Zikali ceased, and thrusting his hideous head to within an inch or two of that of the dying man, he glowered at him with his fierce and fiery eyes. Then he began to whisper into the king's ear, who quivered at his words, as the victim quivers beneath the torturer's looks.

At that moment the end of the candle fell into the bottle which was of clear white glass, and there burned for a little while dully before it went out. Never shall I forget the scene illumined by its blue and ghastly light. The dying man lying on the low couch, rocking his head to and fro; the wizard bending over him like some grey vampire bat sucking the life-blood from his helpless throat. The terror in the eyes of the one, the insatiable hate in the eyes of the other. Oh! it was awful!

"Macumazahn," gasped Cetewayo in a rattling whisper, "help me, Macumazahn. I say that I am poisoned by this Zikali, who hates me. Oh! drive away the ghosts! Drive them away!"

I looked at him and at his tormentor squatted by him like a mocking fiend, and as I looked the candle went out.

Then my nerve broke, the cold sweat poured from my face and I fled from the hut as a man might from a scene in hell, followed by the low mocking laugh of Zikali.

Outside the women and others were gathered in the gloom. I told them to go to the king, who was dying, and blundered up the slope to search for some white man. No one was to be found, but a Kaffir messenger by the office told me that Malimati was still away and had been sent for. So I returned to my wagon and lay down in it exhausted, for what more could I do?

It was a rough night. Thunder muttered and rain fell in driving gusts. I dozed off, only to be awakened by a sound of wailing. Then I knew that the king was dead, for this was the Isililo, the cry of mourning. I wondered whether the murderers—for that he was poisoned I had no doubt—were among those who wailed.

Towards dawn the storm rolled off and the night grew serene and clear, for a waning moon was shining in the sky. The heat of that stiffing place oppressed me; my blood seemed to be afire. I knew that there was a stream in a gorge about half a mile away, for it had been pointed out to me. I longed for a swim in cool water, who, to tell truth, had found none for some days, and bethought me that I would bathe in this stream before I trekked from that hateful spot, for to me it had become hateful. Calling my driver, who was awake and talking with the voorloopers, for they knew what was passing at the kraal and were alarmed, I told them to get the oxen ready to start as I would be back presently. Then I set off for the stream and, after a longish walk, scrambled down a steep ravine to its banks, following a path made by Kaffir women going to draw water. Arrived there at last I found that it was in flood and rising rapidly, at least so I judged from the sound, for in that deep, tree-hung place the light was too faint to allow me to see anything. So I sat down waiting for the dawn and wishing that I had not come because of the mosquitoes.

At length it broke and the mists lifted, showing that the spot was one of great beauty. Opposite to me was a waterfall twenty or thirty feet high, over which the torrent rushed into a black pool below. Everywhere grew tall ferns and beyond these graceful trees, from whose leaves hung raindrops. In the centre of the stream on the edge of the fall was a rock not a dozen feet away from me, round which the water foamed. Something was squatted on this rock, at first I could not see what because of the mist, but thought that it was a grey-headed baboon, or some other animal, and regretted that I had not brought a gun with me. Presently I became aware that it must be a man, for, in a chanting voice, it began to speak or pray in Zulu, and hidden behind a flowering bush, I could hear the words. They were to this effect—

"O my Spirit, here where thou foundest me when I was young, hundreds of years ago" (he said hundreds, but I suppose he meant tens), "I come back to thee. In this pool I dived and beneath the waters found thee, my Snake, and thou didst wind thyself about my body and about my heart" (here I understood that the speaker was alluding to his initiation as a witch-doctor which generally includes, or used to include, the finding of a snake in a river that coils itself about the neophyte). "About my body and in my heart thou hast dwelt from that sun to this, giving me wisdom and good and evil counsel, and that which thou hast counselled, I have done. Now I return thee whence thou camest, there to await me in the new birth.

"O Spirits of my fathers, toiling through many years I have avenged you on the House of Senzangacona, and never again will there be a king of the Zulus, for the last of them lies dead by my hand. O my murdered wives and my children, I have offered up to you a mighty sacrifice, a sacrifice of thousands upon thousands.

"O Umkulu-kulu, Great One of the heavens, who sentest me to earth, I have done thy work upon the earth and bring back to thee thy harvest of the seed that thou hast sown, a blood-red harvest, O Umkulu-kulu. Be still, be still, my Snake, the sun arises, and soon, soon shalt thou rest in the water that wast thine from the beginning of the world!"

The voice ceased, and presently a spear of light piercing the mists, lit upon the speaker. It was Zikali and about him was wound a great yellow-bellied snake, of which the black head with flickering tongue waved above his head and seemed from time to time to lick him on the brow. (I suppose it had come to him from the water, for its skin glittered as though with wet.) He stood up on tottering feet, staring at the red eye of the rising sun, then crying, *"Finished, finished with joy!"* with a loud and dreadful laughter, he plunged into the foaming pool beneath.

Such was the end of Zikali the Wizard, Opener of Roads, the "Thing-that-should-never-have-been-born," and such was the vengeance that he worked upon the great House of Senzangacona, bringing it to naught and with it the nation of the Zulus.

The Ivory Child

Table of Contents

Allan Gives a Shooting Lesson

Now I, Allan Quatermain, come to the story of what was, perhaps, one of the strangest of all the adventures which have befallen me in the course of a life that so far can scarcely be called tame or humdrum.

Amongst many other things it tells of the war against the Black Kendah people and the dead of Jana, their elephant god. Often since then I have wondered if this creature was or was not anything more than a mere gigantic beast of the forest. It seems improbable, even impossible, but the reader of future days may judge of this matter for himself.

Also he can form his opinion as to the religion of the White Kendah and their pretensions to a certain degree of magical skill. Of this magic I will make only one remark: If it existed at all, it was by no means infallible. To take a single instance, Harût and Marût were convinced by divination that I, and I only, could kill Jana, which was why they invited me to Kendahland. Yet in the end it was Hans who killed him. Jana nearly killed me!

Now to my tale.

In another history, called "The Holy Flower," I have told how I came to England with a young gentleman of the name of Scroope, partly to see him safely home after a hunting accident, and partly to try to dispose of a unique orchid for a friend of mine called Brother John by the white people, and Dogeetah by the natives, who was popularly supposed to be mad, but, in fact, was very sane indeed. So sane was he that he pursued what seemed to be an absolutely desperate quest for over twenty years, until, with some humble assistance on my part, he brought it to a curiously successful issue. But all this tale is told in "The Holy Flower," and I only allude to it here, that is at present, to explain how I came to be in England.

While in this country I stayed for a few days with Scroope, or, rather, with his fiancée and her people, at a fine house in Essex. (I called it Essex to avoid the place being identified, but really it was one of the neighbouring counties.) During my visit I was taken to see a much finer place, a splendid old castle with brick gateway towers, that had been wonderfully well restored and turned into a most luxurious modern dwelling. Let us call it "Ragnall," the seat of a baron of that name.

I had heard a good deal about Lord Ragnall, who, according to all accounts, seemed a kind of Admirable Crichton. He was said to be wonderfully handsome, a great scholar—he had taken a double first at college; a great athlete—he had been captain of the Oxford boat at the University race; a very promising speaker who had already made his mark in the House of Lords; a sportsman who had shot tigers and other large game in India; a poet who had published a successful volume of verse under a pseudonym; a good solider until he left the Service; and lastly, a man of enormous wealth, owning, in addition to his estates, several coal mines and an entire town in the north of England.

"Dear me!" I said when the list was finished, "he seems to have been born with a whole case of gold spoons in his mouth. I hope one of them will not choke him," adding: "Perhaps he will be unlucky in love."

"That's just where he is most lucky of all," answered the young lady to whom I was talking—it was Scroope's fiancée, Miss Manners—"for he is engaged to a lady that, I am told, is the loveliest, sweetest, cleverest girl in all England, and they absolutely adore each other."

"Dear me!" I repeated. "I wonder what Fate *has* got up its sleeve for Lord Ragnall and his perfect lady-love?"

I was doomed to find out one day.

So it came about that when, on the following morning, I was asked if I would like to see the wonders of Ragnall Castle, I answered "Yes." Really, however, I wanted to have a look at Lord Ragnall himself, if possible, for the account of his many perfections had impressed the imagination of a poor colonist like myself, who had never found an opportunity of setting his eyes upon a kind of human angel. Human devils I had met in plenty, but never a single angel—at least, of the male sex. Also there was always the possibility that I might get a glimpse of the still more angelic lady to whom he was engaged, whose name, I understood, was the Hon. Miss Holmes. So I said that nothing would please me more than to see this castle.

Thither we drove accordingly through the fine, frosty air, for the month was December. On reaching the castle, Mr. Scroope was told that Lord Ragnall, whom he knew well, was out shooting somewhere in the park, but that, of course, he could show his friend over the place. So we went in, the three of us, for Miss Manners, to whom Scroope was to be married very shortly, had driven us over in her pony carriage. The porter at the gateway towers took us to the main door of the castle and handed us over to another man, whom he addressed as Mr. Savage, whispering to me that he was his lordship's personal attendant.

I remember the name, because it seemed to me that I had never seen anyone who looked much less savage. In truth, his appearance was that of a duke in disguise, as I imagine dukes to be, for I never set eyes on one. His dress—he wore a black morning cut-away coat—was faultless. His manners were exquisite, polite to the verge of irony, but with a hint of haughty pride in the background. He was handsome also, with a fine nose and a hawk-like eye, while a touch of baldness added to the general effect. His age may have been anything between thirty-five and forty, and the way he deprived me of my hat and stick, to which I strove to cling, showed, I thought, resolution of character. Probably, I reflected to myself, he considers me an unusual sort of person who might damage the pictures and other objects of art with the stick, and not seeing his way how to ask me to give it up without suggesting suspicion, has hit upon the expedient of taking my hat also.

In after days Mr. Samuel Savage informed me that I was quite right in this surmise. He said he thought that, judging from my somewhat unconventional appearance, I might be one of the dangerous class of whom he had been reading in the papers, namely, a "hanarchist." I write the word as he pronounced it, for here comes the curious thing. This man, so flawless, so well instructed in some respects, had a fault which gave everything away. His h's were uncertain. Three of them would come quite right, but the fourth, let us say, would be conspicuous either by its utter absence or by its unwanted appearance. He could speak, when describing the Ragnall pictures, in rotund and flowing periods that would scarcely have disgraced the pen of Gibbon. Then suddenly that "h" would appear or disappear, and the illusion was over. It was like a sudden shock of cold water down the back. I never discovered the origin of his family; it was a matter of which he did not speak, perhaps because he was vague about it himself; but if an earl of Norman blood had married a handsome Cockney kitchenmaid of native ability, I can quite imagine that Samuel Savage might have been a child of the union. For the rest he was a good man and a faithful one, for whom I have a high respect.

On this occasion he conducted us round the castle, or, rather, its more public rooms, showing us many treasures and, I should think, at least two hundred pictures by eminent and departed artists, which gave him an opportunity of exhibiting a peculiar, if somewhat erratic, knowledge of history. To tell the truth, I began to wish that it were a little less full in detail, since on a December day those large apartments felt uncommonly cold. Scroope and Miss Manners seemed to keep warm, perhaps with the inward fires of mutual admiration, but as I had no one to admire except Mr.

Savage, a temperature of about 35 degrees produced its natural effect upon me.

At length we took a short cut from the large to the little gallery through a warmed and comfortable room, which I understood was Lord Ragnall's study. Halting for a moment by one of the fires, I observed a picture on the wall, over which a curtain was drawn, and asked Mr. Savage what it might be.

"That, sir," he replied with a kind of haughty reserve, "is the portrait of her future ladyship, which his lordship keeps for his private heye."

Miss Manners sniggered, and I said:

"Oh, thank you. What an ill-omened kind of thing to do!"

Then, observing through an open door the hall in which my hat had been taken from me, I lingered and as the others vanished in the little gallery, slipped into it, recovered my belongings, and passed out to the garden, purposing to walk there till I was warm again and Scroope reappeared. While I marched up and down a terrace, on which, I remember, several very cold-looking peacocks were seated, like conscientious birds that knew it was their duty to be ornamental, however low the temperature, I heard some shots fired, apparently in a clump of ilex oaks which grew about five hundred yards away, and reflected to myself that they seemed to be those of a small rifle, not of a shotgun.

My curiosity being excited as to what was to be an almost professional matter, I walked towards the grove, making a circuit through a shrubbery. At length I found myself near to the edge of a glade, and perceived, standing behind the shelter of a magnificent ilex, two men. One of these was a young keeper, and the other, from his appearance, I felt sure must be Lord Ragnall himself. Certainly he was a splendid-looking man, very tall, very broad, very handsome, with a peaked beard, a kind and charming face, and large dark eyes. He wore a cloak upon his shoulders, which was thrown back from over a velvet coat, and, except for the light double-barrelled rifle in his hand, looked exactly like a picture by Van Dyck which Mr. Savage had just informed me was that of one of his lordship's ancestors of the time of Charles I.

Standing behind another oak, I observed that he was trying to shoot wood-pigeons as they descended to feed upon the acorns, for which the hard weather had made them greedy. From time to time these beautiful blue birds appeared and hovered a moment before they settled, whereon the sportsman fired and—they flew away. *Bang! Bang* went the double-barrelled rifle, and off fled the pigeon.

"Damn!" said the sportsman in a pleasant, laughing voice; "that's the twelfth I have missed, Charles."

"You hit his tail, my lord. I saw a feather come out. But, my lord, as I told you, there ain't no man living what can kill pigeons on the wing with a bullet, even when they seem to sit still in the air."

"I have heard of one, Charles. Mr. Scroope has a friend from Africa staying with him who, he swears, could knock over four out of six."

"Then, my lord, Mr. Scroope has a friend what lies," replied Charles as he handed him the second rifle.

This was too much for me. I stepped forward, raising my hat politely, and said:

"Sir, forgive me for interrupting you, but you are not shooting at those wood-pigeons in the right way. Although they seem to hover just before they settle, they are dropping much faster than you think. Your keeper was mistaken when he said that you knocked a feather out of the tail of that last bird at which you fired two barrels. In both cases you shot at least a foot above it, and what fell was a leaf from the ilex tree."

There was a moment's silence, which was broken by Charles, who ejaculated in a thick voice:

"Well, of all the cheek!"

Lord Ragnall, however, for it was he, looked first angry and then amused.

"Sir," he said, "I thank you for your advice, which no doubt is excellent, for it is certainly true that I have missed every pigeon which I tried to shoot with these confounded little rifles. But if you could demonstrate in practice what you so kindly set out in precept, the value of your counsel would be enhanced."

Thus he spoke, mimicking, I have no doubt (for he had a sense of humour), the manner of my address, which nervousness had made somewhat pompous.

"Give me the rifle," I answered, taking off my greatcoat.

He handed it me with a bow.

"Mind what you are about," growled Charles. "That there thing is full cocked and 'air-triggered."

I withered, or, rather, tried to wither him with a glance, but this unbelieving keeper only stared back at me with insolence in his round and bird-like eyes. Never before had I felt quite so angry with a menial. Then a horrible doubt struck me. Supposing I should miss! I knew very little of the manner of flight of English wood-pigeons, which are not difficult to miss with a bullet, and nothing at all of these particular rifles, though a glance at them showed me that they were exquisite weapons of their sort and by a great maker. If I muffed the thing now, how should I bear the scorn of Charles and the polite amusement of his noble master? Almost I prayed that no more pigeons would put in an appearance, and thus that the issue of my supposed skill might be left in doubt.

But this was not to be. These birds came from far in ones or twos to search for their favourite food, and the fact that others had been scared away did not cause them to cease from coming. Presently I heard Charles mutter:

"Now, then, look out, guv'nor. Here's your chance of teaching his lordship how to do it, though he does happen to be the best shot in these counties."

While he spoke two pigeons appeared, one a little behind the other, coming down very straight. As they reached the opening in the ilex grove they hovered, preparing to alight, for of us they could see nothing, one at a distance of about fifty and the other of, say, seventy yards away. I took the nearest, got on to it, allowing for the drop and the angle, and touched the trigger of the rifle, which fell to my shoulder very sweetly. The bullet struck that pigeon on the crop, out of which fell a shower of acorns that it had been eating, as it sank to the ground stone dead. Number two pigeon, realizing danger, began to mount upwards almost straight. I fired the second barrel, and by good luck shot its head off. Then I snatched the other rifle, which Charles had been loading automatically, from his outstretched hand, for at that moment I saw two more pigeons coming. At the first I risked a difficult shot and hit it far back, knocking out its tail, but bringing it, still fluttering, to the ground. The other, too, I covered, but when I touched the trigger there was a click, no more.

This was my opportunity of coming even with Charles, and I availed myself of it.

"Young man," I said, while he gaped at me open-mouthed, "you should learn to be careful with rifles, which are dangerous weapons. If you give one to a shooter that is not loaded, it shows that you are capable of anything."

Then I turned, and addressing Lord Ragnall, added:

"I must apologize for that third shot of mine, which was infamous, for I committed a similar fault to that against which I warned you, sir, and did not fire far enough ahead. However, it may serve to show your attendant the difference between the tail of a pigeon and an oak leaf," and I pointed to one of the feathers of the poor bird, which was still drifting to the ground.

"Well, if this here snipe of a chap ain't the devil in boots!" exclaimed Charles to himself.

But his master cut him short with a look, then lifted his hat to me and said:

"Sir, the practice much surpasses the precept, which is unusual. I congratulate you upon a skill that almost partakes of the marvellous, unless, indeed, chance——" And he stopped.

"It is natural that you should think so," I replied; "but if more pigeons come, and

Mr. Charles will make sure that he loads the rifle, I hope to undeceive you."

At this moment, however, a loud shout from Scroope, who was looking for me, reinforced by a shrill cry uttered by Miss Manners, banished every pigeon within half a mile, a fact of which I was not sorry, since who knows whether I should have it all, or any, of the next three birds?

"I think my friends are calling me, so I will bid you good morning," I said awkwardly.

"One moment, sir," he exclaimed. "Might I first ask you your name? Mine is Ragnall—Lord Ragnall."

"And mine is Allan Quatermain," I said.

"Oh!" he answered, "that explains matters. Charles, this is Mr. Scroope's friend, the gentleman that you said—exaggerated. I think you had better apologize."

But Charles was gone, to pick up the pigeons, I suppose.

At this moment Scroope and the young lady appeared, having heard our voices, and a general explanation ensued.

"Mr. Quatermain has been giving me a lesson in shooting pigeons on the wing with a small-bore rifle," said Lord Ragnall, pointing to the dead birds that still lay upon the ground.

"He is competent to do that," said Scroope.

"Painfully competent," replied his lordship. "If you don't believe me, ask the under-keeper."

"It is the only thing I can do," I explained modestly. "Rifle-shooting is my trade, and I have made a habit of practising at birds on the wing with ball. I have no doubt that with a shot-gun your lordship would leave me nowhere, for that is a game at which I have had little practice, except when shooting for the pot in Africa."

"Yes," interrupted Scroope, "you wouldn't have any chance at that, Allan, against one of the finest shots in England."

"I'm not so sure," said Lord Ragnall, laughing pleasantly. "I have an idea that Mr. Quatermain is full of surprises. However, with his leave, we'll see. If you have a day to spare, Mr. Quatermain, we are going to shoot through the home coverts to-morrow, which haven't been touched till now, and I hope you will join us."

"It is most kind of you, but that is impossible," I answered with firmness. "I have no gun here."

"Oh, never mind that, Mr. Quatermain. I have a pair of breech-loaders" —these were new things at that date—"which have been sent down to me to try. I am going to return them, because they are much too short in the stock for me. I think they would just suit you, and you are quite welcome to the use of them."

Again I excused myself, guessing that the discomfited Charles would put all sorts of stories about concerning me, and not wishing to look foolish before a party of grand strangers, no doubt chosen for their skill at this particular form of sport.

"Well, Allan," exclaimed Scroope, who always had a talent for saying the wrong thing, "you are quite right not to go into a competition with Lord Ragnall over high pheasants."

I flushed, for there was some truth in his blundering remark, whereon Lord Ragnall said with ready tact:

"I asked Mr. Quatermain to shoot, not to a shooting match, Scroope, and I hope he'll come."

This left me no option, and with a sinking heart I had to accept.

"Sorry I can't ask you too, Scroope," said his lordship, when details had been arranged, "but we can only manage seven guns at this shoot. But will you and Miss Manners come to dine and sleep to-morrow evening? I should like to introduce your future wife to my future wife," he added, colouring a little.

Miss Manners being devoured with curiosity as to the wonderful Miss Holmes, of whom she had heard so much but never actually seen, accepted at once, before her lover could get out a word, whereon Scroope volunteered to bring me over in the morning and load for me. Being possessed by a terror that I should be handed over to the care of the unsympathetic Charles, I replied that I should be very grateful, and so the thing was settled.

On our way home we passed through a country town, of which I forget the name, and the sight of a gunsmith's shop there reminded me that I had no cartridges. So I stopped to order some, as, fortunately, Lord Ragnall had mentioned that the guns he was going to lend me were twelve-bores. The tradesman asked me how many cartridges I wanted, and when I replied "a hundred," stared at me and said:

"If, as I understood, sir, you are going to the big winter shoot at Ragnall to-morrow, you had better make it three hundred and fifty at least. I shall be there to watch, like lots of others, and I expect to see nearly two hundred fired by each gun at the last Lake stand."

"Very well," I answered, fearing to show more ignorance by further discussion. "I will call for the cartridges on my way to-morrow morning. Please load them with three drachms of powder."

"Yes, sir, and an ounce and an eighth of No. 5 shot, sir? That's what all the gentlemen use."

"No," I answered, "No. 3; please be sure as to that. Good evening."

The gunsmith stared at me, and as I left the shop I heard him remark to his assistant:

"That African gent must think he's going out to shoot ostriches with buck shot. I expect he ain't no good, whatever they may say about him."

Allan Makes a Bet

On the following morning Scroope and I arrived at Castle Ragnall at or about a quarter to ten. On our way we stopped to pick up my three hundred and fifty cartridges. I had to pay something over three solid sovereigns for them, as in those days such things were dear, which showed me that I was not going to get my lesson in English pheasant shooting for nothing. The gunsmith, however, to whom Scroope gave a lift in his cart to the castle, impressed upon me that they were dirt cheap, since he and his assistant had sat up most of the night loading them with my special No. 3 shot.

As I climbed out of the vehicle a splendid-looking and portly person, arrayed in a velvet coat and a scarlet waistcoat, approached with the air of an emperor, followed by an individual in whom I recognized Charles, carrying a gun under each arm.

"That's the head-keeper," whispered Scroope; "mind you treat him respectfully."

Much alarmed, I took off my hat and waited.

"Do I speak to Mr. Allan Quatermain?" said his majesty in a deep and rumbling voice, surveying me the while with a cold and disapproving eye.

I intimated that he did.

"Then, sir," he went on, pausing a little at the "sir," as though he suspected me of being no more than an African colleague of his own, "I have been ordered by his lordship to bring you these guns, and I hope, sir, that you will be careful of them, as they are here on sale or return. Charles, explain the working of them there guns to this foreign gentleman, and in doing so keep the muzzles up *or* down. They ain't loaded, it's true, but the example is always useful."

"Thank you, Mr. Keeper," I replied, growing somewhat nettled, "but I think that I am already acquainted with most that there is to learn about guns."

"I am glad to hear it, sir," said his majesty with evident disbelief. "Charles, I understand that Squire Scroope is going to load for the gentleman, which I hope he knows how to do with safety. His lordship's orders are that you accompany them and carry the cartridges. And, Charles, you will please keep count of the number fired and what is killed dead, not reckoning runners. I'm sick of them stories of runners."

These directions were given in a portentous stage aside which we were not supposed to hear. They caused Scroope to snigger and Charles to grin, but in me they raised a feeling of indignation.

I took one of the guns and looked at it. It was a costly and beautifully made weapon of the period, with an under-lever action.

"There's nothing wrong with the gun, sir," rumbled Red Waistcoat. "If you hold it straight it will do the rest. But keep the muzzle up, sir, keep it up, for I know what the bore is without studying the same with my eye. Also perhaps you won't take it amiss if I tell you that here at Ragnall we hates a low pheasant. I mention it because the last gentleman who came from foreign parts—he was French, he was—shot nothing all day but one hen bird sitting just on the top of the brush, two beaters, his lordship's hat, and a starling."

At this point Scroope broke into a roar of idiotic laughter. Charles, from whom Fortune decreed that I was not to escape, after all, turned his back and doubled up as though seized with sudden pain in the stomach, and I grew absolutely furious.

"Confound it, Mr. Keeper," I explained, "what do you mean by lecturing me? Attend to your business, and I'll attend to mine."

At this moment who should appear from behind the angle of some building—we were talking in the stableyard, near the gun-room—but Lord Ragnall himself. I could see that he had overheard the conversation, for he looked angry.

"Jenkins," he said, addressing the keeper, "do what Mr. Quatermain has said and attend to your own business. Perhaps you are not aware that he has shot more lions, elephants, and other big game than you have cats. But, however that may be, it is not your place to try to instruct him or any of my guests. Now go and see to the beaters."

"Beg pardon, my lord," ejaculated Jenkins, his face, that was as florid as his waistcoat, turning quite pale; "no offence meant, my lord, but elephants and lions don't fly, my lord, and those accustomed to such ground varmin are apt to shoot low, my lord. Beaters all ready at the Hunt Copse, my lord."

Thus speaking he backed himself out of sight. Lord Ragnall watched him go, then said with a laugh:

"I apologize to you, Mr. Quatermain. That silly old fool was part of my inheritance, so to speak; and the joke of it is that he is himself the worst and most dangerous shot I ever saw. However, on the other hand, he is the best rearer of pheasants in the county, so I put up with him. Come in, now, won't you? Charles will look after your guns and cartridges."

So Scroope and I were taken through a side entrance into the big hall and there introduced to the other members of the shooting party, most of whom were staying at the castle. They were famous shots. Indeed, I had read of the prowess of some of them in *The Field*, a paper that I always took in Africa, although often enough, when I was on my distant expeditions, I did not see a copy of it for a year at a time.

To my astonishment I found that I knew one of these gentlemen. We had not, it is true, met for a dozen years; but I seldom forget a face, and I was sure that I could not be mistaken in this instance. That mean appearance, those small, shifty grey eyes, that red, pointed nose could belong to nobody except Van Koop, so famous in his day in South Africa in connexion with certain gigantic and most successful frauds that the law seemed quite unable to touch, of which frauds I had been one of the many victims to the extent of £250, a large sum for me.

The last time we met there had been a stormy scene between us, which ended in my declaring in my wrath that if I came across him on the veld I should shoot him at sight. Perhaps that was one of the reasons why Mr. van Koop vanished from South Africa, for I may add that he was a cur of the first water. I believe that he had only just entered the room, having driven over from wherever he lived at some distance from Ragnall. At any rate, he knew nothing of my presence at this shoot. Had he known I am quite sure that he would have been absent. He turned, and seeing me, ejaculated: "Allan Quatermain, by heaven!" beneath his breath, but in such a tone of astonishment that it attracted the attention of Lord Ragnall, who was standing near.

"Yes, Mr. van Koop," I answered in a cheerful voice, "Allan Quatermain, no other, and I hope you are as glad to see me as I am to see you."

"I think there is some mistake," said Lord Ragnall, staring at us. "This is Sir Junius Fortescue, who used to be Mr. Fortescue."

"Indeed," I replied. "I don't know that I ever remember his being called by that particular name, but I do know that we are old— friends."

Lord Ragnall moved away as though he did not wish to continue the conversation, which no one else had overheard, and Van Koop sidled up to me.

"Mr. Quatermain," he said in a low voice, "circumstances have changed with me since last we met."

"So I gather," I replied; "but mine have remained much the same, and if it is convenient to you to repay me that £250 you owe me, with interest, I shall be much obliged. If not, I think I have a good story to tell about you."

"Oh, Mr. Quatermain," he answered with a sort of smile which made me feel inclined to kick him, "you know I dispute that debt."

"Do you?" I exclaimed. "Well, perhaps you will dispute the story also. But the question is, will you be believed when I give the proofs?"

"Ever heard of the Statute of Limitations, Mr. Quatermain?" he asked with a sneer.

"Not where character is concerned," I replied stoutly. "Now, what are you going to do?"

He reflected for a moment, and answered:

"Look here, Mr. Quatermain, you were always a bit of a sportsman, and I'll make you an offer. If I kill more birds than you do to-day, you shall promise to hold your tongue about my affairs in South Africa; and if you kill more than I do, you shall still hold your tongue, but I will pay you that £250 and interest for six years."

I also reflected for a moment, knowing that the man had something up his sleeve. Of course, I could refuse and make a scandal. But that was not in my line, and would not bring me nearer my £250, which, if I chanced to win, might find its way back to me.

"All right, done!" I said.

"What is your bet, Sir Junius?" asked Lord Ragnall, who was approaching again.

"It is rather a long story," he answered, "but, to put it shortly, years ago, when I was travelling in Africa, Mr. Quatermain and I had a dispute as to a sum of £5 which he thought I owed him, and to save argument about a trifle we have agreed that I should shoot against him for it to-day."

"Indeed," said Lord Ragnall rather seriously, for I could see that he did not believe Van Koop's statement as to the amount of the bet; perhaps he had heard more than we thought. "To be frank, Sir Junius, I don't much care for betting—for that's what it comes to—here. Also I think Mr. Quatermain said yesterday that he had never shot pheasants in England, so the match seems scarcely fair. However, you gentlemen know your own business best. Only I must tell you both that if money is concerned, I shall have to set someone whose decision will be final to count your birds and report the number to me."

"Agreed," said Van Koop, or, rather, Sir Junius; but I answered nothing, for, to tell the truth, already I felt ashamed of the whole affair.

As it happened, Lord Ragnall and I walked together ahead of the others, to the first covert, which was half a mile or more away.

"You have met Sir Junius before?" he said to me interrogatively.

"I have met Mr. van Koop before," I answered, "about twelve years since, shortly after which he vanished from South Africa, where he was a well-known and very successful—speculator."

"To reappear here. Ten years ago he bought a large property in this neighbourhood. Three years ago he became a baronet."

"How did a man like Van Koop become a baronet?" I inquired.

"By purchase, I believe."

"By purchase! Are honours in England purchased?"

"You are delightfully innocent, Mr. Quatermain, as a hunter from Africa should be," said Lord Ragnall, laughing. "Your friend——"

"Excuse me, Lord Ragnall, I am a very humble person, not so elevated, indeed, as that gamekeeper of yours; therefore I should not venture to call Sir Junius, late Mr. van Koop, my friend, at least in earnest."

He laughed again.

"Well, the individual with whom you make bets subscribed largely to the funds of his party. I am telling you what I know to be true, though the amount I do not know. It has been variously stated to be from fifteen to fifty thousand pounds, and, perhaps by coincidence, subsequently was somehow created a baronet."

I stared at him.

"That's all the story," he went on. "I don't like the man myself, but he is a wonderful pheasant shot, which passes him everywhere. Shooting has become a kind of fetish in these parts, Mr. Quatermain. For instance, it is a tradition on this estate that we must kill more pheasants than on any other in the country, and therefore I have to ask the best guns, who are not always the best fellows. It annoys me, but it seems that I must do what was done before me."

"Under those circumstances I should be inclined to give up the thing altogether, Lord Ragnall. Sport as sport is good, but when it becomes a business it grows hateful. I know, who have had to follow it as a trade for many years."

"That's an idea," he replied reflectively. "Meanwhile, I do hope that you will win back your—£5 from Sir Junius. He is so vain that I would gladly give £50 to see you do so."

"There is little chance of that," I said, "for, as I told you, I have never shot pheasants before. Still, I'll try, as you wish it."

"That's right. And look here, Mr. Quatermain, shoot well forward of them. You see, I am venturing to advise you now, as you advised me yesterday. Shot does not travel so fast as ball, and the pheasant is a bird that is generally going much quicker than you think. Now, here we are. Charles will show you your stand. Good luck to you."

Ten minutes later the game began outside of a long covert, all the seven guns being posted within sight of each other. So occupied was I in watching the preliminaries, which were quite new to me, that I allowed first a hare and then a hen pheasant to depart without firing at them, which hen pheasant, by the way, curved round and was beautifully killed by Van Koop, who stood two guns off upon my right.

"Look here, Allan," said Scroope, "if you are going to beat your African friend you had better wake up, for you won't do it by admiring the scenery or that squirrel on a tree."

So I woke up. Just at that moment there was a cry of "cock forward." I thought it meant a cock pheasant, and was astonished when I saw a beautiful brown bird with a long beak flitting towards me through the tops of the oak trees.

"Am I to shoot at that?" I asked.

"Of course. It is a woodcock," answered Scroope.

By this time the brown bird was rocking past me within ten yards. I fired and killed it, for where it had been appeared nothing but a cloud of feathers. It was a quick and clever shot, or so I thought. But when Charles stepped out and picked from the ground only a beak and a head, a titter of laughter went down the whole line of guns and loaders.

"I say, old chap," said Scroope, "if you will use No. 3 shot, let your birds get a little farther off you."

The incident upset me so much that immediately afterwards I missed three easy pheasants in succession, while Van Koop added two to his bag.

Scroope shook his head and Charles groaned audibly. Now that I was not in competition with his master he had become suddenly anxious that I should win, for in some mysterious way the news of that bet had spread, and my adversary was not popular amongst the keeper class.

"Here you come again," said Scroope, pointing to an advancing pheasant.

It was an extraordinarily high pheasant, flushed, I think, outside the covert by a stop, so high that, as it travelled down the line, although three guns fired at it, including Van Koop, none of them seemed to touch it. Then I fired, and remembering Lord Ragnall's advice, far in front. Its flight changed. Still it travelled through the air, but with the momentum of a stone to fall fifty yards to my right, dead.

"That's better!" said Scroope, while Charles grinned all over his round face, muttering:

"Wiped his eye that time."

This shot seemed to give me confidence, and I improved considerably, though, oddly enough, I found that it was the high and difficult pheasants which I killed and the easy ones that I was apt to muff. But Van Koop, who was certainly a finished artist, killed both.

At the next stand Lord Ragnall, who had been observing my somewhat indifferent performance, asked me to stand back with him behind the other guns.

"I see the tall ones are your line, Mr. Quatermain," he said, "and you will get some here."

On this occasion we were placed in a dip between two long coverts which lay about three hundred yards apart. That which was being beaten proved full of pheasants, and the shooting of those picked guns was really a thing to see. I did quite well here, nearly, but not altogether, as well as Lord Ragnall himself, though that is saying a great deal, for he was a lovely shot.

"Bravo!" he said at the end of the beat. "I believe you have got a chance of winning your £5, after all."

When, however, at luncheon, more than an hour later, I found that I was thirty pheasants behind my adversary, I shook my head, and so did everybody else. On the whole, that luncheon, of which we partook in a keeper's house, was a very pleasant meal, though Van Koop talked so continuously and in such a boastful strain that I saw it irritated our host and some of the other gentlemen, who were very pleasant people. At last he began to patronize me, asking me how I had been getting on with my "elephant-potting" of late years.

I replied, "Fairly well."

"Then you should tell our friends some of your famous stories, which I promise I won't contradict," he said, adding: "You see, they are different from us, and have no experience of big-game shooting."

"I did not know that you had any, either, Sir Junius," I answered, nettled. "Indeed, I thought I remembered your telling me in Africa that the only big game you had ever shot was an ox sick with the red- water. Anyway, shooting is a business with me, not an amusement, as it is to you, and I do not talk shop."

At this he collapsed amid some laughter, after which Scroope, the most loyal of friends, began to repeat exploits of mine till my ears tingled, and I rose and went outside to look at the weather.

It had changed very much during luncheon. The fair promise of the morning had departed, the sky was overcast, and a wind, blowing in strong gusts, was rising rapidly, driving before it occasional scurries of snow.

"My word," said Lord Ragnall, who had joined me, "the Lake covert— that's our great stand here, you know—will take some shooting this afternoon. We ought to kill seven hundred pheasants in it with this team, but I doubt if we shall get five. Now, Mr. Quatermain, I am going to stand Sir Junius Fortescue and you back in the covert, where you will have the best of it, as a lot of pheasants will never face the lake against this wind. What is more, I am coming with you, if I may, as six guns are enough for this beat, and I don't mean to shoot any more to-day."

"I fear that you will be disappointed," I said nervously.

"Oh, no, I sha'n't," he answered. "I tell you frankly that if only you could have a season's practice, in my opinion you would make the best pheasant shot of the lot of us. At present you don't quite understand the ways of the birds, that's all; also those guns are strange to you. Have a glass of cherry brandy; it will steady your nerves."

I drank the cherry brandy, and presently off we went. The covert we were going to shoot, into which we had been driving pheasants all the morning, must have been nearly a mile long. At the top end it was broad, narrowing at the bottom to a width of about two hundred yards. Here it ran into a horse-shoe shaped piece of water that was about fifty yards in breadth. Four of the guns were placed round the bow of this water, but on its farther side, in such a position that the pheasants should stream over them to yet another covert behind at the top of a slope, Van Koop and I, however, were ordered to take our places, he to the right and I to the left, about seventy yards up the tongue in little glades in the woodland, having the lake to our right and our left respectively. I noticed with dismay that we were so set that the guns below us on its farther side could note all that we did or did not do; also that a little band of watchers, among whom I recognized my friend the gunsmith, were gathered in a place where, without interfering with us, they could see the sport. On our way to the boat, however, which was to row us across the water, an incident happened that put me in very good spirits and earned some applause.

I was walking with Lord Ragnall, Scroope and Charles, about sixty yards clear of a belt of tall trees, when from far away on the other side of the trees came a cry of "Partridges over!" in the hoarse voice of the red-waistcoated Jenkins, who was engaged in superintending the driving in of some low scrub before he joined his army at the top of the covert.

"Look out, Mr. Quatermain, they are coming this way," said Lord Ragnall, while Charles thrust a loaded gun into my hand.

Another moment and they appeared over the tree-tops, a big covey of them in a long, straggling line, travelling at I know not what speed, for a fierce gust from the rising gale had caught them. I fired at the first bird, which fell at my feet. I fired again, and another fell behind me. I snatched up the second gun and killed a third as it passed over me high up. Then, wheeling round, I covered the last retreating bird, and lo! it too fell, a very long shot indeed.

"By George!" said Scroope, "I never saw that done before," while Ragnall stared and Charles whistled.

But now I will tell the truth and expose all my weakness. The second bird was not the one I aimed at. I was behind it and caught that which followed. And in my vanity I did not own up, at least not till that evening.

The four dead partridges—there was not a runner among them—having been collected amidst many congratulations, we went on and were punted across the lake to the covert. As we entered the boat I observed that, in addition to the great bags, Charles was carrying a box of cartridges under his arm, and asked him where he got it from.

He replied, from Mr. Popham—that was the gunsmith's name—who had brought it with him in case I should not have enough. I made no remark, but as I knew I had quite half of my cartridges left out of the three hundred and fifty that I had bought, I wondered to myself what kind of a shoot this was going to be.

Well, we took up our stands, and while we were doing so, suddenly the wind increased to a tearing gale, which seemed to me to blow from all points of the compass in turn. Rooks flying homewards, and pigeons disturbed by the beaters were swept over us like drifting leaves; wild duck, of which I got one, went by like arrows; the great bare oaks tossed their boughs and groaned; while not far off a fir tree was blown down, falling with a splash into the water.

"It's a wild afternoon," said Lord Ragnall, and as he spoke Van Koop came from his stand, looking rather scared, and suggested that the shoot should be given up.

Lord Ragnall asked me what I wished to do. I replied that I would rather go on, but that I was in his hands.

"I think we are fairly safe in these open places, Sir Junius," he said; "and as the pheasants have been so much disturbed already, it does not much matter if they are blown about a bit. But if you are of another opinion, perhaps you had better get out of it and stand with the others over the lake. I'll send for my guns and take your place."

On hearing this Van Koop changed his mind and said that he would go on.

So the beat began. At first the wind blew from behind us, and pheasants in increasing numbers passed over our heads, most of them rather low, to the guns on the farther side of the water, who, skilled though they were, did not make very good work with them. We had been instructed not to fire at birds going forward, so I let these be. Van Koop, however, did not interpret the order in the same spirit, for he loosed at several, killing one or two and missing others.

"That fellow is no sportsman," I heard Lord Ragnall remark. "I suppose it is the bet."

Then he sent Charles to ask him to desist.

Shortly after this the gale worked round to the north and settled there, blowing with ever-increasing violence. The pheasants, however, still flew forward in the shelter of the trees, for they were making for the covert on the hill, where they had been bred. But when they got into the open and felt the full force of the wind, quite four out of six of them turned and came back at a most fearful pace, many so high as to be almost out of shot.

For the next three-quarters of an hour or more—as I think I have explained, the beat was a very long one—I had such covert shooting as I suppose I shall never see again. High above those shrieking trees, or over the lake to my left, flashed the wind-driven pheasants in an endless procession. Oddly enough, I found that this wild work suited me, for as time went on and the pheasants grew more and more impossible, I shot better and better. One after another down they came far behind me with a crash in the brushwood or a splash in the lake, till the guns grew almost too hot to hold. There were so many of them that I discovered I could pick my shots; also that nine out of ten were caught by the wind and curved at a certain angle, and that the time to fire was just before they took the curve. The excitement was great and the sport splendid, as anyone will testify who has shot December pheasants breaking back over the covert and in a tearing gale. Van Koop also was doing very well, but the guns in front got comparatively little shooting. They were forced to stand there, poor fellows, and watch our performance from afar.

As the thing drew towards an end the birds came thicker and thicker, and I shot, as I have said, better and better. This may be judged from the fact that, notwithstanding their height and tremendous pace, I killed my last thirty pheasants with thirty-five cartridges. The final bird of all, a splendid cock, appeared by himself out of nothingness when we thought that all was done. I think it must have been flushed from the covert on the hill, or been turned back just as it reached it by the resistless strength of the storm. Over it came, so high above us that it looked quite small in the dark snow-scud.

"Too far—no use!" said Lord Ragnall, as I lifted the gun.

Still, I fired, holding I know not how much in front, and lo! that pheasant died in mid air, falling with a mighty splash near the bank of the lake, but at a great distance behind us. The shot was so remarkable that everyone who saw it, including most of the beaters, who had passed us by now, uttered a cheer, and the red-waistcoated old Jenkins, who had stopped by us, remarked: "Well, bust me if that bain't a master one!"

Scroope made me angry by slapping me so hard upon the back that it hurt, and nearly caused me to let off the other barrel of the gun. Charles seemed to become one great grin, and Lord Ragnall, with a brief congratulatory "Never enjoyed a shoot so much in my life," called to the men who were posted behind us to pick up all the dead pheasants, being careful to keep mine apart from those of Sir Junius Fortescue.

"You should have a hundred and forty-three at this stand," he said, "allowing for every possible runner. Charles and I make the same total."

I remarked that I did not think there were many runners, as the No. 3 shot had served me very well, and getting into the boat was rowed to the other side, where I received more congratulations. Then, as all further shooting was out of the question because of the weather, we walked back to the castle to tea.

As I emptied my cup Lord Ragnall, who had left the room, returned and asked us to come and see the game. So we went, to find it laid out in endless lines upon the snow-powdered grass in the quadrangle of the castle, arranged in one main and two separate lots.

"Those are yours and Sir Junius's," said Scroope. "I wonder which of you has won. I'll put a sovereign on you, old fellow."

"Then you're a donkey for your pains," I answered, feeling vexed, for at that moment I had forgotten all about the bet.

I do not remember how many pheasants were killed altogether, but the total was much smaller than had been hoped for, because of the gale.

"Jenkins," said Lord Ragnall presently to Red Waistcoat, "how many have you to the credit of Sir Junius Fortescue?"

"Two hundred and seventy-seven, my lord, twelve hares, two woodcocks, and three pigeons."

"And how many to that of Mr. Quatermain?" adding: "I must remind you both, gentlemen, that the birds have been picked as carefully as possible and kept unmixed, and therefore that the figures given by Jenkins must be considered as final."

"Quite so," I answered, but Van Koop said nothing. Then, while we all waited anxiously, came the amazing answer:

"Two hundred and seventy-seven pheasants, my lord, same number as those of Sir Junius, Bart., fifteen hares, three pigeons, four partridges, one duck, and a beak—I mean a woodcock."

"Then it seems you have won your £5, Mr. Quatermain, upon which I congratulate you," said Lord Ragnall.

"Stop a minute," broke in Van Koop. "The bet was as to pheasants; the other things don't count."

"I think the term used was 'birds,'" I remarked. "But to be frank, when I made it I was thinking of pheasants, as no doubt Sir Junius was also. Therefore, if the counting is correct, there is a dead heat and the wager falls through."

"I am sure we all appreciate the view you take of the matter," said Lord Ragnall, "for it might be argued another way. In these circumstances Sir Junius keeps his £5 in his pocket. It is unlucky for you, Quatermain," he added, dropping the "mister," "that the last high pheasant you shot can't be found. It fell into the lake, you remember, and, I suppose, swam ashore and ran."

"Yes," I replied, "especially as I could have sworn that it was quite dead."

"So could I, Quatermain; but the fact remains that it isn't there."

"If we had all the pheasants that we think fall dead our bags would be much bigger than they are," remarked Van Koop, with a look of great relief upon his face, adding in his horrid, patronizing way: "Still, you shot uncommonly well, Quatermain. I'd no idea you would run me so close."

I felt inclined to answer, but didn't. Only Lord Ragnall said:

"Mr. Quatermain shot more than well. His performance in the Lake covert was the most brilliant that I have ever seen. When you went in there together, Sir Junius, you were thirty ahead of him, and you fired seventeen more cartridges at the stand."

Then, just as we turned to go, something happened. The round-eyed Charles ran puffing into the quadrangle, followed by another man with a dog, who had been specially set to pick my birds, and carrying in his hand a much-bedraggled cock pheasant without a tail.

"I've got him, my lord," he gasped, for he had run very fast; "the little gent's—I mean that which he killed in the clouds with the last shot he fired. It had gone right down into the mud and stuck there. Tom and me fished him up with a pole."

Lord Ragnall took the bird and looked at it. It was almost cold, but evidently freshly killed, for the limbs were quite flexible.

"That turns the scale in favour of Mr. Quatermain," he said, "so, Sir Junius, you had better pay your money and congratulate him, as I do."

"I protest," exclaimed Van Koop, looking very angry and meaner than usual. "How am I to know that this was Mr. Quatermain's pheasant? The sum involved is more than £5 and I feel it is my duty to protest."

"Because my men say so, Sir Junius; moreover, seeing the height from which the bird fell, their story is obviously true."

Then he examined the pheasant further, pointing out that it appeared to have only one wound—a shot through the throat almost exactly at the root of the beak, of which shot there was no mark of exit. "What sized shot were you using, Sir Junius?" he asked.

"No. 4 at the last stand."

"And you were using No. 3, Mr. Quatermain. Now, was any other gun using No. 3?"

All shook their heads.

"Jenkins, open that bird's head. I think the shot that killed it will be found in the brain."

Jenkins obeyed, using a penknife cleverly enough. Pressed against the bone of the skull he found the shot.

"No. 3 it is, sure enough, my lord," he said.

"You will agree that settles the matter, Sir Junius," said Lord Ragnall. "And now, as a bet has been made here it had better be paid."

"I have not enough money on me," said Van Koop sulkily.

"I think your banker is mine," said Lord Ragnall quietly, "so you can write a cheque in the house. Come in, all of you, it is cold in this wind."

So we went into the smoking-room, and Lord Ragnall, who, I could see, was annoyed, instantly fetched a blank cheque from his study and handed it to Van Koop in rather a pointed manner.

He took it, and turning to me, said:

"I remember the capital sum, but how much is the interest? Sorry to trouble you, but I am not very good at figures."

"Then you must have changed a good deal during the last twelve years, Sir Junius," I could not help saying. "Still, never mind the interest, I shall be quite satisfied with the principal."

So he filled up the cheque for £250 and threw it down on the table before me, saying something about its being a bother to mix up business with pleasure.

I took the draft, saw that it was correct though rather illegible, and proceeded to dry it by waving it in the air. As I did so it came into my mind that I would not touch the money of this successful scamp, won back from him in such a way.

Yielding to a perhaps foolish impulse, I said:

"Lord Ragnall, this cheque is for a debt which years ago I wrote off as lost. At luncheon to-day you were talking of a Cottage Hospital for which you are trying to get up an endowment fund in this neighbourhood, and in answer to a question from you Sir Junius Fortescue said that he had not as yet made any subscription to its fund. Will you allow me to hand you Sir Junius's subscription—to be entered in his name, if you please?" And I passed him the cheque, which was drawn to myself or bearer.

He looked at the amount, and seeing that it was not £5, but £250, flushed, then asked:

"What do you say to this act of generosity on the part of Mr. Quatermain, Sir Junius?"

There was no answer, because Sir Junius had gone. I never saw him again, for years ago the poor man died quite disgraced. His passion for semi-fraudulent speculations reasserted itself, and he became a bankrupt in conditions which caused him to leave the country for America, where he was killed in a railway accident while travelling as an immigrant. I have heard, however, that he was not asked to shoot at Ragnall any more.

The cheque was passed to the credit of the Cottage Hospital, but not, as I had requested, as a subscription from Sir Junius Fortescue. A couple of years later, indeed, I learned that this sum of money was used to build a little room in that institution to accommodate sick children, which room was named the Allan Quatermain ward.

Now, I have told this story of that December shoot because it was the beginning of my long and close friendship with Ragnall.

When he found that Van Koop had gone away without saying good-bye, Lord Ragnall made no remark. Only he took my hand and shook it.

I have only to add that, although, except for the element of competition which entered into it, I enjoyed this day's shooting very much indeed, when I came to count up its cost I felt glad that I had not been asked to any more such entertainments. Here it is, taken from an old note-book:

Cartridges, including those not used and given to Charles	£4	0	0
Game License	3	0	0
Tip to Red Waistcoat (keeper)	2	0	0
Tip to Charles	0	10	0
Tip to man who helped Charles to find pheasant	0	5	0
Tip to man who collected pheasants behind me	0	10	0
	£10	5	0

Truly pheasant shooting in England is, or was, a sport for the rich!

Miss Holmes

Two and a half hours passed by, most of which time I spent lying down to rest and get rid of a headache caused by the continual, rapid firing and the roar of the gale, or both; also in rubbing my shoulder with ointment, for it was sore from the recoil of the guns. Then Scroope appeared, as, being unable to find my way about the long passages of that great old castle, I had asked him to do, and we descended together to the large drawing-room.

It was a splendid apartment, only used upon state occasions, lighted, I should think, with at least two or three hundred wax candles, which threw a soft glow over the panelled and pictured walls, the priceless antique furniture, and the bejewelled ladies who were gathered there. To my mind there never was and never will be any artificial light to equal that of wax candles in sufficient quantity. The company was large; I think thirty sat down to dinner that night, which was given to introduce Lord Ragnall's future wife to the neighbourhood, whereof she was destined to be the leader.

Miss Manners, who was looking very happy and charming in her jewels and fine clothes, joined us at once, and informed Scroope that "she" was just coming; the maid in the cloakroom had told her so.

"Is she?" replied Scroope indifferently. "Well, so long as you have come I don't care about anyone else."

Then he told her she was looking beautiful, and stared at her with such affection that I fell back a step or two and contemplated a picture of Judith vigorously engaged in cutting off the head of Holofernes.

Presently the large door at the end of the room was thrown open and the immaculate Savage, who was acting as a kind of master of the ceremonies, announced in well-bred but penetrating tones, "Lady Longden and the Honourable Miss Holmes." I stared, like everybody else, but for a while her ladyship filled my eye. She was an ample and, to my mind, rather awful-looking person, clad in black satin—she was a widow—and very large diamonds. Her hair was white, her nose was hooked, her dark eyes were penetrating, and she had a bad cold in her head. That was all I found time to notice about her, for suddenly her daughter came into my line of vision.

Truly she was a lovely girl, or rather, young woman, for she must have been two or three-and-twenty. Not very tall, her proportions were rounded and exquisite, and her movements as graceful as those of a doe. Altogether she was doe-like, especially in the fineness of her lines and her large and liquid eyes. She was a dark beauty, with rich brown, waving hair, a clear olive complexion, a perfectly shaped mouth and very red lips. To me she looked more Italian or Spanish than Anglo-Saxon, and I believe that, as a matter of fact, she had some southern blood in her on her father's side. She wore a dress of soft rose colour, and her only ornaments were a string of pearls and a single red camellia. I could see but one blemish, if it were a blemish, in her perfect person, and that was a curious white mark upon her breast, which in its shape exactly resembled the crescent moon.

The face, however, impressed me with other than its physical qualities. It was bright, intelligent, sympathetic and, just now, happy. But I thought it more, I thought it mystical. Something that her mother said to her, probably about her dress, caused her smile to vanish for a moment, and then, from beneath it as it were, appeared this shadow of innate mysticism. In a second it was gone and she was laughing again; but I, who am accustomed to observe, had caught it, perhaps alone of all that company. Moreover, it reminded me of something.

What was it? Ah! I knew. A look that sometimes I had seen upon the face of a certain Zulu lady named Mameena, especially at the moment of her wonderful and tragic death. The thought made me shiver a little; I could not tell why, for certainly, I reflected, this high-placed and fortunate English girl had nothing in common with that fate-driven Child of Storm, whose dark and imperial spirit dwelt in the woman called Mameena. They were as far apart as Zululand is from Essex. Yet it was quite sure that both of them had touch with hidden things.

Lord Ragnall, looking more like a splendid Van Dyck than ever in his evening dress, stepped forward to greet his fiancée and her mother with a courtly bow, and I turned again to continue my contemplation of the stalwart Judith and the very ugly head of Holofernes. Presently I was aware of a soft voice—a very rich and thrilling voice—asking quite close to me:

"Which is he? Oh! you need not answer, dear. I know him from the description."

"Yes," replied Lord Ragnall to Miss Holmes—for it was she—"you are quite right. I will introduce you to him presently. But, love, whom do you wish to take you in to dinner? I can't—your mother, you know; and as there are no titles here to-night, you may make your choice. Would you like old Dr. Jeffreys, the clergyman?"

"No," she replied, with quiet firmness, "I know him; he took me in once before. I wish Mr. Allan Quatermain to take me in. He is interesting, and I want to hear about Africa."

"Very well," he answered, "and he *is*. more interesting than all the rest put together. But, Luna, why are you always thinking and talking about Africa? One might imagine that you were going to live there."

"So I may one day," she answered dreamily. "Who knows where one has lived, or where one will live!" And again I saw that mystic look come into her face.

I heard no more of that conversation, which it is improbable that anyone whose ears had not been sharpened by a lifetime of listening in great silences would have caught at all. To tell the truth, I made myself scarce, slipping off to the other end of the big room in the hope of evading the kind intentions of Miss Holmes. I have a great dislike of being put out of my place, and I felt that among all these local celebrities it was not fitting that I should be selected to take in the future bride on an occasion of this sort. But it was of no use, for presently Lord Ragnall hunted me up, bringing the young lady with him.

"Let me introduce you to Miss Holmes, Quatermain," he said. "She is anxious that you should take her in to dinner, if you will be so kind. She is very interested in—in——"

"Africa," I suggested.

"In Mr. Quatermain, who, I am told, is one of the greatest hunters in Africa," she corrected me, with a dazzling smile.

I bowed, not knowing what to say. Lord Ragnall laughed and vanished, leaving us together. Dinner was announced. Presently we were wending in the centre of a long and glittering procession across the central hall to the banqueting chamber, a splendid room with a roof like a church that was said to have been built in the times of the Plantagenets. Here Mr. Savage, who evidently had been looking out for her future ladyship, conducted us to our places, which were upon the left of Lord Ragnall, who sat at the head of the broad table with Lady Longden on his right. Then the old clergyman, Dr. Jeffreys, a pompous and rather frowsy ecclesiastic, said grace, for grace was still in fashion at such feasts in those days, asking Heaven to make us truly thankful for the dinner we were about to consume.

Certainly there was a great deal to be thankful for in the eating and drinking line, but of all I remember little, except a general vision of silver dishes, champagne, splendour, and things I did not want to eat being constantly handed to me. What I do remember is Miss Holmes, and nothing but Miss Holmes; the charm of her conversation, the light of her beautiful eyes, the fragrance of her hair, her most flattering interest in my unworthy self. To tell the truth, we got on "like fire in the winter grass," as the Zulus say, and when that dinner was over the grass was still burning.

I don't think that Lord Ragnall quite liked it, but fortunately Lady Longden was a talkative person. First she conversed about her cold in the head, sneezing at intervals, poor soul, and being reduced to send for another handkerchief after the entrées. Then she got off upon business matters; to judge from the look of boredom on her host's face, I think it must have been of settlements. Three times did I hear him refer her to the lawyers—without avail. Lastly, when he thought he had escaped, she embarked upon a quite vigorous argument with Dr. Jeffreys about church matters—I gathered that she was "low" and he was "high"—in which she insisted upon his lordship acting as referee.

"Do try and keep your attention fixed, George," I heard her say severely. "To allow it to wander when high spiritual affairs are under discussion (sneeze) is scarcely reverent. Could you tell the man to shut that door? The draught is dreadful. It is quite impossible for you to agree with both of us, as you say you do, seeing that metaphorically Dr. Jeffreys is at one pole and I am at the other." (Sneeze.)

"Then I wish I were at the Tropic of Cancer," I heard him mutter with a groan.

In vain; he had to keep his "attention fixed" on this point for the next three-quarters of an hour. So as Miss Manners was at the other side of me, and Scroope, unhampered by the presence of any prospective mother-in-law, was at the other side of her, for all practical purposes Miss Holmes and I were left alone.

She began by saying:

"I hear you beat Sir Junius Fortescue out shooting to-day, and won a lot of money from him which you gave to the Cottage Hospital. I don't like shooting, and I don't like betting; and it's strange, because you don't look like a man who bets. But I detest Sir Junius Fortescue, and that is a bond of union between us."

"I never said I detested him."

"No, but I am sure you do. Your face changed when I mentioned his name."

"As it happens, you are right. But, Miss Holmes, I should like you to understand that you were also right when you said I did not look like a betting man." And I told her some of the story of Van Koop and the £250.

"Ah!" she said, when I had finished, "I always felt sure he was a horror. And my mother wanted me, just because he pretended to be low church—but that's a secret."

Then I congratulated her upon her approaching marriage, saying what a joyful thing it was now and again to see everything going in real, happy, storybook fashion: beauty, male and female, united by love, high rank, wealth, troops of friends, health of body, a lovely and an ancient home in a settled land where dangers do not come—at present— respect and affection of crowds of dependants, the prospect of a high and useful career of a sort whereof the door is shut to most people, everything in short that human beings who are not actually royalty could desire or deserve. Indeed after my second glass of champagne I grew quite eloquent on these and kindred points, being moved thereto by memories of the misery that is in the world which formed so great a contrast to the lot of this striking and brilliant pair.

She listened to me attentively and answered:

"Thank you for your kind thoughts and wishes. But does it not strike you, Mr. Quatermain, that there is something ill-omened in such talk? I believe that it does; that as you finished speaking it occurred to you that after all the future is as much veiled from all of us as—as the picture which hangs behind its curtain of rose-coloured silk in Lord Ragnall's study is from you."

"How did you know that?" I asked sharply in a low voice. For by the strangest of coincidences, as I concluded my somewhat old-fashioned little speech of compliments, this very reflection had entered my mind, and with it the memory of the veiled picture which Mr. Savage had pointed out to me on the previous morning.

"I can't say, Mr. Quatermain, but I did know it. You were thinking of the picture, were you not?"

"And if I was," I said, avoiding a direct reply, "what of it? Though it is hidden from everybody else, he has only to draw the curtain and see—you."

"Supposing he should draw the curtain one day and see nothing, Mr. Quatermain?"

"Then the picture would have been stolen, that is all, and he would have to search for it till he found it again, which doubtless sooner or later he would do."

"Yes, sooner or later. But where? Perhaps you have lost a picture or two in your time, Mr. Quatermain, and are better able to answer the question than I am."

There was silence for a few moments, for this talk of lost pictures brought back memories which choked me.

Then she began to speak again, low, quickly, and with suppressed passion, but acting wonderfully all the while. Knowing that eyes were on her, her gestures and the expression of her face were such as might have been those of any young lady of fashion who was talking of everyday affairs, such as dancing, or flowers, or jewels. She smiled and even laughed occasionally. She played with the golden salt-cellar in front of her and, upsetting a little of the salt, threw it over her left shoulder, appearing to ask me if I were a victim of that ancient habit, and so on.

But all the while she was talking deeply of deep things, such as I should never have thought would pass her mind. This was the substance of what she said, for I cannot set it all down verbatim; after so many years my memory fails me.

"I am not like other women. Something moves me to tell you so, something very real and powerful which pushes me as a strong man might. It is odd, because I have never spoken to anyone else like that, not to my mother for instance, or even to Lord Ragnall. They would neither of them understand, although they would misunderstand differently. My mother would think I ought to see a doctor—and if you knew that doctor! He," and she nodded towards Lord Ragnall, "would think that my engagement had upset me, or that I had grown rather more religious than I ought to be at my age, and been reflecting too much— well, on the end of all things. From a child I have understood that I am a mystery set in the midst of many other mysteries. It all came to me one night when I was about nine years old. I seemed to see the past and the future, although I could grasp neither. Such a long, long past and such an infinite future. I don't know what I saw, and still see sometimes. It comes in a flash, and is in a flash forgotten. My mind cannot hold it. It is too big for my mind; you might as well try to pack Dr. Jeffreys there into this wineglass. Only two facts remain written on my heart. The first is that there is trouble ahead of me, curious and unusual trouble; and the second, that permanently, continually, I, or a part of me, have something to do with Africa, a country of which I know nothing except from a few very dull books. Also, by the way—this is a new thought—that I have a great deal to do with *you*. That is why I am so interested in Africa and you. Tell me about Africa and yourself now, while we have the chance." And she ended rather abruptly, adding in a louder voice, "You have lived there all your life, have you not, Mr. Quatermain?"

"I rather think your mother would be right—about the doctor, I mean," I said.

"You *say* that, but you don't *believe* it. Oh! you are very transparent, Mr. Quatermain—at least, to me."

So, hurriedly enough, for these subjects seemed to be uncomfortable, even dangerous in a sense, I began to talk of the first thing about Africa that I remembered—namely, of the legend of the Holy Flower that was guarded by a huge ape, of which I had heard from a white man who was supposed to be rather mad, who went by the name of Brother John. Also I told her that there was something in it, as I had with me a specimen of the flower.

"Oh! show it me," she said.

I replied that I feared I could not, as it was locked away in a safe in London, whither I was returning on the morrow. I promised, however, to send her a life-sized water-colour drawing of which I had caused several to be made. She asked me if I were going to look for this flower, and I said that I hoped so if I could make the necessary arrangements. Next she asked me if there chanced to be any other African quests upon which I had set my mind. I replied that there were several. For instance, I had heard vaguely through Brother John, and indirectly from one or two other sources, of the existence of a certain tribe in East Central Africa—Arabs or semi-Arabs—who were reported to worship a child that always remained a child. This child, I took it, was a dwarf; but as I was interested in native religious customs which were infinite in their variety, I should much like to find out the truth of the matter.

"Talking of Arabs," she broke in, "I will tell you a curious story. Once when I was a little girl, eight or nine years of age—it was just before that kind of awakening of which I have spoken to you—I was playing in Kensington Gardens, for we lived in London at the time, in the charge of my nurse-governess. She was talking to some young man who she said was her cousin, and told me to run about with my hoop and not to bother. I drove the hoop across the grass to some elm trees. From behind one of the trees came out two tall men dressed in white robes and turbans, who looked to me like scriptural characters in a picture-book. One was an elderly man with flashing, black eyes, hooked nose, and a long grey beard. The other was much younger, but I do not remember him so well. They were both brown in colour, but otherwise almost like white men; not Negroes by any means. My hoop hit the elder man, and I stood still, not knowing what to say. He bowed politely and picked it up, but did not offer to return it to me. They talked together rapidly, and one of them pointed to the moon-shaped birthmark which you see I have upon my neck, for it was hot weather, and I was wearing a low-cut frock. It was because of this mark that my father named me Luna. The elder of the two said in broken English:

"'What is your name, pretty little girl?'

"I told him it was Luna Holmes. Then he drew from his robe a box made of scented wood, and, opening it, took out some sweetmeat which looked as if it had been frozen, and gave me a piece that, being very fond of sweet, I put into my mouth. Next, he bowled the hoop along the ground into the shadow of the trees—it was evening time and beginning to grow dark—saying, 'Run, catch it, little girl!'

"I began to run, but something in the taste of that sweet caused me to drop it from my lips. Then all grew misty, and the next thing I remember was finding myself in the arms of the younger Eastern, with the nurse and her 'cousin,' a stalwart person like a soldier, standing in front of us.

"'Little girl go ill,' said the elder Arab. 'We seek policeman.'

"'You drop that child,' answered the 'cousin,' doubling his fists. Then I grew faint again, and when I came to myself the two white-robed men had gone. All the way home my governess scolded me for accepting sweets from strangers, saying that if my parents came to know of it, I should be whipped and sent to bed. Of course, I begged her not to tell them, and at last she consented. Do you know, I think you are the first to whom I have ever mentioned the matter, of which I am sure the governess never breathed a word, though after that, whenever we walked in the gardens, her 'cousin' always came to look after us. In the end I think she married him."

"You believe the sweet was drugged?" I asked.

She nodded. "There was something very strange in it. It was a night or two after I had tasted it that I had what just now I called my awakening, and began to think about Africa."

"Have you ever seen these men again, Miss Holmes?"

"No, never."

At this moment I heard Lady Longden say, in a severe voice:

"My dear Luna, I am sorry to interrupt your absorbing conversation, but we are all waiting for you."

So they were, for to my horror I saw that everyone was standing up except ourselves.

Miss Holmes departed in a hurry, while Scroope whispered in my ear with a snigger:

"I say, Allan, if you carry on like that with his young lady, his lordship will be growing jealous of you."

"Don't be a fool," I said sharply. But there was something in his remark, for as Lord Ragnall passed on his way to the other end of the table, he said in a low voice and with rather a forced smile:

"Well, Quatermain, I hope your dinner has not been as dull as mine, although your appetite seemed so poor."

Then I reflected that I could not remember having eaten a thing since the first entrée. So overcome was I that, rejecting all Scroope's attempts at conversation, I sat silent, drinking port and filling up with dates, until not long afterwards we went into the drawing-room, where I sat down as far from Miss Holmes as possible, and looked at a book of views of Jerusalem.

While I was thus engaged, Lord Ragnall, pitying my lonely condition, or being instigated thereto by Miss Holmes, I know not which, came up and began to chat with me about African big-game shooting. Also he asked me what was my permanent address in that country. I told him Durban, and in my turn asked why he wanted to know.

"Because Miss Holmes seems quite crazy about the place, and I expect I shall be dragged out there one day," he replied, quite gloomily. It was a prophetic remark.

At this moment our conversation was interrupted by Lady Longden, who came to bid her future son-in-law good night. She said that she must go to bed, and put her feet in mustard and water as her cold was so bad, which left me wondering whether she meant to carry out this operation in bed. I recommended her to take quinine, a suggestion she acknowledged rather inconsequently by remarking in somewhat icy tones that she supposed I sat up to all hours of the night in Africa. I replied that frequently I did, waiting for the sun to rise next day, for that member of the British aristocracy irritated me.

Thus we parted, and I never saw her again. She died many years ago, poor soul, and I suppose is now freezing her former acquaintances in the Shades, for I cannot imagine that she ever had a friend. They talk a great deal about the influences of heredity nowadays, but I don't believe very much in them myself. Who, for instance, could conceive that persons so utterly different in every way as Lady Longden and her daughter, Miss Holmes, could be mother and child? Our bodies, no doubt, we do inherit from our ancestors, but not our individualities. These come from far away.

A good many of the guests went at the same time, having long distances to drive on that cold frosty night, although it was only just ten o'clock. For as was usual at that period even in fashionable houses, we had dined at seven.

Harût and Marût

After Lord Ragnall had seen his guests to the door in the old-fashioned manner, he returned and asked me if I played cards, or whether I preferred music. I was assuring him that I hated the sight of a card when Mr. Savage appeared in his silent way and respectfully inquired of his lordship whether any gentleman was staying in the house whose Christian name was *Here-come-a-zany*. Lord Ragnall looked at him with a searching eye as though he suspected him of being drunk, and then asked what he meant by such a ridiculous question.

"I mean, my lord," replied Mr. Savage with a touch of offence in his tone, "that two foreign individuals in white clothes have arrived at the castle, stating that they wish to speak at once with a *Mr. Here-come-a-zany* who is staying here. I told them to go away as the butler said he could make nothing of their talk, but they only sat down in the snow and said they would wait for *Here-come-a-zany*."

"Then you had better put them in the old guardroom, lock them up with something to eat, and send the stable-boy for the policeman, who is a zany if ever anybody was. I expect they are after the pheasants."

"Stop a bit," I said, for an idea had occurred to me. "The message may be meant for me, though I can't conceive who sent it. My native name is Macumazana, which possibly Mr. Savage has not caught quite correctly. Shall I go to see these men?"

"I wouldn't do that in this cold, Quatermain," Lord Ragnall answered. "Did they say what they are, Savage?"

"I made out that they were conjurers, my lord. At least when I told them to go away one of them said, 'You will go first, gentleman.' Then, my lord, I heard a hissing sound in my coat-tail pocket and, putting my hand into it, I found a large snake which dropped on the ground and vanished. It quite paralysed me, my lord, and while I stood there wondering whether I was bitten, a mouse jumped out of the kitchenmaid's hair. She had been laughing at their dress, my lord, but *now* she's screaming in hysterics."

The solemn aspect of Mr. Savage as he narrated these unholy marvels was such that, like the kitchenmaid, we both burst into ill-timed merriment. Attracted by our laughter, Miss Holmes, Miss Manners, with whom she was talking, and some of the other guests, approached and asked what was the matter.

"Savage here declares that there are two conjurers in the kitchen premises, who have been producing snakes out of his pocket and mice from the hair of one of the maids, and who want to see Mr. Quatermain," Lord Ragnall answered.

"Conjurers! Oh, do have them in, George," exclaimed Miss Holmes; while Miss Manners and the others, who were getting a little tired of promiscuous conversation, echoed her request.

"By all means," he answered, "though we have enough mice here without their bringing any more. Savage, go and tell your two friends that *Mr. Here-come-a-zany* is waiting for them in the drawing-room, and that the company would like to see some of their tricks."

Savage bowed and departed, like a hero to execution, for by his pallor I could see that he was in a great fright. When he had gone we set to work and cleared a space in the middle of the room, in front of which we arranged chairs for the company to sit on.

"No doubt they are Indian jugglers," said Lord Ragnall, "and will want a place to grow their mango-tree, as I remember seeing them do in Kashmir."

As he spoke the door opened and Mr. Savage appeared through it, walking much faster than was his wont. I noted also that he gripped the pockets of his swallow-tail coat firmly in his hand.

"Mr. Hare-root and Mr. Mare-root," he announced.

"Hare-root and Mare-root!" repeated Lord Ragnall.

"Harût and Marût, I expect," I said. "I think I have read somewhere that they were great magicians, whose names these conjurers have taken." (Since then I have discovered that they are mentioned in the Koran as masters of the Black Art.)

A moment later two men followed him through the doorway. The first was a tall, Eastern-looking person with a grave countenance, a long, white beard, a hooked nose, and flashing, hawk-like eyes. The second was shorter and rather stout, also much younger. He had a genial, smiling face, small, beady-black eyes, and was clean-shaven. They were very light in colour; indeed I have seen Italians who are much darker; and there was about their whole aspect a certain air of power.

Instantly I remembered the story that Miss Holmes had told me at dinner and looked at her covertly, to see that she had turned quite pale and was trembling a little. I do not think that anyone else noticed this, however, as all were staring at the strangers. Moreover she recovered herself in a moment, and, catching my eye, laid her finger on her lips in token of silence.

The men were clothed in thick, fur-lined cloaks, which they took off and, folding them neatly, laid upon the floor, standing revealed in robes of a beautiful whiteness and in large plain turbans, also white.

"High-class Somali Arabs," thought I to myself, noting the while that as they arranged the robes they were taking in every one of us with their quick eyes. One of them shut the door, leaving Savage on this side of it as though they meant him to be present. Then they walked towards us, each of them carrying an ornamental basket made apparently of split reeds, that contained doubtless their conjuring outfit and probably the snake which Savage had found in his pocket. To my surprise they came straight to me, and, having set down the baskets, lifted their hands above their heads, as a person about to dive might do, and bowed till the points of their fingers touched the floor. Next they spoke, not in Arabic as I had expected that they would, but in Bantu, which of course I understood perfectly well.

"I, Harût, head priest and doctor of the White Kendah People, greet you, O Macumazana," said the elder man.

"I, Marût, a priest and doctor of the People of the White Kendah, greet you, O Watcher-by-night, whom we have travelled far to find," said the younger man. Then together,

"We both greet you, O Lord, who seem small but are great, O Chief with a troubled past and with a mighty future, O Beloved of Mameena who has 'gone down' but still speaks from beneath, Mameena who was and is of our company."

At this point it was my turn to shiver and become pale, as any may guess who may have chanced to read the history of Mameena, and the turn of Miss Holmes to watch *me* with animated interest.

"O Slayer of evil men and beasts!" they went on, in their rich-voiced, monotonous chant, "who, as our magic tells us, are destined to deliver our land from the terrible scourge, we greet you, we bow before you, we acknowledge you as our lord and brother, to whom we vow safety among us and in the desert, to whom we promise a great reward."

Again they bowed, once, twice, thrice; then stood silent before me with folded arms.

"What on earth are they saying?" asked Scroope. "I could catch a few words"—he knew a little kitchen Zulu—"but not much."

I told him briefly while the others listened.

"What does Mameena mean?" asked Miss Holmes, with a horrible acuteness. "Is it a woman's name?"

Hearing her, Harût and Marût bowed as though doing reverence to that name. I am sorry to say that at this point I grew confused, though really there was no reason why I should, and muttered something about a native girl who had made trouble in her day.

Miss Holmes and the other ladies looked at me with amused disbelief, and to my dismay the venerable Harût turned to Miss Holmes, and with his inevitable bow, said in broken English:

"Mameena very beautiful woman, perhaps more beautiful than you, lady. Mameena love the white lord Macumazana. She love him while she live, she love him now she dead. She tell me so again just now. You ask white lord tell you pretty story of how he kiss her before she kill herself."

Needless to say all this very misleading information was received by the audience with an attention that I can but call rapt, and in a kind of holy silence which was broken only by a sudden burst of sniggering on the part of Scroope. I favoured him with my fiercest frown. Then I fell upon that venerable villain Harût, and belaboured him in Bantu, while the audience listened as intently as though they understood.

I asked him what he meant by coming here to asperse my character. I asked him who the deuce he was. I asked him how he came to know anything about Mameena, and finally I told him that soon or late I would be even with him, and paused exhausted.

He stood there looking for all the world like a statue of the patriarch Job as I imagine him, and when I had done, replied without moving a muscle and in English:

"O Lord, Zikali, Zulu wizard, friend of mine! All great wizard friend just like all elephant and all snake. Zikali make me know Mameena, and she tell me story and send you much love, and say she wait for you always." (More sniggers from Scroope, and still intenser interest evinced by Miss Holmes and others.) "If you like, I show you Mameena 'fore I go." (Murmurs from Miss Holmes and Miss Manners of "Oh, *please* do!") "But that very little business, for what one long-ago lady out of so many?"

Then suddenly he broke into Bantu, and added: "A jest is a jest, Macumazana, though often there is meaning in a jest, and you shall see Mameena if you will. I come here to ask you to do my people a service for which you shall not lack reward. We, the White Kendah, the People of the Child, are at war with the Black Kendah, our subjects who outnumber us. The Black Kendah have an evil spirit for a god, which spirit from the beginning has dwelt in the largest elephant in all the world, a beast that none can kill, but which kills many and bewitches more. While that elephant, which is named Jana, lives we, the People of the Child, go in terror, for day by day it destroys us. We have learned—how it does not matter—that you alone can kill that elephant. If you will come and kill it, we will show you the place where all the elephants go to die, and you shall take their ivory, many wagon-loads, and grow rich. Soon you are going on a journey that has to do with a flower, and you will visit peoples named the Mazitu and the Pongo who live on an island in a lake. Far beyond the Pongo and across the desert dwell my people, the Kendah, in a secret land. When you wish to visit us, as you will do, journey to the north of that lake where the Pongo dwell, and stay there on the edge of the desert shooting till we come. Now mock me if you will, but do not forget, for these things shall befall in their season, though that time be far. If we meet no more for a while, still do not forget. When you have need of gold or of the ivory that is gold, then journey to the north of the lake where the Pongo dwell, and call on the names of Harût and Marût."

"And call on the names of Harût and Marût," repeated the younger man, who hitherto appeared to take no interest in our talk.

Next, before I could answer, before I could think the thing out indeed, for all this breath from savage and mystical Africa blowing on me suddenly here in an Essex drawing-room, seemed to overwhelm me, the ineffable Harût proceeded in his English conjurer's patter:

"Rich ladies and gentlemen want see trick by poor old wizard from centre Africa. Well, we show them, but please 'member no magic, all quite simple trick. Teach it you if you pay. Please not look too hard, no want you learn how it done. What you like see? Tree grow out of nothing, eh? Good! Please lend me that plate—what you call him—china."

Then the performance began. The tree grew admirably upon the china plate under the cover of an antimacassar. A number of bits of stick danced together on the said plate, apparently without being touched. At a whistle from Marût a second snake crawled out of the pocket of the horrified Mr. Savage, who stood observing these proceedings at a respectful distance, erected itself on its tail upon the plate and took fire till it was consumed to ashes, and so forth.

The show was very good, but to tell the truth I did not take much notice of it, for I had seen similar things before and was engaged in thoughts much excited by what Harût had said to me. At length the pair paused amidst the clapping of the audience, and Marût began to pack up the properties as though all were done. Then Harût observed casually:

"The Lord Macumazana think this poor business and he right. Very poor business, any conjurer do better. All common trick"—here his eye fell upon Mr. Savage who was wriggling uneasily in the background. "What matter with that gentleman? Brother Marût, go see."

Brother Marût went and freed Mr. Savage from two more snakes which seemed to have taken possession of various parts of his garments. Also, amidst shouts of laughter, from a large dead rat which he appeared to draw from his well-oiled hair.

"Ah!" said Harût, as his confederate returned with these prizes, leaving Savage collapsed in a chair, "snake love that gentleman much. He earn great money in Africa. Well, he keep rat in hair; hungry snake always want rat. But as I say, this poor business. Now you like to see some better, eh? Mameena, eh?"

"No," I replied firmly, whereat everyone laughed.

"Elephant Jana we want you kill, eh? Just as he look this minute."

"Yes," I said, "very much indeed, only how will you show it me?"

"That quite easy, Macumazana. You just smoke little Kendah 'bacco and see many things, if you have gift, as I *think* you got, and as I almost *sure* that lady got," and he pointed to Miss Holmes. "Sometimes they things people want see, and sometimes they things people not want see."

"Dakka," I said contemptuously, alluding to the Indian hemp on which natives make themselves drunk throughout great districts of Africa.

"Oh! no, not dakka, that common stuff; this 'bacco much better than dakka, only grow in Kendah-land. You think all nonsense? Well, you see. Give me match please."

Then while we watched he placed some tobacco, at least it looked like tobacco, in a little wooden bowl that he also produced from his basket. Next he said something to his companion, Marût, who drew a flute from his robe made out of a thick reed, and began to play on it a wild and melancholy music, the sound of which seemed to affect my backbone as standing on a great height often does. Presently too Harût broke into a low song whereof I could not understand a word, that rose and fell with the music of the flute. Now he struck a match, which seemed incongruous in the midst of this semi-magical ceremony, and taking a pinch of the tobacco, lit it and dropped it among the rest. A pale, blue smoke arose from the bowl and with it a very sweet odour not unlike that of the tuberoses gardeners grow in hot-houses, but more searching.

"Now you breath smoke, Macumazana," he said, "and tell us what you see. Oh! no fear, that not hurt you. Just like cigarette. Look," and he inhaled some of the vapour and blew it out through his nostrils, after which his face seemed to change to me, though what the change was I could not define.

I hesitated till Scroope said:

"Come, Allan, don't shirk this Central African adventure. I'll try if you like."

"No," said Harût brusquely, "*you* no good."

Then curiosity and perhaps the fear of being laughed at overcame me. I took the bowl and held it under my nose, while Harût threw over my head the antimacassar which he had used in the mango trick, to keep in the fumes I suppose.

At first these fumes were unpleasant, but just as I was about to drop the bowl they seemed to become agreeable and to penetrate to the inmost recesses of my being. The general affect of them was not unlike that of the laughing gas which dentists give, with this difference, that whereas the gas produces insensibility, these fumes seemed to set the mind on fire and to burn away all limitations of time and distance. Things shifted before me. It was as though I were no longer in that room but travelling with inconceivable rapidity.

Suddenly I appeared to stop before a curtain of mist. The mist rolled up in front of me and I saw a wild and wonderful scene. There lay a lake surrounded by dense African forest. The sky above was still red with the last lights of sunset and in it floated the full moon. On the eastern side of the lake was a great open space where nothing seemed to grow and all about this space were the skeletons of hundreds of dead elephants. There they lay, some of them almost covered with grey mosses hanging to their bones, through which their yellow tusks projected as though they had been dead for centuries; others with the rotting hide still on them. I knew that I was looking on a cemetery of elephants, the place where these great beasts went to die, as I have since been told the extinct moas did in New Zealand. All my life as a hunter had I heard rumours of these cemeteries, but never before did I see such a spot even in a dream.

See! There was one dying now, a huge gaunt bull that looked as though it were several hundred years old. It stood there swaying to and fro. Then it lifted its trunk, I suppose to trumpet, though of course I could hear nothing, and slowly sank upon its knees and so remained in the last relaxation of death.

Almost in the centre of this cemetery was a little mound of water- washed rock that had endured when the rest of the stony plain was denuded in past epochs. Suddenly upon that rock appeared the shape of the most gigantic elephant that ever I beheld in all my long experience. It had one enormous tusk, but the other was deformed and broken off short. Its sides were scarred as though with fighting and its eyes shone red and wickedly. Held in its trunk was the body of a woman whose hair hung down upon one side and whose feet hung down upon the other. Clasped in her arms was a child that seemed to be still living.

The rogue, as a brute of this sort is called, for evidently such it was, dropped the corpse to the ground and stood a while, flapping its ears. Then it felt for and picked up the child with its trunk, swung it to and fro and finally tossed it high into the air, hurling it far away. After this it walked to the elephant that I had just seen die, and charged the carcass, knocking it over. Then having lifted its trunk as though to trumpet in triumph, it shambled off towards the forest and vanished.

The curtain of mist fell again and in it, dimly, I thought I saw— well, never mind who or what I saw. Then I awoke.

"Well, did you see anything?" asked a chorus of voices.

I told them what I had seen, leaving out the last part.

"I say, old fellow," said Scroope, "you must have been pretty clever to get all that in, for your eyes weren't shut for more than ten seconds."

"Then I wonder what you would say if I repeated everything," I answered, for I still felt dreamy and not quite myself.

"You see elephant Jana?" asked Harût. "He kill woman and child, eh? Well, he do that every night. Well, that why people of White Kendah want you to kill *him* and take all that ivory which they no dare touch because it in holy place and Black Kendah not let them. So he live still. That what we wish know. Thank you much, Macumazana. You very good look through-distance man. Just what I think. Kendah 'bacco smoke work very well in you. Now, beautiful lady," he added turning to Miss Holmes, "you like look too? Better look. Who knows what you see?"

Miss Holmes hesitated a moment, studying me with an inquiring eye. But I made no sign, being in truth very curious to hear *her* experience.

"Yes," she said.

"I would prefer, Luna, that you left this business alone," remarked Lord Ragnall uneasily. "I think it is time that you ladies went to bed."

"Here is a match," said Miss Holmes to Harût who was engaged in putting more tobacco into the bowl, the suspicion of a smile upon his grave and statuesque countenance. Harût received the match with a low bow and fired the stuff as before. Then he handed the bowl, from which once again the blue smoke curled upwards, to Miss Holmes, and gently and gracefully let the antimacassar fall over it and her head, which it draped as a wedding veil might do. A few seconds later she threw off the antimacassar and cast the bowl, in which the fire was now out, on to the floor. Then she stood up with wide eyes, looking wondrous lovely and, notwithstanding her lack of height, majestic.

"I have been in another world," she said in a low voice as though she spoke to the air, "I have travelled a great way. I found myself in a small place made of stone. It was dark in the place, the fire in that bowl lit it up. There was nothing there except a beautiful statue of a naked baby which seemed to be carved in yellow ivory, and a chair made of ebony inlaid with ivory and seated with string. I stood in front of the statue of the Ivory Child. It seemed to come to life and smile at me. Round its neck was a string of red stones. It took them from its neck and set them upon mine. Then it pointed to the chair, and I sat down in the chair. That was all."

Harût followed her words with an interest that I could see was intense, although he attempted to hide it. Then he asked me to translate them, which I did.

As their full sense came home to him, although his face remained impassive, I saw his dark eyes shine with the light of triumph. Moreover I heard him whisper to Marût words that seemed to mean,

"The Sacred Child accepts the Guardian. The Spirit of the White Kendah finds a voice again."

Then as though involuntarily, but with the utmost reverence, both of them bowed deeply towards Miss Holmes.

A babel of conversation broke out.

"What a ridiculous dream," I heard Lord Ragnall say in a vexed voice. "An ivory child that seemed to come to life and to give you a necklace. Whoever heard such nonsense?"

"Whoever heard such nonsense?" repeated Miss Holmes after him, as though in polite acquiescence, but speaking as an automaton might speak.

"I say," interrupted Scroope, addressing Miss Manners, "this is a drawing-room entertainment and a half, isn't it, dear?"

"I don't know," answered Miss Manners, doubtfully, "it is rather too queer for my taste. Tricks are all very well, but when it comes to magic and visions I get frightened."

"Well, I suppose the show is over," said Lord Ragnall. "Quatermain, would you mind asking your conjurer friends what I owe them?"

Here Harût, who had understood, paused from packing up his properties and answered,

"Nothing, O great Lord, nothing. It is we owe you much. Here we learn what we want know long time. I mean if elephant Jana still kill people of Kendah. Kendah 'bacco no speak to us. Only speak to new spirit. You got great gift, lady, and you too, Macumazana. You not like smoke more Kendah 'bacco and look into past, eh? Better look! Very full, past, learn much there about all us; learn how things begin. Make you understand lot what seem odd to-day. No! Well, one day you look p'raps, 'cause past pull hard and call loud, only no one hear what it say. Good night, O great Lord. Good night, O beautiful lady. Good night, O Macumazana, till we meet again when you come kill elephant Jana. Blessing of the Heaven-Child, who give rain, who protect all danger, who give food, who give health, on you all."

Then making many obeisances they walked backwards to the door where they put on their long cloaks.

At a sign from Lord Ragnall I accompanied them, an office which, fearing more snakes, Mr. Savage was very glad to resign to me. Presently we stood outside the house amidst the moaning trees, and very cold it was there.

"What does all this mean, O men of Africa?" I asked.

"Answer the question yourself when you stand face to face with the great elephant Jana that has in it an evil spirit, O Macumazana," replied Harût. "Nay, listen. We are far from our home and we sought tidings through those who could give it to us, and we have won those tidings, that is all. We are worshippers of the Heavenly Child that is eternal youth and all good things, but of late the Child has lacked a tongue. Yet to-night it spoke again. Seek to know no more, you who in due season will know all things."

"Seek to know no more," echoed Marût, "who already, perhaps, know too much, lest harm should come to you, Macumazana."

"Where are you going to sleep to-night?" I asked.

"We do not sleep here," answered Harût, "we walk to the great city and thence find our way to Africa, where we shall meet you again. You know that we are no liars, common readers of thought and makers of tricks, for did not Dogeetah, the wandering white man, speak to you of the people of whom he had heard who worshipped the Child of Heaven? Go in, Macumazana, ere you take harm in this horrible cold, and take with you this as a marriage gift from the Child of Heaven whom she met to-night, to the beautiful lady stamped with the sign of the young moon who is about to marry the great lord she loves."

Then he thrust a little linen-wrapped parcel into my hand and with his companion vanished into the darkness.

I returned to the drawing-room where the others were still discussing the remarkable performance of the two native conjurers.

"They have gone," I said in answer to Lord Ragnall, "to walk to London as they said. But they have sent a wedding-present to Miss Holmes," and I showed the parcel.

"Open it, Quatermain," he said again.

"No, George," interrupted Miss Holmes, laughing, for by now she seemed to have quite recovered herself, "I like to open my own presents."

He shrugged his shoulders and I handed her the parcel, which was neatly sewn up. Somebody produced scissors and the stitches were cut. Within the linen was a necklace of beautiful red stones, oval-shaped like amber beads and of the size of a robin's egg. They were roughly polished and threaded on what I recognized at once to be hair from an elephant's tail. From certain indications I judged these stones, which might have been spinels or carbuncles, or even rubies, to be very ancient. Possibly they had once hung round the neck of some lady in old Egypt. Indeed a beautiful little statuette, also of red stone, which was suspended from the centre of the necklace, suggested that this was so, for it may well have been a likeness of one of the great gods of the Egyptians, the infant Horus, the son of Isis.

"That is the necklace I saw which the Ivory Child gave me in my dream," said Miss Holmes quietly.

Then with much deliberation she clasped it round her throat.

The Plot

The sequel to the events of this evening may be told very briefly and of it the reader can form his own judgment. I narrate it as it happened.

That night I did not sleep at all well. It may have been because of the excitement of the great shoot in which I found myself in competition with another man whom I disliked and who had defrauded me in the past, to say nothing of its physical strain in cold and heavy weather. Or it may have been that my imagination was stirred by the arrival of that strange pair, Harût and Marût, apparently in search of myself, seven thousand miles away from any place where they can have known aught of an insignificant individual with a purely local repute. Or it may have been that the pictures which they showed me when under the influence of the fumes of their "tobacco"—or of their hypnotism— took an undue possession of my brain.

Or lastly, the strange coincidence that the beautiful betrothed of my host should have related to me a tale of her childhood of which she declared she had never spoken before, and that within an hour the two principal actors in that tale should have appeared before my eyes and hers (for I may state that from the beginning I had no doubt that they were the same men), moved me and filled me with quite natural foreboding. Or all these things together may have tended to a concomitant effect. At any rate the issue was that I could not sleep.

For hour after hour I lay thinking and in an irritated way listening for the chimes of the Ragnall stable-clock which once had adorned the tower of the church and struck the quarters with a damnable reiteration. I concluded that Messrs. Harût and Marût were a couple of common Arab rogues such as I had seen performing at the African ports. Then a quarter struck and I concluded that the elephants' cemetery which I beheld in the smoke undoubtedly existed and that I meant to collar those thousands of pounds' worth of ivory before I died. Then after another quarter I concluded that there was no elephants' cemetery—although by the way my old friend, Dogeetah or Brother John, had mentioned such a thing to me—but that probably there was a tribe, as he had also mentioned, called the Kendah, who worshipped a baby, or rather its effigy.

Well now, as had already occurred to me, the old Egyptians, of whom I was always fond of reading when I got a chance, also worshipped a child, Horus the Saviour. And that child had a mother called Isis symbolized in the crescent moon, the great Nature goddess, the mistress of mysteries to whose cult ten thousand priests were sworn— do not Herodotus and others, especially Apuleius, tell us all about her? And by a queer coincidence Miss Holmes had the mark of a crescent moon upon her breast. And when she was a child those two men, or others very like them, had pointed out that mark to each other. And I had seen them staring hard at it that night. And in her vapour-invoked dream the "Heavenly Child," *alias* Horus, or the double of Horus, the *Ka*, I think the Egyptians called it, had awakened at the sight of her and kissed her and given her the necklace of the goddess, and—all the rest. What did it mean?

I went to sleep at last wondering what on earth it *could* mean, till presently that confounded clock woke me up again and I must go through the whole business once more.

By degrees, this was towards dawn, I became aware that all hope of rest had vanished from me utterly; that I was most painfully awake, and what is more, oppressed by a curious fear to the effect that something was going to happen to Miss Holmes. So vivid did this fear become that at length I arose, lit a candle and dressed myself. As it happened I knew where Miss Holmes slept. Her room, which I had seen her enter, was on the same corridor as mine though at the other end of it near the head of a stair that ran I knew not whither. In my portmanteau that had been sent over from Miss Manners's house, amongst other things was a small double-barrelled pistol which from long habit I always carried with me loaded, except for the caps that were in a little leather case with some spare ammunition attached to the pistol belt. I took it out, capped it and thrust it into my pocket. Then I slipped from the room and stood behind a tall clock in the corridor, watching Miss Holmes's door and reflecting what a fool I should look if anyone chanced to find me.

Half an hour or so later by the light of the setting moon which struggled through a window, I saw the door open and Miss Holmes emerge in a kind of dressing-gown and still wearing the necklace which Harût and Marût had given her. Of this I was sure for the light gleamed upon the red stones.

Also it shone upon her face and showed me without doubt that she was walking in her sleep.

Gliding as silently as a ghost she crossed the corridor and vanished. I followed and saw that she had descended an ancient, twisting stairway which I had noted in the castle wall. I went after her, my stockinged feet making no noise, feeling my way carefully in the darkness of the stair, for I did not dare to strike a match. Beneath me I heard a noise as of someone fumbling with bolts. Then a door creaked on its hinges and there was some light. When I reached the doorway I caught sight of the figure of Miss Holmes flitting across a hollow garden that was laid out in the bottom of the castle moat which had been drained. The garden, as I had observed when we walked through it on the previous day on our way to the first covert that we shot, was bordered by a shrubbery through which ran paths that led to the back drive of the castle.

Across the garden glided the figure of Miss Holmes and after it went I, crouching and taking cover behind every bush as though I were stalking big game, which indeed I was. She entered the shrubbery, moving much more swiftly now, for as she went she seemed to gather speed, like a stone which is rolled down a hill. It was as though whatever might be attracting her, for I felt sure that she was being drawn by something, acted more strongly upon her sleeping will as she drew nearer to it. For a while I lost sight of her in the shadow of the tall trees. Then suddenly I saw her again, standing quite still in an opening caused by the blowing down in the gale of one of the avenue of elms that bordered the back drive. But now she was no longer alone, for advancing towards her were two cloaked figures in whom I recognized Harût and Marût.

There she stood with outstretched arms, and towards her, stealthily as lions stalking a buck, came Harût and Marût. Moreover, between the naked boughs of the fallen elm I caught sight of what looked like the outline of a closed carriage standing upon the drive. Also I heard a horse stamp upon the frosty ground. Round the edge of the little glade I ran, keeping in the dark shadow, as I went cocking the pistol that was in my pocket. Then suddenly I darted out and stood between Harût and Marût and Miss Holmes.

Not a word passed between us. I think that all three of us subconsciously were anxious not to awake the sleeping woman, knowing that if we did so there would be a terrible scene. Only after motioning to me to stand aside, of course in vain, Harût and Marût drew from their robes curved and cruel-looking knives and bowed, for even now their politeness did not forsake them. I bowed back and when I straightened myself those enterprising Easterns found that I was covering the heart of Harût with my pistol. Then with that perception which is part of the mental outfit of the great, they saw that the game was up since I could have shot them both before a knife touched me.

"You have won this time, O Watcher-by-Night," whispered Harût softly, "but another time you will lose. That beautiful lady belongs to us and the People of the White Kendah, for she is marked with the holy mark of the young moon. The call of the Child of Heaven is heard in her heart, and will bring her home to the Child as it has brought her to us to-night. Now lead her hence still sleeping, O brave and clever one, so well named Watcher-by-Night."

Then they were gone and presently I heard the sound of horses being driven rapidly along the drive.

For a moment I hesitated as to whether I would or would not run in and shoot those horses. Two considerations stayed me. The first was that if I did so my pistol would be empty, or even if I shot one horse and retained a barrel loaded, with it I could only kill a single man, leaving myself defenceless against the knife of the other. The second consideration was that now as before I did not wish to wake up Miss Holmes.

I crept to her and not knowing what else to do, took hold of one of her outstretched hands. She turned and came with me at once as though she knew me, remaining all the while fast asleep. Thus we went back to the house, through the still open door, up the stairway straight to her own room, on the threshold of which I loosed her hand. The room was dark and I could see nothing, but I listened until I heard a sound as of a person throwing herself upon the bed and drawing up the blankets. Then knowing that she was safe for a while, I shut the door, which opened outwards as doors of ancient make sometimes do, and set against it a little table that stood in the passage.

Next, after reflecting for a minute, the circumstances being awkward in many ways, I went to my room and lit a candle. Obviously it was my duty to inform Lord Ragnall of what had happened and that as soon as possible. But I had no idea in what part of that huge building his sleeping place might be, nor, for patent reasons, was it desirable that I should disturb the house and so create talk. In this dilemma I remembered that Lord Ragnall's confidential servant, Mr. Savage, when he conducted me to my room on the previous night, which he made a point of doing perhaps because he wished to talk over the matter of the snakes that had found their way into his pockets, had shown me a bell in it which he said rang outside his door. He called it an "emergency bell." I remarked idly that it was improbable that I should have any occasion for its use.

"Who knows, sir?" said Mr. Savage prophetically. "There are folk who say that this old castle is haunted, which after what I have seen to-night I can well believe. If you should chance to meet a ghost looking, let us say, like those black villains, Harum and Scarum, or whatever they call themselves—well, sir, two's better company than one."

I considered that bell but was loath to ring it for the reasons I have given. Then I went outside the room and looked. As I had hoped might be the case, there ran the wire on the face of the wall connected along its length by other wires with the various rooms it passed.

I set to work and followed that wire. It was not an easy job; indeed once or twice it reminded me of that story of the old Greek hero who found his way through a labyrinth by means of a silken thread. I forget whether it were a bull or a lady he was looking for, but with care and perseverance he found one or the other, or it may have been both.

Down staircases and various passages I went with my eye glued upon the wire, which occasionally got mixed up with other wires, till at length it led me through a swing door covered with red baize into what appeared to be a modern annexe to the castle. Here at last it terminated on the spring of an alarming-looking and deep-throated bell that hung immediately over a certain door.

On this door I knocked, hoping that it might be that of Mr. Savage and praying earnestly that it did not enclose the chaste resting-place of the cook or any other female. Too late, I mean after I had knocked, it occurred to me that if so my position would be painful to a degree. However in this particular Fortune stood my friend, which does not always happen to the virtuous. For presently I heard a voice which I recognized as that of Mr. Savage, asking, not without a certain quaver in its tone,

"Who the devil is that?"

"Me," I replied, being flustered.

"'Me' won't do," said the voice. 'Me' might be Harum or it might be Scarum, or it might be someone worse. Who's 'Me'?"

"Allan Quatermain, you idiot," I whispered through the keyhole.

"Anna who? Well, never mind. Go away, Hanna. I'll talk to you in the morning."

Then I kicked the door, and at length, very cautiously, Mr. Savage opened it.

"Good heavens, sir," he said, "what are you doing here, sir? Dressed too, at this hour, and with the handle of a pistol sticking out of your pocket—or is it—the head of a snake?" and he jumped back, a strange and stately figure in a long white nightshirt which apparently he wore over his underclothing.

I entered the room and shut the door, whereon he politely handed me a chair, remarking,

"Is it ghosts, sir, or are you ill, or is it Harum and Scarum, of whom I have been thinking all night? Very cold too, sir, being afraid to pull up the bedclothes for fear lest there might be more reptiles in them." He pointed to his dress-coat hanging on the back of another chair with both the pockets turned inside out, adding tragically, "To think, sir, that this new coat has been a nest of snakes, which I have hated like poison from a child, and me almost a teetotaller!"

"Yes," I said impatiently, "it's Harum and Scarum as you call them. Take me to Lord Ragnall's bedroom at once."

"Ah! sir, burgling, I suppose, or mayhap worse," he exclaimed as he threw on some miscellaneous garments and seized a life-preserver which hung upon a hook. "Now I'm ready, only I hope they have left their snakes behind. I never could bear the sight of a snake, and they seem to know it—the brutes."

In due course we reached Lord Ragnall's room, which Mr. Savage entered, and in answer to a stifled inquiry exclaimed,

"Mr. Allan Quatermain to see you, my lord."

"What is it, Quatermain?" he asked, sitting up in bed and yawning. "Have you had a nightmare?"

"Yes," I answered, and Savage having left us and shut the door, I told him everything as it is written down.

"Great heavens!" he exclaimed when I had finished. "If it had not been for you and your intuition and courage——"

"Never mind me," I interrupted. "The question is—what should be done now? Are you going to try to arrest these men, or will you—hold your tongue and merely cause them to be watched?"

"Really I don't know. Even if we can catch them the whole story would sound so strange in a law-court, and all sorts of things might be suggested."

"Yes, Lord Ragnall, it would sound so strange that I beg you will come at once to see the evidences of what I tell you, before rain or snow obliterates them, bringing another witness with you. Lady Longden, perhaps."

"Lady Longden! Why one might as well write to *The Times*. I have it! There's Savage. He is faithful and can be silent."

So Savage was called in and, while Lord Ragnall dressed himself hurriedly, told the outline of his story under pain of instant dismissal if he breathed a word. Really to watch his face was as good as a play. So astonished was he that all he could ejaculate was—

"The black-hearted villains! Well, they ain't friendly with snakes for nothing."

Then having made sure that Miss Holmes was still in her room, we went down the twisting stair and through the side doorway, locking the door after us. By now the dawn was breaking and there was enough light to enable me in certain places where the snow that fell after the gale remained, to show Lord Ragnall and Savage the impress of the little bedroom slippers which Miss Holmes wore, and of my stockinged feet following after.

In the plantation things were still easier, for every detail of the movements of the four of us could be traced. Moreover, on the back drive was the spoor of the horses and the marks of the wheels of the carriage that had been brought for the purposes of the abduction. Also my great good fortune, for this seemed to prove my theory, we found a parcel wrapped in native linen that appeared to have fallen out of the carriage when Harût and Marût made their hurried escape, as one of the wheels had gone over it. It contained an Eastern woman's dress and veil, intended, I suppose, to be used in disguising Miss Holmes, who thence-forward would have appeared to be the wife or daughter of one of the abductors.

Savage discovered this parcel, which he lifted only to drop it with a yell, for underneath it lay a torpid snake, doubtless one of those that had been used in the performance.

Of these discoveries and many other details, on our return to the house, Lord Ragnall made full notes in a pocket-book, that when completed were signed by all three of us.

There is not much more to tell, that is of this part of the story. The matter was put into the hands of detectives who discovered that the Easterns had driven to London, where all traces of the carriage which conveyed them was lost. They, however, embarked upon a steamer called the *Antelope*, together with two native women, who probably had been provided to look after Miss Holmes, and sailed that very afternoon for Egypt. Thither, of course, it was useless to follow them in those days, even if it had been advisable to do so.

To return to Miss Holmes. She came down to breakfast looking very charming but rather pale. Again I sat next to her and took some opportunity to ask her how she had rested that night.

She replied, Very well and yet very ill, since, although she never remembered sleeping more soundly in her life, she had experienced all sorts of queer dreams of which she could remember nothing at all, a circumstance that annoyed her much, as she was sure that they were most interesting. Then she added,

"Do you know, Mr. Quatermain, I found a lot of mud on my dressing-gown this morning, and my bedroom slippers were also a mass of mud and wet through. How do you account for that? It is just as though I had been walking about outside in my sleep, which is absurd, as I never did such a thing in my life."

Not feeling equal to the invention of any convincing explanation of these phenomena, I upset the marmalade pot on to the table in such a way that some of it fell upon her dress, and then covered my retreat with profuse apologies. Understanding my dilemma, for he had heard something of this talk, Lord Ragnall came to my aid with a startling statement of which I forget the purport, and thus that crisis passed.

Shortly after breakfast Scroope announced to Miss Manners that her carriage was waiting, and we departed. Before I went, as it chanced, I had a few private words with my host, with Miss Holmes, and with the magnificent Mr. Savage. To the last, by the way, I offered a tip which he refused, saying that after all we had gone through together he could not allow "money to come between us," by which he meant, to pass from my pocket to his. Lord Ragnall asked me for both my English and my African addresses, which he noted in his pocket-book. Then he said,

"Really, Quatermain, I feel as though I had known you for years instead of three days; if you will allow me I will add that I should like to know a great deal more of you." (He was destined to do so, poor fellow, though neither of us knew it at the time.) "If ever you come to England again I hope you will make this house your headquarters."

"And if ever you come to South Africa, Lord Ragnall, I hope you will make my four-roomed shanty on the Berea at Durban your headquarters. You will get a hearty welcome there and something to eat, but little more."

"There is nothing I should like better, Quatermain. Circumstances have put me in a certain position in this country, still to tell you the truth there is a great deal about the life of which I grow very tired. But you see I am going to be married, and that I fear means an end of travelling, since naturally my wife will wish to take her place in society and the rest."

"Of course," I replied, "for it is not every young lady who has the luck to become an English peeress with all the etceteras, is it? Still I am not so sure but that Miss Holmes will take to travelling some day, although I *am* sure that she would do better to stay at home."

He looked at me curiously, then asked,

"You don't think there is anything really serious in all this business, do you?"

"I don't know what to think," I answered, "except that you will do well to keep a good eye upon your wife. What those Easterns tried to do last night and, I think, years ago, they may try again soon, or years hence, for evidently they are patient and determined men with much to win. Also it is a curious coincidence that she should have that mark upon her which appeals so strongly to Messrs. Harût and Marût, and, to be brief, she is in some ways different from most young women. As she said to me herself last night, Lord Ragnall, we are surrounded by mysteries; mysteries of blood, of inherited spirit, of this world generally in which it is probable that we all descended from quite a few common ancestors. And beyond these are other mysteries of the measureless universe to which we belong, that may already be exercising their strong and secret influences upon us, as perhaps, did we know it, they have done for millions of years in the Infinite whence we came and whither we go."

I suppose I spoke somewhat solemnly, for he said,

"Do you know you frighten me a little, though I don't quite understand what you mean." Then we parted.

With Miss Holmes my conversation was shorter. She remarked,

"It has been a great pleasure to me to meet you. I do not remember anybody with whom I have found myself in so much sympathy—except one of course. It is strange to think that when we meet again I shall be a married woman."

"I do not suppose we shall ever meet again, Miss Holmes. Your life is here, mine is in the wildest places of a wild land far away."

"Oh! yes, we shall," she answered. "I learned this and lots of other things when I held my head in that smoke last night."

Then we also parted.

Lastly Mr. Savage arrived with my coat. "Goodbye, Mr. Quatermain," he said. "If I forget everything else I shall never forget you and those villains, Harum and Scarum and their snakes. I hope it won't be my lot ever to clap eyes on them again, Mr. Quatermain, and yet somehow I don't feel so sure of that."

"Nor do I," I replied, with a kind of inspiration, after which followed the episode of the rejected tip.

The Bona Fide Gold Mine

Fully two years had gone by since I bade farewell to Lord Ragnall and Miss Holmes, and when the curtain draws up again behold me seated on the stoep of my little house at Durban, plunged in reflection and very sad indeed. Why I was sad I will explain presently.

In that interval of time I had heard once or twice about Lord Ragnall. Thus I received from Scroope a letter telling of his lordship's marriage with Miss Holmes, which, it appeared, had been a very fine affair indeed, quite one of the events of the London season. Two Royalties attended the ceremony, a duke was the best man, and the presents according to all accounts were superb and of great value, including a priceless pearl necklace given by the bridegroom to the bride. A cutting from a society paper which Scroope enclosed dwelt at length upon the splendid appearance of the bridegroom and the sweet loveliness of the bride. Also it described her dress in language which was Greek to me. One sentence, however, interested me intensely.

It ran: "The bride occasioned some comment by wearing only one ornament, although the Ragnall family diamonds, which have not seen the light for many years, are known to be some of the finest in the country. It was a necklace of what appeared to be large but rather roughly polished rubies, to which hung a small effigy of an Egyptian god also fashioned from a ruby. It must be added that although of an unusual nature on such an occasion this jewel suited her dark beauty well. Lady Ragnall's selection of it, however, from the many she possesses was the cause of much speculation. When asked by a friend why she had chosen it, she is reported to have said that it was to bring her good fortune."

Now why did she wear the barbaric marriage gift of Harût and Marût in preference to all the other gems at her disposal, I wondered. The thing was so strange as to be almost uncanny.

The second piece of information concerning this pair reached me through the medium of an old *Times* newspaper which I received over a year later. It was to the effect that a son and heir had been born to Lord Ragnall and that both mother and child were doing well.

So there's the end to a very curious little story, thought I to myself.

Well, during those two years many things befell me. First of all, in company with my old friend Sir Stephen Somers, I made the expedition to Pongoland in search of the wonderful orchid which he desired to add to his collection. I have already written of that journey and our extraordinary adventures, and need therefore allude to it no more here, except to say that during the course of it I was sorely tempted to travel to the territory north of the lake in which the Pongos dwelt. Much did I desire to see whether Messrs. Harût and Marût would in truth appear to conduct me to the land where the wonderful elephant which was supposed to be animated by an evil spirit was waiting to be killed by my rifle. However, I resisted the impulse, as indeed our circumstances obliged me to do. In the end we returned safely to Durban, and here I came to the conclusion that never again would I risk my life on such mad expeditions.

Owing to circumstances which I have detailed elsewhere I was now in possession of a considerable sum of cash, and this I determined to lay out in such a fashion as to make me independent of hunting and trading in the wilder regions of Africa. As usual when money is forthcoming, an opportunity soon presented itself in the shape of a gold mine which had been discovered on the borders of Zululand, one of the first that was ever found in those districts. A Jew trader named Jacob brought it to my notice and offered me a half share if I would put up the capital necessary to work the mine. I made a journey of inspection and convinced myself that it was indeed a wonderful proposition. I need not enter into the particulars nor, to tell the truth, have I any desire to do so, for the subject is still painful to me, further than to say that this Jew and some friends of his panned out visible gold before my eyes and then revealed to me the magnificent quartz reef from which, as they demonstrated, it had been washed in the bygone ages of the world. The news of our discovery spread like wildfire, and as, whatever else I might be, everyone knew that I was honest, in the end a small company was formed with Allan Quatermain, Esq., as the chairman of the Bona Fide Gold Mine, Limited.

Oh! that company! Often to this day I dream of it when I have indigestion.

Our capital was small, £10,000, of which the Jew, who was well named Jacob, and his friends, took half (for nothing of course) as the purchase price of their rights. I thought the proportion large and said so, especially after I had ascertained that these rights had cost them exactly three dozen of square-face gin, a broken-down wagon, four cows past the bearing age and £5 in cash. However, when it was pointed out to me that by their peculiar knowledge and genius they had located and provided the value of a property of enormous potential worth, moreover that this sum was to be paid to them in scrip which would only be realizable when success was assured and not in money, after a night of anxious consideration I gave way.

Personally, before I consented to accept the chairmanship, which carried with it a salary of £100 a year (which I never got), I bought and paid for in cash, shares to the value of £1,000 sterling. I remember that Jacob and his friends seemed surprised at this act of mine, as they had offered to give me five hundred of their shares for nothing "in consideration of the guarantee of my name." These I refused, saying that I would not ask others to invest in a venture in which I had no actual money stake; whereon they accepted my decision, not without enthusiasm. In the end the balance of £4,000 was subscribed and we got to work. Work is a good name for it so far as I was concerned, for never in all my days have I gone through so harrowing a time.

We began by washing a certain patch of gravel and obtained results which seemed really astonishing. So remarkable were they that on publication the shares rose to 10s. premium. Jacob and Co. took advantage of this opportunity to sell quite half of their bonus holding to eager applicants, explaining to me that they did so not for personal profit, which they scorned, but "to broaden the basis of the undertaking by admitting fresh blood."

It was shortly after this boom that the gravel surrounding the rich patch became very gravelly indeed, and it was determined that we should buy a small battery and begin to crush the quartz from which the gold was supposed to flow in a Pactolian stream. We negotiated for that battery through a Cape Town firm of engineers—but why follow the melancholy business in all its details? The shares began to decrease in value. They shrank to their original price of £1, then to 15s., then to 10s. Jacob, he was managing director, explained to me that it was necessary to "support the market," as he was already doing to an enormous extent, and that I as chairman ought to take a "lead in this good work" in order to show my faith in the concern.

I took a lead to the extent of another £500, which was all that I could afford. I admit that it was a shock to such trust in human nature as remained to me when I discovered subsequently that the 1,000 shares which I bought for my £500 had really been the property of Jacob, although they appeared to be sold to me in various other names.

The crisis came at last, for before that battery was delivered our available funds were exhausted, and no one would subscribe another halfpenny. Debentures, it is true, had been issued and taken up to the extent of about £1,000 out of the £5,000 offered, though who bought them remained at the time a mystery to me. Ultimately a meeting was called to consider the question of liquidating the company, and at this meeting, after three sleepless nights, I occupied the chair.

When I entered the room, to my amazement I found that of the five directors only one was present besides myself, an honest old retired sea captain who had bought and paid for 300 shares. Jacob and the two friends who represented his interests had, it appeared, taken ship that morning for Cape Town, whither they were summoned to attend various relatives who had been seized with illness.

It was a stormy meeting at first. I explained the position to the best of my ability, and when I had finished was assailed with a number of questions which I could not answer to the satisfaction of myself or of anybody else. Then a gentleman, the owner of ten shares, who had evidently been drinking, suggested in plain language that I had cheated the shareholders by issuing false reports.

I jumped up in a fury and, although he was twice my size, asked him to come and argue the question outside, whereon he promptly went away. This incident excited a laugh, and then the whole truth came out. A man with coloured blood in him stood up and told a story which was subsequently proved to be true. Jacob had employed him to "salt" the mine by mixing a heavy sprinkling of gold in the gravel we had first washed (which the coloured man swore he did in innocence), and subsequently had defrauded him of his wages. That was all. I sank back in my chair overcome. Then some good fellow in the audience, who had lost money himself in the affair and whom I scarcely knew, got up and made a noble speech which went far to restore my belief in human nature.

He said in effect that it was well known that I, Allan Quatermain, after working like a horse in the interests of the shareholders, had practically ruined myself over this enterprise, and that the real thief was Jacob, who had made tracks for the Cape, taking with him a large cash profit resulting from the sale of shares. Finally he concluded by calling for "three cheers for our honest friend and fellow sufferer, Mr. Allan Quatermain."

Strange to say the audience gave them very heartily indeed. I thanked them with tears in my eyes, saying that I was glad to leave the room as poor as I had ever been, but with a reputation which my conscience as well as their kindness assured me was quite unblemished.

Thus the winding-up resolution was passed and that meeting came to an end. After shaking hands with my deliverer from a most unpleasant situation, I walked homewards with the lightest heart in the world. My money was gone, it was true; also my over-confidence in others had led me to make a fool of myself by accepting as fact, on what I believed to be the evidence of my eyes, that which I had not sufficient expert knowledge to verify. But my honour was saved, and as I have again and again seen in the course of life, money is nothing when compared with honour, a remark which Shakespeare made long ago, though like many other truths this is one of which a full appreciation can only be gained by personal experience.

Not very far from the place where our meeting had been held I passed a side street then in embryo, for it had only one or two houses situated in their gardens and a rather large and muddy sluit of water running down one side at the edge of the footpath. Save for two people this street was empty, but that pair attracted my attention. They were a white man, in whom I recognized the stout and half-intoxicated individual who had accused me of cheating the company and then departed, and a withered old Hottentot who at that distance, nearly a hundred yards away, much reminded me of a certain Hans.

This Hans, I must explain, was originally a servant of my father, who was a missionary in the Cape Colony, and had been my companion in many adventures. Thus in my youth he and I alone escaped when Dingaan murdered Retief and his party of Boers,] and he had been one of my party in our quest for the wonderful orchid, the record of which I have written down in "The Holy Flower."

Hans had his weak points, among which must be counted his love of liquor, but he was a gallant and resourceful old fellow as indeed he had amply proved upon that orchid-seeking expedition. Moreover he loved me with a love passing the love of women. Now, having acquired some money in a way I need not stop to describe—for is it not written elsewhere?—he was settled as a kind of little chief on a farm not very far from Durban, where he lived in great honour because of the fame of his deeds.

The white man and Hans, if Hans it was, were engaged in violent altercation whereof snatches floated to me on the breeze, spoken in the Dutch tongue.

"You dirty little Hottentot!" shouted the white man, waving a stick, "I'll cut the liver out of you. What do you mean by nosing about after me like a jackal?" And he struck at Hans, who jumped aside.

"Son of a fat white sow," screamed Hans in answer (for the moment I heard his voice I knew that it was Hans), "did you dare to call the Baas a thief? Yes, a thief, O Rooter in the mud, O Feeder on filth and worms, O Hog of the gutter—the Baas, the clipping of whose nail is worth more than you and all your family, he whose honour is as clear as the sunlight and whose heart is cleaner than the white sand of the sea."

"Yes, I did," roared the white man; "for he got my money in the gold mine."

"Then, hog, why did you run away. Why did you not wait to tell him so outside that house?"

"I'll teach you about running away, you little yellow dog," replied the other, catching Hans a cut across the ribs.

"Oh! you want to see me run, do you?" said Hans, skipping back a few yards with wonderful agility. "Then look!"

Thus speaking he lowered his head and charged like a buffalo. Fair in the middle he caught that white man, causing him to double up, fly backwards and land with a most resounding splash in the deepest part of the muddy sluit. Here I may remark that, as his shins are the weakest, a Hottentot's head is by far the hardest and most dangerous part of him. Indeed it seems to partake of the nature of a cannon ball, for, without more than temporary disturbance to its possessor, I have seen a half-loaded wagon go over one of them on a muddy road.

Having delivered this home thrust Hans bolted round a corner and disappeared, while I waited trembling to see what happened to his adversary. To my relief nearly a minute later he crept out of the sluit covered with mud and dripping with water and hobbled off slowly down the street, his head so near his feet that he looked as though he had been folded in two, and his hands pressed upon what I believe is medically known as the diaphragm. Then I also went upon my way roaring with laughter. Often I have heard Hottentots called the lowest of mankind, but, reflected I, they can at any rate be good friends to those who treat them well—a fact of which I was to have further proof ere long.

By the time I reached my house and had filled my pipe and sat myself down in the dilapidated cane chair on the veranda, that natural reaction set in which so often follows rejoicing at the escape from a great danger. It was true that no one believed I had cheated them over that thrice-accursed gold mine, but how about other matters?

I mused upon the Bible narrative of Jacob and Esau with a new and very poignant sympathy for Esau. I wondered what would become of my Jacob. Jacob, I mean the original, prospered exceedingly as a result of his deal in porridge, and, as thought I, probably would his artful descendant who so appropriately bore his name. As a matter of fact I do not know what became of him, but bearing his talents in mind I think it probable that, like Van Koop, under some other patronymic he has now been rewarded with a title by the British Government. At any rate I had eaten the porridge in the shape of worthless but dearly purchased shares, after labouring hard at the chase of the golden calf, while brother Jacob had got my inheritance, or rather my money. Probably he was now counting it over in sovereigns upon the ship and sniggering as he thought of the shareholders' meeting with me in the chair. Well, he was a thief and would run his road to whatever end is appointed for thieves, so why should I bother my head more about him? As I had kept my honour—let him take my savings.

But I had a son to support, and now what was I to do with scarcely three hundred pounds, a good stock of guns and this little Durban property left to me in the world? Commerce in all its shapes I renounced once and for ever. It was too high—or too low—for me; so it would seem that there remained to me only my old business of professional hunting. Once again I must seek those adventures which I had forsworn when my evil star shone so brightly over a gold mine. What was it to be? Elephants, I supposed, since these are the only creatures worth killing from a money point of view. But most of my old haunts had been more or less shot out. The competition of younger professionals, of wandering backveld Boers and even of poaching natives who had obtained guns, was growing severe. If I went at all I should have to travel farther afield.

Whilst I meditated thus, turning over the comparative advantages or disadvantages of various possible hunting grounds in my mind, my attention was caught by a kind of cough that seemed to proceed from the farther side of a large gardenia bush. It was not a human cough, but rather resembled that made by a certain small buck at night, probably to signal to its mate, which of course it could not be as there were no buck within several miles. Yet I knew it came from a human throat, for had I not heard it before in many an hour of difficulty and danger?

"Draw near, Hans," I said in Dutch, and instantly out of a clump of aloes that grew in front of the pomegranate hedge, crept the withered shape of the old Hottentot, as a big yellow snake might do. Why he should choose this method of advance instead of that offered by the garden path I did not know, but it was quite in accordance with his secretive nature, inherited from a hundred generations of ancestors who spent their lives avoiding the observation of murderous foes.

He squatted down in front of me, staring in a vacant way at the fierce ball of the westering sun without blinking an eyelid, just as a vulture does.

"You look to me as though you had been fighting, Hans," I said. "The crown of your hat is knocked out; you are splashed with mud and there is the mark of a stick upon your left side."

"Yes, Baas. You are right as usual, Baas. I had a quarrel with a man about sixpence that he owed me, and knocked him over with my head, forgetting to take my hat off first. Therefore it is spoiled, for which I am sorry, as it was quite a new hat, not two years old. The Baas gave it me. He bought it in a store at Utrecht when we were coming back from Pongoland."

"Why do you lie to me?" I asked "You have been fighting a white man and for more than sixpence. You knocked him into a sluit and the mud splashed up over you."

"Yes, Baas, that is so. Your spirit speaks truly to you of the matter. Yet it wanders a little from the path, since I fought the white man for less than sixpence. I fought him for love, which is nothing at all."

"Then you are even a bigger fool than I took you for, Hans. What do you want now?"

"I want to borrow a pound, Baas. The white man will take me before the magistrate, and I shall be fined a pound, or fourteen days in the *trunk* (i.e. jail). It is true that the white man struck me first, but the magistrate will not believe the word of a poor old Hottentot against his, and I have no witness. He will say, 'Hans, you were drunk again. Hans, you are a liar and deserve to be flogged, which you will be next time. Pay a pound and ten shillings more, which is the price of good white justice, or go to the *trunk* for fourteen days and make baskets there for the great Queen to use.' Baas, I have the price of the justice which is ten shillings, but I want to borrow the pound for the fine."

"Hans, I think that just now you are better able to lend me a pound than I am to lend one to you. My bag is empty, Hans."

"Is it so, Baas? Well, it does not matter. If necessary I can make baskets for the great white Queen to put her food in, for fourteen days, or mats on which she will wipe her feet. The *trunk* is not such a bad place, Baas. It gives time to think of the white man's justice and to thank the Great One in the Sky, because the little sins one did not do have been found out and punished, while the big sins one did do, such as—well, never mind, Baas—have not been found out at all. Your reverend father, the Predikant, always taught me to have a thankful heart, Baas, and when I remember that I have only been in the *trunk* for three months altogether who, if all were known, ought to have been there for years, I remember his words, Baas."

"Why should you go to the *trunk* at all, Hans, when you are rich and can pay a fine, even if it were a hundred pounds?"

"A month or two ago it is true I was rich, Baas, but now I am poor. I have nothing left except ten shillings."

"Hans," I said severely, "you have been gambling again; you have been drinking again. You have sold your property and your cattle to pay your gambling debts and to buy square-face gin."

"Yes, Baas, and for no good it seems; though it is not true that I have been drinking. I sold the land and the cattle for £650, Baas, and with the money I bought other things."

"What did you buy?" I said.

He fumbled first in one pocket of his coat and then in the other, and ultimately produced a crumpled and dirty-looking piece of paper that resembled a bank-note. I took and examined this document and next minute nearly fainted. It certified that Hans was the proprietor of I know not how many debentures or shares, I forget which they were, in the Bona Fide Gold Mine, Limited, that same company of which I was the unlucky chairman, in consideration for which he had paid a sum of over six hundred and fifty pounds.

"Hans," I said feebly, "from whom did you buy this?"

"From the baas with the hooked nose, Baas. He who was named Jacob, after the great man in the Bible of whom your father, the Predikant, used to tell us, that one who was so slim and dressed himself up in a goatskin and gave his brother mealie porridge when he was hungry, after he had come in from shooting buck, Baas, and got his farm and cattle, Baas, and then went to Heaven up a ladder, Baas."

"And who told you to buy them, Hans?"

"Sammy, Baas, he who was your cook when we went to Pongoland, he who hid in the mealie-pit when the slavers burned Beza-Town and came out half cooked like a fowl from the oven. The Baas Jacob stopped at Sammy's hotel, Baas, and told him that unless he bought bits of paper like this, of which he had plenty, you would be brought before the magistrate and sent to the *trunk*, Baas. So Sammy bought some, Baas, but not many for he had only a little money, and the Baas Jacob paid him for all he ate and drank with other bits of paper. Then Sammy came to me and showed me what it was my duty to do, reminding me that your reverend father, the Predikant, had left you in my charge till one of us dies, whether you were well or ill and whether you got better or got worse—just like a white wife, Baas. So I sold the farm and the cattle to a friend of the Baas Jacob's, at a very low price, Baas, and that is all the story."

I heard and, to tell the honest truth, almost I wept, since the thought of the sacrifice which this poor old Hottentot had made for my sake on the instigation of a rogue utterly overwhelmed me.

"Hans," I asked recovering myself, "tell me what was that new name which the Zulu captain Mavovo gave you before he died, I mean after you had fired Beza-Town and caught Hassan and his slavers in their own trap?"

Hans, who had suddenly found something that interested him extremely out at sea, perhaps because he did not wish to witness my grief, turned round slowly and answered:

"Mavovo named me Light-in-Darkness, and by that name the Kafirs know me now, Baas, though some of them call me Lord-of-the-Fire."

"Then Mavovo named you well, for indeed, Hans, you shine like a light in the darkness of my heart. I whom you think wise am but a fool, Hans, who has been tricked by a *vernuker*, a common cheat, and he has tricked you and Sammy as well. But as he has shown me that man can be very vile, you have shown me that he can be very noble; and, setting the one against the other, my spirit that was in the dust rises up once more like a withered flower after rain. Light-in-Darkness, although if I had ten thousand pounds I could never pay you back— since what you have given me is more than all the gold in the world and all the land and all the cattle—yet with honour and with love I will try to pay you," and I held out my hand to him.

He took it and pressed it against his wrinkled old forehead, then answered:

"Talk no more of that, Baas, for it makes me sad, who am so happy. How often have you forgiven me when I have done wrong? How often have you not flogged me when I should have been flogged for being drunk and other things—yes, even when once I stole some of your powder and sold it to buy square-face gin, though it is true I knew it was bad powder, not fit for you to use? Did I thank you then overmuch? Why therefore should you thank me who have done but a little thing, not really to help you but because, as you know, I love gambling, and was told that this bit of paper would soon be worth much more than I gave for it. If it had proved so, should I have given you that money? No, I should have kept it myself and bought a bigger farm and more cattle."

"Hans," I said sternly, "if you lie so hard, you will certainly go to hell, as the Predikant, my father, often told you."

"Not if I lie for you, Baas, or if I do it doesn't matter, except that then we should be separated by the big kloof written of in the Book, especially as there I should meet the Baas Jacob, as I very much want to do for a reason of my own."

Not wishing to pursue this somewhat unchristian line of thought, I inquired of him why he felt happy.

"Oh! Baas," he answered with a twinkle in his little black eyes, "can't you guess why? Now you have very little money left and I have none at all. Therefore it is plain that we must go somewhere to earn money, and I am glad of that, Baas, for I am tired of sitting on that farm out there and growing mealies and milking cows, especially as I am too old to marry, Baas, as you are tired of looking for gold where there isn't any and singing sad songs in that house of meeting yonder like you did this afternoon. Oh! the Great Father in the skies knew what He was about when He sent the Baas Jacob our way. He beat us for our good, Baas, as He does always if we could only understand."

I reflected to myself that I had not often heard the doctrine of the Church better or more concisely put, but I only said:

"That is true, Hans, and I thank you for the lesson, the second you have taught me to-day. But where are we to go to, Hans? Remember, it must be elephants."

He suggested some places; indeed he seemed to have come provided with a list of them, and I sat silent making no comment. At length he finished and squatted there before me, chewing a bit of tobacco I had given him, and looking up at me interrogatively with his head on one side, for all the world like a dilapidated and inquisitive bird.

"Hans," I said, "do you remember a story I told you when you came to see me a year or more ago, about a tribe called the Kendah in whose country there is said to be a great cemetery of elephants which travel there to die from all the land about? A country that lies somewhere to the north-east of the lake island on which the Pongo used to dwell?"

"Yes, Baas."

"And you said, I think, that you had never heard of such a people."

"No, Baas, I never said anything at all. I have heard a good deal about them."

"Then why did you not tell me so before, you little idiot?" I asked indignantly.

"What was the good, Baas? You were hunting gold then, not ivory. Why should I make you unhappy, and waste my own breath by talking about beautiful things which were far beyond the reach of either of us, far as that sky?"

"Don't ask fool's questions but tell me what you know, Hans. Tell me at once."

"This, Baas: When we were up at Beza-Town after we came back from killing the gorilla-god, and the Baas Stephen your friend lay sick, and there was nothing else to do, I talked with everyone I could find worth talking to, and they were not many, Baas. But there was one very old woman who was not of the Mazitu race and whose husband and children were all dead, but whom the people in the town looked up to and feared because she was wise and made medicines out of herbs, and told fortunes. I used to go to see her. She was quite blind, Baas, and fond of talking with me—which shows how wise she was. I told her all about the Pongo gorilla-god, of which already she knew something. When I had done she said that he was as nothing compared with a certain god that she had seen in her youth, seven tens of years ago, when she became marriageable. I asked her for that story, and she spoke it thus:

"Far away to the north and east live a people called the Kendah, who are ruled over by a sultan. They are a very great people and inhabit a most fertile country. But all round their country the land is desolate and manless, peopled only by game, for the reason that they will suffer none to dwell there. That is why nobody knows anything about them: he that comes across the wilderness into that land is killed and never returns to tell of it.

"She told me also that she was born of this people, but fled because their sultan wished to place her in his house of women, which she did not desire. For a long while she wandered southwards, living on roots and berries, till she came to desert land and at last, worn out, lay down to die. Then she was found by some of the Mazitu who were on an expedition seeking ostrich feathers for war-plumes. They gave her food and, seeing that she was fair, brought her back to their country, where one of them married her. But of her own land she uttered only lying words to them because she feared that if she told the truth the gods who guard its secrets would be avenged on her, though now when she was near to death she dreaded them no more, since even the Kendah gods cannot swim through the waters of death. That is all she said about her journey because she had forgotten the rest."

"Bother her journey, Hans. What did she say about her god and the Kendah people?"

"This, Baas: that the Kendah have not one god but two, and not one ruler but two. They have a good god who is a child-fetish" (here I started) "that speaks through the mouth of an oracle who is always a woman. If that woman dies the god does not speak until they find another woman bearing certain marks which show that she holds the spirit of the god. Before the woman dies she always tells the priests in what land they are to look for her who is to come after her; but sometimes they cannot find her and then trouble falls because 'the Child has lost its tongue,' and the people become the prey of the other god that never dies."

"And what is that god, Hans?"

"That god, Baas, is an elephant" (here I started again), "a very bad elephant to which human sacrifice is offered. I think, Baas, that it is the devil wearing the shape of an elephant, at least that is what she said. Now the sultan is a worshipper of the god that dwells in the elephant Jana" (here I positively whistled) "and so are most of the people, indeed all those among them who are black. For once far away in the beginning the Kendah were two peoples, but the lighter-coloured people who worshipped the Child came down from the north and conquered the black people, bringing the Child with them, or so I understood her, Baas, thousands and thousands of years ago when the world was young. Since then they have flowed on side by side like two streams in the same channel, never mixing, for each keeps its own colour. Only, she said, that stream which comes from the north grows weaker and that from the south more strong."

"Then why does not the strong swallow up the weak?"

"Because the weak are still the pure and the wise, Baas, or so the old vrouw declared. Because they worship the good while the others worship the devil, and as your father the Predikant used to say, Good is the cock which always wins the fight at the last, Baas. Yes, when he seems to be dead he gets up again and kicks the devil in the stomach and stands on him and crows, Baas. Also these northern folk are mighty magicians. Through their Child-fetish they give rain and fat seasons and keep away sickness, whereas Jana gives only evil gifts that have to do with cruelty and war and so forth. Lastly, the priests who rule through the Child have the secrets of wealth and ancient knowledge, whereas the sultan and his followers have only the might of the spear. This was the song which the old woman sang to me, Baas."

"Why did you not tell me of these matters when we were at Beza-Town and I could have talked with her myself, Hans?"

"For two reasons, Baas. The first was that I feared, if I told you, you would wish to go on to find these people, whereas I was tired of travelling and wanted to come to Natal to rest. The second was that on the night when the old woman finished telling me her story, she was taken sick and died, and therefore it would have been no use to bring you to see her. So I saved it up in my head until it was wanted. Moreover, Baas, all the Mazitu declared that old woman to be the greatest of liars."

"She was not altogether a liar, Hans. Hear what I have learned," and I told him of the magic of Harût and Marût and of the picture that I had seemed to see of the elephant Jana and of the prayer that Harût and Marût had made to me, to all of which he listened quite stolidly. It is not easy to astonish a Hottentot's brain, which often draws no accurate dividing-line between the possible and what the modern world holds to be impossible.

"Yes, Baas," he said when I had finished, "then it seems that the old woman was not such a liar after all. Baas, when shall we start after that hoard of dead ivory, and which way will you go? By Kilwa or through Zululand? It should be settled soon because of the seasons."

After this we talked together for a long while, for with pockets as empty as mine were then, the problem seemed difficult, if not insoluble.

Lord Ragnall's Story

That night Hans slept at my house, or rather outside of it in the garden, or upon the stoep, saying that he feared arrest if he went to the town, because of his quarrel with the white man. As it happened, however, the other party concerned never stirred further in the business, probably because he was too drunk to remember who had knocked him into the sluit or whether he had gravitated thither by accident.

On the following morning we renewed our discussion, debating in detail every possible method of reaching the Kendah people by help of such means as we could command. Like that of the previous night it proved somewhat abortive. Obviously such a long and hazardous expedition ought to be properly financed and—where was the money? At length I came to the conclusion that if we went at all it would be best, in the circumstances, for Hans and myself to start alone with a Scotch cart drawn by oxen and driven by a couple of Zulu hunters, which we could lade with ammunition and a few necessaries.

Thus lightly equipped we might work through Zululand and thence northward to Beza-Town, the capital of the Mazitu, where we were sure of a welcome. After that we must take our chance. It was probable that we should never reach the district where these Kendah were supposed to dwell, but at least I might be able to kill some elephants in the wild country beyond Zululand.

While we were talking I heard the gun fired which announced the arrival of the English mail, and stepping to the end of the garden, saw the steamer lying at anchor outside the bar. Then I went indoors to write a few business letters which, since I had become immersed in the affairs of that unlucky gold mine, had grown to be almost a daily task with me. I had got through several with many groanings, for none were agreeable in their tenor, when Hans poked his head through the window in a silent kind of a way as a big snake might do, and said: "Baas, I think there are two baases out on the road there who are looking for you. Very fine baases whom I don't know."

"Shareholders in the Bona Fide Gold Mine," thought I to myself, then added as I prepared to leave through the back door: "If they come here tell them I am not at home. Tell them I left early this morning for the Congo River to look for the sources of the Nile."

"Yes, Baas," said Hans, collapsing on to the stoep.

I went out through the back door, sorrowing that I, Allan Quatermain, should have reached a rung in the ladder of life whence I shrank from looking any stranger in the face, for fear of what he might have to say to me. Then suddenly my pride asserted itself. After all what was there of which I should be ashamed? I would face these irate shareholders as I had faced the others yesterday.

I walked round the little house to the front garden which was planted with orange trees, and up to a big moonflower bush, I believe *datura* is its right name, that grew near the pomegranate hedge which separated my domain from the road. There a conversation was in progress, if so it may be called. "*Ikona*" (that is: "I don't know"), "*Inkoosi*" (i.e. "Chief"), said some Kafir in a stupid drawl.

Thereon a voice that instantly struck me as familiar, answered:

"We want to know where the great hunter lives."

"*Ikona*," said the Kafir.

"Can't you remember his native name?" asked another voice which was also familiar to me, for I never forget voices though I am unable to place them at once.

"The great hunter, Here-come-a-zany," said the first voice triumphantly, and instantly there flashed back upon my mind a vision of the splendid drawing-room at

Ragnall Castle and of an imposing majordomo introducing into it two white-robed, Arab-looking men.

"Mr. Savage, by the Heavens!" I muttered. "What in the name of goodness is he doing here?"

"There," said the second voice, "your black friend has bolted, and no wonder, for who can be called by such a name? If you had done what I told you, Savage, and hired a white guide, it would have saved us a lot of trouble. Why will you always think that you know better than anyone else?"

"Seemed an unnecessary expense, my lord, considering we are travelling incog., my lord."

"How long shall we travel 'incog.' if you persist in calling me my lord at the top of your voice, Savage? There is a house beyond those trees; go in and ask where——"

By this time I had reached the gate which I opened, remarking quietly,

"How do you do, Lord Ragnall? How do you do, Mr. Savage? I thought that I recognized your voices on the road and came to see if I was right. Please walk in; that is, if it is I whom you wish to visit."

As I spoke I studied them both, and observed that while Savage looked much the same, although slightly out of place in these strange surroundings, the time that had passed since we met had changed Lord Ragnall a good deal. He was still a magnificent-looking man, one of those whom no one that had seen him would ever forget, but now his handsome face was stamped with some new seal of suffering. I felt at once that he had become acquainted with grief. The shadow in his dark eyes and a certain worn expression about the mouth told me that this was so.

"Yes, Quatermain," he said as he took my hand, "it is you whom I have travelled seven thousand miles to visit, and I thank God that I have been so fortunate as to find you. I feared lest you might be dead, or perhaps far away in the centre of Africa where I should never be able to track you down."

"A week later perhaps you would not have found me, Lord Ragnall," I answered, "but as it happens misfortune has kept me here."

"And misfortune has brought me here, Quatermain."

Then before I had time to answer Savage came up and we went into the house.

"You are just in time for lunch," I said, "and as luck will have it there is a good rock cod and a leg of oribé buck for you to eat. Boy, set two more places."

"One more place, if you please, sir," said Savage. "I should prefer to take my food afterwards."

"You will have to get over that in Africa," I muttered. Still I let him have his way, with the result that presently the strange sight was seen of the magnificent English majordomo standing behind my chair in the little room and handing round the square-face as though it were champagne. It was a spectacle that excited the greatest interest in my primitive establishment and caused Hans with some native hangers-on to gather at the window. However, Lord Ragnall took it as a matter of course and I thought it better not to interfere.

When we had finished we went on to the stoep to smoke, leaving Savage to eat his dinner, and I asked Lord Ragnall where his luggage was. He replied that he had left it at the Customs. "Then," I said, "I will send a native with Savage to arrange about getting it up here. If you do not mind my rough accommodation there is a room for you, and your man can pitch a tent in the garden."

After some demur he accepted with gratitude, and a little later Savage and the native were sent off with a note to a man who hired out a mule-cart.

"Now," I said when the gate had shut behind them, "will you tell me why you have come to Africa?"

"Disaster," he replied. "Disaster of the worst sort."

"Is your wife dead, Lord Ragnall?"

"I do not know. I almost hope that she is. At any rate she is lost to me."

An idea leapt to my mind to the effect that she might have run away with somebody else, a thing which often happens in the world. But fortunately I kept it to myself and only said,

"She was nearly lost once before, was she not?"

"Yes, when you saved her. Oh! if only you had been with us, Quatermain, this would never have happened. Listen: About eighteen months ago she had a son, a very beautiful child. She recovered well from the business and we were as happy as two mortals could be, for we loved each other, Quatermain, and God has blessed us in every way; we were so happy that I remember her telling me that our great good fortune made her feel afraid. One day last September when I was out shooting, she drove in a little pony cart we had, with the nurse, and the child but no man, to call on Mrs. Scroope who also had been recently confined. She often went out thus, for the pony was an old animal and quiet as a sheep.

"By some cursed trick of fate it chanced that when they were passing through the little town which you may remember near Ragnall, they met a travelling menagerie that was going to some new encampment. At the head of the procession marched a large bull elephant, which I discovered afterwards was an ill-tempered brute that had already killed a man and should never have been allowed upon the roads. The sight of the pony cart, or perhaps a red cloak which my wife was wearing, as she always liked bright colours, for some unknown reason seems to have infuriated this beast, which trumpeted. The pony becoming frightened wheeled round and overturned the cart right in front of the animal, but apparently without hurting anybody. Then"—here he paused a moment and with an effort continued—"that devil in beast's shape cocked its ears, stretched out its long trunk, dragged the baby from the nurse's arms, whirled it round and threw it high into the air, to fall crushed upon the kerb. It sniffed at the body of the child, feeling it over with the tip of its trunk, as though to make sure that it was dead. Next, once more it trumpeted triumphantly, and without attempting to harm my wife or anybody else, walked quietly past the broken cart and continued its journey, until outside the town it was made fast and shot."

"What an awful story!" I said with a gasp.

"Yes, but there is worse to follow. My poor wife went off her head, with the shock I suppose, for no physical injury could be found upon her. She did not suffer in health or become violent, quite the reverse indeed for her gentleness increased. She just went off her head. For hours at a time she would sit silent and smiling, playing with the stones of that red necklace which those conjurers gave her, or rather counting them, as a nun might do with the beads of her rosary. At times, however, she would talk, but always to the baby, as though it lay before her or she were nursing it. Oh! Quatermain, it was pitiful, pitiful!

"I did everything I could. She was seen by three of the greatest brain-doctors in England, but none of them was able to help. The only hope they gave was that the fit might pass off as suddenly as it had come. They said too that a thorough change of scene would perhaps be beneficial, and suggested Egypt; that was in October. I did not take much to the idea, I don't know why, and personally should not have acceded to it had it not been for a curious circumstance. The last consultation took place in the big drawing-room at Ragnall. When it was over my wife remained with her mother at one end of the room while I and the doctors talked together at the other, as I thought quite out of her earshot. Presently, however, she called to me, saying in a perfectly clear and natural voice:

"'Yes, George, I will go to Egypt. I should like to go to Egypt.' Then she went on playing with the necklace and talking to the imaginary child.

"Again on the following morning as I came into her room to kiss her, she exclaimed,

"'When do we start for Egypt? Let it be soon.'

"With these sayings the doctors were very pleased, declaring that they showed signs of a returning interest in life and begging me not to thwart her wish.

"So I gave way and in the end we went to Egypt together with Lady Longden, who insisted upon accompanying us although she is a wretched sailor. At Cairo a large dahabeeyah that I had hired in advance, manned by an excellent crew and a guard of four soldiers, was awaiting us. In it we started up the Nile. For a month or more all went well; also to my delight my wife seemed now and again to show signs of returning intelligence. Thus she took some interest in the sculptures on the walls of the temples, about which she had been very fond of reading when in health. I remember that only a few days before the— the catastrophe, she pointed out one of them to me, it was of Isis and the infant Horus, saying, 'Look, George, the holy Mother and the holy Child,' and then bowed to it reverently as she might have done to an altar. At length after passing the First Cataract and the Island of Philæ we came to the temple of Abu Simbel, opposite to which our boat was moored. On the following morning we explored the temple at daybreak and saw the sun strike upon the four statues which sit at its farther end, spending the rest of that day studying the colossal figures of Rameses that are carved upon its face and watching some cavalcades of Arabs mounted upon camels travelling along the banks of the Nile.

"My wife was unusually quiet that afternoon. For hour after hour she sat still upon the deck, gazing first at the mouth of the rock-hewn temple and the mighty figures which guard it and then at the surrounding desert. Only once did I hear her speak and then she said, 'Beautiful, beautiful! Now I am at home.' We dined and as there was no moon, went to bed rather early after listening to the Sudanese singers as they sang one of their weird chanties.

"My wife and her mother slept together in the state cabin of the dahabeeyah, which was at the stern of the boat. My cabin, a small one, was on one side of this, and that of the trained nurse on the other. The crew and the guard were forward of the saloon. A gangway was fixed from the side to the shore and over it a sentry stood, or was supposed to stand. During the night a Khamsin wind began to blow, though lightly as was to be expected at this season of the year. I did not hear it for, as a matter of fact, I slept very soundly, as it appears did everyone else upon the dahabeeyah, including the sentry as I suspect.

"The first thing I remember was the appearance of Lady Longden just at daybreak at the doorway of my cabin and the frightened sound of her voice asking if Luna, that is my wife, was with me. Then it transpired that she had left her cabin clad in a fur cloak, evidently some time before, as the bed in which she had been lying was quite cold. Quatermain, we searched everywhere; we searched for four days, but from that hour to this no trace whatever of her has been found."

"Have you any theory?" I asked.

"Yes, or at least all the experts whom we consulted have a theory. It is that she slipped down the saloon in the dark, gained the deck and thence fell or threw herself into the Nile, which of course would have carried her body away. As you may have heard, the Nile is full of bodies. I myself saw two of them during that journey. The Egyptian police and others were so convinced that this was what had happened that, notwithstanding the reward of a thousand pounds which I offered for any valuable information, they could scarcely be persuaded to continue the search."

"You said that a wind was blowing and I understand that the shores are sandy, so I suppose that all footprints would have been filled in?"

He nodded and I went on. "What is your own belief? Do you think she was drowned?"

He countered my query with another of:

"What do *you* think?"

"I? Oh! although I have no right to say so, I don't think at all. I am quite sure that she was *not* drowned; that she is living at this moment."

"Where?"

"As to that you had better inquire of our friends, Harût and Marût," I answered dryly.

"What have you to go on, Quatermain? There is no clue."

"On the contrary I hold that there are a good many clues. The whole English part of the story in which we were concerned, and the threats those mysterious persons uttered are the first and greatest of these clues. The second is the fact that your hiring of the dahabeeyah regardless of expense was known a long time before your arrival in Egypt, for I suppose you did so in your own name, which is not exactly that of Smith or Brown. The third is your wife's sleep-walking propensities, which would have made it quite easy for her to be drawn ashore under some kind of mesmeric influence. The fourth is that you had seen Arabs mounted on camels upon the banks of the Nile. The fifth is the heavy sleep you say held everybody on board that particular night, which suggests to me that your food may have been drugged. The sixth is the apathy displayed by those employed in the search, which suggests to me that some person or persons in authority may have been bribed, as is common in the East, or perhaps frightened with threats of bewitchment. The seventh is that a night was chosen when a wind blew which would obliterate all spoor whether of men or of swiftly travelling camels. These are enough to begin with, though doubtless if I had time to think I could find others. You must remember too that although the journey would be long, this country of the Kendah can doubtless be reached from the Sudan by those who know the road, as well as from southern or eastern Africa."

"Then you think that my wife has been kidnapped by those villains, Harût and Marût?"

"Of course, though villains is a strong term to apply to them. They might be quite honest men according to their peculiar lights, as indeed I expect they are. Remember that they serve a god or a fetish, or rather, as they believe, a god *in* a fetish, who to them doubtless is a very terrible master, especially when, as I understand, that god is threatened by a rival god."

"Why do you say that, Quatermain?"

By way of answer I repeated to him the story which Hans said he had heard from the old woman at Beza, the town of the Mazitu. Lord Ragnall listened with the deepest interest, then said in an agitated voice:

"That is a very strange tale, but has it struck you, Quatermain, that if your suppositions are correct, one of the most terrible circumstances connected with my case is that our child should have chanced to come to its dreadful death through the wickedness of an elephant?"

"That curious coincidence has struck me most forcibly, Lord Ragnall. At the same time I do not see how it can be set down as more than a coincidence, since the elephant which slaughtered your child was certainly not that called Jana. To suppose because there is a war between an elephant-god and a child-god somewhere in the heart of Africa, that therefore another elephant can be so influenced that it kills a child in England, is to my mind out of all reason."

That is what I said to him, as I did not wish to introduce a new horror into an affair that was already horrible enough. But, recollecting that these priests, Harût and Marût, believed the mother of this murdered infant to be none other than the oracle of their worship (though how this chanced passed my comprehension), and therefore the great enemy of the evil elephant-god, I confess that at heart I felt afraid. If any powers of magic, black or white or both, were mixed up with the matter as my experiences in England seemed to suggest, who could say what might be their exact limits? As, however, it has been demonstrated again and again by the learned that no such thing as African magic exists, this line of thought appeared to be too foolish to follow. So passing it by I asked Lord Ragnall to continue.

"For over a month," he went on, "I stopped in Egypt waiting till emissaries who had been sent to the chiefs of various tribes in the Sudan and elsewhere, returned with the news that nothing whatsoever had been seen of a white woman travelling in the company of natives, nor had they heard of any such woman being sold as a slave. Also through the Khedive, on whom I was able to bring influence to bear by help of the British Government, I caused many harems in Egypt to be visited, entirely without result. After this, leaving the inquiry in the hands of the British Consul and a firm of French lawyers, although in truth all hope had gone, I returned to England whither I had already sent Lady Longden, broken-hearted, for it occurred to me as possible that my wife might have drifted or been taken thither. But here, too, there was no trace of her or of anybody who could possibly answer to her description. So at last I came to the conclusion that her bones must lie somewhere at the bottom of the Nile, and gave way to despair."

"Always a foolish thing to do," I remarked.

"You will say so indeed when you hear the end, Quatermain. My bereavement and the sleeplessness which it caused prayed upon me so much, for now that the child was dead my wife was everything to me, that, I will tell you the truth, my brain became affected and like Job I cursed God in my heart and determined to die. Indeed I should have died by my own hand, had it not been for Savage. I had procured the laudanum and loaded the pistol with which I proposed to shoot myself immediately after it was swallowed so that there might be no mistake. One night only a couple of months or so ago, Quatermain, I sat in my study at Ragnall, with the doors locked as I thought, writing a few final letters before I did the deed. The last of them was just finished about twelve when hearing a noise, I looked up and saw Savage standing before me. I asked him angrily how he came there (I suppose he must have had another key to one of the other doors) and what he wanted. Ignoring the first part of the question he replied:

"'My lord, I have been thinking over our trouble'—he was with us in Egypt—'I have been thinking so much that it has got a hold of my sleep. To-night as you said you did not want me any more and I was tired, I went to bed early and had a dream. I dreamed that we were once more in the shrubbery, as happened some years ago, and that the little African gent who shot like a book, was showing us the traces of those two black men, just as he did when they tried to steal her ladyship. Then in my dream I seemed to go back to bed and that beastly snake which we found lying under the parcel in the road seemed to follow me. When I had got to sleep again, all in the dream, there it was standing on its tail at the end of the bed, hissing till it woke me. Then it spoke in good English and not in African as might have been expected.

"'"Savage," it said, "get up and dress yourself and go at once and tell his lordship to travel to Natal and find Mr. Allan Quatermain" (you may remember that was the African gentleman's name, my lord, which, with so many coming and going in this great house, I had quite forgotten, until I had the dream). "Find Mr. Allan Quatermain," that slimy reptile went on, opening and shutting its mouth for all the world like a Christian making a speech, "for he will have something to tell him as to that which has made a hole in his heart that is now filled with the seven devils. Be quick, Savage, and don't stop to put on your shirt or your tie"—I have not, my lord, as you may see. "He is shut up in the study, but you know how to get into it. If he will not listen to you let him look round the study and he will see something which will tell him that this is a true dream."

"'Then the snake vanished, seeming to wriggle down the left bottom bed-post, and I woke up in a cold sweat, my lord, and did what it had told me.'

"Those were his very words, Quatermain, for I wrote them down afterwards while they were fresh in my memory, and you see here they are in my pocket-book.

"Well, I answered him, rather brusquely I am afraid, for a crazed man who is about to leave the world under such circumstances does not show at his best when disturbed almost in the very act, to the edge of which long agony has brought him. I told him that all his dream of snakes seemed ridiculous, which obviously it was, and was about to send him away, when it occurred to me that the suggestion it conveyed that I should put myself in communication with you was not ridiculous in view of the part you had already played in the story."

"Very far from ridiculous," I interpolated.

"To tell the truth," went on Lord Ragnall, "I had already thought of doing the same thing, but somehow beneath the pressure of my imminent grief the idea was squeezed out of my mind, perhaps because you were so far away and I did not know if I could find you even if I tried. Pausing for a moment before I dismissed Savage, I rose from the desk at which I was writing and began to walk up and down the room thinking what I would do. I am not certain if you saw it when you were at Ragnall, but it is a large room, fifty feet long or so though not very broad. It has two fireplaces, in both of which fires were burning on this night, and it was lit by four standing lamps besides that upon my desk. Now between these fireplaces, in a kind of niche in the wall, and a little in the shadow because none of the lamps was exactly opposite to it, hung a portrait of my wife which I had caused to be painted by a fashionable artist when first we became engaged."

"I remember it," I said. "Or rather, I remember its existence. I did not see it because a curtain hung over the picture, which Savage told me you did not wish to be looked at by anybody but yourself. At the time I remarked to him, or rather to myself, that to veil the likeness of a living woman in such a way seemed to me rather an ill-omened thing to do, though why I should have thought it so I do not quite know."

"You are quite right, Quatermain. I had that foolish fancy, a lover's freak, I suppose. When we married the curtain was removed although the brass rod on which it hung was left by some oversight. On my return to England after my loss, however, I found that I could not bear to look upon this lifeless likeness of one who had been taken from me so cruelly, and I caused it to be replaced. I did more. In order that it might not be disturbed by some dusting housemaid, I myself made it fast with three or four tin-tacks which I remember I drove through the velvet stuff into the panelling, using a fireiron as a hammer. At the time I thought it a good job although by accident I struck the nail of the third finger of my left hand so hard that it came off. Look, it has not quite finished growing again," and he showed the finger on which the new nail was still in process of formation.

"Well, as I walked up and down the room some impulse caused me to look towards the picture. To my astonishment I saw that it was no longer veiled, although to the best of my belief the curtain had been drawn over it as lately as that afternoon; indeed I could have sworn that this was so. I called to Savage to bring the lamp that stood upon my table, and by its light made an examination. The curtain was drawn back, very tidily, being fastened in its place clear of the little alcove by means of a thin brass chain. Also along one edge of it, that which I had nailed to the panelling, the tin-tacks were still in their places; that is, three of them were, the fourth I found afterwards upon the floor.

"'She looks beautiful, doesn't she, my lord,' said Savage, 'and please God so we shall still find her somewhere in the world.'

"I did not answer him, or even remark upon the withdrawal of the curtain, as to which indeed I never made an inquiry. I suppose that it was done by some zealous servant while I was pretending to eat my dinner—there were one or two new ones in the house whose names and appearance I did not know. What impressed itself upon my mind was that the face which I had never expected to see again on the earth, even in a picture, was once more given to my eyes, it mattered not how. This, in my excited state, for laudanum waiting to be swallowed and a pistol at full cock for firing do not induce calmness in a man already almost mad, at any rate until they have fulfilled their offices, did in truth appear to me to be something of the nature of a sign such as that spoken of in Savage's idiotic dream, which I was to find if 'I looked round the study.'

"'Savage,' I said, 'I don't think much of your dreams about snakes that talk to you, but I do think that it might be well to see Mr. Quatermain. To-day is Sunday and I believe that the African mail sails on Friday. Go to town early to-morrow and book passages.'

"Also I told him to see various gunsmiths and bid them send down a selection of rifles and other weapons for me to choose from, as I did not know whither we might wander in Africa, and to make further necessary arrangements. All of these things he did, and—here we are."

"Yes," I answered reflectively, "here you are. What is more, here is your luggage of which there seems to be enough for a regiment," and I pointed to a Scotch cart piled up with baggage and followed by a long line of Kafirs carrying sundry packages upon their heads that, marshalled by Savage, had halted at my gate.

The Start

That evening when the baggage had been disposed of and locked up in my little stable and arrangements were made for the delivery of some cases containing tinned foods, etc., which had proved too heavy for the Scotch cart, Lord Ragnall and I continued our conversation. First, however, we unpacked the guns and checked the ammunition, of which there was a large supply, with more to follow.

A beautiful battery they were of all sorts from elephant guns down, the most costly and best finished that money could buy at the time. It made me shiver to think what the bill for them must have been, while their appearance when they were put together and stood in a long line against the wall of my sitting-room, moved old Hans to a kind of ecstasy. For a long while he contemplated them, patting the stocks one after the other and giving to each a name as though they were all alive, then exclaimed:

"With such weapons as these the Baas could kill the devil himself. Still, let the Baas bring Intombi with him"—a favourite old rifle of mine and a mere toy in size, that had however done me good service in the past, as those who have read what I have written in "Marie" and "The Holy Flower" may remember. "For, Baas, after all, the wife of one's youth often proves more to be trusted than the fine young ones a man buys in his age. Also one knows all her faults, but who can say how many there may be hidden up in new women however beautifully they are tattooed?" and he pointed to the elaborate engraving upon the guns.

I translated this speech to Lord Ragnall. It made him laugh, at which I was glad for up till then I had not seen him even smile. I should add that in addition to these sporting weapons there were no fewer than fifty military rifles of the best make, they were large-bore Sniders that had just then been put upon the market, and with them, packed in tin cases, a great quantity of ammunition. Although the regulations were not so strict then as they are now, I met with a great deal of difficulty in getting all this armament through the Customs. Lord Ragnall however had letters from the Colonial Office to such authorities as ruled in Natal, and on our giving a joint undertaking that they were for defensive purposes only in unexplored territory and not for sale, they were allowed through. Fortunate did it prove for us in after days that this matter was arranged.

That night before we went to bed I narrated to Lord Ragnall all the history of our search for the Holy Flower, which he seemed to find very entertaining. Also I told him of my adventures, to me far more terrible, as chairman of the Bona Fide Gold Mine and of their melancholy end.

"The lesson of which is," he remarked when I had finished, "that because a man is master of one trade, it does not follow that he is master of another. You are, I should judge, one of the finest shots in the world, you are also a great hunter and explorer. But when it comes to companies, Quatermain——! Still," he went on, "I ought to be grateful to that Bona Fide Gold Mine, since I gather that had it not been for it and for your rascally friend, Mr. Jacob, I should not have found you here."

"No," I answered, "it is probable that you would not, as by this time I might have been far in the interior where a man cannot be traced and letters do not reach him."

Then he made a few pointed inquiries about the affairs of the mine, noting my answers down in his pocket-book. I thought this odd but concluded that he wished to verify my statements before entering into a close companionship with me, since for aught he knew I might be the largest liar in the world and a swindler to boot. So I said nothing, even when I heard through a roundabout channel on the morrow that he had sought an interview with the late secretary of the defunct company.

A few days later, for I may as well finish with this matter at once, the astonishing object of these inquiries was made clear to me. One morning I found upon my table a whole pile of correspondence, at the sight of which I groaned, feeling sure that it must come from duns and be connected with that infernal mine. Curiosity and a desire to face the worst, however, led me to open the first letter which as it happened proved to be from that very shareholder who had proposed a vote of confidence in me at the winding-up meeting. By the time that it was finished my eyes were swimming and really I felt quite faint. It ran:

"Honoured Sir,—I knew that I was putting my money on the right horse when I said the other day that you were one of the straightest that ever ran. Well, I have got the cheque sent me by the lawyer on your account, being payment in full for every farthing I invested in the Bona Fide Gold Mine, and I can only say that it is uncommonly useful, for that business had pretty well cleaned me out. God bless you, Mr. Quatermain."

I opened another letter, and another, and another. They were all to the same effect. Bewildered I went on to the stoep, where I found Hans with an epistle in his hand which he requested me to be good enough to read. I read it. It was from a well-known firm of local lawyers and said:

"On behalf of Allan Quatermain, Esq., we beg to enclose a draft for the sum of £650, being the value of the interest in the Bona Fide Gold Company, Limited (in liquidation), which stands in your name on the books of the company. Please sign enclosed receipt and return same to us."

Yes, and there was the draft for £650 sterling!

I explained the matter to Hans, or rather I translated the document, adding:

"You see you have got your money back again. But Hans, I never sent it; I don't know where it comes from."

"Is it money, Baas?" asked Hans, surveying the draft with suspicion. "It looks very much like the other bit of paper for which I paid money."

Again I explained, reiterating that I knew nothing of the transaction.

"Well, Baas," he said, "if you did not send it someone did—perhaps your father the reverend Predikant, who sees that you are in trouble and wishes to wash your name white again. Meanwhile, Baas, please put that bit of paper in your pocket-book and keep it for me, for otherwise I might be tempted to buy square-face with it."

"No," I answered, "you can now buy your land back, or some other land, and there will be no need for you to come with me to the country of the Kendah."

Hans thought a moment and then very deliberately began to tear up the draft; indeed I was only just in time to save it from destruction.

"If the Baas is going to turn me off because of this paper," he said, "I will make it small and eat it."

"You silly old fool," I said as I possessed myself of the cheque.

Then the conversation was interrupted, for who should appear but Sammy, my old cook, who began in his pompous language:

"The perfect rectitude of your conduct, Mr. Quatermain, moves me to the deepest gratitude, though indeed I wish that I had put something into the food of the knave Jacob who beguiled us all, that would have caused him internal pangs of a severe if not of a dangerous order. My holding in the gold mine was not extensive, but the unpaid bill of the said Jacob and his friends——"

Here I cut him short and fled, since I saw yet another shareholder galloping to the gate, and behind him two more in a spider. First I took refuge in my room, my idea being to put away that pile of letters. In so doing I observed that there was one still unopened. Half mechanically I took it from the envelope and glanced at its contents. They were word for word identical with those of that addressed to "Mr. Hans, Hottentot," only my name was at the bottom of it instead of that of Hans and the cheque was for £1,500, the amount I had paid for the shares I held in the venture.

Feeling as though my brain were in a melting-pot, I departed from the house into a patch of native bush that in those days still grew upon the slope of the hill behind. Here I sat myself down, as I had often done before when there was a knotty point to be considered, aimlessly watching a lovely emerald cuckoo flashing, a jewel of light, from tree to tree, while I turned all this fairy-godmother business over in my mind.

Of course it soon became clear to me. Lord Ragnall in this case was the little old lady with the wand, the touch of which could convert worthless share certificates into bank-notes of their face value. I remembered now that his wealth was said to be phenomenal and after all the cash capital of the company was quite small. But the question was —could I accept his bounty?

I returned to the house where the first person whom I met was Lord Ragnall himself, just arrived from some interview about the fifty Snider rifles, which were still in bond. I told him solemnly that I wished to speak to him, whereon he remarked in a cheerful voice,

"Advance, friend, and all's well!"

I don't know that I need set out the details of the interview. He waited till I had got through my halting speech of mingled gratitude and expostulation, then remarked:

"My friend, if you will allow me to call you so, it is quite true that I have done this because I wished to do it. But it is equally true that to me it is a small thing—to be frank, scarcely a month's income; what I have saved travelling on that ship to Natal would pay for it all. Also I have weighed my own interest in the matter, for I am anxious that you should start upon this hazardous journey of ours up country with a mind absolutely free from self-reproach or any money care, for thus you will be able to do me better service. Therefore I beg that you will say no more of the episode. I have only one thing to add, namely that I have myself bought up at par value a few of the debentures. The price of them will pay the lawyers and the liquidation fees; moreover they give me a status as a shareholder which will enable me to sue Mr. Jacob for his fraud, to which business I have already issued instructions. For please understand that I have not paid off any shares still standing in his name or in those of his friends."

Here I may add that nothing ever came of this action, for the lawyers found themselves unable to serve any writ upon that elusive person, Mr. Jacob, who by then had probably adopted the name of some other patriarch.

"Please put it all down as a rich man's whim," he concluded.

"I can't call that a whim which has returned £1,500 odd to my pocket that I had lost upon a gamble, Lord Ragnall."

"Do you remember, Quatermain, how you won £250 upon a gamble at my place and what you did with it, which sum probably represented to you twenty or fifty times what it would to me? Also if that argument does not appeal to you, may I remark that I do not expect you to give me your services as a professional hunter and guide for nothing."

"Ah!" I answered, fixing on this point and ignoring the rest, "now we come to business. If I may look upon this amount as salary, a very handsome salary by the way, paid in advance, you taking the risks of my dying or becoming incapacitated before it is earned, I will say no more of the matter. If not I must refuse to accept what is an unearned gift."

"I confess, Quatermain, that I did not regard it in that light, though I might have been willing to call it a retaining fee. However, do not let us wrangle about money any more. We can always settle our accounts when the bill is added up, if ever we reach so far. Now let us come to more important details."

So we fell to discussing the scheme, route and details of our proposed journey. Expenditure being practically no object, there were several plans open to us. We might sail up the coast and go by Kilwa, as I had done on the search for the Holy Flower, or we might retrace the line of our retreat from the Mazitu country which ran through Zululand. Again, we might advance by whatever road we selected with a small army of drilled and disciplined retainers, trusting to force to break a way through to the Kendah. Or we might go practically unaccompanied, relying on our native wit and good fortune to attain our ends. Each of these alternatives had so much to recommend it and yet presented so many difficulties, that after long hours of discussion, for this talk was renewed again and again, I found it quite impossible to decide upon any one of them, especially as in the end Lord Ragnall always left the choice with its heavy responsibilities to me.

At length in despair I opened the window and whistled twice on a certain low note. A minute later Hans shuffled in, shaking the wet off the new corduroy clothes which he had bought upon the strength of his return to affluence, for it was raining outside, and squatted himself down upon the floor at a little distance. In the shadow of the table which cut off the light from the hanging lamp he looked, I remember, exactly like an enormous and antique toad. I threw him a piece of tobacco which he thrust into his corn-cob pipe and lit with a match.

"The Baas called me," he said when it was drawing to his satisfaction, "what does Baas want of Hans?"

"Light in darkness!" I replied, playing on his native name, and proceeded to set out the whole case to him.

He listened without a word, then asked for a small glass of gin, which I gave him doubtfully. Having swallowed this at a gulp as though it were water, he delivered himself briefly to this effect:

"I think the Baas will do well not to go to Kilwa, since it means waiting for a ship, or hiring one; also there may be more slave- traders there by now who will bear him no love because of a lesson he taught them a while ago. On the other hand the road through Zululand is open, though it be long, and there the name of Macumazana is one well known. I think also that the Baas would do well not to take too many men, who make marching slow, only a wagon or two and some drivers which might be sent back when they can go no farther. From Zululand messengers can be dispatched to the Mazitu, who love you, and Bausi or whoever is king there to-day will order bearers to meet us on the road, until which time we can hire other bearers in Zululand. The old woman at Beza-Town told me, moreover, as you will remember, that the Kendah are a very great people who live by themselves and will allow none to enter their land, which is bordered by deserts. Therefore no force that you could take with you and feed upon a road without water would be strong enough to knock down their gates like an elephant, and it seems better that you should try to creep through them like a wise snake, although they appear to be shut in your face. Perhaps also they will not be shut since did you not say that two of their great doctors promised to meet you and guide you through them?"

"Yes," I interrupted, "I dare say it will be easier to get in than to get out of Kendahland."

"Last of all, Baas, if you take many men armed with guns, the black part of the Kendah people of whom I told you will perhaps think you come to make war, whatever the white Kendah may say, and kill us all, whereas if we be but a few perchance they will let us pass in peace. I think that is all, Baas. Let the Baas and the Lord Igeza forgive me if my words are foolish."

Here I should explain that "Igeza" was the name which the natives had given to Lord Ragnall because of his appearance. The word means a handsome person in the Zulu tongue. Savage they called "Bena," I don't know why. "Bena" in Zulu means to push out the breast and it may be that the name was a round-about allusion to the proud appearance of the dignified Savage, or possibly it had some other recondite signification. At any rate Lord Ragnall, Hans and myself knew the splendid Savage thenceforward by the homely appellation of Beans. His master said it suited him very well because he was so green.

"The advice seems wise, Hans. Go now. No, no more gin," I answered.

As a matter of fact careful consideration convinced us it was so wise that we acted on it down to the last detail.

So it came about that one fine afternoon about a fortnight later, for hurry as we would our preparations took a little time, we trekked for Zululand over the sandy roads that ran from the outskirts of Durban. Our baggage and stores were stowed in two half-tented wagons, very good wagons since everything we had with us was the best that money could buy, the after-part of which served us as sleeping-places at night. Hans sat on the *voor-kisse* or driving-seat of one of the wagons; Lord Ragnall, Savage and I were mounted upon "salted" horses, that is, horses which had recovered from and were therefore supposed to be proof against the dreadful sickness, valuable and docile animals which were trained to shooting.

At our start a little contretemps occurred. To my amazement I saw Savage, who insisted upon continuing to wear his funereal upper servant's cut-away coat, engaged with grim determination in mounting his steed from the wrong side. He got into the saddle somehow, but there was worse to follow. The horse, astonished at such treatment, bolted a little way, Savage sawing at its mouth. Lord Ragnall and I cantered after it past the wagons, fearing disaster. All of a sudden it swerved violently and Savage flew into the air, landing heavily in a sitting posture.

"Poor Beans!" ejaculated Lord Ragnall as we sped forward. "I expect there is an end of his journeyings."

To our surprise, however, we saw him leap from the ground with the most marvellous agility and begin to dance about slapping at his posterior parts and shouting,

"Take it off! Kill it!"

A few seconds later we discovered the reason. The horse had shied at a sleeping puff adder which was curled up in the sand of that little frequented road, and on this puff adder Savage had descended with so much force, for he weighed thirteen stone, that the creature was squashed quite flat and never stirred again. This, however, he did not notice in his agitation, being convinced indeed that it was hanging to him behind like a bulldog.

"Snakes! my lord," he exclaimed, when at last after careful search we demonstrated to him that the adder had died before it could come into action.

"I hate 'em, my lord, and they haunts" (he said 'aunts) "me. If ever I get out of this I'll go and live in Ireland, my lord, where they say there ain't none. But it isn't likely that I shall," he added mournfully, "for the omen is horrid."

"On the contrary," I answered, "it is splendid, for you have killed the snake and not the snake you. 'The dog it was that died,' Savage."

After this the Kafirs gave Savage a second very long name which meant "He-who-sits-down-on-snakes-and-makes-them-flat." Having remounted him on his horse, which was standing patiently a few yards away, at length we got off. I lingered a minute behind the others to give some directions to my old Griqua gardener, Jack, who snivelled at parting with me, and to take a last look at my little home. Alack! I feared it might be the last indeed, knowing as I did that this was a dangerous enterprise upon which I found myself embarked, I who had vowed that I would be done with danger.

With a lump in my throat I turned from the contemplation of that peaceful dwelling and happy garden in which each tree and plant was dear to me, and waving a good-bye to Jack, cantered on to where Ragnall was waiting for me.

"I am afraid this is rather a sad hour for you, who are leaving your little boy and your home," he said gently, "to face unknown perils."

"Not so sad as others I have passed," I answered, "and perils are my daily bread in every sense of the word. Moreover, whatever it is for me it is for you also."

"No, Quatermain. For me it is an hour of hope; a faint hope, I admit, but the only one left, for the letters I got last night from Egypt and England report that no clue whatsoever has been found, and indeed that the search for any has been abandoned. Yes, I follow the last star left in my sky and if it sets I hope that I may set also, at any rate to this world. Therefore I am happier than I have been for months, thanks to you," and he stretched out his hand, which I shook.

It was a token of friendship and mutual confidence which I am glad to say nothing that happened afterwards ever disturbed for a moment.

The Meeting in the Desert

Now I do not propose to describe all our journey to Kendahland, or at any rate the first part thereof. It was interesting enough in its way and we met with a few hunting adventures, also some others. But there is so much to tell of what happened to us after we reached the place that I have not the time, even if I had the inclination to set all these matters down. Let it be sufficient, then, to say that although owing to political events the country happened to be rather disturbed at the time, we trekked through Zululand without any great difficulty. For here my name was a power in the land and all parties united to help me. Thence, too, I managed to dispatch three messengers, half-bred border men, lean fellows and swift of foot, forward to the king of the Mazitu, as Hans had suggested that I should do, advising him that his old friends, Macumazana, Watcher-by-Night, and the yellow man who was named Light-in-Darkness and Lord-of-the-Fire, were about to visit him again.

As I knew we could not take the wagons beyond a certain point where there was a river called the Luba, unfordable by anything on wheels, I requested him, moreover, to send a hundred bearers with whatever escort might be necessary, to meet us on the banks of that river at a spot which was known to both of us. These words the messengers promised to deliver for a fee of five head of cattle apiece, to be paid on their return, or to their families if they died on the road, which cattle we purchased and left in charge of a chief, who was their kinsman. As it happened two of the poor fellows did die, one of them of cold in a swamp through which they took a short cut, and the other at the teeth of a hungry lion. The third, however, won through and delivered the message.

After resting for a fortnight in the northern parts of Zululand, to give time to our wayworn oxen to get some flesh on their bones in the warm bushveld where grass was plentiful even in the dry season, we trekked forward by a route known to Hans and myself. Indeed it was the same which we had followed on our journey from Mazituland after our expedition in search for the Holy Flower.

We took with us a small army of Zulu bearers. This, although they were difficult to feed in a country where no corn could be bought, proved fortunate in the end, since so many of our cattle died from tsetse bite that we were obliged to abandon one of the wagons, which meant that the goods it contained must be carried by men. At length we reached the banks of the river, and camped there one night by three tall peaks of rock which the natives called "The Three Doctors," where I had instructed the messengers to tell the Mazitu to meet us. For four days we remained here, since rains in the interior had made the river quite impassable. Every morning I climbed the tallest of the "Doctors" and with my glasses looked over its broad yellow flood, searching the wide, bush-clad land beyond in the hope of discovering the Mazitu advancing to meet us. Not a man was to be seen, however, and on the fourth evening, as the river had now become fordable, we determined that we would cross on the morrow, leaving the remaining wagon, which it was impossible to drag over its rocky bottom, to be taken back to Natal by our drivers.

Here a difficulty arose. No promise of reward would induce any of our Zulu bearers even to wet their feet in the waters of this River Luba, which for some reason that I could not extract from them they declared to be *tagati*, that is, bewitched, to people of their blood. When I pointed out that three Zulus had already undertaken to cross it, they answered that those men were half-breeds, so that for them it was only half bewitched, but they thought that even so one or more of them would pay the penalty of death for this rash crime.

It chanced that this happened, for, as I have said, two of the poor fellows did die, though not, I think, owing to the magical properties of the waters of the Luba. This is how African superstitions are kept alive. Sooner or later some saying of the sort fulfils itself and then the instance is remembered and handed down for generations, while other instances in which nothing out of the common has occurred are not heeded, or are forgotten.

This decision on the part of those stupid Zulus put us in an awkward fix, since it was impossible for us to carry over all our baggage and ammunition without help. Therefore glad was I when before dawn on the fifth morning the nocturnal Hans crept into the wagon, in the after part of which Ragnall and I were sleeping, and informed us that he heard men's voices on the farther side of the river, though how he could hear anything above that roar of water passed my comprehension.

At the first break of dawn again we climbed the tallest of the "Doctor" rocks and stared into the mist. At length it rolled away and there on the farther side of the river I saw quite a hundred men who by their dress and spears I knew to be Mazitu. They saw me also and raising a cheer, dashed into the water, groups of them holding each other round the middle to prevent their being swept away. Thereupon our silly Zulus seized their spears and formed up upon the bank. I slid down the steep side of the "Great Doctor" and ran forward, calling out that these were friends who came.

"Friends or foes," answered their captain sullenly, "it is a pity that we should walk so far and not have a fight with those Mazitu dogs."

Well, I drove them off to a distance, not knowing what might happen if the two peoples met, and then went down to the bank. By now the Mazitu were near, and to my delight at the head of them I perceived no other than my old friend, their chief general, Babemba, a one-eyed man with whom Hans and I had shared many adventures. Through the water he plunged with great bounds and reaching the shore, greeted me literally with rapture.

"O Macumazana," he said, "little did I hope that ever again I should look upon your face. Welcome to you, a thousand welcomes, and to you too, Light-in-Darkness, Lord-of-the-Fire, Cunning-one whose wit saved us in the battle of the Gate. But where is Dogeetah, where is Wazeela, and where are the Mother and the Child of the Flower?"

"Far away across the Black Water, Babemba," I answered. "But here are two others in place of them," and I introduced him to Ragnall and Savage by their native names of Igeza and Bena.

He contemplated them for a moment, then said:

"This," pointing to Ragnall, "is a great lord, but this," pointing to Savage, who was much the better dressed of the two, "is a cock of the ashpit arrayed in an eagle's feathers," a remark I did not translate, but one which caused Hans to snigger vacuously.

While we breakfasted on food prepared by the "Cock of the Ashpit," who amongst many other merits had that of being an excellent cook, I heard all the news. Bausi the king was dead but had been succeeded by one of his sons, also named Bausi, whom I remembered. Beza-Town had been rebuilt after the great fire that destroyed the slavers, and much more strongly fortified than before. Of the slavers themselves nothing more had been seen, or of the Pongo either, though the Mazitu declared that their ghosts, or those of their victims, still haunted the island in the lake. That was all, except the ill tidings as to two of our messengers which the third, who had returned with the Mazitu, reported to us.

After breakfast I addressed and sent away our Zulus, each with a handsome present from the trade goods, giving into their charge the remaining wagon and our servants, none of whom, somewhat to my relief, wished to accompany us farther. They sang their song of good-bye, saluted and departed over the rise, still looking hungrily behind them at the Mazitu, and we were very pleased to see the last of them without bloodshed or trouble.

When we had watched the white tilt of the wagon vanish, we set to work to get ourselves and our goods across the river. This we accomplished safely, for the Mazitu worked for us like friends and not as do hired men. On the farther bank, however, it took us two full days so to divide up the loads that the bearers could carry them without being overladen.

At length all was arranged and we started. Of the month's trek that followed there is nothing to tell, except that we completed it without notable accidents and at last reached the new Beza-Town, which much resembled the old, where we were accorded a great public reception. Bausi II himself headed the procession which met us outside the south gate on that very mound which we had occupied in the great fight, where the bones of the gallant Mavovo and my other hunters lay buried. Almost did it seem to me as though I could hear their deep voices joining in the shouts of welcome.

That night, while the Mazitu feasted in our honour, we held an *indaba* in the big new guest house with Bausi II, a pleasant-faced young man, and old Babemba. The king asked us how long we meant to stay at Beza-Town, intimating his hope that the visit would be prolonged. I replied, but a few days, as we were travelling far to the north to find a people called the Kendah whom we wished to see, and hoped that he would give us bearers to carry our goods as far as the confines of their country. At the name of Kendah a look of astonishment appeared upon their faces and Babemba said:

"Has madness seized you, Macumazana, that you would attempt this thing? Oh surely you must be mad."

"You thought us mad, Babemba, when we crossed the lake to Rica Town, yet we came back safely."

"True, Macumazana, but compared to the Kendah the Pongo were but as the smallest star before the face of the sun."

"What do you know of them then?" I asked. "But stay—before you answer, I will speak what I know," and I repeated what I had learned from Hans, who confirmed my words, and from Harût and Marût, leaving out, however, any mention of their dealings with Lady Ragnall.

"It is all true," said Babemba when I had finished, "for that old woman of whom Light-in-the-Darkness speaks, was one of the wives of my uncle and I knew her well. Hearken! These Kendah are a terrible nation and countless in number and of all the people the fiercest. Their king is called Simba, which means Lion. He who rules is always called Simba, and has been so called for hundreds of years. He is of the Black Kendah whose god is the elephant Jana, but as Light-in-Darkness has said, there are also the White Kendah who are Arab men, the priests and traders of the people. The Kendah will allow no stranger within their doors; if one comes they kill him by torment, or blind him and turn him out into the desert which surrounds their country, there to die. These things the old woman who married my uncle told me, as she told them to Light-in-Darkness, also I have heard them from others, and what she did not tell me, that the White Kendah are great breeders of the beasts called camels which they sell to the Arabs of the north. Go not near them, for if you pass the desert the Black Kendah will kill you; and if you escape these, then their king, Simba, will kill you; and if you escape him, then their god Jana will kill you; and if you escape him, then their white priests will kill you with their magic. Oh! long before you look upon the faces of those priests you will be dead many times over."

"Then why did they ask me to visit them, Babemba?"

"I know not, Macumazana, but perhaps because they wished to make an offering of you to the god Jana, whom no spear can harm; no, nor even your bullets that pierce a tree."

"I am willing to make trial of that matter," I answered confidently, "and any way we must go to see these things for ourselves."

"Yes," echoed Ragnall, "we must certainly go," while even Savage, for I had been translating to them all this while, nodded his head although he looked as though he would much rather stay behind.

"Ask him if there are any snakes there, sir," he said, and foolishly enough I put the question to give me time to think of other things.

"Yes, O Bena. Yes, O Cock of the Ashpit," replied Babemba. "My uncle's Kendar wife told me that one of the guardians of the shrine of the White Kendah is such a snake as was never seen elsewhere in the world."

"Then say to him, sir," said Savage, when I had translated almost automatically, "that shrine ain't a church where *I* shall go to say my prayers."

Alas! poor Savage little knew the future and its gifts.

Then we came to the question of bearers. The end of it was that after some hesitation Bausi II, because of his great affection for us, promised to provide us with these upon our solemnly undertaking to dismiss them at the borders of the desert, "so that they might escape our doom," as he remarked cheerfully.

Four days later we started, accompanied by about one hundred and twenty picked men under the command of old Babemba himself, who, he explained, wished to be the last to see us alive in the world. This was depressing, but other circumstances connected with our start were calculated to weigh even more upon my spirit. Thus the night before we left Hans arrived and asked me to "write a paper" for him. I inquired what he wanted me to put in the paper. He replied that as he was going to his death and had property, namely the £650 that had been left in a bank to his credit, he desired to make a "white man's will" to be left in the charge of Babemba. The only provision of the said will was that I was to inherit his property, if I lived. If I died, which, he added, "of course you must, Baas, like the rest of us," it was to be devoted to furnishing poor black people in hospital with something comforting to drink instead of the "cow's water" that was given to them there. Needless to say I turned him out at once, and that testamentary deposition remained unrecorded. Indeed it was unnecessary, since, as I reminded him, on my advice he had already made a will before we left Durban, a circumstance that he had quite forgotten.

The second event, which occurred about an hour before our departure, was, that hearing a mighty wailing in the market-place where once Hans and I had been tied to stakes to be shot to death with arrows, I went out to see what was the matter. At the gateway I was greeted by the sight of about a hundred old women plastered all over with ashes, engaged in howling their loudest in a melancholy unison. Behind these stood the entire population of Beza-Town, who chanted a kind of chorus.

"What the devil are they doing?" I asked of Hans.

"Singing our death-song, Baas," he replied stolidly, "as they say that where we are going no one will take the trouble to do so, and it is not right that great lords should die and the heavens above remain uninformed that they are coming."

"That's cheerful," I remarked, and wheeling round, asked Ragnall straight out if he wished to persevere in this business, for to tell the truth my nerve was shaken.

"I must," he answered simply, "but there is no reason why you and Hans should, or Savage either for the matter of that."

"Oh! I'm going where you go," I said, "and where I go Hans will go. Savage must speak for himself."

This he did and to the same effect, being a very honest and faithful man. It was the more to his credit since, as he informed me in private, he did not enjoy African adventure and often dreamed at nights of his comfortable room at Ragnall whence he superintended the social activities of that great establishment.

So we departed and marched for the matter of a month or more through every kind of country. After we had passed the head of the great lake wherein lay the island, if it really was an island, where the Pongo used to dwell (one clear morning through my glasses I discerned the mountain top that marked the former residence of the Mother of the Flower, and by contrast it made me feel quite homesick), we struck up north, following a route known to Babemba and our guides. After this we steered by the stars through a land with very few inhabitants, timid and nondescript folk who dwelt in scattered villages and scarcely understood the art of cultivating the soil, even in its most primitive form.

A hundred miles or so farther on these villages ceased and thenceforward we only encountered some nomads, little bushmen who lived on game which they shot with poisoned arrows. Once they attacked us and killed two of the Mazitu with those horrid arrows, against the venom of which no remedy that we had in our medicine chest proved of any avail. On this occasion Savage exhibited his courage if not his discretion, for rushing out of our thorn fence, after missing a bushmen with both barrels at a distance of five yards—he was, I think, the worst shot I ever saw—he seized the little viper with his hands and dragged him back to camp. How Savage escaped with his life I do not know, for one poisoned arrow went through his hat and stuck in his hair and another just grazed his leg without drawing blood.

This valorous deed was of great service to us, since we were able through Hans, who knew something of the bushmen's language, to explain to our prisoner that if we were shot at again he would be hung. This information he contrived to shout, or rather to squeak and grunt, to his amiable tribe, of which it appeared he was a kind of chief, with the result that we were no more molested. Later, when we were clear of the bushmen country, we let him depart, which he did with great rapidity.

By degrees the land grew more and more barren and utterly devoid of inhabitants, till at last it merged into desert. At the edge of this desert which rolled away without apparent limit we came, however, to a kind of oasis where there was a strong and beautiful spring of water that formed a stream which soon lost itself in the surrounding sand. As we could go no farther, for even if we had wished to do so, and were able to find water there, the Mazitu refused to accompany us into the desert, not knowing what else to do, we camped in the oasis and waited.

As it happened, the place was a kind of hunter's paradise, since every kind of game, large and small, came to the water to drink at night, and in the daytime browsed upon the saltish grass that at this season of the year grew plentifully upon the edge of the wilderness.

Amongst other creatures there were elephants in plenty that travelled hither out of the bushlands we had passed, or sometimes emerged from the desert itself, suggesting that beyond this waste there lay fertile country. So numerous were these great beasts indeed that for my part I hoped earnestly that it would prove impossible for us to continue our journey, since I saw that in a few months I could collect an enormous amount of ivory, enough to make me comparatively rich, if only I were able to get it away. As it was we only killed a few of them, ten in all to be accurate, that we might send back the tusks as presents to Bausi II. To slaughter the poor animals uselessly was cruel, especially as being unaccustomed to the sight of man, they were as easy to approach as cows. Even Savage slew one—by carefully aiming at another five paces to its left.

For the rest we lived on the fat of the land and, as meat was necessary to us, had as much sport as we could desire among the various antelope.

For fourteen days or so this went on, till at length we grew thoroughly tired of the business, as did the Mazitu, who were so gorged with flesh that they began to desire vegetable food. Twice we rode as far into the desert as we dared, for our horses remained to us and had grown fresh again after the rest, but only to return without information. The place was just a vast wilderness strewn with brown stones beautifully polished by the wind-driven sand of ages, and quite devoid of water.

After our second trip, on which we suffered severely from thirst, we held a consultation. Old Babemba said that he could keep his men no longer, even for us, as they insisted upon returning home, and inquired what we meant to do and why we sat here "like a stone." I answered that we were waiting for some of the Kendah who had bid me to shoot game hereabouts until they arrived to be our guides. He remarked that the Kendah to the best of his belief lived in a country that was still hundreds of miles away and that, as they did not know of our presence, any communication across the desert being impossible, our proceedings seemed to be foolish.

I retorted that I was not quite so sure of this, since the Kendah seemed to have remarkable ways of acquiring information.

"Then, Macumazana, I fear that you will have to wait by yourselves until you discover which of us is right," he said stolidly.

Turning to Ragnall, I asked him what he would do, pointing out that to journey into the desert meant death, especially as we did not know whither we were going, and that to return alone, without the stores which we must abandon, through the country of the bushmen to Mazituland, would also be a risky proceeding. However, it was for him to decide.

Now he grew much perturbed. Taking me apart again he dwelt earnestly upon his secret reasons for wishing to visit these Kendah, with which of course I was already acquainted, as indeed was Savage.

"I desire to stay here," he ended.

"Which means that we must all stay, Ragnall, since Savage will not desert you. Nor will Hans desert me although he thinks us mad. He points out that I came to seek ivory and here about is ivory in plenty for the trouble of taking."

"I might remain alone, Quatermain——" he began, but I looked at him in such a way that he never finished the sentence.

Ultimately we came to a compromise. Babemba, on behalf of the Mazitu, agreed to wait three more days. If nothing happened during that period we on our part agreed to return with them to a stretch of well-watered bush about fifty miles behind us, which we knew swarmed with elephants, that by now were growing shy of approaching our oasis where there was so much noise and shooting. There we would kill as much ivory as we could carry, an operation in which they were willing to assist for the fun of it, and then go back with them to Mazituland.

The three days went by and with every hour that passed my spirits rose, as did those of Savage and Hans, while Lord Ragnall became more and more depressed. The third afternoon was devoted to a jubilant packing of loads, for in accordance with the terms of our bargain we were to start backwards on our spoor at dawn upon the morrow. Most happily did I lay myself down to sleep in my little bough shelter that night, feeling that at last I was rid of an uncommonly awkward adventure. If I thought that we could do any good by staying on, it would have been another matter. But as I was certain that there was no earthly chance of our finding among the Kendah—if ever we reached them—the lady who had tumbled in the Nile in Egypt, well, I was glad that Providence had been so good as to make it impossible for us to commit suicide by thirst in a desert, or otherwise. For, notwithstanding my former reasonings to the contrary, I was now convinced that this was what had happened to poor Ragnall's wife.

That, however, was just what Providence had not done. In the middle of the night, to be precise, at exactly two in the morning, I was awakened by Hans, who slept at the back of my shanty, into which he had crept through a hole in the faggots, exclaiming in a frightened voice,

"Open your eyes and look, Baas. There are two *spooks* waiting to see you outside, Baas."

Very cautiously I lifted myself a little and stared out into the moonlight. There, seated about five paces from the open end of the hut were the "spooks" sure enough, two white-robed figures squatting silent and immovable on the ground. At first I was frightened. Then I bethought me of thieves and felt for my Colt pistol under the rug that served me as a pillow. As I got hold of the handle, however, a deep voice said:

"Is it your custom, O Macumazana, Watcher-by-Night, to receive guests with bullets?"

Now thought I to myself, who is there in the world who could see a man catch hold of the handle of a pistol in the recesses of a dark place and under a blanket at night, except the owner of that voice which I seemed to remember hearing in a certain drawing-room in England?

"Yes, Harût," I answered with an unconcerned yawn, "when the guests come in such a doubtful fashion and in the middle of the night. But as you are here at last, will you be so good as to tell us why you have kept us waiting all this time? Is that your way of fulfilling an engagement?"

"O Lord Macumazana," answered Harût, for of course it was he, in quite a perturbed tone, "I offer to you our humble apologies. The truth is that when we heard of your arrival at Beza-Town we started, or tried to start, from hundreds of miles away to keep our tryst with you here as we promised we would do. But we are mortal, Macumazana, and accidents intervened. Thus, when we had ascertained the weight of your baggage, camels had to be collected to carry it, which were grazing at a distance. Also it was necessary to send forward to dig out a certain well in the desert where they must drink. Hence the delay. Still, you will admit that we have arrived in time, five, or at any rate four hours before the rising of that sun which was to light you on your homeward way."

"Yes, you have, O Prophets, or O Liars, whichever you may be," I exclaimed with pardonable exasperation, for really their knowledge of my private affairs, however obtained, was enough to anger a saint. "So as you are here at last, come in and have a drink, for whether you are men or devils, you must be cold out there in the damp."

In they came accordingly, and, not being Mohammedans, partook of a tot of square-face from a bottle which I kept locked in a box to put Hans beyond the reach of temptation.

"To your health, Harût and Marût," I said, drinking a little out of the pannikin and giving the rest to Hans, who gulped the fiery liquor down with a smack of his lips. For I will admit that I joined in this unholy midnight potation to gain time for thought and to steady my nerve.

"To your health, O Lord Macumazana," the pair answered as they swallowed their tots, which I had made pretty stiff, and set down their pannikins in front of them with as much reverence as though these had been holy vessels.

"Now," I said, throwing a blanket over my shoulders, for the air was chilly, "now let us talk," and taking the lantern which Hans had thoughtfully lighted, I held it up and contemplated them.

There they were, Harût and Marût without doubt, to all appearance totally unchanged since some years before I had seen them at Ragnall in England. "What are you doing here?" I asked in a kind of fiery indignation inspired by my intense curiosity. "How did you get out of England after you had tried to steal away the lady to whom you sent the necklace? What did you do with that lady after you had beguiled her from the boat at Abu-Simbel? In the name of your Holy Child, or of Shaitan of the Mohammedans, or of Set of the Egyptians, answer me, lest I should make an end of both of you, which I can do here without any questions being asked," and I whipped out my pistol.

"Pardon us," said Harût with a grave smile, "but if you were to do as you say, Lord Macumazana, many questions would be asked which *you* might find it hard to answer. So be pleased to put that death-dealer back into its place, and to tell us before we reply to you, what you know of Set of the Egyptians."

"As much or as little as you do," I replied.

Both bowed as though this information were of the most satisfactory order. Then Harût went on: "In reply to your requests, O Macumazana, we left England by a steamboat and in due course after long journeyings we reached our own country. We do not understand your allusions to a place called Abu-Simbel on the Nile, whence, never having been there, we have taken no lady. Indeed, we never meant to take that lady to whom we sent a necklace in England. We only meant to ask certain questions of her, as she had the gift of vision, when you appeared and interrupted us. What should we want with white ladies, who have already far too many of our own?"

"I don't know," I replied, "but I do know that you are the biggest liars I ever met."

At these words, which some might have thought insulting, Harût and Marût bowed again as though to acknowledge a great compliment. Then Harût said:

"Let us leave the question of ladies and come to matters that have to do with men. You are here as we told you that you would be at a time when you did not believe us, and we here to meet *you*, as we told you that we would be. How we knew that you were coming and how we came do not matter at all. Believe what you will. Are you ready to start with us, O Lord Macumazana, that you may bring to its death the wicked elephant Jana which ravages our land, and receive the great reward of ivory? If so, your camel waits."

"One camel cannot carry four men," I answered, avoiding the question.

"In courage and skill you are more than many men, O Macumazana, yet in body you are but one and not four."

"If you think that I am going with you alone, you are much mistaken, Harût and Marût," I exclaimed. "Here with me is my servant without whom I do not stir," and I pointed to Hans, whom they contemplated gravely. "Also there is the Lord Ragnall, who in this land is named Igeza, and his servant who here is named Bena, the man out of whom you drew snakes in the room in England. They also must accompany us."

At this news the impassive countenances of Harût and Marût showed, I thought, some signs of disturbance. They muttered together in an unknown tongue. Then Harût said:

"Our secret land is open to you alone, O Macumazana, for one purpose only—to kill the elephant Jana, for which deed we promise you a great reward. We do not wish to see the others there."

"Then you can kill your own elephant, Harût and Marût, for not one step do I go with you. Why should I when there is as much ivory here as I want, to be had for the shooting?"

"How if we take you, O Macumazana?"

"How if I kill you both, O Harût and Marût? Fools, here are many brave men at my command, and if you or any with you want fighting it shall be given you in plenty. Hans, bid the Mazitu stand to their arms and summon Igeza and Bena."

"Stay, Lord," said Harût, "and put down that weapon," for once more I had produced the pistol. "We would not begin our fellowship by shedding blood, though we are safer from you than you think. Your companions shall accompany you to the land of the Kendah, but let them know that they do so at their own risk. Learn that it is revealed to us that if they go in there some of them will pass out again as spirits but not as men."

"Do you mean that you will murder them?"

"No. We mean that yonder are some stronger than us or any men, who will take their lives in sacrifice. Not yours, Macumazana, for that, it is decreed, is safe, but those of two of the others, which two we do not know."

"Indeed, Harût and Marût, and how am I to be sure that any of us are safe, or that you do not but trick us to your country, there to kill us with treachery and steal our goods?"

"Because we swear it by the oath that may not be broken; we swear it by the Heavenly Child," both of them exclaimed solemnly, speaking with one voice and bowing till their foreheads almost touched the ground.

I shrugged my shoulders and laughed a little.

"You do not believe us," went on Harût, "who have not heard what happens to those who break this oath. Come now and see something. Within five paces of your hut is a tall ant-heap upon which doubtless you have been accustomed to stand and overlook the desert." (This was true, but how did they guess it, I wondered.) "Go climb that ant-heap once more."

Perhaps it was rash, but my curiosity led me to accept this invitation. Out I went, followed by Hans with a loaded double-barrelled rifle, and scrambled up the ant-heap which, as it was twenty feet high and there were no trees just here, commanded a very fine view of the desert beyond.

"Look to the north," said Harût from its foot.

I looked, and there in the bright moonlight five or six hundred yards away, ranged rank by rank upon a slope of sand and along the crest of the ridge beyond, I saw quite two hundred kneeling camels, and by each camel a tall, white-robed figure who held in his hand a long lance to the shaft of which, not far beneath the blade, was attached a little flag. For a while I stared to make sure that I was not the victim of an illusion or a mirage. Then when I had satisfied myself that these were indeed men and camels I descended from the ant-heap.

"You will admit, Macumazana," said Harût politely, "that if we had meant you any ill, with such a force it would have been easy for us to take a sleeping camp at night. But these men come here to be your escort, not to kill or enslave you or yours. And, Macumazana, we have sworn to you the oath that may not be broken. Now we go to our people. In the morning, after you have eaten, we will return again unarmed and alone."

Then like shadows they slipped away.

Charge!

Ten minutes later the truth was known and every man in the camp was up and armed. At first there were some signs of panic, but these with the help of Babemba we managed to control, setting the men to make the best preparations for defence that circumstances would allow, and thus occupying their minds. For from the first we saw that, except for the three of us who had horses, escape was impossible. That great camel corps could catch us within a mile.

Leaving old Babemba in charge of his soldiers, we three white men and Hans held a council at which I repeated every word that had passed between Harût and Marût and myself, including their absolute denial of their having had anything to do with the disappearance of Lady Ragnall on the Nile.

"Now," I asked, "what is to be done? My fate is sealed, since for purposes of their own, of which probably we know nothing, these people intend to take me with them to their country, as indeed they are justified in doing, since I have been fool enough to keep a kind of assignation with them here. But they don't want anybody else. Therefore there is nothing to prevent you Ragnall, and you Savage, and you Hans, from returning with the Mazitu."

"Oh! Baas," said Hans, who could understand English well enough although he seldom spoke it, "why are you always bothering me with such *praatjes*?"—(that is, chatter). "Whatever you do I will do, and I don't care what you do, except for your own sake, Baas. If I am going to die, let me die; it doesn't at all matter how, since I must go soon and make report to your reverend father, the Predikant. And now, Baas, I have been awake all night, for I heard those camels coming a long while before the two spook men appeared, and as I have never heard camels before, could not make out what they were, for they don't walk like giraffes. So I am going to sleep, Baas, there in the sun. When you have settled things, you can wake me up and give me your orders," and he suited the action to the word, for when I glanced at him again he was, or appeared to be, slumbering, just like a dog at its master's feet.

I looked at Ragnall in interrogation.

"I am going on," he said briefly.

"Despite the denial of these men of any complicity in your wife's fate?" I asked. "If their words are true, what have you to gain by this journey, Ragnall?"

"An interesting experience while it lasts; that is all. Like Hans there, if what they say *is*. true, my future is a matter of complete indifference to me. But I do not believe a word of what they say. Something tells me that they know a great deal which they do not choose to repeat—about my wife I mean. That is why they are so anxious that I should not accompany you."

"You must judge for yourself," I answered doubtfully, "and I hope to Heaven that you are judging right. Now, Savage, what have you decided? Remember before you reply that these uncanny fellows declare that if we four go, two of us will never return. It seems impossible that they can read the future, still, without doubt, they *are* most uncanny."

"Sir," said Savage, "I will take my chance. Before I left England his lordship made a provision for my old mother and my widowed sister and her children, and I have none other dependent upon me. Moreover, I won't return alone with those Mazitu to become a barbarian, for how could I find my way back to the coast without anyone to guide me? So I'll go on and leave the rest to God."

"Which is just what we have all got to do," I remarked. "Well, as that is settled, let us send for Babemba and tell him."

This we did accordingly. The old fellow received the news with more resignation than I had anticipated. Fixing his one eye upon me, he said:

"Macumazana, these words are what I expected from you. Had any other man spoken them I should have declared that he was quite mad. But I remember that I said this when you determined to visit the Pongo, and that you came back from their country safe and sound, having done wonderful things there, and that it was the Pongo who suffered, not you. So I believe it will be again, so far as you are concerned, Macumazana, for I think that some devil goes with you who looks after his own. For the others I do not know. They must settle the matter with their own devils, or with those of the Kendah people. Now farewell, Macumazana, for it comes to me that we shall meet no more. Well, that happens to all at last, and it is good to have known you who are so great in your own way. Often I shall think of you as you will think of me, and hope that in a country beyond that of the Kendah I may hear from your lips all that has befallen you on this and other journeys. Now I go to withdraw my men before these white-robed Arabs come on their strange beasts to seize you, lest they should take us also and there should be a fight in which we, being the fewer, must die. The loads are all in order ready to be laden on their strange beasts. If they declare that the horses cannot cross the desert, leave them loose and we will catch them and take them home with us, and since they are male and female, breed young ones from them which shall be yours when you send for them, or Bausi the king's if you never send. Nay, I want no more presents who have the gun and the powder and the bullets you gave me, and the tusks of ivory for Bausi the king, and what is best of all, the memory of you and of your courage and wisdom. May these and the gods you worship befriend you. From yonder hill we will watch till we see that you have gone. Farewell," and waiting for no answer, he departed with the tears running from his solitary eye.

Ten minutes later the Mazitu bearers had also saluted us and gone, leaving us seated in that deserted camp surrounded by our baggage, and so far as I was concerned, feeling most lonely. Another ten minutes went by which we occupied in packing our personal belongings. Then Hans, who was now washing out the coffee kettle at a little distance, looked up and said:

"Here come the spook-men, Baas, the whole regiment of them." We ran and looked. It was true. Marshalled in orderly squadrons, the camels with their riders were sweeping towards us, and a fine sight the beasts made with their swaying necks and long, lurching gait. About fifty yards away they halted just where the stream from our spring entered the desert, and there proceeded to water the camels, twenty of them at a time. Two men, however, in whom I recognized Harût and Marût, walked forward and presently were standing before us, bowing obsequiously.

"Good morning, Lord," said Harût to Ragnall in his broken English. "So you come with Macumazana to call at our poor house, as we call at your fine one in England. You think we got the beautiful lady you marry, she we give old necklace. That is not so. No white lady ever in Kendahland. We hear story from Macumazana and believe that lady drowned in Nile, for you 'member she walk much in her sleep. We very sorry for you, but gods know their business. They leave when they will leave, and take when they will take. You find her again some day more beautiful still and with her soul come back."

Here I looked at him sharply. I had told him nothing about Lady Ragnall having lost her wits. How then did he know of the matter? Still I thought it best to hold my peace. I think that Harût saw he had made some mistake, for leaving the subject of Lady Ragnall, he went on:

"You very welcome, O Lord, but it right tell you this most dangerous journey, since elephant Jana not like strangers, and," he continued slowly, "think no elephant like your blood, and all elephants brothers. What one hate rest hate everywhere in world. See it in your face that you already suffer great hurt from elephant, you or someone near you. Also some of Kendah very fierce people and love fighting, and p'raps there war in the land while you there, and in war people get killed."

"Very good, my friend," said Ragnall, "I am prepared to take my chance of these things. Either we all go to your country together, as Macumazana has explained to you, or none of us go."

"We understand. That is our bargain and we no break word," replied Harût.

Then he turned his benevolent gaze upon Savage, and said: "So you come too, Mr. Bena. That your name here, eh? Well, you learn lot things in Kendahland, about snakes and all rest."

Here the jovial-looking Marût whispered something into the ear of his companion, smiling all over his face and showing his white teeth as he did so. "Oh!" went on Harût, "my brother tells me you meet one snake already, down in country called Natal, but sit on him so hard, that he grow quite flat and no bite."

"Who told him that?" gasped Savage.

"Oh! forget. Think Macumazana. No? Then p'raps you tell him in sleep, for people talk much in sleep, you know, and some other people got good ears and hear long way. Or p'raps little joke Harût. You 'member, he first-rate conjurer. P'raps he send that snake. No trouble if know how. Well, we show you much better snake Kendahland. But you no sit on *him*, Mr. Bena."

To me, I know not why, there was something horrible in all this jocosity, something that gave me the creeps as always does the sight of a cat playing with a mouse. I felt even then that it foreshadowed terrible things. How *could* these men know the details of occurrences at which they were not present and of which no one had told them? Did that strange "tobacco" of theirs really give them some clairvoyant power, I wondered, or had they other secret methods of obtaining news? I glanced at poor Savage and perceived that he too felt as I did, for he had turned quite pale beneath his tan. Even Hans was affected, for he whispered to me in Dutch: "These are not men; these are devils, Baas, and this journey of ours is one into hell."

Only Ragnall sat stern, silent, and apparently quite unmoved. Indeed there was something almost sphinx-like about the set and expression of his handsome face. Moreover, I felt sure that Harût and Marût recognized the man's strength and determination and that he was one with whom they must reckon seriously. Beneath all their smiles and courtesies I could read this knowledge in their eyes; also that it was causing them grave anxiety. It was as though they knew that here was one against whom their power had no avail, whose fate was the master of their fate. In a sense Harût admitted this to me, for suddenly he looked up and said in a changed voice and in Bantu:

"You are a good reader of hearts, O Macumazana, almost as good as I am. But remember that there is One Who writes upon the book of the heart, Who is the Lord of us who do but read, and that what He writes, that will befall, strive as we may, for in His hands is the future."

"Quite so," I replied coolly, "and that is why I am going with you to Kendahland and fear you not at all."

"So it is and so let it be," he answered. "And now, Lords, are you ready to start? For long is the road and who knows what awaits us ere we see its end?"

"Yes," I replied, "long is the road of life and who knows what awaits us ere we see its end—and after?"

Three hours later I halted the splendid white riding-camel upon which I was mounted, and looked back from the crest of a wave of the desert. There far behind us on the horizon, by the help of my glasses, I could make out the site of the camp we had left and even the tall ant-hill whence I had gazed in the moonlight at our mysterious escort which seemed to have sprung from the desert as though by magic.

This was the manner of our march: A mile or so ahead of us went a picket of eight or ten men mounted on the swiftest beasts, doubtless to give warning of any danger. Next, three or four hundred yards away, followed a body of about fifty Kendah, travelling in a double line, and behind these the baggage men, mounted like everyone else, and leading behind them strings of camels laden with water, provisions, tents of skin and all our goods, including the fifty rifles and the ammunition that Ragnall had brought from England. Then came we three white men and Hans, each of us riding as swift and fine a camel as Africa can breed. On our right at a distance of about half a mile, and also on our left, travelled other bodies of the Kendah of the same numerical strength as that ahead, while the rear was brought up by the remainder of the company who drove a number of spare camels.

Thus we journeyed in the centre of a square whence any escape would have been impossible, for I forgot to say that our keepers Harût and Marût rode exactly behind us, at such a distance that we could call to them if we wished.

At first I found this method of travelling very tiring, as does everyone who is quite unaccustomed to camel-back. Indeed the swing and the jolt of the swift creature beneath me seemed to wrench my bones asunder to such an extent that at the beginning I had once or twice to be lifted from the saddle when, after hours of torture, at length we camped for the night. Poor Savage suffered even more than I did, for the motion reduced him to a kind of jelly. Ragnall, however, who I think had ridden camels before, felt little inconvenience, and the same may be said of Hans, who rode in all sorts of positions, sometimes sideways like a lady, and at others kneeling on the saddle like a monkey on a barrel-organ. Also, being very light and tough as rimpis, the swaying motion did not seem to affect him.

By degrees all these troubles left us to such an extent that I could cover my fifty miles a day, more or less, without even feeling tired. Indeed I grew to like the life in that pure and sparkling desert air, perhaps because it was so restful. Day after day we journeyed on across the endless, sandy plain, watching the sun rise, watching it grow high, watching it sink again. Night after night we ate our simple food with appetite and slept beneath the glittering stars till the new dawn broke in glory from the bosom of the immeasurable East.

We spoke but little during all this time. It was as though the silence of the wilderness had got hold of us and sealed our lips. Or perhaps each of us was occupied with his own thoughts. At any rate I know that for my part I seemed to live in a kind of dreamland, thinking of the past, reflecting much upon the innumerable problems of this passing show called life, but not paying much heed to the future. What did the future matter to me, who did not know whether I should have a share of it even for another month, or week, or day, surrounded as I was by the shadow of death? No, I troubled little as to any earthly future, although I admit that in this oasis of calm I reflected upon that state where past, present and future will all be one; also that those reflections, which were in their essence a kind of unshaped prayer, brought much calm to my spirit.

With the regiment of escort we had practically no communication; I think that they had been forbidden to talk to us. They were a very silent set of men, finely-made, capable persons, of an Arab type, light rather than dark in colour, who seemed for the most part to communicate with each other by signs or in low-muttered words. Evidently they looked upon Harût and Marût with great veneration, for any order which either of these brethren gave, if they were brethren, was obeyed without dispute or delay. Thus, when I happened to mention that I had lost a pocket-knife at one of our camping-places two days' journey back, three of them, much against my wish, were ordered to return to look for it, and did so, making no question. Eight days later they rejoined us much exhausted and having lost a camel, but with the knife, which they handed to me with a low bow; and I confess that I felt ashamed to take the thing.

Nor did we exchange many further confidences with Harût and Marût. Up to the time of our arrival at the boundaries of the Kendah country, our only talk with them was of the incidents of travel, of where we should camp, of how far it might be to the next water, for water-holes or old wells existed in this desert, of such birds as we saw, and so forth. As to other and more important matters a kind of truce seemed to prevail. Still, I observed that they were always studying us, and especially Lord Ragnall, who rode on day after day, self-absorbed and staring straight in front of him as though he looked at something we could not see.

Thus we covered hundreds of miles, not less than five hundred at the least, reckoning our progress at only thirty miles a day, including stoppages. For occasionally we stopped at the water-holes or small oases, where the camels drank and rested. Indeed, these were so conveniently arranged that I came to the conclusion that once there must have been some established route running across these wastelands to the south, of which the traditional knowledge remained with the Kendah people. If so, it had not been used for generations, for save those of one or two that had died on the outward march, we saw no skeletons of camels or other beasts, or indeed any sign of man. The place was an absolute wilderness where nothing lived except a few small mammals at the oases and the birds that passed over it in the air on their way to more fertile regions. Of these, by the way, I saw many that are known both to Europe and Africa, especially ducks and cranes; also storks that, for aught I can say, may have come from far- off, homely Holland.

At last the character of the country began to change. Grass appeared on its lower-lying stretches, then bushes, then occasional trees and among the trees a few buck. Halting the caravan I crept out and shot two of these buck with a right and left, a feat that caused our grave escort to stare in a fashion which showed me that they had never seen anything of the sort done before.

That night, while we were eating the venison with relish, since it was the first fresh meat that we had tasted for many a day, I observed that the disposition of our camp was different from its common form. Thus it was smaller and placed on an eminence. Also the camels were not allowed to graze where they would as usual, but were kept within a limited area while their riders were arranged in groups outside of them. Further, the stores were piled near our tents, in the centre, with guards set over them. I asked Harût and Marût, who were sharing our meal, the reason of these alterations.

"It is because we are on the borders of the Kendah country," answered old Harût. "Four days' more march will bring us there, Macumazana."

"Then why should you take precautions against your own people? Surely they will welcome you."

"With spears perhaps. Macumazana, learn that the Kendah are not one but two people. As you may have heard before, we are the White Kendah, but there are also Black Kendah who outnumber us many times over, though in the beginning we from the north conquered them, or so says our history. The White Kendah have their own territory; but as there is no other road, to reach it we must pass through that of the Black Kendah, where it is always possible that we may be attacked, especially as we bring strangers into the land."

"How is it then that the Black Kendah allow you to live at all, Harût, if they are so much the more numerous?"

"Because of fear, Macumazana. They fear our wisdom and the decrees of the Heavenly Child spoken through the mouth of its oracle, which, if it is offended, can bring a curse upon them. Still, if they find us outside our borders they may kill us, if they can, as we may kill them if we find them within our borders."

"Indeed, Harût. Then it looks to me as though there were a war breeding between you."

"A war is breeding, Macumazana, the last great war in which either the White Kendah or the Black Kendah must perish. Or perhaps both will die together. Maybe that is the real reason why we have asked you to be our guest, Macumazana," and with their usual courteous bows, both of them rose and departed before I could reply.

"You see how it stands," I said to Ragnall. "We have been brought here to fight for our friends, Harût, Marût and Co., against their rebellious subjects, or rather the king who reigns jointly with them."

"It looks like it," he replied quietly, "but doubtless we shall find out the truth in time and meanwhile speculation is no good. Do you go to bed, Quatermain, I will watch till midnight and then wake you."

That night passed in safety. Next day we marched before the dawn, passing through country that grew continually better watered and more fertile, though it was still open plain but sloping upwards ever more steeply. On this plain I saw herds of antelopes and what in the distance looked like cattle, but no human being. Before evening we camped where there was good water and plenty of food for the camels.

While the camp was being set Harût came and invited us to follow him to the outposts, whence he said we should see a view. We walked with him, a matter of not more than a quarter of a mile to the head of that rise up which we had been travelling all day, and thence perceived one of the most glorious prospects on which my eyes have fallen in all great Africa. From where we stood the land sloped steeply for a matter of ten or fifteen miles, till finally the fall ended in a vast plain like to the bottom of a gigantic saucer, that I presume in some far time of the world's history was once an enormous lake. A river ran east and west across this plain and into it fell tributaries. Far beyond this river the contours of the country rose again till, many, many miles away, there appeared a solitary hill, tumulus-shaped, which seemed to be covered with bush.

Beyond and surrounding this hill was more plain which with the aid of my powerful glasses was, we could see, bordered at last by a range of great mountains, looking like a blue line pencilled across the northern distance. To the east and west the plain seemed to be illimitable. Obviously its soil was of a most fertile character and supported numbers of inhabitants, for everywhere we could see their kraals or villages. Much of it to the west, however, was covered with dense forest with, to all appearance, a clearing in its midst.

"Behold the land of the Kendah," said Harût. "On this side of the River Tava live the Black Kendah, on the farther side, the White Kendah."

"And what is that hill?"

"That is the Holy Mount, the Home of the Heavenly Child, where no man may set foot"—here he looked at us meaningly—"save the priests of the Child."

"What happens to him if he does?" I asked.

"He dies, my Lord Macumazana."

"Then it is guarded, Harût?"

"It is guarded, not with mortal weapons, Macumazana, but by the spirits that watch over the Child."

As he would say no more on this interesting matter, I asked him as to the numbers of the Kendah people, to which he replied that the Black Kendah might number twenty thousand men of arm-bearing age, but the White Kendah not more than two thousand.

"Then no wonder you want spirits to guard your Heavenly Child," I remarked, "since the Black Kendah are your foes and with you warriors are few."

At this moment our conversation was interrupted by the arrival of a picket on a camel, who reported something to Harût which appeared to disturb him. I asked him what was the matter.

"That is the matter," he said, pointing to a man mounted on a rough pony who just then appeared from behind some bushes about half a mile away, galloping down the slope towards the plain. "He is one of the scouts of Simba, King of the Black Kendah, and he goes to Simba's town in yonder forest to make report of our arrival.

Return to camp, Macumazana, and eat, for we must march with the rising of the moon."

As soon as the moon rose we marched accordingly, although the camels, many of which were much worn with the long journey, scarcely had been given time to fill themselves and none to rest. All night we marched down the long slope, only halting for half an hour before daylight to eat something and rearrange the loads on the baggage beasts, which now, I noticed, were guarded with extra care. When we were starting again Marût came to us and remarked with his usual smile, on behalf of his brother Harût, who was otherwise engaged, that it might be well if we had our guns ready, since we were entering the land of the elephant Jana and "who knew but that we might meet him?"

"Or his worshippers on two legs," I suggested, to which his only reply was a nod.

So we got our repeating rifles, some of the first that were ever made, serviceable but rather complicated weapons that fired five cartridges. Hans, however, with my permission, armed himself with the little Purdey piece that was named "Intombi," the singe-barrelled, muzzle- loading gun which had done me so much service in earlier days, and even on my last journey to Pongoland. He said that he was accustomed to it and did not understand these new-fangled breechloaders, also that it was "lucky." I consented as I did not think that it made much difference with what kind of rifle Hans was provided. As a marksman he had this peculiarity: up to a hundred yards or so he was an excellent shot, but beyond that distance no good at all.

A quarter of an hour later, as the dawn was breaking, we passed through a kind of *nek* of rough stones bordering the flat land, and emerged into a compact body on to the edge of the grassy plain. Here the word was given to halt for a reason that became clear to me so soon as I was out of the rocks. For there, marching rapidly, not half a mile away, were some five hundred white-robed men. A large proportion of these were mounted, the best being foot-soldiers, of whom more were running up every minute, appearing out of bush that grew upon the hill-side, apparently to dispute our passage. These people, who were black-faced with fuzzy hair upon which they wore no head-dress, all seemed to be armed with spears.

Presently from out of the mass of them two horsemen dashed forward, one of whom bore a white flag in token that they came to parley. Our advance guard allowed them to pass and they galloped on, dodging in and out between the camels with wonderful skill till at length they came to where we were with Harût and Marût, and pulling up their horses so sharply that the animals almost sat down on their haunches, saluted by raising their spears. They were very fine-looking fellows, perfectly black in colour with a negroid cast of countenance and long frizzled hair which hung down on to their shoulders. Their clothing was light, consisting of hide riding breeches that resembled bathing drawers, sandals, and an arrangement of triple chains which seemed to be made of some silvery metal that hung from their necks across the breast and back. Their arms consisted of a long lance similar to that carried by the White Kendah, and a straight, cross-handled sword suspended from a belt. This, as I ascertained afterwards, was the regulation cavalry equipment among these people. The footmen carried a shorter spear, a round leather shield, two throwing javelins or assegais, and a curved knife with a horn handle.

"Greeting, Prophets of the Child!" cried one of them. "We are messengers from the god Jana who speaks through the mouth of Simba the King."

"Say on, worshippers of the devil Jana. What word has Simba the King for us?" answered Harût.

"The word of war, Prophet. What do you beyond your southern boundary of the Tava river in the territory of the Black Kendah, that was sealed to them by pact after the battle of a hundred years ago? Is not all the land to the north as far as the mountains and beyond the mountains enough for you? Simba the King let you go out, hoping that the desert would swallow you, but return you shall not."

"That we shall know presently," replied Harût in a suave voice. "It depends upon whether the Heavenly Child or the devil Jana is the more powerful in the land. Still, as we would avoid bloodshed if we may, we desire to explain to you, messengers of King Simba, that we are here upon a peaceful errand. It was necessary that we should convey the white lords to make an offering to the Child, and this was the only road by which we could lead them to the Holy Mount, since they come from the south. Through the forests and the swamps that lie to the east and west camels cannot travel."

"And what is the offering that the white men would make to the Child, Prophet? Oh! we know well, for like you we have our magic. The offering that they must make is the blood of Jana our god, which you have brought them here to kill with their strange weapons, as though any weapon could prevail against Jana the god. Now, give to us these white men that we may offer them to the god, and perchance Simba the King will let you go through."

"Why?" asked Harût, "seeing that you declare that the white men cannot harm Jana, to whom indeed they wish no harm. To surrender them to you that they may be torn to pieces by the devil Jana would be to break the law of hospitality, for they are our guests. Now return to Simba the King, and say to Simba that if he lifts a spear against us the threefold curse of the Child shall fall upon him and upon you his people: The curse of Heaven by storm or by drought. The curse of famine. The curse of war. I the prophet have spoken. Depart."

Watching, I could see that this ultimatum delivered by Harût in a most impressive voice, and seconded as it was by the sudden and simultaneous lifting of the spears of all our escort that were within hearing, produced a considerable effect upon the messengers. Their faces grew afraid and they shrank a little. Evidently the "threefold curse of the Child" suggested calamities which they dreaded. Making no answer, they wheeled their horses about and galloped back to the force that was gathering below as swiftly as they had come.

"We must fight, my Lord Macumazana," said Harût, "and if we would live, conquer, as I know that we shall do."

Then he issued some orders, of which the result was that the caravan adopted a wedge-shaped formation like to that of a great flock of wildfowl on the wing. Harût stationed himself almost at the apex of the triangle. I with Hans and Marût were about the centre of the line, while Ragnall and Savage were placed opposite to us in the right line, the whole width of the wedge being between us. The baggage camels and their leaders occupied the middle space between the lines and were followed by a small rear-guard.

At first we white men were inclined to protest at this separation, but when Marût explained to us that its object was to give confidence to the two divisions of the force and also to minimize the risk of destruction or capture of all three of us, of course we had nothing more to say. So we just shook hands, and with as much assurance as we could command wished each other well through the job.

Then we parted, poor Savage looking very limp indeed, for this was his first experience of war. Ragnall, however, who came of an old fighting stock, seemed to be happy as a king. I who had known so many battles, was the reverse of happy, for inconveniently enough there flashed into my mind at this juncture the dying words of the Zulu captain and seer, Mavovo, which foretold that I too should fall far away in war; and I wondered whether this were the occasion that had been present to his foreseeing mind.

Only Hans seemed quite unconcerned. Indeed I noted that he took the opportunity of the halt to fill and light his large corn-cob pipe, a bit of bravado in the face of Providence for which I could have kicked him had he not been perched in his usual monkey fashion on the top of a very tall camel. The act, however, excited the admiration of the Kendah, for I heard one of them call to the others:

"Look! He is not a monkey after all, but a man—more of a man than his master."

The arrangements were soon made. Within a quarter of an hour of the departure of the messengers Harût, after bowing thrice towards the Holy Mountain, rose in his stirrups and shaking a long spear above his head, shouted a single word:

"Charge!"

Allan Is Captured

The ride that followed was really quite exhilarating. The camels, notwithstanding their long journey, seemed to have caught some of the enthusiasm of the war-horse as described in the Book of Job; indeed I had no idea that they could travel at such a rate. On we swung down the slope, keeping excellent order, the forest of tall spears shining and the little lancer-like pennons fluttering on the breeze in a very gallant way. In silence we went save for the thudding of the hoofs of the camels and an occasional squeal of anger as some rider drove his lance handle into their ribs. Not until we actually joined battle did a single man open his lips. Then, it is true, there went up one simultaneous and mighty roar of:

"The Child! Death to Jana! The Child! The Child!"

But this happened a few minutes later.

As we drew near the enemy I saw that they had massed their footmen in a dense body, six or eight lines thick. There they stood to receive the impact of our charge, or rather they did not all stand, for the first two ranks were kneeling with long spears stretched out in front of them. I imagine that their appearance must have greatly resembled that of the Greek phalanx, or that of the Swiss prepared to receive cavalry in the Middle Ages. On either side of this formidable body, which by now must have numbered four or five hundred men, and at a distance perhaps of a quarter of a mile from them, were gathered the horsemen of the Black Kendah, divided into two bodies of nearly equal strength, say about a hundred horse in each body.

As we approached, our triangle curved a little, no doubt under the direction of Harût. A minute or so later I saw the reason. It was that we might strike the foot-soldiers not full in front but at an angle. It was an admirable manœuvre, for when presently we did strike, we caught them swiftly on the flank and crumpled them up. My word! we went through those fellows like a knife through butter; they had as much chance against the rush of our camels as a brown-paper screen has against a typhoon. Over they rolled in heaps while the White Kendah spitted them with their lances.

"The Child is top dog! My money on the Child," reflected I in irreverent ecstasy. But that exultation was premature, for those Black Kendah were by no means all dead. Presently I saw that scores of them had appeared among the camels, which they were engaged in stabbing, or trying to stab, in the stomach with their spears. Also I had forgotten the horsemen. As our charge slackened owing to the complication in front, these arrived on our flanks like two thunderbolts. We faced about and did our best to meet the onslaught, of which the net result was that both our left and right lines were pierced through about fifty yards behind the baggage camels. Luckily for us the very impetuosity of the Black Kendah rush deprived it of most of the fruits of victory, since the two squadrons, being unable to check their horses, ended by charging into each other and becoming mixed in inextricable confusion. Then, I do not know who gave the order, we wheeled our camels in and fell upon them, a struggling, stationary mass, with the result that many of them were speared, or overthrown and trampled.

"I have said we, but that is not quite correct, at any rate so far as Marût, Hans, I and about fifteen camelmen were concerned. How it happened I could not tell in that dust and confusion, but we were cut off from the main body and presently found ourselves fighting desperately in a group at which Black Kendah horsemen were charging again and again. We made the best stand we could. By degrees the bewildered camels sank under the repeated spear-thrusts of the enemy, all except one, oddly enough that ridden by Hans, which by some strange chance was never touched. The rest of us were thrown or tumbled off the camels and continued the fight from behind their struggling bodies.

That is where I came in. Up to this time I had not fired a single shot, partly because I do not like missing, which it is so easy to do from the back of a swaying camel, and still more for the reason that I had not the slightest desire to kill any of these savage men unless I was obliged to do so in self-defence. Now, however, the thing was different, as I was fighting for my life. Leaning against my camel, which was dying and beating its head upon the ground, groaning horribly the while, I emptied the five cartridges of the repeater into those Black Kendah, pausing between each shot to take aim, with the result that presently five riderless horses were galloping loose about the veld.

The effect was electrical, since our attackers had never seen anything of the kind before. For a while they all drew off, which gave me time to reload. Then they came on again and I repeated the process. For a second time they retreated and after consultation which lasted for a minute or more, made a third attack. Once more I saluted them to the best of my ability, though on this occasion only three men and a horse fell. The fifth shot was a clean miss because they came on in such a scattered formation that I had to turn from side to side to fire.

Now at last the game was up, for the simple reason that I had no more cartridges save two in my double-barrelled pistol. It may be asked why. The answer is, want of foresight. Too many cartridges in one's pocket are apt to chafe on camel-back and so is a belt full of them. In those days also the engagements were few in which a man fired over fifteen. I had forty or fifty more in a bag, which bag Savage with his usual politeness had taken and hung upon his saddle without saying a word to me. At the beginning of the action I found this out, but could not then get them from him as he was separated from me. Hans, always careless in small matters, was really to blame as he ought to have seen that I had the cartridges, or at any rate to have carried them himself. In short, it was one of those accidents that will happen. There is nothing more to be said.

After a still longer consultation our enemies advanced on us for the fourth time, but very slowly. Meanwhile I had been taking stock of the position. The camel corps, or what was left of it, oblivious of our plight which the dust of conflict had hidden from them, was travelling on to the north, more or less victorious. That is to say, it had cut its way through the Black Kendah and was escaping unpursued, huddled up in a mob with the baggage animals safe in its centre. The Black Kendah themselves were engaged in killing our wounded and succouring their own; also in collecting the bodies of the dead. In short, quite unintentionally, we were deserted. Probably, if anybody thought about us at all in the turmoil of desperate battle, they concluded that we were among the slain.

Marût came up to me, unhurt, still smiling and waving a bloody spear.

"Lord Macumazana," he said, "the end is at hand. The Child has saved the others, or most of them, but us it has abandoned. Now what will you do? Kill yourself, or if that does not please you, suffer me to kill you? Or shoot on until you must surrender?"

"I have nothing to shoot with any more," I answered. "But if we surrender, what will happen to us?"

"We shall be taken to Simba's town and there sacrificed to the devil Jana—I have not time to tell you how. Therefore I propose to kill myself."

"Then I think you are foolish, Marût, since once we are dead, we are dead; but while we are alive it is always possible that we may escape from Jana. If the worst comes to the worst I have a pistol with two bullets in it, one for you and one for me."

"The wisdom of the Child is in you," he replied. "I shall surrender with you, Macumazana, and take my chance."

Then he turned and explained things to his followers, who spoke together for a moment. In the end these took a strange and, to my mind, a very heroic decision. Waiting till the attacking Kendah were quite close to us, with the exception of three men, who either because they lacked courage or for some other reason, stayed with us, they advanced humbly as though to make submission. A number of the Black Kendah dismounted and ran up, I suppose to take them prisoners. The men waited till these were all round them. Then with a yell of "The Child!" they sprang forward, taking the enemy unawares and fighting like demons, inflicted great loss upon them before they fell themselves covered with wounds.

"Brave men indeed!" said Marût approvingly. "Well, now they are all at peace with the Child, where doubtless we shall find them ere long."

I nodded but answered nothing. To tell the truth, I was too much engaged in nursing the remains of my own courage to enter into conversation about that of other people.

This fierce and cunning stratagem of desperate men which had cost their enemies so dear, seemed to infuriate the Black Kendah.

At us came the whole mob of them—we were but six now—roaring "Jana! Jana!" and led by a grey-beard who, to judge from the number of silver chains upon his breast and his other trappings, seemed to be a great man among them. When they were about fifty yards away and I was preparing for the worst, a shot rang out from above and behind me. At the same instant Greybeard threw his arms wide and letting fall the spear he held, pitched from his horse, evidently stone dead. I glanced back and saw Hans, the corn-cob pipe still in his mouth and the little rifle, "Intombi," still at his shoulder. He had fired from the back of the camel, I think for the first time that day, and whether by chance or through good marksmanship, I do not know, had killed this man.

His sudden and unexpected end seemed to fill the Black Kendah with grief and dismay. Halting in their charge they gathered round him, while a fierce-looking middle-aged man, also adorned with much barbaric finery, dismounted to examine him.

"That is Simba the King," said Marût, "and the slain one is his uncle, Goru, the great general who brought him up from a babe."

"Then I wish I had another cartridge left for the nephew," I began and stopped, for Hans was speaking to me.

"Good-bye, Baas," he said, "I must go, for I cannot load 'Intombi' on the back of this beast. If you meet your reverend father the Predikant before I do, tell him to make a nice place ready for me among the fires."

Then before I could get out an answer, Hans dragged his camel round; as I have said, it was quite uninjured. Urging it to a shambling gallop with blows of the rifle stock, he departed at a great rate, not towards the home of the Child but up the hill into a brake of giant grass mingled with thorn trees that grew quite close at hand. Here with startling suddenness both he and the camel vanished away.

If the Black Kendah saw him go, of which I am doubtful, for they all seemed to be lost in consultation round their king and the dead general, Goru, they made no attempt to follow him. Another possibility is that they thought he was trying to lead them into some snare or ambush.

I do not know what they thought because I never heard them mention Hans or the matter of his disappearance, if indeed they ever realized that there was such a person. Curiously enough in the case of men who had just shown themselves so brave, this last accident of the decease of Goru coming on the top of all their other casualties, seemed to take the courage out of them. It was as though they had come to the conclusion that we with our guns were something more than mortal.

For several minutes they debated in evident hesitation. At last from out of their array rode a single man, in whom I recognized one of the envoys who had met us in the morning, carrying in his hand a white flag as he had done before. Thereon I laid down my rifle in token that I would not fire at him, which indeed I could not do having nothing to fire. Seeing this he came to within a few yards and halting, addressed Marût.

"O second Prophet of the Child," he said, "these are the words of Simba the King: Your god has been too strong for us to-day, though in a day to come it may be otherwise. I thought I had you in a pit; that you were the bucks and I the hunter. But, though with loss, you have escaped out of the pit," and the speaker glanced towards our retreating force which was now but a cloud of dust in the far distance, "while I the hunter have been gored by your horns," and again he glanced at the dead that were scattered about the plain. "The noblest of the buck, the white bull of the herd," and he looked at me, who in any other circumstances would have felt complimented, "and you, O Prophet Marût, and one or two others, besides those that I have slain, are however still in the pit and your horn is a magic horn," here he pointed to my rifle, "which pierces from afar and kills dead all by whom it is touched."

"So I caught those gentry well in the middle," thought I to myself, "and with soft-nosed bullets!"

"Therefore I, Simba the King, make you an offer. Yield yourselves and I swear that no spear shall be driven through your hearts and no knife come near your throats. You shall only be taken to my town and there be fed on the best and kept as prisoners, till once more there is peace between the Black Kendah and the White. If you refuse, then I will ring you round and perhaps in the dark rush on you and kill you all. Or perhaps I will watch you from day to day till you, who have no water, die of thirst in the heat of the sun. These are my words to which nothing may be added and from which nothing shall be taken away."

Having finished this speech he rode back a few yards out of earshot, and waited.

"What will you answer, Lord Macumazana?" asked Marût.

I replied by another question. "Is there any chance of our being rescued by your people?"

He shook his head. "None. What we have seen to-day is but a small part of the army of the Black Kendah, one regiment of foot and one of horse, that are always ready. By to-morrow thousands will be gathered, many more than we can hope to deal with in the open and still less in their strongholds, also Harût will believe that we are dead. Unless the Child saves us we shall be left to our fate."

"Then it seems that we are indeed in a pit, as that black brute of a king puts it, Marût, and if he does what he says and rushes us at sundown, everyone of us will be killed. Also I am thirsty already and there is nothing to drink. But will this king keep his word? There are other ways of dying besides by steel."

"I think that he will keep his word, but as that messenger said, he will not add to his word. Choose now, for see, they are beginning to hedge us round."

"What do you say, men?" I asked of the three who had remained with us.

"We say, Lord, that we are in the hands of the Child, though we wish now that we had died with our brothers," answered their spokesman fatalistically.

So after Marût and I had consulted together for a little as to the form of his reply, he beckoned to the messenger and said:

"We accept the offer of Simba, although it would be easy for this lord to kill him now where he stands, namely, to yield ourselves as prisoners on his oath that no harm shall come to us. For know that if harm does come, the vengeance will be terrible. Now in proof of his good faith, let Simba draw near and drink the cup of peace with us, for we thirst."

"Not so," said the messenger, "for then that white lord might kill him with his tube. Give me the tube and Simba shall come."

"Take it," I said magnanimously, handing him the rifle, which he received in a very gingerly fashion. After all, I reflected, there is nothing much more useless than a rifle without ammunition.

Off he went holding the weapon at arm's length, and presently Simba himself, accompanied by some of his men, one of whom carried a skin of water and another a large cup hollowed from an elephant's tusk, rode up to us. This Simba was a fine and rather terrifying person with a large moustache and a chin shaved except for a little tuft of hair which he wore at its point like an Italian. His eyes were big and dark, frank-looking, yet now and again with sinister expression in the corners of them. He was not nearly so black as most of his followers; probably in bygone generations his blood had been crossed with that of the White Kendah. He wore his hair long without any head-dress, held in place by a band of gold which I suppose represented a crown. On his forehead was a large white scar, probably received in some battle. Such was his appearance.

He looked at me with great curiosity, and I have often wondered since what kind of an impression I produced upon him. My hat had fallen off, or I had knocked it off when I fired my last cartridge into his people, and forgotten to replace it, and my intractable hair, which was longer than usual, had not been recently brushed. My worn Norfolk jacket was dyed with blood from a wounded or dying man who had tumbled against me in the scrimmage when the cavalry charged us, and my right leg and boot were stained in a similar fashion from having rubbed against my camel where a spear had entered it. Altogether I must have appeared a most disreputable object.

Some indication of his opinion was given, however, in a remark, which of course I pretended not to understand, that I overheard him make to one of his officers:

"Truly," he said, "we must not always look to the strong for strength. And yet this little white porcupine is strength itself, for see how much damage he has wrought us. Also consider his eyes that appear to pierce everything. Jana himself might fear those eyes. Well, time that grinds the rocks will tell us all."

All of this I caught perfectly, my ears being very sharp, although he thought that he spoke out of my hearing, for after spending a month in their company I understood the Kendah dialect of Bantu very well.

Having delivered himself thus he rode nearer and said:

"You, Prophet Marût, my enemy, have heard the terms of me, Simba the King, and have accepted them. Therefore discuss them no more. What I have promised I will keep. What I have given I give, neither greater nor less by the weight of a hair."

"So be it, O King," answered Marût with his usual smile, which nothing ever seemed to disturb. "Only remember that if those terms are broken either in the letter or in the spirit, especially the spirit" (that is the best rendering I can give of his word), "the manifold curses of the Child will fall upon you and yours. Yes, though you kill us all by treachery, still those curses will fall."

"May Jana take the Child and all who worship it," exclaimed the king with evident irritation.

"In the end, O King, Jana will take the Child and its followers—or the Child will take Jana and his followers. Which of these things must happen is known to the Child alone, and perchance to its prophets. Meanwhile, for every one of those of the Child I think that three of the followers of Jana, or more, lie dead upon this field. Also the caravan is now out of your reach with two of the white lords and many of such tubes which deal death, like that which we have surrendered to you. Therefore because we are helpless, do not think that the Child is helpless. Jana must have been asleep, O King, or you would have set your trap better."

I thought that this coolly insolent speech would have produced some outburst, but in fact it seemed to have an opposite effect. Making no reply to it, Simba said almost humbly:

"I come to drink the cup of peace with you and the white lord, O Prophet. Afterwards we can talk. Give me water, slave."

Then a man filled the great ivory cup with water from the skin he carried. Simba took it and having sprinkled a little upon the ground, I suppose as an offering, drank from the cup, doubtless to show that it was not poisoned. Watching carefully, I made sure that he swallowed what he drank by studying the motions of his throat. Then he handed the cup with a bow to Marût, who with a still deeper bow passed it to me. Being absolutely parched I absorbed about a pint of it, and feeling a new man, passed the horn to Marût, who swallowed the rest. Then it was filled again for our three White Kendah, the King first tasting the water as before, after which Marût and I had a second pull.

When at length our thirst was satisfied, horses were brought to us, serviceable and docile little beasts with sheepskins for saddles and loops of hide for stirrups. On these we mounted and for the next three hours rode across the plain, surrounded by a strong escort and with an armed Black Kendah running on each side of our horses and holding in his hand a thong attached to the ring of the bridle, no doubt to prevent any attempt to escape.

Our road ran past but not through some villages whence we saw many women and children staring at us, and through beautiful crops of mealies and other sorts of grain that in this country were now just ripening. The luxuriant appearance of these crops suggested that the rains must have been plentiful and the season all that could be desired. From some of the villages by the track arose a miserable sound of wailing. Evidently their inhabitants had already heard that certain of their menkind had fallen in that morning's fight.

At the end of the third hour we began to enter the great forest which I had seen when first we looked down on Kendahland. It was filled with splendid trees, most of them quite strange to me, but perhaps because of the denseness of their overshadowing crowns there was comparatively no undergrowth. The general effect of the place was very gloomy, since little light could pass through the interlacing foliage of the tops of those mighty trees.

Towards evening we came to a clearing in this forest, it may have been four or five miles in diameter, but whether it was natural or artificial I am not sure. I think, however, that it was probably the former for two reasons: the hollow nature of the ground, which lay a good many feet lower than the surrounding forest, and the wonderful fertility of the soil, which suggested that it had once been deposited upon an old lake bottom. Never did I see such crops as those that grew upon that clearing; they were magnificent.

Wending our way along the road that ran through the tall corn, for here every inch was cultivated, we came suddenly upon the capital of the Black Kendah, which was known as Simba Town. It was a large place, somewhat different from any other African settlement with which I am acquainted, inasmuch as it was not only stockaded but completely surrounded by a broad artificial moat filled with water from a stream that ran through the centre of the town, over which moat there were four timber bridges placed at the cardinal points of the compass. These bridges were strong enough to bear horses or stock, but so made that in the event of attack they could be destroyed in a few minutes.

Riding through the eastern gate, a stout timber structure on the farther side of the corresponding bridge, where the king was received with salutes by an armed guard, we entered one of the main streets of the town which ran from north to south and from east to west. It was broad and on either side of it were the dwellings of the inhabitants set close together because the space within the stockade was limited. These were not huts but square buildings of mud with flat roofs of some kind of cement. Evidently they were built upon the model of Oriental and North African houses of which some debased tradition remained with these people. Thus a stairway or ladder ran from the interior to the roof of each house, whereon its inhabitants were accustomed, as I discovered afterwards, to sleep during a good part of the year, also to eat in the cool of the day. Many of them were gathered there now to watch us pass, men, women, and children, all except the little ones decently clothed in long garments of various colours, the women for the most part in white and the men in a kind of bluish linen.

I saw at once that they had already heard of the fight and of the considerable losses which their people had sustained, for their reception of us prisoners was most unfriendly. Indeed the men shook their fists at us, the women screamed out curses, while the children stuck out their tongues in token of derision or defiance. Most of these demonstrations, however, were directed at Marût and his followers, who only smiled indifferently. At me they stared in wonder not unmixed with fear.

A quarter of a mile or so from the gate we came to an inner enclosure, that answered to the South African cattle kraal, surrounded by a dry ditch and a timber palisade outside of which was planted a green fence of some shrub with long white thorns. Here we passed through more gates, to find ourselves in an oval space, perhaps five acres in extent. Evidently this served as a market ground, but all around it were open sheds where hundreds of horses were stabled. No cattle seemed to be kept there, except a few that with sheep and goats were driven in every day for slaughter purposes at a shambles at the north end, from the great stock kraals built beyond the forest to the south, where they were safe from possible raiding by the White Kendah.

A tall reed fence cut off the southern end of this marketplace, outside of which we were ordered to dismount. Passing through yet another gate we found within the fence a large hut or house built on the same model as the others in the town, which Marût whispered to me was that of the king. Behind it were smaller houses in which lived his queen and women, good-looking females, who advanced to meet him with obsequious bows. To the right and left were two more buildings of about equal size, one of which was occupied by the royal guard and the other was the guest-house whither we were conducted.

It proved to be a comfortable dwelling about thirty feet square but containing only one room, with various huts behind it that served for cooking and other purposes. In one of these the three camelmen were placed. Immediately on our arrival food was brought to us, a lamb or kid roasted whole upon a wooden platter, and some green mealie-cobs boiled upon another platter; also water to drink and wash with in earthenware jars of sun-dried clay.

I ate heartily, for I was starving. Then, as it was useless to attempt precautions against murder, without any talk to my fellow prisoner, for which we were both too tired, I threw myself down on a mattress stuffed with corn husks in a corner of the hut, drew a skin rug over me and, having commended myself to the protection of the Power above, fell fast asleep.

The First Curse

The next thing I remember was feeling upon my face the sunlight that poured through a window-place which was protected by immovable wooden bars. For a while I lay still, reflecting as memory returned to me upon all the events of the previous day and upon my present unhappy position. Here I was a prisoner in the hands of a horde of fierce savages who had every reason to hate me, for though this was done in self-defence, had I not killed a number of their people against whom personally I had no quarrel? It was true that their king had promised me safety, but what reliance could be put upon the word of such a man? Unless something occurred to save me, without doubt my days were numbered. In this way or in that I should be murdered, which served me right for ever entering upon such a business.

The only satisfactory point in the story was that, for the present at any rate, Ragnall and Savage had escaped, though doubtless sooner or later fate would overtake them also. I was sure that they had escaped, since two of the camelmen with us had informed Marût that they saw them swept away surrounded by our people and quite unharmed. Now they would be grieving over my death, since none survived who could tell them of our capture, unless the Black Kendah chose to do so, which was not likely. I wondered what course they would take when Ragnall found that his quest was vain, as of course must happen. Try to get out of the country, I suppose, as I prayed they might succeed in doing, though this was most improbable.

Then there was Hans. He of course would attempt to retrace our road across the desert, if he had got clear away. Having a good camel, a rifle and some ammunition, it was just possible that he might win through, as he never forgot a path which he had once travelled, though probably in a week's time a few bones upon the desert would be all that remained of him. Well, as he had suggested, perhaps we should soon be talking the event over in some far sphere with my father—and others. Poor old Hans!

I opened my eyes and looked about me. The first thing I noticed was that my double-barrelled pistol, which I had placed at full cock beside me before I went to sleep, was gone, also my large clasp-knife. This discovery did not tend to raise my spirits, since I was now quite weaponless. Then I observed Marût seated on the floor of the hut staring straight in front of him, and noted that at length even he had ceased to smile, but that his lips were moving as though he were engaged in prayer or meditation.

"Marût," I said, "someone has been in this place while we were asleep and stolen my pistol and knife."

"Yes, Lord," he answered, "and my knife also. I saw them come in the middle of the night, two men who walked softly as cats, and searched everything."

"Then why did you not wake me?"

"What would have been the use, Lord? If we had caught hold of the men, they would have called out and we should have been murdered at once. It was best to let them take the things, which after all are of no good to us here."

"The pistol might have been of some good," I replied significantly.

"Yes," he said, nodding, "but at the worst death is easy to find."

"Do you think, Marût, that we could manage to let Harût and the others know our plight? That smoke which I breathed in England, for instance, seemed to show me far-off things—if we could get any of it."

"The smoke was nothing, Lord, but some harmless burning powder which clouded your mind for a minute, and enabled you to see the thoughts that were in *our* minds. *We* drew the pictures at which you looked. Also here there is none."

"Oh!" I said, "the old trick of suggestion; just what I imagined. Then there's an end of that, and as the others will think that we are dead and we cannot communicate with them, we have no hope except in ourselves."

"Or the Child," suggested Marût gently.

"Look here!" I said with irritation. "After you have just told me that your smoke vision was a mere conjurer's trick, how do you expect me to believe in your blessed Child? Who is the Child? What is the Child, and—this is more important—what can it do? As your throat is going to be cut shortly you may as well tell me the truth."

"Lord Macumazana, I will. Who and what the Child is I cannot say because I do not know. But it has been our god for thousands of years, and we believe that our remote forefathers brought it with them when they were driven out of Egypt at some time unknown. We have writings concerning it done up in little rolls, but as we cannot read them they are of no use to us. It has an hereditary priesthood, of which Harût my uncle, for he is my uncle, is the head. We believe that the Child is God, or rather a symbol in which God dwells, and that it can save us in this world and the next, for we hold that man is an immortal spirit. We believe also that through its Oracle—a priestess who is called Guardian of the Child—it can declare the future and bring blessings or curses upon men, especially upon our enemies. When the Oracle dies we are helpless since the Child has no 'mouth' and our enemies prevail against us. This happened a long while ago, and the last Oracle having declared before her death that her successor was to be found in England, my uncle and I travelled thither disguised as conjurers and made search for many years. We thought that we had found the new Oracle in the lady who married the Lord Igeza, because of that mark of the new moon upon her neck. After our return to Africa, however, for as I have spoken of this matter I may as well tell you all," here he stared me full in the eyes and spoke in a clear metallic voice which somehow no longer convinced me, "we found that we had made a mistake, for the real Oracle, a mere girl, was discovered among our own people, and has now been for two years installed in her office. Without doubt the last Guardian of the Child was wandering in her mind when she told us that story before her death as to a woman in England, a country of which she had heard through Arabs. That is all."

"Thank you," I replied, feeling that it would be useless to show any suspicion of his story. "Now will you be so good as to tell me who and what is the god, or the elephant Jana, whom you have brought me here to kill? Is the elephant a god, or is the god an elephant? In either case what has it to do with the Child?"

"Lord, Jana among us Kendah represents the evil in the world, as the Child represents the good. Jana is he whom the Mohammedans call Shaitan and the Christians call Satan, and our forefathers, the old Egyptians, called Set."

"Ah!" thought I to myself, "now we have got it. Horus the Divine Child, and Set the evil monster, with whom it strives everlastingly."

"Always," went on Marût, "there has been war between the Child and Jana, that is, between Good and Evil, and we know that in the end one of them must conquer the other."

"The whole world has known that from the beginning," I interrupted. "But who and what is this Jana?"

"Among the Black Kendah, Lord, Jana is an elephant, or at any rate his symbol is an elephant, a very terrible beast to which sacrifices are made, that kills all who do not worship him if he chances to meet them. He lives farther on in the forest yonder, and the Black Kendah make use of him in war, for the devil in him obeys their priests."

"Indeed, and is this elephant always the same?"

"I cannot tell you, but for many generations it has been the same, for it is known by its size and by the fact that one of its tusks is twisted downwards."

"Well," I remarked, "all this proves nothing, since elephants certainly live for at least two hundred years, and perhaps much longer. Also, after they become 'rogues' they acquire every kind of wicked and unnatural habit, as to which I could tell you lots of stories. Have you seen this elephant?"

"No, Macumazana," he answered with a shiver. "If I had seen it should I have been alive to-day? Yet I fear I am fated to see it ere long, not alone," and again he shivered, looking at me in a very suggestive manner.

At this moment our conversation was interrupted by the arrival of two Black Kendahs who brought us our breakfast of porridge and a boiled fowl, and stood there while we ate it. For my part I was not sorry, as I had learned all I wanted to know of the theological opinions and practice of the land, and had come to the conclusion that the terrible devil-god of the Black Kendah was merely a rogue elephant of unusual size and ferocity, which under other circumstances it would have given me the greatest pleasure to try to shoot.

When we had finished eating, that is soon, for neither of our appetites was good that morning, we walked out of the house into the surrounding compound and visited the camelmen in their hut. Here we found them squatted on the ground looking very depressed indeed. When I asked them what was the matter they replied, "Nothing," except that they were men about to die and life was pleasant. Also they had wives and children whom they would never see again.

Having tried to cheer them up to the best of my ability, which I fear I did without conviction, for in my heart I agreed with their view of the case, we returned to the guest-house and mounted the stair which led to the flat roof. Hence we saw that some curious ceremony was in progress in the centre of the market-place. At that distance we could not make out the details, for I forgot to say that my glasses had been stolen with the pistol and knife, probably because they were supposed to be lethal weapons or instruments of magic.

A rough altar had been erected, on which a fire burned. Behind it the king, Simba, was seated on a stool with various councillors about him. In front of the altar was a stout wooden table, on which lay what looked like the body of a goat or a sheep. A fantastically dressed man, assisted by other men, appeared to be engaged in inspecting the inside of this animal with, we gathered, unsatisfactory results, for presently he raised his arms and uttered a loud wail. Then the creature's viscera were removed from it and thrown upon the fire, while the rest of the carcass was carried off.

I asked Marût what he thought they were doing. He replied dejectedly:

"Consulting their Oracle; perhaps as to whether we should live or die, Macumazana."

Just then the priest in the strange, feathered attire approached the king, carrying some small object in his hand. I wondered what it could be, till the sound of a report reached my ears and I saw the man begin to jump round upon one leg, holding the other with both his hands at the knee and howling loudly.

"Ah!" I said, "that pistol was full cocked, and the bullet got him in the foot."

Simba shouted out something, whereon a man picked up the pistol and threw it into the fire, round which the others gathered to watch it burn.

"You wait," I said to Marût, and as I spoke the words the inevitable happened.

Off went the other barrel of the pistol, which hopped out of the fire with the recoil like a living thing. But as it happened one of the assistant priests was standing in front of the mouth of that barrel, and he also hopped once, but never again, for the heavy bullet struck him somewhere in the body and killed him. Now there was consternation. Everyone ran away, leaving the dead man lying on the ground. Simba led the rout and the head-priest brought up the rear, skipping along upon one leg.

Having observed these events, which filled me with an unholy joy, we descended into the house again as there was nothing more to see, also because it occurred to me that our presence on the roof, watching their discomfiture, might irritate these savages. About ten minutes later the gate of the fence round the guest-house was thrown open, and through it came four men carrying on a stretcher the body of the priest whom the bullet had killed, which they laid down in front of our door. Then followed the king with an armed guard, and after him the befeathered diviner with his foot bound up, who supported himself upon the shoulders of two of his colleagues. This man, I now perceived, wore a hideous mask, from which projected two tusks in imitation of those of an elephant. Also there were others, as many as the space would hold.

The king called to us to come out of the house, which, having no choice, we did. One glance at him showed me that the man was frantic with fear, or rage, or both.

"Look upon your work, magicians!" he said in a terrible voice, pointing first to the dead priest, then to the diviner's wounded foot.

"It is no work of ours, King Simba," answered Marût. "It is your own work. You stole the magic weapon of the white lord and made it angry, so that it has revenged itself upon you."

"It is true," said Simba, "that the tube has killed one of those who took it away from you and wounded the other" (here was luck indeed). "But it was you who ordered it to do so, magicians. Now, hark! Yesterday I promised you safety, that no spear should pierce your hearts and no knife come near your throats, and drank the cup of peace with you. But you have broken the pact, working us more harm, and therefore it no longer holds, since there are many other ways in which men can die. Listen again! This is my decree. By your magic you have taken away the life of one of my servants and hurt another of my servants, destroying the middle toe of his left foot. If within three days you do not give back the life to him who seems to be dead, and give back the toe to him who seems to be hurt, as you well can do, then you shall join those whom you have slain in the land of death, how I will not tell you."

Now when I heard this amazing sentence I gasped within myself, but thinking it better to keep up my rôle of understanding nothing of their talk, I preserved an immovable countenance and left Marût to answer. This, to his credit be it recorded, he did with his customary pleasant smile.

"O King," he said, "who can bring the dead back to life? Not even the Child itself, at any rate in this world, for there is no way."

"Then, Prophet of the Child, you had better find a way, or, I repeat, I send you to join them," he shouted, rolling his eyes.

"What did my brother, the great Prophet, promise to you but yesterday, O King, if you harmed us?" asked Marût. "Was it not that the three great curses should fall upon your people? Learn now that if so much as one of us is murdered by you, these things shall swiftly come to pass. I, Marût, who am also a Prophet of the Child, have said it."

Now Simba seemed to go quite mad, so mad that I thought all was over. He waved his spear and danced about in front of us, till the silver chains clanked upon his breast. He vituperated the Child and its worshippers, who, he declared, had worked evil on the Black Kendah for generations. He appealed to his god Jana to avenge these evils, "to pierce the Child with his tusks, to tear it with his trunk, and to trample it with his feet," all of which the wounded diviner ably seconded through his horrid mask.

There we stood before him, I leaning against the wall of the house with an air of studied nonchalance mingled with mild interest, at least that is what I meant to do, and Marût smiling sweetly and staring at the heavens. Whilst I was wondering what exact portion of my frame was destined to become acquainted with that spear, of a sudden Simba gave it up. Turning to his followers, he bade them dig a hole in the corner of our little enclosure and set the dead man in it, "with his head out so that he may breathe," an order which they promptly executed.

Then he issued a command that we should be well fed and tended, and remarking that if the departed was not alive and healthy on the third morning from that day, we should hear from him again, he and his company stalked off, except those men who were occupied with the interment.

Soon this was finished also. There sat the deceased buried to the neck with his face looking towards the house, a most disagreeable sight. Presently, however, matters were improved in this respect by one of the sextons fetching a large earthenware pot and several smaller pots full of food and water. The latter they set round the head, I suppose for the sustenance of the body beneath, and then placed the big vessel inverted over all, "to keep the sun off our sleeping brother," as I heard one say to the other.

This pot looked innocent enough when all was done, like one of those that gardeners in England put over forced rhubarb, no more. And yet, such is the strength of the imagination, I think that on the whole I should have preferred the object underneath naked and unadorned. For instance, I have forgotten to say that the heads of those of the White Kendah who had fallen in the fight had been set up on poles in front of Simba's house. They were unpleasant to contemplate, but to my mind not so unpleasant as that pot.

As a matter of fact, this precaution against injury from the sun to the late diviner proved unnecessary, since by some strange chance from that moment the sun ceased to shine. Quite suddenly clouds arose which gradually covered the whole sky and the weather began to turn very cold, unprecedentedly so, Marût informed me, for the time of year, which, it will be remembered, in this country was the season just before harvest. Obviously the Black Kendah thought so also, since from our seats on the roof, whither we had retreated to be as far as possible from the pot, we saw them gathered in the market-place, staring at the sky and talking to each other.

The day passed without any further event, except the arrival of our meals, for which we had no great appetite. The night came, earlier than usual because of the clouds, and we fell asleep, or rather into a series of dozes. Once I thought that I heard someone stirring in the huts behind us, but as it was followed by silence I took no more notice. At length the light broke very slowly, for now the clouds were denser than ever. Shivering with the cold, Marût and I made a visit to the camel-drivers, who were not allowed to enter our house. On going into their hut we saw to our horror that only two of them remained, seated stonily upon the floor. We asked where the third was. They replied they did not know. In the middle of the night, they said, men had crept in, who seized, bound and gagged him, then dragged him away. As there was nothing to be said or done, we returned to breakfast filled with horrid fears.

Nothing happened that day except that some priests arrived, lifted the earthenware pot, examined their departed colleague, who by now had become an unencouraging spectacle, removed old dishes of food, arranged more about him, and went off. Also the clouds grew thicker and thicker, and the air more and more chilly, till, had we been in any northern latitude, I should have said that snow was pending. From our perch on the roof-top I observed the population of Simba Town discussing the weather with ever-increasing eagerness; also that the people who were going out to work in the fields wore mats over their shoulders.

Once more darkness came, and this night, notwithstanding the cold, we spent wrapped in rugs, on the roof of the house. It had occurred to us that kidnapping would be less easy there, as we could make some sort of a fight at the head of the stairway, or, if the worst came to the worst, dive from the parapet and break our necks. We kept watch turn and turn about. During my watch about midnight I heard a noise going on in the hut behind us; scuffling and a stifled cry which turned my blood cold. About an hour later a fire was lighted in the centre of the market-place where the sheep had been sacrificed, and by the flare of it I could see people moving. But what they did I could not see, which was perhaps as well.

Next morning only one of the camelmen was left. This remaining man was now almost crazy with fear, and could give no clear account of what had happened to his companion.

The poor fellow implored us to take him away to our house, as he feared to be left alone with "the black devils." We tried to do so, but armed guards appeared mysteriously and thrust him back into his own hut.

This day was an exact repetition of the others. The same inspection of the deceased and renewal of his food; the same cold, clouded sky, the same agitated conferences in the market-place.

For the third time darkness fell upon us in that horrible place. Once more we took refuge on the roof, but this night neither of us slept. We were too cold, too physically miserable, and too filled with mental apprehensions. All nature seemed to be big with impending disaster. The sky appeared to be sinking down upon the earth. The moon was hidden, yet a faint and lurid light shone now in one quarter of the horizon, now in another. There was no wind, but the air moaned audibly. It was as though the end of the world were near as, I reflected, probably might be the case so far as we were concerned. Never, perhaps, have I felt so spiritually terrified as I was during the dreadful inaction of that night. Even if I had known that I was going to be executed at dawn, I think that by comparison I should have been light-hearted. But the worst part of the business was that I knew nothing. I was like a man forced to walk through dense darkness among precipices, quite unable to guess when my journey would end in space, but enduring all the agonies of death at every step.

About midnight again we heard that scuffle and stifled cry in the hut behind us.

"He's gone," I whispered to Marût, wiping the cold sweat from my brow.

"Yes," answered Marût, "and very soon we shall follow him, Macumazana."

I wished that his face were visible so that I could see if he still smiled when he uttered those words.

An hour or so later the usual fire appeared in the marketplace, round which the usual figures flitted dimly. The sight of them fascinated me, although I did not want to look, fearing what I might see. Luckily, however, we were too far off to discern anything at night.

While these unholy ceremonies were in progress the climax came, that is so far as the weather was concerned. Of a sudden a great gale sprang up, a gale of icy wind such as in Southern Africa sometimes precedes a thunderstorm. It blew for half an hour or more, then lulled. Now lightning flashed across the heavens, and by the glare of it we perceived that all the population of Simba Town seemed to be gathered in the market-place. At least there were some thousands of them, talking, gesticulating, pointing at the sky.

A few minutes later there came a great crash of thunder, of which it was impossible to locate the sound, for it rolled from everywhere. Then suddenly something hard struck the roof by my side and rebounded, to be followed next moment by a blow upon my shoulder which nearly knocked me flat, although I was well protected by the skin rugs.

"Down the stair!" I called. "They are stoning us," and suited the action to the word.

Ten seconds later we were both in the room, crouched in its farther corner, for the stones or whatever they were seemed to be following us. I struck a match, of which fortunately I had some, together with my pipe and a good pocketful of tobacco—my only solace in those days—and, as it burned up, saw first that blood was running down Marût's face, and secondly, that these stones were great lumps of ice, some of them weighing several ounces, which hopped about the floor like live things.

"Hailstorm!" remarked Marût with his accustomed smile.

"Hell storm!" I replied, "for whoever saw hail like that before?"

Then the match burnt out and conversation came to an end for the reason that we could no longer hear each other speak. The hail came down with a perpetual, rattling roar, that in its sum was one of the most terrible sounds to which I ever listened. And yet above it I thought that I could catch another, still more terrible, the wail of hundreds of people in agony. After the first few minutes I began to be afraid that the roof would be battered in, or that the walls would crumble beneath this perpetual fire of the musketry of heaven. But the cement was good and the place well built.

So it came about that the house stood the tempest, which had it been roofed with tiles or galvanized iron I am sure it would never have done, since the lumps of ice must have shattered one and pierced the other like paper. Indeed I have seen this happen in a bad hailstorm in Natal which killed my best horse. But even that hail was as snowflakes compared to this.

I suppose that this natural phenomenon continued for about twenty minutes, not more, during ten of which it was at its worst. Then by degrees it ceased, the sky cleared and the moon shone out beautifully. We climbed to the roof again and looked. It was several inches deep in jagged ice, while the market-place and all the country round appeared in the bright moonlight to be buried beneath a veil of snow.

Very rapidly, as the normal temperature of that warm land reasserted itself, this snow or rather hail melted, causing a flood of water which, where there was any fall, began to rush away with a gurgling sound. Also we heard other sounds, such as that from the galloping hoofs of many of the horses which had broken loose from their wrecked stables at the north end of the market-place, where in great number they had been killed by the falling roofs or had kicked each other to death, and a wild universal wail that rose from every quarter of the big town, in which quantities of the worst-built houses had collapsed. Further, lying here and there about the market-place we could see scores of dark shapes that we knew to be those of men, women and children, whom those sharp missiles hurled from heaven had caught before they could escape and slain or wounded almost to death. For it will be remembered that perhaps not fewer than two thousand people were gathered on this market-place, attending the horrid midnight sacrifice and discussing the unnatural weather when the storm burst upon them suddenly as an avalanche.

"The Child is small, yet its strength is great. Behold the first curse!" said Marût solemnly.

I stared at him, but as he chose to believe that a very unusual hailstorm was a visitation from heaven I did not think it worth while arguing the point. Only I wondered if he really did believe this. Then I remembered that such an event was said to have afflicted the old Egyptians in the hour of their pride because they would not "let the people go." Well, these blackguardedly Black Kendah were certainly worse than the Egyptians can ever have been; also they would not let *us* go. It was not wonderful therefore that Marût should be the victim of phantasies on the matter.

Not until the following morning did we come to understand the full extent of the calamity which had overtaken the Black Kendah. I think I have said that their crops this year were magnificent and just ripening to harvest. From our roof on previous days we could see a great area of them stretching to the edge of the forest. When the sun rose that morning this area had vanished, and the ground was covered with a carpet of green pulp. Also the forest itself appeared suddenly to have experienced the full effects of a northern winter. Not a leaf was left upon the trees, which stood their pointing their naked boughs to heaven.

No one who had not seen it could imagine the devastating fury of that storm. For example, the head of the diviner who was buried in the court-yard awaiting resurrection through our magic was, it may be recalled, covered with a stout earthenware pot. Now that pot had shattered into sherds and the head beneath was nothing but bits of broken bone which it would have been impossible for the very best magic to reconstruct to the likeness of a human being.

Calamity indeed stalked naked through the land.

Jana

No breakfast was brought to us that morning, probably for the reason that there was none to bring. This did not matter, however, seeing that plenty of food accumulated from supper and other meals stood in a corner of the house practically untouched. So we ate what we could and then paid our usual visit to the hut in which the camelmen had been confined. I say had been, for now it was quite empty, the last poor fellow having vanished away like his companions.

The sight of this vacuum filled me with a kind of fury.

"They have all been murdered!" I said to Marût.

"No," he replied with gentle accuracy. "They have been sacrificed to Jana. What we have seen on the market-place at night was the rite of their sacrifice. Now it will be our turn, Lord Macumazana."

"Well," I exclaimed, "I hope these devils are satisfied with Jana's answer to their accursed offerings, and if they try their fiendish pranks on us——"

"Doubtless there will be another answer. But, Lord, the question is, will that help us?"

Dumb with impotent rage I returned to the house, where presently the remains of the reed gate opened. Through it appeared Simba the King, the diviner with the injured foot walking upon crutches, and others of whom the most were more or less wounded, presumably by the hailstones. Then it was that in my wrath I put off the pretence of not understanding their language and went for them before they could utter a single word.

"Where are our servants, you murderers?" I asked, shaking my fist at them. "Have you sacrificed them to your devil-god? If so, behold the fruits of sacrifice!" and I swept my arm towards the country beyond. "Where are your crops?" I went on. "Tell me on what you will live this winter?" (At these words they quailed. In their imagination already they saw famine stalking towards them.) "Why do you keep us here? Is it that you wait for a worse thing to befall you? Why do you visit us here now?" and I paused, gasping with indignation.

"We came to look whether you had brought back to life that doctor whom you killed with your magic, white man," answered the king heavily.

I stepped to the corner of the court-yard and, drawing aside a mat that I had thrown there, showed them what lay beneath.

"Look then," I said, "and be sure that if you do not let us go, as yonder thing is, so shall all of you be before another moon has been born and died. Such is the life we shall give to evil men like you."

Now they grew positively terrified.

"Lord," said Simba, for the first time addressing me by a title of respect, "your magic is too strong for us. Great misfortune has fallen upon our land. Hundreds of people are dead, killed by the ice-stones that you have called down. Our harvest is ruined, and there is but little corn left in the storepits now when we looked to gather the new grain. Messengers come in from the outlying land telling us that nearly all the sheep and goats and very many of the cattle are slain. Soon we shall starve."

"As you deserve to starve," I answered. "Now—will you let us go?"

Simba stared at me doubtfully, then began to whisper into the ear of the lamed diviner. I could not catch what they said, so I watched their faces. That of the diviner whose head I was glad to see had been cut by a hailstone so that both ends of him were now injured, told me a good deal. His mask had been ugly, but now that it was off the countenance beneath was far uglier. Of a negroid type, pendulous- lipped, sensuous and loose-eyed, he was indeed a hideous fellow, yet very cunning and cruel-looking, as men of his class are apt to be. Humbled as he was for the moment, I felt sure that he was still plotting evil against us, somewhat against the will of his master. The issue showed that I was right. At length Simba spoke, saying:

"We had intended, Lord, to keep you and the priest of the Child here as hostages against mischief that might be worked on us by the followers of the Child, who have always been our bitter enemies and done us much undeserved wrong, although on our part we have faithfully kept the pact concluded in the days of our grandfathers. It seems, however, that fate, or your magic, is too strong for us, and therefore I have determined to let you go. To-night at sundown we will set you on the road which leads to the ford of the River Tava, which divides our territory from that of the White Kendah, and you may depart where you will, since our wish is that never again may we see your ill- omened faces."

At this intelligence my heart leapt in joy that was altogether premature. But, preserving my indignant air, I exclaimed:

"To-night! Why to-night? Why not at once? It is hard for us to cross unknown rivers in the dark."

"The water is low, Lord, and the ford easy. Moreover, if you started now you would reach it in the dark; whereas if you start at sundown, you will reach it in the morning. Lastly, we cannot conduct you hence until we have buried our dead."

Then, without giving me time to answer, he turned and left the place, followed by the others. Only at the gateway the diviner wheeled round on his crutches and glared at us both, muttering something with his thick lips; probably it was curses.

"At any rate they are going to set us free," I said to Marût, not without exultation, when they had all vanished.

"Yes, Lord," he replied, "but *where* are they going to set us free? The demon Jana lives in the forests and the swamps by the banks of the Tava River, and it is said that he ravages at night."

I did not pursue the subject, but reflected to myself cheerfully that this mystic rogue-elephant was a long way off and might be circumvented, whereas that altar of sacrifice was extremely near and very difficult to avoid.

Never did a thief with a rich booty in view, or a wooer having an assignation with his lady, wait for sundown more eagerly than I did that day. Hour after hour I sat upon the house-top, watching the Black Kendah carrying off the dead killed by the hailstones and generally trying to repair the damage done by the terrific tempest. Watching the sun also as it climbed down the cloudless sky, and literally counting the minutes till it should reach the horizon, although I knew well that it would have been wiser after such a night to prepare for our journey by lying down to sleep.

At length the great orb began to sink in majesty behind the tattered western forest, and, punctual to the minute, Simba, with a mounted escort of some twenty men and two led horses, appeared at our gate. As our preparations, which consisted only of Marût stuffing such food as was available into the breast of his robe, were already made, we walked out of that accursed guest-house and, at a sign from the king, mounted the horses. Riding across the empty market-place and past the spot where the rough stone altar still stood with charred bones protruding from the ashes of its extinguished fire—were they those of our friends the camel-drivers? I wondered—we entered the north street of the town.

Here, standing at the doors of their houses, were many of the inhabitants who had gathered to watch us pass. Never did I see hate more savage than was written on those faces as they shook their fists at us and muttered curses not loud but deep.

No wonder! for they were all ruined, poor folk, with nothing to look forward to but starvation until long months hence the harvest came again for those who would live to gather it. Also they were convinced that we, the white magician and the prophet of their enemy the Child, had brought this disaster on them. Had it not been for the escort I believe they would have fallen on us and torn us to pieces. Considering them I understood for the first time how disagreeable real unpopularity *can be*. But when I saw the actual condition of the fruitful gardens without in the waning daylight, I confess that I was moved to some sympathy with their owners. It was appalling. Not a handful of grain was there left to gather, for the corn had been not only "laid" but literally cut to ribbons by the hail.

After running for some miles through the cultivated land the road entered the forest. Here it was dark as pitch, so dark that I wondered how our guides found their way. In that blackness dreadful apprehensions seized me, for I became convinced that we had been brought here to be murdered. Every minute I expected to feel a knife-thrust in my back. I thought of digging my heels into the horse's sides and trying to gallop off anywhere, but abandoned the idea, first because I could not desert Marût, of whom I had lost touch in the gloom, and secondly because I was hemmed in by the escort. For the same reason I did not try to slip from the horse and glide away into the forest. There was nothing to be done save to go on and await the end.

It came at last some hours later. We were out of the forest now, and there was the moon rising, past her full but still very bright. Her light showed me that we were on a wild moorland, swampy, with scattered trees growing here and there, across which what seemed to be a game track ran down hill. That was all I could make out. Here the escort halted, and Simba the King said in a sullen voice:

"Dismount and go your ways, evil spirits, for we travel no farther across this place which is haunted. Follow the track and it will lead you to a lake. Pass the lake and by morning you will come to the river beyond which lies the country of your friends. May its waters swallow you if you reach them. For learn, there is one who watches on this road whom few care to meet."

As he finished speaking men sprang at us and, pulling us from the horses, thrust us out of their company. Then they turned and in another minute were lost in the darkness, leaving us alone.

"What now, friend Marût?" I asked.

"Now, Lord, all we can do is to go forward, for if we stay here Simba and his people will return and kill us at the daylight. One of them said so to me."

"Then, 'come on, Macduff,'" I exclaimed, stepping out briskly, and though he had never read Shakespeare, Marût understood and followed.

"What did Simba mean about 'one on the road whom few care to meet'?" I asked over my shoulder when we had done half a mile or so.

"I think he meant the elephant Jana," replied Marût with a groan.

"Then I hope Jana isn't at home. Cheer up, Marût. The chances are that we shall never meet a single elephant in this big place."

"Yet many elephants have been here, Lord," and he pointed to the ground. "It is said that they come to die by the waters of the lake and this is one of the roads they follow on their death journey, a road that no other living thing dare travel."

"Oh!" I exclaimed. "Then after all that was a true dream I had in the house in England."

"Yes, Lord, because my brother Harût once lost his way out hunting when he was young and saw what his mind showed you in the dream, and what we shall see presently, if we live to come so far."

I made no reply, both because what he said was either true or false, which I should ascertain presently, and because I was engaged in searching the ground with my eyes. He was right; many elephants had travelled this path—one quite recently. I, a hunter of those brutes, could not be deceived on this point. Once or twice also I thought that I caught sight of the outline of some tall creature moving silently through the scattered thorns a couple of hundred yards or so to our right. It might have been an elephant or a giraffe, or perhaps nothing but a shadow, so I said nothing. As I heard no noise I was inclined to believe the latter explanation. In any case, what was the good of speaking? Unarmed and solitary amidst unknown dangers, our position was desperate, and as Marût's nerve was already giving out, to emphasize its horrors to him would be mere foolishness.

On we trudged for another two hours, during which time the only living thing that I saw was a large owl which sailed round our heads as though to look at us, and then flew away ahead.

This owl, Marût informed me, was one of "Jana's spies" that kept him advised of all that was passing in his territory. I muttered "Bosh" and tramped on. Still I was glad that we saw no more of the owl, for in certain circumstances such dark fears are catching.

We reached the top of a rise, and there beneath us lay the most desolate scene that ever I have seen. At least it would have been the most desolate if I did not chance to have looked on it before, in the drawing-room of Ragnall Castle! There was no doubt about it. Below was the black, melancholy lake, a large sheet of water surrounded by reeds. Around, but at a considerable distance, appeared the tropical forest. To the east of the lake stretched a stony plain. At the time I could make out no more because of the uncertain light and the distance, for we had still over a mile to go before we reached the edge of the lake.

The aspect of the place filled me with tremblings, both because of its utter uncanniness and because of the inexplicable truth that I had seen it before. Most people will have experienced this kind of moral shock when on going to some new land they recognize a locality as being quite familiar to them in all its details. Or it may be the rooms of a house hitherto unvisited by them. Or it may be a conversation of which, when it begins, they already foreknow the sequence and the end, because in some dim state, when or how who can say, they have taken part in that talk with those same speakers. If this be so even in cheerful surroundings and among our friends or acquaintances, it is easy to imagine how much greater was the shock to me, a traveller on such a journey and in such a night.

I shrank from approaching the shores of this lake, remembering that as yet all the vision was not unrolled. I looked about me. If we went to the left we should either strike the water, or if we followed its edge, still bearing to the left, must ultimately reach the forest, where probably we should be lost. I looked to the right. The ground was strewn with boulders, among which grew thorns and rank grass, impracticable for men on foot at night. I looked behind me, meditating retreat, and there, some hundreds of yards away behind low, scrubby mimosas mixed with aloe-like plants, I saw something brown toss up and disappear again that might very well have been the trunk of an elephant. Then, animated by the courage of despair and a desire to know the worst, I began to descend the elephant track towards the lake almost at a run.

Ten minutes or so more brought us to the eastern head of the lake, where the reeds whispered in the breath of the night wind like things alive. As I expected, it proved to be a bare, open space where nothing seemed to grow. Yes, and all about me were the decaying remains of elephants, hundreds of them, some with their bones covered in moss, that may have lain here for generations, and others more newly dead. They were all old beasts as I could tell by the tusks, whether male or female. Indeed about me within a radius of a quarter of a mile lay enough ivory to make a man very rich for life, since although discoloured, much of it seemed to have kept quite sound, like human teeth in a mummy case. The sight gave me a new zest for life. If only I could manage to survive and carry off that ivory! I would. In this way or in that I swore that I would! Who could possibly die with so much ivory to be had for the taking? Not that old hunter, Allan Quatermain.

Then I forgot about the ivory, for there in front of me, just where it should be, just as I had seen it in the dream-picture, was the bull elephant dying, a thin and ancient brute that had lived its long life to the last hour. It searched about as though to find a convenient resting-place, and when this was discovered, stood over it, swaying to and fro for a full minute. Then it lifted its trunk and trumpeted shrilly thrice, singing its swan-song, after which it sank slowly to its knees, its trunk outstretched and the points of its worn tusks resting on the ground. Evidently it was dead.

I let my eyes travel on, and behold! about fifty yards beyond the dead bull was a mound of hard rock. I watched it with gasping expectation and—yes, on the top of the mound something slowly materialized. Although I knew what it must be well enough, for a while I could not see quite clearly because there were certain little clouds about and one of them had floated over the face of the moon. It passed, and before me, perhaps a hundred and forty paces away, outlined clearly against the sky, I perceived the devilish elephant of my vision.

Oh! what a brute was that! In bulk and height it appeared to be half as big again as any of its tribe which I had known in all my life's experience. It was enormous, unearthly; a survivor perhaps of some ancient species that lived before the Flood, or at least a very giant of its kind. Its grey-black sides were scarred as though with fighting. One of its huge tusks, much worn at the end, for evidently it was very old, gleamed white in the moonlight. The other was broken off about halfway down its length. When perfect it had been malformed, for it curved downwards and not upwards, also rather out to the right.

There stood this mammoth, this leviathan, this *monstrum horrendum, informe, ingens*, as I remember my old father used to call a certain gigantic and misshapen bull that we had on the Station, flapping a pair of ears that looked like the sides of a Kafir hut, and waving a trunk as big as a weaver's beam—whatever a weaver's beam may be—an appalling and a petrifying sight.

I squatted behind the skeleton of an elephant which happened to be handy and well covered with moss and ferns and watched the beast, fascinated, wishing that I had a large-bore rifle in my hand. What became of Marût I do not exactly know, but I think that he lay down on the ground.

During the minute or so that followed I reflected a good deal, as we do in times of emergency, often after a useless sort of a fashion. For instance, I wondered why the brute appeared thus upon yonder mound, and the thought suggested itself to me that it was summoned thither from some neighbouring lair by the trumpet call of the dying elephant. It occurred to me even that it was a kind of king of the elephants, to which they felt bound to report themselves, as it were, in the hour of their decease. Certainly what followed gave some credence to my fantastical notion which, if there were anything in it, might account for this great graveyard at that particular spot.

After standing for a while in the attitude that I have described, testing the air with its trunk, Jana, for I will call him so, lumbered down the mound and advanced straight to where the elephant that I had thought to be dead was kneeling. As a matter of fact it was not quite dead, for when Jana arrived it lifted its trunk and curled it round that of Jana as though in affectionate greeting, then let it fall to the ground again. Thereon Jana did what I had seen it do in my dream or vision at Ragnall, namely, attacked it, knocking it over on to its side, where it lay motionless; quite dead this time.

Now I remembered that the vision was not accurate after all, since in it I had seen Jana destroy a woman and a child, who on the present occasion were wanting. Since then I have thought that this was because Harût, clairvoyantly or telepathically, had conveyed to me, as indeed Marût declared, a scene which he had witnessed similar to that which I was witnessing, but not identical in its incidents. Thus it happened, perhaps, that while the act of the woman and the child was omitted, in our case there was another act of the play to follow of which I had received no inkling in my Ragnall experience. Indeed, if I had received it, I should not have been there that night, for no inducement on earth would have brought me to Kendahland.

This was the act. Jana, having prodded his dead brother to his satisfaction, whether from viciousness or to put it out of pain, I cannot say, stood over the carcass in an attitude of grief or pious meditation. At this time, I should mention, the wind, which had been rustling the hail-stripped reeds at the lake border, had died away almost, but not completely; that is to say, only a very faint gust blew now and again, which, with a hunter's instinct, I observed with satisfaction drew *from* the direction of Jana towards ourselves. This I knew, because it struck on my forehead, which was wet with perspiration, and cooled the skin.

Presently, however, by a cursed spite of fate, one of these gusts—a very little one—came from some quarter behind us, for I felt it in my back hair, that was as damp as the rest of me. Just then I was glancing to my right, where it seemed to me that out of the corner of my eye I had caught sight of something passing among the stones at a distance of a hundred yards or so, possibly the shadow of a cloud or another elephant. At the time I did not ascertain which it was, since a faint rattle from Jana's trunk reconcentrated all my faculties on him in a painfully vivid fashion.

I looked to see that all the contemplation had departed from his attitude, now as alert as that of a fox-terrier which imagines he has seen a rat. His vast ears were cocked, his huge bulk trembled, his enormous trunk sniffed the air.

"Great Heavens!" thought I to myself, "he has winded us!" Then I took such consolation as I could from the fact that the next gust once more struck upon my forehead, for I hoped he would conclude that he had made a mistake.

Not a bit of it! Jana as far too old a bird—or beast—to make any mistake. He grunted, got himself going like a luggage train, and with great deliberation walked towards us, smelling at the ground, smelling at the air, smelling to the right, to the left, and even towards heaven above, as though he expected that thence might fall upon him vengeance for his many sins. A dozen times as he came did I cover him with an imaginary rifle, marking the exact spots where I might have hoped to send a bullet to his vitals, in a kind of automatic fashion, for all my real brain was contemplating my own approaching end.

I wondered how it would happen. Would he drive that great tusk through me, would he throw me into the air, or would he kneel upon my poor little body, and avenge the deaths of his kin that had fallen at my hands? Marût was speaking in a rattling whisper:

"His priests have told Jana to kill us; we are about to die," he said. "Before I die I want to say that the lady, the wife of the lord——"

"Silence!" I hissed. "He will hear you," for at that instant I took not the slightest interest in any lady on the earth. Fiercely I glared at Marût and noted even then how pitiful was his countenance. There was no smile there now. All its jovial roundness had vanished. It had sunk in; it was blue and ghastly with large, protruding eyes, like to that of a man who had been three days dead.

I was right—Jana *had* heard. Low as the whisper was, through that intense silence it had penetrated to his almost preternatural senses. Forward he came at a run for twenty paces or more with his trunk held straight out in front of him. Then he halted again, perhaps the length of a cricket pitch away, and smelt as before.

The sight was too much for Marût. He sprang up and ran for his life towards the lake, purposing, I suppose, to take refuge in the water. Oh! how he ran. After him went Jana like a railway engine—express this time—trumpeting as he charged. Marût reached the lake, which was quite close, about ten yards ahead, and plunging into it with a bound, began to swim.

Now, I thought, he may get away if the crocodiles don't have him, for that devil will scarcely take to the water. But this was just where I made a mistake, for with a mighty splash in went Jana too. Also he was the better swimmer. Marût soon saw this and swung round to the shore, by which manœuvre he gained a little as he could turn quicker than Jana.

Back they came, Jana just behind Marût, striking at him with his great trunk.

They landed, Marût flew a few yards ahead doubling in and out among the rocks like a hare and, to my horror, making for where I lay, whether by accident or in a mad hope of obtaining protection, I do not know.

It may be asked why I had not taken the opportunity to run also in the opposite direction. There are several answers. The first was that there seemed to be nowhere to run; the second, that I felt sure, if I did run, I should trip up over the skeletons of those elephants or the stones; the third, that I did not think of it at once; the fourth, that Jana had not yet seen me, and I had no craving to introduce myself to him personally; and the fifth and greatest, that I was so paralysed with fear that I did not feel as though I could lift myself from the ground. Everything about me seemed to be dead, except my powers of observation, which were painfully alive.

Of a sudden Marût gave up. Less than a stone's throw from me he wheeled round and, facing Jana, hurled at him some fearful and concentrated curse, of which all that I could distinguish were the words: "The Child!"

Oddly enough it seemed to have an effect upon the furious rogue, which halted in its rush and, putting its four feet together, slid a few paces nearer and stood still. It was just as though the beast had understood the words and were considering them. If so, their effect was to rouse him to perfect madness. He screamed terribly; he lashed his sides with his trunk; his red and wicked eyes rolled; foam flew from the cavern of his open mouth; he danced upon his great feet, a sort of hideous Scottish reel. Then he charged!

I shut my eyes for a moment. When I opened them again it was to see poor Marût higher in the air than ever he flew before. I thought that he would never come down, but he did at last with an awesome thud. Jana went to him and very gently, now that he was dead, picked him up in his trunk. I prayed that he might carry him away to some hiding- place and leave me in peace. But not so. With slow and stately strides, rocking the deceased Marût up and down in his trunk, as a nurse might rock a baby, he marched on to the very stone where I lay, behind which I suppose he had seen or smelt me all the time.

For quite a long while, it seemed more than a century, he stood over me, studying me as though I interested him very much, the water of the lake trickling in a refreshing stream from his great ears on to my back. Had it not been for that water I think I should have fainted, but as it was I did the next best thing—pretended to be dead. Perhaps this monster would scorn to touch a dead man. Watching out of the corner of my eye, I saw him lift one vast paw that was the size of an arm-chair and hold it over me.

Now good-bye to the world, thought I. Then the foot descended as a steam-hammer does, but also as a steam-hammer sometimes does when used to crack nuts, stopped as it touched my back, and presently came to earth again alongside of me, perhaps because Jana thought the foothold dangerous. At any rate, he took another and better way. Depositing the remains of Marût with the most tender care beside me, as though the nurse were putting the child to bed, he unwound his yards of trunk and began to feel me all over with its tip, commencing at the back of my neck. Oh! the sensation of that clammy, wriggling tip upon my spinal column!

Down it went till it reached the seat of my trousers. There it pinched, presumably to ascertain whether or no I were malingering, a most agonizing pinch like to that of a pair of blacksmith's tongs. So sharp was it that, although I did not stir, who was aware that the slightest movement meant death, it tore a piece out of the stout cloth of my breeches, to say nothing of a portion of the skin beneath. This seemed to astonish the beast, for it lifted the tip of its trunk and shifted its head, as though to examine the fragment by the light of the moon.

Now indeed all was over, for when it saw blood upon that cloth——! I put up one short, piteous prayer to Heaven to save me from this terrible end, and lo, it was answered!

For just as Jana, the results of the inspection being unsatisfactory, was cocking his ears and making ready to slay me, there rang out the short, sharp report of a rifle fired within a few yards. Glancing up at the instant, I saw blood spurt from the monster's left eye, where evidently the bullet had found a home.

He felt at his eye with his trunk; then, uttering a scream of pain, wheeled round and rushed away.

The Chase

I suppose that I swooned for a minute or two. At any rate I remember a long and very curious dream, such a dream as is evolved by a patient under laughing gas, that is very clear and vivid at the time but immediately afterwards slips from the mind's grasp as water does from the clenched hand. It was something to the effect that all those hundreds of skeleton elephants rose and marshalled themselves before me, making obeisance to me by bending their bony knees, because, as I quite understood, I was the only human being that had ever escaped from Jana. Moreover, on the foremost elephant's skull Hans was perched like a mahout, giving words of command, to their serried ranks and explaining to them that it would be very convenient if they would carry their tusks, for which they had no further use, and pile them in a certain place—I forget where—that must be near a good road to facilitate their subsequent transport to a land where they would be made into billiard balls and the backs of ladies' hair-brushes. Next, through the figments of that retreating dream, I heard the undoubted voice of Hans himself, which of course I knew to be absurd as Hans was lost and doubtless dead, saying:

"If you are alive, Baas, please wake up soon, as I have finished reloading Intombi, and it is time to be going. I think I hit Jana in the eye, but so big a beast will soon get over so little a thing as that and look for us, and the bullet from Intombi is too small to kill him, Baas, especially as it is not likely that either of us could hit him in the other eye."

Now I sat up and stared. Yes, there was Hans himself looking just the same as usual, only perhaps rather dirtier, engaged in setting a cap on to the nipple of the little rifle Intombi.

"Hans," I said in a hollow voice, "why the devil are you here?"

"To save you from the devil, of course, Baas," he replied aptly. Then, resting the gun against the stone, the old fellow knelt down by my side and, throwing his arms around me, began to blubber over me, exclaiming:

"Just in time, Baas! Only just in time, for as usual Hans made a mess of things and judged badly—I'll tell you afterwards. Still, just in time, thanks be to your reverend father, the Predikant. Oh! if he had delayed me for one more minute you would have been as flat as my nose, Baas. Now come quickly. I've got the camel tied up there, and he can carry two, being fat and strong after four days' rest with plenty to eat. This place is haunted, Baas, and that king of the devils, Jana, will be back after us presently, as soon as he has wiped the blood out of his eye."

I didn't make any remark, having no taste for conversation just then, but only looked at poor Marût, who lay by me as though he was sleeping.

"Oh, Baas," said Hans, "there is no need to trouble about him, for his neck is broken and he's quite dead. Also it is as well," he added cheerfully. "For, as your reverend father doubtless remembered, the camel could never carry three. Moreover, if he stops here, perhaps Jana will come back to play with him instead of following us."

Poor Marût! This was his requiem as sung by Hans.

With a last glance at the unhappy man to whom I had grown attached in a way during our time of joint captivity and trial, I took the arm of the old Hottentot, or rather leant upon his shoulder, for at first I felt too weak to walk by myself, and picked my path with him through the stones and skeletons of elephants across the plateau eastwards, that is, away from the lake. About two hundred yards from the scene of our tragedy was a mound of rock similar to that on which Jana had appeared, but much smaller, behind which we found the camel, kneeling as a well-trained beast of the sort should do and tethered to a stone.

As we went, in brief but sufficient language Hans told me his story. It seemed that after he had shot the Kendah general it came into his cunning, foreseeing mind that he might be of more use to me free than as a companion in captivity, or that if I were killed he might in that case live to bring vengeance on my slayers. So he broke away, as has been described, and hid till nightfall on the hill-side. Then by the light of the moon he tracked us, avoiding the villages, and ultimately found a place of shelter in a kind of cave in the forest near to Simba Town, where no people lived. Here he fed the camel at night, concealing it at dawn in the cave. The days he spent up a tall tree, whence he could watch all that went on in the town beneath, living meanwhile on some food which he carried in a bag tied to the saddle, helped out by green mealies which he stole from a neighbouring field.

Thus he saw most of what passed in the town, including the desolation wrought by the fearful tempest of hail, which, being in their cave, both he and the camel escaped without harm. On the next evening from his post of outlook up the tree, where he had now some difficulty in hiding himself because the hail had stripped off all its leaves, he saw Marût and myself brought from the guest-house and taken away by the escort. Descending and running to the cave, he saddled the camel and started in pursuit, plunging into the forest and hiding there when he perceived that the escort were leaving us.

Here he waited until they had gone by on their return journey. So close did they pass to him that he could overhear their talk, which told him they expected, or rather were sure, that we should be destroyed by the elephant Jana, their devil god, to whom the camelmen had been already sacrificed. After they had departed he remounted and followed us. Here I asked him why he had not overtaken us before we came to the cemetery of elephants, as I presumed he might have done, since he stated that he was close in our rear. This indeed was the case, for it was the head of the camel I saw behind the thorn trees when I looked back, and not the trunk of an elephant as I had supposed.

At the time he would give me no direct answer, except that he grew muddled as he had already suggested, and thought it best to keep in the background and see what happened. Long afterwards, however, he admitted to me that he acted on a presentiment.

"It seemed to me, Baas," he said, "that your reverend father was telling me that I should do best to let you two go on and not show myself, since if I did so we should all three be killed, as one of us must walk whom the other two could not desert. Whereas if I left you as you were, one of you would be killed and the other escape, and that the one to be killed would not be *you*, Baas. All of which came about as the Spirit spoke in my head, for Marût was killed, who did not matter, and—you know the rest, Baas."

To return to Hans' story. He saw us march down to the borders of the lake, and, keeping to our right, took cover behind the knoll of rock, whence he watched also all that followed. When Jana advanced to attack us Hans crept forward in the hope, a very wild one, of crippling him with the little Purdey rifle. Indeed, he was about to fire at the hind leg when Marût made his run for life and plunged into the lake. Then he crawled on to lead me away to the camel, but when he was within a few yards the chase returned our way and Marût was killed.

From that moment he waited for an opportunity to shoot Jana in the only spot where so soft a bullet would, as he knew, have the faintest chance of injuring him vitally—namely, in the eye—for he was sure that its penetration would not be sufficient to reach the vitals through that thick hide and the mass of flesh behind. With an infinite and wonderful patience he waited, knowing that my life or death hung in the balance. While Jana held his foot over me, while he felt me with his trunk, still Hans waited, balancing the arguments for and against firing upon the scales of experience in his clever old mind, and in the end coming to a right and wise conclusion.

At length his chance came, the brute exposed his eye, and by the light of the clear moon Hans, always a very good shot at a distance when it was not necessary to allow for trajectory and wind, let drive and *hit*. The bullet did not get to the brain as he had hoped; it had not strength for that, but it destroyed this left eye and gave Jana such pain that for a while he forgot all about me and everything else except escape.

Such was the Hottentot's tale as I picked it up from his laconic, colourless, Dutch *patois* sentences, then and afterwards; a very wonderful tale I thought. But for him, his fidelity and his bushman's cunning, where should I have found myself before that moon set?

We mounted the camel after I had paused a minute to take a pull from a flask of brandy which remained in the saddlebags. Although he loved strong drink so well Hans had saved it untouched on the mere chance that it might some time be of service to me, his master. The monkey- like Hottentot sat in front and directed the camel, while I accommodated myself as best I could on the sheepskins behind. Luckily they were thick and soft, for Jana's pinch was not exactly that of a lover.

Off we went, picking our way carefully till we reached the elephant track beyond the mound where Jana had appeared, which, in the light of faith, we hoped would lead us to the River Tava. Here we made better progress, but still could not go very fast because of the holes made by the feet of Jana and his company. Soon we had left the cemetery behind us, and lost sight of the lake which I devoutly trusted I might never see again.

Now the track ran upwards from the hollow to a ridge two or three miles away. We reached the crest of this ridge without accident, except that on our road we met another aged elephant, a cow with very poor tusks, travelling to its last resting place, or so I suppose. I don't know which was the more frightened, the sick cow or the camel, for camels hate elephants as horses hate camels until they get used to them. The cow bolted to the right as quickly as it could, which was not very fast, and the camel bolted to the left with such convulsive bounds that we were nearly thrown off its back. However, being an equable brute, it soon recovered its balance, and we got back to the track beyond the cow.

From the top of the rise we saw that before us lay a sandy plain lightly clothed in grass, and, to our joy, about ten miles away at the foot of a very gentle slope, the moonlight gleamed upon the waters of a broad river. It was not easy to make out, but it was there, we were both sure it was there; we could not mistake the wavering, silver flash. On we went for another quarter of a mile, when something caused me to turn round on the sheepskin and look back.

Oh Heavens! At the very top of the rise, clearly outlined against the sky, stood Jana himself with his trunk lifted. Next instant he trumpeted, a furious, rattling challenge of rage and defiance.

"Allemagte! Baas," said Hans, "the old devil is coming to look for his lost eye, and has seen us with that which remains. He has been travelling on our spoor."

"Forward!" I answered, bringing my heels into the camel's ribs.

Then the race began. The camel was a very good camel, one of the real running breed; also, as Hans said, it was comparatively fresh, and may, moreover, have been aware that it was near to the plains where it had been bred. Lastly, the going was now excellent, soft to its spongy feet but not too deep in sand, nor were there any rocks over which it could fall. It went off like the wind, making nothing of our united weights which did not come to more than two hundred pounds, or a half of what it could carry with ease, being perhaps urged to its top speed by the knowledge that the elephant was behind. For mile after mile we rushed down the plain. But we did not

go alone, for Jana came after us like a cruiser after a gunboat. Moreover, swiftly as
we travelled, he travelled just a little swifter, gaining say a few yards in every
hundred. For the last mile before we came to the river bank, half an hour later
perhaps, though it seemed to be a week, he was not more than fifty paces to our rear.
I glanced back at him, and in the light of the moon, which was growing low, he bore
a strange resemblance to a mud cottage with broken chimneys (which were his ears
flapping on each side of him), and the yard pump projecting from the upper window.

"We shall beat him now, Hans," I said looking at the broad river which was now
close at hand.

"Yes, Baas," answered Hans doubtfully and in jerks. "This is very good camel,
Baas. He runs so fast that I have no inside left, I suppose because he smells his wife
over that river, to say nothing of death behind him. But, Baas, I am not sure; that
devil Jana is still faster than the camel, and he wants to settle for his lost eye, which
makes him lively. Also I see stones ahead, which are bad for camels. Then there is the
river, and I don't know if camels can swim, but Jana can as Marût learned. Do you
think, Baas, that you could manage to sting him up with a bullet in his knee or that
great trunk of his, just to give him something to think about besides ourselves?"

Thus he prattled on, I believe to occupy my mind and his own, till at length,
growing impatient, I replied:

"Be silent, donkey. Can I shoot an elephant backwards over my shoulder with a
rifle meant for springbuck? Hit the camel! Hit it hard!"

Alas! Hans was right! There *were* stones at the verge of the river, which doubtless
it had washed out in periods of past flood, and presently we were among them. Now
a camel, so good on sand that is its native heath, is a worthless brute among stones,
over which it slips and flounders. But to Jana these appeared to offer little or no
obstacle. At any rate he came over them almost if not quite as fast as before. By the
time that we reached the brink of the water he was not more than ten yards behind.
I could even see the blood running down from the socket of his ruined eye.

Moreover, at the sight of the foaming but shallow torrent, the camel, a creature
unaccustomed to water, pulled up in a mulish kind of way and for a moment refused
to stir. Luckily at this instant Jana let off one of his archangel kind of trumpetings
which started our beast again, since it was more afraid of elephants than it was of
water.

In we went and were presently floundering among the loose stones at the bottom
of the river, which was nowhere over four feet deep, with Jana splashing after us not
more than five yards behind. I twisted myself round and fired at him with the rifle.
Whether I hit him or no I could not say, but he stopped for a few seconds, perhaps
because he remembered the effect of a similar explosion upon his eye, which gave us
a trifling start. Then he came on again in his steam-engine fashion.

When we were about in the middle of the river the inevitable happened. The
camel fell, pitching us over its head into the stream. Still clinging to the rifle I picked
myself up and began half to swim half to wade towards the farther shore, catching
hold of Hans with my free hand. In a moment Jana was on to that camel. He gored
it with his tusks, he trampled it with his feet, he got it round the neck with his trunk,
dragging nearly the whole bulk of it out of the water. Then he set to work to pound
it down into the mud and stones at the bottom of the river with such a persistent
thoroughness, that he gave us time to reach the other bank and climb up a stout tree
which grew there, a sloping, flat-topped kind of tree that was fortunately easy to
ascend, at least for a man. Here we sat gasping, perhaps about thirty feet above the
ground level, and waited.

Presently Jana, having finished with the camel, followed us, and without any
difficulty located us in that tree. He walked all round it considering the situation.
Then he wound his huge trunk about the bole of the tree and, putting out his
strength, tried to pull it over. It was an anxious moment, but this particular child of

the forest had not grown there for some hundreds of years, withstanding all the shocks of wind, weather and water, in order to be laid low by an elephant, however enormous. It shook a little—no more. Abandoning this attempt as futile, Jana next began to try to dig it up by driving his tusk under its roots. Here, too, he failed because they grew among stones which evidently jarred him.

Ceasing from these agricultural efforts with a deep rumble of rage, he adopted yet a third expedient. Rearing his huge bulk into the air he brought down his forefeet with all the tremendous weight of his great body behind them on to the sloping trunk of the tree just below where the branches sprang, perhaps twelve or thirteen feet above the ground. The shock was so heavy that for a moment I thought the tree would be uprooted or snapped in two. Thank Heaven! it held, but the vibration was such that Hans and I were nearly shaken out of the upper branches, like autumn apples from a bough. Indeed, I think I should have gone had not the monkey-like Hans, who had toes to cling with as well as fingers, gripped me by the collar.

Thrice did Jana repeat this manœuvre, and at the third onslaught I saw to my horror that the roots were loosening. I heard some of them snap, and a crack appeared in the ground not far from the bole. Fortunately Jana never noted these symptoms, for abandoning a plan which he considered unavailing, he stood for a while swaying his trunk and lost in gentle thought.

"Hans," I whispered, "load the rifle quick! I can get him in the spine or the other eye."

"Wet powder won't go off, Baas," groaned Hans. "The water got to it in the river."

"No," I answered, "and it is all your fault for making me shoot at him when I could take no aim."

"It would have been just the same, Baas, for the rifle went under water also when we fell from the camel, and the cap would have been damp, and perhaps the powder too. Also the shot made Jana stop for a moment."

This was true, but it was maddening to be obliged to sit there with an empty gun, when if I had but one charge, or even my pistol, I was sure that I could have blinded or crippled this satanic pachyderm.

A few minutes later Jana played his last card. Coming quite close to the trunk of the tree he reared himself up as before, but this time stretched out his forelegs so that these and his body were supported on the broad bole. Then he elongated his trunk and with it began to break off boughs which grew between us and him.

"I don't think he can reach us," I said doubtfully to Hans, "that is, unless he brings a stone to stand on."

"Oh! Baas, pray be silent," answered Hans, "or he will understand and fetch one."

Although the idea seemed absurd, on the whole I thought it well to take the hint, for who knew how much this experienced beast did or did not understand? Then, as we could go no higher, we wriggled as far as we dared along our boughs and waited.

Presently Jana, having finished his clearing operations, began to lengthen his trunk to its full measure. Literally, it seemed to expand like a telescope or an indiarubber ring. Out it came, foot after foot, till its snapping tip was waving within a few inches of us, just short of my foot and Han's head, or rather felt hat. One final stretch and he reached the hat, which he removed with a flourish and thrust into the red cavern of his mouth. As it appeared no more I suppose he ate it. This loss of his hat moved Hans to fury. Hurling horrible curses at Jana he drew his butcher's knife and made ready.

Once more the sinuous brown trunk elongated itself. Evidently Jana had got a better hold with his hind legs this time, or perhaps had actually wriggled himself a few inches up the tree. At any rate I saw to my dismay that there was every prospect of my making a second acquaintance with that snapping tip. The end of the trunk was lying along my bough like a huge brown snake and creeping up, up, up.

"He'll get us," I muttered.

Hans said nothing but leaned forward a little, holding on with his left hand. Next instant in the light of the rising sun I saw a knife flash, saw also that the point of it had been driven through the lower lip of Jana's trunk, pinning it to the bough like a butterfly to a board.

My word! what a commotion ensued! Up the trunk came a scream which nearly blew me away. Then Jana, with a wriggling motion, tried to unnail himself as gently as possible, for it was clear that the knife point hurt him, but could not do so because Hans still held the handle and had driven the blade deep into the wood. Lastly he dragged himself downwards with such energy that something had to go, that something being the skin and muscle of the lower lip, which was cut clean through, leaving the knife erect in the bough.

Over he went backwards, a most imperial cropper. Then he picked himself up, thrust the tip of his trunk into his mouth, sucked it as one does a cut finger, and finally, roaring in defeated rage, fled into the river, which he waded, and back upon his tracks towards his own home. Yes, off he went, Hans screaming curses and demands that he should restore his hat to him, and very seldom in all my life have I seen a sight that I thought more beautiful than that of his whisking tail.

"Now, Baas," chuckled Hans, "the old devil has got a sore nose as well as a sore eye by which to remember us. And, Baas, I think we had better be going before he has time to think and comes back with a long stick to knock us out of this tree."

So we went, in double-quick time I can assure you, or at any rate as fast as my stiff limbs and general condition would allow. Fortunately we had now no doubt as to our direction, since standing up through the mists of dawn with the sunbeams resting on its forest-clad crest, we could clearly see the strange, tumulus-shaped hill which the White Kendah called the Holy Mount, the Home of the Child. It appeared to be about twenty miles away, but in reality was a good deal farther, for when we had walked for several hours it seemed almost as distant as ever.

In truth that was a dreadful trudge. Not only was I exhausted with all the terrors I had passed and our long midnight flight, but the wound where Jana had pinched out a portion of my frame, inflamed by the riding, had now grown stiff and intolerably sore, so that every step gave me pain which sometimes culminated in agony. Moreover, it was no use giving in, foodless as we were, for Marût had carried the provisions, and with the chance of Jana returning to look us up. So I stuck to it and said nothing.

For the first ten miles the country seemed uninhabited; doubtless it was too near the borders of the Black Kendah to be popular as a place of residence. After this we saw herds of cattle and a few camels, apparently untended; perhaps their guards were hidden away in the long grass. Then we came to some fields of mealies that were, I noticed, quite untouched by the hailstorm, which, it would seem, had confined its attentions to the land of the Black Kendah. Of these we ate thankfully enough. A little farther on we perceived huts perched on an inaccessible place in a kloof. Also their inhabitants perceived us, for they ran away as though in a great fright.

Still we did not try to approach the huts, not knowing how we should be received. After my sojourn in Simba Town I had become possessed of a love of life in the open.

For another two hours I limped forward with pain and grief—by now I was leaning on Hans' shoulder—up an endless, uncultivated rise clothed with euphorbias and fern-like cycads. At length we reached its top and found ourselves within a rifle shot of a fenced native village. I suppose that its inhabitants had been warned of our coming by runners from the huts I have mentioned. At any rate the moment we appeared the men, to the number of thirty or more, poured out of the south gate armed with spears and other weapons and proceeded to ring us round and behave in a very threatening manner. I noticed at once that, although most of them were comparatively light in colour, some of these men partook of the negro characteristics of the Black Kendah from whom we had escaped, to such an extent indeed that this blood was clearly predominant in them. Still, it was also clear that they were deadly foes of this people, for when I shouted out to them that we were the friends of Harût and those who worshipped the Child, they yelled back that we were liars. No friends of the Child, they said, came from the country of the Black Kendah, who worshipped the devil Jana. I tried to explain that least of all men in the world did we worship Jana, who had been hunting us for hours, but they would not listen.

"You are spies of Simba's, the smell of Jana is upon you" (this may have been true enough), they yelled, adding: "We will kill you, white- faced goat. We will kill you, little yellow monkey, for none who are not enemies come here from the land of the Black Kendah."

"Kill us then," I answered, "and bring the curse of the Child upon you. Bring famine, bring hail, bring war!"

These words were, I think, well chosen; at any rate they induced a pause in their murderous intentions. For a while they hesitated, all talking together at once. At last the advocates of violence appeared to get the upper hand, and once more a number of the men began to dance about us, waving their spears and crying out that we must die who came from the Black Kendah.

I sat down upon the ground, for I was so exhausted that at the time I did not greatly care whether I died or lived, while Hans drew his knife and stood over me, cursing them as he had cursed at Jana. By slow degrees they drew nearer and nearer. I watched them with a kind of idle curiosity, believing that the moment when they came within actual spear-thrust would be our last, but, as I have said, not greatly caring because of my mental and physical exhaustion.

I had already closed my eyes that I might not see the flash of the falling steel, when an exclamation from Hans caused me to open them again. Following the line of the knife with which he pointed, I perceived a troop of men on camels emerging from the gates of the village at full speed. In front of these, his white garments fluttering on the wind, rode a bearded and dignified person in whom I recognized Harût, Harût himself, waving a spear and shouting as he came. Our assailants heard and saw him also, then flung down their weapons as though in dismay either at his appearance or his words, which I could not catch. Harût guided his rushing camel straight at the man who I presume was their leader, and struck at him with his spear, as though in fury, wounding him in the shoulder and causing him to fall to the ground. As he struck he called out:

"Dog! Would you harm the guests of the Child?"

Then I heard no more because I fainted away.

The Dweller in the Cave

After this it seemed to me that I dreamed a long and very troubled dream concerning all sorts of curious things which I cannot remember. At last I opened my eyes and observed that I lay on a low bed raised about three inches above the floor, in an Eastern-looking room, large and cool. It had window-places in it but no windows, only grass mats hung upon a rod which, I noted inconsequently, worked on a rough, wooden hinge, or rather pin, that enabled the curtain to be turned back against the wall.

Through one of these window-places I saw at a little distance the slope of the forest-covered hill, which reminded me of something to do with a child—for the life of me I could not remember what. As I lay wondering over the matter I heard a shuffling step which I recognized, and, turning, saw Hans twiddling a new hat made of straw in his fingers.

"Hans," I said, "where did you get that new hat?"

"They gave it me here, Baas," he answered. "The Baas will remember that the devil Jana ate the other."

Then I did remember more or less, while Hans continued to twiddle the hat. I begged him to put it on his head because it fidgeted me, and then inquired where we were.

"In the Town of the Child, Baas, where they carried you after you had seemed to die down yonder. A very nice town, where there is plenty to eat, though, having been asleep for three days, you have had nothing except a little milk and soup, which was poured down your throat with a spoon whenever you seemed to half wake up for a while."

"I was tired and wanted a long rest, Hans, and now I feel hungry. Tell me, are the lord and Bena here also, or were they killed after all?"

"Yes, Baas, they are safe enough, and so are all our goods. They were both with Harût when he saved us down by the village yonder, but you went to sleep and did not see them. They have been nursing you ever since, Baas."

Just then Savage himself entered, carrying some soup upon a wooden tray and looking almost as smart as he used to do at Ragnall Castle.

"Good day, sir," he said in his best professional manner. "Very glad to see you back with us, sir, and getting well, I trust, especially after we had given you and Mr. Hans up as dead."

I thanked him and drank the soup, asking him to cook me something more substantial as I was starving, which he departed to do. Then I sent Hans to find Lord Ragnall, who it appeared was out walking in the town. No sooner had they gone than Harût entered looking more dignified than ever and, bowing gravely, seated himself upon the mat in the Eastern fashion.

"Some strong spirit must go with you, Lord Macumazana," he said, "that you should live today, after we were sure that you had been slain."

"That's where you made a mistake. Your magic was not of much service to you there, friend Harût."

"Yet my magic, as you call it, though I have none, was of some service after all, Macumazana. As it chanced I had no opportunity of breathing in the wisdom of the Child for two days from the hour of our arrival here, because I was hurt on the knee in the fight and so weary that I could not travel up the mountain and seek light from the eyes of the Child. On the third day, however, I went and the Oracle told me all. Then I descended swiftly, gathered men and reached those fools in time to keep you from harm. They have paid for what they did, Lord."

"I am sorry, Harût, for they knew no better; and, Harût, although I saved myself, or rather Hans saved me, we have left your brother behind, and with him the others."

"I know. Jana was too strong for them; you and your servant alone could prevail against him."

"Not so, Harût. He prevailed against us; all we could do was to injure his eye and the tip of his trunk and escape from him."

"Which is more than any others have done for many generations, Lord. But doubtless as the beginning was, so shall the end be. Jana, I think, is near his death and through you."

"I don't know," I repeated. "Who and what is Jana?"

"Have I not told you that he is an evil spirit who inhabits the body of a huge elephant?"

"Yes, and so did Marût; but I think that he is just a huge elephant with a very bad temper of his own. Still, whatever he is, he will take some killing, and I don't want to meet him again by that horrible lake."

"Then you will meet him elsewhere, Lord. For if you do not go to look for Jana, Jana will come to look for you who have hurt him so sorely. Remember that henceforth, wherever you go in all this land, it may happen that you will meet Jana."

"Do you mean to say that the brute comes into the territory of the White Kendah?"

"Yes, Macumazana, at times he comes, or a spirit wearing his shape comes; I know not which. What I do know is that twice in my life I myself have seen him upon the Holy Mount, though how he came or how he went none can tell."

"Why was he wandering there, Harût?"

"Who can say, Lord? Tell me why evil wanders through the world and I will answer your question. Only I repeat—let those who have harmed Jana beware of Jana."

"And let Jana beware of me if I can meet him with a decent gun in my hand, for I have a score to settle with the beast. Now, Harût, there is another matter. Just before he was killed Marût, your brother, began to tell me something about the wife of the Lord Ragnall. I had no time to listen to the end of his words, though I thought he said that she was upon yonder Holy Mount. Did I hear aright?"

Instantly Harût's face became like that of a stone idol, impenetrable, impassive.

"Either you misunderstood, Lord," he answered, "or my brother raved in his fear. Wherever she may be, that beautiful lady is not upon the Holy Mount, unless there is another Holy Mount in the Land of Death. Moreover, Lord, as we are speaking of this matter, let me tell you the forest upon that Mount must be trodden by none save the priest of the Child. If others set foot there they die, for it is watched by a guardian more terrible even than Jana, nor is he the only one. Ask me nothing of that guardian, for I will not answer, and, above all, if you or your comrades value life, let them not seek to look upon him."

Understanding that it was quite useless to pursue this subject farther at the moment, I turned to another, remarking that the hailstorm which had smitten the country of the Black Kendah was the worst that I had ever experienced.

"Yes," answered Harût, "so I have learned. That was the first of the curses which the Child, through my mouth, promised to Simba and his people if they molested us upon our road. The second, you will remember, was famine, which for them is near at hand, seeing that they have little corn in store and none left to gather, and that most of their cattle are dead of the hail."

"If they have no corn while, as I noted, you have plenty which the storm spared, will not they, who are many in number but near to starving, attack you and take your corn, Harût?"

"Certainly they will do so, Lord, and then will fall the third curse, the curse of war.

All this was foreseen long ago, Macumazana, and you are here to help us in that war. Among your goods you have many guns and much powder and lead. You shall teach our people how to use those guns, that with them we may destroy the Black Kendah."

"I think not," I replied quietly. "I came here to kill a certain elephant, and to receive payment for my service in ivory, not to fight the Black Kendah, of whom I have already seen enough. Moreover, the guns are not my property but that of the Lord Ragnall, who perhaps will ask his own price for the use of them."

"And the Lord Ragnall, who came here against our will, is, as it chances, our property and we may ask your own price for his life. Now, farewell for a while, since you, who are still sick and weak, have talked enough. Only before I go, as your friend and that of those with you, I will add one word. If you would continue to look upon the sun, let none of you try to set foot in the forest upon the Holy Mount. Wander where you will upon its southern slopes, but strive not to pass the wall of rock which rings the forest round."

Then he rose, bowed gravely and departed, leaving me full of reflections.

Shortly afterwards Savage and Hans returned, bringing me some meat which the former had cooked in an admirable fashion. I ate of it heartily, and just as they were carrying off the remains of the meal Ragnall himself arrived. Our greeting was very warm, as might be expected in the case of two comrades who never thought to speak to each other again on this side of the grave. As I had supposed, he was certain that Hans and I had been cut off and killed by the Black Kendah, as, after we were missed, some of the camelmen asserted that they had actually seen us fall. So he went on, or rather was carried on by the rush of the camels, grieving, since, it being impossible to attempt to recover our bodies or even to return, that was the only thing to do, and in due course reached the Town of the Child without further accident. Here they rested and mourned for us, till some days later Harût suddenly announced that we still lived, though how he knew this they could not ascertain. Then they sallied out and found us, as has been told, in great danger from the ignorant villagers who, until we appeared, had not even heard of our existence.

I asked what they had done and what information they had obtained since their arrival at this place. His answer was: Nothing and none worth mentioning. The town appeared to be a small one of not much over two thousand inhabitants, all of whom were engaged in agricultural pursuits and in camel-breeding. The herds of camels, however, they gathered, for the most part were kept at outlying settlements on the farther side of the cone-shaped mountain. As they were unable to talk the language the only person from whom they could gain knowledge was Harût, who spoke to them in his broken English and told them much what he had told me, namely that the upper mountain was a sacred place that might only be visited by the priests, since any uninitiated person who set foot there came to a bad end. They had not seen any of these priests in the town, where no form of worship appeared to be practised, but they had observed men driving small numbers of sheep or goats up the flanks of the mountain towards the forest.

Of what went on upon this mountain and who lived there they remained in complete ignorance. It was a case of stalemate. Harût would not tell them anything nor could they learn anything for themselves. He added in a depressed way that the whole business seemed very hopeless, and that he had begun to doubt whether there was any tidings of his lost wife to be gained among the Kendah, White or Black.

Now I repeated to him Marût's dying words, of which most unhappily I had never heard the end. These seemed to give him new life since they showed that tidings there was of some sort, if only it could be extracted. But how might this be done? How, how?

For a whole week things went on thus. During this time I recovered my strength completely, except in one particular which reduced me to helplessness. The place on my thigh where Jana had pinched out a bit of the skin healed up well enough, but the inflammation struck inwards to the nerve of my left leg, where once I had been injured by a lion, with the result that whenever I tried to move I was tortured by pains of a sciatic nature. So I was obliged to lie still and to content myself with being carried on the bed into a little garden which surrounded the mud-built and white-washed house that had been allotted to us as a dwelling-place.

There I lay hour after hour, staring at the Holy Mount which began to spring from the plain within a few hundred yards of the scattered township. For a mile or so its slopes were bare except for grass on which sheep and goats were grazed, and a few scattered trees. Studying the place through glasses I observed that these slopes were crowned by a vertical precipice of what looked like lava rock, which seemed to surround the whole mountain and must have been quite a hundred feet high. Beyond this precipice, which to all appearance was of an unclimbable nature, began a dense forest of large trees, cedars I thought, clothing it to the very top, that is so far as I could see.

One day when I was considering the place, Harût entered the garden suddenly and caught me in the act.

"The House of the god is beautiful," he said, "is it not?"

"Very," I answered, "and of a strange formation. But how do those who dwell on it climb that precipice?"

"It cannot be climbed," he answered, "but there is a road which I am about to travel who go to worship the Child. Yet I have told you, Macumazana, that any strangers who seek to walk that road find death. If they do not believe me, let them try," he added meaningly.

Then, after many inquiries about my health, he informed me that news had reached him to the effect that the Black Kendah were mad at the loss of their crops which the hail had destroyed and because of the near prospect of starvation.

"Then soon they will be wishing to reap yours with spears," I said.

"That is so. Therefore, my Lord Macumazana, get well quickly that you may be able to scare away these crows with guns, for in fourteen days the harvest should begin upon our uplands. Farewell and have no fears, for during my absence my people will feed and watch you and on the third night I shall return again."

After Harût's departure a deep depression fell upon all of us. Even Hans was depressed, while Savage became like a man under sentence of execution at a near but uncertain date. I tried to cheer him up and asked him what was the matter.

"I don't know, Mr. Quatermain," he answered, "but the fact is this is a 'ateful and un'oly 'ole" (in his agitation he quite lost grip of his h's, which was always weak), "and I am sure that it is the last I shall ever see, except one."

"Well, Savage," I said jokingly, "at any rate there don't seem to be any snakes here."

"No, Mr. Quatermain. That is, I haven't met any, but they crawl about me all night, and whenever I see that prophet man he talks of them to me. Yes, he talks of them and nothing else with a sort of cold look in his eyes that makes my back creep. I wish it was over, I do, who shall never see old England again," and he went away, I think to hide his very painful and evident emotion.

That evening Hans returned from an expedition on which I had sent him with instructions to try to get round the mountain and report what was on its other side. It had been a complete failure, as after he had gone a few miles men appeared who ordered him back. They were so threatening in their demeanour that had it not been for the little rifle, Intombi, which he carried under pretence of shooting buck, a weapon that they regarded with great awe, they would, he thought, have killed him. He added that he had been quite unsuccessful in his efforts to collect any news of value from man, woman or child, all of whom, although very polite, appeared to have orders to tell him nothing, concluding with the remark that he considered the White Kendah bigger devils than the Black Kendah, inasmuch as they were more clever.

Shortly after this abortive attempt we debated our position with earnestness and came to a certain conclusion, of which I will speak in its place.

If I remember right it was on this same night of our debate, after Harût's return from the mountain, that the first incident of interest happened. There were two rooms in our house divided by a partition which ran almost up to the roof. In the left-hand room slept Ragnall and Savage, and in that to the right Hans and I. Just at the breaking of dawn I was awakened by hearing some agitated conversation between Savage and his master. A minute later they both entered my sleeping place, and I saw in the faint light that Ragnall looked very disturbed and Savage very frightened.

"What's the matter?" I asked.

"We have seen my wife," answered Ragnall.

I stared at him and he went on:

"Savage woke me by saying that there was someone in the room. I sat up and looked and, as I live, Quatermain, standing gazing at me in such a position that the light of dawn from the window-place fell upon her, was my wife."

"How was she dressed?" I asked at once.

"In a kind of white robe cut rather low, with her hair loose hanging to her waist, but carefully combed and held outspread by what appeared to be a bent piece of ivory about a foot and a half long, to which it was fastened by a thread of gold."

"Is that all?"

"No. Upon her breast was that necklace of red stones with the little image hanging from its centre which those rascals gave her and she always wore."

"Anything more?"

"Yes. In her arms she carried what looked like a veiled child. It was so still that I think it must have been dead."

"Well. What happened?"

"I was so overcome I could not speak, and she stood gazing at me with wide-opened eyes, looking more beautiful than I can tell you. She never stirred, and her lips never moved—that I will swear. And yet both of us heard her say, very low but quite clearly: 'The mountain, George! Don't desert me. Seek me on the mountain, my dear, my husband.'"

"Well, what next?"

"I sprang up and she was gone. That's all."

"Now tell me what *you* saw and heard, Savage."

"What his lordship saw and heard, Mr. Quatermain, neither more nor less. Except that I was awake, having had one of my bad dreams about snakes, and saw her come through the door."

"Through the door! Was it open then?"

"No, sir, it was shut and bolted. She just came through it as if it wasn't there. Then I called to his lordship after she had been looking at him for half a minute or so, for I couldn't speak at first. There's one more thing, or rather two. On her head was a little cap that looked as though it had been made from the skin of a bird, with a gold snake rising up in front, which snake was the first thing I caught sight of, as of course it would be, sir. Also the dress she wore was so thin that through it I could see her shape and the sandals on her feet, which were fastened at the instep with studs of gold."

"I saw no feather cap or snake," said Ragnall.

"Then that's the oddest part of the whole business," I remarked. "Go back to your room, both of you, and if you see anything more, call me. I want to think things over."

They went, in a bewildered sort of fashion, and I called Hans and spoke with him in a whisper, repeating to him the little that he had not understood of our talk, for as I have said, although he never spoke it, Hans knew a great deal of English.

"Now, Hans," I said to him, "what is the use of you? You are no better than a fraud. You pretend to be the best watchdog in Africa, and yet a woman comes into this house under your nose and in the grey of the morning, and you do not see her. Where is your reputation, Hans?"

The old fellow grew almost speechless with indignation, then he spluttered his answer:

"It was not a woman, Baas, but a spook. Who am I that I should be expected to catch spooks as though they were thieves or rats? As it happens I was wide awake half an hour before the dawn and lay with my eyes fixed upon that door, which I bolted myself last night. It never opened, Baas; moreover, since this talk began I have been to look at it. During the night a spider has made its web from door-post to door-post, and that web is unbroken. If you do not believe me, come and see for yourself. Yet they say the woman came through the doorway and therefore through the spider's web. Oh! Baas, what is the use of wasting thought upon the ways of spooks which, like the wind, come and go as they will, especially in this haunted land from which, as we have all agreed, we should do well to get away."

I went and examined the door for myself, for by now my sciatica, or whatever it may have been, was so much better that I could walk a little. What Hans said was true. There was the spider's web with the spider sitting in the middle. Also some of the threads of the web were fixed from post to post, so that it was impossible that the door could have been opened or, if opened, that anyone could have passed through the doorway without breaking them. Therefore, unless the woman came through one of the little window-places, which was almost incredible as they were high above the ground, or dropped from the smoke-hole in the roof, or had been shut into the place when the door was closed on the previous night, I could not see how she had arrived there. And if any one of these incredible suppositions was correct, then how did she get out again with two men watching her?

There were only two solutions to the problem—namely, that the whole occurrence was hallucination, or that, in fact, Ragnall and Savage had seen something unnatural and uncanny. If the latter were correct I only wished that I had shared the experience, as I have always longed to see a ghost. A real, indisputable ghost would be a great support to our doubting minds, that is if we *knew* its owner to be dead.

But—this was another thought—if by any chance Lady Ragnall were still alive and a prisoner upon that mountain, what they had seen was no ghost, but a shadow or *simulacrum* of a living person projected consciously or unconsciously by that person for some unknown purpose. What could the purpose be? As it chanced the answer was not difficult, and to it the words she was reported to have uttered gave a cue. Only a few hours ago, just before we turned in indeed, as I have said, we had been discussing matters. What I have not said is that in the end we arrived at the conclusion that our quest here was wild and useless and that we should do well to try to escape from the place before we became involved in a war of extermination between two branches of an obscure tribe, one of which was quite and the other semi-savage.

Indeed, although Ragnall still hung back a little, it had been arranged that I should try to purchase camels in exchange for guns, unless I could get them for nothing which might be less suspicious, and that we should attempt such an escape under cover of an expedition to kill the elephant Jana.

Supposing such a vision to be possible, then might it not have come, or been sent to deter us from this plan? It would seem so.

Thus reflecting I went to sleep worn out with useless wonderment, and did not wake again till breakfast time. That morning, when we were alone together, Ragnall said to me:

"I have been thinking over what happened, or seemed to happen last night. I am not at all a superstitious man, or one given to vain imaginings, but I am sure that Savage and I really did see and hear the spirit or the shadow of my wife. Her body it could not have been as you will admit, though how she could utter, or seem to utter, audible speech without one is more than I can tell. Also I am sure that she is captive upon yonder mountain and came to call me to rescue her. Under these circumstances I feel that it is my duty, as well as my desire, to give up any idea of leaving the country and try to find out the truth."

"And how will you do that," I asked, "seeing that no one will tell us anything?"

"By going to see for myself."

"It is impossible, Ragnall. I am too lame at present to walk half a mile, much less to climb precipices."

"I know, and that is one of the reasons why I did not suggest that you should accompany me. The other is that there is no object in all of us risking our lives. I wished to face the thing alone, but that good fellow Savage says that he will go where I go, leaving you and Hans here to make further attempts if we do not return. Our plan is to slip out of the town during the night, wearing white dresses like the Kendah, of which I have bought some for tobacco, and make the best of our way up the slope by starlight that is very bright now. When dawn comes we will try to find the road through that precipice, or over it, and for the rest trust to Providence."

Dismayed at this intelligence, I did all I could to dissuade him from such a mad venture, but quite without avail, for never did I know a more determined or more fearless man than Lord Ragnall. He had made up his mind and there was an end of the matter. Afterwards I talked with Savage, pointing out to him all the perils involved in the attempt, but likewise without avail. He was more depressed than usual, apparently on the ground that "having seen the ghost of her ladyship" he was sure he had not long to live. Still, he declared that where his master went he would go, as he preferred to die with him rather than alone.

So I was obliged to give in and with a melancholy heart to do what I could to help in the simple preparations for this crazy undertaking, realizing all the while that the only real help must come from above, since in such a case man was powerless. I should add that after consultation, Ragnall gave up the idea of adopting a Kendah disguise which was certain to be discovered, also of starting at night when the town was guarded.

That very afternoon they went, going out of the town quite openly on the pretext of shooting partridges and small buck on the lower slopes of the mountain, where both were numerous, as Harût had informed us we were quite at liberty to do. The farewell was somewhat sad, especially with Savage, who gave me a letter he had written for his old mother in England, requesting me to post it if ever again I came to a civilized land.

I did my best to put a better spirit in him but without avail. He only wrung my hand warmly, said that it was a pleasure to have known such a "real gentleman" as myself, and expressed a hope that I might get out of this hell and live to a green old age amongst Christians. Then he wiped away a tear with the cuff of his coat, touched his hat in the orthodox fashion and departed. Their outfit, I should add, was very simple: some food in bags, a flask of spirits, two double-barrelled guns that would shoot either shot or ball, a bull's-eye lantern, matches and their pistols.

Hans walked with them a little way and, leaving them outside the town, returned.

"Why do you look so gloomy, Hans?" I asked.

"Because, Baas," he answered, twiddling his hat, "I had grown to be fond of the white man, Bena, who was always very kind to me and did not treat me like dirt as low-born whites are apt to do. Also he cooked well, and now I shall have to do that work which I do not like."

"What do you mean, Hans? The man isn't dead, is he?"

"No, Baas, but soon he will be, for the shadow of death is in his eyes."

"Then how about Lord Ragnall?"

"I saw no shadow in his eyes; I think that he will live, Baas."

I tried to get some explanation of these dark sayings out of the Hottentot, but he would add nothing to his words.

All the following night I lay awake filled with heavy fears which deepened as the hours went on. Just before dawn we heard a knocking on our door and Ragnall's voice whispering to us to open. Hans did so while I lit a candle, of which we had a good supply. As it burned up Ragnall entered, and from his face I saw at once that something terrible had happened. He went to the jar where we kept our water and drank three pannikin-fuls, one after the other. Then without waiting to be asked, he said:

"Savage is dead," and paused a while as though some awful recollection overcame him. "Listen," he went on presently. "We worked up the hill- side without firing, although we saw plenty of partridges and one buck, till just as twilight was closing in, we came to the cliff face. Here we perceived a track that ran to the mouth of a narrow cave or tunnel in the lava rock of the precipice, which looked quite unclimbable. While we were wondering what to do, eight or ten white- robed men appeared out of the shadows and seized us before we could make any resistance. After talking together for a little they took away our guns and pistols, with which some of them disappeared. Then their leader, with many bows, indicated that we were at liberty to proceed by pointing first to the mouth of the cave, and next to the top of the precipice, saying something about '*ingane*,' which I believe means a little child, does it not?"

I nodded, and he went on:

"After this they all departed down the hill, smiling in a fashion that disturbed me. We stood for a while irresolute, until it became quite dark. I asked Savage what he thought we had better do, expecting that he would say 'Return to the town.' To my surprise, he answered:

"'Go on, of course, my lord. Don't let those brutes say that we white men daren't walk a step without our guns. Indeed, in any case I mean to go on, even if your lordship won't.'

"Whilst he spoke he took a bull's-eye lantern from his foodbag, which had not been interfered with by the Kendah, and lit it. I stared at him amazed, for the man seemed to be animated by some tremendous purpose. Or rather it was as though a force from without had got hold of his will and were pushing him on to an unknown end. Indeed his next words showed that this was so, for he exclaimed:

"'There is something drawing me into that cave, my lord. It may be death; I think it is death, but whatever it be, go I must. Perhaps you would do well to stop outside till I have seen.'

"I stepped forward to catch hold of the man, who I thought had gone mad, as perhaps was the case. Before I could lay my hands on him he had run rapidly to the mouth of the cave. Of course I followed, but when I reached its entrance the star of light thrown forward by the bull's-eye lantern showed me that he was already about eight yards down the tunnel. Then I heard a terrible hissing noise and Savage exclaiming: 'Oh! my God!' twice over. As he spoke the lantern fell from his hand, but did not go out, because, as you know, it is made to burn in any position. I leapt forward and picked it from the ground, and while I was doing so became aware that Savage was running still farther into the depths of the cave. I lifted the lantern above my head and looked.

"This was what I saw: About ten paces from me was Savage with his arms outstretched and dancing—yes, dancing—first to the right and then to the left, with a kind of horrible grace and to the tune of a hideous hissing music. I held the lantern higher and perceived that beyond him, lifted eight or nine feet into the air, nearly to the roof of the tunnel in fact, was the head of the hugest snake of which I have ever heard. It was as broad as the bottom of a wheelbarrow—were it cut off I think it would fill a large wheelbarrow—while the neck upon which it was supported was quite as thick as my middle, and the undulating body behind it, which stretched far away into the darkness, was the size of an eighteen-gallon cask and glittered green and grey, lined and splashed with silver and with gold.

"It hissed and swayed its great head to the right, holding Savage with cold eyes that yet seemed to be on fire, whereon he danced to the right. It hissed again and swayed its head to the left, whereon he danced to the left. Then suddenly it reared its head right to the top of the cave and so remained for a few seconds, whereon Savage stood still, bending a little forward, as though he were bowing to the reptile. Next instant, like a flash it struck, for I saw its white fangs bury themselves in the back of Savage, who with a kind of sigh fell forward on to his face. Then there was a convulsion of those shining folds, followed by a sound as of bones being ground up in a steam-driven mortar.

"I staggered against the wall of the cave and shut my eyes for a moment, for I felt faint. When I opened them again it was to see something flat, misshapen, elongated like a reflection in a spoon, something that had been Savage lying on the floor, and stretched out over it the huge serpent studying me with its steely eyes. Then I ran; I am not ashamed to say I ran out of that horrible hole and far into the night."

"Small blame to you," I said, adding: "Hans, give me some square-face neat." For I felt as queer as though I also had been in that cave with its guardian.

"There is very little more to tell," went on Ragnall after I had drunk the hollands. "I lost my way on the mountain-side and wandered for many hours, till at last I blundered up against one of the outermost houses of the town, after which things were easy. Perhaps I should add that wherever I went on my way down the mountain it seemed to me that I heard people laughing at me in an unnatural kind of voice. That's all."

After this we sat silent for a long while, till at length Hans said in his unmoved tone:

"The light has come, Baas. Shall I blow out the candle, which it is a pity to waste? Also, does the Baas wish me to cook the breakfast, now that the snake devil is making his off Bena, as I hope to make mine off him before all is done. Snakes are very good to eat, Baas, if you know how to dress them in the Hottentot way."

Hans Steals the Keys

A few hours later some of the White Kendah arrived at the house and very politely delivered to us Ragnall's and poor Savage's guns and pistols, which they said they had found lying in the grass on the mountain-side, and with them the bull's-eye lantern that Ragnall had thrown away in his flight; all of which articles I accepted without comment. That evening also Harût called and, after salutations, asked where Bena was as he did not see him. Then my indignation broke out:

"Oh! white-bearded father of liars," I said, "you know well that he is in the belly of the serpent which lives in the cave of the mountain."

"What, Lord!" exclaimed Harût addressing Ragnall in his peculiar English, "have you been for walk up to hole in hill? Suppose Bena want see big snake. He always very fond of snake, you know, and they very fond of him. You 'member how they come out of his pocket in your house in England? Well, he know all about snake now."

"You villain!" exclaimed Ragnall, "you murderer! I have a mind to kill you where you are."

"Why you choke me, Lord, because snake choke your man? Poor snake, he only want dinner. If you go where lion live, lion kill you. If you go where snake live, snake kill you. I tell you not to. You take no notice. Now I tell you all—go if you wish, no one stop you. Perhaps you kill snake, who knows? Only you no take gun there, please. That not allowed. When you tired of this town, go see snake. Only, 'member that not right way to House of Child. There another way which you never find."

"Look here," said Ragnall, "what is the use of all this foolery? You know very well why we are in your devilish country. It is because I believe you have stolen my wife to make her the priestess of your evil religion whatever it may be, and I want her back."

"All this great mistake," replied Harût blandly. "We no steal beautiful lady you marry because we find she not right priestess. Also Macumazana here not to look for lady but to kill elephant Jana and get pay in ivory like good business man. You, Lord, come with him as friend though we no ask you, that all. Then you try find temple of our god and snake which watch door kill your servant. Why we not kill *you*, eh?"

"Because you are afraid to," answered Ragnall boldly. "Kill me if you can and take the consequences. I am ready."

Harût studied him not without admiration.

"You very brave man," he said, "and we no wish kill you and p'raps after all everything come right in end. Only Child know about that. Also you help us fight Black Kendah by and by. So, Lord, you quite safe unless you big fool and go call on snake in cave. He very hungry snake and soon want more dinner. You hear, Light-in-Darkness, Lord-of- the-Fire," he added suddenly turning on Hans who was squatted near by twiddling his hat with a face that for absolute impassiveness resembled a deal board. "You hear, he very hungry snake, and you make nice tea for him."

Hans rolled his little yellow eyes without even turning his head until they rested on the stately countenance of Harût, and answered in Bantu:

"I hear, Liar-with-the-White-Beard, but what have I to do with this matter? Jana is my enemy who would have killed Macumazana, my master, not your dirty snake. What is the good of this snake of yours? If it were any good, why does it not kill Jana whom you hate? And if it is no good, why do you not take a stick and knock it on the head? If you are afraid I will do so for you if you pay me. That for your snake," and very energetically he spat upon the floor.

"All right," said Harût, still speaking in English, "you go kill snake. Go when you like, no one say no. Then we give you new name. Then we call you Lord-of-the-Snake."

As Hans, who now was engaged in lighting his corn-cob pipe, did not deign to answer these remarks, Harût turned to me and said:

"Lord Macumazana, your leg still bad, eh? Well, I bring you some ointment what make it quite well; it holy ointment come from the Child. We want you get well quick."

Then suddenly he broke into Bantu. "My Lord, war draws near. The Black Kendah are gathering all their strength to attack us and we must have your aid. I go down to the River Tava to see to certain matters, as to the reaping of the outlying crops and other things. Within a week I will be back; then we must talk again, for by that time, if you will use the ointment that I have given you, you will be as well as ever you were in your life. Rub it on your leg, and mix a piece as large as a mealie grain in water and swallow it at night. It is not poison, see," and taking the cover off a little earthenware pot which he produced he scooped from it with his finger some of the contents, which looked like lard, put it on his tongue and swallowed it.

Then he rose and departed with his usual bows.

Here I may state that I used Harût's prescription with the most excellent results. That night I took a dose in water, very nasty it was, and rubbed my leg with the stuff, to find that next morning all pain had left me and that, except for some local weakness, I was practically quite well. I kept the rest of the salve for years, and it proved a perfect specific in cases of sciatica and rheumatism. Now, alas! it is all used and no recipe is available from which it can be made up again.

The next few days passed uneventfully. As soon as I could walk I began to go about the town, which was nothing but a scattered village much resembling those to be seen on the eastern coasts of Africa. Nearly all the men seemed to be away, making preparations for the harvest, I suppose, and as the women shut themselves up in their houses after the Oriental fashion, though the few that I saw about were unveiled and rather good-looking, I did not gather any intelligence worth noting.

To tell the truth I cannot remember being in a more uninteresting place than this little town with its extremely uncommunicative population which, it seemed to me, lived under a shadow of fear that prevented all gaiety. Even the children, of whom there were not many, crept about in a depressed fashion and talked in a low voice. I never saw any of them playing games or heard them shouting and laughing, as young people do in most parts of the world. For the rest we were very well looked after. Plenty of food was provided for us and every thought taken for our comfort. Thus a strong and quiet pony was brought for me to ride because of my lameness. I had only to go out of the house and call and it arrived from somewhere, all ready saddled and bridled, in charge of a lad who appeared to be dumb. At any rate when I spoke to him he would not answer.

Mounted on this pony I took one or two rides along the southern slopes of the mountain on the old pretext of shooting for the pot. Hans accompanied me on these occasions, but was, I noted, very silent and thoughtful, as though he were hunting something up and down his tortuous intelligence. Once we got quite near to the mouth of the cave or tunnel where poor Savage had met his horrid end. As we stood studying it a white-robed man whose head was shaved, which made me think he must be a priest, came up and asked me mockingly why we did not go through the tunnel and see what lay beyond, adding, almost in the words of Harût himself, that none would attempt to interfere with us as the road was open to any who could travel it. By way of answer I only smiled and put him a few questions about a very beautiful breed of goats with long silky hair, some of which he seemed to be engaged in herding. He replied that these goats were sacred, being the food of "one who dwelt in the Mountain who only ate when the moon changed."

When I inquired who this person was he said with his unpleasant smile that I had better go through the tunnel and see for myself, an invitation which I did not accept.

That evening Harût appeared unexpectedly, looking very grave and troubled. He was in a great hurry and only stayed long enough to congratulate me upon the excellent effects of his ointment, since "no man could fight Jana on one leg."

I asked him when the fight with Jana was to come off. He replied:

"Lord, I go up to the Mountain to attend the Feast of the First- fruits, which is held at sunrise on the day of the new moon. After the offering the Oracle will speak and we shall learn when there will be war with Jana, and perchance other things."

"May we not attend this feast, Harût, who are weary of doing nothing here?"

"Certainly," he answered with his grave bow. "That is, if you come unarmed; for to appear before the Child with arms is death. You know the road; it runs through yonder cave and the forest beyond the cave. Take it when you will, Lord."

"Then if we can pass the cave we shall be welcome at the feast?"

"You will be very welcome. None shall hurt you there, going or returning. I swear it by the Child. Oh! Macumazana," he added, smiling a little, "why do you talk folly, who know well that one lives in yonder cave whom none may look upon and love, as Bena learned not long ago? You are thinking that perhaps you might kill this Dweller in the cave with your weapons. Put away that dream, seeing that henceforth those who watch you have orders to see that none of you leave this house carrying so much as a knife. Indeed, unless you promise me that this shall be so you will not be suffered to set foot outside its garden until I return again. Now do you promise?"

I thought a while and, drawing the two others aside out of hearing, asked them their opinion.

Ragnall was at first unwilling to give any such promise, but Hans said:

"Baas, it is better to go free and unhurt without guns and knives than to become a prisoner once, as you were among the Black Kendah. Often there is but a short step between the prison and the grave."

Both Ragnall and I acknowledged the force of this argument and in the end we gave the promise, speaking one by one.

"It is enough," said Harût; "moreover, know, Lord, that among us White Kendah he who breaks an oath is put across the River Tava unarmed to make report thereof to Jana, Father of Lies. Now farewell. If we do not meet at the Feast of the First-fruits on the day of the new moon, whither once more I invite you, we can talk together here after I have heard the voice of the Oracle."

Then he mounted a camel which awaited him outside the gate and departed with an escort of twelve men, also riding camels.

"There is some other road up that mountain, Quatermain," said Ragnall. "A camel could sooner pass through the eye of a needle than through that dreadful cave, even if it were empty."

"Probably," I answered, "but as we don't know where it is and I dare say it lies miles from here, we need not trouble our heads on the matter. The cave is *our* only road, which means that there is *no* road."

That evening at supper we discovered that Hans was missing; also that he had got possession of my keys and broken into a box containing liquor, for there it stood open in the cooking-hut with the keys in the lock.

"He has gone on the drink," I said to Ragnall, "and upon my soul I don't wonder at it; for sixpence I would follow his example."

Then we went to bed. Next morning we breakfasted rather late, since when one has nothing to do there is no object in getting up early. As I was preparing to go to the cook-house to boil some eggs, to our astonishment Hans appeared with a kettle of coffee.

"Hans," I said, "you are a thief."

"Yes, Baas," answered Hans.

"You have been at the gin box and taking that poison."

"Yes, Baas, I have been taking poison. Also I took a walk and all is right now. The Baas must not be angry, for it is very dull doing nothing here. Will the Baases eat porridge as well as eggs?"

As it was no use scolding him I said that we would. Moreover, there was something about his manner which made me suspicious, for really he did not look like a person who has just been very drunk.

After we had finished breakfast he came and squatted down before me. Having lit his pipe he asked suddenly:

"Would the Baases like to walk through that cave to-night? If so, there will be no trouble."

"What do you mean?" I asked, suspecting that he was still drunk.

"I mean, Baas, that the Dweller-in-the-cave is fast asleep."

"How do you know that, Hans?"

"Because I am the nurse who put him to sleep, Baas, though he kicked and cried a great deal. He is asleep; he will wake no more. Baas, I have killed the Father of Serpents."

"Hans," I said, "now I am sure that you are still drunk, although you do not show it outside."

"Hans," added Ragnall, to whom I had translated as much of this as he did not understand, "it is too early in the day to tell good stories. How could you possibly have killed that serpent without a gun—for you took none with you—or with it either for that matter?"

"Will the Baases come and take a walk through the cave?" asked Hans with a snigger.

"Not till I am quite sure that you are sober," I replied; then, remembering certain other events in this worthy's career, added; "Hans, if you do not tell us the story at once I will beat you."

"There isn't much story, Baas," replied Hans between long sucks at his pipe, which had nearly gone out, "because the thing was so easy. The Baas is very clever and so is the Lord Baas, why then can they never see the stones that lie under their noses? It is because their eyes are always fixed upon the mountains between this world and the next. But the poor Hottentot, who looks at the ground to be sure that he does not stumble, ah! he sees the stones. Now, Baas, did you not hear that man in a night shirt with his head shaved say that those goats were food for One who dwelt in the mountain?"

"I did. What of it, Hans?"

"Who would be the One who dwelt in the mountain except the Father of Snakes in the cave, Baas? Ah, now for the first time you see the stone that lay at your feet all the while. And, Baas, did not the bald man add that this One in the mountain was only fed at new and full moon, and is not to-morrow the day of new moon, and therefore would he not be very hungry on the day before new moon, that is, last night?"

"No doubt, Hans; but how can you kill a snake by feeding it?"

"Oh! Baas, you may eat things that make you ill, and so can a snake. Now you will guess the rest, so I had better go to wash the dishes."

"Whether I guess or do not guess," I replied sagely, the latter being the right hypothesis, "the dishes can wait, Hans, since the Lord there has not guessed; so continue."

"Very well, Baas. In one of those boxes are some pounds of stuff which, when mixed with water, is used for preserving skins and skulls."

"You mean the arsenic crystals," I said with a flash of inspiration.

"I don't know what you call them, Baas. At first I thought they were hard sugar and stole some once, when the real sugar was left behind, to put into the coffee—without telling the Baas, because it was my fault that the sugar was left behind."

"Great Heavens!" I ejaculated, "then why aren't we all dead?"

"Because at the last moment, Baas, I thought I would make sure, so I put some of the hard sugar into hot milk and, when it had melted, I gave it to that yellow dog which once bit me in the leg, the one that came from Beza-Town, Baas, that I told you had run away. He was a very greedy dog, Baas, and drank up the milk at once. Then he gave a howl, twisted about, foamed at the mouth and died and I buried him at once. After that I threw some more of the large sugar mixed with mealies to the fowls that we brought with us for cooking. Two cocks and a hen swallowed them by mistake for the corn. Presently they fell on their backs, kicked a little and died. Some of the Mazitu, who were great thieves, stole those dead fowls, Baas. After this, Baas, I thought it best not to use that sugar in the coffee, and later on Bena told me that it was deadly poison. Well, Baas, it came into my mind that if I could make that great snake swallow enough of this poison, he, too, might die.

"So I stole your keys, as I often do, Baas, when I want anything, because you leave them lying about everywhere, and to deceive you first opened one of the boxes that are full of square-face and brandy and left it open, for I wished you to think that I had just gone to get drunk like anybody else. Then I opened another box and got out two one-pound tins of the sugar which kills dogs and fowls. Half a pound of it I melted in boiling water with some real sugar to make the stuff sweet, and put it into a bottle. The rest I tied with string in twelve little packets in the soft paper which is in one of the boxes, and put them in my pocket. Then I went up the hill, Baas, to the place where I saw those goats are kraaled at night behind a reed fence. As I had hoped, no one was watching them because there are no tigers so near this town, and man does not steal the goats that are sacred. I went into the kraal and found a fat young ewe which had a kid. I dragged it out and, taking it behind some stones, I made its leg fast with a bit of cord and poured this stuff out of the bottle all over its skin, rubbing it in well. Then I tied the twelve packets of hard poison- sugar everywhere about its body, making them very fast deep in the long hair so that they could not tumble or rub off.

"After this I untied the goat, led it near to the mouth of the cave and held it there for a time while it kept on bleating for its kid. Next I took it almost up to the cave, wondering how I should drive it in, for I did not wish to enter there myself, Baas. As it happened I need not have troubled about that. When the goat was within five yards of the cave, it stopped bleating, stood still and shivered. Then it began to go forward with little jumps, as though it did not want to go, yet must do so. Also, Baas, I felt as though *I* wished to go with it. So I lay down and put my heels against a rock, leaving go of the goat.

"For now, Baas, I did not care where that goat went so long as I could keep out of the hole where dwelt the Father of Serpents that had eaten Bena. But it was all right, Baas; the goat knew what it had to do and did it, jumping straight into the cave. As it entered it turned its head and looked at me. I could see its eyes in the starlight, and, Baas, they were dreadful. I think it knew what was coming and did not like it at all. And yet it had to walk on because it could not help it. Just like a man going to the devil, Baas!

"Holding on to the stone I peered after it, for I had heard something stirring in the cave making a soft noise like a white lady's dress upon the floor. There in the blackness I saw two little sparks of fire, which were the eyes of the serpent, Baas. Then I heard a sound of hissing like four big kettles boiling all at once, and a little bleat from the goat. After this there was a noise as of men wrestling, followed by another noise as of bones breaking, and lastly, yet another sucking noise as of a pump that won't draw up the water. Then everything grew nice and quiet and I went some way off, sat down a little to one side of the cave, and waited to see if anything happened.

"It must have been nearly an hour later that something did begin to happen,

Baas. It was as though sacks filled with chaff were being beaten against stone walls there in the cave. Ah! thought I to myself, your stomach is beginning to ache, Eater-up-of-Bena, and, as that goat had little horns on its head—to which I tied two of the bags of the poison, Baas—and, like all snakes, no doubt you have spikes in your throat pointing downwards, you won't be able to get it up again. Then —I expect this was after the poison-sugar had begun to melt nicely in the serpent's stomach, Baas—there was a noise as though a whole company of girls were dancing a war-dance in the cave to a music of hisses.

"And then—oh! then, Baas, of a sudden that Father of Serpents came out. I tell you, Baas, that when I saw him in the bright starlight my hair stood up upon my head, for never has there been such another snake in the whole world. Those that live in trees and eat bucks in Zululand, of whose skins men make waistcoats and slippers, are but babies compared to this one. He came out, yard after yard of him. He wriggled about, he stood upon his tail with his head where the top of a tree might be, he made himself into a ring, he bit at stones and at his own stomach, while I hid behind my rock praying to your reverend father that he might not see me. Then at last he rushed away down the hill, faster than any horse could gallop.

"Now I hoped that he had gone for good and thought of going myself. Still I feared to do so lest I should meet him somewhere, so I made up my mind to wait till daylight. It was as well, Baas, for about half an hour later he came back again. Only now he could not jump, he could only crawl. Never in my life did I see a snake look so sick, Baas. Into the cave he went and lay there hissing. By degrees the hissing grew very faint, till at length they died away altogether. I waited another half-hour, Baas, and then I grew so curious that I thought that I would go to look in the cave.

"I lit the little lantern I had with me and, holding it in one hand and my stick in the other, I crept into the hole. Before I had crawled ten paces I saw something white stretched along the ground. It was the belly of the great snake, Baas, which lay upon its back quite dead.

"I know that it was dead, for I lit three wax matches, setting them to burn upon its tail and it never stirred, as any live snake will do when it feels fire. Then I came home, Baas, feeling very proud because I had outwitted that great-grandfather of all snakes who killed Bena my friend, and had made the way clear for us to walk through the cave.

"That is all the story, Baas. Now I must go to wash those dishes," and without waiting for any comment off he went, leaving us marvelling at his wit, resource and courage.

"What next?" I asked presently.

"Nothing till to-night," answered Ragnall with determination, "when I am going to look at the snake which the noble Hans has killed and whatever lies beyond the cave, as you will remember Harût invited us to do unmolested, if we could."

"Do you think Harût will keep his word, Ragnall?"

"On the whole, yes, and if he doesn't I don't care. Anything is better than sitting here in this suspense."

"I agree as to Harût, because we are too valuable to be killed just now, if for no other reason; also as to the suspense, which is unendurable. Therefore I will walk with you to look at that snake, Ragnall, and so no doubt will Hans. The exercise will do my leg good."

"Do you think it wise?" he asked doubtfully; "in your case, I mean."

"I think it most unwise that we should separate any more. We had better stand or fall altogether; further, we do not seem to have any luck apart."

The Sanctuary and the Oath

That evening shortly after sundown the three of us started boldly from our house wearing over our clothes the Kendah dresses which Ragnall had bought, and carrying nothing save sticks in our hands, some food and the lantern in our pockets. On the outskirts of the town we were met by certain Kendah, one of whom I knew, for I had often ridden by his side on our march across the desert.

"Have any of you arms upon you, Lord Macumazana?" he asked, looking curiously at us and our white robes.

"None," I answered. "Search us if you will."

"Your word is sufficient," he replied with the grave courtesy of his people. "If you are unarmed we have orders to let you go where you wish however you may be dressed. Yet, Lord," he whispered to me, "I pray you do not enter the cave, since One lives there who strikes and does not miss, One whose kiss is death. I pray it for your own sakes, also for ours who need you."

"We shall not wake him who sleeps in the cave," I answered enigmatically, as we departed rejoicing, for now we had learned that the Kendah did not yet know of the death of the serpent.

An hour's walk up the hill, guided by Hans, brought us to the mouth of the tunnel. To tell the truth I could have wished it had been longer, for as we drew near all sorts of doubts assailed me. What if Hans really had been drinking and invented this story to account for his absence? What if the snake had recovered from a merely temporary indisposition? What if it had a wife and family living in that cave, every one of them thirsting for vengeance?

Well, it was too late to hesitate now, but secretly I hoped that one of the others would prefer to lead the way. We reached the place and listened. It was silent as a tomb. Then that brave fellow Hans lit the lantern and said:

"Do you stop here, Baases, while I go to look. If you hear anything happen to me, you will have time to run away," words that made me feel somewhat ashamed of myself.

However, knowing that he was quick as a weasel and silent as a cat, we let him go. A minute or two later suddenly he reappeared out of the darkness, for he had turned the metal shield over the bull's-eye of the lantern, and even in that light I could see that he was grinning.

"It is all right, Baas," he said. "The Father of Serpents has really gone to that land whither he sent Bena, where no doubt he is now roasting in the fires of hell, and I don't see any others. Come and look at him."

So in we went and there, true enough, upon the floor of the cave lay the huge reptile stone dead and already much swollen. I don't know how long it was, for part of its body was twisted into coils, so I will only say that it was by far the most enormous snake that I have ever seen. It is true that I have heard of such reptiles in different parts of Africa, but hitherto I had always put them down as fabulous creatures transformed into and worshipped as local gods. Also this particular specimen was, I presume, of a new variety, since, according to Ragnall, it both struck like the cobra or the adder, and crushed like the boa-constrictor. It is possible, however, that he was mistaken on this point; I do not know, since I had no time, or indeed inclination, to examine its head for the poison fangs, and when next I passed that way it was gone.

I shall never forget the stench of that cave. It was horrible, which is not to be wondered at seeing that probably this creature had dwelt there for centuries, since these large snakes are said to be as long lived as tortoises, and, being sacred, of course it had never lacked for food. Everywhere lay piles of cast bones, amongst one of which I noticed fragments of a human skull, perhaps that of poor Savage. Also the projecting rocks in the place were covered with great pieces of snake skin, doubtless rubbed off by the reptile when once a year it changed its coat.

For a while we gazed at the loathsome and still glittering creature, then pushed on fearful lest we should stumble upon more of its kind. I suppose that it must have been solitary, a kind of serpent rogue, as Jana was an elephant rogue, for we met none and, if the information which I obtained afterwards may be believed, there was no species at all resembling it in the country. What its origin may have been I never learned. All the Kendah could or would say about it was that it had lived in this hole from the beginning and that Black Kendah prisoners, or malefactors, were sometimes given to it to kill, as White Kendah prisoners were given to Jana.

The cave itself proved to be not very long, perhaps one hundred and fifty feet, no more. It was not an artificial but a natural hollow in the lava rock, which I suppose had once been blown through it by an outburst of steam. Towards the farther end it narrowed so much that I began to fear there might be no exit. In this I was mistaken, however, for at its termination we found a hole just large enough for a man to walk in upright and so difficult to climb through that it became clear to us that certainly this was not the path by which the White Kendah approached their sanctuary.

Scrambling out of this aperture with thankfulness, we found ourselves upon the slope of a kind of huge ditch of lava which ran first downwards for about eighty paces, then up again to the base of the great cone of the inner mountain which was covered with dense forest.

I presume that the whole formation of this peculiar hill was the result of a violent volcanic action in the early ages of the earth. But as I do not understand such matters I will not dilate upon them further than to say that, although comparatively small, it bore a certain resemblance to other extinct volcanoes which I had met with in different parts of Africa.

We climbed down to the bottom of the ditch that from its general appearance might have been dug out by some giant race as a protection to their stronghold, and up its farther side to where the forest began on deep and fertile soil. Why there should have been rich earth here and none in the ditch is more than we could guess, but perhaps the presence of springs of water in this part of the mount may have been a cause. At any rate it was so.

The trees in this forest were huge and of a variety of cedar, but did not grow closely together; also there was practically no undergrowth, perhaps for the reason that their dense, spreading tops shut out the light. As I saw afterwards both trunks and boughs were clothed with long grey moss, which even at midday gave the place a very ghostly appearance. The darkness beneath those trees was intense, literally we could not see an inch before our faces. Yet rather than stand still we struggled on, Hans leading the way, for his instincts were quicker than ours. The steep rise of the ground beneath our feet told us that we were going uphill, as we wished to do, and from time to time I consulted a pocket compass I carried by the light of a match, knowing from previous observations that the top of the Holy Mount lay due north.

Thus for hour after hour we crept up and on, occasionally butting into the trunk of a tree or stumbling over a fallen bough, but meeting with no other adventures or obstacles of a physical kind. Of moral, or rather mental, obstacles there were many, since to all of us the atmosphere of this forest was as that of a haunted house. It may have been the embracing darkness, or the sough of the night wind amongst the boughs and mosses, or the sense of the imminent dangers that we had passed and that still awaited us. Or it may have been unknown horrors connected with this place of which some spiritual essence still survived, for without doubt localities preserve such influences, which can be felt by the sensitive among living things, especially in favouring conditions of fear and gloom. At any rate I never experienced more subtle and yet more penetrating terrors than I did upon that night, and afterwards Ragnall confessed to me that my case was his own. Black as it was I thought that I saw apparitions, among them glaring eyes and that of the elephant Jana standing in front of me with his trunk raised against the bole of a cedar. I could have sworn that I saw him, nor was I reassured when Hans whispered to me below his breath, for here we did not seem to dare to raise our voices:

"Look, Baas. Is it Jana glowing like hot iron who stands yonder?"

"Don't be a fool," I answered. "How can Jana be here and, if he were here, how could we see him in the night?" But as I said the words I remembered Harût had told us that Jana had been met with on the Holy Mount "in the spirit or in the flesh." However this may be, next instant he was gone and we beheld him or his shadow no more. Also we thought that from time to time we heard voices speaking all around us, now here, now there and now in the tree tops above our heads, though what they said we could not catch or understand.

Thus the long night wore away. Our progress was very slow, but guided by occasional glimpses at the compass we never stopped but twice, once when we found ourselves apparently surrounded by tree boles and fallen boughs, and once when we got into swampy ground. Then we took the risk of lighting the lantern, and by its aid picked our way through these difficult places. By degrees the trees grew fewer so that we could see the stars between their tops. This was a help to us as I knew that one of them, which I had carefully noted, shone at this season of the year directly over the cone of the mountain, and we were enabled to steer thereby.

It must have been not more than half an hour before the dawn that Hans, who was leading—we were pushing our way through thick bushes at the time—halted hurriedly, saying:

"Stop, Baas, we are on the edge of a cliff. When I thrust my stick forward it stands on nothing."

Needless to say we pulled up dead and so remained without stirring an inch, for who could say what might be beyond us? Ragnall wished to examine the ground with the lantern. I was about to consent, though doubtfully, when suddenly I heard voices murmuring and through the screen of bushes saw lights moving at a little distance, forty feet or more below us. Then we gave up all idea of making further use of the lantern and crouched still as mice in our bushes, waiting for the dawn.

It came at last. In the east appeared a faint pearly flush that by degrees spread itself over the whole arch of the sky and was welcomed by the barking of monkeys and the call of birds in the depths of the dew-steeped forest. Next a ray from the unrisen sun, a single spear of light shot suddenly across the sky, and as it appeared, from the darkness below us arose a sound of chanting, very low and sweet to hear. It died away and for a little while there was silence broken only by a rustling sound like to that of people taking their seats in a dark theatre. Then a woman began to sing in a beautiful, contralto voice, but in what language I do not know, for I could not catch the words, if these were words and not only musical notes.

I felt Ragnall trembling beside me and in a whisper asked him what was the matter. He answered, also in a whisper:

"I believe that is my wife's voice."

"If so, I beg you to control yourself," I replied.

Now the skies began to flame and the light to pour itself into a misty hollow beneath us like streams of many-coloured gems into a bowl, driving away the shadows. By degrees these vanished; by degrees we saw everything. Beneath us was an amphitheatre, on the southern wall of which we were seated, though it was not a wall but a lava cliff between forty and fifty feet high which served as a wall. The amphitheatre itself, however, almost exactly resembled those of the ancients which I had seen in pictures and Ragnall had visited in Italy, Greece, and Southern France.

It was oval in shape and not very large, perhaps the flat space at the bottom may have covered something over an acre, but all round this oval ran tiers of seats cut in the lava of the crater. For without doubt this was the crater of an extinct volcano.

Moreover, in what I will call the arena, stood a temple that in its main outlines, although small, exactly resembled those still to be seen in Egypt. There was the gateway or pylon; there the open outer court with columns round it supporting roofed cloisters, which, as we ascertained afterwards, were used as dwelling-places by the priests. There beyond and connected with the first by a short passage was a second rather smaller court, also open to the sky, and beyond this again, built like all the rest of the temple of lava blocks, a roofed erection measuring about twelve feet square, which I guessed at once must be the sanctuary.

This temple was, as I have said, small, but extremely well proportioned, every detail of it being in the most excellent taste though unornamented by sculpture or painting. I have to add that in front of the sanctuary door stood a large block of lava, which I concluded was an altar, and in front of this a stone seat and a basin, also of stone, supported upon a very low tripod. Further, behind the sanctuary was a square house with window-places.

At the moment of our first sight of this place the courts were empty, but on the benches of the amphitheatre were seated about three hundred persons, male and female, the men to the north and the women to the south. They were all clad in pure white robes, the heads of the men being shaved and those of the women veiled, but leaving the face exposed. Lastly, there were two roadways into the amphitheatre, one running east and one west through tunnels hollowed in the encircling rock of the crater, both of which roads were closed at the mouths of the tunnels by massive wooden double doors, seventeen or eighteen feet in height. From these roadways and their doors we learned two things. First, that the cave where had lived the Father of Serpents was, as I had suspected, not the real approach to the shrine of the Child, but only a blind; and, secondly, that the ceremony we were about to witness was secret and might only be attended by the priestly class or families of this strange tribe.

Scarcely was it full daylight when from the cells of the cloisters round the outer court issued twelve priests headed by Harût himself, who looked very dignified in his white garment, each of whom carried on a wooden platter ears of different kinds of corn. Then from the cells of the southern cloister issued twelve women, or rather girls, for all were young and very comely, who ranged themselves alongside of the men. These also carried wooden platters, and on them blooming flowers.

At a sign they struck up a religious chant and began to walk forward through the passage that led from the first court to the second. Arriving in front of the altar they halted and one by one, first a priest and then a priestess, set down the platters of offerings, piling them above each other into a cone. Next the priests and the priestesses ranged themselves in lines on either side of the altar, and Harût took a platter of corn and a platter of flowers in his hands. These he held first towards that quarter of the sky in which swam the invisible new moon, secondly towards the rising sun, and thirdly towards the doors of the sanctuary, making genuflexions and uttering some chanted prayer, the words of which we could not hear.

A pause followed, that was succeeded by a sudden outburst of song wherein all the audience took part. It was a very sonorous and beautiful song or hymn in some language which I did not understand, divided into four verses, the end of each verse being marked by the bowing of every one of those many singers towards the east, towards the west, and finally towards the altar.

Another pause till suddenly the doors of the sanctuary were thrown wide and from between them issued—the goddess Isis of the Egyptians as I have seen her in pictures! She was wrapped in closely clinging draperies of material so thin that the whiteness of her body could be seen beneath. Her hair was outspread before her, and she wore a head- dress or bonnet of glittering feathers from the front of which rose a little golden snake. In her arms she bore what at that distance seemed to be a naked child. With her came two women, walking a little behind her and supporting her arms, who also wore feather bonnets but without the golden snake, and were clad in tight-fitting, transparent garments.

"My God!" whispered Ragnall, "it is my wife!"

"Then be silent and thank Him that she is alive and well," I answered.

The goddess Isis, or the English lady—in that excitement I did not reck which—stood still while the priests and priestesses and all the audience, who, gathered on the upper benches of the amphitheatre, could see her above the wall of the inner court, raised a thrice- repeated and triumphant cry of welcome. Then Harût and the first priestess lifted respectively an ear of corn and a flower from the two topmost platters and held these first to the lips of the child in her arms and secondly to her lips.

This ceremony concluded, the two attendant women led her round the altar to the stone chair, upon which she seated herself. Next fire was kindled in the bowl on the tripod in front of the chair, how I could not see; but perhaps it was already smouldering there. At any rate it burnt up in a thin blue flame, on to which Harût and the head priestess threw something that caused the flame to turn to smoke. Then Isis, for I prefer to call her so while describing this ceremony, was caused to bend her head forward, so that it was enveloped in the smoke exactly as she and I had done some years before in the drawing-room at Ragnall Castle. Presently the smoke died away and the two attendants with the feathered head-dresses straightened her in the chair where she sat still holding the babe against her breast as she might have done to nurse it, but with her head bent forward like that of a person in a swoon.

Now Harût stepped forward and appeared to speak to the goddess at some length, then fell back again and waited, till in the midst of an intense silence she rose from her seat and, fixing her wide eyes on the heavens, spoke in her turn, for although we heard nothing of what she said, in that clear, morning light we could see her lips moving. For some minutes she spoke, then sat down again upon the chair and remained motionless, staring straight in front of her. Harût advanced again, this time to the front of the altar, and, taking his stand upon a kind of stone step, addressed the priests and priestesses and all the encircling audience in a voice so loud and clear that I could distinguish and understand every word he said.

"The Guardian of the heavenly Child, the Nurse decreed, the appointed Nurturer, She who is the shadow of her that bore the Child, She who in her day bears the symbol of the Child and is consecrated to its service from of old, She whose heart is filled with the wisdom of the Child and who utters the decrees of Heaven, has spoken. Hearken now to the voice of the Oracle uttered in answer to the questions of me, Harût, the head priest of the Eternal Child during my life-days. Thus says the Oracle, the Guardian, the Nurturer, marked like all who went before her with the holy mark of the new moon. She on whom the spirit, flitting from generation to generation, has alighted for a while. 'O people of the White Kendah, worshippers of the Child in this land and descendants of those who for thousands of years worshipped the Child in a more ancient land until the barbarians drove it thence with the remnant that remained. War is upon you, O people of the White Kendah. Jana the evil one; he whose other name is Set, he whose other name is Satan, he who for this while lives in the shape of an elephant, he who is worshipped by the thousands whom once you conquered, and whom still you bridle by my might, comes up against you. The Darkness wars against the Daylight, the Evil wars against the Good. My curse has fallen upon the people of Jana, my hail has smitten them, their corn and their cattle; they have no food to eat. But they are still strong for war and there is food in your land. They come to take your corn; Jana comes to trample your god. The Evil comes to destroy the Good, the Night to Devour the Day. It is the last of many battles. How shall you conquer, O People of the Child? Not by your own strength, for you are few in number and Jana is very strong. Not by the strength of the Child, for the Child grows weak and old, the days of its dominion are almost done, and its worship is almost outworn. Here alone that worship lingers, but new gods, who are still the old gods, press on to take its place and to lead it to its rest.'

"How then shall you conquer that, when the Child has departed to its own place, a remnant of you may still remain? In one way only—so says the Guardian, the Nurturer of the Child speaking with the voice of the Child; by the help of those whom you have summoned to your aid from far. There were four of them, but one you have suffered to be slain in the maw of the Watcher in the cave. It was an evil deed, O sons and daughters of the Child, for as the Watcher is now dead, so ere long many of you who planned this deed must die who, had it not been for that man's blood, would have lived on a while. Why did you do this thing? That you might keep a secret, the secret of the theft of a woman, that you might continue to act a lie which falls upon your head like a stone from heaven.

"Thus saith the Child: 'Lift no hand against the three who remain, and what they shall ask, that give, for thus alone shall some of you be saved from Jana and those who serve him, even though the Guardian and the Child be taken away and the Child itself returned to its own place.' These are the words of the Oracle uttered at the Feast of the First-fruits, the words that cannot be changed and mayhap its last."

Harût ceased, and there was silence while this portentous message sank into the minds of his audience. At length they seemed to understand its ominous nature and from them all there arose a universal, simultaneous groan. As it died away the two attendants dressed as goddesses assisted the personification of the Lady Isis to rise from her seat and, opening the robes upon her breast, pointed to something beneath her throat, doubtless that birthmark shaped like the new moon which made her so sacred in their eyes since she who bore it and she alone could fill her holy office.

All the audience and with them the priests and priestesses bowed before her. She lifted the symbol of the Child, holding it high above her head, whereon once more they bowed with the deepest veneration. Then still holding the effigy aloft, she turned and with her two attendants passed into the sanctuary and doubtless thence by a covered way into the house beyond. At any rate we saw her no more.

As soon as she was gone the congregation, if I may call it so, leaving their seats, swarmed down into the outer court of the temple through its eastern gate, which was now opened. Here the priests proceeded to distribute among them the offerings taken from the altar, giving a grain of corn to each of the men to eat and a flower to each of the women, which flower she kissed and hid in the bosom of her robe. Evidently it was a kind of sacrament.

Ragnall lifted himself a little upon his hands and knees, and I saw that his eyes glowed and his face was very pale.

"What are you going to do?" I asked.

"Demand that those people give me back my wife, whom they have stolen. Don't try to stop me, Quatermain, I mean what I say."

"But, but," I stammered, "they never will and we are but three unarmed men."

Hans lifted up his little yellow face between us.

"Baas," he hissed, "I have a thought. The Lord Baas wishes to get the lady dressed like a bird as to her head and like one for burial as to her body, who is, he says, his wife. But for us to take her from among so many is impossible. Now what did that old witch-doctor Harût declare just now? He declared, speaking for his fetish, that by our help alone the White Kendah can resist the hosts of the Black Kendah and that no harm must be done to us if the White Kendah would continue to live. So it seems, Baas, that we have something to sell which the White Kendah must buy, namely our help against the Black Kendah, for if we will not fight for them, they believe that they cannot conquer their enemies and kill the devil Jana. Well now, supposing that the

Baas says that our price is the white woman dressed like a bird, to be delivered over to us when we have defeated the Black Kendah and killed Jana—after which they will have no more use for her. And supposing that the Baas says that if they refuse to pay that price we will burn all our powder and cartridges so that the rifles are no use? Is there not a path to walk on here?"

"Perhaps," I answered. "Something of the sort was working in my mind but I had no time to think it out."

Turning, I explained the idea to Ragnall, adding:

"I pray you not to be rash. If you are, not only may we be killed, which does not so much matter, but it is very probable that even if they spare us they will put an end to your wife rather than suffer one whom they look upon as holy and who is necessary to their faith in its last struggle to be separated from her charge of the Child."

This was a fortunate argument of mine and one which went home.

"To lose her now would be more than I could bear," he muttered.

"Then will you promise to let me try to manage this affair and not to interfere with me and show violence?"

He hesitated a moment and answered:

"Yes, I promise, for you two are cleverer than I am and—I cannot trust my judgment."

"Good," I said, assuming an air of confidence which I did not feel. "Now we will go down to call upon Harût and his friends. I want to have a closer look at that temple."

So behind our screen of bushes we wriggled back a little distance till we knew that the slope of the ground would hide us when we stood up. Then as quickly as we could we made our way eastwards for something over a quarter of a mile and after this turned to the north. As I expected, beyond the ring of the crater we found ourselves on the rising, tree-clad bosom of the mountain and, threading our path through the cedars, came presently to that track or roadway which led to the eastern gate of the amphitheatre. This road we followed unseen until presently the gateway appeared before us. We walked through it without attracting any attention, perhaps because all the people were either talking together, or praying, or perhaps because like themselves we were wrapped in white robes. At the mouth of the tunnel we stopped and I called out in a loud voice:

"The white lords and their servant have come to visit Harût, as he invited them to do. Bring us, we pray you, into the presence of Harût."

Everyone wheeled round and stared at us standing there in the shadow of the gateway tunnel, for the sun behind us was still low. My word, how they did stare! A voice cried:

"Kill them! Kill these strangers who desecrate our temple."

"What!" I answered. "Would you kill those to whom your high-priest has given safe-conduct; those moreover by whose help alone, as your Oracle has just declared, you can hope to slay Jana and destroy his hosts?"

"How do they know that?" shouted another voice. "They are magicians!"

"Yes," I remarked, "all magic does not dwell in the hearts of the White Kendah. If you doubt it, go to look at the Watcher in the Cave whom your Oracle told you is dead. You will find that it did not lie."

As I spoke a man rushed through the gates, his white rob streaming on the wind, shouting as he emerged from the tunnel:

"O Priests and Priestesses of the Child, the ancient serpent is dead. I whose office it is to feed the serpent on the day of the new moon have found him dead in his house."

"You hear," I interpolated calmly. "The Father of Snakes is dead. If you want to know how, I will tell you. We looked on it and it died."

They might have answered that poor Savage also looked on it with the result that *he* died, but luckily it did not occur to them to do so. On the contrary, they just stood still and stared at us like a flock of startled sheep.

Presently the sheep parted and the shepherd in the shape of Harût appeared looking, I reflected, the very picture of Abraham softened by a touch of the melancholia of Job, that is, as I have always imagined those patriarchs. He bowed to us with his usual Oriental courtesy, and we bowed back to him. Hans' bow, I may explain, was of the most peculiar nature, more like a *skulpat*, as the Boers call a land-tortoise, drawing its wrinkled head into its shell and putting it out again than anything else. Then Harût remarked in his peculiar English, which I suppose the White Kendah took for some tongue known only to magicians:

"So you get here, eh? Why you get here, how the devil you get here, eh?"

"We got here because you asked us to do so if we could," I answered, "and we thought it rude not to accept your invitation. For the rest, we came through a cave where you kept a tame snake, an ugly-looking reptile but very harmless to those who know how to deal with snakes and are not afraid of them as poor Bena was. If you can spare the skin I should like to have it to make myself a robe."

Harût looked at me with evident respect, muttering:

"Oh, Macumazana, you what you English call cool, quite cool! Is that all?"

"No," I answered. "Although you did not happen to notice us, we have been present at your church service, and heard and seen everything. For instance, we saw the wife of the lord here whom you stole away in Egypt, her that, being a liar, Harût, you swore you never stole. Also we heard her words after you had made her drunk with your tobacco smoke."

Now for once in his life Harût was, in sporting parlance, knocked out. He looked at us, then turning quite pale, lifted his eyes to heaven and rocked upon his feet as though he were about to fall.

"How you do it? How you do it, eh?" he queried in a weak voice.

"Never you mind how we did it, my friend," I answered loftily. "What we want to know is when you are going to hand over that lady to her husband."

"Not possible," he answered, recovering some of his tone. "First we kill you, first we kill her, she Nurse of the Child. While Child there, she stop there till she die."

"See here," broke in Ragnall. "Either you give me my wife or someone else will die. You will die, Harût. I am a stronger man than you are and unless you promise to give me my wife I will kill you now with this stick and my hands. Do not move or call out if you want to live."

"Lord," answered the old man with some dignity, "I know you can kill me, and if you kill me, I think I say thank you who no wish to live in so much trouble. But what good that, since in one minute then you die too, all of you, and lady she stop here till Black Kendah king take her to wife or she too die?"

"Let us talk," I broke in, treading warningly upon Ragnall's foot. "We have heard your Oracle and we know that you believe its words. It is said that we alone can help you to conquer the Black Kendah. If you will not promise what we ask, we will not help you. We will burn our powder and melt our lead, so that the guns we have cannot speak with Jana and with Simba, and after that we will do other things that I need not tell you. But if you promise what we ask, then we will fight for you against Jana and Simba and teach your men to use the fifty rifles which we have here with us, and by our help you shall conquer. Do you understand?"

He nodded and stroking his long beard, asked:

"What you want us promise, eh?"

"We want you to promise that after Jana is dead and the Black Kendah are driven away, you will give up to us unharmed that lady whom you have stolen. Also that you will bring her and us safely out of your country by the roads you know, and meanwhile that you will let this lord see his wife."

"Not last, no," replied Harût, "that not possible. That bring us all to grave. Also no good, 'cause her mind empty. For rest, you come to other place, sit down and eat while

I talk with priests. Be afraid nothing; you quite safe."

"Why should we be afraid? It is you who should be afraid, you who stole the lady and brought Bena to his death. Do you not remember the words of your own Oracle, Harût?"

"Yes, I know words, but how *you* know them *that* I not know," he replied.

Then he issued some orders, as a result of which a guard formed itself about us and conducted us through the crowd and along the passage to the second court of the temple, which was now empty. Here the guard left us but remained at the mouth of the passage, keeping watch. Presently women brought us food and drink, of which Hans and I partook heartily though Ragnall, who was so near to his lost wife and yet so far away, could eat but little. Mingled joy because after these months of arduous search he found her yet alive, and fear lest she should again be taken from him for ever, deprived him of all appetite.

While we ate, priests to the number of about a dozen, who I suppose had been summoned by Harût, were admitted by the guard and, gathering out of earshot of us between the altar and the sanctuary, entered on an earnest discussion with him. Watching their faces I could see that there was a strong difference of opinion between them, about half taking one view on the matter of which they disputed, and half another. At length Harût made some proposition to which they all agreed. Then the door of the sanctuary was opened with a strange sort of key which one of the priests produced, showing a dark interior in which gleamed a white object, I suppose the statue of the Child. Harût and two others entered, the door being closed behind them. About five minutes later they appeared again and others, who listened earnestly and after renewed consultation signified assent by holding up the right hand. Now one of the priests walked to where we were and, bowing, begged us to advance to the altar. This we did, and were stood in a line in front of it, Hans being set in the middle place, while the priests ranged themselves on either side. Next Harût, having once more opened the door of the sanctuary, took his stand a little to the right of it and addressed us, not in English but in his own language, pausing at the end of each sentence that I might translate to Ragnall.

"Lords Macumazana and Igeza, and yellow man who is named Light-in-Darkness," he said, "we, the head priests of the Child, speaking on behalf of the White Kendah people with full authority so to do, have taken counsel together and of the wisdom of the Child as to the demands which you make of us. Those demands are: First, that after you have killed Jana and defeated the Black Kendah we should give over to you the white lady who was born in a far land to fill the office of Guardian of the Child, as is shown by the mark of the new moon upon her breast, but who, because for the second time we could not take her, became the wife of you, the Lord Igeza. Secondly, that we should conduct you and her safely out of our land to some place whence you can return to your own country. Both of these things we will do, because we know from of old that if once Jana is dead we shall have no cause to fear the Black Kendah any more, since we believe that then they will leave their home and go elsewhere, and therefore that we shall no longer need an Oracle to declare to us in what way Heaven will protect us from Jana and from them. Or if another Oracle should become necessary to us, doubtless in due season she will be found. Also we admit that we stole away this lady because we must, although she was the wife of one of you. But if we swear this, you on your part must also swear that you will stay with us till the end of the war, making our cause your cause and, if need be, giving your lives for us in battle. You must swear further that none of you will attempt to see or to take hence that lady who is named Guardian of the Child until we hand her over to you unharmed. If you will not swear these things, then since no blood may be shed in this holy place, here we will ring you round until you die of hunger and of thirst, or if you escape from this temple, then we will fall upon you and put you to death and fight our own battle with Jana as best we may."

"And if we make these promises how are we to know that you will keep yours?" I interrupted.

"Because the oath that we shall give you will be the oath of the Child that may not be broken."

"Then give it," I said, for although I did not altogether like the security, obviously it was the best to be had.

So very solemnly they laid their right hands upon the altar and "in the presence of the Child and the name of the Child and of all the White Kendah people," repeated after Harût a most solemn oath of which I have already given the substance. It called down on their heads a very dreadful doom in this world and the next, should it be broken either in the spirit or the letter; the said oath, however, to be only binding if we, on our part, swore to observe their terms and kept our engagement also in the spirit and the letter.

Then they asked us to fulfil our share of the pact and very considerately drew out of hearing while we discussed the matter; Harût, the only one of them who understood a word of English, retiring behind the sanctuary. At first I had difficulties with Ragnall, who was most unwilling to bind himself in any way. In the end, on my pointing out that nothing less than our lives were involved and probably that of his wife as well, also that no other course was open to us, he gave way, to my great relief.

Hans announced himself ready to swear anything, adding blandly that words mattered nothing, as afterwards we could do whatever seemed best in our own interests, whereon I read him a short moral lecture on the heinousness of perjury, which did not seem to impress him very much.

This matter settled, we called back the priests and informed them of our decision. Harût demanded that we should affirm it "by the Child," which we declined to do, saying that it was our custom to swear only in the name of our own God. Being a liberal-minded man who had travelled, Harût gave way on the point. So I swore first to the effect that I would fight for the White Kendah to the finish in consideration of the promises that they had made to us. I added that I would not attempt either to see or to interfere with the lady here known as the Guardian of the Child until the war was over or even to bring our existence to her knowledge, ending up, "so help me God," as I had done several times when giving evidence in a court of law.

Next Ragnall with a great effort repeated my oath in English, Harût listening carefully to every word and once or twice asking me to explain the exact meaning of some of them.

Lastly Hans, who seemed very bored with the whole affair, swore, also repeating the words after me and finishing on his own account with "so help me the reverend Predikant, the Baas's father," a form that he utterly declined to vary although it involved more explanations. When pressed, indeed, he showed considerable ingenuity by pointing out to the priests that to his mind my poor father stood in exactly the same relation to the Power above us as their Oracle did to the Child. He offered generously, however, to throw in the spirits of his grandfather and grandmother and some extraordinary divinity they worshipped, I think it was a hare, as an additional guarantee of good faith. This proposal the priests accepted gravely, whereon Hans whispered into my ear in Dutch:

"Those fools do not remember that when pressed by dogs the hare often doubles on its own spoor, and that your reverend father will be very pleased if I can play them the same trick with the white lady that they played with the Lord Igeza."

I only looked at him in reply, since the morality of Hans was past argument. It might perhaps be summed up in one sentence: To get the better of his neighbour in his master's service, honestly if possible; if not, by any means that came to his hand down to that of murder. At the bottom of his dark and mysterious heart Hans worshipped only one god, named Love, not of woman or child, but of my humble self. His principles were those of a rather sly but very high-class and exclusive dog, neither better nor worse. Still, when all is said and done, there are lower creatures in the world than high-class dogs. At least so the masters whom they adore are apt to think, especially if their watchfulness and courage have often saved them from death or disaster.

The Embassy

The ceremonies were over and the priests, with the exception of Harût and two who remained to attend upon him, vanished, probably to inform the male and female hierophants of their result, and through these the whole people of the White Kendah. Old Harût stared at us for a little while, then said in English, which he always liked to talk when Ragnall was present, perhaps for the sake of practice:

"What you like do now, eh? P'r'aps wish fly back to Town of Child, for suppose this how you come. If so, please take me with you, because that save long ride."

"Oh! no," I answered. "We walked here through that hole where lived the Father of Snakes who died of fear when he saw us, and just mixed with the rest of you in the court of the temple."

"Good lie," said Harût admiringly, "very first-class lie! Wonder how you kill great snake, which we all think never die, for he live there hundred, hundred years; our people find him there when first they come to this country, and make him kind of god. Well, he nasty beast and best dead. I say, you like see Child? If so, come, for you our brothers now, only please take off hat and not speak.

I intimated that we should "like see Child," and led by Harût we entered the little sanctuary which was barely large enough to hold all of us. In a niche of the end wall stood the sacred effigy which Ragnall and I examined with a kind of reverent interest. It proved to be the statue of an infant about two feet high, cut, I imagine, from the base of a single but very large elephant's tusk, so ancient that the yellowish ivory had become rotten and was covered with a multitude of tiny fissures. Indeed, for its appearance I made up my mind that several thousands of years must have passed since the beast died from which this ivory was taken, especially as it had, I presume, always been carefully preserved under cover.

The workmanship of the object was excellent, that of a fine artist who, I should think, had taken some living infant for his model, perhaps a child of the Pharaoh of the day. Here I may say at once that there could be no doubt of its Egyptian origin, since on one side of the head was a single lock of hair, while the fourth finger of the right hand was held before the lips as though to enjoin silence. Both of these peculiarities, it will be remembered, are characteristic of the infant Horus, the child of Osiris and Isis, as portrayed in bronzes and temple carvings. So at least Ragnall, who recently had studied many such effigies in Egypt, informed me later. There was nothing else in the place except an ancient, string-seated chair of ebony, adorned with inlaid ivory patterns; an effigy of a snake in porcelain, showing that serpent worship was in some way mixed up with their religion; and two rolls of papyrus, at least that is what they looked like, which were laid in the niche with the statue. These rolls, to my disappointment, Harût refused to allow us to examine or even to touch.

After we had left the sanctuary I asked Harût when this figure was brought to their land. He replied that it came when they came, at what date he could not tell us as it was so long ago, and that with it came the worship and the ceremonies of their religion.

In answer to further questions he added that this figure, which seemed to be of ivory, contained the spirits which ruled the sun and the moon, and through them the world. This, said Ragnall, was just a piece of Egyptian theology, preserved down to our own times in a remote corner of Africa, doubtless by descendants of dwellers on the Nile who had been driven thence in some national catastrophe, and brought away with them their faith and one of the effigies of their gods. Perhaps they fled at the time of the Persian invasion by Cambyses.

After we had emerged from this deeply interesting shrine, which was locked behind us, Harût led us, not through the passage connecting it with the stone house that we knew was occupied by Ragnall's wife in her capacity as Guardian of the Child, or a latter-day personification of Isis, Lady of the Moon, at which house he cast many longing glances, but back through the two courts and the pylon to the gateway of the temple. Here on the road by which we had entered the place, a fact which we did not mention to him, he paused and addressed us.

"Lords," he said, "now you and the People of the White Kendah are one; your ends are their ends, your fate is their fate, their secrets are your secrets. You, Lord Igeza, work for a reward, namely the person of that lady whom we took from you on the Nile."

"How did you do that?" interrupted Ragnall when I had interpreted.

"Lord, we watched you. We knew when you came to Egypt; we followed you in Egypt, whither we had journeyed on our road to England once more to seek our Oracles, till the day of our opportunity dawned. Then at night we called her and she obeyed the call, as she must do whose mind we have taken away—ask me not how—and brought her to dwell with us, she who is marked from her birth with the holy sign and wears upon her breast certain charmed stones and a symbol that for thousands of years have adorned the body of the Child and those of its Oracles. Do you remember a company of Arabs whom you saw riding on the banks of the Great River on the day before the night when she was lost to you? We were with that company and on our camels we bore her thence, happy and unharmed to this our land, as I trust, when all is done, we shall bear her back again and you with her."

"I trust so also, for you have wrought me a great wrong," said Ragnall briefly, "perhaps a greater wrong than I know at present, for how came it that my boy was killed by an elephant?"

"Ask that question of Jana and not of me," Harût answered darkly. Then he went on: "You also, Lord Macumazana, work for a reward, the countless store of ivory which your eyes have beheld lying in the burial place of elephants beyond the Tava River. When you have slain Jana who watches the store, and defeated the Black Kendah who serve him, it is yours and we will give you camels to bear it, or some of it, for all cannot be carried, to the sea where it can be taken away in ships. As for the yellow man, I think that he seeks no reward who soon will inherit all things."

"The old witch-doctor means that I am going to die," remarked Hans expectorating reflectively. "Well, Baas, I am quite ready, if only Jana and certain others die first. Indeed I grow too old to fight and travel as I used to do, and therefore shall be glad to pass to some land where I become young again."

"Stuff and rubbish!" I exclaimed, then turned and listened to Harût who, not understanding our Dutch conversation, was speaking once more.

"Lords," he said, "these paths which run east and west are the real approach to the mountain top and the temple, not that which, as I suppose, led you through the cave of the old serpent. The road to the west, which wanders round the base of the hill to a pass in those distant mountains and thence across the deserts to the north, is so easy to stop that by it we need fear no attack. With this eastern road the case is, however, different, as I shall now show you, if you will ride with me."

Then he gave some orders to two attendant priests who departed at a run and presently reappeared at the head of a small train of camels which had been hidden, I know not where. We mounted and, following the road across a flat piece of ground, found that not more than half a mile away was another precipitous ridge of rock which had presumably once formed the lip of an outer crater. This ridge, however, was broken away for a width of two or three hundred yards, perhaps by some outrush of lava, the road running through the centre of the gap on which schanzes had been built here and there for purposes of defence. Looking at these I saw that they were very old and inefficient and asked when they had been erected. Harût replied about a century before when the last war took place with the Black Kendah, who had been finally driven off at this spot, for then the White Kendah were more numerous than at present.

"So Simba knows this road?" I said.

"Yes, Lord, and Jana knows it also, for he fought in that war and still at times visits us here and kills any whom he may meet. Only to the temple he has never dared to come."

Now I wondered whether we had really seen Jana in the forest on the previous night, but coming to the conclusion that it was useless to investigate the matter, made no inquiries, especially as these would have revealed to Harût the route by which we approached the temple. Only I pointed out to him that proper defences should be put up here without delay, that is if they meant to make a stronghold of the mountain.

"We do, Lord," he answered, "since we are not strong enough to attack the Black Kendah in their own country or to meet them in pitched battle on the plain. Here and in no other place must be fought the last fight between Jana and the Child. Therefore it will be your task to build walls cunningly, so that when they come we may defeat Jana and the hosts of the Black Kendah."

"Do you mean that this elephant will accompany Simba and his soldiers, Harût?"

"Without doubt, Lord, since he has always done so from the beginning. Jana is tame to the king and certain priests of the Black Kendah, whose forefathers have fed him for generations, and will obey their orders. Also he can think for himself, being an evil spirit and invulnerable."

"His left eye and the tip of his trunk are not invulnerable," I remarked, "though from what I saw of him I should say there is no doubt about his being able to think for himself. Well, I am glad the brute is coming as I have an account to settle with him."

"As he, Lord, who does not forget, has an account to settle with you and your servant, Light-in-Darkness," commented Harût in an unpleasant and suggestive tone.

Then after we had taken a few measurements and Ragnall, who understands such matters, had drawn a rough sketch of the place in his pocket-book to serve as data for our proposed scheme of fortifications, we pursued our journey back to the town, where we had left all our stores and there were many things to be arranged. It proved to be quite a long ride, down the eastern slope of the mountain which was easy to negotiate, although like the rest of this strange hill it was covered with dense cedar forests that also seemed to me to have defensive possibilities. Reaching its foot at length we were obliged to make a detour by certain winding paths to avoid ground that was too rough for the camels, so that in the end we did not come to our own house in the Town of the Child till about midday.

Glad enough were we to reach it, since all three of us were tired out with our terrible night journey and the anxious emotions that we had undergone. Indeed, after we had eaten we lay down and I rejoiced to see that, notwithstanding the state of mental excitement into which the discovery of his wife had plunged him, Ragnall was the first of us to fall asleep.

About five o'clock we were awakened by a messenger from Harût, who requested our attendance on important business at a kind of meeting- house which stood at a little distance on an open place where the White Kendah bartered produce. Here we found Harût and about twenty of the headmen seated in the shade of a thatched roof, while behind them, at a respectful distance, stood quite a hundred of the White Kendah. Most of these, however, were women and children, for as I have said the greater part of the male population was absent from the town because of the commencement of the harvest.

We were conducted to chairs, or rather stools of honour, and when we two had seated ourselves, Hans taking his stand behind us, Harût rose and informed us that an embassy had arrived from the Black Kendah which was about to be admitted.

Presently they came, five of them, great, truculent-looking fellows of a surprising blackness, unarmed, for they had not been allowed to bring their weapons in to the town, but adorned with the usual silver chains across their breasts to show their rank, and other savage finery. In the man who was their leader I recognized one of those messengers who had accosted us when first we entered their territory on our way from the south, before that fight in which I was taken prisoner. Stepping forward and addressing himself to Harût, he said:

"A while ago, O Prophet of the Child, I, the messenger of the god Jana, speaking through the mouth of Simba the King, gave to you and your brother Marût a certain warning to which you did not listen. Now Jana has Marût, and again I come to warn you, Harût."

"If I remember right," interrupted Harût blandly, "I think that on that occasion two of you delivered the message and that the Child marked one of you upon the brow. If Jana has my brother, say, where is yours?"

"We warned you," went on the messenger, "and you cursed us in the name of the Child."

"Yes," interrupted Harût again, "we cursed you with three curses. The first was the curse of Heaven by storm or drought, which has fallen upon you. The second was the curse of famine, which is falling upon you; and the third was the curse of war, which is yet to fall on you."

"It is of war that we come to speak," replied the messenger, diplomatically avoiding the other two topics which perhaps he found it awkward to discuss.

"That is foolish of you," replied the bland Harût, "seeing that the other day you matched yourselves against us with but small success. Many of you were killed but only a very few of us, and the white lord whom you took captive escaped out of your hands and from the tusks of Jana who, I think, now lacks an eye. If he is a god, how comes it that he lacks an eye and could not kill an unarmed white man?"

"Let Jana answer for himself, as he will do ere long, O Harût. Meanwhile, these are the words of Jana spoken through the mouth of Simba the King: The Child has destroyed my harvest and therefore I demand this of the people of the Child—that they give me three-fourths of their harvest, reaping the same and delivering it on the south bank of the River Tava. That they give me the two white lords to be sacrificed to me. That they give the white lady who is Guardian of the Child to be a wife of Simba the King, and with her a hundred virgins of your people. That the image of the Child be brought to the god Jana in the presence of his priests and Simba the King. These are the demands of Jana spoken through the mouth of Simba the King."

Watching, I saw a thrill of horror shake the forms of Harût and of all those with him as the full meaning of these, to them, most impious requests sank into their minds. But he only asked very quietly:

"And if we refuse the demands, what then?"

"Then," shouted the messenger insolently, "then Jana declares war upon you, the last war of all, war till every one of your men be dead and the Child you worship is burnt to grey ashes with fire. War till your women are taken as slaves and the corn which you refuse is stored in our grain pits and your land is a waste and your name forgotten. Already the hosts of Jana are gathered and the trumpet of Jana calls them to the fight. To-morrow or the next day they advance upon you, and ere the moon is full not one of you will be left to look upon her."

Harût rose, and walking from under the shed, turned his back upon the envoys and stared at the distant line of great mountains which stood out far away against the sky. Out of curiosity I followed him and observed that these mountains were no longer visible. Where they had been was nothing but a line of black and heavy cloud. After looking for a while he returned and addressing the envoys, said quite casually:

"If you will be advised by me, friends, you will ride hard for the river. There is such rain upon the mountains as I have never seen before, and you will be fortunate if you cross it before the flood comes down, the greatest flood that has happened in our day."

This intelligence seemed to disturb the messengers, for they too stepped out of the shed and stared at the mountains, muttering to each other something that I could not understand. Then they returned and with a fine appearance of indifference demanded an immediate answer to their challenge.

"Can you not guess it?" answered Harût. Then changing his tone he drew himself to his full height and thundered out at them: "Get you back to your evil spirit of a god that hides in the shape of a beast of the forest and to his slave who calls himself a king, and say to them: 'Thus speaks the Child to his rebellious servants, the Black Kendah dogs: Swim my river when you can, which will not be yet, and come up against me when you will; for whenever you come I shall be ready for you. You are already dead, O Jana. You are already dead, O Simba the slave. You are scattered and lost, O dogs of the Black Kendah, and the home of such of you as remain shall be far away in a barren land, where you must dig deep for water and live upon the wild game because there little corn will grow.' Now begone, and swiftly, lest you stop here for ever."

So they turned and went, leaving me full of admiration for the histrionic powers of Harût.

I must add, however, that being without doubt a keen observer of the weather conditions of the neighbourhood, he was quite right about the rain upon the mountains, which by the way never extended to the territory of the People of the Child. As we heard afterwards, the flood came down just as the envoys reached the river; indeed, one of them was drowned in attempting its crossing, and for fourteen days after this it remained impassable to an army.

That very evening we began our preparations to meet an attack which was now inevitable. Putting aside the supposed rival powers of the tribal divinities worshipped under the names of the Child and Jana, which, while they added a kind of Homeric interest to the contest, could, we felt, scarcely affect an issue that must be decided with cold steel and other mortal weapons, the position of the White Kendah was serious indeed. As I think I have said, in all they did not number more than about two thousand men between the ages of twenty and fifty- five, or, including lads between fourteen and twenty and old men still able-bodied between fifty-five and seventy, say two thousand seven hundred capable of some sort of martial service. To these might be added something under two thousand women, since among this dwindling folk, oddly enough, from causes that I never ascertained, the males out-numbered the females, which accounted for their marriage customs that were, by comparison with those of most African peoples, monogamous. At any rate only the rich among them had more than one wife, while the poor or otherwise ineligible often had none at all, since inter-marriage with other races and above all with the Black Kendah dwelling beyond the river was so strictly taboo that it was punishable with death or expulsion.

Against this little band the Black Kendah could bring up twenty thousand men, besides boys and aged persons who with the women would probably be left to defend their own country, that is, not less than ten to one. Moreover, all of these enemies would be fighting with the courage of despair, since quite three-fourths of their crops with many of their cattle and sheep had been destroyed by the terrific hail- burst that I have described. Therefore, since no other corn was available in the surrounding land, where they dwelt alone encircled by deserts, either they must capture that of the White Kendah, or suffer terribly from starvation until a year later when another harvest ripened.

The only points I could see in favour of the People of the Child were that they would fight on the vantage ground of their mountain stronghold, a formidable position if properly defended. Also they would have the benefit of the skill and knowledge of Ragnall and myself. Lastly, the enemy must face our rifles. Neither the White nor the Black Kendah, I should say, possessed any guns, except a few antiquated flintlock weapons that the former had captured from some nomadic tribe and kept as curiosities. Why this was the case I do not know, since undoubtedly at times the White Kendah traded in camels and corn with Arabs who wandered as far as the Sudan, or Egypt, nomadic tribes to whom even then firearms were known, although perhaps rarely used by them. But so it was, possibly because of some old law or prejudice which forbade their introduction into the country, or mayhap of the difficulty of procuring powder and lead, or for the reason that they had none to teach them the use of such new-fangled weapons.

Now it will be remembered that, on the chance of their proving useful, Ragnall, in addition to our own sporting rifles, had brought with him to Africa fifty Snider rifles with an ample supply of ammunition, the same that I had trouble in passing through the Customs at Durban, all of which had arrived safely at the Town of the Child. Clearly our first duty was to make the best possible use of this invaluable store. To that end I asked Harût to select seventy-five of the boldest and most intelligent young men among his people, and to hand them over to me and Hans for instruction in musketry. We had only fifty rifles but I drilled seventy-five men, or fifty per cent. more, that some might be ready to replace any who fell.

From dawn to dark each day Hans and I worked at trying to convert these Kendah into sharpshooters. It was no easy task with men, however willing, who till then had never held a gun, especially as I must be very sparing of the ammunition necessary to practice, of which of course our supply was limited. Still we taught them how to take cover, how to fire and to cease from firing at a word of command, also to hold the rifles low and waste no shot. To make marksmen of them was more than I could hope to do under the circumstances.

With the exception of these men nearly the entire male population were working day and night to get in the harvest. This proved a very difficult business, both because some of the crops were scarcely fit and because all the grain had to be carried on camels to be stored in and at the back of the second court of the temple, the only place where it was likely to be safe. Indeed in the end a great deal was left unreaped. Then the herds of cattle and breeding camels which grazed on the farther sides of the Holy Mount must be brought into places of safety, glens in the forest on its slope, and forage stacked to feed them. Also it was necessary to provide scouts to keep watch along the river.

Lastly, the fortifications in the mountain pass required unceasing labour and attention. This was the task of Ragnall, who fortunately in his youth, before he succeeded unexpectedly to the title, was for some years an officer in the Royal Engineers and therefore thoroughly understood that business. Indeed he understood it rather too well, since the result of his somewhat complicated and scientific scheme of defence was a little confusing to the simple native mind. However, with the assistance of all the priests and of all the women and children who were not engaged in provisioning the Mount, he built wall after wall and redoubt after redoubt, if that is the right word, to say nothing of the shelter trenches he dug and many pitfalls, furnished at the bottom with sharp stakes, which he hollowed out wherever the soil could be easily moved, to discomfit a charging enemy.

Indeed, when I saw the amount of work he had concluded in ten days, which was not until I joined him on the mountain, I was quite astonished.

About this time a dispute arose as to whether we should attempt to prevent the Black Kendah from crossing the river which was now running down, a plan that some of the elders favoured. At last the controversy was referred to me as head general and I decided against anything of the sort. It seemed to me that our force was too small, and that if I took the rifle-men a great deal of ammunition might be expended with poor result. Also in the event of any reverse or when we were finally driven back, which must happen, there might be difficulty about remounting the camels, our only means of escape from the horsemen who would possibly gallop us down. Moreover the

Tava had several fords, any one of which might be selected by the enemy. So it was arranged that we should make our first and last stand upon the Holy Mount.

On the fourteenth night from new moon our swift camel-scouts who were posted in relays between the Tava and the Mount reported that the Black Kendah were gathered in thousands upon the farther side of the river, where they were engaged in celebrating magical ceremonies. On the fifteenth night the scouts reported that they were crossing the river, about five thousand horsemen and fifteen thousand foot soldiers, and that at the head of them marched the huge god-elephant Jana, on which rode Simba the King and a lame priest (evidently my friend whose foot had been injured by the pistol), who acted as a mahout. This part of the story I confess I did not believe, since it seemed to me impossible that anyone could ride upon that mad rogue, Jana. Yet, as subsequent events showed, it was in fact true. I suppose that in certain hands the beast became tame. Or perhaps it was drugged.

Two nights later, for the Black Kendah advanced but slowly, spreading themselves over the country in order to collect such crops as had not been gathered through lack of time or because they were still unripe, we saw flames and smoke arising from the Town of the Child beneath us, which they had fired. Now we knew that the time of trial had come and until near midnight men, women and children worked feverishly finishing or trying to finish the fortifications and making every preparation in our power.

Our position was that we held a very strong post, that is, strong against an enemy unprovided with big guns or even firearms, which, as all other possible approaches had been blocked, was only assailable by direct frontal attack from the east. In the pass we had three main lines of defence, one arranged behind the other and separated by distances of a few hundred yards. Our last refuge was furnished by the walls of the temple itself, in the rear of which were camped the whole White Kendah tribe, save a few hundred who were employed in watching the herds of camels and stock in almost inaccessible positions on the northern slopes of the Mount.

There were perhaps five thousand people of both sexes and every age gathered in this camp, which was so well provided with food and water that it could have stood a siege of several months. If, however, our defences should be carried there was no possibility of escape, since we learned from our scouts that the Black Kendah, who by tradition and through spies were well acquainted with every feature of the country, had detached a party of several thousand men to watch the western road and the slopes of the mountain, in case we should try to break out by that route. The only one remaining, that which ran through the cave of the serpent, we had taken the precaution of blocking up with great stones, lest through it our flank should be turned.

In short, we were rats in a trap and where we were there we must either conquer or die—unless indeed we chose to surrender, which for most of us would mean a fate worse than death.

Allan Quatermain Misses

I had made my last round of the little corps that I facetiously named "The Sharpshooters," though to tell the truth at shooting they were anything but sharp, and seen that each man was in his place behind a wall with a reserve man squatted at the rear of every pair of them, waiting to take his rifle if either of these should fall. Also I had made sure that all of them had twenty rounds of ammunition in their skin pouches. More I would not serve out, fearing lest in excitement or in panic they might fire away to the last cartridge uselessly, as before now even disciplined white troops have been known to do. Therefore I had arranged that certain old men of standing who could be trusted should wait in a place of comparative safety behind the line, carrying all our reserve ammunition, which amounted, allowing for what had been expended in practice, to nearly sixty rounds per rifle. This they were instructed to deliver from their wallets to the firing line in small lots when they saw that it was necessary and not before.

It was, I admit, an arrangement apt to miscarry in the heat of desperate battle, but I could think of none better, since it was absolutely necessary that no shot should be wasted.

After a few words of exhortation and caution to the natives who acted as sergeants to the corps, I returned to a bough shelter that had been built for us behind a rock to get a few hours' sleep, if that were possible, before the fight began.

Here I found Ragnall, who had just come in from his inspection. This was of a much more extensive nature than my own, since it involved going round some furlongs of the rough walls and trenches that he had prepared with so much thought and care, and seeing that the various companies of the White Kendah were ready to play their part in the defence of them.

He was tired and rather excited, too much so to sleep at once. So we talked a little while, first about the prospects of the morrow's battle, as to which we were, to say the least of it, dubious, and afterwards of other things. I asked him if during his stay in this place, while I was below at the town or later, he had heard or seen anything of his wife.

"Nothing," he answered. "These priests never speak of her, and if they did Harût is the only one of them that I can really understand. Moreover, I have kept my word strictly and, even when I had occasion to see to the blocking of the western road, made a circuit on the mountain-top in order to avoid the neighbourhood of that house where I suppose she lives Oh! Quatermain, my friend, my case is a hard one, as you would think if the woman you loved with your whole heart were shut up within a few hundred yards of you and no communication with her possible after all this time of separation and agony. What makes it worse is, as I gathered from what Harût said the other day, that she is still out of her mind."

"That has some consolations," I replied, "since the mindless do not suffer. But if such is the case, how do you account for what you and poor Savage saw that night in the Town of the Child? It was not altogether a phantasy, for the dress you described was the same we saw her wearing at the Feast of the First-fruits."

"I don't know what to make of it, Quatermain, except that many strange things happen in the world which we mock at as insults to our limited intelligence because we cannot understand them." (Very soon I was to have another proof of this remark.) "But what are you driving at? You are keeping something back."

"Only this, Ragnall. If your wife were utterly mad I cannot conceive how it came about that she searched you out and spoke to you even in a vision—for the thing was not an individual dream since both you and Savage saw her. Nor did she actually visit you in the flesh, as the door never opened and the spider's web across it was not broken. So it comes to this: either some part of her is not mad but can still exercise sufficient will to project itself upon your senses, or she is dead and her disembodied spirit did this thing. Now we know that she is not dead, for we have seen her and Harût has confessed as much. Therefore I maintain that, whatever may be her temporary state, she must still be fundamentally of a reasonable mind, as she is of a natural body. For instance, she may only be hypnotized, in which case the spell will break one day."

"Thank you for that thought, old fellow. It never occurred to me and it gives me new hope. Now listen! If I should come to grief in this business, which is very likely, and you should survive, you will do your best to get her home; will you not? Here is a codicil to my will which I drew up after that night of dream, duly witnessed by Savage and Hans. It leaves to you whatever sums may be necessary in this connexion and something over for yourself. Take it, it is best in your keeping, especially as if you should be killed it has no value."

"Of course I will do my best," I answered as I put away the paper in my pocket. "And now don't let us take any more thought of being killed, which may prevent us from getting the sleep we want. I don't mean to be killed if I can help it. I mean to give those beggars, the Black Kendah, such a doing as they never had before, and then start for the coast with you and Lady Ragnall, as, God willing, we shall do. Good night."

After this I slept like a top for some hours, as I believe Ragnall did also. When I awoke, which happened suddenly and completely, the first thing that I saw was Hans seated at the entrance to my little shelter smoking his corn-cob pipe, and nursing the single-barrelled rifle, Intombi, on his knee. I asked him what the time was, to which he replied that it lacked two hours to dawn. Then I asked him why he had not been sleeping. He replied that he had been asleep and dreamed a dream. Idly enough I inquired what dream, to which he replied:

"Rather a strange one, Baas, for a man who is about to go into battle. I dreamed that I was in a large place that was full of quiet. It was light there, but I could not see any sun or moon, and the air was very soft and tasted like food and drink, so much so, Baas, that if anyone had offered me a cup quite full of the best 'Cape smoke' I should have told him to take it away. Then, Baas, suddenly I saw your reverend father, the Predikant, standing beside me and looking just as he used to look, only younger and stronger and very happy, and so of course knew at once that I was dead and in hell. Only I wondered where the fire that does not go out might be, for I could not see it. Presently your reverend father said to me: 'Good day, Hans. So you have come here at last. Now tell me, how has it gone with my son, the Baas Allan? Have you looked after him as I told you to do?'

"I answered: 'I have looked after him as well as I could, O reverend sir. Little enough have I done; still, not once or twice or three times only have I offered up my life for him as was my duty, and yet we both have lived.' And that I might be sure he heard the best of me, as was but natural, I told him the times, Baas, making a big story out of small things, although all the while I could see that he knew exactly just where I began to lie and just where I stopped from lying. Still he did not scold me, Baas; indeed, when I had finished, he said:

"'Well done, O good and faithful servant,' words that I think I have heard him use before when he was alive, Baas, and used to preach to us for such a long time on Sunday afternoons. Then he asked: 'And how goes it with Baas Allan, my son, now, Hans?' to which I replied:

"'The Baas Allan is going to fight a very great battle in which he may well fall, and if I could feel sorry here, which I can't, I should weep, O reverend sir, because I have died before that battle began and therefore cannot stand at his side in the battle and be killed for him as a servant should for his master!'

"'You will stand at his side in the battle,' said your [missing line in printed version—JB] do as it is fitting that you should. And afterwards, Hans, you will make report to me of how the battle went and of what honour my son has won therein. Moreover, know this, Hans, that though while you live in the world you seem to see many other things, they are but dreams, since in all the world there is but one real thing, and its name is Love, which if it be but strong enough, the stars themselves must obey, for it is the king of every one of them, and all who dwell in them worship it day and night under many names for ever and for ever, Amen.'

"What he meant by that I am sure I don't know, Baas, seeing that I have never thought much of women, at least not for many years since my last old vrouw went and drank herself to death after lying in her sleep on the baby which I loved much better than I did her, Baas.

"Well, before I could ask him, or about hell either, he was gone like a whiff of smoke from a rifle mouth in a strong wind."

Hans paused, puffed at his pipe, spat upon the ground in his usual reflective way and asked:

"Is the Baas tired of the dream or would he like to hear the rest?"

"I should like to hear the rest," I said in a low voice, for I was strangely moved.

"Well, Baas, while I was standing in that place which was so full of quiet, turning my hat in my hands and wondering what work they would set me to there among the devils, I looked up. There I saw coming towards me two very beautiful women, Baas, who had their arms round each other's necks. They were dressed in white, with the little hard things that are found in shells hanging about them, and bright stones in their hair. And as they came, Baas, wherever they set a foot flowers sprang up, very pretty flowers, so that all their path across the quiet place was marked with flowers. Birds too sang as they passed, at least I think they were birds though I could not see them."

"What were they like, Hans?" I whispered.

"One of them, Baas, the taller I did not know. But the other I knew well enough; it was she whose name is holy, not to be mentioned. Yet I must mention that name; it was the Missie Marie herself as last we saw her alive many, many years ago, only grown a hundred times more beautiful."

Now I groaned, and Hans went on:

"The two White Ones came up to me, and stood looking at me with eyes that were more soft than those of bucks. Then the Missie Marie said to the other: 'This is Hans of whom I have so often told you, O Star.'"

Here I groaned again, for how did this Hottentot know that name, or rather its sweet rendering?

"Then she who was called Star asked, 'How goes it with one who is the heart of all three of us, O Hans?' Yes, Baas, those Shining Ones joined *me*, the dirty little Hottentot in my old clothes and smelling of tobacco, with themselves when they spoke of you, for I knew they were speaking of you, Baas, which made me think I must be drunk, even there in the quiet place. So I told them all that I had told your reverend father, and a very great deal more, for they seemed never to be tired of listening. And once, when I mentioned that sometimes, while pretending to be asleep, I had heard you praying aloud at night for the Missie Marie who died for you, and for another who had been your wife whose name I did not remember but who had also died, they both cried a little, Baas. Their tears shone like crystals and smelt like that stuff in a little glass tube which Harût said that he brought from some far land when he put a drop or two on your handkerchief, after you were faint from the pain in your leg at the house yonder. Or perhaps it was the flowers that smelt, for where the tears fell there sprang up white lilies shaped like two babes' hands held together in prayer."

Hearing this, I hid my face in my hands lest Hans should see human tears unscented with attar of roses, and bade him continue.

"Baas, the White One who was called Star, asked me of your son, the young Baas Harry, and I told her that when last I had seen him he was strong and well and would make a bigger man than you were, whereat she sighed and shook her head. Then the Missie Marie said: 'Tell the Baas, Hans, that I also have a child which he will see one day, but it is not a son.'

"After this they, too, said something about Love, but what it was I cannot remember, since even as I repeat this dream to you it is beginning to slip away from me fast as a swallow skimming the water. Their last words, however, I do remember. They were: 'Say to the Baas that we who never met in life, but who here are as twin sisters, wait and count the years and count the months and count the days and count the hours and count the minutes and count the seconds until once more he shall hear our voices calling to him across the night.' That's what they say, Baas. Then they were gone and only the flowers remained to show that they had been standing there.

"Now I set off to bring you the message and travelled a very long way at a great rate; if Jana himself had been after me I could not have gone more fast. At last I got out of that quiet place and among mountains where there were dark kloofs, and there in the kloofs I heard Zulu impis singing their war-song; yes, they sang the *ingoma* or something very like it. Now suddenly in the pass of the mountains along which I sped, there appeared before me a very beautiful woman whose skin shone like the best copper coffee kettle after I have polished it, Baas. She was dressed in a leopard-like moocha and wore on her shoulders a fur kaross, and about her neck a circlet of blue beads, and from her hair there rose one crane's feather tall as a walking-stick, and in her hand she held a little spear. No flowers sprang beneath her feet when she walked towards me and no birds sang, only the air was filled with the sound of a royal salute which rolled among the mountains like the roar of thunder, and her eyes flashed like summer lightning."

Now I let my hands fall and stared at him, for well I knew what was coming.

"'Stand, yellow man!' she said, 'and give me the royal salute.'

"So I gave her the *Bayéte*, though who she might be I did not know, since I did not think it wise to stay to ask her if it were hers of right, although I should have liked to do so. Then she said: 'The Old Man on the plain yonder and those two pale White Ones have talked to you of their love for your master, the Lord Macumazana. I tell you, little Yellow Dog, that they do not know what love can be. There is more love for him in my eyes alone than they have in all that makes them fair. Say it to the Lord Macumazana that, as I know well, he goes down to battle and that the Lady Mameena will be with him in the battle as, though he saw her not, she has been with him in other battles, and will be with him till the River of Time has run over the edge of the world and is lost beyond the sun. Let him remember this when Jana rushes on and death is very near to him to-day, and let him look—for then perchance he shall see me. Begone now, Yellow Dog, to the heels of your master, and play your part well in the battle, for of what you do or leave undone you shall give account to me. Say that Mameena sends her greetings to the Lord Macumazana and that she adds this, that when the Old Man and the White ones told you that Love is the secret blood of the worlds which makes them to be they did not lie. Love reigns and I, Mameena, am its priestess, and the heart of Macumazana is my holy house.'

"Then, Baas, I tumbled off a precipice and woke up here; and, Baas, as we may not light a fire I have kept some coffee hot for you buried in warm ashes," and without another word he went to fetch that coffee, leaving me shaken and amazed.

For what kind of a dream was it which revealed to an old Hottentot all these mysteries and hidden things about persons whom he had never seen and of whom I had never spoken to him? My father and my wife Marie might be explained, for with these he had been mixed up, but how about Stella and above all Mameena, although of course it was possible that he had heard of the latter, who made some stir in her time? But to hit her off as he had done in all her pride, splendour, and dominion of desire!

Well, that was his story which, perhaps fortunately, I lacked time to analyse or brood upon, since there was much in it calculated to unnerve a man just entering the crisis of a desperate fray. Indeed a minute or so later, as I was swallowing the last of the coffee, messengers arrived about some business, I forget what, sent by Ragnall I think, who had risen before I woke. I turned to give the pannikin to Hans, but he had vanished in his snake-like fashion, so I threw it down upon the ground and devoted my mind to the question raised in Ragnall's message.

Next minute scouts came in who had been watching the camp of the Black Kendah all night.

These were sleeping not more than half a mile away, in an open place on the slope of the hill with pickets thrown out round them, intending to advance upon us, it was said, as soon as the sun rose, since because of their number they feared lest to march at night should throw them into confusion and, in case of their falling into an ambush, bring about a disaster. Such at least was the story of two spies whom our people had captured.

There had been some question as to whether we should not attempt a night attack upon their camp, of which I was rather in favour. After full debate, however, the idea had been abandoned, owing to the fewness of our numbers, the dislike which the White Kendah shared with the Black of attempting to operate in the dark, and the well chosen position of our enemy, whom it would be impossible to rush before we were discovered by their outposts. What I hoped in my heart was that they might try to rush us, notwithstanding the story of the two captured spies, and in the gloom, after the moon had sunk low and before the dawn came, become entangled in our pitfalls and outlying entrenchments, where we should be able to destroy a great number of them. Only on the previous afternoon that cunning old fellow, Hans, had pointed out to me how advantageous such an event would be to our cause and, while agreeing with him, I suggested that probably the Black Kendah knew this as well as we did, as the prisoners had told us.

Yet that very thing happened, and through Hans himself. Thus: Old Harût had come to me just one hour before the dawn to inform me that all our people were awake and at their stations, and to make some last arrangements as to the course of the defence, also about our final concentration behind the last line of walls and in the first court of the temple, if we should be driven from the outer entrenchments. He was telling me that the Oracle of the Child had uttered words at the ceremony that night which he and all the priests considered were of the most favourable import, news to which I listened with some impatience, feeling as I did that this business had passed out of the range of the Child and its Oracle. As he spoke, suddenly through the silence that precedes the dawn, there floated to our ears the unmistakable sound of a rifle. Yes, a rifle shot, half a mile or so away, followed by the roaring murmur of a great camp unexpectedly alarmed at night.

"Who can have fired that?" I asked. "The Black Kendah have no guns."

He replied that he did not know, unless some of my fifty men had left their posts.

While we were investigating the matter, scouts rushed in with the intelligence that the Black Kendah, thinking apparently that they were being attacked, had broken camp and were advancing towards us. We passed a warning all down the lines and stood to arms. Five minutes later, as I stood listening to that approaching roar, filled with every kind of fear and melancholy foreboding such as the hour and the occasion might well have evoked, through the gloom, which was dense, the moon being hidden behind the hill, I thought I caught sight of something running towards me like a crouching man. I lifted my rifle to fire but, reflecting that it might be no more than a hyena and fearing to provoke a fusilade from my half-trained company, did not do so.

Next instant I was glad indeed, for immediately on the other side of the wall behind which I was standing I heard a well-known voice gasp out:

"Don't shoot, Baas, it is I."

"What have you been doing, Hans?" I said as he scrambled over the wall to my side, limping a little as I fancied.

"Baas," he puffed, "I have been paying the Black Kendah a visit. I crept down between their stupid outposts, who are as blind in the dark as a bat in daytime, hoping to find Jana and put a bullet into his leg or trunk. I didn't find him, Baas, although I heard him. But one of their captains stood up in front of a watchfire, giving a good shot. My bullet found *him*, Baas, for he tumbled back into the fire making the sparks fly this way and that. Then I ran and, as you see, got here quite safely."

"Why did you play that fool's trick?" I asked, "seeing that it ought to have cost you your life?"

"I shall die just when I have to die, not before, Baas," he replied in the intervals of reloading the little rifle. "Also it was the trick of a wise man, not of a fool, seeing that it has made the Black Kendah think that we were attacking them and caused them to hurry on to attack *us* in the dark over ground that they do not know. Listen to them coming!"

As he spoke a roar of sound told us that the great charge had swept round a turn there was in the pass and was heading towards us up the straight. Ivory horns brayed, captains shouted orders, the very mountains shook beneath the beating of thousands of feet of men and horses, while in one great yell that echoed from the cliffs and forests went up the battle-cry of "*Jana! Jana!*"—a mixed tumult of noise which contrasted very strangely with the utter silence in our ranks.

"They will be among the pitfalls presently," sniggered Hans, shifting his weight nervously from one leg on to the other. "Hark! they are going into them."

It was true. Screams of fear and pain told me that the front ranks had begun to fall, horse and foot together, into the cunningly devised snares of which with so much labour we had dug many, concealing them with earth spread over thin wickerwork, or rather interlaced boughs. Into them went the forerunners, to be pierced by the sharp, fire- hardened stakes set at the bottom of each pit. Vainly did those who were near enough to understand their danger call to the ranks behind to stop. They could not or would not comprehend, and had no room to extend their front. Forward surged the human torrent, thrusting all in front of it to death by wounds or suffocation in those deadly holes, till one by one they were filled level with the ground by struggling men and horses, over whom the army still rushed on.

How many perished there I do not know, but after the battle was over we found scarcely a pit that was not crowded to the brim with dead. Truly this device of Ragnall's, for if I had conceived the idea, which was unfamiliar to the Kendah, it was he who had carried it out in so masterly a fashion, had served us well.

Still the enemy surged on, since the pits were only large enough to hold a tithe of them, till at length, horsemen and footmen mixed up together in inextricable confusion, their mighty mass became faintly visible quite close to us, a blacker blot upon the gloom.

Then my turn came. When they were not more than fifty yards away from the first wall, I shouted an order to my riflemen to fire, aiming low, and set the example by loosing both barrels of an elephant gun at the thickest of the mob. At that distance even the most inexperienced shots could not miss such a mark, especially as those bullets that went high struck among the oncoming troops behind, or caught the horsemen lifted above their fellows. Indeed, of the first few rounds I do not think that one was wasted, while often single balls killed or injured several men.

The result was instantaneous. The Black Kendah who, be it remembered, were totally unaccustomed to the effects of rifle fire and imagined that we only possessed two or three guns in all, stopped their advance as though paralyzed. For a few seconds there was silence, except for the intermittent crackle of the rifles as my men loaded and fired. Next came the cries of the smitten men and horses that were falling everywhere, and then—the unmistakable sound of a stampede.

"They have gone. That was too warm for them, Baas," chuckled Hans exultingly.

"Yes," I answered, when I had at length succeeded in stopping the firing, "but I expect they will come back with the light. Still, that trick of yours has cost them dear, Hans."

By degrees the dawn began to break. It was, I remember, a particularly beautiful dawn, resembling a gigantic and vivid rose opening in the east, or a cup of brightness from which many coloured wines were poured all athwart the firmament. Very peaceful also, for not a breath of wind was stirring. But what a scene the first rays of the sun revealed upon that narrow stretch of pass in front of us. Everywhere the pitfalls and trenches were filled with still surging heaps of men and horses, while all about lay dead and wounded men, the red harvest of our rifle fire. It was dreadful to contrast the heavenly peace above and the hellish horror beneath.

We took count and found that up to this moment we had not lost a single man, one only having been slightly wounded by a thrown spear. As is common among semi-savages, this fact filled the White Kendah with an undue exultation. Thinking that as the beginning was so the end must be, they cheered and shouted, shaking each other's hands, then fell to eating the food which the women brought them with appetite, chattering incessantly, although as a general rule they were a very silent people. Even the grave Harût, who arrived full of congratulations, seemed as high-spirited as a boy, till I reminded him that the real battle had not yet commenced.

The Black Kendah had fallen into a trap and lost some of their number, that was all, which was fortunate for us but could scarcely affect the issue of the struggle, since they had many thousands left. Ragnall, who had come up from his lines, agreed with me. As he said, these people were fighting for life as well as honour, seeing that most of the corn which they needed for their sustenance was stored in great heaps either in or to the rear of the temple behind us. Therefore they must come on until they won or were destroyed. How with our small force could we hope to destroy this multitude? That was the problem which weighed upon our hearts.

About a quarter of an hour later two spies that we had set upon the top of the precipitous cliffs, whence they had a good view of the pass beyond the bend, came scrambling down the rocks like monkeys by a route that was known to them. These boys, for they were no more, reported that the Black Kendah were reforming their army beyond the bend of the pass, and that the cavalry were dismounting and sending their horses to the rear, evidently because they found them useless in such a place. A little later solitary men appeared from behind the bend, carrying bundles of long sticks to each of which was attached a piece of white cloth, a proceeding that excited my curiosity.

Soon its object became apparent. Swiftly these men, of whom in the end there may have been thirty or forty, ran to and fro, testing the ground with spears in search for pitfalls. I think they only found a very few that had not been broken into, but in front of these and also of those that were already full of men and horses they set up the flags as a warning that they should be avoided in the advance. Also they removed a number of their wounded.

We had great difficulty in restraining the White Kendah from rushing out to attack them, which of course would only have led us into a trap in our turn, since they would have fled and conducted their pursuers into the arms of the enemy. Nor would I allow my riflemen to fire, as the result must have been many misses and a great waste of ammunition which ere long would be badly wanted. I, however, did shoot two or three, then gave it up as the remainder took no notice whatever.

When they had thoroughly explored the ground they retired until, a little later, the Black Kendah army began to appear, marching in serried regiments and excellent order round the bend, till perhaps eight or ten thousand of them were visible, a very fierce and awe- inspiring *impi*. Their front ranks halted between three and four hundred yards away, which I thought farther off than it was advisable to open fire on them with Snider rifles held by unskilled troops. Then came a pause, which at length was broken by the blowing of horns and a sound of exultant shouting beyond the turn of the pass.

Now from round this turn appeared the strangest sight that I think my eyes had ever seen. Yes, there came the huge elephant, Jana, at a slow, shambling trot. On his back and head were two men in whom, with my glasses, I recognized the lame priest whom I already knew too well and Simba, the king of the Black Kendah, himself, gorgeously apparelled and waving a long spear, seated in a kind of wooden chair. Round the brute's neck were a number of bright metal chains, twelve in all, and each of these chains was held by a spearman who ran alongside, six on one side and six on the other. Lastly, ingeniously fastened to the end of his trunk were three other chains to which were attached spiked knobs of metal.

On he came as docilely as any Indian elephant used for carrying teak logs, passing through the centre of the host up a wide lane which had been left, I suppose for his convenience, and intelligently avoiding the pitfalls filled with dead. I thought that he would stop among the first ranks. But not so. Slackening his pace to a walk he marched forwards towards our fortifications. Now, of course, I saw my chance and made sure that my double-barrelled elephant rifle was ready and that Hans held a second rifle, also double-barrelled and of similar calibre, full-cocked in such a position that I could snatch it from him in a moment.

"I am going to kill that elephant," I said. "Let no one else fire. Stand still and you shall see the god Jana die."

Still the enormous beast floundered forward; up to that moment I had never realized how truly huge it was, not even when it stood over me in the moonlight about to crush me with its foot. Of this I am sure, that none to equal it ever lived in Africa, at least in any times of which I have knowledge.

"Fire, Baas," whispered Hans, "it is near enough."

But like the Frenchman and the cock pheasant, I determined to wait until it stopped, wishing to finish it with a single ball, if only for the prestige of the thing.

At length it did stop and, opening its cavern of a mouth, lifted its great trunk and trumpeted, while Simba, standing up in his chair, began to shout out some command to us to surrender to the god Jana, "the Invincible, the Invulnerable."

"I will show you if you are invulnerable, my boy," said I to myself, glancing round to make sure that Hans had the second rifle ready and catching sight of Ragnall and Harût and all the White Kendah standing up in their trenches, breathlessly awaiting the end, as were the Black Kendah a few hundred yards away. Never could there have been a fairer shot and one more certain to result in a fatal wound. The brute's head was up and its mouth was open. All I had to do was to send a hard- tipped bullet crashing through the palate to the brain behind. It was so easy that I would have made a bet that I could have finished him with one hand tied behind me.

I lifted the heavy rifle. I got the sights dead on to a certain spot at the back of that red cave. I pressed the trigger; the charge boomed —and nothing happened! I heard no bullet strike and Jana did not even take the trouble to close his mouth.

An exclamation of "O-oh!" went up from the watchers. Before it had died away the second bullet followed the first, with the same result or rather lack of result, and another louder "O-oh!" arose. Then Jana tranquilly shut his mouth, having finished trumpeting, and as though to give me a still better target, turned broadside on and stood quite still.

With an inward curse I snatched the second rifle and aiming behind the ear at a spot which long experience told me covered the heart let drive again, first one barrel and then the other.

Jana never stirred. No bullet thudded. No mark of blood appeared upon his hide. The horrible thought overcame me that I, Allan Quatermain, I the famous shot, the renowned elephant-hunter, had four times missed this haystack of a brute from a distance of forty yards. So great was my shame that I think I almost fainted. Through a kind of mist I heard various ejaculations:

"Great Heavens!" said Ragnall.

"*Allemagte!*" remarked Hans.

"The Child help us!" muttered Harût.

All the rest of them stared at me as though I were a freak or a lunatic. Then somebody laughed nervously, and immediately everybody began to laugh. Even the distant army of the Black Kendah became convulsed with roars of unholy merriment and I, Allan Quatermain, was the centre of all this mockery, till I felt as though I were going mad. Suddenly the laughter ceased and once more Simba the King began to roar out something about "Jana the Invincible and Invulnerable," to which the White Kendah replied with cries of "Magic" and "Bewitched! Bewitched!"

"Yes," yelled Simba, "no bullet can touch Jana the god, not even those of the white lord who was brought from far to kill him."

Hans leaped on to the top of the wall, where he danced up and down like an intoxicated monkey, and screamed:

"Then where is Jana's left eye? Did not my bullet put it out like a lamp? If Jana is invulnerable, why did my bullet put out his left eye?"

Hans ceased from dancing on the wall and steadying himself, lifted the little rifle Intombi, shouting:

"Let us see whether after all this beast is a god or an elephant."

Then he touched the trigger, and simultaneously with the report, I heard the bullet clap and saw blood appear on Jana's hide just by the very spot over the heart at which I had aimed without result. Of course, the soft ball driven from a small-bore rifle with a light charge of powder was far too weak to penetrate to the vitals. Probably it did not do much more than pierce through the skin and an inch or two of flesh behind it.

Still, its effects upon this "invulnerable" god were of a marked order. He whipped round; he lifted his trunk and screamed with rage and pain. Then off he lumbered back towards his own people, at such a pace that the attendants who held the chains on either side of him were thrown over and forced to leave go of him, while the king and the priest upon his back could only retain their seats by clinging to the chair and the rope about his neck.

The result was satisfactory so far as the dispelling of magical illusions went, but it left me in a worse position than before, since it now became evident that what had protected Jana from my bullets was nothing more supernatural than my own lack of skill. Oh! never in my life did I drink of such a cup of humiliation as it was my lot to drain to the dregs in this most unhappy hour. Almost did I hope that I might be killed at once.

And yet, and yet, how was it possible that with all my skill I should have missed this towering mountain of flesh four times in succession. The question is one to which I have never discovered any answer, especially as Hans hit it easily enough, which at the time I wished heartily he had not done, since his success only served to emphasize my miserable failure. Fortunately, just then a diversion occurred which freed my unhappy self from further public attention. With a shout and a roar the great army of the Black Kendah woke into life.

The advance had begun.

Allan Weeps

On they came, slowly and steadily, preceded by a cloud of skirmishers —a thousand or more of these—who kept as open an order as the narrow ground would allow and carried, each of them, a bundle of throwing spears arranged in loops or sockets at the back of the shield. When these men were about a hundred yards away we opened fire and killed a great number of them, also some of the marshalled troops behind. But this did not stop them in the least, for what could fifty rifles do against a horde of brave barbarians who, it seemed, had no fear of death? Presently their spears were falling among us and a few casualties began to occur, not many, because of the protecting wall, but still some. Again and again we loaded and fired, sweeping away those in front of us, but always others came to take their places. Finally at some word of command these light skirmishers vanished, except whose who were dead or wounded, taking shelter behind the advancing regiments which now were within fifty yards of us.

Then, after a momentary pause another command was shouted out and the first regiment charged in three solid ranks. We fired a volley point blank into them and, as it was hopeless for fifty men to withstand such an onslaught, bolted during the temporary confusion that ensued, taking refuge, as it had been arranged that we should do, at a point of vantage farther down the line of fortifications, whence we maintained our galling fire.

Now it was that the main body of the White Kendah came into action under the leadership of Ragnall and Harût. The enemy scrambled over the first wall, which we had just vacated, to find themselves in a network of other walls held by our spearmen in a narrow place where numbers gave no great advantage.

Here the fighting was terrible and the loss of the attackers great, for always as they carried one entrenchment they found another a few yards in front of them, out of which the defenders could only be driven at much cost of life.

Two hours or more the battle went on thus. In spite of the desperate resistance which we offered, the multitude of the Black Kendah, who I must say fought magnificently, stormed wall after wall, leaving hundreds of dead and wounded to mark their difficult progress. Meanwhile I and my riflemen rained bullets on them from certain positions which we had selected beforehand, until at length our ammunition began to run low.

At half-past eight in the morning we were driven back over the open ground to our last entrenchment, a very strong one just outside of the eastern gate of the temple which, it will be remembered, was set in a tunnel pierced through the natural lava rock. Thrice did the Black Kendah come on and thrice we beat them off, till the ditch in front of the wall was almost full of fallen. As fast as they climbed to the top of it the White Kendah thrust them through with their long spears, or we shot them with our rifles, the nature of the ground being such that only a direct frontal attack was possible.

In the end they drew back sullenly, having, as we hoped, given up the assault. As it turned out, this was not so. They were only resting and waiting for the arrival of their reserve. It came up shouting and singing a war-song, two thousand strong or more, and presently once more they charged like a flood of water. We beat them back. They reformed and charged a second time and we beat them back.

Then they took another counsel. Standing among the dead and dying at the base of the wall, which was built of loose stones and earth, where we could not easily get at them because of the showers of spears which were rained at anyone who showed himself, they began to undermine it, levering out the bottom stones with stakes and battering them with poles.

In five minutes a breach appeared, through which they poured tumultuously. It was hopeless to withstand that onslaught of so vast a number. Fighting desperately, we were driven down the tunnel and through the doors that were opened to us, into the first court of the temple. By furious efforts we managed to close these doors and block them with stones and earth. But this did not avail us long, for, bringing brushwood and dry grass, they built a fire against them that soon caught the thick cedar wood of which they were made.

While they burned we consulted together. Further retreat seemed impossible, since the second court of the temple, save for a narrow passage, was filled with corn which allowed no room for fighting, while behind it were gathered all the women and children, more than two thousand of them. Here, or nowhere, we must make our stand and conquer or die. Up to this time, compared with what which we had inflicted upon the Black Kendah, of whom a couple of thousand or more had fallen, our loss was comparatively slight, say two hundred killed and as many more wounded. Most of such of the latter as could not walk we had managed to carry into the first court of the temple, laying them close against the cloister walls, whence they watched us in a grisly ring.

This left us about sixteen hundred able-bodied men or many more than we could employ with effect in that narrow place. Therefore we determined to act upon a plan which we had already designed in case such an emergency as ours should arise. About three hundred and fifty of the best men were to remain to defend the temple till all were slain. The rest, to the number of over a thousand, were to withdraw through the second court and the gates beyond to the camp of the women and children. These they were to conduct by secret paths that were known to them to where the camels were kraaled, and mounting as many as possible of them on the camels to fly whither they could. Our hope was that the victorious Black Kendah would be too exhausted to follow them across the plain to the distant mountains. It was a dreadful determination, but we had no choice.

"What of my wife?" Ragnall asked hoarsely.

"While the temple stands she must remain in the temple," replied Harût. "But when all is lost, if I have fallen, do you, White Lord, go to the sanctuary with those who remain and take her and the Ivory Child and flee after the others. Only I lay this charge on you under pain of the curse of Heaven, that you do not suffer the Ivory Child to fall into the hands of the Black Kendah. First must you burn it with fire or grind it to dust with stones. Moreover, I give this command to all in case of the priests in charge of it should fail me, that they set flame to the brushwood that is built up with the stacks of corn, so that, after all, those of our enemies who escape may die of famine."

Instantly and without murmuring, for never did I see more perfect discipline than that which prevailed among these poor people, the orders given by Harût, who in addition to his office as head priest was a kind of president of what was in fact a republic, were put in the way of execution. Company by company the men appointed to escort the women and children departed through the gateway of the second court, each company turning in the gateway to salute us who remained, by raising their spears, till all were gone. Then we, the three hundred and fifty who were left, marshalled ourselves as the Greeks may have done in the Pass of Thermopylæ.

First stood I and my riflemen, to whom all the remaining ammunition was served out; it amounted to eight rounds per man. Then, ranged across the court in four lines, came the spearmen armed with lances and swords under the immediate command of Harût. Behind these, near the gate of the second court so that at the last they might attempt the rescue of the priestess, were fifty picked men, captained by Ragnall, who, I forgot to say, was wounded in two places, though not badly, having received a spear thrust in the left shoulder and a sword cut to the left thigh during his desperate defence of the entrenchment.

By the time that all was ready and every man had been given to drink from the great jars of water which stood along the walls, the massive wooden doors began to burn through, though this did not happen for quite half an hour after the enemy had begun to attempt to fire them. They fell at length beneath the battering of poles, leaving only the mound of earth and stones which we had piled up in the gateway after the closing of the doors. This the Black Kendah, who had raked out the burning embers, set themselves to dig away with hands and sticks and spears, a task that was made very difficult to them by about a score of our people who stabbed at them with their long lances or dashed them down with stones, killing and disabling many. But always the dead and wounded were dragged off while others took their places, so that at last the gateway was practically cleared. Then I called back the spearmen who passed into the ranks behind us, and made ready to play my part.

I had not long to wait. With a rush and a roar a great company of the Black Kendah charged the gateway. Just as they began to emerge into the court I gave the word to fire, sending fifty Snider bullets tearing into them from a distance of a few yards. They fell in a heap; they fell like corn before the scythe, not a man won through. Quickly we reloaded and waited for the next rush. In due course it came and the dreadful scene repeated itself. Now the gateway and the tunnel beyond were so choked with fallen men that the enemy must drag these out before they could charge any more. It was done under the fire of myself, Hans and a few picked shots—somehow it was done.

Once more they charged, and once more were mown down. So it went on till our last cartridge was spent, for never did I see more magnificent courage than was shown by those Black Kendah in the face of terrific loss. Then my people threw aside their useless rifles and arming themselves with spears and swords fell back to rest, leaving Harût and his company to take their place. For half an hour or more raged that awful struggle, since the spot being so narrow, charge as they would, the Black Kendah could not win through the spears of despairing warriors defending their lives and the sanctuary of their god. Nor, the encircling cliffs being so sheer, could they get round any other way.

At length the enemy drew back as though defeated, giving us time to drag aside our dead and wounded and drink more water, for the heat in the place was now overwhelming. We hoped against hope that they had given up the attack. But this was far from the case; they were but making a new plan.

Suddenly in the gateway there appeared the huge bulk of the elephant Jana, rushing forward at speed and being urged on by men who pricked it with spears behind. It swept through the defenders as though they were but dry grass, battering those in front of it with its great trunk from which swung the iron balls that crushed all on whom they fell, and paying no more heed to the lance thrusts than it might have done to the bites of gnats. On it came, trumpeting and trampling, and after it in a flood flowed the Black Kendah, upon whom our spearmen flung themselves from either side.

At the time I, followed by Hans, was just returning from speaking with Ragnall at the gate of the second court. A little before I had retired exhausted from the fierce and fearful fighting, whereon he took my place and repelled several of the Black Kendah charges, including the last. In this fray he received a further injury, a knock on the head from a stick or stone which stunned him for a few minutes, whereon some of our people had carried him off and set him on the ground with his back against one of the pillars of the second gate. Being told that he was hurt I ran to see what was the matter. Finding to my joy that it was nothing very serious, I was hurrying to the front again when I looked up and saw that devil Jana charging straight towards me, the throng of armed men parting on each side of him, as rough water does before the leaping prow of a storm-driven ship.

To tell the truth, although I was never fond of unnecessary risks, I rejoiced at the sight. Not even all the excitement of that hideous and prolonged battle had obliterated from my mind the burning sense of shame at the exhibition which I had made of myself by missing this beast with four barrels at forty yards.

Now, thought I to myself with a kind of exultant thrill, now, Jana, I will wipe out both my disgrace and you. This time there shall be no mistake, or if there is, let it be my last.

On thundered Jana, whirling the iron balls among the soldiers, who fled to right and left leaving a clear path between me and him. To make quite sure of things, for I was trembling a little with fatigue and somewhat sick from the continuous sight of bloodshed, I knelt down upon my right knee, using the other as a prop for my left elbow, and since I could not make certain of a head shot because of the continual whirling of the huge trunk, got the sight of my big-game rifle dead on to the beast where the throat joins the chest. I hoped that the heavy conical bullet would either pierce through to the spine or cut one of the large arteries in the neck, or at least that the tremendous shock of its impact would bring him down.

At about twenty paces I fired and hit—not Jana but the lame priest who was fulfilling the office of mahout, perched upon his shoulders many feet above the point at which I had aimed. Yes! I hit him in the head, which was shattered like an eggshell, so that he fell lifeless to the ground.

In perfect desperation again I aimed, and fired when Jana was not more than thirty feet away. This time the bullet must have gone wide to the left, for I saw a chip fly from the end of the animal's broken and deformed tusk, which stuck out in that direction several feet clear of its side.

Then I gave up all hope. There was no time to gain my feet and escape; indeed I did not wish to do so, who felt that there are some failures which can only be absolved by death. I just knelt there, waiting for the end.

In an instant the giant creature was almost over me. I remember looking up at it and thinking in a queer sort of a way—perhaps it was some ancestral memory—that I was a little ape-like child about to be slain by a primordial elephant, thrice as big as any that now inhabit the earth. Then something appeared to happen which I only repeat to show how at such moments absurd and impossible things seem real to us.

The reader may remember the strange dream which Hans had related to me that morning.

One incident of this phantasy was that he had met the spirit of the Zulu lady Mameena, whom I knew in bygone years, and that she bade him tell me she would be with me in the battle and that I was to look for her when death drew near to me and "Jana thundered on," for then perchance I should see her.

Well, no doubt in some lightning flash of thought the memory of these words occurred to me at this juncture, with the ridiculous result that my subjective intelligence, if that is the right term, actually created the scene which they described. As clearly, or perhaps more clearly than ever I saw anything else in my life, I appeared to behold the beautiful Mameena in her fur cloak and her blue beads, standing between Jana and myself with her arms folded upon her breast and looking exactly as she did in the tremendous moment of her death before King Panda. I even noted how the faint breeze stirred a loose end of her outspread hair and how the sunlight caught a particular point of a copper bangle on her upper arm.

So she stood, or rather seemed to stand, quite still; and as it happened, at that moment the giant Jana, either because something had frightened him, or perhaps owing to the shock of my bullet striking on his tusk having jarred the brain, suddenly pulled up, sliding along a little with all his four feet together, till I thought he was going to sit down like a performing elephant. Then it appeared to me as though

Mameena turned round very slowly, bent towards me, whispering something which I could not hear although her lips moved, looked at me sweetly with those wonderful eyes of hers and vanished away.

A fraction of a second later all this vision had gone and something that was no vision took its place. Jana had recovered himself and was at me again with open mouth and lifted trunk. I heard a Dutch curse and saw a little yellow form; saw Hans, for it was he, thrust the barrels of my second elephant rifle almost into that red cave of a mouth, which however they could not reach, and fire, first one barrel, then the other.

Another moment, and the mighty trunk had wrapped itself about Hans and hurled him through the air to fall on to his head and arms thirty or forty feet away.

Jana staggered as though he too were about to fall; recovered himself, swerved to the right, perhaps to follow Hans, stumbled on a few paces, missing me altogether, then again came to a standstill. I wriggled myself round and, seated on the pavement of the court, watched what followed, and glad am I that I was able to do so, for never shall I behold such another scene.

First I saw Ragnall run up with a rifle and fire two barrels at the brute's head, of which he took no notice whatsoever. Then I saw his wife, who in this land was known as the Guardian of the Child, issuing from the portals of the second court, dressed in her goddess robes, wearing the cap of bird's feathers, attended by the two priestesses also dressed as goddesses, as we had seen her on the morning of sacrifice, and holding in front of her the statue of the Ivory Child.

On she came quite quietly, her wide, empty eyes fixed upon Jana. As she advanced the monster seemed to grow uneasy. Turning his head, he lifted his trunk and thrust it along his back until it gripped the ankle of the King Simba, who all this while was seated there in his chair making no movement.

With a slow, steady pull he dragged Simba from the chair so that he fell upon the ground near his left foreleg. Next very composedly he wound his trunk about the body of the helpless man, whose horrified eyes I can see to this day, and began to whirl him round and round in the air, gently at first but with a motion that grew ever more rapid, until the bright chains on the victim's breast flashed in the sunlight like a silver wheel. Then he hurled him to the ground, where the poor king lay a mere shattered pulp that had been human.

Now the priestess was standing in front of the beast-god, apparently quite without fear, though her two attendants had fallen back. Ragnall sprang forward as though to drag her away, but a dozen men leapt on to him and held him fast, either to save his life or for some secret reason of their own which I never learned.

Jana looked down at her and she looked up at Jana. Then he screamed furiously and, shooting out his trunk, snatched the Ivory Child from her hands, whirled it round as he had whirled Simba, and at last dashed it to the stone pavement as he had dashed Simba, so that its substance, grown brittle on the passage of the ages, shattered into ten thousand fragments.

At this sight a great groan went up from the men of the White Kendah, the women dressed as goddesses shrieked and tore their robes, and Harût, who stood near, fell down in a fit or faint.

Once more Jana screamed. Then slowly he knelt down, beat his trunk and the clattering metal balls upon the ground thrice, as though he were making obeisance to the beautiful priestess who stood before him, shivered throughout his mighty bulk, and rolled over—dead!

The fighting ceased. The Black Kendah, who all this while had been pressing into the court of the temple, saw and stood stupefied. It was as though in the presence of events to them so pregnant and terrible men could no longer lift their swords in war.

A voice called: "The god is dead! The king is dead! Jana has slain Simba and has himself been slain! Shattered is the Child; spilt is the blood of Jana! Fly, People of the Black Kendah; fly, for the gods are dead and your land is a land of ghosts!"

From every side was this wail echoed: "Fly, People of the Black Kendah, for the gods are dead!"

They turned; they sped away like shadows, carrying their wounded with them, nor did any attempt to stay them. Thirty minutes later, save for some desperately hurt or dying men, not one of them was left in the temple or the pass beyond. They had all gone, leaving none but the dead behind them.

The fight was finished! The fight that had seemed lost was won!

I dragged myself from the ground. As I gained my tottering feet, for now that all was over I felt as if I were made of running water, I saw the men who held Ragnall loose their grip of him. He sprang to where his wife was and stood before her as though confused, much as Jana had stood, Jana against whose head he rested, his left hand holding to the brute's gigantic tusk, for I think that he also was weak with toil, terror, loss of blood and emotion.

"Luna," he gasped, "Luna!"

Leaning on the shoulder of a Kendah man, I drew nearer to see what passed between them, for my curiosity overcame my faintness. For quite a long while she stared at him, till suddenly her eyes began to change. It was as though a soul were arising in their emptiness as the moon arises in the quiet evening sky, giving them light and life. At length she spoke in a slow, hesitating voice, the tones of which I remembered well enough, saying:

"Oh! George, that dreadful brute," and she pointed to the dead elephant, "has killed our baby. Look at it! Look at it! We must be everything to each other now, dear, as we were before it came—unless God sends us another."

Then she burst into a flood of weeping and fell into his arms, after which I turned away. So, to their honour be it said, did the Kendah, leaving the pair alone behind the bulk of dead Jana.

Here I may state two things: first, that Lady Ragnall, whose bodily health had remained perfect throughout, entirely recovered her reason from that moment. It was as though on the shattering of the Ivory Child some spell had been lifted off her. What this spell may have been I am quite unable to explain, but I presume that in a dim and unknown way she connected this effigy with her own lost infant and that while she held and tended it her intellect remained in abeyance. If so, she must also have connected its destruction with the death of her own child which, strangely enough, it will be remembered, was likewise killed by an elephant. The first death that occurred in her presence took away her reason, the second seeming death, which also occurred in her presence, brought it back again!

Secondly, from the moment of the destruction of her boy in the streets of the English country town to that of the shattering of the Ivory Child in Central Africa her memory was an utter blank, with one exception. This exception was a dream which a few days later she narrated to Ragnall in my presence. That dream was that she had seen him and Savage sleeping together in a native house one night. In view of a certain incident recorded in this history I leave the reader to draw his own conclusions as to this curious incident. I have none to offer, or if I have I prefer to keep them to myself.

Leaving Ragnall and his wife, I staggered off to look for Hans and found him lying senseless near the north wall of the temple. Evidently he was beyond human help, for Jana seemed to have crushed most of his ribs in his iron trunk. We carried him to one of the priest's cells and there I watched him till the end, which came at sundown.

Before he died he became quite conscious and talked with me a good deal.

"Don't grieve about missing Jana, Baas," he said, "for it wasn't you who missed him but some devil that turned your bullets. You see, Baas, he was bewitched against you white men. When you look at him closely you will find that the Lord Igeza missed him also" (strange as it may seem, this proved to be the case), "and when you managed to hit the tip of his tusk with the last ball the magic was wearing off him, that's all. But, Baas, those Black Kendah wizards forgot to bewitch him against the little yellow man, of whom they took no account. So I hit him sure enough every time I fired at him, and I hope he liked the taste of my bullets in that great mouth of his. He knew who had sent them there very well. That's why he left you alone and made for me, as I had hoped he would. Oh! Baas, I die happy, quite happy since I have killed Jana and he caught me and not you, me who was nearly finished anyhow. For, Baas, though I didn't say anything about it, a thrown spear struck my groin when I went down among the Black Kendah this morning. It was only a small cut, which bled little, but as the fighting went on something gave way and my inside began to come through it, though I tied it up with a bit of cloth, which of course means death in a day or two." (Subsequent examination showed me that Hans's story of this wound was perfectly true. He could not have lived for very long.)

"Baas," he went on after a pause, "no doubt I shall meet that Zulu lady Mameena to-night. Tell me, is she really entitled to the royal salute? Because if not, when I am as much a spook as she is I will not give it to her again. She never gave me my titles, which are good ones in their way, so why should I give her the *Bayéte*, unless it is hers by right of blood, although I am only a little 'yellow dog' as she chose to call me?"

As this ridiculous point seemed to weigh upon his mind I told him that Mameena was not even of royal blood and in nowise entitled to the salute of kings.

"Ah!" he said with a feeble grin, "then now I shall know how to deal with her, especially as she cannot pretend that I did not play my part in the battle, as she bade me do. Did you see anything of her when Jana charged, Baas, because I thought I did?"

"I seemed to see something, but no doubt it was only a fancy."

"A fancy? Explain to me, Baas, where truths end and fancies begin and whether what we think are fancies are not sometimes the real truths. Once or twice I have thought so of late, Baas."

I could not answer this riddle, so instead I gave him some water which he asked for, and he continued:

"Baas, have you any messages for the two Shining ones, for her whose name is holy and her sister, and for the child of her whose name is holy, the Missie Marie, and for your reverend father, the Predikant? If so, tell it quickly before my head grows too empty to hold the words."

I will confess, however foolish it may seem, that I gave him certain messages, but what they were I shall not write down. Let them remain secret between me and him. Yes, between me and him and perhaps those to whom they were to be delivered. For after all, in his own words, who can know exactly where fancies end and truth begin, and whether at times fancies are not the veritable truths in this universal mystery of which the individual life of each of us is so small a part?

Hans repeated what I had spoken to him word for word, as a native does, repeated it twice over, after which he said he knew it by heart and remained silent for a long while. Then he asked me to lift him up in the doorway of the cell so that he might look at the sun setting for the last time, "for, Baas," he added, "I think I am going far beyond the sun."

He stared at it for a while, remarking that from the look of the sky there should be fine weather coming, "which will be good for your journey towards the Black Water, Baas, with all that ivory to carry."

I answered that perhaps I should never get the ivory from the graveyard of the elephants, as the Black Kendah might prevent this.

"No, no, Baas," he replied, "now that Jana is dead the Black Kendah will go away. I know it, I know it!"

Then he wandered for a space, speaking of sundry adventures we had shared together, till quite before the last indeed, when his mind returned to him.

"Baas," he said, "did not the captain Mavovo name me Light-in- Darkness, and is not that my name? When you too enter the Darkness, look for that Light; it will be shining very close to you."

He only spoke once more. His words were:

"Baas, I understand now what your reverend father, the Predikant, meant when he spoke to me about Love last night. It had nothing to do with women, Baas, at least not much. It was something a great deal bigger, Baas, something as big as what I feel for you!"

Then Hans died with a smile on his wrinkled face.

I wept!

Homewards

There is not much more to write of this expedition, or if that statement be not strictly true, not much more that I wish to write, though I have no doubt that Ragnall, if he had a mind that way, could make a good and valuable book concerning many matters on which, confining myself to the history of our adventure, I have scarcely touched. All the affinities between this Central African Worship of the Heavenly Child and its Guardian and that of Horus and Isis in Egypt from which it was undoubtedly descended, for instance. Also the part which the great serpent played therein, as it may be seen playing a part in every tomb upon the Nile, and indeed plays a part in our own and other religions. Further, our journey across the desert to the Red Sea was very interesting, but I am tired of describing journeys—and of making them.

The truth is that after the death of Hans, like to Queen Sheba when she had surveyed the wonders of Solomon's court, there was no more spirit in me. For quite a long while I did not seem to care at all what happened to me or to anybody else. We buried him in a place of honour, exactly where he shot Jana before the gateway of the second court, and when the earth was thrown over his little yellow face I felt as though half my past had departed with him into that hole. Poor drunken old Hans, where in the world shall I find such another man as you were? Where in the world shall I find so much love as filled the cup of that strange heart of yours?

I dare say it is a form of selfishness, but what every man desires is something that cares for him *alone*, which is just why we are so fond of dogs. Now Hans was a dog with a human brain and he cared for me alone. Often our vanity makes us think that this has happened to some of us in the instance of one or more women. But honest and quiet reflection may well cause us to doubt the truth of such supposings. The woman who as we believed adored us solely has probably in the course of her career adored others, or at any rate other things.

To take but one instance, that of Mameena, the Zulu lady whom Hans thought he saw in the Shades. She, I believe, did me the honour to be very fond of me, but I am convinced that she was fonder still of her ambition. Now Hans never cared for any living creature, or for any human hope or object, as he cared for me. There was no man or woman whom he would not have cheated, or even murdered for my sake. There was no earthly advantage, down to that of life itself, that he would not, and in the end did not forgo for my sake; witness the case of his little fortune which he invested in my rotten gold mine and thought nothing of losing—for my sake.

That is love *in excelsis*, and the man who has succeeded in inspiring it in any creature, even in a low, bibulous, old Hottentot, may feel proud indeed. At least I am proud and as the years go by the pride increases, as the hope grows that somewhere in the quiet of that great plain which he saw in his dream, I may find the light of Hans's love burning like a beacon in the darkness, as he promised I should do, and that it may guide and warm my shivering, new-born soul before I dare the adventure of the Infinite.

Meanwhile, since the sublime and the ridiculous are so very near akin, I often wonder how he and Mameena settled that question of her right to the royal salute. Perhaps I shall learn one day—indeed already I have had a hint of it. If so, even in the blaze of a new and universal Truth, I am certain that their stories will differ wildly.

Hans was quite right about the Black Kendah. They cleared out, probably in search of food, where I do not know and I do not care, though whether this were a temporary or permanent move on their part remains, and so far as I am concerned is likely to remain, veiled in obscurity. They were great blackguards, though extraordinarily fine soldiers, and what became of them is a matter of complete indifference to me. One thing is certain, however, a very large percentage of them never migrated at all, for something over three thousand of their bodies did our people have to bury in the pass and about the temple, a purpose for which all the pits and trenches we had dug came in very useful. Our loss, by the way, was five hundred and three, including those who died of wounds. It was a great fight and, except for those who perished in the pitfalls during the first rush, all practically hand to hand.

Jana we interred where he fell because we could not move him, within a few feet of the body of his slayer Hans. I have always regretted that I did not take the exact measurements of this brute, as I believe the record elephant of the world, but I had no time to do so and no rule or tape at hand. I only saw him for a minute on the following morning, just as he was being tumbled into a huge hole, together with the remains of his master, Simba the King. I found, however, that the sole wounds upon him, save some cuts and scratches from spears, were those inflicted by Hans—namely, the loss of one eye, the puncture through the skin over the heart made when he shot at him for the second time with the little rifle Intombi, and two neat holes at the back of the mouth through which the bullets from the elephant gun had driven upwards to the base of the brain, causing his death from hæmorrhage on that organ.

I asked the White Kendah to give me his two enormous tusks, unequalled, I suppose, in size and weight in Africa, although one was deformed and broken. But they refused. These, I presume, they wished to keep, together with the chains off his breast and trunk, as mementoes of their victory over the god of their foes. At any rate they hewed the former out with axes and removed the latter before tumbling the carcass into the grave. From the worn-down state of the teeth I concluded that this beast must have been extraordinarily old, how old it is impossible to say.

That is all I have to tell of Jana. May he rest in peace, which certainly he will not do if Hans dwells anywhere in his neighbourhood, in the region which the old boy used to call that of the "fires that do not go out." Because of my horrible failure in connection with this beast, the very memory of which humiliates me, I do not like to think of it more than I can help.

For the rest the White Kendah kept faith with us in every particular. In a curious and semi-religious ceremony, at which I was not present, Lady Ragnall was absolved from her high office of Guardian or Nurse to a god whereof the symbol no longer existed, though I believe that the priests collected the tiny fragments of ivory, or as many of them as could be found, and preserved them in a jar in the sanctuary. After this had been done women stripped the Nurse of her hallowed robes, of the ancient origin of which, by the way, I believe that none of them, except perhaps Harût, had any idea, any more than they knew that the Child represented the Egyptian Horus and his lady Guardian the moon- goddess Isis. Then, dressed in some native garments, she was handed over to Ragnall and thenceforth treated as a stranger-guest, like ourselves, being allowed, however, to live with her husband in the same house that she had occupied during all the period of her strange captivity. Here they abode together, lost in the mutual bliss of this wonderful reunion to which they had attained through so much bodily and spiritual darkness and misery, until a month or so later we started upon our journey across the mountains and the great desert that lay beyond them.

Only once did I find any real opportunity of private conversation with Lady Ragnall.

This happened after her husband had recovered from the hurts he received in the battle, on an occasion when he was obliged to separate from her for a day in order to attend to some matter in the Town of the Child. I think it had to do with the rifles used in the battle, which he had presented to the White Kendah. So, leaving me to look after her, he went, unwillingly enough, who seemed to hate losing sight of his wife even for an hour.

I took her for a walk in the wood, to that very point indeed on the lip of the crater whence we had watched her play her part as priestess at the Feast of the First-fruits. After we had stood there a while we went down among the great cedars, trying to retrace the last part of our march through the darkness of that anxious night, whereof now for the first time I told her all the story.

Growing tired of scrambling among the fallen boughs, at length Lady Ragnall sat down and said:

"Do you know, Mr. Quatermain, these are the first words we have really had since that party at Ragnall before I was married, when, as you may have forgotten, you took me in to dinner."

I replied that there was nothing I recollected much more clearly, which was both true and the right thing to say, or so I supposed.

"Well," she said slowly, "you see that after all there was something in those fancies of mine which at the time you thought would best be dealt with by a doctor—about Africa and the rest, I mean."

"Yes, Lady Ragnall, though of course we should always remember that coincidence accounts for many things. In any case they are done with now."

"Not quite, Mr. Quatermain, even as you mean, since we have still a long way to go. Also in another sense I believe that they are but begun."

"I do not understand, Lady Ragnall."

"Nor do I, but listen. You know that of anything which happened during those months I have no memory at all, except of that one dream when I seemed to see George and Savage in the hut. I remember my baby being killed by that horrible circus elephant, just as the Ivory Child was killed or rather destroyed by Jana, which I suppose is another of your coincidences, Mr. Quatermain. After that I remember nothing until I woke up and saw George standing in front of me covered with blood, and you, and Jana dead, and the rest."

"Because during that time your mind was gone, Lady Ragnall."

"Yes, but where had it gone? I tell you, Mr. Quatermain, that although I remember nothing of what was passing about me then, I do remember a great deal of what seemed to be passing either long ago or in some time to come, though I have said nothing of it to George, as I hope you will not either. It might upset him."

"What do you remember?" I asked.

"That's the trouble; I can't tell you. What was once very clear to me has for the most part become vague and formless. When my mind tries to grasp it, it slips away. It was another life to this, quite a different life; and there was a great story in it of which I think what we have been going through is either a sequel or a prologue. I see, or saw, cities and temples with people moving about them, George and you among them, also that old priest, Harût. You will laugh, but my recollection is that you stood in some relationship to me, either that of father or brother."

"Or perhaps a cousin," I suggested.

"Or perhaps a cousin," she repeated, smiling, "or a great friend; at any rate something very intimate. As for George, I don't know what he was, or Harût either. But the odd thing is that little yellow man, Hans, whom I only saw once living for a few minutes that I can remember, comes more clearly back to my mind than any of you. He was a dwarf, much stouter than when I saw him the other day, but very like. I recall him curiously dressed with feathers and holding an ivory rod, seated upon a stool at the feet of a great personage—a king, I think. The king asked him questions, and everyone listened to his answers. That is all, except that the scenes seemed to be flooded with sunlight."

"Which is more than this place is. I think we had better be moving, Lady Ragnall, or you will catch a chill under these damp cedars."

I said this because I did not wish to pursue the conversation. I considered it too exciting under all her circumstances, especially as I perceived that mystical look gathering on her face and in her beautiful eyes, which I remembered noting before she was married.

She read my thoughts and answered with a laugh:

"Yes, it is damp; but you know I am very strong and damp will not hurt me. For the rest you need not be afraid, Mr. Quatermain. I did not lose my mind. It was taken from me by some power and sent to live elsewhere. Now it has been given back and I do not think it will be taken again in that way."

"Of course it won't," I exclaimed confidently. "Whoever dreamed of such a thing?"

"*You* did," she answered, looking me in the eyes. "Now before we go I want to say one more thing. Harût and the head priestess have made me a present. They have given me a box full of that herb they called tobacco, but of which I have discovered the real name is Taduki. It is the same that they burned in the bowl when you and I saw visions at Ragnall Castle, which visions, Mr. Quatermain, by another of your coincidences, have since been translated into facts."

"I know. We saw you breathe that smoke again as priestess when you uttered the prophecy as Oracle of the Child at the Feast of the First-fruits. But what are you going to do with this stuff, Lady Ragnall? I think you have had enough of visions just at present."

"So do I, though to tell you the truth I like them. I am going to keep it and do nothing—as yet. Still, I want you always to remember one thing—don't laugh at me"—here again she looked me in the eyes—"that there is a time coming, some way off I think, when I and you—no one else, Mr. Quatermain—will breathe that smoke again together and see strange things."

"No, no!" I replied, "I have given up tobacco of the Kendah variety; it is too strong for me."

"Yes, yes!" she said, "for something that is stronger than the Kendah tobacco will make you do it—when I wish."

"Did Harût tell you that, Lady Ragnall?"

"I don't know," she answered confusedly. "I think the Ivory Child told me; it used to talk to me often. You know that Child isn't really destroyed. Like my reason that seemed to be lost, it has only gone backwards or forwards where you and I shall see it again. You and I and no others—unless it be the little yellow man. I repeat that I do not know when that will be. Perhaps it is written in those rolls of papyrus, which they have given me also, because they said they belonged to me who am 'the first priestess and the last.' They told me, however, or perhaps," she added, passing her hand across her forehead, "it was the Child who told me, that I was not to attempt to read them or have them read, until after a great change in my life. What the change will be I do not know."

"And had better not inquire, Lady Ragnall, since in this world most changes are for the worse."

"I agree, and shall not inquire. Now I have spoken to you like this because I felt that I must do so. Also I want to thank you for all you have done for me and George. Probably we shall not talk in such a way again; as I am situated the opportunity will be lacking, even if the wish is present. So once more I thank you from my heart. Until we meet again—I mean really meet—good-bye," and she held her right hand to me in such a fashion that I knew she meant me to kiss it.

This I did very reverently and we walked back to the temple almost in silence.

That month of rest, or rather the last three weeks of it, since for the first few days after the battle I was quite prostrate, I occupied in various ways, amongst others in a journey with Harût to Simba Town. This we made after our spies had assured us that the Black Kendah were really gone somewhere to the south-west, in which direction fertile and unoccupied lands were said to exist about three hundred miles away. It was with very strange feelings that I retraced our road and looked once more upon that wind-bent tree still scored with the marks of Jana's huge tusk, in the boughs of which Hans and I had taken refuge from the monster's fury. Crossing the river, quite low now, I travelled up the slope down which we raced for our lives and came to the melancholy lake and the cemetery of dead elephants.

Here all was unchanged. There was the little mount worn by his feet, on which Jana was wont to stand. There were the rocks behind which I had tried to hide, and near to them some crushed human bones which I knew to be those of the unfortunate Marût. These we buried with due reverence on the spot where he had fallen, I meanwhile thanking God that my own bones were not being interred at their side, as but for Hans would have been the case—if they were ever interred at all. All about lay the skeletons of dead elephants, and from among these we collected as much of the best ivory as we could carry, namely about fifty camel loads. Of course there was much more, but a great deal of the stuff had been exposed for so long to sun and weather that it was almost worthless.

Having sent this ivory back to the Town of the Child, which was being rebuilt after a fashion, we went on to Simba Town through the forest, dispatching pickets ahead of us to search and make sure that it was empty. Empty it was indeed; never did I see such a place of desolation.

The Black Kendah had left it just as it stood, except for a pile of corpses which lay around and over the altar in the market-place, where the three poor camelmen were sacrificed to Jana, doubtless those of wounded men who had died during or after the retreat. The doors of the houses stood open, many domestic articles, such as great jars resembling that which had been set over the head of the dead man whom we were commanded to restore life, and other furniture lay about because they could not be carried away. So did a great quantity of spears and various weapons of war, whose owners being killed would never want them again. Except a few starved dogs and jackals no living creature remained in the town. It was in its own way as waste and even more impressive than the graveyard of elephants by the lonely lake.

"The curse of the Child worked well," said Harût to me grimly. "First, the storm; the hunger; then the battle; and now the misery of flight and ruin."

"It seems so," I answered. "Yet that curse, like others, came back to roost, for if Jana is dead and his people fled, where are the Child and many of its people? What will you do without your god, Harût?"

"Repent us of our sins and wait till the Heavens send us another, as doubtless they will in their own season," he replied very sadly.

I wonder whether they ever did and, if so, what form that new divinity put on.

I slept, or rather did not sleep, that night in the same guest-house in which Marût and I had been imprisoned during our dreadful days of fear, reconstructing in my mind every event connected with them. Once more I saw the fires of sacrifice flaring upon the altar and heard the roar of the dancing hail that proclaimed the ruin of the Black Kendah as loudly as the trumpet of a destroying angel. Very glad was I when the morning came at length and, having looked my last upon Simba Town, I crossed the moats and set out homewards through the forest whereof the stripped boughs also spoke of death, though in the spring these would grow green again.

Ten days later we started from the Holy Mount, a caravan of about a hundred camels, of which fifty were laden with the ivory and the rest ridden by our escort under the command of Harût and our three selves. But there was an evil fate upon this ivory, as on everything else that had to do with Jana. Some weeks later in the desert a great sandstorm overtook us in which we barely escaped with our lives. At the height of the storm the ivory-laden camels broke loose, flying before it. Probably they fell and were buried beneath the sand; at any rate of the fifty we only recovered ten.

Ragnall wished to pay me the value of the remaining loads, which ran into thousands of pounds, but I would not take the money, saying it was outside our bargain. Sometimes since then I have thought that I was foolish, especially when on glancing at that codicil to his will in after days, the same which he had given me before the battle, I found that he had set me down for a legacy of £10,000. But in such matters every man must follow his own instinct.

The White Kendah, an unemotional people especially now when they were mourning for their lost god and their dead, watched us go without any demonstration of affection, or even of farewell. Only those priestesses who had attended upon the person of Lady Ragnall while she played a divine part among them wept when they parted from her, and uttered prayers that they might meet her again "in the presence of the Child."

The pass through the great mountains proved hard to climb, as the foothold for the camels was bad. But we managed it at last, most of the way on foot, pausing a little while on their crest to look our last for ever at the land which we had left, where the Mount of the Child was still dimly visible. Then we descended their farther slope and entered the northern desert.

Day after day and week after week we travelled across that endless desert by a way known to Harût on which water could be found, the only living things in all its vastness, meeting with no accidents save that of the sandstorm in which the ivory was lost. I was much alone during that time, since Harût spoke little and Ragnall and his wife were wrapped up in each other.

At length, months later, we struck a little port on the Red Sea, of which I forget the Arab name, a place as hot as the infernal regions. Shortly afterwards, by great good luck, two trading vessels put in for water, one bound for Aden, in which I embarked en route for Natal, and the other for the port of Suez, whence Ragnall and his wife could travel overland to Alexandria.

Our parting was so hurried at the last, as is often the way after long fellowship, that beyond mutual thanks and good wishes we said little to one another. I can see them now standing with their arms about each other watching me disappear. Concerning their future there is so much to tell that of it I shall say nothing; at any rate here and now, except that Lady Ragnall was right. We did not part for the last time.

As I shook old Harût's hand in farewell he told me that he was going on to Egypt, and I asked him why.

"Perchance to look for another god, Lord Macumazana," he answered gravely, "whom now there is no Jana to destroy. We may speak of that matter if we should meet again."

Such are some of the things that I remember about this journey, but to tell truth I paid little attention to them and many others.

For oh! my heart was sore because of Hans.

The Ancient Allan

Table of Contents

An Old Friend

Now I, Allan Quatermain, come to the weirdest (with one or two exceptions perhaps) of all the experiences which it has amused me to employ my idle hours in recording here in a strange land, for after all England is strange to me. I grow elderly. I have, as I suppose, passed the period of enterprise and adventure and I should be well satisfied with the lot that Fate has given to my unworthy self.

To begin with, I am still alive and in health when by all the rules I should have been dead many times over. I suppose I ought to be thankful for that but, before expressing an opinion on the point, I should have to be quite sure whether it is better to be alive or dead. The religious plump for the latter, though I have never observed that the religious are more eager to die than the rest of us poor mortals.

For instance, if they are told that their holy hearts are wrong, they spend time and much money in rushing to a place called Nauheim in Germany, to put them right by means of water-drinking, thereby shortening their hours of heavenly bliss and depriving their heirs of a certain amount of cash. The same thing applies to Buxton in my own neighbourhood and gout, especially when it threatens the stomach or the throat. Even archbishops will do these things, to say nothing of such small fry as deans, or stout and prominent lay figures of the Church.

From common sinners like myself such conduct might be expected, but in the case of those who are obviously poised on the topmost rungs of the Jacobean—I mean, the heavenly—ladder, it is legitimate to inquire why they show such reluctance in jumping off. As a matter of fact the only persons that, individually, I have seen quite willing to die, except now and again to save somebody else whom they were so foolish as to care for more than they did for themselves, have been not those "upon whom the light has shined" to quote an earnest paper I chanced to read this morning, but, to quote again, "the sinful heathen wandering in their native blackness," by which I understand the writer to refer to their moral state and not to their sable skins wherein for the most part they are also condemned to wander, that is if they happen to have been born south of a certain degree of latitude.

To come to facts, the staff of Faith which each must shape for himself, is often hewn from unsuitable kinds of wood, yes, even by the very best among us. Willow, for instance, is pretty and easy to cut, but try to support yourself with it on the edge of a precipice and see where you are. Then of a truth you will long for ironbark, or even homely oak. I might carry my parable further, some allusions to the proper material of which to fashion the helmet of Salvation suggest themselves to me for example, but I won't.

The truth is that we fear to die because all the religions are full of uncomfortable hints as to what may happen to us afterwards as a reward for our deviations from their laws and we half believe in something, whereas often the savage, not being troubled with religion, fears less, because he half believes in nothing. For very few inhabitants of this earth can attain either to complete belief or to its absolute opposite. They can seldom lay their hands upon their hearts, and say they *know* that they will live for ever, or sleep for ever; there remains in the case of most honest men an element of doubt in either hypothesis.

That is what makes this story of mine so interesting, at any rate to me, since it does seem to suggest that whether or no I have a future, as personally I hold to be the case and not altogether without evidence, certainly I have had a past, though, so far as I know, in this world only; a fact, if it be a fact, from which can be deduced all kinds of arguments according to the taste of the reasoner.

And now for my experience, which it is only fair to add, may after all have been no more than a long and connected dream. Yet how was I to dream of lands, events and people whereof I have only the vaguest knowledge, or none at all, unless indeed, as some say, being a part of this world, we have hidden away somewhere in ourselves an acquaintance with everything that has ever happened in the world. However, it does not much matter and it is useless to discuss that which we cannot prove.

Here at any rate is the story.

In a book or a record which I have written down and put away with others under the title of "The Ivory Child," I have told the tale of a certain expedition I made in company with Lord Ragnall. Its object was to search for his wife who was stolen away while travelling in Egypt in a state of mental incapacity resulting from shock caused by the loss of her child under tragic and terrible circumstances. The thieves were the priests of a certain bastard Arab tribe who, on account of a birthmark shaped like the young moon which was visible above her breast, believed her to be the priestess or oracle of their worship. This worship evidently had its origin in Ancient Egypt since, although they did not seem to know it, the priestess was nothing less than a personification of the great goddess Isis, and the Ivory Child, their fetish, was a statue of the infant Horus, the fabled son of Isis and Osiris whom the Egyptians looked upon as the overcomer of Set or the Devil, the murderer of Osiris before his resurrection and ascent to Heaven to be the god of the dead.

I need not set down afresh all that happened to us on this remarkable adventure. Suffice it to say that in the end we recovered the lady and that her mind was restored to her. Before she left the Kendah country, however, the priesthood presented her with two ancient rolls of papyrus, also with a quantity of a certain herb, not unlike tobacco in appearance, which by the Kendah was called *Taduki*. Once, before we took our great homeward journey across the desert, Lady Ragnall and I had a curious conversation about this herb whereof the property is to cause the person who inhales its fumes to become clairvoyant, or to dream dreams, whichever the truth may be. It was used for this purpose in the mystical ceremonies of the Kendah religion when under its influence the priestess or oracle of the Ivory Child was wont to announce divine revelations. During her tenure of this office Lady Ragnall was frequently subjected to the spell of the *Taduki* vapour, and said strange things, some of which I heard with my own ears. Also myself once I experienced its effects and saw a curious vision, whereof many of the particulars were afterwards translated into facts.

Now the conversation which I have mentioned was shortly to the effect, that she, Lady Ragnall, believed a time would come when she or I or both of us, were destined to imbibe these *Taduki* fumes and see wonderful pictures of some past or future existence in which we were both concerned. This knowledge, she declared, had come to her while she was officiating in an apparently mindless condition as the priestess of the Kendah god called the Ivory Child.

At the time I did not think it wise to pursue so exciting a subject with a woman whose mind had been recently unbalanced, and afterwards in the stress of new experiences, I forgot all about the matter, or at any rate only thought of it very rarely.

Once, however, it did recur to me with some force. Shortly after I came to England to spend my remaining days far from the temptations of adventure, I was beguiled into becoming a steward of a Charity dinner and, what was worse, into attending the said dinner. Although its objects were admirable, it proved one of the most dreadful functions in which I was ever called upon to share. There was a vast number of people, some of them highly distinguished, who had come to support the Charity or to show off their Orders, I don't know which, and others like myself, not at all distinguished, just common subscribers, who had no Orders and stood about the crowded room like waiters looking for a job.

At the dinner, which was very bad, I sat at a table so remote that I could hear but little of the interminable speeches, which was perhaps fortunate for me. In these circumstances I drifted into conversation with my neighbour, a queer, wizened, black-bearded man who somehow or other had found out that I was acquainted with the wilder parts of Africa. He proved to be a wealthy scientist whose passion it was to study the properties of herbs, especially of such as grow in the interior of South America where he had been travelling for some years.

Presently he mentioned a root named Yage, known to the Indians which, when pounded up into a paste and taken in the form of pills, had the effect of enabling the patient to see events that were passing at a distance. Indeed he alleged that a vision thus produced had caused him to return home, since in it he saw that some relative of his, I think a twin-sister, was dangerously ill. In fact, however, he might as well have stayed away, as he only arrived in London on the day after her funeral.

As I saw that he was really interested in the subject and observed that he was a very temperate man who did not seem to be romancing, I told him something of my experiences with *Taduki*, to which he listened with a kind of rapt but suppressed excitement. When I affected disbelief in the whole business, he differed from me almost rudely, asking why I rejected phenomena simply because I was too dense to understand them. I answered perhaps because such phenomena were inconvenient and upset one's ideas. To this he replied that all progress involved the upsetting of existent ideas. Moreover he implored me, if the chance should ever come my way, to pursue experiments with *Taduki* fumes and let him know the results.

Here our conversation came to an end for suddenly a band that was braying near by, struck up "God save the Queen," and we hastily exchanged cards and parted. I only mention it because, had it not occurred, I think it probable that I should never have been in a position to write this history.

The remarks of my acquaintance remained in my mind and influenced it so much that when the occasion came, I did as a kind of duty what, however much I was pressed, I am almost sure I should never have done for any other reason, just because I thought that I ought to take an opportunity of trying to discover what was the truth of the matter. As it chanced it was quick in coming.

Here I should explain that I attended the dinner of which I have spoken not very long after a very lengthy absence from England, whither I had come to live when King Solomon's Mines had made me rich. Therefore it happened that between the conclusion of my Kendah adventure some years before and this time I saw nothing and heard little of Lord and Lady Ragnall. Once a rumour did reach me, however, I think through Sir Henry Curtis or Captain Good, that the former had died as a result of an accident. What the accident was my informant did not know and as I was just starting on a far journey at the time, I had no opportunity of making inquiries. My talk with the botanical scientist determined me to do so; indeed a few days later I discovered from a book of reference that Lord Ragnall was dead, leaving no heir; also that his wife survived him.

I was working myself up to write to her when one morning the postman brought me here at the Grange a letter which had "Ragnall Castle" printed on the flap of the envelope. I did not know the writing which was very clear and firm, for as it chanced, to the best of my recollection, I had never seen that of Lady Ragnall. Here is a copy of the letter it contained:

"My dear Mr. Quatermain,—Very strangely I have just seen at a meeting of the Horticultural Society, a gentleman who declares that a few days ago he sat next to you at some public dinner. Indeed I do not think there can be any doubt for he showed me your card which he had in his purse with a Yorkshire address upon it.

"A dispute had arisen as to whether a certain variety of Crinum lily was first found in Africa, or Southern America. This gentleman, an authority upon South American flora, made a speech saying that he had never met with it there, but that an acquaintance of his, Mr. Quatermain, to whom he had spoken on the subject, said that he had seen something of the sort in the interior of Africa." (This was quite true for I remembered the incident.) "At the tea which followed the meeting I spoke to this gentleman whose name I never caught, and to my astonishment learnt that he must have been referring to you whom I believed to be dead, for so we were told a long time ago. This seemed certain, for in addition to the evidence of the name, he described your personal appearance and told me that you had come to live in England.

"My dear friend, I can assure you it is long since I heard anything which rejoiced me so much. Oh! as I write all the past comes back, flowing in upon me like a pent-up flood of water, but I trust that of this I shall soon have an opportunity of talking to you. So let it be for a while.

"Alas! my friend, since we parted on the shores of the Red Sea, tragedy has pursued me. As you will know, for both my husband and I wrote to you, although you did not answer the letters" (I never received them), "we reached England safely and took up our old life again, though to tell you the truth, after my African experiences things could never be quite the same to me, or for the matter of that to George either. To a great extent he changed his pursuits and certain political ambitions which he once cherished, seemed no longer to appeal to him. He became a student of past history and especially of Egyptology, which under all the circumstances you may think strange, as I did. However it suited me well enough, since I also have tastes that way. So we worked together and I can now read hieroglyphics as well as most people. One year he said that he would like to go to Egypt again, if I were not afraid. I answered that it had not been a very lucky place for us, but that personally I was not in the least afraid and longed to return there. For as you know, I have, or think I have, ties with Egypt and indeed with all Africa. Well, we went and had a very happy time, although I was always expecting to see old Harut come round the corner.

"After this it became a custom with us who, since George practically gave up shooting and attending the House of Lords, had nothing to keep us in England, to winter in Egypt. We did this for five years in succession, living in a bungalow which we built at a place in the desert, not far from the banks of the Nile, about half way between Luxor which was the ancient Thebes, and Assouan. George took a great fancy to this spot when first he saw it, and so in truth did I, for, like Memphis, it attracted me so much that I used to laugh and say I believed that once I had something to do with it.

"Now near to our villa that we called 'Ragnall' after this house, are the remains of a temple which were almost buried in the sand. This temple George obtained permission to excavate. It proved to be a long and costly business, but as he did not mind spending the money, that was no obstacle. For four winters we worked at it, employing several hundred men. As we went on we discovered that although not one of the largest, the temple, owing to its having been buried by the sand during, or shortly after the Roman epoch, remained much more perfect than we had expected, because the early Christians had never got at it with their chisels and hammers. Before long I hope to show you pictures and photographs of the various courts, etc., so I will not attempt to describe them now.

"It is a temple to Isis—built, or rather rebuilt over the remains of an older temple on a site that seems to have been called Amada, at any rate in the later days, and so named after a city in Nubia, apparently by one of the Amen-hetep Pharaohs who had conquered it. Its style is beautiful, being of the best period of the Egyptian Renaissance under the last native dynasties.

"At the beginning of the fifth winter, at length we approached the sanctuary, a difficult business because of the retaining walls that had to be built to keep the sand from flowing down as fast as it was removed, and the great quantities of stuff that must be carried off by the tramway. In so doing we came upon a shallow grave which appeared to have been hastily filled in and roughly covered over with paving stones like the rest of the court, as though to conceal its existence. In this grave lay the skeleton of a large man, together with the rusted blade of an iron sword and some fragments of armour. Evidently he had never been mummified, for there were no wrappings, canopic jars, *ushapti* figures or funeral offerings. The state of the bones showed us why, for the right forearm was cut through and the skull smashed in; also an iron arrow-head lay among the ribs. The man had been buried hurriedly after a battle in which he had met his death. Searching in the dust beneath the bones we found a gold ring still on one of the fingers. On its bezel was engraved the cartouche of 'Peroa, beloved of Ra.' Now Peroa probably means Pharaoh and perhaps he was Khabasha who revolted against the Persians and ruled for a year or two, after which he is supposed to have been defeated and killed, though of his end and place of burial there is no record. Whether these were the remnants of Khabasha himself, or of one of his high ministers or generals who wore the King's cartouche upon his ring in token of his office, of course I cannot say.

"When George had read the cartouche he handed me the ring which I slipped upon the first finger of my left hand, where I still wear it. Then leaving the grave open for further examination, we went on with the work, for we were greatly excited. At length, this was towards evening, we had cleared enough of the sanctuary, which was small, to uncover the shrine that, if not a monolith, was made of four pieces of granite so wonderfully put together that one could not see the joints. On the curved architrave as I think it is called, was carved the symbol of a winged disc, and beneath in hieroglyphics as fresh as though they had only been cut yesterday, an inscription to the effect that Peroa, Royal Son of the Sun, gave this shrine as an 'excellent eternal work,' together with the statues of the Holy Mother and the Holy Child to the 'emanations of the great Goddess Isis and the god Horus,' Amada, Royal Lady, being votaress or high-priestess.

"We only read the hieroglyphics very hurriedly, being anxious to see what was within the shrine that, the cedar door having rotted away, was filled with fine, drifted sand. Basketful by basketful we got it out and then, my friend, there appeared the most beautiful life-sized statue of Isis carved in alabaster that ever I have seen. She was seated on a throne-like chair and wore the vulture cap on which traces of colour remained. Her arms were held forward as though to support a child, which perhaps she was suckling as one of the breasts was bare. But if so, the child had gone. The execution of the statue was exquisite and its tender and mystic face extraordinarily beautiful, so life-like also that I think it must have been copied from a living model. Oh! my friend, when I looked upon it, which we did by the light of the candles, for the sun was sinking and shadows gathered in that excavated hole, I felt—never mind what I felt—perhaps *you* can guess who know my history.

"While we stared and stared, I longing to go upon my knees, I knew not why, suddenly I felt a faint trembling of the ground. At the same moment, the head overseer of the works, a man called Achmet, rushed up to us, shouting out—'Back! Back! The wall has burst. The sand runs!'

"He seized me by the arm and dragged me away beside of and behind the grave, George turning to follow. Next instant I saw a kind of wave of sand, on the crest of which appeared the stones of the wall, curl over and break. It struck the shrine, overturned and shattered it, which makes me think it was made of four pieces, and shattered also the alabaster statue within, for I saw its head strike George upon the back and throw him forward. He reeled and fell into the open grave which in another moment was filled and covered with the debris that seemed to grip me to my middle in its flow. After this I remembered nothing more until hours later I found myself lying in our house.

"Achmet and his Egyptians had done nothing; indeed none of them could be persuaded to approach the place till the sun rose because, as they said, the old gods of the land whom they looked upon as devils, were angry at being disturbed and would kill them as they had killed the Bey, meaning George. Then, distracted as I was, I went myself for there was no other European there, to find that the whole site of the sanctuary was buried beneath hundreds of tons of sand, that, beginning at the gap in the broken wall, had flowed from every side. Indeed it would have taken weeks to dig it out, since to sink a shaft was impracticable and so dangerous that the local officials refused to allow it to be attempted. The end of it was that an English bishop came up from Cairo and consecrated the ground by special arrangement with the Government, which of course makes it impossible that this part of the temple should be further disturbed. After this he read the Burial Service over my dear husband.

"So there is the end of a very terrible story which I have written down because I do not wish to have to talk about it more than is necessary when we meet. For, dear Mr. Quatermain, we shall meet, as I always knew that we should—yes, even after I heard that you were dead. You will remember that I told you so years ago in Kendah Land and that it would happen after a great change in my life, though what that change might be I could not say. . . ."

This is the end of the letter except for certain suggested dates for the visit which she took for granted I should make to Ragnall.

Ragnall Castle

When I had finished reading this amazing document I lit my pipe and set to work to think it over. The hypothetical inquirer might ask why I thought it amazing. There was nothing odd in a dilettante Englishman of highly cultivated mind taking to Egyptology and, being, as it chanced, one of the richest men in the kingdom, spending a fraction of his wealth in excavating temples. Nor was it strange that he should have happened to die by accident when engaged in that pursuit, which I can imagine to be very fascinating in the delightful winter climate of Egypt. He was not the first person to be buried by a fall of sand. Why, only a little while ago the same fate overtook a nursery-governess and the child in her charge who were trying to dig out a martin's nest in a pit in this very parish. Their operations brought down a huge mass of the overhanging bank beneath which the sand-vein had been hollowed by workmen who deserted the pit when they saw that it had become unsafe. Next day I and my gardeners helped to recover their bodies, for their whereabouts was not discovered until the following morning, and a sad business it was.

Yet, taken in conjunction with the history of this couple, the whole Ragnall affair was very strange. When but a child Lady Ragnall, then the Hon. Miss Holmes, had been identified by the priests of a remote African tribe as the oracle of their peculiar faith, which we afterwards proved to be derived from old Egypt, in short the worship of Isis and Horus. Subsequently they tried to steal her away and through the accident of my intervention, failed. Later on, after her marriage when shock had deprived her of her mind, these priests renewed the attempt, this time in Egypt, and succeeded. In the end we rescued her in Central Africa, where she was playing the part of the Mother-goddess Isis and even wearing her ancient robes. Next she and her husband came home with their minds turned towards a branch of study that took them back to Egypt. Here they devote themselves to unearthing a temple and find out that among all the gods of Egypt, who seem to have been extremely numerous, it was dedicated to Isis and Horus, the very divinities with whom they recently they had been so intimately concerned if in traditional and degenerate forms.

Moreover that was not the finish of it. They come to the sanctuary. They discover the statue of the goddess with the child gone, as their child was gone. A disaster occurs and both destroys and buries Ragnall so effectually that nothing of him is ever seen again: he just vanishes into another man's grave and remains there.

A common sort of catastrophe enough, it is true, though people of superstitious mind might have thought that it looked as though the goddess, or whatever force was behind the goddess, was working vengeance on the man who desecrated her ancient shrine. And, by the way, though I cannot remember whether or no I mentioned it in "The Ivory Child," I recall that the old priest of the Kendah, Harut, once told me he was sure Ragnall would meet with a violent death. This seemed likely enough in that country under our circumstances there, still I asked him why. He answered,

"Because he has laid hands on that which is holy and not meant for man," and he looked at Lady Ragnall.

I remarked that all women were holy, whereon he replied that he did not think so and changed the subject.

Well, Ragnall, who had married the lady who once served as the last priestess of Isis upon earth, was killed, whereas she, the priestess, was almost miraculously preserved from harm. And—oh! the whole story was deuced odd and that is all. Poor Ragnall! He was a great English gentleman and one whom when first I knew him, I held to be the most fortunate person I ever met, endowed as he was with every advantage of mind, body and estate. Yet in the end this did not prove to be the case. Well, while he lived he was a good friend and a good fellow and none can hope for a better epitaph in a world where all things are soon forgotten.

And now, what was I to do? To tell the truth I did not altogether desire to reopen this chapter in past history, or to have to listen to painful reminiscences from the lips of a bereaved woman. Moreover, beautiful as she had been, for doubtless she was *passee* now, and charming as of course she remained—I do not think I ever knew anyone who was quite so charming—there was something about Lady Ragnall which alarmed me. She did not resemble any other woman. Of course no woman is ever quite like another, but in her case the separateness, if I may so call it, was very marked. It was as though she had walked out of a different age, or even world, and been but superficially clothed with the attributes of our own. I felt that from the first moment I set eyes upon her and while reading her letter the sensation returned with added force.

Also for me she had a peculiar attraction and not one of the ordinary kind. It is curious to find oneself strangely intimate with a person of whom after all one does not know much, just as if one really knew a great deal that was shut off by a thin but quite impassable door. If so, I did not want to open that door for who could tell what might be on the other side of it? And intimate conversations with a lady in whose company one has shared very strange experiences, not infrequently lead to the opening of every kind of door.

Further I had made up my mind some time ago to have no more friendships with women who are so full of surprises, but to live out the rest of my life in a kind of monastery of men who have few surprises, being creatures whose thoughts are nearly always open and whose actions can always be foretold.

Lastly there was that *Taduki* business. Well, there at any rate I was clear and decided. No earthly power would induce me to have anything more to do with *Taduki* smoke. Of course I remembered that Lady Ragnall once told me kindly but firmly that I would if she wished. But that was just where she made a mistake. For the rest it seemed unkind to refuse her invitation now when she was in trouble, especially as I had once promised that if ever I could be of help, she had only to command me. No, I must go. But if that word—*Taduki*—were so much as mentioned I would leave again in a hurry. Moreover it would not be, for doubtless she had forgotten all about the stuff by now, even if it were not lost.

The end of it was that as I did not wish to write a long letter entering into all that Lady Ragnall had told me, I sent her a telegram, saying that if convenient to her, I would arrive at the Castle on the following Saturday evening and adding that I must be back here on the Tuesday afternoon, as I had guests coming to stay with me on that day. This was perfectly true as the season was mid-November and I was to begin shooting my coverts on the Wednesday morning, a function that once fixed, cannot be postponed.

In due course an answer arrived—"Delighted, but hoped that you would have been able to stay longer."

Behold me then about six o'clock on the said Saturday evening being once more whirled by a splendid pair of horses through the gateway arch of Ragnall Castle. The carriage stopped beneath the portico, the great doors flew open revealing the glow of the hall fire and lights within, the footman sprang down from the box and two other footmen descended the steps to assist me and my belongings out of the carriage. These, I remember, consisted of a handbag with my dress clothes and a yellow-backed novel.

So one of them took the handbag and the other had to content himself with the novel, which made me wish I had brought a portmanteau as well, if only for the look of the thing. The pair thus burdened, escorted me up the steps and delivered me over to the butler who scanned me with a critical eye. I scanned him also and perceived that he was a very fine specimen of his class. Indeed his stately presence so overcame me that I remarked nervously, as he helped me off with my coat, that when last I was here another had filled his office.

"Indeed, Sir," he said, "and what was his name, Sir?"

"Savage," I replied.

"And where might he be now, Sir?"

"Inside a snake!" I answered. "At least he was inside a snake but now I hope he is waiting upon his master in Heaven."

The man recoiled a little, pulling off my coat with a jerk. Then he coughed, rubbed his bald head, stared and recovering himself with an effort, said,

"Indeed, Sir! I only came to this place after the death of his late lordship, when her ladyship changed all the household. Alfred, show this gentleman up to her ladyship's boudoir, and William, take his— baggage—to the blue room. Her ladyship wishes to see you at once, Sir, before the others come."

So I went up the big staircase to a part of the Castle that I did not remember, wondering who "the others" might be. Almost could I have sworn that the shade of Savage accompanied me up those stairs; I could feel him at my side.

Presently a door was thrown open and I was ushered into a room somewhat dimly lit and full of the scent of flowers. By the fire near a tea-table, stood a lady clad in some dark dress with the light glinting on her rich-hued hair. She turned and I saw that she still wore the necklace of red stones, and beneath it on her breast a single red flower. For this was Lady Ragnall; about that there was no doubt at all, so little doubt indeed that I was amazed. I had expected to see a stout, elderly woman whom I should only know by the colour of her eyes and her voice, and perhaps certain tricks of manner. But, this was the mischief of it, I could not perceive any change, at any rate in that light. She was just the same! Perhaps a little fuller in figure, which was an advantage; perhaps a little more considered in her movements, perhaps a little taller or at any rate more stately, and that was all.

These things I learned in a flash. Then with a murmured "Mr. Quatermain, my Lady," the footman closed the door and she saw me.

Moving quickly towards me with both her hands outstretched, she exclaimed in that honey-soft voice of hers,

"Oh! my dear friend——" stopped and added, "Why, you haven't changed a bit."

"Fossils wear well," I replied, "but that is just what I was thinking of you."

"Then it is very rude of you to call me a fossil when I am only approaching that stage. Oh! I am glad to see you. I *am* glad!" and she gave me both the outstretched hands.

Upon my word I felt inclined to kiss her and have wondered ever since if she would have been very angry. I am not certain that she did not divine the inclination. At any rate after a little pause she dropped my hands and laughed. Then she said,

"I must tell you at once. A most terrible catastrophe has happened——"

Instantly it occurred to me that she had forgotten having informed me by letter of all the details of her husband's death. Such things chance to people who have once lost their memory. So I tried to look as sympathetic as I felt, sighed and waited.

"It's not so bad as all that," she said with a little shake of her head, reading my thought as she always had the power to do from the first moment we met. "We can talk about *that* afterwards. It's only that I hoped we were going to have a quiet two days, and now the Atterby-Smiths are coming, yes, in half an hour. Five of them!"

"The Atterby-Smiths!" I exclaimed, for somehow I too felt disappointed. "Who are the Atterby-Smiths?"

"Cousins of George's, his nearest relatives. They think he ought to have left them everything. But he didn't, because he could never bear the sight of them. You see his property was unentailed and he left it all to me. Now the entire family is advancing to suggest that I should leave it to them, as perhaps I might have done if they had not chosen to come just now."

"Why didn't you put them off?" I asked.

"Because I couldn't," she answered with a little stamp of her foot, "otherwise do you suppose they would have been here? They were far too clever. They telegraphed after lunch giving the train by which they were to arrive, but no address save Charing Cross. I thought of moving up to the Berkeley Square house, but it was impossible in the time, also I didn't know how to catch you. Oh! it's *most* vexatious."

"Perhaps they are very nice," I suggested feebly.

"Nice! Wait till you have seen them. Besides if they had been angels I did not want them just now. But how selfish I am! Come and have some tea. And you can stop longer, that is if you live through the Atterby- Smiths who are worse than both the Kendah tribes put together. Indeed I wish old Harut were coming instead. I should like to see Harut again, wouldn't you?" and suddenly the mystical look I knew so well, gathered on her face.

"Yes, perhaps I should," I replied doubtfully. "But I must leave by the first train on Tuesday morning; it goes at eight o'clock. I looked it up."

"Then the Atterby-Smiths leave on Monday if I have to turn them out of the house. So we shall get one evening clear at any rate. Stop a minute," and she rang the bell.

The footman appeared as suddenly as though he had been listening at the door.

"Alfred," she said, "tell Moxley" (he, I discovered, was the butler) "that when Mr. and Mrs. Atterby-Smith, the two Misses Atterby-Smith and the young Mr. Atterby-Smith arrive, they are to be shown to their rooms. Tell the cook also to put off dinner till half-past eight, and if Mr. and Mrs. Scroope arrive earlier, tell Moxley to tell them that I am sorry to be a little late, but that I was delayed by some parish business. Now do you understand?"

"Yes, my Lady," said Alfred and vanished.

"He doesn't understand in the least," remarked Lady Ragnall, "but so long as he doesn't show the Atterby-Smiths up here, in which case he can go away with them on Monday, I don't care. It will all work out somehow. Now sit down by the fire and let's talk. We've got nearly an hour and twenty minutes and you can smoke if you like. I learnt to in Egypt," and she took a cigarette from the mantelpiece and lit it.

That hour and twenty minutes went like a flash, for we had so much to say to each other that we never even got to the things we wanted to say. For instance, I began to tell her about King Solomon's Mines, which was a long story; and she to tell me what happened after we parted on the shores of the Red Sea. At least the first hour and a quarter went, when suddenly the door opened and Alfred in a somewhat frightened voice announced—"Mr. and Mrs. Atterby-Smith, the Misses Atterby-Smith and Mr. Atterby-Smith junior."

Then he caught sight of his mistress's eye and fled.

I looked and felt inclined to do likewise if only there had been another door. But there wasn't and that which existed was quite full. In the forefront came A.-S. senior, like a bull leading the herd. Indeed his appearance was bull-like as my eye, travelling from the expanse of white shirt-front (they were all dressed for dinner) to his red and massive countenance surmounted by two horn-like tufts of carroty hair, informed me at a glance. Followed Mrs. A.-S., the British matron incarnate. Literally there seemed to be acres of her; black silk below and white skin above on which set in filigree floated big green stones, like islands in an ocean. Her countenance too, though stupid was very stern and frightened me. Followed the progeny of this formidable pair. They were tall and thin, also red haired. The girls, whose age I could not guess in the least, were exactly like each other, which was not strange as afterwards I discovered that they were twins. They had pale blue eyes and somehow reminded me of fish. Both of them were dressed in green and wore topaz necklaces. The young man who seemed to be about one or two and twenty, had also pale blue eyes, in one of which he wore an eye-glass, but his hair was sandy as though it had been bleached, parted in the middle and oiled down flat.

For a moment there was a silence which I felt to be dreadful. Then in a big, pompous voice A.-S. *pere* said,

"How do you do, my dear Luna? As I ascertained from the footman that you had not yet gone to dress, I insisted upon his leading us here for a little private conversation after we have been parted for so many years. We wished to offer you our condolences in person on your and our still recent loss."

"Thank you," said Lady Ragnall, "but I think we have corresponded on the subject which is painful to me."

"I fear that we are interrupting a smoking party, Thomas," said Mrs. A.-S. in a cold voice, sniffing at the air for all the world like a suspicious animal, whereon the five of them stared at Lady Ragnall's cigarette which she held between her fingers.

"Yes," said Lady Ragnall. "Won't you have one? Mr. Quatermain, hand Mrs. Smith the box, please."

I obeyed automatically, proffering it to the lady who nearly withered me with a glance, and then to each to each in turn. To my relief the young man took one.

"Archibald," said his mother, "you are surely not going to make your sisters' dresses smell of tobacco just before dinner."

Archibald sniggered and replied,

"A little more smoke will not make any difference in this room, Ma."

"That is true, darling," said Mrs. A.-S. and was straightway seized with a fit of asthma.

After this I am sure I don't know what happened, for muttering something about its being time to dress, I rushed from the room and wandered about until I could find someone to conduct me to my own where I lingered until I heard the dinner-bell ring. But even this retreat was not without disaster, for in my hurry I trod upon one of the young lady's dresses; I don't know whether it was Dolly's or Polly's (they were named Dolly and Polly) and heard a dreadful crack about her middle as though she were breaking in two. Thereon Archibald giggled again and Dolly and Polly remarked with one voice—they always spoke together,

"Oh! clumsy!"

To complete my misfortunes I missed my way going downstairs and strayed to and fro like a lost lamb until I found myself confronted by a green baize door which reminded me of something. I stood staring at it till suddenly a vision arose before me of myself following a bell wire through that very door in the darkness of the night when in search for the late Mr. Savage upon a certain urgent occasion. Yes, there could be no doubt about it, for look! there was the wire, and strange it seemed to me that I should live to behold it again. Curiosity led me to push the door open just to ascertain if my memory served me aright about the exact locality of the room. Next moment I regretted it for I fell straight into the arms of either Polly or Dolly.

"Oh!" said she, "I've just been sewn up."

I reflected that this was my case also in another sense, but asked feebly if she knew the way downstairs.

She didn't; neither of us did, till at length we met Mrs. Smith coming to look for her.

If I had been a burglar she could not have regarded me with graver suspicions. But at any rate *she* knew the way downstairs. And there to my joy I found my old friend Scroope and his wife, both of them grown stout and elderly, but as jolly as ever, after which the Smith family ceased to trouble me.

Also there was the rector of the parish, Dr. Jeffreys and an absurdly young wife whom he had recently married, a fluffy-headed little thing with round eyes and a cheerful, perky manner. The two of them together looked exactly like a turkey-cock and a chicken. I remembered him well enough and to my astonishment he remembered me, perhaps because Lady Ragnall, when she had hastily invited him to meet the Smith family, mentioned that I was coming. Lastly there was the curate, a dark, young man who seemed to be always brooding over the secrets of time and eternity, though perhaps he was only thinking about his dinner or the next day's services.

Well, there we stood in that well-remembered drawing-room in which first I had made the acquaintance of Harut and Marut; also of the beautiful Miss Holmes as Lady Ragnall was then called. The Scroopes, the Jeffreys and I gathered in one group and the Atterby-Smiths in another like a force about to attack, while between the two, brooding and indeterminate, stood the curate, a neutral observer.

Presently Lady Ragnall arrived, apologizing for being late. For some reason best known to herself she had chosen to dress as though for a great party. I believe it was out of mischief and in order to show Mrs. Atterby-Smith some of the diamonds she was firmly determined that family should never inherit. At any rate there she stood glittering and lovely, and smiled upon us.

Then came dinner and once more I marched to the great hall in her company; Dr. Jeffreys got Mrs. Smith; Papa Smith got Mrs. Jeffreys who looked like a Grecian maiden walking into dinner with the Minotaur; Scroope got one of the Miss Smiths, she who wore a pink bow, the gloomy curate got the other with a blue bow, and Archibald got Mrs. Scroope who departed making faces at us over his shoulder.

"You look very grand and nice," I said to Lady Ragnall as we followed the others at a discreet distance.

"I am glad," she answered, "as to the nice, I mean. As for the grand, that dreadful woman is always writing to me about the Ragnall diamonds, so I thought that she should see some of them for the first and last time. Do you know I haven't worn these things since George and I went to Court together, and I daresay shall never wear them again, for there is only one ornament I care for and I have got *that* on under my dress."

I stared and her and with a laugh said that she was very mischievous.

"I suppose so," she replied, "but I detest those people who are pompous and rude and have spoiled my party. Do you know I had half a mind to come down in the dress that I wore as Isis in Kendah Land. I have got it upstairs and you shall see me in it before you go, for old time's sake. Only it occurred to me that they might think me mad, so I didn't. Dr. Jeffreys, will you say grace, please?"

Well, it was a most agreeable dinner so far as I was concerned, for I sat between my hostess and Mrs. Scroope and the rest were too far off for conversation. Moreover as Archibald developed an unexpected quantity of small talk, and Scroope on the other side amused himself by filling pink-bow Miss Smith's innocent mind with preposterous stories about Africa, as had happened to me once before at this table, Lady Ragnall and I were practically left undisturbed.

"Isn't it strange that we should find ourselves sitting here again after all these years, except that you are in my poor mother's place? Oh! when that scientific gentleman convinced me the other day that you whom I had heard were dead, were not only alive and well but actually in England, really I could have embraced him."

I thought of an answer but did not make it, though as usual she read my mind for I saw her smile.

"The truth is," she went on, "I am an only child and really have no friends, though of course being—well, you know," and she glanced at the jewels on her breast, "I have plenty of acquaintances."

"And suitors," I suggested.

"Yes," she replied blushing, "as many as Penelope, not one of whom cares twopence about me any more than I care for them. The truth is, Mr. Quatermain, that nobody and nothing interest me, except a spot in the churchyard yonder and another amid ruins in Egypt."

"You have had sad bereavements," I said looking the other way.

"Very sad and they have left life empty. Still I should not complain for I have had my share of good. Also it isn't true to say that nothing interests me. Egypt interests me, though after what has happened I do not feel as though I could return there. All Africa interests me and," she added dropping her voice, "I can say it because I know you will not misunderstand, you interest me, as you have always done since the first moment I saw you."

"*I!*" I exclaimed, staring at my own reflection in a silver plate which made me look—well, more unattractive than usual. "It's very kind of you to say so, but I can't understand why I should. You have seen very little of me, Lady Ragnall, except in that long journey across the desert when we did not talk much, since you were otherwise engaged."

"I know. That's the odd part of it, for I feel as though I had seen you for years and years and knew everything about you that one human being can know of another. Of course, too, I do know a good lot of your life through George and Harut."

"Harut was a great liar," I said uneasily.

"Was he? I always thought him painfully truthful, though how he got at the truth I do not know. Anyhow," she added with meaning, "don't suppose I think the worse of you because others have thought so well. Women who seem to be all different, generally, I notice, have this in common. If one or two of them like a man, the rest like him also because something in him appeals to the universal feminine instinct, and the same applies to their dislike. Now men, I think, are different in that respect."

"Perhaps because they are more catholic and charitable," I suggested, "or perhaps because they like those who like them."

She laughed in her charming way, and said,

"However these remarks do not apply to you and me, for as I think I told you once before in that cedar wood in Kendah Land where you feared lest I should catch a chill, or become—odd again, it is another you with whom something in me seems to be so intimate."

"That's fortunate for your sake," I muttered, still staring at and pointing to the silver plate.

Again she laughed. "Do you remember the *Taduki* herb?" she asked. "I have plenty of it safe upstairs, and not long ago I took a whiff of it, only a whiff because you know it had to be saved."

"And what did you see?"

"Never mind. The question is what shall we *both* see?"

"Nothing," I said firmly. "No earthly power will make me breathe that unholy drug again."

"Except me," she murmured with sweet decision. "No, don't think about leaving the house. You can't, there are no Sunday trains. Besides you won't if I ask you not."

"'In vain is the net spread in the sight of any bird,'" I replied, firm as a mountain.

"Is it? Then why are so many caught?"

At that moment the Bull of Bashan—I mean Smith, began to bellow something at his hostess from the other end of the table and our conversation came to an end.

"I say, old chap," whispered Scroope in my ear when we stood up to see the ladies out. "I suppose you are thinking of marrying again. Well, you might do worse," and he glanced at the glittering form of Lady Ragnall vanishing through the doorway behind her guests.

"Shut up, you idiot!" I replied indignantly.

"Why?" he asked with innocence. "Marriage is an honourable estate, especially when there is lots of the latter. I remember saying something of the sort to you years ago and at this table, when as it happened you also took in her ladyship. Only there was George in the wind then; now it has carried him away."

Without deigning any reply I seized my glass and went to sit down between the canon and the Bull of Bashan.

Allan Gives His Word

Mr. Atterby-Smith proved on acquaintance to be even worse than unfond fancy painted him. He was a gentleman in a way and of good family whereof the real name was Atterby, the Smith having been added to secure a moderate fortune left to him on that condition. His connection with Lord Ragnall was not close and through the mother's side. For the rest he lived in some south-coast watering-place and fancied himself a sportsman because he had on various occasions hired a Scottish moor or deer forest. Evidently he had never done anything nor earned a shilling during all his life and was bringing his family up to follow in his useless footsteps. The chief note of his character was that intolerable vanity which so often marks men who have nothing whatsoever about which to be vain. Also he had a great idea of his rights and what was due to him, which he appeared to consider included, upon what ground I could not in the least understand, the reversal of all the Ragnall properties and wealth. I do not think I need say any more about him, except that he bored me to extinction, especially after his fourth glass of port.

Perhaps, however, the son was worse, for he asked questions without number and when at last I was reduced to silence, lectured me about shooting. Yes, this callow youth who was at Sandhurst, instructed me, Allan Quatermain, how to kill elephants, he who had never seen an elephant except when he fed it with buns at the Zoo. At last Mr. Smith, who to Scroope's great amusement had taken the end of the table and assumed the position of host, gave the signal to move and we adjourned to the drawing-room.

I don't know what had happened but there we found the atmosphere distinctly stormy. The ample Mrs. Smith sat in a chair fanning herself, which caused the barbaric ornaments she wore to clank upon her fat arm. Upon either side of her, pale and indeterminate, stood Polly and Dolly each pretending to read a book. Somehow the three of them reminded me of a coat-of-arms seen in a nightmare, British Matron *sejant* with Modesty and Virtue as supporters. Opposite, on the other side of the fire and evidently very angry, stood Lady Ragnall, *regardant*.

"Do I understand you to say, Luna," I heard Mrs. A.-S. ask in resonant tones as I entered the room, "that you actually played the part of a heathen goddess among these savages, clad in a transparent bed-robe?"

"Yes, Mrs. Atterby-Smith," replied Lady Ragnall, "and a nightcap of feathers. I will put it on for you if you won't be shocked. Or perhaps one of your daughters——"

"Oh!" said both the young ladies together, "please be quiet. Here come the gentlemen."

After this there was a heavy silence broken only by the stifled giggles in the background of Mrs. Scroope and the canon's fluffy- headed wife, who to do her justice had some fun in her. Thank goodness the evening, or rather that part of it did not last long, since presently Mrs. Atterby-Smith, after studying me for a long while with a cold eye, rose majestically and swept off to bed followed by her offspring.

Afterwards I ascertained from Mrs. Scroope that Lady Ragnall had been amusing herself by taking away my character in every possible manner for the benefit of her connections, who were left with a general impression that I was the chief of a native tribe somewhere in Central Africa where I dwelt in light attire surrounded by the usual accessories. No wonder, therefore, that Mrs. A.-S. thought it best to remove her "Twin Pets," as she called them, out of my ravening reach.

Then the Scroopes went away, having arranged for me to lunch with them on the morrow, an invitation that I hastily accepted, though I heard Lady Ragnall mutter—"Mean!" beneath her breath. With them departed the canon and his wife and the curate, being, as they said, "early birds with duties to perform." After this Lady Ragnall paid me out by going to bed, having instructed Moxley to show us to the smoking room, "where," she whispered as she said good night, "I hope you will enjoy yourself."

Over the rest of the night I draw a veil. For a solid hour and three- quarters did I sit in that room between this dreadful pair, being alternately questioned and lectured. At length I could stand it no longer and while pretending to help myself to whiskey and soda, slipped through the door and fled upstairs.

I arrived late to breakfast purposely and found that I was wise, for Lady Ragnall was absent upstairs, recovering from "a headache." Mr. A.-Smith was also suffering from a headache downstairs, the result of champagne, port and whisky mixed, and all his family seemed to have pains in their tempers. Having ascertained that they were going to the church in the park, I departed to one two miles away and thence walked straight on to the Scroopes' where I had a very pleasant time, remaining till five in the afternoon. I returned to tea at the Castle where I found Lady Ragnall so cross that I went to church again, to the six o'clock service this time, only getting back in time to dress for dinner. Here I was paid out for I had to take in Mrs. Atterby-Smith. Oh! what a meal was that. We sat for the most part in solemn silence broken only by requests to pass the salt. I observed with satisfaction, however, that things were growing lively at the other end of the table where A.-Smith *pere* was drinking a good deal too much wine. At last I heard him say,

"We had hoped to spend a few days with you, my dear Luna. But as you tell us that your engagements make this impossible"—and he paused to drink some port, whereon Lady Ragnall remarked inconsequently,

"I assure you the ten o'clock train is far the best and I have ordered the carriage at half-past nine, which is not very early."

"As your engagements make this impossible," he repeated, "we would ask for the opportunity of a little family conclave with you to-night."

Here all of them turned and glowered at me.

"Certainly," said Lady Ragnall, "'the sooner 'tis over the sooner to sleep.' Mr. Quatermain, I am sure, will excuse us, will you not? I have had the museum lit up for you, Mr. Quatermain. You may find some Egyptian things there that will interest you."

"Oh, with pleasure!" I murmured, and fled away.

I spent a very instructive two hours in the museum, studying various Egyptian antiquities including a couple of mummies which rather terrified me. They looked so very corpse-like standing there in their wrappings. One was that of a lady who was a "Singer of Amen," I remember. I wondered where she was singing now and what song. Presently I came to a glass case which riveted my attention, for above it was a label bearing the following words: "Two Papyri given to Lady Ragnall by the priests of the Kendah Tribe in Africa." Within were the papyri unrolled and beneath each of the documents, its translation, so far as they could be translated for they were somewhat broken. No. 1, which was dated, "In the first year of Peroa," appeared to be the official appointment of the Royal Lady Amada, to be the prophetess to the temple of Isis and Horus the Child, which was also called Amada, and situated on the east bank of the Nile above Thebes. Evidently this was the same temple of which Lady Ragnall had written to me in her letter, where her husband had met his death by accident, a coincidence which made me start when I remembered how and where the document had come into her hands and what kind of office she filled at the time.

The second papyrus, or rather its translation, contained a most comprehensive curse upon any man who ventured to interfere with the personal sanctity of this same Royal Lady of Amada, who, apparently in virtue of her office, was doomed to perpetual celibacy like the vestal virgins. I do not remember all the terms of the curse, but I know that it invoked the vengeance of Isis the Mother, Lady of the Moon, and Horus the Child upon anyone who should dare such a desecration, and in so many words doomed him to death by violence "far from his own country where first he had looked on Ra," (i.e. the sun) and also to certain spiritual sufferings afterwards.

The document gave me the idea that it was composed in troubled days to protect that particularly sacred person, the Prophetess of Isis whose cult, as I have since learned, was rising in Egypt at the time, from threatened danger, perhaps at the hands of some foreign man. It occurred to me even that this Princess, for evidently she was a descendant of kings, had been appointed to a most sacred office for that very purpose. Men who shrink from little will often fear to incur the direct curse of widely venerated gods in order to obtain their desires, even if they be not their own gods. Such were my conclusions about this curious and ancient writing which I regret I cannot give in full as I neglected to copy it at the time.

I may add that it seemed extremely strange to me that it and the other which dealt with a particular temple in Egypt should have passed into Lady Ragnall's hands over two thousand years later in a distant part of Africa, and that subsequently her husband should have been killed in her presence whilst excavating the very temple to which they referred, whence too in all probability they were taken. Moreover, oddly enough Lady Ragnall had herself for a while filled the role of Isis in a shrine whereof these two papyri had been part of the sacred appurtenances for unknown ages, and one of her official titles there was Prophetess and Lady of the Moon, whose symbol she wore upon her breast.

Although I have always recognized that there are a great many more things in the world than are dreamt of in our philosophy, I say with truth and confidence that I am not a superstitious man. Yet I confess that these papers and the circumstances connected with them, made me feel afraid.

Also they made me wish that I had not come to Ragnall Castle.

Well, the Atterby-Smiths had so far effectually put a stop to any talk of such matters and even if Lady Ragnall should succeed in getting rid of them by that morning train, as to which I was doubtful, there remained but a single day of my visit during which it ought not to be hard to stave off the subject. Thus I reflected, standing face to face with those mummies, till presently I observed that the Singer of Amen who wore a staring, gold mask, seemed to be watching me with her oblong painted eyes. To my fancy a sardonic smile gathered in them and spread to the mouth.

"That's what *you* think," this smile seemed to say, "as once before you thought that Fate could be escaped. Wait and see, my friend. Wait and see!"

"Not in this room any way," I remarked aloud, and departed in a hurry down the passage which led to the main staircase.

Before I reached its end a remarkable sight caused me to halt in the shadow. The Atterby-Smith family were going to bed *en bloc*. They marched in single file up the great stair, each of them carrying a hand candle. Papa led and young Hopeful brought up the rear. Their countenances were full of war, even the twins looked like angry lambs, but something written on them informed me that they had suffered defeat recent and grievous. So they vanished up the stairway and out of my ken for ever.

When they had gone I started again and ran straight into Lady Ragnall. If her guests had been angry, it was clear that *she* was furious, almost weeping with rage, indeed. Moreover, she turned and rent me.

"You are a wretch," she said, "to run away and leave me all day long with those horrible people. Well, they will never come here again, for I have told them that if they do the servants have orders to shut the door in their faces."

Not knowing what to say I remarked that I had spent a most instructive evening in the museum, which seemed to make her angrier than ever. At any rate she whisked off without even saying "good night" and left me standing there. Afterwards I learned that the A.-S.'s had calmly informed Lady Ragnall that she had stolen their property and demanded that "as an act of justice" she should make a will leaving everything she possessed to them, and meanwhile furnish them with an allowance of L4,000 a year. What I did not learn were the exact terms of her answer.

Next morning Alfred, when he called me, brought me a note from his mistress which I fully expected would contain a request that I should depart by the same train as her other guests. Its real contents, however, were very different.

"My dear Friend," it ran, "I am so ashamed of myself and so sorry for my rudeness last night, for which I deeply apologise. If you knew all that I had gone through at the hands of those dreadful mendicants, you would forgive me.—L.R."

"P.S.—I have ordered breakfast at 10. Don't go down much before, for your own sake."

Somewhat relieved in my mind, for I thought she was really angry with me, not altogether without cause, I rose, dressed and set to work to write some letters. While I was doing so I heard the wheels of a carriage beneath and opening my window, saw the Atterby-Smith family in the act of departing in the Castle bus. Smith himself seemed to be still enraged, but the others looked depressed. Indeed I heard the wife of his bosom say to him,

"Calm yourself, my dear. Remember that Providence knows what is best for us and that beggars on horseback are always unjust and ungrateful."

To which her spouse replied,

"Hold your infernal tongue, will you," and then began to rate the servants about the luggage.

Well, off they went. Glaring through the door of the bus, Mr. Smith caught sight of me leaning out of the window, seeing which I waved my hand to him in adieu. His only reply to this courtesy was to shake his fist, though whether at me or at the Castle and its inhabitants in general, I neither know nor care.

When I was quite sure that they had gone and were not coming back again to find something they had forgotten, I went downstairs and surprised a conclave between the butler, Moxley, and his satellites, reinforced by Lady Ragnall's maid and two other female servants.

"Gratuities!" Moxley was exclaiming, which I thought a fine word for tips, "not a smell of them! His gratuities were—'Damn your eyes, you fat bottle-washer,' being his name for butler. *My* eyes, mind you, Ann, not Alfred's or William's, and that because he had tumbled over his own rugs. Gentleman! Why, I name him a hog with his litter."

"Hogs don't have litters, Mr. Moxley," observed Ann smartly.

"Well, young woman, if there weren't no hogs, there'd be no litters, so there! However, he won't root about in this castle no more, for I happened to catch a word or two of what passed between him and her Ladyship last night. He said straight out that she was making love to that little Mr. Quatermain who wanted her money, and probably not for the first time as they had forgathered in Africa. A gentleman, mind you, Ann, who although peculiar, I like, and who, the keeper Charles tells me, is the best shot in the whole world."

"And what did she say to that?" asked Ann.

"What did she say? What didn't she say, that's the question. It was just as though all the furniture in the room got up and went for them Smiths. Well, having heard enough, and more than I wanted, I stepped off with the tray and next minute out they all come and grab the bedroom candlesticks. That's all and there's her Ladyship's bell. Alfred, don't stand gaping there but go and light the hot-plates."

So they melted away and I descended from the landing, indignant but laughing. No wonder that Lady Ragnall lost her temper!

Ten minutes later she arrived in the dining-room, waving a lighted ribbon that disseminated perfume.

"What on earth are you doing?" I asked.

"Fumigating the house," she said. "It is unnecessary as I don't think they were infectious, but the ceremony has a moral significance—like incense. Anyway it relieves my feelings."

Then she laughed and threw the remains of the ribbon into the fire, adding,

"If you say a word about those people I'll leave the room."

I think we had one of the jolliest breakfasts I ever remember. To begin with we were both hungry since our miseries of the night before had prevented us from eating any dinner. Indeed she swore that she had scarcely tasted food since Saturday. Then we had such a lot to talk about. With short intervals we talked all that day, either in the house or while walking through the gardens and grounds. Passing through the latter I came to the spot on the back drive where once I had saved her from being abducted by Harut and Marut, and as I recognized it, uttered an exclamation. She asked me why and the end of it was that I told her all that story which to this moment she had never heard, for Ragnall had thought well to keep it from her.

She listened intently, then said,

"So I owe you more than I knew. Yet, I'm not sure, for you see I was abducted after all. Also if I had been taken there, probably George would never have married me or seen me again, and that might have been better for him."

"Why?" I asked. "You were all the world to him."

"Is any woman ever all the world to a man, Mr. Quatermain?"

I hesitated, expecting some attack.

"Don't answer," she went on, "it would be too long and you wouldn't convince me who have been in the East. However, he was all the world to me. Therefore his welfare was what I wished and wish, and I think he would have had more of it if he had never married me."

"Why?" I asked again.

"Because I brought him no good luck, did I? I needn't go through all the story as you know it. And in the end it was through me that he was killed in Egypt."

"Or through the goddess Isis," I broke in rather nervously.

"Yes, the goddess Isis, a part I have played in my time, or something like it. And he was killed in the temple of the goddess Isis. And those papyri of which you read the translations in the museum, which were given to me in Kendah Land, seem to have come from that same temple. And—how about the Ivory Child? Isis in the temple evidently held a child in her arms, but when we found her it had gone. Supposing this child was the same as that of which I was guardian! It might have been, since the papyri came from that temple. What do you think?"

"I don't think anything," I answered, "except that it is all very odd. I don't even understand what Isis and the child Horus represent. They were not mere images either in Egypt or Kendah Land. There must be an idea behind them somewhere."

"Oh! there was. Isis was the universal Mother, Nature herself with all the powers, seen and unseen, that are hidden in Nature; Love personified also, although not actually the queen of Love like Hathor, her sister goddess. The Horus child, whom the old Egyptians called Heru-Hennu, signified eternal regeneration, eternal youth, eternal strength and beauty. Also he was the Avenger who overthrew Set, the Prince of Darkness, and thus in a way opened the Door of Life to men."

"It seems to me that all religions have much in common," I said.

"Yes, a great deal. It was easy for the old Egyptians to become Christian, since for many of them it only meant worshipping Isis and Horus under new and holier names. But come in, it grows cold."

We had tea in Lady Ragnall's boudoir and after it had been taken away our conversation died. She sat there on the other side of the fire with a cigarette between her lips, looking at me through the perfumed smoke till I began to grow uncomfortable and to feel that a crisis of some sort was at hand. This proved perfectly correct, for it was. Presently she said,

"We took a long journey once together, Mr. Quatermain, did we not?"

"Undoubtedly," I answered, and began to talk of it until she cut me short with a wave of her hand, and went on,

"Well, we are going to take a longer one together after dinner to-night."

"What! Where! How!" I exclaimed much alarmed.

"I don't know where, but as for how—look in that box," and she pointed to a little carved Eastern chest made of rose or sandal wood, that stood upon a table between us.

With a groan I rose and opened it. Inside was another box made of silver. This I opened also and perceived that within lay bundles of dried leaves that looked like tobacco, from which floated an enervating and well-remembered scent that clouded my brain for a moment. Then I shut down the lids and returned to my seat.

"*Taduki*," I murmured.

"Yes, *Taduki*, and I believe in perfect order with all its virtue intact."

"Virtue!" I exclaimed. "I don't think there is any virtue about that hateful and magical herb which I believe grew in the devil's garden. Moreover, Lady Ragnall, although there are few things in the world that I would refuse you, I tell you at once that nothing will induce me to have anything more to do with it."

She laughed softly and asked why not.

"Because I find life so full of perplexities and memories that I have no wish to make acquaintance with any more, such as I am sure lie hid by the thousand in that box."

"If so, don't you think that they might clear up some of those which surround you to-day?"

"No, for in such things there is no finality, since whatever one saw would also require explanation."

"Don't let us argue," she replied. "It is tiring and I daresay we shall need all our strength to-night."

I looked at her speechless. Why could she not take No for an answer? As usual she read my thought and replied to it.

"Why did not Adam refuse the apple that Eve offered him?" she inquired musingly. "Or rather why did he eat it after many refusals and learn the secret of good and evil, to the great gain of the world which thenceforward became acquainted with the dignity of labour?"

"Because the woman tempted him," I snapped.

"Quite so. It has always been her business in life and always will be. Well, I am tempting you now, and not in vain."

"Do you remember who was tempting the woman?"

"Certainly. Also that he was a good school-master since he caused the thirst for knowledge to overcome fear and thus laid the foundation- stone of all human progress. That allegory may be read two ways, as one of a rise from ignorance instead of a fall from innocence."

"You are too clever for me with your perverted notions. Also, you said we were not to argue. I have therefore only to repeat that I will not eat your apple, or rather, breathe your *Taduki*."

"Adam over again," she replied, shaking her head. "The same old beginning and the same old end, because you see at last you will do exactly what Adam did."

Here she rose and standing over me, looked me straight in the eyes with the curious result that all my will power seemed to evaporate. Then she sat down again, laughing softly, and remarked as though to herself,

"Who would have thought that Allan Quatermain was a moral coward!"

"Coward," I repeated. "Coward!"

"Yes, that's the right word. At least you were a minute ago. Now courage has come back to you. Why, it's almost time to dress for dinner, but before you go, listen.

I have some power over you, my friend, as you have some power over me, for I tell you frankly if you wished me very much to do anything, I should have to do it; and the same applies conversely. Now, to-night we are, as I believe, going to open a great gate and to see wonderful things, glorious things that will thrill us for the rest of our lives, and perhaps suggest to us what is coming after death. You will not fail me, will you?" she continued in a pleading voice. "If you do I must try alone since no one else will serve, and then I *know*—how I cannot say—that I shall be exposed to great danger. Yes, I think that I shall lose my mind once more and never find it again this side the grave. You would not have that happen to me, would you, just because you shrink from digging up old memories?"

"Of course not," I stammered. "I should never forgive myself."

"Yes, of course not. There was really no need for me to ask you. Then you promise you will do all I wish?" and once more she looked at me, adding, "Don't be ashamed, for you remember that I have been in touch with hidden things and am not quite as other women are. You will recollect I told you that which I have never breathed to any other living soul, years ago on that night when first we met."

"I promise," I answered and was about to add something, I forget what, when she cut me short, saying,

"That's enough, for I know your word is rather better than your bond. Now dress as quickly as you can or the dinner will be spoiled."

Through the Gates

Short as was the time at my disposal before the dinner-gong sounded, it proved ample for reflection. With every article of attire that I discarded went some of that boudoir glamour till its last traces vanished with my walking-boots. I was fallen indeed. I who had come to this place so full of virtuous resolutions, could now only reflect upon the true and universal meaning of our daily prayer that we might be kept from temptation. And yet what had tempted me? For my life's sake I could not say. The desire to please a most charming woman and to keep her from making solitary experiments of a dangerous nature, I suppose, though whether they should be less dangerous carried out jointly remained to be seen. Certainly it was not any wish to eat of her proffered apple of Knowledge, for already I knew a great deal more than I cared for about things in general. Oh! the truth was that woman is the mightiest force in the world, at any rate where the majority of us poor men is concerned. She commanded and I must obey.

I grew desperate and wondered if I could escape. Perhaps I might slip out of the back door and run for it, without my great coat or hat although the night was so cold and I should probably be taken up as a lunatic. No, it was impossible for I had forged a chain that might not be broken. I had passed my word of honour. Well, I was in for it and after all what was there of which I need be afraid that I should tremble and shrink back as though I were about to run away with somebody's wife, or rather to be run away with quite contrary to my own inclination? Nothing at all. A mere nonsensical ordeal much less serious than a visit to the dentist.

Probably that stuff had lost its strength by now—that is, unless it had grown more powerful by keeping, as is the case with certain sorts of explosives. And if it had not, the worst to be expected was a silly dream, followed perhaps by headache. That is, unless I did not chance to wake up again at all in this world, which was a most unpleasant possibility. Another thing, suppose I woke and she didn't! What should I say then? Of a certainty I should find myself in the dock. Yes, and there were further dreadful eventualities, quite conceivable, every one of them, the very thought of which plunged me into a cold perspiration and made me feel so weak that I was obliged to sit down.

Then I heard the gong; to me it sounded like the execution bell to a prisoner under sentence of death. I crept downstairs feebly and found Lady Ragnall waiting for me in the drawing-room, clothed with gaiety as with a garment. I remember that it made me most indignant that she could be so happy in such circumstances, but I said nothing. She looked me up and down and remarked,

"Really from your appearance you might have seen the Ragnall ghost, or be going to be married against your will, or—I don't know what. Also you have forgotten to fasten your tie."

I looked in the glass. It was true, for there hung the ends down my shirt front. Then I struggled with the wretched thing until at last she had to help me, which she did laughing softly. Somehow her touch gave me confidence again and enabled me to say quite boldly that I only wanted my dinner.

"Yes," she replied, "but you are not to eat much and you must only drink water. The priestesses in Kendah Land told me that this was necessary before taking *Taduki* in its strongest form, as we are going to do to-night. You know the prophet Harut only gave us the merest whiff in this room years ago."

I groaned and she laughed again.

That dinner with nothing to drink, although to avoid suspicion I let Moxley fill my glass once or twice, and little to eat for my appetite had vanished, went by like a bad dream. I recall no more about it until I heard Lady Ragnall tell Moxley to see that there was a good fire in the museum where we were going to study that night and must not be disturbed.

Another minute and I was automatically opening the door for her. As she passed she paused to do something to her dress and whispered,

"Come in a quarter of an hour. Mind—no port which clouds the intellect."

"I have none left to cloud," I remarked after her.

Then I went back and sat by the fire feeling most miserable and staring at the decanters, for never in my life do I remember wanting a bottle of wine more. The big clock ticked and ticked and at last chimed the quarter, jarring on my nerves in that great lonely banqueting hall. Then I rose and crept upstairs like an evil-doer and it seemed to me that the servants in the hall looked on me with suspicion, as well they might.

I reached the museum and found it brilliantly lit, but empty except for the cheerful company of the two mummies who also appeared to regard me with gleaming but doubtful eyes. So I sat down there in front of the fire, not even daring to smoke lest tobacco should complicate *Taduki*.

Presently I heard a low sound of laughter, looked up and nearly fell backwards, that is, metaphorically, for the chair prevented such a physical collapse.

It was not wonderful since before me, like a bride of ancient days adorned for her husband, stood the goddess Isis—white robes, feathered headdress, ancient bracelets, gold-studded sandals on bare feet, scented hair, ruby necklace and all the rest. I stared, then there burst from me words which were the last I meant to say,

"Great Heavens! how beautiful you are."

"Am I?" she asked. "I am glad," and she glided across the room and locked the door.

"Now," she said, returning, "we had better get to business, that is unless you would like to worship the goddess Isis a little first, to bring yourself into a proper frame of mind, you know."

"No," I replied, my dignity returning to me. "I do not wish to worship any goddess, especially when she isn't a goddess. It was not a part of the bargain."

"Quite so," she said, nodding, "but who knows what you will be worshipping before an hour is over? Oh! forgive me for laughing at you, but I can't help it. You are so evidently frightened."

"Who wouldn't be frightened?" I answered, looking with gloomy apprehension at the sandal-wood box which had appeared upon a case full of scarabs. "Look here, Lady Ragnall," I added, "why can't you leave all this unholy business alone and let us spend a pleasant evening talking, now that those Smith people have gone? I have lots of stories about my African adventures which would interest you."

"Because I want to hear my own African adventures, and perhaps yours too, which I am sure will interest me a great deal more," she exclaimed earnestly. "You think it is all foolishness, but it is not. Those Kendah priestesses told me much when I seemed to be out of my mind. For a long time I did not remember what they said, but of late years, especially since George and I began to excavate that temple, plenty has come back to me bit by bit, fragments, you know, that make me desire to learn the rest as I never desired anything else on earth. And the worst of it has always been that from the beginning I have known—and know—that this can only happen with you and through you, why I cannot say, or have forgotten. That's what sent me nearly wild with joy when I heard that you were not only alive, but in this country. You won't disappoint me, will you? There is nothing I can offer you which would have any value for you, so I can only beg you not to disappoint me—well, because I am your friend."

I turned away my head, hesitating, and when I looked up again I saw that her beautiful eyes were full of tears. Naturally that settled the matter, so I only said,

"Let us get on with the affair. What am I to do? Stop a bit. I may as well provide against eventualities," and going to a table I took a sheet of notepaper and wrote:

"Lady Ragnall and I, Allan Quatermain, are about to make an experiment with an herb which we discovered some years ago in Africa. If by any chance this should result in accident to either or both of us, the Coroner is requested to understand that it is not a case of murder or of suicide, but merely of unfortunate scientific research."

This I dated, adding the hour, 9.47 P.M., and signed, requesting her to do the same.

She obeyed with a smile, saying it was strange that one who had lived a life of such constant danger as myself, should be so afraid to die.

"Look here, young lady," I replied with irritation, "doesn't it occur to you that *I* may be afraid lest *you* should die—and *I* be hanged for it," I added by an afterthought.

"Oh! I see," she answered, "that is really very nice of you. But, of course, you would think like that; it is your nature."

"Yes," I replied. "Nature, not merit."

She went to a cupboard which formed the bottom of one of the mahogany museum cases, and extracted from it first of all a bowl of ancient appearance made of some black stone with projecting knobs for handles that were carved with the heads of women wearing ceremonial wigs; and next a low tripod of ebony or some other black wood. I looked at these articles and recognized them. They had stood in front of the sanctuary in the temple in Kendah Land, and over them I had once seen this very woman dressed as she was to-night, bend her head in the magic smoke before she had uttered the prophecy of the passing of the Kendah god.

"So you brought these away too," I said.

"Yes," she replied with solemnity, "that they might be ready at the appointed hour when we needed them."

Then she spoke no more for a while, but busied herself with certain rather eerie preparations. First she set the tripod and its bowl in an open space which I was glad to note was at some distance from the fire, since if either of us fell into that who would there be to take us off before cremation ensued? Then she drew up a curved settee with a back and arms, a comfortable-looking article having a seat that sloped backwards like those in clubs, and motioned to me to sit down. This I did with much the same sensations that are evoked by taking one's place upon an operation-table.

Next she brought that accursed *Taduki* box, I mean the inner silver one, the contents of which I heartily wished I had thrown upon the fire, and set it down, open, near the tripod. Lastly she lifted some glowing embers of wood from the grate with tongs, and dropped them into the stone bowl.

"I think that's all. Now for the great adventure," she said in a voice that was at once rapt and dreamy.

"What am I to do?" I asked feebly.

"That is quite simple," she replied, as she sat herself down beside me well within reach of the *Taduki* box, the brazier being between us with its tripod stand pressed against the edge of the couch, and in its curve, so that we were really upon each side of it. "When the smoke begins to rise thickly you have only to bend your head a little forward, with your shoulders still resting against the settee, and inhale until you find your senses leaving you, though I don't know that this is necessary for the stuff is subtle. Then throw your head back, go to sleep and dream."

"What am I to dream about?" I inquired in a vacuous way, for my senses were leaving me already.

"You will dream, I think, of past events in which both of us played a part, at least I hope so. I dreamt of them before in Kendah Land, but then I was not myself, and for the most part they are forgotten. Moreover, I learned that we can only see them all when we are together. Now speak no more."

This command, by the way, at once produced in me an intense desire for prolonged conversation. It was not to be gratified, however, for at that moment she stood up again facing the tripod and me, and began to sing in a rich and thrilling voice. What she sang I do not know for I could not understand the language, but I presume it was some ancient chant that she learned in Kendah Land. At any rate, there she stood, a lovely and inspired priestess clad in her sacerdotal robes, and sang, waving her arms and fixing her eyes upon mine. Presently she bent down, took a little of the *Taduki* weed and with words of incantation, dropped it upon the embers in the bowl. Twice she did this, then sat herself upon the couch and waited.

A clear flame sprang up and burned for thirty seconds or so, I suppose while it consumed the volatile oils in the weed. Then it died down and smoke began to come, white, rich and billowy, with a very pleasant odour resembling that of hot-house flowers. It spread out between us like a fan, and though its veil I heard her say,

"The gates are wide. Enter!"

I knew what she meant well enough, and though for a moment I thought of cheating, there is no other word for it, knew also that she had detected the thought and was scorning me in her mind. At any rate I felt that I must obey and thrust my head forward into the smoke, as a green ham is thrust into a chimney. The warm vapour struck against my face like fog, or rather steam, but without causing me to choke or my eyes to smart. I drew it down my throat with a deep inhalation—once, twice, thrice, then as my brain began to swim, threw myself back as I had been instructed to do. A deep and happy drowsiness stole over me, and the last thing I remember was hearing the clock strike the first two strokes of the hour of ten. The third stroke I heard also, but it sounded like to that of the richest-throated bell that ever boomed in all the world. I remember becoming aware that it was the signal for the rolling up of some vast proscenium, revealing behind it a stage that was the world—nothing less.

What did I see? What did I see? Let me try to recall and record.

First of all something chaotic. Great rushes of vapour driven by mighty winds; great seas, for the most part calm. Then upheavals and volcanoes spouting fire. Then tropic scenes of infinite luxuriance. Terrific reptiles feeding on the brinks of marshes, and huge elephant- like animals moving between palms beyond. Then, in a glade, rough huts and about them a jabbering crowd of creatures that were only half human, for sometimes they stood upright and sometimes ran on their hands and feet. Also they were almost covered with hair which was all they had in the way of clothes, and at the moment that I met them, were terribly frightened by the appearance of a huge mammoth, if that is the right name for it, which walked into the glade and looked at us. At any rate it was a beast of the elephant tribe which I judged to be nearly twenty feet high, with enormous curving tusks.

The point of the vision was that I recognized myself among those hairy jabberers, not by anything outward and visible, but by something inward and spiritual. Moreover, I was being urged by a female of the race, I can scarcely call her a woman, to justify my existence by tackling the mammoth in her particular interest, or to give her up to someone who would. In the end I tackled it, rushing forward with a weapon, I think it was a sharp stone tied to a stick, though how I could expect to hurt a beast twenty feet high with such a thing is more than I can understand, unless perhaps the stone was poisoned.

At any rate the end was sudden. I threw the stone, whereat a great trunk shot out from between the tusks and caught me. Round and round I went in the air, reflecting as I did so, for I suppose at the time my normal consciousness had not quite left me, that this was my first encounter with the elephant Jana, also that it was very foolish to try to oblige a female regardless of personal risk. . . .

All became dark, as no doubt it would have done, but presently, that is after a lapse of a great many thousands of years, or so it appeared to me, light grew again.

This time I was a black man living in something not unlike a Kaffir kraal on the top of a hill.

There was shouting below and enemies attacked us; a woman rushed out of a hut and gave me a spear and a shield, the latter made of wood with white spots on it, and pointed to the path of duty which ran down the hill. I followed in company with others, though without enthusiasm, and presently met a roaring giant of a man at the bottom. I stuck my spear into him and he stuck his into me, through the stomach, which hurt me most abominably. After this I retired up the hill where the woman pulled the spear out and gave it to another man. I remember no more.

Then followed a whole maze of visions, but really I cannot disentangle them. Nor is it worth while doing so since after all they were only of the nature of an overture, jumbled incidents of former lives, real or imaginary, or so I suppose, having to do, all of them, with elementary things, such as hunger and wounds and women and death.

At length these broken fragments of the past were swept away out of my consciousness and I found myself face to face with something connected and tangible, not too remote or unfamiliar for understanding. It was the beginning of the real story.

I, please remember always that I knew it was I, Allan, and no one else, that is, the same personality or whatever it may be which makes each man different from any other man, saw myself in a chariot drawn by two horses with arched necks and driven by a charioteer who sat on a little seat in front. It was a highly ornamented, springless vehicle of wood and gilded, something like a packing-case with a pole, or as we should call it in South Africa, a disselboom, to which the horses were harnessed. In this cart I stood arrayed in flowing robes fastened round my middle by a studded belt, with strips of coloured cloth wound round my legs and sandals on my feet. To my mind the general effect of the attire was distinctly feminine and I did not like it at all.

I was glad to observe, however, that the I of those days was anything but feminine. Indeed I could never have believed that once I was so good-looking, even over two thousand years ago. I was not very tall but extremely stalwart, burly almost, with an arm that as I could observe, since it projected from the sleeve of my lady's gown, would have done no discredit to a prize-fighter, and a chest like a bull.

The face also I admired very much. The brow was broad; the black eyes were full and proud-looking, the features somewhat massive but well- cut and highly intelligent; the mouth firm and shapely, with lips that were perhaps a trifle too thick; the hair—well, there was rather a failure in the hair, at least according to modern ideas, for it curled so beautifully as to suggest that one of my ancestors might have fallen in love with a person of negroid origin. However there was lots of it, hanging down almost to the shoulders and bound about the brow by a very neat fillet of blue cloth with silver studs. The colour of my skin, I was glad to note, was by no means black, only a light and pleasing brown such as might have been produced by sunburn. My age, I might add, was anywhere between five and twenty and five and thirty, perhaps nearer the latter than the former, at any rate, the very prime of life.

For the rest, I held in my left hand a very stout, long bow of black wood which seemed to have seen much service, with a string of what looked like catgut, on which was set a broad-feathered, barbed arrow. This I kept in place with the fingers of my right hand, on one of which I observed a handsome gold ring with strange characters carved upon the bezel.

Now for the charioteer.

He was black as night, black as a Sunday hat, with yellow rolling eyes set in a countenance of extraordinary ugliness and I may add, extraordinary humour. His big, wide mouth with thick lips ran up the left side of his face towards an ear that was also big and projecting. His hair, that had a feather stuck in it, was real nigger wool covering a skull like a cannon ball and I should imagine as hard. This head, by the way, was set plumb upon the shoulders, as though it had been driven down between them by a pile hammer. They were very broad shoulders suggesting enormous strength, but the gaily-clad body beneath, which was supported by two bowed legs and large, flat feet, was that of a dwarf who by the proportions of his limbs Nature first intended for a giant; yes, an Ethiopian dwarf.

Looking through this remarkable exterior, as it were, I recognized that inside of it was the soul, or animating principle, of—whom do you think? None other than my beloved old servant and companion, the Hottentot Hans whose loss I had mourned for years! Hans himself who died for me, slaying the great elephant, Jana, in Kendah Land, the elephant I could not hit, and thereby saving my life. Oh! although I had been obliged to go back to the days of I knew not what ancient empire to do so in my trance, or whatever it was, I could have wept with joy at finding him again, especially as I knew by instinct that as he loved the Allan Quatermain of to-day, so he loved this Egyptian in a wheeled packing-case, for I may as well say at once that such was my nationality in the dream.

Now I looked about me and perceived that my chariot was the second of a cavalcade. Immediately in front of it was one infinitely more gorgeous in which stood a person who even if I had not known it, I should have guessed to be a king, and who, as a matter of fact, was none other than the King of kings, at that time the absolute master of most of the known world, though what his name may have been, I have no notion. He wore a long flowing robe of purple silk embroidered with gold and bound in at the waist by a jewelled girdle from which hung the private, sacred seal; the little "White Seal" that, as I learned afterwards, was famous throughout the earth.

On his head was a stiff cloth cap, also purple in colour, round which was fastened a fillet of light blue stuff spotted with white. The best idea that I can give of its general appearance is to liken it to a tall hat of fashionable shape, without a brim, slightly squashed in so that it bulged at the top, and surrounded by a rather sporting necktie. Really, however, it was the *kitaris* or headdress of these monarchs worn by them alone. If anyone else had put on that hat, even by mistake in the dark, well, his head would have come off with it, that is all.

This king held a bow in his hand with an arrow set upon its string, just as I did, for we were out hunting, and as I shall have to narrate presently, lions are no respecters of persons. By his side, leaning against the back of the chariot, was a tall, sharp-pointed wand of cedar wood with a knob of some green precious stone, probably an emerald, fashioned to the likeness of an apple. This was the royal sceptre. Immediately behind the chariot walked several great nobles. One of them carried a golden footstool, another a parasol, furled at the moment; another a spare bow and a quiver of arrows, and another a jewelled fly-whisk made of palm fibre.

The king, I should add, was young, handsome with a curled beard and clear-cut, high-bred looking features; his face, however, was bad, cruel and stamped with an air of weariness, or rather, satiety, which was emphasized by the black circles beneath his fine dark eyes. Moreover pride seemed to emanate from him and yet there was something in his bearing and glances which suggested fear. He was a god who knows that he is mortal and is therefore afraid lest at any moment he may be called upon to lose his godship in his mortality.

Not that he dreaded the perils of the chase; he was too much of a man for that. But how could he tell lest among all that crowd of crawling nobles, there was not one who had a dagger ready for his back, or a phial of poison to mix with his wine or water? He with all the world in the hollow of his hand, was filled with secret terrors which as I learned since first I seemed to see him thus, fulfilled themselves at the appointed time. For this man of blood was destined to die in blood, though not by murder.

The cavalcade halted. Presently a fat eunuch glittering in his gold- wrought garments like some bronzed beetle in the sunlight, came waddling back towards me.

He was odious and I knew that we hated each other.

"Greeting, Egyptian," he said, mopping his brow with his sleeve for the sun was hot. "An honour for you! A great honour! The King of kings commands your presence. Yes, he would speak with you with his own lips, and with that abortion of a servant of yours also. Come! Come swiftly!"

"Swift as an arrow, Houman," I answered laughing, "seeing that for three moons I, like an arrow, have rested upon the string and flown no nearer to his Majesty."

"Three moons!" screeched the eunuch. "Why, many wait three years and many go to the grave still waiting; bigger men than you, Egyptian, though I hear you do claim to be of royal blood yonder on the Nile. But talk not of arrows flying towards the most High, for surely it is ill-omened and might earn you another honour, that of the string," and he made a motion suggestive of a cord encircling his throat. "Man, leave your bow behind! Would you appear before the King armed? Yes, and your dagger also."

"Perchance a lion might appear before the King and he does not leave his claws and teeth behind," I answered drily as I divested myself of my weapons.

Then we started, the three of us, leaving the chariot in charge of a soldier.

"Draw your sleeves over your hands," said the eunuch. "None must appear before the King showing his hands, and, dwarf, since you have no sleeves, thrust yours into your robe."

"What am I to do with my feet?" he answered in a thick, guttural voice. "Will it offend the King of kings to see my feet, most noble eunuch?"

"Certainly, certainly," answered Houman, "since they are ugly enough to offend even me. Hide them as much as possible. Now we are near, down on your faces and crawl forward slowly on your knees and elbows, as I do. Down, I say!"

So down I went, though with anger in my heart, for be it remembered that I, the modern Allan Quatermain, knew every thought and feeling that passed through the mind of my prototype.

It was as though I were a spectator at a play, with this difference. I could read the motives and reflections of this former *ego* as well as observe his actions. Also I could rejoice when he rejoiced, weep when he wept and generally feel all that he felt, though at the same time I retained the power of studying him from my own modern standpoint and with my own existing intelligence. Being two we still were one, or being one we still were two, whichever way you like to put it. Lastly I lacked these powers with reference to the other actors in the piece. Of these I knew just as much, or as little as my former self knew, that is if he ever really existed. There was nothing unnatural in my faculties where they were concerned. I had no insight into their souls any more than I have into those of the people about me to-day. Now I hope that I have made clear my somewhat uncommon position with reference to these pages from the Book of the Past.

Well, preceded by the eunuch and followed by the dwarf, I crawled though the sand in which grew some thorny plants that pricked my knees and fingers, towards the person of the Monarch of the World. He had descended from his chariot by help of a footstool, and was engaged in drinking from a golden cup, while his attendants stood around in various attitudes of adoration, he who had handed him the cup being upon his knees. Presently he looked up and saw us.

"Who are these?" he asked in a high voice that yet was not unmusical, "and why do you bring them into my presence?"

"May it please the King," answered our guide, knocking his head upon the ground in a very agony of humiliation, "may it please the King——"

"It would please me better, dog, if you answered my question. Who are they?"

"May it please the King, this is the Egyptian hunter and noble, Shabaka."

"I hear," said his Majesty with a gleam of interest in his tired eyes, "and what does this Egyptian here?"

"May it please the King, the King bade me bring him to the presence, but now when the chariots halted."

"I forgot; you are forgiven. But who is that with him? Is it a man or an ape?"

Here I screwed my head round and saw that my slave in his efforts to obey the eunuch's instructions and hide his feet, had made himself into a kind of ball, much as a hedgehog does, except that his big head appeared in front of the ball.

"O King, that I understand is the Egyptian's servant and charioteer."

Again he looked interested, and exclaimed,

"Is it so? Then Egypt must be a stranger country than I thought if such ape-men live there. Stand up, Egyptian, and bid your ape stand up also, for I cannot hear men who speak with their mouths in the dust."

So I rose and saluted by lifting both my hands and bowing as I had observed others do, trying, however, to keep them covered by my sleeves. The King looked me up and down, then said briefly,

"Set out your name and the business that brought you to my city."

"May the King live for ever," I replied. "As this lord said," and I pointed to the eunuch——

"He is not a lord but a dog," interrupted the Monarch, "who wears the robe of women. But continue."

"As this dog who wears the robe of women said"—here the King laughed, but the eunuch, Houman, turned green with rage and glowered at me—"my name is Shabaka. I am a descendant of the Ethiopian king of Egypt of that same name."

"It seems from all I hear that there are too many descendants of kings in Egypt. When I visit that land which perhaps soon I must do with an army at my back," here he stared at me coldly, "it may be well to lessen their number. There is a certain Peroa for instance."

He paused, but I made no answer, since Peroa was my father's cousin and of the fallen Royal House; also the protector of my youth.

"Well, Shabaka," he went on, "in Persia royal blood is common also, though some of us think it looks best when it is shed. What else are you?"

"A slayer of royal beasts, O King of kings, a hunter of lions and of elephants," (this statement interested me, Allan Quatermain, intensely, showing me as it did that our tastes are very persistent); "also when I am at home, a breeder of cattle and a grower of grain."

"Good trades, all of them, Shabaka. But why came you here?"

"Idernes the satrap of Egypt, servant of the King of kings, sought for one who would travel to the East because the King of kings desired to hear of the hunting of lions in the lands that lie to the south of Egypt towards the beginnings of the great river. Then I, who desired to see new countries, said, 'Here am I. Send me.' So I came and for three moons have dwelt in the royal city, but till this hour have scarcely so much as seen the face of the great King, although by many messengers I have announced my presence, showing them the letters of Idernes giving me safe-conduct. Therefore I propose to-morrow or the next day to return to Egypt."

The King said a word and a scribe appeared whom he commanded to take note of my words and let the matter be inquired of, since some should suffer for this neglect, a saying at which I saw Houman and certain of the nobles turn pale and whisper to each other.

"Now I remember," he exclaimed, "that I did desire Idernes to send me an Egyptian hunter. Well, you are here and we are about to hunt the lion of which there are many in yonder reeds, hungry and fierce beasts, since for three days they have been herded in so that they can kill no food. How many lions have you slain, Shabaka?"

"Fifty and three in all, O King, not counting the cubs."

He stared at me, answering with a sneer,

"You Egyptians have large mouths. I have always heard it of you. Well, to-day we will see whether you can kill a fifty-fourth. In an hour when the sun begins to sink, the hounds will be loosed in yonder reeds and since the water is behind them, the lions will come out, and then we shall see."

Now I saw that the King thought me to be a liar and the blood rose to my head.

"Why wait till the sun begins to sink, O King of kings?" I said. "Why not enter the reeds, as is our fashion in the Land of Kush, and rouse the lions from sleep in their own lair?"

Now the King laughed outright and called in a loud voice to his courtiers,

"Do ye hear this boasting Egyptian, who talks of entering the reeds and facing the lions in their lair, a thing that no man dare do where none can see to shoot? What say ye now? Shall we ask him to prove his words?"

Some great lord stepped forward, one who was a hunter though he looked little like it, for the scent on his hair reached me from four paces away and there was paint upon his face.

"Yes, O King," he said in a mincing voice, "let him enter and kill a lion. But if he fail, then let a lion kill him. There are some hungry in the palace den and it is not fit that the King's ears should be filled with empty words by foreigners from Egypt."

"So be it," said the King. "Egyptian, you have brought it on your own head. Prove that you can do what you say and I will give you great honour. Fail, and to the lions with him who lies of lions. Still," he added, "it is not right that you should go alone. Choose therefore one of these lords to keep you company; he who would put you to the test, if you will."

Now I looked at the scented noble who turned pale beneath his paint. Then I looked at the fat eunuch, Houman, who opened his mouth and gasped like a fish, and when I had looked, I shook my head and said as though to myself,

"Not so, no woman and no eunuch shall be my companion on this quest," whereat the King and all the rest laughed out loud. "The dwarf and I will go alone."

"The dwarf!" said the King. "Can he hunt lions also?"

"No, O King, but perchance he can smell them, for otherwise how shall I find them in that thicket within an hour?"

"Perchance they can smell him. How is the ape-man named?" asked the King.

"Bes, O King, after the god of the Egyptians whom he resembles."

"Dare you accompany your master on this hunt, O Bes?" inquired the King.

Then Bes looked up, rolling his yellow eyes, and answered in his thick and guttural voice,

"I am my master's slave and dare I refuse to accompany him? If I did he might kill me, as the King of kings kills his slaves. It is better to die with honour by the teeth of a lion, than with dishonour beneath the whip of a master. So at least we think in Ethiopia."

"Well spoken, dwarf Bes!" exclaimed the King. "So would I have all men think throughout the East. Let the words of this Ethiop be written down and copies of them sent to the satraps of all the provinces that they may be read to the peoples of the earth. I the King have decreed it."

The Wager

While the scribes were at their work I bowed before the King and prayed his leave and I and the dwarf Bes might get to ours.

"Go," he said, "and return here within an hour. If you do not return tidings of your death shall be sent to the satrap of Egypt to be told to your wives."

"I thank the King, but it is needless, for I have no wives, which are ill company for a hunter."

"Strange," he said, "since many women would be glad to name such a man their husband, at least here among us Easterns."

Walking backwards and bowing as we went, Bes and I returned to our chariot. There we stripped off our outer garments till Bes was naked save for his waistcloth and I was clad only in a jerkin. Then I took my bow, my arrows and my knife, and Bes took two spears, one light for throwing and the other short, broad and heavy for stabbing. Thus armed we passed back before the Easterns who stared at us, and advanced to the edge of the thicket of tall reeds that was full of lions.

Here Bes took dust and threw it into the air that we might learn from which quarter the light wind blew.

"We will go against the breeze, Lord," he said, "that I may smell the lions before they smell us."

I nodded, and answered,

"Hearken, Bes. Well may it be that we kill no lions in this place where it is hard to shoot. Yet I would not return to be thrown to wild beasts by yonder evil king. Therefore if we fail in this or in any other way, do you kill me, if you still live."

He rolled his eyes and grinned.

"Not so, Master. Then we will win through the reeds and lie hid in their edge till darkness comes, for in them those half-men will never dare to seek for us. Afterwards we will swim the water and disguise ourselves as jugglers and try to reach the coast, and so back to Egypt, having learned much. Never stretch out your hand to Death till he stretches out his to you, which he will do soon enough, Master."

Again I nodded and said,

"And if a lion should kill me, Bes, what then?"

"Then, Master, I will kill that lion if I can and go report the matter to the King."

"And if he should wish to throw you to the beasts, Bes, what then?"

"Then, first I will drag him down to the greatest of all beasts, he who waits to devour evil-doers in the Under-world, be they kings or slaves," and he stretched out his long arms and made a motion as of clutching a man by the throat. "Oh! have no fear, Master, I can break him like a stick, and afterwards we will talk the matter over among the dead, for I shall swallow my tongue and die also. It is a good trick, Master, which I wish you would learn."

Then he took my hand and kissed it and we entered the reeds, I, who was a hunter, feeling more happy than I had done since we set foot in the East.

Yet the quest was desperate for the reeds were tall and often I could not see more than a bow's length in front of me. Presently, however, we found a path made perchance by game coming down to drink, or by crocodiles coming up to sleep, and followed it, I with an arrow on my string and Bes with the throwing spear in his right hand and the stabbing spear in his left, half a pace ahead of me. On we crept, Bes drawing in the air through his great nostrils as a hound might do, till suddenly he stopped and sniffed towards the north.

"I smell lion near," he whispered, searching among the reed stems with his eyes.

"I see lion," he whispered again, and pointed, but I could see nothing save the stems of the reeds.

"Rouse him," I whispered back, "and I will shoot as he bounds."

Then Bes poised the spear, shook it till it quivered, and threw. There was a roar and a lioness appeared with the spear fast in her flank. I loosed the arrow but it cut into the thick reeds and stuck there.

"Forward!" whispered Bes, "for where woman is, there look for man. The lion will be near."

We crept on, Bes stopping to cut the arrow from a reed and set it back in the quiver, for it was a good arrow made by himself. But now he shifted the broad spear to his right hand and in his left held his knife. We heard the wounded lioness roar not far away.

"She calls her man to help her," whispered Bes, and as the words left his lips the reeds down wind began to sway, for we were smelt.

They swayed, they parted and, half seen, half hid between their stems, appeared the head of a great, black-maned lion. I drew the string and shot, this time not in vain, for I heard the arrow thud upon his hide. Then before I could set another he was on us, reared upon his hind legs and roaring. As I drew my dagger he struck at me, but I bent down and his paw went over my head. Then his weight came against me and I fell beneath him, stabbing him in the belly as I fell. I saw his mighty jaws open to crush my head. Then they shut again and through them burst a whine like that of a hurt dog.

Bes had driven his spear into the lion's breast, so deep that the point of it came out through the back. Still he was not dead, only now it was Bes he sought. The dwarf ran at him as he reared up again, and casting his great arms about the brute's body, wrestled with him as man with man.

Then it was, for the first time I think, that I learned all the Ethiopian's strength. For he, a dwarf, threw that lion on its back and thrusting his big head beneath the jaws, struggled with it madly. I was up, the knife still in my hand, and oh! I too was strong. Into the throat I drove it, dragging it this way and that, and lo! the lion moaned and died and his blood gushed out over both of us. Then Bes sat up and laughed, and I too laughed, since neither of us had more than scratches and we had done what men could scarcely do.

"Do you remember, Master," said Bes when he had finished laughing, as he wiped his brow with some damp moss, "how, once far away up the Nile you charged a mad elephant with a spear and saved me who had fallen, from being trampled to death?"

I, Shabaka, answered that I did. (And I, Allan Quatermain, observing all these things in my psychic trance in the museum of Ragnall Castle, reflected that I also remembered how a certain Hans had saved me from a certain mad elephant, to wit, Jana, not so long before, which just shows how things come round.)

"Yes," went on Bes, "you saved me from that elephant, though it seemed death to you. And, Master, I will tell you something now. That very morning I had tried to poison you, only you would not wait to eat because the elephants were near."

"Did you?" I asked idly. "Why?"

"Because two years before you captured me in battle with some of my people, and as I was misshapen, or for pity's sake, spared my life and made me your slave. Well, I who had been a chief, a very great chief, Master, did not wish to remain a slave and did wish to avenge my people's blood. Therefore I tried to poison you, and that very day you saved my life, offering for it your own."

"I think it was because I wanted the tusks of the elephant, Bes."

"Perhaps, Master, only you will remember that this elephant was a young cow and had no tusks worth anything. Still had it carried tusks, it might have been so, since one white tusk is worth many black dwarfs. Well, to-day I have paid you back. I say it lest you should forget that had it not been for me, that lion would have eaten you."

"Yes, Bes, you have paid me back and I thank you."

"Master, hitherto I always thought you one who worshipped Maat, goddess of Truth. Now I see that you worship the god of Lies, whoever he may be, that god who dwells in the breasts of women and most men, but has no name. For, Master, it was *you* who saved *me* from the lion and not I you, since you cut its throat at the last. So that debt of mine is still to pay and by the great Grasshopper which we worship in my country, who is much better than all the gods of the Egyptians put together, I swear that I will pay it soon, or mayhap ten thousand years hence. At the last it shall be paid."

"Why do you worship a grasshopper and why is he better than the gods of the Egyptians?" I asked carelessly, for I was tired and his talk amused me while we rested.

"We worship the Grasshopper, Master, because he jumps with men's spirits from one life to another, or from this world to the next, yes, right through the blue sky. And he is better than your Egyptian gods because they leave you to find your own way there, and then eat you alive, that is if you have tried to poison people, as of course we have all done. But, Master, we are fresh again now, so let us be going, for the hour will soon be finished. Also when she has eaten the spear handle, that lioness may return."

"Yes," I said; "let us go and report to the King of kings that we have killed a lion."

"Master, it is not enough. Even common kings believe little that they do not see, wherefore it is certain that a King of kings will believe nothing and still more certain that he will not come here to look. So as we cannot carry the lion, we must take a bit of it," and straightway he cut off the end of the brute's tail.

Following the crocodile path, presently we reached the edge of the reeds opposite to the camp where the King now sat in state beneath a purple pavilion that had been reared, eating a meal, with his courtiers standing at a distance and looking very hungry.

Out of the reeds bounded Bes, naked and bloody, waving the lion's tail and singing some wild Ethiopian chant, while I, also bloody and half naked, for the lion's claws had torn my jerkin off me, followed with bow unstrung.

The King looked up and saw us.

"What! Do you live, Egyptian?" he asked. "Of a surety I thought that by now you would be dead."

"It was the lion that died, O King," I answered, pointing to Bes who, having ceased from his song, was jumping about carrying the beast's tail in his mouth as a dog carries a bone.

"It seems that this Egyptian has killed a lion," said the King to one of his lords, him of the painted face and scented hair.

"May be please the King," he answered, bowing, "a tail is not the whole beast and may have been taken thither, or cut from a lion lying dead already. The King knows that the Egyptians are great liars."

So he spoke because he was jealous of the deed.

"These men look as though they had met a live one, not one that is dead," said the King, scanning our blood-stained shapes. "Still, as you doubt it, you will wish to put the matter to the proof. Therefore, Cousin, take six men with you, enter the reeds and search. In that soft ground it will be easy to follow their footmarks."

"It is dangerous, O King," began the prince, for such he was, no less.

"And therefore the task will be the more to your taste, Cousin. Go now, and be swift."

So six hunters were called and the prince went, cursing me beneath his breath as he passed us. For he was terribly afraid, and with reason. Suddenly Bes ceased from his antics and prostrating himself, cried,

"A boon, O King. This noble lord throws doubt upon my master's word. Suffer that I may lead him to where the lion lies dead, since otherwise wandering in those reeds the great King's cousin might come to harm and the great King be grieved."

"I have many cousins," said the King. "Still go if you wish, Dwarf."

So Bes ran after the prince and catching him up, tapped him on the shoulder with the lion's tail to point out the way. Then they vanished into the reeds and I went to the chariot to wash off the blood from my body and clothes. As I fastened my robe I heard a sound of roaring, then one scream, after which all grew still. Now I drew near to the reeds and stood between them and the King's camp.

Presently on their edge appeared Bes dancing and singing as before, but this time he held a lion's tail in either hand. After him came the six hunters dragging between them the body of the lion we had killed. They staggered with it towards the King, and I followed.

"I see the dwarf," he said. "I see the dead lion and I see the hunters. But where is my cousin? Make report, O Bes."

"O King of kings," replied Bes, "the mighty prince your cousin lies flat yonder beneath the body of that lion's wife. She sprang upon him and killed him, and I sprang upon her and killed her with my spear. Here is her tail, O King of kings."

"Is this true?" he asked of the hunters.

"It is true, O King," answered their captain. "The lioness, which was wounded, leapt upon the prince, choosing him although he was behind us all. Then this dwarf leapt upon the lioness, being behind the prince and nearest to him, and drove his spear through her shoulders to her heart. So we brought the first lion as the King commanded us, since we could carry no more."

The face of the King grew red with rage.

"Seven of my people and one black dwarf!" he exclaimed. "Yet the lioness kills my cousin and the dwarf kills the lioness. Such is the tale that will go to Egypt concerning the hunters of the King of the world. Seize those men, Guards, and let them be fed to the wild beasts in the palace dens."

At once the unfortunates were seized and led away. Then the King called Bes to him, and taking the gold chain he wore about his neck, threw it over his head, thereby, though I knew nothing of it at the time, conferring upon him some noble rank. Next he called to me and said,

"It would seem that you are skilled in the use of the bow and in the hunting of lions, Egyptian. Therefore I will honour you, for this afternoon your chariot shall drive with my chariot, and we will hunt side by side. Moreover, I will lay you a wager as to which of us will kill the most lions, for know, Shabaka, that I also am skilled in the use of the bow, more skilled than any among the millions of my subjects."

"Then, O King, it is of little use for me to match myself against you, seeing that I have met men who can shoot better than I do, or, since in the East all must speak nothing but the truth, not being liars as the dead prince said we Egyptians are, one man."

"Who was that man, Shabaka?"

"The Prince Peroa, O King."

The King frowned as though the name displeased him, then answered,

"Am I not greater than this Peroa and cannot I therefore shoot better?"

"Doubtless, O King of kings, and therefore how can I who shoot worse than Peroa, match myself against you?"

"For which reason I will give you odds, Shabaka. Behold this rope of rose-hued pearls I wear. They are unequalled in the whole world, for twenty years the merchants sought them in the days of my father; half of them would buy a satrapy. I wager them"—here the listening nobles gasped and the fat eunuch, Houman, held up his hands in horror.

"Against what, O King?"

"Your slave Bes, to whom I have taken a fancy."

Now I trembled and Bes rolled his yellow eyes.

"Your pardon, O King of kings," I said, "but it is not enough. I am a hunter and to such, priceless pearls are of little use. But to me that dwarf is of much use in my hunting."

"So be it, Shabaka, then I will add to the wager. If you win, together with the pearls I will give you the dwarf's weight in solid gold."

"The King is bountiful," I answered, "but it is not enough, for even if I win against one who can shoot better than Peroa, which is impossible, what should I do with so much gold? Surely for the sake of it I should be murdered or ever I saw the coasts of Egypt."

"What shall I add then?" asked the King. "The most beauteous maiden in the House of Women?"

I shook my head. "Not so, O King, for then I must marry who would remain single."

"There is no need, you might sell her to your friend, Peroa. A satrapy?"

"Not so, O King, for then I must govern it, which would keep me from my hunting, until it pleased the King to take my head."

"By the name of the holy ones I worship what then do you ask added to the pearls and the pure gold?"

Now I tried to bethink me of something that the King could not grant, since I had no wish for this match which my heart warned me would end in trouble. As no thought came to me I looked at Bes and saw that he was rolling his eyes towards the six doomed hunters who were being led away, also in pretence of driving off a fly, pointing to them with one of the lion tails. Then I remembered that a decree once uttered by the King of the East could not be altered, and saw a road of escape.

"O King," I said, "together with the pearls and the gold I ask that the lives of those six hunters be added to the wager, to be spared if by chance I should win."

"Why?" asked the King amazed.

"Because they are brave men, O King, and I would not see the bones of such cracked by tame beasts in a cage."

"Is my judgment registered?" asked the King.

"Not yet, O King," answered the head scribe.

"Then it has no weight and can be suspended without the breaking of the law. Shabaka, thus stands our wager. If I kill more lions than you do this day, or, should but two be slain, I kill the first, or should none be slain, I plant more arrows in their bodies, I take your slave, Bes the dwarf, to be my slave. But should you have the better of me in any of these ways, then I give to you this girdle of rose pearls and the weight of the dwarf Bes in gold and the six hunters free of harm, to do with what you will. Let it be recorded, and to the hunt."

Soon Bes and I were in our chariot which by command took place in line with that of the King, but at a distance of some thirty steps. Bending over the dwarf who drove, I spoke with him, saying,

"Our luck is ill to-day, Bes, seeing that before the end of it we may well be parted."

"Not so, Master, our luck is good to-day seeing that before the end of it you will be the richer by the finest pearls in the whole world, by my weight in pure gold (and Master, I am twice as heavy as the king thought and will stuff myself with twenty pounds of meat before the weighing, if I have the chance, or at least with water, though in this hot place that will not last for long), and by six picked huntsmen, brave men as you thought, who will serve to escort us and our treasure to the coast."

"First I must win the match, Bes."

"Which you could do with one eye blinded, Master, and a sore finger. Kings think that they can shoot because all the worms that crawl about them and are named men, dare not show themselves their betters. Oh! I have heard tales in yonder city. There have been days when this Lord of the world has missed six lions with as many arrows, and they seated smiling in his face, being but tamed brutes brought from far in cages of wood, yes, smiling like cats in the sun. Look you, Master, he drinks too much wine and sits up too late in his Women's house—there are three hundred of them there, Master—to shoot as you and I can. If you doubt it, look at his eyes and hands. Oh! the pearls and the gold and the men are yours, and that painted prince who mocked us is where he ought to be—dead in the mud.

"Did I tell you how I managed that, Master? As you know better than I do, lions hate those that have on them the smell of their own blood. Therefore, while I pointed out the way to him, I touched the painted prince with the bleeding tail of that which we killed, pretending that it was by chance, for which he cursed me, as well he might. So when we came to the dead lion and, as I had expected, met there the lioness you had wounded, she charged through the hunters at him who smelt of her husband, and bit his head off."

"But, Bes, you smelt of him also, and worse."

"Yes, Master, but that painted cousin of the King came first. I kept well behind him, pretending to be afraid," and he chuckled quietly, adding, "I expect that he is now telling an angry tale about me to Osiris, or to the Grasshopper that takes him there, as it may happen."

"These Easterns worship neither Osiris, nor your Grasshopper, Bes, but a flame of fire."

"Then he is telling the tale to the fire, and I hope that it will get tired and burn him."

So we talked merrily enough because we had done great deeds and thought that we had outwitted the Easterns and the King, not knowing all their craft. For none had told us that that man who hunted with the King and yet dared to draw arrow upon the quarry before the King should be put to death as one who had done insult to his Majesty. This that royal fox remembered and therefore was sure that he would win the wager.

Now the chariots turned and passing down a path came to an open space that was cleared of reeds. Here they halted, that of the King and my own side by side with ten paces between them, and those of the court behind. Meanwhile huntsmen with dogs entered the great brake far away to the right and left of us, also in front, so that the lions might be driven backwards and forwards across the open space.

Soon we heard the hounds baying on all sides. Then Bes made a sucking noise with his great lips and pointed to the edge of the reeds in front of us some sixty paces away. Looking, I saw a yellow shape creeping along between their dark stems, and although the shot was far, forgetting all things save I was a hunter and there was my game, I drew the arrow to my ear, aimed and loosed, making allowance for its fall and for the wind.

Oh! that shot was good. It struck the lion in the body and pierced him through. Out he came, roaring, rolling, and tearing at the ground. But by now I had another arrow on the string, and although the King lifted his bow, I loosed first. Again it struck, this time in the throat, and that lion groaned and died.

The King looked at me angrily, and from the court behind rose a murmur of wonder mingled with wrath, wonder at my marksmanship, and wrath because I had dared to shoot before the King.

"The wager looks well for us," muttered Bes, but I bade him be silent, for more lions were stirring.

Now one leapt across the open space, passing in front of the King and within thirty paces of us. He shot and missed it, sending his shaft two spans above its back. Then I shot and drove the arrow through it just where the head joins the neck, cutting the spine, so that it died at once.

Again that murmur went up and the King struck the charioteer on the head with his clenched fist, crying out that he had suffered the horses to move and should be scourged for causing his hand to shake.

This charioteer, although he was a lord—since in the East men of high rank waited on the King like slaves and even clipped his nails and beard—craved pardon humbly, admitting his fault.

"It is a lie," whispered Bes. "The horses never stirred. How could they with those grooms holding their heads? Nevertheless, Master, the pearls are as good as round your neck."

"Silence," I answered. "As we have heard, in the East all men speak the truth; it is only Egyptians who lie. Also in the East men's necks are encircled with bowstrings as well as pearls, and ears are long."

The hounds continued to bay, drawing nearer to us. A lioness bounded out of the reeds, ran towards the King's chariot and as though amazed, sat down like a dog, so near that a man might have hit it with a stone. The King shot short, striking it in the fore-paw only, whereon it shook out the arrow and rushed back into the reeds, while the court behind cried,

"May the King live for ever! The beast is dead."

"We shall see if it is dead presently," said Bes, and I nodded.

Another lion appeared to the right of the King. Again he shot and missed it, whereon he began to curse and to swear in his own royal oaths, and the charioteer trembled. Then came the end.

One of the hounds drew quite close and roused the lioness that had been pricked in the foot. She turned and killed it with a blow of her paw, then, being mad, charged straight at the King's chariot. The horses reared, lifting the grooms off their feet. The King shot wildly and fell backwards out of the chariot, as even Kings of the world must do when they have nothing left to stand on. The lioness saw that he was down and leapt at him, straight over the chariot. As she leapt I shot at her in the air and pierced her through the loins, paralysing her, so that although she fell down near the King, she could not come at him to kill him.

I sprang from my chariot, but before I could reach the lioness hunters had run up with spears and stabbed her, which was easy as she could not move.

The King rose from the ground, for he was unharmed, and said in a loud voice,

"Had not that shaft of mine gone home, I think that the East would have bowed to another lord to-night."

Now, forgetting that I was speaking to the King of the earth, forgetting the wager and all besides, I exclaimed,

"Nay, your shaft missed; mine went home," whereon one of the courtiers cried,

"This Egyptian is a liar, and calls the King one!"

"A liar?" I said astonished. "Look at the arrow and see from whose quiver it came," and I drew one from my own of the Egyptian make and marked with my mark.

Then a tumult broke out, all the courtiers and eunuchs talking at once, yet all bowing to the mud-stained person of the King, like ears of wheat to a tree in a storm. Not wishing to urge my claims further, for my part I returned to the chariot and the hunting being done, as I supposed, unstrung my bow which I prized above all things, and set it in its case.

While I was thus employed the eunuch Houman approached me with a sickly smile, saying,

"The King commands your presence, Egyptian, that you may receive your reward."

I nodded, saying that I would come, and he returned.

"Bes," I said when he was out of hearing, "my heart sinks. I do not trust that King who I think means mischief."

"So do I, Master. Oh! we have been great fools. When a god and a man climb a tree together, the man should allow the god to come first to the top, and thence tell the world that he is a god."

"Yes," I answered, "but who ever sees Wisdom until she is flying away? Now perhaps, the god being the stronger, will cast down the man."

Then both together we advanced towards the King, leaving the chariot in charge of soldiers. He was seated on a gilded chair which served him as a throne, and behind him were his officers, eunuchs and attendants, though not all of them, since at a little distance some of them were engaged in beating the lord who had served as his charioteer upon the feet with rods. We prostrated ourselves before him and waited till he spoke. At length he said,

"Shabaka the Egyptian, we made a wager with you, of which you will remember the terms. It seems that you have won the wager, since you slew two lions, whereas we, the King, slew but one, that which leapt upon us in the chariot."

Here Bes groaned at my side and I looked up.

"Fear nothing," he went on, "it shall be paid." Here he snatched off the girdle of priceless, rose-hued pearls and threw it in my face.

"At the palace too," he went on, "the dwarf shall be set in the scales and his full weight in pure gold shall be given to you. Moreover, the lives of the six hunters are yours, and with them the men themselves."

"May the King live for ever!" I exclaimed, feeling that I must say something.

"I hope so," he answered cruelly, "but, Egyptian, you shall not, who have broken the laws of the land."

"In what way, O King?" I asked.

"By shooting at the lions before the King had time to draw his bow, and by telling the King that he lied to his face, for both of which things the punishment is death."

Now my heart swelled till I thought it would burst with rage. Then of a sudden, a certain spirit entered into me and I rose to my feet and said,

"O King, you have declared that I must die and as this is so, I will kneel to you no more who soon shall sup at the table of Osiris, and there be far greater than any king, going before him with clean hands. Is it not your law that he who is condemned to die has first the right to set out his case for the honour of his name?"

"It is," said the King, I think because he was curious to hear what I had to say. "Speak on."

"O King, although my blood is as high as your own, of that I say nothing, for at the wish of your satrap I came to the East from Egypt as a hunter, to show you how we of Egypt kill lions and other beasts. For three months I have waited in the royal city seeking admission to the presence of the King, and in vain. At length I was bidden to this hunt when I was about to depart to my own land, and being taunted by your servants, entered the reeds with my slave, and there slew a lion. Then it pleased you to thrust a wager upon me which I did not wish to take, as to which of us would shoot the most lions; a wager as I now understand you did not mean that I should win, whatever might be my skill, since you thought I knew that I must shoot at nothing till you had first shot and killed the beasts or scared them away.

"So I matched myself against you, as hunter against hunter, for in the field, as before the gods, all are equal, not as a slave against a king who is determined to avenge defeat by death. We were posted and the lions came. I shot at those which appeared opposite to me, or upon my side, leaving those that appeared opposite to you, or on your side unshot at, as is the custom of hunters. My skill, or my fortune, was better than yours and I killed, whereas you missed or only wounded. In the end a lioness sprang at you and I shot it lest it should kill you; as could easily be proved by the arrow in its body. Now you say that I must die because I have broken some laws of yours which men should be ashamed to make, and to save your honour, pay me what I have won, knowing that pearls and gold and slaves are of no value to a dying man and can be taken back again. That is all the story.

"Yet I would add one word. You Easterns have two sayings which you teach to your children; that they should learn to shoot with the bow, and to tell the truth. O King, they are my last lessons to you. Learn to shoot with the bow—which you cannot do, and to tell the truth which you have not done. Now I have spoken and am ready to die and I thank you for the patience with which you have heard my words, that, as the King does *not* live for ever, I hope one day to repeat to you more fully beyond the grave."

Now at this bold speech of mine all those nobles and attendants gasped, for never had they heard such words addressed to his Majesty. The King turned red as though with shame, but made no answer, only he asked of those about him.

"What fate for this man?"

"Death, O King!" they cried with one voice.

"What death?" he asked again.

Then his Councillors consulted together and one of them answered,

"The slowest known to our law, *death by the boat.*"

Hearing this and not knowing what was meant, it came into my mind that I was to be turned adrift in a boat and there left to starve.

"Behold the reward of good hunting!" I mocked in my rage. "O King, because of this deed of shame I call upon you the curse of all the gods of all the peoples. Henceforth may your sleep be ever haunted by evil dreams of what shall follow the last sleep, and in the end may you also die in blood."

The King opened his mouth as though to answer, but from it came nothing but a low cry of fear. Then guards rushed up and seized me.

The Doom of the Boat

The guards led me to my chariot and thrust me into it, and with me Bes. I asked them if they would murder him also, to which the eunuch, Houman, answered No, since he had committed no crime, but that he must go with me to be weighed. Then soldiers took the horses by the bridles and led them, while others, having first snatched away my bow and all our other weapons, surrounded the chariot lest we should escape. So Bes and I were able to talk together in a Libyan tongue that none of them understood, even if they heard our words.

"Your life is spared," I said to him, "that the King may take you as a slave."

"Then he will take an ill slave, Master, since I swear by the Grasshopper that within a moon I will find means to kill him, and afterwards come to join you in a land where men hunt fair."

I smiled and Bes went on,

"Now I wish I had time to teach you that trick of swallowing your own tongue, since perhaps you will need it in this boat of which they talk."

"Did you not say to me an hour or two ago, Bes, that we are fools to stretch out our hands to Death until he stretches out his to us? I will not die until I must—now."

"Why 'now,' Master, seeing that only this afternoon you bade me kill you rather than let you be thrown to the wild beasts?" he asked peering at me curiously.

"Do you remember the old hermit, the holy Tanofir, who dwells in a cell over the sepulchre of the Apis bulls in the burial ground of the desert near to Memphis, Bes?"

"The magician and prophet who is the brother of your grandfather, Master, and the son of a king; he who brought you up before he became a hermit? Yes, I know him well, though I have seldom been very near to him because his eyes frighten me, as they frightened Cambyses the Persian when Tanofir cursed him and foretold his doom after he had stabbed the holy Apis, saying that by a wound from that same sword in his own body he should die himself, which thing came to pass. As they have frightened many another man also."

"Well, Bes, when yonder king told me that I must die, fear filled me who did not wish to die thus, and after the fear came a blackness in my mind. Then of a sudden in that blackness I saw a picture of Tanofir, my great uncle, seated in a sepulchre looking towards the East. Moreover I heard him speak, and to me, saying, 'Shabaka, my foster-son, fear nothing. You are in great danger but it will pass. Speak to the great King all that rises in your heart, for the gods of Vengeance make use of your tongue and whatever you prophesy to him shall be fulfilled.' So I spoke the words you heard and I feared nothing."

"Is it so, Master? Then I think that the holy Tanofir must have entered my heart also. Know that I was minded to leap upon that king and break his neck, so that all three of us might end together. But of a sudden something seemed to tell me to leave him alone and let things go as they are fated. But how can the holy Tanofir who grows blind with age, see so far?"

"I do not know, Bes, save that he is not as are other men, for in him is gathered all the ancient wisdom of Egypt. Moreover he lives with the gods while still upon earth, and like the gods can send his *Ka*, as we Egyptians call the spirit, or invisible self which companions all from the cradle to the grave and afterwards, whither he will. So doubtless to-day he sent it hither to me whom he loves more than anything on earth. Also I remember that before I entered on this journey he told me that I should return safe and sound. Therefore, Bes, I say I fear nothing."

"Nor do I, Master. Yet if you see me do strange things, or hear me speak strange words, take no note of them, since I shall be but playing a part as I think wisest."

After this we talked of that day's adventure with the lions, and of others that we had shared together, laughing merrily all the while, till the soldiers stared at us as though we were mad. Also the fat eunuch, Houman, who was mounted on an ass, rode up and said,

"What, Egyptian who dared to twist the beard of the Great King, you laugh, do you? Well, you will sing a different song in the boat to that which you sing in the chariot. Think of my words on the eighth day from this."

"I will think of them, Eunuch," I answered, looking at him fiercely in the eyes, "but who knows what kind of a song you will be singing before the eighth day from this?"

"What I do is done under the authority of the ancient and holy Seal of Seals," he answered in a quavering voice, touching the little cylinder of white shell which I had noted upon the person of the King, but that now hung from a gold chain about the eunuch's neck.

Then he made the sign which Easterns use to avert evil and rode off again, looking very frightened.

So we came to the royal city and went up to a wonderful palace. Here we were taken from the chariot and led into a room where food and drink in plenty were given to me as though I were an honoured guest, which caused me to wonder. Bes also, seated on the ground at a distance, ate and drank, for his own reasons filling himself to the throat as though he were a wineskin, until the serving slaves mocked at him for a glutton.

When we had finished eating, slaves appeared bearing a wooden framework from which hung a great pair of scales. Also there appeared officers of the King's Treasury, carrying leather bags which they opened, breaking the seals to show that the contents were pure gold coin. They set a number of these bags on one of the scales, and then ordered Bes to seat himself in the other. So much heavier did he prove than they expected him to be, that they were obliged to send back to the Treasury to fetch more bags of gold, for although Bes was so short in height, his weight was that of a large man. One of the treasurers grumbled, saying he should have been weighed before he had eaten and drunk. But the officer to whom he spoke grinned and answered that it mattered little, since the King was heir to criminals and that these bags would soon return to the Treasury, only they would need washing first, a remark that made me wonder.

At length, when the scales were even, the six hunters whose lives I had won and who had been given to me as slaves, were brought in and ordered to shoulder the bags of gold. I too was seized and my hands were bound behind me. Then I was led out in charge of the eunuch Houman, who informed me with a leer that it would be his duty to attend to my comfort till the end. With him were four black men all dressed in the same way. These, he said, were the executioners. Lastly came Bes watched by three of the king's guards armed with spears, lest he should attempt to rescue me or to do anyone a mischief.

Now my heart began to sink and I asked Houman what was to happen to me.

"This, O Egyptian slayer of lions. You will be laid upon a bed in a little boat upon the river and another boat will be placed over you, for these boats are called the Twins, Egyptian, in such a fashion that your head and your hands will project at one end and your feet at the other. There you will be left, comfortable as a baby in its cradle, and twice every day the best of food and drink will be brought to you. Should your appetite fail, moreover, it will be my duty to revive it by pricking your eyes with the point of a knife until it returns. Also after each meal I shall wash your face, your hands and your feet with milk and honey, lest the flies that buzz about them should suffer hunger, and to preserve your skin from burning by the sun. Thus slowly you will grow weaker and at length fall asleep. The last one who went into the boat—he, unlucky man, had by accident wandered into the court of the House of Women and seen some of the ladies there unveiled —only lived for twelve days, but you, being so strong, may hope to last for eighteen. Is there anything more that I can tell you? If so, ask it quickly for we draw near to the river."

Now when I heard this and understood all the horror of my fate, I forgot the vision of my great uncle, the holy Tanofir, and his comfortable prophecies, and my heart failed me altogether, so that I stood stock still.

"What, Lion-hunter and Bearder of kings, do you think it is too early to go to bed?" mocked this devilish eunuch. "On with you!" and he began to beat me about the face with the handle of his fly-whisk.

Then my manhood came back to me.

"When did the King tell you to touch me, you fatted swine?" I roared, and turning, since I could not reach him with my bound hands, kicked him in the body with all my strength, so that he fell down, writhing and screaming with agony. Indeed, had not the executioners leapt upon me, I would have trampled the life out of him where he lay. But they held me fast and presently, after he had been sick, Houman recovered enough to come forward leaning on the shoulders of two guards. Only now he mocked me no more.

We reached a quay just as the sun was setting. There in charge of a one-eyed black slave, a little square-ended boat floated at the river's edge, while on the quay itself lay a similar but somewhat shorter boat, bottom uppermost. Now the hunters whom I had won in the wager, with many glances of compassion, for they were brave men and knew that it was I who had saved their lives, placed the bags of gold in the bottom of the floating boat, and on the top of these a mattress stuffed with straw. Then the girdle of rose-hued pearls was made fast about my middle, my hands were untied, I was seized by the executioners and laid on my back on the mattress, and my wrists and ankles were fixed by cords to iron rings that were screwed to the thwarts of the boat. After this the other, shorter boat was laid over me in such a manner that it did not touch me, leaving my head, my hands and my feet exposed as the eunuch had said.

While this wicked work was going forward Bes sat on the quay, watching, till presently, after I had been made fast and covered up, he burst into shouts of laughter, clapped his hands and began to dance about as though with joy, till the eunuch, who had now recovered somewhat from my kick, grew curious and asked him why he behaved thus.

"O noble Eunuch," he answered, "once I was free and that man made me a slave, so that for many years I have been obliged to toil for him whom I hate. Moreover, often he has beaten me and starved me, which was why you saw me eat so much not long ago, and threatened to kill me, and now at last I have my revenge upon him who is about to die miserably. That is why I laugh and sing and dance and clap my hands, O most noble Eunuch, I who shall become the follower and servant of the glorious King of all the earth, and perhaps your friend, too, O Eunuch of eunuchs, whose sacred person my brutal master dared to kick."

"I understand," said Houman smiling, though with a twisted face, "and will make report of all you say to the King, and ask him to grant that you shall sometimes prick this Egyptian in the eye. Now go spit in his face and tell him what you think of him."

So Bes waded into the water which was quite shallow here, and spat into my face, or pretended to, while amid a torrent of vile language, he interpolated certain words in the Libyan tongue, which meant,

"O my most beloved father, mother, and other relatives, have no fear. Though things look very black, remember the vision of the holy Tanofir, who doubtless allows these things to happen to you to try your faith by direct order of the gods. Be sure that I will not leave you to perish, or if there should be no escape, that I will find a way to put you out of your misery and to avenge you. Yes, yes, I will yet see that accursed swine, Houman, take your place in this boat. Now I go to the Court to which it seems that this gold chain gives me a right of entry, or so the eunuch says, but soon I will be back again."

Then followed another stream or most horrible abuse and more spitting, after which he waded back to land and embraced Houman, calling him his best friend.

They went, leaving me alone in the boat save for the guard upon the quay who, now that darkness had come, soon grew silent. It was lonely, very lonely, lying there staring at the empty sky with only the stinging gnats for company, and soon my limbs began to ache. I thought of the poor wretches who had suffered in this same boat and wondered if their lot would be my lot.

Bes was faithful and clever, but what could a single dwarf do among all these black-hearted fiends? And if he could do nothing, oh! if he could do nothing!

The seconds seemed minutes, the minutes seemed hours, and the hours seemed years. What then would the days be, passed in torture and agony while waiting for a filthy death? Where now were the gods I had worshipped and—was there any god? Or was man but a self-deceiver who created gods instead of the gods creating him, because he did not love to think of an eternal blackness in which he would soon be swallowed up and lost? Well, at least that would mean sleep, and sleep is better than torment of mind or body.

It came to me, I think, who was so weary. At any rate I opened my eyes to see that the low moon had vanished and that some of the stars which I knew as a hunter who had often steered his way by them, had moved a little. While I was wondering idly why they moved, I heard the tramp of soldiers on the quay and the voice of an officer giving a command. Then I felt the boat being drawn in by the cord with which it was attached to the quay. Next the other boat that lay over me was lifted off, the ropes that bound we were undone and I was set upon my feet, for already I was so stiff that I could scarcely stand. A voice which I recognised as that of the eunuch Houman, addressed me in respectful tones, which made me think I must be dreaming.

"Noble Shabaka," said the voice, "the Great King commands your presence at his feast."

"Is it so?" I answered in my dream. "Then my absence from their feast will vex the gnats of the river," a saying at which Houman and others with him laughed obsequiously.

Next I heard the bags of gold being removed from the boat, after which we walked away, guards supporting me by either elbow until I found my strength again, and Houman following just behind, perhaps because he feared my foot if he went in front.

"What has chanced, Eunuch," I asked presently, "that I am disturbed from the bed where I was sleeping so well?"

"I do not know, Lord," he answered. "I only know that the King of kings has suddenly commanded that you should be brought before him as a guest clothed in a robe of honour, even if to do so, you must be awakened from your rest, yes, to his own royal table, for he holds a feast this night. Lord," he went on in a whining voice, "if perchance fortune should have changed her face to you, I pray you bear no malice to those who, when she frowned, were forced, yes, under the private Seal of Seals, against their will to carry out the commands of the King. Be just, O Lord Shabaka."

"Say no more. I will try to be just," I answered. "But what is justice in the East? I only know of it in Egypt."

Now we reached one of the doors of the palace and I was taken to a chamber where slaves who were waiting, washed and anointed me with scents, after which they clad me in a beautiful robe of silk, setting the girdle of rose-hued pearls about me.

When they had finished, preceded by Houman I was led to a great pillared hall closed in with silk hangings, where many feasted. Through them I went to a dais at the head of the hall where between half-drawn curtains surrounded by cup-bearers and other officers, the King sat in all his glory upon a cushioned golden throne. He had a glittering wine-cup in his hand and at a glance I saw that he was drunk, as it is the fashion for these Easterns to be at their great feasts, for he looked happy and human which he did not do when he was sober. Or perchance, as sometimes I thought afterwards, he only pretended to be drunk. Also I saw something else, namely, Bes, wondrously attired with the gold chain about his neck and wearing a red headdress. He was seated on the carpet before the throne, and saying things that made the King laugh and even caused the grave officers behind to smile.

I came to the dais and at a little sign from Bes who yet did not seem to see me, such a sign as he often made when he caught sight of game before I did, I prostrated myself. The King looked at me, then asked,

"Who is this?" adding, "Oh, I remember, the Egyptian whose arrows do not miss, the wonderful hunter whom Idernes sent to me from Memphis, which I hope to visit ere long. We quarrelled, did we not, Egyptian, something about a lion?"

"Not so, King," I answered. "The King was angry and with justice, because I could not kill a lion before it frightened his horses."

This I said because my hours in the boat had made me humble, also because the words came to my lips.

"Yes, yes, something like that, or at least you lie well. Whatever it may have been, it is done with now, a mere hunters' difference," and taking from his side his long sceptre that was headed with the great emerald, he stretched it out for me to touch in token of pardon.

Then I knew that I was safe for he to whom the King has extended his sceptre is forgiven all crimes, yes, even if he had attempted the royal life. The Court knew it also, for every man who saw bowed towards me, yes, even the officers behind the King. One of the cup- bearers too brought me a goblet of the King's own wine, which I drank thankfully, calling down health on the King.

"That was a wonderful shot of yours, Egyptian," he said, "when you sent an arrow through the lioness that dared to attack my Majesty. Yes, the King owes his life to you and he is grateful as you shall learn. This slave of yours," and he pointed to Bes in his gaudy attire, "has brought the whole matter to my mind whence it had fallen, and, Shabaka," here he hiccupped, "you may have noted how differently things look to the naked eye and when seen through a wine goblet. He has told me a wonderful story—what was the story, Dwarf?"

"May it please the great King," answered Bes, rolling his big eyes, "only a little tale of another king of my own country whom I used to think great until I came to the East and learned what kings could be. That king had a servant with whom he used to hunt, indeed he was my own father. One day they were out together seeking a certain elephant whose tusks were bigger than those of any other. Then the elephant charged the king and my father, at the risk of his life, killed it and claimed the tusks, as is the custom among the Ethiopians. But the king who greatly desired those tusks, caused my father to be poisoned that he might take them as his heir. Only before he died, my father, who could talk the elephant language, told all the other elephants of this wickedness, at which they were very angry, because they knew well that from the beginning of time their tusks have belonged to him who killed them, and the elephants are a people who do not like ancient laws to be altered. So the elephants made a league together and when the king next went out hunting, taking heed of nothing else they rushed at the king and tore him into pieces no bigger than a finger, and then killed the prince his son, who was behind him. That is the tale of the elephants who love Law, O King."

"Yes, yes," said his Majesty, waking up from a little doze, "but what became of the great tusks? I should like to have them."

"I inherited them as my father's son, O King, and gave them to my master, who doubtless will send them to you when he gets back to Egypt."

"A strange tale," said the King. "A very strange tale which seems to remind me of something that happened not long ago. What was it? Well, it does not matter. Egyptian, do you seek any reward for that shot of yours at the lioness? If so, it shall be given to you. Have you a grudge against anyone, for instance?"

"O King," I answered, "I do seek justice against a certain man. This evening I was led to the bank of the river in charge of the eunuch Houman, who desired to take me for a row in a boat. On the road, for no offence he struck me on the head with the handle of his fly-whip. See, here are the marks of it, O King. Unless the King commanded him to strike me which I do not remember, I seek justice against this eunuch."

Now the King grew very angry and cried,

"What! Did the dog dare to strike a freeborn noble Egyptian?"

Here Houman threw himself upon his face in terror and began to babble out I know not what about the punishment of the boat, which was unlucky for him, for it put the matter into the King's mind.

"The boat!" he cried. "Ah! yes, the boat; being so fat you will fit it well, Eunuch. To the boat with him, and before he enters it a hundred blows upon the feet with the rods," and he pointed at him with his sceptre.

Then guards sprang upon Houman and dragged him away. As he went he clutched at Bes, but hissing something into his ear, the dwarf bit him through the hand till he let go. So Houman departed and the King's guests laughed at the sight, for he had worked mischief to many.

When he had gone the King stared at me and asked,

"But why did I disturb you from your sleep, Egyptian? Oh! I remember. This dwarf says that he has seen the fairest woman in the whole world, and the most learned, some lady of Egypt, but that he does not know her name, that you alone know her name. I disturbed you that you might tell it to me but if you have forgotten it, you can go back to your bed and rest there till it returns to you. There are plenty of boats in the river, Egyptian."

"The fairest and most learned woman in the world?" I said astonished. "Who can that be, unless he means the lady Amada?" and I paused, wishing I had bitten out my tongue before I spoke, for I smelt a trap.

"Yes, Master," said Bes in a clear voice. "That was the name, the lady Amada."

"Who is this lady Amada?" asked the King, seeming to grow suddenly sober. "And what is she like?"

"I can tell you that, O King," said Bes. "She is like a willow shaken in the wind for slenderness and grace. She has eyes like those of a buck at gaze; she has lips like rosebuds; she has hair black as the night and soft as silk, the odour of which floats round her like that of flowers. She has a voice that whispers like the evening wind, and yet is rich as honey. Oh! she is beautiful as a goddess and when men see her their hearts melt like wax in the sun and for a long while they can look upon no other woman, not till the next day indeed if they meet her in the evening," and Bes smacked his thick lips and gazed upwards.

"By the holy Fire," laughed the King, "I feel my heart melting already. Say, Shabaka, what do you know of this Amada? Is she married or a maiden?"

Now I answered because I must, for after all that boat was not far away, nor did I dare to lie.

"She is married, O King of kings, to the goddess Isis whom she loves alone."

"A woman married to a woman, or rather to the Queen of women," he answered laughing, "well, that matters little."

"Nay, O King, it matters much since she is under the protection of Isis and inviolate."

"That remains to be seen, Shabaka. I think that I would dare the wrath of every false goddess in heaven to win such a prize. Learned also, you say, Shabaka."

"Aye, O King, full of learning to the finger tips, a prophetess also, one in whom the divine fire burns like a lamp in a vase of alabaster, one to whom visions come and who can read the future and the past."

"Still better," said the King. "One, then, who would be a fitting consort for the King of kings, who wearies of fat, round-eyed, sweetmeat-sucking fools whereof there are hundreds yonder," and he pointed towards the House of Women. "Who is this maid's father?"

"He is dead but she is the niece of the Prince Peroa, and by birth the Royal Lady of Egypt, O King."

"Good, then she is well born also. Hearken, O Shabaka, to-morrow you start back to Egypt, bearing letters from me to my vassal Peroa, and to my Satrap Idernes, bidding Peroa to hand over this lady Amada to Idernes and bidding Idernes to send her to the East with all honour and without delay, that she may enter my household as one of my wives."

Now I was filled with rage and horror, and about to refuse this mission when Bes broke in swiftly,

"Will the King of kings be pleased to give command as to my master's safe and honourable escort to Egypt?"

"It is commanded with all things necessary for Shabaka the Egyptian and the dwarf his servant, with the gold and gems and slaves he won from me in a wager, and everything else that is his. Let it be recorded."

Scribes sprang forward and wrote the King's words down, while like one in a dream I thought to myself that they could not now be altered. The King watched them sleepily for a while, then seemed to wake up and grow clear-minded again. At least he said to me,

"Fortune has shown you smiles and frowns to-day, Egyptian, and the smiles last. Yet remember that she has teeth behind her lips wherewith to tear out the throat of the faithless. Man, if you play me false or fail in your mission, be sure that you shall die and in such a fashion that will make you think of yonder boat as a pleasant bed, and with you this woman Amada and her uncle Peroa, and all your kin and hers; yes," he added with a burst of shrewdness, "and even that abortion of a dwarf to whom I have listened because he amused me, but who perhaps is more cunning than he seems."

"O King of kings," I said, "I will not be false." But I did not add to whom I would be true.

"Good. Ere long I shall visit Egypt, as I have told you, and there I shall pass judgment on you and others. Till then, farewell. Fear nothing, for you have my safe-conduct. Begone, both of you, for you weary me. But first drink and keep the cup, and in exchange, give me that bow of yours which shoots so far and straight."

"It is the King's," I answered as I pledged him in the golden, jewelled cup which a butler had handed to me.

Then the curtain fell in front of the throne and chamberlains came forward to lead me and Bes back to our lodging, one of whom took the cup and bore it in front of us.

Down the hall we went between the feasting nobles who all bowed to one to whom the Great King had shown favour, and so out of the palace through the quiet night back to the house where I had dwelt while waiting audience of the King. Here the chamberlains bade me farewell, giving the cup to Bes to carry, and saying that on the morrow early my gold should be brought to me together with all that was needed for my journey, also one who would receive the bow I had promised to the King, which had already been returned to my lodgings with everything that was ours. Then they bowed and went.

We entered the house, climbing a stair to an upper chamber. Here Bes barred the door and the shutters, making sure that none could see or hear us.

Then he turned, threw his arms about me, kissed my hand and burst into tears.

Bes Steals the Signet

"Oh! my Master," gulped Bes, "I weep because I am tired, so take no notice. The day was long and during it twice at least there has been but the twinkling of an eyelid, but the thickness of a finger nail, but the weight of a hair between you and death."

"Yes," I said, "and you were the eyelid, the finger nail and the hair."

"No, Master, not I, but something beyond me. The tool carves the statue and the hand holds the tool but the spirit guides the hand. Not once only since the sun rose has my mind been empty as a drum. Then something struck on it, perhaps the holy Tanofir, perhaps another, and it knew what note to sound. So it was when I cursed you in the boat. So it was when I walked back with the eunuch, meaning to kill him on the road, and then remembered that the death of one vile eunuch would not help you at all, whereas alive he could bring me to the presence of the King, if I paid him, as I did out of the gold in your purse which I carried. Moreover he earned his hire, for when the King grew dull, wine not yet having taken a hold on him, it was he who brought me to his mind as one who might amuse him, being so ugly and different from others, if only for a few minutes, after the women dancers had failed to do so."

"And what happened then, Bes?"

"Then I was fetched and did my juggling tricks with that snake I caught and tamed, which is in my pouch now. You should not hate it any more, Master, for it played your game well. After this the King began to talk to me and I saw that his mind was ill at ease about you whom he knew that he had wronged. So I told him that story of an elephant that my father killed to save a king—it grew up in my mind like a toadstool in the night, Master, did this story of an ungrateful king and what befell him. Then the King became still more unquiet in his heart about you and asked the eunuch, Houman, where you were, to which he answered that by his order you were sleeping in a boat and might not be disturbed. So that arrow of mine missed its mark because the King did not like to eat his own words and cause you to be brought from out the boat, whither he had sent you. Now when everything seemed lost, some god, or perhaps the holy Tanofir who is ever present with me to see that I have not forgotten him, put it into the King's mouth to begin to talk about women and to ask me if I had ever seen any fairer than those dancers whom I met going out as I came in. I answered that I had not noticed them much because they were so ugly, as indeed all women had seemed to me since once upon the banks of Nile I had looked upon one who was as Hathor herself for beauty. The King asked me who this might be and I answered that I did not know since I had never dared to ask the name of one whom even my master held to be as a goddess, although as boy and girl they had been brought up together.

"Then the King saw his opportunity to ease his conscience and inquired of an old councillor if there were not a law which gave the king power to alter his decree if thereby he could satisfy his soul and acquire knowledge. The councillor answered that there was such a law and began to give examples of its working, till the King cut him short and said that by virtue of it he commanded that you should be brought out of your bed in the boat and led before him to answer a question.

"So you were sent for, Master, but I did not go with the messengers, fearing lest if I did the King would forget all about the matter before you came. Therefore I stayed and amused him with tales of hunting, till I could not think of any more, for you were long in coming. Indeed I began to fear lest he should declare the feast at an end. But at the last, just as he was yawning and spoke to one of his councillors, bidding him send to the House of Women that they might make ready to receive him there, you came, and the rest you know."

Now I looked at Bes and said,

"May the blessing of all the gods of all the lands be on your head, since had it not been for you I should now lie in torment in that boat. Hearken, friend: If ever we reach Egypt again, you will set foot on it, not as a slave but as a free man. You will be rich also, Bes, that is, if we can take the gold I won with us, since half of it is yours."

Bes squatted down upon the floor and looked up at me with a strange smile on his ugly face.

"You have given me three things, Master," he said. "Gold, which I do not want at present; freedom, which I do not want at present and mayhap, never shall while you live and love me; and the title of friend. This I do want, though why I should care to hear it from your lips I am not sure, seeing that for a long while I have known that it was spoken in your heart. Since you have said it, however, I will tell you something which hitherto I have hid even from you. I have a right to that name, for if your blood is high, O Shabaka, so is mine. Know that this poor dwarf whom you took captive and saved long years ago was more than the petty chief which he declared himself to be. He was and is by right the King of the Ethiopians and that throne with all its wealth and power he could claim to-morrow if he would."

"The King of the Ethiopians!" I said. "Oh! friend Bes, I pray you to remember that we no longer stand in yonder court lying for our lives."

"I speak no lie, O Shabaka, I before you am King of the Ethiopians. Moreover, I laid that kingship down of my own will and should I so desire, can take it up again when I will, since the Ethiopians are faithful to their kings."

"Why?" I asked, astonished.

"Master, for so I will still call you who am not yet upon the land of Egypt where you have promised me freedom, do you remember anything strange about the people of that tribe from among whom you and the Egyptian soldiers captured me by surprise, because they wished to drive you and your following from their country?"

Now I thought and answered,

"Yes, one thing. I saw no women in their camp, nor any sign of children. This I know because I gave orders that such were to be spared and it was reported to me that there were none, so I supposed that they had fled away."

"There were none to fly, Master. That tribe was a brotherhood which had abjured women. Look on me now. I am misshapen, hideous, am I not? Born thus, it is said, because before my birth my mother was frightened by a dwarf. Yet the law of the Ethiopians is that their kings must marry within a year of their crowning. Therefore I chose a woman to be the queen whom I had long desired in secret. She scorned me, vowing that not for all the thrones of all the world would she be mated to a monster, and that if it were done by force she would kill herself, a saying that went abroad throughout the land. I said that she had spoken well and sent her in safety from the country, after which I too laid down my crown and departed with some who loved me, to form a brotherhood of women-haters further down the Nile, beyond the borders of Ethiopia. There the Egyptian force of which you were in command, attacked us unprepared, and you made me your slave. That is all."

"But why did you do this, Bes, seeing that maidens are many and all would not have thought thus?"

"Because I wished for that one only, Master; also I feared lest I should become the father of a breed of twisted dwarfs. So I who was a king am now a slave, and yet, who knows which way the Grasshopper will jump? One day from a slave I may again grow into a king. And now let us seek that wherein kings are as slaves and slaves as kings—sleep."

So we lay down and slept, I thanking the gods that my bed was not yonder in the boat upon the great river.

When I woke refreshed, though after all I had gone through on the yesterday my brain still swam a little, the light was pouring through the carved work of the shuttered windows. By it I saw Bes seated on the floor engaged in doing something to his bow, which, as I have said, had been restored to us with our other weapons, and asked him sleepily what it was.

"Master," he said, "yonder King demanded your bow and therefore a bow must be sent to him. But there is no need for it to be that with which you shot the lions, which, too, you value above anything you have, seeing that it came down to you from your forefather who was a Pharaoh of Egypt, and has been your companion from boyhood ever since you were strong enough to draw it. As you may remember I copied that bow out of a somewhat lighter wood, which I could bend with ease, and it is the copy that we will give to the King. Only first I must set your string upon it, for that may have been noted; also make one or two marks that are on your bow which I am finishing now, having begun the task with the dawn."

"You are clever," I said laughing, "and I am glad. The holy Tanofir, looking on my bow, once had a vision. It was that an arrow loosed from it would drink the blood of a great king and save Egypt. But what king and when, he did not see."

The dwarf nodded and answered,

"I have heard that tale and so have others. Therefore I play this trick since it is better that yonder palace dweller should get the arrow than the bow. There, it is finished to the last scratch, and none, save you and I, would know them apart. Till we are clear of this cursed land your bow is mine, Master, and you must find you another of the Eastern make."

"Master," I repeated after him. "Say, Bes, did I dream or did you in truth tell me last night that you are by birth and right the king of a great country?"

"I told you that, Master and it is true, no dream, since joy and suffering mixed unseal the lips and from them comes that at times which the heart would hide. Now I ask a favour of you, that you will speak no more of this matter either to me or to any other, man or woman, unless I should speak of it first. Let it be as though it were indeed a dream."

"It is granted," I said as I rose and clothed myself, not in my own garments which had been taken from me in the palace, but in the splendid silken robes that had been set upon me after I was loosed from the boat. When this was done and I had washed and combed my long, curling hair, we descended to a lower chamber and called for the woman of the house to bring us food, of which I ate heartily. As we finished our meal we heard shouts in the street outside of, "Make way for the servants of the King!" and looking through the window-place, saw a great cavalcade approaching, headed by two princes on horseback.

"Now I pray that yonder Tyrant has not changed his mind and that these do not come to take me back to the boat," I said in a low voice.

"Have no fear, Master," answered Bes, "seeing that you have touched his sceptre and drunk from his cup which he gave to you. After these things no harm can happen to you in any land he rules. Therefore be at ease and deal with these fellows proudly."

A minute later two princes entered followed by slaves who bore many things, among them those hide bags filled with gold that had been set beneath me in the boat. The elder of them bowed, greeting me with the title of "Lord," and I bowed back to him. Then he handed me certain rolls tied up with silk and sealed, which he said I was to deliver as the King had commanded to the King's Satrap in Egypt, and to the Prince Peroa. Also he gave me other letters addressed to the King's servants on the road and written on tablets of clay in a writing I could not read, with all of which I touched my forehead in the Eastern fashion.

After this he told me that by noon all would be ready for my journey which I should make with the rank of the King's Envoy, duly provisioned and escorted by his servants, with liberty to use the royal horses from post to post. Then he ordered the slaves to bring in the gifts which the King sent to me, and these were many, including even suits of flexible armour that would turn any sword-thrust or arrow.

I thanked him, saying that I would be ready to start by noon, and asked whether the King wished to see me before I rode. He replied that he had so wished, but that as he was suffering in his head from the effects of the sun, he could not. He bade me, however, remember all that he had said to me and to be sure that the beauteous lady Amada, of whom I had spoken, was sent to him without delay. In that case my reward should be great; but if I failed to fulfil his commands, then his wrath would be greater and I should perish miserably as he had promised.

I bowed and made no answer, after which he and his companions opened the bags of gold to show me that it was there, offering to weigh it again against my servant, the dwarf, so that I could see that nothing had been taken away.

I replied that the King's word was truer than any scale, whereon the bags were tied up again and sealed. Then I produced the bow, or rather its counterfeit, and having shown it to the princes, wrapped it and six of my own arrows in a linen cloth, to be taken to the King, with a message that though hard to draw it was the deadliest weapon in the world. The elder of them took it, bowed and bade me farewell, saying that perhaps we should meet again ere long in Egypt, if my gods gave me a safe journey. So we parted and I was glad to see the last of them.

Scarcely had they gone when the six hunters whom I had won in the wager and thereby saved from death, entered the chamber and fell upon their knees before me, asking for orders as to making ready my gear for the journey. I inquired of them if they were coming also, to which their spokesman replied that they were my slaves to do what I commanded.

"Do you desire to come?" I inquired.

"O Lord Shabaka," answered their spokesman, "we do, though some of us must leave wives and children behind us."

"Why?" I asked.

"For two reasons, Lord. Here we are men disgraced, though through no fault of our own and if you were to leave us in this land, soon the anger of the King would find us out and we should lose not only our wives and children, but with them our lives. Whereas in another land we may get other wives and more children, but never shall we get another life. Therefore we would leave those dear ones to our friends, knowing that soon the women will forget and find other husbands, and that the children will grow up to whatever fate is appointed them, thinking of us, their fathers, as dead. Secondly we are hunters by trade, and we have seen that you are a great hunter, one whom we shall always be proud to serve in the chase or in war, one, too, who went out of his path to save our lives, because he saw that we had been unjustly doomed to a cruel death. Therefore we desire nothing better than to be your slaves, hoping that perchance we may earn our liberty from you in days to come by our good service."

"Is that the wish of all of you?" I asked.

Speaking one by one, they said that it was, though tears rose in the eyes of some of them who were married at the thought of parting from their women and their little ones, who, it seemed might not be brought with them because they were the people of the King and had not been named in the bet. Moreover, horses could not be found for so many, nor could they travel fast.

"Come then," I said, "and know that while you are faithful to me, I will be good to you, men of my own trade, and perhaps in the end set you free in a land where brave fellows are not given to be torn to pieces by wild beasts at the word of any kind. But if you fail me or betray me, then either I will kill you, or sell you to those who deal in slaves, to work at the oar, or in the mines till you die."

"Henceforth we have no lord but you, O Shabaka," they said, and one after another took my hand and pressed it to their foreheads, vowing to be true to me in all things while we lived.

So I bade them begone to bid farewell to those they loved and return again within half an hour of noon, never expecting, to tell the truth, that they would come. Indeed I did this to give them the opportunity of escaping if they saw fit, and hiding themselves where they would. But as I have often noted, the trade of hunting breeds honesty in the blood and at the hour appointed all of these men appeared, one of them with a woman who carried a child in her arms, clinging to him and weeping bitterly. When her veil slipped aside I saw that she was young and very fair to look on.

So at noon we left the city of the Great King in the charge of two of his officers who brought me his thanks for the bow I had sent him, which he said he should treasure above everything he possessed, a saying at which Bes rolled his yellow eyes and grinned. We were mounted on splendid stallions from the royal stables and clad in the shirts of mail that had been presented to us, though when we were clear of the city we took these off because of the heat, also because that which Bes wore chafed him, being too long for his squat shape. Our goods together with the bags of gold were laden on sumpter horses which were led by my six hunter slaves. Four picked soldiers brought up the rear, mighty men from the King's own bodyguard, and two of the royal postmen who served us as guides. Also there were cooks and grooms with spare horses.

Thus we started in state and a great crowd watched us go. Our road ran by the river which we must cross in barges lower down, so that in a few minutes we came to that quay whither I had been led on the previous night to die. Yes, there were the watching guards, and there floated the hateful double boat, at the prow of which appeared the tortured face of the eunuch Houman, who rolled his head from side to side to rid himself of the torment of the flies. He caught sight of us and began to scream for pity and forgiveness, whereat Bes smiled. The officers halted our cavalcade and one of them approaching me said,

"It is the King's command, O Lord Shabaka, that you should look upon this villain who traduced you to the King and afterwards dared to strike you. If you will, enter the water and blind him, that your face may be the last thing he sees before he passes into darkness."

I shook my head, but Bes into whose mind some thought had come, whispered to me,

"I wish to speak with yonder eunuch, so give me leave and fear nothing. I will do him no hurt, only good, if I find the chance."

Then I said to the officer,

"It is not for great lords to avenge themselves upon the fallen. Yet my slave here was also wronged and would say a word to yonder Houman."

"So be it," said the officer, "only let him be careful not to hurt him too sorely, lest he should die before the time and escape his punishment."

Then Bes tucked up his robes and waded into the river, flourishing a great knife, while seeing him come, Houman began to scream with fear. He reached the boat and bent over the eunuch, talking to him in a low voice. What he did there I could not see because his cloak was spread out on either side of the man's head. Presently, however, I caught sight of the flash of a knife and heard yells of agony followed by groans, whereat I called to him to return and let the fellow be. For when I remembered that his fate was near to being my own, those sounds made me sick at heart and I grew angry with Bes, though the cruel Easterns only laughed.

At length he came back grinning and washing the blade of his knife in the water. I spoke fiercely to him in my own language, and still he grinned on, making no answer. When we were mounted again and riding away from that horrible boat with its groaning prisoner, watching Bes whose behaviour and silence I could not understand, I saw him sweep his hand across his great mouth and thrust it swiftly into his bosom. After this he spoke readily enough, though in a low voice lest someone who understood Egyptian should overhear him.

"You are a fool, Master," he said, "to think that I should wish to waste time in torturing that fat knave."

"Then why did you torture him?" I asked.

"Because my god, the Grasshopper, when he fashioned me a dwarf, gave me a big mouth and good teeth," he answered, whereon I stared at him, thinking that he had gone mad.

"Listen, Master. I did not hurt Houman. All I did was to cut his cords nearly through from the under side, so that when night comes he can break them and escape, if he has the wit. Now, Master, you may not have noticed, but I did, that before the King doomed you to death by the boat yesterday, he took a certain round, white seal, a cylinder with gods and signs cut on it, which hung by a gold chain from his girdle, and gave it to Houman to be his warrant for all he did. This seal Houman showed to the Treasurer whereon they produced the gold that was weighed in the scales against me, and to others when he ordered the boat to be prepared for you to lie in. Moreover he forgot to return it, for when he himself was dragged off to the boat by direct command of the King, I caught sight of the chain beneath his robe. Can you guess the rest?"

"Not quite," I answered, for I wished to hear the tale in his own words.

"Well, Master, when I was walking with Houman after he had put you in the boat, I asked him about this seal. He showed it to me and said that he who bore it was for the time the king of all the Empire of the East. It seems that there is but one such seal which has descended from ancient days from king to king, and that of it every officer, great or small, has an impress in all lands. If the seal is produced to him, he compares it with the impress and should the two agree, he obeys the order that is brought as though the King had given it in person. When we reached the Court doubtless Houman would have returned the seal, but seeing that the King was, or feigned to be drunk, waited for fear lest it should be lost, and with it his life. Then he was seized as you saw, and in his terror forgot all about the seal, as did the King and his officers."

"But, surely, Bes, those who took Houman to the boat would have removed it."

"Master, even the most clear-sighted do not see well at night. At any rate my hope was that they had not done so, and that is why I waded out to prick the eyes of Houman. Moreover, as I had hoped, so it was; there beneath his robe I saw the chain. Then I spoke to him, saying,

"'I am come to put out your eyes, as you deserve, seeing how you have treated my master. Still I will spare you at a price. Give me the King's ancient white seal that opens all doors, and I will only make a pretence of blinding you. Moreover I will cut your cords nearly through, so that when the night comes you can break them, roll into the river and escape.'

"'Take it if you can,' he said, 'and use it to injure or destroy that accursed one.'"

"So you took it, Bes."

"Yes, Master, but not easily. Remember, it was on a chain about the man's neck, and I could not draw it over his head, for, like his hands, his throat was tied by a cord, as you remember yours was."

"I remember very well," I said, "for my throat is still sore from the rope that ran to the same staples to which my hands were fastened."

"Yes, Master, and therefore if I drew the chain off his neck, it would still have been on the ropes. I thought of trying to cut it with the knife, but this was not easy because it is thick, and if I had dragged it up on the blade of the knife it would have been seen, for many eyes were watching me, Master. Then I took another counsel. While I pretended to be putting out the eyes of Houman, I bent down and getting the chain between my teeth I bit it through. One tooth broke— see, but the next finished the business. I ate through the soft gold, Master, and then sucked up the chain and the round white seal into my mouth, and that is why I could not answer you just now, because my cheeks were full of chain. So we have the King's seal that all the subject countries know and obey. It may be useful, yonder in Egypt, and at least the gold is of value."

"Clever!" I exclaimed, "very clever. But you have forgotten something, Bes. When that knave escapes, he will tell the whole story and the King will send after us and kill us who have stolen his royal seal."

"I don't think so, Master. First, it is not likely that Houman will escape. He is very fat and soft and already suffers much. After a day in the sun also he will be weak. Moreover I do not think that he can swim, for eunuchs hate the water. So if he gets out of the boat it is probable that he will drown in the river, since he dare not wade to the quay where the guards will be waiting. But if he does escape by swimming across the river, he will hide for his life's sake and never be seen again, and if by chance he is caught, he will say that the seal fell into the water when he was taken to the boat, or that one of the guards had stolen it. What he will not say is that he had bargained it away with someone who in return, cut his cords, since for that crime he must die by worse tortures than those of the boat. Lastly we shall ride so fast that with six hours' start none will catch us. Or if they do I can throw away the chain and swallow the seal."

As Bes said, so it happened. The fate of Houman I never learned, and of the theft of the seal I heard no more until a proclamation was issued to all the kingdoms that a new one was in use. But this was not until long afterwards when it had served my turn and that of Egypt.

The Lady Amada

Now day by day, hour by hour and minute by minute every detail of that journey appeared before me, but to set it all down is needless. As I, Allan Quatermain, write the record of my vision, still I seem to hear the thunder of our horses' hoofs while we rushed forward at full gallop over the plains, over the mountain passes and by the banks of rivers. The speed at which we travelled was wonderful, for at intervals of about forty miles were post-houses and at these, whatever might be the hour of day or night, we found fresh horses from the King's stud awaiting us. Moreover, the postmasters knew that we were coming, which astonished me until we discovered that they had been warned of our arrival by two King's messengers who travelled ahead of us.

These men, it would seem, although our officers and guides professed ignorance of the matter, must have left the King's palace at dawn on the day of our departure, whereas we did not mount in the city till a little after noon. Therefore they had six hours good start of us, and what is more, travelled lighter than we did, having no sumpter beasts with them, and no cooks or servants. Moreover, always they had the pick of the horses and chose the three swiftest beasts, leading the third in case one of their own should founder or meet with accident. Thus it came about that we never caught them up although we covered quite a hundred miles a day. Only once did I see them, far off upon the skyline of a mountain range which we had to climb, but by the time we had reached its crest they were gone.

At length we came to the desert without accident and crossed it, though more slowly. But even here the King had his posts which were in charge of Arabs who lived in tents by wells of water, or sometimes where there was none save what was brought to them. So still we galloped on, parched by the burning sand beneath and the burning sand above, and reached the borders of Egypt.

Here, upon the very boundary line, the two officers halted the cavalcade saying that their orders were to return thence and make report to the King. There then we parted, Bes and I with the six hunters who still chose to cling to me, going forward and the officers of the King with the guides and servants going back. The good horses that we rode from the last post they gave to us by the King's command, together with the sumpter beasts, since horses broken to the saddle were hard to come by in Egypt where they were trained to draw chariots. These we took, sending back my thanks to the King, and started on once more, Bes leading that beast which bore the gold and the hunters serving as a guard.

Indeed I was glad to see the last of those Easterns although they had brought us safely and treated us well, for all the while I was never sure but that they had some orders to lead us into a trap, or perhaps to make away with us in our sleep and take back the gold and the priceless, rose-hued pearls, any two of which were worth it all. But such was not their command nor did they dare to steal them on their own account, since then, even if they escaped the vengeance of the King, their wives and all their families would have paid the price.

Now we entered Egypt near the Salt Lakes that are not far from the head of the Gulf, crossing the canal that the old Pharaohs had dug, which proved easy for it was silted up. Before we reached it we found some peasant folk labouring in their gardens and I heard one of them call to another,

"Here come more of the Easterns. What is toward, think you, neighbour?"

"I do not know," answered the other, "but when I passed down the canal this morning, I saw a body of the Great King's guards gathering from the fort. Doubtless it is to meet these men of whose coming the other two who went by fifty hours ago, have warned the officers."

"Now what does that mean?" I asked of Bes.

"Neither more nor less than we have heard, Master. The two King's messengers who have gone ahead of us all the way from the city, have told the officer of the frontier fort that we are coming, so he has advanced to the ford to meet us, for what purpose I do not know."

"Nor do I," I said, "but I wish we could take another road, if there were one."

"There is none, Master, for above and below the canal is full of water and the banks are too steep for horses to climb. Also we must show no doubt or fear."

He thought a while, then added,

"Take the royal seal, Master. It may be useful."

He gave it to me, and I examined it more closely than I had done before. It was a cylinder of plain white shell hung on a gold chain, that which Bes had bitten through, but now mended again by taking out the broken link. On this cylinder were cut figures; as I think of a priest presenting a noble to a god, over whom was the crescent of the moon, while behind the god stood a man or demon with a tall spear. Also between the figures were mystic signs, meaning I know not what. The workmanship of the carving was grown shallow with time and use for the cylinder seemed to be very ancient, a sacred thing that had descended from generation to generation and was threaded through with a bar of silver on which it turned.

I put the seal which was like no other that I had seen, being the work of an early and simpler age, round my neck beneath my mail and we went on.

Descending the steep bank of the canal we came to the ford where the sand that had silted in was covered by not more than a foot of water. As we entered it, on the top of the further bank appeared a body of about thirty armed and mounted men, one of whom carried the Great King's banner, on which I noted was blazoned the very figures that were cut upon the cylinder. Now it was too late to retreat, so we rode through the water and met the soldiers. Their officer advanced, crying,

"In the name of the Great King, greeting, my lord Shabaka!"

"In the name of the Great King, greeting!" I answered. "What would you with Shabaka, Officer of the King?"

"Only to do him honour. The word of the King has reached us and we come to escort you to the Court of Idernes, the Satrap of the King and Governor of Egypt who sits at Sais."

"That is not my road, Officer. I travel to Memphis to deliver the commands of the King to my cousin, Peroa, the ruler of Egypt under the King. Afterwards, perchance, I shall visit the high Idernes."

"To whom our commands are to take you now, my lord Shabaka, not afterwards," said the officer sternly, glancing round at his armed escort.

"I come to give commands, not to receive them, Captain of the King."

"Seize Shabaka and his servants," said the officer briefly, whereon the soldiers rode forward to surround us.

I waited till they were near at hand. Then suddenly I plunged my hand beneath my robe and drew out the small, white seal which I held before the eyes of the officer, saying,

"Who is it that dares to lay a finger upon the holder of the King's White Seal? Surely that man is ready for death."

The officer stared at it, then leapt from his horse and flung himself face downwards on the ground, crying,

"It is the ancient signet of the Kings of the East, given to their first forefather by Samas the Sungod, on which hangs the fortunes of the Great House! Pardon, my lord Shabaka."

"It is granted," I answered, "because what you did you did in ignorance. Now go to the Satrap Idernes and say to him that if he would have speech with the bearer of the King's seal which all must obey, he will find him at Memphis. Farewell," and with Bes and the six hunters I rode through the guards, none striving to hinder me.

"That was well done, Master," said Bes.

"Yes," I said. "Those two messengers who went ahead of us brought orders to the frontier guard of Idernes that I should be taken to him as a prisoner. I do not know why, but I think because things are passing in Egypt of which we know nothing and the King did not desire that I should see the Prince Peroa and give him news that I might have gathered. Mayhap we have been outwitted, Bes, and the business of the lady Amada is but a pretext to pick a quarrel suddenly before Peroa can strike the first blow."

"Perhaps, Master, for these Easterns are very crafty. But, Master, what happens to those who make a false use of the King's ancient, sacred signet? I think they have cut the ropes which tie them to earth," and he looked upwards to the sky rolling his yellow eyes.

"They must find new ropes, Bes, and quickly, before they are caught. Hearken. You have sat upon a throne and I can speak out to you. Think you that my cousin, the Prince Peroa, loves to be the servant of this distant, Eastern king, he who by right is Pharaoh of Egypt? Peroa must strike or lose his niece and perchance his life. Forward, that we may warn him."

"And if he will not strike, Master, knowing the King's might and being somewhat slow to move?"

"Then, Bes, I think that you and I had best go hunting far away in those lands you know, where even the Great King cannot follow us."

"And where, if only I can find a woman who does not make me ill to look on, and whom I do not make ill, I too can once more be a king, Master, and the lord of many thousand brave armed men. I must speak of that matter to the holy Tanofir."

"Who doubtless will know what to advise you, Bes; or, if he dies not, I shall."

For a while we rode on in silence, each thinking his own thoughts. Then Bes said,

"Master, before so very long we shall reach the Nile, and having with us gold in plenty can buy boats and hire crews. It comes into my mind that we should do well for our own safety and comfort to start at once on a hunting journey far from Egypt; in the land of the Ethiopians, Master. There perchance I could gather together some of the wise men in whose hands I left the rule of my kingdom, and submit to them this question of a woman to marry me. The Ethiopians are a faithful people, Master, and will not reject me because I have spent some years seeing the world afar, that I might learn how to rule them better."

"I have remembered that it cannot be, Bes," I said.

"Why not, Master?"

"For this reason. You left your country because of a woman? I cannot leave mine again because of a woman."

Bes rolled his eyes around as though he thought to see that woman in the desert. Not discovering her, he stared upwards and there found light.

"Is she perchance named the lady Amada, Master?"

I nodded.

"So. The lady Amada who you told the Great King is the most beautiful one in the whole world, causing the fire of Love to burn up in his royal heart, and with it many other things of which we do not know at present."

"*You* told him, Bes," I said angrily.

"I told him of a beautiful one; I did not tell him her name, Master, and although I never thought of it at the time, perhaps she will be angry with him who told her name."

Now fear took hold of me, and Bes saw it in my face.

"Do not be afraid, Master. If there is trouble I will swear that I told the Great King that lady's name."

"Yes, Bes, but how would that fit in with the story, seeing that I was brought out of the boat for this very purpose?"

"Quite easily, Master, since I will say that you were led from the boat to confirm my tale. Oh! she will be angry with me, no doubt, but in Egypt even a dwarf cannot be killed because he has declared a certain lady to be the most beautiful in the world. But, Master, tell me, when did you learn to love her?"

"When we were boy and girl, Bes. We used to play together, being cousins, and I used to hold her hand. Then suddenly she refused to let me hold her hand any more, and I being quite grown up then, though she was younger, understood that I had better go away."

"I should have stopped where I was, Master."

"No, Bes. She was studying to be a priestess and my great uncle, the holy Tanofir, told me that I had better go away. So I went down south hunting and fighting in command of the troops, and met you, Bes."

"Which perhaps was better for you, Master, than to stop to watch the lady Amada acquire learning. Still, I wonder whether the holy Tanofir is *always* right. You see, Master, he thinks a great deal of priests and priestesses, and is so very old that he has forgotten all about love and that without it there never would have been a holy Tanofir."

"The holy Tanofir thinks of souls, not of bodies, Bes."

"Yes, Master. Still, oil is of no use without a lamp, or a soul without a body, at least here underneath the sun, or so we were taught who worship the Grasshopper. But, Master, when you came back from all your hunting, what happened then?"

"Then I found, Bes, that the lady Amada, having acquired all the learning possible, had taken her first vows to Isis, which she said she would not break for any man on earth although she might have done so without crime. Therefore, although I was dear to her, as a brother would have been had she had one, and she swore that she had never even thought of another man, she refused so much as to think of marrying who dreamed only of the heavenly perfections of the lady Isis."

"Ump!" said Bes. "We Ethiopians have Priestesses of the Grasshopper, or the Grasshopper's wife, but they do not think of her like that. I hope that one day something stronger than herself will not cause the lady Amada to break her vows to the heavenly Isis. Only then, perhaps, it may be for the sake of another man who did not go off to the East on account of such fool's talk. But here is a village and the horses are spent. Let us stop and eat, as I suppose even the lady Amada does sometimes."

On the following afternoon we crossed the Nile, and towards sunset entered the vast and ancient city of Memphis. On its white walls floated the banners of the Great King which Bes pointed out to me, saying that wherever we went in the whole world, it seemed that we could never be free from those accursed symbols.

"May I live to spit upon them and cast them into the moat," I answered savagely, for as I drew near to Amada they grew ten times more hateful to me than they had been before.

In truth I was nearer to Amada than I thought, for after we had passed the enclosure of the temple of Ptah, the most wonderful and the mightiest in the whole world, we came to the temple of Isis. There near to the pylon gate we met a procession of her priests and priestesses advancing to offer the evening sacrifice of song and flowers, clad, all of them, in robes of purest white. It was a day of festival, so singers went with them. After the singers came a band of priestesses bearing flowers, in front of whom walked another priestess shaking a *sistrum* that made a little tinkling music.

Even at a distance there was something about the tall and slender shape of this priestess that stirred me. When we came nearer I saw why, for it was Amada herself. Through the thin veil she wore I could see her dark and tender eyes set beneath the broad brow that was so full of thought, and the sweet, curved mouth that was like no other woman's. Moreover there could be no doubt since the veil parting above her breast showed the birth-mark for which she was famous, the mark of the young moon, the sign of Isis.

I sprang from my horse and ran towards her. She looked up and saw me. At first she frowned, then her face grew wondering, then tender, and I thought that her red lips shaped my name. Moreover in her confusion she let the *sistrum* fall.

I muttered "Amada!" and stepped forward, but priests ran between us and thrust me away. Next moment she had recovered the *sistrum* and passed on with her head bowed. Nor did she lift her eyes to look back.

"Begone, man!" cried a priest, "Begone, whoever you may be. Because you wear Eastern armour do you think that you can dare the curse of Isis?"

Then I fell back, the holy image of the goddess passed and the procession vanished through the pylon gate. I, Shabaka the Egyptian, stood by my horse and watched it depart. I was happy because the lady Amada was alive, well, and more beautiful than ever; also because she had shown signs of joy and confusion at seeing me again. Yet I was unhappy because I met her still filling a holy office which built a wall between us, also because it seemed to me an evil omen that I should have been repelled from her by a priest of Isis who talked of the curse of the goddess. Moreover the sacred statue, I suppose by accident, turned towards me as it passed and perhaps by the chance of light, seemed to frown upon me.

Thus I thought as Shabaka hundreds of years before the Christian era, but as Allan Quatermain the modern man, to whom it was given so marvellously to behold all these things and who in beholding them, yet never quite lost the sense of his own identity of to-day, I was amazed. For I knew that this lady Amada was the same being though clad in different flesh, as that other lady with whom I had breathed the magical *Taduki* fumes which had power to rend the curtain of the past, or, perhaps, only to breed dreams of what it might have been.

To the outward eye, indeed she was different, as I was different, taller, more slender, larger-eyed, with longer and slimmer hands than those of any Western woman, and on the whole even more beautiful and alluring. Moreover that mysterious look which from time to time I had seen on Lady Ragnall's face, was more constant on that of the lady Amada. It brooded in the deep eyes and settled in a curious smile about the curves of the lips, a smile that was not altogether human, such a smile as one might wear who had looked on hidden things and heard voices that spoke beyond the limits of the world.

Somehow neither then nor at any other time during all my dream, could I imagine this Amada, this daughter of a hundred kings, whose blood might be traced back through dynasty on dynasty, as nothing but a woman who nurses children upon her breast. It was as though something of our common nature had been bred out of her and something of another nature whereof we have no ken, had entered to fill its place. And yet these two women were the same, that I *knew*, or at any rate, much of them was the same, for who can say what part of us we leave behind as we flit from life to life, to find it again elsewhere in the abysms of Time and Change? One thing too was quite identical—the birthmark of the new moon above the breast which the priests of the Kendah had declared was always the seal that marked their prophetess, the guardian of the Holy Child.

When the procession had quite departed and I could no longer hear the sound of singing, I remounted and rode on to my house, or rather to that of my mother, the great lady Tiu, which was situated beneath the wall of the old palace facing towards the Nile. Indeed my heart was full of this mother of mine whom I loved and who loved me, for I was her only child, and my father had been long dead; so long that I could not remember him. Eight months had gone by since I saw her face and in eight months who knew what might have happened? The thought made me cold for she, who was aged and not too strong, perhaps had been gathered to Osiris. Oh! if that were so!

I shook my tired horse to a canter, Bes riding ahead of me to clear a road through the crowded street in which, at this hour of sundown, all the idlers of Memphis seemed to have gathered. They stared at me because it was not common to see men riding in Memphis, and with little love, since from my dress and escort they took me to be some envoy from their hated master, the Great King of the East. Some even threatened to bar the way; but we thrust through and presently turned into a thoroughfare of private houses standing in their own gardens. Ours was the third of these. At its gate I leapt from my horse, pushed open the closed door and hastened in to seek and learn.

I had not far to go for, there in the courtyard, standing at the head of our modest household and dressed in her festal robes, was my mother, the stately and white-haired lady Tiu, as one stands who awaits the coming of an honoured guest. I ran to her and kneeling, kissed her hand, saying,

"My mother! My mother, I have come safe home and greet you."

"I greet you also, my son," she answered, bending down and kissing me on the brow, "who have been in far lands and passed so many dangers. I greet you and thank the guardian gods who have brought you safe home again. Rise, my son."

I rose and kissed her on the face, then looked at the servants who were bowing their welcome to me, and said,

"How comes it, Lady of the House, that all are gathered here? Did you await some guest?"

"We awaited you, my son. For an hour have we stood here listening for the sound of your feet."

"Me!" I exclaimed. "That is strange, seeing that I have ridden fast and hard from the East, tarrying only a few minutes, and those since I entered Memphis, when I met——" and I stopped.

"Met whom, Shabaka?"

"The lady Amada walking in the procession of Isis."

"Ah! the lady Amada. The mother waits that the son may stop to greet the lady Amada!"

"But *why* did you wait, my mother? Who but a spirit or a bird of the air could have told you that I was coming, seeing that I sent no messenger before me?"

"You must have done so, Shabaka, since yesterday one came from the holy Tanofir, our relative who dwells in the desert in the burial-ground of Sekera. He bore a message from Tanofir to me, telling me to make ready since before sundown to-night you, my son, would be with me, having escaped great dangers, accompanied by the dwarf Bes, your servant, and six strange Eastern men. So I made ready and waited; also I prepared lodging for the six strange men in the outbuildings behind the house and sent a thank offering to the temple. For know, my son, I have suffered much fear for you."

"And not without cause, as you will say when I tell you all," I answered laughing. "But how Tanofir knew that I was coming is more than I can guess. Come, my mother, greet Bes here, for had it not been for him, never should I have lived to hold your hand again."

So she greeted him and thanked him, whereon Bes rolled his eyes and muttered something about the holy Tanofir, after which we entered the house. Thence I despatched a messenger to the Prince Peroa saying that if it were his pleasure I would wait on him at once, seeing that I had much to tell him. This done I bathed and caused my hair and beard to be trimmed and, discarding the Eastern garments, clothed myself in those of Egypt, and so felt that I was my own man again. Then I came out refreshed and drank a cup of Syrian wine and the night having fallen, sat down by my mother in the chamber with a lamp between us, and, holding her hand, told her something of my story, showing her the sacks of gold that had come with me safely from the East, and the chain of priceless, rose-hued pearls that I had won in a wager from the Great King.

Now when she learned how Bes by his wit had saved me from a death of torment in the boat, my mother clapped her hands to summon a servant and sent for Bes, and said to him,

"Bes, hitherto I have looked on you as a slave taken by my son, the noble Shabaka, in one of his far journeys that it pleases him to make to fight and to hunt. But henceforth I look upon you as a friend and give you a seat at my table. Moreover it comes into my mind that although so strangely shaped by some evil god, perhaps you are more than you seem to be."

Now Bes looked at me to see if I had told my mother anything, and when I shook my head answered,

"I thank you, O Lady of the House, who have but done my duty to my master. Still it is true that as a goatskin often holds good wine, so a dwarf should not always be judged by what can be seen of him."

Then he went away.

"It seems that we are rich again, Son, who have been somewhat poor of late years," said my mother, looking at the bags of gold. "Also, there are the pearls which doubtless are worth more than the gold. What are you going to do with them, Shabaka?"

"I thought of offering them as a gift to the lady Amada," I replied hesitatingly, "that is unless you——"

"I? No, I am too old for such gems. Yet, Son, it might be well to keep them for a time, seeing that while they are your own they may give you more weight in the eyes of the Prince Peroa and others. Whereas if you gave them the lady Amada and she took them, perchance it might only be to see them return to the East, whither you tell me she is summoned by one whose orders may not be disobeyed."

Now I turned white with rage and answered,

"While I live, Mother, Amada shall never go to the East to be the woman of yonder King."

"While you live, Son. But those who cross the will of a great king, are apt to die. Also this is a matter which her uncle, the Prince Peroa, must decide as policy dictates. Now as ever the woman is but a pawn in the game. Oh! my son," she went on, "do not pin all your heart to the robe of this Amada. She is very fair and very learned, but is she one who will love? Moreover, if so she is a priestess and it would be difficult for her to wed who is sworn to Isis. Lastly, remember this: If Egypt were free, she would be its heiress, not her uncle, Peroa. For hers is the true blood, not his. Would he, therefore, be willing to give her to any man who, according to the ancient custom, through her would acquire the right to rule?"

"I do not seek to rule, Mother; I only seek to wed Amada whom I love."

"Amada whom you love and whose name you, or rather your servant Bes, which is the same thing since it will be held that he did it by your order, gave to the King of the East, or so I understand. Here is a pretty tangle, Shabaka, and rather would I be without all that gold and those priceless pearls than have the task of its unravelling."

Before I could answer and explain all the truth to her, the curtain was swung aside and through it came a messenger from the Prince Peroa, who bade me come to eat with him at once at the palace, since he must see me this night.

So my mother having set the rope of rose-hued pearls in a double chain about my neck, I kissed her and went, with Bes who was also bidden. Outside a chariot was waiting into which we entered.

"Now, Master," said Bes to me as we drove to the palace, "I almost wish that we were back in another chariot hunting lions in the East."

"Why?" I asked.

"Because then, although we had much to fear, there was no woman in the story. Now the woman has entered it and I think that our real troubles are about to begin. Oh! to-morrow I go to seek counsel of the holy Tanofir."

"And I come with you," I answered, "for I think it will be needed."

The Messengers

We descended at the great gate of the palace and were led through empty halls that were no longer used now when there was no king in Egypt, to the wing of the building in which dwelt the Prince Peroa. Here we were received by a chamberlain, for the Prince of Egypt still kept some state although it was but small, and had about him men who bore the old, high-sounding titles of the "Officers of Pharaoh."

The chamberlain led me and Bes to an ante-chamber of the banqueting hall and left us, saying that he would summon the Prince who wished to see me before he ate. This, however, was not necessary since while he spoke Peroa, who as I guessed had been waiting for me, entered by another door. He was a majestic-looking man of middle age, for grey showed in his hair and beard, clad in white garments with a purple hem and wearing on his brow a golden circlet, from the front of which rose the *uraeus* in the shape of a hooded snake that might be worn by those of royal blood alone. His face was full of thought and his black and piercing eyes looked heavy as though with sleeplessness. Indeed I could see that he was troubled. His gaze fell upon us and his features changed to a pleasant smile.

"Greeting, Cousin Shabaka," he said. "I am glad that you have returned safe from the East, and burn to hear your tidings. I pray that they may be good, for never was good news more needed in Egypt."

"Greeting, Prince," I answered, bowing my knee. "I and my servant here are returned safe, but as for our tidings, well, judge of them for yourself," and drawing the letter of the Great King from my robe, I touched my forehead with the roll and handed it to him.

"I see that you have acquired the Eastern customs, Shabaka," he said as he took it. "But here in my own house which once was the palace of our forefathers, the Pharaohs of Egypt, by your leave I will omit them. Amen be my witness," he added bitterly, "I cannot bear to lay the letter of a foreign king against my brow in token of my country's vassalage."

Then he broke the silk of the seals and read, and as he read his face grew black with rage.

"What!" he cried, casting down the roll and stamping on it. "What! Does this dog of an Eastern king bid me send my niece, by birth the Royal Princess of Egypt, to be his toy until he wearies of her? First I will choke her with my own hands. How comes it, Shabaka, that you care to bring me such a message? Were I Pharaoh now I think your life would pay the price."

"As it would certainly have paid the price, had I not done so. Prince, I brought the letter because I must. Also a copy of it has gone, I believe, to Idernes the Satrap at Sais. It is better to face the truth, Prince, and I think that I may be of more service to you alive than dead. If you do not wish to send the lady Amada to the King, marry her to someone else, after which he will seek her no more."

He looked at me shrewdly and said,

"To whom then? I cannot marry her, being her uncle and already married. Do you mean to yourself, Shabaka?"

"I have loved the lady Amada from a child, Prince," I answered boldly. "Also I have high blood in me and having brought much gold from the East, am rich again and one accustomed to war."

"So you have brought gold from the East! How? Well, you can tell me afterwards. But you fly high. You, a Count of Egypt, wish to marry the Royal Lady of Egypt, for such she is by birth and rank, which, if ever Egypt were free again, would give you a title to the throne."

"I ask no throne, Prince. If there were one to fill I should be content to leave that to you and your heirs."

"So you say, no doubt honestly. But would the children of Amada say the same? Would you even say it if you were her husband, and would she say it? Moreover she is a priestess, sworn not to wed, though perhaps that trouble might be overcome, if she wishes to wed, which I doubt. Mayhap you might discover. Well, you are hungry and worn with long travelling. Come, let us eat, and afterwards you can tell your story. Amada and the others will be glad to hear it, as I shall. Follow me, Count Shabaka."

So we went to the lesser banqueting-hall, I filled with joy because I should see Amada, and yet, much afraid because of that story which I must tell. Gathered there, waiting for the Prince, we found the Princess his wife, a large and kindly woman, also his two eldest daughters and his young son, a lad of about sixteen. Moreover, there were certain officers, while at the tables of the lower hall sat others of the household, men of smaller rank, and their wives, since Peroa still maintained some kind of a shadow of the Court of old Egypt.

The Princess and the others greeted me, and Bes also who had always been a favourite with them, before he went to take his seat at the lowest table, and I greeted them, looking all the while for Amada whom I did not see. Presently, however, as we took our places on the couches, she entered dressed, not as a priestess, but in the beautiful robes of a great lady of Egypt and wearing on her head the *uraeus* circlet that signified her royal blood. As it chanced the only seat left vacant was that next to myself, which she took before she recognized me, for she was engaged in asking pardon for her lateness of the Prince and Princess, saying that she had been detained by the ceremonies at the temple. Seeing suddenly that I was her neighbour, she made as though she would change her place, then altered her mind and stayed where she was.

"Greeting, Cousin Shabaka," she said, "though not for the first time to-day. Oh! my heart was glad when looking up, outside the temple, I caught sight of you clad in that strange Eastern armour, and knew that you had returned safe from your long wanderings. Yet afterwards I must do penance for it by saying two added prayers, since at such a time my thoughts should have been with the goddess only."

"Greeting, Cousin Amada," I answered, "but she must be a jealous goddess who grudges a thought to a relative—and friend—at such a time."

"She is jealous, Shabaka, as being the Queen of women she must be who demands to reign alone in the hearts of her votaries. But tell me of your travels in the East and how you came by that rope of wondrous pearls, if indeed there can be pearls so large and beautiful."

This at the time I had little chance of doing, however, since the young Princess on the other side of her began to talk to Amada about some forthcoming festival, and the Prince's son next to me who was fond of hunting, to question me about sport in the East and when, unhappily, I said that I had shot lions there, gave me no peace for the rest of that feast. Also the Princess opposite was anxious to learn what food noble people ate in the East, and how it was cooked and how they sat at table, and what was the furniture of their rooms and did women attend feasts as in Egypt, and so forth. So it came about that what between these things and eating and drinking, which, being well-nigh starved, I was obliged to do, for, save a cup of wine, I had taken nothing in my mother's house, I found little chance of talking with the lovely Amada, although I knew that all the while she was studying me out of the corners of her large eyes. Or perhaps it was the rose-hued pearls she studied, I was not sure.

Only one thing did she say to me when there was a little pause while the cup went round, and she pledged me according to custom and passed it on. It was,

"You look well, Shabaka, though somewhat tired, but sadder than you used, I think."

"Perhaps because I have seen things to sadden me, Amada. But you too look well but somewhat lovelier than you used, I think, if that be possible."

She smiled and blushed as she replied,

"The Eastern ladies have taught you how to say pretty things. But you should not waste them upon me who have done with women's vanities and have given myself to learning and—religion."

"Have learning and religion no vanities of their own?" I began, when suddenly the Prince gave a signal to end the feast.

Thereon all the lower part of the hall went away and the little tables at which we ate were removed by servants, leaving us only wine-cups in our hands which a butler filled from time to time, mixing the wine with water. This reminded me of something, and having asked leave, I beckoned to Bes, who still lingered near the door, and took from him that splendid, golden goblet which the Great King had given me, that by my command he had brought wrapped up in linen and hidden beneath his robe. Having undone the wrappings I bowed and offered it to the Prince Peroa.

"What is this wondrous thing?" asked the Prince, when all had finished admiring its workmanship. "Is it a gift that you bring me from the King of the East, Shabaka?"

"It is a gift from myself, O Prince, if you will be pleased to accept it," I answered, adding, "Yet it is true that it comes from the King of the East, since it was his own drinking-cup that he gave me in exchange for a certain bow, though not the one he sought, after he had pledged me."

"You seem to have found much favour in the eyes of this king, Shabaka, which is more than most of us Egyptians do," he exclaimed, then went on hastily, "Still, I thank you for your splendid gift, and however you came by it, shall value it much."

"Perhaps my cousin Shabaka will tell us his story," broke in Amada, her eyes still fixed upon the rose-hued pearls, "and of how he came to win all the beauteous things that dazzle our eyes to-night."

Now I thought of offering her the pearls, but remembering my mother's words, also that the Princess might not like to see another woman bear off such a prize, did not do so. So I began to tell my story instead, Bes seated on the ground near to me by the Prince's wish, that he might tell his.

The tale was long for in it was much that went before the day when I saw myself in the chariot hunting lions with the King of kings, which I, the modern man who set down all this vision, now learned for the first time. It told of the details of my journey to the East, of my coming to the royal city and the rest, all of which it is needless to repeat. Then I came to the lion hunt, to my winning of the wager, and all that happened to me; of my being condemned to death, of the weighing of Bes against the gold, and of how I was laid in the boat of torment, a story at which I noticed Amada turn pale and tremble.

Here I ceased, saying that Bes knew better than I what had chanced at the Court while I was pinned in the boat, whereon all present cried out to Bes to take up the tale. This he did, and much better than I could have done, bringing out many little things which made the scene appear before them, as Ethiopians have the art of doing. At last he came to the place in his story where the king asked him if he had ever seen a woman fairer than the dancers, and went on thus:

"O Prince, I told the Great King that I had; that there dwelt in Egypt a lady of royal blood with eyes like stars, with hair like silk and long as an unbridled horse's tail, with a shape like to that of a goddess, with breath like flowers, with skin like milk, with a voice like honey, with learning like to that of the god Thoth, with wit like a razor's edge, with teeth like pearls, with majesty of bearing like to that of the king himself, with fingers like rosebuds set in pink seashells, with motion like that of an antelope, with grace like that of a swan floating upon water, and—I don't remember the rest, O Prince."

"Perhaps it is as well," exclaimed Peroa. "But what did the King say then?"

"He asked her name, O Prince."

"And what name did you give to this wondrous lady who surpasses all the goddesses in loveliness and charm, O dwarf Bes?" inquired Amada much amused.

"What name, O High-born One? Is it needful to ask? Why, what name could I give but your own, for is there any other in the world of whom a man whose heart is filled with truth could speak such things?"

Now hearing this I gasped, but before I could speak Amada leapt up, crying,

"Wretch! You dared to speak my name to this king! Surely you should be scourged till your bones are bare."

"And why not, Lady? Would you have had me sit still and hear those fat trollops of the East exalted above you? Would you have had me so disloyal to your royal loveliness?"

"You should be scourged," repeated Amada stamping her foot. "My Uncle, I pray you cause this knave to be scourged."

"Nay, nay," said Peroa moodily. "Poor simple man, he knew no better and thought only to sing your praises in a far land. Be not angry with the dwarf, Niece. Had it been Shabaka who gave your name, the thing would be different. What happened next, Bes?"

"Only this, Prince," said Bes, looking upwards and rolling his eyes, as was his fashion when unloading some great lie from his heart. "The King sent his servants to bring my master from the boat, that he might inquire of him whether he had always found me truthful. For, Prince, those Easterns set much store by truth which here in Egypt is worshipped as a goddess. There they do not worship her because she lives in the heart of every man, and some women."

Now all stared at Bes who continued to stare at the ceiling, and I rose to say something, I know not what, when suddenly the doors opened and through them appeared heralds, crying,

"Hearken, Peroa, Prince of Egypt by grace of the Great King. A message from the Great King. Read and obey, O Peroa, Prince of Egypt by grace of the Great King!"

As they cried thus from between them emerged a man whose long Eastern robes were stained with the dust of travel. Advancing without salute he drew out a roll, touched his forehead with it, bowing deeply, and handed it to the prince, saying,

"Kiss the Word. Read the Word. Obey the Word, O servant of our Master, the King of kings, beneath whose feet we are all but dust."

Peroa took the roll, made a semblance of lifting it to his forehead, opened and read it. As he did so I saw the veins swell upon his neck and his eyes flash, but he only said,

"O Messenger, to-night I feast, to-morrow an answer shall be given to you to convey to the Satrap Idernes. My servants will find you food and lodging. You are dismissed."

"Let the answer be given early lest you also should be dismissed, O Peroa," said the man with insolence.

Then he turned his back upon the prince, as one does on an inferior, and walked away, accompanied by the herald.

When they were gone and the doors had been shut, Peroa spoke in a voice that was thick with fury, saying,

"Hearken, all of you, to the words of the writing."

Then he read it.

"From the King of kings, the Ruler of all the earth, to Peroa, one of his servants in the Satrapy of Egypt,

"Deliver over to my servant Idernes without delay, the person of Amada, a lady of the blood of the old Pharaohs of Egypt, who is your relative and in your guardianship, that she may be numbered among the women of my house."

Now all present looked at each other, while Amada stood as though she had been frozen into stone. Before she could speak, Peroa went on,

"See how the King seeks a quarrel against me that he may destroy me and bray Egypt in his mortar, and tan it like a hide to wrap about his feet. Nay, hold your peace, Amada. Have no fear. You shall not be sent to the East; first will I kill you with my own hands. But what answer shall we give, for the matter is urgent and on it hang all our lives? Bethink you, Idernes has a great force yonder at Sais, and if I refuse outright, he will attack us, which indeed is what the King means him to do before we can make preparation. Say then, shall we fight, or shall we fly to Upper Egypt, abandoning Memphis, and there make our stand?"

Now the Councillors present seemed to find no answer, for they did not know what to say. But Bes whispered in my ear,

"Remember, Master, that you hold the King's seal. Let an answer be sent to Idernes under the White Seal, bidding him wait on you."

Then I rose and spoke.

"O Peroa," I said, "as it chances I am the bearer of the private signet of the Great King, which all men must obey in the north and in the south, in the east and in the west, wherever the sun shines over the dominions of the King. Look on it," and taking the ancient White Seal from about my neck, I handed it to him.

He looked and the Councillors looked. Then they said almost with one voice,

"It is the White Seal, the very signet of the Great Kings of the East," and they bowed before the dreadful thing.

"How you came by this we do not know, Shabaka," said Peroa. "That can be inquired of afterwards. Yet in truth it seems to be the old Signet of signets, that which has come down from father to son for countless generations, that which the King of kings carries on his person and affixes to his private orders and to the greatest documents of State, which afterwards can never be recalled, that of which a copy is emblazoned on his banner."

"It is," I answered, "and from the King's person it came to me for a while. If any doubt, let the impress be brought, that is furnished to all the officers throughout the Empire, and let the seal be set in the impress."

Now one of the officers rose and went to bring the impress which was in his keeping, but Peroa continued,

"If this be the true seal, how would you use it, Shabaka, to help us in our present trouble?"

"Thus, Prince," I answered. "I would send a command under the seal to Idernes to wait upon the holder of the seal here in Memphis. He will suspect a trap and will not come until he has gathered a great army. Then he will come, but meanwhile, you, Prince, can also collect an army."

"That needs gold, Shabaka, and I have little. The King of kings takes all in tribute."

"I have some, Prince, to the weight of a heavy man, and it is at the service of Egypt."

"I thank you, Shabaka. Believe me, such generosity shall not go unrewarded," and he glanced at Amada who dropped her eyes. "But if we can collect the army, what then?"

"Then you can put Memphis into a state of defence. Then too when Idernes comes I will meet him and, as the bearer of the seal, command him under the seal to retreat and disperse his army."

"But if he does, Shabaka, it will only be until he has received fresh orders from the Great King, whereon he will advance again."

"No, Prince, *he* will not advance, or that army either. For when they are in retreat we will fall on them and destroy them, and declare you, O Prince, Pharaoh of Egypt, though what will happen afterwards I do not know."

When they heard this all gasped. Only Amada whispered,

"Well said!" and Bes clapped his big hands softly in the Ethiopian fashion.

"A bold counsel," said Peroa, "and one on which I must have the night to think. Return here, Shabaka, an hour after sunrise to-morrow, by which time I can gather all the wisest men in Memphis, and we will discuss this matter. Ah! here is the impress. Now let the seal be tried."

A box was brought and opened. In it was a slab of wood on which was an impress of the King's seal in wax, surrounded by those of other seals certifying that it was genuine. Also there was a writing describing the appearance of the seal. I handed the signet to Peroa who, having compared it with the description in the writing, fitted it to the impress on the wax.

"It is the same," he said. "See, all of you."

They looked and nodded. Then he would have given it back to me but I refused to take it, saying,

"It is not well that this mighty symbol should hang about the neck of a private man whence it might be stolen or lost."

"Or who might be murdered for its sake," interrupted Peroa.

"Yes, Prince. Therefore take it and hide it in the safest and most secret place in the palace, and with it these pearls that are too priceless to be flaunted about the streets of Memphis at night, unless indeed——" and I turned to look for Amada, but she was gone.

So the seal and the pearls were taken and locked in the box with the impress and borne away. Nor was I sorry to see the last of them, wisely as it happened. Then I bade the Prince and his company good night, and presently was driving homeward with Bes in the chariot.

Our way led us past some large houses once occupied by officers of the Court of Pharaoh, but now that there was no Court, fallen into ruins. Suddenly from out of these houses sprang a band of men disguised as common robbers, whose faces were hidden by cloths with eye-holes cut in them. They seized the horses by the bridles, and before we could do anything, leapt upon us and held us fast. Then a tall man speaking with a foreign accent, said,

"Search that officer and the dwarf. Take from them the seal upon a gold chain and a rope of rose-hued pearls which they have stolen. But do them no harm."

So they searched us, the tall man himself helping and, aided by others, holding Bes who struggled with them, and searched the chariot also, by the light of the moon, but found nothing. The tall man muttered that I must be the wrong officer, and at a sign they left us and ran away.

"That was a wise thought of mine, Bes, which caused me to leave certain ornaments in the palace," I said. "As it is they have taken nothing."

"Yes, Master," he answered, "though I have taken something from them," a saying that I did not understand at the time. "Those Easterns whom we met by the canal told Idernes about the seal, and he ordered this to be done. That tall man was one of the messengers who came to-night to the palace."

"Then why did they not kill us, Bes?"

"Because murder, especially of one who holds the seal, is an ugly business, that is easily tracked down, whereas thieves are many in Memphis and who troubles about them when they have failed? Oh! the Grasshopper, or Amen, or both, have been with us to-night."

So I thought although I said nothing, for since we had come off scatheless, what did it matter? Well, this. It showed me that the signet of the Great King was indeed to be dreaded and coveted, even here in Egypt. If Idernes could get it into his possession, what might he not do with it? Cause himself to be proclaimed Pharaoh perhaps and become the forefather of an independent dynasty. Why not, when the Empire of the East was taxed with a great war elsewhere? And if this was so why should not Peroa do the same, he who had behind him all Old Egypt, maddened with its wrongs and foreign rule?

That same night before I slept, but after Bes and I had hidden away the bags of gold by burying them beneath the clay floor, I laid the whole matter before my mother who was a very wise woman. She heard me out, answering little, then said,

"The business is very dangerous, and of its end I will not speak until I have heard the counsel of your great-uncle, the holy Tanofir. Still, things having gone so far, it seems to me that boldness may be the best course, since the great King has his Grecian wars to deal with, and whatever he may say, cannot attack Egypt yet awhile. Therefore if Peroa is able to overcome Idernes and his army he may cause himself to be proclaimed Pharaoh and make Egypt free if only for a time."

"Such is my mind, Mother."

"Not all your mind, Son, I think," she answered smiling, "for you think more of the lovely Amada than of these high policies, at any rate to-night. Well, marry your Amada if you can, though I misdoubt me somewhat of a woman who is so lost in learning and thinks so much about her soul. At least if you marry her and Egypt should become free, as it was for thousands of years, you will be the next heir to the throne as husband of the Great Royal Lady."

"How can that be, Mother, seeing that Peroa has a son?"

"A vain youth with no more in him than a child's rattle. If once Amada ceases to think about her soul she will begin to think about her throne, especially if she has children. But all this is far away and for the present I am glad that neither she nor the thieves have got those pearls, though perhaps they might be safer here than where they are. And now, my son, go rest for you need it, and dream of nothing, not even Amada, who for her part will dream of Isis, if at all. I will wake you before the dawn."

So I went, being too tired to talk more, and slept like a crocodile in the sun, till, as it seemed to me, but a few minutes later I saw my mother standing over me with a lamp, saying that it was time to rise. I rose, unwillingly enough, but refreshed, washed and dressed myself, by which time the sun had begun to appear. Then I ate some food and, calling Bes, made ready to start for the palace.

"My son," said my mother, the lady Tiu, before we parted, "while you have been sleeping I have been thinking, as is the way of the old. Peroa, your cousin, will be glad enough to make use of you, but he does not love you over much because he is jealous of you and fears lest you should become his rival in the future. Still he is an honest man and will keep a bargain which he once has made. Now it seems that above everything on earth you desire Amada on whom you have set your heart since boyhood, but who has always played with you and spoken to you with her arm stretched out. Also life is short and may come to an end any day, as you should know better than most men who have lived among dangers, and therefore it is well that a man should take what he desires, even if he finds afterwards that the rose he crushes to his breast has thorns. For then at least he will have smelt the rose, not only have looked on and longed to smell it. Therefore, before you hand over your gold, and place your wit and strength at the service of Peroa, make your bargain with him; namely, that if thereby you save Amada from the King's House of Women and help to set Peroa on the throne, he shall promise her to you free of any priestly curse, you giving her as dowry the priceless rose-hued pearls that are worth a kingdom. So you will get your rose till it withers, and if the thorns prick, do not blame me, and one day you may become a king—or a slave, Amen knows which."

Now I laughed and said that I would take her counsel who desired Amada and nothing else. As for all her talk about thorns, I paid no heed to it, knowing that she loved me very much and was jealous of Amada who she thought would take her place with me.

Shabaka Plights His Troth

Bes and I went armed to the palace, walking in the middle of the road, but now that the sun was up we met no more robbers. At the gate a messenger summoned me alone to the presence of Peroa, who, he said, wished to talk with me before the sitting of the Council. I went and found him by himself.

"I hear that you were attacked last night," he said after greeting me.

I answered that I was and told him the story, adding that it was fortunate I had left the White Seal and the pearls in safe keeping, since without doubt the would-be thieves were Easterns who desired to recover them.

"Ah! the pearls," he said. "One of those who handled them, who was once a dealer in gems, says that they are without price, unmatched in the whole world, and that never in all his life has he seen any to equal the smallest of them."

I replied that I believed this was so. Then he asked me of the value of the gold of which I had spoken. I told him and it was a great sum, for gold was scarce in Egypt. His eyes gleamed for he needed wealth to pay soldiers.

"And all this you are ready to hand over to me, Shabaka?"

Now I bethought me of my mother's words, and answered,

"Yes, Prince, at a price."

"What price, Shabaka?"

"The price of the hand of the Royal Lady, Amada, freed from her vows. Moreover, I will give her the pearls as a marriage dowry and place at your service my sword and all the knowledge I have gained in the East, swearing to stand or fall with you."

"I thought it, Shabaka. Well, in this world nothing is given for nothing and the offer is a fair one. You are well born, too, as well as myself, and a brave and clever man. Further, Amada has not taken her final vows and therefore the high priests can absolve her from her marriage to the goddess, or to her son Horus, whichever it may be, for I do not understand these mysteries. But, Shabaka, if Fortune should chance to go with us and I should became the first Pharaoh of a new dynasty in Egypt, he who was married to the Royal Princess of the true blood might become a danger to my throne and family."

"I shall not be that man, Prince, who am content with my own station, and to be your servant."

"And my son's, Shabaka? You know that I have but one lawful son."

"And your son's, Prince."

"You are honest, Shabaka, and I believe you. But how about your sons, if you have any, and how about Amada herself? Well, in great businesses something must be risked, and I need the gold and the rest which I cannot take for nothing, for you won them by your skill and courage and they are yours. But how you won the seal you have not told us, nor is there time for you to do so now."

He thought a little, walking up and down the chamber, then went on,

"I accept your offer, Shabaka, so far as I can."

"So far as you can, Prince?"

"Yes; I can give you Amada in marriage and make that marriage easy, but only if Amada herself consents. The will of a Royal Princess of Egypt of full age cannot be forced, save by her father if he reigns as Pharaoh, and I am not her father, but only her guardian. Therefore it stands thus. Are you willing to fulfil your part of the bargain, save only as regards the pearls, if she does not marry you, and to take your chance of winning Amada as a man wins a woman, I on my part promising to do all in my power to help your suit?"

Now it was my turn to think for a moment. What did I risk? The gold and perhaps the pearls, no more, for in any case I should fight for Peroa against the Eastern king whom I hated, and through him for Egypt. Well, these came to me by chance, and if they went by chance what of it? Also I was not one who desired to wed a woman, however much I worshipped her, if she desired to turn her back on me. If I could win her in fair love—well. If not, it was my misfortune, and I wanted her in no other way. Lastly, I had reason to think that she looked on me more favourably than she had ever done on any other man, and that if it had not been for what my mother called her soul and its longings, she would have given herself to me before I journeyed to the East. Indeed, once she had said as much, and there was something in her eyes last night which told me that in her heart she loved me, though with what passion at the time I did not know. So very swiftly I made up my mind and answered,

"I understand and I accept. The gold shall be delivered to you to-day, Prince. The pearls are already in your keeping to await the end."

"Good!" he exclaimed. "Then let the matter be reduced to writing and at once, that afterwards neither of us may have cause to complain of the other."

So he sent for his secret scribe and dictated to him, briefly but clearly, the substance of our bargain, nothing being added, and nothing taken away. This roll written on papyrus was afterwards copied twice, Peroa taking one copy, I another, and a third being deposited according to custom, in the library of the temple of Ptah.

When all was done and Peroa and I had touched each other's breasts and given our word in the name of Amen, we went to the hall in which we had dined, where those whom the Prince had summoned were assembled. Altogether there were about thirty of them, great citizens of Memphis, or landowners from without who had been called together in the night. Some of these men were very old and could remember when Egypt had a Pharaoh of its own before the East set its heel upon her neck, of noble blood also.

Others were merchants who dealt with all the cities of Egypt; others hereditary generals, or captains of fleets of ships; others Grecians, officers of mercenaries who were supposed to be in the pay of the King of kings, but hated him, as did all the Greeks. Then there were the high priests of Ptah, of Amen, of Osiris and others who were still the most powerful men in the land, since there was no village between Thebes and the mouths of the Nile in which they had not those who were sworn to the service of their gods.

Such was the company representing all that remained or could be gathered there of the greatness of Egypt the ancient and the fallen.

To these when the doors had been closed and barred and trusty watchmen set to guard them, Peroa expounded the case in a low and earnest voice. He showed them that the King of the East sought a new quarrel against Egypt that he might grind her to powder beneath his heel, and that he did this by demanding the person of Amada, his own niece and the Royal Lady of Egypt, to be included in his household like any common woman. If she were refused then he would send a great army under pretext of taking her, and lay the land waste as far as Thebes. And if she were granted some new quarrel would be picked and in the person of the royal Amada all of them be for ever shamed.

Next he showed the seal, telling them that I—who was known to many of them, at least by repute—had brought it from the East, and repeating to them the plan that I had proposed upon the previous night. After this he asked their counsel, saying that before noon he must send an answer to Idernes, the King's Satrap at Sais.

Then I was called upon to speak and, in answer to questions, answered frankly that I had stolen the ancient White Seal from the King's servant who carried it as a warrant for the King's private vengeance on one who had bested him. How I did not mention. I told them also of the state of the Great King's empire and that I had heard that he was about to enter upon a war with the Greeks which would need all its strength, and that therefore if they wished to strike for liberty the time was at hand.

Then the talk began and lasted for two hours, each man giving his judgment according to precedence, some one way and some another. When all had done and it became clear that there were differences of opinion, some being content to live on in slavery with what remained to them and others desiring to strike for freedom, among whom were the high priests who feared lest the Eastern heretics should utterly destroy their worship, Peroa spoke once more.

"Elders of Egypt," he said briefly, "certain of you think one way, and certain another, but of this be sure, such talk as we have held together cannot be hid. It will come to the ears of spies and through them to those of the Great King, and then all of us alike are doomed. If you refuse to stir, this very day I with my family and household and the Royal Lady Amada, and all who cling to me, fly to Upper Egypt and perhaps beyond it to Ethiopia, leaving you to deal with the Great King, as you will, or to follow me into exile. That he will attack us there is no doubt, either over the pretext of Amada or some other, since Shabaka has heard as much from his own lips. Now choose."

Then, after a little whispering together, every man of them voted for rebellion, though some of them I could see with heavy hearts, and bound themselves by a great oath to cling together to the last.

The matter being thus settled such a letter was written to Idernes as I had suggested on the night before, and sealed with the Signet of signets. Of the yielding up of Amada it said nothing, but commanded Idernes, under the private White Seal that none dared disobey, to wait upon the Prince Peroa at Memphis forthwith, and there learn from him, the Holder of the Seal, what was the will of the Great King. Then the Council was adjourned till one hour after noon, and most of them departed to send messengers bearing secret word to the various cities and nomes of Egypt.

Before they went, however, I was directed to wait upon my relative, the holy Tanofir, whom all acknowledged to be the greatest magician in Egypt, and to ask of him to seek wisdom and an oracle from his Spirit as to the future and whether in it we should fare well or ill. This I promised to do.

When most of the Council were gone the messengers of Idernes were summoned, and came proudly, and with them, or rather before them, Bes for whom I had sent as he was not present at the Council.

"Master," he whispered to me, "the tallest of those messengers is the man who captained the robbers last night. Wait and I will prove it."

Peroa gave the roll to the head messenger, bidding him bear it to the Satrap in answer to the letter which he had delivered to him. The man took it insolently and thrust it into his robe, as he did so revealing a silver chain that had been broken and knotted together, and asked whether there were words to bear besides those written in the roll. Before Peroa could answer Bes sprang up saying,

"O Prince, a boon, the boon of justice on this man. Last night he and others with him attacked my master and myself, seeking to rob us, but finding nothing let us go."

"You lie, Abortion!" said the Eastern.

"Oh! I lie, do I?" mocked Bes. "Well, let us see," and shooting out his long arm, he grasped the chain about the messenger's neck and broke it with a jerk. "Look, O Prince," he said, "you may have noted last night, when that man entered the hall, that there hung about his neck this chain to which was tied a silver key."

"I noted it," said Peroa.

"Then ask him, O Prince, where is the key now."

"What is that to you, Dwarf?" broke in the man. "The key is my mark of office as chief butler to the High Satrap. Must I always bear it for your pleasure?"

"Not when it has been taken from you, Butler," answered Bes. "See, here it is," and from his sleeve he produced the key hanging to a piece of the chain. "Listen, O Prince," he said. "I struggled with this man and the key was in my left hand though he did not know it at the time, and with it some of the chain. Compare them and judge. Also his mask slipped and I saw his face and knew him again."

Peroa laid the pieces of the chain together and observed the workmanship which was Eastern and rare. Then he clapped his hands, at which sign armed men of his household entered from behind him.

"It is the same," he said. "Butler of Idernes, you are a common thief."

The man strove to answer, but could not for the deed was proved against him.

"Then, O Prince," asked Bes, "what is the punishment of those thieves who attack passers-by with violence in the streets of Memphis, for such I demand on him?"

"The cutting off of the right hand and scourging," answered Peroa, at which words the butler turned to fly. But Bes leapt on him like an ape upon a bird, and held him fast.

"Seize that thief," said Peroa to his servants, "and let him receive fifty blows with the rods. His hand I spare because he must travel."

They laid the man down and the rods having been fetched, gave him the blows until at the thirtieth he howled for mercy, crying out that it was true and that it was he who had captained the robbers, words which Peroa caused to be written down. Then he asked him why he, a messenger from the Satrap, had robbed in the streets of Memphis, and as he refused to answer, commanded the officer of justice to lay on. After three more blows the man said,

"O Prince, this was no common robbery for gain. I did what I was commanded to do, because yonder noble had about him the ancient White Seal of the Great King which he showed to certain of the Satrap's servants by the banks of the canal. That seal is a holy token, O Prince, which, it is said, has descended for twice a thousand years in the family of the Great King, and as the Satrap did not know how it had come into the hands of the noble Shabaka, he ordered me to obtain it if I could."

"And the pearls too, Butler?"

"Yes, O Prince, since those gems are a great possession with which any Satrap could buy a larger satrapy."

"Let him go," said Peroa, and the man rose, rubbing himself and weeping in his pain.

"Now, Butler," he went on, "return to your master with a grateful heart, since you have been spared much that you deserve. Say to him that he cannot steal the Signet, but that if he is wise he will obey it, since otherwise his fate may be worse than yours, and to all his servants say the same. Foolish man, how can you, or your master, guess what is in the mind of the Great King, or for what purpose the Signet of signets is here in Egypt? Beware lest you fall into a pit, all of you together, and let Idernes beware lest he find himself at the very bottom of that pit."

"O Prince, I will beware," said the humbled butler, "and whatever is written over the seal, that I will obey, like many others."

"You are wise," answered Peroa; "I pray for his own sake that the Satrap Idernes may be as wise. Now begone, thanking whatever god you worship that your life is whole in you and that your right hand remains upon your wrist."

So the butler and those with him prostrated themselves before Peroa and bowed humbly to me and even to Bes because in their hearts now they believed that we were clothed by the Great King with terrible powers that might destroy them all, if so we chose. Then they went, the butler limping a little and with no pride left in him.

"That was good work," said Peroa to me afterwards when we were alone, "for now yonder knave is frightened and will frighten his master."

"Yes," I answered, "you played that pipe well, Prince. Still, there is no time to lose, since before another moon this will all be reported in the East, whence a new light may arise and perchance a new signet."

"You say you stole the White Seal?" he asked.

"Nay, Prince, the truth is that Bes bought it—in a certain fashion— and I used it. Perhaps it is well that you should know no more at present."

"Perhaps," he answered, and we parted, for he had much to do.

That afternoon the Council met again. At it I gave over the gold and by help of it all was arranged. Within a week ten thousand armed men would be in Memphis and a hundred ships with their crews upon the Nile; also a great army would be gathering in Upper Egypt, officered for the most part by Greeks skilled in war. The Greek cities too at the mouths of the Nile would be ready to revolt, or so some of their citizens declared, for they hated the Great King bitterly and longed to cast off his yoke.

For my part, I received the command of the bodyguard of Peroa in which were many Greeks, and a generalship in the army; while to Bes, at my prayer, was given the freedom of the land which he accepted with a smile, he who was a king in his own country.

At length all was finished and I went out into the palace garden to rest myself before I rode into the desert to see my great uncle, the holy Tanofir. I was alone, for Bes had gone to bring our horses on which we were to ride, and sat myself down beneath a palm-tree, thinking of the great adventure on which we had entered with a merry heart, for I loved adventures.

Next I thought of Amada and was less merry. Then I looked up and lo! she stood before me, unaccompanied and wearing the dress, not of a priestess, but of an Egyptian lady with the little circlet of her rank upon her hair. I rose and bowed to her and we began to walk together beneath the palms, my heart beating hard within me, for I knew that my hour had come to speak.

Yet it was she who spoke the first, saying,

"I hear that you have been playing a high part, Shabaka, and doing great things for Egypt."

"For Egypt and for you who are Egypt," I answered.

"So I should have been called in the old days, Cousin, because of my blood and the rank it gives, though now I am but as any other lady of the land."

"And so you shall be called in days to come, Amada, if my sword and wit can win their way."

"How so, Cousin, seeing that you have promised certain things to my uncle Peroa and his son?"

"I have promised those things, Amada, and I will abide by my promise; but the gods are above all, and who knows what they may decree?"

"Yes, Cousin, the gods are above all, and in their hands we will let these matters rest, provoking them in no manner and least of all by treachery to our oaths."

We walked for a little way in silence. Then I spoke.

"Amada, there are more things than thrones in the world."

"Yes, Cousin, there is that in which all thrones end—death, which it seems we court."

"And, Amada, there is that in which all thrones begin—love, which I court from you."

"I have known it long," she said, considering me gravely, "and been grateful to you who are more to me than any man has been or ever will be. But, Shabaka, I am a priestess bound to set the holy One I serve above a mortal."

"That holy One was wed and bore a child, Amada, who avenged his father, as I trust that we shall avenge Egypt. Therefore she looks with a kind eye upon wives and mothers. Also you have not taken your final vows and can be absolved."

"Yes," she said softly.

"Then, Amada, will you give yourself into my keeping?"

"I think so, Shabaka, though it has been in my mind for long, as you know well, to give myself only to learning and the service of the heavenly Lady. My heart calls me to you, it is true, day and night it calls, how loudly I will not tell; yet I would not yield myself to that alone. But Egypt calls me also, since I have been shown in a dream while I watched in the sanctuary, that you are the only man who can free her, and I think that this dream came from on high. Therefore I will give myself, but not yet."

"Not yet," I said dismayed. "When?"

"When I have been absolved from my vows, which must be done on the night of the next new moon, which is twenty-seven days from this. Then, if nothing comes between us during those twenty-seven days, it shall be announced that the Royal Lady of Egypt is to wed the noble Shabaka."

"Twenty-seven days! In such times much may happen in them, Amada. Still, except death, what can come between us?"

"I know of nothing, Shabaka, whose past is shadowless as the noon."

"Or I either," I replied.

Now we were standing in the clear sunlight, but as I said the words a wind stirred the palm-trees and the shadow from one of them fell full upon me, and she who was very quick, noted it.

"Some might take that for an omen," she said with a little laugh, pointing to the line of the shadow. "Oh! Shabaka, if you have aught to confess, say it now and I will forgive it. But do not leave me to discover it afterwards when I may not forgive. Perchance during your journeyings in the East——"

"Nothing, nothing," I exclaimed joyfully, who during all that time had scarcely spoken to a youthful woman.

"I am glad that nothing happened in the East that could separate us, Shabaka, though in truth my thought was not your own, for there are more things than women in the world. Only it seems strange to me that you should return to Egypt laden with such priceless gifts from him who is Egypt's greatest enemy."

"Have I not told you that I put my country before myself? Those gifts were won fairly in a wager, Amada, whereof you heard the story but last night. Moreover you know the purpose to which they are to be put," I replied indignantly.

"Yes, I know and now I am sure. Be not angry, Shabaka, with her who loves you truly and hopes ere long to call you husband. But till that day take it not amiss if I keep somewhat aloof from you, who must break with the past and learn to face a future of which I did not dream."

For the rest she stretched out her hand and I kissed it, for while she was still a priestess her lips she would not suffer me to touch. Another moment and smiling happily, she had glided away, leaving me alone in the garden.

Then it was for the first time that I bethought me of the warnings of Bes and remembered that it was I, not he, who had told the Great King the name of the most beautiful woman in Egypt, although in all innocence. Yes, I remembered, and felt as if all the shadows on the earth had wrapped me round. I thought of finding her, but she had gone whither I knew not in that great palace. So I determined that the next time we were alone I would tell her of the matter, explaining all, and with this thought I comforted myself who did not know that until many days were past we should be alone no more.

After this I went home and told my mother all my joy, for in truth there was no happier man in Egypt. She listened, then answered, smiling a little.

"When your father wished to take me to wife, Shabaka, it was not my hand that I gave him to kiss, and as you know, I too have the blood of kings in me. But then I was not a priestess of Isis, so doubtless all is well. Only in twenty-seven days much may happen, as you said to Amada. Now I wonder why did she——? Well, no matter, since priestesses are not like other women who only think of the man they have won and of naught before or after. The blessing of the gods and mine be on you both, my son," and she went away to attend to her household matters.

As we rode to Sekera to find the holy Tanofir I told Bes also, adding that I had forgotten to reveal that it was I who had spoken Amada's name to the king, but that

I intended to do so ere long.

Bes rolled his eyes and answered,

"If I were you, Master, as I had forgotten, I should continue to forget, for what is welcome in one hour is not always welcome in another. Why speak of the matter at all, which is one hard to explain to a woman, however wise and royal? I have already said that *I* spoke the name to the King and that you were brought from the boat to say whether I was noted for my truthfulness. Is not that enough?"

While I considered, Bes went on,

"You may remember, Master, that when I told, well—the truth about this story, the lady Amada asked earnestly that I should be scourged, even to the bones. Now if you should tell another truth which will make mine dull as tarnished silver, she will not leave me even my bones, for I shall be proved a liar, and what will happen to you I am sure I do not know. And, Master, as I am no longer a slave here in Egypt, to say nothing of what I may be elsewhere, I have no fancy for scourgings, who may not kiss the hand that smites me as you can."

"But, Bes," I said, "what is, is and may always be learned in this way or in that."

"Master, if what is were always learned, I think the world would fall to pieces, or at least there would be no men left on it. Why should this matter be learned? It is known to you and me alone, leaving out the Great King who probably has forgotten as he was drunk at the time. Oh! Master, when you have neither bow nor spear at hand, it is not wise to kick a sleeping lion in the stomach, for then he will remember its emptiness and sup off you. Beside, when first I told you that tale I made a mistake. I did tell the Great King, as I now remember quite clearly, that the beautiful lady was named Amada, and he only sent for you to ask if I spoke the truth."

"Bes," I exclaimed, "you worshippers of the Grasshopper wear virtue easily."

"Easily as an old sandal, Master, or rather not at all, since the Grasshopper has need of none. For ages they have studied the ways of those who worship the gods of Egypt, and from them have learned——"

"What?"

"Amongst other things, Master, that woman, being modest, is shocked at the sight of the naked Truth."

The Holy Tanofir

We entered the City of Graves that is called Sekera. In the centre towered pyramids that hid the bones of ancient and forgotten kings, and everywhere around upon the desert sands was street upon street of monuments, but save for a priest or two hurrying to patter his paid office in the funeral chapels of the departed, never a living man. Bes looked about him and sniffed with his wide nostrils.

"Is there not death enough in the world, Master," he asked, "that the living should wish to proclaim it in this fashion, rolling it on their tongues like a morsel they are loth to swallow, because it tastes so good? Oh! what a waste is here. All these have had their day and yet they need houses and pyramids and painted chambers in which to sleep, whereas if they believed the faith they practised, they would have been content to give their bones to feed the earth they fed on, and fill heaven with their souls."

"Do your people thus, Bes?"

"For the most part, Master. Our dead kings and great ones we enclose in pillars of crystal, but we do this that they may serve a double purpose. One is that the pillars may support the roof of their successors, and the other, that those who inherit their goods may please themselves by reflecting how much handsomer they are than those who went before them. For no mummy looks really nice, Master, at least with its wrappings off, and our kings are put naked into the crystal."

"And what becomes of the rest, Bes?"

"Their bodies go to the earth or the water and the Grasshopper carries off their souls to—where, Master?"

"I do not know, Bes."

"No, Master, no one knows, except the lady Amada and perhaps the holy Tanofir. Here I think is the entrance to his hole," and he pulled up his beast with a jerk at what looked like the doorway of a tomb.

Apparently we were expected, for a tall and proud-looking girl clad in white and with extraordinarily dark eyes, appeared in the doorway and asked in a soft voice if we were the noble Shabaka and Bes, his slave.

"I am Shabaka," I answered, "and this is Bes, who is not my slave but a free citizen of Egypt."

The girl contemplated the dwarf with her big eyes, then said,

"And other things, I think."

"What things?" inquired Bes with interest, as he stared at this beautiful lady.

"A very brave and clever man and one perhaps who is more than he seems to be?"

"Who has been telling you about me?" exclaimed Bes anxiously.

"No one, O Bes, at least not that I can remember."

"Not that you can remember! Then who and what are you who learn things you know not how?"

"I am named Karema and desert-bred, and my office is that of Cup to the holy Tanofir."

"If hermits drink from such a cup I shall turn hermit," said Bes, laughing. "But how can a woman be a man's cup and what kind of a wine does he drink from her?"

"The wine of wisdom, O Bes," she replied colouring a little, for like many Arabs of high blood she was very fair in hue.

"Wine of wisdom," said Bes. "From such cups most drink the wine of folly, or sometimes of madness."

"The holy Tanofir awaits you," she interrupted, and turning, entered the doorway.

A little way down the passage was a niche in which stood three lamps ready lighted. One of these she took and gave the others to us. Then we followed her down a steep incline of many steps, till at length we found ourselves in a hot and enormous hall hewn from the living rock and filled with blackness.

"What is this place?" said Bes, who looked frightened, and although he spoke in a low whisper, our guide overheard him and turning, answered,

"This is the burial place of the Apis bulls. See, here lies the last, not yet closed in," and holding up her lamp she revealed a mighty sarcophagus of black granite set in a niche of the mausoleum.

"So they make mummies of bulls as well as of men," groaned Bes. "Oh! what a land. But when I have seen the holy Tanofir it was in a brick cell beneath the sky."

"Doubtless that was at night, O Bes," answered Karema, "for in such a house he sleeps, spending his days in the Apis tomb, because of all the evil that is worked beneath the sun."

"Hump," said Bes, "I should have thought that more was worked beneath the moon, but doubtless the holy Tanofir knows better, or being asleep does not mind."

Now in front of each of the walled-up niches was a little chapel, and at the fourth of these whence a light came, the maiden stopped, saying,

"Enter. Here dwells the holy Tanofir. He tended this god during its life-days in his youth, and now that the god is dead he prays above its bones."

"Prays to the bones of a dead bull in the dark! Well, give me a live grasshopper in the light; he is more cheerful," muttered Bes.

"O Dwarf," cried a deep and resounding voice from within the chapel, "talk no more of things you do not understand. I do not pray to the bones of a dead bull, as you in your ignorance suppose. I pray to the spirit whereof this sacred beast was but one of the fleshly symbols, which in this haunted place you will do well not to offend."

Then for once I saw Bes grow afraid, for his great jaw dropped and he trembled.

"Master," he said to me, "when next you visit tombs where maidens look into your heart and hermits hear your very thoughts, I pray you leave me behind. The holy Tanofir I love, if from afar, but I like not his house, or his——" Here he looked at Karema who was regarding him with a sweet smile over the lamp flame, and added, "There is something the matter with me, Master; I cannot even lie."

"Cease from talking follies, O Shabaka and Bes, and enter," said the tremendous voice from within.

So we entered and saw a strange sight. Against the back wall of the chapel which was lit with lamps, stood a life-sized statue of Maat, goddess of Law and Truth, fashioned of alabaster. On her head was a tall feather, her hair was covered with a wig, on her neck lay a collar of blue stones; on her arms and wrists were bracelets of gold. A tight robe draped her body. In her right hand that hung down by her side, she held the looped Cross of Life, and in her left which was advanced, a long, lotus-headed sceptre, while her painted eyes stared fixedly at the darkness. Crouched upon the ground, at the feet of the statue, scribe fashion, sat my great-uncle Tanofir, a very aged man with sightless eyes and long hands, so thin that one might see through them against the lamp-flame. His head was shaven, his beard was long and white; white too was his robe. In front of him was a low altar, on which stood a shallow silver vessel filled with pure water, and on either side of it a burning lamp.

We knelt down before him, or rather I knelt, for Bes threw himself flat upon his face.

"Am I the King of kings whom you have so lately visited, that you should prostrate yourselves before me?" said Tanofir in his great voice, which, coming from so frail and aged a man seemed most unnatural. "Or is it to the goddess of Truth beyond that you bow yourselves? If so, that is well, since one, if not both of you, greatly needs her pardon and her help. Or is it to the sleeping god beyond who holds the whole world on his horns? Or is it to the darkness of this hallowed place which causes you to remember the nearness of the awaiting tomb?"

"Nay, my Uncle," I said, "we would greet you, no more, who are so worthy of our veneration, seeing we believe, both of us, that you saved us yonder in the East, from that tomb of which you speak, or rather from the jaws of lions or a cruel death by torments."

"Perchance I did, I or the gods of which I am the instrument. At least I remember that I sent you certain messages in answer to a prayer for help that reached me, here in my darkness. For know that since we parted I have gone quite blind so that I must use this maiden's eyes to read what is written in yonder divining-cup. Well, it makes the darkness of this sepulchre easier to bear and prepares me for my own. 'Tis full a hundred and twenty years since first I looked upon the light, and now the time of sleep draws near. Come hither, my nephew, and kiss me on the brow, remembering in your strength that a day will dawn when as I am, so shall you be, if the gods spare you so long."

So I kissed him, not without fear, for the old man was unearthly. Then he sent Karema from the place and bade me tell him my story, which I did. Why he did this I cannot say, since he seemed to know it already and once or twice corrected me in certain matters that I had forgotten, for instance as to the exact words that I had used to the Great King in my rage and as to the fashion in which I was tied in the boat. When I had done, he said,

"So you gave the name of Amada to the Great King, did you? Well, you could have done nothing else if you wished to go on living, and therefore cannot be blamed. Yet before all is finished I think it will bring you into trouble, Shabaka, since among many gifts, the gods did not give that of reason to women. If so, bear it, since it is better to have trouble and be alive than to have none and be dead, that is, for those whose work is still to do in the world. And you, or rather Bes, stole the White Signet of signets of which, although it is so simple and ancient, there is not the like for power in the whole world. That was well done since it will be useful for a while. And now Peroa has determined to rebel against the King, which also is well done. Oh! trouble not to tell me of that business for I know all. But what would you learn of me, Shabaka?"

"I am instructed to learn from you the end of these great matters, my Uncle."

"Are you mad, Shabaka, that you should think me a god who can read the future?"

"Not at all, my Uncle, who know that you can if you will."

"Call the maiden," he said.

So Bes went out and brought her in.

"Be seated, Karema, there in front of the altar, and look into my eyes."

She obeyed and presently seemed to go to sleep for her head nodded. Then he said,

"Wake, woman, look into the water in the bowl upon the altar and tell me what you see."

She appeared to wake, though I perceived that this was not really so, for she seemed a different woman with a fixed face that frightened me, and wide and frozen eyes. She stared into the silver bowl, then spoke in a new voice, as though some spirit used her tongue.

"I see myself crowned a queen in a land I hate," she said coldly, a saying at which I gasped. "I am seated on a throne beside yonder dwarf," a saying at which Bes gasped. "Although so hideous, this dwarf is a great man with a good heart, a cunning mind and the courage of a lion. Also his blood is royal."

Here Bes rolled his eyes and smiled, but Tanofir did not seem in the least astonished, and said,

"Much of this is known to me and the rest can be guessed. Pass on to what will happen in Egypt, before the spirit leaves you."

"There will be war in Egypt," she answered. "I see fightings; Shabaka and others lead the Egyptians. The Easterns are driven away or slain. Peroa rules as Pharaoh, I see him on his throne. Shabaka is driven away in his turn, I see him travelling south with the dwarf and with myself, looking very sad. Time passes. I see the moons float by; I see messengers reach Shabaka, sent by Peroa and you O holy Tanofir; they tell of trouble in Egypt. I see Shabaka and the dwarf coming north at the head of a great army of black men armed with bows. With them I come rejoicing, for my heart seems to shine. He reaches a temple on the Nile about which is camped another great army, a countless army of Easterns under the command of the King of kings. Shabaka and the dwarf give battle to that army and the fray is desperate. They destroy it, they drive it into the Nile; the Nile runs red with blood. The Great King falls, an arrow from the bow of Shabaka is in his heart. He enters the temple, a conqueror, and there lies Peroa, dying or dead. A veiled priestess is there before an image, I cannot see her face. Shabaka looks on her. She stretches out her arms to him, her eyes burn with woman's love, her breast heaves, and above the image frowns and threatens. All is done, for Tanofir, Master of spirits, you die, yonder in the temple on the Nile, and therefore I can see no more. The power that comes through you, has left me."

Then once more she became as a woman asleep.

"You have heard, Shabaka and Bes," said Tanofir quietly and stroking his long white beard, "and what that maiden seemed to read in the water you may believe or disbelieve as you will."

"What do you believe, O holy Tanofir?" I asked.

"The only part of the story whereof I am sure," he replied, evading a direct answer, "is that which said that I shall die, and that when I am dead I shall no longer be able to cause the maiden Karema to see visions. For the rest I do not know. These things may happen or they may not. But," he added with a note of warning in his voice, "whether they happen or not, my counsel to you both is that you say nothing of them beforehand."

"What then shall we report to those who bid me seek the oracle of your wisdom, O Tanofir?"

"You can tell them that my wisdom declared that the omens were mixed with good and evil, but that time would show the truth. Hush now, the maiden is about to awake and must not be frightened. Also it is time for me to be led from this sepulchre to where I sleep, for I think that Ra has set and I am weary. Oh! Shabaka, why do you seek to peer into the future, which from day to day will unroll itself as does a scroll? Be content with the present, man, and take what Fate gives you of good or ill, not seeking to learn what offerings he hides beneath his robe in the days and the years and the centuries to come."

"Yet you have sought to learn those things, O Tanofir, and not in vain."

"Aye and what have they made of me? A blind old hermit weighed down with the weight of years and holding in my fingers but some few threads that with pain and grief I have plucked from the fringe of Wisdom's robe. Be warned by me, Nephew. While you are a man, live the life of a man, and when you become a spirit, live the life of a spirit. But do not seek to mix the two together like oil and wine, and thus spoil both. I am glad to learn, O Bes, that you are going to make a king's, or a slave's wife, whichever it may be, of this maiden, seeing that I love her well and hold this trade unwholesome for her. She will be better bearing babes than reading visions in a diviner's cup, and I will pray the gods that they may not be dwarfs as you are, but take on the likeness of their mother, who tells me that she is fair. Hush! she stirs.

"Karema, are you awake? Good. Then lead me from the sepulchre, that I may make my evening prayer beneath the stars. Go, Shabaka and Bes, you are brave men, both of you, and I am glad to have the one for nephew and the other for pupil. My greetings to your mother, Tiu. She is a good woman and a true, one to whom you will do well to hearken. To the lady Amada also, and bid her study her beauteous face in a mirror and not be holy overmuch, since too great holiness often thwarts itself and ends in trouble for the unholy flesh. Still she loves pearls like other women, does she not, and even the statue of Isis likes to be adorned. As for you, Bes, though I think that is not your name, do not lie except when you are obliged, for jugglers who play with too many knives are apt to cut their fingers. Also give no more evil counsel to your Master on matters that have to do with woman. Now farewell. Let me hear how fortune favours you from time to time, Shabaka, for you take part in a great game, such as I loved in my youth before I became a holy hermit. Oh! if they had listened to me, things would have been different in Egypt to-day. But it was written otherwise, and as ever, women were the scribes. Good night, good night, good night! I am glad that my thought reached you yonder in the East, and taught you what to say and do. It is well to be wise sometimes, for others' sake, but not for our own, oh! not for our own."

"Master," said Bes as we ambled homewards beneath the stars, "the holy Tanofir is a man for thought to feed on, since having climbed to the topmost peak of holiness, he does not seem to like its cold air and warns off those who would follow in his footsteps."

"Then he might have spared himself the pains in your case, Bes, or in my own for that matter, since we shall never come so high."

"No, Master, and I am glad to have his leave to stay lower down, since that hot place of dead bulls is not one which I wish to inhabit in my age, making use of a maiden to stare into a pot of water, and there read marvels, which I could invent better for myself after a jug or two of wine. Oh! the holy Tanofir is quite right. If these things are going to happen let them happen, for we cannot change them by knowing of them beforehand. Who wishes to know, Master, if his throat will be cut?"

"Or that he will be married," I suggested.

"Just so, Master, seeing that such prophecies end in becoming truths because we make them true, feeling that we must. Thus, now I must marry yonder Karema if she will marry me for fear lest I should prove the holy Tanofir to be what he called me—a liar."

I laughed and then asked Bes if he had taken note of what the seeress said of our flight south and our return thence with a great army of black men armed with bows.

"Yes, Master," he answered gravely, "and I think this army can be none other than that of the Ethiopians of whom by right I am the King. This very night I send messengers to tell those who rule in my place that I still live and am changing my mind on the matter of marriage. Also that if I do change it I may return to them, the wisest man who ever wore the crown of Ethiopia, having journeyed all about the world and collected much knowledge."

"Perhaps, Bes, those who rule in your place may not wish to give it up to you. Perhaps they will kill you."

"Have no fear, Master; as I have told you, the Ethiopians are a faithful people. Moreover they know that such a deed would bring the curse of the Grasshopper on them, since then the locusts would appear and eat up all their land, and when they were starving their enemies would attack them. Lastly they are a very tall folk and simple-minded and would not wish to miss the chance of being ruled over by the wisest dwarf in all the world, if only because it would be something new to them, Master."

Again I laughed thinking that Bes was jesting according to his fashion. But when that night, chancing to go round the corner of the house, I came upon him with a circlet of feathers round his head and his big bow in his hand, addressing three great black men who knelt before him as though he were a god, I changed my mind. As I withdrew he caught sight of me and said,

"I pray you, my lord Shabaka, stay one moment." Then he spoke to the three men in his own language, translating sentence by sentence to me what he said to them. Briefly it was this:—

"Say to the Lords and Councillors of the Ancient Kingdom that I, the Karoon" (for such it seemed was his title) "have a friend named the lord Shabaka, he whom you see before you, who again and again has saved my life, nursing me in his arms as a mother nurses her babe, and who is, after me, the bravest and the wisest man in all the world. Say to them that if indeed I double myself by marriage and return having fulfilled the law, I will beg this mighty prince to accompany me, and that if he consents that will be the most joyful day which the Ethiopians have seen for a thousand years, since he will teach them wisdom and lead their armies in great and glorious battles. Let the priests of the Grasshopper pray therefore that he may consent to do so. Now salute the mighty lord Shabaka who can send one arrow through all three of you and two more behind, and depart, tarrying not day or night till you reach the land of Ethiopia. Then when you have delivered the message of Karoon to the Captains and the Councillors, return, or let others return and seek me out wherever I may be, bringing of the gold of Ethiopia and other gifts, together with their answer, seeing that I and the lord Shabaka who have the world beneath our feet, will not come to a land where we are not welcome."

So these great men saluted me as though I were the King of kings himself, after which they rubbed their foreheads in the dust before Bes, said something which I did not understand, leapt to their feet, crying "Karoon" and sprang away into the night.

"It is good to have been a slave, Master," said Bes when they had gone, "since it teaches one that it is even better to be a king, at least sometimes."

Here I may add that during the days which followed Bes was often absent. When I asked him where he had gone, he would answer, to drink in the wisdom of the holy Tanofir by help of a certain silver vessel that the maiden Karema held to his lips. From all of which I gathered that he was wooing the lady who had called herself the Cup of Tanofir, and wondered how the business went, though as he said no more I did not ask him.

Indeed I had little time to talk with Bes about such light matters, since things moved apace in Memphis. Within six days all the great lords left in Upper Egypt were sworn to the revolt under the leadership of Peroa, and hour by hour their vassals or hired mercenaries flowed into the city. These it was my duty to weld into an army, and at this task I toiled without cease, separating them into regiments and drilling them, also arranging for the arming and victualling of the boats of war. Then news came that Idernes was advancing from Sais with a great force of Easterns, all the garrison of Lower Egypt indeed, as his messengers said, to answer the summons conveyed to him under the private Seal of seals.

Of Amada during this time I saw little, only meeting her now and again at the table of Peroa, or elsewhere in public. For the rest it pleased her to keep away from me. Once or twice I tried to find her alone, only to discover that she was engaged in the service of the goddess. Once, too, as she left Peroa's table, I whispered into her ear that I wished to speak with her. But she shook her head, saying,

"After the new moon, Shabaka. Then you shall speak with me as much as you wish."

Thus it came about that never could I find opportunity to tell her of that matter of what had happened at the court of the Great King. Still every morning she sent me some token, flowers or trifling gifts, and once a ring that must have belonged to her forefathers, since on its bezel was engraved the royal *uraeus*, together with the signs of long life and health, which ring I wore hung about my neck but not upon my finger, fearing lest that emblem of royalty might offend Peroa or some of his House, if they chanced to see it. So in answer I also sent her flowers and other gifts, and for the rest was content to wait.

All of which things my mother noted with a smile, saying that the lady Amada showed a wonderful discretion, such as any man would value in a wife of so much beauty, which also must be most pleasing to her mistress, the goddess Isis. To this I answered that I valued it less as a lover than I might do as a husband. My mother smiled again and spoke of something else.

Thus things went on while the storm-clouds gathered over Egypt.

One night I could not sleep. It was that of the new moon and I knew that during those hours of darkness, before the solemn conclave of the high priests, with pomp and ceremony in the sanctuary of the temple, Amada had undergone absolution of her vows to Isis and been given liberty to wed as other women do. Indeed my mother, in virtue of her rank as a Singer of Amen, had been present at the rite, and returning, told me all that happened.

She described how Amada had appeared, clad as a priestess, how she had put up her prayer to the four high priests seated in state, demanding to be loosed from her vow "for the sake of her heart and of Egypt."

Then one of the high priests, he of Amen, I think, as the chief of them all, had advanced to the statue of the goddess Isis and whispered the prayer to it, whereon after a pause the goddess nodded thrice in the sight of all present, thereby signifying her assent. This done the high priest returned and proclaimed the absolution in the ancient words "for the sake of the suppliant's heart and of Egypt" and with it the blessing of the goddess on her union, adding, however, the formula, "at thy prayer, daughter and spouse, I, the goddess Isis, cut the rope that binds thee to me on earth. Yet if thou should'st tie it again, know that it may never more be severed, for if thou strivest so to do, it shall strangle thee in whatever shape thou livest on the earth throughout the generations, and with thee the man thou choosest and those who give thee to him. Thus saith Isis the Queen of Heaven."

"What does that mean?" I asked my mother.

"It means, my son, that if, having broken her vows to Isis, a woman should repeat them and once more enter the service of the goddess, and then for the second time seek to break them, she and the man for whom she did this thing would be like flies in a spider's web, and that not only in this life, but in any other that may be given to them in the world."

"It seems that Isis has a long arm," I said.

"Without doubt a very long arm, my son, since Isis, by whatever name she is called, is a power that does not die or forget."

"Well, Mother, in this case she can have no reason to remember, since never again will Amada be her priestess."

"I think not, Shabaka. Yet who can be sure of what a woman will or will not do, now or hereafter? For my part I am glad that I have served Amen and not Isis, and that after I was wed."

The Slaying of Idernes

Whilst I was still talking to my mother I received an urgent summons to the palace. I went and in a little ante-chamber met Amada alone, who, I could see, was waiting there for me. She was arrayed in her secular dress and wore the insignia of royalty, looking exceedingly beautiful. Moreover, her whole aspect had changed, for now she was no longer a priestess sworn to mysteries, but just a lovely and a loving woman.

"It is done, Shabaka," she whispered, "and thou art mine and I am thine."

Then I opened my arms and she sank upon my breast and for the first time I kissed her on the lips, kissed her many times and oh! my heart almost burst with joy. But all too fleeting was that sweet moment of love's first fruits, whereon I had sown the seed so many years ago, for while we yet clung together, whispering sweet things into each other's ears, I heard a voice calling me and was forced to go away before I had even time to ask when we might be wed.

Within the Council was gathered. The news before it was that the Satrap Idernes lay camped upon the Nile with some ten thousand men, not far from the great pyramids, that is, within striking distance of Memphis. Moreover his messengers announced that he purposed to visit the Prince Peroa that day with a small guard only, to inquire into this matter of the Signet, for which visit he demanded a safe-conduct sworn in the name of the Great King and in those of the gods of Egypt and the East. Failing this he would at once attack Memphis notwithstanding any commands that might be given him under the Signet, which, until he beheld it with his own eyes, he believed to be a forgery.

The question was—what answer should be sent to him? The debate that followed proved long and earnest. Some were in favour of attacking Idernes at once although his camp was reported to be strongly entrenched and flanked on one side by the Nile and on the other by the rising ground whereon stood the great sphinx and the pyramids. Others, among whom I was numbered, thought otherwise, for I hold that some evil god led me to give counsel that day which, if it were good for Egypt was most ill for my own fortunes. Perchance this god was Isis, angry at the loss of her votary.

I pointed out that by receiving Idernes Peroa would gain time which would enable a body of three thousand men, if not more, who were advancing down the Nile, to join us before they were perhaps cut off from the city, and thus give us a force as large as his, or larger. Also I showed that having summoned Idernes under the Signet, we should put ourselves in the wrong if we refused to receive him and instead attacked him at once.

A third party was in favour of allowing him to enter Memphis with his guard and then making him prisoner or killing him. As to this I pointed out again that not only would it involve the breaking of a solemn oath, which might bring the curse of the gods upon our cause and proclaim us traitors to the world, but it would also be foolish since Idernes was not the only general of the Easterns and if we cut off him and his escort, it would avail us little for then the rest of the Easterns would fight in a just cause.

So in the end it was agreed that the safe-conduct should be sent and that Peroa should receive Idernes that very day at a great feast given in his honour. Accordingly it was sent in the ancient form, the oaths being taken before the messengers that neither he nor those with him who must not number more than twenty men, would be harmed in Memphis and that he would be guarded on the road back until he reached the outposts of his own camp.

This done, I was despatched up the Nile bank in a chariot accompanied only by Bes, to hurry on the march of those troops of which I have spoken, so that they might reach Memphis by sundown. Before I went, however, I had some words alone with Peroa. He told me that my immediate marriage with the lady Amada would be announced at the feast that night. Thereon I prayed him to deliver to Amada the rope of priceless rose-hued pearls which was in his keeping, as my betrothal gift, with the prayer that she would wear them at the feast for my sake. There was no time for more.

The journey up Nile proved long for the road was bad being covered with drifted sand in some places and deep in mud from the inundation waters in others. At length I found the troops just starting forward after their rest, and rejoiced to see that there were more of them than I had thought. I told the case to their captains, who promised to make a forced march and to be in Memphis two hours before midnight.

As we drove back Bes said to me suddenly,

"Do you know why you could not find me this morning?"

I answered that I did not.

"Because a good slave should always run a pace ahead of his master, to clear the road and tell him of its pitfalls. I was being married. The Cup of the holy Tanofir is now by law and right Queen of the Ethiopians. So when you meet her again you must treat her with great respect, as I do already."

"Indeed, Bes," I said laughing, "and how did you manage that business? You must have wooed her well during these days which have been so full for both of us."

"I did not woo her over much, Master; indeed, the time was lacking. I wooed the holy Tanofir, which was more important."

"The holy Tanofir, Bes?" I exclaimed.

"Yes, Master. You see this beautiful Cup of his is after all—his beautiful Cup. Her mind is the shadow of his mind and from her he pours out his wisdom. So I told him all the case. At first he was angry, for, notwithstanding the words he spoke to you and me, when it came to a point the holy Tanofir, being after all much like other men, did not wish to lose his Cup. Indeed had he been a few score of years younger I am not sure but that he would have forgotten some of his holiness because of her. Still he came to see matters in the true light at last—for your sake, Master, not for mine, since his wisdom told him it was needful that I should become King of the Ethiopians again, to do which I must be married. At any rate he worked upon the mind of that Cup of his—having first settled that she should procure a younger sister of her own to fill her place—in such fashion that when at length I spoke to her on the matter, she did not say no."

"No doubt because she was fond of you for yourself, Bes. A woman would not marry even to please the holy Tanofir."

"Oh! Master," he replied in a new voice, a very sad voice, "I would that I could think so. But look at me, a misshapen dwarf, accursed from birth. Could a fair lady like this Karema wed such a one for his own sake?"

"Well, Bes, there might be other reasons besides the holy Tanofir," I said hurriedly.

"Master, there were no other reasons, unless the Cup, when it is awake, remembers what it has held in trance, which I do not believe. I wooed her as I was, not telling her that I am also King of the Ethiopians, or any more than I seem to be. Moreover the holy Tanofir told her nothing, for he swore as much to me and he does not lie."

"And what did she say to you, Bes?" I asked, for I was curious.

"She lied fast enough, Master. She said—well, what she said when first we met her, that there was more in me than the eye saw and that she who had lived so much with spirits looked to the spirit rather than to the flesh, and that dwarf or no she loved me and desired nothing better than to marry me and be my true and faithful wife and helpmeet. She lied so well that once or twice almost I believed her. At any rate I took her at her word, not altogether for myself, believe me, Master, but because without doubt what the holy Tanofir has shown us will come to pass, and it is necessary to you that I should be married."

"You married her to help me, Bes?"

"That is so, Master—after all, but a little thing, seeing that she is beautiful, well born and very pleasant, and I am fond of her. Also I do her no wrong for she has bought more than she bargained for, and if she has any that are not dwarfs, her children may be kings. I do not think," he added reflectively, "that even the faithful Ethiopians could accept a second dwarf as their king. One is very well for a change, but not two or three. The stomach of a tall people would turn against them."

I took Bes's hand and pressed it, understanding the depth of his love and sacrifice. Also some spirit—doubtless it came from the holy Tanofir—moved me to say,

"Be comforted, Bes, for I am sure of this. Your children will be strong and straight and tall, more so than any of their forefathers that went before them."

This indeed proved to be the case, for their father's deformity was but an accident, not born in his blood.

"Those are good-omened words, Master, for which I thank you, though the holy Tanofir said the like when he wed us with the sacred words this morning and gave us his blessing, endowing my wife with certain gifts of secret wisdom which he said would be of use to her and me."

"Where is she now, Bes?"

"With the holy Tanofir, Master, until I fetch her, training her younger sister to be a diviner's worthy Cup. Only perhaps I shall never send, seeing that I think there will be fighting soon."

"Yes, Bes, but being newly married you will do well to leave it to others."

"No, no, Master. Battle is better than wives. Moreover, could you think that I would leave you to stand alone in the fray? Why if I did and harm came to you I should die of shame or hang myself and then Karema would never be a queen. So both her trades would be gone, since after marriage she cannot be a Cup, and her heart would break. But here are the gates of Memphis, so we will forget love and think of war."

An hour later I and my mother, the lady Tiu, stood in the banqueting hall of the palace with many others, and learned that the Satrap Idernes and his escort had reached Memphis and would be present at the feast. A while later trumpets blew and a glittering procession entered the hall. At the head of it was Peroa who led Idernes by the hand. This Eastern was a big, strong man with tired and anxious eyes, such as I had noted were common among the servants of the Great King who from day to day never knew whether they would fill a Satrapy or a grave. He was clad in gorgeous silks and wore a cap upon his head in which shone a jewel, but beneath his robes I caught the glint of mail.

As he came into the hall and noted the number and quality of the guests and the stir and the expectant look upon their faces, he started as though he were afraid, but recovering himself, murmured some courteous words to his host and advanced towards the seat of honour which was pointed out to him upon the Prince's right. After these two followed the wife of Peroa with her son and daughters. Then, walking alone in token of her high rank, appeared Amada, the Royal Lady of Egypt, wonderfully arrayed. Now, however, she wore no emblems of royalty, either because it was not thought wise that these should be shown in the presence of the Satrap, or because she was about to be given in marriage to one who was not royal. Indeed, as I noted with joy, her only ornament was the rope of rose-hued pearls which were arranged in a double row upon her breast.

She searched me out with her eyes, smiled, touching the pearls with her finger, and passed on to her place next to the daughters of Peroa, at one end of the head table which was shaped like a horse's hoof.

After her came the nobles who had accompanied Idernes, grave Eastern men. One of these, a tall captain with eyes like a hawk, seemed familiar to me. Nor was I mistaken, for Bes, who stood behind me and whose business it would be to wait on me at the feast, whispered in my ear,

"Note that man. He was present when you were brought before the Great King from the boat and saw and heard all that passed."

"Then I wish he were absent now," I whispered back, for at the words a sudden fear shot through me, of what I could not say.

By degrees all were seated in their appointed places. Mine was by that of my mother at a long table that stood as it were across the ends of the high table but at a little distance from them, so that I was almost opposite to Peroa and Idernes and could see Amada, although she was too far away for me to be able to speak to her.

The feast began and at first was somewhat heavy and silent, since, save for the talk of courtesy, none spoke much. At length wine, whereof I noted that Idernes drank a good deal, as did his escort, but Peroa and the Egyptians little, loosened men's tongues and they grew merrier. For it was the custom of the people of the Great King to discuss both private and public business when full of strong drink, but of the Egyptians when they were quite sober. This was well known to Peroa and many of us, especially to myself who had been among them, which was one of the reasons why Idernes had been asked to meet us at a feast, where we might have the advantage of him in debate.

Presently the Satrap noted the splendid cup from which he drank and asked some question concerning it of the hawk-eyed noble of whom I have spoken. When it had been answered he said in a voice loud enough for me to overhear,

"Tell me, O Prince Peroa, was this cup ever that of the Great King which it so much resembles?"

"So I understand, O Idernes," answered Peroa. "That is, until it became mine by gift from the lord Shabaka, who received it from the Great King."

An expression of horror appeared upon the face of the Satrap and upon those of his nobles.

"Surely," he answered, "this Shabaka must hold the King's favours lightly if he passes them on thus to the first-comer. At the least, let not the vessel which has been hallowed by the lips of the King of kings be dishonoured by the humblest of his servants. I pray you, O Prince, that I may be given another cup."

So a new goblet was brought to him, Peroa trying to pass the matter off as a jest by appealing to me to tell the story of the cup. Then I said while all listened,

"O Prince, the most high Satrap is mistaken. The King of kings did not give me the cup, I bought it from him in exchange for a certain famous bow, and therefore held it not wrong to pass it on to you, my lord."

Idernes made no answer and seemed to forget the matter.

A while later, however, his eye fell upon Amada and the rose-hued pearls she wore, and again he asked a question of the hawk-eyed captain, then said,

"Think me not discourteous, O Prince, if I seem to look upon yonder lovely lady which in our country, where women do not appear in public, we should think it an insult to do. But on her fair breast I see certain pearls like to some that are known throughout the world, which for many years have been worn by those who sit upon the throne of the East. I would ask if they are the same, or others?"

"I do not know, O Idernes," answered Peroa; "I only know that the lord Shabaka brought them from the East. Inquire of him, if it be your pleasure."

"Shabaka again——" began Idernes, but I cut him short, saying,

"Yes, O Satrap, Shabaka again. I won those pearls in a bet from the Great King, and with them a certain weight of gold. This I think you knew before, since your messenger of a while ago was whipped for trying to steal them, which under the rods he said he did by command, O Satrap."

To this bold speech Idernes made no answer. Only his captains frowned and many of the Egyptians murmured approval.

After this the feast went on without further incident for a while, the Easterns always drinking more wine, till at length the tables were cleared and all of the meaner sort departed from the hall, save the butlers and the personal servants such as Bes, who stood behind the seats of their masters. There came a silence such as precedes the bursting of a storm, and in the midst of it Idernes spoke, somewhat thickly.

"I did not come here, O Peroa," he said, "from the seat of government at Sais to eat your meats and drink your wine. I came to speak of high matters with you."

"It is so, O Satrap," answered Peroa. "And now what may be your will? Would you retire to discuss them with me and my Councillors?"

"Where is the need, O Peroa, seeing that I have naught to say which may not be heard by all?"

"As it pleases you. Speak on, O Satrap."

"I have been summoned here, Prince Peroa, by a writing under what seems to be the Signet of signets—the ancient White Seal that for generations unknown has been worn by the forefathers of the King of kings. Where is this Signet?"

"Here," said the Prince, opening his robe. "Look on it, Satrap, and let your lords look, but let none of you dare to touch it."

Idernes looked long and earnestly, and so did some of his people, especially the lord with the hawk eyes. Then they stared at each other bewildered and whispered together.

"It seems to be the very Seal—the White Seal itself!" exclaimed Idernes at length. "Tell me now, Peroa. How came this sacred thing that dwells in the East hither into Egypt?"

"The lord Shabaka brought it to me with certain letters from the Great King, O Satrap."

"Shabaka for the third time, by the holy Fire!" cried Idernes. "He brought the cup; he brought the famous pearls; he brought the gold, and he brought the Signet of signets. What is there then that he did not bring? Perchance he has the person of the King of kings himself in his keeping!"

"Not that, O Satrap, only the commands of the King of kings which are prepared ready to deliver to you under the White Seal that you acknowledge."

"And what may they be, Egyptian?"

"This, O Satrap: That you and all the army which you have brought with you retire to Sais and thence out of Egypt as quickly as you may, or pay for disobedience with your lives."

Now Idernes and his captains gasped.

"Why this is rebellion!" he said.

"No, O Satrap, only the command of the Great King given under the White Seal," and drawing a roll from his breast, Peroa laid it on his brow and cast it down before Idernes, adding,

"Obey the writing and the Signet, or by virtue of my commission, as soon as you are returned to your army and your safe-conduct is expired, I fall upon you and destroy you."

Idernes looked about him like a wolf in a trap, then asked,

"Do you mean to murder me here?"

"Not so," answered Peroa, "for you have our safe-conduct and Egyptians are honourable men. But you are dismissed your office and ordered to leave Egypt."

Idernes thought a little while, then said,

"If I leave Egypt, there is at least one whom I am commanded to take with me under orders and writings that you will not dispute, a maiden named Amada whom the Great King would number among his women. I am told it is she who sits yonder—a jewel indeed, fair as the pearls upon her breast which thus will return into the King's keeping. Let her be handed over, for she rides with me at once."

Now in the midst of an intense silence Peroa answered,

"Amada, the Royal Lady of Egypt, cannot be sent to dwell in the House of Women of the Great King without the consent of the lord Shabaka, whose she is."

"Shabaka for the fourth time!" said Idernes, glaring at me. "Then let Shabaka come too. Or his head in a basket will suffice, since that will save trouble afterwards, also some pain to Shabaka. Why, now I remember. It was this very Shabaka whom the Great King condemned to death by the boat for a crime against his Majesty, and who bought his life by promising to deliver to him the fairest and most learned woman in the world—the lady Amada of Egypt. And thus does the knave keep his oath!"

Now I leapt to my feet, as did most of those present. Only Amada kept her seat and looked at me.

"You lie!" I cried, "and were it not for your safe-conduct I would kill you for the lie."

"I lie, do I?" sneered Idernes. "Speak then, you who were present, and tell this noble company whether I lie," and he pointed to the hawk- eyed lord.

"He does not lie," said the Captain. "I was in the Court of the Great King and heard yonder Shabaka purchase pardon by promising to hand over his cousin, the lady Amada, to the King. The pearls were entrusted to him as a gift to her and I see she wears them. The gold also of which mention has been made was to provide for her journey in state to the East, or so I heard. The cup was his guerdon, also a sum for his own purse."

"It is false," I shouted. "The name of Amada slipped my lips by chance —no more."

"So it slipped your lips by chance, did it?" sneered Idernes. "Now, if you are wise, you will suffer the lady Amada to slip your hand, and not by chance. But let us have done with this cunning knave. Prince, will you hand over yonder fair woman, or will you not?"

"Satrap, I will not," answered Peroa. "The demand is an insult put forward to force us to rebellion, since there is no man in Egypt who will not be ready to die in defence of the Royal Lady of Egypt."

This statement was received with a shout of applause by every Egyptian in the hall. Idernes waited until it had died away, then said,

"Prince Peroa and Egyptians, you have conveyed to me certain commands sealed with the Signet of signets, which I think was stolen by yonder Shabaka. Now hearken; until this matter is made clear I will obey those commands thus far. I will return with my army to Sais and there wait until I have received the orders of the Great King, after report made to him. If so much as an arrow is shot at us on our march, it will be open rebellion, as the price of which Egypt shall be crushed as she was never crushed before, and every one of you here present shall lose his head, save only the lady Amada who is the property of the Great King. Now I thank you for your hospitality and demand that you escort me and those with me back to my camp, since it seems that here we are in the midst of enemies."

"Before you go, Idernes," I shouted, "know that you and your lying captain shall pay with your lives for your slander on me."

"Many will pay with their lives for this night's work, O thief of pearls and seals," answered the Satrap, and turning, left the hall with his company.

Now I searched for Amada, but she also had gone with the ladies of Peroa's household who feared lest the feast should end in blows and bloodshed, also lest she should be snatched away. Indeed of all the women in the hall, only my mother remained.

"Search out the lady Amada," I said to her, "and tell her the truth."

"Yes, my son," she answered thoughtfully; "but what is the truth? I understood it was Bes who first gave the name of the lady Amada to the Great King. Now we learn from your own lips that it was you. Wise would you have been, my son, if you had bitten out your tongue before you said it, since this is a matter that any woman may well misunderstand."

"Her name was surprised out of me, Mother. It was Bes who spoke to the King of the beauty of a certain lady of Egypt."

"And I think, my son, it was Bes who told Peroa and his guests that he and not you had given the King her name, which you do not seem to have denied. Well, doubtless both of you are to blame for foolishness, no more, since well I know that you would have died ten times over rather than buy your life at the price of the honour of the Lady of Egypt. This I will say to her as soon as I may, praying that it may not be too late, and afterwards you shall tell me everything, which you would have done well to do at first, if Bes, as I think, had not been over cunning after the fashion of black people, and counselled you otherwise. See, Peroa calls you and I must go, for there are greater matters afoot than that of who let slip the name of the lady Amada to the King of kings."

So she went and there followed a swift council of war, the question being whether we were to strike at the Satrap's army or to allow it to retreat to Sais. In my turn I was asked for my judgment of the issue, and answered,

"Strike and at once, since we cannot hope to storm Sais, which is far away. Moreover such strength as we have is now gathered and if it is idle and perhaps unpaid, will disperse again. But if we can destroy Idernes and his army, it will be long before the King of kings, who is sending all his multitudes against the Greeks, can gather another, and during this time Egypt may again become a nation and able to protect herself under Peroa her own Pharaoh."

In the end I, and those who thought like me, prevailed, so that before the dawn I was sailing down the Nile with the fleet, having two thousand men under my command. Also I took with me the six hunters whom I had won from the Great King, since I knew them to be faithful, and thought that their knowledge of the Easterns and their ways might be of service. Our orders were to hold a certain neck of land between the river and the hills where the army of Idernes must pass, until Peroa and all his strength could attack him from behind.

Four hours later, the wind being very favourable to us, we reached that place and there took up our station and having made all as ready as we could, rested.

In the early afternoon Bes awakened me from the heavy sleep into which I had fallen, and pointed to the south. I looked and through the desert haze saw the chariots of Idernes advancing in ordered ranks, and after them the masses of his footmen.

Now we had no chariots, only archers, and two regiments armed with long spears and swords. Also the sailors on the boats had their slings and throwing javelins. Lastly the ground was in our favour since it sloped upwards and the space between the river and the hills was narrow, somewhat boggy too after the inundation of the Nile, which meant that the chariots must advance in a column and could not gather sufficient speed to sweep over us.

Idernes and his captains noted all this also, and halted. Then they sent a herald forward to ask who we were and to command us in the name of the Great King to make way for the army of the Great King.

I answered that we were Egyptians, ordered by Peroa to hold the road against the Satrap who had done affront to Egypt by demanding that its Royal Lady should be given over to him to be sent to the East as a woman-slave, and that if the Satrap wished to clear a road, he could come and do so. Or if it pleased him he could go back towards Memphis, or stay where he was, since we did not wish to strike the first blow. I added this,

"I who speak on behalf of the Prince Peroa, am the lord Shabaka, that same man whom but last night the Satrap and a certain captain of his named a liar. Now the Easterns are brave men and we of Egypt have always heard that among them none is braver than Idernes who gained his advancement through courage and skill in war. Let him therefore come out together with the lord who named me a liar, armed with swords only, and I, who being a liar must also be a coward, together with my servant, a black dwarf, will meet them man to man in the sight of both the armies, and fight them to the death. Or if it pleases Idernes better, let him not come and I will seek him and kill him in the battle, or by him be killed."

The herald, having taken stock of me and of Bes at whom he laughed, returned with the message.

"Will he come, think you, Master?" asked Bes.

"Mayhap," I answered, "since it is a shame for an Eastern to refuse a challenge from any man whom he calls barbarian, and if he did so it might cost him his life afterwards at the hands of the Great King. Also if he should fall there are others to take his command, but none who can wipe away the stain upon his honour."

"Yes," said Bes; "also they will think me a dwarf of no account, which makes the task of killing you easy. Well, they shall see."

Now when I sent this challenge I had more in my mind than a desire to avenge myself upon Idernes and his captain for the public shame they had put upon me. I wished to delay the attack of their host upon our little band and give time for the army of Peroa to come up behind. Moreover, if I fell it did not greatly matter, except as an omen, seeing that I had good officers under me who knew all my plans.

We saw the herald reach the Satrap's army and after a while return towards us again, which made us think my challenge had been refused, especially as with him was an officer who, I took it, was sent to spy out our strength. But this was not so, for the man said,

"The Satrap Idernes has sworn by the Great King to kill the thief of the Signet and send his head to the Great King, and fears that if he waits to meet him in battle, he may slip away. Therefore he is minded to accept your challenge, O Shabaka, and put an end to you, and indeed under the laws of the East he may not refuse. But a noble of the Great King may not fight against a black slave save with a whip, so how can that noble accept the challenge of the dwarf Bes?"

"Quite well," answered Bes, "seeing that I am no slave but a free citizen of Egypt. Moreover, in my own country of Ethiopia I am of royal blood. Lastly, tell the man this, that if he does not come and afterwards falls into my hands or into those of the lord Shabaka, he who talks of whips shall be scourged with them till his life creeps out from between his bare bones."

Thus spoke Bes, rolling his great eyes and looking so terrible that the herald and the officer fell back a step or two. Then I told them that if my offer did not please them, I myself would fight, first Idernes and then the noble. So they returned.

The end of it was that we saw Idernes and his captain advancing, followed by a guard of ten men. Then after I had explained all things to my officers, I also advanced with Bes, followed by a guard of ten picked men. We met between the armies on a little sandy plain at the foot of the rise and there followed talk between the captains of our guards as to arms and so forth, but we four said nothing to each other, since the time for words was past. Only Bes and I sat down upon the sand and spoke a little together of Amada and Karema and of how they would receive the news of our victory or deaths.

"It does not much matter, Master," said Bes at last, "seeing that if we die we shall never know, and if we live we shall learn for ourselves."

At length all was arranged and we stood up to face each other, the four of us being armed in the same way. For as did Idernes and the hawk-eyed lord, Bes and I wore shirts of mail and helms, those that we had brought with us from the East. For weapons we had short and heavy swords, small shields and knives at our girdles.

"Look your last upon the sun, Thieves," mocked Idernes, "for when you see it again, it shall be with blind eyes from the points of spears fastened to the gateway pillars of the Great King's palace."

"Liars you have lived and liars you shall die," shouted Bes, but I said nothing.

Now the agreement was that when the word had been given Idernes and I, and the noble and Bes, should fight together, but if they killed one of us, or we killed one of them, the two who survived might fall together on the remaining man. Remembering this, as he told me afterwards, at the signal Bes leapt forward like a flash with working face and foam upon his lips, and before ever I could come to Idernes, how I know not, had received the blow of the Eastern lord upon his shield and without striking back, had gripped him in his long arms and wrapped him round with his bowed legs. In an instant they were on the ground, Bes uppermost, and I heard the sound of blow upon blow struck with knife or sword, I knew not which, upon the Eastern's mail, followed by a shout of victory from the Egyptians which told me that Bes had slain him.

Now Idernes and I were smiting at each other. He was a taller and a bigger man than myself, but older and one who had lived too well. Therefore I thought it wise to keep him at a distance and tire him, which I did by retreating and catching his sword-cuts on my shield, only smiting back now and again.

"He runs! He runs!" shouted the Easterns. "O Idernes, beware the dwarf!"

"Stand away, Bes," I called; "this is my game," and he obeyed, as often he had done when we were hunting together.

Now a shrewd blow from Idernes cut through my helm and staggered me, and another before I could recover myself, shore the shield from my hand, whereat the Easterns shouted more loudly than before. Then fear of defeat entered into me and made me mad, for this Satrap was a great fighter. With a shout of "Egypt!" I went at him like a wounded lion and soon it was his turn to stagger back. But alas! I struck too hard, for my sword snapped upon his mail.

"The knife!" screamed Bes; "the knife!"

I hurled the sword hilt in the Satrap's face and drew the dagger from my belt. Then I ran in beneath his guard and stabbed and stabbed and stabbed. He gripped me and we went down side by side, rolling over each other. The gods know how it ended, for things were growing dim to me when some thrust of mine found a rent in his mail made when the sword broke and he became weak. His spirit weakened also, for he gasped,

"Spare my life, Egyptian, and my treasure is yours. I swear it by the Fire."

"Not for all the treasure in the world, Slanderer," I panted back and drove the dagger home to the hilt thrice, until he died. Then I staggered to my feet, and when the armies saw that it was I who rose while Idernes lay still a roar of triumph went up from the Egyptians, answered by a roar of rage from the Easterns.

With a cry of "Well done, Master!" Bes leapt upon the dead man and hewed his head from him, as already he had served the hawk-eyed noble. Then gripping one head in each hand he held them up for the Easterns to see.

"Men of the Great King," I said, "bear us witness that we have fought fairly, man to man, when we need not have done so."

The ten of the Satrap's guard stood silent, but my own shouted,

"Back, Shabaka! The Easterns charge!"

I looked and saw them coming like waves of steel, then supported by my men and preceded by Bes who danced in front shaking the severed heads, I ran back to my own ranks where one gave me wine to drink and threw water over my hurts which were but slight. Scarcely was it done when the battle closed in and soon in it I forgot the deaths of Idernes and the Eastern liar.

Amada Returns to Isis

We fought a very terrible fight that evening there by the banks of Nile. Our position was good, but we were outnumbered by four or five to one, and the Easterns and their mercenaries were mad at the death of the Satrap by my hand. Time upon time they came on furiously, charging up the slope like wild bulls. For the most part we relied upon our archers to drive them back, since our half-trained troops could scarcely hope to stand against the onset of veterans disciplined in war. So taking cover behind the rocks we rained arrows on them, shooting the horses in the chariots, and when these were down, pouring our shafts upon the footmen behind. Myself I took my great black bow and drew it thrice, and each time I saw a noble fall, for no mail could withstand the arrows which it sent, and of that art I was a master. None in Egypt could shoot so far or so straight as I did, save perhaps Peroa himself. I had no time to do more since always I must be moving up and down the line encouraging my men.

Three times we drove them back, after which they grew cunning. Ceasing from a direct onslaught and keeping what remained of their chariots in reserve, they sent one body of men to climb along the slope of the hill where the rocks gave them cover from our arrows, and another to creep through the reeds and growing crops upon the bank of the river where we could not see to shoot them well, although the slingers in the ships did them some damage.

Thus they attacked us on either flank, and while we were thus engaged their centre made a charge. Then came the bitterest of the fighting for now the bows were useless, and it was sword against sword and spear against spear. Once we broke and I thought that they were through. But I led a charge against them and drove them back a little way. Still the issue was doubtful till I saw Bes rush past me grinning and leaping, and with him a small body of Greeks whom we held in reserve, and I think that the sight of the terrible dwarf whom they thought a devil, frightened the Easterns more than did the Greeks.

At any rate, shouting out something about an evil spirit whom the Egyptians worshipped, by which I suppose they meant that god after whom Bes was named, they retreated, leaving many dead but taking their wounded with them, for they were unbroken.

At the foot of the slope they reformed and took counsel, then sat down out of bowshot as though to rest. Now I guessed their plan. It was to wait till night closed in, which would be soon for the sun was sinking, and then, when we could not see to shoot, either rush through us by the weight of numbers, or march back to where the cliffs were lower and climb them, thus passing us on the higher open land.

Now we also took counsel, though little came of it, since we did not know what to do. We were too few to attack so great an army, nor if we climbed the cliffs could we hope to withstand them in the desert sands, or to hold our own against them if they charged in the dark. If this happened it seemed that all we could do would be to fight as long as we could, after which the survivors of us must take refuge on our boats. So it came to this, that we should lose the battle and the greater part of the Easterns would win back to Sais, unless indeed the main army under Peroa came to our aid.

Whilst we talked I caused the wounded to be carried to the ships before it grew too dark to move them. Bes went with them. Presently he returned, running swiftly.

"Master," he said, "the evening wind is blowing strong and stirs the sand, but from a mast-head through it I caught sight of Peroa's banners. The army comes round the bend of the river not four furlongs away. Now charge and those Easterns will be caught between the hammer and the stone, for while they are meeting us they will not look behind."

So I went down the lines of our little force telling them the good news and showing them my plan. They listened and understood. We formed up, those who were left of us, not more than a thousand men perhaps, and advanced. The Easterns laughed when they saw us coming down the slope, for they thought that we were mad and that they would kill us every one, believing as they did that Peroa had no other army. When we were within bowshot we began to shoot, though sparingly, for but few arrows were left. Galled by our archery they marshalled their ranks to charge us again. With a shout we leapt forward to meet them, for now from the higher ground I saw the chariots of Peroa rushing to our rescue.

We met, we fought. Surely there had been no such fighting since the days of Thotmes and Rameses the Great. Still they drove us back till unseen and unsuspected the chariots and the footmen of Peroa broke on them from behind, broke on them like a desert storm. They gave, they fled this way and that, some to the banks of the Nile, some to the hills. By the light of the setting sun we finished it and ere the darkness closed in the Great King's army was destroyed, save for the fugitives whom we hunted down next day.

Yes, in that battle perished ten thousand of the Easterns and their mercenaries, and upon its field at dawn we crowned Peroa Pharaoh of Egypt, and he named me the chief general of his army. There, too, fell over a thousand of my men and among them those six hunters whom I had won in the wager with the Great King and brought with me from the East. Throughout the fray they served me as a bodyguard, fighting furiously, who knew that they could hope for no mercy from their own people. One by one they were slain, the last two of them in the charge at sunset. Well, they were brave and faithful to me, so peace be on their spirits. Better to die thus than in the den of lions.

In triumph we returned to Memphis, I bringing in the rear-guard and the spoils. Before Pharaoh and I parted a messenger brought me more good news. Sure tidings had come that the King of kings had been driven by revolt in his dominions to embark upon a mighty war with Syria, Greece and Cyprus and other half-conquered countries, in which, doubtless by agreement, the fires of insurrection had suddenly burned up. Also already Peroa's messengers had departed to tell them of what was passing on the Nile.

"If this be true," said Peroa when he had heard all, "the Great King will have no new army to spare for Egypt."

"It is so, Pharaoh," I answered. "Yet I think he will conquer in this great war and that within two years you must be prepared to meet him face to face."

"Two years are long, Shabaka, and in them, by your help, much may be done."

But as it chanced he was destined to be robbed of that help, and this by the work of Woman the destroyer.

It happened thus. Amidst great rejoicings Pharaoh reached Memphis and in the vast temple of Amen laid down our spoils in the presence of the god, thousands of right hands hewn from the fallen, thousands of swords and other weapons and tens of chariots, together with much treasure of which a portion was given to the god. The high priests blessed us in the name of Amen and of the other gods; the people blessed us and threw flowers in our path; all the land rejoiced because once more it was free.

There too that day in the temple with ancient form and ceremonial Peroa was crowned Pharaoh of Egypt. Sceptres and jewels that had been hid for generations were brought out by those who knew the secret of their hiding-places; the crowns that had been worn by old Pharaohs, were set upon his head; yes, the double crown of the Upper and the Lower Land. Thus in a Memphis mad with joy at the casting off of the foreign yoke, he was anointed the first of a new dynasty, and with him his queen.

I too received honours, for the story of the slaying of Idernes at my hands and of how I held the pass had gone abroad, so that next to Pharaoh, I was looked upon as the greatest man in Egypt. Nor was Bes forgotten, since many of the common people thought that he was a spirit in the form of a dwarf whom the gods had sent to aid us with his strength and cunning. Indeed at the close of the ceremony voices cried out in the multitude of watchers, demanding that I who was to marry the Royal Lady of Egypt should be named next in succession to the throne.

The Pharaoh heard and glanced first at his son and then at me, doubtfully, whereon, covered with confusion, I slipped away.

The portico of the temple was deserted, since all, even the guards, had crowded into the vast court to watch the coronation. Only in the shadow, seated against the pedestal of one of the two colossal statues in front of the outer pylon gate and looking very small beneath its greatness, was a man wrapped in a dark cloak whom noting vaguely I took to be a beggar. As I passed him, he plucked at my robe, and I stopped to search for something to give to him but could find naught.

"I have nothing, Father," I said laughing, "except the gold hilt of my sword."

"Do not part with that, Son," answered a deep voice, "for I think you will need it before all is over."

Then while I stared at him he threw back his hood and I saw that beneath was the ancient withered face and the long white beard of my great-uncle, the holy Tanofir, the hermit and magician.

"Great things happen yonder, Shabaka. So great that I have come from my sepulchre to see, or rather, being blind, to listen, who thrice in my life days have known the like before," and he pointed to the glittering throng in the court within. "Yes," he went on, "I have seen Pharaohs crowned and Pharaohs die—one of them at the hand of a conqueror. What will happen to this Pharaoh, think you, Shabaka?"

"You should be better able to answer that question than I, who am no prophet, my Uncle."

"How, my Nephew, seeing that your dwarf has borne away my magic Cup? I do not grudge her to him for he is a brave dwarf and clever, who may yet prove a good prop to you, as he has done before, and to Egypt also. But she has gone and the new vessel is not yet shaped to my liking. So how can I answer?"

"Out of the store of wisdom gathered in your breast."

"So! my Nephew. Well, my store of wisdom tells me that feasts are sometimes followed by want and rejoicings by sorrow and victories by defeat, and splendid sins by repentance and slow climbing back to good again. Also that you will soon take a long journey. Where is the Royal Lady Amada? I did not hear her step among those who passed in to the Crowning. But even my hearing has grown somewhat weak of late, except in the silence of the night, Shabaka."

"I do not know, my Uncle, who have only been in Memphis one hour. But what do you mean? Doubtless she prepares herself for the feast where I shall meet her."

"Doubtless. Tell me, what passes at the temple of Isis? As I crept past the pylon feeling my way with my beggar's staff, I thought—but how can you know who have only been in Memphis an hour? Yet surely I heard voices just now calling out that you, Shabaka, should be named as the next successor to the throne of Egypt. Was it so?"

"Yes, holy Tanofir. That is why I have left who was vexed and am sworn to seek no such honour, which indeed I do not desire."

"Just so, Nephew. Yet gifts have a way of coming to those who do not desire them and the last vision that I saw before my Cup left me, or rather that she saw, was of you wearing the Double Crown. She said that you looked very well in it, Shabaka. But now begone, for hark, here comes the procession with the new-anointed Pharaoh whose royal robe you won for him yonder in the pass, when you smote down Idernes and held his legions. Oh! it was well done and my new Cup, though faulty, was good enough to show me all. I felt proud of you, Shabaka, but begone, begone! 'A gift for the poor old beggar! A gift, my lords, for the poor blind beggar who has had none since the last Pharaoh was crowned in Egypt and finds it hard to live on memories!'"

At our house I found my mother just returned from the Coronation, but Bes I did not find and guessed that he had slipped away to meet his new-made wife, Karema. My mother embraced me and blessed me, making much of me and my deeds in the battle; also she doctored such small hurts as I had. I put the matter by as shortly as I could and asked her if she had seen aught of Amada. She answered that she had neither seen nor heard of her which I was sure she thought strange, as she began to talk quickly of other things. I said to her what I had said to the holy Tanofir, that doubtless she was making ready for the feast since I could not find her at the Crowning.

"Or saying good-bye to the goddess," answered my mother nodding, "since there are some who find it even harder to fall from heaven to earth than to climb from earth to heaven, and after all you are but a man, my son."

Then she slipped away to attire herself, leaving me wondering, because my mother was shrewd and never spoke at random.

There was the holy Tanofir, too, with his talk about the temple of Isis, and he also did not speak at random. Oh! now I felt as I had done when the shadow of the palm-tree fell on me yonder in the palace garden.

The mood passed for my blood still tingled with the glory of that great fight, and my heart shut its doors to sadness, knowing as I did, that I was the most praised man in Memphis that day. Indeed had I not, I should have learned it when with my mother I entered the great banqueting-hall of the palace somewhat late, for she was long in making ready.

The first thing I saw there was Bes gorgeously arrayed in Eastern silks that he had plundered from the Satrap's tent, standing on a table so that all might see and hear him, and holding aloft in one hand the grisly head of Idernes and in the other that of the hawk-eyed noble whom he had slain, while in his thick, guttural voice he told the tale of that great fray. Catching sight of me, he called aloud,

"See! Here comes the man! Here comes the hero to whom Egypt owes its liberty and Pharaoh his crown."

Thereon all the company and the soldiers and servants who were gathered about the door began to shout and acclaim me, till I wished that I could vanish away as the holy Tanofir was said to be able to do. Since this was impossible I rushed at Bes who leapt from the table like a monkey and, still waving the heads and talking, slipped from the hall, I know not how, followed by the loud laughter of the guests.

Then heralds announced the coming of Pharaoh and all grew silent. He and his company entered with pomp and we, his subjects, prostrated ourselves in the ancient fashion.

"Rise, my guests," he cried. "Rise, my people. Above all do you rise, Shabaka, my beloved cousin, to whom Egypt and I owe so much."

So we rose and I took my seat in a place of honour having my mother at my side, and looked about me for Amada, but in vain. There was the carven chair upon which she should have been among those of the princesses, but it was empty. At first I thought that she was late, but when time went by and she did not appear, I asked if she were ill, a question that none seemed able to answer.

The feast went on with all the ancient ceremonies that attended the crowning of a Pharaoh of Egypt, since there were old men who remembered these, also the scribes and priests had them written in their books.

I took no heed of them and will not set them down. At length Pharaoh pledged his subjects, and his subjects pledged Pharaoh. Then the doors were opened and through them came a company of white-robed, shaven priests bearing on a bier the body of a dead man wrapped in his mummy-cloths. At first some laughed for this rite had not been performed in Egypt since she passed into the hands of the Great Kings of the East and therefore was strange to them. Then they grew silent since after all it was solemn to see those death-bearing priests flitting in and out between the great columns, now seen and now lost in the shadows, and to listen to their funeral chants.

In the hush my mother whispered to me that this body was that of the last Pharaoh of Egypt brought from his tomb, but whether this were so I cannot say for certain. At length they brought the mummy which was crowned with a snake-headed circlet of the royal *uraeus* and still draped with withered funeral wreaths, and stood it on its feet opposite to Peroa just behind and between my mother and me in such a fashion that it cut off the light from us.

The faint and heavy smell of the embalmer's spices struck upon my nostrils, a dead flower from the chaplets fell upon my head and, glancing over my shoulder, I saw the painted or enamelled eyes in the gilded mask staring at me. The thing filled me with fear, I knew not of what. Not of death, surely, for that I had faced a score of times of late and thought nothing of it. Indeed I am not sure that it was fear I felt, but rather a deep sense of the vanity of all things. It seemed to come home to me—Shabaka or Allan Quatermain, for in my dream the inspiration or whatever it might be, struck through the spirit that animated both of us—as it had never done before, that everything is *nothing*, that victory and love and even life itself have no meaning; that naught really exists save the soul of man and God, of whom perchance that soul is a part sent forth for a while to do His work through good and ill. The thought lifted me up and yet crushed me, since for a moment all that makes a man passed away, and I felt myself standing in utter loneliness, naked before the glory of God, watched only by the flaming stars that light his throne. Yes, and at that moment suddenly I learned that all the gods are but one God, having many shapes and called by many names.

Then I heard the priests saying,

"Pharaoh the Osiris greets Pharaoh the living on the Earth and sends to him this message—'As I am, so shalt thou be, and where I am, there thou shalt dwell through all the ages of Eternity.'"

Then Pharaoh the living rose and bowed to Pharaoh the dead and Pharaoh the dead was taken away back to his Eternal House and I wondered whether his Ka or his spirit, or whatever is the part of him that lives on, were watching us and remembering the feasts whereof he had partaken in his pomp in this pillared hall, as his forefathers had done before him for hundreds or thousands of years.

Not until the mummy had gone and the last sound of the chanting of the priests had died, did the hearts of the feasters grow light again. But soon they forgot, as men alive always forget death and those whom Time has devoured, for the wine was good and strong and the eyes of the women were bright and victory had crowned our spears, and for a while Egypt was once more free.

So it went on till Pharaoh rose and departed, the great gold earrings in his ears jingling as he walked, and the trumpets sounding before and after him. I too rose to go with my mother when a messenger came and bade me wait upon Pharaoh, and with me the dwarf Bes. So we went, leaving an officer to conduct my mother to our home. As I passed her she caught me by the sleeve and whispered in my ear,

"My son, whatever chances to you, be brave and remember that the world holds more than women."

"Yes," I answered, "it holds death and God, or they hold it," though what put the words into my mind I do not know, since I did not understand and had no time to ask her meaning.

The messenger led us to the door of Peroa's private chamber, the same in which I had seen him on my return from the East. Here he bade me enter, and Bes to wait without. I went in and found two men and a woman in the chamber, all standing very silent. The men were Pharaoh who still wore his glorious robe and Double Crown, and the high priest of Isis clothed in white; the other was the lady Amada also clothed in the snowy robes of Isis.

At the sight of her thus arrayed my heart stopped and I stood silent because I could not speak. She too stood silent and I saw that beneath her thin veil her beautiful face was set and pale as that of an alabaster statue. Indeed she might have been not a lovely living woman, but the goddess Isis herself whose symbols she bore about her.

"Shabaka," said Pharaoh at length, "the Royal Lady of Egypt, Amada, priestess of Isis, has somewhat to say to you."

"Let the Royal Lady of Egypt speak on to her servant and affianced husband," I answered.

"Count Shabaka, General of the armies," she began in a cold clear voice like to that of one who repeats a lesson, "learn that you are no more my affianced husband and that I who am gathered again to Isis the divine, am no more your affianced wife."

"I do not understand. Will it please you to be more plain?" I said faintly.

"I will be more plain, Count Shabaka, more plain than you have been with me. Since we speak together for the last time it is well that I should be plain. Hear me. When first you returned from the East, in yonder hall you told us of certain things that happened to you there. Then the dwarf your servant took up the tale. He said that he gave my name to the Great King. I was wroth as well I might be, but even when I prayed that he should be scourged, you did not deny that it was he who gave my name to the King, although Pharaoh yonder said that if you had spoken the name it would have been another matter."

"I had no time," I answered, "for just then the messengers came from Idernes and afterwards when I sought you you were gone."

"Had you then no time," she asked coldly, "beneath the palms in the garden of the palace when we were affianced? Oh! there was time in plenty but it did not please you to tell me that you had bought safety and great gifts at the price of the honour of the Lady of Egypt whose love you stole."

"You do not understand!" I exclaimed wildly.

"Forgive me, Shabaka, but I understand very well indeed, since from your own words I learned at the feast given to Idernes that 'the name of Amada' slipped your lips by chance and thus came to the ears of the Great King."

"The tale that Idernes and his captain told was false, Lady, and for it Bes and I took their lives with our own hands."

"It had perhaps been better, Shabaka, if you had kept them living that they might confess that it was false. But doubtless you thought them safer dead, since dead men cannot speak, and for this reason challenged them to single combat."

I gasped and could not answer for my mind seemed to leave me, and she went on in a gentler voice,

"I do not wish to speak angrily to you, my cousin Shabaka, especially when you have just wrought such great deeds for Egypt. Moreover by the law I serve I may speak angrily to no man. Know then that on learning the truth, since I could love none but you according to the flesh and therefore can never give myself in marriage to another, I sought refuge in the arms of the goddess whom for your sake I had deserted. She was pleased to receive me, forgetting my treason. On this very day for the second time I took the oaths which may no more be broken, and that I may dwell where I shall never see you more, Pharaoh here has been pleased, at my request to name me high priestess and prophetess of Isis and to appoint me as a dwelling-place her temple at Amada where I was born far away in Upper Egypt. Now all is said and done, so farewell."

"All is not said and done," I broke out in fury. "Pharaoh, I ask your leave to tell the full story of this business of the naming of the lady Amada to the King of kings, and that in the presence of the dwarf Bes. Even a slave is allowed to set out his tale before judgment is passed upon him."

Peroa glanced at Amada who made no sign, then said,

"It is granted, General Shabaka."

So Bes was called into the chamber and having looked about him curiously, seated himself upon the ground.

"Bes," I said, "you have heard nothing of what has passed." (Here I was mistaken, for as he told me afterwards he had heard everything through the door which was not quite closed.) "It is needful, Bes, that you should repeat truly all that happened at the court of the King of kings before and after I was brought from the boat."

Bes obeyed, telling the tale very well, so well that all listened earnestly, without error moreover. When he had finished I also told my story and how, shaken by all I had gone through and already weak from the torment of the boat, the name of Amada was surprised from me who never dreamed that the King would at once make demand of her, and who would have perished a thousand times rather than such a thing should happen. I added what I had learned afterwards from our escort, that this name was already well known to the Great King who meant to make use of it as a cause of quarrel with Egypt. Further, that he had let me escape from a death by horrible torments because of some dream that he had dreamed while he rested before the banquet, in which a god appeared and told him that it was an evil thing to slay a man because that man had bested him at a hunting match and one of which heaven would keep an account. Still because of the law of his land he must find a public pretext for loosing one whom he had once condemned, and therefore chose this matter of the lady Amada whom he pretended to send me to bring to him.

When I had finished, as Amada still remained silent, Pharaoh asked of Bes how it came about that he told one story on the night of our return and another on this night.

"Because, O Pharaoh," answered Bes rolling his eyes, "for the first time in my life I have been just a little too clever and shot my arrow just a little too far. Hearken, Pharaoh, and Royal Lady, and High Priest. I knew that my master loves the lady Amada and knew also that she is quick of tongue and temper, one who readily takes offence even if thereby she breaks her own heart and so brings her life to ruin, and with it perchance her country. Therefore, knowing women whom I have studied in my own land, I saw in this matter just such a cause of offence as she would lay hold of, and counselled my master to keep silent as to the story of the naming of her before the King. Some evil spirit made him listen to this bad counsel, so far at least, that when I lied as to what had chanced, for which lie the lady Amada prayed that I might be scourged till my bones broke through the skin, he did not at once tell all the truth. Nor did he do so afterwards because he feared that if he did I should in fact be scourged, for my master and I love each other. Neither of us wishes to see the other scourged, though such is my lot to-night," and he glanced at Amada. "I have said."

Then at last Amada spoke.

"Had I known all this story from the first, perhaps I should not have done what I have done to-day and perhaps I should have forgiven and forgotten, for in truth even if the dwarf still lies, I believe your word, O Shabaka, and understand how all came about. But now it is too late to change. Say, O Priest of the Mother, is it not too late?"

"It is too late," said the priest solemnly, "seeing that if such vows as yours are broken for the second time, O Prophetess, the curse of the goddess will pursue you and him for whom they were broken, yes, through this life and all other lives that perchance may be given to you upon the earth or elsewhere."

"Pharaoh," I cried in despair, "I made a bond with you. It is recorded in writing and sealed. I have kept my part of the bond; my treasure you have spent; your enemies I have slain; your army I have commanded not so ill. Will you not keep yours and bid the priests release this lady from her vow and give her to me to whom she was promised? Or must I believe that you refuse, not because of goddesses and vows, but because yonder is the Royal Lady of Egypt, the true heiress to the throne who might perchance bear children, which as prophetess of Isis she can never do. Yes, because of this and because of certain cries that came to your ears in the hour of your crowning before Amen-ra and all the gods?"

Peroa flushed as he heard me and answered,

"You speak roughly, Cousin, and were you any other man I might be tempted to answer roughly. But I know that you suffer and therefore I forgive. Nay, you must believe no such things. Rather must you remember that in this bond of which you speak, it was set down that I only promised you the lady Amada with her own consent, and this she has withdrawn."

"Then, Pharaoh, hearken! To-morrow I leave Egypt for another land, giving you back your generalship and sheathing the sword that I had hoped to wield in its defence and yours when the last great day of trial by battle comes, as come it will. I tell you that I go to return no more, unless the lady Amada yonder shall summon me back to fight for her and you, promising herself to me in guerdon."

"That can never be," said Amada.

Then I became aware of another presence in the room, though how and when it appeared I do not know, but I suppose that it had crept in while we were lost in talk. At least between me and Pharaoh, crouched upon the ground, was the figure of a man wrapped in a beggar's cloak. It threw back the hood and there appeared the ashen face and snowy beard of the holy Tanofir.

"You know me, Pharaoh," he said in his deep, solemn voice. "I am Tanofir, the King's son; Tanofir the hermit, Tanofir the seer. I have heard all that passes, it matters not how and I come to you with a message, I who read men's hearts. Of vows and goddesses and women I say nothing. But this I say to you, that if you break the spirit of your bond and suffer yonder Shabaka to go hence with a bitter heart, trouble shall come on you. All the Great King's armies did not die yonder by the banks of Nile, and mayhap one day he will journey to bury the bones of those who fell, and with them *yours*, O Pharaoh. I do not think that you will listen to me to-night, and I am sure that yonder lady, full of the new-fanned flame of the jealous goddess, will not listen. Still let her take counsel and remember my words: In the hour of desperate danger let her send to Shabaka and demand his help, promising in return what he has asked and remembering that if Isis loves her, that goddess was born upon the Nile and loves Egypt more."

"Too late, too late, *too late*!" wailed Amada

Then she burst into tears and turning fled away with the high priest. Pharaoh went also leaving me and Bes alone. I looked for the holy Tanofir to speak with him, but he too was gone.

"It is time to sleep, Master," said Bes, "for all this talk is more wearisome than any battle. Why! what is this that has your name upon it?" and he picked a silk-wrapped package from the floor and opened it.

Within were the priceless rose-hued pearls!

Shabaka Fights the Crocodile

"Where to?" I said to Bes when we were outside the palace, for I was so broken with grief that I scarcely knew what I did.

"To the house of the lady Tiu, I think, Master, since there you must make preparations for your start on the morrow, also bid her farewell. Oh!" he went on in a kind of rapture which afterwards I knew was feigned though at the time I did not think about it, "Oh! how happy should you be who now are free from all this woman-coil, with life new and fresh before you. Reflect, Master, on the hunting we will have yonder in Ethiopia. No more cares, no more plannings for the welfare of Egypt, no more persuading of the doubtful to take up arms, no more desperate battle-ventures with your country's honour on your sword- point. And if you must see women—well, there are plenty in Ethiopia who come and go lightly as an evening breeze laden with the odour of flowers, and never trouble in the morning."

"At any rate *you* are not free from such coils, Bes," I said and in the moonlight I saw his great face fall in.

"No, Master, I am tying them about my throat. See, such is the way of the world, or of the gods that rule the world, I know not which. For years I have been happy and free, I have enjoyed adventures and visited strange countries and have gathered learning, till I think I am the wisest man upon the Nile, at the side of one whom I loved and holding nothing at risk, except my own life which mattered no more than that of a gnat dancing in the sun. Now all is changed. I have a wife whom I love also, more than I can tell you," and he sighed, "but who still must be looked after and obeyed—yes, obeyed. Further, soon I shall have a people and a crown to wear, and councillors and affairs of state, and an ancient religion to support and the Grasshopper itself knows what besides. The burden has rolled from your back to mine, Master, making my heart which was so light, heavy, and oh! I wish it had stopped where it was."

Even then I laughed, sad as I was, for truth lived in the philosophy of Bes.

"Master," he went on in a changed voice, "I have been a fool and my folly has worked you ill. Forgive me since I acted for the best, only until the end no one ever knows what is the best. Now here is the house and I go to meet my wife and to make certain arrangements. By dawn perhaps you will be ready to start to Ethiopia."

"Do you really desire that I should accompany you there, Bes?"

"Certainly, Master. That is unless you should desire that I accompany you somewhere else instead, by sea southward for instance. If so, I do not know that I would refuse, since Ethiopia will not run away and there is much of the world that I should still like to visit. Only then there is Karema to be thought about, who expects, or, when she learns all, soon will expect, to be a queen," he added doubtfully.

"No, Bes, I am too tired to make new plans, so let us go to Ethiopia and not disappoint Karema, who after holding a cup so long naturally would like to try a sceptre."

"I think that is wisest, Master; at any rate the holy Tanofir thinks it wisest, and he is the voice of Fate. Oh! why do we trouble who after all, every one of us, are nothing but pieces upon the board of Fate."

Then he turned and left me and I entered the house where I found my mother sitting, still in her festal robes, like one who waits. She looked at my face, then asked what troubled me. I sat down on a stool at her feet and told her everything.

"Much as I thought," she said when I had finished. "These over-learned women are strange fish to catch and hold, and too much soul is like too much sail upon a boat when the desert wind begins to blow across the Nile. Well, do not let us blame her or Bes, or Peroa who is already anxious for his dynasty and would rather that Amada were a priestess than your wife, or even the goddess Isis, who no doubt is anxious for her votaries. Let us rather blame the Power that is behind the veil, or to it bow our heads, seeing that we know nothing of the end for which it works. So Egypt shuts her doors on you, my Son, and whither away? Not to the East again, I trust, for there you would soon grow shorter by a head."

"I go to Ethiopia, my Mother, where it seems that Bes is a great man and can shelter me."

"So we go to Ethiopia, do we? Well, it is a long journey for an old woman, but I weary of Memphis where I have lived for so many years and doubtless the sands of the south make good burial grounds."

"We!" I exclaimed. "We?"

"Surely, my Son, since in losing a wife you have again found a mother and until I die we part no more."

When I heard this my eyes filled with tears. My conscience smote me also because of late, and indeed for years past, I had thought so much of Amada and so little of my mother. And now it was Amada who had cast me out, unjustly, without waiting to learn the truth, because at the worst I, who worshipped her, had saved myself from death in slow torment by speaking her name, while my mother, forgetting all, took me to her bosom again as she had done when I was a babe. I knew not what to say, but remembering the pearls, I drew them out and placed them round my mother's neck.

She looked at the wonderful things and smiled, then said,

"Such gems as these become white locks and withered breasts but ill. Yet, my Son, I will keep them for you till you find a wife, if not Amada, then another."

"If not Amada, I shall never find a wife," I said bitterly, whereat she smiled.

Then she left me to make ready before she slept a while.

Work as we would noon had passed two hours, on the following day, before we were prepared to start, for there was much to do. Thus the house must be placed in charge of friends and the means of travel collected. Also a messenger came from Pharaoh praying me for his and Egypt's sake to think again before I left them, and an answer sent that go I must, whither the holy Tanofir would know if at any time Pharaoh desired to learn. In reply to this came another messenger who brought me parting gifts from Pharaoh, a chain of honour, a title of higher nobility, a commission as his envoy to whatever land I wandered, and so forth, which I must acknowledge. Lastly as we were leaving the house to seek the boat which Bes had made ready on the Nile, there came yet another messenger at the sight of whom my heart leapt, for he was priest of Isis.

He bowed and handed me a roll. I opened it with a trembling hand and read:

"From the Prophetess of Isis whose house is at Amada, aforetime Royal Lady of Egypt, to the Count Shabaka,

"I learn, O my Cousin, that you depart from Egypt and knowing the reason my heart is sore. Believe me, my Cousin, I love you well, better than any who lives upon the earth, nor will that love ever change, since the goddess who holds my future in her hands, knows of what we are made and is not jealous of the past. Therefore she will not be wroth at the earthly love of one who is gathered to her heavenly arms. Her blessing and mine be on you and if we see each other no more face to face in the world, may we meet again in the halls of Osiris. Farewell, beloved Shabaka. Oh! why did you suffer that black master of lies, the dwarf Bes, to persuade you to hide the truth from me?"

So the writing ended and below it were two stains still wet, which I knew were caused by tears. Moreover, wrapped in a piece of silk and fastened to the scroll was a little gold ring graven with the royal *uraeus* that Amada had always worn from childhood. Only on the previous night I had noted it on the first finger of her right hand.

I took my stylus and my waxen tablets and wrote on one of them:

"Had you been a man, Amada, and not a woman, I think you would have judged me differently but, learned priestess and prophetess as you are, a woman you remain. Perchance a time may come when once more you will turn to me in the hour of your need; if so and I am living, I will come. Yea, if I am dead I think that I still shall come, since nothing can really part us. Meanwhile by day and by night I wear your ring and whenever I look on it I think of Amada the woman whose lips have pressed my own, and forget Amada the priestess who for her soul's sake has been pleased to break the heart of the man who loved her and whom she misjudged so sorely in her pride and anger."

This tablet I wrapped up and sealed, using clay and her own ring to make the seal, and gave it for delivery to the priest.

At length we drew near to the river and here, gathered on the open land, I found the most of those who had fought with me in the battle against the Easterns, and with them a great concourse of others from the city. These collected round me, some of them wounded and hobbling upon crutches, praying me not to go, as did the others who foresaw sorrow to Egypt from my loss. But I broke away from them almost in tears and with my mother hid myself beneath the canopy of the boat. Here Bes was waiting, also his beautiful wife who, although she seemed sad at leaving Egypt, smiled a greeting to us while the steersmen and rowers of the boat, tall Ethiopians every one of them, rose and gave me a General's salute. Then, as the wind served, we hoisted the sail and glided away up Nile, till presently the temples and palm-groves of Memphis were lost to sight.

Of that long, long journey there is no need to tell. Up the Nile we travelled slowly, dragging the boat past the cataracts till Egypt was far behind us. In the end, many days after we had passed the mouth of another river that was blue in colour which flowed from the northern mountain lands down into the Nile, we came to a place where the rapids were so long and steep that we must leave the boat and travel overland. Drawing near to it at sunset I saw a multitude of people gathered on the sand and beyond them a camp in which were set many beautiful pavilions that seemed to be broidered with silk and gold, as were the banners that floated above them whereon appeared the effigy of a grasshopper, also done in gold with silver legs.

"It seems that my messengers travelled in safety," said Bes to me, "for know, that yonder are some of my subjects who have come here to meet us. Now, Master, I must no longer call you master since I fear I am once more a king. And you must no longer call me Bes, but Karoon. Moreover, forgive me, but when you come into my presence you must bow, which I shall like less than you do, but it is the custom of the Ethiopians. Oh! I would that you were the king and that I were your friend, for henceforth good-bye to ease and jollity."

I laughed, but Bes did not laugh at all, only turned to his wife who already ruled him as though he were indeed a slave, and said, "Lady Karema, make yourself as beautiful as you can and forget that you have ever been a Cup or anything useful, since henceforth you must be a queen, that is if you please my people."

"And what happens if I do not please them, Husband?" asked Karema opening her fine eyes.

"I do not quite know, Wife. Perhaps they may refuse to accept me, at which I shall not weep. Or perhaps they may refuse to accept you, at which of course I should weep very much, for you see you are so very white and, heretofore, all the queens of the Ethiopians have been black."

"And if they refuse to accept me because I am white, or rather brown, instead of black like oiled marble, what then, O Husband?"

"Then—oh! then I cannot say, O Wife. Perhaps they will send you back to your own country. Or perhaps they will separate us and place you in a temple where you will live alone in all honour. I remember that once they did that to a white woman, making a goddess of her until she died of weariness. Or perhaps—well, I do not know."

Then Karema grew angry.

"Now I wish I had remained a Cup," she said, "and the servant of the holy Tanofir who at least taught me many secret things, instead of coming to dwell among black barbarians in the company of a dwarf who, even if he be a king, it seems has no power to protect the wife whom he has chosen."

"Why will women always grow wroth before there is need?" asked Bes humbly. "Surely it would be time to rate me when any of these things had happened."

"If any of them do happen, Husband, I shall say much worse things than that," she replied, but the talk went no further, for at this moment our boat grounded and singing a wild song, many of those who waited rushed into the water to drag it to the bank.

Then Bes stood up on the prow, waving his bow and there arose a mighty shout of, "*Karoon! Karoon!* It is he, it is he returned after many years!"

Twice they shouted thus and then, every one of them, threw themselves face downwards in the sand.

"Yes, my people," cried Bes, "it is I, Karoon, who having been miraculously preserved from many dangers in far lands by the help of the Grasshopper in heaven, and, as my messengers will have told you, of my beloved friend, lord Shabaka the Egyptian, who has deigned to come to dwell with us for a while, have at length returned to Ethiopia that I may shed my wisdom on you like the sun and pour it on your heads like melted honey. Moreover, mindful of our laws which aforetime I defied and therefore left you, I have searched the whole world through till I found the most beautiful woman that it contained, and made her my wife. She too has deigned to come to this far country to be your queen. Advance, fair Karema, and show yourself to these my Ethiopians."

So Karema stepped forward and stood on the prow of the boat by the side of Bes, and a strange couple they looked. The Ethiopians who had risen, considered her gravely, then one of them said,

"Karoon called her beautiful, but in truth she is almost white and very ugly."

"At least she is a woman," said another, "for her shape is female."

"Yes, and he has married her," remarked a third, "and even a king may choose his own wife sometimes. For in such matters who can judge another's taste?"

"Cease," said Bes in a lordly way. "If you do not think her beautiful to-night, you will to-morrow. And now let us land and rest."

So we landed and while I did so I took note of these Ethiopians. They were great men, black as charcoal with thick lips, white teeth and flat noses. Their eyes were large and the whites of them somewhat yellow, their hair curled like wool, their beards were short and on their faces they wore a continual smile. Of dress most of them had little, but their elders or leaders wore lion and leopard skins and some were clad in a kind of silken tunic belted about the middle. All were armed for war with long bows, short swords and small shields round in shape and made from the hide of the hippopotamus or of the unicorn. Gold was plentiful amongst them since even the humblest wore bracelets of that metal, while about the necks of the chieftains it was wound in great torques, also sometimes on their ankles. They wore sandals on their feet and some of them had ostrich feathers stuck in their hair, a few also had grasshoppers fashioned of gold bound on the top of their heads, and these I took to be the priests. There were no women in their number.

As the sun was sinking we were led at once to a very beautiful tent made of woven flax and ornamented as I have described, where we found food made ready for us in plenty, milk in bowls and the flesh of sheep and oxen boiled and roasted. Bes, however, was taken to a place apart, which made Karema even more angry than she was before.

Scarcely had we finished eating when a herald rushed into the tent crying, "Prostrate yourselves! Yea, be prostrated, the Grasshopper comes! Karoon comes."

Here I must say that I found that the title of Karoon meant "Great Grasshopper," but Karema who did not know this, asked indignantly why she should prostrate herself to a grasshopper. Indeed she refused to do so even when Bes entered the pavilion wonderfully attired in a gorgeous-coloured robe of which the train was held by two huge men. So absurd did he look that my mother and I must bow very deeply to hide our laughter while Karema said,

"It would be better, Husband, if you found children to carry your robe instead of two giants. Moreover, if it is meant to copy the colours of a grasshopper, 'tis badly done, since grasshoppers are green and you are gold and scarlet. Also they do not wear feathers set awry upon their heads."

Bes rolled his eyes as though in agony, then turning, bade his attendants be gone. They obeyed, though doubtfully as though they did not like to leave him alone with us, whereon he let down the flap of the pavilion, threw off his gorgeous coverings and said,

"You must learn to understand, Wife, that our customs are different from those of Egypt. There I was happy as a slave and you were held to be beautiful as the Cup of the holy Tanofir, also learned. Here I am wretched as a king and you are held to be ugly, also ignorant as a stranger. Oh! do not answer, I pray you, but learn that all goes well. For the time you are accepted as my wife, subject to the decision of a council of matrons, aged relatives of my family, who will decide when we reach the City of the Grasshopper whether or not you shall be acknowledged as the Queen of the Ethiopians. No, no, I pray you say nothing since I must go away at once, as according to the law of the Ethiopians the time has come for the Grasshopper to sleep, alone, Karema, as you are not yet acknowledged as my wife. You also can sleep with the lady Tiu and for Shabaka a tent is provided. Rest sweetly, Wife. Hark! They fetch me."

"Now, if I had my way," said Karema, "I would rest in that boat going back to Egypt. What say you, lord Shabaka?"

But I made no answer who followed Bes out of the tent, leaving her to talk the matter over with my mother. Here I found a crowd of his people waiting to convey him to sleep and watching, saw them place him in another tent round which they ranged themselves, playing upon musical instruments. After this someone came and led me to my own place where was a good bed in which I lay down to sleep. This however I could not do for a long while because of my own laughter and the noise of the drums and horns that were soothing Bes to his rest. For now I understood why he had preferred to be a slave in Egypt rather than a king in Ethiopia.

In the morning I rose before the dawn and went out to the river-bank to bathe. While I was making ready to wash myself, who should appear but Bes, followed, but at a distance, by a number of his people.

"Never have I spent such a night, Master," he said, "at least not since you took me prisoner years ago, since by law I may not stop those horns and musical instruments. Now, however, also according to the law of the Ethiopians, I am my own lord until the sun rises. So I have come here to gather some of those blue lilies which she loves as a present for Karema, because I fear that she is angry and must be appeased."

"Certainly she is very angry," I said, "or at least was so when I left her last night. Oh! Bes, why did you let your people tell her that she was ugly?"

"How can I help it, Master? Have you not always heard that the Ethiopians are chiefly famous for one thing, namely that they speak nothing but the truth. To them she, being different, seems to be ugly. Therefore when they say that she is ugly, they speak the truth."

"If so, it is a truth that she does not like, Bes, as I have no doubt she will tell you by and by. Do they think me ugly also?"

"Yes, they do, Master; but they think also that you look like a man who can draw a bow and use a sword, and that goes far with the Ethiopians. Of your mother they say nothing because she is old and they venerate the aged whom the Grasshopper is waiting to carry away."

Now I began to laugh again and went with Bes to gather the lilies. These grew at the end of a mass of reeds woven together by the pressure of the current and floating on the water. Bes lay down upon his stomach while his people watched from a distance on the bank amazed into silence, and stretched out his long arms to reach the blue lotus flowers. Suddenly the reeds gave way beneath him just as he had grasped two of the flowers and was dragging at them, so that he fell into the river.

Next instant I saw a swirl in the brown water and perceived a huge crocodile. It rushed at Bes open-mouthed. Being a good swimmer he twisted his body in order to avoid it, but I heard the great teeth close with a snap on the short leathern garment which he wore about his middle.

"The devil has me! Farewell!" he cried and vanished beneath the water.

Now, as I have said, I was almost stripped for bathing, but had not yet taken off my short sword which was girded round me by a belt. In an instant I drew it and amidst the yells of horror of the Ethiopians who had seen all from the bank, I plunged into the river. There are few able to swim as I could and I had the art of diving with my eyes open and remaining long beneath the surface without drawing breath, for this I had practised from a child.

Immediately I saw the great reptile sinking to the mud and dragging Bes with him to drown him there. But here the river was very deep and with a few swift strokes I was able to get under the crocodile. Then with all my strength I stabbed upwards, driving the sword far into the soft part of the throat. Feeling the pain of the sharp iron the beast let go of Bes and turned on me. How it happened I do not know but presently I found myself upon its back and was striking at its eyes. One thrust at least went home, for the blinded brute rose to the surface, bearing me with him, and oh! the sweetness of the air as I breathed again.

Thus we appeared, I riding the crocodile like a horse and stabbing furiously, while close by was Bes rolling his yellow eyes but helpless, for he had no weapon. Still the devil was not dead although blood streamed from him, only mad with pain and rage. Nor could the shouting Ethiopians help me since they had only bows and dared not shoot lest their shafts should pierce me. The crocodile began to sink again, snapping furiously at my legs. Then I bethought me of a trick I had seen practised by natives on the Nile.

Waiting till its huge jaws were open I thrust my arm between them, grasping the short sword in such fashion that the hilt rested on its tongue and the point against the roof of its mouth. It tried to close its jaws and lo! the good iron was fixed between them, holding them wide open. Then I withdrew my hand and floated upwards with nothing worse than a cut upon the wrist from one of its sharp fangs. I appeared upon the surface and after me the crocodile spouting blood and wallowing in its death agonies. I remembered no more till I found myself lying on the bank surrounded by a multitude with Bes standing over me. Also in the shallow water was the crocodile dead, my sword still fixed between its jaws.

"Are you harmed, Master" cried Bes in a voice of agony.

"Very little I think," I answered, sitting up with the blood pouring from my arm. Bes thrust aside Karema who had come lightly clothed from her tent, saying,

"All is well, Wife. I will bring you the lilies presently."

Then he flung his arms about me, kissed my hands and my brow and turning to the crowd, shouted,

"Last night you were disputing as to whether this Egyptian lord should be allowed to dwell with me in the land of Ethiopia. Which of you disputes it now?"

"No one!" they answered with a roar. "He is not a man but a god. No man could have done such a deed."

"So it seems," answered Bes quietly. "At least none of you even tried to do it. Yet he is not a god but only that kind of man who is called a hero. Also he is my brother, and while I reign in Ethiopia either he shall reign at my side, or I go away with him."

"It shall be so, Karoon!" they shouted with one voice. And after this I was carried back to the tent.

In front of it my mother waited and kissed me proudly before them all, whereat they shouted again.

So ended this adventure of the crocodile, except that presently Bes went back and recovered the two lilies for Karema, this time from a boat, which caused the Ethiopians to call out that he must love her very much, though not as much as he did me.

That afternoon, borne in litters, we set out for the City of the Grasshopper, which we reached on the fourth day. As we drew near the place regiments of men to the number of twelve thousand or more, came out to meet us, so that at last we arrived escorted by an army who sang their songs of triumph and played upon their musical instruments until my head ached with the noise.

This city was a great place whereof the houses were built of mud and thatched with reeds. It stood upon a wide plain and in its centre rose a natural, rocky hill upon the crest of which, fashioned of blocks of gleaming marble and roofed with a metal that shone as gold, was the temple of the Grasshopper, a columned building very like to those of Egypt. Round it also were other public buildings, among them the palace of the Karoon, the whole being surrounded by triple marble walls as a protection from attack by foes. Never had I seen anything so beautiful as that hill with its edifices of shining white roofed with gold or copper and gleaming in the sun.

Descending from my litter I walked to those of my mother and Karema, for Bes in his majesty might not be approached, and said as much to them.

"Yes, Son," answered my mother, "it is worth while to have travelled so far to see such a sight. I shall have a fine sepulchre, Son."

"I have seen it all before," broke in Karema.

"When?" I asked.

"I do not know. I suppose it must have been when I was the Cup of the holy Tanofir. At least it is familiar to me. Already I weary of it, for who can care for a land or a city where they think white people hideous and scarcely allow a wife to go near her husband, save between midnight and dawn when they cease from their horrible music?"

"It will be your part to change these customs, Karema."

"Yes," she exclaimed, "certainly that will be my part," after which I went back to my litter.

The Summons

Now at the gates of the City of the Grasshopper we were royally received. The priests came out to meet us, pushing a colossal image of their god before them on a kind of flat chariot, and I remember wondering what would be the value of that huge golden locust, if it were melted down. Also the Council came, very ancient men all of them, since the Ethiopians for the most part lived more than a hundred years. Perhaps that is why they were so glad to welcome Bes since they were too old to care about retaining power in their own hands as they had done during his long absence. For save Bes there was no other man living of the true royal blood who could take the throne.

Then there were thousands of women, broad-faced and smiling whose black skins shone with scented oils, for they wore little except a girdle about their waists and many ornaments of gold. Thus their earrings were sometimes a palm in breadth and many of them had great gold rings through their noses, such as in Egypt are put in those of bulls. My mother laughed at them, but Karema said that she thought them hideous and hateful.

They were a strange people, these Ethiopians, like children, most of them, being merry and kind and never thinking of one thing for more than a minute. Thus one would see them weep and laugh almost in the same breath. But among them was an upper class who had great learning and much ancient knowledge. These men made their laws wherein there was always sense under what seemed to be folly, designed the temples, managed the mines of gold and other metals and followed the arts. They were the real masters of the land, the rest were but slaves content to live in plenty, for in that fertile soil want never came near them, and to do as they were bid.

Thus they passed from the cradle to the grave amidst song and flowers, carrying out their light, allotted tasks, and for the rest, living as they would and loving those they would, especially their children, of whom they had many. By nature and tradition the men were warriors and hunters, being skilled in the use of the bow and always at war when they could find anyone to fight. Indeed when we came among them their trouble was that they had no enemies left, and at once they implored Bes to lead them out to battle since they were weary of herding kine and tilling fields.

All of these things I found out by degrees, also that they were a great people who could send out an army of seventy thousand men and yet leave enough behind them to defend their land. Of the world beyond their borders the most of them knew little, but the learned men of whom I have spoken, a great deal, since they travelled to Egypt and elsewhere to study the customs of other countries. For the rest their only god was the Grasshopper and like that insect they skipped and chirruped through life and when the winter of death came sprang away to another of which they knew nothing, leaving their young behind them to bask in the sun of unborn summers. Such were the Ethiopians.

Now of all the ceremonies of the reception of Bes and his re-crowning as Karoon, I knew little, for the reason that the tooth of the crocodile poisoned my blood and made me very ill, so that I remained for a moon or more lying in a fine room in the palace where gold seemed to be as plentiful as earthen pots are in Egypt, and all the vessels were of crystal. Had it not been for the skill of the Ethiopian leeches and above all for the nursing of my mother, I think that I must have died. She it was who withstood them when they wished to cut off my arm, and wisely, for it recovered and was as strong as it had ever been. In the end I grew well again and from the platform in front of the temple was presented to the people by Bes as his saviour and the next greatest to him in the kingdom, nor shall I ever forget the shoutings with which I was received.

Karema also was presented as his wife, having passed the Ordeal of the Matrons, but only, I think, because it was found that she was in the way to give an heir to the throne. For to them her beauty was ugliness, nor could they understand how it came about that their king, who contrary to the general customs of the land, was only allowed one wife lest the children should quarrel, could have chosen a lady who was not black. So they received her in silence with many whisperings which made Karema very angry.

When in due course, however, the child came and proved to be a son black as the best of them and of perfect shape, they relented towards her and after the birth of a second, grew to love her. But she never forgave and loved them not at all. Nor was she over-fond of these children of hers because they were so black which, she said, showed how poisonous was the blood of the Ethiopians. And indeed this is so, for often I have noticed that if an Ethiopian weds with one of another colour, their offspring is black down to the third or fourth generation. Therefore Karema longed for Egypt notwithstanding the splendour in which she dwelt.

So greatly did she long that she had recourse to the magic lore which she had learned from the holy Tanofir, and would sit for hours gazing into water in a crystal bowl, or sometimes into a ball of crystal without the water, trying to see visions therein that had to do with what passed in Egypt. Moreover in time much of her gift returned to her and she did see many things which she repeated to me, for she would tell no one else of them, not even her husband.

Thus she saw Amada kneeling in a shrine before the statue of Isis and weeping: a picture that made me sad. Also she saw the holy Tanofir brooding in the darkness of the Cave of the Bulls, and read in his mind that he was thinking of us, though what he thought she could not read. Again she saw Eastern messengers delivering letters to Pharaoh and knew from his face that he was disturbed and that Egypt was threatened with calamities. And so forth.

Soon the news of her powers of divination spread abroad, so that all the Ethiopians grew to fear her as a seeress and thenceforth, whatever they may have thought, none of them dared to say that she was ugly. Further, her gift was real, since if she told me of a certain thing such as that messengers were approaching, in due course they would arrive and make clear much that she had not been able to understand in her visions.

Now from the time that I grew strong again and as soon as Bes was firmly seated on his throne, he and I set to work to train and drill the army of the Ethiopians, which hitherto had been little more than a mob of men carrying bows and swords. We divided it into phalanxes after the Greek fashion, and armed these bodies with long lances, swords, and large shields in the place of the small ones they had carried before. Also we trained the archers, teaching them to advance in open order and shoot from cover, and lastly chose the best soldiers to be captains and generals. So it came about that at the end of the two years that I spent in Ethiopia there was a force of sixty thousand men or more whom I should not have been afraid to match against any troops in the world, since they were of great strength and courage, and, as I have said, by nature lovers of war. Also their bows being longer and more powerful, they could shoot arrows farther than the Easterns or the Egyptians.

The Ethiopian lords wondered why their King and I did these things, since they saw no enemy against which so great an army could be led to battle. On that matter Bes and I kept our own counsel, telling them only that it was good for the men to be trained to war, since, hearing of their wealth, one day the King of kings might attempt to invade their country. So month by month I laboured at this task, leading armies into distant regions to accustom them to travelling far afield, carrying with them what was necessary for their sustenance.

So it went on until a sad thing happened, since on returning from one of these forays in which I had punished a tribe that had murdered some Ethiopian hunters and we had taken many thousands of their cattle, I found my mother dying. She had been smitten by a fever which was common at that season of the year, and being old and weak had no strength to throw it off.

As medicine did not help her, the priests of the Grasshopper prayed day and night in their temple for her recovery. Yes, there they prayed to a golden locust standing on an altar in a sanctuary that was surrounded by crystal coffins wherein rested the flesh of former kings of the land. To me the sight was pitiful, but Bes asked me what was the difference between praying to a locust and praying to images with the heads of beasts, or to a dwarf shaped as he was like we did in Egypt, and I could not answer him.

"The truth is, Brother," he said, for so he called me now, "that all peoples in the world do not offer petitions to what they see and have been taught to revere, but to something beyond of which to them it is a sign. But why the Ethiopians should have chosen a grasshopper as a symbol of God who is everywhere, is more than I can tell. Still they have done so for thousands of years."

When I came to my mother's bedside she was wandering and I saw that she could not live long. In a little while, however, her mind cleared so that she knew me and tears of joy ran down her pale cheeks because I had returned before she died. She reminded me that she had always said that she would find a grave in Ethiopia, and asked to be buried and not kept above ground in crystal, as was the custom there. Then she said that she had been dreaming of my father and of me; also that she did not think that I need fret myself overmuch about Amada, since she was sure that before long I should kiss her on the lips.

I asked if she meant that I should marry her and that we should be happy and fortunate. She replied that she supposed that I should marry her, but of the rest would say nothing. Indeed her face grew troubled, as though some thought hurt her, and leaving the matter of Amada she bade Karema bring me the rose-hued pearls, blessed me, prayed for our reunion in the halls of Osiris, and straightway died.

So I caused her to be embalmed after the Egyptian fashion and enclosed in a coffin of crystal with a scarab on her heart that Karema had discovered somewhere in the city, for always she was searching for things that reminded her of Egypt, whereof many were to be found brought from time to time by travellers or strangers. Then with such ceremony as we could without the services of the priests of Osiris, Karema and I buried her in a tomb that Bes had caused to be made near to the steps of the temple of the Grasshopper, while Bes and his nobles watched from a distance.

And so farewell to my beloved mother, the lady Tiu.

After she was gone I grew very sad and lonely. While she lived I had a home, but now I was an exile, a stranger in a strange land with no one of my own people to talk to except Karema, with whom, as there were gossips even in Ethiopia, I thought it well not to talk too much. There was Bes it was true, but now he was a great king and the time of kings is not their own. Moreover Bes was Bes and an Ethiopian and I was I and an Egyptian, and therefore notwithstanding our love and brotherhood, we could never be like men of the same blood and country.

I grew weary of Ethiopia with its useless gold and damp eternal green and heat, and longed for the sand and the keen desert air. Bes noted it and offered me wives, but I shrank from these black women however buxom and kindly, and wished for no offspring of their race whom afterwards I could never leave. To Egypt I had sworn not to return unless one voice called me and it remained silent. What then was I to do, being no longer content to discipline and command an army that I might not lead into battle?

At length I made up my mind. By nature I was a hunter as much as a soldier; I would beg from Bes a band of brave men whom I knew, lovers of adventure who sought new things, and with them strike down south, following the path of the elephants to wherever the gods might lead us. Doubtless in the end it would be to death, but what matter when there is nothing for which one cares to live?

While I was brooding over these plans Karema read my mind, perhaps because it was her own, perhaps by help of her strange arts, which I do not know. At least one day when I was sitting alone looking at the city beneath from one of the palace window-places, she came to me looking very beautiful and very mystic in the white robes she always loved to wear, and said,

"My lord Shabaka, you tire of this land of honey and sweetness and soft airs and flowers and gold and crystal and black people who grin and chatter and are not pleasant to be near, is it not so?"

"Yes, Queen," I answered.

"Do not call me queen, my lord Shabaka, for I weary of that name, as we both do of the rest. Call me Karema the Arab, or Karema the Cup, which you will, but by the name of Thoth, god of learning, do *not* call me queen."

"Karema then," I said. "Well, how do you know that I tire of all this, Karema?"

"How could you do otherwise who are not a barbarian and who have Egypt in your heart, and Egypt's fate and——" here she looked me straight in the eye's, "Egypt's Lady. Besides, I measure you by myself."

"You at least should be happy, Karema, who are great and rich and beloved, and the wife of a King who is one of the best of men, and the mother of children."

"Yes, Shabaka, I should be but I am not, for who can live on sweetmeats only, especially when they like what is sour? See now how strangely we are made. When I was a girl, the daughter of an Arab chief, well bred and well taught as it chanced, I tired of the hard life of the desert and the narrow minds about me, I who longed for wisdom and to know great men. Then I became the Cup of the holy Tanofir and wisdom was all about me, strange wisdom from another world, rough, sharp wisdom from Tanofir, and the quiet wisdom of the dead among whom I dwelt. I wearied of that also, Shabaka. I was beautiful and knew it and I longed to shine in a Court, to be admired among men, to be envied of women, to rule. My husband came my way. He was clever with a great heart. He was your friend and therefore I was sure that he must be loyal and true. He was, or might be, a king, as I knew, though he thought that I did not. I married him and the holy Tanofir laughed but he did not say me nay, and I became a queen. And now I wish sometimes that I were dead, or back holding the cup of the holy Tanofir with the wisdom of the heavens flowing round me and the soft darkness of the tombs about me. It seems that in this world we never can be content, Shabaka."

"No, Karema, we only think that we should be if things were otherwise than they are. But how can I help you, Karema?"

"Least of all by going away and leaving me alone," she answered with the tears starting to her eyes.

Looking at her, I began to think that the best thing I could do would be to go away and at once, but as ever she read my thought, shook her head and laughed.

"No, no, I have put on my yoke and will carry it to the end. Have I not two black children and a husband who is a hero, a wit and a mountebank in one, and a throne and more gold and crystal than I ever wish to see again even in a dream, and shall I not cling to these good things? If you went I should only be a little more unhappy than before, that is all. Not for my sake do I ask you to stay, but for your own."

"How for my own, Karema? I have done all that I can do here. I have built the army afresh from cook-boys to generals. Bes needs me no longer who has you, his children and his country, and I die of weariness."

"You can stop to make use of that army you have built afresh, Shabaka."

"Against whom? There are none to fight."

"Against the Great King of the East. Listen. My gift of vision has grown strong and clear of late. Only to-day I have seen a meeting between Pharaoh, the holy Tanofir and the lady Amada. They were all disturbed, I know not at what, and the end of it was that Amada wrote in a roll and gave the writing to messengers, who I think even now are speeding southward—to you, Shabaka. Nay, do not look doubtfully on me, it is true."

"Then you did well to tell me, Karema, for within a moon of this day I should have been where perhaps no messengers would have found me. Now I will wait and let it be your part to prepare the mind of Bes. Do you think that he would give me an army to lead to Egypt, if there were need?"

She nodded and answered,

"He would do so for three reasons. The first is because he loves you, the second because he too wearies of Ethiopia and this rich, fat life of peace, and the third, because I shall tell him that he must."

"Then why trouble to speak of the other two?" I said laughing.

So I stayed on in the City of the Grasshopper, and busied myself with the questions of how to transport and feed a great army that must hold the field for six months or a year; also with the setting of hundreds of skilled men to the making of bows, arrows, swords and shields. Nor did Bes say me no in these matters. Indeed he helped them forward by issuing the orders as his own, wherein I saw the hand of Karema.

Three months went by and I began to think that Karema's power had been at fault, or that her vision was one that came from her lips and not from her heart, to keep me in Ethiopia. But again she read my mind and smiled.

"Not so, Shabaka," she said. "Those messengers have come to trouble and are detained by a petty tribe beyond our borders over some matter of a woman. Ten days ago the frontier guards marched to set them free."

So again I waited and at length the messengers came, three of them Egyptians and three men of Ethiopia who dwelt in Egypt to learn its wisdom, reporting that as Karema had said, through the foolishness of a servant they had been held prisoner by an Arab chief and thus delayed. Then they delivered the writings which they had kept safe. One was from Pharaoh to the Karoon of Ethiopia; one from the holy Tanofir to Karema; and one from the lady Amada to myself.

With a trembling hand I broke the silk and seals and read. It ran thus:

"Shabaka, my Cousin,

"You departed from Egypt saying that never would you return unless I, Amada the priestess, called you, and I told you that I should never call. You said, moreover, that if you came at my call you would demand me in guerdon, and I told you that never would I give myself to you who was doubly sworn to Isis. Yet now I call and now I say that if you come and conquer and I yet live, then, if you still will it, I am yours. Thus stands the case: The Great King advances upon Egypt with an army countless as the sands, nor can Egypt hope to battle against him unaided and alone. He comes to make of her a slave, to kill her children, to burn her temples, to sack her cities and to defile her gods with blasphemies. Moreover he comes to seize me and to drag me away to shame in his House of Women.

"Therefore for the sake of the gods, for Egypt's sake and for my own, I pray you come and save us. Moreover I still love you, Shabaka, yes, more a thousand times, then ever I did, though whether you still love me I know not. For that love's sake, therefore, I am ready to break my vows to Isis and to dare her vengeance, if she should desire to be avenged upon me who would save her and her worship, praying that it may fall on my head and not on yours. This will I do by the counsel of the holy Tanofir, by command of Pharaoh, and with the consent of the high priests of Egypt.

"Now I, Amada, have written. Choose, Shabaka, beloved of my heart."

Such was the letter that caused my head to swim and set my soul on fire. Still I said nothing, but thrust it into my robe and waited. Presently Bes, who had been reading in his roll, looked up and spoke, saying,

"Are you minded to see arrows fly and swords shine in war, Brother? If so, here is opportunity. Pharaoh writes to me above his own seal, seeking an alliance between Egypt and Ethiopia. He says that the King of kings invades him and that if he conquers Egypt he has sworn to travel on and conquer Ethiopia also, since he learns that it is now ruled by a certain dwarf who once stole his White Signet, and by a certain Egyptian who once killed his Satrap, Idernes."

"What says the Karoon?" I asked.

Bes rolled his eyes and turning to Karema, asked,

"What says the Karoon's wife?"

Karema laid down the roll she had been studying and answered,

"She says that she has received a command from her master the holy Tanofir to wait upon him forthwith, for reasons that he will explain when she arrives, or to brave his curse upon her, her children, her country and her husband, and not only his but that of the spirits who serve him."

"The curse of the holy Tanofir is not a thing to mock at," said Bes, "as I who revere him, know as well as any man."

"No, Husband, and therefore I leave for Egypt as soon as may be. It seems that my sister is dead, this year past, and the holy Tanofir has no one to hold his cup."

"And what shall I do?" asked Bes.

"That is for you to say, Husband. But if you will, you can stay here and guard our children, giving the command of your army to the lord Shabaka."

Now, for we were alone, Bes twisted himself about, rolling his eyes and laughing as he used to do before he became Karoon of Ethiopia.

"O-ho-ho! Wife," he said, "so you are to go to Egypt, leaving me to play the nurse to babes, and my brother here is to command my armies, leaving me to look after the old men and the women. Nay, I think otherwise. I think that I shall come also, that is if my brother wishes it. Did he not save my life and is it not his and with it all I have? Oh! have done. Once more we will stand side by side in the battle, Brother, and afterwards let Fate do as it will with us. Tell me now, what is the tale of archers and of swordsmen with which we can march against the Great King with whom, like you, I have a score to settle?"

"Seventy and five thousand," I answered.

"Good! On the fifth day from now the army marches for Egypt."

Tanofir Finds His Broken Cup

March we did, but on the fifteenth day, not the fifth, since there was much to make ready. First the Council of the Ethiopians must be consulted and through them the people. In the beginning there was trouble over the matter, since many were against a distant war, and this even after Bes had urged that it was better to attack than wait to be attacked. For they answered, and justly, that here in Ethiopia distance and the desert were their shields, since the King of kings, however great his strength, would be weary and famished before he set foot within their borders.

In the end the knot was cut with a sword, for when the army came to learn of the dispute, from the generals down to the common soldiers, every man clamoured to be led to war, since, as I have said, these Ethiopians were fighters all of them, and near at hand there were none left with whom they could fight. So when the Council came to see that they must choose between war abroad and revolt at home, they gave way, bargaining only that the children of the Karoon should not leave the land so that if aught befell him, there would be some of the true blood left to succeed.

Also the Grasshopper was consulted by the priests who found the omens favourable. Indeed I was told that this great golden locust sat up upon its hind legs upon the altar and waved its feelers in the air, which only happened when wonderful fortune was about to bless the land. The tale reminded me of the nodding of the statues of our own gods in Egypt when a new Pharaoh was presented to them, and of that of Isis when Amada put up her prayer to the divine Mother. To tell the truth, I suspected Karema of having some hand in the business. However, so it happened.

At length we set forth, a mighty host, Bes commanding the swordsmen and I, under him, the archers, of whom there were more than thirty thousand men, and glad was I when all the farewells were said and we were free of the weeping crowds of women. At first Bes and Karema were somewhat sad at parting from their children, but in a little while they grew gay again since the one longed for battle and the other for the sands of Egypt.

Now of our advance I need say little, except that it was slow, though none dared to bar the road of so mighty an array. Since we must go on foot, we were not able to cover more than five leagues a day, for even after we reached the river boats could not be found for so many, though Karema travelled in one with her ladies. Also cattle and corn must always be sent forward for food. Still we crept on to Egypt without sickness, accident, or revolt.

When we drew near to its frontiers messengers met us from Pharaoh bearing letters in answer to those which we had sent with the tidings of our coming. These contained little but ill news. It seemed that the Great King with a countless host had taken all the cities of the Delta and, after a long siege, had captured Memphis and put it to the sack, and that the army of Egypt, fighting desperately by land and upon the Nile was being driven southwards towards Thebes. Pharaoh added that he proposed to make his last stand at the strong city of Amada, since he doubted whether the troops from Lower Egypt would not rather surrender to the Easterns than retreat further up the Nile. He thanked and blessed us for our promised aid and prayed that it might come in time to save Egypt from slavery and himself from death.

Also there was a letter for me from Amada in which she said,

"Oh! come quickly. Come quickly, beloved Shabaka, lest of me you should find but bones for never will I fall living into the hands of the Great King. We are sore pressed and although Amada has been made very strong, it can stand but a little while against such a countless multitude armed with all the engines of war."

For Karema, too, there were messages from the holy Tanofir of the same meaning, saying that unless we appeared within a moon of their receipt, all was lost.

We read and took counsel. Then we pressed forward by double marches, sending swift runners forward to bid Pharaoh and his army hold on to the last spear and arrow.

On the twenty-fifth day from the receipt of this news we came to the great frontier city which we found in tumult for its citizens were mad with fear. Here we rested one night and ate of the food that was gathered there in plenty. Then leaving a small rear-guard of five thousand men who were tired out, to hold the place, we pressed onwards, for Amada was still four days' march away. On the morning of the fourth day we were told that it was falling, or had fallen, and when at length we came in sight of the place we saw that it was beleaguered by an innumerable host of Easterns, while on the Nile was a great fleet of Grecian and Cyprian mercenaries. Moreover, heralds from the King of kings reached us, saying:

"Surrender, Barbarians, or before the second day dawns you shall sleep sound, every one of you."

To these we answered that we would take counsel on the matter and that perhaps on the morrow we would surrender, since when we had marched from Ethiopia, we did not know how great was the King's strength, having been deceived as to it by the letters of the Pharaoh. Meanwhile that the King of kings would do well to let us alone, since we were brave men and meant to die hard, and it would be better for him to leave us to march back to Ethiopia, rather than lose an army in trying to kill us.

With these words which were spoken by Bes himself, the messengers departed. One of them however, who seemed to be a great lord, called in a loud voice to his companions, saying it was hard that nobles should have to do the errands, not of a man but of an ape who would look better hanging to a pole. Bes made no answer, only rolled his yellow eyes and said when the lord was out of hearing,

"Now by the Grasshopper and all the gods of Egypt I swear that in payment for this insult I will choke the Nile with the army of the Great King, and hang that knave to a pole from the prow of the royal ship." Which last thing I hope he did.

When the embassy had gone Bes gave orders that the whole army should eat and lie down to sleep.

"I am sure," said he, "that the Great King will not attack us at once, since he will hope that we shall flee away during the night, having seen his strength."

So the Ethiopians filled themselves and then lay down to sleep, which these people can do at any time, even if not tired as they were. But while they rested Bes and I and Karema, with some of the generals consulted together long and earnestly. For in truth we knew not what to do. But a league away lay the town of Amada beset by hundreds of thousands of the Easterns so that none could come in or out, and within its walls were the remains of Pharaoh's army, not more than twenty thousand men, all told, if what we heard were true. On the Nile also was the great Grecian and Cyprian fleet, two hundred vessels and more, though as we could see by the light of the setting sun the most of these were made fast to the western bank where the Egyptians could not come at them.

For the rest our position was good, being on high desert beyond the cultivated land which bordered the eastern bank. But in front of us, separating us from the southern army of the King, stretched a swamp hard to cross, so that we could not hope to make an attack by night as there was no moon. Lastly, the main Eastern strength, to the number of two hundred thousand or more, lay to the north beyond Amada.

All these things we considered, talking low and earnestly there in the tent, till it grew so dark that we could not see each other's faces while behind us slumbered our army that now numbered some seventy thousand men.

"We are in a trap," said Bes at length. "If we await attack they will weigh us down with numbers. If we flee they have camels and horses and will overtake us; also ships of which we have none. If we attack it must be without cover through swamp where we shall be bogged.

"Meanwhile Pharaoh is perishing within yonder walls of Amada which the engines batter down. By the Grasshopper! I know not what to do. It seems that our journey is vain and that few of us will see Ethiopia more; also that Egypt is sped."

I made no answer, for here my generalship failed me and I had nothing to say. The captains, too, were silent, only woman-like, Karema wept a little, and I too went near to weeping who thought of Amada penned in yonder temple like a lamb that awaits the butcher's knife.

Suddenly, coming from the door of the tent which I thought was closed, I heard a deep voice say,

"I have ever noted that those of Ethiopian blood are melancholy after sundown, though of Egyptians I had thought better things."

Now about this voice there was something familiar to me, still I said nothing, nor did the others, for to speak the truth, all of us were frightened and thought that we must dream. For how could any thing that breathed approach this tent through a triple line of sentries? So we sat still, staring at the darkness, till presently in that darkness appeared a glow of light, such as comes from the fire-flies of Ethiopia. It grew and grew while we gasped with fear, till presently it took shape, and the shape it took was that of the ancient withered face, the sightless eyes, and the white beard of the holy Tanofir. Yes, there not two feet from the ground seemed to float the head of the holy Tanofir, limned in faint flame, which I suppose must have been reflected on to it from the light of some camp-fire without.

"O my beloved master!" cried Karema, and threw herself towards him.

"O my beloved Cup!" answered Tanofir. "Glad am I to know you well and unshattered."

Then a torch was lit and lo! there before us, wrapped in his dark cloak sat the holy Tanofir.

"Whence come you, my Great-uncle?" I asked amazed.

"From less far than you do, Nephew," he answered. "Namely out of Amada yonder. Oh! ask me not how. It is easy if you are a blind old beggar who knows the path. And by the way, if you have aught to eat I should be glad of a bite and a sup, since in Amada food has been scarce for this last month, and to-night there is little left."

Karema sped from the tent and presently returned with bread and wine of which Tanofir partook almost greedily.

"This is the first strong drink that I have tasted for many a year," he said as he drained the goblet; "but better a broken vow than broken wits when one has much to plan and do. At least I hope the gods will think so when I meet them presently. There—I am strong again. Now, say, what is your force?"

We told him.

"Good. And what is your plan?"

We shook our heads, having none.

"Bes," he said sternly, "I think you grow dull since you became a king —or perhaps it is marriage that makes you so. Why, in bygone years schemes would have come so fast that they would have choked each other between those thick lips of yours. And Shabaka, tell me, have you lost all your generalship whereof once you had plenty, in the soft air of Ethiopia? Or is it that even the shadow of marriage makes *you* dull? Well, I must turn to the woman, for that is always the lot of man. Your plan, Karema, and quickly for there is no time to lose."

Now the face of Karema grew fixed and her eyes dreamy as she spoke in a slow, measured voice like one who knows not what she says.

"My plan is to destroy the armies of the Great King and to relieve the city of Amada."

"A very good plan," said holy Tanofir, "but the question is, how?"

"I think," went on Karema, "that about a league above this place there is a spot where at this season the Nile can be forded by tall men without the wetting of their shoulders. First then, I would send five thousand swordsmen across that ford and let them creep down on the navy of the Great King where the sailors revel in safety, or sleep sound, and fire the ships. The wind blows strongly from the south and the flames will leap fast from one of them to the other. Most of their crews will be burned and the rest can be slain by our five thousand."

"Good, very good," said the holy Tanofir, "but not enough, seeing that on the eastern bank is gathered the host of over two hundred thousand men. Now how will you deal with *them*, Karema?"

"I seem to see a road yonder beyond the swamp. It runs on the edge of the desert but behind the sand-hills. I would send the archers of whom there are more than thirty thousand, under the command of Shabaka along that road which leads them past Amada. On its farther side are low hills strewn with rocks. Here I would let the archers take cover and wait for the breaking of the dawn. Then beneath them they will see the most of the Eastern host and with such bows as ours they can sweep the plain from the hills almost to the Nile, and having a hundred arrows to a man, should slaughter the Easterns by the ten thousand, for when these turn to charge a shaft should pierce through two together."

"Good again," said Tanofir. "But what of the army of the Great King which lies upon this side of Amada?"

"I think that before the dawn, believing us so few, it will advance and with the first light begin to thread the swamp, and therefore we must keep five thousand archers to gall it as it comes. Still it will win through, though with loss, and find us waiting for it here shoulder to shoulder, rank upon rank with locked shields, against which horse and foot shall break in vain, for who shall drive a wedge through the Ethiopian squares that Shabaka has trained and that Bes, the Karoon, commands? I say that they shall roll back like waves from a cliff; yes, again and again, growing ever fewer till the clamour of battle and the shouts of fear and agony reach their ears from beyond Amada where Shabaka and the archers do their work and the sight of the burning ships strikes terror in them and they fly."

"Good again," said the holy Tanofir. "But still many on both fronts will be left, for this army of Easterns is very vast. And how will you deal with these, O Karema?"

"On these I would have Pharaoh with all his remaining strength pour from the northern and the southern gates of Amada, for so shall they be caught like wounded lions between two wild bulls and torn and trampled and utterly destroyed. Only I know not how to tell Pharaoh what he must do, and when."

"Good again," said the holy Tanofir, "very good. And as for the telling of Pharaoh, well, I shall see him presently. It is strange, my chipped Cup which I had almost thrown away as useless, that although broken, you still hold so much wisdom. For know, wonderful though it may seem, that just such plans as you have spoken have grown up in my own mind, only I wished to learn if you thought them wise."

Then he laughed a little and Karema stretched her arms as one does who awakes from sleep, rubbed her eyes and asked if he would not eat more food.

In an instant Tanofir was speaking again in a quick, clear voice.

"Bes, or King," he said, "doubtless you will do your wife's will. Therefore let the host be aroused and stand to its arms. As it chances I have four men without who can be trusted. Two of these will guide the five thousand to the ford and across it; also down upon the ships. The other two will guide Shabaka and the archers along the road which Karema remembers so well; perhaps she trod it as a child. For my part I return to Amada to make sure that Pharaoh does his share and at the right time.

For mark, unless all this is carried through to-night Amada will fall to-morrow, a certain priestess will die, and you, Bes, and your soldiers will never look on Ethiopia again. Is it agreed?"

I nodded who did not wish to waste time in words, and Bes rolled his eyes and answered,

"When one can think of nothing, it is best to follow the counsel of those who can think of something; also to hunt rather than to be hunted. Especially is this so if that something comes from the holy Tanofir or his broken Cup. Generals, you have heard. Rouse the host and bid them stand to their arms company by company!"

The generals leapt away into the darkness like arrows from a bow, and presently we heard the noise of gathering men.

"Where are these guides of yours, holy Tanofir?" asked Bes.

Tanofir beckoned over his shoulder, and out of the gloom, one by one, four men stole into the tent. They were strange, quiet men, but I can say no more of them since their faces were veiled, nor as it chances, did I ever see any of them after the battle, in which I suppose that they were killed. Or perhaps they appeared after—well, never mind!

"You have heard," said Tanofir, whereupon all four of them bowed their mysterious veiled heads.

"Now, my Brother," whispered Bes into my ear, "tell me, I pray you, how did four men who were not in the tent, hear what was said in this tent, and how did they come through the guards who have orders to kill anyone who does not know the countersign, especially men whose faces are wrapped in napkins?"

"I do not know," I answered, whereon Bes groaned, only Karema smiled a little as though to herself.

"Then, having heard, obey," said the holy Tanofir, whereon the four veiled ones bowed again.

"Will you not give them their orders, O most Venerable?" inquired Bes doubtfully.

"I think it is needless," said Tanofir in a dry voice. "Why try to teach those who know?"

"Will you not offer them something to eat, since they also must be hungry?" I asked of Karema.

"Fool, be silent," she replied, looking on me with contempt. "Do the— friends—of Tanofir need to eat?"

"I should have thought so after being beleaguered for a month in a starving town. If the master wants to eat, why should not his men?" I murmured.

Then a thought struck me and I was silent.

A general returned and reported that the orders had been executed and that all the army was afoot.

"Good," said Bes. "Then start forthwith with five thousand men, and burn those ships, according to the plan laid down by the Queen Karema, which you heard her speak but now," and he named certain regiments that he should take with him, those of the general's own command, adding: "Save some of the ships if you can, and afterwards cross the Nile in them with your men, and join yourself either to my force or to that of the lord Shabaka, according to what you see. May the Grasshopper give you victory and wisdom."

The general saluted and asked,

"Who guides us to and across the ford of the great river?"

Two of the veiled men stepped forward whereon the general muttered into my ear,

"I like not the look of them. I pray the Grasshopper they do not guide us across the River of Death."

"Have no fear, General," said the holy Tanofir from the other end of the tent. "If you and your men play their parts as well as the guides will play theirs, the ships are already burned together with their companies. Only take fire with you."

So that general departed with the two guides, looking somewhat frightened, and soon was marching up Nile at the head of five thousand swordsmen.

Now Bes looked at me and said,

"It seems that you had better be gone also, my Brother, with the archers. Perchance the holy Tanofir will show you whither."

"No, no," answered Tanofir, "my guides will show him. Look not so doubtful, Shabaka. Did I fail you when you were in the grip of the King of kings in the East, and only your own life and that of Bes were at stake?"

"I do not know," I answered.

"You do not know, but I know, as I think do Bes and Karema, since the one received the messages which the other sent. Well, if I did not fail you then, shall I fail you now when Egypt is at stake? Follow these guides I give you, and——" here he took hold of the quiver of arrows that lay beside me on the ground, and as certainly as though he could see it with his blind eyes, touched one of them, on the shaft of which were two black and a white feather, "remember my words after you have loosed this arrow from your great black bow and noted where it strikes."

Then I turned to Bes and asked,

"Where do we meet again?"

"I cannot say, Brother," he answered. "In Amada if that may be. If not, at the Table of Osiris, or in the fields of the Grasshopper, or in the blackness which swallows all, gods and men together."

"Does Karema come with me or bide with you?" I asked again.

"She does neither," interrupted Tanofir, "she accompanies me to Amada, where I have need of her and she will be more safe. Oh! fear nothing, for every hermit however poor, still carries his staff and his cup, even if it be cracked."

Then I shook Bes by the hand and went my way, wondering if I were awake or dreaming, and the last thing I saw in that tent was the beautiful face of Karema smiling at me. This I took to be a good omen, since I knew that it was the heart of the holy Tanofir which smiled, and that her eyes were but its mirror.

Already my thirty thousand archers were marshalling, and having made sure that there was ample store of arrows and that all their gourds were filled with water, I set myself at their head while in front of me walked the two veiled guides. I looked upon them doubtfully, since it seemed dangerous to trust an army to unknown men who for aught I knew, might lead us into the midst of our foes. Then I remembered that they were vouched for by the holy Tanofir, my own great-uncle whom I trusted above any man on earth, and took heart again.

How had he come into our tent, I wondered, and how, blind as he was, would he get back into Amada with Karema, if he took her? Well, who could account for the goings or the comings of the holy Tanofir, who was more of a spirit than a man? Perhaps it was not really he whom we had seen, but what we Egyptians called his *Ka* or Double which can pass to and fro at will. Only do *Kas* eat? Of this matter I knew only that offerings of food and drink are made to them in tombs. So leaving the holy Tanofir to guard himself, I turned my mind to our own business, which was to surprise the army of the Great King.

Skirting the swamp we came to rough and higher ground and though I could see little in that darkness, I knew that we were walking up a hill. Presently we crossed its crest and descending for three bowshots or so, I felt that my feet were on a road. Now the guides turned to the left and after them in a long line came my army of thirty thousand archers. In utter silence we went since we had no beasts with us and our sandalled feet made little noise; moreover orders had been passed down the line that the man who made a sound should die.

For two hours or more we marched thus, then bore to the left again and climbed a slope, by which time I judged we must be well past the town of Amada. Here suddenly the guides halted and we after them at whispered words of command. One of them took me by the cloak, led me forward a little way to the crest of the ridge, and pointed with his white-sleeved arm. I looked and there beneath me, well within bowshot, were thousands of the watchfires of the King's army, flaring, some of them, in the strong wind. For a full league those fires burned and we were opposite to the midmost of them.

"See now, General Shabaka," said the guide, speaking for the first time in a curious hissing whisper such as might come from a man who had no lips, "beneath you sleeps the Eastern host, which being so great, has not thought it needful to guard this ridge. Now marshal your archers in a fourfold line in such fashion that at the first break of dawn they can take cover behind the rocks and shoot, every man of them without piercing his fellow. Do you bide here with the centre where your standard can be seen by all to north and south. I and my companion will lead your vanguard farther on to where the ridge draws nearer to the Nile, so that with their arrows they can hold back and slay any who strive to escape down stream. The rest is in your hands, for we are guides, not generals. Summon your captains and issue your commands."

So we went back again and I called the officers together and told them what they were to do, then despatched them to their regiments.

Presently the vanguard of ten thousand men drew away and vanished, and with them the white-robed guides on whom I never looked again. Then I marshalled my centre as well as I could in the gloom, and bade them lie down to rest and sleep if they were able; also, within thirty minutes of the sunrise, to eat and drink a little of the food they carried, to see that every bow was ready and that the arrows were loosened in every quiver. This done, with a few whom I trusted to serve me as messengers and guard, I crept up to the brow of the hill or slope, and there we laid us down and watched.

The Battle—and After

Two hours went by and I knew by the stars that the dawn could not be far away. My eyes were fixed upon the Nile and on the lights that hung to the prows of the Great King's ships. Where were those who had been sent to fire them, I wondered, for of them I saw nothing. Well, their journey would be long as they must wade the river. Perhaps they had not yet arrived, or perhaps they had miscarried. At least the fleet seemed very quiet. None were alarmed there and no sentry challenged.

At length it grew near to dawn and behind me I heard the gentle stir of the Ethiopians arising and eating as they had been bidden, whereon I too ate and drank a little, though never had I less wished for food. The East brightened and far up the Nile of a sudden there appeared what at first I took to be a meteor or a lantern waving in the wind that now was blowing its strongest, as it does at this season of the year just at the time of dawn. Yet that lantern seemed to travel fast and lo! now I saw that it was fire running up the rigging of a ship.

It leapt from rope to rope and from sail to sail till they blazed fiercely, and in other ships also nearer to us, flame appeared that grew to a great red sheet. Our men had not failed; the navy of the King of kings was burning! Oh! how it burned fanned by the breath of that strong wind. From vessel to vessel leapt the fire like a thing alive, for all of them were drawn up on the bank with prows fastened in such fashion that they could not readily be made loose. Some broke away indeed, but they were aflame and only served to spread the fire more quickly. Before the rim of the sun appeared for a league or more there was nothing but blazing ships from which rose a hideous crying, and still more and more took fire lower down the line.

I had no time to watch for now I must be up and doing. The sky grew grey, there was light enough to see though faintly. I cast my eyes about me and perceived that no place in the world could have been better for archery. In front the hill was steep for a hundred paces or more and scattered over with thousands of large stones behind which bowmen might take shelter. Then came a gentle slope of loose sand up which attackers would find it hard to climb. Then the long flat plain whereon the Easterns were camped, and beyond it, scarce two furlongs away, the banks of Nile.

Indeed the place was ill-chosen for so great an army, nor could it have held them all, had not the camping ground been a full league in length, and even so they were crowded. Out of the mist their tents appeared, thousands of them, farther than my eye could reach, and almost opposite to me, near to the banks of the river, was a great pavilion of silk and gold that I guessed must shelter the majesty of the King of kings. Indeed this was certain since now I saw that over it floated his royal banner which I knew so well, I who had stolen the little White Signet of signets from which it was taken. Truly the holy Tanofir, or his Cup, Karema, or his messengers, or the spirits with whom he dwelt, I know not which, had a general's eye and knew how to plan an ambuscade.

So, thought I to myself as I ran back to my army to meet the gathered captains and set all things in order. It was soon done for they were ready, as were the fierce Ethiopians fresh from their rest and food, and stringing their bows, every one of them, or loosening the arrows in their quivers. As I came they lifted their hands in salute, for speak they dared not and I sent a whisper down their ranks, that this day they must fight and conquer, or fall for the glory of Ethiopia and their king. Then I gave my orders and before the sun rose and revealed them they crept forward in a fourfold line and took shelter behind the stones, lying there invisible on their bellies until the moment came.

The red rim of Ra appeared glorious in the East, and I, from behind the rocks that

I had chosen, sat down and watched. Oh! truly Tanofir or the gods of Egypt were ordering things aright for us. The huge camp was awake now and aware of what was happening on the Nile. They could not see well because of the tall reeds upon the river's rim and therefore, without order or discipline, by the thousand and the ten thousand, for their numbers were countless, some with arms and some without, they ran to the slope of sand beneath our station and began to climb it to have a better view of the burning ships.

The sun leapt up swiftly as it does in Egypt. His glowing edge appeared over the crest of the hill though the hollows beneath were still filled with shadow. The moment was at hand. I waited till I had counted ten, glancing to the right and left of me to see that all were ready and to suffer the crowd to thicken on the slope, but not to reach the lowest rocks, whither they were climbing. Then I gave the double signal that had been agreed.

Behind me the banner of the golden Grasshopper was raised upon a tall pole and broke upon the breeze. That was the first signal whereat every man rose to his knees and set shaft on string. Next I lifted my bow, the black bow, the ancient bow that few save I could bend, and drew it to my ear.

Far away, out of arrow-reach as most would have said, floated the Great King's standard over his pavilion. At this I aimed, making allowance for the wind, and shot. The shaft leapt forward, seen in the sunlight, lost in the shadow, seen in the sunlight again and lastly seen once more, pinning that golden standard against its pole!

At the sight of the omen a roar went up that rolled to right and left of us, a roar from thirty thousand throats. Now it was lost in a sound like to the hissing of thunder rain in Ethiopia, the sound of thirty thousand arrows rushing through the wind. Oh! they were well aimed, those arrows for I had not taught the Ethiopians archery in vain.

How many went down before them? The gods of Egypt know alone. I do not. All I know is that the long slope of sand which had been crowded with standing men, was now thick with fallen men, many of whom lay as though they were asleep. For what mail could resist the iron-pointed shafts driven by the strong bows of the Ethiopians?

And this was but a beginning, for, flight after flight, those arrows sped till the air grew dark with them. Soon there were no more to shoot at on the slope, for these were down, and the order went to lift the bows and draw upon the camp, and especially upon the parks of baggage beasts. Presently these were down also, or rushing maddened to and fro.

At last the Eastern generals saw and understood. Orders were shouted and in a mad confusion the scores of thousands who were unharmed, rushed back towards the banks of Nile where our shafts could not reach them. Here they formed up in their companies and took counsel. It was soon ended, for all the vast mass of them, preceded by a cloud of archers, began to advance upon the hill.

Now I passed a command to the Ethiopians, of whom so far not one had fallen, to lie low and wait. On came the glittering multitude of Easterns, gay with purple and gold, their mail and swords shining in the risen sun. On they came by squadron and by company, more than the eye could number. They reached the sand slope thick with their own dead and wounded and paused a little because they could see no man, since the black bodies of the Ethiopians were hid behind the black stones and the black bows did not catch the light.

Then from a gorgeous group that I guessed hid the person of the Great King surrounded by his regiment of guards, ten thousand of them who were called Immortals, messengers sprang forth screaming the order to charge. The host began to climb the slippery sand slope but still I held my hand till their endless lines were within fifty paces of us and their arrows rattled harmlessly against our stones. Then I caused the banner of the Grasshopper that had been lowered, to be lifted thrice, and at the third lifting once more thirty thousand arrows rushed forth to kill.

They went down, they went down in lines and heaps, riddled through and through. But still others came on for they fought under the eye of the Great King, and to fly meant death with shame and torture. We could not kill them all, they were too many. We could not kill the half of them. Now their foremost were within ten paces of us and since we must stand up to shoot, our men began to fall, also pierced with arrows. I caused the blast of retreat to be sounded on the ivory horn and step by step we drew back to the crest of the ridge, shooting as we went. On the crest we re-formed rapidly in a double line standing as close as we could together and my example was followed all down the ranks to right and left. Then I bethought me of a plan that I had taught these archers again and again in Ethiopia.

With the flag I signalled a command to stop shooting and also passed the word down the line, so that presently no more arrows flew. The Easterns hesitated, wondering whether this were a trap, or if we lacked shafts, and meanwhile I sent messengers with certain orders to the vanguard, who sped away at speed behind the hill, running as they never ran before. Presently I heard a voice below cry out,

"The Great King commands that the barbarians be destroyed. Let the barbarians be destroyed!"

Now with a roar they came on like a flood. I waited till they were within twenty paces of us, and shouted, "Shoot and fall!"

The first line shot and oh! fearful was its work, for not a shaft missed those crowded hosts and many pinned two together. My archers shot and fell down, setting new arrows to the string as they fell, whereon the second line also shot over them. Then up we sprang and loosed again, and again fell down, whereon the second line once more poured in its deadly hail.

Now the Easterns stayed their advance, for their front ranks lay prone, and those behind must climb over them if they could. Yes, standing there in glittering groups they rocked and hesitated although their officers struck them with swords and lances to drive them forward. Once more our front rank rose and loosed, and once more we dropped and let the shafts of the second speed over us. It was too much, flesh and blood could not bear more of those arrows. Thousands upon thousands were down and the rest began to flee in confusion.

Then at my command the ivory horns sounded the charge. Every man slung his bow upon his back and drew his short sword.

"On to them!" I cried and leapt forward.

Like a black torrent we rushed down the hill, leaping over the dead and wounded. The retreat became a rout since before these ebon, great- eyed warriors the soft Easterns did not care to stand. They fled screaming,

"These are devils! These are devils!"

We were among them now, hacking and stabbing with the short swords upon their heads and backs. There was no need to aim the blow, they were so many. Like a huddled mob of cattle they turned and fled down Nile. But my orders had reached the vanguard and these, hidden in the growing crops on the narrow neck of swampy land between the hills and the Nile, met them with arrows as they came, also raked them from the steep cliff side. Their chariot wheels sank into the mud till the horses were slain; their footmen were piled in heaps about them, till soon there was a mighty wall of dead and dying. And our centre and rearguard came up behind. Oh! we slew and slew, till before the sun was an hour high over half the army of the Great King was no more. Then we re-formed, having suffered but little loss, and drank of the water of the Nile.

"All is not done," I cried.

For the Immortals still remained behind us, gathered in massed ranks about their king. Also there were many thousands of others between these and the walls of Amada, and to the south of the city yet a second army, that with which Bes had been left to deal, with what success I knew not.

"Ethiopians," I shouted, "cease crying Victory, since the battle is about to begin. Strike, and at once before the Easterns find their heart again."

So we advanced upon the Immortals, all of us, for now the vanguard had joined our strength.

In long lines we advanced over that blood-soaked plain, and as we came the Great King loosed his remaining chariots against us. It availed him nothing, since the horses could not face our arrows whereof, thanks be to the gods! I had prepared so ample a store, carried in bundles by lads. Scarce a chariot reached our lines, and those that did were destroyed, leaving us unbroken.

The chariots were done with and their drivers dead, but there still frowned the squares of the Immortals. We shot at them till nearly all our shafts were spent, and, galled to madness, they charged. We did not wait for the points of those long spears, but ran in beneath them striking with our short swords, and oh! grim and desperate was that battle, since the Easterns were clad in mail and the Ethiopians had but short jerkins of bull's hide.

Fight as we would we were driven back. The fray turned against us and we fell by hundreds. I bethought me of flight to the hills, since now we were outnumbered and very weary. But behold! when all seemed lost a great shouting rose from Amada and through her opened gates poured forth all that remained of the army of Pharaoh, perhaps eighteen or twenty thousand men. I saw, and my heart rose again.

"Stand firm!" I cried. "Stand firm!" and lo! we stood.

The Egyptians were on them now and in their midst I saw Pharaoh's banner. By degrees the battle swayed towards the banks of Nile, we to the north, the Egyptians to the south and the Easterns between us. They were trying to turn our flank; yes, and would have done it, had there not suddenly appeared upon the Nile a fleet of ships. At first I thought that we were lost, for these ships were from Greece and Cyprus, till I saw the banner of the Grasshopper wave from a prow, and knew that they were manned by our five thousand who had gone out to burn the fleet, and had saved these vessels. They beached and from their crowded holds poured the five thousand, or those that were left of them, and ranging themselves upon the bank, raised their war-shout and attacked the ends of the Easterns' lines.

Now we charged for the last time and the Egyptians charged from the south. Ha-ha! the ranks of the Immortals were broken at length. We were among them. I saw Pharaoh, his *uraeus* circlet on his helm. He was wounded and sore beset. A tall Immortal rushed at him with a spear and drove it home.

Pharaoh fell.

I leapt over him and killed that Eastern with a blow upon the neck, but my sword shattered on his armour. The tide of battle rolled up and swept us apart and I saw Pharaoh being carried away. Look! yonder was the Great King himself standing in a golden chariot, the Great King in all his glory whom last I had seen far away in the East. He knew me and shot at me with a bow, the bow he thought my own, shouting, "Die, dog of an Egyptian!"

His arrow pierced my helm but missed my head. I strove to come at him but could not.

The real rout began. The Immortals were broken like an earthen jar. They retreated in groups fighting desperately and of these the thickest was around the Great King. He whom I hated was about to escape me. He still had horses; he would fly down Nile, gain his reserves and so away back to the East, where he would gather new and yet larger armies, since men in millions were at his command. Then he would return and destroy Egypt when perchance there were no Ethiopians to help her, and perhaps after all drag Amada to his House of Women. See, they were breaking through and already I was far away with a wound in my breast, a hurt leg and a shattered sword.

What could I do? My arrows were spent and the bearers had none left to give me.

No, there was one still in the quiver. I drew it out. On its shaft were two black feathers and one white. Who had spoken of that arrow? I remembered, Tanofir. I was to think of certain things that he had said when I noted what it pierced. I unslung my bow, strung it and set that arrow on the string.

By now the Great King was far away, out of reach for most archers. His chariot forging ahead amidst the remnant of his guards and the nobles who attended on his sacred person, travelled over a little rise where doubtless once there had been a village, long since rotted down to its parent clay. The sunlight glinted on his shining armour and silken robe, whereof the back was toward me.

I aimed, I drew, I loosed! Swift and far the shaft sped forward. By Osiris! it struck him full between the shoulders, and lo! the King of kings, the Monarch of the World, lurched forward, fell on to the rail of his chariot, and rolled to the ground. Next instant there arose a roar of, "The King is dead! The Great King is dead! *Fly, fly, fly!*"

So they fled and after them thundered the pursuers slaying and slaying till they could lift their arms no more. Oh! yes, some escaped though the men of Thebes and country folk murdered many of them and but a few ever won back to the East to tell the tale of the blotting out of the mighty army of the King of kings and of the doom dealt to him by the great black bow of Shabaka the Egyptian.

I stood there gasping, when suddenly I heard a voice at my side. It said,

"You seem to have done very well, Brother, even better than we did yonder on the other side of the town, though some might think that fray a thing whereof to make a song. Also that last shot of yours was worthy of a good archer, for I marked it, I marked it. A great lord was laid low thereby. Let us go and see who it was."

I threw my arm round the bull neck of Bes and leaning on him, advanced to where the King lay alone save for the fallen about him.

"This man is not yet sped," said Bes. "Let us look upon his face," and he turned him over, and stretched him there upon the sand with the arrow standing two spans beyond his corselet.

"Why," said Bes, "this is a certain High one with whom we had dealings in the East!" and he laughed thickly.

Then the Great King opened his eyes and knew us and on his dying features came a look of hate.

"So you have conquered, Egyptian," he said. "Oh! if only I had you again in the East, whence in my folly I let you go——"

"You would set me in your boat, would you not, whence by the wisdom of Bes I escaped."

"More than that," he gasped.

"I shall not serve you so," I went on. "I shall leave you to die as a warrior should upon a fair fought field. But learn, tyrant and murderer, that the shaft which overthrew you came from the black bow you coveted and thought you had received, and that this hand loosed it —not at hazard."

"I guessed it," he whispered.

"Know, too, King, that the lady Amada whom you also coveted, waits to be my wife; that your mighty army is destroyed, and that Egypt is free by the hands of Shabaka the Egyptian and Bes the dwarf."

"Shabaka the Egyptian," he muttered, "whom I held and let go because of a dream and for policy. So, Shabaka, you will wed Amada whom I desired because I could not take her, and doubtless you will rule in Egypt, for Pharaoh, I think, is as I am to-day. O Shabaka, you are strong and a great warrior, but there is something stronger than you in the world—that which men call Fate. Such success as yours offends the gods. Look on me, Shabaka, look on the King of kings, the Ruler of the earth, lying shamed in the dust before you, and, accursed Shabaka! do not call yourself happy until you see death as near as I do now."

Then he threw his arms wide and died.

We called to soldiers to bear his body and having set the pursuit, with that royal clay entered into Amada in triumph. It was not a very great town and the temple was its finest building and thither we wended. In the outer court we found Pharaoh lying at the point of death, for from many wounds his life drained out with his flowing blood, nor could the leeches help him.

"Greeting, Shabaka," he said, "you and the Ethiopians have saved Egypt. My son is slain in the battle and I too am slain, and who remains to rule her save you, you and Amada? Would that you had married her at once, and never left my side. But she was foolish and headstrong and I—was jealous of you, Shabaka. Forgive me, and farewell."

He spoke no more although he lived a little while.

Karema came from the inner court. She greeted her husband, then turned and said,

"Lord Shabaka, one waits to welcome you."

I rested myself upon her shoulder, for I could not walk alone.

"What happened to the army of the Karoon?" I asked as we went slowly.

"That happened, Lord, which the holy Tanofir foretold. The Easterns attacked across the swamp, thinking to bear us down by numbers. But the paths were too narrow and their columns were bogged in the mud. Still they struggled on against the arrows to its edge and there the Ethiopians fell on them and being lighter-footed and without armour, had the mastery of them, who were encumbered by their very multitude. Oh! I saw it all from the temple top. Bes did well and I am proud of him, as I am proud of you."

"It is of the Ethiopians that you should be proud, Karema, since with one to five they have won a great battle."

We came to the end of the second court where was a sanctuary.

"Enter," said Karema and fell back.

I did so and though the cedar door was left a little ajar, at first could see nothing because of the gloom of the place. By degrees my eyes grew accustomed to the darkness and I perceived an alabaster statue of the goddess Isis of the size of life, who held in her arms an ivory child, also lifesize. Then I heard a sigh and, looking down, saw a woman clad in white kneeling at the feet of the statue, lost in prayer. Suddenly she rose and turned and the ray of light from the door ajar fell upon her. It was Amada draped only in the transparent robe of a priestess, and oh! she was beautiful beyond imagining, so beautiful that my heart stood still.

She saw me in my battered mail and the blood flowed up to her breast and brow and in her eyes there came a light such as I had never known in them before, the light that is lit only by the torch of woman's love. Yes, no longer were hers the eyes of a priestess; they were the eyes of a woman who burns with mortal passion.

"Amada," I whispered, "Amada found at last."

"Shabaka," she whispered back, "returned at last, to me, your home," and she stretched out her arms toward me.

But before I could take her into mine, she uttered a little cry and shrank away.

"Oh! not here," she said, "not here in the presence of this Holy One who watches all that passes in heaven and earth."

"Then perchance, Amada, she has watched the freeing of Egypt on yonder field to-day, and knows for whose sake it was done."

"Hearken, Shabaka. I am your guerdon. Moreover as a woman I am yours. There is naught I desire so much as to feel your kiss upon me. For it and it alone I am ready to risk my spirit's death and torment. But for you I fear. Twice have I sworn myself to this goddess and she is very jealous of those who rob her of her votaries. I fear that her curse will fall not only on me, but on you also, and not only for this life but for all lives that may be given to us. For your own sake, I pray you leave me. I hear that

Pharaoh my uncle is dead or dying, and doubtless they will offer you the throne. Take it, Shabaka, for in it I ask no share. Take it and leave me to serve the goddess till my death."

"I too serve a goddess," I answered hoarsely, "and she is named Love, and you are her priestess. Little I care for Isis who serve the goddess Love. Come, kiss me here and now, ere perchance I die. Kiss me who have waited long enough, and so let us be wed."

One moment she paused, swaying in the wind of passion, like a tall reed on the banks of Nile, and then, ah! then she sank upon my breast and pressed her lips against my own.

AND AFTER

For a few moments I, Shabaka, seemed to be lost in a kind of delirium and surrounded by a rose-hued mist. Then I, Allan Quatermain, heard a sharp quick sound as of a clock striking, and looked up. It was a lock, a beautiful old clock on a mantelpiece opposite to me and the hands showed that it had just struck the hour of ten.

Now I remembered that centuries ago, as I was dropping asleep, I did not know why, I had seen that clock and those hands in the same position and known that it was striking the second stroke of ten. Oh! what did it all mean? Had thousands of years gone by or—only eight seconds?

There was a weight upon my shoulder. I glanced round to see what it was and discovered the beautiful head of Lady Ragnall who was sweetly sleeping there. Lady Ragnall! and in that very strange dream which I had dreamed she was the priestess called Amada. Look, there was the mark of the new moon above her breast. And not a second ago I had been in a shrine with Amada dressed as Lady Ragnall was to-night, in circumstances so intimate that it made me blush to think of them. Lady Ragnall! Amada!—Amada! Lady Ragnall! A shrine! A boudoir! Oh! I must be going mad!

I could not disturb her, it would have been—well, unseemly. So I, Shabaka, or Allan Quatermain, just sat still feeling curiously comfortable, and tried to piece things together, when suddenly Amada— I mean Lady Ragnall woke.

"I wonder," she said without lifting her head from my shoulder, "what happened to the holy Tanofir. I think that I heard him outside the shine giving directions for the digging of Pharaoh's grave at that spot, and saying that he must do so at once as his time was very short. Yes, and I wished that he would go away. Oh! my goodness!" she exclaimed, and suddenly sprang up.

I too rose and we stood facing each other.

Between us, in front of the fire stood the tripod and the bowl of black stone at the bottom of which lay a pinch of white ashes, the remains of the *Taduki*. We stared at it and at each other.

"Oh! where have we been, Shaba—I mean, Mr. Quatermain?" she gasped, looking at me round-eyed.

"I don't know," I answered confusedly. "To the East I suppose. That is —it was all a dream."

"A dream!" she said. "What nonsense! Tell me, were you or were you not in a sanctuary just now with me before the statue of Isis, the same that fell on George two years ago and killed him, and did you or did you not give me a necklace of wonderful rosy pearls which we put upon the neck of the statue as a peace-offering because I had broken my vows to the goddess—those that you won from the Great King?"

"No," I answered triumphantly, "I did nothing of the sort. Is it likely that I should have taken those priceless pearls into battle? I gave them to Karema to keep after my mother returned them to me on her death-bed; I remember it distinctly."

"Yes, and Karema handed them to me again as your love-token when she appeared in the city with the holy Tanofir, and what was more welcome at the moment—something to eat. For we were near starving, you know. Well, I threw them over your neck and my own in the shrine to be the symbol of our eternal union. But afterwards we thought that it might be wise to offer them to the goddess—to appease her, you know. Oh! how dared we plight our mortal troth there in her very shrine and presence, and I her twice-sworn servant? It was insult heaped on sacrilege."

"At a guess, because love is stronger than fear," I replied. "But it seems that you dreamed a little longer than I did. So perhaps you can tell me what happened afterwards. I only got as far as—well, I forget how far I got," I added, for at that moment full memory returned and I could not go on.

She blushed to her eyes and grew disturbed.

"It is all mixed up in my mind too," she exclaimed. "I can only remember something rather absurd—and affectionate. You know what strange things dreams are."

"I thought you said it wasn't a dream."

"Really I don't know what it was. But—your wound doesn't hurt you, does it? You were bleeding a good deal. It stained me here," and she touched her breast and looked down wonderingly at her sacred, ancient robe as though she expected to see that it was red.

"As there is no stain now it *must* have been a dream. But my word! that was a battle," I answered.

"Yes, I watched it from the pylon top, and oh! it was glorious. Do you remember the charge of the Ethiopians against the Immortals? Why of course you must as you led it. And then the fall of Pharaoh Peroa—he was George, you know. And the death of the Great King, killed by your black bow; you were a wonderful shot even then, you see. And the burning of the ships, how they blazed! And—a hundred other things."

"Yes," I said, "it came off. The holy Tanofir was a good strategist— or his Cup was, I don't know which."

"And you were a good general, and so for the matter of that was Bes. Oh! what agonies I went through while the fight hung doubtful. My heart was on fire, yes, I seemed to burn for——" and she stopped.

"For whom?" I asked.

"For Egypt of course, and when, reflected in the alabaster, I saw you enter that shrine, where you remember I was praying for your success— and safety, I nearly died of joy. For you know I had been, well, attached to you—to Shabaka, I mean—all the time—that's my part of the story which I daresay you did not see. Although I seemed so cold and wayward I could love, yes, in that life I knew how to love. And Shabaka looked, oh! a hero with his rent mail and the glory of triumph in his eyes. He was very handsome, too, in his way. But what nonsense I am talking."

"Yes, great nonsense. Still, I wish we were sure how it ended. It is a pity that you forget, for I am crazed with curiosity. I suppose there is no more *Taduki*, is there?"

"Not a scrap," she answered firmly, "and if there were it would be fatal to take it twice on the same day. We have learned all there is to learn. Perhaps it is as well, though I should like to know what happened after our—our marriage."

"So we *were* married, were we?"

"I mean," she went on ignoring my remark, "whether you ruled long in Egypt. For you, or rather Shabaka, did rule. Also whether the Easterns returned and drove us out, or what. You see the Ivory Child went away somehow, for we found it again in Kendah Land only a few years ago."

"Perhaps we retired to Ethiopia," I suggested, "and the worship of the Child continued in some part of that country after the Ethiopian kingdom passed away."

"Perhaps, only I don't think Karema would ever have gone back to Ethiopia unless she was obliged. You remember how she hated the place. No, not even to see those black children of hers. Well, as we can never tell, it is no use speculating."

"I thought there *was* more *Taduki*," I remarked sadly. "I am sure I saw some in the coffer."

"Not one bit," she answered still more firmly than before, and, stretching out her hand, she shut down the lid of the coffer before I could look into it. "It may be best so, for as it stands the story had a happy ending and I don't want to learn, oh! I don't want to learn how the curse of Isis fell on you and me."

"So you believe in that?"

"Yes, I do," she answered with passion, "and what is more, I believe it is working still, which perhaps is why we have all come down in the world, you and I and George and Hans, yes, and even old Harut whom we knew in Kendah Land, who, I think, was the holy Tanofir. For as surely as I live I *know* beyond possibility of doubt that whatever we may be called to-day, you were the General Shabaka and I was the priestess Amada, Royal Lady of Egypt, and between us and about us the curse of Isis wavers like a sword. That is why George was killed and that is why—but I feel very tired, I think I had better go to bed."

As I recall that I have explained, I was obliged to leave Ragnall Castle early the next morning to keep a shooting engagement. O heavens! to keep a shooting engagement!

But whatever Amada, I mean Lady Ragnall, said, there *was* plenty more *Taduki*, as I have good reason to know.

Allan Quatermain.

She and Allan

Table of Contents

Note by the Late Mr. Allan Quatermain

My friend, into whose hands I hope that all these manuscripts of mine will pass one day, of this one I have something to say to you.

A long while ago I jotted down in it the history of the events that it details with more or less completeness. This I did for my own satisfaction. You will have noted how memory fails us as we advance in years; we recollect, with an almost painful exactitude, what we experienced and saw in our youth, but the happenings of our middle life slip away from us or become blurred, like a stretch of low-lying landscape overflowed by grey and nebulous mist. Far off the sun still seems to shine upon the plains and hills of adolescence and early manhood, as yet it shines about us in the fleeting hours of our age, that ground on which we stand to-day, but the valley between is filled with fog. Yes, even its prominences, which symbolise the more startling events of that past, often are lost in this confusing fog.

It was an appreciation of these truths which led me to set down the following details (though of course much is omitted) of my brief intercourse with the strange and splendid creature whom I knew under the names of *Ayesha*, or *Híya*, or *She-who-commands*; not indeed with any view to their publication, but before I forgot them that, if I wished to do so, I might re-peruse them in the evening of old age to which I hope to attain.

Indeed, at the time the last thing I intended was that they should be given to the world even after my own death, because they, or many of them, are so unusual that I feared lest they should cause smiles and in a way cast a slur upon my memory and truthfulness. Also, as you will read, as to this matter I made a promise and I have always tried to keep my promises and to guard the secrets of others. For these reasons I proposed, in case I neglected or forgot to destroy them myself, to leave a direction that this should be done by my executors. Further, I have been careful to make no allusion *whatever* to them either in casual conversation or in anything else that I may have written, my desire being that this page of my life should be kept quite private, something known only to myself. Therefore, too, I never so much as hinted of them to anyone, not even to yourself to whom I have told so much.

Well, I recorded the main facts concerning this expedition and its issues, simply and with as much exactness as I could, and laid them aside. I do not say that I never thought of them again, since amongst them were some which, together with the problems they suggested, proved to be of an unforgettable nature.

Also, whenever any of Ayesha's sayings or stories which are not preserved in these pages came back to me, as has happened from time to time, I jotted them down and put them away with this manuscript. Thus among these notes you will find a history of the city of Kôr as she told it to me, which I have omitted here. Still, many of these remarkable events did more or less fade from my mind, as the image does from an unfixed photograph, till only their outlines remained, faint if distinguishable.

To tell the truth, I was rather ashamed of the whole story in which I cut so poor a figure. On reflection it was obvious to me, although honesty had compelled me to set out all that is essential exactly as it occurred, adding nothing and taking nothing away, that I had been the victim of very gross deceit. This strange woman, whom I had met in the ruins of a place called Kôr, without any doubt had thrown a glamour over my senses and at the moment almost caused me to believe much that is quite unbelievable.

For instance, she had told me ridiculous stories as to interviews between herself and certain heathen goddesses, though it is true that, almost with her next breath, these she qualified or contradicted. Also, she had suggested that her life had been prolonged far beyond our mortal span, for hundreds and hundreds of years, indeed; which, as Euclid says, is absurd, and had pretended to supernatural powers, which is still more absurd. Moreover, by a clever use of some hypnotic or mesmeric power, she had feigned to transport me to some place beyond the earth and in the Halls of Hades to show me what is veiled from the eyes of man, and not only me, but the savage warrior Umhlopekazi, commonly called Umslopogaas of the Axe, who, with Hans, a Hottentot, was my companion upon that adventure. There were like things equally incredible, such as her appearance, when all seemed lost, in the battle with the troll-like Rezu. To omit these, the sum of it was that I had been shamefully duped, and if anyone finds himself in that position, as most people have at one time or another in their lives, Wisdom suggests that he had better keep the circumstances to himself.

Well, so the matter stood, or rather lay in the recesses of my mind— and in the cupboard where I hide my papers—when one evening someone, as a matter of fact it was Captain Good, an individual of romantic tendencies who is fond, sometimes I think too fond, of fiction, brought a book to this house which he insisted over and over again really I must peruse.

Ascertaining that it was a novel I declined, for to tell the truth I am not fond of romance in any shape, being a person who has found the hard facts of life of sufficient interest as they stand.

Reading I admit I like, but in this matter, as in everything else, my range is limited. I study the Bible, especially the Old Testament, both because of its sacred lessons and of the majesty of the language of its inspired translators; whereof that of Ayesha, which I render so poorly from her flowing and melodious Arabic, reminded me. For poetry I turn to Shakespeare, and, at the other end of the scale, to the Ingoldsby Legends, many of which I know almost by heart, while for current affairs I content myself with the newspapers.

For the rest I peruse anything to do with ancient Egypt that I happen to come across, because this land and its history have a queer fascination for me, that perhaps has its roots in occurrences or dreams of which this is not the place to speak. Lastly now and again I read one of the Latin or Greek authors in a translation, since I regret to say that my lack of education does not enable me to do so in the original. But for modern fiction I have no taste, although from time to time I sample it in a railway train and occasionally am amused by such excursions into the poetic and unreal.

So it came about that the more Good bothered me to read this particular romance, the more I determined that I would do nothing of the sort. Being a persistent person, however, when he went away about ten o'clock at night, he deposited it by my side, under my nose indeed, so that it might not be overlooked. Thus it came about that I could not help seeing some Egyptian hieroglyphics in an oval on the cover, also the title, and underneath it your own name, my friend, all of which excited my curiosity, especially the title, which was brief and enigmatic, consisting indeed of one word, "*She*."

I took up the work and on opening it the first thing my eye fell upon was a picture of a veiled woman, the sight of which made my heart stand still, so painfully did it remind me of a certain veiled woman whom once it had been my fortune to meet. Glancing from it to the printed page one word seemed to leap at me. It was *Kôr*! Now of veiled women there are plenty in the world, but were there also two Kôrs?

Then I turned to the beginning and began to read. This happened in the autumn when the sun does not rise till about six, but it was broad daylight before I ceased from reading, or rather rushing through that book.

Oh! what was I to make of it? For here in its pages (to say nothing of old Billali, who, by the way lied, probably to order, when he told Mr. Holly that no white man had visited his country for many generations, and those gloomy, man-eating

Amahagger scoundrels) once again I found myself face to face with *She-who-commands*, now rendered as *She-who- must-be-obeyed*, which means much the same thing—in her case at least; yes, with Ayesha the lovely, the mystic, the changeful and the imperious.

Moreover the history filled up many gaps in my own limited experiences of that enigmatical being who was half divine (though, I think, rather wicked or at any rate unmoral in her way) and yet all woman. It is true that it showed her in lights very different from and higher than those in which she had presented herself to me. Yet the substratum of her character was the same, or rather of her characters, for of these she seemed to have several in a single body, being, as she said of herself to me, "not One but Many and not Here but Everywhere."

Further, I found the story of Kallikrates, which I had set down as a mere falsehood invented for my bewilderment, expanded and explained. Or rather not explained, since, perhaps that she might deceive, to me she had spoken of this murdered Kallikrates without enthusiasm, as a handsome person to whom, because of an indiscretion of her youth, she was bound by destiny and whose return—somewhat to her sorrow—she must wait. At least she did so at first, though in the end when she bared her heart at the moment of our farewell, she vowed she loved him only and was "appointed" to him "by a divine decree."

Also I found other things of which I knew nothing, such as the Fire of Life with its fatal gift of indefinite existence, although I remember that like the giant Rezu whom Umslopogaas defeated, she did talk of a "Cup of Life" of which she had drunk, that might have been offered to my lips, had I been politic, bowed the knee and shown more faith in her and her supernatural pretensions.

Lastly I saw the story of her end, and as I read it I wept, yes, I confess I wept, although I feel sure that she will return again. Now I understood why she had quailed and even seemed to shrivel when, in my last interview with her, stung beyond endurance by her witcheries and sarcasms, I had suggested that even for her with all her powers, Fate might reserve one of its shrewdest blows. Some prescience had told her that if the words seemed random, Truth spoke through my lips, although, and this was the worst of it, she did not know what weapon would deal the stroke or when and where it was doomed to fall.

I was amazed, I was overcome, but as I closed that book I made up my mind, first that I would continue to preserve absolute silence as to Ayesha and my dealings with her, as, during my life, I was bound by oath to do, and secondly that I would *not* cause my manuscript to be destroyed. I did not feel that I had any right to do so in view of what already had been published to the world. There let it lie to appear one day, or not to appear, as might be fated. Meanwhile my lips were sealed. I would give Good back his book without comment and—buy another copy!

One more word. It is clear that I did not touch more than the fringe of the real Ayesha. In a thousand ways she bewitched and deceived me so that I never plumbed her nature's depths. Perhaps this was my own fault because from the first I shewed a lack of faith in her and she wished to pay me back in her own fashion, or perhaps she had other private reasons for her secrecy. Certainly the character she discovered to me differed in many ways from that which she revealed to Mr. Holly and to Leo Vincey, or Kallikrates, whom, it seems, once she slew in her jealousy and rage.

She told me as much as she thought it fit that I should know, and no more!

Allan Quatermain.

The Grange, Yorkshire.

The Talisman

I believe it was the old Egyptians, a very wise people, probably indeed much wiser than we know, for in the leisure of their ample centuries they had time to think out things, who declared that each individual personality is made up of six or seven different elements, although the Bible only allows us three, namely, body, soul, and spirit. The body that the man or woman wore, if I understand their theory aright which perhaps I, an ignorant person, do not, was but a kind of sack or fleshly covering containing these different principles. Or mayhap it did not contain them all, but was simply a house as it were, in which they lived from time to time and seldom all together, although one or more of them was present continually, as though to keep the place warmed and aired.

This is but a casual illustrative suggestion, for what right have I, Allan Quatermain, out of my little reading and probably erroneous deductions, to form any judgment as to the theories of the old Egyptians? Still these, as I understand them, suffice to furnish me with the text that man is not one, but many, in which connection it may be remembered that often in Scripture he is spoken of as being the home of many demons, seven, I think. Also, to come to another far-off example, the Zulus talk of their witch-doctors as being inhabited by "a multitude of spirits."

Anyhow of one thing I am quite sure, we are not always the same. Different personalities actuate us at different times. In one hour passion of this sort or the other is our lord; in another we are reason itself. In one hour we follow the basest appetites; in another we hate them and the spirit arising through our mortal murk shines within or above us like a star. In one hour our desire is to kill and spare not; in another we are filled with the holiest compassion even towards an insect or a snake, and are ready to forgive like a god. Everything rules us in turn, to such an extent indeed, that sometimes one begins to wonder whether we really rule anything.

Now the reason of all this homily is that I, Allan, the most practical and unimaginative of persons, just a homely, half-educated hunter and trader who chances to have seen a good deal of the particular little world in which his lot was cast, at one period of my life became the victim of spiritual longings.

I am a man who has suffered great bereavements in my time such as have seared my soul, since, perhaps because of my rather primitive and simple nature, my affections are very strong. By day or night I can never forget those whom I have loved and whom I believe to have loved me.

For you know, in our vanity some of us are apt to hold that certain people with whom we have been intimate upon the earth, really did care for us and, in our still greater vanity—or should it be called madness?—to imagine that they still care for us after they have left the earth and entered on some new state of society and surroundings which, if they exist, inferentially are much more congenial than any they can have experienced here. At times, however, cold doubts strike us as to this matter, of which we long to know the truth. Also behind looms a still blacker doubt, namely whether they live at all.

For some years of my lonely existence these problems haunted me day by day, till at length I desired above everything on earth to lay them at rest in one way or another. Once, at Durban, I met a man who was a spiritualist to whom I confided a little of my perplexities. He laughed at me and said that they could be settled with the greatest ease. All I had to do was to visit a certain local medium who for a fee of one guinea would tell me everything I wanted to know. Although I rather grudged the guinea, being more than usually hard up at the time, I called upon this person, but over the results of that visit, or rather the lack of them, I draw a veil.

My queer and perhaps unwholesome longing, however, remained with me and would not be abated. I consulted a clergyman of my acquaintance, a good and spiritually-minded man, but he could only shrug his shoulders and refer me to the Bible, saying, quite rightly I doubt not, that with what it reveals I ought to be contented. Then I read certain mystical books which were recommended to me. These were full of fine words, undiscoverable in a pocket dictionary, but really took me no forwarder, since in them I found nothing that I could not have invented myself, although while I was actually studying them, they seemed to convince me. I even tackled Swedenborg, or rather samples of him, for he is very copious, but without satisfactory results. [Ha!— JB]

Then I gave up the business.

Some months later I was in Zululand and being near the Black Kloof where he dwelt, I paid a visit to my acquaintance of whom I have written elsewhere, the wonderful and ancient dwarf, Zikali, known as "The-Thing-that-should-never-have-been-born," also more universally among the Zulus as "Opener-of-Roads." When we had talked of many things connected with the state of Zululand and its politics, I rose to leave for my waggon, since I never cared for sleeping in the Black Kloof if it could be avoided.

"Is there nothing else that you want to ask me, Macumazahn?" asked the old dwarf, tossing back his long hair and looking at—I had almost written through—me.

I shook my head.

"That is strange, Macumazahn, for I seem to see something written on your mind—something to do with spirits."

Then I remembered all the problems that had been troubling me, although in truth I had never thought of propounding them to Zikali.

"Ah! it comes back, does it?" he exclaimed, reading my thought. "Out with it, then, Macumazahn, while I am in a mood to answer, and before I grow tired, for you are an old friend of mine and will so remain till the end, many years hence, and if I can serve you, I will."

I filled my pipe and sat down again upon the stool of carved red-wood which had been brought for me.

"You are named 'Opener-of-Roads,' are you not, Zikali?" I said.

"Yes, the Zulus have always called me that, since before the days of Chaka. But what of names, which often enough mean nothing at all?"

"Only that *I* want to open a road, Zikali, that which runs across the River of Death."

"Oho!" he laughed, "it is very easy," and snatching up a little assegai that lay beside him, he proffered it to me, adding, "Be brave now and fall on that. Then before I have counted sixty the road will be wide open, but whether you will see anything on it I cannot tell you."

Again I shook my head and answered,

"It is against our law. Also while I still live I desire to know whether I shall meet certain others on that road after my time has come to cross the River. Perhaps you who deal with spirits, can prove the matter to me, which no one else seems able to do."

"Oho!" laughed Zikali again. "What do my ears hear? Am I, the poor Zulu cheat, as you will remember once you called me, Macumazahn, asked to show that which is hidden from all the wisdom of the great White People?"

"The question is," I answered with irritation, "not what you are asked to do, but what you can do."

"That I do not know yet, Macumazahn. Whose spirits do you desire to see? If that of a woman called Mameena is one of them, I think that perhaps I whom she loved——"

"She is *not* one of them, Zikali. Moreover, if she loved you, you paid back her love with death."

"Which perhaps was the kindest thing I could do, Macumazahn, for reasons that you may be able to guess, and others with which I will not trouble you. But if not hers, whose? Let me look, let me look! Why, there seems to be two of them, head-wives, I mean, and I thought that white men only took one wife. Also a multitude of others; their faces float up in the water of your mind. An old man with grey hair, little children, perhaps they were brothers and sisters, and some who may be friends. Also very clear indeed that Mameena whom you do not wish to see. Well, Macumazahn, this is unfortunate, since she is the only one whom I can show you, or rather put you in the way of finding. Unless indeed there are other Kaffir women——"

"What do you mean?" I asked.

"I mean, Macumazahn, that only black feet travel on the road which I can open; over those in which ran white blood I have no power."

"Then it is finished," I said, rising again and taking a step or two towards the gate.

"Come back and sit down, Macumazahn. I did not say so. Am I the only ruler of magic in Africa, which I am told is a big country?"

I came back and sat down, for my curiosity, a great failing with me, was excited.

"Thank you, Zikali," I said, "but I will have no dealings with more of your witch-doctors."

"No, no, because you are afraid of them; quite without reason, Macumazahn, seeing that they are all cheats except myself. I am the last child of wisdom, the rest are stuffed with lies, as Chaka found out when he killed every one of them whom he could catch. But perhaps there might be a white doctor who would have rule over white spirits."

"If you mean missionaries——" I began hastily.

"No, Macumazahn, I do not mean your praying men who are cast in one mould and measured with one rule, and say what they are taught to say, not thinking for themselves."

"Some of them think, Zikali."

"Yes, and then the others fall on them with big sticks. The real priest is he to whom the Spirit comes, not he who feeds upon its wrappings, and speaks through a mask carved by his father's fathers. I am a priest like that, which is why all my fellowship have hated me."

"If so, you have paid back their hate, Zikali, but cease to cast round the lion, like a timid hound, and tell me what you mean. Of whom do you speak?"

"That is the trouble, Macumazahn. I do not know. This lion, or rather lioness, lies hid in the caves of a very distant mountain and I have never seen her—in the flesh."

"Then how can you talk of what you have never seen?"

"In the same way, Macumazahn, that your priests talk of what they have never seen, because they, or a few of them, have knowledge of it. I will tell you a secret. All seers who live at the same time, if they are great, commune with each other because they are akin and their spirits meet in sleep or dreams. Therefore I know of a mistress of our craft, a very lioness among jackals, who for thousands of years has lain sleeping in the northern caves and, humble though I am, she knows of me."

"Quite so," I said, yawning, "but perhaps, Zikali, you will come to the point of the spear. What of her? How is she named, and if she exists will she help me?"

"I will answer your question backwards, Macumazahn. I think that she will help you if you help her, in what way I do not know, because although witch-doctors sometimes work without pay, as I am doing now, Macumazahn, witch-doctoresses never do. As for her name, the only one that she has among our company is 'Queen,' because she is the first of all of them and the most beauteous among women. For the rest I can tell you nothing, except that she has always been and I suppose, in this shape or in that, will always be while the world lasts, because she has found the secret of life unending."

"You mean that she is immortal, Zikali," I answered with a smile.

"I do not say that, Macumazahn, because my little mind cannot shape the thought of immortality. But when I was a babe, which is far ago, she had lived so long that scarce would she knew the difference between then and now, and already in her breast was all wisdom gathered. I know it, because although, as I have said, we have never seen each other, at times we walk together in our sleep, for thus she shares her loneliness, and I think, though this may be but a dream, that last night she told me to send you on to her to seek an answer to certain questions which you would put to me to-day. Also to me she seemed to desire that you should do her a service; I know not what service."

Now I grew angry and asked,

"Why does it please you to fool me, Zikali, with such talk as this? If there is any truth in it, show me where the woman called *Queen* lives and how I am to come to her."

The old wizard took up the little assegai which he had offered to me and with its blade raked our ashes from the fire that always burnt in front of him. While he did so, he talked to me, as I thought in a random fashion, perhaps to distract my attention, of a certain white man whom he said I should meet upon my journey and of his affairs, also of other matters, none of which interested me much at the time. These ashes he patted down flat and then on them drew a map with the point of his spear, making grooves for streams, certain marks for bush and forest, wavy lines for water and swamps and little heaps for hills.

When he had finished it all he bade me come round the fire and study the picture across which by an after-thought he drew a wandering furrow with the edge of the assegai to represent a river, and gathered the ashes in a lump at the northern end to signify a large mountain.

"Look at it well, Macumazahn," he said, "and forget nothing, since if you make this journey and forget, you die. Nay, no need to copy it in that book of yours, for see, I will stamp it on your mind."

Then suddenly he gathered up the warm ashes in a double handful and threw them into my face, muttering something as he did so and adding aloud,

"There, now you will remember."

"Certainly I shall," I answered, coughing, "and I beg that you will not play such a joke upon me again."

As a matter of fact, whatever may have been the reason, I never forgot any detail of that extremely intricate map.

"That big river must be the Zambesi," I stuttered, "and even then the mountain of your Queen, if it be her mountain, is far away, and how can I come there alone?"

"I don't know, Macumazahn, though perhaps you might do so in company. At least I believe that in the old days people used to travel to the place, since I have heard a great city stood there once which was the heart of a mighty empire."

Now I pricked up my ears, for though I believed nothing of Zikali's story of a wonderful Queen, I was always intensely interested in past civilisations and their relics. Also I knew that the old wizard's knowledge was extensive and peculiar, however he came by it, and I did not think that he would lie to me in this matter. Indeed to tell the truth, then and there I made up my mind that if it were in any way possible, I would attempt this journey.

"How did people travel to the city, Zikali?"

"By sea, I suppose, Macumazahn, but I think that you will be wise not to try that road, since I believe that on the sea side the marshes are now impassable and you will be safer on your feet."

"You want me to go on this adventure, Zikali. Why? I know you never do anything without motive."

"Oho! Macumazahn, you are clever and see deeper into the trunk of a tree than most. Yes, I want you to go for three reasons. First, that you may satisfy your soul on certain matters and I would help you to do so. Secondly, because I want to satisfy mine, and thirdly, because I know that you will come back safe to be a prop to me in things that will happen in days unborn. Otherwise I would have told you nothing of this story, since it is necessary to me that you should remain living beneath the sun."

"Have done, Zikali. What is it that you desire?"

"Oh! a great deal that I shall get, but chiefly two things, so with the rest I will not trouble you. First I desire to know to know whether these dreams of mine of a wonderful white witch-doctoress, or witch, and of my converse with her are indeed more than dreams. Next I would learn whether certain plots of mine at which I have worked for years, will succeed."

"What plots, Zikali, and how can my taking a distant journey tell you anything about them?"

"You know them well enough, Macumazahn; they have to do with the overthrow of a Royal House that has worked me bitter wrong. As to how your journey can help me, why, thus. You shall promise to me to ask of this Queen whether Zikali, Opener-of-Roads, shall triumph or be overthrown in that on which he has set his heart."

"As you seem to know this witch so well, why do you not ask her yourself, Zikali?"

"To ask is one thing, Macumazahn. To get an answer is another. I have asked in the watches of the night, and the reply was, 'Come hither and perchance I will tell you.' 'Queen,' I said, 'how can I come save in the spirit, who am an ancient and a crippled dwarf scarcely able to stand upon my feet?'

"'Then send a messenger, Wizard, and be sure that he is white, for of black savages I have seen more than enough. Let him bear a token also that he comes from you and tell me of it in your sleep. Moreover let that token be something of power which will protect him on the journey.'

"Such is the answer that comes to me in my dreams, Macumazahn."

"Well, what token will you give me, Zikali?"

He groped about in his robe and produced a piece of ivory of the size of a large chessman, that had a hole in it, through which ran a plaited cord of the stiff hairs from an elephant's tail. On this article, which was of a rusty brown colour, he breathed, then having whispered to it for a while, handed it to me.

I took the talisman, for such I guessed it to be, idly enough, held it to the light to examine it, and started back so violently that almost I let it fall. I do not quite know why I started, but I think it was because some influence seemed to leap from it to me. Zikali started also and cried out,

"Have a care, Macumazahn. Am I young that I can bear bring dashed to the ground?"

"What do you mean?" I asked, still staring at the thing which I perceived to be a most wonderfully fashioned likeness of the old dwarf himself as he appeared before me crouched upon the ground. There were the deepset eyes, the great head, the toad-like shape, the long hair, all.

"It is a clever carving, is it not, Macumazahn? I am skilled in that art, you know, and therefore can judge of carving."

"Yes, I know," I answered, bethinking me of another statuette of his which he had given to me on the morrow of the death of her from whom it was modelled. "But what of the thing?"

"Macumazahn, it has come down to me through the ages. As you may have heard, all great doctors when they die pass on their wisdom and something of their knowledge to another doctor of spirits who is still living on the earth, that nothing may be lost, or as little as possible. Also I have learned that to such likenesses as these may be given the strength of him or her from whom they were shaped."

Now I bethought me of the old Egyptians and their *Ka* statues of which I had read, and that these statues, magically charmed and set in the tombs of the departed, were supposed to be inhabited everlastingly by the Doubles of the dead endued with more power even than ever these possessed in life. But of this I said nothing to Zikali, thinking that it would take too much explanation, though I wondered very much how he had come by the same idea.

"When that ivory is hung over your heart, Macumazahn, where you must always wear it, learn that with it goes the strength of Zikali; the thought that would have been his thought and the wisdom that is his wisdom, will be your companions, as much as though he walked at your side and could instruct you in every peril. Moreover north and south and east and west this image is known to men who, when they see it, will bow down and obey, opening a road to him who wears the medicine of the Opener-of-Roads."

"Indeed," I said, smiling, "and what is this colour on the ivory?"

"I forget, Macumazahn, who have had it a great number of years, ever since it descended to me from a forefather of mine, who was fashioned in the same mould as I am. It looks like blood, does it not? It is a pity that Mameena is not still alive, since she whose memory was so excellent might have been able to tell you," and as he spoke, with a motion that was at once sure and swift, he threw the loop of elephant hair over my head.

Hastily I changed the subject, feeling that after his wont this old wizard, the most terrible man whom ever I knew, who had been so much concerned with the tragic death of Mameena, was stabbing at me in some hidden fashion.

"You tell me to go on this journey," I said, "and not alone. Yet for companion you give me only an ugly piece of ivory shaped as no man ever was," here I got one back at Zikali, "and from the look of it, steeped in blood, which ivory, if I had my way, I would throw into the camp fire. Who, then, am I to take with me?"

"Don't do that, Macumazahn—I mean throw the ivory into the fire— since I have no wish to burn before my time, and if you do, you who have worn it might burn with me. At least certainly you would die with the magic thing and go to acquire knowledge more quickly than you desire. No, no, and do not try to take it off your neck, or rather try if you will."

I did try, but something seemed to prevent me from accomplishing my purpose of giving the carving back to Zikali as I wished to do. First my pipe got in the way of my hand, then the elephant hairs caught in the collar of my coat; then a pang of rheumatism to which I was accustomed from an old lion-bite, developed of a sudden in my arm, and lastly I grew tired of bothering about the thing.

Zikali, who had been watching my movements, burst out into one of his terrible laughs that seemed to fill the whole kloof and to re-echo from its rocky walls. It died away and he went on, without further reference to the talisman or image.

"You asked whom you were to take with you, Macumazahn. Well, as to this I must make inquiry of those who know. Man, my medicines!"

From the shadows in the hut behind darted out a tall figure carrying a great spear in one hand and in the other a catskin bag which with a salute he laid down at the feet of his master. This salute, by the way, was that of a Zulu word which means "Lord" or "Home" of Ghosts.

Zikali groped in the bag and produced from it certain knuckle-bones.

"A common method," he muttered, "such as every vulgar wizard uses, but one that is quick and, as the matter concerned is small, will serve my turn. Let us see now, whom you shall take with you, Macumazahn."

Then he breathed upon the bones, shook them up in his thin hands and with a quick turn of the wrist, threw them into the air. After this he studied them carefully, where they lay among the ashes which he had raked out of the fire, those that he had used for the making of his map.

"Do you know a man named Umslopogaas, Macumazahn, the chief of a tribe that is called The People of the Axe, whose titles of praise are Bulalio or the Slaughterer, and Woodpecker, the latter from the way he handles his ancient axe? He is a savage fellow, but one of high blood and higher courage, a great captain in his way, though he will never come to anything, save a glorious death—in your company, I think, Macumazahn." (Here he studied the bones again for a while.) "Yes, I am sure, in your company, though not upon this journey."

"I have heard of him," I answered cautiously. "It is said in the land that he is a son of Chaka, the great king of the Zulus."

"Is it, Macumazahn? And is it said also that he was the slayer of Chaka's brother, Dingaan, also the lover of the fairest woman that the Zulus have ever seen, who was called Nada the Lily? Unless indeed a certain Mameena, who, I seem to remember, was a friend of yours, may have been even more beautiful?"

"I know nothing of Nada the Lily," I answered.

"No, no, Mameena, 'the Waiting Wind,' has blown over her fame, so why should you know of one who has been dead a long while? Why also, Macumazahn, do you always bring women into every business? I begin to believe that although you are so strict in a white man's fashion, you must be too fond of them, a weakness which makes for ruin to any man. Well, now, I think that this wolf-man, this axe-man, this warrior, Umslopogaas should be a good fellow to you on your journey to visit the white witch, Queen—another woman by the way, Macumazahn, and therefore one of whom you should be careful. Oh! yes, he will come with you—because of a man called Lousta and a woman named Monazi, a wife of his who hates him and does—not hate Lousta. I am almost sure that he will come with you, so do not stop to ask questions about him."

"Is there anyone else?" I inquired.

Zikali glanced at the bones again, poking them about in the ashes with his toe, then replied with a yawn,

"You seem to have a little yellow man in your service, a clever snake who knows how to creep through grass, and when to strike and when to lie hidden. I should take him too, if I were you."

"You know well that I have such a man, Zikali, a Hottentot named Hans, clever in his way but drunken, very faithful too, since he loved my father before me. He is cooking my supper in the waggon now. Are there to be any others?"

"No, I think you three will be enough, with a guard of soldiers from the People of the Axe, for you will meet with fighting and a ghost or two. Umslopogaas has always one at his elbow named Nada, and perhaps you have several. For instance, there was a certain Mameena whom I always seem to feel about me when you are near, Macumazahn.

"Why, the wind is rising again, which is odd on so still an evening. Listen to how it wails, yes, and stirs your hair, though mine hangs straight enough. But why do I talk of ghosts, seeing that you travel to seek other ghosts, white ghosts, beyond my ken, who can only deal with those who were black?

"Good-night, Macumazahn, good-night. When you return from visiting the white Queen, that Great One beneath those feet I, Zikali, who am also great in my way, am but a grain of dust, come and tell me her answer to my question.

"Meanwhile, be careful always to wear that pretty little image which I have given you, as a young lover sometimes wears a lock of hair cut from the head of some fool-girl that he thinks is fond of him. It will bring you safety and luck, Macumazahn, which, for the most part, is more than the lock of hair does to the lover. Oh! it is a strange world, full of jest to those who can see the strings that work it. I am one of them, and perhaps, Macumazahn, you are another, or will be before all is done—or begun.

"Good-night, and good fortune to you on your journeyings, and, Macumazahn, although you are so fond of women, be careful not to fall in love with that white Queen, because it would make others jealous; I mean some who you have lost sight of for a while, also I think that being under a curse of her own, she is not one whom you can put into your sack. *Oho! Oho-ho!* Slave, bring me my blanket, it grows cold, and my medicine also, that which protects me from the ghosts, who are thick to-night. Macumazahn brings them, I think. *Oho-ho!*"

I turned to depart but when I had gone a little way Zikali called me back again and said, speaking very low,

"When you meet this Umslopogaas, as you will meet him, he who is called the Woodpecker and the Slaughterer, say these words to him,

"'A bat has been twittering round the hut of the Opener-of-Roads, and to his ears it squeaked the name of a certain Lousta and the name of a woman called Monazi. Also it twittered another greater name that may not be uttered, that of an elephant who shakes the earth, and said that this elephant sniffs the air with his trunk and grows angry, and sharpens his tusks to dig a certain Woodpecker out of his hole in a tree that grows near the Witch Mountain. Say, too, that the Opener-of- Roads thinks that this Woodpecker would be wise to fly north for a while in the company of one who watches by night, lest harm should come to a bird that pecks at the feet of the great and chatters of it in his nest.'"

Then Zikali waved his hand and I went, wondering into what plot I had stumbled.

The Messengers

I did not rest as I should that night who somehow was never able to sleep well in the neighbourhood of the Black Kloof. I suppose that Zikali's constant talk about ghosts, with his hints and innuendoes concerning those who were dead, always affected my nerves till, in a subconscious way, I began to believe that such things existed and were hanging about me. Many people are open to the power of suggestion, and I am afraid that I am one of them.

However, the sun which has such strength to kill noxious things, puts an end to ghosts more quickly even than it does to other evil vapours and emanations, and when I woke up to find it shining brilliantly in a pure heaven, I laughed with much heartiness over the whole affair.

Going to the spring near which we were outspanned, I took off my shirt to have a good wash, still chuckling at the memory of all the hocus-pocus of my old friend, the Opener-of-Roads.

While engaged in this matutinal operation I struck my hand against something and looking, observed that it was the hideous little ivory image of Zikali, which he had set about my neck. The sight of the thing and the memory of his ridiculous talk about it, especially of its assertion that it had come down to him through the ages, which it could not have done, seeing that it was a likeness of himself, irritated me so much that I proceeded to take it off with the full intention of throwing it into the spring.

As I was in the act of doing this, from a clump of reeds mixed with bushes, quite close to me, there came a sound of hissing, and suddenly above them appeared the head of a great black *immamba*, perhaps the deadliest of all our African snakes, and the only one I know which will attack man without provocation.

Leaving go of the image, I sprang back in a great hurry towards where my gun lay. Then the snake vanished and making sure that it had departed to its hole, which was probably at a distance, I returned to the pool, and once more began to take off the talisman in order to consign it to the bottom of the pool.

After all, I reflected, it was a hideous and probably a blood-stained thing which I did not in the least wish to wear about my neck like a lady's love-token.

Just as it was coming over my head, suddenly from the other side of the bush that infernal snake popped up again, this time, it was clear, really intent on business. It began to move towards me in the lightning-like way *immambas* have, hissing and flicking its tongue.

I was too quick for my friend, however, for snatching up the gun that I had lain down beside me, I let it have a charge of buckshot in the neck which nearly cut it in two, so that it fell down and expired with hideous convulsive writhings.

Hearing the shot Hans came running from the waggon to see what was the matter. Hans, I should say, was that same Hottentot who had been the companion of most of my journeyings since my father's day. He was with me when as a young fellow I accompanied Retief to Dingaan's kraal, and like myself, escaped the massacre. Also we shared many other adventures, including the great one in the Land of the Ivory Child where he slew the huge elephant-god, Jana, and himself was slain. But of this journey we did not dream in those days.

For the rest Hans was a most entirely unprincipled person, but as the Boers say, "as clever as a waggonload of monkeys." Also he drank when he got the chance. One good quality he had, however; no man was ever more faithful, and perhaps it would be true to say that neither man nor woman ever loved me, unworthy, quite so well.

In appearance he rather resembled an antique and dilapidated baboon; his face was wrinkled like a dried nut and his quick little eyes were bloodshot. I never knew what his age was, any more than he did himself, but the years had left him tough as whipcord and absolutely untiring. Lastly he was perhaps the best hand at following a spoor that ever I knew and up to a hundred and fifty yards or so, a very deadly shot with a rifle especially when he used a little single- barrelled, muzzle-loading gun of mine made by Purdey which he named *Intombi* or Maiden. Of that gun, however, I have written in "The Holy Flower" and elsewhere.

"What is it, Baas?" he asked. "Here there are no lions, nor any game."

"Look the other side of the bush, Hans."

He slipped round it, making a wide circle with his usual caution, then, seeing the snake which was, by the way, I think, the biggest *immamba* I ever killed, suddenly froze, as it were, in a stiff attitude that reminded me of a pointer when it scents game. Having made sure that it was dead, he nodded and said,

"Black *'mamba*, or so you would call it, though I know it for something else."

"What else, Hans?"

"One of the old witch-doctor Zikali's spirits which he sets at the mouth of this kloof to warn him of who comes or goes. I know it well, and so do others. I saw it listening behind a stone when you were up the kloof last evening talking with the Opener-of-Roads."

"Then Zikali will lack a spirit," I answered, laughing, "which perhaps he will not miss amongst so many. It serves him right for setting the brute on me."

"Quite so, Baas. He will be angry. I wonder why he did it?" he added suspiciously, "seeing that he is such a friend of yours."

"He didn't do it, Hans. These snakes are very fierce and give battle, that is all."

Hans paid no attention to my remark, which probably he thought only worthy of a white man who does not understand, but rolled his yellow, bloodshot eyes about, as though in search of explanations. Presently they fell upon the ivory that hung about my neck, and he started.

"Why do you wear that pretty likeness of the Great One yonder over your heart, as I have known you do with things that belonged to women in past days, Baas? Do you know that it is Zikali's Great Medicine, nothing less, as everyone does throughout the land? When Zikali sends an order far away, he always sends that image with it, for then he who receives the order knows that he must obey or die. Also the messenger knows that he will come to no harm if he does not take it off, because, Baas, the image is Zikali himself, and Zikali is the image. They are one and the same. Also it is the image of his father's father's father—or so he says."

"That is an odd story," I said.

Then I told Hans as much as I thought advisable of how this horrid little talisman came into my possession.

Hans nodded without showing any surprise.

"So we are going on a long journey," he said. "Well, I thought it was time that we did something more than wander about these tame countries selling blankets to stinking old women and so forth, Baas. Moreover, Zikali does not wish that you should come to harm, doubtless because he does wish to make use of you afterwards—oh! it's safe to talk now when that spirit is away looking for another snake. What were you doing with the Great Medicine, Baas, when the *'mamba* attacked you?"

"Taking it off to throw it into the pool, Hans, as I do not like the thing. I tried twice and each time the *immamba* appeared."

"Of course it appeared, Baas, and what is more, if you had taken that Medicine off and thrown it away *you* would have disappeared, since the *'mamba* would have killed you. Zikali wanted to show you that, Baas, and that is why he set the snake at you."

"You are a superstitious old fool, Hans."

"Yes, Baas, but my father knew all about that Great Medicine before me, for he was a bit of a doctor, and so does every wizard and witch for a thousand miles or more. I tell you, Baas, it is known by all though no one ever talks about it, no, not even the king himself. Baas, speaking to you, not with the voice of Hans the old drunkard, but with that of the Predikant, your reverend father, who made so good a Christian of me and who tells me to do so from up in Heaven where the hot fires are which the wood feeds of itself, I beg you not to try to throw away the Medicine again, or if you wish to do so, to leave me behind on this journey. For you see, Baas, although I am now so good, almost like one of those angels with the pretty goose's wings in the pictures, I feel that I should like to grow a little better before I go to the Place of Fires to make report to your reverend father, the Predikant."

Thinking of how horrified my dear father would be if he could hear all this string of ridiculous nonsense and learn the result of his moral and religious lessons on raw Hottentot material, I burst out laughing. But Hans went on as gravely as a judge,

"Wear the Great Medicine, Baas, wear it; part with the liver inside you before you part with that, Baas. It may not be as pretty or smell as sweet as a woman's hair in a little gold bottle, but it is much more useful. The sight of the woman's hair will only make you sick in your stomach and cause you to remember a lot of things which you had much better forget, but the Great Medicine, or rather Zikali who is in it, will keep the assegais and sickness out of you and turn back bad magic on to the heads of those who sent it, and always bring us plenty to eat and perhaps, if we are lucky, a little to drink too sometimes."

"Go away," I said, "I want to wash."

"Yes, Baas, but with the Baas's leave I will sit on the other side of that bush with the gun—not to look at the Baas without his clothes, because white people are always so ugly that it makes me feel ill to see them undressed, also because—the Baas will forgive me—but because they smell. No, not for that, but just to see that no other snake comes."

"Get out of the road, you dirty little scoundrel, and stop your impudence," I said, lifting my foot suggestively.

Thereon he scooted with a subdued grin round the other side of the bush, whence as I knew well he kept his eye fixed on me to be sure that I made no further attempt to take off the Great Medicine.

Now of this talisman I may as well say at once that I am no believer in it or its precious influences. Therefore, although it was useful sometimes, notably twice when Umslopogaas was concerned, I do not know whether personally I should have done better or worse upon that journey if I had thrown it into the pool.

It is true, however, that until quite the end of this history when it became needful to do so to save another, I never made any further attempt to remove it from my neck, not even when it rubbed a sore in my skin, because I did not wish to offend the prejudices of Hans.

It is true, moreover, that this hideous ivory had a reputation which stretched very far from the place where it was made and was regarded with great reverence by all kinds of queer people, even by the Amahagger themselves, of whom presently, as they say in pedigrees, a fact of which I found sundry proofs. Indeed, I saw a first example of it when a little while later I met that great warrior, Umslopogaas, Chief of the People of the Axe.

For, after determining firmly, for reasons which I will set out, that I would not visit this man, in the end I did so, although by then I had given up any idea of journeying across the Zambesi to look for a mysterious and non-existent witch-woman, as Zikali had suggested that I should do. To begin with I knew that his talk was all rubbish and, even if it were not, that at the bottom of it was some desire of the Opener-of-Roads that I should make a path for him to travel towards an indefinite but doubtless evil object of his own. Further, by this time I had worn through that mood of mine which had caused me to yearn for correspondence with the departed and a certain knowledge of their existence.

I wonder whether many people understand, as I do, how entirely distinct and how variable are these moods which sway us, or at any rate some of us, at sundry periods of our lives. As I think I have already suggested, at one time we are all spiritual; at another all physical; at one time we are sure that our lives here are as a dream and a shadow and that the real existence lies elsewhere; at another that these brief days of ours are the only business with which we have to do and that of it we must make the best. At one time we think our loves much more immortal than the stars; at another that they are mere shadows cast by the baleful sun of desire upon the shallow and fleeting water we call Life which seems to flow out of nowhere into nowhere. At one time we are full of faith, at another all such hopes are blotted out by a black wall of Nothingness, and so on *ad infinitum*. Only very stupid people, or humbugs, are or pretend to be, always consistent and unchanging.

To return, I determined not only that I would not travel north to seek that which no living man will ever find, certainty as to the future, but also, to show my independence of Zikali, that I would not visit this chief, Umslopogaas. So, having traded all my goods and made a fair profit (on paper), I set myself to return to Natal, proposing to rest awhile in my little house at Durban, and told Hans my mind.

"Very good, Baas," he said. "I, too, should like to go to Durban. There are lots of things there that we cannot get here," and he fixed his roving eye upon a square-faced gin bottle, which as it happened was filled with nothing stronger than water, because all the gin was drunk. "Yet, Baas, we shall not see the Berea for a long while."

"Why do you say that?" I asked sharply.

"Oh! Baas, I don't know, but you went to visit the Opener-of-Roads, did you not, and he told you to go north and lent you a certain Great Medicine, did he not?"

Here Hands proceeded to light his corncob pipe with an ash from the fire, all the time keeping his beady eyes fixed upon that part of me where he knew the talisman was hung.

"Quite true, Hans, but now I mean to show Zikali that I am not his messenger, for south or north or east or west. So to-morrow morning we cross the river and trek for Natal."

"Yes, Baas, but then why not cross it this evening? There is still light."

"I have said that we will cross it to-morrow morning," I answered with that firmness which I have read always indicates a man of character, "and I do not change my word."

"No, Baas, but sometimes other things change besides words. Will the Baas have that buck's leg for supper, or the stuff out of a tin with a dint in it, which we bought at a store two years ago? The flies have got at the buck's leg, but I cut out the bits with the maggots on it and ate them myself."

Hans was right, things do change, especially the weather. That night, unexpectedly, for when I turned in the sky seemed quite serene, there came a terrible rain long before it was due, which lasted off and on for three whole days and continued intermittently for an indefinite period. Needless to say the river, which it would have been so easy to cross on this particular evening, by the morning was a raging torrent, and so remained for several weeks.

In despair at length I trekked south to where a ford was reported, which, when reached, proved impracticable.

I tried another, a dozen miles further on, which was very hard to come to over boggy land. It looked all right and we were getting across finely, when suddenly one of the wheels sank in an unsuspected hole and there we stuck. Indeed, I believe the waggon, or bits of it, would have remained in the neighbourhood of that ford to this day, had I not managed to borrow some extra oxen belonging to a Christian Kaffir, and with their help to drag it back to the bank whence we had started.

As it happened I was only just in time, since a new storm which had burst further up the river, brought it down in flood again, a very heavy flood.

In this country, England, where I write, there are bridges everywhere and no one seems to appreciate them. If they think of them at all it is to grumble about the cost of their upkeep. I wish they could have experienced what a lack of them means in a wild country during times of excessive rain, and the same remark applied to roads. You should think more of your blessings, my friends, as the old woman said to her complaining daughter who had twins two years running, adding that they might have been triplets.

To return—after this I confessed myself beaten and gave up until such time as it should please Providence to turn off the water-tap. Trekking out of sight of that infernal river which annoyed me with its constant gurgling, I camped on a comparatively dry spot that overlooked a beautiful stretch of rolling veld. Towards sunset the clouds lifted and I saw a mile or two away a most extraordinary mountain on the lower slopes of which grew a dense forest. Its upper part, which was of bare rock, looked exactly like the seated figure of a grotesque person with the chin resting on the breast. There was the head, there were the arms, there were the knees. Indeed, the whole mass of it reminded me strongly of the effigy of Zikali which was tied about my neck, or rather of Zikali himself.

"What is that called?" I said to Hans, pointing to this strange hill, now blazing in the angry fire of the setting sun that had burst out between the storm clouds, which made it appear more ominous even than before.

"That is the Witch Mountain, Baas, where the Chief Umslopogaas and a blood brother of his who carried a great club used to hunt with the wolves. It is haunted and in a cave at the top of it lie the bones of Nada the Lily, the fair woman whose name is a song, she who was the love of Umslopogaas."

"Rubbish," I said, though I had heard something of all that story and remembered that Zikali had mentioned this Nada, comparing her beauty to that of another whom once I knew.

"Where then lives the Chief Umslopogaas?"

"They say that his town is yonder on the plain, Baas. It is called the Place of the Axe and is strongly fortified with a river round most of it, and his people are the People of the Axe. They are a fierce people, and all the country round here is uninhabited because Umslopogaas has cleaned out the tribes who used to live in it, first with his wolves and afterwards in war. He is so strong a chief and so terrible in battle that even Chaka himself was afraid of him, and they say that he brought Dingaan the King to his end because of a quarrel about this Nada. Cetywayo, the present king, too leaves him alone and to him he pays no tribute."

Whilst I was about to ask Hans from whom he had collected all this information, suddenly I heard sounds, and looking up, saw three tall men clad in full herald's dress rushing towards us at great speed.

"Here come some chips from the Axe," said Hans, and promptly bolted into the waggon.

I did not bolt because there was no time to do so without loss of dignity, but, although I wished I had my rifle with me, just sat still upon my stool and with great deliberation lighted my pipe, taking not the slightest notice of the three savage-looking fellows.

These, who I noted carried axes instead of assegais, rushed straight at me with the axes raised in such a fashion that anyone unacquainted with the habits of Zulu warriors of the old school, might have thought that they intended nothing short of murder.

As I expected, however, within about six feet of me they halted suddenly and stood there still as statues. For my part I went on lighting my pipe as though I did not see them and when at length I was obliged to lift my head, surveyed them with an air of mild interest.

Then I took a little book out of my pocket, it was my favourite copy of the Ingoldsby Legends—and began to read.

The passage which caught my eye, if "axe" be substituted for "knife" was not inappropriate. It was from "The Nurse's Story," and runs,

"But, oh! what a thing 'tis to see and to know That the bare knife is raised in the hand of the foe, Without hope to repel or to ward off the blow!"

This proceeding of mine astonished them a good deal who felt that they had, so to speak, missed fire. At last the soldier in the middle said,

"Are you blind, White Man?"

"No, Black Fellow," I answered, "but I am short-sighted. Would you be so good as to stand out of my light?" a remark which puzzled them so much that all three drew back a few paces.

When I had read a little further I came to the following lines,

"'Tis plain, As anatomists tell us, that never again, Shall life revisit the foully slain When once they've been cut through the jugular vein."

In my circumstances at that moment this statement seemed altogether too suggestive, so I shut up the book and remarked,

"If you are wanderers who want food, as I judge by your being so thin, I am sorry that I have little meat, but my servants will give you what they can."

"Ow!" said the spokesman, "he calls us wanderers! Either he must be a very great man or he is mad."

"You are right. I am a great man," I answered, yawning, "and if you trouble me too much you will see that I can be mad also. Now what do you want?"

"We are messengers from the great Chief Umslopogaas, Captain of the People of the Axe, and we want tribute," answered the man in a somewhat changed tone.

"Do you? Then you won't get it. I thought that only the King of Zululand had a right to tribute, and your Captain's name is not Cetywayo, is it?"

"Our Captain is King here," said the man still more uncertainly.

"Is he indeed? Then away with you back to him and tell this King of whom I have never heard, though I have a message for a certain Umslopogaas, that Macumazahn, Watcher-by-Night, intends to visit him to-morrow, if he will send a guide at the first light to show the best path for the waggon."

"Hearken," said the man to his companions, "this is Macumazahn himself and no other. Well, we thought it, for who else would have dared——"

Then they saluted with their axes, calling me "Chief" and other fine names, and departed as they had come, at a run, calling out that my message should be delivered and that doubtless Umslopogaas would send the guide.

So it came about that, quite contrary to my intention, after all circumstances brought me to the Town of the Axe. Even to the last moment I had not meant to go there, but when the tribute was demanded I saw that it was best to do so, and having once passed my word it could not be altered. Indeed, I felt sure that in this event there would be trouble and that my oxen would be stolen, or worse.

So Fate having issued its decree, of which Hans's version was that Zikali, or his Great Medicine, had so arranged things, I shrugged my shoulders and waited.

Umslopogaas of the Axe

Next morning at the dawn guides arrived from the Town of the Axe, bringing with them a yoke of spare oxen, which showed that its Chief was really anxious to see me. So, in due course we inspanned and started, the guides leading us by a rough but practicable road down the steep hillside to the saucer-like plain beneath, where I saw many cattle grazing. Travelling some miles across this plain, we came at last to a river of no great breadth that encircled a considerable Kaffir town on three sides, the fourth being protected by a little line of koppies which were joined together with walls. Also the place was strongly fortified with fences and in every other way known to the native mind.

With the help of the spare oxen we crossed the river safely at the ford, although it was very full, and on the further side were received by a guard of men, tall, soldierlike fellows, all of them armed with axes as the messengers had been. They led us up to the cattle enclosure in the centre of the town, which although it could be used to protect beasts in case of emergency, also served the practical purpose of a public square.

Here some ceremony was in progress, for soldiers stood round the kraal while heralds pranced and shouted. At the head of the place in front of the chief's big hut was a little group of people, among whom a big, gaunt man sat upon a stool clad in a warrior's dress with a great and very long axe hafted with wire-lashed rhinoceros horn, laid across his knees.

Our guides led me, with Hans sneaking after me like a dejected and low-bred dog (for the waggon had stopped outside the gate), across the kraal to where the heralds shouted and the big man sat yawning. At once I noted that he was a very remarkable person, broad and tall and spare of frame, with long, tough-looking arms and a fierce face which reminded me of that of the late King Dingaan. Also he had a great hole in his head above the temple where the skull had been driven in by some blow, and keen, royal-looking eyes.

He looked up and seeing me, cried out,

"What! Has a white man come to fight me for the chieftainship of the People of the Axe? Well, he is a small one."

"No," I answered quietly, "but Macumazahn, Watcher-by-Night, has come to visit you in answer to your request, O Umslopogaas; Macumazahn whose name was known in this land before yours was told of, O Umslopogaas."

The Chief heard and rising from his seat, lifted the big axe in salute.

"I greet you, O Macumazahn," he said, "who although you are small in stature, are very great indeed in fame. Have I not heard how you conquered Bangu, although Saduko slew him, and of how you gave up the six hundred head of cattle to Tshoza and the men of the Amangwane who fought with you, the cattle that were your own? Have I not heard how you led the Tulwana against the Usutu and stamped flat three of Cetywayo's regiments in the days of Panda, although, alas! because of an oath of mine I lifted no steel in that battle, I who will have nothing to do with those that spring from the blood of Senzangacona— perhaps because I smell too strongly of it, Macumazahn. Oh! yes, I have heard these and many other things concerning you, though until now it has never been my fortune to look upon your face, O Watcher-by-Night, and therefore I greet you well, Bold one, Cunning one, Upright one, Friend of us Black People."

"Thank you," I answered, "but you said something about fighting. If there is to be anything of the sort, let us get it over. If you want to fight, I am quite ready," and I tapped the rifle which I carried.

The grim Chief broke into a laugh and said,

"Listen. By an ancient law any man on this day in each year may fight me for this Chieftainship, as I fought and conquered him who held it before me, and take it from me with my life and the axe, though of late none seems to like the business. But that law was made before there were guns, or men like Macumazahn who, it is said, can hit a lizard on a wall at fifty paces. Therefore I tell you that if you wish to fight me with a rifle, O Macumazahn, I give in and you may have the chieftainship," and he laughed again in his fierce fashion.

"I think it is too hot for fighting either with guns or axes, and Chieftainships are honey that is full of stinging bees," I answered.

Then I took my seat on a stool that had been brought for me and placed by the side of Umslopogaas, after which the ceremony went on.

The heralds cried out the challenge to all and sundry to come and fight the Holder of the Axe for the chieftainship of the Axe without the slightest result, since nobody seemed to desire to do anything of the sort. Then, after a pause, Umslopogaas rose, swinging his formidable weapon round his head and declared that by right of conquest he was Chief of the Tribe for the ensuing year, an announcement that everybody accepted without surprise.

Again the heralds summoned all and sundry who had grievances, to come forward and to state them and receive redress.

After a little pause there appeared a very handsome woman with large eyes, particularly brilliant eyes that rolled as though they were in search of someone. She was finely dressed and I saw by the ornaments she wore that she held the rank of a chief's wife.

"I, Monazi, have a complaint to make," she said, "as it is the right of the humblest to do on this day. In succession to Zinita whom Dingaan slew with her children, I am your *Inkosikaas*, your head- wife, O Umslopogaas."

"That I know well enough," said Umslopogaas, "what of it?"

"This, that you neglect me for other women, as you neglected Zinita for Nada the Beautiful, Nada the witch. I am childless, as are all your wives because of the curse that this Nada left behind her. I demand that this curse should be lifted from me. For your sake I abandoned Lousta the Chief, to whom I was betrothed, and this is the end of it, that I am neglected and childless."

"Am I the Heavens Above that I can cause you to bear children, woman?" asked Umslopogaas angrily. "Would that you had clung to Lousta, my blood-brother and my friend, whom you lament, and left me alone."

"That still may chance, if I am not better treated," answered Monazi with a flash of her eyes. "Will you dismiss yonder new wife of yours and give me back my place, and will you lift the curse of Nada off me, or will you not?"

"As to the first," answered Umslopogaas, "learn, Monazi, that I will not dismiss my new wife, who at least is gentler-tongued and truer- hearted than you are. As to the second, you ask that which it is not in my power to give, since children are the gift of Heaven, and barrenness is its bane. Moreover, you have done ill to bring into this matter the name of one who is dead, who of all women was the sweetest and most innocent. Lastly, I warn you before the people to cease from your plottings or traffic with Lousta, lest ill come of them to you, or him, even though he be my blood-brother, or to both."

"Plottings!" cried Monazi in a shrill and furious voice. "Does Umslopogaas talk of plottings? Well, I have heard that Chaka the Lion left a son, and that this son has set a trap for the feet of him who sits on Chaka's throne. Perchance that king has heard it also; perchance the People of the Axe will soon have another Chief."

"Is it thus?" said Umslopogaas quietly. "And if so, will he be named Lousta?"

Then his smouldering wrath broke out and in a kind of roaring voice he went on,

"What have I done that the wives of my bosom should be my betrayers, those who would give me to death? Zinita betrayed me to Dingaan and in reward was slain, and my children with her. Now would you, Monazi, betray me to Cetywayo—though in truth there is naught to betray? Well, if so, bethink you and let Lousta bethink him of what chanced to Zinita, and of what chances to those who stand before the axe of Umslopogaas. What have I done, I say, that women should thus strive to work me ill?"

"This," answered Monazi with a mocking laugh, "that you have loved one of them too well. If he would live in peace, he who has wives should favour all alike. Least of anything should he moan continually over one who is dead, a witch who has left a curse behind her and thus insulted and do wrong to the living. Also he would be wise to attend to the matters of his own tribe and household and to cease from ambitions that may bring him to the assegai, and them with him."

"I have heard your counsel, Wife, so now begone!" said Umslopogaas, looking at her very strangely, and it seemed to me not without fear.

"Have you wives, Macumazahn?" he asked of me in a low voice when she was out of hearing.

"Only among the spirits," I answered.

"Well for you then; moreover, it is a bond between us, for I too have but one true wife and she also is among the spirits. But go rest a while, and later we will talk."

So I went, leaving the Chief to his business, thinking as I walked away of a certain message with which I was charged for him and of how into that message came names that I had just heard, namely that of a man called Lousta and of a woman called Monazi. Also I thought of the hints which in her jealous anger and disappointment at her lack of children, this woman had dropped about a plot against him who sat on the throne of Chaka, which of course must mean King Cetywayo himself.

I came to the guest-hut, which proved to be a very good place and clean; also in it I found plenty of food made ready for me and for my servants. After eating I slept for a time as it is always my fashion to do when I have nothing else on hand, since who knows for how long he may be kept awake at night? Indeed, it was not until the sun had begun to sink that a messenger came, saying that the Chief desired to see me if I had rested. So I went to his big hut which stood alone with a strong fence set round it at a distance, so that none could come within hearing of what was said, even at the door of the hut. I observed also that a man armed with an axe kept guard at the gateway in this fence round which he walked from time to time.

The Chief Umslopogaas was seated on a stool by the door of his hut with his rhinoceros-horn-handled axe which was fastened to his right wrist by a thong, leaning against his thigh, and a wolfskin hanging from his broad shoulders. Very grim and fierce he looked thus, with the red light of the sunset playing on him. He greeted me and pointed to another stool on which I sat myself down. Apparently he had been watching my eyes, for he said,

"I see that like other creatures which move at night, such as leopards and hyenas, you take note of all, O Watcher-by-Night, even of the soldier who guards this place and of where the fence is set and of how its gate is fashioned."

"Had I not done so I should have been dead long ago, O Chief."

"Yes, and because it is not my nature to do so as I should, perchance I shall soon be dead. It is not enough to be fierce and foremost in the battle, Macumazahn. He who would sleep safe and of whom, when he dies, folk will say 'He has eaten' (i.e., he has lived out his life), must do more than this. He must guard his tongue and even his thoughts! he must listen to the stirring of rats in the thatch and look for snakes in the grass; he must trust few, and least of all those who sleep upon his bosom. But those who have the Lion's blood in them or who are prone to charge like a buffalo, often neglect these matters and therefore in the end they fall into a pit."

"Yes," I answered, "especially those who have the lion's blood in them, whether that lion be man or beast."

This I said because of the rumours I had heard that this Slaughterer was in truth the son of Chaka. Therefore not knowing whether or no he were playing on the word "lion," which was Chaka's title, I wished to draw him, especially as I saw in his face a great likeness to Chaka's brother Dingaan, whom, it was whispered, this same Umslopogaas had slain. As it happened I failed, for after a pause he said,

"Why do you come to visit me, Macumazahn, who have never done so before?"

"I do not come to visit you, Umslopogaas. That was not my intention. You brought me, or rather the flooded rivers and you together brought me, for I was on my way to Natal and could not cross the drifts."

"Yet I think you have a message for me, White Man, for not long ago a certain wandering witch-doctor who came here told me to expect you and that you had words to say to me."

"Did he, Umslopogaas? Well, it is true that I have a message, though it is one that I did not mean to deliver."

"Yet being here, perchance you will deliver it, Macumazahn, for those who have messages and will not speak them, sometimes come to trouble."

"Yes, being here, I will deliver it, seeing that so it seems to be fated. Tell me, do you chance to know a certain Small One who is great, a certain Old One whose brain is young, a doctor who is called Opener-of-Roads?"

"I have heard of him, as have my forefathers for generations."

"Indeed, and if it pleases you to tell me, Umslopogaas, what might be the names of those forefathers of yours, who have heard of this doctor for generations? They must have been short-lived men and as such I should like to know of them."

"That you cannot," replied Umslopogaas shortly, "since they are *hlonipa* (i.e. not to be spoken) in this land."

"Indeed," I said again. "I thought that rule applied only to the names of kings, but of course I am but an ignorant white man who may well be mistaken on such matters of your Zulu customs."

"Yes, O Macumazahn, you may be mistaken or—you may not. It matters nothing. But what of this message of yours?"

"It came at the end of a long story, O Bulalio. But since you seek to know, these were the words of it, so nearly as I can remember them."

Then sentence by sentence I repeated to him all that Zikali had said to me when he called me back after bidding me farewell, which doubtless he did because he wished to cut his message more deeply into the tablets of my mind.

Umslopogaas listened to every syllable with a curious intentness, and then asked me to repeat it all again, which I did.

"Lousta! Monazi!" he said slowly. "Well, you heard those names to-day, did you not, White Man? And you heard certain things from the lips of this Monazi who was angry, that give colour to that talk of the Opener-of-Roads. It seems to me," he added, glancing about him and speaking in a low voice, "that what I suspected is true and that without doubt I am betrayed."

"I do not understand," I replied indifferently. "All this talk is dark to me, as is the message of the Opener-of-Roads, or rather its meaning. By whom and about what are you betrayed?"

"Let that snake sleep. Do not kick it with your foot. Suffice it you to know that my head hangs upon this matter; that I am a rat in a forked stick, and if the stick is pressed on by a heavy hand, then where is the rat?"

"Where all rats go, I suppose, that is, unless they are wise rats that bite the hand which holds the stick before it is pressed down."

"What is the rest of this story of yours, Macumazahn, which was told before the Opener-of-Roads gave you that message? Does it please you to repeat it to me that I may judge of it with my ears?"

"Certainly," I answered, "on one condition, that what the ears hear, the heart shall keep to itself alone."

Umslopogaas stooped and laid his hand upon the broad blade of the weapon beside him, saying,

"By the Axe I swear it. If I break the oath be the Axe my doom."

Then I told him the tale, as I have set it down already, thinking to myself that of it he would understand little, being but a wild warrior-man. As it chanced, however, I was mistaken, for he seemed to understand a great deal, perchance because such primitive natures are in closer touch with high and secret things than we imagine; perchance for other reasons with which I became acquainted later.

"It stands thus," he said when I had finished, "or so I think. You, Macumazahn, seek certain women who are dead to learn whether they still live, or are really dead, but so far have failed to find them. Still seeking, you asked the counsel of Zikali, Opener-of-Roads, he who among other titles is also called 'Home of Spirits.' He answered that he could not satisfy your heart because this tree was too tall for him to climb, but that far to the north there lives a certain white witch who has powers greater than his, being able to fly to the top of any tree, and to this white witch he bade you go. Have I the story right thus far?"

I answered that he had.

"Good! Then Zikali went on to choose you companions for your journey, but two, leaving out the guards or servants. I, Umhlopekazi, called Bulalio the Slaughterer, called the Woodpecker also, was one of these, and that little yellow monkey of a man whom I saw with you to-day, called Hansi, was the other. Then you made a mock of Zikali by determining not to visit me, Umhlopekazi, and not to go north to find the great white Queen of whom he had told you, but to return to Natal. Is that so?"

I said it was.

"Then the rain fell and the winds blew and the rivers rose in wrath so that you could not return to Natal, and after all by chance, or by fate, or by the will of Zikali, the wizard of wizards, you drifted here to the kraal of me, Umhlopekazi, and told me this story."

"Just so," I answered.

"Well, White Man, how am I to know that all this is not but a trap for my feet which already seem to feel cords between the toes of both of them? What token do you bring, O Watcher-by-Night? How am I to know that the Opener-of-Roads really sent me this message which has been delivered so strangely by one who wished to travel on another path? The wandering witch-doctor told me that he who came would bear some sign."

"I can't say," I answered, "at least in words. But," I added after reflection, "as you ask for a token, perhaps I might be able to show you something that would bring proof to your heart, if there were any secret place——"

Umslopogaas walked to the gateway of the fence and saw that the sentry was at his post. Then he walked round the hut casting an eye upon its roof, and muttered to me as he returned.

"Once I was caught thus. There lived a certain wife of mine who set her ear to the smoke-hole and so brought about the death of many, and among them of herself and of our children. Enter. All is safe. Yet if you talk, speak low."

So we went into the hut taking the stools with us, and seated ourselves by the fire that burned there on to which Umslopogaas threw chips of resinous wood.

"Now," he said.

I opened my shirt and by the clear light of the flame showed him the image of Zikali which hung about my neck. He stared at it, though touch it he would not. Then he stood up and lifting his great axe, he saluted the image with the word "*Makosi!*" the salute that is given to great wizards because they are supposed to be the home of many spirits.

"It is the big Medicine, the Medicine itself," he said, "that which has been known in the land since the time of Senzangacona, the father of the Zulu Royal House, and as it is said, before him."

"How can that be?" I asked, "seeing that this image represents Zikali, Opener-of-Roads, as an old man, and Senzangacona died many years ago?"

"I do not know," he answered, "but it is so. Listen. There was a certain Mopo, or as some called him, Umbopo, who was Chaka's body- servant and my foster-father, and he told me that twice this Medicine," and he pointed to the image, "was sent to Chaka, and that each time the Lion obeyed the message that came with it. A third time it was sent, but he did not obey the message and then—where was Chaka?"

Here Umslopogaas passed his hand across his mouth, a significant gesture amongst the Zulus.

"Mopo," I said, "yes, I have heard the story of Mopo, also that Chaka's body became *his* servant in the end, since Mopo killed him with the help of the princes Dingaan and Umhlangana. Also I have heard that this Mopo still lives, though not in Zululand."

"Does he, Macumazahn?" said Umslopogaas, taking snuff from a spoon and looking at me keenly over the spoon. "You seem to know a great deal, Macumazahn; too much as some might think."

"Yes," I answered, "perhaps I do know too much, or at any rate more than I want to know. For instance, O fosterling of Mopo and son of— was the lady named Baleka?—I know a good deal about *you*."

Umslopogaas stared at me and laying his hand upon the great axe, half rose. Then he sat down again.

"I think that this," and I touched the image of Zikali upon my breast, "would turn even the blade of the axe named Groan-maker," I said and paused. As nothing happened, I went on, "For instance, again I think I know—or have I dreamed it?—that a certain chief, whose mother's name I believe was Baleka—by the way, was she not one of Chaka's 'sisters'?—has been plotting against that son of Panda who sits upon the throne, and that his plots have been betrayed, so that he is in some danger of his life."

"Macumazahn," said Umslopogaas hoarsely, "I tell you that did you not wear the Great Medicine on your breast, I would kill you where you sit and bury you beneath the floor of the hut, as one who knows—too much."

"It would be a mistake, Umslopogaas, one of the many that you have made. But as I *do* wear the Medicine, the question does not arise, does it?"

Again he made no answer and I went on, "And now, what about this journey to the north? If indeed I must make it, would you wish to accompany me?"

Umslopogaas rose from the stool and crawled out of the hut, apparently to make some inspection. Presently he returned and remarked that the night was clear although there were heavy storm clouds on the horizon, by which I understood him to convey in Zulu metaphor that it was safe for us to talk, but that danger threatened from afar.

"Macumazahn," he said, "we speak under the blanket of the Opener-of- Roads who sits upon your heart, and whose sign you bring to me, as he sent me word that you would, do we not?"

"I suppose so," I answered. "At any rate we speak as man to man, and hitherto the honour of Macumazahn has not been doubted in Zululand. So if you have anything to say, Chief Bulalio, say it at once, for I am tired and should like to eat and rest."

"Good, Macumazahn. I have this to say. I who am the son of one who was greater than he, have plotted to seize the throne of Zululand from him who sits upon that throne. It is true, for I grew weary of my idleness as a petty chief. Moreover, I should have succeeded with the help of Zikali, who hates the House of Senzangacona, though me, who am of its blood, he does not hate, because ever I have striven against that House. But it seems from his message and those words spoken by an angry woman, that I have been betrayed, and that to-night or to-morrow night, or by the next moon, the slayers will be upon me, smiting me before I can smite, at which I cannot grumble."

"By whom have you been betrayed, Umslopogaas?"

"By that wife of mine, as I think, Macumazahn. Also by Lousta, my blood-brother, over whom she has cast her net and made false to me, so that he hopes to win her whom he has always loved and with her the Chieftainship of the Axe. Now what shall I do?—Tell me, you whose eyes can see in the dark."

I thought a moment and answered, "I think that if I were you, I would leave this Lousta to sit in my place for a while as Chief of the People of the Axe, and take a journey north, Umslopogaas. Then if trouble comes from the Great House where a king sits, it will come to Lousta who can show that the People of the Axe are innocent and that you are far away."

"That is cunning, Macumazahn. There speaks the Great Medicine. If I go north, who can say that I have plotted, and if I leave my betrayer in my place, who can say that I was a traitor, who have set him where I used to sit and left the land upon a private matter? And now tell me of this journey of yours."

So I told him everything, although until that moment I had not made up my mind to go upon this journey, I who had come here to his kraal by accident, or so it seemed, and by accident had delivered to him a certain message.

"You wish to consult a white witch-doctoress, Macumazahn, who according to Zikali lives far to the north, as to the dead. Now I too, though perchance you will not think it of a black man, desire to learn of the dead; yes, of a certain wife of my youth who was sister and friend as well as wife, whom too I loved better than all the world. Also I desire to learn of a brother of mine whose name I never speak, who ruled the wolves with me and who died at my side on yonder Witch- Mountain, having made him a mat of men to lie on in a great and glorious fight. For of him as of the woman I think all day and dream all night, and I would know if they still live anywhere and I may look to see them again when I have died as a warrior should and as I hope to do. Do you understand, Watcher-by-Night?"

I answered that I understood very well, as his case seemed to be like my own.

"It may happen," went on Umslopogaas, "that all this talk of the dead who are supposed to live after they are dead, is but as the sound of wind whispering in the reeds at night, that comes from nowhere and goes nowhere and means nothing. But at least ours will be a great journey in which we shall find adventure and fighting, since it is well known in the land that wherever Macumazahn goes there is plenty of both. Also it seems well for reasons that have been spoken of between us, as Zikali says, that I should leave the country of the Zulus for a while, who desire to die a man's death at the last and not to be trapped like a jackal in a pit. Lastly I think that we shall agree well together though my temper is rough at times, and that neither of us will desert the other in trouble, though of that little yellow dog of yours I am not so sure."

"I answer for him," I replied. "Hans is a true man, cunning also when once he is away from drink."

Then we spoke of plans for our journey, and of when and where we should meet to make it, talking till it was late, after which I went to sleep in the guest-hut.

The Lion and the Axe

Next day early I left the town of the People of the Axe, having bid a formal farewell to Umslopogaas, saying in a voice that all could hear that as the rivers were still flooded, I proposed to trek to the northern parts of Zululand and trade there until the weather was better. Our private arrangement, however, was that on the night of the next full moon, which happened about four weeks later, we should meet at the eastern foot of a certain great, flat-topped mountain known to both of us, which stands to the north of Zululand but well beyond its borders.

So northward I trekked, slowly to spare my oxen, trading as I went. The details do not matter, but as it happened I met with more luck upon that journey than had come my way for many a long year. Although I worked on credit since nearly all my goods were sold, as owing to my repute I could always do in Zululand, I made some excellent bargains in cattle, and to top up with, bought a large lot of ivory so cheap that really I think it must have been stolen.

All of this, cattle, and ivory together, I sent to Natal in charge of a white friend of mine whom I could trust, where the stuff was sold very well indeed, and the proceeds paid to my account, the "trade" equivalents being duly remitted to the native vendors.

In fact, my good fortune was such that if I had been superstitious like Hans, I should have been inclined to attribute it to the influence of Zikali's "Great Medicine." As it was I knew it to be one of the chances of a trader's life and accepted it with a shrug as often as I had been accustomed to do in the alternative of losses.

Only one untoward incident happened to me. Of a sudden a party of the King's soldiers under the command of a well-known *Induna* or Councillor, arrived and insisted upon searching my waggon, as I thought at first in connection with that cheap lot of ivory which had already departed to Natal. However, never a word did they say of ivory, nor indeed was a single thing belonging to me taken by them.

I was very indignant and expressed my feelings to the *Induna* in no measured terms. He on his part was most apologetic, and explained that what he did he was obliged to do "by the King's orders." Also he let it slip that he was seeking for a certain "evil-doer" who, it was thought, might be with me without my knowing his real character, and as this "evil-doer," whose name he would not mention, was a very fierce man, it had been necessary to bring a strong guard with him.

Now I bethought me of Umslopogaas, but merely looked blank and shrugged my shoulders, saying that I was not in the habit of consorting with evil-doers.

Still unsatisfied, the *Induna* questioned me as to the places where I had been during this journey of mine in the Zulu country. I told him with the utmost frankness, mentioning among others—because I was sure that already he knew all my movements well—the town of the People of the Axe.

Then he asked me if I had seen its Chief, a certain Umslopogaas or Bulalio. I answered, Yes, that I had met him there for the first time and thought him a very remarkable man.

With this the *Induna* agreed emphatically, saying that perhaps I did not know *how* remarkable. Next he asked me where he was now, to which I replied that I had not the faintest idea, but I presumed in his kraal where I had left him. The *Induna* explained that he was *not* in his kraal; that he had gone away leaving one Lousta and his own head wife Monazi to administer the chieftainship for a while, because, as he stated, he wished to make a journey.

I yawned as if weary of the subject of this chief, and indeed of the whole business. Then the *Induna* said that I must come to the King and repeat to him all the words that I had spoken. I replied that I could not possibly do so as, having finished my trading, I had arranged to go north to shoot elephants. He answered that elephants lived a long while and would not die while I was visiting the King.

Then followed an argument which grew heated and ended in his declaring that to the King I must come, even if he had to take me there by force.

I sat silent, wondering what to say or do and leant forward to pick a piece of wood out of the fire wherewith to light my pipe. Now my shirt was not buttoned and as it chanced this action caused the ivory image of Zikali that hung about my neck to appear between its edges. The *Induna* saw it and his eyes grew big with fear.

"Hide that!" he whispered, "hide that, lest it should bewitch me. Indeed, already I feel as though I were being bewitched. It is the Great Medicine itself."

"That will certainly happen to you," I said, yawning again, "if you insist upon my taking a week's trek to visit the Black One, or interfere with me in any way now or afterwards," and I lifted my hand towards the talisman, looking him steadily in the face.

"Perhaps after all, Macumazahn, it is not necessary for you to visit the King," he said in an uncertain voice. "I will go and make report to him that you know nothing of this evil-doer."

And he went in such a hurry that he never waited to say good-bye. Next morning before the dawn I went also and trekked steadily until I was clear of Zululand.

In due course and without accident, for the weather, which had been so wet, had now turned beautifully fine and dry, we came to the great, flat-topped hill that I have mentioned, trekking thither over high, sparsely-timbered veld that offered few difficulties to the waggon. This peculiar hill, known to such natives as lived in those parts by a long word that means "Hut-with-a-flat-roof," is surrounded by forest, for here trees grow wonderfully well, perhaps because of the water that flows from its slopes. Forcing our way through this forest, which was full of game, I reached its eastern foot and there camped, five days before that night of full moon on which I had arranged to meet Umslopogaas.

That I should meet him I did not in the least believe, firstly because I thought it very probable that he would have changed his mind about coming, and secondly for the excellent reason that I expected he had gone to call upon the King against his will, as I had been asked to do. It was evident to me that he was up to his eyes in some serious plot against Cetywayo, in which he was the old dwarf Zikali's partner, or rather, tool; also that his plot had been betrayed, with the result that he was "wanted" and would have little chance of passing safely through Zululand. So taking one thing with another I imagined that I had seen his grim face and his peculiar, ancient-looking axe for the last time.

To tell the truth I was glad. Although at first the idea had appealed to me a little, I did not want to make this wild-goose, or wild-witch chase through unknown lands to seek for a totally fabulous person who dwelt far across the Zambesi. I had, as it were, been forced into the thing, but if Umslopogaas did not appear, my obligations would be at an end and I should return to Natal at my leisure. First, however, I would do a little shooting since I found that a large herd of elephants haunted this forest. Indeed I was tempted to attack them at once, but did not do so since, as Hans pointed out, if we were going north it would be difficult to carry the ivory, especially if we had to leave the waggon, and I was too old a hunter to desire to kill the great beasts for the fun of the thing.

So I just sat down and rested, letting the oxen feed throughout the hours of light on the rich grasses which grew upon the bottom-most slopes of the big mountain where we were camped by a stream, not more than a hundred yards above the timber line.

At some time or other there had been a native village at this spot; probably the

Zulus had cleaned it out in long past years, for I found human bones black with age lying in the long grass. Indeed, the cattle-kraal still remained and in such good condition that by piling up a few stones here and there on the walls and closing the narrow entrances with thorn bushes, we could still use it to enclose our oxen at night. This I did for fear lest there should be lions about, though I had neither seen nor heard them.

So the days went by pleasantly enough with lots to eat, since whenever we wanted meat I had only to go a few yards to shoot a fat buck at a spot whither they trekked to drink in the evening, till at last came the time of full moon. Of this I was also glad, since, to tell the truth, I had begun to be bored. Rest is good, but for a man who has always led an active life too much of it is very bad, for then he begins to think and thought in large doses is depressing.

Of the fire-eating Umslopogaas there was no sign, so I made up my mind that on the morrow I would start after those elephants and when I had shot—or failed to shoot—some of them, return to Natal. I felt unable to remain idle any more; it never was my gift to do so, which is perhaps why I employ my ample leisure here in England in jotting down such reminiscences as these.

Well, the full moon came up in silver glory and after I had taken a good look at her for luck, also at all the veld within sight, I turned in. An hour or two later some noise from the direction of the cattle- kraal woke me up. As it did not recur, I thought that I would go to sleep again. Then an uneasy thought came to me that I could not remember having looked to see whether the entrance was properly closed, as it was my habit to do. It was the same sort of troublesome doubt which in a civilised house makes a man get out of bed and go along the cold passages to the sitting-room to see whether he has put out the lamp. It always proves that he *has* put it out, but that does not prevent a repetition of the performance next time the perplexity arises.

I reflected that perhaps the noise was caused by the oxen pushing their way through the carelessly-closed entrance, and at any rate that I had better go to see. So I slipped on my boots and a coat and went without waking Hans or the boys, only taking with me a loaded, single- barrelled rifle which I used for shooting small buck, but no spare cartridges.

Now in front of the gateway of the cattle-kraal, shading it, grew a single big tree of the wild fig order. Passing under this tree I looked and saw that the gateway was quite securely closed, as now I remembered I had noted at sunset. Then I started to go back but had not stepped more than two or three paces when, in the bright moonlight, I saw the head of my smallest ox, a beast of the Zulu breed, suddenly appear over the top of the wall. About this there would have been nothing particularly astonishing, had it not been for the fact that this head belonged to a dead animal, as I could tell from the closed eyes and the hanging tongue.

"What in the name of goodness——" I began to myself, when my reflections were cut short by the appearance of another head, that of one of the biggest lions I ever saw, which had the ox by the throat, and with the enormous strength that is given to these creatures, by getting its back beneath the body, was deliberately hoisting it over the wall, to drag it away to devour at its leisure.

There was the brute within twelve feet of me, and what is more, it saw me as I saw it, and stopped, still holding the ox by the throat.

"What a chance for Allan Quatermain! Of course he shot it dead," one can fancy anyone saying who knows me by repute, also that by the gift of God I am handy with a rifle. Well, indeed, it should have been, for even with the small-bore piece that I carried, a bullet ought to have pierced through the soft parts of its throat to the brain and to have killed that lion as dead as Julius Cæsar. Theoretically the thing was easy enough; indeed, although I was startled for a moment, by the time that I had the rifle to my shoulder I had little fear of the issue, unless there was a miss-fire, especially as the beast seemed so astonished that it remained quite still.

Then the unexpected happened as generally it does in life, particularly in hunting, which, in my case, is a part of life. I fired, but by misfortune the bullet struck the tip of the horn of that confounded ox, which tip either was or at that moment fell in front of the spot on the lion's throat whereat half-unconsciously I had aimed. Result: the ball was turned and, departing at an angle, just cut the skin of the lion's neck deeply enough to hurt it very much and to make it madder than all the hatters in the world.

Dropping the ox, with a most terrific roar it came over the wall at me —I remember that there seemed to be yards of it—I mean of the lion— in front of which appeared a cavernous mouth full of gleaming teeth.

I skipped back with much agility, also a little to one side, because there was nothing else to do, reflecting in a kind of inconsequent way, that after all Zikali's Great Medicine was not worth a curse. The lion landed on my side of the wall and reared itself upon its hind legs before getting to business, towering high above me but slightly to my left.

Then I saw a strange thing. A shadow thrown by the moon flitted past me—all I noted of it was the distorted shape of a great, lifted axe, probably because the axe came first. The shadow fell and with it another shadow, that of a lion's paw dropping to the ground. Next there was a most awful noise of roaring, and wheeling round I saw such a fray as never I shall see again. A tall, grim, black man was fighting the great lion, that now lacked one paw, but still stood upon its hind legs, striking at him with the other.

The man, who was absolutely silent, dodged the blow and hit back with the axe, catching the beast upon the breast with such weight that it came to the ground in a lopsided fashion, since now it had only one fore-foot on which to light.

The axe flashed up again and before the lion could recover itself, or do anything else, fell with a crash upon its skull, sinking deep into the head. After this all was over, for the beast's brain was cut in two.

"I am here at the appointed time, Macumazahn," said Umslopogaas, for it was he, as with difficulty he dragged his axe from the lion's severed skull, "to find you watching by night as it is reported that you always do."

"No," I retorted, for his tone irritated me, "you are late, Bulalio, the moon has been up some hours."

"I said, O Macumazahn, that I would meet you on the *night* of the full moon, not at the rising of the moon."

"That is true," I replied, mollified, "and at any rate you came at a good moment."

"Yes," he answered, "though as it happens in this clear light the thing was easy to anyone who can handle an axe. Had it been darker the end might have been different. But, Macumazahn, you are not so clever as I thought, since otherwise you would not have come out against a lion with a toy like that," and he pointed to the little rifle in my hand.

"I did not know that there was a lion, Umslopogaas."

"That is why you are not so clever as I thought, since of one sort or another there is always a lion which wise men should be prepared to meet, Macumazahn."

"You are right again," I replied.

At that moment Hans arrived upon the scene, followed at a discreet distance by the waggon boys, and took in the situation at a glance.

"The Great Medicine of the Opener-of-Roads has worked well," was all he said.

"The great medicine of the Opener-of-Heads has worked better," remarked Umslopogaas with a little laugh and pointing to his red axe. "Never before since she came into my keeping has *Inkosikaas* (i.e. 'Chieftainess,' for so was this famous weapon named) sunk so low as to drink the blood of beasts. Still, the stroke was a good one so she need not be ashamed. But, Yellow Man, how comes it that you who, I have been told, are cunning, watch your master so ill?"

"I was asleep," stuttered Hans indignantly.

"Those who serve should never sleep," replied Umslopogaas sternly. Then he turned and whistled, and behold! out of the long grass that grew at a little distance, emerged twelve great men, all of them bearing axes and wearing cloaks of hyena skins, who saluted me by raising their axes.

"Set a watch and skin me this beast by dawn. It will make us a mat," said Umslopogaas, whereon again they saluted silently and melted away.

"Who are these?" I asked.

"A few picked warriors whom I brought with me, Macumazahn. There were one or two more, but they got lost on the way."

Then we went to the waggon and spoke no more that night.

Next morning I told Umslopogaas of the visit I had received from the *Induna* of the King who wished me to come to the royal kraal. He nodded and said,

"As it chances certain thieves attacked me on my journey, which is why one or two of my people remain behind who will never travel again. We made good play with those thieves; not one of them escaped," he added grimly, "and their bodies we threw into a river where are many crocodiles. But their spears I brought away and I think that they are such as the King's guard use. If so, his search for them will be long, since the fight took place where no man lives and we burned the shields and trappings. Oho! he will think that the ghosts have taken them."

That morning we trekked on fast, fearing lest a regiment searching for these "thieves" should strike and follow our spoor. Luckily the ox that the lion had killed was one of some spare cattle which I was driving with me, so its loss did not inconvenience us. As we went Umslopogaas told me that he had duly appointed Lousta and his wife Monazi to rule the tribe during his absence, an office which they accepted doubtfully, Monazi acting as Chieftainess and Lousta as her head *Induna* or Councillor.

I asked him whether he thought this wise under all the circumstances, seeing that it had occurred to me since I made the suggestion, that they might be unwilling to surrender power on his return, also that other domestic complications might ensue.

"It matters little, Macumazahn," he said with a shrug of his great shoulders, "for of this I am sure, that I have played my part with the People of the Axe and to stop among them would have meant my death, who am a man betrayed. What do I care who love none and now have no children? Still, it is true that I might have fled to Natal with the cattle and there have led a fat and easy life. But ease and plenty I do not desire who would live and fall as a warrior should.

"Never again, mayhap, shall I see the Ghost-Mountain where the wolves ravened and the old Witch sits in stone waiting for the world to die, or sleep in the town of the People of the Axe. What do I want with wives and oxen while I have *Inkosikaas* the Groan-maker and she is true to me?" he added, shaking the ancient axe above his head so that the sun gleamed upon the curved blade and the hollow gouge or point at the back beyond the shaft socket. "Where the Axe goes, there go the strength and virtue of the Axe, O Macumazahn."

"It is a strange weapon," I said.

"Aye, a strange and an old, forged far away, says Zikali, by a warrior-wizard hundreds of years ago, a great fighter who was also the first of smiths and who sits in the Under-world waiting for it to return to his hand when its work is finished beneath the sun. That will be soon, Macumazahn, since Zikali told me that I am the last Holder of the Axe."

"Did you then see the Opener-of-Roads?" I asked.

"Aye, I saw him. He it was who told me which way to go to escape from Zululand. Also he laughed when he heard how the flooded rivers brought you to my kraal, and sent you a message in which he said that the spirit of a snake had told him that you tried to throw the Great Medicine into a pool, but were stopped by that snake, whilst it was still alive. This, he said, you must do no more, lest he should send another snake to stop *you*."

"Did he?" I replied indignantly, for Zikali's power of seeing or learning about things that happened at a distance puzzled and annoyed me.

Only Hans grinned and said,

"I told you so, Baas."

On we travelled from day to day, meeting with such difficulties and dangers as are common on roadless veld in Africa, but no more, for the grass was good and there was plenty of game, of which we shot what we wanted for meat. Indeed, here in the back regions of what is known as Portuguese South East Africa, every sort of wild animal was so numerous that personally I wished we could turn our journey into a shooting expedition.

But of this Umslopogaas, whom hunting bored, would not hear. In fact, he was much more anxious than myself to carry out our original purpose. When I asked him why, he answered because of something Zikali had told him. What this was he would not say, except that in the country whither we wandered he would fight a great fight and win much honour.

Now Umslopogaas was by nature a fighting man, one who took a positive joy in battle, and like an old Norseman, seemed to think that thus only could a man decorously die. This amazed me, a peaceful person who loves quiet and a home. Still, I gave way, partly to please him, partly because I hoped that we might discover something of interest, and still more because, having once undertaken an enterprise, my pride prompted me to see it through.

Now while he was preparing to draw his map in the ashes, or afterwards, I forget which, Zikali had told me that when we drew near to the great river we should come to a place on the edge of bush-veld that ran down to the river, where a white man lived, adding, after casting his bones and reading from them, that he thought this white man was a "trek-Boer." This, I should explain, means a Dutchman who has travelled away from wherever he lived and made a home for himself in the wilderness, as some wandering spirit and the desire to be free of authority often prompt these people to do. Also, after another inspection of his enchanted knuckle-bones, he had declared that something remarkable would happen to this man or his family, while I was visiting him. Lastly in that map he drew in the ashes, the details of which were impressed so indelibly upon my memory, he had shown me where I should find the dwelling of this white man, of whom and of whose habitation doubtless he knew through the many spies who seemed to be at the service of all witch-doctors, and more especially of Zikali, the greatest among them.

Travelling by the sun and the compress I had trekked steadily in the exact direction which he indicated, to find that in this useful particular he was well named the "Opener-of-Roads," since always before me I found a practicable path, although to the right or to the left there would have been none. Thus when we came to mountains, it was at a spot where we discovered a pass; when we came to swamps it was where a ridge of high ground ran between, and so forth. Also such tribes as we met upon our journey always proved of a friendly character, although perhaps the aspect of Umslopogaas and his fierce band whom, rather irreverently, I named his twelve Apostles, had a share in inducing this peaceful attitude.

So smooth was our progress and so well marked by water at certain intervals, that at last I came to the conclusion that we must be following some ancient road which at a forgotten period of history, had run from south to north, or *vice versâ*. Or rather, to be honest, it was the observant Hans who made this discovery from various indications which had escaped my notice. I need not stop to detail them, but one of these was that at certain places the water-holes on a high, rather barren land had been dug out, and in one or more instances, lined with stones after the fashion of an ancient well. Evidently we were following an old trade route made, perhaps, in forgotten ages when Africa was more civilised than it is now.

Passing over certain high, misty lands during the third week of our trek, where frequently at this season of the year the sun never showed itself before ten o'clock and disappeared at three or four in the afternoon, and where twice we were held up for two whole days by dense fog, we came across a queer nomadic people who seemed to live in movable grass huts and to keep great herds of goats and long-tailed sheep.

These folk ran away from us at first, but when they found that we did them no harm, became friendly and brought us offerings of milk, also of a kind of slug or caterpillar which they seemed to eat. Hans, who was a great master of different native dialects, discovered a tongue, or a mixture of tongues, in which he could make himself understood to some of them.

They told him that in their day they had never seen a white man, although their fathers' fathers (an expression by which they meant their remote ancestors) had known many of them. They added, however, that if we went on steadily towards the north for another seven days' journey, we should come to a place where a white man lived, one, they had heard, who had a long beard and killed animals with guns, as we did.

Encouraged by this intelligence we pushed forward, now travelling down hill out of the mists into a more genial country. Indeed, the veld here was beautiful, high, rolling plains like those of the East African plateau, covered with a deep and fertile chocolate-coloured soil, as we could see where the rains had washed out dongas. The climate, too, seemed to be cool and very healthful. Altogether it was a pity to see such lands lying idle and tenanted only by countless herds of game, for there were not any native inhabitants, or at least we met none.

On we trekked, our road still sloping slightly down hill, till at length we saw far away a vast sea of bush-veld which, as I guessed correctly, must fringe the great Zambesi River. Moreover we, or rather Hans, whose eyes were those of a hawk, saw something else, namely buildings of a more or less civilised kind, which stood among trees by the side of a stream several miles on this side of the great belt of bush.

"Look, Baas," said Hans, "those wanderers did not lie; there is the house of the white man. I wonder if he drinks anything stronger than water," he added with a sigh and a kind of reminiscent contraction of his yellow throat.

As it happened, he did.

Inez

We had sighted the house from far away shortly after sunrise and by midday we were there. As we approached I saw that it stood almost immediately beneath two great baobab trees, babyan trees we call them in South Africa, perhaps because monkeys eat their fruit. It was a thatched house with whitewashed walls and a stoep or veranda round it, apparently of the ordinary Dutch type. Moreover, beyond it, at a little distance were other houses or rather shanties with waggon sheds, etc., and beyond and mixed up with these a number of native huts. Further on were considerable fields green with springing corn; also we saw herds of cattle grazing on the slopes. Evidently our white man was rich.

Umslopogaas surveyed the place with a soldier's eye and said to me,

"This must be a peaceful country, Macumazahn, where no attack is feared, since of defences I see none."

"Yes," I answered, "why not, with a wilderness behind it and bush-veld and a great river in front?"

"Men can cross rivers and travel through bush-veld," he answered, and was silent.

Up to this time we had seen no one, although it might have been presumed that a waggon trekking towards the house was a sufficiently unusual sight to have attracted attention.

"Where can they be?" I asked.

"Asleep, Baas, I think," said Hans, and as a matter of fact he was right. The whole population of the place was indulging in a noonday siesta.

At last we came so near to the house that I halted the waggon and descended from the driving-box in order to investigate. At this moment someone did appear, the sight of whom astonished me not a little, namely, a very striking-looking young woman. She was tall, handsome, with large dark eyes, good features, a rather pale complexion, and I think the saddest face that I ever saw. Evidently she had heard the noise of the waggon and had come out to see what caused it, for she had nothing on her head, which was covered with thick hair of a raven blackness. Catching sight of the great Umslopogaas with his gleaming axe and of his savage-looking bodyguard, she uttered an exclamation and not unnaturally turned to fly.

"It's all right," I sang out, emerging from behind the oxen, and in English, though before the words had left my lips I reflected that there was not the slightest reason to suppose that she would understand them. Probably she was Dutch, or Portuguese, although by some instinct I had addressed her in English.

To my surprise she answered me in the same tongue, spoken, it is true, with a peculiar accent which I could not place, as it was neither Scotch nor Irish.

"Thank you," she said. "I, sir, was frightened. Your friends look——" Here she stumbled for a word, then added, "terrocious."

I laughed at this composite adjective and answered,

"Well, so they are in a way, though they will not harm you or me. But, young lady, tell me, can we outspan here? Perhaps your husband——"

"I have no husband, I have only a father, sir," and she sighed.

"Well, then, could I speak to your father? My name is Allan Quatermain and I am making a journey of exploration, to find out about the country beyond, you know."

"Yes, I will go to wake him. He is asleep. Everyone sleeps here at midday—except me," she said with another sigh.

"Why do you not follow their example?" I asked jocosely, for this young woman puzzled me and I wanted to find out about her.

"Because I sleep little, sir, who think too much. There will be plenty of time to sleep soon for all of us, will there not?"

I stared at her and inquired her name, because I did not know what else to say.

"My name is Inez Robertson," she answered. "I will go to wake my father. Meanwhile please unyoke your oxen. They can feed with the others; they look as though they wanted rest, poor things." Then she turned and went into the house.

"Inez Robertson," I said to myself, "that's a queer combination. English father and Portuguese mother, I suppose. But what can an Englishman be doing in a place like this? If it had been a trek-Boer I should not have been surprised." Then I began to give directions about out-spanning.

We had just got the oxen out of the yokes, when a big, raw-boned, red- bearded, blue-eyed, roughly-clad man of about fifty years of age appeared from the house, yawning. I threw my eye over him as he advanced with a peculiar rolling gait, and formed certain conclusions. A drunkard who has once been a gentleman, I reflected to myself, for there was something peculiarly dissolute in his appearance, also one who has had to do with the sea, a diagnosis which proved very accurate.

"How do you do, Mr. Allan Quatermain, which I think my daughter said is your name, unless I dreamed it, for it is one that I seem to have heard before," he exclaimed with a broad Scotch accent which I do not attempt to reproduce. "What in the name of blazes brings you here where no real white man has been for years? Well, I am glad enough to see you any way, for I am sick of half-breed Portuguese and niggers, and snuff-and-butter girls, and gin and bad whisky. Leave your people to attend to those oxen and come in and have a drink."

"Thank you, Mr. Robertson——"

"Captain Robertson," he interrupted. "Man, don't look astonished. You mightn't guess it, but I commanded a mail-steamer once and should like to hear myself called rightly again before I die."

"I beg your pardon—Captain Robertson, but myself, I don't drink anything before sundown. However, if you have something to eat——?"

"Oh yes, Inez—she's my daughter—will find you a bite. Those men of yours," and he also looked doubtfully at Umslopogaas and his savage company, "will want food as well. I'll have a beast killed for them; they look as if they could eat it, horns and all. Where are my people? All asleep, I suppose, the lazy lubbers. Wait a bit, I'll wake them up."

Going to the house he snatched a great sjambok cut from hippopotamus hide, from where it hung on a nail in the wall, and ran towards the group of huts which I have mentioned, roaring out the name Thomaso, also a string of oaths such as seamen use, mixed with others of a Portuguese variety. What happened there I could not see because boughs were in the way, but presently I heard blows and screams, and caught sight of people, all dark-skinned, flying from the huts.

A little later a fat, half-breed man—I should say from his curling hair that his mother was a negress and his father a Portuguese— appeared with some other nondescript fellows and began to give directions in a competent fashion about our oxen, also as to the killing of a calf. He spoke in bastard Portuguese, which I could understand, and I heard him talk of Umslopogaas to whom he pointed, as "that nigger," after the fashion of such cross-bred people who choose to consider themselves white men. Also he made uncomplimentary remarks about Hans, who of course understood every word he said. Evidently Thomaso's temper had been ruffled by this sudden and violent disturbance of his nap.

Just then our host appeared puffing with his exertions and declaring that he had stirred up the swine with a vengeance, in proof of which he pointed to the sjambok that was reddened with blood.

"Captain Robertson," I said, "I wish to give you a hint to be passed on to Mr. Thomaso, if that is he. He spoke of the Zulu soldier there as a nigger, etc. Well, he is a chief of a high rank and rather a terrible fellow if roused. Therefore I recommend Mr. Thomaso not to let him understand that he is insulting him."

"Oh! that's the way of these 'snuff-and-butters' one of whose grandmothers once met a white man," replied the Captain, laughing, "but I'll tell him," and he did in Portuguese.

His retainer listened in silence, looking at Umslopogaas rather sulkily. Then we walked into the house. As we went the Captain said,

"Señor Thomaso—he calls himself Señor—is my manager here and a clever man, honest too in his way and attached to me, perhaps because I saved his life once. But he has a nasty temper, as have all these cross-breeds, so I hope he won't get wrong with that native who carries a big axe."

"I hope so too, for his own sake," I replied emphatically.

The Captain led the way into the sitting-room; there was but one in the house. It proved a queer kind of place with rude furniture seated with strips of hide after the Boer fashion, and yet bearing a certain air of refinement which was doubtless due to Inez, who, with the assistance of a stout native girl, was already engaged in setting the table. Thus there was a shelf with books, Shakespeare was one of these, I noticed—over which hung an ivory crucifix, which suggested that Inez was a Catholic. On the walls, too, were some good portraits, and on the window-ledge a jar full of flowers. Also the forks and spoons were of silver, as were the mugs, and engraved with a tremendous coat-of-arms and a Portuguese motto.

Presently the food appeared, which was excellent and plentiful, and the Captain, his daughter and I sat down and ate. I noted that he drank gin and water, an innocent-looking beverage but strong as he took it. It was offered to me, but like Miss Inez, I preferred coffee.

During the meal and afterwards while we smoked upon the veranda, I told them as much as I thought desirable of my plans. I said that I was engaged upon a journey of exploration of the country beyond the Zambesi, and that having heard of this settlement, which, by the way, was called Strathmuir, as I gathered after a place in far away Scotland where the Captain had been born and passed his childhood, I had come here to inquire as to how to cross the great river, and about other things.

The Captain was interested, especially when I informed him that I was that same "Hunter Quatermain" of whom he had heard in past years, but he told me that it would be impossible to take the waggon down into the low bush-veld which we could see beneath us, as there all the oxen would die of the bite of the tsetse fly. I answered that I was aware of this and proposed to try to make an arrangement to leave it in his charge till I returned.

"That might be managed, Mr. Quatermain," he answered. "But, man, will you ever return? They say there are queer folk living on the other side of the Zambesi, savage men who are cannibals, Amahagger I think they call them. It was they who in past years cleaned out all this country, except a few river tribes who live in floating huts or on islands among the reeds, and that's why it is so empty. But this happened long ago, much before my time, and I don't suppose they will ever cross the river again."

"If I might ask, what brought you here, Captain?" I said, for the point was one on which I felt curious.

"That which brings most men to wild places, Mr. Quatermain—trouble. If you want to know, I had a misfortune and piled up my ship. There were some lives lost and, rightly or wrongly, I got the sack. Then I started as a trader in a God-forsaken hole named Chinde, one of the Zambesi mouths, you know, and did very well, as we Scotchmen have a way of doing.

"There I married a Portuguese lady, a real lady of high blood, one of the old sort. When my girl, Inez, was about twelve years old I got into more trouble, for my wife died and it pleased a certain relative of hers to say that it was because I had neglected her. This ended in a row and the truth is that I killed him—in fair fight, mind you. Still, kill him I did though I scarcely knew that I had done it at the time, after which the place grew too hot to hold me. So I sold up and swore that I would have no more to do with what they are pleased to call civilisation on the East Coast.

"During my trading I had heard that there was fine country up this way, and here I came and settled years ago, bringing my girl and Thomaso, who was one of my managers, also a few other people with me. And here I have been ever since, doing very well as before, for I trade a lot of ivory and other things and grow stuff and cattle, which I sell to the River natives. Yes, I am a rich man now and could go to live on my means in Scotland, or anywhere."

"Why don't you?" I asked.

"Oh! for many reasons. I have lost touch with all that and become half wild and I like this life and the sunshine and being my own master. Also, if I did, things might be raked up against me, about that man's death. Also, though I daresay it will make you think badly of me for it, Mr. Quatermain, I have ties down there," and he waved is hand towards the village, if so it could be called, "which it wouldn't be easy for me to break. A man may be fond of his children, Mr. Quatermain, even if their skins ain't so white as they ought to be. Lastly I have habits—you see, I am speaking out to you as man to man —which might get me into trouble again if I went back to the world," and he nodded his fine, capable-looking head in the direction of the bottle on the table.

"I see," I said hastily, for this kind of confession bursting out of the man's lonely heart when what he had drunk took a hold of him, was painful to hear. "But how about your daughter, Miss Inez?"

"Ah!" he said, with a quiver in his voice, "there you touch it. She ought to go away. There is no one for her to marry here, where we haven't seen a white man for years, and she's a lady right enough, like her mother. But who is she to go to, being a Roman Catholic whom my own dour Presbyterian folk in Scotland, if any of them are left, would turn their backs on? Moreover, she loves me in her own fashion, as I love her, and she wouldn't leave me because she thinks it her duty to stay and knows that if she did, I should go to the devil altogether. Still—perhaps you might help me about her, Mr. Quatermain, that is if you live to come back from your journey," he added doubtfully.

I felt inclined to ask how I could possibly help in such a matter, but thought it wisest to say nothing. This, however, he did not notice, for he went on,

"Now I think I will have a nap, as I do my work in the early morning, and sometimes late at night when my brain seems to clear up again, for you see I was a sailor for many years and accustomed to keeping watches. You'll look after yourself, won't you, and treat the place as your own?" Then he vanished into the house to lie down.

When I had finished my pipe I went for a walk. First I visited the waggon where I found Umslopogaas and his company engaged in cooking the beast that had been given them, Zulu fashion; Hans with his usual cunning had already secured a meal, probably from the servants, or from Inez herself; at least he left them and followed me. First we went down to the huts, where we saw a number of good-looking young women of mixed blood, all decently dressed and engaged about their household duties. Also we saw four or five boys and girls, to say nothing of a baby in arms, fine young people, one or two of whom were more white than coloured.

"Those children are very like the Baas with the red beard," remarked Hans reflectively.

"Yes," I said, and shivered, for now I understood the awfulness of this poor man's case. He was the father of a number of half-breeds who tied him to this spot as anchors tie a ship. I went on rather hastily past some sheds to a long, low building which proved to be a store. Here the quarter-blood called Thomaso, and some assistants were engaged in trading with natives from the Zambesi swamps, men of a kind that I had never seen, but in a way more civilised than many further south. What they were selling or buying, I did not stop to see, but I noticed that the store was full of goods of one sort or another, including a great deal of ivory, which, as I supposed, had come down the river from inland.

Then we walked on to the cultivated fields where we saw corn growing very well, also tobacco and other crops. Beyond this were cattle kraals and in the distance we perceived a great number of cattle and goats feeding on the slopes.

"This red-bearded Baas must be very rich in all things," remarked the observant Hans when we had completed our investigations.

"Yes," I answered, "rich and yet poor."

"How can a man be both rich and yet poor, Baas?" asked Hans.

Just at that moment some of the half-breed children whom I have mentioned, ran past us more naked than dressed and whooping like little savages. Hans contemplated them gravely, then said,

"I think I understand now, Baas. A man may be rich in things he loves and yet does not want, which makes him poor in other ways."

"Yes," I answered, "as you *are*, Hans, when you take too much to drink."

Just then we met the stately Miss Inez returning from the store, carrying some articles in a basket, soap, I think, and tea in a packet, amongst them. I told Hans to take the basket and bear it to the house for her. He went off with it and, walking slowly, we fell into conversation.

"Your father must do very well here," I said, nodding at the store with the crowd of natives round it.

"Yes," she answered, "he makes much money which he puts in a bank at the coast, for living costs us nothing and there is great profit in what he buys and sells, also in the crops he grows and in the cattle. But," she added pathetically, "what is the use of money in a place like this?"

"You can get things with it," I answered vaguely.

"That is what my father says, but what does he get? Strong stuff to drink; dresses for those women down there, and sometimes pearls, jewels and other things for me which I do not want. I have a box full of them set in ugly gold, or loose which I cannot use, and if I put them on, who is there to see them? That clever half-breed, Thomaso— for he is clever in his way, faithful too—or the women down there—no one else."

"You do not seem to be happy, Miss Inez."

"No. I cannot tell how unhappy others are, who have met none, but sometimes I think that I must be the most miserable woman in the world."

"Oh! no," I replied cheerfully, "plenty are worse off."

"Then, Mr. Quatermain, it must be because they cannot feel. Did you ever have a father whom you loved?"

"Yes, Miss Inez. He is dead, but he was a very good man, a kind of saint. Ask my servant, the little Hottentot Hans; he will tell you about him."

"Ah! a very good man. Well, as you may have guessed, mine is not, though there is much good in him, for he has a kind heart, and a big brain. But the drink and those women down there, they ruin him," and she wrung her hands.

"Why don't you go away?" I blurted out.

"Because it is my duty to stop. That is what my religion teaches me, although of it I know little except through books, who have seen no priest for years except one who was a missionary, a Baptist, I think, who told me that my faith was false and would lead me to hell. Yes, not understanding how I lived, he said that, who did not know that hell is here. No, I cannot go, who hopes always that still God and the Saints will show me how to save my father, even though it be with my blood. And now I have said too much to you who are quite a stranger. Yet, I do not know why, I feel that you will not betray me, and what is more, that you will help me if you can, since you are not one of those who drink, or——" and she waved her hand towards the huts.

"I have my faults, Miss Inez," I answered.

"Yes, no doubt, else you would be a saint, not a man, and even the saints had their faults, or so I seem to remember, and became saints by repentance and conquering them. Still, I am sure that you will help me if you can."

Then with a sudden flash of her dark eyes that said more than all her words, she turned and left me.

Here's a pretty kettle of fish, thought I to myself as I strolled back to the waggon to see how things were going on there, and how to get the live fish out of the kettle before they boil or spoil is more than I know. I wonder why fate is always finding me such jobs to do.

Even as I thought thus a voice in my heart seemed to echo that poor girl's words—because it is your duty—and to add others to them—woe betide him who neglects his duty. I was appointed to try to hook a few fish out of the vast kettle of human woe, and therefore I must go on hooking. Meanwhile this particular problem seemed beyond me. Perhaps Fate would help, I reflected. As a matter of fact, in the end Fate did, if Fate is the right word to use in this connection.

The Sea-Cow Hunt

Now it had been my intention to push forward across the river at once, but here luck, or our old friend, Fate, was against me. To begin with several of Umslopogaas' men fell sick with a kind of stomach trouble, arising no doubt from something they had eaten. This, however, was not their view, or that of Umslopogaas himself. It happened that one of these men, Goroko by name, who practised as a witch-doctor in his lighter moments, naturally suspected that a spell had been cast upon them, for such people see magic in everything.

Therefore he organised a "smelling-out" at which Umslopogaas, who was as superstitious as the rest, assisted. So did Hans, although he called himself a Christian, partly out of curiosity, for he was as curious as a magpie, and partly from fear lest some implication should be brought against him in his absence. I saw the business going on from a little distance, and, unseen myself, thought it well to keep an eye upon the proceedings in case anything untoward should occur. This I did with Miss Inez, who had never witnessed anything of the sort, as a companion.

The circle, a small one, was formed in the usual fashion; Goroko rigged up in the best witch-doctor's costume that he could improvise, duly came under the influence of his "Spirit" and skipped about, waving a wildebeeste's tail, and so forth.

Finally to my horror he broke out of the ring, and running to a group of spectators from the village, switched Thomaso, who was standing among them with a lordly and contemptuous air, across the face with the gnu's tail, shouting out that he was the wizard who had poisoned the bowels of the sick men. Thereon Thomaso, who although he could be insolent, like most crossbreeds was not remarkable for courage, seeing the stir that this announcement created amongst the fierce-faced Zulus and fearing developments, promptly bolted, none attempting to follow him.

After this, just as I thought that everything was over and that the time had come for me to speak a few earnest words to Umslopogaas, pointing out that matters must go no further as regards Thomaso, whom I knew that he and his people hated, Goroko went back to the circle and was seized with a new burst of inspiration.

Throwing down his whisk, he lifted his arms above his head and stared at the heavens. Then he began to shout out something in a loud voice which I was too far off to catch. Whatever it may have been, evidently it frightened his hearers, as I could see from the expressions on their faces. Even Umslopogaas was alarmed, for he let his axe fall for a moment, rose as though to speak, then sat down again and covered his eyes with his hands.

In a minute it was over; Goroko seemed to become normal, took some snuff and as I guessed, after the usual fashion of these doctors, began to ask what he had been saying while the "Spirit" possessed him, which he either had, or affected to have, forgotten. The circle, too, broke up and its members began to talk to each other in a subdued way, while Umslopogaas remained seated on the ground, brooding, and Hans slipped away in his snake-like fashion, doubtless in search of me.

"What was it all about, Mr. Quatermain?" asked Inez.

"Oh! a lot of nonsense," I said. "I fancy that witch-doctor declared that your friend Thomaso put something into those men's food to make them sick."

"I daresay that he did; it would be just like him, Mr. Quatermain, as I know that he hates them, especially Umslopogaas, of whom I am very fond. He brought me some beautiful flowers this morning which he had found somewhere, and made a long speech which I could not understand."

The idea of Umslopogaas, that man of blood and iron, bringing flowers to a young lady, was so absurd that I broke out laughing and even the sad-faced Inez smiled. Then she left me to see about something and I went to speak to Hans and asked him what had happened.

"Something rather queer, I think, Baas," he answered vacuously, "though I did not quite understand the last part. The doctor, Goroko, smelt out Thomaso as the man who had made them sick, and though they will not kill him because we are guests here, those Zulus are very angry with Thomaso and I think will beat him if they get a chance. But that is only the small half of the stick," and he paused.

"What is the big half, then?" I asked with irritation.

"Baas, the Spirit in Goroko——"

"The jackass in Goroko, you mean," I interrupted. "How can you, who are a Christian, talk such rubbish about spirits? I only wish that my father could hear you."

"Oh! Baas, your reverend father, the Predikant, is now wise enough to know all about Spirits and that there are some who come into black witch-doctors though they turn up their noses at white men and leave them alone. However, whatever it is that makes Goroko speak, got hold of him so that his lips said, though he remembered nothing of it afterwards, that soon this place would be red with blood—that there would be a great killing here, Baas. That is all."

"Red with blood! Whose blood? What did the fool mean?"

"I don't know, Baas, but what you call the jackass in Goroko, declared that those who are 'with the Great Medicine'—meaning what you wear, Baas—will be quite safe. So I hope that it will not be our blood; also that you will get out of this place as soon as you can."

Well, I scolded Hans because he believed in what this doctor said, for I could see that he did believe it, then went to question Umslopogaas, whom I found looking quite pleased, which annoyed me still more.

"What is it that Goroko has been saying and why do you smile, Bulalio?" I asked.

"Nothing much, Macumazahn, except that the man who looks like tallow that has gone bad, put something in our food which made us sick, for which I would kill him were he not Red-beard's servant and that it would frighten the lady his daughter. Also he said that soon there will be fighting, which is why I smiled, who grow weary of peace. We came out to fight, did we not?"

"Certainly not," I answered. "We came out to make a quiet journey in strange lands, which is what I mean to do."

"Ah! well, Macumazahn, in strange lands one meets strange men with whom one does not always agree, and then *Inkosikaas* begins to talk," and he whirled the great axe round his head, making the air whistle as it was forced through the gouge at its back.

I could get no more out of him, so having extracted a promise from him that nothing should happen to Thomaso who, I pointed out, was probably quite unjustly accused, I went away.

Still, the whole incident left a disagreeable impression on my mind, and I began to wish that we were safe across the Zambesi without more trouble. But we could not start at once because two of the Zulus were still not well enough to travel and there were many preparations to be made about the loads, and so forth, since the waggon must be left behind. Also, and this was another complication—Hans had a sore upon his foot, resulting from the prick of a poisonous thorn, and it was desirable that this should be quite healed before we marched.

So it came about that I was really glad when Captain Robertson suggested that we should go down to a certain swamp formed, I gathered, by some small tributary of the Zambesi to take part in a kind of hippopotamus battue. It seemed that at this season of the year these great animals always frequented the place in numbers, also that by barring a neck of deep water through which they gained it, they, or a proportion of them, could be cut off and killed.

This had been done once or twice in the past, though not of late, perhaps because Captain Robertson had lacked the energy to organise such a hunt. Now he wished to do so again, taking advantage of my presence, both because of the value of the hides of the sea-cows which were cut up to be sent to the coast and sold as *sjamboks* or whips, and because of the sport of the thing. Also I think he desired to show me that he was not altogether sunk in sloth and drink.

I fell in with the idea readily enough, since in all my hunting life I had never seen anything of the sort, especially as I was told that the expedition would not take more than a week and I reckoned that the sick men and Hans would not be fit to travel sooner. So great preparations were made. The riverside natives, whose share of the spoil was to be the carcases of the slain sea-cows, were summoned by hundreds and sent off to their appointed stations to beat the swamps at a signal given by the firing of a great pile of reeds. Also many other things were done upon which I need not enter.

Then came the time for us to depart to the appointed spot over twenty miles away, most of which distance it seemed we could trek in the waggon. Captain Robertson, who for the time had cut off his gin, was as active about the affair as though he were once more in command of a mail-steamer. Nothing escaped his attention; indeed, in the care which he gave to details he reminded me of the captain of a great ship that is leaving port, and from it I learned how able a man he must once have been.

"Does your daughter accompany us?" I asked on the night before we started.

"Oh! no," he answered, "she would only be in the way. She will be quite safe here, especially as Thomaso, who is no hunter, remains in charge of the place with some of the older natives to look after the women and children."

Later I saw Inez herself, who said that she would have liked to come, although she hated to see great beasts killed, but that her father was against it because he thought she might catch fever. So she supposed that she had better remain where she was.

I agreed, though in my heart I was doubtful, and said that I would leave Hans, whose foot was not as yet quite well, and with whom she had made friends as she had done with Umslopogaas, to look after her. Also there would be with him the two great Zulus who were now recovering from their attack of stomach sickness, so that she would have nothing to fear. She answered with her slow smile that she feared nothing, still, she would have liked to come with us. Then we parted, as it proved for a long time.

It was quite a ceremony. Umslopogaas, "in the name of the Axe" solemnly gave over Inez to the charge of his two followers, bidding them guard her with so much earnestness that I began to suspect he feared something which he did not choose to mention. My mind went back indeed to the prophecy of the witch-doctor Goroko, of which it was possible that he might be thinking, but as while he spoke he kept his fierce eyes fixed upon the fat and pompous quarter-breed, Thomaso, I concluded that here was the object of his doubts.

It might have occurred to him that this Thomaso would take the opportunity of her father's absence to annoy Inez. If so I was sure that he was mistaken for various reasons, of which I need only quote one, namely, that even if such an idea had ever entered his head, Thomaso was far too great a coward to translate it into action. Still, suspecting something, I also gave Hans instructions to keep a sharp eye on Inez and generally to watch the place, and if he saw anything suspicious, to communicate with us at once.

"Yes, Baas," said Hans, "I will look after 'Sad-Eyes'"—for so with their usual quickness of observation our Zulus had named Inez—"as though she were my grandmother, though what there is to fear for her, I do not know. But, Baas, I would much rather come and look after you, as your reverend father, the Predikant, told me to do always, which is my duty, not girl-herding, Baas. Also my foot is now quite well and—I want to shoot sea-cows, and——" Here he paused.

"And what, Hans?"

"And Goroko said that there was going to be much fighting and if there should be fighting and you should come to harm because I was not there to protect you, what would your reverend father think of me then?"

All of which meant two things: that Hans never liked being separated from me if he could help it, and that he much preferred a shooting trip to stopping alone in this strange place with nothing to do except eat and sleep. So I concluded, though indeed I did not get quite to the bottom of the business. In reality Hans was putting up a most gallant struggle against temptation.

As I found out afterwards, Captain Robertson had been giving him strong drink on the sly, moved thereto by sympathy with a fellow toper. Also he had shown him where, if he wanted it, he could get more, and Hans always wanted gin very badly indeed. To leave it within his reach was like leaving a handful of diamonds lying about in the room of a thief. This he knew, but was ashamed to tell me the truth, and thence came much trouble.

"You will stop here, Hans, look after the young lady and nurse your foot," I said sternly, whereon he collapsed with a sigh and asked for some tobacco.

Meanwhile Captain Robertson, who I think had been taking a stirrup cup to cheer him on the road, was making his farewells down in what was known as "the village," for I saw him there kissing a collection of half-breed children, and giving Thomaso instructions to look after them and their mothers. Returning at length, he called to Inez, who remained upon the veranda, for she always seemed to shrink from her father after his visits to the village, to "keep a stiff upper lip" and not feel lonely, and commanded the cavalcade to start.

So off we went, about twenty of the village natives, a motley crew armed with every kind of gun, marching ahead and singing songs. Then came the waggon with Captain Robertson and myself seated on the driving-box, and lastly Umslopogaas and his Zulus, except the two who had been left behind.

We trekked along a kind of native road over fine veld of the same character as that on which Strathmuir stood, having the lower-lying bush-veld which ran down to the Zambesi on our right. Before nightfall we came to a ridge whereon this bush-veld turned south, fringing that tributary of the great river in the swamps of which we were to hunt for sea-cows. Here we camped and next morning, leaving the waggon in charge of my *voorlooper* and a couple of the Strathmuir natives, for the driver was to act as my gun-bearer—we marched down into the sea of bush-veld. It proved to be full of game, but at this we dared not fire for fearing of disturbing the hippopotami in the swamps beneath, whence in that event they might escape us back to the river.

About midday we passed out of the bush-veld and reached the place where the drive was to be. Here, bordered by steep banks covered with bush, was swampy ground not more than two hundred yards wide, down the centre of which ran a narrow channel of rather deep water, draining a vast expanse of morass above. It was up this channel that the sea-cows travelled to the feeding ground where they loved to collect at that season of the year.

There with the assistance of some of the riverside natives we made our preparations under the direction of Captain Robertson. The rest of these men, to the number of several hundreds, had made a wide détour to the head of the swamps, miles away, whence they were to advance at a certain signal. These preparations were simple. A quantity of thorn trees were cut down and by means of heavy stones fastened to their trunks, anchored in the narrow channel of deep water. To their tops, which floated on the placid surface, were tied a variety of rags which we had brought with us, such as old red flannel shirts, gay-coloured but worn-out blankets, and I know not what besides. Some of these fragments also were attached to the anchored ropes under water.

Also we selected places for the guns upon the steep banks that I have mentioned, between which this channel ran. Foreseeing what would happen, I chose one for myself behind a particularly stout rock and what is more, built a stone wall to the height of several feet on the landward side of it, as I guessed that the natives posted near to me would prove wild in their shooting.

These labours occupied the rest of that day, and at night we retired to higher ground to sleep. Before dawn on the following morning we returned and took up our stations, some on one side of the channel and some on the other which we had to reach in a canoe brought for the purpose by the river natives.

Then, before the sun rose, Captain Robertson fired a huge pile of dried reeds and bushes, which was to give the signal to the river natives far away to begin their beat. This done, we sat down and waited, after making sure that every gun had plenty of ammunition ready.

As the dawn broke, by climbing a tree near my *schanze* or shelter, I saw a good many miles away to the south a wide circle of little fires, and guessed that the natives were beginning to burn the dry reeds of the swamp. Presently these fires drew together into a thin wall of flame. Then I knew that it was time to return to the *schanze* and prepare. It was full daylight, however, before anything happened.

Watching the still channel of water, I saw ripples on it and bubbles of air rising. Suddenly there appeared the head of a great bull- hippopotamus which, having caught sight of our rag barricade, either above or below water, had risen to the surface to see what it might be. I put a bullet from an eight-bore rifle through its brain, whereon it sank, as I guessed, stone dead to the bottom of the channel, thus helping to increase the barricade by the bulk of its great body. Also it had another effect. I have observed that sea-cows cannot bear the smell and taint of blood, which frightens them horribly, so that they will expose themselves to almost any risk, rather than get it into their nostrils.

Now, in this still water where there was no perceptible current, the blood from the dead bull soon spread all about so that when the herd, following their leader, began to arrive they were much alarmed. Indeed, the first of them on winding or tasting it, turned and tried to get back up the channel where, however, they met others following, and there ensued a tremendous confusion. They rose to the surface, blowing, snorting, bellowing and scrambling over each other in the water, while continually more and more arrived behind them, till there was a perfect pandemonium in that narrow place.

All our guns opened fire wildly upon the mass; it was like a battle and through the smoke I caught sight of the riverside natives who were acting as beaters, advancing far away, fantastically dressed, screaming with excitement and waving spears, or sometimes torches of flaming reeds. Most of these were scrambling along the banks, but some of the bolder spirits advanced over the lagoon in canoes, driving the hippopotami towards the mouth of the channel by which alone they could escape into the great swamps below and so on to the river. In all my hunting experience I do not think I ever saw a more remarkable scene. Still, in a way, to me it was unpleasant, for I flatter myself that I am a sportsman and a battle of this sort is not sport as I understand the term.

At length it came to this; the channel for quite a long way was literally full of hippopotami—I should think there must have been a hundred of them or more of all sorts and sizes, from great bulls down to little calves. Some of these were killed, not many, for the shooting of our gallant company was execrable and almost at hazard. Also for every sea-cow that died, of which number I think that Captain Robertson and myself accounted for most—many were only wounded.

Still, the unhappy beasts, crazed with noise and fire and blood, did not seem to dare to face our frail barricade, probably for the reason that I have given. For a while they remained massed together in the water, or under it, making a most horrible noise. Then of a sudden they seemed to take a resolution. A few of them broke back towards the burning reeds, the screaming beaters and the advancing canoes. One of these, indeed, a wounded bull, charged a canoe, crushed it in its huge jaws and killed the rower, how exactly I do not know, for his body was never found. The majority of them, however, took another counsel, for emerging from the water on either side, they began to scramble towards us along the steep banks, or even to climb up them with surprising agility. It was at this point in the proceedings that I congratulated myself earnestly upon the solid character of the water-worn rock which I had selected as a shelter.

Behind this rock together with my gun-bearer and Umslopogaas, who, as he did not shoot, had elected to be my companion, I crouched and banged away at the unwieldy creatures as they advanced. But fire fast as I might with two rifles, I could not stop the half of them—they were drawing unpleasantly near. I glanced at Umslopogaas and even then was amused to see that probably for the first time in his life that redoubtable warrior was in a genuine fright.

"This is madness, Macumazahn," he shouted above the din. "Are we to stop here and be stamped flat by a horde of water-pigs?"

"It seems so," I answered, "unless you prefer to be stamped flat outside—or eaten," I added, pointing to a great crocodile that had also emerged from the channel and was coming along towards us with open jaws.

"By the Axe!" shouted Umslopogaas again, "I—a warrior—will not die thus, trodden on like a slug by an ox."

Now I have mentioned a tree which I climbed. In his extremity Umslopogaas rushed for that tree and went up it like a lamplighter, just as the crocodile wriggled past its trunk, snapping at his retreating legs.

After this I took no more note of him, partly because of the advancing sea-cows, and more for the reason that one of the village natives posted above me, firing wildly, put a large round bullet through the sleeve of my coat. Indeed, had it not been for the wall which I built that protected us, I am certain that both my bearer and I would have been killed, for afterwards I found it splashed over with lead from bullets which had struck the stones.

Well, thanks to the strength of my rock and to the wall, or as Hans said afterwards, to Zikali's Great Medicine, we escaped unhurt. The rush went by me; indeed, I killed one sea-cow so close that the powder from the rifle actually burned its hide. But it did go by, leaving us untouched. All, however, were not so fortunate, since of the village natives two were trampled to death, while a third had his leg broken.

Also, and this was really amusing—a bewildered bull charging at full speed, crashed into the trunk of Umslopogaas' tree, and as it was not very thick, snapped it in two. Down came the top in which the dignified chief was ensconced like a bird in a nest, though at that moment there was precious little dignity about him. However, except for scratches he was not hurt, as the hippopotamus had other business in urgent need of attention and did not stop to settle with him.

"Such are the things which happen to a man who mixes himself up with matters of which he knows nothing," said Umslopogaas sententiously to me afterwards. But all the same he could never bear any allusion to this tree-climbing episode in his martial career, which, as it happened, had taken place in full view of his retainers, among whom it remained the greatest of jokes. Indeed, he wanted to kill a man, the wag of the party, who gave him a slang name which, being translated, means "*He-who-is-so-brave-that-he-dares-to-ride-a-water-horse-up-a- tree.*"

It was all over at last, for which I thanked Providence devoutly. A good many of the sea-cows were dead, I think twenty-one was out exact bag, but the majority of them had escaped in one way or another, many as I fear, wounded. I imagine that at the last the bulk of the herd overcame its fears and swimming through our screen, passed away down the channel. At any rate they were gone, and having ascertained that there was nothing to be done for the man who had been trampled on my side of the channel, I crossed it in the canoe with the object of returning quietly to our camp to rest.

But as yet there was to be no quiet for me, for there I found Captain Robertson, who I think had been refreshing himself out of a bottle and was in a great state of excitement about a native who had been killed near him who was a favourite of his, and another whose leg was broken. He declared vehemently that the hippopotamus which had done this had been wounded and rushed into some bushes a few hundred yards away, and that he meant to take vengeance upon it. Indeed, he was just setting off to do so.

Seeing his agitated state I thought it wisest to follow him. What happened need not be set out in detail. It is sufficient to say that he found that hippopotamus and blazed both barrels at it in the bushes, hitting it, but not seriously. Out lumbered the creature with its mouth open, wishing to escape. Robertson turned to fly as he was in its path, but from one cause or another, tripped and fell down. Certainly he would have been crushed beneath its huge feet had I not stepped in front of him and sent two solid eight-bore bullets down that yawning throat, killing it dead within three feet of where Robertson was trying to rise, and I may add, of myself.

This narrow escape sobered him, and I am bound to say that his gratitude was profuse.

"You are a brave man," he said, "and had it not been for you by now I should be wherever bad people go. I'll not forget it, Mr. Quatermain, and if ever you want anything that John Robertson can give, why, it's yours."

"Very well," I answered, being seized by an inspiration, "I do want something that you can give easily enough."

"Give it a name and it's yours, half my place, if you like."

"I want," I went on as I slipped new cartridges into the rifle, "I want you to promise to give up drink for your daughter's sake. That's what nearly did for you just now, you know."

"Man, you ask a hard thing," he said slowly. "But by God I'll try for her sake and for yours too."

Then I went to help to set the leg of the injured man, which was all the rest I got that morning.

The Oath

We spent three more days at that place. First it was necessary to allow time to elapse before the gases which generated in their great bodies caused those of the sea-cows which had been killed in the water, to float. Then they must be skinned and their thick hides cut into strips and pieces to be traded for *sjamboks* or to make small native shields for which some of the East Coast tribes will pay heavily.

All this took a long while, during which I amused, or disgusted myself in watching those river natives devouring the flesh of the beasts. The lean, what there was of it, they dried and smoked into a kind of "biltong," but a great deal of the fat they ate at once. I had the curiosity to weigh a lump which was given to one thin, hungry-looking fellow. It scaled quite twenty pounds. Within four hours he had eaten it to the last ounce and lay there, a distended and torpid log. What would not we white people give for such a digestion!

At last all was over and we started homewards, the man with a broken leg being carried in a kind of litter. On the edge of the bush-veld we found the waggon quite safe, also one of Captain Robertson's that had followed us from Strathmuir in order to carry the expected load of hippopotamus' hides and ivory. I asked my *voorlooper* if anything had happened during our absence. He answered nothing, but on the previous evening after dark, he had seen a glow in the direction of Strathmuir which lay on somewhat lower ground about twenty miles away, as though numerous fires had been lighted there. It struck him so much, he added, that he climbed a tree to observe it better. He did not think, however, that any building had been burned there, as the glow was not strong enough for that.

I suggested that it was caused by some grass fire or reed-burning, to which he replied indifferently that he did not think so as the line of the glow was not sufficiently continuous.

There the matter ended, though I confess that the story made me anxious, for what exact reason I could not say. Umslopogaas also, who had listened to it, for our talk was in Zulu, looked grave, but made no remark. But as since his tree-climbing experience he had been singularly silent, of this I thought little.

We had trekked at a time which we calculated would bring us to Strathmuir about an hour before sundown, allowing for a short halt half way. As my oxen were got in more quickly than those of the other waggon after this outspan, I was the first away, followed at a little distance by Umslopogaas, who preferred to walk with his Zulus. The truth was that I could not get that story about the glow of fires out of my mind and was anxious to push on, which had caused me to hurry up the inspanning.

Perhaps we had covered a couple of miles of the ten or twelve which still lay between us and Strathmuir, when far off on the crest of one of the waves of the veld which much resembled those of the swelling sea frozen while in motion, I saw a small figure approaching us at a rapid trot. Somehow that figure suggested Hans to my mind, so much so that I fetched my glasses to examine it more closely. A short scrutiny through them convinced me that Hans it was, Hans and no other, advancing at a great pace.

Filled with uneasiness, I ordered the driver to flog up the oxen, with the result that in a little over five minutes we met. Halting the waggon, I leapt from the waggon-box and calling to Umslopogaas who had kept up with us at a slow, swinging trot, went to Hans, who, when he saw me, stood still at a little distance, swinging his apology for a hat in his hand, as was his fashion when ashamed or perplexed.

"What is the matter, Hans?" I asked when we were within speaking distance.

"Oh! Baas, everything," he answered, and I noticed that he kept his eyes fixed upon the ground and that his lips twitched.

"Speak, you fool, and in Zulu," I said, for by now Umslopogaas had joined me.

"Baas," he answered in that tongue, "a terrible thing has come about at the farm of Red-Beard yonder. Yesterday afternoon at the time when people are in the habit of sleeping there till the sun grows less hot, a body of great men with fierce faces who carried big spears—perhaps there were fifty of them, Baas—crept up to the place through the long grass and growing crops, and attacked it."

"Did you see them come?" I asked.

"No, Baas. I was watching at a little distance as you bade me do and the sun being hot, I shut my eyes to keep out the glare of it, so that I did not see them until they had passed me and heard the noise."

"You mean that you were asleep or drunk, Hans, but go on."

"Baas, I do not know," he answered shamefacedly, "but after that I climbed a tall tree with a kind of bush at the top of it" (I ascertained afterwards that this was a sort of leafy-crowned palm), "and from it I saw everything without being seen."

"What did you see, Hans?" I asked him.

"I saw the big men run up and make a kind of circle round the village. Then they shouted, and the people in the village came out to see what was the matter. Thomaso and some of the men caught sight of them first and ran away fast into the hillside at the back where the trees grow, before the circle was complete. Then the women and the children came out and the big men killed them with their spears—all, all!"

"Good God!" I exclaimed. "And what happened at the house and to the lady?"

"Baas, some of the men had surrounded that also and when she heard the noise the lady Sad-Eyes came out on to the stoep and with her came the two Zulus of the Axe who had been left sick but were now quite recovered. A number of the big men ran as though to take her, but the two Zulus made a great fight in front of the little steps to the stoep, having their backs protected by the stoep, and killed six of them before they themselves were killed. Also Sad-Eyes shot one with a pistol she carried, and wounded another so that the spear fell out of his hand.

"Then the rest fell on her and tied her up, setting her in a chair on the stoep where two remained to watch her. They did her no hurt, Baas; indeed, they seemed to treat her as gently as they could. Also they went into the house and there they caught that tall fat yellow girl who always smiles and is called Janee, she who waits upon the Lady Sad-Eyes, and brought her out to her. I think they told her, Baas, that she must look after her mistress and that if she tried to run away she would be killed, for afterwards I saw Janee bring her food and other things."

"And then, Hans?"

"Then, Baas, most of the great men rested a while, though some of them went through the store gathering such things as they liked, blankets, knives and iron cooking-pots, but they set fire to nothing, nor did they try to catch the cattle. Also they took dry wood from the pile and lit big fires, eight or nine of them, and when the sun set they began to feast."

"What did they feast on, Hans, if they took no cattle?" I asked with a shiver, for I was afraid of I knew not what.

"Baas," answered Hans, turning his head away and looking at the ground, "they feasted on the children whom they had killed, also on some of the young women. These tall soldiers are men-eaters, Baas."

At this horrible intelligence I turned faint and felt as though I was going to fall, but recovering myself, signed to him to go on with his story.

"They feasted quite nicely, Baas," he continued, "making no noise. Then some of them slept while others watched, and that went on all night. As soon as it was dark, but before the moon rose, I slid down the tree and crept round to the back of the house without being seen or heard, as I can, Baas. I got into the house by the back door and crawled to the window of the sitting-room. It was open and peeping through I saw Sad-Eyes still tied to the seat on the stoep not more than a pace away, while the girl Janee crouched on the floor at her feet—I think she was asleep or fainting.

"I made a little noise, like a night-adder hissing, and kept on making it, till at last Sad-Eyes turned her head. Then I spoke in a very low whisper, for fear lest I should wake the two guards who were dozing on either side of her wrapped in their blankets, saying, 'It is I, Hans, come to help you.' 'You cannot,' she answered, also speaking very low. 'Get to your master and tell him and my father to follow. These men are called Amahagger and live far away across the river. They are going to take me to their home, as I understand, to rule them, because they want a white woman to be a queen over them who have always been ruled by a certain white queen, against whom they have rebelled. I do not think they mean to do me any harm, unless perhaps they want to marry me to their chief, but of this I am not sure from their talk which I understand badly. Now go, before they catch you.'

"'I think you might get away,' I whispered back. 'I will cut your bonds. When you are free, slip through the window and I will guide you.'

"'Very well, try it,' she said.

"So I drew my knife and stretched out my arm. But then, Baas, I showed myself a fool—if the Great Medicine had still been there I might have known better. I forgot the starlight which shone upon the blade of the knife. That girl Janee came out of her sleep or swoon, lifted her head and saw the knife. She screamed once, then at a word from her mistress was silent. But it was enough, for it woke up the guards who glared about them and threatened Janee with their great spears, also they went to sleep no more, but began to talk together, though what they said I could not hear, for I was hiding on the floor of the room. After this, knowing that I could do no good and might do harm and get myself killed, I crept out of the house as I had crept in, and crawled back to my tree."

"Why did you not come to me?" I asked.

"Because I still hoped I might be able to help Sad-Eyes, Baas. Also I wanted to see what happened, and I knew that I could not bring you here in time to be any good. Yet it is true I thought of coming though I did not know the road."

"Perhaps you were right."

"At the first dawn," continued Hans, "the great men who are called Amahagger rose and ate what was left over from the night before. Then they gathered themselves together and went to the house. Here they found a large chair, that seated with *rimpis* in which the Baas Red- Beard sits, and lashed two poles to the chair. Beneath the chair they tied the garments and other things of the Lady Sad-Eyes which they made Janee gather as Sad-Eyes directed her. This done, very gently they sat Sad-Eyes herself in the chair, bowing while they made her fast. After this eight of them set the poles upon their shoulders, and they all went away at a trot, heading for the bush-veld, driving with them a herd of goats which they had stolen from the farm, and making Janee run by the chair. I saw everything, Baas, for they passed just beneath my tree. Then I came to seek you, following the outward spoor of the waggons which I could not have done well at night. That is all, Baas."

"Hans," I said, "you have been drinking and because of it the lady Sad-Eyes is taken a prisoner by cannibals; for had you been awake and watching, you might have seen them coming and saved her and the rest. Still, afterwards you did well, and for the rest you must answer to Heaven."

"I must tell your reverend father, the Predikant, Baas, that the white master, Red-Beard, gave me the liquor and it is rude not to do as a great white master does, and drink it up. I am sure he will understand, Baas," said Hans abjectly.

I thought to myself that it was true and that the spear which Robertson cast had fallen upon his own head, as the Zulus say, but I made no answer, lacking time for argument.

"Did you say," asked Umslopogaas, speaking for the first time, "that my servants killed only six of these men-eaters?"

Hans nodded and answered, "Yes, six. I counted the bodies."

"It was ill done, they should have killed six each," said Umslopogaas moodily. "Well, they have left the more for us to finish," and he fingered the great axe.

Just then Captain Robertson arrived in his waggon, calling out anxiously to know what was the matter, for some premonition of evil seemed to have struck him. My heart sank at the sight of him, for how was I to tell such a story to the father of the murdered children and of the abducted girl?

In the end I felt that I could not. Yes, I turned coward and saying that I must fetch something out of the waggon, bolted into it, bidding Hans go forward and repeat his tale. He obeyed unwillingly enough and looking out between the curtains of the waggon tent I saw all that happened, though I could not hear the words that passed.

Robertson had halted the oxen and jumping from the waggon-box strode forward and met Hans, who began to speak with him, twitching his hat in his hands. Gradually as the tale progressed, I saw the Captain's face freeze into a mask of horror. Then he began to argue and deny, then to weep—oh! it was a terrible sight to see that great man weeping over those whom he had lost, and in such a fashion.

After this a kind of blind rage seized him and I thought he was going to kill Hans, who was of the same opinion, for he ran away. Next he staggered about, shaking his fists, cursing and shouting, till presently he fell of a heap and lay face downwards, beating his head against the ground and groaning.

Now I went to him and sat up.

"That's a pretty story, Quatermain, which this little yellow monkey has been gibbering at me. Man, do you understand what he says? He says that all those half-blood children of mine are dead, murdered by savages from over the Zambesi, yes, and eaten, too, with their mothers. Do you take the point? Eaten like lambs. Those fires your man saw last night were the fires on which they were cooked, my little *so-and-so* and *so-and-so*," and he mentioned half a dozen different names. "Yes, cooked, Quatermain. And that isn't all of it, they have taken Inez too. They didn't eat her, but they have dragged her off a captive for God knows what reason. I couldn't understand. The whole ship's crew is gone, except the captain absent on leave and the first officer, Thomaso, who deserted with some Lascar stokers, and left the women and children to their fate. My God, I'm going mad. I'm going mad! If you have any mercy in you, give me something to drink."

"All right," I said, "I will. Sit here and wait a minute."

Then I went to the waggon and poured out a stiff tot of spirits into which I put an amazing doze of bromide from a little medicine chest I always carry with me, and thirty drops of chlorodyne on the top of it. All this compound I mixed up with a little water and took it to him in a tin cup so that he could not see the colour.

He drank it at a gulp and throwing the pannikin aside, sat down on the veld, groaning while the company watched him at a respectful distance, for Hans had joined the others and his tale had spread like fire in drought-parched grass.

In a few minutes the drugs began to take effect upon Robertson's tortured nerves, for he rose and said quietly,

"What now?"

"Vengeance, or rather justice," I answered.

"Yes," he exclaimed, "vengeance. I swear that I will be avenged, or die—or both."

Again I saw my opportunity and said, "You must swear more than that, Robertson. Only sober men can accomplish great things, for drink destroys the judgment. If you wish to be avenged for the dead and to rescue the living, you must be sober, or I for one will not help you."

"Will you help me if I do, to the end, good or ill, Quatermain?" he added.

I nodded.

"That's as much as another's oath," he muttered. "Still, I will put my thought in words. I swear by God, by my mother—like these natives— and by my daughter born in honest marriage, that I will never touch another drop of strong drink, until I have avenged those poor women and their little children, and rescued Inez from their murderers. If I do you may put a bullet through me."

"That's all right," I said in an offhand fashion, though inwardly I glowed with pride at the success of my great idea, for at the time I thought it great, and went on,

"Now let us get to business. The first thing to do is to trek to Strathmuir and make preparations; the next to start upon the trail. Come to sit on the waggon with me and tell me what guns and ammunition you have got, for according to Hans those savages don't seem to have touched anything, except a few blankets and a herd of goats."

He did as I asked, telling me all he could remember. Then he said,

"It is a strange thing, but now I recall that about two years ago a great savage with a high nose, who talked a sort of Arabic which, like Inez, I understand, having lived on the coast, turned up one day and said he wanted to trade. I asked him what in, and he answered that he would like to buy some children. I told him that I was not a slave- dealer. Then he looked at Inez, who was moving about, and said that he would like to buy her to be a wife for his Chief, and offered some fabulous sum in ivory and in gold, which he said should be paid before she was taken away. I snatched his big spear from his hand, broke it over his head and gave him the best hiding with its shaft that he had ever heard of. Then I kicked him off the place. He limped away but when he was out of reach, turned and called out that one day he would come again with others and take her, meaning Inez, without leaving the price in ivory and gold. I ran for my gun, but when I got back he had gone and I never thought of the matter again from that day to this."

"Well, he kept his promise," I said, but Robertson made no answer, for by this time that thundering dose of bromide and laudanum had taken effect on him and he had fallen asleep, of which I was glad, for I thought that this sleep would save his sanity, as I believe it did for a while.

We reached Strathmuir towards sunset, too late to think of attempting the pursuit that day. Indeed, during our trek, I had thought the matter out carefully and come to the conclusion that to try to do so would be useless. We must rest and make preparations; also there was no hope of our overtaking these brutes who already had a clear twelve hours' start, by a sudden spurt. They must be run down patiently by following their spoor, if indeed they could be run down at all before they vanished into the vast recesses of unknown Africa. The most we could do this night was to get ready.

Captain Robertson was still sleeping when we passed the village and of this I was heartily glad, since the remains of a cannibal feast are not pleasant to behold, especially when they are——! Indeed, of these I determined to be rid at once, so slipping off the waggon with Hans and some of the farm boys, for none of the Zulus would defile themselves by touching such human remnants—I made up two of the smouldering fires, the light of which the *voorlooper* had seen upon the sky, and on to them cast, or caused to be cast, those poor fragments. Also I told the farm natives to dig a big grave and in it to place the other bodies and generally to remove the traces of murder.

Then I went on to the house, and not too soon. Seeing the waggons arrive and having made sure that the Amahagger were gone, Thomaso and the other cowards emerged from their hiding-places and returned. Unfortunately for the former the first person he met was Umslopogaas, who began to revile the fat half-breed in no measured terms, calling him dog, coward, and other opprobrious names, such as deserter of women and children, and so forth—all of which someone translated.

Thomaso, an insolent person, tried to swagger the matter out, saying that he had gone to get assistance. Infuriated at this lie, Umslopogaas leapt upon him with a roar and though he was a strong man, dealt with him as a lion does with a buck. Lifting him from his feet, he hurled him to the ground, then as he strove to rise and run, caught him again and as it seemed to me, was about to break his back across his knee. Just at this juncture I arrived.

"Let the man go," I shouted to him. "Is there not enough death here already?"

"Yes," answered Umslopogaas, "I think there is. Best that this jackal should live to eat his own shame," and he cast Thomaso to the ground, where he lay groaning.

Robertson, who was still asleep in the waggon, woke up at the noise, and descended from it, looking dazed. I got him to the house and in doing so made my way past, or rather between the bodies of the two Zulus and of the six men whom they had killed, also of him whom Inez had shot. Those Zulus had made a splendid fight for they were covered with wounds, all of them in front, as I found upon examination.

Having made Robertson lie down upon his bed, I took a good look at the slain Amahagger. They were magnificent men, all of them; tall, spare and shapely with very clear-cut features and rather frizzled hair. From these characteristics, as well as the lightness of their colour, I concluded that they were of a Semitic or Arab type, and that the admixture of their blood with that of the Bantus was but slight, if indeed there were any at all. Their spears, of which one had been cut through by a blow of a Zulu's axe, were long and broad, not unlike to those used by the Masai, but of finer workmanship.

By this time the sun was setting and thoroughly tired by all that I had gone through, I went into the house to get something to eat, having told Hans to find food and prepare a meal. As I sat down Robertson joined me and I made him also eat. His first impulse was to go to the cupboard and fetch the spirit bottle; indeed, he rose to do so.

"Hans is making coffee," I said warningly.

"Thank you," he answered, "I forgot. Force of habit, you know."

Here I may state that never from that moment did I see him touch another drop of liquor, not even when I drank my modest tot in front of him. His triumph over temptation was splendid and complete, especially as the absence of his accustomed potations made him ill for some time and of course depressed his spirits, with painful results that were apparent in due course.

In fact, the man became totally changed. He grew gloomy but resourceful, also full of patience. Only one idea obsessed him—to rescue his daughter and avenge the murder of his people; indeed, except his sins, he thought of and found interest in nothing else. Moreover, his iron constitution cast off all the effects of his past debauchery and he grew so strong that although I was pretty tough in those days, he could out-tire me.

To return; I engaged him in conversation and with his help made a list of what we should require on our vendetta journey, all of which served to occupy his mind. Then I sent him to bed, saying that I would call him before dawn, having first put a little more bromide into his third cup of coffee. After this I turned in and notwithstanding the sight of those remains of the cannibal feast and the knowledge of the dead men who lay outside my window, I slept like a top.

Indeed, it was the Captain who awakened me, not I the Captain, saying that daylight was on the break and we had better be stirring. So we went down to the Store, where I was thankful to find that everything had been tidied up in accordance with my directions.

On our way Robertson asked me what had become of the remains, whereon I pointed to the smouldering ashes of one of the great fires. He went to it and kneeling down, said a prayer in broad Scotch, doubtless one that he had learned at his mother's knee. Then he took some of the ashes from the edge of the pyre—for such it was—and threw them into the glowing embers where, as he knew, lay all that was left of those who had sprung from him. Also he tossed others of them into the air, though what he meant by this I did not understand and never asked. Probably it was some rite indicative of expiation or of revenge, or both, which he had learned from the savages among whom he had lived so long.

After this we went into the Store and with the help of some of the natives, or half-breeds, who had accompanied us on the sea-cow expedition, selected all the goods we wanted, which we sent to the house.

As we returned thither I saw Umslopogaas and his men engaged, with the usual Zulu ceremonies, in burying their two companions in a hole they had made in the hillside. I noted, however, that they did not inter their war-axes or their throwing-spears with them as usual, probably because they thought that these might be needed. In place of them they put with the dead little models roughly shaped of bits of wood, which models they "killed" by first breaking them across.

I lingered to watch the funeral and heard Goroko, the witch-doctor, make a little speech.

"O Father and Chief of the Axe," he said, addressing Umslopogaas, who stood silent leaning on his weapon and watching all, a portentous figure in the morning mist, "O Father, O Son of the Heavens" (this was an allusion to the royal blood of Umslopogaas of which the secret was well known, although it would never have been spoken aloud in Zululand), "O Slaughterer (Bulalio), O Woodpecker who picks at the hearts of men; O King-Slayer; O Conqueror of the Halakazi; O Victor in a hundred fights; O Gatherer of the Lily-bloom that faded in the hand; O Wolf-man, Captain of the Wolves that ravened; O Slayer of Faku; O Great One whom it pleases to seem small, because he must follow his blood to the end appointed——"

This was the opening of the speech, the "*bonga*-ing" or giving of Titles of Praise to the person addressed, of which I have quoted but a sample, for there were many more of them that I have forgotten. Then the speaker went on,

"It was told to me, though of it I remember nothing, that when my Spirit was in me a while ago I prophesied that this place would flow with blood, and lo! the blood has flowed, and with it that of these our brothers," and he gave the names of the two dead Zulus, also those of their forefathers for several generations.

"It seems, Father, that they died well, as you would have wished them to die, and as doubtless they desired to die themselves, leaving a tale behind them, though it is true that they might have died better, killing more of the men-eaters, as it is certain they would have done, had they not been sick inside. They are finished; they have gone beyond to await us in the Under-world among the ghosts. Their story is told and soon to their children they will be but names whispered in honour after the sun has set. Enough of them who have showed us how to die as our fathers did before them."

Goroko paused a while, then added with a waving of his hands,

"My Spirit comes to me again and I know that these our brothers shall not pass unavenged. Chief of the Axe, great glory awaits the Axe, for it shall feed full. I have spoken."

"Good words!" grunted Umslopogaas. Then he saluted the dead by raising *Inkosikaas* and came to me to consult about our journey.

Pursuit

After all we did not get away much before noon, because first there was a great deal to be done. To begin with the loads had to be arranged. These consisted largely of ammunition, everything else being cut down to an irreducible minimum. To carry them we took two donkeys there were on the place, also half a dozen pack oxen, all of which animals were supposed to be "salted"—that is, to have suffered and recovered from every kind of sickness, including the bite of the deadly tsetse fly. I suspected, it is true, that they would not be proof against further attacks, still, I hoped that they would last for some time, as indeed proved to be the case.

In the event of the beasts failing us, we took also ten of the best of those Strathmuir men who had accompanied us on the sea-cow trip, to serve as bearers when it became necessary. It cannot be said that these snuff-and-butter fellows—for most, if not all of them had some dash of white blood in their veins—were exactly willing volunteers. Indeed, if a choice had been left to them, they would, I think, have declined this adventure.

But there was no choice. Their master, Robertson, ordered them to come and after a glance at the Zulus they concluded that the command was one which would be enforced and that if they stopped behind, it would not be as living men. Also some of them had lost wives or children in the slaughter, which, if they were not very brave, filled them with a desire for revenge. Lastly, they could all shoot after a fashion and had good rifles; moreover if I may say so, I think that they put confidence in my leadership. So they made the best of a bad business and got themselves ready.

Then arrangements must be made about the carrying on of the farm and store during our absence. These, together with my waggon and oxen, were put in the charge of Thomaso, since there was no one else who could be trusted at all—a very battered and crestfallen Thomaso, by the way. When he heard of it he was much relieved, since I think he feared lest he also should be expected to take part in the hunt of the Amahagger man-eaters. Also it may have occurred to him that in all probability none of us would ever come back at all, in which case by a process of natural devolution, he might find himself the owner of the business and much valuable property. However, he swore by sundry saints—for Thomaso was nominally a Catholic—that he would look after everything as though it were his own, as no doubt he hoped it might become.

"Hearken, fat pig," said Umslopogaas, Hans obligingly translating so that there might be no mistake, "if I come back, and come back I shall who travel with the Great Medicine—and find even one of the cattle of the white lord, Macumazahn, Watcher-by-Night, missing, or one article stolen from his waggon, or the fields of your master not cultivated or his goods wasted, I swear by the Axe that I will hew you into pieces with the axe; yes, if to do it I have to hunt you from where the sun rises to where it sets and down the length of the night between. Do you understand, fat pig, deserter of women and children, who to save yourself could run faster than a buck?"

Thomaso replied that he understood very clearly indeed, and that, Heaven helping him, all should be kept safe and sound. Still, I was sure that in his manly heart he was promising great gifts to the saints if they would so arrange matters that Umslopogaas and his axe were never seen at Strathmuir again, and reflecting that after all the Amahagger had their uses. However, as I did not trust him in the least, much against their will, I left my driver and *voorlooper* to guard my belongings.

At last we did get off, pursued by the fervent blessings of Thomaso and the prayers of the others that we would avenge their murdered relatives. We were a curious and motley procession. First went Hans, because at following a spoor he was, I believe, almost unequalled in Africa, and with him, Umslopogaas, and three of his Zulus to guard against surprise. These were followed by Captain Robertson, who seemed to prefer to walk alone and whom I thought it best to leave undisturbed. Then I came and after me straggled the Strathmuir boys with the pack animals, the cavalcade being closed by the remaining Zulus under the command of Goroko. These walked last in case any of the mixed-bloods should attempt to desert, as we thought it quite probable that they would.

Less than an hour's tramp brought us to the bush-veld where I feared that our troubles might begin, since if the Amahagger were cunning, they would take advantage of it to confuse or hide their spoor. As it chanced, however, they had done nothing of the sort and a child could have followed their march. Just before nightfall we came to their first halting-place where they had made a fire and eaten one of the herd of farm goats which they had driven away with them, although they left the cattle, I suppose, because goats are docile and travel well.

Hans showed us everything that had happened; where the chair in which Inez was carried was set down, where she and Janee had been allowed to walk that she might stretch her stiff limbs, the dregs of some coffee that evidently Janee had made in a saucepan, and so forth.

He even told us the exact number of the Amahagger, which he said totalled forty-one, including the man whom Inez had wounded. His spoor he distinguished from that of the others both by an occasional drop of blood and because he walked lightly on his right foot, doubtless for the reason that he wished to avoid jarring his wound, which was on that side.

At this spot we were obliged to stay till daybreak, since it was impossible to follow the spoor by night, a circumstance that gave the cannibals a great advantage over us.

The next two days were repetitions of the first, but on the fourth we passed out of the bush-veld into the swamp country that bordered the great river. Here our task was still easy since the Amahagger had followed one of the paths made by the river-dwellers who had their habitations on mounds, though whether these were natural or artificial I am not sure, and sometimes on floating islands.

On our second day in the reeds we came upon a sad sight. To our left stood one of these mound villages, if a village it could be called, since it consisted only of four or five huts inhabited perhaps by twenty people. We went up to it to obtain information and stumbled across the body of an old man lying in the pathway. A few yards further on we found the ashes of a big fire and by it such remains as we had seen at Strathmuir. Here there had been another cannibal feast. The miserable huts were empty, but as at Strathmuir, had not been burnt.

We were going away when the acute ears of Hans caught the sound of groans. We searched about and in a clump of reeds near the foot of the mound, found an old woman with a great spear wound just above her skinny thigh piercing deep into the vitals, but of a nature which is not immediately mortal. One of Robertson's people who understood the language of these swamp-dwellers well, spoke to her. She told him that she wanted water. It was brought and she drank copiously. Then in answer to his questions she began to talk.

She said that the Amahagger had attacked the village and killed all who could not escape. They had eaten a young woman and three children. She had been wounded by a spear and fled away into the place where we found her, where none of them took the trouble to follow her as she "was not worth eating."

By my direction the man asked her whether she knew anything of these Amahagger. She replied that her grandfathers had, though she had heard nothing of them since she was a child, which must have been seventy years before. They were a fierce people who lived far up north across the Great River, the remnants of a race that had once "ruled the world."

Her grandfathers used to say that they were not always cannibals, but had become so long before because of a lack of food and now had acquired the taste. It was for this purpose that they still raided to get other people to eat, since their ruler would not allow them to eat one another. The flesh of cattle they did not care for, although they had plenty of them, but sometimes they ate goats and pigs because they said they tasted like man. According to her grandfathers they were a very evil people and full of magic.

All of this the old woman told us quite briskly after she had drunk the water, I think because her wound had mortified and she felt no pain. Her information, however, as is common with the aged, dealt entirely with the far past; of the history of the Amahagger since the days of her forebears she knew nothing, nor had she seen anything of Inez. All she could tell us was that some of them had attacked her village at dawn and that when she ran out of the hut she was speared.

While Robertson and I were wondering what we should do with the poor old creature whom it seemed cruel to leave here to perish, she cleared up the question by suddenly expiring before our eyes. Uttering the name of someone with whom, doubtless, she had been familiar in her youth, three or four times over, she just sank down and seemed to go to sleep and on examination we found that she was dead. So we left her and went on.

Next day we came to the edge of the Great River, here a sheet of placid running water about a mile across, for at this time of the year it was low. Perceiving quite a big village on our left, we went to it and made enquiries, to find that it had not been attacked by the cannibals, probably because it was too powerful, but that three nights before some of their canoes had been stolen, in which no doubt these had crossed the river.

As the people of this village had traded with Robertson at Strathmuir, we had no difficulty in obtaining other canoes from them in which to cross the Zambesi in return for one of our oxen that I could see was already sickening from tsetse bite. These canoes were large enough to take the donkeys that were patient creatures and stood still, but the cattle we could not get into them for fear of an upset. So we killed the two driven beasts that were left to us and took them with us as dead meat for food, while the three remaining pack oxen we tried to swim across, dragging them after the canoes with hide *reims* round their horns. As a result two were drowned, but one, a bold-hearted and enterprising animal, gained the other bank.

Here again we struck a sea of reeds in which, after casting about, Hans once more found the spoor of the Amahagger. That it was theirs beyond doubt was proved by the circumstance that on a thorny kind of weed we found a fragment of a cotton dress which, because of the pattern stamped on it, we all recognised as one that Inez had been wearing. At first I thought that this had been torn off by the thorns, but on examination we became certain that it had been placed there purposely, probably by Janee, to give us a clue. This conclusion was confirmed when at subsequent periods of the hunt we found other fragments of the same garment.

Now it would be useless for me to set out the details of this prolonged and arduous chase which in all endured for something over three weeks. Again and again we lost the trail and were only able to recover it by long and elaborate search, which occupied much time. Then, after we escaped from the reeds and swamps, we found ourselves upon stony uplands where the spoor was almost impossible to follow, indeed, we only rediscovered it by stumbling across the dead body of that cannibal whom Inez had wounded. Evidently he had perished from his hurt, which I could see had mortified. From the state of his remains we gathered that the raiders must be about two days' march ahead of us.

Striking their spoor again on softer ground where the impress of their feet remained—at any rate to the cunning sight of Hans—we followed them down across great valleys wherein trees grew sparsely, which valleys were separated from each other by ridges of high and barren land. On these belts of rocky soil our difficulties were great, but here twice we were put on the right track by more fragments torn from the dress of Inez.

At length we lost the spoor altogether; not a sign of it was to be found. We had no idea which way to go. All about us appeared these valleys covered with scattered bush running this way and that, so that we could not tell which of them to follow or to cross. The thing seemed hopeless, for how could we expect to find a little body of men in that immensity? Hans shook his head and even the fierce and steadfast Robertson was discouraged.

"I fear my poor lassie is gone," he said, and relapsed into brooding as had become his wont.

"Never say die! It's dogged as does it!" I replied cheerfully in the words of Nelson, who also had learned what it meant to hunt an enemy over trackless wastes, although his were of water.

I walked to the top of the rise where we were encamped, and sat down alone to think matters over. Our condition was somewhat parlous; all our beasts were now dead, even the second donkey, which was the last of them, having perished that morning, and been eaten, for food was scanty since of late we had met with little game. The Strathmuir men, who now must carry the loads, were almost worn out and doubtless would have deserted, except for the fact that there was no place to which they could go. Even the Zulus were discouraged, and said they had come away from home across the Great River to fight, not to run about in wildernesses and starve, though Umslopogaas made no complaint, being buoyed up by the promise of his soothsayer, Goroko, that battle was ahead of him in which he would win great glory.

Hans, however, remained cheerful, for the reason, as he remarked vacuously, that the Great Medicine was with us and that therefore, however bad things seemed to be, all in fact was well; an argument that carried no conviction to my soul.

It was on a certain evening towards sunset that I went away thus alone. I looked about me, east and west and north. Everywhere appeared the same bush-clad valleys and barren rises, miles upon miles of them. I bethought me of the map that old Zikali had drawn in the ashes, and remembered that it showed these valleys and rises and that beyond them there should be a great swamp, and beyond the swamp a mountain. So it seemed that we were on the right road to the home of his white Queen, if such a person existed, or at any rate we were passing over country similar to that which he had pictured or imagined.

But at this time I was not troubling my head about white queens. I was thinking of poor Inez. That she was alive a few days before we knew from the fragments of her dress. But where was she now? The spoor was utterly lost on that stony ground, or if any traces of it remained a heavy deluge of rain had washed them away. Even Hans had confessed himself beaten.

I stared about me helplessly, and as I did so a flying ray of light from the setting sun reflected downwards from a storm-cloud, fell upon a white patch on the crest of one of the distant land-waves. It struck me that probably limestone outcropped at this spot, as indeed proved to be the case; also that such a patch of white would be a convenient guide for any who were travelling across that sea of bush. Further, some instinct within seemed to impel me to steer for it, although I had all but made up my mind to go in a totally different direction many more points to the east. It was almost as though a voice were calling to me to take this path and no other. Doubtless this was an effect produced by weariness and mental overstrain. Still, there it was, very real and tangible, one that I did not attempt to combat.

So next morning at the dawn I headed north by west, laying my course for that white patch and for the first time breaking the straight line of our advance. Captain Robertson, whose temper had not been bettered by prolonged and frightful anxiety, or I may add, by his unaccustomed abstinence, asked me rather roughly why I was altering the course.

"Look here, Captain," I answered, "if we were at sea and you did something of the sort, I should not put such a question to you, and if by any chance I did, I should not expect you to answer. Well, by your own wish I am in command here and I think that the same argument holds."

"Yes," he replied. "I suppose you have studied your chart, if there is any of this God-forsaken country, and at any rate discipline is discipline. So steam ahead and don't mind me."

The others accepted my decision without comment; most of them were so miserable that they did not care which way we went, also they were good enough to repose confidence in my judgment.

"Doubtless the Baas has reasons," said Hans dubiously, "although the spoor, when last we saw it, headed towards the rising sun and as the country is all the same, I do not see why those man-eaters should have returned."

"Yes," I said, "I have reasons," although in fact I had none at all.

Hans surveyed me with a watery eye as though waiting for me to explain them, but I looked haughty and declined to oblige.

"The Baas has reasons," continued Hans, "for taking us on what I think to be the wrong side of that great ridge, there to hunt for the spoor of the men-eaters, and they are so deep down in his mind that he cannot dig them up for poor old Hans to look at. Well, the Baas wears the Great Medicine and perhaps it is there that the reasons sit. Those Strathmuir fellows say that they can go no further and wish to die. Umslopogaas has just gone to them with his axe to tell them that he is ready to help them to their wish. Look, he has got there, for they are coming quickly, who after all prefer to live."

Well, we started for my white patch of stones which no one else had noticed and of which I said nothing to anyone, and reached it by the following evening, to find, as I expected, that it was a lime outcrop.

By now we were in a poor way, for we had practically nothing left to eat, which did not tend to raise the spirits of the party. Also that lime outcrop proved to be an uninteresting spot overlooking a wide valley which seemed to suggest that there were other valleys of a similar sort beyond it, and nothing more.

Captain Robertson sat stern-faced and despondent at a distance muttering into his beard, as had become a habit with him. Umslopogaas leaned upon his axe and contemplated the heavens, also occasionally the Strathmuir men who cowered beneath his eye. The Zulus squatted about sharing such snuff as remained to them in economic pinches. Goroko, the witch-doctor, engaged himself in consulting his "Spirit," by means of bone-throwing, upon the humble subject of whether or no we should succeed in killing any game for food to-morrow, a point on which I gathered that his "Spirit" was quite uncertain. In short, the gloom was deep and universal and the sky looked as though it were going to rain.

Hans became sarcastic. Sneaking up to me in his most aggravating way, like a dog that means to steal something and cover up the theft with simulated affection, he pointed out one by one all the disadvantages of our present position. He indicated *per contra*, that if *his* advice had been followed, his conviction was that even if we had not found the man-eaters and rescued the lady called Sad-Eyes, our state would have been quite different. He was sure, he added, that the valley which he had suggested we should follow, was one full of game, inasmuch as he had seen their spoor at its entrance.

"Then why did you not say so?" I asked.

Hans sucked at his empty corn-cob pipe, which was his way of indicating that he would like me to give him some tobacco, much as a dog groans heavily under the table when he wants a bit to eat, and answered that it was not for him to point out things to one who knew everything, like the great Macumazahn, Watcher-by-Night, his honoured master. Still, the luck did seem to have gone a bit wrong. The privations could have been put up with (here he sucked very loudly at the empty pipe and looked at mine, which was alight), everything could have been put up with, if only there had been a chance of coming even with those men-eaters and rescuing the Lady Sad-Eyes, whose face haunted his sleep. As it was, however, he was convinced that by following the course I had mapped out we had lost their spoor finally and that probably they were now three days' march away in another direction. Still, the Baas had said that he had his reasons, and that of course was enough for him, Hans, only if the Baas would condescend to tell him, he would as a matter of curiosity like to know what the reasons were.

At that moment I confess that, much as I was attached to him, I should have liked to murder Hans, who, I felt, believing that he had me "on toast," to use a vulgar phrase, was taking advantage of my position to make a mock of me in his sly, Hottentot way.

I tried to continue to look grand, but felt that the attitude did not impress. Then I stared about me as though taking counsel with the Heavens, devoutly hoping that the Heavens would respond to my mute appeal. As a matter of fact they did.

"There is my reason, Hans," I said in my most icy voice, and I pointed to a faint line of smoke rising against the twilight sky on the further side of the intervening valley.

"You will perceive, Hans," I added, "that those Amahagger cannibals have forgotten their caution and lit a fire yonder, which they have not done for a long time. Perhaps you would like to know why this has happened. If so I will tell you. It is because for some days past I have purposely lost their spoor, which they knew we were following, and lit fires to puzzle them. Now, thinking that they have done with us, they have become incautious and shown us where they are. That is my reason, Hans."

He heard and, although of course he did not believe that I had lost the spoor on purpose, stared at me till I thought his little eyes were going to drop out of his head. But even in his admiration he contrived to convey an insult as only a native can.

"How wonderful is the Great Medicine of the Opener-of-Roads, that it should have been able thus to instruct the Baas," he said. "Without doubt the Great Medicine is right and yonder those men-eaters are encamped, who might just as well as have been anywhere else within a hundred miles."

"Drat the Great Medicine," I replied, but beneath my breath, then added aloud,

"Be so good, Hans, as to go to Umslopogaas and to tell him that Macumazahn, or the Great Medicine, proposes to march at once to attack the camp of the Amahagger, and—here is some tobacco."

"Yes, Baas," answered Hans humbly, as he snatched the tobacco and wriggled away like a worm.

Then I went to talk with Robertson.

The end of it was that within an hour we were creeping across that valley towards the spot where I had seen the line of smoke rising against the twilight sky.

Somewhere about midnight we reached the neighbourhood of this place. How near or how far we were from it, we could not tell since the moon was invisible, as of course the smoke was in the dark. Now the question was, what should we do?

Obviously there would be enormous advantages in a night attack, or at least in locating the enemy, so that it might be carried out at dawn before he marched. Especially was this so, since we were scarcely in a condition even if we could come face to face with them, to fight these savages when they were prepared and in the light of day. Only we two white men, with Hans, Umslopogaas and his Zulus, could be relied upon in such a case, since the Strathmuir mixed-bloods had become entirely demoralised and were not to be trusted at a pinch. Indeed, tired and half starving as we were, none of us was at his best. Therefore a surprise seemed our only chance. But first we must find those whom we wished to surprise.

Ultimately, after a hurried consultation, it was agreed that Hans and I should go forward and see if we could locate the Amahagger. Robertson wished to come too, but I pointed out that he must remain to look after his people, who, if he left them, might take the opportunity to melt away in the darkness, especially as they knew that heavy fighting was at hand. Also if anything happened to me it was desirable that one white man should remain to lead the party. Umslopogaas, too, volunteered, but knowing his character, I declined his help. To tell the truth, I was almost certain that if we came upon the men-eaters, he would charge the whole lot of them and accomplish a fine but futile end after hacking down a number of cannibal barbarians, whose extinction or escape remained absolutely immaterial to our purpose, namely, the rescue of Inez.

So it came about that Hans and I started alone, I not at all enjoying the job. I suppose that there lurks in my nature some of that primeval terror of the dark, which must continually have haunted our remote forefathers of a hundred or a thousand generations gone and still lingers in the blood of most of us. At any rate even if I am named the Watcher-by-Night, greatly do I prefer to fight or to face peril in the sunlight, though it is true that I would rather avoid both at any time.

In fact, I wished heartily that the Amahagger were at the other side of Africa, or in heaven, and that I, completely ignorant of the person called Inez Robertson, were seated smoking the pipe of peace on my own stoep in Durban. I think that Hans guessed my state of mind, since he suggested that he should go alone, adding with his usual unveiled rudeness, that he was quite certain that he would do much better without me, since white men always made a noise.

"Yes," I replied, determined to give him a Roland for his Oliver, "I have no doubt you would—under the first bush you came across, where you would sleep till dawn, and then return and say that you could not find the Amahagger."

Hans chuckled, quite appreciating the joke, and having thus mutually affronted each other, we started on our quest.

The Swamp

Neither Hans nor I carried rifles that we knew would be in the way on our business, which was just to scout. Moreover, one is always tempted to shoot if a gun is at hand, and this I did not want to do at present. So, although I had my revolver in case of urgent necessity, my only other weapon was a Zulu axe, that formerly had belonged to one of those two men who died defending Inez on the veranda at Strathmuir, while Hans had nothing but his long knife. Thus armed, or unarmed, we crept forward towards that spot whence, as we conjectured, we had seen the line of smoke rising some hours before.

For about a quarter of a mile we went on thus without seeing or hearing anything, and a difficult job it was in that gloom among the scattered trees with no light save such as the stars gave us. Indeed, I was about to suggest that we had better abandon the enterprise until daybreak when Hans nudged me, whispering,

"Look to the right between those twin thorns."

I obeyed and following the line of sight which he had indicated, perceived, at a distance of about two hundred yards a faint glow, so faint indeed that I think only Hans would have noticed it. Really it might have been nothing more than the phosphorescence rising from a heap of fungus, or even from a decaying animal.

"The fire of which we saw the smoke that has burnt to ashes," whispered Hans again. "I think that they have gone, but let us look."

So we crawled forward very cautiously to avoid making the slightest noise; so cautiously, indeed, that it must have taken us nearly half an hour to cover those two hundred yards.

At length we were within about forty yards of that dying fire and, afraid to go further, came to a stand—or rather, a lie-still—behind some bushes until we knew more. Hans lifted his head and sniffed with his broad nostrils; then he whispered into my ear, but so low that I could scarcely hear him.

"Amahagger there all right, Baas, I smell them."

This of course was possible, since what wind there was blew from the direction of the fire, although I whose nose is fairly keen could smell nothing at all. So I determined to wait and watch a while, and indicated my decision to Hans, who, considering our purpose accomplished, showed signs of wishing to retreat.

Some minutes we lay thus, till of a sudden this happened. A branch of resinous wood of which the stem had been eaten through by the flames, fell upon the ashes of the fire and burnt up with a brilliant light. In it we saw that the Amahagger were sleeping in a circle round the fire wrapped in their blankets.

Also we saw another thing, namely that nearer to us, not more than a dozen yards away, indeed, was a kind of little tent, also made of fur rugs or blankets, which doubtless sheltered Inez. Indeed, this was evident from the fact that at the mouth of it, wrapped up in something, lay none other than her maid, Janee, for her face being towards us, was recognised by us both in the flare of the flaming branch. One more thing we noted, namely, that two of the cannibals, evidently a guard, were sleeping between us and the little tent. Of course they ought to have been awake, but fatigue had overcome them and there they slumbered, seated on the ground, their heads hanging forward almost upon their knees.

An idea came to me. If we could kill those men without waking the others in that gloom, it might be possible to rescue Inez at once. Rapidly I weighed the *pros* and *cons* of such an attempt. Its advantages, if successful, were that the object of our pursuit would be carried through without further trouble and that it was most doubtful whether we should ever get such a chance again. If we returned to fetch the others and attacked in force, the probability was that those Amahagger, or one of them, would hear some sound made by the advance of a number of men, and fly into the darkness; or, rather than lose Inez, they might kill her. Or if they stood and fought, she might be slain in the scrimmage. Or, as after all we had only about a dozen effectives, for the Strathmuir bearers could not be relied upon, they might defeat and kill us whom they outnumbered by two or three to one.

These were the arguments for the attempt. Those for not making it were equally obvious. To begin with it was one of extraordinary risk; the two guards or someone else behind them might wake up—for such people, like dogs, mostly sleep with one eye open, especially when they knew that they are being pursued. Or if they did not we might bungle the business so that they raised an outcry before they grew silent for ever, in which case both of us and perhaps Inez also would probably pay the penalty before we could get away.

Such was the horned dilemma upon one point or other of which we ran the risk of being impaled. For a full minute or more I considered the matter with an earnestness almost amounting to mental agony, and at last all but came to the conclusion that the danger was too enormous. It would be better, notwithstanding the many disadvantages of that plan, to go back and fetch the others.

But then it was that I made one of my many mistakes in life. Most of us do more foolish things than wise ones and sometimes I think that in spite of a certain reputation for caution and far-sightedness, I am exceptionally cursed in this respect. Indeed, when I look back upon my past, I can scarcely see the scanty flowers of wisdom that decorate its path because of the fat, ugly trees of error by which it is overshadowed.

On that occasion, forgetting past experiences where Hans was concerned, my natural tendency to blunder took the form of relying upon another's judgment instead of on my own. Although I had formed a certain view as to what should be done, the *pros* and *cons* seemed so evenly balanced that I determined to consult the little Hottentot and accept his verdict. This, after all, was but a form of gambling like pitch and toss, since, although it is true Hans was a clever, or at any rate a cunning man according to his lights, and experienced, it meant that I was placing my own judgment in abeyance, which no one considering a life-and-death enterprise should do, taking the chance of that of another, whatever it might be. However, not for the first time, I did so—to my grief.

In the tiniest of whispers with my lips right against his smelly head, I submitted the problem to Hans, asking him what we should do, go on or go back. He considered a while, then answered in a voice which he contrived to make like the drone of a night beetle.

"Those men are fast asleep, I know it by their breathing. Also the Baas has the Great Medicine. Therefore I say go on, kill them and rescue Sad-Eyes."

Now I saw that the Fates to which I had appealed had decided against me and that I must accept their decree. With a sick and sinking heart—for I did not at all like the business—I wondered for a moment what had led Hans to take this view, which was directly opposite to any I had expected from him. Of course his superstition about the Great Medicine had something to do with it, but I felt convinced that this was not all.

Even then I guessed that two arguments appealed to him, of which the first was that he desired, if possible, to put an end to this intolerable and unceasing hunt which had worn us all out, no matter what that end might be. The second and more powerful, however, was, I believed, and rightly, that the idea of this stealthy, midnight blow appealed irresistibly to the craft of his half-wild nature in which the strains of the leopard and the snake seemed to mingle with that of the human being. For be it remembered that notwithstanding his veneer of civilisation, Hans was a savage whose forefathers for countless ages had preserved themselves alive by means of such attacks and stratagems.

The die having been cast, in the same infinitesimal whispers we made our arrangements, which were few and simple. They amounted to this— that we were to creep on to the men and each of us to kill that one who was opposite to him, I with the axe and Hans with his knife, remembering that it must be done with a single stroke—that is, if they did not wake up and kill us—after which we were to get Inez out of her shelter, dressed or undressed, and make off with her into the darkness where we were pretty sure of being able to baffle pursuit until we reached our own camp.

Provided that we could kill the two guards in the proper fashion— rather a large proviso, I admit—the thing was simple as shelling peas which, notwithstanding the proverb, in my experience is not simple at all, since generally the shells crack the wrong way and at least one of the peas remained in the pod. So it happened in this case, for Janee, whom we had both forgotten, remained in the pod.

I am sure I don't know why we overlooked her; indeed, the error was inexcusable, especially as Hans had already experienced her foolishness and she was lying there before our eyes. I suppose that our minds were so concentrated upon the guard-killing and the tragic and impressive Inez that there was no room in them for the stolid and matter-of-fact Janee. At any rate she proved to be the pea that would not come out of the pod.

Often in my life I have felt terrified, not being by nature one of those who rejoices in dangers and wild adventures for their own sake, which only the stupid do, but who has, on the contrary, been forced to undertake them by the pressure of circumstances, a kind of hydraulic force that no one can resist, and who, having undertaken, has been carried through them, triumphing over the shrinkings of his flesh by some secret reserve of nerve power. Almost am I tempted to call it spirit-power, something that lives beyond and yet inspires our frail and fallible bodies.

Well, rarely have I been more frightened than I was at this moment. Actually I hung back until I saw that Hans slithering through the grass like a thick yellow snake with the great knife in his right hand, was quite a foot ahead of me. Then my pride came to the rescue and I spurted, if one can spurt upon one's stomach, and drew level with him. After this we went at a pace so slow that any able-bodied snail would have left us standing still. Inch by inch we crept forward, lying motionless a while after each convulsive movement, once for quite a long time, since the left-hand cannibal seemed about to wake up, for he opened his mouth and yawned. If so, he changed his mind and rolling from a sitting posture on to his side, went to sleep much more soundly than before.

A minute or so later the right-hand ruffian, my man, also stirred, so sharply that I thought he had heard something. Apparently, however, he was only haunted by dreams resulting from an evil life, or perhaps by the prescience of its end, for after waving his arm and muttering something in a frightened voice, he too, wearied out, poor devil, sank back into sleep.

At last we were on them, but paused because we could not see exactly where to strike and knew, each of us, that our first blow must be the last and fatal. A cloud had come up and dimmed what light there was, and we must wait for it to pass. It was a long wait, or so it seemed.

At length that cloud did pass and in faint outline I saw the classical head of my Amahagger bowed in deep sleep. With a heart beating as it does only in the fierce extremities of love or war, I hissed like a snake, which was our agreed signal. Then rising to my knees, I lifted the Zulu axe and struck with all my strength.

The blow was straight and true; Umslopogaas himself could not have dealt a better. The victim in front of me uttered no sound and made no movement; only sank gently on to his side, and there lay as dead as though he had never been born.

It appeared that Hans had done equally well, since the other man kicked out his long legs, which struck me on the knees. Then he also became strangely still. In short, both of them were stone dead and would tell no stories this side of Judgment Day.

Recovering my axe, which had been wrenched from my hand, I crept forward and opened the curtain-like rugs or blankets, I do not know which they were, that covered Inez. I heard her stir at once. The movement had wakened her, since captives sleep lightly.

"Make no noise, Inez," I whispered. "It is I, Allan Quatermain, come to rescue you. Slip out and follow me; do you understand?"

"Yes, quite," she whispered back and began to rise.

At this moment a blood-curdling yell seemed to fill earth and heaven, a yell at the memory of which even now I feel faint, although I am writing years after its echoes died away.

I may as well say at once that it came from Janee who, awaking suddenly, had perceived against the background of the sky, Hans standing over her, looking like a yellow devil with a long knife in his hand, which she thought was about to be used to murder her.

So, lacking self-restraint, she screamed in the most lusty fashion, for her lungs were excellent, and—the game was up.

Instantly every man sleeping round the fire leapt to his feet and rushed in the direction of the echoes of Janee's yell. It was impossible to get Inez free of her tent arrangement or to do anything, except whisper to her,

"Feign sleep and know nothing. We will follow you. Your father is with us."

Then I bolted back into the bushes, which Hans had reached already.

A minute or two later when we were clear of the hubbub and nearing our own camp, Hans remarked to me sententiously,

"The Great Medicine worked well, Baas, but not quite well enough, for what medicine can avail against a woman's folly?"

"It was our own folly we should blame," I answered. "We ought to have known that fool-girl would shriek, and taken precautions."

"Yes, Baas, we ought to have killed her too, for nothing else would have kept her quiet," replied Hans in cheerful assent. "Now we shall have to pay for our mistake, for the hunt must go on."

At this moment we stumbled across Robertson and Umslopogaas who, with the others, and every living thing within a mile or two had also heard Janee's yell, and briefly told our story. When he learned how near we had been to rescuing his daughter, Robertson groaned, but Umslopogaas only said,

"Well, there are two less of the men-eaters left to deal with. Still, for once your wisdom failed you, Macumazahn. When you had found the camp you should have returned, so that we might all attack it together. Had we done so, before the dawn there would not have been one of them left."

"Yes," I answered, "I think that my wisdom did fail me, if I have any to fail. But come; perhaps we may catch them yet."

So we advanced, Hans and I showing the road. But when we reached the place it was too late, for all that remained of the Amahagger, or of Inez and Janee, were the two dead men whom we had killed, and in that darkness pursuit was impossible. So we went back to our own camp to rest and await the dawn before taking up the trail, only to find ourselves confronted with a new trouble. All the Strathmuir half-breeds whom we had left behind as useless, had taken advantage of our absence and that of the Zulus, to desert. They had just bolted back upon our tracks and vanished into the sea of bush. What became of them I do not know, as we never saw them again, but my belief is that these cowardly fellows all perished, for certainly not one of them reached Strathmuir.

Fortunately for us, however, they departed in such a hurry that they left all their loads behind them, and even some of the guns they carried. Evidently Janee's yell was the last straw which broke the back of such nerve as remained to them. Doubtless they believed it to be the signal of attack by hordes of cannibals.

As there was nothing to said or done, since any pursuit of these curs was out of the question, we made the best of things as they were. It proved a simple business. From the loads we selected such articles as were essential, ammunition for the most part, to carry ourselves—and the rest we abandoned, hiding it under a pile of stones in case we should ever come that way again.

The guns they had thrown aside we distributed among the Zulus who had none, though the thought that they possessed them, so far as I was concerned, added another terror to life. The prospect of going into battle with those wild axemen letting off bullets in every direction was not pleasant, but fortunately when that crisis came, they cast them away and reverted to the weapons to which they were accustomed.

Now all this sounds much like a tale of disaster, or at any rate of failure. It is, however, wonderful by what strange ways good results are brought about, so much so that at times I think that these seeming accidents must be arranged by an Intelligence superior to our own, to fulfil through us purposes of which we know nothing, and frequently, be it admitted, of a nature sufficiently obscure. Of course this is a fatalistic doctrine, but then, as I have said before, within certain limits I am a fatalist.

To take the present case, for instance, the whole Inez episode at first sight might appear to be an excrescence on my narrative, of which the object is to describe how I met a certain very wonderful woman and what I heard and experienced in her company. Yet it is not really so, since had it not been for the Inez adventure, it is quite clear that I should never have reached the home of this woman, if woman she were, or have seen her at all. Before long this became very obvious to me, as shall be told.

From the night upon which Hans and I failed to rescue Inez we had no more difficulty in following the trail of the cannibals, who thenceforward were never more than a few hours ahead of us and had no time to be careful or to attempt to hide their spoor. Yet so fast did they travel that do what we would, burdened and wearied as we were, it proved impossible to overtake them.

For the first three days the track ran on through scattered, rolling bush-veld of the character that I have described, but tending continually down hill. When we broke camp on the morning of the fourth day, eating a hasty meal at dawn (for now game had become astonishingly plentiful, so that we did not lack food) the rising sun showed beneath us an endless sea of billowy mist stretching in every direction far as the sight could carry.

To the north, however, it did come to an end, for there, as I judged fifty or sixty miles away, rose the grim outline of what looked like a huge fortress, which I knew must be one of those extraordinary mountain formations, probably owing their origin to volcanic action, that are to be met with here and there in the vast expanses of Central and Eastern Africa. Being so distant it was impossible to estimate its size, which I guessed must be enormous, but in looking at it I bethought me of that great mountain in which Zikali said the marvellous white Queen lived, and wondered whether it could be the same, as from my memory of his map upon the ashes, it well might be, that is, if such a place existed at all. If so the map had shown it as surrounded by swamps and—well, surely that mist hid the face of a mighty swamp?

It did indeed, since before nightfall, following the spoor of those Amahagger, we had plunged into a morass so vast that in all my experience I have never seen or heard of its like. It was a veritable ocean of papyrus and other reeds, some of them a dozen or more feet high, so that it was impossible to see a yard in any direction.

Here it was that the Amahagger ahead of us proved our salvation, since without them to guide us we must soon have perished. For through that gigantic swamp there ran a road, as I think an ancient road, since in one or two places I saw stone work which must have been laid by man. Yet it was not a road which it would have been possible to follow without a guide, seeing that it also was overgrown with reeds. Indeed, the only difference between it and the surrounding swamp was that on the road the soil was comparatively firm, that is to say, one seldom sank into it above the knee, whereas on either side of it quagmires were often apparently bottomless, and what is more, partook of the nature of quicksand.

This we found out soon after we entered the swamp, since Robertson, pushing forward with the fierce eagerness which seemed to consume him, neglected to keep his eye upon the spoor and stepped off the edge on to land that appeared to be exactly similar to its surface. Instantly he began to sink in greasy and tenacious mud. Umslopogaas and I were only twenty yards behind, yet by the time we reached him in answer to his shouts, already he was engulfed up to his middle and going down so rapidly that in another minute he would have vanished altogether. Well, we got him out but not with ease, for that mud clung to him like the tentacles of an octopus. After this we were more careful.

Nor did this road run straight; on the contrary, it curved about and sometimes turned at right angles, doubtless to avoid a piece of swamp over which it had proved impossible for the ancients to construct a causeway, or to follow some out-crop of harder soil beneath.

The difficulties of that horrible place are beyond description, and indeed can scarcely be imagined. First there was that of a kind of grass which grew among the roots of the reeds and had edges like to those of knives. As Robertson and I wore gaiters we did not suffer so much from it, but the poor Zulus with their bare legs were terribly cut about and in some cases lame.

Then there were the mosquitoes which lived here by the million and all seemed anxious for a bite; also snakes of a peculiarly deadly kind were numerous. A Zulu was bitten by one of them of so poisonous a nature that he died within three minutes, for the venom seemed to go straight to his heart. We threw his body into the swamp, where it vanished at once.

Lastly there was the all-pervading stench and the intolerable heat of the place, since no breath of air could penetrate that forest of reeds, while a minor trouble was that of the multitude of leeches which fastened on to our bodies. By looking one could see the creatures sitting on the under side of leaves with their heads stretched out waiting to attack anything that went by. As wayfarers there could not have been numerous, I wondered what they had lived on for the last few thousand years. By the way, I found that paraffin, of which we had a small supply for our hand-lamps, rubbed over all exposed surfaces, was to some extent a protection against these blood-sucking worms and the gnats, although it did make one go about smelling like a dirty oil tin.

During the day, except for the occasional rush of some great iguana or other reptile, and the sound of the wings of the flocks of wildfowl passing over us from time to time, the march was deathly silent. But at night it was different, for then the bull-frogs boomed incessantly, as did the bitterns, while great swamp owls and other night-flying birds uttered their weird cries. Also there were mysterious sucking noises caused, no doubt, by the sinking of areas of swamp, with those of bursting bubbles of foul, up-rushing gas.

Strange lights, too, played about, will-o'-the-wisps or St. Elmo fires, as I believe they are called, that frightened the Zulus very much, since they believed them to be spirits of the dead. Perhaps this superstition had something to do with their native legend that mankind was "torn out of the reeds." If so, they may have imagined that the ghosts of men went back to the reeds, of which there were enough here to accommodate those of the entire Zulu nation. Any way they were much scared; even the bold witch-doctor, Goroko, was scared and went through incantations with the little bag of medicines he carried to secure protection for himself and his companions.

Indeed, I think even the iron Umslopogaas himself was not as comfortable as he might have been, although he did inform me that he had come out to fight and did not care whether it were with man, or wizard, or spirit.

In short, of all the journeys that I have made, with the exception of the passage of the desert on our way to King Solomon's Mines, I think that through this enormous swamp was the most miserable. Heartily did I curse myself for ever having undertaken such a quest in a wild attempt to allay that sickness, or rather to quench that thirst of the soul which, I imagine, at times assails most of those who have hearts and think or dream.

For this was at the bottom of the business: this it was which had delivered me into the hands of Zikali, Opener-of-Roads, who, as now I am sure, was merely making use of me for his private occult purposes. He desired to consult the distant Oracle, if such a person existed, as to great schemes of his own, and therefore, to attain his end, made use of my secret longings which I had been so foolish as to reveal to him, quite careless of what happened to me in the process. [A bit narrow and uncharitable, this view. It seems to me that Zikali is taking a big risk in giving him the Great Medicine.—JB]

Well, I was in for the business and must follow it to the finish whatever that might be. After all it was very interesting and if there were anything in what Zikali said (if there were not I could not conceive what object he had in sending me on such a wild-goose chase through this home of geese and ducks), it might become more interesting still. For being pretty well fever-proof I did not think I should die in that morass, as of course nine white men out of ten would have done, and, beyond it lay the huge mountain which day by day grew larger and clearer.

Nor did Hans, who, with a childlike trust, pinned his faith to the Great Medicine. This, he remarked, was the worst veld through which he had ever travelled, but as the Great Medicine would never consent to be buried in that stinking mud, he had no doubt that we should come safely through it some time. I replied that this wonderful medicine of his had not saved one of our companions who had now made a grave in the same mud.

"No, Baas," he said, "but those Zulus have nothing to do with the Medicine which was given to you, and to me who accompanied you when we saw the Opener-of-Roads. Therefore perhaps they will all die, except Umslopogaas, whom you were told to take with you. If so, what does it matter, since there are plenty of Zulus, although there be but one Macumazahn or one Hans? Also the Baas may remember that he began by offending a snake and therefore it is quite natural that this snake's brother should have bitten the Zulu."

"If you are right, he should have bitten me, Hans."

"Yes, Baas, and so no doubt he would have done had you not been protected by the Great Medicine, and me too had not my grandfather been a snake-charmer, to say nothing of the smell of the Medicine being on me as well. The snakes know those that they should bite, Baas."

"So do the mosquitoes," I answered, grabbing a handful of them. "The Great Medicine has no effect upon them."

"Oh! yes, Baas, it has, since though it pleases them to bite, the bites do us no harm, or at least not much, and all are made happy. Still, I wish we could get out of these reeds of which I never want to see another, and Baas, please keep your rifle ready for I think I hear a crocodile stirring there."

"No need, Hans," I remarked sarcastically. "Go and tell him that I have the Great Medicine."

"Yes, Baas, I will; also that if he is very hungry, there are some Zulus camped a few yards further down the road," and he went solemnly to the reeds a little way off and began to talk to them.

"You infernal donkey!" I murmured, and drew my blanket over my head in a vain attempt to keep out the mosquitoes and smoking furiously with the same object, tried to get to sleep.

At last the swamp bottom began to slope upwards a little, with the result that as the land dried through natural drainage, the reeds grew thinner by degrees, until finally they ceased and we found ourselves on firmer ground; indeed, upon the lowest slopes of the great mountain that I have mentioned, that now towered above us, forbidden and majestic.

I had made a little map in my pocket-book of the various twists and turns of the road through that vast Slough of Despond, marking them from hour to hour as we followed its devious wanderings. On studying this at the end of that part of our journey I realised afresh how utterly impossible it would have been for us to thread that misty maze where a few false steps would always have meant death by suffocation, had it not been for the spoor of those Amahagger travelling immediately ahead of us who were acquainted with its secrets. Had they been friendly guides they could not have done us a better turn.

What I wondered was why they had not tried to ambush us in the reeds, since our fires must have shown them that we were close upon their heels. That they did try to burn us out was clear from certain evidences that I found, but fortunately at this season of the year in the absence of a strong wind the rank reeds were too green to catch fire. For the rest I was soon to learn the reason of their neglect to attack us in that dense cover.

They were waiting for a better opportunity!

The Attack

We won out of the reeds at last, for which I fervently thanked God, since to have crossed that endless marsh unguided, with the loss of only one man, seemed little less than miraculous. We emerged from them late in the afternoon and being wearied out, stopped for a while to rest and eat of the flesh of a buck that I had been fortunate enough to shoot upon their fringe. Then we pushed forward up the slope, proposing to camp for the night on the crest of it a mile or so away where I thought we should escape from the deadly mist in which we had been enveloped for so long, and obtain a clear view of the country ahead.

Following the bank of a stream which here ran down into the marsh, we came at length to this crest just as the sun was sinking. Below us lay a deep valley, a fold, as it were, in the skin of the mountain, well but not densely bushed. The woods of this valley climbed up the mountain flank for some distance above it and then gave way to grassy slopes that ended in steep sides of rock, which were crowned by a black and frowning precipice of unknown height.

There was, I remember, something very impressive about this towering natural wall, which seemed to shut off whatever lay beyond the gaze of man, as though it veiled an ancient mystery. Indeed, the aspect of it thrilled me, I knew not why. I observed, however, that at one point in the mighty cliff there seemed to be a narrow cleft down which, no doubt, lava had flowed in a remote age, and it occurred to me that up this cleft ran a roadway, probably a continuation of that by which we had threaded the swamp. The fact that through my glasses I could see herds of cattle grazing on the slopes of the mountain went to confirm this view, since cattle imply owners and herdsmen, and search as I would, I could find no native villages on the slopes. The inference seemed to be that those owners dwelt beyond or within the mountain.

All of these things I saw and pointed out to Robertson in the light of the setting sun.

Meanwhile Umslopogaas had been engaged in selecting the spot where we were to camp for the night. Some soldierlike instinct, or perchance some prescience of danger, caused him to choose a place particularly suitable to defence. It was on a steep-sided mound that more or less resembled a gigantic ant-heap. Upon one side this mound was protected by the stream which because of a pool was here rather deep, while at the back of it stood a collection of those curious and piled-up water-worn rocks that are often to be found in Africa. These rocks, lying one upon another like the stones of a Cyclopean wall, curved round the western side of the mound, so that practically it was only open for a narrow space, say thirty or forty feet, upon that face of it which looked on to the mountain.

"Umslopogaas expects battle," remarked Hans to me with a grin, "otherwise with all this nice plain round us he would not have chosen to camp in a place which a few men could hold against many. Yes, Baas, he thinks that those cannibals are going to attack us."

"Stranger things have happened," I answered indifferently, and having seen to the rifles, went to lie down, observing as I did so that the tired Zulus seemed already to be asleep. Only Umslopogaas did not sleep. On the contrary, he stood leaning on his axe staring at the dim outlines of the opposing precipice.

"A strange mountain, Macumazahn," he said, "compared to it that of the Witch, beneath which my kraal lies, is but a little baby. I wonder what we shall find within it. I have always loved mountains, Macumazahn, ever since a dead brother of mine and I lived with the wolves in the Witch's lap, for on them I have had the best of my fighting."

"Perhaps it is not done with yet," I answered wearily.

"I hope not, Macumazahn, since some is due for us, after all these days of mud and stench. Sleep a while now, Macumazahn, for that head of yours which you use so much, must need rest. Fear not, I and the little yellow man who do not think as much as you do, will keep watch and wake you if there is need, as mayhap there will be before the dawn. Here none can come at us except in front, and the place is narrow."

So I lay down and slept as soundly as ever I had done in my life, for a space of four or five hours I suppose. Then, by some instinct perhaps, I awoke suddenly, feeling much refreshed in that sweet mountain air, a new man indeed, and in the moonlight saw Umslopogaas striding towards me.

"Arise, Macumazahn," he said, "I hear men stirring below us."

At this moment Hans slipped past him, whispering,

"The cannibals are coming, Baas, a good number of them. I think they mean to attack before dawn."

Then he passed behind me to warn the Zulus. As he went by, I said to him,

"If so, Hans, now is the time for your Great Medicine to show what it can do."

"The Great Medicine will look after you and me all right, Baas," he replied, pausing and speaking in Dutch, which Umslopogaas did not understand, "but I expect there will be fewer of those Zulus to cook for before the sun grows hot. Their spirits will be turned into snakes and go back into the reeds from which they say they were 'torn out,'" he added over his shoulder.

I should explain that Hans acted as cook to our party and it was a grievance with him that the Zulus ate so much of the meat which he was called upon to prepare. Indeed, there is never much sympathy between Hottentots and Zulus.

"What is the little yellow man saying about us?" asked Umslopogaas suspiciously.

"He is saying that if it comes to battle, you and your men will make a great fight," I replied diplomatically.

"Yes, we will do that, Macumazahn, but I thought he said that we should be killed and that this pleased him."

"Oh dear no!" I answered hastily. "How could he be pleased if that happened, since then he would be left defenceless, if he were not killed too. Now, Umslopogaas, let us make a plan for this fight."

So, together with Robertson, rapidly we discussed the thing. As a result, with the help of the Zulus, we dragged together some loose stones and the tops of three small thorn trees which we had cut down, and with them made a low breastwork, sufficient to give us some protection if we lay down to shoot. It was the work of a few minutes since we had prepared the material when we camped in case an emergency should arise.

Behind this breastwork we gathered and waited, Robertson and I being careful to get a little to the rear of the Zulus, who it will be remembered had the rifles which the Strathmuir bastards had left behind them when they bolted, in addition to their axes and throwing assegais. The question was how these cannibals would fight. I knew that they were armed with long spears and knives but I did not know if they used those spears for thrusting or for throwing. In the former case it would be difficult to get at them with the axes because they must have the longer reach. Fortunately as it turned out, they did both.

At length all was ready and there came that long and trying wait, the most disagreeable part of a fight in which one grows nervous and begins to reflect earnestly upon one's sins. Clearly the Amahagger, if they really intended business, did not mean to attack till just before dawn, after the common native fashion, thinking to rush us in the low and puzzling light. What perplexed me was that they should wish to attack us at all after having let so many opportunities of doing so go by. Apparently these men were now in sight of their own home, where no doubt they had many friends, and by pushing on could reach its shelter before us, especially as they knew the roads and we did not.

They had come out for a secret purpose that seemed to have to do with the abduction of a certain young white woman for reasons connected with their tribal statecraft or ritual, which is the kind of thing that happens not infrequently among obscure and ancient African tribes. Well, they had abducted their young woman and were in sight of safety and success in their objects, whatever these might be. For what possible reason, then, could they desire to risk a fight with the outraged friends and relatives of that young woman?

It was true that they outnumbered us and therefore had a good chance of victory, but on the other hand, they must know that it would be very dearly won, and if it were not won, that we should retake their captive, so that all their trouble would have been for nothing. Further they must be as exhausted and travel-worn as we were ourselves and in no condition to face a desperate battle.

The problem was beyond me and I gave it up with the reflection that either this threatened attack was a mere feint to delay us, or that behind it was something mysterious, such as a determination to prevent us at all hazards from discovering the secrets of that mountain stronghold.

When I put the riddle to Hans, who was lying next to me, he was ready with another solution.

"They are men-eaters, Baas," he said, "and being hungry, wish to eat us before they get to their own land where doubtless they are not allowed to eat each other."

"Do you think so," I answered, "when we are so thin?" and I surveyed Hans' scraggy form in the moonlight.

"Oh! yes, Baas, we should be quite good boiled—like old hens, Baas. Also it is the nature of cannibals to prefer thin man to fat beef. The devil that is in them gives them that taste, Baas, just as he makes me like gin, or you turn your head to look at pretty women, as those Zulus say you always did in their country, especially at a certain witch who was named Mameena and whom you kissed before everybody——"

Here I turned my head to look at Hans, proposing to smite him with words, or physically, since to have this Mameena myth, of which I have detailed the origin in the book called *Child of Storm*, re-arise out of his hideous little mouth was too much. But before I could get out a syllable he held up his finger and whispered,

"Hush! the dawn breaks and they come. I hear them."

I listened intently but could distinguish nothing. Only straining my eyes, presently I thought that about a hundred yards down the slope beneath us in the dim light I caught sight of ghostlike figures flitting from tree to tree; also that these figures were drawing nearer.

"Look out!" I said to Robertson on my right, "I believe they are coming."

"Man," he answered sternly, "I hope so, for whom else have I wanted to meet all these days?"

Now the figures vanished into a little fold of the ground. A minute or so later they re-appeared upon its hither side where such light as there was from the fading stars and the gathering dawn fell full upon them, for here were no trees. I looked and a thrill of horror went through me, for with one glance I recognised that these were *not the men whom we had been following*. To begin with, there were many more of them, quite a hundred, I should think, also they had painted shields, wore feathers in their hair, and generally so far as I could judge, seemed to be fat and fresh.

"We have been led into an ambush," I said first in Zulu to Umslopogaas immediately in front, and then in English to Robertson.

"If so, man, we must just do the best we can," answered the latter, "but God help my poor daughter, for those other devils will have taken her away, leaving their brethren to make an end of us."

"It is so, Macumazahn," broke in Umslopogaas. "Well, whatever the end of it, we shall have a better fight. Now do you give the word and we will obey."

The savages, for so I call them, although I admit that cannibals or not, they looked more like high-class Arabs than savages, came on in perfect silence, hoping, I suppose, to catch us asleep. When they were about fifty yards away, running in a treble line with spears advanced, I called out "Fire!" in Zulu, and set the example by loosing off both barrels of my express rifle at men whom I had picked out as leaders, with results that must have been more satisfactory to me than to the two Amahagger whose troubles in this world came to an end.

There followed a tremendous fusillade, the Zulus banging off their guns wildly, but even at that distance managing for the most part to shoot over the enemy's heads. Captain Robertson and Hans, however, did better and the general result was that the Amahagger, who appeared to be unaccustomed to firearms, retreated in a hurry to a fold of the ground whence they had emerged. Before the last of them got there I loaded again, so that two more stopped behind. Altogether we had put nine or ten of them out of action.

Now I hoped that they would give the business up. But this was not so, for being brave fellows, after a pause of perhaps five minutes, once more they charged in a body, hoping to overwhelm us. Again we greeted them with bullets and knocked out several, whereon the rest threw a volley of their long spears at us. I was glad to see them do this although one of the Zulus got his death from it, while two more were wounded. I myself had a very narrow escape, for a spear passed between my neck and shoulder. Each of them carried but one of these weapons and I knew that if they used them up in throwing, only their big knives would remain to them with which to attack us.

After this discharge of spears which was kept up for some time, they rushed at us and there followed a great fight. The Zulus, throwing down their guns, rose to their feet and holding their little fighting shields which had been carried in their mats, in the left hand, wielded their axes with the right. Umslopogaas, who stood in the centre of them, however, had no shield and swung his great axe with both arms. This was the first time that I had seen him fight and the spectacle was in a way magnificent. Again and again the axe crashed down and every time it fell it left one dead beneath the stroke, till at length those Amahagger shrank back out of his reach.

Meanwhile Robertson, Hans and I, standing on some stones at the back, kept up a continual fire upon them, shooting over the heads of the Zulus, who were playing their part like men. Yes, they shrank back, leaving many dead behind them. Then a captain tried to gather them for another rush, and once more they moved forward. I killed that captain with a revolver shot, for my rifle had become too hot to hold, and at the sight of his fall, they broke and ran back into the little hollow where our bullets could not reach them.

So far we had held our own, but at a price, for three of the Zulus were now dead and three more wounded, one of them severely, the other two but enough to cripple them. In fact, now there were left of them but three untouched men, and Umslopogaas, so that in all for fighting purposes we were but seven. What availed it that we had killed a great number of these Amahagger, when we were but seven? How could seven men withstand such another onslaught?

There in the pale light of the dawn we looked at each other dismayed.

"Now," said Umslopogaas, leaning on his red axe, "there remains but one thing to do, make a good end, though I would that it were in a greater cause. At least we must either fight or fly," and he looked down at the wounded.

"Think not of us, Father," murmured one of them, the man who had a mortal hurt. "If it is best, kill us and begone that you may live to bear the Axe in years to come."

"Well spoken!" said Umslopogaas, and again stood still a while, then added, "The word is with you, Macumazahn, who are our captain."

I set out the situation to Robertson and Hans as briefly as I could, showing that there was a chance of life if we ran, but so far as I could see, none if we stayed.

"Go if you like, Quatermain," answered the Captain, "but I shall stop and die here, for since my girl is gone I think I'm better dead."

I motioned to Hans to speak.

"Baas," he answered, "the Great Medicine is here with us upon the earth and your reverend father, the Predikant, is with us in the sky, so I think we had better stop here and do what we can, especially as I do not want to see those reeds any more at present."

"So do I," I said briefly, giving no reasons.

So we made ready for the next attack which we knew would be the last, strengthening our little wall and dragging the dead Amahagger up against it as an added protection. As we were thus engaged the sun rose and in its first beams, some miles away on the opposing slopes of the mountain looking tiny against the black background of the precipice, we saw a party of men creeping forward. Lifting my glasses I studied it and perceived that in its midst was a litter.

"There goes your daughter," I said, and handed the glasses to Robertson.

"Oh! my God," he answered, "those villains have outwitted us after all."

Another minute and the litter, or rather the chair with its escort, had vanished into the shadow of the great cliffs, probably up some pass which we could not see.

Next moment our thoughts were otherwise engaged, since from various symptoms we gathered that the attack was about to be renewed. Spears upon which shone the light of the rising sun, appeared above the edge of the ground-fold that I have mentioned, which to the east increased to a deep, bush-clad ravine. Also there were voices as of leaders encouraging their men to a desperate effort.

"They are coming," I said to Robertson.

"Yes," he answered, "they are coming and we are going. It's a queer end to the thing we call life, isn't it, Quatermain, and hang it all! I wonder what's beyond? Not much for me, I expect, but whatever it is could scarcely be worse than what I've gone through here below in one way and another."

"There's hope for all of us," I replied as cheerfully as I could, for the man's deep depression disturbed me.

"Mayhap, Quatermain, for who knows the infinite mercy of whatever made us as we are? My old mother used to preach of it and I remember her words now. But in my case I expect it will stop at hope, or sleep, and if it wasn't for Inez, I'd not mind so much, for I tell you I've had enough of the world and life. Look, there's one of them. Take that, you black devil!" and lifting his rifle he aimed and fired at an Amahagger who appeared upon the edge of the fold of ground. What is more he hit him, for I saw the man double up and fall backwards.

Then the game began afresh, for the cannibals (I suppose they were cannibals like their brethren) crept out of shelter, advancing on their stomachs or their hands and knees, so as to offer a smaller mark, and dragging between them a long and slender tree-trunk with which clearly they intended to batter down our wall.

Of course I blazed away at them, pretty carefully too, for I was determined that what I believed to be the last exercise of the gift of shooting that has been given to me, should prove a record. Therefore I selected my men and even where I would hit them, and as subsequent examination showed, I made no mistakes in the seven or eight shots that I fired. But all the while, like poor Captain Robertson, I was thinking of other things; namely, where I was bound for presently and if I should meet certain folk there and what was the meaning of this show called Life, which unless it leads somewhere, according to my judgment has none at all. Until these questions were solved, however, my duty was to kill as many of those ruffians as I could, and this I did with finish and despatch.

Robertson and Hans were firing also, with more or less success, but there were too many to be stopped by our three rifles. Still they came on till at length their fierce faces were within a few yards of our little parapet and Umslopogaas had lifted his great axe to give them greeting. They paused a moment before making their final rush, and so did we to slip in fresh cartridges.

"Die well, Hans," I said, "and if you get there first, wait for me on the other side."

"Yes, Baas, I always meant to do that, though not yet. We are not going to die this time, Baas. Those who have the Great Medicine don't die; it is the others who die, like that fellow," and he pointed to an Amahagger who went reeling round and round with a bullet from his Winchester through the middle, for he had fired in the midst of his remarks.

"Curse—I mean bless—the Great Medicine," I said as I lifted my rifle to my shoulder.

At that moment all those Amahagger—there were about sixty of them left—became seized with a certain perturbation. They stood still, they stared towards the fold of ground out of which they had emerged; they called to each other words which I did not catch, and then—they turned to run.

Umslopogaas saw, and with a leader's instinct, acted. Springing over the parapet, followed by his remaining Zulus of the Axe, he leapt upon them with a roar. Down they went before *Inkosikaas*, like corn before a sickle. The thing was marvellous to see, it was like the charge of a leopard, so swift was the rush and so lightning-like were the strokes or rather the pecks of that flashing axe, for now he was tapping at their heads or spines with the gouge-like point upon its back. Nor were these the only victims, for those brave followers of his also did their part. In a minute all who remained upon their feet of the Amahagger were in full flight, vanishing this way and that among the trees. Hans fired a parting shot after the last of them, then sat down upon a stone and finding his corn-cob pipe, proceeded to fill it.

"The Great Medicine, Baas," he began sententiously, "or perhaps your reverend father, the Predikant——" Here he paused and pointed doubtfully with the bowl of the pipe towards the fold in the ground, adding, "Here it is, but I think it must be your reverend father, not the Great Medicine, yes, the Predikant himself, returned from Heaven, the Place of Fires!"

Looking vaguely in the direction indicated, for I could not conceive what he meant and thought that the excitement must have made him mad, I perceived a venerable old man with a long white beard and clothed in a flowing garment, also white, who reminded me of Father Christmas at a child's party, walking towards us and radiating benignancy. Also behind him I perceived a whole forest of spear points emerging from the gully. He seemed to take it for granted that we should not shoot at him, for he came on quite unconcerned, carefully picking his way among the corpses. When he was near enough he stopped and said in a kind of Arabic which I could understand,

"I greet you, Strangers, in the name of her I serve. I see that I am just in time, but this does not surprise me, since she said that it would be so. You seem to have done very well with these dogs," and he prodded a dead Amahagger with his sandalled foot. "Yes, very well indeed. You must be great warriors."

Then he paused and we stared at each other.

Through the Mountain Wall

"These do not seem to be friends of yours," I said, pointing to the fallen. "And yet," I added, nodding towards the spearmen who were now emerging from the gully, "they are very like your friends."

"Puppies from the same litter are often alike, yet when they grow up sometimes they fight each other," replied Father Christmas blandly. "At least these come to save and not to kill you. Look! they kill the others!" and he pointed to them making an end of some of the wounded men. "But who are these?" and he glanced with evident astonishment, first at the fearsome-looking Umslopogaas and then at the grotesque Hans. "Nay, answer not, you must be weary and need rest. Afterwards we can talk."

"Well, as a matter of fact we have not yet breakfasted," I replied. "Also I have business to attend to here," and I glanced at our wounded.

The old fellow nodded and went to speak to the captains of his force, doubtless as to the pursuit of the enemy, for presently I saw a company spring forward on their tracks. Then, assisted by Hans and the remaining Zulus, of whom one was Goroko, I turned to attend to our own people. The task proved lighter than I expected, since the badly injured man was dead or dying and the hurts of the two others were in their legs and comparatively slight, such as Goroko could doctor in his own native fashion.

After this, taking Hans to guard my back, I went down to the stream and washed myself. Then I returned and ate, wondering the while that I could do so with appetite after the terrible dangers which we had passed. Still, we had passed them, and Robertson, Umslopogaas with three of his men, I and Hans were quite unharmed, a fact for which I returned thanks in silence but sincerely enough to Providence.

Hans also returned thanks in his own fashion, after he had filled himself, not before, and lit his corn-cob pipe. But Robertson made no remark; indeed, when he had satisfied his natural cravings, he rose and walking a few paces forward, stood staring at the cleft in the mountain cliff into which he had seen the litter vanish that bore his daughter to some fate unknown.

Even the great fight that we had fought and the victory we had won against overpowering odds did not appear to impress him. He only glared at the mountain into the heart of which Inez had been raped away, and shook his fist. Since she was gone all else went for nothing, so much so that he did not offer to assist with the wounded Zulus or show curiosity about the strange old man by whom we had been rescued.

"The Great Medicine, Baas," said Hans in a bewildered way, "is even more powerful than I thought. Not only has it brought us safely through the fighting and without a scratch, for those Zulus there do not matter and there will be less cooking for me to do now that they are gone; it has also brought down your reverend father the Predikant from the Place of Fires in Heaven, somewhat changed from what I remember him, it is true, but still without doubt the same. When I make my report to him presently, if he can understand my talk, I shall——"

"Stop your infernal nonsense, you son of a donkey," I broke in, for at this moment old Father Christmas, smiling more benignly than before, re-appeared from the kloof into which he had vanished and advanced towards us bowing with much politeness.

Having seated himself upon the little wall that we had built up, he contemplated us, stroking his beautiful white beard, then said, addressing me,

"Of a certainty you should be proud who with a few have defeated so many. Still, had I not been ordered to come at speed, I think that by now you would have been as those are," and he looked towards the dead Zulus who were laid out at a distance like men asleep, while their companions sought for a place to bury them.

"Ordered by whom?" I asked.

"There is only one who can order," he answered with mild astonishment. "'She-who-commands, She-who-is-everlasting'!"

It occurred to me that this must be some Arabic idiom for the Eternal Feminine, but I only looked vague and said,

"It would appear that there are some whom this exalted everlasting She cannot command; those who attacked us; also those who have fled away yonder," and I waved my hand towards the mountain.

"No command is absolute; in every country there are rebels, even, as I have heard, in Heaven above us. But, Wanderer, what is your name?"

"Watcher-by-Night," I answered.

"Ah! a good name for one who must have watched well by night, and by day too, to reach this country living where She-who-commands says that no man of your colour has set foot for many generations. Indeed, I think she told me once that two thousand years had gone by since she spoke to a white man in the City of Kôr."

"Did she indeed?" I exclaimed, stifling a cough.

"You do not believe me," he went on, smiling. "Well, She-who-commands can explain matters for herself better than I who was not alive two thousand years ago, so far as I remember. But what must I call him with the Axe?"

"Warrior is his name."

"Again a good name, as to judge by the wounds on them, certain of those rebels I think are now telling each other in Hell. And this man, if indeed he be a man——" he added, looking doubtfully at Hans.

"Light-in-Darkness is his name."

"I see, doubtless because his colour is that of the winter sun in thick fog, or a bad egg broken into milk. And the other white man who mutters and whose brow is like a storm?"

"He is called Avenger; you will learn why later on," I answered impatiently, for I grew tired of this catechism, adding, "And what are you called and, if you are pleased to tell it to us, upon what errand do you visit us in so fortunate an hour?"

"I am named Billali," he answered, "the servant and messenger of She-who-commands, and I was sent to save you and to bring you safely to her."

"How can this be, Billali, seeing that none knew of our coming?"

"Yet She-who-commands knew," he said with his benignant smile. "Indeed, I think that she learned of it some moons ago through a message that was sent to her and so arranged all things that you should be guided safely to her secret home; since otherwise how would you have passed a great pathless swamp with the loss, I think she said, of but one man whom a snake bit?"

Now I stared at the old fellow, for how could he know of the death of this man, but thought it useless to pursue the conversation further.

"When you are rested and ready," he went on, "we will start. Meanwhile I leave you that I may prepare litters to carry those wounded men, and you also, Watcher-by-Night, if you wish." Then with a dignified bow, for everything about this old fellow was stately, he turned and vanished into the kloof.

The next hour or so was occupied in the burial of the dead Zulus, a ceremony in which I took no part beyond standing up and raising my hat as they were borne away, for as I have said somewhere, it is best to leave natives alone on these occasions. Indeed, I lay down, reflecting that strangely enough there seemed to be something in old Zikali's tale of a wonderful white Queen who lived in a mountain fastness, since there was the mountain as he had drawn it on the ashes, and the servants of that Queen who, apparently, had knowledge of our coming, appeared in the nick of time to rescue us from one of the tightest fixes in which ever I found myself.

Moreover, the antique and courteous individual called Billali, spoke of her as

"She-who-is-everlasting." What the deuce could he mean by that, I wondered? Probably that she was very old and therefore disagreeable to look on, which I confessed to myself would be a disappointment.

And how did she know that we were coming? I could not guess and when I asked Robertson, he merely shrugged his shoulders and intimated that he took no interest in the matter. The truth is that nothing moved the man, whose whole soul was wrapped in one desire, namely to rescue, or avenge, the daughter against whom he knew he had so sorely sinned.

In fact, this loose-living but reformed seaman was becoming a monomaniac, and what is more, one of the religious type. He had a Bible with him that had been given to him by his mother when he was a boy, and in this he read constantly; also he was always on his knees and at night I could hear him groaning and praying aloud. Doubtless now that the chains of drink had fallen off him, the instincts and the blood of the dour old Covenanters from whom he was descended, were asserting themselves. In a way this was a good thing though for some time past I had feared lest it should end in his going mad, and certainly as a companion he was more cheerful in his unregenerate days.

Abandoning speculation as useless and taking my chance of being murdered where I lay, for after all Billali's followers were singularly like the men with whom we had been fighting and for aught I knew might be animated by identical objects—I just went to sleep, as I can do at any time, to wake up an hour or so later feeling wonderfully refreshed. Hans, who when I closed my eyes was already asleep slumbering at my feet curled up like a dog on a spot where the sun struck hotly, roused me by saying:

"Awake, Baas, they are here!"

I sprang up, snatching at my rifle, for I thought that he meant that we were being attacked again, to see Billali advancing at the head of a train of four litters made of bamboo with grass mats for curtains and coverings, each of which was carried by stalwart Amahagger, as I supposed that they must be. Two of these, the finest, Billali indicated were for Robertson and myself, and the two others for the wounded. Umslopogaas and the remaining Zulus evidently were expected to walk, as was Hans.

"How did you make these so quickly," I asked, surveying their elegant and indeed artistic workmanship.

"We did not make them, Watcher-by-Night, we brought them with us folded up. She-who-commands looked in her glass and said that four would be needed, besides my own which is yonder, two for white lords and two for wounded black men, which you see is the number required."

"Yes," I answered vaguely, marvelling what kind of a glass it was that gave the lady this information.

Before I could inquire upon the point Billali added,

"You will be glad to learn that my men caught some of those rebels who dared to attack you, eight or ten of them who had been hurt by your missiles or axe-cuts, and put them to death in the proper fashion— yes, quite the proper fashion," and he smiled a little. "The rest had gone too far where it would have been dangerous to follow them among the rocks. Enter now, my lord Watcher-by-Night, for the road is steep and we must travel fast if we would reach the place where She-who-commands is camped in the ancient holy city, before the moon sinks behind the cliffs to-night."

So having explained matters to Robertson and Umslopogaas, who announced that nothing would induce *him* to be carried like an old woman, or a corpse upon a shield, and seen that the hurt Zulus were comfortably accommodated, Robertson and I got into our litters, which proved to be delightfully easy and restful.

Then when our gear was collected by the hook-nosed bearers to whom we were obliged to trust, though we kept with us our rifles and a certain amount of ammunition, we started. First went a number of Billali's spearmen, then came the litters with the wounded alongside of which Umslopogaas and his three uninjured Zulus talked or trotted, then another litter containing Billali, then my own by which ran Hans, and Robertson's, and lastly the rest of the Amahagger and the relief bearers.

"I see now, Baas," said Hans, thrusting his head between my curtains, "that yonder Whitebeard cannot be your reverend father, the Predikant, after all."

"Why not?" I asked, though the fact was fairly obvious.

"Because, Baas, if he were, he would not have left Hans, of whom he always thought so well, to run in the sun like a dog, while he and others travel in carriages like great white ladies."

"You had better save your breath instead of talking nonsense, Hans," I said, "since I believe that you have a long way to go."

In fact, it proved to be a very long way indeed, especially as after we began to breast the mountain, we must travel slowly. We started about ten o'clock in the morning, for the fight which after all did not take long—had, it will be remembered, begun shortly after dawn, and it was three in the afternoon before we reached the base of the towering cliff which I have mentioned.

Here, at the foot of a remarkable, isolated column of rock, on which I was destined to see a strange sight in the after days, we halted and ate of the remaining food which we had brought with us, while the Amahagger consumed their own, that seemed to consist largely of curdled milk, such as the Zulus call *maas*, and lumps of a kind of bread.

I noted that they were a very curious people who fed in silence and on whose handsome, solemn faces one never saw a smile. Somehow it gave me the creeps to look at them. Robertson was affected in the same way, for in one of the rare intervals of his abstraction he remarked that they were "no canny." Then he added,

"Ask yon old wizard who might be one of the Bible prophets come to life—what those man-eating devils have done with my daughter."

I did so, and Billali answered,

"Say that they have taken her away to make a queen of her, since having rebelled against their own queen, they must have another who is white. Say too that She-who-commands will wage war on them and perhaps win her back, unless they kill her first."

"Ah!" Robertson repeated when I had translated, "unless they kill her first—or worse." Then he relapsed into his usual silence.

Presently we started on again, heading straight for what looked like a sheer wall of black rock a thousand feet or more in height, up a path so steep that Robertson and I got out and walked, or rather scrambled, in order to ease the bearers. Billali, I noticed, remained in his litter. The convenience of the bearers did not trouble him; he only ordered an extra gang to the poles. I could not imagine how we were to negotiate this precipice. Nor could Umslopogaas, who looked at it and said,

"If we are to climb that, Macumazahn, I think that the only one who will live to get to the top will be that little yellow monkey of yours," and he pointed with his axe at Hans.

"If I do," replied that worthy, much nettled, for he hated to be called a "yellow monkey" by the Zulus, "be sure that I will roll down stones upon any black butcher whom I see sprawling upon the cliff below."

Umslopogaas smiled grimly, for he had a sense of humour and could appreciate a repartee even when it hit him hard. Then we stopped talking for the climb took all our breath.

At length we came to the cliff face where, to all appearance, our journey must end. Suddenly, however, out of the blind black wall in front of us started the apparition of a tall man armed with a great spear and wearing a white robe, who challenged us hoarsely.

Suddenly he stood before us, as a ghost might do, though whence he came we could not see. Presently the mystery was explained. Here in the cliff face there was a cleft, though one invisible even from a few paces away, since its outer edge projected over the inner wall of rock. Moreover, this opening was not above four feet in width, a mere split in the huge mountain mass caused by some titanic convulsion in past ages. For it was a definite split since, once entered, far, far above could be traced a faint line of light coming from the sky, although the gloom of the passage was such that torches, which were stored at hand, must be used by those who threaded it. One man could have held the place against a hundred—until he was killed. Still, it was guarded, not only at the mouth where the warrior had appeared, but further along at every turn in the jagged chasm, and these were many.

Into this grim place we went. The Zulus did not like it at all, for they are a light-loving people and I noted that even Umslopogaas seemed scared and hung back a little. Nor did Hans, who with his usual suspicion, feared some trap; nor, for the matter of that, did I, though I thought it well to appear much interested. Only Robertson seemed quite indifferent and trudged along stolidly after a man carrying a torch.

Old Billali put his head out of the litter and shouted back to me to fear nothing, since there were no pitfalls in the path, his voice echoing strangely between those narrow walls of measureless height.

For half an hour or more we pursued this dreary, winding path round the corners of which the draught tore in gusts so fierce that more than once the litters with the wounded men and those who bore them were nearly blown over. It was safe enough, however, since on either side of us, smooth and without break, rose the sheer walls of rock over which lay the tiny ribbon of blue sky. At length the cleft widened somewhat and the light grew stronger, making the torches unnecessary.

Then of a sudden we came to its end and found ourselves upon a little plateau in the mountainside. Behind us for a thousand feet or so rose the sheer rock wall as it did upon the outer face, while in front and beneath, far beneath, was a beautiful plain circular in shape and of great extent, which plain was everywhere surrounded, so far as I could see, by the same wall of rock. In short, notwithstanding its enormous size, without doubt it was neither more nor less than the crater of a vast extinct volcano. Lastly, not far from the centre of this plain was what appeared to be a city, since through my glasses I could see great walls built of stone, and what I thought were houses, all of them of a character more substantial than any that I had discovered in the wilds of Africa.

I went to Billali's litter and asked him who lived in the city.

"No one," he answered, "it has been dead for thousands of years, but She-who-commands is camped there at present with an army, and thither we go at once. Forward, bearers."

So, Robertson and I having re-entered our litters, we started on down hill at a rapid pace, for the road, though steep, was safe and kept in good order. All the rest of that afternoon we travelled and by sunset reached the edge of the plain, where we halted a while to rest and eat, till the light of the growing moon grew strong enough to enable us to proceed. Umslopogaas came up and spoke to me.

"Here is a fortress indeed, Macumazahn," he said, "since none can climb that fence of rock in which the holes seem to be few and small."

"Yes," I answered, "but it is one out of which those who are in, would find it difficult to get out. We are buffaloes in a pit, Umslopogaas."

"That is so," he answered, "I have thought it already. But if any would meddle with us we still have our horns and can toss for a while."

Then he went back to his men.

The sunset in that great solemn place was a wonderful thing to see. First of all the measureless crater was filled with light like a bowl with fire. Then as the great orb sank behind the western cliff, half of the plain became quite dark while shadows seemed to rush forward over the eastern part of its surface, till that too was swallowed up in gloom and for a little while there remained only a glow reflected from the cliff face and from the sky above, while on the crest of the parapet of rock played strange and glorious fires. Presently these too vanished and the world was dark.

Then the half moon broke from behind a bank of clouds and by its silver, uncertain light we struggled forward across the flat plain, rather slowly now, for even the iron muscles of those bearers grew tired. I could not see much of it, but I gathered that we were passing through crops, very fine crops to judge by their height, as doubtless they would be upon this lava soil; also once or twice we splashed through streams.

At length, being tired and lulled by the swaying of the litter and by the sound of a weird, low chant that the bearers had set up now that they neared home and were afraid of no attack, I sank into a doze. When I awoke again it was to find that the litter had halted and to hear the voice of Billali say,

"Descend, White Lords, and come with your companions, the black Warrior and the yellow man who is named Light-in-Darkness. She-who-commands desires to see you at once before you eat and sleep, and must not be kept waiting. Fear not for the others, they will be cared for till you return."

The White Witch

I descended from the litter and told the others what the old fellow had said. Robertson did not want to come, and indeed refused to do so until I suggested to him that such conduct might prejudice a powerful person against us. Umslopogaas was indifferent, putting, as he remarked, no faith in a ruler who was a woman.

Only Hans, although he was so tired, acquiesced with some eagerness, the fact being that his brain was more alert and that he had all the curiosity of the monkey tribe which he so much resembled in appearance, and wanted to see this queen whom Zikali revered.

In the end we started, conducted by Billali and by men who carried torches whereof the light showed me that we were passing between houses, or at any rate walls that had been those of houses, and along what seemed to be a paved street.

Walking under what I took to be a great arch or portico, we came into a court that was full of towering pillars but unroofed, for I could see the stars above. At its end we entered a building of which the doorway was hung with mats, to find that it was lighted with lamps and that all down its length on either side guards with long spears stood at intervals.

"Oh, Baas," said Hans hesitatingly, "this is the mouth of a trap," while Umslopogaas glared about him suspiciously, fingering the handle of his great axe.

"Be silent," I answered. "All this mountain is a trap, therefore another does not matter, and we have our pistols."

Walking forward between the double line of guards who stood immovable as statues, we came to some curtains hung at the end of a long, narrow hall which, although I know little of such things, were, I noted, made of rich stuff embroidered in colours and with golden threads. Before these curtains Billali motioned us to halt.

After a whispered colloquy with someone beyond carried on through the join of the curtains, he vanished between them, leaving us alone for five minutes or more. At length they opened and a tall and elegant woman with an Arab cast of countenance and clad in white robes, appeared and beckoned to us to enter. She did not speak or answer when I spoke to her, which was not wonderful as afterwards I discovered that she was a mute. We went in, I wondering very much what we were going to see.

On the further side of the curtains was a room of no great size illumined with lamps of which the light fell upon sculptured walls. It looked to me as though it might once have been the inmost court or a sanctuary of some temple, for at its head was a dais upon which once perhaps had stood the shrine or statue of a god. On this dais there was now a couch and on the couch—a goddess!

There she sat, straight and still, clothed in shining white and veiled, but with her draperies so arranged that they emphasised rather than concealed the wonderful elegance of her tall form. From beneath the veil, which was such as a bride wears, appeared two plaits of glossy, raven hair of great length, to the end of each of which was suspended a single large pearl. On either side of her stood a tall woman like to her who had led us through the curtains, and on his knees in front, but to the right, knelt Billali.

About this seated personage there was an air of singular majesty, such as might pervade a queen as fancy paints her, though she had a nobler figure than any queen I ever saw depicted. Mystery seemed to flow from her; it clothed her like the veil she wore, which of course heightened the effect. Beauty flowed from her also; although it was shrouded I knew that it was there, no veil or coverings could obscure it—at least, to my imagination. Moreover she breathed out power also; one felt it in the air as one feels a thunderstorm before it breaks, and it seemed to me that this power was not quite human, that it drew its strength from afar and dwelt a stranger to the earth.

To tell the truth, although my curiosity, always strong, was enormously excited and though now I felt glad that I had attempted this journey with all its perils, I was horribly afraid, so much afraid that I should have liked to turn and run away. From the beginning I knew myself to be in the presence of an unearthly being clothed in soft and perfect woman's flesh, something alien, too, and different from our human race.

What a picture it all made! There she sat, quiet and stately as a perfect marble statue; only her breast, rising and falling beneath the white robe, showed that she was alive and breathed as others do. Another thing showed it also—her eyes. At first I could not see them through the veil, but presently either because I grew accustomed to the light, or because they brightened as those of certain animals have power to do when they watch intently, it ceased to be a covering to them. Distinctly I saw them now, large and dark and splendid with a tinge of deep blue in the iris; alluring and yet awful in their majestic aloofness which seemed to look through and beyond, to embrace all without seeking and without effort. Those eyes were like windows through which light flows from within, a light of the spirit.

I glanced round to see the effect of this vision upon my companions. It was most peculiar. Hans had sunk to his knees; his hands were joined in the attitude of prayer and his ugly little face reminded me of that of a big fish out of water and dying from excess of air. Robertson, startled out of his abstraction, stared at the royal-looking woman on the couch with his mouth open.

"Man," he whispered, "I've got them back although I have touched nothing for weeks, only this time they are lovely. For yon's no human lady, I feel it in my bones."

Umslopogaas stood great and grim, his hands resting on the handle of his tall axe; and he stared also, the blood pulsing against the skin that covered the hole in his head.

"Watcher-by-Night," he said to me in his deep voice, but also speaking in a whisper, "this chieftainess is not one woman, but all women. Beneath those robes of hers I seem to see the beauty of one who has 'gone Beyond,' of the Lily who is lost to me. Do you not feel it thus, Macumazahn?"

Now that he mentioned it, certainly I did; indeed, I had felt it all along although amid the rush of sensations this one had scarcely disentangled itself in my mind. I looked at the draped shape and saw— well, never mind whom I saw; it was not one only but several in sequence; also a woman who at that time I did not know although I came to know her afterwards, too well, perhaps, or at any rate quite enough to puzzle me. The odd thing was that in this hallucination the personalities of these individuals seemed to overlap and merge, till at last I began to wonder whether they were not parts of the same entity or being, manifesting itself in sundry shapes, yet springing from one centre, as different coloured rays flow from the same crystal, while the beams from their source of light shift and change. But the fancy is too metaphysical for my poor powers to express as clearly as I would. Also no doubt it was but a hallucination that had its origin, perhaps, in the mischievous brain of her who sat before us.

At length she spoke and her voice sounded like silver bells heard over water in a great calm. It was low and sweet, oh! so sweet that at its first notes for a moment my senses seemed to swoon and my pulse to stop. It was to me that she addressed herself.

"My servant here," and ever so slightly she turned her head towards the kneeling Billali, "tells me that you who are named Watcher-in-the- Night, understand the tongue in which I speak to you. Is it so?"

"I understand Arabic of a kind well enough, having learned it on the East Coast and from Arabs in past years, but not such Arabic as you use, O——" and I paused.

"Call me *Hiya*," she broke in, "which is my title here, meaning, as you know, She, or Woman. Or if that does not please you, call me Ayesha. It would rejoice me after so long to hear the name I bore spoken by the lips of one of my colour and of gentle blood."

I blushed at the compliment so artfully conveyed, and repeated stupidly enough, "—Not such Arabic as you use, O—Ayesha."

"I thought that you would like the sound of the word better than that of *Hiya*, though afterwards I will teach you to pronounce it as you should, O—have you any other name save Watcher-by-Night, which seems also to be a title?"

"Yes," I answered. "Allan."

"—O—Allan. Tell me of these," she went on quickly, indicating my companions with a sweep of her slender hand, "for they do not speak Arabic, I think. Or stay, I will tell you of them and you shall say if I do so rightly. This one," and she nodded towards Robertson, "is a man bemused. There comes from him a colour which I see if you cannot, and that colour betokens a desire for revenge, though I think that in his time he has desired other things also, as I remember men always did from the beginning, to their ruin. Human nature does not change, Allan, and wine and women are ancient snares. Enough of him for this time. The little yellow one there is afraid of me, as are all of you. That is woman's greatest power, although she is so weak and gentle, men are still afraid of her just because they are so foolish that they cannot understand her. To them after a million years she still remains the Unknown and to us all the Unknown is also the awful. Do you remember the proverb of the Romans that says it well and briefly?"

I nodded, for it was one of the Latin tags that my father had taught me.

"Good. Well, he is a little wild man, is he not, nearer to the apes from whose race our bodies come? But do you know that, Allan?"

I nodded again, and said,

"There are disputes upon the point, Ayesha."

"Yes, they had begun in my day and we will discuss them later. Still, I say—nearer to the ape than you or I, and therefore of interest, as the germ of things is always. Yet he has qualities, I think; cunning, and fidelity and love which in its round is all in all. Do you understand, Allan, that love is all in all?"

I answered warily that it depended upon what she meant by love, to which she replied that she would explain afterwards when we had leisure to talk, adding,

"What this little yellow monkey understands by it at least has served you well, or so I believe. You shall tell me the tale of it some day. Now of the last, this Black One. Here I think is a man indeed, a warrior of warriors such as there used to be in the early world, if a savage. Well, believe me, Allan, savages are often the best. Moreover, all are still savage at heart, even you and I. For what is termed culture is but coat upon coat of paint laid on to hide our native colour, and often there is poison in the paint. That axe of his has drunk deep, I think, though always in fair fight, and I say that it shall drink deeper yet. Have I read these men aright, Allan?"

"Not so ill," I answered.

"I thought it," she said with a musical laugh, "although at this place I rust and grow dull like an unused sword. Now you would rest. Go—all of you. To-morrow you and I will talk alone. Fear nothing for your safety; you are watched by my slaves and I watch my slaves. Until to-morrow, then, farewell. Go now, eat and sleep, as alas we all must do who linger on this ball of earth and cling to a life we should do well to lose. Billali, lead them hence," and she waved her hand to signify that the audience was ended.

At this sign Hans, who apparently was still much afraid, rose from his knees and literally bolted through the curtains. Robertson followed him. Umslopogaas stood a moment, drew himself up and lifting the great axe, cried *Bayéte*, after which he too turned and went.

"What does that word mean, Allan?" she asked.

I explained that it was the salutation which the Zulu people only give to kings.

"Did I not say that savages are often the best?" she exclaimed in a gratified voice. "The white man, your companion, gave me no salute, but the Black One knows when he stands before a woman who is royal."

"He too is of royal blood in his own land," I said.

"If so, we are akin, Allan."

Then I bowed deeply to her in my best manner and rising from her couch for the first time she stood up, looking very tall and commanding, and bowed back.

After this I went to find the others on the further side of the curtains, except Hans, who had run down the long narrow hall and through the mats at its end. We followed, marching with dignity behind Billali and between the double line of guards, who raised their spears as we passed them, and on the further side of the mats discovered Hans, still looking terrified.

"Baas," he said to me as we threaded our way through the court of columns, "in my life I have seen all kinds of dreadful things and faced them, but never have I been so much afraid as I am of that white witch. Baas, I think that she is the devil of whom your reverend father, the Predikant, used to talk so much, or perhaps his wife."

"If so, Hans," I answered, "the devil is not so black as he is painted. But I advise you to be careful of what you say as she may have long ears."

"It doesn't matter at all what one says, Baas, because she reads thoughts before they pass the lips. I felt her doing it there in that room. And do you be careful, Baas, or she will eat up your spirit and make you fall in love with her, who, I expect, is very ugly indeed, since otherwise she would not wear a veil. Whoever saw a pretty woman tie up her head in a sack, Baas?"

"Perhaps she does this because she is so beautiful, Hans, that she fears the hearts of men who look upon her would melt."

"Oh, no, Baas, all women want to melt men's hearts; the more the better. They seem to have other things in their minds, but really they think of nothing else until they are too old and ugly, and it takes them a long while to be sure of that."

So Hans went on talking his shrewd nonsense till, following so far as I could see, the same road as that by which we had come, we reached our quarters, where we found food prepared for us, broiled goat's flesh with corncakes and milk, I think it was; also beds for us two white men covered with skin rugs and blankets woven of wool.

These quarters, I should explain, consisted of rooms in a house built of stone of which the walls had once been painted. The roof of the house was gone now, for we could see the stars shining above us, but as the air was very soft in this sheltered plain, this was an advantage rather than otherwise. The largest room was reserved for Robertson and myself, while another at the back was given to Umslopogaas and his Zulus, and a third to the two wounded men.

Billali showed us these arrangements by the light of lamps and apologised that they were not better because, as he explained, the place was a ruin and there had been no time to build us a house. He added that we might sleep without fear as we were guarded and none would dare to harm the guests of She-who-commands, on whom he was sure we, or at any rate I and the black Warrior, had produced an excellent impression. Then he bowed himself out, saying that he would return in the morning, and left us to our own devices.

Robertson and I sat down on stools that had been set for us, and ate, but he seemed so overcome by his experiences, or by his sombre thoughts, that I could not draw him into conversation. All he remarked was that we had fallen into queer company and that those who supped with Satan needed a long spoon. Having delivered himself of this sentiment he threw himself upon the bed, prayed aloud for a while as had become his fashion, to be "protected from warlocks and witches," amongst other things, and went to sleep.

Before I turned in I visited Umslopogaas's room to see that all was well with him and his people, and found him standing in the doorway staring at the star-spangled sky.

"Greeting, Macumazahn," he said, "you who are white and wise and I am black and a fighter have seen many strange things beneath the sun, but never such a one as we have looked upon to-night. Who and what is that chieftainess, Macumazahn?"

"I do not know," I said, "but it is worth while to have lived to see her, even though she be veiled."

"Nor do I, Macumazahn. Nay, I do know, for my heart tells me that she is the greatest of all witches and that you will do well to guard your spirit lest she should steal it away. If she were not a witch, should I have seemed to behold the shape of Nada the Lily who was the wife of my youth, beneath those white robes of hers, and though the tongue in which she spoke was strange to me, to hear the murmur of Nada's voice between her lips, of Nada who has gone further from me than those stars. It is good that you wear the Great Medicine of Zikali upon your breast, Macumazahn, for perhaps it will shield you from harm at those hands that are shaped of ivory."

"Zikali is another of the tribe," I answered, laughing, "although less beautiful to see. Also I am not afraid of any of them, and from this one, if she be more than some white woman whom it pleases to veil herself, I shall hope to gather wisdom."

"Yes, Macumazahn, such wisdom as Spirits and the dead have to give."

"Mayhap, Umslopogaas, but we came here to seek Spirits and the dead, did we not?"

"Aye," answered Umslopogaas, "these and war, and I think that we shall find enough of all three. Only I hope that war will come the first, lest the Spirits and the dead should bewitch me and take away my skill and courage."

Then we parted, and too tired even to wonder any more, I threw myself down on my bed and slept.

I was awakened when the sun was already high, by the sound of Robertson, who was on his knees, praying aloud as usual, a habit of his which I confess got on my nerves. Prayer, in my opinion, is a private matter between man and his Creator, that is, except in church; further, I did not in the least wish to hear all about Robertson's sins, which seemed to have been many and peculiar. It is bad enough to have to bear the burden of one's own transgressions without learning of those of other people, that is, unless one is a priest and must do so professionally. So I jumped up to escape and make arrangements for a wash, only to butt into old Billali, who was standing in the doorway contemplating Robertson with much interest and stroking his white beard.

He greeted me with his courteous bow and said,

"Tell your companion, O Watcher, that it is not necessary for him to go upon his knees to She-who-commands—and must be obeyed," he added with emphasis, "when he is not in her presence, and that even then he would do well to keep silent, since so much talking in a strange tongue might trouble her."

I burst out laughing and answered,

"He does not go upon his knees and pray to She-who-commands, but to the Great One who is in the sky."

"Indeed, Watcher. Well, here we only know a Great One who is upon the earth, though it is true that perhaps she visits the skies sometimes."

"Is it so, Billali?" I answered incredulously. "And now, I would ask you to take me to some place where I can bathe."

"It is ready," he replied. "Come."

So I called to Hans, who was hanging about with a rifle on his arm, to follow with a cloth and soap, of which fortunately we had a couple of pieces left, and we started along what had once been a paved roadway running between stone houses, whereof the time-eaten ruins still remained on either side.

"Who and what is this Queen of yours, Billali?" I asked as we went. "Surely she is not of the Amahagger blood."

"Ask it of herself, O Watcher, for I cannot tell you. All I know is that I can trace my own family for ten generations and that my tenth forefather told his son on his deathbed, for the saying has come down through his descendants—that when he was young She-who-commands had ruled the land for more scores of years than he could count months of life."

I stopped and stared at him, since the lie was so amazing that it seemed to deprive me of the power of motion. Noting my very obvious disbelief he continued blandly,

"If you doubt, ask. And now here is where you may bathe."

Then he led me through an arched doorway and down a wrecked passage to what very obviously once had been a splendid bath-house such as some I have seen pictures of that were built by the Romans. Its size was that of a large room; it was constructed of a kind of marble with a sloping bottom that varied from three to seven feet in depth, and water still ran in and out of it through large glazed pipes. Moreover round it was a footway about five feet across, from which opened chambers, unroofed now, that the bathers used as dressing-rooms, while between these chambers stood the remains of statues. One at the end indeed, where an alcove had protected it from sun and weather, was still quite perfect, except for the outstretched arms which were gone (the right hand I noticed lying at the bottom of the bath). It was that of a nude young woman in the attitude of diving, a very beautiful bit of work, I thought, though of course I am no judge of sculpture. Even the smile mingled with trepidation upon the girl's face was most naturally portrayed.

This statue showed two things, that the bath was used by females and that the people who built it were highly civilised, also that they belonged to an advanced if somewhat Eastern race, since the girl's nose was, if anything, Semitic in character, and her lips, though prettily shaped, were full. For the rest, the basin was so clean that I presume it must have been made ready for me or other recent bathers, and at its bottom I discovered gratings and broken pipes of earthenware which suggested that in the old days the water could be warmed by means of a furnace.

This relic of a long-past civilisation excited Hans even more than it did myself, since having never seen anything of the sort, he thought it so strange that, as he informed me, he imagined that it must have been built by witchcraft. In it I had a most delightful and much- needed bath. Even Hans was persuaded to follow my example—a thing I had rarely known him to do before—and seated in its shallowest part, splashed some water over his yellow, wrinkled anatomy. Then we returned to our house, where I found an excellent breakfast had been provided which was brought to us by tall, silent, handsome women who surveyed us out of the corners of their eyes, but said nothing.

Shortly after I had finished my meal, Billali, who had disappeared, came back again and said that She-who-commands desired my presence as she would speak with me; also that I must come alone. So, after attending to the wounded, who both seemed to be getting on well, I went, followed by Hans armed with his rifle, though I only carried my revolver. Robertson wished to accompany me, as he did not seem to care about being left alone with the Zulus in that strange place, but this Billali would not allow. Indeed, when he persisted, two great men stepped forward and crossed their spears before him in a somewhat threatening fashion. Then at my entreaty, for I feared lest trouble should arise, he gave in and returned to the house.

Following our path of the night before, we walked up a ruined street which I could see was only one of scores in what had once been a very great city, until we came to the archway that I have mentioned, a large one now overgrown with plants that from their yellow, sweet- scented bloom I judged to be a species of wallflower, also with a kind of houseleek or saxifrage.

Here Hans was stopped by guards, Billali explaining to me that he must await my return, an order which he obeyed unwillingly enough. Then I went on down the narrow passage, lined as before by guards who stood silent as statues, and came to the curtains at the end. Before these at a motion from Billali, who did not seem to dare to speak in this place, I stood still and waited.

Allan Hears a Strange Tale

For some minutes I remained before those curtains until, had it not been for something electric in the air which got into my bones, a kind of force that, perhaps in my fancy only, seemed to pervade the place, I should certainly have grown bored. Indeed I was about to ask my companion why he did not announce our arrival instead of standing there like a stuck pig with his eyes shut as though in prayer or meditation, when the curtains parted and from between them appeared one of those tall waiting women whom we had seen on the previous night. She contemplated us gravely for a few moments, then moved her hand twice, once forward, towards Billali as a signal to him to retire, which he did with great rapidity, and next in a beckoning fashion towards myself to invite me to follow her.

I obeyed, passing between the thick curtains which she fastened in some way behind me, and found myself in the same roofed and sculptured room that I have already described. Only now there were no lamps, such light as penetrated it coming from an opening above that I could not see, and falling upon the dais at its head, also on her who sat upon the dais.

Yes, there she was in her white robes and veil, the point and centre of a little lake of light, a wondrous and in a sense a spiritual vision, for in truth there was something about her which was not of the world, something that drew and yet frightened me. Still as a statue she sat, like one to whom time is of no account and who has grown weary of motion, and on either side of her yet more still, like caryatides supporting a shrine, stood two of the stately women who were her attendants.

For the rest a sweet and subtle odour pervaded the chamber which took hold of my senses as *hasheesh* might do, which I was sure proceeded from her, or from her garments, for I could see no perfumes burning. She spoke no word, yet I knew she was inviting me to come nearer and moved forward till I reached a curious carved chair that was placed just beneath the dais, and there halted, not liking to sit down without permission.

For a long while she contemplated me, for as before I could feel her eyes searching me from head to foot and as it were looking through me as though she would discover my very soul. Then at length she moved, waving those two ivory arms of hers outwards with a kind of swimming stroke, whereon the women to right and left of her turned and glided away, I know not whither.

"Sit, Allan," she said, "and let us talk, for I think we have much to say to each other. Have you slept well? And eaten?—though I fear that the food is but rough. Also was the bath made ready for you?"

"Yes, Ayesha," I answered to all three questions, adding, for I knew not what to say, "It seems to be a very ancient bath."

"When I last saw it," she replied, "it was well enough with statues standing round it worked by a sculptor who had seen beauty in his dreams. But in two thousand years—or is it more?—the tooth of Time bites deep, and doubtless like all else in this dead place it is now a ruin."

I coughed to cover up the exclamation of disbelief that rose to my lips and remarked blandly that two thousand years was certainly a long time.

"When you say one thing, Allan, and mean another, your Arabic is even more vile than usual and does not serve to cloak your thought."

"It may be so, Ayesha, for I only know that tongue as I do many other of the dialects of Africa by learning it from common men. My own speech is English, in which, if you are acquainted with it, I should prefer to talk."

"I know not English, which doubtless is some language that has arisen since I left the world. Perhaps later you shall teach it to me. I tell you, you anger me whom it is not well to anger, because you believe nothing that passes my lips and yet do not dare to say so."

"How can I believe one, Ayesha, who if I understand aright, speaks of having seen a certain bath two thousand years ago, whereas one hundred years are the full days of man? Forgive me therefore if I cannot believe what I know to be untrue."

Now I thought that she would be very angry and was sorry that I had spoken. But as it happened she was not.

"You must have courage to give me the lie so boldly—and I like courage," she said, "who have been cringed to for so long. Indeed, I know that you are brave, who have heard how you bore yourself in the fight yesterday, and much else about you. I think that we shall be friends, but—seek no more."

"What else should I seek, Ayesha?" I asked innocently.

"Now you are lying again," she said, "who know well that no man who is a man sees a woman who is beautiful and pleases him, without wondering whether, should he desire it, she could come to love him, that is, if she be young."

"Which at least is not possible if she has lived two thousand years. Then naturally she would prefer to wear a veil," I said boldly, seeking to avoid the argument into which I saw she wished to drag me.

"Ah!" she answered, "the little yellow man who is named Light-in- Darkness put that thought into your heart, I think. Oh, do not trouble as to how I know it, who have many spies here, as he guessed well enough. So a woman who has lived two thousand years must be hideous and wrinkled, must she? The stamp of youth and loveliness must long have fled from her; of that you, the wise man, are sure. Very well. Now you tempt me to do what I had determined I would not do and you shall pluck the fruit of that tree of curiosity which grows so fast within you. Look, Allan, and say whether I am old and hideous, even though I have lived two thousand years upon the earth and mayhap many more."

Then she lifted her hands and did something to her veil, so that for a moment—only one moment—her face was revealed, after which the veil fell into its place.

I looked, I saw, and if that chair had lacked a back I believe that I should have fallen out of it to the ground. As for what I saw—well, it cannot be described, at any rate by me, except perhaps as a flash of glory.

Every man has dreamed of perfect beauty, basing his ideas of it perhaps on that of some woman he has met who chanced to take his fancy, with a few accessories from splendid pictures or Greek statues thrown in, *plus* a garnishment of the imagination. At any rate I have, and here was that perfect beauty multiplied by ten, such beauty, that at the sight of it the senses reeled. And yet I repeat that it is not to be described.

I do not know what the nose or the lips were like; in fact, all that I can remember with distinctness is the splendour of the eyes, of which I had caught some hint through her veil on the previous night. Oh, they were wondrous, those eyes, but I cannot tell their colour save that the groundwork of them was black. Moreover they seemed to be more than eyes as we understand them. They were indeed windows of the soul, out of which looked thought and majesty and infinite wisdom, mixed with all the allurements and the mystery that we are accustomed to see or to imagine in woman.

Here let me say something at once. If this marvellous creature expected that the revelation of her splendour was going to make me her slave; to cause me to fall in love with her, as it is called, well, she must have been disappointed, for it had no such effect. It frightened and in a sense humbled me, that is all, for I felt myself to be in the presence of something that was not human, something alien to me as a man, which I could fear and even adore as humanity would adore that which is Divine, but with which I had no desire to mix. Moreover, was it divine, or was it something very different? I did not know, I only knew that it was not for me; as soon should I have thought of asking for a star to set within my lantern.

I think that she felt this, felt that her stroke had missed, as the French say, that is if she meant to strike at all at this moment. Of this I am not certain, for it was in a changed voice, one with a suspicion of chill in it that she said with a little laugh,

"Do you admit now, Allan, that a woman may be old and still remain fair and unwrinkled?"

"I admit," I answered, although I was trembling so much that I could hardly speak with steadiness, "that a woman may be splendid and lovely beyond anything that the mind of man can conceive, whatever her age, of which I know nothing. I would add this, Ayesha, that I thank you very much for having revealed to me the glory that is hid beneath your veil."

"Why?" she asked, and I thought that I detected curiosity in her question.

"For this reason, Ayesha. Now there is no fear of my troubling you in such a fashion as you seemed to dread a little while ago. As soon would a man desire to court the moon sailing in her silver loveliness through heaven."

"The moon! It is strange that you should compare me to the moon," she said musingly. "Do you know that the moon was a great goddess in Old Egypt and that her name was Isis and—well, once I had to do with Isis? Perhaps you were there and knew it, since more lives than one are given to most of us. I must search and learn. For the rest, all have not thought as you do, Allan. Many, on the contrary, love and seek to win the Divine."

"So do I at a distance, Ayesha, but to come too near to it I do not aspire. If I did perhaps I might be consumed."

"You have wisdom," she replied, not without a note of admiration in her voice. "The moths are few that fear the flame, but those are the moths which live. Also I think that you have scorched your wings before and learned that fire hurts. Indeed, now I remember that I have heard of three such fires of love through which you have flown, Allan, though all of them are dead ashes now, or shine elsewhere. Two burned in your youth when a certain lady died to save you, a great woman that, is it not so? And the third, ah! she was fire indeed, though of a copper hue. What was her name? I cannot remember, but I think it had something to do with the wind, yes, with the wind when it wails."

I stared at her. Was this Mameena myth to be dug up again in a secret place in the heart of Africa? And how the deuce did she know anything about Mameena? Could she have been questioning Hans or Umslopogaas? No, it was not possible, for she had never seen them out of my presence.

"Perhaps," she went on in a mocking voice, "perhaps once again you disbelieve, Allan, whose cynic mind is so hard to open to new truths. Well, shall I show you the faces of these three? I can," and she waved her hand towards some object that stood on a tripod to the right of her in the shadow—it looked like a crystal basin. "But what would it serve when you who know them so well, believed that I drew their pictures out of your own soul? Also perchance but one face would appear and that one strange to you. [Lady Ragnall perhaps?—JB]

"Have you heard, Allan, that among the wise some hold that not all of us is visible at once here on earth within the same house of flesh; that the whole self in its home above, separates itself into sundry parts, each of which walks the earth in different form, a segment of life's circle that can never be dissolved and must unite again at last?"

I shook my head blankly, for I had never heard anything of the sort.

"You have still much to learn, Allan, although doubtless there are some who think you wise," she went on in the same mocking voice. "Well, I hold that this doctrine is built upon a rock of truth; also," she added after studying me for a minute, "that in your case these three women do not complete that circle. I think there is a fourth who as yet is strange to you in this life, though you have known her well enough in others."

I groaned, imagining that she alluded to herself, which was foolish of me, for at once she read my mind and went on with a rather acid little laugh,

"No, no, not the humble slave who sits before you, whom, as you have told me, it would please you to reject as unworthy were she brought to you in offering, as in the old days was done at the courts of the great kings of the East. O fool, fool! who hold yourself so strong and do not know that if I chose, before yon shadow had moved a finger's breadth, I could bring you to my feet, praying that you might be suffered to kiss my robe, yes, just the border of my robe."

"Then I beg of you not to choose, Ayesha, since I think that when there is work to be done by both of us, we shall find more comfort side by side than if I were on the ground seeking to kiss a garment that doubtless then it would delight you to snatch away."

At these words her whole attitude seemed to change. I could see her lovely shape brace itself up, as it were, beneath her robes and felt in some way that her mind had also changed; that it had rid itself of mockery and woman's pique and like a shifting searchlight, was directed upon some new objective.

"Work to be done," she repeated after me in a new voice. "Yes, I thank you who bring it to my mind, since the hours pass and that work presses. Also I think there is a bargain to be made between us who are both of the blood that keeps bargains, even if they be not written on a roll and signed and sealed. Why do you come to me and what do you seek of me, Allan, Watcher-in-the-Night? Say it and truthfully, for though I may laugh at lies and pass them by when they have to do with the eternal sword-play which Nature decrees between man and woman, until these break apart or, casting down the swords, seek arms in which they agree too well, when they have to do with policy and high purpose and ambition's ends, why then I avenge them upon the liar."

Now I hesitated, as what I had to tell her seemed so foolish, indeed so insane, while she waited patiently as though to give me time to shape my thoughts. Speaking at last because I must, I said,

"I come to ask you, Ayesha, to show me the dead, if the dead still live elsewhere."

"And who told you, Allan, that I could show you the dead, if they are not truly dead? There is but one, I think, and if you are his messenger, show me his token. Without it we do not speak together of this business."

"What token?" I asked innocently, though I guessed her meaning well enough.

She searched me with her great eyes, for I felt, and indeed saw them on me through the veil, then answered,

"I think—nay, let me be sure," and half rising from the couch, she bent her heard over the tripod that I have described, and stared into what seemed to be a crystal bowl. "If I read aright," she said, straightening herself presently, "it is a hideous thing enough, the carving of an abortion of a man such as no woman would care to look on lest her babe should bear its stamp. It is a charmed thing also that has virtues for him who wears it, especially for you, Allan, since something tells me that it is dyed with the blood of one who loved you. If you have it, let it be revealed, since without it I do not talk with you of these dead you seek."

Now I drew Zikali's talisman from its hiding-place and held it towards her.

"Give it to me," she said.

I was about to obey when something seemed to warn me not to do so.

"Nay," I answered, "he who lent me this carving for a while, charged me that except in emergency and to save others, I must wear it night and day till I returned it to his hand, saying that if I parted from it fortune would desert me. I believe none of this talk and tried to be rid of it, whereon death drew near to me from a snake, such a snake as I see you wear about you, which doubtless also has poison in its fangs, if of another sort, Ayesha."

"Draw near," she said, "and let me look. Man, be not afraid."

So I rose from my chair and knelt before her, hoping secretly that no one would see me in that ridiculous position, which the most unsuspicious might misinterpret. I admit, however, that it proved to have compensations, since even through the veil I saw her marvellous eyes better than I had done before, and something of the pure outline of her classic face; also the fragrance of her hair was wonderful.

She took the talisman in her hand and examined it closely.

"I have heard of this charm and it is true that the thing has power," she said, "for I can feel it running through my veins, also that it is a shield of defence to him who wears it. Yes, and now I understand what perplexed me somewhat, namely, how it came about that when you vexed me into unveiling—but let that matter be. The wisdom was not your own, but another's, that is all. Yes, the wisdom of one whose years have borne him beyond the shafts that fly from woman's eyes, the ruinous shafts which bring men down to doom and nothingness. Tell me, Allan, is this the likeness of him who gave it to you?"

"Yes, Ayesha, the very picture, as I think, carved by himself, though he said that it is ancient, and others tell that it has been known in the land for centuries."

"So perchance has he," she answered drily, "since some of our company live long. Now tell me this wizard's names. Nay, wait awhile for I would prove that indeed you are his messenger with whom I may talk about the dead, and other things, Allan. You can read Arabic, can you not?"

"A little," I answered.

Then from a stool at her side she took paper, or rather papyrus and a reed pen, and on her knee wrote something on the sheet which she gave to me folded up.

"Now tell me the names," she said, "and then let us see if they tally with what I have written, for if so you are a true man, not a mere wanderer or a spy."

"The principal names of this doctor are Zikali, the Opener-of-Roads, the 'Thing-that-should-never-have-been-born,'" I answered.

"Read the writing, Allan," she said.

I unfolded the sheet and read Arabic words which meant, "Weapons, Cleaver-of-Rocks, One-at-whom-dogs-bark-and-children-wail."

"The last two are near enough," she said, "but the first is wrong."

"Nay, Ayesha, since in this man's tongue the word 'Zikali' means 'Weapons'"; intelligence at which she clapped her hands as a merry girl might do. "The man," I went on, "is without doubt a great doctor, one who sees and knows things that others do not, but I do not understand why this token carved in his likeness should have power, as you say it has."

"Because with it goes his spirit, Allan. Have you never heard of the Egyptians, a very wise people who, as I remember, declared that man has a *Ka* or Double, a second self, that can either dwell in his statue or be sent afar?"

I answered that I had heard this.

"Well the *Ka* of this Zikali goes with that hideous image of him, which is perhaps why you have come safe through many dangers and why also I seemed to dream so much of him last night. Tell me now, what does Zikali want of me whose power he knows very well?"

"An oracle, the answer to a riddle, Ayesha."

"Then set it out another time. So you decide to see the dead, and this old dwarf, who is a home of wisdom, desires an oracle from one who is greater than he. Good. And what are you, or both of you, prepared to pay for these boons? Know, Allan, that I am a merchant who sells my favours dear. Tell me then, will you pay?"

"I think that it depends upon the price," I answered cautiously. "Set out the price, Ayesha."

"Be not afraid, O cunning dealer," she mocked. "I do not ask your soul or even that love of yours which you guard so jealously, since these things I could take without the asking. Nay, I ask only what a brave and honest man may give without shame: your help in war, and perhaps," she added with a softer tone, "your friendship. I think, Allan, that I like you well, perhaps because you remind me of another whom I knew long ago."

I bowed at the compliment, feeling proud and pleased at the prospect of a friendship with this wonderful and splendid creature, although I was aware that it had many dangers. Then I sat still and waited. She also waited, brooding.

"Listen," she said after a while, "I will tell you a story and when you have heard it you shall answer, even if you do not believe it, but not before. Does it please you to listen to something of the tale of my life which I am moved to tell you, that you may know with whom you have to deal?"

Again I bowed, thinking to myself that I knew nothing that would please me more, who was eaten up with a devouring curiosity about this woman.

Now she rose from her couch and descending off the dais, began to walk up and down the chamber. I say, to walk, but her movements were more like the gliding of an eagle through the air or the motion of a swan upon still water, so smooth were they and gracious. As she walked she spoke in a low and thrilling voice.

"Listen," she said again, "and even if my story seems marvellous to you, interrupt, and above all, mock me not, lest I should grow angry, which might be ill for you. I am not as other women are, O Allan, who having conquered the secrets of Nature," here I felt an intense desire to ask what secrets, but remembered and held my tongue, "to my sorrow have preserved my youth and beauty through many ages. Moreover in the past, perhaps in payment for my sins, I have lived other lives of which some memory remains with me.

"By my last birth I am an Arab lady of royal blood, a descendant of the Kings of the East. There I dwelt in the wilderness and ruled a people, and at night I gathered wisdom from the stars and the spirits of the earth and air. At length I wearied of it all and my people too wearied of me and besought me to depart, for, Allan, I would have naught to do with men, yet men went mad because of my beauty and slew each other out of jealousy. Moreover other peoples made war upon my people, hoping to take me captive that I might be a wife to their kings. So I left them, and being furnished with great wealth in hoarded gold and jewels, together with a certain holy man, my master, I wandered through the world, studying the nations and their worships. At Jerusalem I tarried and learned of Jehovah who is, or was, its God.

"At Paphos in the Isle of Chitim I dwelt a while till the folk of that city thought that I was Aphrodite returned to earth and sought to worship me. For this reason and because I made a mock of Aphrodite, I, who, as I have said, would have naught to do with men, she through her priests cursed me, saying that her yoke should lie more heavily upon my neck from age to age than on that of any woman who had breathed beneath the sun.

"It was a wondrous scene," she added reflectively, "that of the cursing, since for every word I gave back two. Moreover I told the hoary villain of a high-priest to make report to his goddess that long after she was dead in the world, I would live on, for the spirit of prophecy was on me in that hour. Yet the curse fell in its season, since in her day, doubt it or not, Aphrodite had strength, as indeed under other names she has and will have while the world endures, and for aught I know, beyond it. Do they worship her now in any land, Allan?"

"No, only her statues because of their beauty, though Love is always worshipped."

"Yes, who can testify to that better than you yourself, Allan, if he who is called Zikali tells me the truth concerning you in the dreams he sends? As for the statues, I saw some of them as they left the master's hand in Greece, and when I told him that he might have found a better model, once I was that model. If this marble still endures, it must be the most famous of them all, though perchance Aphrodite has shattered it in her jealous rage. You shall tell me of these statues afterwards; mine had a mark on the left shoulder like to a mole, but the stone was imperfect, not my flesh, as I can prove if you should wish."

Thinking it better not to enter on a discussion as to Ayesha's shoulder, I remained silent and she went on.

"I dwelt in Egypt also, and there, to be rid of men who wearied me with their sighs and importunities, also to acquire more wisdom of which she was the mistress, I entered the service of the goddess Isis, Queen of Heaven, vowing to remain virgin for ever. Soon I became her high-priestess and in her most sacred shrines upon the Nile, I communed with the goddess and shared her power, since from me her daughter, she withheld none of her secrets. So it came about that though Pharaohs held the sceptre, it was I who ruled Egypt and brought it and Sidon to their fall, it matters not how or why, as it was fated that I must do. Yes, kings would come to seek counsel from me where I sat throned, dressed in the garb of Isis and breathing out her power. Yet, my task accomplished, of it all I grew weary, as men will surely do of the heavens that they preach, should they chance to find them."

I wondered what this "task" might be, but only asked, "Why?"

"Because in their pictured heaven all things lie to their hands and man, being man, cannot be happy without struggle, and woman, being woman, without victory over others. What is cheaply bought, or given, has no value, Allan; to be enjoyed, it must first be won. But I bade you not to break my thought."

I asked pardon and she went on,

"Then it was that the shadow of the curse of Aphrodite fell upon me, yes, and of the curse of Isis also, so that these twin maledictions have made me what I am, a lost soul dwelling in the wilderness waiting the fulfilment of a fate whereof I know not the end. For though I have all wisdom, all knowledge of the Past and much power together with the gift of life and beauty, the future is as dark to me as night without its moon and stars.

"Hearken, this chanced to me. Though it be to my shame I tell it you that all may be clear. At a temple of Isis on the Nile where I ruled, there was a certain priest, a Greek by birth, vowed like myself to the service of the goddess and therefore to wed none but her, the goddess herself—that is, in the spirit. He was named Kallikrates, a man of courage and of beauty, such an one as those Greeks carved in the statues of their god Apollo. Never, I think, was a man more beautiful in face and form, though in soul he was not great, as often happens to men who have all else, and well-nigh always happens to women, save myself and perhaps one or two others that history tells of, doubtless magnifying their fabled charms.

"The Pharaoh of that day, the last of the native blood, him whom the Persians drove to doom, had a daughter, the Princess of Egypt, Amenartas by name, a fair woman in her fashion, though somewhat swarthy. In her youth this Amenartas became enamoured of Kallikrates and he of her, when he was a captain of the Grecian Mercenaries at Pharaoh's Court. Indeed, she brought blood upon his hands because of her, wherefore he fled to Isis for forgiveness and for peace. Thither in after time she followed him and again urged her love.

"Learning of the thing and knowing it for sacrilege, I summoned this priest and warned him of his danger and of the doom which awaited him should he continue in that path. He grew affrighted. He flung himself upon the ground before me with groans and supplications, and kissing my feet, vowed most falsely to me that his dealings with the royal Amenartas were but a veil and that it was I whom he worshipped. His unhallowed words filled me with horror and sternly I bade him begone and do penance for his crime, saying that I would pray the goddess on behalf of him.

"He went, leaving me alone lost in thought in the darkening shrine. Then sleep fell on me and in my sleep I dreamed a dream, or saw a vision. For suddenly there stood before me a woman beauteous as myself clad in nothing save a golden girdle and a veil of gossamer.

"'O Ayesha,' she said in a honeyed voice, 'priestess of Isis of the Egyptians, sworn to the barren worship of Isis and fed on the ashes of her unprofitable wisdom, know that I am Aphrodite of the Greeks whom many times thou hast mocked and defied, and Queen of the breathing world, as Isis is Queen of the world that is dead. Now because thou didst despise me and pour contempt upon my name, I smite thee with my strength and lay a curse upon thee. It is that thou shalt love and desire this man who but now hath kissed thy feet, ever longing till the world's end to kiss his lips in payment, although thou art as far above him as the moon thou servest is above the Nile. Think not that thou shalt escape my doom, for know that however strong the spirit, here upon the earth the flesh is stronger still and of all flesh I am the queen.'

"Then she laughed softly and smiting me across the eyes with a lock of her scented hair, was gone.

"Allan, I awoke from my sleep and a great trouble fell upon me, for I who had never loved before now was rent with a rage of love and for this man who till that moment had been naught to me but as some beauteous image of gold and ivory. I longed for him, my heart was racked with jealousy because of the Egyptian who favoured him, an eating flame possessed my breast. I grew mad. There in the shrine of Isis the divine I cast myself upon my knees and cried to Aphrodite to return and give me him I sought, for whose sake I would renounce all else, even if I must pour my wisdom into a beauteous, empty cup. Yes, thus I prayed and lay upon the ground and wept until, outworn, once more sleep fell upon me.

"Now in the darkness of the holy place once more there came a dream or vision, since before me in her glory stood the goddess Isis crowned with the crescent of the young moon and holding in her hand the jewelled *sistrum* that is her symbol, from which came music like to the melody of distant bells. She gazed at me and in her great eyes were scorn and anger.

"'O Ayesha, Daughter of Wisdom,' she said in a solemn voice, 'whom I, Isis, had come to look upon rather as a child than a servant, since in none other of my priestesses was such greatness to be found, and whom in a day to be I had purposed to raise to the very steps of my heavenly throne, thou hast broken thine oath and, forsaking me, hast worshipped false Aphrodite of the Greeks who is mine enemy. Yea, in the eternal war between the spirit and the flesh, thou hast chosen the part of flesh. Therefore I hate thee and add my doom to that which Aphrodite laid upon thee, which, hadst thou prayed to me and not to her, I would have lifted from thy heart.

"'Hearken! The Grecian whom thou hast chosen, by Aphrodite's will, thou shalt love as the Pathian said. More, thy love shall bring his blood upon thy hands, nor mayest thou follow him to the grave. For I will show thee the Source of Life and thou shalt drink of it to make thyself more fair even than thou art and thus outpace thy rival, and when thy lover is dead, in a desolate place thou shalt wait in grief and solitude till he is born again and find thee there.

"'Yet shall this be but the beginning of thy sorrows, since through all time thou shalt pursue thy fate till at length thou canst draw up this man to the height on which thine own soul stands by the ropes of love and loss and suffering. Moreover through it all thou shalt despise thyself, which is man's and woman's hardest lot, thou who having the rare feast of spirit spread out before thee, hast chosen to fill thyself from the troughs of flesh.'

"Then, Allan, in my dream I made a proud answer to the goddess, saying, 'Hear me, mighty mistress of many Forms who dost appear in all that lives! An evil fate has fallen upon me, but was it I who chose that fate? Can the leaf contend against the driving gale? Can the falling stone turn upwards to the sky, or when Nature draws it, can the tide cease to flow? A goddess whom I have offended, that goddess whose strength causes the whole world to be, has laid her curse upon me and because I have bent before the storm, as bend I must, or break, another goddess whom I serve, thou thyself, Mother Isis, hast added to the curse. Where then is Justice, O Lady of the Moon?'

"'Not here, Woman,' she answered. 'Yet far away Justice lives and shall be won at last and mayhap because thou art so proud and high- stomached, it is laid upon thee to seek her blinded eyes through many an age. Yet at last I think thou shalt set thy sins against her weights and find the balance even. Therefore cease from questioning the high decrees of destiny which thou canst not understand and be content to suffer, remembering that all joy grows from the root of pain. Moreover, know this for thy comfort, that the wisdom which thou hast shall grow and gather on thee and with it thy beauty and thy power; also that at the last thou shalt look upon my face again, in token whereof I leave to thee my symbol, the *sistrum* that I bear, and with it this command. Follow that false priest of mine wherever he may go and avenge me upon him, and if thou lose him there, wait while the generations pass till he return again. Such and no other is thy destiny.'

"Allan, the vision faded and when I awoke the lights of dawn played upon the image of the goddess in the sanctuary. They played, moreover, upon the holy jewelled thing that in my dream her hand had held, the *sistrum* of her worship, shaped like the loop of life, the magic symbol that she had vowed to me, wherewith goes her power, which henceforth was mine.

"I took it and followed after the priest Kallikrates, to whom thenceforward I was bound by passion's ties that are stronger than all the goddesses in this wide universe."

Here I, Allan, could contain myself no longer and asked, "What for?" then, fearing her wrath, wished that I had been silent.

But she was not angry, perhaps because this tale of her interviews with goddesses, doubtless fabled, had made her humble, for she answered quietly,

"By Aphrodite, or by Isis, or both of them I did not know. All I knew was that I *must* seek him, then and evermore, as seek I do to-day and shall perchance through æons yet unborn. So I followed, as I was taught and commanded, the *sistrum* being my guide, how it matters not, and giving me the means, and so at last I came to this ancient land whereof the ruin in which you sit was once known as Kôr."

Allan Misses Opportunity

All the while that she was talking thus the Lady or the Queen or the Witch-woman, Ayesha, had been walking up and down the place from the curtains to the foot of the dais, sweeping me with her scented robes as she passed to and fro, and as she walked she waved her arms as an orator might do to emphasise the more moving passages of her tale. Now at the end of it, or what I took to be the end, she stepped on to the dais and sank upon the couch as if exhausted, though I think her spirit was weary rather than her body.

Here she sat awhile, brooding, her chin resting on her hand, then suddenly looked up and fixing her glance upon me—for I could see the flash of it through her thin veil—said,

"What think you of this story, Allan? Do you believe it and have you ever heard its like?"

"*Never*," I answered with emphasis, "and of course I believe every word. Only there are one or two questions that with your leave I would wish to ask, Ayesha."

"By which you mean, Allan, that you believe nothing, being by nature without faith and doubtful of all that you cannot see and touch and handle. Well, perhaps you are wise, since what I have told you is not all the truth. For example, it comes back to me now that it was not in the temple on the Nile, or indeed upon the Earth, that I saw the vision of Aphrodite and of Isis, but elsewhere; also that it was here in Kôr that I was first consumed by passion for Kallikrates whom hitherto I had scorned. In two thousand years one forgets much, Allan. Out with your questions and I will answer them, unless they be too long."

"Ayesha," I said humbly, reflecting to myself that my questions would, at any rate, be shorter than her varying tale, "even I who am not learned have heard of these goddesses of whom you speak, of the Grecian Aphrodite who rose from the sea upon the shores of Cyprus and dwelt at Paphos and elsewhere——"

"Yes, doubtless like most men you have heard of her and perchance also have been struck across the eyes with her hair, like your betters before you," she interrupted with sarcasm.

"——Also," I went on, avoiding argument, "I have heard of Isis of the Egyptians, Lady of the Moon, Mother of Mysteries, Spouse of Osiris whose child was Horus the Avenger."

"Aye, and I think will hear more of her before you have done, Allan, for now something comes back to me concerning you and her and another. I am not the only one who has broken the oaths of Isis and received her curse, Allan, as *you* may find out in the days to come. But what of these heavenly queens?"

"Only this, Ayesha; I have been taught that they were but phantasms fabled by men with many another false divinity, and could have sworn that this was true. And yet you talk of them as real and living, which perplexes me."

"Being dull of understanding doubtless it perplexes you, Allan. Yet if you had imagination you might understand that these goddesses are great Principles of Nature; Isis, of throned Wisdom and strait virtue, and Aphrodite, of Love, as it is known to men and women who, being human, have it laid upon them that they must hand on the torch of Life in their little hour. Also you would know that such Principles can seem to take shape and form and at certain ages of the world appear to their servants visible in majesty, though perchance to-day others with changed names wield their sceptres and work their will. Now you are answered on this matter. So to the next."

Privately I did not feel as though I were answered at all and I was sure that I know nothing of the kind she indicated, but thinking it best to leave the subject, I went on,

"If I understood rightly, Ayesha, the events which you have been pleased first to describe to me, and then to qualify or contradict, took place when the Pharaohs reigned. Now no Pharaoh has sat upon the throne of Egypt for near two thousand years, for the last was a Grecian woman whom the Romans conquered and drove to death. And yet, Ayesha, you speak as though you have lived all through that gulf of time, and in this there must be error, because it is impossible. Therefore I suppose you to mean that this history has come down to you in writing, or perhaps in dreams. I believe that even in such far-off times there were writers of romance, and we all know of what stuff dreams are made. At least this thought comes to me," I added hurriedly, fearing lest I had said too much, "and one so wise as you are, I repeat, knows well that a woman who says she has lived two thousand years must be mad or—suffer from delusions, because I repeat, it is impossible."

At these quite innocent remarks she sprang to her feet in a rage that might truly be called royal in every sense.

"Impossible! Romance! Dreams! Delusions! Mad!" she cried in a ringing voice. "Oh! of a truth you weary me, and I have a mind to send you whither you will learn what is impossible and what is not. Indeed, I would do it, and now, only I need your services, and if I did there would be none left for me to talk with, since your companion is moonstruck and the others are but savages of whom I have seen enough.

"Hearken, fool! *Nothing* is impossible. Why do you seek, you who talk of the impossible, to girdle the great world in the span of your two hands and to weigh the secrets of the Universe in the balance of your petty mind and, of that which you cannot understand, to say that it is not? Life you admit because you see it all about you. But that it should endure for two thousand years, which after all is but a second's beat in the story of the earth, that to you is 'impossible,' although in truth the buried seed or the sealed-up toad can live as long. Doubtless, also, you have some faith which promises you this same boon to all eternity, after the little change called Death.

"Nay, Allan, it is possible enough, like to many other things of which you do not dream to-day that will be common to the eyes of those who follow after you. Mayhap you think it impossible that I should speak with and learn of you from yonder old black wizard who dwells in the country whence you came. And yet whenever I will I do so in the night because he is in tune with me, and what I do shall be done by all men in the years unborn. Yes, they shall talk together across the wide spaces of the earth, and the lover shall hear her lover's voice although great seas roll between them. Nor perchance will it stop at this; perchance in future time men shall hold converse with the denizens of the stars, and even with the dead who have passed into silence and the darkness. Do you hear and understand me?"

"Yes, yes," I answered feebly.

"You lie, as you are too prone to do. You hear but you do not understand nor believe, and oh! you vex me sorely. Now I had it in my mind to tell you the secret of this long life of mine; long, mark you, but not endless, for doubtless I must die and change and return again, like others, and even to show you how it may be won. But you are not worthy in your faithlessness."

"No, no, I am not worthy," I answered, who at that moment did not feel the least desire to live two thousand years, perhaps with this woman as a neighbour, rating me from generation to generation. Yet it is true, that now when I am older and a certain event cannot be postponed much longer, I do often regret that I neglected to take this unique chance, if in truth there was one, of prolonging an existence which after all has its consolations—especially when one has made one's pile. Certainly it is a case, a flagrant case, of neglected opportunities, and my only consolation for having lost them is that this was due to the uprightness of my nature which made it so hard for me to acquiesce in alternative statements that I had every cause to disbelieve and thus to give offence to a very powerful and petulant if attractive lady.

"So that is done with," she went on with a little stamp of indignation, "as soon you will be also, who, had you not crossed and doubted me, might have lived on for untold time and become one of the masters of the world, as I am."

Here she paused, choked, I think, with her almost childish anger, and because I could not help it, I said,

"Such place and power, if they be yours, Ayesha, do not seem to bring you much reward. If I were a master of the world I do not think that I should choose to dwell unchangingly among savages who eat men and in a pile of ruins. But perhaps the curses of Aphrodite and of Isis are stronger masters still?" and I paused inquiringly.

This bold argument—for now I see that it was bold—seemed to astonish and even bewilder my wonderful companion.

"You have more wisdom than I thought," she said reflectively, "who have come to understand that no one is really lord of anything, since above there is always a more powerful lord who withers all his pomp and pride to nothingness, even as the great kings learned in olden days, and I, who am higher than they are, am learning now. Hearken. Troubles beset me wherein I would have your help and that of your companions, for which I will pay each of you the fee that he desires. The brooding white man who is with you shall free his daughter and unharmed; though that *he* will be unharmed I do not promise. The black savage captain shall fight his fill and gain the glory that he seeks, also something that he seeks still more. The little yellow man asks nothing save to be with his master like a dog and to satisfy at once his stomach and his apish curiosity. You, Allan, shall see those dead over whom you brood at night, though the other guerdon that you might have won is now passed from your reach because you mock me in your heart."

"What must we do to gain these things?" I asked. "How can we humble creatures help one who is all powerful and who has gathered in her breast the infinite knowledge of two thousand years?"

"You must make war under my banner and rid me of my foes. As for the reason, listen to the end of my tale and you shall learn."

I reflected that it was a marvellous thing that this queen who claimed supernatural powers should need our help in a war, but thinking it wiser to keep my meditations to myself, said nothing. As a matter of fact I might just as well have spoken, since as usual she read my thoughts.

"You are thinking that it is strange, Allan, that I, the Mighty and Undying, should seek your aid in some petty tribal battle, and so it would be were my foes but common savages. But they are more; they are men protected by the ancient god of this immemorial city of Kôr, a great god in his day whose spirit still haunts these ruins and whose strength still protects the worshippers who cling to him and practise his unholy rites of human sacrifice."

"How was this god named?" I asked.

"*Rezu* was his name, and from him came the Egyptian Re or Ra, since in the beginning Kôr was the mother of Egypt and the conquering people of Kôr took their god with them when they burst into the valley of the Nile and subdued its peoples long before the first Pharaoh, Menes, wore Egypt's crown."

"Ra was the sun, was he not?" I asked.

"Aye, and Rezu also was a sun-god whom from his throne in the fires of the Lord of Day, gave life to men, or slew them if he willed with his thunderbolts of drought and pestilence and storm. He was no gentle king of heaven, but one who demanded blood-sacrifice from his worshippers, yes, even that of maids and children. So it came about that the people of Kôr, who saw their virgins slain and eaten by the priests of Rezu, and their infants burned to ashes in the fires that his rays lit, turned themselves to the worship of the gentle moon, the goddess whom they named *Lulala*, while some of them chose Truth for their queen, since Truth, they said, was greater and more to be desired than the fierce Sun-King or even the sweet Moon-Lady, Truth, who sat above them both throned in the furthest stars of Heaven. Then the demon, Rezu, grew wroth and sent a pestilence upon Kôr and its subject lands and slew their people, save those who clung to him in the great apostasy, and with them some others who served Lulala and Truth the Divine, that escaped I know not how."

"Did you see this great pestilence?" I asked, much interested.

"Nay, it befell generations before I came to Kôr. One Junis, a priest, wrote a record of it in the caves yonder where I have my home and where is the burying-place of the countless thousands that it slew. In my day Kôr, of which, should you desire to hear it, I will tell you the history, was a ruin as it is now, though scattered in the lands amidst the tumbled stones which once built up her subject cities, a people named the Amahagger dwelt in Households, or Tribes and there sacrificed men by fire and devoured them, following the rites of the demon Rezu. For these were the descendants of those who escaped the pestilence. Also there were certain others, children of the worshippers of Lulala whose kingdom is the moon, and of Truth the Queen, who clung to the gentle worship of their forefathers and were ever at war with the followers of Rezu."

"What brought *you* to Kôr, Ayesha?" I asked irrelevantly.

"Have I not said that I was led hither by the command and the symbol of great Isis whom I serve? Also," she added after a pause, "that I might find a certain pair, one of whom had broken his oaths to her, tempted thereto by the other."

"And did you find them, Ayesha?" I asked.

"Aye, I found them, or rather they found me, and in my presence the goddess executed her decree upon her false priest and drove his temptress back to the world."

"That must have been dreadful for you, Ayesha, since I understood that you also—liked this priest."

She sprang from her couch and in a low, hissing voice which resembled the sound made by an angry snake and turned my blood cold to hear, exclaimed,

"Man, do you dare to mock me? Nay, you are but a blundering, curious fool, and it is well for you that this is so, since otherwise like Kallikrates, never should you leave Kôr living. Cease from seeking that which you may not learn. Suffice it for you to know that the doom of Isis fell upon the lost Kallikrates, her priest forsworn, and that on me also fell her doom, who must dwell here, dead yet living, till he return again and the play begins afresh.

"Stranger," she went on in a softer voice, "perchance your faith, whate'er it be, parades a hell to terrify its worshippers and give strength to the arms of its prophesying priests, who swear they hold the keys of doom or of the eternal joys. I see you sign assent" (I had nodded at her extremely accurate guess) "and therefore can understand that in such a hell as this, here upon the earth I have dwelt for some two thousand years, expiating the crime of Powers above me whereof I am but the hand and instrument, since those Powers which decreed that I should love, decree also that I must avenge that love."

She sank down upon the couch as though exhausted by emotion, of which I could only guess the reasons, hiding her face in her hands. Presently she let them fall again and continued,

"Of these woes ask me no more. They sleep till the hour of their resurrection, which I think draws nigh; indeed, I thought that you perchance——But let that be. 'Twas near the mark; nearer, Allan, than you know, not in it! Therefore leave them to their sleep as I would if I might—ah! if I might, whose companions they are throughout the weary ages. Alas! that through the secret which was revealed to me I remain undying on the earth who in death might perhaps have found a rest, and being human although half divine, must still busy myself with the affairs of earth.

"Look you, Wanderer, after that which was fated had happened and I remained in my agony of solitude and sorrow, after, too, I had drunk of the cup of enduring life and like the Prometheus of old fable, found myself bound to this changeless rock, whereon day by day the vultures of remorse tear out my living heart which in the watches of the night is ever doomed to grow again within my woman's breast, I was plunged into petty troubles of the flesh, aye and welcomed them because their irk at times gave me forgetfulness. When the savage dwellers in this land came to know that a mighty one had arisen among them who was the servant of the Lady of the Moon, those of them who still worshipped their goddess Lulala, gathered themselves about me, while those of them who worshipped Rezu sought to overthrow me.

"'Here,' they said, 'is the goddess Lulala come to earth. In the name of Rezu let us slay her and make an end,' for these fools thought that I could be killed. Allan, I conquered them, but their captain, who also is named Rezu and whom they held and hold to be an emanation of the god himself walking the earth, I could not conquer."

"Why not?" I asked.

"For this reason, Allan. In some past age his god showed him the same secret that was shown to me. He too had drunk of the Cup of Life and lives on unharmed by Time, so that being in strength my equal, no spear of mine can reach his heart clad in the armour of his evil god."

"Then what spear can?" I inquired helplessly, who was bewildered.

"None at all, Allan, yet an *axe* may, as you shall hear, or so I think. For many generations there has been peace of a sort between the worshippers of Lulala who dwell with me in the Plain of Kôr, or rather of myself, since to these people *I* am Lulala, and the worshippers of Rezu, who dwell in the strongholds beyond the mountain crest. But of late years their chief Rezu, having devastated the lands about, has grown restless and threatened to attack on Kôr, which is not strong enough to stand against him. Moreover he has sought for a white queen to rule under him, purposing to set her up to mock my majesty."

"Is that why those cannibals carried away the daughter of my companion, the Sea-Captain who is named Avenger?" I asked.

"It is, Allan, since presently he will give it out that I am dead or fled, if he has not done so already, and that this new queen has arisen in my place. Thereby he hopes to draw away many who cling to me ere he advances upon Kôr, carrying with him this girl veiled as I am, so that none may know the difference between us, since not a man of them has ever looked upon my face, Allan. Therefore this Rezu must die, if die he can; otherwise, although it is impossible that he should harm me, he may slay or draw away my people and leave me with none to rule in this place where by the decree of Fate I must dwell on until he whom I seek returns. You are thinking in your heart that such savages would be little loss and this is so, but still they serve as slaves to me in my loneliness. Moreover I have sworn to protect them from the demon Rezu and they have trusted in me and therefore my honour is at stake, for never shall it be said that those who trusted in She-who-commands, were overthrown because they put faith in one who was powerless."

"What do you mean about an axe, Ayesha?" I asked. "Why can an axe alone kill Rezu?"

"The thing is a mystery, O Allan, of which I may not tell you all, since to do so I must reveal secrets which I have determined you shall not learn. Suffice it to you to know that when this Rezu drank of the Cup of Life he took with him his axe. Now this axe was an ancient weapon rumoured to have been fashioned by the gods and, as it chanced, that axe drew to itself more and stronger life than did Rezu, how, it does not matter, if indeed the tale be more than a fable. At least this I know is true, for he who guarded the Gate of Life, a certain Noot, a master of mysteries, and mine also in my day of youth, who being a philosopher and very wise, chose never to pass that portal which was open to him, said it to me himself ere he went the way of flesh.

He told this Rezu also that now he had naught to fear save his own axe and therefore he counselled him to guard it well, since if it was lifted against him in another's hands it would bring him down to death, which nothing else could do. Like to the heel of Achilles whereof the great Homer sings—have you read Homer, Allan?"

"In a translation," I answered.

"Good, then you will remember the story. Like to the heel of Achilles, I say, that axe would be the only gate by which death could enter his invulnerable flesh, or rather it alone could make the gate."

"How did Noot know that?" I asked.

"I cannot say," she answered with irritation. "Perchance he did not know it. Perchance it is all an idle tale, but at least it is true that Rezu believed and believes it, and what a man believes is true for him and will certainly befall. If it were otherwise, what is the use of faith which in a thousand forms supports our race and holds it from the horrors of the Pit? Only those who believe nothing inherit what they believe—nothing, Allan."

"It may be so," I replied prosaically, "but what happened about the axe?"

"In the end it was lost, or as some say stolen by a woman whom Rezu had deserted, and therefore he walks the world in fear from day to day. Nay, ask no more empty questions" (I had opened my mouth to speak) "but hear the end of the tale. In my trouble concerning Rezu I remembered this wild legend of the axe and since, when lost in a forest every path that may lead to safety should be explored, I sent my wisdom forth to make inquiry concerning it, as I who am great, have the power to do, of certain who are in tune with me throughout this wide land of Africa. Amongst others, I inquired of that old wizard whom you named Zikali, Opener of Roads, and he gave me an answer that there lived in his land a certain warrior who ruled a tribe called the People of the Axe by right of the Axe, of which axe none, not even he, knew the beginning or the legend. On the chance, though it was a small one, I bade the wizard send that warrior here with his axe. Last night he stood before me and I looked upon him and the axe, which at least is ancient and has a story. Whether it be the same that Rezu bore I do not know who never saw it, yet perchance he who bears it now is prepared to hold it aloft in battle even against Rezu, though he be terrible to see, and then we shall learn."

"Oh! yes," I answered, "he is quite prepared, for that is his nature. Also among this man's people, the holder of the Axe is thought to be unconquerable."

"Yet some must have been conquered who held it," she replied musingly. "Well, you shall tell me that tale later. Now we have talked long and you are weary and astonished. Go, eat and rest yourself. To-night when the moon rises I will come to where you are, not before, for I have much that must be done, and show you those with whom you must fight against Rezu, and make a plan of battle."

"But I do not want to fight," I answered, "who have fought enough and came here to seek wisdom, not bloodshed."

"First the sacrifice, then the reward," she answered, "that is if any are left to be rewarded. Farewell."

Robertson Is Lost

So I went and was conducted by Billali, the old chamberlain, for such seemed to be his office, who had been waiting patiently without all this while, back to our rest-house. On my way I picked up Hans, whom I found sitting outside the arch, and found that as usual that worthy had been keeping his eyes and ears open.

"Baas," he said, "did the White Witch tell you that there is a big *impi* encamped over yonder outside the houses, in what looks like a great dry ditch, and on the edge of the plain beyond?"

"No, Hans, but she said that this evening she would show us those in whose company we must fight."

"Well, Baas, they are there, some thousands of them, for I crept through the broken walls like a snake and saw them. And, Baas, I do not think they are men, I think that they are evil spirits who walk at night only."

"Why, Hans?"

"Because when the sun is high, Baas, as it is now, they are all sleeping. Yes, there they lie abed, fast asleep, as other people do at night, with only a few sentries out on guard, and these are yawning and rubbing their eyes."

"I have heard that there are folk like that in the middle of Africa where the sun is very hot, Hans," I answered, "which perhaps is why She-who-commands is going to take us to see them at night. Also these people, it seems, are worshippers of the moon."

"No, Baas, they are worshippers of the devil and that White Witch is his wife."

"You had better keep your thoughts to yourself, Hans, for whatever she is I think that she can read thoughts from far away, as you guessed last night. Therefore I would not have any if I were you."

"No, Baas, or if I must think, henceforth, it shall be only of gin which in this place is also far away," he replied, grinning.

Then we came to the rest-house where I found that Robertson had already eaten his midday meal and like the Amahagger gone to sleep, while apparently Umslopogaas had done the same; at least I saw nothing of him. Of this I was glad, since that wondrous Ayesha seemed to draw vitality out of me and after my long talk with her I felt very tired. So I too ate and then went to lie down under an old wall in the shade at a little distance, and to reflect upon the marvellous things that I had heard.

Here be it said at once that I believed nothing of them, or at least very little indeed. All the involved tale of Ayesha's long life I dismissed at once as incredible. Clearly she was some beautiful woman who was more or less mad and suffered from megalomania; probably an Arab, who had wandered to this place for reasons of her own, and become the chieftainess of a savage tribe whose traditions she had absorbed and reproduced as personal experiences, again for reasons of her own.

For the rest, she was now threatened by another tribe and knowing that we had guns and could fight from what happened on the yesterday, wished naturally enough for our assistance in the coming battle. As for the marvellous chief Rezu, or rather for his supernatural attributes and all the cock-and-bull story about an axe—well, it was humbug like the rest, and if she believed in it she must be more foolish than I took her to be—even if she were unhinged on certain points. For the rest, her information about myself and Umslopogaas doubtless had reached her from Zikali in some obscure fashion, as she herself acknowledged.

But heavens! how beautiful she was! That flash of loveliness when out of pique or coquetry she lifted her veil, blinded like the lightning. But thank goodness, also like the lightning it frightened; instinctively one felt that it was very dangerous, even to death, and with it I for one wished no closer acquaintance. Fire may be lovely and attractive, also comforting at a proper distance, but he who sits on the top of it is cremated, as many a moth has found.

So I argued, knowing well enough all the while that if this particular human—or inhuman—fire desired to make an holocaust of me, it could do so easily enough, and that in reality I owed my safety so far to a lack of that desire on its part. The glorious Ayesha saw nothing to attract her in an insignificant and withered hunter, or at any rate in his exterior, though with his mind she might find some small affinity. Moreover to make a fool of him just for the fun of it would not serve her purpose, since she needed his assistance in a business that necessitated clear wits and unprejudiced judgment.

Lastly she had declared herself to be absorbed in some tiresome complication with another man, of which it was rather difficult to follow the details. It is true that she described him as a handsome but somewhat empty-headed person whom she had last seen two thousand years ago, but probably this only meant that she thought poorly of him because he had preferred some other woman to herself, while the two thousand years were added to the tale to give it atmosphere.

The worst of scandals becomes romantic and even respectable in two thousand years; witness that of Cleopatra with Cæsar, Mark Antony and other gentlemen. The most virtuous read of Cleopatra with sympathy, even in boarding-schools, and it is felt that were she by some miracle to be blotted out of the book of history, the loss would be enormous. The same applied to Helen, Phryne, and other bad lots. In fact now that one comes to think of it, most of the attractive personages in history, male or female, especially the latter, were bad lots. When we find someone to whose name is added "the good" we skip. No doubt Ayesha, being very clever, appreciated this regrettable truth, and therefore moved her murky entanglements of the past decade or so back for a couple of thousand years, as many of us would like to do.

There remained the very curious circumstance of her apparent correspondence with old Zikali who lived far away. This, however, after all was not inexplicable. In the course of a great deal of experience I have observed that all the witch-doctor family, to which doubtless she belonged, have strange means of communication.

In most instances these are no doubt physical, carried on by help of messengers, or messages passed from one to the other. But sometimes it is reasonable to assume what is known as telepathy, as their link of intercourse. Between two such highly developed experts as Ayesha and Zikali, it might for the sake of argument safely be supposed that it was thus they learned each other's mind and co-operated in each other's projects, though perhaps this end was effected by commoner methods.

Whatever its interpretations, the issue of the business seemed to be that I was to be let in for more fighting. Well, in any case this could not be avoided, since Robertson's daughter, Inez, had to be saved at all costs, if it could possibly be done, even if we lost our lives in the attempt. Therefore fight we must, so there was nothing more to be said. Also without doubt this adventure was particularly interesting and I could only hope that good luck, or Zikali's Great Medicine, or rather Providence, would see me through it safely.

For the rest the fact that our help was necessary to her in this war- like venture showed me clearly enough that all this wonderful woman's pretensions to supernatural powers were the sheerest nonsense. Had they been otherwise she would not have needed our help in her tribal fights, notwithstanding the rubbish she talked about the chief, Rezu, who according to her account of him, must resemble one of the fabulous "trolls," half-human and half-ghostly evil creatures, of whom I have read in the Norse Sagas, who could only be slain by some particular hero armed with a particular weapon.

Reflecting thus I went to sleep and did not wake until the sun was setting. Finding that Hans was also sleeping at my feet just like a faithful dog, I woke him up and we went back together to the rest- house, which we reached as the darkness fell with extraordinary swiftness, as it does in those latitudes, especially in a place surrounded by cliffs.

Not finding Robertson in the house, I concluded that he was somewhere outside, possibly making a reconnaissance on his own account, and told Hans to get supper ready for both of us. While he was doing so, by aid of the Amahagger lamps, Umslopogaas suddenly appeared in the circle of light, and looking about him, said,

"Where is Red-Beard, Macumazahn?"

I answered that I did not know and waited, for I felt sure that he had something to say.

"I think that you had better keep Red-Beard close to you, Macumazahn," he went on. "This afternoon, when you had returned from visiting the white doctoress and having eaten, had gone to sleep under the wall yonder, I saw Red-Beard come out of the house carrying a gun and a bag of cartridges. His eyes rolled wildly and he turned first this way and then that, sniffing at the air, like a buck that scents danger. Then he began to talk aloud in his own tongue and as I saw that he was speaking with his Spirit, as those do who are mad, I went away and left him."

"Why?" I asked.

"Because, as you know, Macumazahn, it is a law among us Zulus never to disturb one who is mad and engaged in talking with his Spirit. Moreover, had I done so, probably he would have shot me, nor should I have complained who would have thrust myself in where I had no right to be."

"Then why did you not come to call me, Umslopogaas?"

"Because then he might have shot you, for, as I have seen for some time he is inspired of heaven and knows not what he does upon the earth, thinking only of the Lady Sad-Eyes who has been stolen away from him, as is but natural. So I left him walking up and down, and when I returned later to look, saw that he was gone, as I thought into this walled hut. Now when Hansi tells me that he is not here, I have come to speak to you about him."

"No, certainly he is not here," I said, and I went to look at the bed where Robertson slept to see if it had been used that evening.

Then for the first time I saw lying on it a piece of paper torn from a pocketbook and addressed to myself. I seized and read it. It ran thus:

"The merciful Lord has sent me a vision of Inez and shown me where she is over the cliff-edge away to the west, also the road to her. In my sleep I heard her talking to me. She told me that she is in great danger—that they are going to marry her to some brute—and called to me to come at once and save her; yes, and to come alone without saying anything to anyone. So I am going at once. Don't be frightened or trouble about me. All will be well, all will be quite well. I will tell you the rest when we meet."

Horrorstruck I translated this insane screed to Umslopogaas and Hans. The former nodded gravely.

"Did I not tell you that he was talking with his Spirit, Macumazahn?" (I had rendered "the merciful Lord" as the Good Spirit.) "Well, he has gone and doubtless his Spirit will take care of him. It is finished."

"At any rate we cannot, Baas," broke in Hans, who I think feared that I might send him out to look for Robertson. "I can follow most spoors, but not on such a night as this when one could cut the blackness into lumps and build a wall of it."

"Yes," I answered, "he has gone and nothing can be done at present," though to myself I reflected that probably he had not gone far and would be found when the moon rose, or at any rate on the following morning.

Still I was most uneasy about the man who, as I had noted for a long while, was losing his balance more and more. The shock of the barbarous and dreadful slaughter of his half-breed children and of the abduction of Inez by these grim, man-eating savages began the business, and I think that it was increased and accentuated by his sudden conversion to complete temperance after years of heavy drinking.

When I persuaded him to this course I was very proud of myself, thinking that I had done a clever thing, but now I was not so sure. Perhaps it would have been better if he had continued to drink something, at any rate for a while, but the trouble is that in such cases there is generally no half-way house. A man, or still more a woman, given to this frailty either turns aggressively sober or remains very drunken. At any rate, even if I had made a mess of it, I had acted for the best and could not blame myself.

For the rest it was clear that in his new phase the religious associations of his youth had re-asserted themselves with remarkable vigour, for I gathered that he had been brought up almost as a Calvinist, and in the rush of their return, had overset his equilibrium. As I have said, he prayed night and day without any of those reserves which most people prefer in their religious exercises, and when he talked of matters outside our quest, his conversation generally revolved round the devil, or hell and its torments, which, to say the truth, did not make him a cheerful companion. Indeed in this respect I liked him much better in his old, unregenerate days, being, I fear, myself a somewhat worldly soul.

Well, the sum of it was that the poor fellow had gone mad and given us the slip, and as Hans said, to search for him at once in that darkness was impossible. Indeed, even if it had been lighter, I do not think that it would have been safe among these Amahagger nightbirds whom I did not trust. Certainly I could not have asked Hans to undertake the task, and if I had, I do not think he would have gone since he was afraid of the Amahagger. Therefore there was nothing to be done except wait and hope for the best.

So I waited till at last the moon came and with it Ayesha, as she had promised. Clad in a rich, dark cloak she arrived in some pomp, heralded by Billali, followed by women, also cloaked, and surrounded by a guard of tall spearmen. I was seated outside the house, smoking, when suddenly she arrived from the shadows and stood before me.

I rose respectfully and bowed, while Umslopogaas, Goroko and the other Zulus who were with me, gave her the royal salute, and Hans cringed like a dog that is afraid of being kicked.

After a swift glance at them, as I guessed by the motion of her veiled head, she seemed to fix her gaze upon my pipe that evidently excited her curiosity, and asked me what it was. I explained as well as I could, expatiating on the charms of smoking.

"So men have learned another useless vice since I left the world, and one that is filthy also," she said, sniffing at the smoke and waving her hand before her face, whereon I dropped the pipe into my pocket, where, being alight, it burnt a hole in my best remaining coat.

I remember the remark because it showed me what a clever actress she was who, to keep up her character of antiquity, pretended to be astonished at a habit with which she must have been well acquainted, although I believe that it was unknown in the ancient world.

"You are troubled," she went on, swiftly changing the subject, "I read it in your face. One of your company is missing. Who is it? Ah! I see, the white man you name Avenger. Where is he gone?"

"That is what I wish to ask you, Ayesha," I said.

"How can I tell you, Allan, who in this place lack any glass into which to look for things that pass afar. Still, let me try," and pressing her hands to her forehead, she remained silent for perhaps a minute, then spoke slowly.

"I think that he has gone over the mountain lip towards the worshippers of Rezu. I think that he is mad; sorrow and something else which I do not understand have turned his brain; something that has to do with the Heavens. I think also that we shall recover him living, if only for a little while, though of this I cannot be sure since it is not given to me to read the future, but only the past, and sometimes the things that happen in the present though they be far away."

"Will you send to search for him, O Ayesha?" I asked anxiously.

"Nay, it is useless, for he is already distant. Moreover those who went might be taken by the outposts of Rezu, as perchance has happened to your companion wandering in his madness. Do you know what he went to seek?"

"More or less," I answered and translated to her the letter that Robertson had left for me.

"It may be as the man writes," she commented, "since the mad often see well in their dreams, though these are not sent by a god as he imagines. The mind in its secret places knows all things, O Allan, although it seems to know little or nothing, and when the breath of vision or the fury of a soul distraught blows away the veils or burns through the gates of distance, then for a while it sees and learns, since, whatever fools may think, often madness is true wisdom. Now follow me with the little yellow man and the Warrior of the Axe. Stay, let me look upon that axe."

I interpreted her wish to Umslopogaas who held it out to her but refused to loose it from his wrist to which it was attached by the leathern thong.

"Does the Black One think that I shall cut him down with his own weapon, I who am so weak and gentle?" she asked, laughing.

"Nay, Ayesha, but it is his law not to part with this Drinker of Lives, which he names 'Chieftainess and Groan-maker,' and clings to closer by day and night than a man does to his wife."

"There he is wise, Allan, since a savage captain may get more wives but never such another axe. The thing is ancient," she added musingly after examining its every detail, "and who knows? It may be that whereof the legend tells which is fated to bring Rezu to the dust. Now ask this fierce-eyed Slayer whether, armed with his axe he can find courage to face the most terrible of all men and the strongest, one who is a wizard also, of whom it is prophesied that only by such an axe as this can he be made to bite the dust."

I obeyed. Umslopogaas laughed grimly and answered,

"Say to the White Witch that there is no man living upon the earth whom I would not face in war, I who have never been conquered in fair fight, though once a chance blow brought me to the doors of death," and he touched the great hole in his forehead. "Say to her also that I have no fear of defeat, I from whom doom is, as I think, still far away, though the Opener-of-Roads has told me that among a strange people I shall die in war at last, as I desire to do, who from my boyhood have lived in war."

"He speaks well," she answered with a note of admiration in her voice. "By Isis, were he but white I would set him to rule these Amahagger under me. Tell him, Allan, that if he lays Rezu low he shall have a great reward."

"And tell the White Witch, Macumazahn," Umslopogaas replied when I had translated, "that I seek no reward, save glory only, and with it the sight of one who is lost to me but with whom my heart still dwells, if indeed this Witch has strength to break the wall of blackness that is built between me and her who is 'gone down.'"

"Strange," reflected Ayesha when she understood, "that this grim Destroyer should yet be bound by the silken bonds of love and yearn for one whom the grave has taken. Learn from it, Allan, that all humanity is cast in the same mould, since my longings and your longings are his also, though the three of us be far apart as are the sun and the moon and the earth, and as different in every other quality. Yet it is true that sun and moon and earth are born of the same black womb of chaos. Therefore in the beginning they were identical, as doubtless they will be in the end when, their journeyings done, they rush together to light space with a flame at which the mocking gods that made them may warm their hands. Well, so it is with men, Allan, whose soul-stuff is drawn from the gulf of Spirit by Nature's hand, and, cast upon the cold air of this death- driven world, freezes into a million shapes each different to the other and yet, be sure, the same. Now talk no more, but follow me. Slave" (this was addressed to Billali), "bid the guards lead on to the camp of the servants of Lulala."

So we went through the silent ruins. Ayesha walked, or rather glided a pace or two ahead, then came Umslopogaas and I side by side, while at our heels followed Hans, very close at our heels since he did not wish to be out of reach of the virtue of the Great Medicine and incidentally of the protection of axe and rifle.

Thus we marched surrounded by the solemn guard for something between a quarter and half a mile, till at length we climbed the debris of a mighty wall that once had encompassed the city, and by the moonlight saw beneath us a vast hollow which clearly at some unknown time had been the bed of an enormous moat and filled with water.

Now, however, it was dry and all about its surface were dotted numerous camp-fires round which men were moving, also some women who appeared to be engaged in cooking food. At a little distance too, upon the further edge of the moat-like depression were a number of white- robed individuals gathered in a circle about a large stone upon which something was stretched that resembled the carcase of a sheep or goat, and round these a great number of spectators.

"The priests of Lulala who make sacrifice to the moon, as they do night by night, save when she is dead," said Ayesha, turning back towards me as though in answer to the query which I had conceived but left unuttered.

What struck me about the whole scene was its extraordinary animation and briskness. All the folk round the fires and outside of them moved about quickly and with the same kind of liveliness which might animate a camp of more natural people at the rising of the sun. It was as though they had just got up full of vigour to commence their daily, or rather their nightly round, which in truth was the case, since as Hans discovered, by habitude these Amahagger preferred to sleep during the day unless something prevented them, and to carry on the activities of life at night. It only remains to add that there seemed to be a great number of them, for their fires following the round of the dry moat, stretched further than I could see.

Scrambling down the crumpled wall by a zig-zag pathway, we came upon the outposts of the army beneath us who challenged, then seeing with whom they had to do, fell flat upon their faces, leaving their great spears, which had iron spikes on their shafts like to those of the Masai, sticking in the ground beside them.

We passed on between some of the fires and I noted how solemn and gloomy, although handsome, were the countenances of the folk by whom these were surrounded. Indeed, they looked like denizens of a different world to ours, one alien to the kindly race of men. There was nothing social about these Amahagger, who seemed to be a people labouring under some ancient ancestral curse of which they could never shake off the memory. Even the women rarely smiled; their clear-cut, stately countenances remained stern and set, except when they glowered at us incuriously. Only when Ayesha passed they prostrated themselves like the rest.

We went on through them and across the moat, climbing its further slope and here suddenly came upon a host of men gathered in a hollow square, apparently in order to receive us. They stood in ranks of five or six deep and their spear-points glimmering in the moonlight looked like long bands of level steel. As we entered the open side of the square all these spears were lifted. Thrice they were lifted and at each uplifting there rose a deep-throated cry of *Hiya*, which is the Arabic for She, and I suppose was a salutation to Ayesha.

She swept on taking no heed, till we came to the centre of the square where a number of men were gathered who prostrated themselves in the usual fashion.

Motioning to them to rise she said,

"Captains, this very night within two hours we march against Rezu and the sun-worshippers, since otherwise as my arts tell me, they march against us. She-who-commands is immortal, as your fathers have known from generation to generation, and cannot be destroyed; but you, her servants, can be destroyed, and Rezu, who also has drunk of the Cup of Life, out-numbers you by three to one and prepares a queen to set up in my place over his own people and such of you as remain. As though," she added with a contemptuous laugh, "any woman of a day could take my place."

She paused and the spokesman of the captains said,

"We hear, O Hiya, and we understand. What wouldst thou have us do, O Lulala-come-to-earth? The armies of Rezu are great and from the beginning he has hated thee and us, also his magic is as thy magic and his length of days as thy length of days. How then can we who are few, three thousand men at the most, match ourselves against Rezu, Son of the Sun? Would it not be better that we should accept the terms of Rezu, which are light, and acknowledge him as our king?"

As she heard these words I saw the tall shape of Ayesha quiver beneath her robes, as I think, not with fear but with rage, because the meaning of them was clear enough, namely that rather than risk a battle with Rezu, these people were contemplating surrender and her own deposition, if indeed she could be deposed. Still she answered in a quiet voice,

"It seems that I have dealt too gently with you and with your fathers, Children of Lulala, whose shadow I am here upon the earth, so that because you only see the scabbard, you have forgotten the sword within and that it can shine forth and smite. Well, why should I be wrath because the brutish will follow the law of brutes, though it be true that I am minded to slay you where you stand? Hearken! Were I less merciful I would leave you to the clutching hands of Rezu, who would drag you one by one to the stone of sacrifice and there offer up your hearts to his god of fire and devour your bodies with his heat. But I bethink me of your wives and children and of your forefathers whom I knew in the dead days, and therefore, if I may, I still would save you from yourselves and your heads from the glowing pot.

"Take counsel together now and say—Will you fight against Rezu, or will you yield? If that is your desire, speak it, and by to-morrow's sun I will begone, taking these with me," and she pointed to us, "whom I have summoned to help us in the war. Aye, I will begone, and when you are stretched upon the stone of sacrifice, and your women and children are the slaves of the men of Rezu, then shall you cry,

"'Oh, where is Hiya whom our fathers knew? Oh, will she not return and save us from this hell?'

"Yes, so shall you cry but there shall come no answer, since then she will have departed to her own habitations in the moon and thence appear no more. Now consult together and answer swiftly, since I weary of you and your ways."

The captains drew apart and began to talk in low voices, while Ayesha stood still, apparently quite unconcerned, and I considered the situation.

It was obvious to me that these people were almost in rebellion against their strange ruler, whose power over them was of a purely moral nature, one that emanated from her personality alone. What I wondered was, being what she seemed to be, why she thought it worth while to exercise it at all. Then I remembered her statement that here and nowhere else she must abide for some secret reason, until a certain mystical gentleman with a Greek name came to fetch her away from this appointed *rendezvous*. Therefore I supposed she had no choice, or rather, suffering as she did from hallucinations, believed herself to have no choice and was obliged to put up with a crowd of disagreeable savages in quarters which were sadly out of repair.

Presently the spokesman returned, saluted with his spear, and asked,

"If we go up to fight against Rezu, who will lead us in the battle, O Hiya?"

"My wisdom shall be your guide," she answered, "this white man shall be your General and there stands the warrior who shall meet Rezu face to face and bring him to the dust," and she pointed to Umslopogaas leaning upon his axe and watching them with a contemptuous smile.

This reply did not seem to please the man for he withdrew to consult again with his companions. After a debate which I suppose was animated for the Amahagger, men of few words who did not indulge in oratory, all of them advanced on us and the spokesman said,

"The choice of a General does not please us, Hiya. We know that the white man is brave because of the fight he made against the men of Rezu over the mountain yonder; also that he and his followers have weapons that deal death from afar. But there is a prophecy among us of which none know the beginning, that he who commands in the last great battle between Lulala and Rezu must produce before the eyes of the People of Lulala a certain holy thing, a charm of power, without which defeat will be the portion of Lulala. Of this holy thing, this spirit-haunted shape of power, we know the likeness and the fashion, for these have come down among our priests, though who told it to them we cannot tell, but of it I will say this only, that it speaks both of the spirit and the body, of man and yet of more than man."

"And if this wondrous charm, this talisman of might, cannot be shown by the white lord here, what then?" asked Ayesha coldly.

"Then, Hiya, this is the word of the People of Lulala, that we will not serve under him in the battle, and this also is their word that we will not go up against Rezu. That thou art mighty we know well, Hiya, also that thou canst slay if thou wilt, but we know also that Rezu is mightier and that against him thou hast no power. Therefore kill us if thou dost so desire, until thy heart is satisfied with death. For it is better that we should perish thus than upon the altar of sacrifice wearing the red-hot crowns of Rezu."

"So say we all," exclaimed the rest of the company when he had finished.

"The thought comes to me to begin to satisfy my heart with thy coward blood and that of thy companions," said Ayesha contemptuously. Then she paused and turning to me, added, "O Watcher-by-Night, what counsel? Is there aught that will convince these chicken-hearted ones over whom I have spread my feathers for so long?"

I shook my head blankly, whereat they murmured together and made as though they would go.

Then it was that Hans, who understood something of Arabic as he did of most African tongues, pulled my sleeve and whispered in my ear.

"The Great Medicine, Baas! Show them Zikali's Great Medicine."

Here was an idea. The description of the article required, a "spirit-haunted shape of power" that spoke "both of the spirit and the body of man and yet of more than man," was so vague that it might mean anything or nothing. And yet——

I turned to Ayesha and prayed her to ask them if what they wanted should be produced, whether they would follow me bravely and fight Rezu to the death. She did so and with one voice they replied,

"Aye, bravely and to the death, him and the Bearer of the Axe of whom also our legend tells."

Then with deliberation I opened my shirt and holding out the image of Zikali as far as the chain of elephant hair would allow, I asked,

"Is this the holy thing, the charm of power, of which your legend tells, O People of the Amahagger and worshippers of Lulala?"

The spokesman glanced at it, then snatching a brand from a watch-fire that burnt near by held it over the carving and stared, and stared again; and as he did, so did the others bending over him.

"Dog! would you singe my beard?" I cried in affected rage, and seizing the brand from his hand I smote him with it over the head.

But he took no heed of the affront which I had offered to him merely to assert my authority. Still for a few moments he stared although the sparks from the wood were frizzling in his greasy hair, then of a sudden went down on his face before me, as did all the others and cried out,

"It is the Holy Thing! It is the spirit-haunted Shape of Power itself, and we the Worshippers of Lulala will follow thee to the death, O white lord, Watcher-by-Night. Yes, where thou goest and he goes who bears the Axe, thither will we follow till not one of us is left upon his feet."

"Then that's settled," I said, yawning, since it is never wise to show concern about anything before savages. Indeed personally I had no wish to be the leader of this very peculiar tribe in an adventure of which I knew nothing, and therefore had hoped that they would leave that honour to someone else. Then I turned and told Umslopogaas what had passed, a tale at which he only shrugged his great shoulders, handling his axe as though he were minded to try its edge upon some of these "Dark-lovers," as he named the Amahagger people because of their nocturnal habits.

Meanwhile Ayesha gave certain orders. Then she came to me and said,

"These men march at once, three thousand strong, and by dawn will camp on the northern mountain crest. At sunrise litters will come to bear you and those with you if they will, to join them, which you should do by midday. In the afternoon marshall them as you think wise, for the battle will take place in the small hours of the following morning, since the People of Lulala only fight at night. I have said."

"Do you not come with us?" I asked, dismayed.

"Nay, not in a war against Rezu, why it matters not. Yet my Spirit will go with you, for I shall watch all that passes, how it matters not and perchance you may see it there—I know not. On the third day from to-morrow we shall meet again in the flesh or beyond it, but as I think in the flesh, and you can claim the reward which you journeyed here to seek. A place shall be prepared for the white lady whom Rezu would have set up as a rival queen to me. Farewell, and farewell also to yonder Bearer of the Axe that shall drink the blood of Rezu, also to the little yellow man who is rightly named Light-in-Darkness, as you shall learn ere all is done."

Then before I could speak she turned and glided away, swiftly surrounded by her guards, leaving me astonished and very uncomfortable.

Allan's Vision

The old chamberlain, Billali, conducted us back to our camp. As we went he discoursed to me of these Amahagger, of whom it seemed he was himself a developed specimen, one who threw back, perhaps tens of generations, to some superior ancestor who lived before they became debased. In substance he told me that they were a wild and lawless lot who lived amongst ruins or in caves, or some of them in swamp dwellings, in small separate communities, each governed by its petty headman who was generally a priest of their goddess Lulala.

Originally they and the people of Rezu were the same, in times when they worshipped the sun and the moon jointly, but "thousands of years" ago, as he expressed it, they had separated, the Rezuites having gone to dwell to the north of the Great Mountain, whence they continually threatened the Lulalaites whom, had it not been for She-who-commands, they would have destroyed long before. The Rezuites, it seemed, were habitual cannibals, whereas the Lulalaite branch of the Amahagger only practised cannibalism occasionally when by a lucky chance they got hold of strangers. "Such as yourself, Watcher-by-Night, and your companions," he added with meaning. If their crime were discovered, however, Hiya, She-who-commands, punished it by death.

I asked if she exercised an active rule over these people. He answered that she did not, as she lacked sufficient interest in them; only when she was angry with individuals she would destroy some of them by "her arts," as she had power to do if she chose. Most of them indeed had never seen her and only knew of her existence by rumour. To them she was a spirit or a goddess who inhabited the ancient tombs that lay to the south of the old city whither she had come because of the threatened war with Rezu, whom alone she feared, he did not know why. He told me again, moreover, that she was the greatest magician who had ever been, and that it was certain she did not die, since their forefathers knew her generations ago. Still she seemed to be under some curse, like the Amahagger themselves, who were the descendants of those who had once inhabited Kôr and the country round it, as far as the sea-coast and for hundreds of miles inland, having been a mighty people in their day before a great plague destroyed them.

For the rest he thought that she was a very unhappy woman who "lived with her own soul mourning the dead" and consorting with none upon the earth.

I asked him why she stayed here, whereat he shook his head and replied, he supposed because of the "curse," since he could conceive of no other reason. He informed me also that her moods varied very much. Sometimes she was fierce and active and at others by comparison mild and low-spirited. Just now she was passing through one of the latter stages, perhaps because of the Rezu trouble, for she did not wish her people to be destroyed by this terrible person; or perhaps for some other reason with which he was not acquainted.

When she chose, she knew all things, except the distant future. Thus she knew that we were coming, also the details of our march and that we should be attacked by the Rezuites who were going out to meet their returning company that had been sent afar to find a white queen. Therefore she had ordered him to go with soldiers to our assistance. I asked why she went veiled, and he replied, because of her beauty which drove even savage men mad, so that in old days she had been obliged to kill a number of them.

That was all he seemed to know about her, except that she was kind to those who served her well, like himself, and protected them from evil of every sort.

Then I asked him about Rezu. He answered that he was a dreadful person, undying, it was said, like She-who-commands, though he had never seen the man himself and never wanted to do so. His followers being cannibals and having literally eaten up all those that they could reach, were now desirous of conquering the people of Lulala that they might eat them also at their leisure. Each other they did not eat, because dog does not eat dog, and therefore they were beginning to grow hungry, although they had plenty of grain and cattle of which they used the milk and hides.

As for the coming battle, he knew nothing about it or what would happen, save that She-who-commands said that it would go well for the Lulalaites under my direction. She was so sure that it would go well, that she did not think it worth while to accompany the army, for she hated noise and bloodshed.

It occurred to me that perhaps she was afraid that she too would be taken captive and eaten, but I kept my reflection to myself.

Just then we arrived at our camp-house, where Billali bade me farewell, saying that he wished to rest as he must be back at dawn with litters, when he hoped to find us ready to start. Then he departed. Umslopogaas and Hans also went away to sleep, leaving me alone who, having taken my repose in the afternoon, did not feel drowsy at the moment. So lovely was the night indeed that I made up my mind to take a little walk during the midnight hours, after the manner of the Amahagger themselves, for having now been recognised as Generalissimo of their forces, I had little fear of being attacked, especially as I carried a pistol in my pocket. So off I set strolling slowly down what seemed to have been a main street of the ancient city, which in its general appearance resembled excavated Pompeii, only on an infinitely larger scale.

As I went I meditated on the strange circumstances in which I found myself. Really they tempted me to believe that I was suffering from delusions and perhaps all the while in fact lay stretched upon a bed in the delirium of fever. That marvellous woman, for instance—even rejecting her tale of miraculously extended life, which I did—what was I to make of her? I did not know, except that wondrous as she was, it remained clear that she claimed a great deal more power than she possessed. This was evident from her tone in the interview with the captains, and from the fact that she had shuffled off the command of her tribe on to my shoulders. If she were so mighty, why did she not command it herself and bring her celestial, or infernal, powers to bear upon the enemy? Again, I could not say, but one fact emerged, namely that she was as interesting as she was beautiful, and uncommonly clever into the bargain.

But what a task was this that she had laid upon me, to lead into battle, with a foe of unascertained strength, a mob of savages probably quite undisciplined, of whose fighting qualities I knew nothing and whom I had no opportunity of organising. The affair seemed madness and I could only hope that luck or destiny would take me through somehow.

To tell the truth, I believed it would, for I had grown almost as superstitious about Zikali and his Great Medicine as was Hans himself. Certainly the effect of it upon those captains was very odd, or would have been had not the explanation come to me in a flash. On the first night of our meeting, as I have described, I showed this talisman to Ayesha, as a kind of letter of credentials, and now I could see that it was she who had arranged all the scene with the captains, or their tribal magician, in order to get her way about my appointment to the command.

Everything about her conduct bore this out, even her feigning ignorance of the existence of the charm and the leaving of it to Hans to suggest its production, which perhaps she did by influencing his mind subconsciously. No doubt more or less it fitted in with one of those nebulous traditions which are so common amongst ancient savage races, and therefore once shown to her confederate, or confederates, would be accepted by the common people as a holy sign, after which the rest was easy.

Such an obvious explanation involved the death of any illusions I might still cherish about this Arab lady, Ayesha, and it is true that I parted with them with regret, as we all do when we think we have discovered something wonderful in the female line. But there it was, and to bother any more about her, her history and aims, seemed useless.

So dismissing her and all present anxieties from my mind, I began to look about me and to wonder at the marvellous scene which unfolded itself before me in the moonlight. That I might see it better, although I was rather afraid of snakes which might hide among the stones, by an easy ascent I climbed a mount of ruins and up the broad slope of a tumbled massive wall, which from its thickness I judged must have been that of some fort or temple. On the crest of this wall, some seventy or eighty feet above the level of the streets, I sat down and looked about me.

Everywhere around me stretched the ruins of the great city, now as fallen and as deserted as Babylon herself. The majestic loneliness of the place was something awful. Even the vision of companies and battalions of men crossing the plain towards the north with the moonlight glistening on their spear-points, did little to lessen this sense of loneliness. I knew that these were the regiments which I was destined to command, travelling to the camp where I must meet them. But in such silence did they move that no sound came from them even in the deathly stillness of the perfect night, so that almost I was tempted to believe them to be the shadow-ghosts of some army of old Kôr.

They vanished, and musing thus I think I must have dozed. At any rate it seemed to me that of a sudden the city was as it had been in the days of its glory. I saw it brilliant with a hundred colours; everywhere was colour, on the painted walls and roofs, the flowering trees that lined the streets and the bright dresses of the men and women who by thousands crowded them and the marts and squares. Even the chariots that moved to and fro were coloured as were the countless banners which floated from palace walls and temple tops.

The enormous place teemed with every activity of life; brides being borne to marriage and dead men to burial; squadrons marching, clad in glittering armour; merchants chaffering; white-robed priests and priestesses passing in procession (who or what did they worship? I wondered); children breaking out of school; grave philosophers debating in the shadow of a cool arcade; a royal person making a progress preceded by runners and surrounded by slaves, and lastly the multitudes of citizens going about the daily business of life.

Even details were visible, such as those of officers of the law chasing an escaped prisoner who had a broken rope tied to his arm, and a collision between two chariots in a narrow street, about the wrecks of which an idle mob gathered as it does to-day if two vehicles collide, while the owners argued, gesticulating angrily, and the police and grooms tried to lift a fallen horse on to its feet. Only no sound of the argument or of anything else reached me. I saw, and that was all. The silence remained intense, as well it might do, since those chariots must have come to grief thousands upon thousands of years ago.

A cloud seemed to pass before my eyes, a thin, gauzy cloud which somehow reminded me of the veil that Ayesha wore. Indeed at the moment, although I could not see her, I would have sworn that she was present at my side, and what is more, that she was mocking me who had set her down as so impotent a trickstress, which doubtless was part of the dream.

At any rate I returned to my normal state, and there about me were the miles of desolate streets and the thousands of broken walls, and the black blots of roofless houses and the wide, untenanted plain bounded by the battlemented line of encircling mountain crests, and above all, the great moon shining softly in a tender sky.

I looked and thrilled, though oppressed by the drear and desolate beauty of the scene around me, descended the wall and the ruined slope and made my way homewards, afraid even of my own shadow. For I seemed to be the only living thing among the dead habitations of immemorial Kôr.

Reaching our camp I found Hans awake and watching for me.

"I was just coming to look for you, Baas," he said. "Indeed I should have done so before, only I knew that you had gone to pay a visit to that tall white 'Missis' who ties up her head in a blanket, and thought that neither of you would like to be disturbed."

"Then you thought wrong," I answered, "and what is more, if you had made that visit I think it might have been one from which you would never have come back."

"Oh yes, Baas," sniggered Hans. "The tall white lady would not have minded. It is you who are so particular, after the fashion of men whom Heaven made very shy."

Without deigning to reply to the gibes of Hans I went to lie down, wondering what kind of a bed poor Robertson occupied that night, and soon fell asleep, as fortunately for myself I have the power to do, whatever my circumstances at the moment. Men who can sleep are those who do the work of the world and succeed, though personally I have had more of the work than of the success.

I was awakened at the first grey dawn by Hans, who informed me that Billali was waiting outside with litters, also that Goroko had already made his incantations and doctored Umslopogaas and his two men for war after the Zulu fashion when battle was expected. He added that these Zulus had refused to be left behind to guard and nurse their wounded companions, and said that rather than do so, they would kill them.

Somehow, he informed me, in what way he could not guess, this had come to the ears of the White Lady who "hid her face from men because it was so ugly," and she had sent women to attend to the sick ones, with word that they should be well cared for. All of this proved to be true enough, but I need not enter into the details.

In the end off we went, I in my litter following Billali's, with an express and a repeating rifle and plenty of ammunition for both, and Hans, also well armed, in that which had been sent for Umslopogaas, who preferred to walk with Goroko and the two other Zulus.

For a little while Hans enjoyed the sensation of being carried by somebody else, and lay upon the cushions smoking with a seraphic smile and addressing sarcastic remarks to the bearers, who fortunately did not understand them. Soon, however, he wearied of these novel delights and as he was still determined not to walk until he was obliged, climbed on to the roof of the litter, astride of which he sat as though it were a horse, looking for all the world like a toy monkey on a horizontal stick.

Our road ran across the level, fertile plain but a small portion of which was cultivated, though I could see that at some time or other, when its population was greater, every inch of it had been under crop. Now it was largely covered by trees, many of them fruit-bearing, between which meandered streams of water which once, I think, had been irrigation channels.

About ten o'clock we reached the foot of the encircling cliffs and began the climb of the escarpment, which was steep, tortuous and difficult. By noon we reached its crest and here found all our little army encamped and, except for the sentries, sleeping, as seemed to be the invariable custom of these people in the daytime.

I caused the chief captains to be awakened and with them made a circuit of the camp, reckoning the numbers of the men which came to about 3,250 and learning what I could concerning them and their way of fighting. Then, accompanied by Umslopogaas and Hans with the Zulus as a guard, also by three of the head-captains of the Amahagger, I walked forward to study the lie of the land.

Coming to the further edge of the escarpment, I found that at this place two broad-based ridges, shaped like those that spring from the boles of certain tropical forest trees, ran from its crest to the plain beneath at a gentle slope. Moreover I saw that on this plain between the ends of the ridges an army was encamped which, by the aid of my glasses, I examined and estimated to number at least ten thousand men.

This army, the Amahagger captains informed me, was that of Rezu, who, they said, intended to commence his attack at dawn on the following morning, since the People of Rezu, being sun-worshippers, would never fight until their god appeared above the horizon. Having studied all there was to see I asked the captains to set out their plan of battle, if they had a plan.

The chief of them answered that it was to advance halfway down the right-hand ridge to a spot where there was a narrow flat piece of ground, and there await attack, since at this place their smaller numbers would not so much matter, whereas these made it impossible for them to assail the enemy.

"But suppose that Rezu should choose to come up to the other ridge and get behind you. What would happen then?" I inquired.

He replied that he did not know, his ideas of strategy being, it was clear, of a primitive order.

"Do your people fight best at night or in the day?" I went on.

He said undoubtedly at night, indeed in all their history there was no record of their having done so in the daytime.

"And yet you propose to let Rezu join battle with you when the sun is high, or in other words to court defeat," I remarked.

Then I went aside and discussed things for a while with Umslopogaas and Hans, after which I returned and gave my orders, declining all argument. Briefly these were that in the dusk before the rising of the moon, our Amahagger must advance down the right-hand ridge in complete silence, and hide themselves among the scrub which I saw grew thickly near its root. A small party, however, under the leadership of Goroko, whom I knew to be a brave and clever captain, was to pass halfway down the left-hand ridge and there light fires over a wide area, so as to make the enemy think that our whole force had encamped there. Then at the proper moment which I had not yet decided upon, we would attack the army of Rezu.

The Amahagger captains did not seem pleased with this plan which I think was too bold for their fancy, and began to murmur together. Seeing that I must assert my authority at once, I walked up to them and said to their chief man,

"Hearken, my friend. By your own wish, not mine, I have been appointed your general and I expect to be obeyed without question. From the moment that the advance begins you will keep close to me and to the Black One, and if so much as one of your men hesitates or turns back, you will die," and I nodded towards the axe of Umslopogaas. "Moreover, afterwards She-who-commands will see that others of you die, should you escape in the fight."

Still they hesitated. Thereon without another word, I produced Zikali's Great Medicine and held it before their eyes, with the result that the sight of this ugly thing did what even the threat of death could not do. They went flat on the ground, every one of them, and swore by Lulala and by She-who-commands, her priestess, that they would do all I said, however mad it seemed to them.

"Good," I answered. "Now go back and make ready, and for the rest, by this time to-morrow we shall know who is or is not mad."

From that moment till the end I had no more trouble with these Amahagger.

I will get on quickly with the story of this fight whereof the preliminary details do not matter. At the proper time Goroko went off with two hundred and fifty men and one of the two Zulus to light the fires and, at an agreed signal, namely the firing of two shots in rapid succession by myself, to begin shouting and generally make as much noise as they could.

We also went off with the remaining three thousand, and before the moon rose, crept as quietly as ghosts down the right-hand ridge. Being such a silent folk who were accustomed to move at night and could see in the dark almost as well as cats, the Amahagger executed this manœuvre splendidly, wrapping their spear-blades in bands of dry grass lest light should glint on them and betray our movements. So in due course we came to the patch of bush where the ridge widened out about five hundred yards from the plain beneath, and there lay down in four companies or regiments, each of them about seven hundred and fifty strong.

Now the moon had risen, but because of the mist which covered the surface of the plain, we could see nothing of the camp of Rezu which we knew must be within a thousand yards of us, unless indeed it had been moved, as the silence seemed to suggest.

This circumstance gave me much anxiety, since I feared lest abandoning their reputed habits, these Rezuites were also contemplating a night attack. Umslopogaas, too, was disturbed on the subject, though because of Goroko and his men whose fires began to twinkle on the opposing ridge something over a mile away, they could not pass up there without our knowledge.

Still, for aught I knew there might be other ways of scaling this mountain. I did not trust the Amahagger, who declared that none existed, since their local knowledge was slight as they never visited these northern slopes because of their fear of Rezu. Supposing that the enemy gained the crest and suddenly assaulted us in the rear! The thought of it made me feel cold down the back.

While I was wondering how I could find out the truth, Hans, who was squatted behind a bush, suddenly rose and gave the rifle he was carrying to the remaining Zulu.

"Baas," he said, "I am going to look and find out what those people are doing, if they are still there, and then you will know how and when to attack them. Don't be afraid for me, Baas, it will be easy in that mist and you know I can move like a snake. Also if I should not come back, it does not matter and it will tell you that they *are* there."

I hesitated who did not wish to expose the brave little Hottentot to such risks. But when he understood, Umslopogaas said,

"Let the man go. It is his gift and duty to spy, as it is mine to smite with the axe, and yours to lead, Macumazahn. Let him go, I say."

I nodded my head, and having kissed my hand in his silly fashion in token of much that he did not wish to say, Hans slipped out of sight, saying that he hoped to be back within an hour. Except for his great knife, he went unarmed, who feared that if he took a pistol he might be tempted to fire it and make a noise.

The Midnight Battle

That hour went by very slowly. Again and again I consulted my watch by the light of the moon, which was now rising high in the heavens, and thought that it would never come to an end. Listen as I would, there was nothing to be heard, and as the mist still prevailed the only thing I could see except the heavens, was the twinkling of the fires lit by Goroko and his party.

At length it was done and there was no sign of Hans. Another half hour passed and still no sign of Hans.

"I think that Light-in-Darkness is dead or taken prisoner," said Umslopogaas.

I answered that I feared so, but that I would give him another fifteen minutes and then, if he did not appear, I proposed to order an advance, hoping to find the enemy where we had last seen them from the top of the mountain.

The fifteen minutes went by also, and as I could see that the Amahagger captains who sat at a little distance were getting very nervous, I picked up my double-barrelled rifle and turned round so that I faced up hill with a view of firing it as had been agreed with Goroko, but in such a fashion that the flashes perhaps would not be seen from the plain below. For this purpose I moved a few yards to the left to get behind the trunk of a tree that grew there, and was already lifting the rifle to my shoulder, when a yellow hand clasped the barrel and a husky voice said,

"Don't fire yet, Baas, as I want to tell you my story first."

I looked down and there was the ugly face of Hans wearing a grin that might have frightened the man in the moon.

"Well," I said with cold indifference, assumed I admit to hide my excessive joy at his safe return, "tell on, and be quick about it. I suppose you lost your way and never found them."

"Yes, Baas, I lost my way for the fog was very thick down there. But in the end I found them all right, by my nose, Baas, for those man- eating people smell strong and I got the wind of one of their sentries. It was easy to pass him in the mist, Baas, so easy that I was tempted to cut his throat as I went, but I didn't for fear lest he should make a noise. No, I walked on right into the middle of them, which was easy too, for they were all asleep, wrapped up in blankets. They hadn't any fires perhaps because they didn't want them to be seen, or perhaps because it is so hot down in that low land, I don't know which.

"So I crept on taking note of all I saw, till at last I came to a little hill of which the top rose above the level of the mist, so that I could see on it a long hut built of green boughs with the leaves still fresh upon them. Now I thought that I would crawl up to the hut since it came into my mind that Rezu himself must be sleeping there and that I might kill him. But while I stood hesitating I heard a noise like to that made by an old woman whose husband had thrown a blanket over her head to keep her quiet, or to that of a bee in a bottle, a sort of droning noise that reminded me of something.

"I thought a while and remembered that when Red Beard was on his knees praying to Heaven, as is his habit when he has nothing else to do, Baas, he makes a noise just like that. I crept towards the sound and presently there I found Red Beard himself tied upon a stone and looking as mad as a buffalo bull stuck in a swamp, for he shook his head and rolled his eyes about, just as though he had had two bottles of bad gin, Baas, and all the while he kept saying prayers. Now I thought that I would cut him loose, and bent over him to do so, when by ill-luck he saw my face and began to shout, saying,

"'Go away, you yellow devil. I know you have come to take me to hell, but you are too soon, and if my hands were loose I would twist your head off your shoulders.'

"He said this in English, Baas, which as you know I can understand quite well, after which I was sure that I had better leave him alone. Whilst I was thinking, there came out of the hut above two old men dressed in night-shirts, such as you white people wear, with yellow things upon their heads that had a metal picture of the sun in front of them."

"Medicine-men," I suggested.

"Yes, Baas, or Predikants of some sort, for they were rather like your reverend father when he dressed himself up and went into a box to preach. Seeing them I slipped back a little way to where the mist began, lay down and listened. They looked at Red Beard, for his shouts at me had brought them out, but he took no notice of them, only went on making a noise like a beetle in a tin can.

"'It is nothing,' said one of the Predikants to the other in the same tongue that these Amahagger use. 'But when is he to be sacrificed? Soon, I hope, for I cannot sleep because of the noise he makes.'

"'When the edge of the sun appears, not before,' answered the other Predikant. 'Then the new queen will be brought out of the hut and this white man will be sacrificed to her.'

"'I think it is a pity to wait so long,' said the first Predikant, 'for never shall we sleep in peace until the red-hot pot is on his head.'

"'First the victory, then the feast,' answered the second Predikant, 'though he will not be so good to eat as that fat young woman who was with the new queen.'

"Then, Baas, they both smacked their lips and one of them went back towards the hut. But the other did not go back. No, he sat down on the ground and glowered at Baas Red-Beard upon the stone. More, he struck him on the face to make him quiet.

"Now, Baas, when I saw this and remembered that they had said that they had eaten Janee whom I liked although she was such a fool, the spirit in me grew so very angry and I thought that I would give this old *skellum* (i.e. rascal) of a Predikant a taste of sacrifice himself, after which I purposed to creep to the hut and see if I could get speech with the Lady Sad-Eyes, if she was there.

"So I wriggled up behind the Predikant as he sat glowering over Red- Beard, and stuck my knife into his back where I thought it would kill him at once. But it didn't, Baas, for he fell on to his face and began to make a noise like a wounded hyena before I could finish him. Then I heard a sound of shouts, and to save my life was obliged to run away into the mist, without loosing Red-Beard or seeing Lady Sad-Eyes. I ran very hard, Baas, making a wide circle to the left, and so at last got back here. That's all, Baas."

"And quite enough, too," I answered, "though if they did not see you, the death of the Medicine-man may frighten them. Poor Janee! Well, I hope to come even with those devils before they are three hours older."

Then I called up Umslopogaas and the Amahagger captains and told them the substance of the story, also that Hans had located the army, or part of it.

The end of it was that we made up our minds to attack at once; indeed I insisted on this, as I was determined if I could to save that unfortunate man, Robertson, who, from Hans' account, evidently was now quite mad and raving. So I fired the two shots as had been arranged and presently heard the sound of distant shoutings on the slope of the opposing ridge. A few minutes later we started, Umslopogaas and I leading the vanguard and the Amahagger captains following with the three remaining companies.

Now the reader, presuming the existence of such a person, will think that everything is sure to go right; that this cunning old fellow, Allan Quatermain, is going to surprise and wipe the floor with those Rezuites, who were already beguiled by the trick he had instructed Goroko to play. That after this he will rescue Robertson who doubtless shortly recovers his mind, also Inez with the greatest ease, in fact that everything will happen as it ought to do if this were a romance instead of a mere record of remarkable facts. But being the latter, as it happened, matters did not work out quite in this convenient way.

To begin with, when those Amahagger told me that the Rezuites never fought in the dark or before the sun was well up, either they lied or they were much mistaken, for at any rate on this occasion they did the exact contrary. All the while that we thought we were stalking them, they were stalking us. The Goroko manœuvre had not deceived them in the least, since from their spies they knew its exact significance.

Here, I may add that those spies were in our own ranks, traitors, in short, who were really in the pay of Rezu and possibly belonged to his abominable faith, some of whom slipped away from time to time to the enemy to report our progress and plans, so far as they knew them.

Further, what Hans had stumbled on was a mere rear guard left around the place of sacrifice and the hut where Inez was confined. The real army he never found at all. That was divided into two bodies and hidden in bush to the right and left of the ridge which we were descending just at the spot where it joined the plain beneath, and into the jaws of these two armies we marched gaily.

Now that hypothetical reader will say, "Why didn't that silly old fool, Allan, think of all these things? Why didn't he remember that he was commanding a pack of savages with whom he had no real acquaintance, among whom there were sure to be traitors, especially as they were of the same blood as the Rezuites, and take precautions?"

Ah! my dear reader, I will only answer that I wish you had handled the job yourself, and enjoyed the opportunity of seeing what *you* could do in the circumstances. Do you suppose I didn't think of all these points? Of course I did. But have you ever heard of the difficulty of making silk purses out of sows' ears, or of turning a lot of gloomy and disagreeable barbarians whom you had never even drilled, into trustworthy and efficient soldiers ready to fight three times their own number and beat them?

Also I beg to observe that I did get through somehow, as you shall learn, which is more than you might have done, Mr. Wisdom, though I admit, not without help from another quarter. It is all very well for you to sit in your armchair and be sapient and turn up your learned nose, like the gentlemen who criticise plays and poems, an easy job compared to the writing of them. From all of which, however, you will understand that I am, to tell the truth, rather ashamed of what followed, since *qui s'excuse, s'accuse.*

As we slunk down that hill in the moonlight, a queer-looking crowd, I admit also that I felt very uncomfortable. To begin with I did not like that remark of the Medicine-man which Hans reported, to the effect that the feast must come after the victory, especially as he had said just before that Robertson was to be sacrificed as the sun rose, which would seem to suggest that the "victory" was planned to take place before that event.

While I was ruminating upon this subject, I looked round for Hans to cross-examine him as to the priest's exact words, only to find that he had slunk off somewhere. A few minutes later he reappeared running back towards us swiftly and, I noticed, taking shelter behind tree trunks and rocks as he came.

"Baas," he gasped, for he was out of breath, "be careful, those Rezu men are on either side ahead. I went forward and ran into them. They threw many spears at me. Look!" and he showed a slight cut on his arm from which blood was flowing.

Instantly I understood that we were ambushed and began to think very hard indeed. As it chanced we were passing across a large flat space upon the ridge, say seven or eight acres in extent, where the bush grew lightly, though owing to the soil being better, the trees were tall.

On the steep slope below this little plain it seemed to be denser and there it was, according to Hans, that the ambush was set. I halted my regiment and sent back messengers to the others that they were to halt also as they came up, on the pretext of giving them a rest before they were marshalled and we advanced to the battle.

Then I told Umslopogaas what Hans said and asked him to send out his Zulu soldier whom he could trust, to see if he could obtain confirmation of the report. This he did at once. Also I asked him what he thought should be done, supposing that it was true.

"Form the Amahagger into a ring or a square and await attack," he answered.

I nodded, for that was my own opinion, but replied,

"If they were Zulus, the plan would be good. But how do we know that these men will stand?"

"We know nothing, Macumazahn, and therefore can only try. If they run it must be up-hill."

Then I called the captains and told them what was toward, which seemed to alarm them very much. Indeed one or two of them wanted to retreat at once, but I said I would shoot the first man who tried to do so. In the end they agreed to my plan and said that they would post their best soldiers above, at the top of the square, with the orders to stop any attempt at a flight up the mountain.

After this we formed up the square as best we could, arranging it in a rather rough, four-fold line. While we were doing this we heard some shouts below and presently the Zulu returned, who reported that all was as Hans had said and that Rezu's men were moving round us, having discovered, as he thought, that we had halted and escaped their ambush.

Still the attack did not develop at once, for the reason that the Rezu army was crawling up the steep flanks of the spur on either side of the level piece of ground, with a view of encircling us altogether, so as to make a clean sweep of our force. As a matter of fact, considered from our point of view, this was a most fortunate move, since thereby they stopped any attempt at a retreat on the part of our Amahagger, whose bolt-hole was now blocked.

When we had done all we could, we sat down, or at least I did, and waited. The night, I remember, was strangely still, only from the slopes on either side of our plateau came a kind of rustling sound which in fact was caused by the feet of Rezu's people, as they marched to surround us.

It ceased at last and the silence grew complete, so much so that I could hear the teeth of some of our tall Amahagger chattering with fear, a sound that gave me little confidence and caused Umslopogaas to remark that the hearts of these big men had never grown; they remained "as those of babies." I told the captains to pass the word down the ranks that those who stood might live, but those who fled would certainly die. Therefore if they wished to see their homes again they had better stand and fight like men. Otherwise most of them would be killed and the rest eaten by Rezu. This was done, and I observed that the message seemed to produce a steadying effect upon our ranks.

Suddenly all around us, from below, from above and on either side there broke a most awful roar which seemed to shape itself into the word, *Rezu*, and next minute also from above, below and either side, some ten thousand men poured forth upon our square.

In the moonlight they looked very terrible with their flowing white robes and great gleaming spears. Hans and I fired some shots, though for all the effect they produced, we might as well have pelted a breaker with pebbles. Then, as I thought that I should be more useful alive than dead, I retreated within the square, Umslopogaas, his Zulu, and Hans coming with me.

On the whole our Amahagger stood the attack better than I expected. They beat back the first rush with considerable loss to the enemy, also the second after a longer struggle. Then there was a pause during which we re-formed our ranks, dragging the wounded men into the square.

Scarcely had we done this when with another mighty shout of "Rezu!" the enemy attacked again—that was about an hour after the battle had begun. But now they had changed their tactics, for instead of trying to rush all sides of the square at once, they concentrated their efforts on the western front, that which faced towards the plain below.

On they came, and among them in the forefront of the battle, now and again I caught sight of a gigantic man, a huge creature who seemed to me to be seven feet high and big in proportion. I could not see him clearly because of the uncertain moonlight, but I noted his fierce aspect, also that he had an enormous beard, black streaked with grey, that flowed down to his middle, and that his hair hung in masses upon his shoulders.

"Rezu himself!" I shouted to Umslopogaas.

"Aye, Macumazahn, Rezu himself without doubt, and I rejoice to see him for he will be a worthy foe to fight. Look! he carries an axe as I do. Now I must save my strength for when we come face to face I shall need it all."

I thought that I would spare Umslopogaas this exertion and watched my opportunity to put a bullet through this giant. But I could never get one. Once when I had covered him an Amahagger rushed in front of my gun so that I could not shoot, and when a second chance came a little cloud floated over the face of the moon and made him invisible. After that I had other things to which to attend, since, as I expected would happen, the western face of our square gave, and yelling like devils, the enemy began to pour in through the gap.

A cold thrill went through me for I saw that the game was up. To re- form these undisciplined Amahagger was impossible; nothing was to be expected except panic, rout and slaughter. I cursed my folly for ever having had anything to do with the business, while Hans screamed to me in a thin voice that the only chance was for us three and the Zulu to bolt and hide in the bush.

I did not answer him because, apart from any nasty pride, the thing was impossible, for how could we get through those struggling masses of men which surrounded us on every side? No, my clock had struck, so I went on making a kind of mental sandwich of prayers and curses; prayers for my soul and forgiveness for my sins, and curses on the Amahagger and everything to do with them, especially Zikali and the woman called Ayesha, who, between them, had led me into this affair.

"Perhaps the Great Medicine of Zikali," piped Hans again as he fired a rifle at the advancing foe.

"Hang the Great Medicine," I shouted back, "and Ayesha with it. No wonder she declined to take a hand in this business."

As I spoke the words I saw old Billali, who not being a man of war was keeping as close to us as he could, go flat onto his venerable face, and reflected that he must have got a thrown spear through him. Casting a hurried glance at him to see if he were done for or only wounded, out of the corner of my eye I caught sight of something diaphanous which gleamed in the moonlight and reminded me of I knew not what at the moment.

I looked round quickly to see what it might be and lo! there, almost at my side was the veiled Ayesha herself, holding in her hand a little rod made of black wood inlaid with ivory not unlike a field marshal's baton, or a sceptre.

I never saw her come and to this day I do not know how she did so; she was just there and what is more she must have put luminous paint or something else on her robes, for they gleamed with a sort of faint, phosphorescent fire, which in the moonlight made her conspicuous all over the field of battle. Nor did she speak a single word, she only waved the rod, pointed with it towards the fierce hordes who were drawing near to us, killing as they came, and began to move forward with a gliding motion.

Now from every side there went up a roar of *"She-who-commands! She-who-commands!"* while the people of Rezu in front shouted *"Lulala! Lulala!* Fly, Lulala is upon us with the witchcrafts of the moon!"

She moved forward and by some strange impulse, for no order was given, we all began to move after her. Yes, the ranks that a minute before were beginning to give way to wild panic, became filled with a marvellous courage and moved after her.

The men of Rezu also, and I suppose with them Rezu himself, for I saw no more of him at that time, began to move uncommonly fast over the edge of the plateau towards the plain beneath. In fact they broke into flight and leaping over dead and dying, we rushed after them, always following the gleaming robe of Ayesha, who must have been an extremely agile person, since without any apparent exertion she held her place a few steps ahead of us.

There was another curious circumstance about this affair, namely, that terrified though they were, those Rezuites, after the first break, soon seemed to find it impossible to depart with speed. They kept turning round to look behind them at that following vision, as though they were so many of Lot's wives. Moreover, the same fate overtook many of them which fell upon that scriptural lady, since they appeared to become petrified and stood there quite still, like rabbits fascinated by a snake, until our people came up and killed them.

This slaying went on all down the last steep slope of the ridge, on which I suppose at least two-thirds of the army of Rezu must have perished, since our Amahagger showed themselves very handy men when it came to exterminating foes who were too terror-struck to fight, and, exhilarated by the occupation, gained courage every moment.

The Slaying of Rezu

At last we were on the plain, the bemused remnant of Rezu's army still doubling before us like a mob of game pursued by wild dogs. Here we halted to re-form our ranks; it seemed to me, although still she spoke no word, that some order reached me from the gleaming Ayesha that I should do this. The business took twenty minutes or so, and then, numbering about two thousand five hundred strong, for the rest had fallen in the fight of the square, we advanced again.

Now there came that dusk which often precedes the rising of the sun, and through it I could see that the battle was not yet over, since gathered in front of us was still a force about equal to our own. Ayesha pointed towards it with her wand and we leapt forward to the attack. Here the men of Rezu stood awaiting us, for they seemed to overcome their terror with the approach of day.

The battle was fierce, a very strange battle in that dim, uncertain light, which scarcely showed us friend from foe. Indeed I am not sure that we should have won it, since Ayesha was no longer visible to give our Amahagger confidence, and as the courage of the Rezuites increased, so theirs seemed to lessen with the passing of the night.

Fortunately, however, just as the issue hung doubtful, there was a shout to our left and looking, I made out the tall shape of Goroko, the witch-doctor, with the other Zulu, followed by his two hundred and fifty men, and leaping on to the flank of the line of Rezu.

That settled the business. The enemy crumpled up and melted, and just then the first lights of dawn appeared in the sky. I looked about me for Ayesha, but she had gone, where to I knew not, though at the moment I feared that she must have been killed in the mêlée.

Then I gave up looking and thinking, since now or never was the time for action. Signalling and shouting to those hatchet-faced Amahagger to advance, accompanied by Umslopogaas with Goroko who had joined us, and Hans, I sprang forward to give them an example, which, to be just to them, they took.

"This is the mound on which Red-Beard should be," cried Hans as we faced a little slope.

I ran up it and through the gloom which precedes the actual dawn, saw a group of men gathered round something, as people collect about a street accident.

"Red-Beard on the stone. They are killing him," screeched Hans again.

It was so; at least several white-robed priests were bending over a prostrate figure with knives in their hands, while behind stood the huge fellow whom I took to be Rezu, staring towards the east as though he were waiting for the rim of the sun to appear before he gave some order. At that very moment it did appear, just a thin edge of bright light on the horizon, and he turned, shouting the order.

Too late! For we were on them. Umslopogaas cut down one of the priests with his axe, and the men about me dealt with the others, while Hans with a couple of sweeps of his long knife, severed the cords with which Robertson was tied.

The poor man who in the growing light I could see was raving mad, sprang up, calling out something in Scotch about "the deil." Seizing a great spear which had fallen from the hand of one of the priests, he rushed furiously at the giant who had given the order, and with a yell drove it at his heart. I saw the spear snap, from which I concluded that this man, whom rightly I took to be Rezu, wore some kind of armour.

Next instant the axe he held, a great weapon, flashed aloft and down went Robertson before its awful stroke, stone dead, for as we found out afterwards, he was cloven almost in two. At the sight of the death of my poor friend rage took hold of me. In my hand was a double- barrelled rifle, an Express loaded with hollow-pointed bullets. I covered the giant and let drive, first with one barrel and then with the other, and what is more, distinctly I heard both bullets strike upon him.

Yet he did not fall. He rocked a little, that is all, then turned and marched off towards a hut, that whereof Hans had told me, which stood about fifty yards away.

"Leave him to me," shouted Umslopogaas. "Steel cuts where bullets cannot pierce," and with a bound like to that of a buck, the great Zulu leapt away after him.

I think that Rezu meant to enter the hut for some purpose of his own, but Umslopogaas was too hard upon his tracks. At any rate he ran past it and down the other slope of the little hill on to the plain behind where the remnants of his army were trying to re-form. There in front of them the giant turned and stood at bay.

Umslopogaas halted also, waiting for us to come up, since, cunning old warrior as he was, he feared lest should he begin the fight before that happened, the horde of them would fall on him. Thirty seconds later we arrived and found him standing still with bent body, small shield advanced and the great axe raised as though in the act of striking, a wondrous picture outlined as it was against the swiftly rising-sun.

Some ten paces away stood the giant leaning on the axe he bore, which was not unlike to that with which woodmen fell big trees. He was an evil man to see and at this, my first full sight of him, I likened him in my mind to Goliath whom David overthrew. Huge he was and hairy, with deep-set, piercing eyes and a great hooked nose. His face seemed thin and ancient also, when with a motion of the great head, he tossed his long locks back from about it, but his limbs were those of a Hercules and his movements full of a youthful vigour. Moreover his aspect as a whole was that of a devil rather than of a man; indeed the sight of it sickened me.

"Let me shoot him," I cried to Umslopogaas, for I had reloaded the rifle as I ran.

"Nay, Watcher-by-Night," answered the Zulu without moving his head, "rifle has had its chance and failed. Now let us see what axe can do. If I cannot kill this man, I will be borne hence feet first who shall have made a long journey for nothing."

Then the giant began to talk in a low, rumbling voice that reverberated from the slope of the little hill behind us.

"Who are you?" he asked, speaking in the same tongue that the Amahagger use, "who dare to come face to face with Rezu? Black hound, do you not know that I cannot be slain who have lived a year for every week of your life's days, and set my foot upon the necks of men by thousands. Have you not seen the spear shatter and the iron balls melt upon my breast like rain-drops, and would you try to bring me down with that toy you carry? My army is defeated—I know it. But what matters that when I can get me more? Because the sacrifice was not completed and the white queen was not wed, therefore my army was defeated by the magic of Lulala, the White Witch who dwells in the tombs. But *I* am not defeated who cannot be slain until I show my back, and then only by a certain axe which long ago has rusted into dust."

Now of this long speech Umslopogaas understood nothing, so I answered for him, briefly enough, but to the point, for there flashed into my mind all Ayesha's tale about an axe.

"A certain axe!" I cried. "Aye, a certain axe! Well, look at that which is held by the Black One, the captain who is named Slaughterer, the ancient axe whose title is Chieftainess, because if so she wills, she takes the lives of all. Look at it well, Rezu, Giant and Wizard, and say whether it is not that which your forefather lost, that which is destined to bring you to your doom?"

Thus I spoke, very loudly that all might hear, slowly also, pausing between each word because I wished to give time for the light to strengthen, seeing as I did that the rays of the rising sun struck upon the face of the giant, whereas the eyes of Umslopogaas were less dazzled by it.

Rezu heard, and stared at the axe which Umslopogaas held aloft, causing it to quiver slightly by an imperceptible motion of his arm. As he stared I saw his hideous face change, and that on it for the first time gathered a look of something resembling fear. Also his followers behind him who were also studying the axe, began to murmur together.

For here I should say that as though by common consent the battle had been stayed; we no longer attacked and the enemy no longer ran. They, or whose who were left of them, stood still as though they felt that the real and ultimate issue of the fight depended upon the forthcoming duel between these two champions, though of that issue they had little doubt since, as I learned afterwards, they believed their king to be invulnerable.

For quite a while Rezu went on staring. Then he said aloud as if he were thinking to himself.

"It is like, very like. The horn haft is the same; the pointed gouge is the same; the blade shaped like the young moon is the same. Almost could I think that before me shook the ancient holy axe. Nay, the gods have taken that back long ago and this is but a trick of the witch, Lulala of the Caves."

Thus he spoke, but still for a moment hesitated.

"Umslopogaas," I said in the deep silence that followed, "hear me."

"I hear you," he answered without turning his head or moving his arms. "What counsel, Watcher-by-Night?"

"This, Slaughterer. Strike not at that man's face and breast, for there I think he is protected by witchcraft or by armour. Get behind him and strike at his back. Do you understand?"

"Nay, Macumazahn, I understand not. Yet I will do your bidding because you are wiser than I and utter no empty words. Now be still."

Then Umslopogaas threw the axe into the air and caught it as it fell, and as he did so began to chant his own praises Zulu fashion.

"Oho!" he said, "I am the child of the Lion, the Black-maned Lion, whose claws never loosened of their prey. I am the Wolf-king, he who hunted with the wolves upon the Witch-mountain with my brother, Bearer of the Club named Watcher-of-the-Fords, I am he who slew him called the Unconquered, Chief of the People of the Axe, he who bore the ancient Axe before me; I am he who smote the Halakazi tribe in their caves and won me Nada the Lily to wife. I am he who took to the King Dingaan a gift that he loved little, and afterward with Mopo, my foster-sire, hurled this Dingaan down to death. I am the Royal One, named Bulalio the Slaughterer, named Woodpecker, named Umhlopekazi the Captain, before whom never yet man has stood in fair and open fight. Now, thou Wizard Rezu, now thou Giant, now thou Ghost-man, come on against me and before the sun has risen by a hand's breadth, all those who watch shall see which of us is better at the game of war. Come on, then! Come on, for I say that my blood boils over and my feet grow cold. Come on, thou grinning dog, thou monster grown fat with eating the flesh of men, thou hook-beaked vulture, thou old, grey-whiskered wolf!"

Thus he changed in his fierce, boastful way, while his two remaining Zulus clapped their hands and sentence by sentence echoed his words, and Goroko, the witch-doctor, muttered incantations behind him.

While he sang thus Umslopogaas began to stir. First only his head and shoulders moved gently, swaying from side to side like a reed shaken in the wind or a snake about to strike. Then slowly he put out first one foot and next the other and drew them back again, as a dancer might do, tempting Rezu to attack.

But the giant would not, his shield held before him, he stood still and waited to see what this black warrior would do.

The snake struck. Umslopogaas darted in and let drive with the long axe. Rezu raised his shield above his head and caught the blow. From the clank it made I knew that this shield which seemed to be of hide, was lined with iron. Rezu smote back, but before the blow could fall the Zulu was out of his reach. This taught me how great was the giant's strength, for though the stroke was heavy, like the steel- hatted axe he bore, still when he saw that it had missed he checked the weapon in mid air, which only a mighty man could have done.

Umslopogaas saw these things also and changed his tactics. His axe was six or eight inches longer in the haft than that of Rezu, and therefore he could reach where Rezu could not, for the giant was short-armed. He twisted it round in his hand so that the moon-shaped blade was uppermost, and keeping it almost at full length, began to peck with the gouge-shaped point on the back at the head and arms of Rezu, that as I knew was a favourite trick of his in fight from which he won his name of "Woodpecker." Rezu defended his head with his shield as best he could against the sharp points of steel which flashed all about him.

Twice it seemed to me that the Zulu's pecks went home upon the giant's breast, but if so they did no harm. Either Rezu's thick beard, or armour beneath it stopped them from penetrating his body. Still he roared out as though with pain, or fury, or both, and growing mad, charged at Umslopogaas and smote with all his strength.

The Zulu caught the blow upon his shield, through which it shore as though the tough hide were paper. Stay the stroke it could not, yet it turned its direction, so that the falling axe slid past Umslopogaas's shoulder, doing him no hurt. Next instant, before Rezu could strike again, the Zulu threw the severed shield into his face and seizing the axe with both hands, leapt in and struck. It was a mighty blow, for I saw the rhinoceros-horn handle of the famous axe bend like a drawn bow, and it went home with a dull thud full upon Rezu's breast. He shook, but no more. Evidently the razor edge of *Inkosikaas* had failed to pierce. There was a sound as though a hollow tree had been smitten and some strands of the long beard, shorn off, fell to the ground, but that was all.

"*Tagati!* (bewitched),*"* cried the watching Zulus. "That stroke should have cut him in two!" while I thought to myself that this man knew how to make good armour.

Rezu laughed aloud, a bellowing kind of laugh, while Umslopogaas sprang back astonished.

"Is it thus!" he cried in Zulu. "Well, all wizards have some door by which their Spirit enters and departs. I must find the door, I must find the door!"

So he spoke and with springing movements tried to get past Rezu, first to the right and then to the left, all the while keeping out of reach. But Rezu ever turned and faced him, as he did so retreating step by step down the slope of the little hill and striking whenever he found a chance, but without avail, for always Umslopogaas was beyond his reach. Also the sunlight which now grew strong, dazzled him, or so I thought. Moreover he seemed to tire somewhat—or so I thought also.

At any rate he determined to make an end of the play, for with a swift motion, as Umslopogaas had done, he threw away his shield and grasping the iron handle of his axe with both hands, charged the Zulu like a bull. Umslopogaas leapt back out of reach. Then suddenly he turned and ran up the rise. Yes, Bulalio the Slaughterer ran!

A roar of mockery went up from the sun-worshippers behind, while our Amahagger laughed and Goroko and the two Zulus stared astonished and ashamed. Only I read his mind aright and wondered what guile he had conceived.

He ran, and Rezu ran after him, but never could he catch the swiftest- footed man in Zululand. To and fro he followed him, for Umslopogaas was taking a zig-zag path towards the crest of the slope, till at length Rezu stopped breathless. But Umslopogaas still ran another twenty yards or so until he reached the top of the slope and there halted and wheeled round.

For ten seconds or more he stood drawing his breath in great gasps, and, looking at his face, I saw that it had become as the face of a wolf. His lips were drawn up into a terrible grin, showing the white teeth between; his cheeks seemed to have fallen in and his eyes glared, while the skin over the hole in his forehead beat up and down.

There he stood, gathering himself together for some mighty effort.

"Run on!" shouted the spectators. "Run back to Kôr, black dog!"

Umslopogaas knew that they were mocking him, but he took no heed, only bent down and rubbed his sweating hand in the grit of the dry earth. Then he straightened himself and charged down on Rezu.

I, Allan Quatermain, have seen many things in battle, but never before or since did I see aught like to this charge. It was swift as that of a lioness, so swift that the Zulu's feet scarcely seemed to touch the ground. On he sped like a thrown spear, till, when within about a dozen feet of Rezu who stood staring at him, he bent his frame almost double and leapt into the air.

Oh! what a leap was that. Surely he must have learnt it from the lion, or the spring-buck. High he rose and now I saw his purpose; it was to clear the tall shape of Rezu. Aye, and he cleared him with half a foot to spare, and as he passed above, smote downwards with the axe so that the blow fell upon the back of Rezu's head. Moreover it went home this time, for I saw the red blood stream and Rezu fell forward on his face. Umslopogaas landed far beyond him, ran a little way because he must, then wheeled round and charged again.

Rezu was rising, but before he gained his feet, the axe *Inkosikaas* thundered down where the neck joins the shoulder and sank in. Still, so great was his strength that Rezu found his feet and smote out wildly. But now his movements were slow and again Umslopogaas got behind him, smiting at his back. Once, twice, thrice, he smote, and at the third blow it seemed as though the massive spine were severed, for his weapon fell from Rezu's hand and slowly he sank down to the ground, and lay there, a huddled heap.

Believing that all was over I ran to where he lay with Umslopogaas standing over him, as it seemed to me, utterly exhausted, for he supported himself by the axe and tottered upon his feet. But Rezu was not yet dead. He opened his cavernous eyes and glared at the Zulu with a look of hellish hate.

"*Thou* hast not conquered me, Black One," he gasped. "It is thine axe which gave thee victory; the ancient, holy axe that once was mine until the woman stole it, yes, that and the craft of the Witch of the Caves who told thee to smite where the Spirit of Life which I feared to enter wholly, had not kissed my flesh, and there only left me mortal. Wolf of a black man, may we meet elsewhere and fight this fray again. Ah! would that I could get these hands about thy throat and take thee with me down into the Darkness. But Lulala wins if only for a while, since her fate, I think, shall be worse than mine. Ah! I see the magic beauty that she boasts turn to shameful——"

Here of a sudden life left him and throwing his great arms wide, a last breath passed bubbling from his lips.

As I stooped to examine the man's huge and hairy carcase that to me looked only half human, with a thunder of feet our Amahagger rushed down upon us and thrusting me aside, fell upon the body of their ancient foe like hounds upon a helpless fox, and with hands and spears and knives literally tore and hacked it limb from limb, till no semblance of humanity remained.

It was impossible to stop them; indeed I was too outworn with labours and emotions to make any such attempt. This I regret the more since I lost the opportunity of making an examination of the body of this troll-like man, and of ascertaining what kind of armour it was he wore beneath that great beard of his, which was strong enough to stop my bullets, and even the razor edge of the axe *Inkosikaas* driven with all the might of the arms of the Zulu, Bulalio. For when I looked again at the sickening sight the giant was but scattered fragments and the armour, whatever it might have been, was gone, rent to little pieces and carried off, doubtless, by the Amahagger, perhaps to be divided between them to serve as charms.

So of Rezu I know only that he was the hugest, most terrible-looking man I have ever seen, one too who carried his vast strength very late in life, since from the aspect of his countenance I imagine that he must have been nigh upon seventy years of age, though his supposed unnatural antiquity of course was nothing but a fable put about by the natives for their own purposes.

Presently Umslopogaas seemed to recover from the kind of faint into which he had fallen and opening his eyes, looked about him. The first person they fell on was old Billali who stood stroking his white beard and contemplating the scene with an air which was at once philosophic and satisfied. This seemed to anger Umslopogaas, for he cried,

"I think it was you, ancient bag of words and sweeper of paths for the feet of the great, who made a mock of me but now, when you thought that I fled before the horns of yonder man-eating bull—" and he nodded towards the fragments of what once had been Rezu. "Find now his axe and though I am weak and weary, I will wash away the insult with your blood."

"What does this glorious black hero say, Watcher-by-Night?" asked Billali in his most courteous tones.

I told him word by word, whereon Billali lifted his hands in horror, turned and fled. Nor did I see him again until we arrived at Kôr.

At the sight of the fall of their giant chief Rezu whom they believed to be invulnerable, his followers, who were watching the fray, set up a great wailing, a most mournful and uncanny noise to hear. Then, as I think did the hosts of the Philistines when David brought down Goliath by his admirable shot with a stone, they set out for their homes wherever these may have been, at an absolutely record pace and in the completest disarray.

Our Amahagger followed them for a while, but soon were left standing still. So they contented themselves with killing any wounded they could find and returned. I did not accompany them; indeed the battle being won, metaphorically I washed my hands of them, and in my thoughts consigned them to a certain locality as a people of whom it might well be said that manners they had none and their customs were simply beastly. Also, although fierce and cruel, these night-bats were not good fighting men and in short never did I wish to have to do with such another company.

Moreover, a very different matter pressed. The object of this business so far as I was concerned, had been to rescue poor Inez, since had it not been for her sake, never would I have consented to lead those Amahagger against their fellow blackguards, the Rezuites.

But where was Inez? If Hans had understood the medicine-man aright, she was, or had been, in the hut, where it was my earnest hope that she still remained, since otherwise the hunt must be continued. This at any rate was easy to discover. Calling Hans, who was amusing himself by taking long shots at the flying enemy, so that they might not forget him, as he said, and the Zulus, I walked up the slope to the hut, or rather booth of boughs, for it was quite twenty feet long by twelve or fifteen broad.

At its eastern end was a doorway or opening closed with a heavy curtain. Here I paused full of tremors, and listened, for to tell the truth I dreaded to draw that curtain, fearing what I might see within. Gathering up my courage at length I tore it aside and, a revolver in my hand, looked in. At first after the strong light without, for the sun was now well up, I could see nothing, since those green boughs and palm leaves were very closely woven. As my eyes grew accustomed to the gloom, however, I perceived a glittering object seated on a kind of throne at the end of the booth, while in a double row in front knelt six white-robed women who seemed to wear chains about their necks and carried large knives slung round their middles. On the floor between these women and the throne lay a dead man, a priest of some sort as I gathered from his garb, who still held a huge spear in his hand. So silent were the figure on the throne and those that knelt before it, that at first I thought that all of them must be dead.

"Lady Sad-Eyes," whispered Hans, "and her bride-women. Doubtless that old Predikant came to kill her when he saw that the battle was lost, but the bride-women killed him with their knives."

Here I may state that Hans' suppositions proved to be quite correct, which shows how quick and deductive was his mind. The figure on the throne was Inez; the priest in his disappointed rage *had* come to kill her, and the bride-women had killed *him* with their knives before he could do so.

I bade the Zulus tear down the curtain and pull away some of the end boughs, so as to let in more light. Then we advanced up the place, holding our pistols and spears in readiness. The kneeling women turned their heads to look at us and I saw that they were all young and handsome in their fashion, although fierce-faced. Also I saw their hands go to the knives they wore. I called to them to let these be and come out, and that if they did so they had nothing to fear. But if they understood, they did not heed my words.

On the contrary while Hans and I covered them with our pistols, fearing lest they should stab the person on the throne whom we took to be Inez, at some word from one of them, they bowed simultaneously towards her, then at another word, suddenly they drew the knives and plunged them to their own hearts!

It was a dreadful sight and one of which I never saw the like. Nor to this day do I know why the deed was done, unless perhaps the women were sworn to the service of the new queen and feared that if they failed to protect her, they would be doomed to some awful end. At any rate we got them out dead or dying, for their blows had been strong and true, and not one of them lived for more than a few minutes.

Then I advanced to the figure on the throne, or rather foot-stooled chair of black wood inlaid with ivory, which sat so silent and motionless that I was certain it was that of a dead woman, especially when I perceived that she was fastened to the chair with leather straps, which were sewn over with gold wire. Also she was veiled and, with one exception, made up, if I may use the term, exactly to resemble the lady Ayesha, even down to the two long plaits of black hair, each finished with some kind of pearl and to the sandalled feet.

The exception was that about her hung a great necklace of gold ornaments from which were suspended pendants also of gold representing the rayed disc of the sun in rude but bold and striking workmanship.

I went to her and having cut the straps, since I could not stop to untie their knots, lifted the veil.

Beneath it was Inez sure enough, and Inez living, for her breast rose and fell as she breathed, but Inez senseless. Her eyes were wide open, yet she was quite senseless. Probably she had been drugged, or perhaps some of the sights of horror which she saw, had taken away her mind. I confess that I was glad that this was so, who otherwise must have told her the dreadful story of her father's end.

We bore her out and away from that horrible place, apparently quite unhurt, and laid her under the shadow of a tree till a litter could be procured. I could do no more who knew not how to treat her state, and had no spirits with me to pour down her throat.

This was the end of our long pursuit, and thus we rescued Inez, whom the Zulus called the Lady Sad-Eyes.

The Spell

Of our return to Kôr I need say nothing, except that in due course we reached that interesting ruin. The journey was chiefly remarkable for one thing, that on this occasion, I imagine for the first and last time in his life, Umslopogaas consented to be carried in a litter, at least for part of the way. He was, as I have said, unwounded, for the axe of his mighty foe had never once so much as touched his skin. What he suffered from was shock, a kind of collapse, since, although few would have thought it, this great and utterly fearless warrior was at bottom a nervous, highly-strung man.

It is only the nervous that climb the highest points of anything, and this is true of fights as of all others. That fearful fray with Rezu had been a great strain on the Zulu. As he put it himself, "the wizard had sucked the strength" out of him, especially when he found that owing to his armour he could not harm him in front, and owing to his cunning could not get at him behind. Then it was that he conceived the desperate expedient of leaping over his head and smiting backwards as he leapt, a trick, he told me, that he had once played years before when he was young, in order to break a shield ring and reach one who stood in its centre.

In this great leap over Rezu's head Umslopogaas knew that he must succeed, or be slain, which in turn would mean my death and that of the others. For this reason he faced the shame of seeming to fly in order to gain the higher ground, whence alone he could gather the speed necessary to such a terrific spring.

Well, he made it and thereby conquered, and this was the end, but as he said, it had left him, "weak as a snake when it crawls out of its hole into the sun after the long winter sleep."

Of one thing, Umslopogaas added, he was thankful, namely that Rezu had never succeeded in getting his arms round him, since he was quite certain that if he had he would have broken him "as a baboon breaks a mealie-stalk." No strength, not even his, could have resisted the iron might of that huge, gorilla-like man.

I agreed with him who had noted Rezu's vast chest and swelling muscles, also the weight of the blows that he struck with the steel- hafted axe (which, by the way, when I sought for it, was missing, stolen, I suppose, by one of the Amahagger).

Whence did that strength come, I wondered, in one who from his face appeared to be old? Was there perchance, after all, some truth in the legend of Samson and did it dwell in that gigantic beard and those long locks of his? It was impossible to say and probably the man was but a Herculean freak, for that he was as strong as Hercules all the stories that I heard afterwards of his feats, left little room for doubt.

About one thing only was I certain in connection with him, namely, that the tales of his supernatural abilities were the merest humbug. He was simply one of the representatives of the family of "strong men," of whom examples are still to be seen doing marvellous feats all over the earth.

For the rest, he was dead and broken up by those Amahagger blood- hounds before I could examine him, or his body-armour either, and there was an end of him and his story. But when I looked at the corpse of poor Robertson, which I did as we buried it where he fell, and saw that though so large and thick-set, it was cleft almost in two by a single blow of Rezu's axe, I came to understand what the might of this savage must have been.

I say savage, but I am not sure that this is a right description of Rezu. Evidently he had a religion of a sort, also imagination, as was shown by the theft of the white woman to be his queen; by his veiling of her to resemble Ayesha whom he dreaded; by the intended propitiatory sacrifice; by the guard of women sworn to her service who slew the priest that tried to kill her, and afterwards committed suicide when they had failed in their office, and by other things. All this indicated something more than savagery, perhaps survivals from a forgotten civilisation, or perhaps native ability on the part of an individual ruler. I do not know and it matters nothing.

Rezu is dead and the world is well rid of him, and those who want to learn more of his people can go to study such as remain of them in their own habitat, which for my part I never wish to visit any more.

During our journey to Kôr poor Inez never stirred. Whenever I went to look at her in the litter, I found her lying there with her eyes open and a fixed stare upon her face which frightened me very much, since I began to fear lest she should die. However I could do nothing to help her, except urge the bearers to top speed. So swiftly did we travel down the hill and across the plain that we reached Kôr just as the sun was setting. As we crossed the moat I perceived old Billali coming to meet us. This he did with many bows, keeping an anxious eye upon the litter which he had learned contained Umslopogaas. Indeed his attitude and that of the Amahagger towards the two of us, and even Hans, thenceforward became almost abject, since after our victory over Rezu and his death beneath the axe, they looked upon us as half divine and treated us accordingly.

"O mighty General," he said, "She-who-commands bids me conduct the lady who is sick to the place that has been made ready for her, which is near your own so that you may watch over her if you will."

I wondered how Ayesha knew that Inez was sick, but being too tired to ask questions, merely bade him lead on. This he did, taking us to another ruined house next to our own quarters which had been swept, cleaned and furnished after a fashion, and moreover cleverly roofed in with mats, so that it was really quite comfortable. Here we found two middle-aged women of a very superior type, who, Billali informed me, were by trade nurses of the sick. Having seen her laid upon her bed, I committed Inez to their charge, since the case was not one that I dared to try to doctor myself, not knowing what drug of the few I possessed should be administered to her. Moreover Billali comforted me with the information that soon She-who-commands would visit her and "make her well again," as she could do.

I answered that I hoped so and went to our quarters where I found an excellent meal ready cooked and with it a stone flagon, of the contents of which Billali said we were all three to drink by the command of Ayesha, who declared that it would take away our weariness.

I tried the stuff, which was pale yellow in colour like sherry and, for aught I knew, might be poison, to find it most comforting, though it did not seem to be very strong to the taste. Certainly, too, its effects were wonderful, since presently all my great weariness fell from me like a discarded cloak, and I found myself with a splendid appetite and feeling better and stronger than I had done for years. In short that drink was a "cocktail" of the best, one of which I only wish I possessed the recipe, though Ayesha told me afterwards that it was distilled from quite harmless herbs and not in any sense a spirit.

Having discovered this, I gave some of it to Hans, also to Umslopogaas, who was with the wounded Zulus, who, we found, were progressing well towards complete recovery, and lastly to Goroko who also was worn out. On all of these the effect of that magical brew proved most satisfactory.

Then, having washed, I ate a splendid dinner, though in this respect Hans, who was seated on the ground nearby, far outpassed my finest efforts.

"Baas," he said, "things have gone very well with us when they might have gone very ill. The Baas Red-Beard is dead, which is a good thing, since a madman would have been difficult to look after, and a brain full of moonshine is a bad companion for any one. Oh! without doubt he is better dead, though your reverend father the

Predikant will have a hard job looking after him there in the Place of Fires."

"Perhaps," I said with a sigh, "since it is better to be dead than to live a lunatic. But what I fear is that the lady his daughter will follow him."

"Oh, no! Baas," replied Hans cheerfully, "though I daresay that she will always be a little mad also, because you see it is in her blood and doubtless she has looked on dreadful things. But the Great Medicine will see to it that she does not die after we have taken so much trouble and gone into such big dangers to save her. That Great Medicine is very wonderful, Baas. First of all it makes you General over those Amahagger who without you would never have fought, as the Witch who ties up her head in a cloth knew well enough. Then it brings us safe through the battle and gives strength to Umslopogaas to kill the old man-eating giant."

"Why did it not give *me* strength to kill him, Hans? I let him have two Express bullets on his chest, which hurt him no more than a tap upon the horns with a dancing stick would hurt a bull-buffalo."

"Oh! Baas, perhaps you missed him, who because you hit things sometimes, think that you do so always."

Having waited to see if I would rise to this piece of insolence, which of course I did not, he went on by way of letting me down easily, "Or perhaps he wore very good armour under his beard, for I saw some of those Amahagger who pulled his hair off and cut him to pieces, go away with what looked like little bits of brass. Also the Great Medicine meant that he should be killed by Umslopogaas and not by you, since otherwise Umslopogaas would have been sad for the rest of his life, whereas now he will walk about the world as proud as a cock with two tails and crow all night as well as all day. Then, Baas, when Rezu broke the square and the Amahagger began to run, without doubt it was the Great Medicine which changed their hearts and made them brave again, so that they charged at the right moment when they saw it going forward on your breast, and instead of being eaten up, ate up the cannibals."

"Indeed! I thought that the Lady who dwells yonder had something to do with that business. Did you see her, Hans?"

"Oh, yes! I saw her, Baas, and I think that without doubt she lifted the cloth from over her head and when the people of Rezu saw how ugly was the face beneath, it did frighten them a little. But doubtless the Great Medicine put that thought into her also, for, Baas, what could a silly woman do in such a case? Did you ever know of a woman who was of any use in a battle, or for anything else except to nurse babies, and this one does not even do that, no doubt because being so hideous under that sheet, no man can be found to marry her."

Now I looked up by chance and in the light of the lamps saw Ayesha standing in the room, which she had entered through the open doorway, within six feet of Hans' back indeed.

"Be sure Baas," he went on, "that this bundle of rags is nothing but a common old cheat who frightens people by pretending to be a spook, as, if she dared to say that it was she who made those stinking Amahagger charge, and not the Great Medicine of the Opener-of-Roads, I would tell her to her face."

Now I was too paralysed to speak, and while I was reflecting that it was fortunate Ayesha did not understand Dutch, she moved a little so that one of the lamps behind her caused her shadow to fall on to the back of the squatting Hans and over it on to the floor beyond. He saw it and stared at the distorted shape of the hooded head, then slowly screwed his neck round and looked upwards behind him.

For a moment he went on staring as though he were frozen, then uttering a wild yell, he scrambled to his feet, bolted out of the house and vanished into the night.

"It seems, Allan," said Ayesha slowly, "that yonder yellow ape of yours is very bold at throwing sticks when the leopardess is not beneath the tree. But when she comes it is otherwise with him. Oh! make no excuse, for I know well that he was speaking ill things of me, because being curious, as apes are, he burns to learn what is behind my veil, and being simple, believes that no woman would hide her face unless its fashion were not pleasing to the nice taste of men."

Then, to my relief, she laughed a little, softly, which showed me that she had a sense of humour, and went on, "Well, let him be, for he is a good ape and courageous in his fashion, as he showed when he went out to spy upon the host of Rezu, and stabbed the murderer-priest by the stone of sacrifice."

"How can you know the words of Hans, Ayesha," I asked, "seeing that he spoke in a tongue which you have never learned?"

"Perchance I read faces, Allan."

"Or backs," I suggested, remembering that his was turned to her.

"Or backs, or voices, or hearts. It matters little which, since read I do. But have done with such childish talk and lead me to this maiden who has been snatched from the claws of Rezu and a fate that is worse than death. Do you understand, Allan, that ere the demon Rezu took her to wife, the plan was to sacrifice her own father to her and then eat him as the woman with her was eaten, and before her eyes? Now the father is dead, which is well, as I think the little yellow man said to you—nay, start not, I read it from his back [Ha!—JB]—since had he lived whose brain was rotted, he would have raved till his death's day. Better, therefore, that he should die like a man fighting against a foe unconquerable by all save one. But she still lives."

"Aye, but mindless, Ayesha."

"Which, in great trouble such as she has passed, is a blessed state, O Allan. Bethink you, have there not been days, aye and months, in your own life when you would have rejoiced to sleep in mindlessness? And should we not, perchance, be happier, all of us, if like the beasts we could not remember, foreknow and understand? Oh! men talk of Heaven, but believe me, the real Heaven is one of dreamless sleep, since life and wakefulness, however high their scale and on whatever star, mean struggle, which being so oft mistaken, must breed sorrow—or remorse that spoils all. Come now."

So I preceded her to the next ruined house where we found Inez lying on the bed still clothed in her barbaric trappings, although the veil had been drawn off her face. There she lay, wide-eyed and still, while the women watched her. Ayesha looked at her a while, then said to me,

"So they tricked her out to be Ayesha's mock and image, and in time accepted by those barbarians as my very self, and even set the seals of royalty on her," and she pointed to the gold discs stamped with the likeness of the sun. "Well, she is a fair maiden, white and gently bred, the first such that I have seen for many an age. Nor did she wish this trickery. Moreover she has taken no hurt; her soul has sunk deep into a sea of horror and that is all, whence doubtless it can be drawn again. Yet I think it best that for a while she should remember naught, lest her brain break, as did her father's, and therefore no net of mine shall drag her back to memory. Let that return gently in future days, and then of it not too much, for so shall all this terror become to her a void in which sad shapes move like shadows, and as shadows are soon forgot and gone, no more to be held than dreams by the awakening sense. Stand aside, Allan, and you women, leave us for a while."

I obeyed, and the women bowed and went. Then Ayesha drew up her veil, and knelt down by the bed of Inez, but in such a fashion that I could not see her face although I admit that I tried to do so. I could see, however, that she set her lips against those of Inez and as I gathered by her motions, seemed to breathe into her lips. Also she lifted her hands and placing one of them upon the heart of Inez, for a minute or more swayed the other from side to side above her eyes, pausing at times to touch her upon the forehead with her finger-tips.

Presently Inez stirred and sat up, whereon Ayesha took a vessel of milk which stood upon the floor and held it to her lips. Inez drank to the last drop, then sank on to the bed again. For a while longer Ayesha continued the motions of her hands, then let fall her veil and rose.

"Look, I have laid a spell upon her," she said, beckoning to me to draw near.

I did so and perceived that now the eyes of Inez were shut and that she seemed to be plunged in a deep and natural sleep.

"So she will remain for this night and that day which follows," said Ayesha, "and when she wakes it will be, I think, to believe herself once more a happy child. Not until she sees her home again will she find her womanhood, and then all this story will be forgotten by her. Of her father you must tell her that he died when you went out to hunt the river-beasts together, and if she seeks for certain others, that they have gone away. But I think that she will ask little more when she learns that he is dead, since I have laid that command upon her soul."

"Hypnotic suggestion," thought I to myself, "and I only hope to heaven that it will work."

Ayesha seemed to guess what was passing through my mind, for she nodded and said,

"Have no fear, Allan, for I am what the black axe-bearer and the little yellow man called a 'witch' which means, as you who are instructed know, one who has knowledge of medicine and other things and who holds a key to some of the mysteries that lie hid in Nature."

"For instance," I suggested, "of how to transport yourself into a battle at the right moment, and out of it again—also at the right moment."

"Yes, Allan, since watching from afar, I saw that those Amahagger curs were about to flee and that I was needed there to hearten them and to put fear into the army of Rezu. So I came."

"But how did you come, Ayesha?"

She laughed as she answered,

"Perhaps I did not come at all. Perhaps you only thought I came; since I seemed to be there the rest matters nothing."

As I still looked unconvinced she went on,

"Oh! foolish man, seek not to learn of that which is too high for you. Yet listen. You in your ignorance suppose that the soul dwells within the body, do you not?"

I answered that I had always been under this impression.

"Yet, Allan, it is otherwise, for the body dwells within the soul."

"Like the pearl in an oyster," I suggested.

"Aye, in a sense, since the pearl which to you is beautiful, is to the oyster a sickness and a poison, and so is the body to the soul whose temple it troubles and defiles. Yet round it is the white and holy soul that ever seeks to bring the vile body to its own purity and colour, yet oft-times fails. Learn, Allan, that flesh and spirit are the deadliest foes joined together by a high decree that they may forget their hate and perfect each other, or failing, be separate to all eternity, the spirit going to its own place and the flesh to its corruption."

"A strange theory," I said.

"Aye, Allan, and one which is so new to you that never will you understand it. Yet it is true and I set it out for this reason. The soul of man, being at liberty and not cooped within his narrow breast, is in touch with that soul of the Universe, which men know as God Whom they call by many names. Therefore it has all knowledge and perhaps all power, and at times the body within it, if it be a wise body, can draw from this well of knowledge and abounding power. So at least can I. And now you will understand why I am so good a doctoress and how I came to appear in the battle, as you said, at the right time, and to leave it when my work was done."

"Oh! yes," I answered, "I quite understand. I thank you much for putting it so plainly."

She laughed a little, appreciating my jest, looked at the sleeping Inez, and said,

"The fair body of this lady dwells in a large soul, I think, though one of a somewhat sombre hue, for souls have their colours, Allan, and stain that which is within them. She will never be a happy woman."

"The black people named her Sad-Eyes," I said.

"Is it so? Well, I name her Sad-Heart, though for such often there is joy at last. Meanwhile she will forget; yes, she will forget the worst and how narrow was the edge between her and the arms of Rezu."

"Just the width of the blade of the axe, *Inkosikaas*," I answered. "But tell me, Ayesha, why could not that axe cut and why did my bullets flatten or turn aside when these smote the breast of Rezu?"

"Because his front-armour was good, Allan, I suppose," she replied indifferently, "and on his back he wore none."

"Then why did you fill my ears with such a different tale about that horrible giant having drunk of a Cup of Life, and all the rest?" I asked with irritation.

"I have forgotten, Allan. Perhaps because the curious, such as you are, like to hear tales even stranger than their own, which in the days to be may become their own. Therefore you will be wise to believe only what I do, and of what I tell you, nothing."

"I don't," I exclaimed exasperated.

She laughed again and replied,

"What need to say to me that which I know already? Yet perhaps in the future it may be different, since often by the alchemy of the mind the fables of our youth are changed into the facts of our age, and we come to believe in anything, as your little yellow man believes in some savage named Zikali, and those Amahagger believe in the talisman round your neck, and I who am the maddest of you all, believe in Love and Wisdom, and the black warrior, Umslopogaas, believes in the virtue of that great axe of his, rather than in those of his own courage and of the strength that wields it. Fools, every one of us, though perchance I am the greatest fool among them. Now take me to the warrior, Umslopogaas, whom I would thank, as I thank you, Allan, and the little yellow man, although he jeers at me with his sharp tongue, not knowing that if I were angered, with a breath I could cause him to cease to be."

"Then why did you not choose Rezu to cease to be, and his army also, Ayesha?"

"It seems that I have done these things through the axe of Umslopogaas and by the help of your generalship, Allan. Why then, waste my own strength when yours lay to my hand?"

"Because you had no power over Rezu, Ayesha, or so you told me."

"Have I not said that my words are snowflakes, meant to melt and leave no trace, hiding my thoughts as this veil hides my beauty? Yet as the beauty is beneath the veil, perchance there is truth beneath the words, though not that truth you think. So you are well answered, and for the rest, I wonder whether Rezu thought I had no power over him when yonder on the mountain spur he saw me float down upon his companies like a spirit of the night. Well, perchance some day I shall learn this and many other things."

I made no answer, since what was the use of arguing with a woman who told me frankly that all she said was false. So, although I longed to ask her why these Amahagger had such reverence for the talisman that Hans called the Great Medicine, since now I guessed that her first explanations concerning it were quite untrue, I held my tongue.

Yet as we went out of the house, by some coincidence she alluded to this very matter.

"I wish to tell you, Allan," she said, "why it was those Amahagger would not accept you as a General till their eyes had seen that which you wear upon your breast. Their tale of a legend of this very thing seemed that of savages or of their cunning priests, not to be believed by a wise man such as you are, like some others that you have heard in Kôr. Yet it has in it a grain of truth, for as it chanced a little while ago, about a hundred years ago, I think, the old wizard whose picture is cut upon the wood, came to visit her who held my place before me as ruler of this tribe—she was very like me and as I believe, my mother, Allan—because of her repute for wisdom.

"At that time I have heard there was a question of war between the worshippers of Lulala and the grandfather of Rezu. But this Zikali told the People of Lulala that they must not fight the People of Rezu until in a day to come a white man should visit Kôr and bring with him a piece of wood on which was cut the image of a dwarf like to that of Zikali himself. Then and not before they must fight and conquer the People of Rezu. Now this story came down among them and you who may have thought the first tale magical, will understand it in its simplicity: is it not so, you wise Allan?"

"Oh! yes," I answered, "except that I do not see how Zikali can have come here a hundred years ago, since men do not live as long, although he pretends to have done so."

"No, Allan, nor do I, but perhaps it was his father, or his grandfather who came, since being observant, you will have noted that if the parent is mis-formed, so often are the descendants; also that the pretence of wizardry at times comes down with the blood."

Again I made no answer for I saw that Ayesha was fooling me, and before she could exhaust that amusement we reached the place where Umslopogaas and his men were gathered round a camp fire. He sat silent, but Goroko with much animation was telling the story of the fight in picturesque and colourful language, or that part of it which he had seen, for the benefit of the two wounded men who took no share in it and who, lying on their blankets with heads thrust forward, were listening with eagerness to the entrancing tale. Suddenly they caught sight of Ayesha, and those of the party who could stand sprang to their feet, while one and all they gave her the royal salute of *Bayéte*.

She waited till the sound had died away. Then she said,

"I come to thank you and your men, O Wielder of the Axe, who have shown yourself very great in battle, and to say to you that my Spirit tells me that every one of you, yes, even those who are still sick, will come safe to your own land again and live out your years with honour."

Again they saluted at this pleasing intelligence, when I had translated it to them, for of course they knew no Arabic. Then she went on,

"I am told, Umslopogaas, Son of the Lion, as a certain king was named in your land, that the fight you made against Rezu was a very great fight, and that such a leap as yours above his head when you smote him with the axe on the hinder parts where he wore no armour, and brought him to his death, has not been seen before, nor will be again."

I rendered the words, and Umslopogaas, preferring truth to modesty, replied emphatically that this was the case.

"Because of that fight and that leap," Ayesha went on, "as for other deeds that you have done and will do, my Spirit tells me that your name will live in story for many generations. Yet of what use is fame to the dead? Therefore I make you an offer. Bide here with me and you shall rule these Amahagger, and with them the remnant of the People of Rezu. Your cattle shall be countless and your wives the fairest in the land, and your children many, for I will lift a certain curse from off you so that no more shall you be childless. Do you accept, O Holder of the Axe?"

When he understood, Umslopogaas, after pondering a moment, asked if I meant to stay in this land and marry the white chieftainess who spoke such wise words and could appear and disappear in the battle at her will, and like a mountain-top hid her head in a cloud, which was his way of alluding to her veil.

I answered at once and with decision that I intended to do nothing of the sort and immediately regretted my words, since, although I spoke in Zulu, I suppose she read their meaning from my face. At any rate she understood the drift of them.

"Tell him, Allan," she said with a kind of icy politeness, "that you will not stop here and marry me, because if ever I chose a husband he would not be a little man at the doors of whose heart so many women's hands have knocked—yes, even those that are black—and not, I think, in vain. One, moreover, who holds himself so clever that he believes he has nothing left to learn, and in every flower of truth that is shown to him, however fair, smells only poison, and beneath, nurturing it, sees only the gross root of falsehood planted in corruption. Tell him these things, Allan, if it pleases you."

"It does not please me," I answered in a rage at her insults.

"Nor is it needful, Allan, since if I caught the meaning of that barbarous tongue you use aright, you have told him already. Well, let the jest pass, O man who least of all things desires to be Ayesha's husband, and whom Ayesha least of all things desires as her spouse, and ask the Axe-bearer nothing since I perceive that without you he will not stay at Kôr. Nor indeed is it fated that he should do so, for now my Spirit tells me what it hid from me when I spoke a moment gone, that this warrior shall die in a great fight far away and that between then and now much sorrow waits him who save that of one, knows not how to win the love of women. Let him say moreover what reward he desires since if I can give it to him, it shall be his."

Again I translated. Umslopogaas received her prophecies in stoical silence, and as I thought with indifference, and only said in reply,

"The glory that I have won is my reward and the only boon I seek at this queen's hands is that if she can she should give me sight of a woman for whom my heart is hungry, and with it knowledge that this woman lives in that land whither I travel like all men."

When she heard these words Ayesha said,

"True, I had forgotten. Your heart also is hungry, I think, Allan, for the vision of sundry faces that you see no more. Well, I will do my best, but since only faith fulfils itself, how can I who must strive to pierce the gates of darkness for one so unbelieving, know that they will open at my word? Come to me, both of you, at the sunset to-morrow."

Then as though to change the subject, she talked to me for a long while about Kôr, of which she told me a most interesting history, true or false, that I omit here.

At length, as though suddenly she had grown tired, waving her hand to show that the conversation was ended, Ayesha went to the wounded men and touched them each in turn.

"Now they will recover swiftly," she said, and leaving the place was gone into the darkness.

The Gate of Death

Before turning in I examined these wounded men for myself. The truth is that I was anxious to learn their exact condition in order that I might make an estimate as to when it would be possible for us to leave this valley or crater bottom of Kôr, of which I was heartily tired. Who could desire to stay in a place where he had not only been involved in a deal of hard, doubtful, and very dangerous fighting from which all personal interest was absent, but where also he was meshed in a perfect spider's web of bewilderment, and exposed to continual insult into the bargain?

For that is what it came to; this Ayesha took every opportunity to jeer at and affront me. And why? Just because I had conceived doubts, which somehow she discovered, of the amazing tales with which it had amused her to stuff me, as a farmer's wife does a turkey poult with meal pellets. How could she expect me, a man, after all, of some experience, to believe such lies, which, not half an hour before, in the coolest possible fashion she had herself admitted to be lies and nothing else, told for the mere pleasure of romancing?

The immortal Rezu, for instance, who had drunk of the Cup of Life or some such rubbish, now turned out to be nothing but a brawny savage descended from generations of chiefs also called Rezu. Moreover the immemorial Ayesha, who also had drunk of Cups of Life, and according to her first story, had lived in this place for thousands of years, had come here with a mother, who filled the same mystic rôle before her for the benefit of an extremely gloomy and disagreeable tribe of Semitic savages. Yet she was cross with me because I had not swallowed her crude and indigestible mixture of fable and philosophy without a moment's question.

At least I supposed that this was the reason, though another possible explanation did come into my mind. I had refused to be duly overcome by her charms, not because I was unimpressed, for who could be, having looked upon that blinding beauty even for a moment? but rather because, after sundry experiences, I had at last attained to some power of judgment and learned what it is best to leave alone. Perhaps this had annoyed her, especially as no white man seemed to have come her way for a long while and the fabulous Kallikrates had not put in his promised appearance.

Also it was unfortunate that in one way or another—how did she do it, I wondered—she had interpreted Umslopogaas' question to me about marrying her, and my compromising reply. Not that for one moment, as I saw very clearly, did she wish to marry me. But that fact, intuition suggested to my mind, did not the least prevent her from being angry because I shared her views upon this important subject.

Oh! the whole thing was a bore and the sooner I saw the last of that veiled lady and the interesting but wearisome ruins in which she dwelt, the better I should be pleased, although apparently I must trek homewards with a poor young woman who was out of her mind, leaving the bones of her unfortunate father behind me. I admitted to myself, however, that there were consolations in the fact that Providence had thus decreed, for Robertson since he gave up drink had not been a cheerful companion, and two mad people would really have been more than I could manage.

To return, for these reasons I examined the two wounded Zulus with considerable anxiety, only to discover another instance of the chicanery which it amused this Ayesha to play off upon me. For what did I find? That they were practically well. Their hurts, which had never been serious, had healed wonderfully in that pure air, as those of savages have a way of doing, and they told me themselves that they felt quite strong again. Yet with colossal impudence Ayesha had managed to suggest to my mind that she was going to work some remarkable cure upon them, who were already cured.

Well, it was of a piece with the rest of her conduct and there was nothing to do except go to bed, which I did with much gratitude that my resting place that night was not of another sort. The last thing I remember was wondering how on earth Ayesha appeared and disappeared in the course of that battle, a problem as to which I could find no solution, though, as in the case of the others, I was sure that one would occur to me in course of time.

I slept like a top, so soundly indeed that I think there was some kind of soporific in the pick-me-up which looked like sherry, especially as the others who had drunk of it also passed an excellent night.

About ten o'clock on the following morning I awoke feeling particularly well and quite as though I had been enjoying a week at the seaside instead of my recent adventures, which included an abominable battle and some agonising moments during which I thought that my number was up upon the board of Destiny.

I spent the most of that day lounging about, eating, talking over the details of the battle with Umslopogaas and the Zulus and smoking more than usual. (I forgot to say that these Amahagger grew some capital tobacco of which I had obtained a supply, although like most Africans, they only used it in the shape of snuff.) The truth was that after all my marvellings and acute anxieties, also mental and physical exertions, I felt like the housemaid who caused to be cut upon her tombstone that she had gone to a better land where her ambition was to do nothing "for ever and ever." I just wanted to be completely idle and vacuous-minded for at least a month, but as I knew that all I could expect in that line was a single bank holiday, like a City clerk on the spree, of it I determined to make the most.

The result was that before the evening I felt very bored indeed. I had gone to look at Inez, who was still fast asleep, as Ayesha said would be the case, but whose features seemed to have plumped up considerably. The reason of this I gathered from her Amahagger nurses, was that at certain intervals she had awakened sufficiently to swallow considerable quantities of milk, or rather cream, which I hoped would not make her ill. I had chatted with the wounded Zulus, who were now walking about, more bored even than I was myself, and heaping maledictions on their ancestral spirits because they had not been well enough to take part in the battle against Rezu.

I even took a little stroll to look for Hans, who had vanished in his mysterious fashion, but the afternoon was so hot and oppressive with coming thunder, that soon I came back again and fell into a variety of reflections that I need not detail.

While I was thus engaged and meditating, not without uneasiness, upon the ordeal that lay before me after sunset, for I felt sure that it would be an ordeal, Hans appeared and said that the Amahagger *impi* or army was gathered on that spot where I had been elected to the proud position of their General. He added that he believed—how he got this information I do not know—that the White Lady was going to hold a review of them and give them the rewards that they had earned in the battle.

Hearing this, Umslopogaas and the other Zulus said that they would like to see this review if I would accompany them. Although I did not want to go nor indeed desired ever to look at another Amahagger, I consented to save the trouble of argument, on condition that we should do so from a distance.

So, including the wounded men, we strolled off and presently came to the crumbled wall of the old city, beyond which lay the great moat now dry, that once had encircled it with water.

Here on the top of this wall we sat down where we could see without being seen, and observed the Amahagger companies, considerably reduced during the battle, being marshalled by their captains beneath us and about a couple of hundred yards away. Also we observed several groups of men under guard. These we took to be prisoners captured in the fight with Rezu, who, as Hans remarked with a smack of his lips, were probably awaiting sacrifice.

I said I hoped not and yawned, for really the afternoon was intensely hot and the weather most peculiar. The sun had vanished behind clouds, and vapours filled the still air, so dense that at times it grew almost dark; also when these cleared for brief intervals, the landscape in the grey, unholy light looked distorted and unnatural, as it does during an eclipse of the sun.

Goroko, the witch-doctor, stared round him, sniffed the air and then remarked ocularly that it was "wizard's weather" and that there were many spirits about. Upon my word I felt inclined to agree with him, for my feelings were very uncomfortable, but I only replied that if so, I should be obliged if he, as a professional, would be good enough to keep them off me. Of course I knew that electrical charges were about, which accounted for my sensations, and wished that I had never left the camp.

It was during one of these periods of dense gloom that Ayesha must have arrived upon the review ground. At least, when it lifted, there she was in her white garments, surrounded by women and guards, engaged apparently in making an oration, for although I could not hear a word, I could see by the motions of her arms that she was speaking.

Had she been the central figure in some stage scene, no limelights could have set her off to better advantage, than did those of the heavens above her. Suddenly, through the blanket of cloud, flowing from a hole in it that looked like an eye, came a blood-red ray which fell full upon her, so that she alone was fiercely visible whilst all around was gloom in which shapes moved dimly. Certainly she looked strange and even terrifying in that red ray which stained her robe till I who had but just come out of battle with its "confused noise," began to think of "the garments rolled in blood" of which I often read in my favourite Old Testament. For crimson was she from head to foot; a tall shape of terror and of wrath.

The eye in heaven shut and the ray went out. Then came one of the spaces of grey light and in it I saw men being brought up, apparently from the groups of prisoners, under guard, and, to the number of a dozen or more, stood in a line before Ayesha.

Then I saw nothing more for a long while, because blackness seemed to flow in from every quarter of the heavens and to block out the scene beneath. At least after a pause of perhaps five minutes, during which the stillness was intense, the storm broke.

It was a very curious storm; in all my experience of African tempests I cannot recall one which it resembled. It began with the usual cold and wailing wind. This died away, and suddenly the whole arch of heaven was alive with little lightnings that seemed to strike horizontally, not downwards to the earth, weaving a web of fire upon the surface of the sky.

By the illumination of these lightnings which, but for the swiftness of their flashing and greater intensity, somewhat resembled a dense shower of shooting stars, I perceived that Ayesha was addressing the men that had been brought before her, who stood dejectedly in a long line with their heads bent, quite unattended, since their guards had fallen back.

"If I were going to receive a reward of cattle or wives, I should look happier than those moon-worshippers, Baas," remarked Hans reflectively.

"Perhaps it would depend," I answered, "upon what the cattle and wives were like. If the cattle had red-water and would bring disease into your herd, or wild bulls that would gore you, and the wives were skinny old widows with evil tongues, then I think you would look as do those men, Hans."

I don't quite know what made me speak thus, but I believe it was some sense of pending death or disaster, suggested, probably, by the ominous character of the setting provided by Nature to the curious drama of which we were witnesses.

"I never thought of that, Baas," commented Hans, "but it is true that all gifts are not good, especially witches' gifts."

As he spoke the little net-like lightnings died away, leaving behind them a gross darkness through which, far above us, the wind wailed again.

Then suddenly all the heaven was turned into one blaze of light, and by it I saw Ayesha standing tall and rigid with her hand pointed towards the line of men in front of her. The blaze went out, to be followed by blackness, and to return almost instantly in a yet fiercer blaze which seemed to fall earthwards in a torrent of fire that concentrated itself in a kind of flame-spout upon the spot where Ayesha stood.

Through that flame or rather in the heart of it, I saw Ayesha and the file of men in front of her, as the great King saw the prophets in the midst of the furnace that had been heated sevenfold. Only these men did not walk about in the fire; no, they fell backwards, while Ayesha alone remained upon her feet with outstretched hand.

Next came more blackness and crash upon crash of such thunder that the earth shook as it reverberated from the mountain cliffs. Never in my life did I hear such fearful thunder. It frightened the Zulus so much, that they fell upon their faces, except Goroko and Umslopogaas, whose pride kept them upon their feet, the former because he had a reputation to preserve as a "Heaven-herd," or Master of tempests.

I confess that I should have liked to follow their example, and lie down, being dreadfully afraid lest the lightning should strike me. But there—I did not.

At last the thunder died away and in the most mysterious fashion that violent tempest came to a sudden end, as does a storm upon the stage. No rain fell, which in itself was surprising enough and most unusual, but in place of it a garment of the completest calm descended upon the earth. By degrees, too, the darkness passed and the westering sun reappeared. Its rays fell upon the place where the Amahagger companies had stood, but now not one of them was to be seen.

They were all gone and Ayesha with them. So completely had they vanished away that I should have thought that we suffered from illusions, were it not for the line of dead men which lay there looking very small and lonesome on the veld; mere dots indeed at that distance.

We stared at each other and at them, and then Goroko said that he would like to inspect the bodies to learn whether lightning killed at Kôr as it did elsewhere, also whether it had smitten them altogether or leapt from man to man. This, as a professional "Heaven-herd," he declared he could tell from the marks upon these unfortunates.

As I was curious also and wanted to make a few observations, I consented. So with the exception of the wounded men, who I thought should avoid the exertion, we scrambled down the débris of the tumbled wall and across the open space beyond, reaching the scene of the tragedy without meeting or seeing anyone.

There lay the dead, eleven of them, in an exact line as they had stood. They were all upon their backs with widely-opened eyes and an expression of great fear frozen upon their faces. Some of these I recognised, as did Umslopogaas and Hans. They were soldiers or captains who had marched under me to attack Rezu, although until this moment I had not seen any of them after we began to descend the ridge where the battle took place.

"Baas," said Hans, "I believe that these were the traitors who slipped away and told Rezu of our plans so that he attacked us on the ridge, instead of our attacking him on the plain as we had arranged so nicely. At least they were none of them in the battle and afterwards I heard the Amahagger talking of some of them."

I remarked that if so the lightning had discriminated very well in this instance.

Meanwhile Goroko was examining the bodies one by one, and presently called out,

"These doomed ones died not by lightning but by witchcraft. There is not a burn upon one of them, nor are their garments scorched."

I went to look and found that it was perfectly true; to all outward appearance the eleven were quite unmarked and unharmed. Except for their frightened air, they might have died a natural death in their sleep.

"Does lightning always scorch?" I asked Goroko.

"Always, Macumazahn," he answered, "that is, if he who has been struck is killed, as these are, and not only stunned. Moreover, most of yonder dead wear knives which should have melted or shattered with the sheaths burnt off them. Yet those knives are as though they had just left the smith's hammer and the whet-stone," and he drew some of them to show me.

Again it was quite true and here I may remark that my experience tallied with that of Goroko, since I have never seen anyone killed by lightning on whom or on whose clothing there was not some trace of its passage.

"*Ow!*" said Umslopogaas, "this is witchcraft, not Heaven-wrath. The place is enchanted. Let us get away lest we be smitten also who have not earned doom like those traitors."

"No need to fear," said Hans, "since with us is the Great Medicine of Zikali which can tie up the lightning as an old woman does a bundle of sticks."

Still I observed that for all his confidence, Hans himself was the first to depart and with considerable speed. So we went back to our camp without more conversation, since the Zulus were scared and I confess that myself I could not understand the matter, though no doubt it admitted of some quite simple explanation.

However that might be, this Kôr was a queer place with its legends, its sullen Amahagger and its mysterious queen, to whom at times, in spite of my inner conviction to the contrary, I was still inclined to attribute powers beyond those that are common even among very beautiful and able women.

This reflection reminded me that she had promised us a further exhibition of those powers and within an hour or two. Remembering this I began to regret that I had ever asked for any such manifestations, for who knew what these might or might not involve?

So much did I regret it that I determined, unless Ayesha sent for us, as she had said she would do, I would conveniently forget the appointment. Luckily Umslopogaas seemed to be of the same way of thinking; at any rate he went off to eat his evening meal without alluding to it at all. So I made up my mind that I would not bring the matter to his notice and having ascertained that Inez was still asleep, I followed his example and dined myself, though without any particular appetite.

As I finished the sun was setting in a perfectly clear sky, so as there was no sign of any messenger, I thought that I would go to bed early, leaving orders that I was not to be disturbed. But on this point my luck was lacking, for just as I had taken off my coat, Hans arrived and said that old Billali was without and had come to take me somewhere.

Well, there was nothing to do but to put it on again. Before I had finished this operation Billali himself arrived with undignified and unusual haste. I asked him what was the matter, and he answered inconsequently that the Black One, the slayer of Rezu, was at the door "with his axe."

"That generally accompanies him," I replied. Then, remembering the cause of Billali's alarm, I explained to him that he must not take too much notice of a few hasty words spoken by an essentially gentle- natured person whose nerve had given way beneath provocation and bodily effort. The old fellow bowed in assent and stroked his beard, but I noticed that while Umslopogaas was near, he clung to me like a shadow. Perhaps he thought that nervous attacks might be recurrent, like those of fever.

Outside the house I found Umslopogaas leaning on his axe and looking at the sky in which the last red rays of evening lingered.

"The sun has set, Macumazahn," he said, "and it is time to visit this white queen as she bade us, and to learn whether she can indeed lead us 'down below' where the dead are said to dwell."

So he had not forgotten, which was disconcerting. To cover up my own doubts I asked him with affected confidence and cheerfulness whether he was not afraid to risk this journey "down below," that is, to the Realm of Death.

"Why should I fear to tread a road that awaits the feet of all of us and at the gate of which we knock day by day, especially if we chance to live by war, as do you and I, Macumazahn?" he inquired with a quiet dignity, which made me feel ashamed.

"Why indeed?" I answered, adding to myself, "though I should much prefer any other highway."

After this we started without more words, I keeping up my spirits by reflecting that the whole business was nonsense and that there could be nothing to dread.

All too soon we passed the ruined archway and were admitted into Ayesha's presence in the usual fashion. As Billali, who remained outside of them, drew the curtains behind us, I observed, to my astonishment, that Hans had sneaked in after me, and squatted down quite close to them, apparently in the hope of being overlooked.

It seemed, as I gathered later, that somehow or other he had guessed, or become aware of the object of our visit, and that his burning curiosity had overcome his terror of the "White Witch." Or possibly he hoped to discover whether or not she were so ugly as he supposed her veil-hidden face to be. At any rate there he was, and if Ayesha noticed him, as I think she did, for I saw by the motion of her head, that she was looking in his direction, she made no remark.

For a while she sat still in her chair contemplating us both. Then she said,

"How comes it that you are late? Those that seek their lost loves should run with eager feet, but yours have tarried."

I muttered some excuse to which she did not trouble to listen, for she went on,

"I think, Allan, that your sandals, which should be winged like to those of the Roman Mercury, are weighted with the grey lead of fear. Well, it is not strange, since you have come to travel through the Gates of Death that are feared by all, even by Ayesha's self, for who knows what he may find beyond them? Ask the Axe-Bearer if he also is afraid."

I obeyed, rendering all that she had said into the Zulu idiom as best I could.

"Say to the Queen," answered Umslopogaas, when he understood, "that I fear nothing, except women's tongues. I am ready to pass the Gates of Death and, if need be, to come back no more. With the white people I know it is otherwise because of some dark teachings to which they listen, that tell of terrors to be, such as we who are black do not dread. Still, we believe that there are ghosts and that the spirits of our fathers live on and as it chances I would learn whether this is so, who above all things desire to met a certain ghost, for which reason I journeyed to this far land.

"Say these things to the white Queen, Macumazahn, and tell her that if she should send me to a place whence there is no return, I who do not love the world, shall not blame her overmuch, though it is true that I should have chosen to die in war. Now I have spoken."

When I had passed on all this speech to Ayesha, her comment on it was,

"This black Captain has a spirit as brave as his body, but how is it with your spirit, Allan? Are you also prepared to risk so much? Learn that I can promise you nothing, save that when I loose the bonds of your mortality and send out your soul to wander in the depths of Death, as I believe that I can do, though even of this I am not certain—you must pass through a gate of terrors that may be closed behind you by a stronger arm than mine. Moreover, what you will find beyond it I do not know, since be sure of this, each of us has his own heaven or his own hell, or both, that soon or late he is doomed to travel. Now will you go forward, or go back? Make choice while there is still time."

At all this ominous talk I felt my heart shrivel like a fire-withered leaf, if I may use that figure, and my blood assume the temperature and consistency of ice-cream.

Earnestly did I curse myself for having allowed my curiosity about matters which we are not meant to understand to bring me to the edge of such a choice. Swiftly I determined to temporise, which I did by asking Ayesha whether she would accompany me upon this eerie expedition.

She laughed a little as she answered,

"Bethink you, Allan. Am I, whose face you have seen, a meet companion for a man who desires to visit the loves that once were his? What would they say or think, if they should see you hand in hand with such a one?"

"I don't know and don't care," I replied desperately, "but this is the kind of journey on which one requires a guide who knows the road. Cannot Umslopogaas go first and come back to tell me how it has fared with him?"

"If the brave and instructed white lord, panoplied in the world's last Faith, is not ashamed to throw the savage in his ignorance out like a feather to test the winds of hell and watch the while to learn whether these blow him back unscorched, or waft him into fires whence there is no return, perchance it might so be ordered, Allan. Ask him yourself, Allan, if he is willing to run this errand for your sake. Or perhaps the little yellow man——" and she paused.

At this point Hans, who having a smattering of Arabic understood something of our talk, could contain himself no longer.

"No, Baas," he broke in from his corner by the curtain, "not *me*. I don't care for hunting spooks, Baas, which leave no spoor that you can follow and are always behind when you think they are in front. Also there are too many of them waiting for me down there and how can I stand up to them until I am a spook myself and know their ways of fighting? Also if you should die when your spirit is away, I want to be left that I may bury you nicely."

"Be silent," I said in my sternest manner. Then, unable to bear more of Ayesha's mockery, for I felt that as usual she was mocking me, I added with all the dignity that I could command,

"I am ready to make this journey through the gate of Death, Ayesha, if indeed you can show me the road. For one purpose and no other I came to Kôr, namely to learn, if so I might, whether those who have died upon the world, live on elsewhere. Now, what must I do?"

The Lesson

"Yes," answered Ayesha, laughing very softly, "for that purpose alone, O truth-seeking Allan, whose curiosity is so fierce that the wide world cannot hold it, did you come to Kôr and not to seek wealth or new lands, or to fight more savages. No, not even to look upon a certain Ayesha, of whom the old wizard told you, though I think you have always loved to try to lift the veil that hides women's hearts, if not their faces. Yet it was I who brought you to Kôr for my own purposes, not your desire, nor Zikali's map and talisman, since had not the white lady who lies sick been stolen by Rezu, never would you have pursued the journey nor found the way hither."

"How could you have had anything to do with that business?" I asked testily, for my nerves were on edge and I said the first thing that came into my mind.

"That, Allan, is a question over which you will wonder for a long while either beneath or beyond the sun, as you will wonder concerning much that has to do with me, which your little mind, shut in its iron box of ignorance and pride, cannot understand to-day.

"For example, you have been wondering, I am sure, how the lightning killed those eleven men whose bodies you went to look on an hour or two ago, and left the rest untouched. Well, I will tell you at once that it was not lightning that killed them, although the strength within me was manifest to you in storm, but rather what that witch- doctor of your following called wizardry. Because they were traitors who betrayed your army to Rezu, I killed them with my wrath and by the wand of my power. Oh! you do not believe, yet perhaps ere long you will, since thus to fulfil your prayer I must also kill you—almost. That is the trouble, Allan. To kill you outright would be easy, but to kill you just enough to set your spirit free and yet leave one crevice of mortal life through which it can creep back again, that is most difficult; a thing that only I can do and even of myself I am not sure."

"Pray do not try the experiment——" I began thoroughly alarmed, but she cut me short.

"Disturb me no more, Allan, with the tremors and changes of your uncertain mind, lest you should work more evil than you think, and making mine uncertain also, spoil my skill. Nay, do not try to fly, for already the net has thrown itself about you and you cannot stir, who are bound like a little gilded wasp in the spider's web, or like birds beneath the eyes of basilisks."

This was true, for I found that, strive as I would, I could not move a limb or even an eyelid. I was frozen to that spot and there was nothing for it except to curse my folly and say my prayers.

All this while she went on talking, but of what she said I have not the faintest idea, because my remaining wits were absorbed in these much-needed implorations.

Presently, of a sudden, I appeared to see Ayesha seated in a temple, for there were columns about her, and behind her was an altar on which a fire burned. All round her, too, were hooded snakes like to that which she wore about her middle, fashioned in gold. To these snakes she sang and they danced to her singing; yes, with flickering tongues they danced upon their tails! What the scene signified I cannot conceive, unless it meant that this mistress of magic was consulting her familiars.

Then that vision vanished and Ayesha's voice began to seem very far away and dreamy, also her wondrous beauty became visible to me through her veil, as though I had acquired a new sense that overcame the limitations of mortal sight. Even in this extremity I reflected it was well that the last thing I looked on should be something so glorious. No, not quite the last thing, for out of the corners of my eyes I saw that Umslopogaas from a sitting position had sunk on to his back and lay, apparently dead, with his axe still gripped tightly and held above his head, as though his arm had been turned to ice.

After this terrible things began to happen to me and I became aware that I was dying. A great wind seemed to catch me up and blow me to and fro, as a leaf is blown in the eddies of a winter gale. Enormous rushes of darkness flowed over me, to be succeeded by vivid bursts of brightness that dazzled like lightning. I fell off precipices and at the foot of them was caught by some fearful strength and tossed to the very skies.

From those skies I was hurled down again into a kind of whirlpool of inky night, round which I spun perpetually, as it seemed for hours and hours. But worst of all was the awful loneliness from which I suffered. It seemed to me as though there were no other living thing in all the Universe and never had been and never would be any other living thing. I felt as though *I* were the Universe rushing solitary through space for ages upon ages in a frantic search for fellowship, and finding none.

Then something seemed to grip my throat and I knew that I had died— for the world floated away from beneath me.

Now fear and every mortal sensation left me, to be replaced by a new and spiritual terror. I, or rather my disembodied consciousness, seemed to come up for judgment, and the horror of it was that I appeared to be my own judge. There, a very embodiment of cold justice, my Spirit, grown luminous, sat upon a throne and to it, with dread and merciless particularity I set out all my misdeeds. It was as if some part of me remained mortal, for I could see my two eyes, my mouth and my hands, but nothing else—and strange enough they looked. From the eyes came tears, from the mouth flowed words and the hands were joined, as though in prayer to that throned and adamantine Spirit which was ME.

It was as though this Spirit were asking how my body had served its purposes and advanced its mighty ends, and in reply—oh! what a miserable tale I had to tell. Fault upon fault, weakness upon weakness, sin upon sin; never before did I understand how black was my record. I tried to relieve the picture with some incidents of attempted good, but that Spirit would not hearken. It seemed to say that it had gathered up the good and knew it all. It was of the evil that it would learn, not of the good that had bettered it, but of the evil by which it had been harmed.

Hearing this there rose up in my consciousness some memory of what Ayesha had said; namely, that the body lived within the temple of the spirit which is oft defied, and not the spirit in the body.

The story was told and I hearkened for the judgment, my own judgment on myself, which I knew would be accepted without question and registered for good or ill. But none came, since ere the balance sank this way or that, ere it could be uttered, I was swept afar.

Through Infinity I was swept, and as I fled faster than the light, the meaning of what I had seen came home to me. I knew, or seemed to know for the first time, that at the last *man must answer to himself*, or perhaps to a divine principle within himself, that out of his own free-will, through long æons and by a million steps, he climbs or sinks to the heights or depths dormant in his nature; that from what he was, springs what he is, and what he is, engenders what he shall be for ever and aye.

Now I envisaged Immortality and splendid and awful was its face. It clasped me to its breast and in the vast circle of its arms I was up- borne, I who knew myself to be without beginning and without end, and yet of the past and of the future knew nothing, save that these were full of mysteries.

As I went I encountered others, or overtook them, making the same journey. Robertson swept past me, and spoke, but in a tongue I could not understand. I noted that the madness had left his eyes and that his fine-cut features were calm and spiritual. The other wanderers I did not know.

I came to a region of blinding light; the thought rose in me that I must have reached the sun, or a sun, though I felt no heat. I stood in a lovely, shining valley about which burned mountains of fire. There were huge trees in that valley, but they glowed like gold and their flowers and fruit were as though they had been fashioned of many-coloured flames.

The place was glorious beyond compare, but very strange to me and not to be described. I sat me down upon a boulder which burned like a ruby, whether with heat or colour I do not know, by the edge of a stream that flowed with what looked like fire and made a lovely music. I stooped down and drank of this water of flames and the scent and the taste of it were as those of the costliest wine.

There, beneath the spreading limbs of a fire-tree I sat, and examined the strange flowers that grew around, coloured like rich jewels and perfumed above imagining. There were birds also which might have been feathered with sapphires, rubies and amethysts, and their song was so sweet that I could have wept to hear it. The scene was wonderful and filled me with exaltation, for I thought of the land where it is promised that there shall be no more night.

People began to appear; men, women, and even children, though whence they came I could not see. They did not fly and they did not walk; they seemed to drift towards me, as unguided boats drift upon the tide. One and all they were very beautiful, but their beauty was not human although their shapes and faces resembled those of men and women made glorious. None were old, and except the children, none seemed very young; it was as though they had grown backwards or forwards to middle life and rested there at their very best.

Now came the marvel; all these uncounted people were known to me, though so far as my knowledge went I had never set eyes on most of them before. Yet I was aware that in some forgotten life or epoch I had been intimate with every one of them; also that it was the fact of my presence and the call of my sub-conscious mind which drew them to this spot. Yet that presence and that call were not visible or audible to them, who, I suppose, flowed down some stream of sympathy, why or whither they did not know. Had I been as they were perchance they would have seen me, as it was they saw nothing and I could not speak and tell them of my presence.

Some of this multitude, however, I knew well enough even when they had departed years and years ago. But about these I noted this, that every one of them was a man or a woman or a child for whom I had felt love or sympathy or friendship. Not one was a person whom I had disliked or whom I had no wish to see again. If they spoke at all I could not hear —or read—their speech, yet to a certain extent I could hear their thoughts.

Many of these were beyond the power of my appreciation on subjects which I had no knowledge, or that were too high for me, but some were of quite simple things such as concern us upon the earth, such as of friendship, or learning, or journeys made or to be made, or art, or literature, or the wonders of Nature, or of the fruits of the earth, as they knew them in this region.

This I noted too, that each separate thought seemed to be hallowed and enclosed in an atmosphere of prayer or heavenly aspiration, as a seed is enclosed in the heart of a flower, or a fruit in its odorous rind, and that this prayer or aspiration presently appeared to bear the thought away, whither I knew not. Moreover, all these thoughts, even of the humblest things, were beauteous and spiritual, nothing cruel or impure or even coarse was to be found among them: they radiated charity, purity and goodness.

Among them I perceived were none that had to do with our earth; this and its affairs seemed to be left far behind these thinkers, a truth that chilled my soul was alien to their company. Worse still, so far as I could discover, although I knew that all these bright ones had been near to me at some hour in the measurements of time and space, not one of their musings dwelt upon me or on aught with which I had to do.

Between me and them there was a great gulf fixed and a high wall built.

Oh, look! One came shining like a star, and from far away came another with dove-like eyes and beautiful exceedingly, and with this last a maiden, whose eyes were as hers who my own heart told me was her mother.

Well, I knew them both; they were those whom I had come to seek, the women who had been mind upon the earth, and at the sight of them my spirit thrilled. Surely they would discover me. Surely at least they would speak of me and feel my presence.

But, although they stayed within a pace or two of where I rested, alas! it was not so. They seemed to kiss and to exchange swift thoughts about many things, high things of which I will not write, and common things; yes, even of the shining robes they wore, but never a one of *me!* I strove to rise and go to them, but could not; I strove to speak and could not; I strove to throw out my thought to them and could not; it fell back upon my head like a stone hurled heavenward.

They were remote from me, utterly apart. I wept tears of bitterness that I should be so near and yet so far; a dull and jealous rage burned in my heart, and this they did seem to feel, or so I fancied; at any rate, apparently by mutual consent, they moved further from me as though something pained them. Yes, my love could not reach their perfected natures, but my anger hurt them.

As I sat chewing this root of bitterness, a man appeared, a very noble man, in whom I recognised my father grown younger and happier-looking, but still my father, with whom came others, men and women whom I knew to be my brothers and sisters who had died in youth far away in Oxfordshire. Joy leapt up in me, for I thought—these will surely know me and give me welcome, since, though here sex has lost its power, blood must still call to blood.

But it was not so. They spoke, or interchanged their thoughts, but not one of me. I read something that passed from my father to them. It was a speculation as to what had brought them all together there, and read also the answer hazarded, that perhaps it might be to give welcome to some unknown who was drawing near from below and would feel lonely and unfriended. Thereon my father replied that he did not see or feel this wanderer, and thought that it could not be so, since it was his mission to greet such on their coming.

Then in an instant all were gone and that lovely, glowing plain was empty, save for myself seated on the ruby-like stone, weeping tears of blood and shame and loss within my soul.

So I sat a long while, till presently I was aware of a new presence, a presence dusky and splendid and arrayed in rich barbaric robes. Straight she came towards me, like a thrown spear, and I knew her for a certain royal and savage woman who on earth was named Mameena, or "Wind-that-wailed." Moreover she divined me, though see me she could not.

"Art there, Watcher-in-the-Night, watching in the light?" she said or thought, I know not which, but the words came to me in the Zulu tongue.

"Aye," she went on, "I know that thou art there; from ten thousand leagues away I felt thy presence and broke from my own place to welcome thee, though I must pay for it with burning chains and bondage. How did those welcome thee whom thou camest out to seek? Did they clasp thee in their arms and press their kisses on thy brow? Or did they shrink away from thee because the smell of earth was on thy hands and lips?"

I seemed to answer that they did not appear to know that I was there.

"Aye, they did not know because their love is not enough, because they have grown too fine for love. But I, the sinner, I knew well, and here am I ready to suffer all for thee and to give thee place within this stormy heart of mine. Forget them, then, and come to rule with me who still am queen in my own house that thou shalt share. There we will live royally and when our hour comes, at least we shall have had our day."

Now before I could reply, some power seemed to seize this splendid creature and whirl her thence so that she departed, flashing these words from her mind to mine,

"For a little while farewell, but remember always that Mameena, the Wailing Wind, being still as a sinful woman in a woman's love and of the earth, earthy, found thee, whom all the rest forgot. O Watcher-in-the-Night, watch in the night for me, for there thou shalt find me, the Child of Storm, again, and yet again."

She was gone and once more I sat in utter solitude upon that ruby stone, staring at the jewelled flowers and the glorious flaming trees and the lambent waters of the brook. What was the meaning of it all, I wondered, and why was I deserted by everyone save a single savage woman, and why had she a power to find me which was denied to all the rest? Well, she had given me an answer, because she was "as a sinful woman with a woman's love and of the earth, earthy," while with the rest it was otherwise. Oh! this was clear, that in the heavens man has no friend among the heavenly, save perhaps the greatest Friend of all Who understands both flesh and spirit.

Thus I mused in this burning world which was still so beautiful, this alien world into which I had thrust myself unwanted and unsought. And while I mused this happened. The fiery waters of the stream were disturbed by something and looking up I saw the cause.

A dog had plunged into them and was swimming towards me. At a glance I knew that dog on which my eyes had not fallen for decades. It was a mongrel, half spaniel and half bull-terrier, which for years had been the dear friend of my youth and died at last on the horns of a wounded wildebeeste that attacked me when I had fallen from my horse upon the veld. Boldly it tackled the maddened buck, thus giving me time to scramble to my rifle and shoot it, but not before the poor hound had yielded its life for mine, since presently it died disembowelled, but licking my hand and forgetful of its agonies. This dog, Smut by name, it was that swam or seemed to swim the brook of fire. It scrambled to the hither shore, it nosed the earth and ran to the ruby stone and stared about it whining and sniffing.

At last it seemed to see or feel me, for it stood upon its hind legs and licked my face, yelping with mad joy, as I could see though I heard nothing. Now I wept in earnest and bent down to hug and kiss the faithful beast, but this I could not do, since like myself it was only shadow.

Then suddenly all dissolved in a cataract of many-coloured flames and I fell down into an infinite gulf of blackness.

Surely Ayesha was talking to me! What did she say? What did she say? I could not catch her words, but I caught her laughter and knew that after her fashion she was making a mock of me. My eyelids were dragged down as though with heavy sleep; it was difficult to lift them. At last they were open and I saw Ayesha seated on her couch before me and —this I noted at once—with her lovely face unveiled. I looked about me, seeking Umslopogaas and Hans. But they were gone as I guessed they must be, since otherwise Ayesha would not have been unveiled. We were quite alone. She was addressing me and in a new fashion, since now she had abandoned the formal "you" and was using the more impressive and intimate "thou," much as is the manner of the French.

"Thou hast made thy journey, Allan," she said, "and what thou hast seen there thou shalt tell me presently. Yet from thy mien I gather this—that thou art glad to look upon flesh and blood again and, after the company of spirits, to find that of mortal woman. Come then and sit beside me and tell thy tale."

"Where are the others?" I asked as I rose slowly to obey, for my head swam and my feet seemed feeble.

"Gone, Allan, who as I think have had enough of ghosts, which is perhaps thy case also. Come, drink this and be a man once more. Drink it to me whose skill and power have brought thee safe from lands that human feet were never meant to tread," and taking a strange-shaped cup from a stool that stood beside her, she offered it to me.

I drank to the last drop, neither knowing nor caring whether it were wine or poison, since my heart seemed desperate at its failure and my spirit crushed beneath the weight of its great betrayal. I suppose it was the former, for the contents of that cup ran through my veins like fire and gave me back my courage and the joy of life.

I stepped to the dais and sat me down upon the couch, leaning against its rounded end so that I was almost face to face with Ayesha who had turned towards me, and thence could study her unveiled loveliness. For a while she said nothing, only eyed me up and down and smiled and smiled, as though she were waiting for that wine to do its work with me.

"Now that thou art a man again, Allan, tell me what thou didst see when thou wast more—or less—than man."

So I told her all, for some power within her seemed to draw the truth out of me. Nor did the tale appear to cause her much surprise.

"There is truth in thy dream," she said when I had finished; "a lesson also."

"Then it was all a dream?" I interrupted.

"Is not everything a dream, even life itself, Allan? If so, what can this be that thou hast seen, but a dream within a dream, and itself containing other dreams, as in the old days the ball fashioned by the eastern workers of ivory would oft be found to contain another ball, and this yet another and another and another, till at the inmost might be found a bead of gold, or perchance a jewel, which was the prize of him who could draw out ball from ball and leave them all unbroken. That search was difficult and rarely was the jewel come by, if at all, so that some said there was none, save in the maker's mind. Yes, I have seen a man go crazed with seeking and die with the mystery unsolved. How much harder, then, is it to come at the diamond of Truth which lies at the core of all our nest of dreams and without which to rest upon they could not be fashioned to seem realities?"

"But was it really a dream, and if so, what were the truth and the lesson?" I asked, determined not to allow her to bemuse or escape me with her metaphysical talk and illustrations.

"The first question has been answered, Allan, as well as I can answer, who am not the architect of this great globe of dreams, and as yet cannot clearly see the ineffable gem within, whose prisoned rays illuminate their substance, though so dimly that only those with the insight of a god can catch their glamour in the night of thought, since to most they are dark as glow-flies in the glare of noon."

"Then what are the truth and the lesson?" I persisted, perceiving that it was hopeless to extract from her an opinion as to the real nature of my experiences and that I must content myself with her deductions from them.

"Thou tellest me, Allan, that in thy dream or vision thou didst seem to appear before thyself seated on a throne and in that self to find thy judge. That is the Truth whereof I spoke, though how it found its way through the black and ignorant shell of one whose wit is so small, is more than I can guess, since I believed that it was revealed to me alone."

(Now I, Allan, thought to myself that I began to see the origin of all these fantasies and that for once Ayesha had made a slip. If she had a theory and I developed that same theory in a hypnotic condition, it was not difficult to guess its fount. However, I kept my mouth shut, and luckily for once she did not seem to read my mind, perhaps because she was too much occupied in spinning her smooth web of entangling words.)

"All men worship their own god," she went on, "and yet seem not to know that this god dwells within them and that of him they are a part. There he dwells and there they mould him to their own fashion, as the potter moulds his clay, though whatever the shape he seems to take beneath their fingers, still he remains the god infinite and unalterable. Still he is the Seeker and the Sought, the Prayer and its Fulfilment, the Love and the Hate, the Virtue and the Vice, since all these qualities the alchemy of his spirit turns into an ultimate and eternal Good. For the god is in all things and all things are in the god, whom men clothe with such diverse garments and whose countenance they hide beneath so many masks.

"In the tree flows the sap, yet what knows the great tree it nurtures of the sap? In the world's womb burns the fire that gives life, yet what of the fire knows the glorious earth it conceived and will destroy; in the heavens the great globes swing through space and rest not, yet what know they of the Strength that sent them spinning and in a time to come will stay their mighty motions, or turn them to another course? Therefore of everything this all-present god is judge, or rather, not one but many judges, since of each living creature he makes its own magistrate to deal out justice according to that creature's law which in the beginning the god established for it and decreed. Thus in the breast of everyone there is a rule and by that rule, at work through a countless chain of lives, in the end he shall be lifted up to Heaven, or bound about and cast down to Hell and death."

"You mean a conscience," I suggested rather feebly, for her thoughts and images overpowered me.

"Aye, a conscience, if thou wilt, and canst only understand that term, though it fits my theme but ill. This is my meaning, that consciences, as thou namest them, are many. I have one; thou, Allan, hast another; that black Axe-bearer has a third; the little yellow man a fourth, and so on through the tale of living things. For even a dog such as thou sawest has a conscience and—like thyself or I—must in the end be its own judge, because of the spark that comes to it from above, the same spark which in me burns as a great fire, and in thee as a smouldering ember of green wood."

"When *you* sit in judgment on yourself in a day to come, Ayesha," I could not help interpolating, "I trust that you will remember that humility did not shine among your virtues."

She smiled in her vivid way—only twice or thrice did I see her smile thus and then it was like a flash of summer lightning illumining a clouded sky, since for the most part her face was grave and even sombre.

"Well answered," she said. "Goad the patient ox enough and even it will grow fierce and paw the ground.

"Humility! What have I to do with it, O Allan? Let humility be the part of the humble-souled and lowly, but for those who reign as I do, and they are few indeed, let there be pride and the glory they have earned. Now I have told thee of the Truth thou sawest in thy vision and wouldst thou hear the Lesson?"

"Yes," I answered, "since I may as well be done with it at once, and doubtless it will be good for me."

"The Lesson, Allan, is one which thou preachest—humility. Vain man and foolish as thou art, thou didst desire to travel the Underworld in search of certain ones who once were all in all to thee—nay, not all in all since of them there were two or more—but at least much. Thus thou wouldst do because, as thou saidest, thou didst seek to know whether they still lived on beyond the gates of Blackness. Yes, thou saidest this, but what thou didst hope to learn in truth was whether they lived on in *thee* and for *thee* only. For thou, thou in thy vanity, didst picture these departed souls as doing naught in that Heaven they had won, save think of thee still burrowing on the earth, and, at times lightening thy labours with kisses from other lips than theirs."

"Never!" I exclaimed indignantly. "Never! it is not true."

"Then I pray pardon, Allan, who only judged of thee by others that were as men are made, and being such, not to be blamed if perchance from time to time, they turned to look on women, who alas! were as they are made. So at least it was when I knew the world, but mayhap since then its richest wine has turned to water, whereby I hope it has been bettered. At the least this was thy thought, that those women who had been thine for an hour, through all eternity could dream of naught else save thy perfections, and hope for naught else than to see thee at their sides through that eternity, or such part of thee as thou couldst spare to each of them. For thou didst forget that where they have gone there may be others even more peerless than thou art and more fit to hold a woman's love, which as we know on earth was ever changeful, and perhaps may so remain where it is certain that new lights must shine and new desires beckon. Dost understand me, Allan?"

"I think so," I answered with a groan. "I understand you to mean that worldly impressions soon wear out and that people who have departed to other spheres may there form new ties and forget the old."

"Yes, Allan, as do those who remain upon this earth, whence these others have departed. Do men and women still re-marry in the world, Allan, as in my day they were wont to do?"

"Of course—it is allowed."

"As many other things, or perchance this same thing, may be allowed elsewhere, for when there are so many habitations from which to choose, why should we always dwell in one of them, however strait the house or poor the prospect?"

Now understanding that I was symbolised by the "strait house" and the "poor prospect" I should have grown angry, had not a certain sense of humour come to my rescue, who remembered that after all Ayesha's satire was profoundly true. Why, beyond the earth, should anyone desire to remain unalterably tied to and inextricably wrapped up in such a personality as my own, especially if others of superior texture abounded about them? Now that I came to think of it, the thing was absurd and not to be the least expected in the midst of a thousand new and vivid interests. I had met with one more disillusionment, that was all.

"Dost understand, Allan," went on Ayesha, who evidently was determined that I should drink this cup to the last drop, "that these dwellers in the sun, or the far planet where thou hast been according to thy tale, saw thee not and knew naught of thee? It may chance therefore that at this time thou wast not in their minds which at others dream of thee continually. Or it may chance that they never dream of thee at all, having quite forgotten thee, as the weaned cub forgets its mother."

"At least there was one who seemed to remember," I exclaimed, for her poisoned mocking stung the words out of me, "one woman and—a dog."

"Aye, the savage, who being Nature's child, a sinner that departed hence by her own act" (how Ayesha knew this I cannot say, I never told her), "has not yet put on perfection and therefore still remembers him whose kiss was last upon her lips. But surely, Allan, it is not thy desire to pass from the gentle, ordered claspings of those white souls for the tumultuous arms of such a one as this. Still, let that be, for who knows what men will or will not do in jealousy and disappointed love? And the dog, it remembered also and even sought thee out, since dogs are more faithful and single-hearted than is mankind. There at least thou hast thy lesson, namely to grow more humble and never to think again that thou holdest all a woman's soul for aye, because once she was kind to thee for a little while on earth."

"Yes," I answered, jumping up in a rage, "as you say, I have my lesson, and more of it than I want. So by your leave, I will now bid you farewell, hoping that when it comes to be *your* turn to learn this lesson, or a worse, Ayesha, as I am sure it will one day, for something tells me so, you may enjoy it more than I have done."

Ayesha's Farewell

Thus I spoke whose nerves were on edge after all that I had seen or, as even then I suspected, seemed to see. For how could I believe that these visions of mine had any higher origin than Ayesha's rather malicious imagination? Already I had formed my theory.

It was that she must be a hypnotist of power, who, after she had put a spell upon her subject, could project into his mind such fancies as she chose together with a selection of her own theories. Only two points remained obscure. The first was—how did she get the necessary information about the private affairs of a humble individual like myself, for these were not known even to Zikali with whom she seemed to be in some kind of correspondence, or to Hans, at any rate in such completeness?

I could but presume that in some mysterious way she drew them from, or rather excited them in my own mind and memory, so that I seemed to see those with whom once I had been intimate, with modifications and in surroundings that her intelligence had carefully prepared. It would not be difficult for a mind like hers familiar, as I gathered it was, with the ancient lore of the Greeks and the Egyptians, to create a kind of Hades and, by way of difference, to change it from one of shadow to one of intense illumination, and into it to plunge the consciousness of him upon whom she had laid her charm of sleep. I had seen nothing and heard nothing that she might not thus have moulded, always given that she had access to the needful clay of facts which I alone could furnish.

Granting this hypothesis, the second point was—what might be the object of her elaborate and most bitter jest? Well, I thought that I could guess. First, she wished to show her power, or rather to make me believe that she had power of a very unusual sort. Secondly, she owed Umslopogaas and myself a debt for our services in the war with Rezu which we had been told would be repaid in this way. Thirdly, I had offended her in some fashion and she took her opportunity of settling the score. Also there was a fourth possibility—that really she considered herself a moral instructress and desired, as she said, to teach me a lesson by showing how futile were human hopes and vanities in respect to the departed and their affections.

Now I do not pretend that all this analysis of Ayesha's motives occurred to me at the moment of my interview with her; indeed, I only completed it later after much careful thought, when I found it sound and good. At that time, although I had inklings, I was too bewildered to form a just judgment.

Further, I was too angry and it was from this bow of my anger that I loosed a shaft at a venture as to some lesson which awaited *her*. Perhaps certain words spoken by the dying Rezu had shaped that shaft. Or perhaps some shadow of her advancing fate fell upon me.

The success of the shot, however, was remarkable. Evidently it pierced the joints of her harness, and indeed went home to Ayesha's heart. She turned pale; all the peach-bloom hues faded from her lovely face, her great eyes seemed to lessen and grow dull and her cheeks to fall in. Indeed, for a moment she looked old, very old, quite an aged woman. Moreover she wept, for I saw two big tears drop upon her white raiment and I was horrified.

"What has happened to you?" I said, or rather gasped.

"Naught," she answered, "save that thou hast hurt me sore. Dost thou not know, Allan, that it is cruel to prophesy ill to any, since such words feathered from Fate's own wing and barbed with venom, fester in the breast and mayhap bring about their own accomplishment. Most cruel of all is it when with them are repaid friendship and gentleness."

I reflected to myself—yes, friendship of the order that is called candid, and gentleness such as is hid in a cat's velvet paw, but contented myself with asking how it was that she who said she was so powerful, came to fear anything at all.

"Because as I have told thee, Allan, there is no armour that can turn the spear of Destiny which, when I heard those words of thine, it seemed to me, I know not why, was directed by thy hand. Look now on Rezu who thought himself unconquerable and yet was slain by the black Axe-bearer and whose bones to-night stay the famine of the jackals. Moreover I am accursed who sought to steal its servant from Heaven to be my love, and how know I when and where vengeance will fall at last? Indeed, it has fallen already on me, who through the long ages amid savages must mourn widowed and alone, but not all of it—oh! I think, not all."

Then she began to weep in good earnest, and watching her, for the first time I understood that this glorious creature who seemed to be so powerful, was after all one of the most miserable of women and as much a prey to loneliness, every sort of passion and apprehensive fear, as can be any common mortal. If, as she said, she had found the secret of life, which of course I did not believe, at least it was obvious that she had lost that of happiness.

She sobbed softly and wept and while she did so the loveliness, which had left her for a little while, returned to her like light to a grey and darkened sky. Oh, how beautiful she seemed with the abundant locks in disorder over her tear-stained face, how beautiful beyond imagining! My heart melted as I studied her; I could think of nothing else except her surpassing charm and glory.

"I pray you, do not weep," I said; "it hurts me and indeed I am sorry if I said anything to give you pain."

But she only shook that glorious hair further about her face and behind its veil wept on.

"You know, Ayesha," I continued, "you have said many hard things to me, making me the target of your bitter wit, therefore it is not strange that at last I answered you."

"And hast thou not deserved them, Allan?" she murmured in soft and broken tones from behind that veil of scented locks.

"Why?" I asked.

"Because from the beginning thou didst defy me, showing in thine every accent that thou heldest me a liar and one of no account in body or in spirit, one not worthy of thy kind look, or of those gentle words which once were my portion among men. Oh! thou hast dealt hardly with me and therefore perchance—I know not—I paid thee back with such poor weapons as a woman holds, though all the while I liked thee well."

Then again she fell to sobbing, swaying herself gently to and fro in her sweet sorrow.

It was too much. Not knowing what else to do to comfort her, I patted her ivory hand which lay upon the couch beside me, and as this appeared to have no effect, I kissed it, which she did not seem to resent. Then suddenly I remembered and let it fall.

She tossed back her hair from her face and fixing her big eyes on me, said gently enough, looking down at her hand,

"What ails thee, Allan?"

"Oh, nothing," I answered; "only I remembered the story you told me about some man called Kallikrates."

She frowned.

"And what of Kallikrates, Allan? Is it not enough that for my sins, with tears, empty longings and repentance, I must wait for him through all the weary centuries? Must I also wear the chains of this Kallikrates, to whom I owe many a debt, when he is far away? Say, didst thou see him in that Heaven of thine, Allan, for there perchance he dwells?"

I shook my head and tried to think the thing out while all the time those wonderful eyes of hers seemed to draw the soul from me. It seemed to me that she bent forward and held up her face to me. Then I lost my reason and also bent forward. Yes, she made me mad, and, save her, I forgot all.

Swiftly she placed her hand upon my heart, saying,

"Stay! What meanest thou? Dost love me, Allan?"

"I think so—that is—yes," I answered.

She sank back upon the couch away from me and began to laugh very softly.

"What words are these," she said, "that they pass thy lips so easily and so unmeant, perchance from long practice? Oh! Allan, I am astonished. Art thou the same man who some few days ago told me, and this unasked, that as soon wouldst thou think of courting the moon as of courting me? Art thou he who not a minute gone swore proudly that never had his heart and his lips wandered from certain angels whither they should not? And now, and now——?"

I coloured to my eyes and rose, muttering,

"Let me be gone!"

"Nay, Allan, why? I see no mark here," and she held up her hand, scanning it carefully. "Thou art too much what thou wert before, except perhaps in thy soul, which is invisible," she added with a touch of malice. "Nor am I angry with thee; indeed, hadst thou not tried to charm away my woe, I should have thought but poorly of thee as a man. There let it rest and be forgotten—or remembered as thou wilt. Still, in answer to thy words concerning my Kallikrates, what of those adored ones that, according to thy tale, but now thou didst find again in a place of light? Because they seemed faithless, shouldst thou be faithless also? Shame on thee, thou fickle Allan!"

She paused, waiting for me to speak.

Well, I could not. I had nothing to say who was utterly disgraced and overwhelmed.

"Thou thinkest, Allan," she went on, "that I have cast my net about thee, and this is true. Learn wisdom from it, Allan, and never again defy a woman—that is, if she be fair, for then she is stronger than thou art, since Nature for its own purpose made her so. Whatever I have done by tears, that ancient artifice of my sex, as in other ways, is for thy instruction, Allan, that thou mayest benefit thereby."

Again I sprang up, uttering an English exclamation which I trust Ayesha did not understand, and again she motioned to me to be seated, saying,

"Nay, leave me not yet since, even if the light fancy of a man that comes and goes like the evening wind and for a breath made me dear to thee, has passed away, there remains certain work which we must do together. Although, thinking of thyself alone, thou hast forgotten it, having been paid thine own fee, one is yet due to that old wizard in a far land who sent thee to visit Kôr and me, as indeed he has reminded me and within an hour."

This amazing statement aroused me from my personal and painful preoccupation and caused me to stare at her blankly.

"Again thou disbelievest me," she said, with a little stamp. "Do so once more, Allan, and I swear I'll bring thee to grovel on the ground and kiss my foot and babble nonsense to a woman sworn to another man, such as never for all thy days thou shalt think of without a blush of shame."

"Oh! no," I broke in hurriedly, "I assure you that you are mistaken. I believe every word you have said, or say or will say; I do in truth."

"Now thou liest. Well, what is one more falsehood among so many? Let it pass."

"What, indeed?" I echoed in eager affirmation, "and as for Zikali's message——" and I paused.

"It was to recall to my mind that he desired to learn whether a certain great enterprise of his will succeed, the details of which he says thou canst tell me. Repeat them to me."

So, glad enough to get away from more dangerous topics, I narrated to her as briefly and clearly as I could, the history of the old witch- doctor's feud with the Royal House of Zululand. She listened, taking in every word, and said,

"So now he yearns to know whether he will conquer or be conquered; and that is why he sent, or thinks that he sent thee on this journey, not for thy sake, Allan, but for his own. I cannot tell thee, for what have I do to with the finish of this petty business, which to him seems so large? Still, as I owe him a debt for luring the Axe-Bearer here to rid me of mine enemy, and thee to lighten my solitude for an hour by the burnishing of thy mind, I will try. Set that bowl before me, Allan," and she pointed to a marble tripod on which stood a basin half full of water, "and come, sit close by me and look into it, telling me what thou seest."

I obeyed her instructions and presently found myself with my head over the basin, staring into the water in the exact attitude of a person who is about to be shampooed.

"This seems rather foolish," I said abjectly, for at that moment I resembled the Queen of Sheba in one particular, if in no other, namely, that there was no more spirit in me. "What am I supposed to do? I see nothing at all."

"Look again," she said, and as she spoke the water grew clouded. Then on it appeared a picture. I saw the interior of a Kaffir hut dimly lighted by a single candle set in the neck of a bottle. To the left of the door of the hut was a bedstead and on it lay stretched a wasted and dying man, in whom, to my astonishment, I recognised Cetywayo, King of the Zulus. At the foot of the bed stood another man—myself grown older by many years, and leaning over the bed, apparently whispering into the dying man's ear, was a grotesque and malevolent figure which I knew to be that of Zikali, Opener-of-Roads, whose glowing eyes were fixed upon the terrified and tortured face of Cetywayo. All was as it happened afterwards, as I have written down in the book called "Finished."

I described what I saw to Ayesha, and while I was doing so the picture vanished away, so that nothing remained save the clear water in the marble bowl. The story did not seem to interest her; indeed, she leaned back and yawned a little.

"Thy vision is good, Allan," she said indifferently, "and wide also, since thou canst see what passes in the sun or distant stars, and pictures of things to be in the water, to say nothing of other pictures in a woman's eyes, all within an hour. Well, this savage business concerns me not and of it I want to know no more. Yet it would appear that here the old wizard who is thy friend, has the answer that he desires. For there in the picture the king he hates lies dying while he hisses in his ear and thou dost watch the end. What more can he seek? Tell him it when ye meet, and tell him also it is my will that in future he should trouble me less, since I love not to be wakened from my sleep to listen to his half-instructed talk and savage vapourings. Indeed, he presumes too much. And now enough of him and his dark plots. Ye have your desires, all of you, and are paid in full."

"Over-paid, perhaps," I said with a sigh.

"Ah, Allan, I think that Lesson thou hast learned pleases thee but little. Well, be comforted for the thing is common. Hast never heard that there is but one morsel more bitter to the taste than desire denied, namely, desire fulfilled? Believe me that there can be no happiness for man until he attains a land where all desire is dead."

"That is what the Buddha preaches, Ayesha."

"Aye, I remember the doctrines of that wise man well, who without doubt had found a key to the gate of Truth, one key only, for, mark thou, Allan, there are many. Yet, man being man must know desires, since without them, robbed of ambitions, strivings, hopes, fears, aye and of life itself, the race must die, which is not the will of the Lord of Life who needs a nursery for his servant's souls, wherein his swords of

Good and Ill shall shape them to his pattern. So it comes about, Allan, that what we think the worst is oft the best for us, and with that knowledge, if we are wise, let us assuage our bitterness and wipe away our tears."

"I have often thought that," I said.

"I doubt it not, Allan, since though it has pleased me to make a jest of thee, I know that thou hast thy share of wisdom, such little share as thou canst gather in thy few short years. I know, too, that thy heart is good and aspires high, and Friend—well, I find in thee a friend indeed, as I think not for the first time, nor certainly for the last. Mark, Allan, what I say, not a lover, but a *friend*, which is higher far. For when passion dies with the passing of the flesh, if there be no friendship what will remain save certain memories that, mayhap, are well forgot? Aye, how would those lovers meet elsewhere who were never more than lovers? With weariness, I hold, as they stared into each other's empty soul, or even with disgust.

"Therefore the wise will seek to turn those with whom Fate mates them into friends, since otherwise soon they will be lost for aye. More, if they are wiser still, having made them friends, they will suffer them to find lovers where they will. Good maxims, are they not? Yet hard to follow, or so, perchance, thou thinkest them—as I do."

She grew silent and brooded a while, resting her chin upon her hand and staring down the hall. Thus the aspect of her face was different from any that I had seen it wear. No longer had it the allure of Aphrodite or the majesty of Hera; rather might it have been that of Athene herself. So wise it seemed, so calm, so full of experience and of foresight, that almost it frightened me.

What was this woman's true story, I wondered, what her real self, and what the sum of her gathered knowledge? Perhaps it was accident, or perhaps, again, she guessed my mind. At any rate her next words seemed in some sense an answer to these speculations. Lifting her eyes she contemplated me a while, then said,

"My friend, we part to meet no more in thy life's day. Often thou wilt wonder concerning me, as to what in truth I am, and mayhap in the end thy judgment will be to write me down some false and beauteous wanderer who, rejected of the world or driven from it by her crimes, made choice to rule among savages, playing the part of Oracle to that little audience and telling strange tales to such few travellers as come her way. Perhaps, indeed, I do play this part among many others, and if so, thou wilt not judge me wrongly.

"Allan, in the old days, mariners who had sailed the northern seas, told me that therein amidst mist and storm float mountains of ice, shed from dizzy cliffs which are hid in darkness where no sun shines. They told me also that whereas above the ocean's breast appears but a blue and dazzling point, sunk beneath it is oft a whole frozen isle, invisible to man.

"Such am I, Allan. Of my being thou seest but one little peak glittering in light or crowned with storm, as heaven's moods sweep over it. But in the depths beneath are hid its white and broad foundations, hollowed by the seas of time to caverns and to palaces which my spirit doth inhabit. So picture me, therefore, as wise and fair, but with a soul unknown, and pray that in time to come thou mayest see it in its splendour.

"Hadst thou been other than thou art, I might have shown thee secrets, making clear to thee the parable of much that I have told thee in metaphor and varying fable, aye, and given thee great gifts of power and enduring days of which thou knowest nothing. But of those who visit shrines, O Allan, two things are required, worship and faith, since without these the oracles are dumb and the healing waters will not flow.

"Now I, Ayesha, am a shrine; yet to me thou broughtest no worship until I won it by a woman's trick, and in me thou hast no faith. Therefore for thee the oracle will not speak and the waters of deliverance will not flow. Yet I blame thee not, who art as thou wast made and the hard world has shaped thee.

"And so we part: Think not I am far from thee because thou seest me not in the days to come, since like that Isis whose majesty alone I still exercise on earth, I, whom men name Ayesha, am in all things. I tell thee that I am not One but Many and, being many, am both Here and Everywhere. When thou standest beneath the sky at night and lookest on the stars, remember that in them mine eyes behold thee; when the soft winds of evening blow, that my breath is on thy brow and when the thunder rolls, that there am I riding on the lightnings and rushing with the gale."

"Do you mean that you are the goddess Isis?" I asked, bewildered. "Because if so why did you tell me that you were but her priestess?"

"Have it as thou wilt, Allan. All sounds do not reach thine ears; all sights are not open to thy eyes and therefore thou art both half deaf and blind. Perchance now that her shrines are dust and her worship is forgot, some spark of the spirit of that immortal Lady whose chariot was the moon, lingers on the earth in this woman's shape of mine, though her essence dwells afar, and perchance her other name is Nature, my mother and thine, O Allan. At the least hath not the World a soul—and of that soul am I not mayhap a part, aye, and thou also? For the rest are not the priest and the Divine he bows to, oft the same?"

It was on my lips to answer, Yes, if the priest is a knave or a self- deceiver, but I did not.

"Farewell, Allan, and let Ayesha's benison go with thee. Safe shalt thou reach thy home, for all is prepared to take thee hence, and thy companions with thee. Safe shalt thou live for many a year, till thy time comes, and then, perchance, thou wilt find those whom thou hast lost more kind than they seemed to be to-night."

She paused awhile, then added,

"Hearken unto my last word! As I have said, much that I have told thee may bear a double meaning, as is the way of parables, to be interpreted as thou wilt. Yet one thing is true. I love a certain man, in the old days named Kallikrates, to whom alone I am appointed by a divine decree, and I await him here. Oh, shouldest thou find him in the world without, tell him that Ayesha awaits him and grows weary in the waiting. Nay, thou wilt never find him, since even if he be born again, by what token would he be known to thee? Therefore I charge thee, keep my secrets well, lest Ayesha's curse should fall on thee. While thou livest tell naught of me to the world thou knowest. Dost thou swear to keep my secrets, Allan?"

"I swear, Ayesha."

"I thank thee, Allan," she answered, and grew silent for a while.

At length Ayesha rose and drawing herself up to the full of her height, stood there majestic. Next she beckoned to me to come near, for I too had risen and left the dais.

I obeyed, and bending down she held her hands over me as though in blessing, then pointed towards the curtains which at this moment were drawn asunder, by whom I do not know.

I went and when I reached them, turned to look my last on her.

There she stood as I had left her, but now her eyes were fixed upon the ground and her face once more was brooding absently as though no such a man as I had ever been. It came into my mind that already she had forgotten me, the plaything of an hour, who had served her turn and been cast aside.

What Umslopogaas Saw

Like one who drams I passed down the outer hall where stood the silent guards as statues might, and out through the archway. Here I paused for a moment, partly to calm my mind in the familiar surroundings of the night, and partly because I thought that I heard someone approaching me through the gloom, and in such a place where I might have many enemies, it was well to be prepared.

As it chanced, however, my imaginary assailant was only Hans, who emerged from some place where he had been hiding; a very disturbed and frightened Hans.

"Oh, Baas," he said in a low and shaky whisper, "I am glad to see you again, and standing on your feet, not being carried with them sticking straight in front of you as I expected."

"Why?" I asked.

"Oh, Baas, because of the things that happened in that place where the tall *vrouw* with her head tied up as though she had tooth-ache, sits like a spider in a web."

"Well, what happened, Hans?" I asked as we walked forward.

"This, Baas. The Doctoress talked and talked at you and Umslopogaas, and as she talked, your faces began to look as though you had drunk half a flask too much of the best gin, such as I wish I had some of here to-night, at once wise and foolish, and full and empty, Baas. Then you both rolled over and lay there quite dead, and whilst I was wondering what I should do and how I should get out your bodies to bury them, the Doctoress came down off her platform and bent, first over you and next over Umslopogaas, whispering into the ears of both of you. Then she took off a snake that looked as though it were made of gold with green eyes, which she wears about her middle beneath the long dish-cloth, Baas, and held it to your lips and next to those of Umslopogaas."

"Well, and what then, Hans?"

"After that all sorts of things came about, Baas, and I felt as though the whole house were travelling through the air, Baas, twice as fast as a bullet does from a rifle. Suddenly, too, the room became filled with fire so hot that it scorched me, and so bright that it made my eyes water, although they can look at the sun without winking. And, Baas, the fire was full of spooks which walked around; yes, I saw some of them standing on your head and stomach, Baas, also on that of Umslopogaas, whilst others went and talked to the white Doctoress as quietly as though they had met her in the market-place and wanted to sell her eggs or butter. Then, Baas, suddenly I saw your reverend father, the Predikant, who looked as though he were red-hot, as doubtless he is in the Place of Fires. I thought he came up to me, Baas, and said, 'Get out of this, Hans. This is no place for a good Hottentot like you, Hans, for here only the very best Christians can bear the heat for long.'

"That finished me, Baas. I just answered that I handed you, the Baas Allan his son, over to his care, hoping that he would see that you did not burn in that oven, whatever happened to Umslopogaas. Then I shut my eyes and mouth and held my nose, and wriggled beneath those curtains as a snake does, Baas, and ran down the hall and across the kraal-yard and through the archway out into the night, where I have been sitting cooling myself ever since, waiting for you to be carried away, Baas. And now you have come alive and with not even your hair burnt off, which shows how wonderful must be the Great Medicine of Zikali, Baas, since nothing else could have saved you in that fire, no, not even your reverend father, the Predikant."

"Hans," I said when he had finished, "you are a very wonderful fellow, for you can get drunk on nothing at all. Please remember, Hans, that you have been drunk to-night, yes, very drunk indeed, and never dare to repeat anything that you thought you saw while you were drunk."

"Yes, Baas, I understand that I was drunk and already have forgotten everything. But, Baas, there is still a bottle full of brandy and if I could have just one more tot I should forget *so* much better!"

By now we had reached our camp and here I found Umslopogaas sitting in the doorway and staring at the sky.

"Good-evening to you, Umslopogaas," I said in my most unconcerned manner, and waited.

"Good-evening, Watcher-by-Night, who I thought was lost in the night, since in the end the night is stronger than any of its watchers."

At this cryptic remark I looked bewildered but said nothing. At length Umslopogaas, whose nature, for a Zulu, was impulsive and lacking in the ordinary native patience, asked,

"Did you make a journey this evening, Macumazahn, and if so, what did you see?"

"Did you have a dream this evening, Umslopogaas?" I inquired by way of answer, "and if so, what was it about? I thought that I saw you shut your eyes in the House of the White One yonder, doubtless because you were weary of talk which you did not understand."

"Aye, Macumazahn, as you suppose I grew weary of that talk which flowed from the lips of the White Witch like the music that comes from a little stream babbling over stones when the sun is hot, and being weary, I fell asleep and dreamed. What I dreamed does not much matter. It is enough to say that I felt as though I were thrown through the air like a stone cast from his sling by a boy who is set upon a stage to scare the birds out of a mealie garden. Further than any stone I went, aye, further than a shooting star, till I reached a wonderful place. It does not much matter what it was like either, and indeed I am already beginning to forget, but there I met everyone I have ever known. I met the Lion of the Zulus, the Black One, the Earth-Shaker, he who had a 'sister' named Baleka, which sister," here he dropped his voice and looked about him suspiciously, "bore a child, which child was fostered by one Mopo, that Mopo who afterwards slew the Black one with the Princes. Now, Macumazahn, I had a score to settle with this Black One, aye, even though our blood be much of the same colour, I had a score to settle with him, because of the slaying of this sister of his, Baleka, together with the Langeni tribe. So I walked up to him and took him by the head-ring and spat in his face and bade him find a spear and shield, and meet me as man to man. Yes, I did this."

"And what happened then, Umslopogaas?" I said, when he paused in his narrative.

"Macumazahn, nothing happened at all. My hand seemed to go through his head-ring and the skull beneath, and to shut upon itself while he went on talking to someone else, a captain whom I recognised, yes, one Faku, whom in the days of Dingaan, the Black One's brother, I myself slew upon the Ghost-Mountain.

"Yes, Macumazahn, and Faku was telling him the tale of how I killed him and of the fight that I and my blood-brother and the wolves made, there on the knees of the old witch who sits aloft on the Ghost Mountain waiting for the world to die, for I could understand their talk, though mine went by them like the wind.

"Macumazahn, they passed away and there came others, Dingaan among them, aye, Dingaan who also knows something of the Witch-Mountain, seeing that there Mopo and I hurled him to his death. With him also I would have had words, but it was the same story, only presently he caught sight of the Black One, yes, of Chaka whom he slew, stabbing him with the little red assegai, and turned and fled, because in that land I think he still fears Chaka, Macumazahn, or so the dream told.

"I went on and met others, men I had fought in my day, most of them, among them was Jikiza, he who ruled the People of the Axe before me whom I slew with his own axe. I lifted the axe and made me ready to fight again, but not one of them took any note of me. There they walked about, or sat drinking beer or taking snuff, but never a sup of the beer or a pinch of the snuff did they offer me, no, not even those among them whom I chanced not to have killed. So I left them and walked on, seeking for Mopo, my foster-father, and a certain man, my blood-brother, by whose side I hunted with the wolves, yes, for them, and for another."

"Well, and did you find them?" I asked.

"Mopo I found not, which makes me think, Macumazahn, that, as once you hinted to me, he whom I thought long dead, perchance still lingers on the earth. But the others I did find . . ." and he ceased, brooding.

Now I knew enough of Umslopogaas's history to be aware that he had loved this man and woman of whom he spoke more than any others on the earth. The "blood-brother," whose name he would not utter, by which he did not mean that he was his brother in blood but one with whom he had made a pact of eternal friendship by the interchange of blood or some such ceremony, according to report, had dwelt with him on the Witch- Mountain where legend told, though this I could scarcely believe, that they had hunted with a pack of hyenas. There, it said also, they fought a great fight with a band send out by Dingaan the king under the command of that Faku whom Umslopogaas had mentioned, in which fight the "Blood-Brother," wielder of a famous club known as Watcher- of-the-Fords, got his death after doing mighty deeds. There also, as I had heard, Nada the Lily, whose beauty was still famous in the land, died under circumstances strange as they were sad.

Naturally, remembering my own experiences, or rather what seemed to be my experiences, for already I had made up my mind that they were but a dream, I was most anxious to learn whether these two who had been so dear to this fierce Zulu, had recognised him.

"Well, and what did they say to you, Umslopogaas?" I asked.

"Macumazahn, they said nothing at all. Hearken! There stood this pair, or sometimes they moved to and fro; my brother, an even greater man than he used to be, with the wolfskin girt about him and the club, Watcher-of-the-Fords, which he alone could wield, upon his shoulder, and Nada, grown lovelier even than she was of old, so lovely, Macumazahn, that my heart rose into my throat when I saw her and stopped my breath. Yes, Macumazahn, there they stood, or walked about arm in arm as lovers might, and looked into each other's eyes and talked of how they had known each other on the earth, for I could understand their words or thoughts, and how it was good to be at rest together where they were."

"You see, they were old friends, Umslopogaas," I said.

"Yes, Macumazahn, very old friends as I thought. So much so that they had never had a word to say of me who also was the old friend of both of them. Aye, my brother, whose name I am sworn not to speak, the woman-hater who vowed he loved nothing save me and the wolves, could smile into the face of Nada the Lily, Nada the bride of my youth, yet never a word of me, while she could smile back and tell him how great a warrior he had been and never a word of me whose deeds she was wont to praise, who saved her in the Halakazi caves and from Dingaan; no, never a word of me although I stood there staring at them."

"I suppose that they did not see you, Umslopogaas."

"That is so, Macumazahn; I am sure that they did not see me, for if they had they would not have been so much at ease. But I saw them and as they would not take heed when I shouted, I ran up calling to my brother to defend himself with his club. Then, as he still took no note, I lifted the axe *Inkosikaas*, making it circle in the light, and smote with all my strength."

"And what happened, Umslopogaas?"

"Only this, Macumazahn, that the axe went straight through my brother from the crown of his head to the groin, cutting him in two, and he just went on talking!

Indeed, he did more, for stooping down he gathered a white lily-bloom which grew there and gave it to Nada, who smelt at it, smiled and thanked him, and then thrust it into her girdle, still thanking him all the while. Yes, she did this for I saw it with my eyes, Macumazahn."

Here the Zulu's voice broke and I think that he wept, for in the faint light I saw him draw his long hand across his eyes, whereon I took the opportunity to turn my back and light a pipe.

"Macumazahn," he went on presently, "it seems that madness took hold of me for a long while, for I shouted and raved at them, thinking that words and rage might hurt where good steel could not, and as I did so they faded away and disappeared, still smiling and talking, Nada smelling at the lily which, having a long stalk, rose up above her breast. After this I rushed away and suddenly met that savage king, Rezu, whom I slew a few days gone. At him I went with the axe, wondering whether he would put up a better fight this second time."

"And did he, Umslopogaas?"

"Nay, but I think he felt me for he turned and fled and when I tried to follow I could not see him. So I ran on and presently who should I find but Baleka, Baleka, Chaka's 'sister' who—repeat it not, Macumazahn—was my mother; and, Macumazahn, *she* saw me. Yes, though I was but little when last she looked on me who now am great and grim, she saw and knew me, for she floated up to me and smiled at me and seemed to press her lips upon my forehead, though I could feel no kiss, and to draw the soreness out of my heart. Then she, too, was gone and of a sudden I fell down through space, having, I suppose, stepped into some deep hole, or perchance a well.

"The next thing I knew was that I awoke in the house of the White Witch and saw you sleeping at my side and the Witch leaning back upon her bed and smiling at me through the thin blanket with which she covers herself up, for I could see the laughter in her eyes.

"Now I grew mad with her because of the things that I had seen in the Place of Dreams, and it came into my heart that it would be well to kill her that the world might be rid of her and her evil magic which can show lies to men. So, being distraught, I sprang up and lifted the axe and stepped towards her, whereon she rose and stood before me, laughing out loud. Then she said something in the tongue I cannot understand, and pointed with her finger, and lo! next moment it was as if giants had seized me and were whirling me away, till presently I found myself breathless but unharmed beyond the arch and—what does it all mean, Macumazahn?"

"Very little, as I think, Umslopogaas, except that this queen has powers to which those of Zikali are as nothing, and can cause visions to float before the eyes of men. For know that such things as you saw, I saw, and in them those whom I have loved also seemed to take no thought of me but only to be concerned with each other. Moreover when I awoke and told this to the queen who is called She-who-commands, she laughed at me as she did at you, and said that it was a good lesson for my pride who in that pride had believed that the dead only thought of the living. But I think that the lesson came from her who wished to humble us, Umslopogaas, and that it was her mind that shaped these visions which we saw."

"I think so too, Macumazahn, but how she knew of all the matters of your life and mine, I do not know, unless perchance Zikali told them to her, speaking in the night-watches as wizards can."

"Nay, Umslopogaas, I believe that by her magic she drew our stories out of our own hearts and then set them forth to us afresh, putting her own colour on them. Also it may be that she drew something from Hans, and from Goroko and the other Zulus with you, and thus paid us the fee that she had promised for our service, but in lung-sick oxen and barren cows, not in good cattle, Umslopogaas."

He nodded and said,

"Though at the time I seemed to go mad and though I know that women are false and men must follow where they lead them, never will I believe that my brother, the woman-hater, and Nada are lovers in the land below and have there forgotten me, the comrade of one of them and the husband of the other. Moreover I hold, Macumazahn, that you and I have met with a just reward for our folly.

"We have sought to look through the bottom of the grave at things which the Great-Great in Heaven above did not mean that men should see, and now that we have seen we are unhappier than we were, since such dreams burn themselves upon the heart as a red-hot iron burns the hide of an ox, so that the hair will never grow again where it has been and the hide is marred.

"To you, Watcher-by-Night, I say, 'Content yourself with your watching and whatever it may bring to you in fame and wealth.' And to myself I say, 'Holder of the Axe, content yourself with the axe and what it may bring to you in fair fight and glory'; and to both of us I say, 'Let the Dead sleep unawakened until we go to join them, which surely will be soon enough.'"

"Good words, Umslopogaas, but they should have been spoken ere ever we set out on this journey."

"Not so, Macumazahn, since that journey we were fated to make to save one who lies yonder, the Lady Sad-Eyes, and, as they tell me, is well again. Also Zikali willed it, and who can resist the will of the Opener-of-Roads? So it is made and we have seen many strange things and won some glory and come to know how deep is the pool of our own foolishness, who thought that we could search out the secrets of Death, and there have only found those of a witch's mind and venom, reflected as in water. And now having discovered all these things I wish to be gone from this haunted land. When do we march, Macumazahn?"

"To-morrow morning, I believe, if the Lady Sad-Eyes and the others are well enough, as She-who-commands says they will be."

"Good. Then I would sleep who am more weary than I was after I had killed Rezu in the battle on the mountain."

"Yes," I answered, "since it is harder to fight ghosts than men, and dreams, if they be bad, are more dreadful than deeds. Good-night, Umslopogaas."

He went, and I too went to see how it fared with Inez. I found that she was fast asleep but in a quite different sleep to that into which Ayesha seemed to have plunged her. Now it was absolutely natural and looking at her lying there upon the bed, I thought how young and healthy was her appearance. The women in charge of her also told me that she had awakened at the hour appointed by She-who-commands, as it seemed, quite well and very hungry, although she appeared to be puzzled by her surroundings. After she had eaten, they added that she had "sung a song," which was probably a hymn, and prayed upon her knees, "making signs upon her breast" and then gone quietly to bed.

My anxiety relieved as regards Inez, I returned to my own quarters. Not feeling inclined for slumber, however, instead of turning in I sat at the doorway contemplating the beauty of the night while I watched the countless fireflies that seemed to dust the air with sparks of burning gold; also the great owls and other fowl that haunt the dark. These had come out in numbers from their hiding-places among the ruins and sailed to and fro like white-winged spirits, now seen and now lost in the gloom.

While I sat thus many reflections came to me as to the extraordinary nature of my experiences during the past few days. Had any man ever known the like, I wondered? What could they mean and what could this marvellous woman Ayesha be? Was she perhaps a personification of Nature itself, as indeed to some extent all women are?

Was she human at all, or was she some spirit symbolising a departed people, faith and civilisation, and haunting the ruins where once she reigned as queen? No, the idea was ridiculous, since such beings do not exist, though it was impossible to doubt that she possessed powers beyond those of common humanity, as she possessed beauty and fascination greater than are given to any other woman.

Of one thing I was certain, however, that the Shades I had seemed to visit had their being in the circle of her own imagination and intelligence. There Umslopogaas was right; we had seen no dead, we had only seen pictures and images that she drew and fashioned.

Why did she do this, I wondered. Perhaps to pretend to powers which she did not possess, perhaps out of sheer elfish mischief, or perhaps, as she asserted, just to teach us a lesson and to humble us in our own sight. Well, if so she had succeeded, for never did I feel so crushed and humiliated as at that moment.

I had seemed to descend, or ascend, into Hades, and there had only seen things that gave me little joy and did but serve to reopen old wounds. Then, on awaking, I had been bewitched; yes, fresh from those visions of the most dear dead, I had been bewitched by the overpowering magic of this woman's loveliness and charm, and made a fool of myself, only to be brought back to my senses by her triumphant mockery. Oh, I was humbled indeed, and yet the odd thing is that I could not feel angry with her, and what is more that, perhaps from vanity, I believed in her profession of friendship towards myself.

Well, the upshot of it was that, like Umslopogaas, more than anything else in the world did I desire to depart from this haunted Kôr and to bury all its recollections in such activities as fortune might bring to me. And yet, and yet it was well to have seen it and to have plucked the flower of such marvellous experience, nor, as I knew even then, could I ever inter the memory of Ayesha the wise, the perfect in all loveliness, and the half-divine in power.

When I awoke the next morning the sun was well up and after I had taken a swim in the old bath and dressed myself, I went to see how it fared with Inez. I found her sitting at the door of her house looking extremely well and with a radiant face. She was engaged in making a chain of some small and beautiful blue flowers of the iris tribe, of which quantities grew about, that she threaded together upon stalks of dry grass.

This chain, which was just finished, she threw over her head so that it hung down upon her white robe, for now she was dressed like an Arab woman though without the veil. I watched her unseen for a little while then came forward and spoke to her. She started at the sight of me and rose as though to run away; then, apparently reassured by my appearance, selected a particularly fine flower and offered it to me.

I saw at once that she did not know me in the least and thought that she had never seen me before, in short, that her mind had gone, exactly as Ayesha had said that it would do. By way of making conversation I asked her if she felt well. She replied, Oh, yes, she had never felt better, then added,

"Daddy has gone on a long journey and will not be back for weeks and weeks."

An idea came to me and I answered,

"Yes, Inez, but I am a friend of his and he has sent me to take you to a place where I hope that we shall find him. Only it is far away, so you also must make a long journey."

She clapped her hands and answered,

"Oh, that will be nice, I do so love travelling, especially to find Daddy, who I expect will have my proper clothes with him, not these which, although they are very comfortable and pretty, seem different to what I used to wear. You look very nice too and I am sure that we shall be great friends, which I am glad of, for I have been rather lonely since my mother went to live with the saints in Heaven, because, you see, Daddy is so busy and so often away, that I do not see much of him."

Upon my word I could have wept when I heard her prattle on thus. It is so terribly unnatural, almost dreadful indeed, to listen to a full grown woman who talks in the accents and expresses the thoughts of a child. However, under all the circumstances I recognised that her calamity was merciful, and remembering that Ayesha had prophesied the recovery of her mind as well as its loss and how great seemed to be her powers in these directions, I took such comfort as I could.

Leaving her I went to see the two Zulus who had been wounded and found to my joy that they were now quite well and fit to travel, for here, too, Ayesha's prophecy had proved good. The other men also were completely rested and anxious to be gone like Umslopogaas and myself.

While I was eating my breakfast Hans announced the venerable Billali, who with a sweeping bow informed me that he had come to inquire when we should be ready to start, as he had received orders to see to all the necessary arrangements. I replied—within an hour, and he departed in a hurry.

But little after the appointed time he reappeared with a number of litters and their bearers, also with a bodyguard of twenty-five picked men, all of whom we recognised as brave fellows who had fought well in the battle. These men and the bearers old Billali harangued, telling them that they were to guide, carry and escort us to the other side of the great swamp, or further if we needed it, and that it was the word of She-who-commands that if so much as the smallest harm came to any one of us, even by accident, they should die every man of them "by the hot-pot," whatever that might be, for I was not sure of the significance of this horror. Then he asked them if they understood. They replied with fervour that they understood perfectly and would lead and guard us as though we were their own mothers.

As a matter of fact they did, and I think would have done so independently of Ayesha's command, since they looked upon Umslopogaas and myself almost as gods and thought that we could destroy them all if we wished, as we had destroyed Rezu and his host.

I asked Billali if he were not coming with us, to which he replied, No, as She-who-commands had returned to her own place and he must follow her at once. I asked him again where her own place might be, to which he answered vaguely that it was everywhere and he stared first at the heavens and then at the earth as though she inhabited most of them, adding that generally it was "in the Caves," though what he meant by that I did not know. Then he said that he was very glad to have met us and that the sight of Umslopogaas killing Rezu was a spectacle that he would remember with pleasure all his life. Also he asked me for a present. I gave him a spare pencil that I possessed in a little German silver case, with which he was delighted. Thus I parted with old Billali, of whom I shall always think with a certain affection.

I noticed even then that he kept very clear indeed of Umslopogaas, thinking, I suppose, that he might take a last opportunity to fulfil his threats and introduce him to his terrible Axe.

Umslopogaas Wears the Great Medicine

A little while later we started, some of us in litters, including the wounded Zulus, who I insisted should be carried for a day or two, and some on foot. Inez I caused to be borne immediately in front of myself so that I could keep an eye upon her. Moreover I put her in the especial charge of Hans, to whom fortunately she took a great fancy at once, perhaps because she remembered subconsciously that she knew him and that he had been kind to her, although when they met after her long sleep, as in my own case, she did not recognise him in the least.

Soon, however, they were again the fastest of friends, so much so that within a day or two the little Hottentot practically filled the place of a maid to her, attending to her every want and looking after her exactly as a nurse does after a child, with the result that it was quite touching to see how she came to depend upon him, "her monkey," as she called him, and how fond he grew of her.

Once, indeed, there was trouble, since hearing a noise, I came up to find Hans bristling with fury and threatening to shoot one of the Zulus, who stupidly, or perhaps rudely, had knocked against the litter of Inez and nearly turned it over. For the rest, the Lady Sad-Eyes, as they called her, had for the time became the Lady Glad-Eyes, since she was merry as the day was long, laughing and singing and playing just as a healthy happy child should do.

Only once did I see her wretched and weep. It was when a kitten which she had insisted on bringing with her, sprang out of the litter and vanished into some bush where it could not be found. Even when she was soon consoled and dried her tears, when Hans explained to her in a mixture of bad English and worse Portuguese, that it had only run away because it wished to get back to its mother which it loved, and that it was cruel to separate it from its mother.

We made good progress and by the evening of the first day were over the crest of the cliff or volcano lip that encircles the great plain of Kôr, and descending rapidly to a sheltered spot on the outer slope where our camp was to be set for the night.

Not very far from this place, as I think I have mentioned, stood, and I suppose still stands, a very curious pinnacle of rock, which, doubtless being of some harder sort, had remained when, hundreds of thousands or millions of years before, the surrounding lava had been washed or had corroded away. This rock pillar was perhaps fifty feet high and as smooth as though it had been worked by man; indeed, I remembered having remarked to Hans, or Umslopogaas—I forget which— when we passed it on our inward journey, that there was a column which no monkey could climb.

As we went by it for the second time, the sun had already disappeared behind the western cliff, but a fierce ray from its sinking orb, struck upon a storm-cloud that hung over us, and thence was reflected in a glow of angry light of which the focus or centre seemed to fall upon the summit of this strange and obelisk-like pinnacle of rock.

At the moment I was out of my litter and walking with Umslopogaas at the end of the line, to make sure that no one straggled in the oncoming darkness. When we had passed the column by some forty or fifty yards, something caused Umslopogaas to turn and look back. He uttered an exclamation which made me follow his example, with the result that I saw a very wonderful thing. For there on the point of the pillar, like St. Simeon Stylites on his famous column, glowing in the sunset rays as though she were on fire, stood Ayesha herself!

It was a strange and in a way a glorious sight, for poised thus between earth and heaven, she looked like some glowing angel rather than a woman, standing as she seemed to do upon the darkness; since the shadows, save for the faintest outline, had swallowed up the column that supported her. Moreover, in the intense, rich light that was focussed on her, we could see every detail of her form and face, for she was unveiled, and even her large and tender eyes which gazed upwards emptily (at this moment they seemed very tender), yes, and the little gold studs that glittered on her sandals and the shine of the snake girdle she wore about her waist.

We stared and stared till I said inconsequently,

"Learn, Umslopogaas, what a liar is that old Billali, who told me that She-who-commands had departed from Kôr to her own place."

"Perhaps this rock edge is her own place, if she be there at all, Macumazahn."

"If she be there," I answered angrily, for my nerves were at once thrilled and torn. "Speak not empty words, Umslopogaas, for where else can she be when we see her with our eyes?"

"Who am I that I should know the ways of witches who, like the winds, are able to go and come as they will? Can a woman run up a wall of rock like a lizard, Macumazahn?"

"Doubtless——" and I began some explanation which I have forgotten, when a passing cloud, or I know not what, cut off the light so that both the pinnacle and she who stood on it became invisible. A minute later it returned for a little while, and there was the point of the needle-shaped rock, but it was empty, as, save for the birds that rested on it, it had been since the beginning of the world.

Then Umslopogaas and I shook our heads and pursued our way in silence.

This was the last that I saw of the glorious Ayesha, if indeed I did see her and not her ghost. Yet it is true that for all the first part of the journey, till we were through the great swamp in fact, from time to time I was conscious, or imagined that I was conscious of her presence. Moreover, once others saw her, or someone who might have been her. It happened thus.

We were in the centre of the great swamp and the trained guides who were leading came to a place where the path forked and were uncertain which road to take. Finally they fixed on the right-hand path and were preparing to follow it together with those who bore the litter of Inez, by the side of which Hans was walking as usual.

At this moment, as Hans told me, the guides went down upon their faces and he saw standing in front of them a white-veiled form who pointed to the left-hand path, and then seemed to be lost in the mist. Without a word the guides rose and followed this left-hand path. Hans stopped the litter till I came up when he told me what had happened, while Inez also began to chatter in her childish fashion about a "White Lady."

I had the curiosity to walk a little way along the right-hand path which they were about to take. Only a few yards further on I found myself sinking in a floating quagmire, from which I extricated myself with much difficulty but just in time for as I discovered afterwards by probing with a pole, the water beneath the matted reeds was deep. That night I questioned the guides upon the subject, but without result, for they pretended to have seen nothing and not to understand what I meant. Of neither of these incidents have I any explanation to offer, except that once contracted, it is as difficult to be rid of the habit of hallucinations as of any other.

It is not necessary that I should give all the details of our long homeward journey. So I will only say that having dismissed our bearers and escorts when we reached higher ground beyond the horrible swamp, keeping one litter for Inez in which the Zulus carried her when she was tired, we accomplished it in complete safety and having crossed the Zambesi, at last one evening reached the house called Strathmuir.

Here we found the waggon and oxen quite safe and were welcomed rapturously by my Zulu driver and the *voorlooper*, who had made up their minds that we were dead and were thinking of trekking homewards. Here also Thomaso greeted us, though I think that, like the Zulus, he was astonished at our safe return and indeed not over-pleased to see us. I told him that Captain Robertson had been killed in a fight in which we had rescued his daughter from the cannibals who had carried her off (information which I cautioned him to keep to himself) but nothing else that I could help.

Also I warned the Zulus through Umslopogaas and Goroko, that no mention was to be made of our adventures, either then or afterwards, since if this were done the curse of the White Queen would fall on them and bring them to disaster and death. I added that the name of this queen and everything that was connected with her, or her doings, must be locked up in their own hearts. It must be like the name of dead kings, not to be spoken. Nor indeed did they ever speak it or tell the story of our search, because they were too much afraid both of Ayesha whom they believed to be the greatest of all witches, and of the axe of their captain, Umslopogaas.

Inez went to bed that night without seeming to recognise her old home, to all appearance just a mindless child as she had been ever since she awoke from her trance at Kôr. Next morning, however, Hans came to tell me that she was changed and that she wished to speak with me. I went, wondering, to find her in the sitting-room, dressed in European clothes which she had taken from where she kept them, and once more a reasoning woman.

"Mr. Quatermain," she said, "I suppose that I must have been ill, for the last thing I remember is going to sleep on the night after you started for the hippopotamus hunt. Where is my father? Did any harm come to him while he was hunting?"

"Alas!" I answered, lying boldly, for I feared lest the truth should take away her mind again, "it did. He was trampled upon by a hippopotamus bull, which charged him, and killed, and we were obliged to bury him where he died."

She bowed her head for a while and muttered some prayer for his soul, then looked at me keenly and said,

"I do not think you are telling me everything, Mr. Quatermain, but something seems to say that this is because it is not well that I should learn everything."

"No," I answered, "you have been ill and out of your mind for quite a long while; something gave you a shock. I think that you learned of your father's death, which you have now forgotten, and were overcome with the news. Please trust to me and believe that if I keep anything back from you, it is because I think it best to do so for the present."

"I trust and I believe," she answered. "Now please leave me, but tell me first where are those women and their children?"

"After your father died they went away," I replied, lying once more.

She looked at me again but made no comment.

Then I left her.

How much Inez ever learned of the true story of her adventures I do not know to this hour, though my opinion is that it was but little. To begin with, everyone, including Thomaso, was threatened with the direst consequences if he said a word to her on the subject; moreover in her way she was a wise woman, one who knew when it was best not to ask questions. She was aware that she had suffered from a fit of aberration or madness and that during this time her father had died and certain peculiar things had happened. There she was content to leave the business and she never again spoke to me upon the subject. Of this I was very glad, as how on earth could I have explained to her about Ayesha's prophecies as to her lapse into childishness and subsequent return to a normal state when she reached her home seeing that I did not understand them myself?

Once indeed she did inquire what had become of Janee to which I answered that she had died during her sickness. It was another lie, at any rate by implication, but I hold that there are occasions when it is righteous to lie. At least these particular falsehoods have never troubled my conscience.

Here I may as well finish the story of Inez, that is, as far as I can. As I have shown she was always a woman of melancholy and religious temperament, qualities that seemed to grow upon her after her return to health. Certainly the religion did, for continually she was engaged in prayer, a development with which heredity may have had something to do, since after he became a reformed character and grew unsettled in his mind, her father followed the same road.

On our return to civilisation, as it chanced, one of the first persons with whom she came in contact was a very earnest and excellent old priest of her own faith. The end of this intimacy was much what might have been expected. Very soon Inez determined to renounce the world, which I think never had any great attractions for her, and entered a sisterhood of an extremely strict Order in Natal, where, added to her many merits, her considerable possessions made her very welcome indeed.

Once in after years I saw her again when she expected before long to become the Mother-Superior of her convent. I found her very cheerful and she told me that her happiness was complete. Even then she did not ask me the true story of what had happened to her during that period when her mind was a blank. She said that she knew something had happened but that as she no longer felt any curiosity about earthly things, she did not wish to know the details. Again I rejoiced, for how could I tell the true tale and expect to be believed, even by the most confiding and simple-minded nun?

To return to more immediate events. When we had been at Strathmuir for a day or two and I thought that her mind was clear enough to judge of affairs, I told Inez that I must journey on to Natal, and asked her what she wished to do. Without a moment's hesitation she replied that she desired to come with me, as now that her father was dead nothing would induce her to continue to live at Strathmuir without friends, or indeed the consolations of religion.

Then she showed me a secret hiding-place cunningly devised in a sort of cellar under the sitting-room floor, where her father was accustomed to keep the spirits of which he consumed so great a quantity. In this hole beneath some bricks, we discovered a large sum in gold stored away, which Robertson had always told his daughter she would find there, in the event of anything happening to him. With the money were his will and securities, also certain mementos of his youth and some love-letters together with a prayer-book that his mother had given him.

These valuables, of which no one knew the existence except herself, we removed and then made our preparations for departure. They were simple; such articles of value as we could carry were packed into the waggon and the best of the cattle we drove with us. The place with the store and the rest of the stock were handed over to Thomaso on a half- profit agreement under arrangement that he should remit the share of Inez twice a year to a bank on the coast, where her father had an account. Whether or not he ever did this I am unable to say, but as no one wished to stop at Strathmuir, I could conceive no better plan because purchasers of property in that district did not exist.

As we trekked away one fine morning I asked Inez whether she was sorry to leave the place.

"No," she replied with energy, "my life there has been a hell and I never wish to see it again."

Now it was after this, on the northern borders of Zululand, that Zikali's Great Medicine, as Hans called it, really played its chief part, for without it I think that we should have been killed, every one of us. I do not propose to set out the business in detail; it is too long and intricate. Suffice it to say, therefore, that it had to do with the plots of Umslopogaas against Cetywayo, which had been betrayed by his wife Monazi and her lover Lousta, both of whom I have mentioned earlier in this record. The result was that a watch for him was kept on all the frontiers, because it was guessed that sooner or later he would return to Zululand; also it had become known that he was travelling in my company.

So it came about that when my approach was reported by spies, a company was gathered under the command of a man connected with the Royal House, and by it we were surrounded. Before attacking, however, this captain sent men to me with the message that with me the King had no quarrel, although I was travelling in doubtful company, and that if I would deliver over to him Umslopogaas, Chief of the People of the Axe, and his followers, I might go whither I wished unharmed, taking my goods with me. Otherwise we should be attacked at once and killed every one of us, since it was not desired that any witnesses should be left of what happened to Umslopogaas. Having delivered this ultimatum and declined any argument as to its terms, the messengers retired, saying that they would return for my answer within half an hour.

When they were out of hearing Umslopogaas, who had listened to their words in grim silence, turned and spoke in such fashion as might have been expected of him.

"Macumazahn," he said, "now I come to the end of an unlucky journey, though mayhap it is not so evil as it seems, since I who went out to seek the dead but to be filled by yonder White Witch with the meat of mocking shadows, am about to find the dead in the only way in which they can be found, namely by becoming of their number."

"It seems that this is the case with all of us, Umslopogaas."

"Not so, Macumazahn. That child of the King will give you safe- conduct. It is I and mine whose blood he seeks, as he has the right to do, since it is true that I would have raised rebellion against the King, I who wearied of my petty lot and knew that by blood his place was mine. In this quarrel you have no share, though you, whose heart is as white as your skin, are not minded to desert me. Moreover, even if you wished to fight, there is one in the waggon yonder whose life is not yours to give. The Lady Sad-Eyes is as a child in your arms and her you must bear to safety."

Now this argument was so unanswerable that I did not know what to say. So I only asked what he meant to do, as escape was impossible, seeing that we were surrounded on every side.

"Make a glorious end, Macumazahn," he said with a smile. "I will go out with those who cling to me, that is with all who remain of my men, since my fate must be theirs, and stand back to back on yonder mound and there wait till these dogs of the King come up against us. Watch a while, Macumazahn, and see how Umslopogaas, Bearer of the Axe, and the warriors of the Axe can fight and die."

Now I was silent for I knew not what to say. There we all stood silent, while minute by minute I watched the shadow creeping forward towards a mark that the head messenger had made with his spear upon the ground, for he had said that when it touched that mark he would return for his answer.

In this rather dreadful silence I heard a dry little cough, which I knew came from the throat of Hans, and to be his method of indicating that he had a remark to make.

"What is it?" I asked with irritation, for it was annoying to see him seated there on the ground fanning himself with the remains of a hat and staring vacantly at the sky.

"Nothing, Baas, or rather, only this, Baas: Those hyenas of Zulus are even more afraid of the Great Medicine than were the cannibals up north, since the maker of it is nearer to them, Baas. You remember, Baas, they knelt to it, as it were, when we were going out of Zululand."

"Well, what of it, now that we are going into Zululand?" I inquired sharply. "Do you want me to show it to them?"